J. R. R. TOLKIEN

The
Book of Lost Tales

PART II

Christopher Tolkien

HarperCollins*Publishers*

HarperCollins*Publishers*
1 London Bridge Street
London SE1 9GF
www.tolkien.co.uk

www.tolkienestate.com

This paperback edition 2015
31

First published in Great Britain by
George Allen & Unwin (Publishers) Ltd 1984

Copyright © The Tolkien Estate Limited
and C.R. Tolkien 1984, 1986

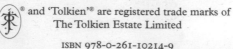
ISBN 978-0-261-10214-9

Printed and bound by
CPI Group (UK) Ltd, Croydon, CR0 4YY

MIX
Paper from
responsible sources
FSC
www.fsc.org   FSC C007454

CONTENTS

PREFACE

This second part of *The Book of Lost Tales* is arranged on the same lines and with the same intentions as the first part, as described in the Foreword to it, pages 10–11. References to the first part are given in the form 'I. 240', to the second as 'p. 240', except where a reference is made to both, e.g. 'I. 222, II. 292'.

As before, I have adopted a consistent (if not necessarily 'correct') system of accentuation for names; and in the cases of *Mim* and *Niniel*, written thus throughout, I give *Mîm* and *Níniel*.

The two pages from the original manuscripts are reproduced with the permission of the Bodleian Library, Oxford, and I wish to express my thanks to the staff of the Department of Western Manuscripts at the Bodleian for their assistance. The correspondence of the original pages to the printed text in this book is as follows:

(1) The page from the manuscript of *The Tale of Tinúviel*. Upper part: printed text page 24 (7 lines up, *the sorest dread*) to page 25 (line 3, *so swiftly.*"). Lower part: printed text page 25 (11 lines up, *the harsh voice*) to page 26 (line 7, *but Tevildo*).

(2) The page from the manuscript of *The Fall of Gondolin*. Upper part: printed text page 189 (line 12, *"Now," therefore said Galdor* to line 20 *if no further.*"). Lower part: printed text page 189 (line 27, *But the others, led by one Legolas Greenleaf*) to page 190 (line 11, *leaving the main company to follow he*).

For differences in the printed text of *The Fall of Gondolin* from the page reproduced see page 201, notes 34–36, and page 203, *Bad Uthwen*; some other small differences not referred to in the notes are also due to later changes made to the text B of the Tale (see pages 146–7).

These pages illustrate the complicated 'jigsaw' of the manuscripts of the *Lost Tales* described in the Foreword to Part I, page 10.

The third volume in this 'History' will contain the alliterative *Lay of the Children of Húrin* (c.1918–1925) and the *Lay of Leithian* (1925–1931), together with the commentary on a part of the latter by C. S. Lewis, and the rewriting of the poem that my father embarked on after the completion of *The Lord of the Rings*.

I

THE TALE OF TINÚVIEL

The *Tale of Tinúviel* was written in 1917, but the earliest extant text is later, being a manuscript in ink over an erased original in pencil; and in fact my father's rewriting of this tale seems to have been one of the last completed elements in the *Lost Tales* (see I. 203–4).

There is also a typescript version of the *Tale of Tinúviel*, later than the manuscript but belonging to the same 'phase' of the mythology: my father had the manuscript before him and changed the text as he went along. Significant differences between the two versions of the tale are given on pp. 41 ff.

In the manuscript the tale is headed: 'Link to the Tale of Tinúviel, also the Tale of Tinúviel.' The *Link* begins with the following passage:

'Great was the power of Melko for ill,' said Eriol, 'if he could indeed destroy with his cunning the happiness and glory of the Gods and Elves, darkening the light of their dwelling and bringing all their love to naught. This must surely be the worst deed that ever he has done.'

'Of a truth never has such evil again been done in Valinor,' said Lindo, 'but Melko's hand has laboured at worse things in the world, and the seeds of his evil have waxen since to a great and terrible growth.'

'Nay,' said Eriol, 'yet can my heart not think of other griefs, for sorrow at the destruction of those most fair Trees and the darkness of the world.'

This passage was struck out, and is not found in the typescript text, but it reappears in almost identical form at the end of *The Flight of the Noldoli* (I. 169). The reason for this was that my father decided that the *Tale of the Sun and Moon*, rather than *Tinúviel*, should follow *The Darkening of Valinor* and *The Flight of the Noldoli* (see I. 203–4, where the complex question of the re-ordering of the *Tales* at this point is discussed). The opening words of the next part of the *Link*, 'Now in the days soon after the telling of this tale', referred, when they were written, to the tale of *The Darkening of Valinor* and *The Flight of the Noldoli*; but it is never made plain to what tale they were to refer when *Tinúviel* had been removed from its earlier position.

The two versions of the *Link* are at first very close, but when Eriol speaks of his own past history they diverge. For the earlier part I give the typescript text alone, and when they diverge I give them both in succession. All discussion of this story of Eriol's life is postponed to Chapter VI.

Now in the days soon after the telling of this tale, behold, winter approached the land of Tol Eressëa, for now had Eriol forgetful of his wandering mood abode some time in old Kortirion. Never in those months did he fare beyond the good tilth that lay without the grey walls of that town, but many a hall of the kindreds of the Inwir and the Teleri received him as their glad guest, and ever more skilled in the tongues of the Elves did he become, and more deep in knowledge of their customs, of their tales and songs.

Then was winter come sudden upon the Lonely Isle, and the lawns and gardens drew on a sparkling mantle of white snows; their fountains were still, and all their bare trees silent, and the far sun glinted pale amid the mist or splintered upon facets of long hanging ice. Still fared Eriol not away, but watched the cold moon from the frosty skies look down upon Mar Vanwa Tyaliéva, and when above the roofs the stars gleamed blue he would listen, yet no sound of the flutes of Timpinen heard he now; for the breath of summer is that sprite, and or ever autumn's secret presence fills the air he takes his grey magic boat, and the swallows draw him far away.

Even so Eriol knew laughter and merriment and musics too, and song, in the dwellings of Kortirion – even Eriol the wanderer whose heart before had known no rest. Came now a grey day, and a wan afternoon, but within was firelight and good warmth and dancing and merry children's noise, for Eriol was making a great play with the maids and boys in the Hall of Play Regained. There at length tired with their mirth they cast themselves down upon the rugs before the hearth, and a child among them, a little maid, said: 'Tell me, O Eriol, a tale!'

'What then shall I tell, O Vëannë?' said he, and she, clambering upon his knee, said: 'A tale of Men and of children in the Great Lands, or of thy home – and didst thou have a garden there such as we, where poppies grew and pansies like those that grow in my corner by the Arbour of the Thrushes?'

I give now the manuscript version of the remainder of the *Link* passage:

Then Eriol told her of his home that was in an old town of Men girt with a wall now crumbled and broken, and a river ran thereby over which a castle with a great tower hung. 'A very high tower indeed,' said he, 'and the moon climbed high or ever he thrust his face above it.' 'Was it then as high as Ingil's Tirin?' said Vëannë, but Eriol said that that he could not guess, for 'twas very many years agone since he had seen that castle or its tower, for 'O Vëannë,' said he, 'I lived there but a while, and not after I was grown to be a boy. My father came of a coastward folk, and the love of the sea that I had never seen was in my bones, and my father whetted my desire, for he told me tales that his father had told him before. Now my mother died in a cruel and hungry siege of that old town, and my father was slain in bitter fight about the walls, and in the end I Eriol escaped to the shoreland of the Western Sea, and mostly have lived upon the bosom of the waves or by its side since those far days.'

Now the children about were filled with sadness at the sorrows that fell on those dwellers in the Great Lands, and at the wars and death, and Vëannë clung to Eriol, saying: 'O Melinon, go never to a war – or hast thou ever yet?'

'Aye, often enough,' said Eriol, 'but not to the great wars of the earthly kings and mighty nations which are cruel and bitter, and many fair lands and lovely things and even women and sweet maids such as thou Vëannë Melinir are whelmed by them in ruin; yet gallant affrays have I seen wherein small bands of brave men do sometimes meet and swift blows are dealt. But behold, why speak we of these things, little one; wouldst not hear rather of my first ventures on the sea?'

Then was there much eagerness alight, and Eriol told them of his wanderings about the western havens, of the comrades he made and the ports he knew, of how he was wrecked upon far western islands until at last upon one lonely one he came on an ancient sailor who gave him shelter, and over a fire within his lonely cabin told him strange tales of things beyond the Western Seas, of the Magic Isles and that most lonely one that lay beyond. Long ago had he once sighted it shining afar off, and after had he sought it many a day in vain.

'Ever after,' said Eriol, 'did I sail more curiously about the western isles seeking more stories of the kind, and thus it is indeed that after many great voyages I came myself by the blessing of the Gods to Tol Eressëa in the end – wherefore I now sit here talking to thee, Vëannë, till my words have run dry.'

Then nonetheless did a boy, Ausir, beg him to tell more of ships and the sea, but Eriol said: 'Nay – still is there time ere Ilfiniol ring

the gong for evening meat: come, one of you children, tell me a
tale that you have heard!' Then Vëannë sat up and clapped her
hands, saying: 'I will tell you the Tale of Tinúviel.'

The typescript version of this passage reads as follows:

Then Eriol told of his home of long ago, that was in an ancient
town of Men girt with a wall now crumbled and broken, for the
folk that dwelt there had long known days of rich and easy peace.
A river ran thereby, o'er which a castle with a great tower hung.
'There dwelt a mighty duke,' said he, 'and did he gaze from the
topmost battlements never might he see the bounds of his wide
domain, save where far to east the blue shapes of the great mountains lay – yet was that tower held the most lofty that stood in the
lands of Men.' 'Was it as high as great Ingil's Tirin?' said Vëannë,
but said Eriol: 'A very high tower indeed was it, and the moon
climbed far or ever he thrust his face above it, yet may I not now
guess how high, O Vëannë, for 'tis many years agone since last I saw
that castle or its steep tower. War fell suddenly on that town amid
its slumbrous peace, nor were its crumbled walls able to withstand
the onslaught of the wild men from the Mountains of the East.
There perished my mother in that cruel and hungry siege, and my
father was slain fighting bitterly about the walls in the last sack. In
those far days was I not yet war-high, and a bondslave was I made.
    'Know then that my father was come of a coastward folk ere he
wandered to that place, and the longing for the sea that I had never
seen was in my bones; which often had my father whetted, telling
me tales of the wide waters and recalling lore that he had learned of
his father aforetime. Small need to tell of my travail thereafter in
thraldom, for in the end I brake my bonds and got me to the
shoreland of the Western Sea – and mostly have I lived upon the
bosom of its waves or by its side since those old days.'
    Now hearing of the sorrows that fell upon the dwellers in the
Great Lands, the wars and death, the children were filled with
sadness, and Vëannë clung to Eriol, saying: 'O Melinon, go thou
never to a war – or hast thou ever yet?'
    'Aye, often enough,' said Eriol, 'yet not to the great wars of the
earthly kings and mighty nations, which are cruel and bitter,
whelming in their ruin all the beauty both of the earth and of those
fair things that men fashion with their hands in times of peace –
nay, they spare not sweet women and tender maids, such as thou,
Vëannë Melinir, for then are men drunk with wrath and the lust of

blood, and Melko fares abroad. But gallant affrays have I seen wherein brave men did sometimes meet, and swift blows were dealt, and strength of body and of heart was proven – but, behold, why speak we of these things, little one? Wouldst not hear rather of my ventures on the sea?'

Then was there much eagerness alight, and Eriol told them of his first wanderings about the western havens, of the comrades he made, and the ports he knew; of how he was one time wrecked upon far western islands and there upon a lonely eyot found an ancient mariner who dwelt for ever solitary in a cabin on the shore, that he had fashioned of the timbers of his boat. 'More wise was he,' said Eriol, 'in all matters of the sea than any other I have met, and much of wizardry was there in his lore. Strange things he told me of regions far beyond the Western Sea, of the Magic Isles and that most lonely one that lies behind. Once long ago, he said, he had sighted it glimmering afar off, and after had he sought it many a day in vain. Much lore he taught me of the hidden seas, and the dark and trackless waters, and without this never had I found this sweetest land, or this dear town or the Cottage of Lost Play – yet it was not without long and grievous search thereafter, and many a weary voyage, that I came myself by the blessing of the Gods to Tol Eressëa at the last – wherefore I now sit here talking to thee, Vëannë, till my words have run dry.'

Then nevertheless did a boy, Ausir, beg him to tell more of ships and the sea, saying: 'For knowest thou not, O Eriol, that that ancient mariner beside the lonely sea was none other than Ulmo's self, who appeareth not seldom thus to those voyagers whom he loves – yet he who has spoken with Ulmo must have many a tale to tell that will not be stale in the ears even of those that dwell here in Kortirion.' But Eriol at that time believed not that saying of Ausir's, and said: 'Nay, pay me your debt ere Ilfrin ring the gong for evening meat – come, one of you shall tell me a tale that you have heard.'

Then did Vëannë sit up and clap her hands, crying: 'I will tell thee the Tale of Tinúviel.'

★

The Tale of Tinúviel

I give now the text of the *Tale of Tinúviel* as it appears in the manuscript. The *Link* is not in fact distinguished or separated in any way from the tale proper, and Vëannë makes no formal opening to it.

'Who was then Tinúviel?' said Eriol. 'Know you not?' said Ausir; 'Tinúviel was the daughter of Tinwë Linto.' 'Tinwelint', said Vëannë, but said the other: ''Tis all one, but the Elves of this house who love the tale do say Tinwë Linto, though Vairë hath said that Tinwë alone is his right name ere he wandered in the woods.'

'Hush thee, Ausir,' said Vëannë, 'for it is my tale and I will tell it to Eriol. Did I not see Gwendeling and Tinúviel once with my own eyes when journeying by the Way of Dreams in long past days?'[1]

'What was Queen Wendelin like (for so do the Elves call her),[2] O Vëannë, if thou sawest her?' said Ausir.

'Slender and very dark of hair,' said Vëannë, 'and her skin was white and pale, but her eyes shone and seemed deep, and she was clad in filmy garments most lovely yet of black, jet-spangled and girt with silver. If ever she sang, or if she danced, dreams and slumbers passed over your head and made it heavy. Indeed she was a sprite that escaped from Lórien's gardens before even Kôr was built, and she wandered in the wooded places of the world, and nightingales went with her and often sang about her. It was the song of these birds that smote the ears of Tinwelint, leader of that tribe of the Eldar that after were the Solosimpi the pipers of the shore, as he fared with his companions behind the horse of Oromë from Palisor. Ilúvatar had set a seed of music in the hearts of all that kindred, or so Vairë saith, and she is of them, and it blossomed after very wondrously, but now the song of Gwendeling's nightingales was the most beautiful music that Tinwelint had ever heard, and he strayed aside for a moment, as he thought, from the host, seeking in the dark trees whence it might come.

And it is said that it was not a moment he hearkened, but many years, and vainly his people sought him, until at length they followed Oromë and were borne upon Tol Eressëa far away, and he saw them never again. Yet after a while as it seemed to him he came upon Gwendeling lying in a bed of leaves gazing at the stars above her and hearkening also to her birds. Now Tinwelint stepping softly stooped and looked upon her, thinking "Lo, here is a fairer being even than the most beautiful of my own folk" – for indeed Gwendeling was not elf or woman but of the children of the Gods; and bending further to touch a tress of her hair he snapped a twig with his foot. Then Gwendeling was up and away laughing softly, sometimes singing distantly or dancing ever just before him, till a swoon of fragrant slumbers fell upon him and he fell face downward neath the trees and slept a very great while.

Now when he awoke he thought no more of his people (and indeed it had been vain, for long now had those reached Valinor) but desired only to see the twilight-lady; but she was not far, for she had remained nigh at hand and watched over him. More of their story I know not, O Eriol, save that in the end she became his wife, for Tinwelint and Gwendeling very long indeed were king and queen of the Lost Elves of Artanor or the Land Beyond, or so it is said here.

Long, long after, as thou knowest, Melko brake again into the world from Valinor, and all the Eldar both those who remained in the dark or had been lost upon the march from Palisor and those Noldoli too who fared back into the world after him seeking their stolen treasury fell beneath his power as thralls. Yet it is told that many there were who escaped and wandered in the woods and empty places, and of these many a wild and woodland clan rallied beneath King Tinwelint. Of those the most were Ilkorindi – which is to say Eldar that never had beheld Valinor or the Two Trees or dwelt in Kôr – and eerie they were and strange beings, knowing little of light or loveliness or of musics save it be dark songs and chantings of a rugged wonder that faded in the wooded places or echoed in deep caves. Different indeed did they become when the Sun arose, and indeed before that already were their numbers mingled with a many wandering Gnomes, and wayward sprites too there were of Lórien's host that dwelt in the courts of Tinwelint, being followers of Gwendeling, and these were not of the kindreds of the Eldalië.

Now in the days of Sunlight and Moonsheen still dwelt Tinwelint in Artanor, and nor he nor the most of his folk went to the Battle of Unnumbered Tears, though that story toucheth not this tale. Yet was his lordship greatly increased after that unhappy field by fugitives that fled to his protection. Hidden was his dwelling from the vision and knowledge of Melko by the magics of Gwendeling the fay, and she wove spells about the paths thereto that none but the Eldar might tread them easily, and so was the king secured from all dangers save it be treachery alone. Now his halls were builded in a deep cavern of great size, and they were nonetheless a kingly and a fair abode. This cavern was in the heart of the mighty forest of Artanor that is the mightiest of forests, and a stream ran before its doors, but none could enter that portal save across the stream, and a bridge spanned it narrow and well-guarded. Those places were not ill albeit the Iron Mountains were not utterly distant beyond whom lay Hisilómë where dwelt Men, and thrall-Noldoli laboured, and few free-Eldar went.

Lo, now I will tell you of things that happened in the halls of Tinwelint after the arising of the Sun indeed but long ere the unforgotten Battle of Unnumbered Tears. And Melko had not completed his designs nor had he unveiled his full might and cruelty.

Two children had Tinwelint then, Dairon and Tinúviel, and Tinúviel was a maiden, and the most beautiful of all the maidens of the hidden Elves, and indeed few have been so fair, for her mother was a fay, a daughter of the Gods; but Dairon was then a boy strong and merry, and above all things he delighted to play upon a pipe of reeds or other woodland instruments, and he is named now among the three most magic players of the Elves, and the others are Tinfang Warble and Ivárë who plays beside the sea. But Tinúviel's joy was rather in the dance, and no names are set with hers for the beauty and subtlety of her twinkling feet.

Now it was the delight of Dairon and Tinúviel to fare away from the cavernous palace of Tinwelint their father and together spend long times amid the trees. There often would Dairon sit upon a tussock or a tree-root and make music while Tinúviel danced thereto, and when she danced to the playing of Dairon more lissom was she than Gwendeling, more magical than Tinfang Warble neath the moon, nor may any see such lilting save be it only in the rose gardens of Valinor where Nessa dances on the lawns of never-fading green.

Even at night when the moon shone pale still would they play and dance, and they were not afraid as I should be, for the rule of Tinwelint and of Gwendeling held evil from the woods and Melko troubled them not as yet, and Men were hemmed beyond the hills.

Now the place that they loved the most was a shady spot, and elms grew there, and beech too, but these were not very tall, and some chestnut trees there were with white flowers, but the ground was moist and a great misty growth of hemlocks rose beneath the trees. On a time of June they were playing there, and the white umbels of the hemlocks were like a cloud about the boles of the trees, and there Tinúviel danced until the evening faded late, and there were many white moths abroad. Tinúviel being a fairy minded them not as many of the children of Men do, although she loved not beetles, and spiders will none of the Eldar touch because of Ungweliantë – but now the white moths flittered about her head and Dairon trilled an eerie tune, when suddenly that strange thing befell.

Never have I heard how Beren came thither over the hills; yet was he braver than most, as thou shalt hear, and 'twas the love of wandering maybe alone that had sped him through the terrors of the Iron Mountains until he reached the Lands Beyond.

Now Beren was a Gnome, son of Egnor the forester who hunted in the darker places³ in the north of Hisilómë. Dread and suspicion was between the Eldar and those of their kindred that had tasted the slavery of Melko, and in this did the evil deeds of the Gnomes at the Haven of the Swans revenge itself. Now the lies of Melko ran among Beren's folk so that they believed evil things of the secret Elves, yet now did he see Tinúviel dancing in the twilight, and Tinúviel was in a silver-pearly dress, and her bare white feet were twinkling among the hemlock-stems. Then Beren cared not whether she were Vala or Elf or child of Men and crept near to see; and he leant against a young elm that grew upon a mound so that he might look down into the little glade where she was dancing, for the enchantment made him faint. So slender was she and so fair that at length he stood heedlessly in the open the better to gaze upon her, and at that moment the full moon came brightly through the boughs and Dairon caught sight of Beren's face. Straightway did he perceive that he was none of their folk, and all the Elves of the woodland thought of the Gnomes of Dor Lómin as treacherous creatures, cruel and faithless, wherefore Dairon dropped his instrument and crying "Flee, flee, O Tinúviel, an enemy walks this wood" he was gone swiftly through the trees. Then Tinúviel in her amaze followed not straightway, for she understood not his words at once, and knowing she could not run or leap so hardily as her brother she slipped suddenly down among the white hemlocks and hid herself beneath a very tall flower with many spreading leaves; and here she looked in her white raiment like a spatter of moonlight shimmering through the leaves upon the floor.

Then Beren was sad, for he was lonely and was grieved at their fright, and he looked for Tinúviel everywhere about, thinking her not fled. Thus suddenly did he lay his hand upon her slender arm beneath the leaves, and with a cry she started away from him and flitted as fast as she could in the wan light, in and about the tree-trunks and the hemlock-stalks. The tender touch of her arm made Beren yet more eager than before to find her, and he followed swiftly and yet not swiftly enough, for in the end she escaped him, and reached the dwellings of her father in fear; nor did she dance alone in the woods for many a day after.

This was a great sorrow to Beren, who would not leave those places, hoping to see that fair elfin maiden dance yet again, and he wandered in the wood growing wild and lonely for many a day and searching for Tinúviel. By dawn and dusk he sought her, but ever more hopefully when the moon shone bright. At last one night he caught a sparkle afar off, and lo, there she was dancing alone on a little treeless knoll and Dairon was not there. Often and often she came there after and danced and sang to herself, and sometimes Dairon would be nigh, and then Beren watched from the wood's edge afar, and sometimes he was away and Beren crept then closer. Indeed for long Tinúviel knew of his coming and feigned otherwise, and for long her fear had departed by reason of the wistful hunger of his face lit by the moonlight; and she saw that he was kind and in love with her beautiful dancing.

Then Beren took to following Tinúviel secretly through the woods even to the entrance of the cave and the bridge's head, and when she was gone in he would cry across the stream, softly saying "Tinúviel", for he had caught the name from Dairon's lips; and although he knew it not Tinúviel often hearkened from within the shadows of the cavernous doors and laughed softly or smiled. At length one day as she danced alone he stepped out more boldly and said to her: "Tinúviel, teach me to dance." "Who art thou?" said she. "Beren. I am from across the Bitter Hills." "Then if thou wouldst dance, follow me," said the maiden, and she danced before Beren away, and away into the woods, nimbly and yet not so fast that he could not follow, and ever and anon she would look back and laugh at him stumbling after, saying "Dance, Beren, dance! as they dance beyond the Bitter Hills!" In this way they came by winding paths to the abode of Tinwelint, and Tinúviel beckoned Beren beyond the stream, and he followed her wondering down into the cave and the deep halls of her home.

When however Beren found himself before the king he was abashed, and of the stateliness of Queen Gwendeling he was in great awe, and behold when the king said: "Who art thou that stumbleth into my halls unbidden?" he had nought to say. Tinúviel answered therefore for him, saying: "This, my father, is Beren, a wanderer from beyond the hills, and he would learn to dance as the Elves of Artanor can dance," and she laughed, but the king frowned when he heard whence Beren came, and he said: "Put away thy light words, my child, and say has this wild Elf of the shadows sought to do thee any harm?"

"Nay, father," said she, "and I think there is not evil in his heart at all, and be thou not harsh with him, unless thou desirest to see thy daughter Tinúviel weep, for more wonder has he at my dancing than any that I have known." Therefore said Tinwelint now: "O Beren son of the Noldoli, what dost thou desire of the Elves of the wood ere thou returnest whence thou camest?"

So great was the amazed joy of Beren's heart when Tinúviel spake thus for him to her father that his courage rose within him, and his adventurous spirit that had brought him out of Hisilómë and over the Mountains of Iron awoke again, and looking boldly upon Tinwelint he said: "Why, O king, I desire thy daughter Tinúviel, for she is the fairest and most sweet of all maidens I have seen or dreamed of."

Then was there a silence in the hall, save that Dairon laughed, and all who heard were astounded, but Tinúviel cast down her eyes, and the king glancing at the wild and rugged aspect of Beren burst also into laughter, whereat Beren flushed for shame, and Tinúviel's heart was sore for him. "Why! wed my Tinúviel fairest of the maidens of the world, and become a prince of the woodland Elves – 'tis but a little boon for a stranger to ask," quoth Tinwelint. "Haply I may with right ask somewhat in return. Nothing great shall it be, a token only of thy esteem. Bring me a Silmaril from the Crown of Melko, and that day Tinúviel weds thee, an she will."

Then all in that place knew that the king treated the matter as an uncouth jest, having pity on the Gnome, and they smiled, for the fame of the Silmarils of Fëanor was now great throughout the world, and the Noldoli had told tales of them, and many that had escaped from Angamandi had seen them now blazing lustrous in the iron crown of Melko. Never did this crown leave his head, and he treasured those jewels as his eyes, and no one in the world, or fay or elf or man, could hope ever to set finger even on them and live. This indeed did Beren know, and he guessed the meaning of their mocking smiles, and aflame with anger he cried: "Nay, but 'tis too small a gift to the father of so sweet a bride. Strange nonetheless seem to me the customs of the woodland Elves, like to the rude laws of the folk of Men, that thou shouldst name the gift unoffered, yet lo! I Beren, a huntsman of the Noldoli, will fulfil thy small desire," and with that he burst from the hall while all stood astonished; but Tinúviel wept suddenly. "'Twas ill done, O my father," she cried, "to send one to his death with thy sorry jesting — for now methinks he will attempt the deed, being maddened by thy scorn, and Melko will slay him, and none will look ever again with such love upon my dancing."

Then said the king: "'Twill not be the first of Gnomes that Melko has slain and for less reason. It is well for him that he lies not bound here in grievous spells for his trespass in my halls and for his insolent speech"; yet Gwendeling said nought, neither did she chide Tinúviel or question her sudden weeping for this unknown wanderer.

Beren however going from before the face of Tinwelint was carried by his wrath far through the woods, until he drew nigh to the lower hills and treeless lands that warned of the approach of the bleak Iron Mountains. Only then did he feel his weariness and stay his march, and thereafter did his greater travails begin. Nights of deep despondency were his and he saw no hope whatever in his quest, and indeed there was little, and soon, as he followed the Iron Mountains till he drew nigh to the terrible regions of Melko's abode, the greatest fears assailed him. Many poisonous snakes were in those places and wolves roamed about, and more fearsome still were the wandering bands of the goblins and the Orcs — foul broodlings of Melko who fared abroad doing his evil work, snaring and capturing beasts, and Men, and Elves, and dragging them to their lord.

Many times was Beren near to capture by the Orcs, and once he escaped the jaws of a great wolf only after a combat wherein he was armed but with an ashen club, and other perils and adventures did he know each day of his wandering to Angamandi. Hunger and thirst too tortured him often, and often he would have turned back had not that been well nigh as perilous as going on; but the voice of Tinúviel pleading with Tinwelint echoed in his heart, and at night time it seemed to him that his heart heard her sometimes weeping softly for him far away in the woodlands of her home: — and this was indeed true.

One day he was driven by great hunger to search amid a deserted camping of some Orcs for scraps of food, but some of these returned unawares and took him prisoner, and they tormented him but did not slay him, for their captain seeing his strength, worn though he was with hardships, thought that Melko might perchance be pleasured if he was brought before him and might set him to some heavy thrall-work in his mines or in his smithies. So came it that Beren was dragged before Melko, and he bore a stout heart within him nonetheless, for it was a belief among his father's kindred that the power of Melko would not abide for ever, but the Valar would hearken at last to the tears of the Noldoli, and would arise and bind Melko and open Valinor once more to the weary Elves, and great joy should come back upon Earth.

Melko however looking upon him was wroth, asking how a Gnome, a thrall by birth of his, had dared to fare away into the woods unbidden, but Beren answered that he was no runagate but came of a kindred of Gnomes that dwelt in Aryador and mingled much there among the folk of Men. Then was Melko yet more angry, for he sought ever to destroy the friendship and intercourse of Elves and Men, and said that evidently here was a plotter of deep treacheries against Melko's lordship, and one worthy of the tortures of the Balrogs; but Beren seeing his peril answered: "Think not, O most mighty Ainu Melko, Lord of the World, that this can be true, for an it were then should I not be here unaided and alone. No friendship has Beren son of Egnor for the kindred of Men; nay indeed, wearying utterly of the lands infested by that folk he has wandered out of Aryador. Many a great tale has my father made to me aforetime of thy splendour and glory, wherefore, albeit I am no renegade thrall, I do desire nothing so much as to serve thee in what small manner I may," and Beren said therewith that he was a great trapper of small animals and a snarer of birds, and had become lost in the hills in these pursuits until after much wandering he had come into strange lands, and even had not the Orcs seized him he would indeed have had no other rede of safety but to approach the majesty of Ainu Melko and beg him to grant him some humble office – as a winner of meats for his table perchance.

Now the Valar must have inspired that speech, or perchance it was a spell of cunning words cast on him in compassion by Gwendeling, for indeed it saved his life, and Melko marking his hardy frame believed him, and was willing to accept him as a thrall of his kitchens. Flattery savoured ever sweet in the nostrils of that Ainu, and for all his unfathomed wisdom many a lie of those whom he despised deceived him, were they clothed sweetly in words of praise; therefore now he gave orders for Beren to be made a thrall of Tevildo Prince of Cats*. Now Tevildo was a

* Footnote in the manuscript: *Tifil (Bridhon) Miaugion or Tevildo (Vardo) Meoita.*

mighty cat – the mightiest of all – and possessed of an evil sprite, as some say, and he was in Melko's constant following; and that cat had all cats subject to him, and he and his subjects were the chasers and getters of meat for Melko's table and for his frequent feasts. Wherefore is it that there is hatred still between the Elves and all cats even now when Melko rules no more, and his beasts are become of little account.

When therefore Beren was led away to the halls of Tevildo, and these were not utterly distant from the place of Melko's throne, he was much afraid, for he had not looked for such a turn in things, and those halls were ill-lighted and were full of growling and of monstrous purrings in the dark. All about shone cats' eyes glowing like green lamps or red or yellow where Tevildo's thanes sat waving and lashing their beautiful tails, but Tevildo himself sat at their head and he was a mighty cat and coal-black and evil to look upon. His eyes were long and very narrow and slanted, and gleamed both red and green, but his great grey whiskers were as stout and as sharp as needles. His purr was like the roll of drums and his growl like thunder, but when he yelled in wrath it turned the blood cold, and indeed small beasts and birds were frozen as to stone, or dropped lifeless often at the very sound. Now Tevildo seeing Beren narrowed his eyes until they seemed to shut, and said: "I smell dog", and he took dislike to Beren from that moment. Now Beren had been a lover of hounds in his own wild home.

"Why," said Tevildo, "do ye dare to bring such a creature before me, unless perchance it is to make meat of him?" But those who led Beren said: "Nay, 'twas the word of Melko that this unhappy Elf wear out his life as a catcher of beasts and birds in Tevildo's employ." Then indeed did Tevildo screech in scorn and said: "Then in sooth was my lord asleep or his thoughts were settled elsewhere, for what use think ye is a child of the Eldar to aid the Prince of Cats and his thanes in the catching of birds or of beasts – as well had ye brought some clumsy-footed Man, for none are there either of Elves or Men that can vie with us in our pursuit." Nonetheless he set Beren to a test, and he bade him go catch three mice, "for my hall is infested with them," said he. This indeed was not true, as might be imagined, yet a certain few there were – a very wild, evil, and magic kind that dared to dwell there in dark holes, but they were larger than rats and very fierce, and Tevildo harboured them for his own private sport and suffered not their numbers to dwindle.

Three days did Beren hunt them, but having nothing wherewith to devise a trap (and indeed he did not lie to Melko saying that he had cunning in such contrivances) he hunted in vain getting nothing better than a bitten finger for all his labour. Then was Tevildo scornful and in great anger, but Beren got no harm of him or his thanes at that time because of Melko's bidding other than a few scratches. Evil however were his days thereafter in the dwellings of Tevildo. They made him a scullion, and his days passed miserably in the washing of floors and vessels, in the scrubbing of tables and the hewing of wood and the drawing of water. Often too would he be set to the turning of spits whereon birds and fat mice were daintily roasted for the cats, yet seldom did he get food or sleep himself, and he became haggard and unkempt, and wished often that never straying out of Hisilómë he had not even caught sight of the vision of Tinúviel.

Now that fair maiden wept for a very great while after Beren's departure and danced no more about the woods, and Dairon grew angry and could not understand her, but she had grown to love the face of Beren peeping through the branches and the crackle of his feet as they followed her through the wood; and his voice that called wistfully "Tinúviel, Tinúviel" across the stream before her father's doors she longed to hear again, and she would not now dance when Beren was fled to the evil halls of Melko and maybe had already perished. So bitter did this thought become at last that that most tender maiden went to her mother, for to her father she dared not go nor even suffer him to see her weep.

"O Gwendeling, my mother," said she, "tell me of thy magic, if thou canst, how doth Beren fare. Is all yet well with him?" "Nay," said Gwendeling. "He lives indeed, but in an evil captivity, and hope is dead in his heart, for behold, he is a slave in the power of Tevildo Prince of Cats."

"Then," said Tinúviel, "I must go and succour him, for none else do I know that will."

Now Gwendeling laughed not, for in many matters she was wise, and forewise, yet it was a thing unthought in a mad dream that any Elf, still less a maiden, the daughter of the king, should fare untended to the halls of Melko, even in those earlier days before the Battle of Tears when Melko's power had not grown great and he veiled his designs and spread his net of lies. Wherefore did Gwendeling softly bid her not to speak such folly; but Tinúviel said: "Then must thou plead with my father for aid, that he send warriors to Angamandi and demand the freedom of Beren from Ainu Melko."

This indeed did Gwendeling do, of love for her daughter, and so wroth was Tinwelint that Tinúviel wished that never had her desire been made known; and Tinwelint bade her nor speak nor think of Beren more, and swore he would slay him an he trod those halls again. Now then Tinúviel pondered much what she might do, and going to Dairon she begged him to aid her, or indeed to fare away with her to Angamandi an he would; but Dairon thought with little love of Beren, and he said: "Wherefore should I go into the direst peril that there is in the world for the sake of a wandering Gnome of the woods? Indeed I have no love for him, for he has destroyed our play together, our music and our dancing." But Dairon moreover told the king of what Tinúviel had desired of him – and this he did not of ill intent but fearing lest Tinúviel fare away to her death in the madness of her heart.

Now[5] when Tinwelint heard this he called Tinúviel and said: "Wherefore, O maiden of mine, does thou not put this folly away from thee, and seek to do my bidding?" But Tinúviel would not answer, and the king bade her promise him that neither would she think more on Beren, nor would she seek in her folly to follow after him to the evil lands whether alone or tempting any of his folk with her. But Tinúviel said that the first she would not promise and the second only in part, for she would not tempt any of the folk of the woodlands to go with her.

Then was her father mightily angry, and beneath his anger not a little amazed and afraid, for he loved Tinúviel; but this was the plan he devised, for he might not shut his daughter for ever in the caverns where only a dim and flickering light ever came. Now above the portals of his cavernous hall was a steep slope falling to the river, and there grew mighty beeches; and one there was that was named Hirilorn, the Queen of Trees, for she was very mighty, and so deeply cloven was her bole that it seemed as if three shafts sprang from the ground together and they were of like size, round and straight, and their grey rind was smooth as silk, unbroken by branch or twig for a very great height above men's heads.

Now Tinwelint let build high up in that strange tree, as high as men could fashion their longest ladders to reach, a little house of wood, and it was above the first branches and was sweetly veiled in leaves. Now that house had three corners and three windows in each wall, and at each corner was one of the shafts of Hirilorn. There then did Tinwelint bid Tinúviel dwell until she would consent to be wise, and when she fared up the ladders of tall pine these were taken from beneath and no way had she to get down again. All that she required was brought to her, and folk would scale the ladders and give her food or whatever else she wished for, and then descending again take away the ladders, and the king promised death to any who left one leaning against the tree or who should try by stealth to place one there at night. A guard therefore was set nigh the tree's foot, and yet came Dairon often thither in sorrow at what he had brought to pass, for he was lonely without Tinúviel; but Tinúviel had at first much pleasure in her house among the leaves, and would gaze out of her little window while Dairon made his sweetest melodies beneath.

But one night a dream of the Valar came to Tinúviel and she dreamt of Beren, and her heart said: "Let me be gone to seek him whom all others have forgot"; and waking, the moon was shining through the trees, and she pondered very deeply how she might escape. Now Tinúviel daughter of Gwendeling was not ignorant of magics or of spells, as may well be believed, and after much thought she devised a plan. The next day she asked those who came to her to bring, if they would, some of the clearest water of the stream below, "but this," she said, "must be drawn at midnight in a silver bowl, and brought to my hand with no word spoken," and after that she desired wine to be brought, "but this," she said, "must be borne hither in a flagon of gold at noon, and he who brings it must sing as he comes," and they did as they were bid, but Tinwelint was not told.

Then said Tinúviel, "Go now to my mother and say to her that her daughter desires a spinning wheel to pass her weary hours," but Dairon secretly she begged fashion her a tiny loom, and he did this even in the little house of Tinúviel in the tree. "But wherewith will you spin and wherewith weave?" said he; and Tinúviel answered: "With spells and magics," but Dairon knew not her design, nor said more to the king or to Gwendeling.

Now Tinúviel took the wine and water when she was alone, and singing a very magical song the while, she mingled them together, and as they lay in the bowl of gold she sang a song of growth, and as they lay in the bowl of silver she sang another song, and the names of all the tallest and longest things upon Earth were set in that song; the beards of the Indravangs, the tail of Karkaras, the body of Glorund, the bole of Hirilorn, and the sword of Nan she named, nor did she forget the chain Angainu that Aulë and Tulkas made or the neck of Gilim the giant, and last and longest of all she spake of the hair of Uinen the lady of the sea that is spread through all the waters. Then did she lave her head with the mingled water and wine, and as she did so she sang a third song, a song of uttermost sleep, and the hair of Tinúviel which was dark and finer than the most delicate threads of twilight began suddenly to grow very fast indeed, and after twelve hours had passed it nigh filled the little room, and then Tinúviel was very pleased and she lay down to rest; and when she awoke the room was full as with a black mist and she was deep hidden under it, and lo! her hair was trailing out of the windows and blowing about the tree boles in the morning. Then with difficulty she found her little shears and cut the threads of that growth nigh to her head, and after that her hair grew only as it was wont before.

Then was the labour of Tinúviel begun, and though she laboured with the deftness of an Elf long was she spinning and longer weaving still, and did any come and hail her from below she bid them be gone, saying: "I am abed, and desire only to sleep," and Dairon was much amazed, and called often up to her, but she did not answer.

Now of that cloudy hair Tinúviel wove a robe of misty black soaked with drowsiness more magical far than even that one that her mother had worn and danced in long long ago before the Sun arose, and therewith she covered her garments of shimmering white, and magic slumbers filled the airs about her; but of what remained she twisted a mighty strand, and this she fastened to the bole of the tree within her house, and then was her labour ended, and she looked out of her window westward to the river. Already the sunlight was fading in the trees, and as dusk filled the woods she began a song very soft and low, and as she sung she cast out her long hair from the window so that its slumbrous mist touched the heads and faces of the guards below, and they listening to her voice fell suddenly into a fathomless sleep. Then did Tinúviel clad in her garments of darkness slip down that rope of hair light as a squirrel, and away she danced to the bridge, and before the bridgewards could cry out she was among them dancing; and as the hem of her black robe touched them they fell asleep, and Tinúviel fled very far away as fast as her dancing feet would flit.

Now when the escape of Tinúviel reached the ears of Tinwelint great was his mingled grief and wrath, and all his court was in uproar, and all the woods ringing with the search, but Tinúviel was already far away drawing nigh to the gloomy foothills where the Mountains of Night begin; and 'tis said that Dairon following after her became utterly lost, and came never back to Elfinesse, but turned towards Palisor, and there plays⁶ subtle magic musics still, wistful and lonely in the woods and forests of the south.

Yet ere long as Tinúviel went forward a sudden dread overtook her at the thought of what she had dared to do and what lay before; then did she turn back for a while, and she wept, wishing Dairon was with her, and it is said that he indeed was not far off, but was wandering lost in the great pines, the Forest of Night, where afterward Túrin slew Beleg by mishap.⁷ Nigh was Tinúviel now to those places, but she entered not that dark region, and regaining heart pressed on, and by reason of the greater magic of her being and because of the spell of wonder and of sleep that fared about her no such dangers assailed her as did Beren before; yet was it a long and evil and weary journey for a maiden to tread.

Now is it to be told to thee, Eriol, that in those days Tevildo had but one trouble in the world, and that was the kindred of the Dogs. Many indeed of these were neither friends nor foes of the Cats, for they had become subject to Melko and were as savage and cruel as any of his animals; indeed from the most cruel and most savage he bred the race of wolves, and they were very dear indeed to him. Was it not the great grey wolf Karkaras Knife-fang, father of wolves, who guarded the gates of Angamandi in those days and long had done so? Many were there however who would neither bow to Melko nor live wholly in fear of him, but dwelt either in the dwellings of Men and guarded them from much evil that had otherwise befallen them or roamed the woods of Hisilómë or passing the mountainous places fared even at times into the region of Artanor and the lands beyond and to the south.

Did ever any of these view Tevildo or any of his thanes or subjects, then there was a great baying and a mighty chase, and albeit seldom was any cat slain by reason of their skill in climbing and in hiding and because of the protecting might of Melko, yet was great enmity between them, and some of those hounds were held in dread among the cats. None however did Tevildo fear, for he was as strong as any among them, and more agile and more swift save only than Huan Captain of Dogs. So swift was Huan that on a time he had tasted the fur of Tevildo, and though Tevildo had paid him for that with a gash from his great claws, yet was the pride of the Prince of Cats unappeased and he lusted to do a great harm to Huan of the Dogs.

Great therefore was the good fortune that befell Tinúviel in meeting with Huan in the woods, although at first she was mortally afraid and fled. But Huan overtook her in two leaps, and speaking soft and deep the tongue of the Lost Elves he bid her be not afraid, and "Wherefore," said he, "do I see an Elfin maiden, and one most fair, wandering alone so nigh to the abodes of the Ainu of Evil? Knowst thou not these are very evil places to be in, little one, even with a companion, and they are death to the lonely?"

"That know I," said she, "and I am not here for the love of wayfaring, but I seek only Beren."

"What knowest thou then," said Huan, "of Beren — or indeed meanest thou Beren son of the huntsman of the Elves, Egnor bo-Rimion, a friend of mine since very ancient days?"

"Nay, I know not even whether my Beren be thy friend, for I seek only Beren from beyond the Bitter Hills, whom I knew in the woods near to my father's home. Now is he gone, and my mother Gwendeling says of her wisdom that he is a thrall in the cruel house of Tevildo Prince of Cats; and whether this be true or yet worse be now befallen him I do not know, and I go to discover him — though plan I have none."

"Then will I make thee one," said Huan, "but do thou trust in me, for I am Huan of the Dogs, chief foe of Tevildo. Rest thee now with me a while within the shadows of the wood, and I will think deeply."

Then Tinúviel did as he said, and indeed she slept long while Huan watched, for she was very weary. But after a while awakening she said: "Lo, I have tarried over long. Come, what is thy thought, O Huan?"

And Huan said: "A dark and difficult matter is this, and no other rede can I devise but this. Creep now if thou hast the heart to the abiding place of that Prince while the sun is high, and Tevildo and the most of his household drowze upon the terraces before his gates. There discover in what manner thou mayst whether Beren be indeed within, as thy mother said to thee. Now I will lie not far hence in the woods, and thou wilt do me a pleasure and aid thy own desires an going before Tevildo, be Beren there or be he not, thou tellest him how thou hast stumbled upon Huan of the Dogs lying sick in the woods at this place. Do not indeed direct him hither, for thou must guide him, if it may be, thyself. Then wilt thou see what I contrive for thee and for Tevildo. Methinks that bearing such tidings Tevildo will not entreat thee ill within his halls nor seek to hold thee there."

In this way did Huan design both to do Tevildo a hurt, or perchance if it might so be to slay him, and to aid Beren whom he guessed in truth to be that Beren son of Egnor whom the hounds of Hisilómë loved. Indeed hearing the name of Gwendeling and knowing thereby that this maiden was a princess of the woodland fairies he was eager to aid her, and his heart warmed to her sweetness.

Now Tinúviel taking heart stole near to the halls of Tevildo, and Huan wondered much at her courage, following unknown to her, as far as he might for the success of his design. At length however she passed beyond his sight, and leaving the shelter of the trees came to a region of long grass dotted with bushes that sloped ever upward toward a shoulder of the hills. Now upon that rocky spur the sun shone, but over all the hills and mountains at its back a black cloud brooded, for there was Angamandi; and Tinúviel fared on not daring to look up at that gloom, for fear oppressed her, and as she went the ground rose and the grass grew more scant and rock-strewn until it came even to a cliff, sheer of one side, and there upon a stony shelf was the castle of Tevildo. No pathway led thereto, and the place where it stood fell towards the woods in terrace after terrace so that none might reach its gates save by many great leaps, and those became ever steeper as the castle drew more nigh. Few were the windows of the house and upon the ground there were none – indeed the very gate was in the air where in the dwellings of Men are wont to be the windows of the upper floor; but the roof had many wide and flat spaces open to the sun.

Now does Tinúviel wander disconsolate upon the lowest terrace and look in dread at the dark house upon the hill, when behold, she came at a bend in the rock upon a lone cat lying in the sun and seemingly asleep. As she approached he opened a yellow eye and blinked at her, and thereupon rising and stretching he stepped up to her and said: "Whither away, little maid – dost not know that you trespass on the sunning ground of his highness Tevildo and his thanes?"

Now Tinúviel was very much afraid, but she made as bold an answer as she was able, saying: "That know I, my lord" – and this pleased the old cat greatly, for he was in truth only Tevildo's doorkeeper – "but I would indeed of your goodness be brought to Tevildo's presence now – nay, even if he sleeps," said she, for the doorkeeper lashed his tail in astonished refusal. "I have words of immediate import for his private ear. Lead me to him, my lord," she pleaded, and thereat the cat purred so loudly that she dared to stroke his ugly head, and this was much larger than her own, being greater than that of any dog that is now on Earth. Thus entreated,

Umuiyan, for such was his name, said: "Come then with me," and seizing Tinúviel suddenly by her garments at the shoulder to her great terror he tossed her upon his back and leaped upon the second terrace. There he stopped, and as Tinúviel scrambled from his back he said: "Well is it for thee that this afternoon my lord Tevildo lieth upon this lowly terrace far from his house, for a great weariness and a desire for sleep has come upon me, so that I fear me I should not be willing to carry thee much farther"; now Tinúviel was robed in her robe of sable mist.

So saying Umuiyan* yawned mightily and stretched himself before he led her along that terrace to an open space, where upon a wide couch of baking stones lay the horrible form of Tevildo himself, and both his evil eyes were shut. Going up to him the doorcat Umuiyan spoke in his ear softly, saying: "A maiden awaits thy pleasure, my lord, who hath news of importance to deliver to thee, nor would she take my refusal." Then did Tevildo angrily lash his tail, half opening an eye — "What is it — be swift," said he, "for this is no hour to come desiring audience of Tevildo Prince of Cats."

"Nay, lord," said Tinúviel trembling, "be not angry; nor do I think that thou wilt when thou hearest, yet is the matter such that it were better not even whispered here where the breezes blow," and Tinúviel cast a glance as it were of apprehension toward the woods.

"Nay, get thee gone," said Tevildo, "thou smellest of dog, and what news of good came ever to a cat from a fairy that had had dealings with the dogs?"

"Why, sir, that I smell of dogs is no matter of wonder, for I have just escaped from one — and it is indeed of a certain very mighty dog whose name thou knowest that I would speak." Then up sat Tevildo and opened his eyes, and he looked all about him, and stretched three times, and at last bade the doorcat lead Tinúviel within; and Umuiyan caught her upon his back as before. Now was Tinúviel in the sorest dread, for having gained what she desired, a chance of entering Tevildo's stronghold and maybe of discovering whether Beren were there, she had no plan more, and knew not what would become of her — indeed had she been able she would have fled; yet now do those cats begin to ascend the terraces towards the castle, and one leap does Umuiyan make bearing Tinúviel upwards and then another, and at the third he

* Written above *Umuiyan* here is the name *Gumniow*, enclosed within brackets.

stumbled so that Tinúviel cried out in fear, and Tevildo said: "What ails thee, Umuiyan, thou clumsy-foot? It is time that thou left my employ if age creeps on thee so swiftly." But Umuiyan said: "Nay, lord, I know not what it is, but a mist is before mine eyes and my head is heavy," and he staggered as one drunk, so that Tinúviel slid from his back, and thereupon he laid him down as if in a dead sleep; but Tevildo was wroth and seized Tinúviel and none too gently, and himself bore her to the gates. Then with a mighty leap he sprang within, and bidding that maiden alight he set up a yell that echoed fearsomely in the dark ways and passages. Forthwith they hastened to him from within, and some he bid descend to Umuiyan and bind him and cast him from the rocks "on the northern side where they fall most sheer, for he is of no use more to me," he said, "for age has robbed him of his sureness of foot"; and Tinúviel quaked to hear the ruthlessness of this beast. But even as he spake he himself yawned and stumbled as with a sudden drowziness, and he bid others to lead Tinúviel away to a certain chamber within, and that was the one where Tevildo was accustomed to sit at meat with his greatest thanes. It was full of bones and smelt evilly; no windows were there and but one door; but a hatchway gave from it upon the great kitchens, and a red light crept thence and dimly lit the place.

Now so adread was Tinúviel when those catfolk left her there that she stood a moment unable to stir, but soon becoming used to the darkness she looked about and espying the hatchway that had a wide sill she sprang thereto, for it was not over high and she was a nimble Elf. Now gazing therethrough, for it was ajar, she saw the wide vaulted kitchens and the great fires that burnt there, and those that toiled always within, and the most were cats – but behold, there by a great fire stooped Beren, and he was grimed with labour, and Tinúviel sat and wept, but as yet dared nothing. Indeed even as she sat the harsh voice of Tevildo sounded suddenly within that chamber: "Nay, where then in Melko's name has that mad Elf fled," and Tinúviel hearing shrank against the wall, but Tevildo caught sight of her where she was perched and cried: "Then the little bird sings not any more; come down or I must fetch thee, for behold, I will not encourage the Elves to seek audience of me in mockery."

Then partly in fear, and part in hope that her clear voice might carry even to Beren, Tinúviel began suddenly to speak very loud and to tell her tale so that the chambers rang; but "Hush, dear maiden," said Tevildo, "if the matter were secret without it is not one for bawling within." Then said Tinúviel: "Speak not thus to me, O cat, mighty Lord of Cats though thou be, for am I not Tinúviel Princess of Fairies that have stepped out of my way to do thee a pleasure?" Now at those words, and she had shouted them even louder than before, a great crash was heard in the kitchens as of a number of vessels of metal and earthenware let suddenly fall, but Tevildo snarled: "There trippeth that fool Beren the Elf. Melko rid me of such folk" – yet Tinúviel, guessing that Beren had heard and been smitten with astonishment, put aside her fears and repented her daring no longer. Tevildo nonetheless was very wroth at her haughty words, and had he not been minded first to discover what good he might get from her tale, it had fared ill with Tinúviel straightway. Indeed from that moment was she in great peril, for Melko and all his vassals held Tinwelint and his folk as outlaws, and great was their joy to ensnare them and cruelly entreat them, so that much favour would Tevildo have gained had he taken Tinúviel before his lord. Indeed, so soon as she named herself, this did he purpose to do when his own business had been done, but of a truth his wits were drowzed that day, and he forgot to marvel more why Tinúviel sat perched upon the sill of the hatchway; nor did he think more of Beren, for his mind was bent only to the tale Tinúviel bore to him. Wherefore said he, dissembling his evil mood, "Nay, Lady, be not angry, but come, delay whetteth my desire – what is it that thou hast for my ears, for they twitch already."

But Tinúviel said: "There is a great beast, rude and violent, and his name is Huan" – and at that name Tevildo's back curved, and his hair bristled and crackled, and the light of his eyes was red – "and," she went on, "it seems to me a shame that such a brute be suffered to infest the woods so nigh even to the abode of the powerful Prince of Cats, my lord Tevildo"; but Tevildo said: "Nor is he suffered, and cometh never there save it be by stealth."

"Howso that may be," said Tinúviel, "there he is now, yet methinks that at last may his [life] be brought utterly to an end, for lo, as I was going through the woods I saw where a great animal lay upon the ground moaning as in sickness – and behold, it was Huan, and some evil spell or malady has him in its grip, and still he lies helpless in a dale not a mile westward in the woods from this hall. Now with this perhaps I would not have troubled your ears, had not the brute when I approached to succour him snarled upon me and essayed to bite me, and meseems that such a creature deserves whatever come to him."

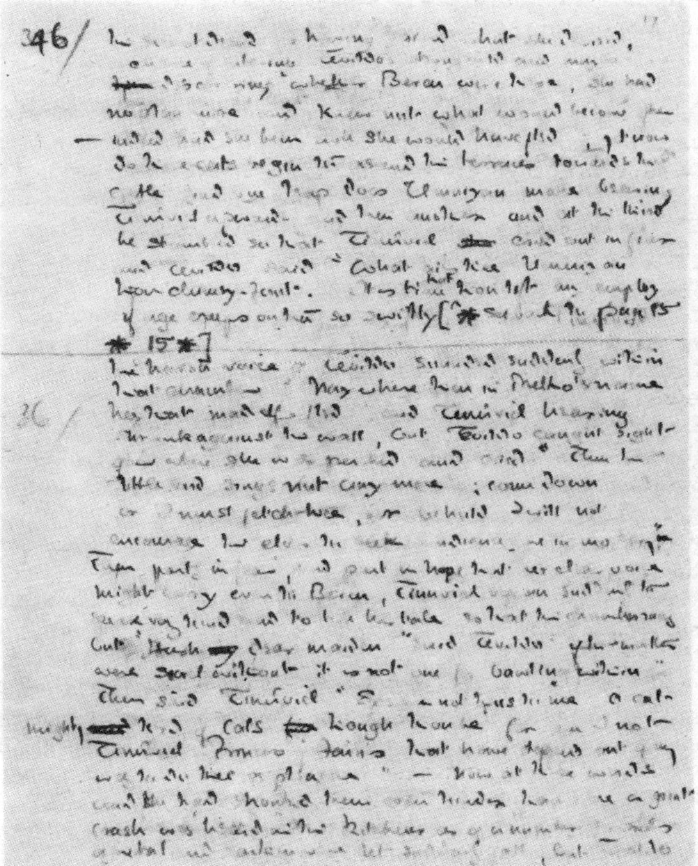

A page from the *Tale of Tinúviel*

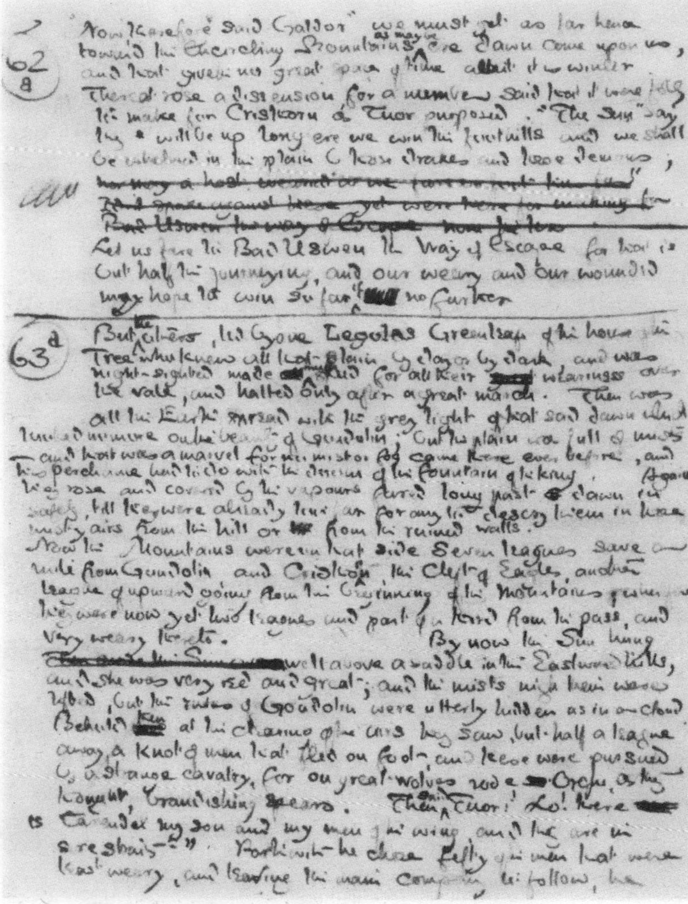

"Now therefore" said Galdor "we must get as far hence toward the Encircling Mountains as may be ere dawn come upon us, and that giveth us great space of time albeit it is winter."

Thereat rose a dissension for a number said that it were folly to make for Cristhorn as Tuor purposed. "The Sun" say they "will be up long ere we win the foothills and we shall be whelmed in the plain by those drakes and those demons; [illegible] Let us fare to Bad Uswen the Way of Escape for that is but half the journeying, and our weary and our wounded may hope to win so far, if no further."

But others, led by Legolas Greenleaf of the house of the Tree who knew all that plain by day or by dark, and was night-sighted made speed for all their weariness over the vale, and halted only after a great march. Then was all the Earth spread with the grey light of that sad dawn which looked no more on the beauty of Gondolin; but the plain was full of mists — and that was a marvel for no mist or fog came there ever before, and this perchance had to do with the doom of the fountain of the king. Again they rose and covered by the vapours fared long past dawn in safety, till they were already far for any to descry them in those misty airs from the hills or from the ruined walls.

Now the Mountains were on that side seven leagues save a mile from Gondolin and Cristhorn the Cleft of Eagles another league of upward going from the beginning of the mountains, for they were now yet two leagues and part of a third from the pass, and very weary thereto. By now the Sun hung well above a saddle in the Eastward hills, and she was very red and great; and the mists nigh them were lifted, but the ruins of Gondolin were utterly hidden as in a cloud. Behold then at the clearing of the airs they saw, but half a league away, a knot of men that fled on foot, and these were pursued by a strange cavalry, for on great wolves rode Orcs, as they thought, brandishing spears. Then said Tuor: "Lo! there is Earendel my son and my men of the wing, and they are in sore straits." Forthwith he chose fifty of the men that were least weary, and leaving the main company to follow, he

A page from the tale of *The Fall of Gondolin*

Now all this that Tinúviel spake was a great lie in whose devising Huan had guided her, and maidens of the Eldar are not wont to fashion lies; yet have I never heard that any of the Eldar blamed her therein nor Beren afterward, and neither do I, for Tevildo was an evil cat and Melko the wickedest of all beings, and Tinúviel was in dire peril at their hands. Tevildo however, himself a great and skilled liar, was so deeply versed in the lies and subtleties of all the beasts and creatures that he seldom knew whether to believe what was said to him or not, and was wont to disbelieve all things save those he wished to believe true, and so was he often deceived by the more honest. Now the story of Huan and his helplessness so pleased him that he was fain to believe it true, and determined at least to test it; yet at first he feigned indifference, saying this was a small matter for such secrecy and might have been spoken outside without further ado. But Tinúviel said she had not thought that Tevildo Prince of Cats needed to learn that the ears of Huan heard the slightest sounds a league away, and the voice of a cat further than any sound else.

Now therefore Tevildo sought to discover from Tinúviel under pretence of mistrusting her tale where exactly Huan might be found, but she made only vague answers, seeing in this her only hope of escaping from the castle, and at length Tevildo, overcome by curiosity and threatening evil things if she should prove false, summoned two of his thanes to him, and one was Oikeroi, a fierce and warlike cat. Then did the three set out with Tinúviel from that place, but Tinúviel took off her magical garment of black and folded it, so that for all its size and density it appeared no more than the smallest kerchief (for so was she able), and thus was she borne down the terraces upon the back of Oikeroi without mishap, and no drowziness assailed her bearer. Now crept they through the woods in the direction she had named, and soon does Tevildo smell dog and bristles and lashes his great tail, but after he climbs a lofty tree and looks down from thence into that dale that Tinúviel had shown to them. There he does indeed see the great form of Huan lying prostrate groaning and moaning, and he comes down in much glee and haste, and indeed in his eagerness he forgets Tinúviel, who now in great fear for Huan lies hidden in a bank of fern. The design of Tevildo and his two companions was to enter that dale silently from different quarters and so come all suddenly upon Huan unawares and slay him, or if he were too stricken to make fight to make sport of him and torment him. This did they now, but even as they leapt out upon him Huan sprang up into the air with a mighty baying, and his jaws closed in the back close to the neck of that cat Oikeroi, and Oikeroi died; but the other thane fled howling up a great tree, and so was Tevildo left alone face to face with Huan, and such an encounter was not much to his mind, yet was Huan upon him too swiftly for flight, and they fought fiercely in that glade, and the noise that Tevildo made was very hideous; but at length Huan had him by the throat, and that cat might well have perished had not his claws as he struck out blindly pierced Huan's eye. Then did Huan give tongue, and Tevildo screeching fearsomely got himself loose with a great wrench and leapt up a tall and smooth tree that stood by, even as his companion had done. Despite his grievous hurt Huan now leaps beneath that tree baying mightily, and Telvido curses him and casts evil words upon him from above.

Then said Huan: "Lo, Tevildo, these are the words of Huan whom thou thoughtest to catch and slay helpless as the miserable mice it is thy wont to hunt — stay for ever up thy lonely tree and bleed to death of thy wounds, or come down and feel again my teeth. But if neither are to thy liking, then tell me where is Tinúviel Princess of Fairies and Beren son of Egnor, for these are my friends. Now these shall be set as ransom against thee — though it be valuing thee far over thy worth."

"As for that cursed Elf, she lies whimpering in the ferns yonder, an my ears mistake not," said Tevildo, "and Beren methinks is being soundly scratched by Miaulë my cook in the kitchens of my castle for his clumsiness there an hour ago."

"Then let them be given to me in safety," said Huan, "and thou mayest return thyself to thy halls and lick thyself unharmed."

"Of a surety my thane who is here with me shall fetch them for thee," said Tevildo, but growled Huan: "Ay, and fetch also all thy tribe and the hosts of the Orcs and the plagues of Melko. Nay, I am no fool; rather shalt thou give Tinúviel a token and she shall fetch Beren, or thou shalt stay here if thou likest not the other way." Then was Tevildo forced to cast down his golden collar — a token no cat dare dishonour, but Huan said: "Nay, more yet is needed, for this will arouse all thy folk to seek thee," and this Tevildo knew and had hoped. So was it that in the end weariness and hunger and fear prevailed upon that proud cat, a prince of the service of Melko, to reveal the secret of the cats and the spell that Melko had entrusted to him; and those were words of magic whereby the stones of his evil house were held together, and whereby he held all beasts of the catfolk under his sway, filling them with an evil power beyond their nature; for long has it been said that Tevildo was an evil fay in beastlike shape. When therefore he had told it Huan laughed till the woods rang, for he knew that the days of the power of the cats were over.

Now sped Tinúviel with the golden collar of Tevildo back to the lowest terrace before the gates, and standing she spake the spell in her clear voice. Then behold, the air was filled with the voices of cats and the house of Tevildo shook; and there came therefrom a host of indwellers and they were shrunk to puny size and were afeared of Tinúviel, who waving the collar of Tevildo spake before them certain of the words that Tevildo had said in her hearing to Huan, and they cowered before her. But she said: "Lo, let all those of the folk of the Elves or of the children of Men that are bound within these halls be brought forth," and behold, Beren was brought forth, but of other thralls there were none, save only Gimli, an aged Gnome, bent in thraldom and grown blind, but whose hearing was the keenest that has been in the world, as all songs say. Gimli came leaning upon a stick and Beren aided him, but Beren was clad in rags and haggard, and he had in his hand a great knife he had caught up in the kitchen, fearing some new ill when the house shook and all the voices of the cats were heard; but when he beheld Tinúviel standing amid the host of cats that shrank from her and saw the great collar of Tevildo, then was he[8] amazed utterly, and knew not what to think. But Tinúviel was very glad, and spoke saying: "O Beren from beyond the Bitter Hills, wilt thou now dance with me – but let it not be here." And she led Beren far away, and all those cats set up a howling and wailing, so that Huan and Tevildo heard it in the woods, but none followed or molested them, for they were afraid, and the magic of Melko was fallen from them.

This indeed they rued afterward when Tevildo returned home followed by his trembling comrade, for Tevildo's wrath was terrible, and he lashed his tail and dealt blows at all who stood nigh. Now Huan of the dogs, though it might seem a folly, when Beren and Tinúviel came to that glade had suffered that evil Prince to return without further war, but the great collar of gold he had set about his own neck, and at this was Tevildo more angry than all else, for a great magic of strength and power lay therein. Little to Huan's liking was it that Tevildo lived still, but now no longer did he fear the cats, and that tribe has fled before the dogs ever since, and the dogs hold them still in scorn since the humbling of Tevildo in the woods nigh Angamandi; and Huan has not done any greater deed. Indeed afterward Melko heard all and he cursed Tevildo and his folk and banished them, nor have they since that day had lord or master or any friend, and their voices wail and screech for their hearts are very lonely and bitter and full of loss, yet there is only darkness therein and no kindliness.

At the time however whereof the tale tells it was Tevildo's chief desire to recapture Beren and Tinúviel and to slay Huan, that he might regain the spell and magic he had lost, for he was in great fear of Melko, and he dared not seek his master's aid and reveal his defeat and the betrayal of his spell. Unwitting of this Huan feared those places, and was in great dread lest those doings come swiftly to Melko's ear, as did most things that came to pass in the world; wherefore now Tinúviel and Beren wandered far away with Huan, and they became great in friendship with him, and in that life Beren grew strong again and his thraldom fell from him, and Tinúviel loved him.

Yet wild and rugged and very lonely were those days, for never a face of Elf or of Man did they see, and Tinúviel grew at last to long sorely for Gwendeling her mother and the songs of sweet magic she was used to sing to her children as twilight fell in the woodlands by their ancient halls. Often she half fancied she heard the flute of Dairon her brother, in pleasant glades' wherein they sojourned, and her heart grew heavy. At length she said to Beren and to Huan: "I must return home," and now is it Beren's heart that is overcast with sorrow, for he loved that life in the woods with the dogs (for by now many others had become joined to Huan), yet not if Tinúviel were not there.

Nonetheless said he: "Never may I go back with thee to the land of Artanor – nor come there ever after to seek thee, sweet Tinúviel, save only bearing a Silmaril; nor may that ever now be achieved, for am I not a fugitive from the very halls of Melko, and in danger of the most evil pains do any of his servants spy me." Now this he said in the grief of his heart at parting with Tinúviel, and she was torn in mind, abiding not the thought of leaving Beren nor yet of living ever thus in exile. So sat she a great while in sad thought and she spoke not, but Beren sat nigh and at length said: "Tinúviel, one thing only can we do – go get a Silmaril"; and she sought thereupon Huan, asking his aid and advice, but he was very grave and saw nothing but folly in the matter. Yet in the end Tinúviel begged of him the fell of Oikeroi that he slew in the affray of the glade; now Oikeroi was a very mighty cat and Huan carried that fell with him as a trophy.

Now doth Tinúviel put forth her skill and fairy-magic, and she sews Beren into this fell and makes him to the likeness of a great cat, and she teaches him how to sit and sprawl, to step and bound and trot in the semblance of a cat, till Huan's very whiskers bristled at the sight, and thereat Beren and Tinúviel laughed. Never however could Beren learn to screech or wail or to purr like any cat that ever walked, nor could Tinúviel awaken a glow in the dead eyes of the catskin – "but we must put up with that," said she, "and thou hast the air of a very noble cat if thou but hold thy tongue."

Then did they bid farewell to Huan and set out for the halls of Melko by easy journeys, for Beren was in great discomfort and heat within the fur of Oikeroi, and Tinúviel's heart became lighter awhile than it had been for long, and she stroked Beren or pulled his tail, and Beren was angry because he could not lash it in answer as fiercely as he wished. At length however they drew near to Angamandi, as indeed the rumblings and deep noises, and the sound of mighty hammerings of ten thousand smiths labouring unceasingly, declared to them. Nigh were the sad chambers where the thrall-Noldoli laboured bitterly under the Orcs and goblins of the hills, and here the gloom and darkness was great so that their hearts fell, but Tinúviel arrayed her once more in her dark garment of deep sleep. Now the gates of Angamandi were of iron wrought hideously and set with knives and spikes, and before them lay the greatest wolf the world has ever seen, even Karkaras Knife-fang who had never slept; and Karkaras growled when he saw Tinúviel approach, but of the cat he took not much heed, for he thought little of cats and they were ever passing in and out.

"Growl not, O Karkaras," said she, "for I go to seek my lord Melko, and this thane of Tevildo goeth with me as escort." Now the dark robe veiled all her shimmering beauty, and Karkaras was not much troubled in mind, yet nonetheless he approached as was his wont to snuff the air of her, and the sweet fragrance of the Eldar that garment might not hide. Therefore straightway did Tinúviel begin a magic dance, and the black strands of her dark veil she cast in his eyes so that his legs shook with a drowziness and he rolled over and was asleep. But not until he was fast in dreams of great chases in the woods of Hisilómë when he was yet a whelp did Tinúviel cease, and then did those twain enter that black portal, and winding down many shadowy ways they stumbled at length into the very presence of Melko.

In that gloom Beren passed well enough as a very thane of

Tevildo, and indeed Oikeroi had aforetime been much about the halls of Melko, so that none heeded him and he slunk under the very chair of the Ainu unseen, but the adders and evil things there lying set him in great fear so that he durst not move.

Now all this fell out most fortunately, for had Tevildo been with Melko their deceit would have been discovered — and indeed of that danger they had thought, not knowing that Tevildo sat now in his halls and knew not what to do should his discomfiture become noised in Angamandi; but behold, Melko espieth Tinúviel and saith: "Who art thou that flittest about my halls like a bat? How camest thou in, for of a surety thou dost not belong here?"

"Nay, that I do not yet," saith Tinúviel, "though I may perchance hereafter, of thy goodness, my lord Melko. Knowest thou not that I am Tinúviel daughter of Tinwelint the outlaw, and he hath driven me from his halls, for he is an overbearing Elf and I give not my love at his command."

Now in truth was Melko amazed that the daughter of Tinwelint came thus of her free will to his dwelling, Angamandi the terrible, and suspecting something untoward he asked what was her desire: "for knowest thou not," saith he, "that there is no love here for thy father or his folk, nor needst thou hope for soft words and good cheer from me."

"So hath my father said," saith she, "but wherefore need I believe him? Behold, I have a skill of subtle dances, and I would dance now before you, my lord, for then methinks I might readily be granted some humble corner of your halls wherein to dwell until such times as you should call for the little dancer Tinúviel to lighten your cares."

"Nay," saith Melko, "such things are little to my mind; but as thou hast come thus far to dance, dance, and after we will see," and with that he leered horribly, for his dark mind pondered some evil.

Then did Tinúviel begin such a dance as neither she nor any other sprite or fay or elf danced ever before or has done since, and after a while even Melko's gaze was held in wonder. Round the hall she fared, swift as a swallow, noiseless as a bat, magically beautiful as only Tinúviel ever was, and now she was at Melko's side, now before him, now behind, and her misty draperies touched his face and waved before his eyes, and the folk that sat about the walls or stood in that place were whelmed one by one in sleep, falling down into deep dreams of all that their ill hearts desired.

Beneath his chair the adders lay like stones, and the wolves before his feet yawned and slumbered, and Melko gazed on enchanted, but he did not sleep. Then began Tinúviel to dance a yet swifter dance before his eyes, and even as she danced she sang in a voice very low and wonderful a song which Gwendeling had taught her long ago, a song that the youths and maidens sang beneath the cypresses of the gardens of Lórien when the Tree of Gold had waned and Silpion was gleaming. The voices of nightingales were in it, and many subtle odours seemed to fill the air of that noisome place as she trod the floor lightly as a feather in the wind; nor has any voice or sight of such beauty ever again been seen there, and Ainu Melko for all his power and majesty succumbed to the magic of that Elf-maid, and indeed even the eyelids of Lórien had grown heavy had he been there to see. Then did Melko fall forward drowzed, and sank at last in utter sleep down from his chair upon the floor, and his iron crown rolled away.

Suddenly Tinúviel ceased. In the hall no sound was heard save of slumbrous breath; even Beren slept beneath the very seat of Melko, but Tinúviel shook him so that he awoke at last. Then in fear and trembling he tore asunder his disguise and freeing himself from it leapt to his feet. Now does he draw that knife that he had from Tevildo's kitchens and he seizes the mighty iron crown, but Tinúviel could not move it and scarcely might the thews of Beren avail to turn it. Great is the frenzy of their fear as in that dark hall of sleeping evil Beren labours as noiselessly as may be to prise out a Silmaril with his knife. Now does he loosen the great central jewel and the sweat pours from his brow, but even as he forces it from the crown lo! his knife snaps with a loud crack.

Tinúviel smothers a cry thereat and Beren springs away with the one Silmaril in his hand, and the sleepers stir and Melko groans as though ill thoughts disturbed his dreams, and a black look comes upon his sleeping face. Content now with that one flashing gem those twain fled desperately from the hall, stumbling wildly down many dark passages till from the glimmering of grey light they knew they neared the gates – and behold! Karkaras lies across the threshold, awake once more and watchful.

Straightway Beren thrust himself before Tinúviel although she said him nay, and this proved in the end ill, for Tinúviel had not time to cast her spell of slumber over the beast again, ere seeing Beren he bared his teeth and growled angrily. "Wherefore this surliness, Karkaras?" said Tinúviel. "Wherefore this Gnome[10] who entered not and yet now issueth in haste?" quoth Knife-fang, and with that he leapt upon Beren, who struck straight between the wolf's eyes with his fist, catching for his throat with the other hand.

Then Karkaras seized that hand in his dreadful jaws, and it was the hand wherein Beren clasped the blazing Silmaril, and both hand and jewel Karkaras bit off and took into his red maw. Great was the agony of Beren and the fear and anguish of Tinúviel, yet even as they expect to feel the teeth of the wolf a new thing strange and terrible comes to pass. Behold now that Silmaril blazeth with a white and hidden fire of its own nature and is possessed of a fierce and holy magic — for did it not come from Valinor and the blessed realms, being fashioned with spells of the Gods and Gnomes before evil came there; and it doth not tolerate the touch of evil flesh or of unholy hand. Now cometh it into the foul body of Karkaras, and suddenly that beast is burnt with a terrible anguish and the howling of his pain is ghastly to hear as it echoeth in those rocky ways, so that all that sleeping court within awakes. Then did Tinúviel and Beren flee like the wind from the gates, yet was Karkaras far before them raging and in madness as a beast pursued by Balrogs; and after when they might draw breath Tinúviel wept over the maimed arm of Beren kissing it often, so that behold it bled not, and pain left it, and was healed by the tender healing of her love; yet was Beren ever after surnamed among all folk Ermabwed the One-handed, which in the language of the Lonely Isle is Elmavoitë.

Now however must they bethink them of escape — if such may be their fortune, and Tinúviel wrapped part of her dark mantle about Beren, and so for a while flitting by dusk and dark amid the hills they were seen by none, albeit Melko had raised all his Orcs of terror against them; and his fury at the rape of that jewel was greater than the Elves had ever seen it yet.

Even so it seems soon to them that the net of the hunters drew ever more tightly upon them, and though they had reached the edge of the more familiar woods and passed the glooms of the forest of Taurfuin, still were there many leagues of peril yet to pass between them and the caverns of the king, and even did they reach ever there it seemed like they would but draw the chase behind them thither and Melko's hate upon all that woodland folk. So great indeed was the hue and cry that Huan learnt of it far away, and he marvelled much at the daring of those twain, and still more that ever they had escaped from Angamandi.

Now goes he with many dogs through the woods hunting Orcs

and thanes of Tevildo, and many hurts he got thus, and many of them he slew or put to fear and flight, until one even at dusk the Valar brought him to a glade in that northward region of Artanor that was called afterward Nan Dumgorthin, the land of the dark idols, but that is a matter that concerns not this tale. Howbeit it was even then a dark land and gloomy and foreboding, and dread wandered beneath its lowering trees no less even than in Taurfuin; and those two Elves Tinúviel and Beren were lying therein weary and without hope, and Tinúviel wept but Beren was fingering his knife.

Now when Huan saw them he would not suffer them to speak or to tell any of their tale, but straightway took Tinúviel upon his mighty back and bade Beren run as best he could beside him, "for," said he, "a great company of the Orcs are drawing swiftly hither, and wolves are their trackers and their scouts." Now doth Huan's pack run about them, and they go very swiftly along quick and secret paths towards the homes of the folk of Tinwelint far away. Thus was it that they eluded the host of their enemies, but had nonetheless many an encounter afterward with wandering things of evil, and Beren slew an Orc that came nigh to dragging off Tinúviel, and that was a good deed. Seeing then that the hunt still pressed them close, once more did Huan lead them by winding ways, and dared not yet straightly to bring them to the land of the woodland fairies. So cunning however was his leading that at last after many days the chase fell far away, and no longer did they see or hear anything of the bands of Orcs; no goblins waylaid them nor did the howling of any evil wolves come upon the airs at night, and belike that was because already they had stepped within the circle of Gwendeling's magic that hid the paths from evil things and kept harm from the regions of the woodelves.

Then did Tinúviel breathe freely once more as she had not done since she fled from her father's halls, and Beren rested in the sun far from the glooms of Angband until the last bitterness of thraldom left him. Because of the light falling through green leaves and the whisper of clean winds and the song of birds once more are they wholly unafraid.

At last came there nevertheless a day whereon waking out of a deep slumber Beren started up as one who leaves a dream of happy things coming suddenly to his mind, and he said: "Farewell, O Huan, most trusty comrade, and thou, little Tinúviel, whom I love, fare thee well. This only I beg of thee, get thee now straight to the safety of thy home, and may good Huan lead thee. But I – lo,

I must away into the solitude of the woods, for I have lost that Silmaril which I had, and never dare I draw near to Angamandi more, wherefore neither will I enter the halls of Tinwelint." Then he wept to himself, but Tinúviel who was nigh and had hearkened to his musing came beside him and said: "Nay, now is my heart changed," and if thou dwellest in the woods, O Beren Ermabwed, then so will I, and if thou wilt wander in the wild places there will I wander also, or with thee or after thee: — yet never shall my father see me again save only if thou takest me to him." Then indeed was Beren glad at her sweet words, and fain would he have dwelt with her as a huntsman of the wild, but his heart smote him for all that she had suffered for him, and for her he put away his pride. Indeed she reasoned with him, saying it would be folly to be stubborn, and that her father would greet them with nought but joy, being glad to see his daughter yet alive — and "maybe," said she, "he will have shame that his jesting has given thy fair hand to the jaws of Karkaras." But Huan also she implored to return with them a space, for "my father owes thee a very great reward, O Huan," saith she, "an he loves his daughter at all."

So came it that those three set forward once again together, and came at last back to the woodlands that Tinúviel knew and loved nigh to the dwellings of her folk and to the deep halls of her home. Yet even as they approach they find fear and tumult among that people such as had not been for a long age, and asking some that wept before their doors they learned that ever since the day of Tinúviel's secret flight ill-fortune had befallen them. Lo, the king had been distraught with grief and had relaxed his ancient wariness and cunning; indeed his warriors had been sent hither and thither deep into the unwholesome woods searching for that maiden, and many had been slain or lost for ever, and war there was with Melko's servants about all their northern and eastern borders, so that the folk feared mightily lest that Ainu upraise his strength and come utterly to crush them and Gwendeling's magic have not the strength to withhold the numbers of the Orcs. "Behold," said they, "now is the worst of all befallen, for long has Queen Gwendeling sat aloof and smiled not nor spoken, looking as it were to a great distance with haggard eyes, and the web of her magic has blown thin about the woods, and the woods are dreary, for Dairon comes not back, neither is his music heard ever in the glades. Behold now the crown of all our evil tidings, for know that there has broken upon us raging from the halls of Evil a great grey wolf filled with an evil spirit, and he fares as though lashed by some hidden madness, and none are safe. Already has he slain many as he runs wildly snapping and yelling through the woods, so that the very banks of the stream that flows before the king's halls has become a lurking-place of danger. There comes the awful wolf oftentimes to drink, looking as the evil Prince himself with bloodshot eyes and tongue lolling out, and never can he slake his desire for water as though some inward fire devours him."

Then was Tinúviel sad at the thought of the unhappiness that had come upon her folk, and most of all was her heart bitter at the story of Dairon, for of this she had not heard any murmur before. Yet could she not wish Beren had come never to the lands of Artanor, and together they made haste to Tinwelint; and already to the Elves of the wood it seemed that the evil was at an end now that Tinúviel was come back among them unharmed. Indeed they scarce had hoped for that.

In great gloom do they find King Tinwelint, yet suddenly is his sorrow melted to tears of gladness, and Gwendeling sings again for joy when Tinúviel enters there and casting away her raiment of dark mist she stands before them in her pearly radiance of old. For a while all is mirth and wonder in that hall, and yet at length the king turns his eyes to Beren and says: "So thou hast returned too – bringing a Silmaril, beyond doubt, in recompense for all the ill thou hast wrought my land; or an thou hast not, I know not wherefore thou art here."

Then Tinúviel stamped her foot and cried so that the king and all about him wondered at her new and fearless mood: "For shame, my father – behold, here is Beren the brave whom thy jesting drove into dark places and foul captivity and the Valar alone saved from a bitter death. Methinks 'twould rather befit a king of the Eldar to reward him than revile him."

"Nay," said Beren, "the king thy father hath the right. Lord," said he, "I have a Silmaril in my hand even now."

"Show me then," said the king in amaze.

"That I cannot," said Beren, "for my hand is not here"; and he held forth his maimed arm.

Then was the king's heart turned to him by reason of his stout and courteous demeanour, and he bade Beren and Tinúviel relate to him all that had befallen either of them, and he was eager to hearken, for he did not fully comprehend the meaning of Beren's words. When however he had heard all yet more was his heart turned to Beren, and he marvelled at the love that had awakened in the heart of Tinúviel so that she had done greater deeds and more daring than any of the warriors of his folk.

"Never again," said he, "O Beren I beg of thee, leave this court nor the side of Tinúviel, for thou art a great Elf and thy name will ever be great among the kindreds." Yet Beren answered him proudly, and said: "Nay, O King, I hold to my word and thine, and I will get thee that Silmaril or ever I dwell in peace in thy halls." And the king entreated him to journey no more into the dark and unknown realms, but Beren said: "No need is there thereof, for behold that jewel is even now nigh to thy caverns," and he made clear to Tinwelint that that beast that ravaged his land was none other than Karkaras, the wolfward of Melko's gates — and this was not known to all, but Beren knew it taught by Huan, whose cunning in the reading of track and slot was greatest among all the hounds, and therein are none of them unskilled. Huan indeed was with Beren now in the halls, and when those twain spoke of a chase and a great hunt he begged to be in that deed; and it was granted gladly. Now do those three prepare themselves to harry that beast, that all the folk be rid of the terror of the wolf, and Beren kept his word, bringing a Silmaril to shine once more in Elfinesse. King Tinwelint himself led that chase, and Beren was beside him, and Mablung the heavy-handed, chief of the king's thanes, leaped up and grasped a spear[12] — a mighty weapon captured in battle with the distant Orcs — and with those three stalked Huan mightiest of dogs, but others they would not take according to the desire of the king, who said: "Four is enough for the slaying even of the Hell-wolf" — but only those who had seen knew how fearsome was that beast, nigh as large as a horse among Men, and so great was the ardour of his breath that it scorched whatsoever it touched. About the hour of sunrise they set forth, and soon after Huan espied a new slot beside the stream, not far from the king's doors, "and," quoth he, "this is the print of Karkaras." Thereafter they followed that stream all day, and at many places its banks were new-trampled and torn and the water of the pools that lay about it was fouled as though some beasts possessed of madness had rolled and fought there not long before.

Now sinks the sun and fades beyond the western trees and darkness is creeping down from Hisilómë so that the light of the forest dies. Even so come they to a place where the spoor swerves from the stream or perchance is lost in its waters and Huan may no longer follow it; and here therefore they encamp, sleeping in turns beside the stream, and the early night wears away.

Suddenly in Beren's watch a sound of great terror leaped up from far away – a howling as of seventy maddened wolves – then lo! the brushwood cracks and saplings snap as the terror draweth near, and Beren knows that Karkaras is upon them. Scarce had he time to rouse the others, and they were but just sprung up and half-awake, when a great form loomed in the wavering moonlight filtering there, and it was fleeing like one mad, and its course was bent towards the water. Thereat Huan gave tongue, and straightway the beast swerved aside towards them, and foam was dripping from his jaws and a red light shining from his eyes, and his face was marred with mingled terror and with wrath. No sooner did he leave the trees than Huan rushed upon him fearless of heart, but he with a mighty leap sprang right over that great dog, for all his fury was kindled suddenly against Beren whom he recognized as he stood behind, and to his dark mind it seemed that there was the cause of all his agony. Then Beren thrust swiftly upward with a spear into his throat, and Huan leapt again and had him by a hind leg, and Karkaras fell as a stone, for at that same moment the king's spear found his heart, and his evil spirit gushed forth and sped howling faintly as it fared over the dark hills to Mandos; but Beren lay under him crushed beneath his weight. Now they roll back that carcase and fall to cutting it open, but Huan licks Beren's face whence blood is flowing. Soon is the truth of Beren's words made clear, for the vitals of the wolf are half-consumed as though an inner fire had long been smouldering there, and suddenly the night is filled with a wondrous lustre, shot with pale and secret colours, as Mablung[13] draws forth the Silmaril. Then holding it out he said: "Behold O King,"[14] but Tinwelint said: "Nay, never will I handle it save only if Beren give it to me." But Huan said: "And that seems like never to be, unless ye tend him swiftly, for methinks he is hurt sorely"; and Mablung and the king were ashamed.

Therefore now they raised Beren gently up and tended him and washed him, and he breathed, but he spoke not nor opened his eyes, and when the sun arose and they had rested a little they bore him as softly as might be upon a bier of boughs back through the woodlands; and nigh midday they drew near the homes of the folk again, and then were they deadly weary, and Beren had not moved nor spoken, but groaned thrice.

There did all the people flock to meet them when their approach was noised among them, and some bore them meat and cool drinks and salves and healing things for their hurts, and but for the harm that Beren had met grēat indeed had been their joy. Now then they covered the leafy boughs whereon he lay with soft raiment, and they bore him away to the halls of the king, and there was Tinúviel awaiting them in great distress; and she fell upon Beren's breast and wept and kissed him, and he awoke and knew her, and after Mablung gave him that Silmaril, and he lifted it above him gazing at its beauty, ere he said slowly and with pain: "Behold, O King, I give thee the wondrous jewel thou didst desire, and it is but a little thing found by the wayside, for once methinks thou hadst one beyond thought more beautiful, and she is now mine." Yet even as he spake the shadows of Mandos lay upon his face, and his spirit fled in that hour to the margin of the world, and Tinúviel's tender kisses called him not back.'

Then did Vëannë suddenly cease speaking, and Eriol sadly said: 'A tale of ruth for so sweet a maid to tell'; but behold, Vëannë wept, and not for a while did she say: 'Nay, that is not all the tale; but here endeth all that I rightly know,' and other children there spake, and one said: 'Lo, I have heard that the magic of Tinúviel's tender kisses healed Beren, and recalled his spirit from the gates of Mandos, and long time he dwelt among the Lost Elves wandering the glades in love with sweet Tinúviel.' But another said: 'Nay, that was not so, O Ausir, and if thou wilt listen I will tell the true and wondrous tale; for Beren died there in Tinúviel's arms even as Vëannë has said, and Tinúviel crushed with sorrow and finding no comfort or light in all the world followed him swiftly down those dark ways that all must tread alone. Now her beauty and tender loveliness touched even the cold heart of Mandos, so that he suffered her to lead Beren forth once more into the world, nor has this ever been done since to Man or Elf, and many songs and stories are there of the prayer of Tinúviel before the throne of Mandos that I remember not right well. Yet said Mandos to those twain: "Lo, O Elves, it is not to any life of perfect joy that I dismiss you, for such may no longer be found in all the world where sits Melko of the evil heart – and know ye that ye will become mortal even as Men, and when ye fare hither again it will be for ever, unless the Gods summon you indeed to Valinor." Nonetheless those twain departed hand in hand, and they fared together through the northern woods, and oftentimes were they seen dancing magic dances down the hills, and their name became heard far and wide.'

And thereat that boy ceased, and Vëannë said: 'Aye, and they did more than dance, for their deeds afterward were very great, and many tales are there thereof that thou must hear, O Eriol Melinon, upon another time of tale-telling. For those twain it is that stories name i·Cuilwarthon, which is to say the dead that live again, and they became mighty fairies in the lands about the north of Sirion. Behold now all is ended – and doth it like thee?' But Eriol said: 'Indeed 'tis a wondrous tale, such as I looked not to hear from the lips of the little maids of Mar Vanwa Tyaliéva,' but Vëannë answered him: 'Nay, but I fashioned it not with words of myself; but it is dear to me – and indeed all the children know of the deeds that it relates – and I have learned it by heart, reading it in the great books, and I do not comprehend all that is set therein.'

'Neither do I,' said Eriol – but suddenly cried Ausir: 'Behold, Eriol, Vëannë has never told thee what befell Huan; nor how he would take no rewards from Tinwelint nor dwell nigh him, but wandered forth again grieving for Tinúviel and Beren. On a time he fell in with Mablung[15] who aided in the chase, and was now fallen much to hunting in lonely parts; and the twain hunted together as friends until the days of Glorund the Drake and of Túrin Turambar, when once more Huan found Beren and played his part in the great deeds of the Nauglafring, the Necklace of the Dwarves.'

'Nay, how could I tell all this,' said Vëannë, 'for behold it is time for the evening meat already'; and soon after the great gong rang.

The second version of the Tale of Tinúviel

As already mentioned (p. 3), there exists a revised version of part of the tale in a typescript (made by my father). This follows the manuscript version closely or very closely on the whole, and in no way alters the style or air of the former; it is therefore unnecessary to give this second version *in extenso*. But the typescript does in places introduce interesting changes, and these are given below (the pages of the corresponding passages in the manuscript version are given in the margin).

The title in the typescript (which begins with the *Link* passage already given, pp. 4–7) was originally 'The Tale of Tynwfiel, Princess of Dor Athro', which was changed to 'The Tale of Tinúviel, the Dancer of Doriath'.

(8)   'Who then was Tinúviel?' said Eriol. 'Knowst thou not,' said Ausir, 'she was the daughter of Singoldo, king of Artanor?' 'Hush

thee, Ausir,' said Vëannë, 'this is my tale, and 'tis a tale of the Gnomes, wherefore I beg that thou fill not Eriol's ear with thy Elfin names. Lo! I will tell this tale only, for did I not see Melian and Tinúviel once long ago with my own eyes when journeying by the Way of Dreams?'

'What then was Queen Melian like,' quoth Eriol, 'if thou hast seen her, O Vëannë?'

'Slender and very dark of hair,' said she, 'and her skin was white and pale, but her eyes shone seeming to hold great depths. Clad she was in filmy garments most lovely yet of the hue of night, jet-spangled and girt with silver. If ever she sang or if ever she danced, dreams and slumbers passed over the heads of those that were nigh, making them heavy as it were with a strong wine of sleep. Indeed she was a sprite that, escaping from Lórien's gardens before even Kôr was built, wandered in the wild places of the world and in every lonely wood. Nightingales fared with her singing about her as she went — and 'twas the song of these birds that smote the ears of Thingol as he marched at the head of that second[16] tribe of the Eldalië which afterward became the Shore-land Pipers, the Solosimpi of the Isle. Now had they come a great way from dim Palisor, and wearily the companies laboured behind the swift-footed horse of Oromë, wherefore the music of the magic birds of Melian seemed to him full of all solace, more beautiful than other melodies of Earth, and he strayed aside for a moment, as he thought, from the host, seeking in the dark trees whence it might come.

And it is said that it was not a moment that he hearkened, but many years, and vainly his people sought him, until at length they must perforce follow Oromë upon Tol Eressëa, and be borne thereon far away leaving him listening to the birds enchanted in the woods of Aryador. That was the first sorrow of the Solosimpi, that after were many; but Ilúvatar in memory of Thingol set a seed of music in the hearts of that folk above all kindreds of the Earth save only the Gods, and after, as all story tells, it blossomed wondrously upon the isle and in glorious Valinor.

Little sorrow, however, had Thingol; for after a little, as him seemed, he came upon Melian lying on a bed of leaves . . .

*

(9)   Long thereafter, as now thou knowest, Melko brake once more into the world from Valinor, and wellnigh all beings therein came under his foul thraldom; nor were the Lost Elves free, nor the errant Gnomes that wandered the mountainous places seeking their stolen treasury. Yet some few there were that led by mighty kings still defied that evil one in fast and hidden places, and if

Turgon King of Gondolin was the most glorious of these, for a while the most mighty and the longest free was Thingol of the Woods.

Now in the after-days of Sunshine and Moonsheen still dwelt Thingol in Artanor and ruled a numerous and hardy folk drawn from all the tribes of ancient Elfinesse – for neither he nor his people went to the dread Battle of Unnumbered Tears – a matter which toucheth not this tale. Yet was his lordship greatly increased after that most bitter field by fugitives seeking a leader and a home. Hidden was his dwelling thereafter from the vision and knowledge of Melko by the cunning magics of Melian the fay, and she wove spells about all the paths that led thereto, so that none but the children of the Eldalië might tread them without straying. Thus was the king guarded against all evils save treachery alone; his halls were built in a deep cavern, vaulted immeasurable, that knew no other entrance than a rocky door, mighty, pillared with stone, and shadowed by the loftiest and most ancient trees in all the shaggy forests of Artanor. A great stream was there that fared a dark and silent course in the deep woods, and this flowed wide and swift before that doorway, so that all who would enter that portal must first cross a bridge hung by the Noldoli of Thingol's service across that water – and narrow it was and strongly guarded. In no wise ill were those forest lands, although not utterly distant were the Iron Mountains and black Hisilómë beyond them where dwelt the strange race of Men, and thrall-Noldoli laboured, and few free-Eldar went.

Two children had Thingol then, Dairon and Tinúviel . . .

*

(10)   'her mother was a fay, a child of Lórien' for manuscript 'her mother was a fay, a daughter of the Gods'.

*

(11)   'Now Beren was a Gnome, son of Egnor the forester' as in manuscript; but *Egnor* changed to *Barahir*. This however was a much later and as it were casual change; Beren's father was still Egnor in 1925.

*

(11)   Manuscript version 'and all the Elves of the woodland thought of the Gnomes of Dor Lómin as treacherous creatures, cruel and faithless' is omitted in the typescript.

*

(13)   *Angband* for manuscript *Angamandi*, and throughout.

*

(14)   Many a combat and an escape had he in those days, and he slew
therein more than once both wolf and the Orc that rode thereon
with nought but an ashen club that he bore; and other perils and
adventures . . .

*

(15)   But Melko looking wroth upon him asked: "How hast thou, O
thrall, dared to fare thus out of the land where thy folk dwells at
my behest, and to wander in the great woods unbidden, leaving
the labours to which thou hast been set?" Then answered Beren
that he was no runagate thrall, but came of a kindred of the
Gnomes that dwelt in Aryador where were many of the folk of
Men. Then was Melko yet more wroth, saying: "Here have we a
plotter of deep treacheries against Melko's lordship, and one
worthy of the tortures of the Balrogs" – for he sought ever to
destroy the friendship and intercourse of Elves and Men, lest they
forget the Battle of Unnumbered Tears and once more arise in
wrath against him. But Beren seeing his peril answered: "Think
not, O most mighty Belcha Morgoth (for such be his names
among the Gnomes), that could be so; for, an it were, then should
I not be here unaided and alone. No friendship has Beren son of
Egnor for the kindred of Men; nay indeed, wearying utterly of the
lands infested by that folk he has wandered out of Aryador.
Whither then should he go but to Angband? For many a great tale
has his father made to him aforetime of thy splendour and thy
glory. Lo, lord, albeit I am no renegade thrall, still do I desire
nothing so much as to serve thee in what small manner I may."
Little of truth was therein, and indeed his father Egnor was the
chiefest foe of Melko in all the kin of the Gnomes that still were
free, save only Turgon king of Gondolin and the sons of Fëanor,
and long days of friendship had he known with the folk of Men,
what time he was brother in arms to Úrin the steadfast; but in
those days he bore another name and Egnor was nought for
Melko. The truth, however, did Beren then tell, saying that he
was a great huntsman, swift and cunning to shoot or snare or to
outrun all birds and beasts. "I was lost unawares in a part of the
hills that were not known to me, O lord," he said, "the while I was
hunting; and wandering far I came to strange lands and knew no
other rede of safety save to fare to Angband, that all can find who
see the black hills of the north from afar. I would myself have fared
to thee and begged of thee some humble office (as a winner of
meats for thy table, perchance) had not these Orcs seized me and
tormented me unjustly."
        Now the Valar must have inspired that speech, or maybe it was
a spell of cunning words cast upon him in compassion by Melian as
he fled from the hall; for indeed it saved his life . . .

Subsequently a part of this passage was emended on the type-script, to read:

. . . and long days of friendship had he known with the folk of Men (as had Beren himself thereafter as brother in arms to Úrin the Steadfast); but in those days the Orcs named him Rog the Fleet, and the name of Egnor was nought to Melko.

At the same time the words 'Now the Valar must have inspired that speech' were changed to 'Now the Valar inspired that speech'.

*

(15)   Thus was Beren set by Melko as a thrall to The Prince of Cats, whom the Gnomes have called Tiberth Bridhon Miaugion, but the Elves Tevildo.

Subsequently *Tiberth* appears for MS *Tevildo* throughout, and in one place the full name *Tiberth Bridhon Miaugion* appears again. In the MS the Gnomish name is *Tifil*.

*

(17)   . . . getting nought but a bitten finger for his toil. Then was Tiberth wroth, and said: "Thou hast lied to my lord, O Gnome, and art fitter to be a scullion than a huntsman, who canst not catch even the mice about my halls." Evil thereafter were his days in the power of Tiberth; for a scullion they made him, and unending labour he had in the hewing of wood and drawing of water, and in the menial services of that noisome abode. Often too was he tormented by the cats and other evil beasts of their company, and when, as happened at whiles, there was an Orc-feast in those halls, he would ofttimes be set to the roasting of birds and other meats upon spits before the mighty fires in Melko's dungeons, until he swooned for the overwhelming heat; yet he knew himself fortunate beyond all hope in being yet alive among those cruel foes of Gods and Elves. Seldom got he food or sleep himself, and he became haggard and half-blind, so that he wished often that never straying out of the wild free places of Hisilómë he had not even caught sight afar off of the vision of Tinúviel.

*

(17)   But Melian laughed not, nor said aught thereto; for in many things was she wise and forewise – yet nonetheless it was a thing unthought in a mad dream that any Elf, still less a maiden, the daughter of that king who had longest defied Melko, should fare alone even to the borders of that sorrowful country amid which lies Angband and the Hells of Iron. Little love was there between the woodland Elves and the folk of Angband even in those days before the Battle of Unnumbered Tears when Melko's power was not grown to its full, and he veiled his designs, and spread his net

of lies. "No help wilt thou get therein of me, little one," said she; "for even if magic and destiny should bring thee safe out of that foolhardiness, yet should many and great things come thereof, and on some many sorrows, and my rede is that thou tell never thy father of thy desire."

But this last word of Melian's did Thingol coming unaware overhear, and they must perforce tell him all, and he was so wroth when he heard it that Tinúviel wished that never had her thoughts been revealed even to her mother.

*

(18)   Indeed I have no love for him, for he has destroyed our play together, our music and our dancing." But Tinúviel said: "I ask it not for him, but for myself, and for that very play of ours together aforetime." And Dairon said: "And for thy sake I say thee nay"; and they spake no more thereof together, but Dairon told the king of what Tinúviel had desired of him, fearing lest that dauntless maiden fare away to her death in the madness of her heart.

*

(18)   . . . he might not shut his daughter for ever in the caves, where the light was only that of torches dim and flickering.

*

(19)   The names of all the tallest and longest things upon Earth were set in that song: the beards of the Indrafangs, the tail of Carcaras, the body of Glorund the drake, the bole of Hirilorn, and the sword of Nan she named, nor did she forget the chain Angainu that Aulë and Tulkas made, or the neck of Gilim the giant that is taller than many elm trees; . . .

Carcaras is spelt thus subsequently in the typescript.

*

(20)   . . . as fast as her dancing feet would flit.

Now when the guards awoke it was late in the morning, and they fled away nor dared to bear the tidings to their lord; and Dairon it was bore word of the escape of Tinúviel to Thingol, for he had met the folk that ran in amazement from the ladders which each morning were lifted to her door. Great was the mingled grief and wrath of the king, and all the deep places of his court were in uproar, and all the woods were ringing with the search; but Tinúviel was already far away dancing madly through the dark woods towards the gloomy foothills and the Mountains of Night. 'Tis said that Dairon sped swiftest and furthest in pursuit, but was wrapped in the deceit of those far places, and became utterly lost, and came never back to Elfinesse, but turned towards Palisor; and there he plays subtle magic musics still, wistful and lonely in the woods and forests of the south.

Now fared Tinúviel forward, and a sudden dread overtook her at the thought of what she had dared to do, and of what lay before her. Then did she turn back for a while, and wept, wishing that Dairon were with her. It is said that he was not indeed at that time far off, and wandered lost in Taurfuin, the Forest of Night, where after Túrin slew Beleg by mishap. Nigh was Tinúviel to those evil places; but she entered not that dark region, and the Valar set a new hope in her heart, so that she pressed on once more.

*

(21) Seldom was any of the cats slain indeed; for in those days they were mightier far in valour and in strength than they have been since those things befell that thou art soon to learn, mightier even than the tawny cats of the southern lands where the sun burns hot. No less too was their skill in climbing and in hiding, and their fleetness was that of an arrow, yet were the free dogs of the northern woods marvellously valiant and knew no fear, and great enmity was between them, and some of those hounds were held in dread even by the greatest of the cats. None, however, did Tiberth fear save only Huan the lord of the Hounds of Hisilómë. So swift was Huan that on a time he had fallen upon Tiberth as he hunted alone in the woods, and pursuing him had overtaken him and nigh rent the fur of his neck from him ere he was rescued by a host of Orcs that heard his cries. Huan got him many hurts in that battle ere he won away, but the wounded pride of Tiberth lusted ever for his death.

Great therefore was the good fortune that befell Tinúviel in meeting with Huan in the woods; and this she did in a little glade nigh to the forest's borders, where the first grasslands begin that are nourished by the upper waters of the river Sirion. Seeing him she was mortally afraid and turned to flee; but in two swift leaps Huan overtook her. Speaking softly the deep tongue of the Lost Elves he bade her be not afeared, and "wherefore," said he, "do I see an Elfin maiden, and one most fair, wandering thus nigh to the places of the Prince of Evil Heart?

*

(22) What is thy thought, O Huan?"

"Little counsel have I for thee," said he, "save that thou goest with all speed back to Artanor and thy father's halls, and I will accompany thee all the way, until those lands be reached that the magic of Melian the Queen does encompass." "That will I never do," said she, "while Beren liveth here, forgotten of his friends." "I thought that such would be thy answer," said he, "but if thou wilt still go forward with thy mad quest, then no counsel have I for thee save a desperate and a perilous one: we must make now all speed towards the ill places of Tiberth's abiding that are yet far off. I will guide thee thither by the most secret ways, and when we are come there thou must creep alone, if thou hast the heart, to the dwelling of that prince at an hour nigh noon when he and most of his household lie drowsing upon the terraces before his gates. There thou mayst perchance discover, if fortune is very kind, whether Beren be indeed within that ill place as thy mother said to thee. But lo, I will lie not far from the foot of the mount whereon Tiberth's hall is built, and thou must say to Tiberth so soon as thou seest him, be Beren there or be he not, that thou hast stumbled upon Huan of the Dogs lying sick of great wounds in a withered dale without his gates. Fear not overmuch, for herein wilt thou both do my pleasure and further thine own desires, as well as may be; nor do I think that when Tiberth hears thy tidings thou wilt be in any peril thyself for a time. Only do thou not direct him to the place that I shall show to thee; thou must offer to guide him thither thyself. Thus thou shalt get free again of his evil house, and shalt see what I contrive for the Prince of Cats." Then did Tinúviel shudder at the thought of what lay before, but she said that this rede would she sooner take than to return home, and they set forth straightway by secret pathways through the woods, and by winding trails over the bleak and stony lands that lay beyond.

At last on a day at morn they came to a wide dale hollowed like a bowl among the rocks. Deep were its sides, but nought grew there save low bushes of scanty leaves and withered grass. "This is the Withered Dale that I spake of," said Huan. "Yonder is the cave where the great

Here the typescript version of the *Tale of Tinúviel* ends, at the foot of a page. I think it is improbable that any more of this version was made.

NOTES

1   For earlier references to Olórë Mallë, the Way of Dreams, see I.18, 27; 211, 225.

2   The distinction made here between the Elves (who call the queen *Wendelin*) and, by implication, the Gnomes (who call her

Gwendeling) is even more explicit in the typescript version, p. 42 ('tis a tale of the *Gnomes*, wherefore I beg that thou fill not Eriol's ears with thy *Elfin* names') and p. 45 ('The Prince of Cats, whom the *Gnomes* have called Tiberth Bridhon Miaugion, but the *Elves* Tevildo'). See I.50–1.

3   The manuscript as originally written read: 'Now Beren was a Gnome, son of a thrall of Melko's, some have said, that laboured in the darker places . . .' See note 4.

4   The manuscript as originally written read: 'I Beren of the Noldoli, son of Egnor the huntsman . . .' See note 3.

5   From this point, and continuing to the words 'forests of the south' on p. 21, the text is written on detached pages placed in the notebook. There is no rejected material corresponding to this passage. It is possible that it existed, and was removed from the book and lost; but, though the book is in a decayed state, it does not seem that any pages were removed here, and I think it more likely that my father simply found himself short of space, as he wrote over the original, erased, version, and (almost certainly) expanded it as he went.

6   The text as originally written read: 'came never back to Ellu, but plays . . .' (for *Ellu* see *Changes to Names* below). As a result of the interpolation 'but turned towards Palisor' Palisor is placed in the south of the world. In the tale of *The Coming of the Elves* (I.114) Palisor is called 'the midmost region' (see also the drawing of the 'World-Ship', I.84), and it seems possible that the word 'south' should have been changed; but it remains in the typescript (p. 47).

7   The *Tale of Turambar*, though composed after the *Tale of Tinúviel*, was in existence when *Tinúviel* was rewritten (see p. 69).

8   From 'amazed utterly' to 'if Tinúviel were not there' (p. 30) the text is written on an inserted page; see note 5 – here also the underlying textual situation is obscure.

9   A short passage of earlier text in pencil becomes visible here, ending: '. . . and Tinúviel grew to long sorely for Wendelin her mother and for the sight of Linwë and for Kapalen making music in pleasant glades.' *Kapalen* must be a name preceding *Tifanto*, itself preceding *Dairon* (see *Changes to Names* below).

10   *this Gnome*: original reading *this man*. This was a slip, but a significant slip (see p. 52), in all probability. It is possible that 'man' was used here, as occasionally elsewhere (e.g. p. 18 'as high as men could fashion their longest ladders', where the reference is to the Elves of Artanor), to mean 'male Elf', but in that case there would seem no reason to change it.

11   Struck out here in the manuscript: 'Beren of the Hills'.

12   'Mablung the heavy-handed, chief of the king's thanes, leaped up and grasped a spear' replaced the original reading 'Tifanto cast aside his pipe and grasped a spear'. Originally the name of Tinúviel's

brother was *Tifanto* throughout the tale. See notes 13–15, and the Commentary, p. 59.

13   *Mablung* replaced *Tifanto*, and again immediately below; see note 12.

14   'O King' replaced 'O father'; see note 12.

15   In this place *Mablung* was the form as first written; see the Commentary, p. 59.

16   It is essential to the narrative of the Coming of the Elves that the Solosimpi were the third and last of the three tribes; 'second' here can only be a slip, if a surprising one.

Changes made to names in
The Tale of Tinúviel

(i)   Manuscript Version

Ilfiniol < *Elfriniol*. In the typescript text the name is *Ilfrin*. See pp. 201–2.

Tinwë Linto, Tinwelint   In the opening passage of the tale (p. 8), where Ausir and Vëannë differ on the forms of Tinwelint's name, the MS is very confused and it is impossible to understand the succeeding stages. Throughout the tale, as originally written, Vëannë calls Tinwelint *Tinto Ellu* or *Ellu*, but in the argument at the beginning it is Ausir who calls him *Tinto Ellu* while Vëannë calls him *Tinto'ellon*. *(Tinto) Ellu* is certainly an 'Elvish' form, but it is corrected throughout the tale to the Gnomish *Tinwelint*, while Ausir's *Tinto Ellu* at the beginning is corrected to *Tinwë Linto*. (At the third occurrence of *Tinwë* in the opening passage the name as originally written was *Linwë*: see I.130.)

In the tales of *The Coming of the Elves* and *The Theft of Melko* in Part One *Ellu* is the name of the second lord of the Solosimpi chosen in Tinwelint's place (afterwards Olwë), but at both occurrences (I.120, 141) this is a later addition (I.130 note 5, 155). Many years later *Ellu* again became Thingol's name (Sindarin *Elu Thingol*, Quenya *Elwë Singollo*, in *The Silmarillion*).

Gwendeling   As the tale was originally written, *Wendelin* was the name throughout (*Wendelin* is found in tales given in Part One, emended from *Tindriel*: I.106–7, 131). It was later changed throughout to the Gnomish form *Gwendeling* (found in the early Gnomish dictionary, I.273, itself changed later to *Gwedhiling*) except in the mouth of Ausir, who uses the 'Elvish' form *Wendelin* (p. 8).

Dairon   < *Tifanto* throughout. For the change of *Tifanto* > *Mablung* at the end of the tale (notes 12–14 above) see the Commentary, p. 59, and for the name *Kapalen* preceding *Tifanto* see note 9.

Dor Lómin   < *Aryador* (p. 11). In the tale of *The Coming of the*

Elves it is said (I.119) that Aryador was the name of Hisilómë among Men; for *Dor Lómin – Hisilómë* see I.112. At subsequent occurrences in this tale *Aryador* was not changed.

Angband was originally twice written, and in one of these cases it was changed to *Angamandi*, in the other (p. 35) allowed to stand; in all other instances *Angamandi* was the form first written. In the manuscript version of the tale Vëannë does not make consistent use of Gnomish or 'Elvish' forms: thus she says *Tevildo* (not *Tifil*), *Angamandi*, *Gwendeling* (< *Wendelin*), *Tinwelint* (< *Tinto (Ellu)*). In the typescript version, on the other hand, Vëannë says *Tiberth*, *Angband*, *Melian* (< *Gwenethlin*), *Thingol* (< *Tinwelint*).

Hirilorn, the Queen of Trees < *Golosbrindi, the Queen of the Forest* (p. 18); *Hirilorn* < *Golosbrindi* at subsequent occurrences.

Uinen < *Önen* (or possibly *Únen*).

Egnor bo-Rimion < *Egnor go-Rimion*. In the tales previously given the patronymic prefix is *go-* (I.146, 155).

Tinwelint < *Tinthellon* (p. 35, the only case). Cf. *Tinto'ellon* mentioned above under *Tinwë Linto*.

i·Cuilwarthon < *i·Guilwarthon*.

(ii)   Typescript Version

Tinúviel < *Tynwfiel* in the title and at every occurrence until the passage corresponding to MS version p. 11 'yet now did he see Tinúviel dancing in the twilight'; there and subsequently the form typed was *Tinúviel*.

Singoldo < *Tinwë Linto* (p. 41).

Melian < *Gwenethlin* at every occurrence until the passage corresponding to MS version p. 12 'the stateliness of Queen Gwendeling'; there and subsequently the form typed was *Melian*.

Thingol < *Tinwelint* at every occurrence until the passage corresponding to MS version p. 12 'by winding paths to the abode of Tinwelint'; there and subsequently the form typed was *Thingol*.

For *Egnor* > *Barahir* see p. 43.

Commentary on
The Tale of Tinúviel

§1.   *The primary narrative*

In this section I shall consider only the conduct of the main story, and leave for the moment such questions as the wider history implied in it, Tinwelint's people and his dwelling, or the geography of the lands that appear in the story.

The story of Beren's coming upon Tinúviel in the moonlit glade in its earliest recorded form (pp. 11–12) was never changed in its central image; and it should be noticed that the passage in *The Silmarillion* (p. 165) is an extremely concentrated and exalted rendering of the scene: many elements not mentioned there were never in fact lost. In a very late reworking of the passage in the *Lay of Leithian**** the hemlocks and the white moths still appear, and Daeron the minstrel is present when Beren comes to the glade. But there are nonetheless the most remarkable differences; and the chief of these is of course that Beren was here no mortal Man, but an Elf, one of the Noldoli, and the absolutely essential element of the story of Beren and Lúthien is not present. It will be seen later (pp. 71–2, 139) that this was not originally so, however: in the now lost (because erased) first form of the *Tale of Tinúviel* he had been a Man (it is for this reason that I have said that the reading *man* in the manuscript (see p. 33 and note 10), later changed to *Gnome*, is a 'significant slip'). Several years after the composition of the tale in the form in which we have it he became a Man again, though at that time (1925–6) my father appears to have hesitated long on the matter of the elvish or mortal nature of Beren.

In the tale there is, necessarily, a quite different reason for the hostility and distrust shown to Beren in Artanor (Doriath) – namely that 'the Elves of the woodland thought of the Gnomes of Dor Lómin as treacherous creatures, cruel and faithless' (see below, p. 65). It seems clear that at this time the history of Beren and his father (Egnor) was only very sketchily devised; there is in any case no hint of the story of the outlaw band led by his father and its betrayal by Gorlim the Unhappy (*The Silmarillion* pp. 162 ff.) before the first form of the *Lay of Leithian*, where the story appears fully formed (the Lay was in being to rather beyond this point by the late summer of 1925). But an association of Beren's father (changed to Beren himself) with Úrin (Húrin) as 'brother in arms' is mentioned in the typescript version of the tale (pp. 44–5); according to the latest of the outlines for *Gilfanon's Tale* (I.240) 'Úrin and Egnor marched with countless battalions' (against the forces of Melko).

In the old story, Tinúviel had no meetings with Beren before the day when he boldly accosted her at last, and it was at that very time that she led him to Tinwelint's cave; they were not lovers, Tinúviel knew nothing of Beren but that he was enamoured of her dancing, and it seems that she brought him before her father as a matter of courtesy, the natural thing to do. The betrayal of Beren to Thingol by Daeron (*The Silmarillion* p. 166) therefore has no place in the old story – there is nothing to betray; and indeed it is not shown in the tale that Dairon knew anything

---

* The long unfinished poem in rhyming couplets in which is told the story of Beren and Lúthien Tinúviel; composed in 1925-31, but parts of it substantially rewritten many years later.

whatsoever of Beren before Tinúviel led him into the cave, beyond having once seen his face in the moonlight.

Despite these radical differences in the narrative structure, it is remarkable how many features of the scene in Tinwelint's hall (pp. 12–13), when Beren stood before the king, endured, while all the inner significance was shifted and enlarged. To the beginning go back, for instance, Beren's abashment and silence, Tinúviel's answering for him, the sudden rising of his courage and uttering of his desire without preamble or hesitation. But the tone is altogether lighter and less grave than it afterwards became; in the jeering laughter of Tinwelint, who treats the matter as a jest and Beren as a benighted fool, there is no hint of what is explicit in the later story: 'Thus he wrought the doom of Doriath, and was ensnared within the curse of Mandos' (*The Silmarillion* p. 167). The Silmarils are indeed famous, and they have a holy power (p. 34), but the fate of the world is not bound up with them (*The Silmarillion* p. 67); Beren is an Elf, if of a feared and distrusted people, and his request lacks the deepest dimension of outrage; and he and Tinúviel are not lovers.

In this passage is the first mention of the Iron Crown of Melko, and the setting of the Silmarils in the Crown; and here again is a detail that was never lost: 'Never did this crown leave his head' (cf. *The Silmarillion* p. 81: 'That crown he never took from his head, though its weight became a deadly weariness').

But from this point Vëannë's story diverges in an altogether unexpected fashion from the later narrative. At no other place in the *Lost Tales* is the subsequent transformation more remarkable than in this, the precursor of the story of the capture of Beren and Felagund and their companions by Sauron the Necromancer, the imprisonment and death of all save Beren in the dungeons of Tol-in-Gaurhoth (the Isle of Werewolves in the river Sirion), and the rescue of Beren and overthrow of Sauron by Lúthien and Huan.

Most notably, what may be referred to as 'the Nargothrond Element' is entirely absent, and in so far as it already existed had as yet made no contact with the story of Beren and Tinúviel (for Nargothrond, not yet so named, at this period see pp. 81, 123–4). Beren has no ring of Felagund, he has no companions on his northward journey, and there is no relationship between (on the one hand) the story of his capture, his speech with Melko, and his dispatch to the house of Tevildo, and (on the other) the events of the later narrative whereby Beren and the band of Elves out of Nargothrond found themselves in Sauron's dungeon. Indeed, all the complex background of legend, of battles and rivalries, oaths and alliances, out of which the story of Beren and Lúthien arises in *The Silmarillion*, is very largely absent. The castle of the Cats 'is' the tower of Sauron on Tol-in-Gaurhoth, but only in the sense that it occupies the same 'space' in the narrative: beyond this there is no point in seeking even shadowy resemblances between the two establishments. The monstrous gormandising cats, their kitchens and their sunning terraces, and their engagingly Elvish-feline names (*Miaugion*, *Miaulë*, *Meoita*) all disappeared without trace. Did Tevildo? It would scarcely be true, I think, to say even that Sauron 'originated' in a cat: in the next phase of the legends the Necromancer (Thû) has no feline attributes. On the other hand it would be wrong to regard it as a simple matter of *replacement* (Thû stepping into the narrative place vacated by Tevildo) without any element of *transformation* of what was previously there. Tevildo's immediate successor is 'the Lord of Wolves', himself a werewolf, and he retains the Tevildo-trait of hating Huan more than any other creature in the world. Tevildo was 'an evil fay in beastlike shape' (p. 29); and the battle between the two great beasts, the hound against the werewolf (originally the hound against the demon in feline form) was never lost.

When the tale returns to Tinúviel in Artanor the situation is quite the reverse: for the story of her imprisonment in the house in Hirilorn and her escape from it never underwent any significant change. The passage in *The Silmarillion* (p. 172) is indeed very brief, but its lack of detail is due to compression rather than to omission based on dissatisfaction; the *Lay of Leithian*, from which the prose account in *The Silmarillion* directly derives, is in this passage so close, in point of narrative detail, to the *Tale of Tinúviel* as to be almost identical with it.

It may be observed that in this part of the story the earliest version had a strength that was diminished later, in that the duration of Tinúviel's imprisonment and her journey to Beren's rescue relates readily enough to that of Beren's captivity, which was intended by his captors to be unending; whereas in the later story there is a great deal of event and movement (with the addition of Lúthien's captivity in Nargothrond) to be fitted into the time when Beren was awaiting his death in the dungeon of the Necromancer.

While the strong element of 'explanatory' beast-fable (concerning cats and dogs) was to be entirely eliminated, and Tevildo Prince of Cats replaced by the Necromancer, Huan nonetheless remained from it as the great Hound of Valinor. His encounter with Tinúviel in the woods, her inability to escape from him, and indeed his love for her from the moment of their meeting (suggested in the tale, p. 23, explicit in *The Silmarillion* p. 173), were already present, though the context of their encounter and the motives of Huan were wholly different from the absence of 'the Nargothrond Element' (Felagund, Celegorm and Curufin).

In the story of the defeat of Tevildo and the rescue of Beren the germ of the later legend is clearly seen, though for the most part only in broad structural resemblances. It is curious to observe that the loud speaking of Tinúviel sitting perched on the sill of the kitchen hatch in the castle of the Cats, so that Beren might hear, is the precursor of her singing on the bridge of Tol-in-Gaurhoth the song that Beren heard in his dungeon (*The Silmarillion* p. 174). Tevildo's intention to hand her over to Melko remained in Sauron's similar purpose (*ibid.*); the killing of the cat

Oikeroi (p. 28) is the germ of Huan's fight with Draugluin – the skin of Huan's dead opponent is put to the same use in either case (pp. 30–1, *The Silmarillion* pp. 178–9); the battle of Tevildo and Huan was to become that of Huan and Wolf-Sauron, and with essentially the same outcome: Huan released his enemy when he yielded the mastery of his dwelling. This last is very notable: the utterance by Tinúviel of the spell which bound stone to stone in the evil castle (p. 29). Of course, when this was written the castle of Tevildo was an adventitious feature in the story – it had no previous history: it was an evil place through and through, and the spell (deriving from Melko) that Tevildo was forced to reveal was the secret of Tevildo's own power over his creatures as well as the magic that held the stones together. With the entry of Felagund into the developing legend and the Elvish watchtower on Tol Sirion (*Minas Tirith: The Silmarillion* pp. 120, 155–6) captured by the Necromancer, the spell is displaced: for it cannot be thought to be the work of Felagund, who built the fortress, since if it had been he would have been able to pronounce it in the dungeon and bring the place down over their heads – a less evil way for them to die. This element in the legend remained, however, and is fully present in *The Silmarillion* (p. 175), though since my father did not actually say there that Sauron told Huan and Lúthien what the words were, but only that he 'yielded himself', one may miss the significance of what happened:

> And she said: 'There everlastingly thy naked self shall endure the torment of his scorn, pierced by his eyes, unless thou yield to me the mastery of thy tower.'
> Then Sauron yielded himself, and Lúthien took the mastery of the isle and all that was there. . . .
> Then Lúthien stood upon the bridge, and declared her power: and the spell was loosed that bound stone to stone, and the gates were thrown down, and the walls opened, and the pits laid bare.

Here again the actual matter of the narrative is totally different in the early and late forms of the legend: in *The Silmarillion* 'many thralls and captives came forth in wonder and dismay . . . for they had lain long in the darkness of Sauron', whereas in the tale the inmates who emerged from the shaken dwelling (other than Beren and the apparently inconsequent figure of the blind slave-Gnome Gimli) were a host of cats, reduced by the breaking of Tevildo's spell to 'puny size'. (If my father had used in the tale names other than Huan, Beren, and Tinúviel, and in the absence of all other knowledge, including that of authorship, it would not be easy to demonstrate from a simple comparison between this part of the Tale and the story as told in *The Silmarillion* that the resemblances were more than superficial and accidental.)

A more minor narrative point may be noticed here. The typescript version would presumably have treated the fight of Huan and Tevildo somewhat differently, for in the manuscript Tevildo and his companion can flee up great trees (p. 28), whereas in the typescript nothing grew in the Withered Dale (where Huan was to lie feigning sick) save 'low bushes of scanty leaves' (p. 48).

In the remainder of the story the congruence between early and late forms is far closer. The narrative structure in the tale may be summarised thus:

- Beren is attired for disguise in the fell of the dead cat Oikeroi.
- He and Tinúviel journey together to Angamandi.
- Tinúviel lays a spell of sleep on Karkaras the wolf-ward of Angamandi.
- They enter Angamandi, Beren slinks in his beast-shape beneath the seat of Melko, and Tinúviel dances before Melko.
- All the host of Angamandi and finally Melko himself are cast into sleep, and Melko's iron crown rolls from his head.
- Tinúviel rouses Beren, who cuts a Silmaril from the crown, and the blade snaps.
- The sleepers stir, and Beren and Tinúviel flee back to the gates, but find Karkaras awake again.
- Karkaras bites off Beren's outthrust hand holding the Silmaril.
- Karkaras becomes mad with the pain of the Silmaril in his belly, for the Silmaril is a holy thing and sears evil flesh.
- Karkaras goes raging south to Artanor.
- Beren and Tinúviel return to Artanor; they go before Tinwelint and Beren declares that a Silmaril is in his hand.
- The hunting of the wolf takes place, and Mablung the Heavy-handed is one of the hunters.
- Beren is slain by Karkaras, and is borne back to the cavern of Tinwelint on a bier of boughs; dying he gives the Silmaril to Tinwelint.
- Tinúviel follows Beren to Mandos, and Mandos permits them to return into the world.

Changing the catskin of Oikeroi to the wolfskin of Draugluin, and altering some other names, this would do tolerably well as a précis of the story in *The Silmarillion*! But of course it is devised as a summary of similarities. There are major differences as well as a host of minor ones that do not appear in it.

Again, most important is the absence of 'the Nargothrond Element'. When this combined with the Beren legend it introduced Felagund as Beren's companion, Lúthien's imprisonment in Nargothrond by Celegorm and Curufin, her escape with Huan the hound of Celegorm, and the attack on Beren and Lúthien as they returned from Tol-in-Gaurhoth by Celegorm and Curufin, now fleeing from Nargothrond (*The Silmarillion* pp. 173–4, 176–8).

The narrative after the conclusion of the episode of 'the Thraldom of Beren' is conducted quite differently in the old story (pp. 30–1), in that here Huan is with Beren and Tinúviel; Tinúviel longs for her home, and Beren is grieved because he loves the life in the woods with the dogs, but he resolves the impasse by determining to obtain a Silmaril, and though Huan thinks their plan is folly he gives them the fell of Oikeroi, clad in which Beren sets out with Tinúviel for Angamandi. In *The Silmarillion* (p. 177) likewise, Beren, after long wandering in the woods with Lúthien (though not with Huan), resolves to set forth again on the quest of the Silmaril, but Lúthien's stance in the matter is different:

'You must choose, Beren, between these two: to relinquish the quest and your oath and seek a life of wandering upon the face of the earth; or to hold to your word and challenge the power of darkness upon its throne. But on either road I shall go with you, and our doom shall be alike.'

There then intervened the attack on Beren and Lúthien by Celegorm and Curufin, when Huan, deserting his master, joined himself to them; they returned together to Doriath, and when they got there Beren left Lúthien sleeping and went back northwards by himself, riding Curufin's horse. He was overtaken on the edge of Anfauglith by Huan bearing Lúthien on his back and bringing from Tol-in-Gaurhoth the skins of Draugluin and of Sauron's bat-messenger Thuringwethil (of whom in the old story there is no trace); attired in these Beren and Lúthien went to Angband. Huan is here their active counsellor.

The later legend is thus more full of movement and incident in this part than is the *Tale of Tinúviel* (though the final form was not achieved all at one stroke, as may be imagined); and in the *Silmarillion* form this is the more marked from the fact that the account is a compression and a summary of the long *Lay of Leithian*.*

In the *Tale of Tinúviel* the account of Beren's disguise is characteristically detailed: his instruction by Tinúviel in feline behaviour, his heat and discomfort inside the skin. Tinúviel's disguise as a bat has however not yet emerged, and whereas in *The Silmarillion* when confronted by

* Cf. Professor T. A. Shippey, *The Road to Middle-earth*, 1982, p. 193: 'In "Beren and Lúthien" as a whole there is too much plot. The other side of that criticism is that on occasion Tolkien has to be rather brisk with his own inventions. Celegorm wounds Beren, and the hound Huan turns on his master and pursues him; "returning he brought to Lúthien a herb out of the forest. With that leaf she staunched Beren's wound, and by her arts and her love she healed him. . . ." The motif of the healing herb is a common one, the centre for instance of the Breton *lai* of *Eliduc* (turned into *conte* by Marie de France). But in that it occupies a whole scene, if not a whole poem. In *The Silmarillion* it appears only to be dismissed in two lines, while Beren's wound is inflicted and healed in five. Repeatedly one has this sense of summary . . .' This sense is eminently justified! In the *Lay of Leithian* the wounding and the healing with the herb occupy some 64 lines. (Cf. my Foreword to *The Silmarillion*, p. 8.)

Carcharoth she 'cast back her foul raiment' and 'commanded him to sleep', here she used once more the magical misty robe spun of her hair: 'the black strands of her dark veil she cast in his eyes' (p. 31). The indifference of Karkaras to the false Oikeroi contrasts with Carcharoth's suspicion of the false Druagluin, of whose death he had heard tidings: in the old story it is emphasised that no news of the discomfiture of Tevildo (and the death of Oikeroi) had yet reached Angamandi.

The encounter of Tinúviel with Melko is given with far more detail than in *The Silmarillion* (here much compressed from its source); notable is the phrase (p. 32) 'he leered horribly, for his dark mind pondered some evil', forerunner of that in *The Silmarillion* (p. 180):

> Then Morgoth looking upon her beauty conceived in his thought an evil lust, and a design more dark than any that had yet come into his heart since he fled from Valinor.

We are never told anything more explicit.

Whether Melko's words to Tinúviel, 'Who art thou that flittest about my halls like a bat?', and the description of her dancing 'noiseless as a bat', were the germ of her later bat-disguise cannot be said, though it seems possible.

The knife with which Beren cut the Silmaril from the Iron Crown has a quite different provenance in the *Tale of Tinúviel*, being a kitchen-knife that Beren took from Tevildo's castle (pp. 29, 33); in *The Silmarillion* it was Angrist, the famous knife made by Telchar which Beren took from Curufin. The sleepers of Angamandi are here disturbed by the sound of the snapping of the knife-blade; in *The Silmarillion* it is the shard flying from the snapped knife and striking Morgoth's cheek that makes him groan and stir.

There is a minor difference in the accounts of the meeting with the wolf as Beren and Tinúviel fled out. In *The Silmarillion* 'Lúthien was spent, and she had not time nor strength to quell the wolf'; in the tale it seems that she might have done so if Beren had not been precipitate. Much more important, there appears here for the first time the conception of the holy power of the Silmarils that burns unhallowed flesh.*

The escape of Tinúviel and Beren from Angamandi and their return to Artanor (pp. 34–6) is treated quite differently in the *Tale of Tinúviel*. In *The Silmarillion* (pp. 182–3) they were rescued by the Eagles and set down on the borders of Doriath; and far more is made of the healing of Beren's wound, in which Huan plays a part. In the old story Huan comes to them later, after their long southward flight on foot. In both accounts there is a discussion between them as to whether or not they should return to her father's hall, but it is quite differently conducted – in the tale it is she who persuades Beren to return, in *The Silmarillion* it is Beren who persuades her.

---

* In an early note there is a reference to 'the sacred Silmarils': I.169, note 2.

There is a curious feature in the story of the Wolf-hunt (pp. 38–9) which may be considered here (see p. 50, notes 12–15). At first, it was Tinúviel's brother who took part in the hunt with Tinwelint, Beren, and Huan, and his name is here *Tifanto*, which was the name throughout the tale before its replacement by *Dairon*.* Subsequently 'Tifanto' – without passing through the stage of 'Dairon' – was replaced by 'Mablung the heavy-handed, chief of the king's thanes', who here makes his first appearance, as the fourth member of the hunt. But earlier in the tale it is told that Tifanto > Dairon, leaving Artanor to seek Tinúviel, became utterly lost, 'and came never back to Elfinesse' (p. 21), and the loss of Tifanto > Dairon is referred to again when Beren and Tinúviel returned to Artanor (pp. 36–7).

Thus on the one hand Tifanto was lost, and it is a grief to Tinúviel on her return to learn of it, but on the other he was present at the Wolf-hunt. *Tifanto* was then changed to *Dairon* throughout the tale, except in the story of the Wolf-hunt, where *Tifanto* was replaced by a new character, *Mablung*. This shows that *Tifanto* was removed from the hunt before the change of name to *Dairon*, but does not explain how, under the name *Tifanto*, he was both lost in the wilds and present at the hunt. Since there is nothing in the MS itself to explain this puzzle, I can only conclude that my father did, in fact, write at first that Tifanto was lost and never came back, and also that he took part in the Wolf-hunt; but observing this contradiction he introduced Mablung in the latter rôle (and probably did this even before the tale was completed, since at the last appearance of Mablung his name was written thus, not emended from *Tifanto*: see note 15). It was subsequent to this that *Tifanto* was emended, wherever it still stood, to *Dairon*.

In the tale the hunt is differently managed from the story in *The Silmarillion* (where, incidentally, Beleg Strongbow was present). It is curious that all (including, as it appears, Huan!) save Beren were asleep when Karkaras came on them ('in Beren's watch', p. 39). In *The Silmarillion* Huan slew Carcharoth and was slain by him, whereas here Karkaras met his death from the king's spear, and the boy Ausir tells at the end that Huan lived on to find Beren again at the time of 'the great deeds of the Nauglafring' (p. 41). Of Huan's destiny, that he should not die 'until he encountered the mightiest wolf that would ever walk the world', and of his being permitted 'thrice only ere his death to speak with words' (*The Silmarillion* p. 173), there is nothing here.

The most remarkable feature of the *Tale of Tinúviel* remains the fact that in its earliest extant form Beren was an Elf; and in this connection very notable are the words of the boy at the end (p. 40):

---

* The idea that Timpinen (Tinfang Warble) was the son of Tinwelint and sister of Tinúviel (see I.106, note 1) had been abandoned. Tifanto/Dairon is now named with Tinfang and Ivárë as 'the three most magic players of the Elves' (p. 10).

Yet said Mandos to those twain: 'Lo, O Elves, it is not to any life of perfect joy that I dismiss you, for such may no longer be found in all the world where sits Melko of the evil heart — and know ye that *ye will become mortal even as Men*, and when ye fare hither again it will be for ever, unless the Gods summon you indeed to Valinor.'

In the tale of *The Coming of the Valar and the Building of Valinor* there occurs the following passage (I.76; commentary I.90):

Thither [i.e. to Mandos] in after days fared the Elves of all the clans who were by illhap slain with weapons or did die of grief for those that were slain — and only so might the Eldar die, and then it was only for a while. There Mandos spake their doom, and there they waited in the darkness, dreaming of their past deeds, until such time as he appointed when they might again be born into their children, and go forth to laugh and sing again.

The same idea occurs in the tale of *The Music of the Ainur* (I.59). The peculiar dispensation of Mandos in the case of Beren and Tinúviel as here conceived is therefore that their whole 'natural' destiny as Elves was changed: having died as Elves might die (from wounds or from grief) they were not reborn as new beings, but returned from Mandos in their own persons — yet now 'mortal even as Men'. The earliest eschatology is too unclear to allow of a satisfactory interpretation of this 'mortality', and the passage in *The Building of Valinor* on the fates of Men (I.77) is particularly hard to understand (see the commentary on it, I.90ff.). But it seems possible that the words 'even as Men' in the address of Mandos to Beren and Tinúviel were included to stress the finality of whatever second deaths they might undergo; their departure would be as final as that of Men, there would be no second return in their own persons, and no reincarnation. They will remain in Mandos ('when ye fare hither again it will be for ever') — unless they are summoned by the Gods to dwell in Valinor. These last words should probably be related to the passage in *The Building of Valinor* concerning the fate of certain Men (I.77):

Few are they and happy indeed for whom at a season doth Nornorë the herald of the Gods set out. Then ride they with him in chariots or upon good horses down into the vale of Valinor and feast in the halls of Valmar, dwelling in the houses of the Gods until the Great End come.

§2. *Places and peoples in the Tale of Tinúviel*

To consider first what can be learned of the geography of the Great Lands from this tale: the early 'dictionary' of the Gnomish language makes it clear that the meaning of *Artanor* was 'the Land Beyond', as it is interpreted in the text (p. 9). Several passages in the *Lost Tales* cast light on this expression. In an outline for Gilfanon's untold tale (I.240) the Noldoli exiled from Valinor

> now fought for the first time with the Orcs and captured the pass of the Bitter Hills; thus they escaped from the Land of Shadows . . . They entered the Forest of Artanor and the Region of the Great Plains . . .

(which latter, I suggested, may be the forerunner of the later Talath Dirnen, the Guarded Plain of Nargothrond). The tale to follow Gilfanon's, according to the projected scheme (I.241), was to be that of Tinúviel, and this outline begins: 'Beren son of Egnor wandered out of Dor Lómin [i.e. Hisilómë, see I.112] into Artanor . . .' In the present tale, it is said that Beren came 'through the terrors of the Iron Mountains until he reached the Lands Beyond' (p. 11), and also (p. 21) that some of the Dogs 'roamed the woods of Hisilómë or passing the mountainous places fared even at times into the region of Artanor and the lands beyond and to the south'. And finally, in the *Tale of Turambar* (p. 72) there is a reference to 'the road over the dark hills of Hithlum into the great forests of the Land Beyond where in those days Tinwelint the hidden king had his abode'.

It is quite clear, then, that Artanor, afterwards called Doriath (which appears in the title to the typescript text of the *Tale of Tinúviel*, together with an earlier form *Dor Athro*, p. 41), lay in the original conception in much the same relation to Hisilómë (the Land of Shadow(s), Dor Lómin, Aryador) as does Doriath to Hithlum (Hisilómë) in *The Silmarillion*: to the south, and divided from it by a mountain-range, the Iron Mountains or Bitter Hills.

In commenting on the tale of *The Theft of Melko and the Darkening of Valinor* I have noticed (I.158–9) that whereas in the *Lost Tales* Hisilómë is declared to be beyond the Iron Mountains, it is also said (in the *Tale of Turambar*, p. 77) that these mountains were so named from Angband, the Hells of Iron, which lay beneath 'their northernmost fastnesses', and that therefore there seems to be a contradictory usage of the term 'Iron Mountains' within the *Lost Tales* – 'unless it can be supposed that these mountains were conceived as a continuous range, the southerly extension (the later Mountains of Shadow) forming the southern fence of Hisilómë, while the northern peaks, being above Angband, gave the range its name'.

Now in the *Tale of Tinúviel* Beren, journeying north from Artanor, 'drew nigh to the lower hills and treeless lands that warned of the approach of the bleak Iron Mountains' (p. 14). These he had previously traversed, coming out of Hisilómë; but now 'he followed the Iron Mountains till he drew nigh to the terrible regions of Melko's abode'.

This seems to support the suggestion that the mountains fencing Hisilómë from the Lands Beyond were continuous with those above Angband; and we may compare the little primitive map (I.81), where the mountain range *f* isolates Hisilómë (*g*): see I.112, 135. The implication is that 'dim' or 'black' Hisilómë had no defence against Melko.

There appear now also the Mountains of Night (pp. 20, 46–7), and it seems clear that the great pinewoods of Taurfuin, the Forest of Night, grew upon those heights (in *The Silmarillion* Dorthonion 'Land of Pines', afterwards named Taur-nu-Fuin). Dairon was lost there, but Tinúviel, though she passed near, did not enter 'that dark region'. There is nothing to show that it was not placed then as it was later – to the east of Ered Wethrin, the Mountains of Shadow. It is also at least possible that the description (in the manuscript version only, p. 23) of Tinúviel, on departing from Huan, leaving 'the shelter of the trees' and coming to 'a region of long grass' is a first intimation of the great plain of Ard-galen (called after its desolation Anfauglith and Dor-nu-Fauglith), especially if this is related to the passage in the typescript version telling of Tinúviel's meeting with Huan 'in a little glade nigh to the forest's borders, where the first grasslands begin that are nourished by the upper waters of the river Sirion' (p. 47).

After their escape from Angamandi Huan found Beren and Tinúviel 'in that northward region of Artanor that was called afterward Nan Dumgorthin, the land of the dark idols' (p. 35). In the Gnomish dictionary *Nan Dumgorthin* is defined as 'a land of dark forest east of Artanor where on a wooded mountain were hidden idols sacrificed to by some evil tribes of renegade men' (*dum* 'secret, not to be spoken', *dumgort*, *dungort* 'an (evil) idol'). In the *Lay of the Children of Húrin* in alliterative verse Túrin and his companion Flinding (later Gwindor), fleeing after the death of Beleg Strongbow, came to this land:

> There the twain enfolded   phantom twilight
> and dim mazes   dark, unholy,
> in Nan Dungorthin   where nameless gods
> have shrouded shrines   in shadows secret,
> more old than Morgoth   or the ancient lords
> the golden Gods   of the guarded West.
> But the ghostly dwellers   of that grey valley
> hindered nor hurt them,   and they held their course
> with creeping flesh   and quaking limb.
> Yet laughter at whiles   with lingering echo,
> as distant mockery   of demon voices
> there harsh and hollow   in the hushed twilight
> Flinding fancied,   fell, unwholesome . . .

There are, I believe, no other references to the gods of Nan Dumgorthin. In the poem the land was placed west of Sirion; and finally, as Nan

Dungortheb 'the Valley of Dreadful Death', it becomes in *The Sil-marillion* (pp. 81, 121) a 'no-land' between the Girdle of Melian and Ered Gorgoroth, the Mountains of Terror. But the description of it in the *Tale of Tinúviel* as a 'northward region of Artanor' clearly does not imply that it lay within the protective magic of Gwendeling, and it seems that this 'zone' was originally less distinctly bounded, and less extensive, than 'the Girdle of Melian' afterwards became. Probably *Artanor* was conceived at this time as a great region of forest in the heart of which was Tinwelint's cavern, and only his immediate domain was protected by the power of the queen:

> Hidden was his dwelling from the vision and knowledge of Melko by the magics of Gwendeling the fay, and she wove spells about the paths thereto that none but the Eldar might tread them easily, and so was the king secured from all dangers save it be treachery alone. (p. 9).

It seems, also, that her protection was originally by no means so complete and so mighty a wall of defence as it became. Thus, although Orcs and wolves disappeared when Beren and Tinúviel 'stepped within the circle of Gwendeling's magic that hid the paths from evil things and kept harm from the regions of the woodelves' (p. 35), the fear is expressed that even if Beren and Tinúviel reached the cavern of King Tinwelint 'they would but draw the chase behind them thither' (p. 34), and Tinwelint's people feared that Melko would 'upraise his strength and come utterly to crush them and Gwendeling's magic have not the strength to withhold the numbers of the Orcs' (p. 36).

The picture of Menegroth beside Esgalduin, accessible only by the bridge (*The Silmarillion* pp. 92–3) goes back to the beginning, though neither cave nor river are named in the tale. But (as will be seen more emphatically in later tales in this book) Tinwelint, the wood-fairy in his cavern, had a long elevation before him, to become ultimately Thingol of the Thousand Caves ('the fairest dwelling of any king that has ever been east of the Sea'). In the beginning, Tinwelint's dwelling was not a subterranean city full of marvels, silver fountains falling into basins of marble and pillars carved like trees, but a rugged cave; and if in the typescript version the cave comes to be 'vaulted immeasureable', it is still illuminated only by the dim and flickering light of torches (pp. 43, 46).

There have been earlier references in the *Lost Tales* to Tinwelint and the place of his dwelling. In a passage added to, but then rejected from, the tale of *The Chaining of Melko* (I.106, note 1) it is said that he was lost in Hisilómë and met Wendelin there; 'loving her he was content to leave his folk and dance for ever in the shadows'. In *The Coming of the Elves* (I.115) 'Tinwë abode not long with his people, and yet 'tis said lives still lord of the scattered Elves of Hisilómë'; and in the same tale (I.118–19) the 'Lost Elves' were still there 'long after when Men were shut in Hisilómë by Melko', and Men called them the Shadow Folk, and feared them. But in the *Tale of Tinúviel* the conception has changed. Tinwelint is now a king ŕuling, not in Hisilómë, but in Artanor.* (It is not said where it was that he came upon Gwendeling.)

In the account (manuscript version only, see pp. 9, 42) of Tinwelint's people there is mention of Elves 'who remained in the dark'; and this obviously refers to Elves who never left the Waters of Awakening. (Of course those who were lost on the march from Palisor also never left 'the dark' (i.e. they never came to the light of the Trees), but the distinction made in this sentence is not between the darkness and the light but between those who *remained* and those who *set out*). On the emergence of this idea in the course of the writing of the *Lost Tales* see I.234. Of Tinwelint's subjects 'the most were Ilkorindi', and they must be those who 'had been lost upon the march from Palisor' (earlier, 'the Lost Elves of Hisilómë').

Here, a major difference in essential conception between the old legend and the form in *The Silmarillion* is apparent. These Ilkorindi of Tinwelint's following ('eerie and strange beings' whose 'dark songs and chantings . . . faded in the wooded places or echoed in deep caves') are described in terms applicable to the wild Avari ('the Unwilling') of *The Silmarillion*; but they are of course actually the precursors of the Grey-elves of Doriath. The term *Eldar* is here equivalent to *Elves* ('all the Eldar both *those who remained in the dark* or had been lost upon the march from Palisor') and is not restricted to those who made, or at least embarked on, the Great Journey; all were Ilkorindi – Dark Elves – if they never passed over the Sea. The later significance of the Great Journey in conferring 'Eldarin' status was an aspect of the elevation of the Grey-elves of Beleriand, bringing about a distinction of the utmost importance within the category of the *Moriquendi* or 'Elves of the Darkness' – the *Avari* (who were not Eldar) and the *Úmanyar* (the Eldar who were 'not of Aman'): see the table 'The Sundering of the Elves' given in *The Silmarillion*. Thus:

Lost Tales		Silmarillion	
	of Kôr	Avari	
Eldar	of the Great Lands (the Darkness): Ilkorindi	Eldar (of the Great Journey)	of Aman / of Middle-earth (Úmanyar)

But among Tinwelint's subjects there were also *Noldoli*, Gnomes. This matter is somewhat obscure, but at least it may be observed that the

---

* In the outlines for *Gilfanon's Tale* the 'Shadow Folk' of Hisilómë have ceased to be Elves and become 'fays' whose origin is unknown: I.237, 239.

manuscript and typescript versions of the *Tale of Tinúviel* do not envisage precisely the same situation.

The manuscript text is perhaps not perfectly explicit on the subject, but it is said (p. 9) that of Tinwelint's subjects *'the most* were Ilkorindi', and that before the rising of the Sun 'already were their numbers mingled with a many wandering Gnomes'. Yet Dairon fled from the apparition of Beren in the forest because 'all the Elves of the woodland thought of the Gnomes of Dor Lómin as treacherous creatures, cruel and faithless' (p. 11); and 'Dread and suspicion was between the Eldar and those of their kindred that had tasted the slavery of Melko, and in this did the evil deeds of the Gnomes at the Haven of the Swans revenge itself' (p. 11). The hostility of the Elves of Artanor to Gnomes was, then, specifically a hostility to the Gnomes of Hisilómë (Dor Lómin), who were suspected of being under the will of Melko (and this is probably a foreshadowing of the suspicion and rejection of Elves escaped from Angband described in *The Silmarillion* p. 156). In the manuscript it is said (p. 9) that *all* the Elves of the Great Lands (those who remained in Palisor, those who were lost on the march, and the Noldoli returned from Valinor) fell beneath the power of Melko, though many escaped and wandered in the wild; and as the manuscript text was first written (see p. 11 and note 3) Beren was 'son of a thrall of Melko's . . . that laboured in the darker places in the north of Hisilómë'. This conception seems reasonably clear, so far as it goes.

In the typescript version it is expressly stated that there were Gnomes 'in Tinwelint's service' (p. 43): the bridge over the forest river, leading to Tinwelint's door, was hung by them. It is not now stated that all the Elves of the Great Lands fell beneath Melko; rather there are named several centres of resistance to his power, in addition to Tinwelint/ Thingol in Artanor: Turgon of Gondolin, the Sons of Fëanor, and Egnor of Hisilómë (Beren's father) – one of the chiefest foes of Melko 'in all the kin of the Gnomes that still were free' (p. 44). Presumably this led to the exclusion in the typescript of the passage telling that the woodland Elves thought of the Gnomes of Dor Lómin as treacherous and faithless (see p. 43), while that concerning the distrust of those who had been Melko's slaves was retained. The passage concerning Hisilómë 'where dwelt Men, and thrall-Noldoli laboured, and few free-Eldar went' (p. 10) was also retained; but Hisilómë, in Beren's wish that he had never strayed out of it, becomes 'the wild free places of Hisilómë' (pp. 17, 45).

This leads to an altogether baffling question, that of the references to the Battle of Unnumbered Tears; and several of the passages just cited bear on it.

The story of 'The Travail of the Noldoli and the Coming of Mankind' that was to have been told by Gilfanon, but which after its opening pages most unhappily never got beyond the stage of outline projections, was to be followed by that of Beren and Tinúviel (see I. 241). After the Battle of Unnumbered Tears there is mention of the Thraldom of the Noldoli, the Mines of Melko, the Spell of Bottomless Dread, the shutting of Men in

Hisilómë, and *then* 'Beren son of Egnor wandered out of Dor Lómin into Artanor . . .' (In *The Silmarillion* the deeds of Beren and Lúthien preceded the Battle of Unnumbered Tears.)

Now in the *Tale of Tinúviel* there is a reference, in both versions, to the 'thrall-Noldoli' who laboured in Hisilómë and of Men dwelling there; and as the passage introducing Beren was first written in the manuscript his father was one of these slaves. It is said, again in both versions, that neither Tinwelint nor the most part of his people went to the battle, but that his lordship was greatly increased by fugitives from it (p. 9); and to the following statement that his dwelling was hidden by the magic of Gwendeling/Melian the typescript adds the word 'thereafter' (p. 43), i.e. after the Battle of Unnumbered Tears. In the changed passage in the typescript referring to Egnor he is one of the chiefest foes of Melko 'in all the kin of the Gnomes *that still were free*'.

All this seems to allow of only one conclusion: the events of the *Tale of Tinúviel* took place *after* the great battle; and this seems to be clinched by the express statement in the typescript: where the manuscript (p. 15) says that Melko 'sought ever to destroy the friendship and intercourse of Elves and Men', the second version adds (p. 44): *'lest they forget the Battle of Unnumbered Tears* and once more arise in wrath against him'.

It is very odd, therefore, that Vëannë should say at the beginning (in the manuscript only, p. 10 and see p. 43) that she will tell 'of things that happened in the halls of Tinwelint *after the arising of the Sun indeed but long ere the unforgotten Battle of Unnumbered Tears*'. (This in any case seems to imply a much longer period between the two events than is suggested in the outlines for *Gilfanon's Tale*: see I.242). This is repeated later (p. 17): 'it was a thing unthought . . . that any Elf . . . should fare untended to the halls of Melko, *even in those earlier days before the Battle of Tears* when Melko's power had not grown great . . .' But it is stranger still that this second sentence is retained in the typescript (p. 45). The typescript version has thus two inescapably contradictory statements:

Melko 'sought ever to destroy the friendship and intercourse of Elves and Men, lest they forget the Battle of Unnumbered Tears' (p. 44);

'Little love was there between the woodland Elves and the folk of Angband even in those days before the Battle of Unnumbered Tears' (p. 45).

Such a radical contradiction within a single text is in the highest degree unusual, perhaps unique, in all the writings concerned with the First Age. But I can see no way to explain it, other than simply accepting it as a radical contradiction; nor indeed can I explain those statements in both versions that the events of the tale took place *before* the battle, since virtually all indications point to the contrary.*

---

* In the *Tale of Turambar* the story of Beren and Tinúviel clearly and necessarily took place *before* the Battle of Unnumbered Tears (pp. 71–2, 140).

§3. *Miscellaneous Matters*

(i) *Morgoth*

Beren addresses Melko as 'most mighty Belcha Morgoth', which are said to be his names among the Gnomes (p. 44). In the Gnomish dictionary *Belcha* is given as the Gnomish form corresponding to *Melko* (see I.260), but *Morgoth* is not found in it: indeed this is the first and only appearance of the name in the *Lost Tales*. The element *goth* is given in the Gnomish dictionary with the meaning 'war, strife'; but if *Morgoth* meant at this period 'Black Strife' it is perhaps strange that Beren should use it in a flattering speech. A name-list made in the 1930s explains *Morgoth* as 'formed from his Orc-name *Goth* "Lord or Master" with *mor* "dark or black" prefixed', but it seems very doubtful that this etymology is valid for the earlier period. This name-list explains *Gothmog* 'Captain of Balrogs' as containing the same Orc-element ('Voice of *Goth* (Morgoth)'); but in the name-list to the tale of *The Fall of Gondolin* (p. 216) the name *Gothmog* is said to mean 'Strife-and-hatred' (*mog-* 'detest, hate' appears in the Gnomish dictionary), which supports the interpretation of *Morgoth* in the present tale as 'Black Strife'.*

(ii) *Orcs and Balrogs*

Despite the reference to 'the wandering bands of the goblins *and* the Orcs' (p. 14, retained in the typescript version), the terms are certainly synonymous in the *Tale of Turambar*. The Orcs are described in the present tale (*ibid.*) as 'foul broodlings of Melko'. In the second version (p. 44) wolf-rider Orcs appear.

Balrogs, mentioned in the tale (p. 15), have appeared in one of the outlines for *Gilfanon's Tale* (I.241); but they had already played an important part in the earliest of the *Lost Tales*, that of *The Fall of Gondolin* (see pp. 212–13).

(iii) *Tinúviel's 'lengthening spell'*

Of the 'longest things' named in this spell (pp. 19–20, 46) two, 'the sword of Nan' and 'the neck of Gilim the giant', seem now lost beyond recall, though they survived into the spell in the *Lay of Leithian*, where the sword of Nan is itself named, *Glend*, and Gilim is called 'the giant of

---

* Nothing is said in any text to suggest that Gothmog played such a role in relation to Morgoth as the interpretation 'Voice of *Goth*' implies, but nor is anything said to contradict it, and he was from the beginning an important figure in the evil realm and in especial relation to Melko (see p. 216). There is perhaps a reminiscence of 'the Voice of Morgoth' in 'the Mouth of Sauron', the Black Númenórean who was the Lieutenant of Barad-dûr (*The Return of the King* V. 10).

Eruman'. *Gilim* in the Gnomish dictionary means 'winter' (see I.260, entry *Melko*), which does not seem particularly appropriate: though a jotting, very difficult to read, in the little notebook used for memoranda in connection with the *Lost Tales* (see I.171) seems to say that Nan was a 'giant of summer of the South', and that he was like an elm.

The *Indravangs* (*Indrafangs* in the typescript) are the 'Longbeards'; this is said in the Gnomish dictionary to be 'a special name of the Nauglath or Dwarves' (see further the *Tale of the Nauglafring*, p. 247).

Karkaras (*Carcaras* in the typescript) 'Knife-fang' is named in the spell since he was originally conceived as the 'father of wolves, who guarded the gates of Angamandi in those days *and long had done so*' (p. 21). In *The Silmarillion* (p. 180) he has a different history: chosen by Morgoth 'from among the whelps of the race of Draugluin' and reared to be the death of Huan, he was set before the gates of Angband in that very time. In *The Silmarillion* (*ibid.*) Carcharoth is rendered 'the Red Maw', and this expression is used in the text of the tale (p. 34): 'both hand and jewel Karkaras bit off and took into his red maw'.

Glorund is the name of the dragon in the *Tale of Turambar* (*Glaurung* in *The Silmarillion*).

In the tale of *The Chaining of Melko* there is no suggestion that Tulkas had any part in the making of the chain (there in the form *Angaino*): I.100.

(iv)   *The influence of the Valar*

There is frequent suggestion that the Valar in some way exercised a direct influence over the minds and hearts of the distant Elves in the Great Lands. Thus it is said (p. 15) that the Valar must have inspired Beren's ingenious speech to Melko, and while this may be no more than a 'rhetorical' flourish, it is clear that Tinúviel's dream of Beren is meant to be accepted as 'a dream of the Valar' (p. 19). Again, 'the Valar set a new hope in her heart' (p. 47); and later in Vëannë's tale the Valar are seen as active 'fates', guiding the destinies of the characters – so the Valar 'brought' Huan to find Beren and Tinúviel in Nan Dumgorthin (p. 35), and Tinúviel says to Tinwelint that 'the Valar alone saved Beren from a bitter death' (p. 37).

TURAMBAR AND THE FOALÓKË

The *Tale of Turambar*, like that of *Tinúviel*, is a manuscript written in ink over a wholly erased original in pencil. But it seems certain that the *extant* form of *Turambar* preceded the *extant* form of *Tinúviel*. This can be deduced in more ways than one, but the order of composition is clearly exemplified in the forms of the name of the King of the Woodland Elves (Thingol). Throughout the manuscript of *Turambar* he was originally *Tintoglin* (and this appears also in the tale of *The Coming of the Elves*, where it was changed to *Tinwelint*, I.115, 131). A note on the manuscript at the beginning of the tale says: 'Tintoglin's name must be altered throughout to *Ellon* or *Tinthellon* = Q. *Ellu*', but the note was struck out, and all through the tale *Tintoglin* was in fact changed to *Tinwelint*.

Now in the *Tale of Tinúviel* the king's name was first given as *Ellu* (or *Tinto Ellu*), and once as *Tinthellon* (pp. 50–1); subsequently it was changed throughout to *Tinwelint*. It is clear that the direction to change *Tintoglin* to *Ellon* or *Tinthellon* = Q. *Ellu*' belongs to the time when the *Tale of Tinúviel* was being, or had been, rewritten, and that the extant *Tale of Turambar* already existed.

There is also the fact that the rewritten *Tinúviel* was followed, at the same time of composition, by the first form of the 'interlude' in which Gilfanon appears (see I.203), whereas at the beginning of *Turambar* there is a reference to Ailios (who was replaced by Gilfanon) concluding the previous tale. On the different arrangement of the tale-telling at this point that my father subsequently introduced but failed to carry through see I.229–30. According to the earlier arrangement, Ailios told his tale on the first night of the feast of Turuhalmë or the Logdrawing, and Eltas followed with the *Tale of Turambar* on the second.

There is evidence that the *Tale of Turambar* was in existence at any rate by the middle of 1919. Humphrey Carpenter discovered a passage, written on a scrap of proof for the Oxford English Dictionary, in an early alphabet of my father's devising; and transliterating it he found it to be from this tale, not far from the beginning. He has told me that my father was using this version of the 'Alphabet of Rúmil' about June 1919 (see *Biography*, p. 100).

When then Ailios had spoken his fill the time for the lighting of candles was at hand, and so came the first day of Turuhalmë to an end; but on the second night Ailios was not there, and being asked by Lindo one Eltas began a tale, and said:

'Now all folk gathered here know that this is the story of Turambar and the Foalókë, and it is,' said he, 'a favourite tale among Men, and tells of very ancient days of that folk before the Battle of Tasarinan when first Men entered the dark vales of Hisilómë.

In these days many such stories do Men tell still, and more have they told in the past especially in those kingdoms of the North that once I knew. Maybe the deeds of other of their warriors have become mingled therein, and many matters beside that are not in the most ancient tale – but now I will tell to you the true and lamentable tale, and I knew it long ere I trod Olórë Mallë in the days before the fall of Gondolin.

In those days my folk dwelt in a vale of Hisilómë and that land did Men name Aryador in the tongues they then used, but they were very far from the shores of Asgon and the spurs of the Iron Mountains were nigh to their dwellings and great woods of very gloomy trees. My father said to me that many of our older men venturing afar had themselves seen the evil worms of Melko and some had fallen before them, and by reason of the hatred of our people for those creatures and of the evil Vala often was the story of Turambar and the Foalókë in their mouths – but rather after the fashion of the Gnomes did they say Turumart and the Fuithlug.

For know that before the Battle of Lamentation and the ruin of the Noldoli there dwelt a lord of Men named Úrin, and hearkening to the summons of the Gnomes he and his folk marched with the Ilkorindi against Melko, but their wives and children they left behind them in the woodlands, and with them was Mavwin wife of Úrin, and her son remained with her, for he was not yet war-high. Now the name of that boy was Túrin and is so in all tongues, but Mavwin do the Eldar call Mavoinë.

Now Úrin and his followers fled not from that battle as did most of the kindreds of Men, but many of them were slain fighting to the last, and Úrin was made captive. Of the Noldoli who fought there all the companies were slain or captured or fled away in rout, save that of Turondo (Turgon) only, and he and his folk cut a path for themselves out of that fray and come not into this tale. Nonetheless the escape of that great company marred the complete victory that otherwise had Melko won over his adversaries, and he desired very greatly to discover whither they had fled; and this he might not do, for his spies availed nothing, and no tortures at that time had power to force treacherous knowledge from the captive Noldoli.

Knowing therefore that the Elves of Kôr thought little of Men, holding them in scant fear or suspicion for their blindness and lack of skill, he would constrain Úrin to take up his employ and go seek after Turondo as a spy of Melko. To this however neither threats of torture nor promises of rich reward would bring Úrin to consent, for he said: "Nay, do as thou wilt, for to no evil work of thine wilt thou ever constrain me, O Melko, thou foe of Gods and Men."

"Of a surety," said Melko in anger, "to no work of mine will I bid thee again, nor yet will I force thee thereto, but upon deeds of mine that will be little to thy liking shalt thou sit here and gaze, nor be able to move foot or hand against them." And this was the torture he devised for the affliction of Úrin the Steadfast, and setting him in a lofty place of the mountains he stood beside him and cursed him and his folk with dread curses of the Valar, putting a doom of woe and a death of sorrow upon them; but to Úrin he gave a measure of vision, so that much of those things that befell his wife and children he might see and be helpless to aid, for magic held him in that high place. "Behold!" said Melko, "the life of Túrin thy son shall be accounted a matter for tears wherever Elves or Men are gathered for the telling of tales"; but Úrin said: "At least none shall pity him for this, that he had a craven for father."

Now after that battle Mavwin got her in tears into the land of Hithlum or Dor Lómin where all Men must now dwell by the word of Melko, save some wild few that yet roamed without. There was Nienóri born to her, but her husband Úrin languished in the thraldom of Melko, and Túrin being yet a small boy Mavwin knew not in her distress how to foster both him and his sister, for Úrin's men had all perished in the great affray, and the strange men who dwelt nigh knew not the dignity of the Lady Mavwin, and all that land was dark and little kindly.

The next short section of the text was struck through afterwards and replaced by a rider on an attached slip. The rejected passage reads:

At that time the rumour [*written above*: memory] of the deeds of Beren Ermabwed had become noised much in Dor Lómin, wherefore it came into the heart of Mavwin, for lack of better counsel, to send Túrin to the court of Tintoglin,[1] begging him to foster this orphan for the memory of Beren, and to teach him the wisdom of fays and of Eldar; now Egnor[2] was akin to Mavwin and he was the father of Beren the One-handed.

The replacement passage reads:

Amended passage to fit better with the story of Tinúviel and the afterhistory of the Nauglafring:

The tale tells however that Úrin had been a friend of the Elves, and in this he was different from many of his folk. Now great had his friendship been with Egnor, the Elf of the greenwood, the huntsman of the Gnomes, and Beren Ermabwed son of Egnor he knew and had rendered him a service once in respect of Damrod his son; but the deeds of Beren of the One Hand in the halls of Tinwelint[3] were remembered still in Dor Lómin. Wherefore it came into the heart of Mavwin, for lack of other counsel, to send Túrin her son to the court of Tinwelint, begging him to foster this orphan for the memory of Úrin and of Beren son of Egnor.[4]

Very bitter indeed was that sundering, and for long [?time] Túrin wept and would not leave his mother, and this was the first of the many sorrows that befell him in life. Yet at length when his mother had reasoned with him he gave way and prepared him in anguish for that journey. With him went two old men, retainers aforetime of his father Úrin, and when all was ready and the farewells taken they turned their feet towards the dark hills, and the little dwelling of Mavwin was lost in the trees, and Túrin blind with tears could see her no more. Then ere they passed out of earshot he cried out: "O Mavwin my mother, soon will I come back to thee" – but he knew not that the doom of Melko lay between them.

Long and very weary and uncertain was the road over the dark hills of Hithlum into the great forests of the Land Beyond where in those days Tinwelint the hidden king had his abode; and Túrin son of Úrin[5] was the first of Men to tread that way, nor have many trodden it since. In perils were Túrin and his guardians of wolves and wandering Orcs that at that time fared even thus far from Angband as the power of Melko waxed and spread over the kingdoms of the North. Evil magics were about them, that often missing their way they wandered fruitlessly for many days, yet in the end did they win through and thanked the Valar therefor – yet maybe it was but part of the fate that Melko wove about their feet, for in after time Túrin would fain have perished as a child there in the dark woods.

Howso that may be, this was the manner of their coming to

Tinwelint's halls; for in the woodlands beyond the mountains they became utterly lost, until at length having no means of sustenance they were like to die, when they were discovered by a wood-ranger, a huntsman of the secret Elves, and he was called Beleg, for he was of great stature and girth as such was among that folk. Then Beleg led them by devious paths through many dark and lonely forestlands to the banks of that shadowed stream before the cavernous doors of Tinwelint's halls. Now coming before that king they were received well for the memory of Úrin the Steadfast, and when also the king heard of the bond tween Úrin and Beren the One-handed⁶ and of the plight of that lady Mavwin his heart became softened and he granted her desire, nor would he send Túrin away, but rather said he: "Son of Úrin, thou shalt dwell sweetly in my woodland court, nor even so as a retainer, but behold as a second child of mine shalt thou be, and all the wisdoms of Gwedheling and of myself shalt thou be taught."

After a time therefore when the travellers had rested he despatched the younger of the two guardians of Túrin back unto Mavwin, for such was that man's desire to die in the service of the wife of Úrin, yet was an escort of Elves sent with him, and such comfort and magics for the journey as could be devised, and moreover these words did he bear from Tinwelint to Mavwin: "Behold O Lady Mavwin wife of Úrin the Steadfast, not for love nor for fear of Melko but of the wisdom of my heart and the fate of the Valar did I not go with my folk to the Battle of Unnumbered Tears, who now am become a safety and a refuge for all who fearing evil may find the secret ways that lead to the protection of my halls. Perchance now is there no other bulwark left against the arrogance of the Vala of Iron, for men say Turgon is not slain, but who knoweth the truth of it or how long he may escape? Now therefore shall thy son Túrin be fostered here as my own child until he is of age to succour thee – then, an he will, he may depart." More too he bid the Lady Mavwin, might she o'ercome the journey, fare back also to his halls, and dwell there in peace; but this when she heard she did not do, both for the tenderness of her little child Nienóri, and for that rather would she dwell poor among Men than live sweetly as an almsguest even among the woodland Elves. It may be too that she clung to that dwelling that Úrin had set her in ere he went to the great war, hoping still faintly for his return, for none of the messengers that had borne the lamentable tidings from that field might say that he was dead, reporting only that none knew where he might be – yet in truth those messengers were few and half-distraught, and now the years were slowly passing since the last blow fell on that most grievous day. Indeed in after days she yearned to look again upon Túrin, and maybe in the end, when Nienóri had grown, had cast aside her pride and fared over the hills, had not these become impassable for the might and great magic of Melko, who hemmed all Men in Hithlum and slew such as dared beyond its walls.

Thus came to pass the dwelling of Túrin in the halls of Tinwelint; and with him was suffered to dwell Gumlin the aged who had fared with him out of Hithlum, and had no heart or strength for the returning. Very much joy had he in that sojourn, yet did the sorrow of his sundering from Mavwin fall never quite away from him; great waxed his strength of body and the stoutness of his feats got him praise wheresoever Tinwelint was held as lord, yet he was a silent boy and often gloomy, and he got not love easily and fortune did not follow him, for few things that he desired greatly came to him and many things at which he laboured went awry. For nothing however did he grieve so much as the ceasing of all messengers between Mavwin and himself, when after a few years as has been told the hills became untraversable and the ways were shut. Now Túrin was seven years old when he fared to the woodland Elves, and seven years he dwelt there while tidings came ever and anon to him from his mother, so that he heard how his sister Nienóri grew to a slender maid and very fair, and how things grew better in Hithlum and his mother more in peace; and then all words ceased, and the years passed.

To ease his sorrow and the rage of his heart, that remembered always how Úrin and his folk had gone down in battle against Melko, Túrin was for ever ranging with the most warlike of the folk of Tinwelint far abroad, and long ere he was grown to first manhood he slew and took hurts in frays with the Orcs that prowled unceasingly upon the confines of the realm and were a menace to the Elves. Indeed but for his prowess much hurt had that folk sustained, and he held the wrath of Melko from them for many years, and after his days they were harassed sorely, and in the end must have been cast into thraldom had not such great and dread events befallen that Melko forgot them.

Now about the courts of Tinwelint there dwelt an Elf called Orgof, and he, as were the most of that king's folk, was an Ilkorin, yet he had Gnome-blood also. Of his mother's side he was nearly akin to the king himself, and was in some favour being a good hunter and an Elf of prowess, yet was he somewhat loose with his tongue and overweening by reason of his favour with the king; yet of nothing was he so fain as of fine raiment and of jewels and of gold and silver ornament, and was ever himself clad most bravely. Now Túrin lying continually in the woods and travailing in far and lonely places grew to be uncouth of raiment and wild of locks, and Orgof made jest of him whensoever the twain sat at the king's board; but Túrin said never a word to his foolish jesting, and indeed at no time did he give much heed to words that were spoken to him, and the eyes beneath his shaggy brows oftentimes looked as to a great distance – so that he seemed to see far things and to listen to sounds of the woodland that others heard not.

On a time Túrin sate at meat with the king, and it was that day twelve years since he had gazed through his tears upon Mavwin standing before the doors and weeping as he made his way among the trees, until their stems had taken her from his sight, and he was moody, speaking curt answers to those that sat nigh him, and most of all to Orgof.

But this fool would not give him peace, making a laugh of his rough clothes and tangled hair, for Túrin had then come new from a long abiding in the woods, and at length he drew forth daintily a comb of gold that he had and offered it to Túrin; and having drunk well, when Túrin deigned not to notice him he said: "Nay, an thou knowst not how to use a comb, hie thee back to thy mother, for she perchance will teach thee – unless in sooth the women of Hithlum be as ugly as their sons and as little kempt." Then a fierce anger born of his sore heart and these words concerning the lady Mavwin blazed suddenly in Túrin's breast, so that he seized a heavy drinking-vessel of gold that lay by his right hand and unmindful of his strength he cast it with great force in Orgof's teeth, saying: "Stop thy mouth therewith, fool, and prate no more." But Orgof's face was broken and he fell back with great weight, striking his head upon the stone of the floor and dragging upon him the table and all its vessels, and he spake nor prated again, for he was dead.

Then all men rose in silence, but Túrin, gazing aghast upon the body of Orgof and the spilled wine upon his hand, turned on his heel and strode into the night; and some that were akin to Orgof drew their weapons half from their sheaths, yet none struck, for the king gave no sign but stared stonily upon the body of Orgof, and very great amaze was in his face. But Túrin laved his hands in the stream without the doors and burst there into tears, saying:

"Lo! Is there a curse upon me, for all I do is ill, and now is it so turned that I must flee the house of my fosterfather an outlaw guilty of blood – nor look upon the faces of any I love again." And in his heart he dared not return to Hithlum lest his mother be bitterly grieved at his disgrace, or perchance he might draw the wrath of the Elves behind him to his folk; wherefore he got himself far away, and when men came to seek him he might not be found.

Yet they did not seek his harm, although he knew it not, for Tinwelint despite his grief and the ill deed pardoned him, and the most of his folk were with him in that, for Túrin had long held his peace or returned courtesy to the folly of Orgof, though stung often enough thereby, for that Elf being not a little jealous was used to barb his words; and now therefore the near kinsmen of Orgof were constrained by fear of Tinwelint and by many gifts to accept the king's doom.

Yet Túrin in unhappiness, believing the hand of all against him and the heart of the king become that of a foe, crept to the uttermost bounds of that woodland realm. There he hunted for his subsistence, being a good shot with the bow, yet he rivalled not the Elves at that, for rather at the wielding of the sword was he mightier than they. To him gathered a few wild spirits, and amongst them was Beleg the huntsman, who had rescued Gumlin and Túrin in the woods aforetime. Now in many adventures were those twain together, Beleg the Elf and Túrin the Man, which are not now told or remembered but which once were sung in many a place. With beast and with goblin they warred and fared at times into far places unknown to the Elves, and the fame of the hidden hunters of the marches began to be heard among Orcs and Elves, so that perchance Tinwelint would soon have become aware of the place of Túrin's abiding, had not upon a time all that band of Túrin's fallen into desperate encounter with a host of Orcs who outnumbered them three times. All were there slain save Túrin and Beleg, and Beleg escaped with wounds, but Túrin was overborne and bound, for such was the will of Melko that he be brought to him alive; for behold, dwelling in the halls of Linwë[7] about which had that fay Gwedheling the queen woven much magic and mystery and such power of spells as can come only from Valinor, whence indeed long time agone she once had brought them, Túrin had been lost out of his sight, and he feared lest he cheat the doom that was devised for him. Therefore now he purposed to entreat him grievously before the eyes of Úrin; but Úrin had called upon the Valar of the West, being taught much concerning them by the

Eldar of Kôr – the Gnomes he had encountered – and his words came, who shall say how, to Manwë Súlimo upon the heights of Taniquetil, the Mountain of the World. Nonetheless was Túrin dragged now many an evil league in sore distress, a captive of the pitiless Orcs, and they made slow journeying, for they followed ever the line of dark hills toward those regions where they rise high and gloomy and their heads are shrouded in black vapours. There are they called Angorodin or the Iron Mountains, for beneath the roots of their northernmost fastnesses lies Angband, the Hells of Iron, most grievous of all abodes – and thither were they now making laden with booty and with evil deeds.

Know then that in those days still was Hithlum and the Lands Beyond full of the wild Elves and of Noldoli yet free, fugitives of the old battle; and some wandered ever wearily, and others had secret and hidden abodes in caves or woodland fastnesses, but Melko sought untiringly after them and most pitilessly did he entreat them of all his thralls did he capture them. Orcs and dragons and evil fays were loosed against them and their lives were full of sorrow and travail, so that those who found not in the end the realms of Tinwelint nor the secret stronghold of the king of the city of stone* perished or were enslaved.

Noldoli too there were who were under the evil enchantments of Melko and wandered as in a dream of fear, doing his ill bidding, for the spell of bottomless dread was on them and they felt the eyes of Melko burn them from afar. Yet often did these sad Elves both thrall and free hear the voice of Ulmo in the streams or by the sea-marge where the waters of Sirion mingled with the waves; for Ulmo, of all the Valar, still thought of them most tenderly and designed with their slender aid to bring Melko's evil to ruin. Then remembering the blessedness of Valinor would they at times cast away their fear, doing good deeds and aiding both Elves and Men against the Lord of Iron.

Now was it that it came into the heart of Beleg the hunter of the Elves to seek after Túrin so soon as his own hurts were healed. This being done in no great number of days, for he had a skill of healing, he made all speed after the band of Orcs, and he had need of all his craft as tracker to follow that trail, for a band of the goblins of Melko go cunningly and very light. Soon was he far beyond any regions known to him, yet for love of Túrin he pressed on, and in this did he show courage greater than the most of that

* Gondolin.

woodland folk, and indeed there are none who may now measure
the depth of fear and anguish that Melko set in the hearts of Men
and of Elves in those sad days. Thus did it fall out that Beleg
became lost and benighted in a dark and perilous region so thick
with pines of giant growth that none but the goblins might find a
track, having eyes that pierced the deepest gloom, yet were many
even of these lost long time in those regions; and they were called
by the Noldoli Taurfuin, the Forest of Night. Now giving himself
up for lost Beleg lay with his back to a mighty tree and listened to
the wind in the gaunt tops of the forest many fathoms above him,
and the moaning of the night airs and the creaking of the branches
was full of sorrow and foreboding, and his heart became utterly
weary.

On a sudden he noticed a little light afar among the trees steady
and pale as it were of a glowworm very bright, yet thinking it
might scarce be glowworm in such a place he crept towards it.
Now the Noldoli that laboured in the earth and aforetime had skill
of crafts in metals and gems in Valinor were the most valued of the
thralls of Melko, and he suffered them not to stray far away, and so
it was that Beleg knew not that these Elves had little lanterns of
strange fashion, and they were of silver and of crystal and a flame
of a pale blue burnt forever within, and this was a secret and the
jewel-makers among them alone knew it nor would they reveal it
even to Melko, albeit many jewels and many magic lights they
were constrained to make for him.

Aided by these lamps the Noldoli fared much at night, and
seldom lost a path had they but once trodden it before. So it was
that drawing near Beleg beheld one of the hill-gnomes stretched
upon the needles beneath a great pine asleep, and his blue lantern
stood glimmering nigh his head. Then Beleg awakened him, and
that Elf started up in great fear and anguish, and Beleg learned
that he was a fugitive from the mines of Melko and named himself
Flinding bo-Dhuilin of an ancient house of the Gnomes. Now
falling into talk Flinding was overjoyed to have speech with a free
Noldo, and told many tales of his flight from the uttermost fastness
of the mines of Melko; and at length said he: "When I thought
myself all but free, lo, I strayed at night unwarily into the midmost
of an Orc-camp, and they were asleep and much spoil and weighted
packs they had, and many captive Elves I thought I descried: and
one there was that lay nigh to a trunk to which he was bound most
grievously, and he moaned and cried out bitterly against Melko,
calling on the names of Úrin and Mavwin; and though at that time

being a craven from long captivity I fled heedlessly, now do I marvel much, for who of the thralls of Angband has not known of Úrin the Steadfast who alone of Men defies Melko chained in torment upon a bitter peak?"

Then was Beleg in great eagerness and sprang to his feet shouting: "'Tis Túrin, fosterson of Tinwelint, even he whom I seek, who was the son of Úrin long ago. – Nay, lead me to this camp, O son of Duilin, and soon shall he be free," but Flinding was much afeared, saying: "Softer words, my Beleg, for the Orcs have ears of cats, and though a day's march lies between me and that encampment who knows whether they be not followed after."

Nonetheless hearing the story of Túrin from Beleg, despite his dread he consented to lead Beleg to that place, and long ere the sun rose on the day or its fainting beams crept into that dark forest they were upon the road, guided by the dancing light of Flinding's swinging lamp. Now it happened that in their journeying their paths crossed that of the Orcs who now were renewing their march, but in a direction other than that they had for long pursued, for now fearing the escape of their prisoner they made for a place where they knew the trees were thinner and a track ran for many a league easy to pursue; wherefore that evening, or ever they came to the spot that Flinding sought, they heard a shouting and a rough singing that was afar in the woods but drawing near; nor did they hide too soon ere the whole of that Orc-band passed nigh to them, and some of the captains were mounted upon small horses, and to one of these was Túrin tied by the wrists so that he must trot or be dragged cruelly. Then did Beleg and Flinding follow timorously after as dusk fell on the forest, and when that band encamped they lurked near until all was quiet save the moaning of the captives. Now Flinding covered his lamp with a pelt and they crept near, and behold the goblins slept, for it was not their wont to keep fire or watch in their bivouacs, and for guard they trusted to certain fierce wolves that went always with their bands as dogs with Men, but slept not when they camped, and their eyes shone like points of red light among the trees. Now was Flinding in sore dread, but Beleg bid him follow, and the two crept between the wolves at a point where there was a great gap between them, and as the luck of the Valar had it Túrin was lying nigh, apart from the others, and Beleg came unseen to his side and would cut his bonds, when he found his knife had dropped from his side in his creeping and his sword he had left behind without the camp. Therefore now, for they dare not risk the creeping forth and back again, do Beleg and Flinding both stout men essay to carry him sleeping soundly in utter weariness stealthily from the camp, and this they did, and it has ever been thought a great feat, and few have done the like in passing the wolf guards of the goblins and despoiling their camps.

Now in the woods at no great distance from the camp they laid him down, for they might not bear him further, seeing that he was a Man and of greater stature than they;[8] but Beleg fetched his sword and would cut his bonds forthwith. The bonds about his wrists he severed first and was cutting those upon the ankles when blundering in the dark he pricked Túrin's foot deeply, and Túrin awoke in fear. Now seeing a form bend over him in the gloom sword in hand and feeling the smart of his foot he thought it was one of the Orcs come to slay him or to torment him – and this they did often, cutting him with knives or hurting him with spears; but now Túrin feeling his hand free leapt up and flung all his weight suddenly upon Beleg, who fell and was half-crushed, lying speechless on the ground; but Túrin at the same time seized the sword and struck it through Beleg's throat or ever Flinding might know what had betid. Then Túrin leapt back and shouting out curses upon the goblins bid them come and slay him or taste of his sword, for he fancied himself in the midst of their camp, and thought not of flight but only of selling his life dear. Now would he have made at Flinding, but that Gnome sprang back, dropping his lamp, so that its cover slipped and the light of it shone forth, and he called out in the tongue of the Gnomes that Túrin should hold his hand and slay not his friends – then did Túrin hearing his speech pause, and as he stood, by the light of the lamp he saw the white face of Beleg lying nigh his feet with pierced throat, and he stood as one stricken to stone, and such was the look upon his face that Flinding dared not speak for a long while. Indeed little mind had he for words, for by that light had he also seen the fate of Beleg and was very bitter in heart. At length however it seemed to Flinding that the Orcs were astir, and so it was, for the shouts of Túrin had come to them; wherefore he said to Túrin: "The Orcs are upon us, let us flee," but Túrin answered not, and Flinding shook him, bidding him gather his wits or perish, and then Túrin did as he was bid but yet as one dazed, and stooping he raised Beleg and kissed his mouth.

Then did Flinding guide Túrin as well as he might swiftly from those regions, and Túrin wandered with him following as he led, and at length for a while they had shaken off pursuit and could breathe again. Now then did Flinding have space to tell Túrin all he knew and of his meeting with Beleg, and the floods of Túrin's tears were loosed, and he wept bitterly, for Beleg had been his comrade often in many deeds; and this was the third anguish that befell Túrin, nor did he lose the mark of that sorrow utterly in all his life; and long he wandered with Flinding caring little whither he went, and but for that Gnome soon would he have been recaptured or lost, for he thought only of the stark face of Beleg the huntsman, lying in the dark forest slain by his hand even as he cut the bonds of thraldom from him.

In that time was Túrin's hair touched with grey, despite his few years. Long time however did Túrin and the Noldo journey together, and by reason of the magic of that lamp fared by night and hid by day and were lost in the hills, and the Orcs found them not.

Now in the mountains there was a place of caves above a stream, and that stream ran down to feed the river Sirion, but grass grew before the doors of the caves, and these were cunningly concealed by trees and such magics as those scattered bands that dwelt therein remembered still. Indeed at this time this place had grown to be a strong dwelling of the folk and many a fugitive swelled them, and there the ancient arts and works of the Noldoli came once more to life albeit in a rude and rugged fashion.

There was smithying in secret and forging of good weapons, and even fashioning of some fair things beside, and the women spun once more and wove, and at times was gold quarried privily in places nigh, where it was found, so that deep in those caverns might vessels of beauty be seen in the flame of secret lights, and old songs were faintly sung. Yet did the dwellers in the caves flee always before the Orcs and never give battle unless compelled by mischance or were they able to so entrap them that all might be slain and none escape alive; and this they did of policy that no tidings reach Melko of their dwelling nor might he suspect any numerous gathering of folk in those parts.

This place however was known to the Noldo Flinding who fared with Túrin; indeed he was once of that people long since, before the Orcs captured him and he was held in thraldom. Thither did he now wend being sure that the pursuit came no longer nigh them, yet went he nonetheless by devious ways, so that it was long ere they drew nigh to that region, and the spies and watchers of the Rodothlim (for so were that folk named) gave warning of their approach, and the folk withdrew before them, such as were abroad from their dwelling. Then they closed their doors and hoped that the strangers might not discover their caves, for they feared and mistrusted all unknown folk of whatever race, so evil were the lessons of that dreadful time.

Now then Flinding and Túrin dared even to the caves' mouths, and perceiving that these twain knew now the paths thereto the Rodothlim sallied and made them prisoners and drew them within their rocky halls, and they were led before the chief, Orodreth. Now the free Noldoli at that time feared much those of their kin who had tasted thraldom, for compelled by fear and torture and spells much treachery had they wrought; even thus did the evil deeds of the Gnomes at Cópas Alqalunten find vengeance,' setting Gnome against Gnome, and the Noldoli cursed the day that ever they first hearkened to the deceit of Melko, rueing utterly their departure from the blessed realm of Valinor.

Nonetheless when Orodreth heard the tale of Flinding and knew it to be true he welcomed him with joy back among the folk, yet was that Gnome so changed by the anguish of his slavery that few knew him again; but for Flinding's sake Orodreth hearkened to the tale of Túrin, and Túrin told of his travails and named Úrin as his sire, nor had the Gnomes yet forgot that name. Then was the heart of Orodreth made kind and he bade them dwell among the Rodothlim and be faithful to him. So came the sojourn of Túrin among the people of the caves, and he dwelt with Flinding bo-Dhuilin and laboured much for the good of the folk, and slew many a wandering Orc, and did doughty deeds in their defence. In return much did he learn of new wisdom from them, for memories of Valinor burnt yet deep in their wild hearts, and greater still was their wisdom than that of such Eldar as had seen never the blest faces of the Gods.

Among that people was a very fair maiden and she was named Failivrin, and her father was Galweg; and this Gnome had a liking for Túrin and aided him much, and Túrin was often with him in ventures and good deeds. Now many a tale of these did Galweg make beside his hearth and Túrin was often at his board, and the heart of Failivrin became moved at the sight of him, and wondered often at his gloom and sadness, pondering what sorrow lay locked in his breast, for Túrin went not gaily being weighted with the death of Beleg that he felt upon his head, and he suffered not his heart to be moved, although he was glad of her sweetness; but he deemed himself an outlawed man and one burdened with a heavy doom of ill. Therefore did Failivrin become sorrowful and wept in secret, and she grew so pale that folk marvelled at the whiteness and delicacy of her face and her bright eyes that shone therein.

Now came a time when the Orc-bands and the evil things of Melko drew ever nigher to the dwelling of this folk, and despite the good spells that ran in the stream beneath it seemed like that their abode would remain no longer hidden. It is said however that during all this time the dwelling of Túrin in the caves and his deeds among the Rodothlim were veiled from Melko's eyes, and that he infested not the Rodothlim for Túrin's sake nor out of design, but rather it was the ever increasing numbers of these creatures and their growing power and fierceness that brought them so far afield. Nonetheless the blindness and ill-fortune that he wove of old clung yet to Túrin, as may be seen.

Each day grew the brows of the chiefs of the Rodothlim more dark, and dreams came to them[10] bidding them arise and depart swiftly and secretly, seeking, if it might be, after Turgon, for with him might yet salvation be found for the Gnomes. Whispers too there were in the stream at eve, and those among them skilled to hear such voices added their foreboding at the councils of the folk. Now at these councils had Túrin won him a place by dint of many valorous deeds, and he gainsaid their fears, trusting in his strength, for he lusted ever for war with the creatures of Melko, and he upbraided the men of the folk, saying: "Lo! Ye have weapons of great excellence of workmanship, and yet are the most of them clean of your foes' blood. Remember ye the Battle of Uncounted Tears and forget not your folk that there fell, nor seek ever to flee, but fight and stand."

Now despite the wisdom of their wisest such bitter words confused their counsels and delayed them, and there were no few of the stout-hearted that found hope in them, being sad at the thought of abandoning those places where they had begun to make an abiding place of peace and goodliness; but Túrin begged Orodreth for a sword, and he had not wielded a sword since the slaying of Beleg, but rather had he been contented with a mighty club. Now then Orodreth let fashion for him a great sword, and it was made by magic to be utterly black save at its edges, and those were shining bright and sharp as but Gnome-steel may be. Heavy it was, and was sheathed in black, and it hung from a sable belt, and Túrin named it Gurtholfin the Wand of Death; and often that blade leapt in his hand of its own lust, and it is said that at times it spake dark words to him. Therewith did he now range the hills, and slew unceasingly, so that Blacksword of the Rodothlim became a name of terror to the Orcs, and for a great season all evil was fended from the caverns of the Gnomes. Hence comes that name of Túrin's among the Gnomes, calling him Mormagli or Mormakil according to their speech, for these names signify black sword.

The greater however did Túrin's valour become so grew the love of Failivrin more deep, and did men murmur against him in his absence she spake for him, and sought ever to minister to him, and her he treated ever courteously and happily, saying he had found a fair sister in the Gnome-lands. By Túrin's deeds however was the ancient counsel of the Rodothlim set aside and their abode made known far and wide, nor was Melko ignorant of it, yet many of the Noldoli now fled to them and their strength waxed and Túrin was held in great honour among them. Then were days of great happiness and for a while men lived openly again and might fare far abroad from their homes in safety, and many boasted of the salvation of the Noldoli, while Melko gathered in secret his great hordes. These did he loose suddenly upon them at unawares, and they gathered their warriors in great haste and went against him, but behold, an army of Orcs descended upon them, and wolves, and Orcs mounted upon wolves; and a great worm was with them whose scales were polished bronze and whose breath was a mingled fire and smoke, and his name was Glorund.[11] All the men of the Rodothlim fell or were taken in that battle, for the foe was numberless, and that was the most bitter affray since the evil field of Nínin-Udathriol.* Orodreth was there sorely hurt and Túrin bore him out of the fight ere yet all was ended, and with the aid of Flinding whose wounds were not great[12] he got him to the caves.

There died Orodreth, reproaching Túrin that he had ever withstood his wise counsels, and Túrin's heart was bitter at the ruin of the folk that was set to his account.[13] Then leaving Lord Orodreth dead Túrin went to the places of Galweg's abiding, and there was Failivrin weeping bitterly at the tidings of her father's death, but Túrin sought to comfort her, and for the pain of her heart and the sorrow of her father's death and of the ruin of her folk she swooned upon his breast and cast her arms about

---

* At the bottom of the manuscript page is written:

  'Nieriltasinwa   the battle of unnumbered tears
  Glorund   Laurundo or Undolaurë'

  Later Glorund and Laurundo were emended to Glorunt and Laurunto.

him. So deep was the ruth of Túrin's heart that in that hour he deemed he loved her very dearly; yet were now he and Flinding alone save for a few aged carles and dying men, and the Orcs having despoiled the field of dead were nigh upon them.

Thus stood Túrin before the doors with Gurtholfin in hand, and Flinding was beside him; and the Orcs fell on that place and ransacked it utterly, dragging out all the folk that lurked therein and all their goods, whatsoever of great or little worth might there lie hid. But Túrin denied the entrance of Galweg's dwelling to them, and they fell thick about him, until a company of their archers standing at a distance shot a cloud of arrows at him. Now he wore chainmail such as all the warriors of the Gnomes have ever loved and still do wear, yet it turned not all those ill shafts, and already was he sore hurt when Flinding fell pierced suddenly through the eye; and soon too had he met his death – and his weird had been the happier thereby – had not that great drake coming now upon the sack bidden them cease their shooting; but with the power of his breath he drove Túrin from those doors and with the magic of his eyes he bound him hand and foot.

Now those drakes and worms are the evillest creatures that Melko has made, and the most uncouth, yet of all are they the most powerful, save it be the Balrogs only. A great cunning and wisdom have they, so that it has been long said amongst Men that whosoever might taste the heart of a dragon would know all tongues of Gods or Men, of birds or beasts, and his ears would catch whispers of the Valar or of Melko such as never had he heard before. Few have there been that ever achieved a deed of such prowess as the slaying of a drake, nor might any even of such doughty ones taste their blood and live, for it is as a poison of fires that slays all save the most godlike in strength. Howso that may be, even as their lord these foul beasts love lies and lust after gold and precious things with a great fierceness of desire, albeit they may not use nor enjoy them.

Thus was it that this *lókë* (for so do the Eldar name the worms of Melko) suffered the Orcs to slay whom they would and to gather whom they listed into a very great and very sorrowful throng of women, maids, and little children, but all the mighty treasure that they had brought from the rocky halls and heaped glistering in the sun before the doors he coveted for himself and forbade them set finger on it, and they durst not withstand him, nor could they have done so an they would.

In that sad band stood Failivrin in horror, and she stretched out her arms towards Túrin, but Túrin was held by the spell of the drake, for that beast had a foul magic in his glance, as have many others of his kind, and he turned the sinews of Túrin as it were to stone, for his eye held Túrin's eye so that his will died, and he could not stir of his own purpose, yet might he see and hear.

Then did Glorund taunt Túrin nigh to madness, saying that lo! he had cast away his sword nor had the heart to strike a blow for his friends — now Túrin's sword lay at his feet whither it had slipped from his unnervéd grasp. Great was the agony of Túrin's heart thereat, and the Orcs laughed at him, and of the captives some cried bitterly against him. Even now did the Orcs begin to drive away that host of thralls, and his heart broke at the sight, yet he moved not; and the pale face of Failivrin faded afar, and her voice was borne to him crying: "O Túrin Mormakil, where is thy heart; O my beloved, wherefore dost thou forsake me?" So great then became Túrin's anguish that even the spell of that worm might not restrain it, and crying aloud he reached for the sword at his feet and would wound the drake with it, but the serpent breathed a foul and heated breath upon him, so that he swooned and thought that it was death.

A long time thereafter, and the tale telleth not how long, he came to himself, and he was lying gazing at the sun before the doors, and his head rested against a heap of gold even as the ransackers had left it. Then said the drake, who was hard by: "Wonderest thou not wherefore I have withheld death from thee, O Túrin Mormakil, who wast once named brave?" Then Túrin remembered all his griefs and the evil that had fallen upon him, and he said: "Taunt me not, foul worm, for thou knowest I would die; and for that alone, methinks, thou slayest me not."

But the drake answered saying: "Know then this, O Túrin son of Úrin, that a fate of evil is woven about thee, and thou mayst not untangle thy footsteps from it whitherever thou goest. Yea indeed, I would not have thee slain, for thus wouldst thou escape very bitter sorrows and a weird of anguish." Then Túrin leaping suddenly to his feet and avoiding that beast's baleful eye raised aloft his sword and cried: "Nay, from this hour shall none name me Túrin if I live. Behold, I will name me a new name and it shall be Turambar!" Now this meaneth Conqueror of Fate, and the form of the name in the Gnome-speech is Turumart. Then uttering these words he made a second time at the drake, thinking indeed to force the drake to slay him and to conquer his fate by death, but the dragon laughed, saying: "Thou fool! An I would, I had slain thee long since and could do so here and now, and if I will not thou canst not do battle with me waking, for my eye can cast once more the binding spell upon thee that thou stand as stone. Nay, get thee gone, O Turambar Conqueror of Fate! First thou must meet thy doom an thou wouldst o'ercome it." But Turambar was filled with shame and anger, and perchance he had slain himself, so great was his madness, although thus might he not hope that ever his spirit would be freed from the dark glooms of Mandos or stray into the pleasant paths of Valinor;[14] but amidst his misery he bethought him of Failivrin's pallid face and he bowed his head, for the thought came into his heart to seek back through all the woods after her sad footsteps even be it to Angamandi and the Hills of Iron. Maybe in that desperate venture he had found a kindly and swift death or perchance an ill one, and maybe he had rescued Failivrin and found happiness, yet not thus was he fated to earn the name he had taken anew, and the drake reading his mind suffered him not thus lightly to escape his tide of ill.

"Hearken to me, O son of Úrin," said he; "ever wast thou a coward at heart, vaunting thyself falsely before men. Perchance thou thinkest it a gallant deed to go follow after a maiden of strange kin, recking little of thine own that suffer now terrible things? Behold, Mavwin who loves thee long has eagerly awaited thy return, knowing that thou hast found manhood a while ago, and she looks for thy succour in vain, for little she knows that her son is an outlaw stained with the blood of his comrades, a defiler of his lord's table. Ill do men entreat her, and behold the Orcs infest now those parts of Hithlum, and she is in fear and peril and her daughter Nienóri thy sister with her."

Then was Turambar aflame with sorrow and with shame for the lies of that worm were barbed with truth, and for the spell of his eyes he believed all that was said. Therefore his old desire to see once more Mavwin his mother and to look upon Nienóri whom he had never seen since his first days[15] grew hot within him, and with a heart torn with sorrow for the fate of Failivrin he turned his feet towards the hills seeking Dor Lómin, and his sword was sheathed. And truly is it said: "Forsake not for anything thy friends – nor believe those who counsel thee to do so" – for of his abandoning of Failivrin in danger that he himself could see came the very direst evil upon him and all he loved; and indeed his heart was confounded and wavered, and he left those places in uttermost shame and weariness. But the dragon gloated upon the hoard and lay coiled upon it, and the fame of that great treasure of golden vessels and of unwrought gold that lay by the caves above the stream fared far and wide about; yet the great worm slept before it, and evil thoughts he had as he pondered the planting of his cunning lies and the sprouting thereof and their growth and fruit, and fumes of smoke went up from his nostrils as he slept.

On a time therefore long afterward came Turambar with great travail into Hisilómë, and found at length the place of the abode of his mother, even the one whence he had been sundered as a child, but behold, it was roofless and the tilth about it ran wild. Then his heart smote him, but he learned of some that dwelt nigh that lighting on better days the Lady Mavwin had departed some years agone to places not far distant where was a great and prosperous dwelling of men, for that region of Hisilómë was fertile and men tilled the land somewhat and many had flocks and herds, though for the most part in the dark days after the great battle men feared to dwell in settled places and ranged the woods and hunted or fished, and so it was with those kindreds about the waters of Asgon whence after arose Tuor son of Peleg.

Hearing these words however Turambar was amazed, and questioned them concerning the wandering into those regions of Orcs and other fierce folk of Melko, but they shook their heads, and said that never had such creatures come hither deep into the land of Hisilómë.[16] "If thou wishest for Orcs then go to the hills that encompass our land about," said they, "and thou wilt not search long. Scarce may the wariest fare in and out so constant is their watch, and they infest the rocky gates of the land that the Children of Men be penned for ever in the Land of Shadows; but men say 'tis the will of Melko that they trouble us not here – and yet it seems to us that thou hast come from afar, and at this we marvel, for long is it since one from other lands might tread this way." Then Turambar was in perplexity at this and he doubted the deceit of the dragon's words, yet he went now in hope to the dwelling of men and the house of his mother, and coming upon homesteads of men he was easily directed thither. Now men looked strangely at his questioning, and indeed they had reason, yet were such as he spoke to in great awe and wonder at him and shrank back from speech with him, for his garb was of the wild woods and his hair was long and his face haggard and drawn as with unquenchable sorrows, and therein burnt fiercely his dark eyes beneath dark brows. A collar of fine gold he wore and his mighty sword was at his side, and men marvelled much at him;

and did any dare to question him he named himself Turambar son of the weary forest,* and that seemed but the more strange to them.

Now came he to the dwelling of Mavwin, and behold it was a fair house, but none dwelt there, and grass was high in the gardens, and there were no kine in the byres nor horses in the sheds, and the pastures about were silent and empty. Only the swallows had dwelling beneath the timbers of the eaves and these made a noise and a bustle as if departure for autumn was at hand, and Turambar sat before the carven doors and wept. And one who was passing on to other dwellings, for a track passed nigh to that homestead, espied him, and coming asked him his grief, and Turambar said that it was bitter for a son sundered for many years from his home to give up all that was dear and dare the dangers of the infested hills to find only the halls of his kindred empty when he returned at last.

"Nay, then this is a very trick of Melko's," said the other, "for of a truth here dwelt the Lady Mavwin wife of Úrin, and yet is she gone two years past very secretly and suddenly, and men say that she seeks her son who is lost, and that her daughter Nienóri goes with her, but I know not the story. This however I know, and many about here do likewise, and cry shame thereon, for know that the guardianship of all her goods and land she gave to Brodda, a man whom she trusted, and he is lord of these regions by men's consent and has to wife a kinswoman of hers. But now she is long away he has mingled her herds and flocks, small as they were, with his mighty ones, branding them with his own marks, yet the dwelling and stead of Mavwin he suffereth to fall to ruin, and men think ill of it but move not, for the power of Brodda has grown to be great."

Then Turambar begged him to set his feet upon the paths to Brodda's halls, and the man did as he desired, so that Turambar striding thither came upon them just as night fell and men sat to meat in that house. Great was the company that night and the light of many torches fell upon them, but the Lady Airin was not there, for men drank overmuch at Brodda's feasts and their songs were fierce and quarrels blazed about the hall, and those things she loved not. Now Turambar smote upon the gates and his heart was black and a great wrath was in him, for the words of the stranger before his mother's doors were bitter to him.

---

* A note on the manuscript referring to this name reads: 'Turumart go-Dhrauthodauros [emended to bo-Dhrauthodavros] or Turambar Rúsitaurion.'

Then did some open to his knocking and Turambar strode into that hall, and Brodda bade him be seated and ordered wine and meats to be set before him, but Turambar would neither eat nor drink, so that men looking askance upon his sullenness asked him who he might be. Then Turambar stepping out into the midst of them before the high place where Brodda sat said: "Behold, I am Turambar son of the forest", and men laughed thereat, but Turambar's eyes were full of wrath. Then said Brodda in doubt: "What wilt thou of me, O son of the wild forest?" But Turambar said: "Lord Brodda, I am come to repay thy stewardship of others' goods," and silence fell in that place; but Brodda laughed, saying again: "But who art thou?" And thereupon Turambar leapt upon the high place and ere Brodda might foresee the act he drew Gurtholfin and seizing Brodda by the locks all but smote his head from off his body, crying aloud: "So dieth the rich man who addeth the widow's little to his much. Lo, men die not all in the wild woods, and am I not in truth the son of Úrin, who having sought back unto his folk findeth an empty hall despoiled." Then was there a great uproar in that hall, and indeed though he was burdened overmuch with his many griefs and wellnigh distraught, yet was this deed of Turambar violent and unlawful. Some were there nonetheless that would not unsheathe their weapons, saying that Brodda was a thief and died as one, but many there were that leapt with swords against Turambar and he was hard put to it, and one man he slew, and it was Orlin. Then came Airin of the long hair in great fear into the halls and at her voice men stayed their hands; but great was her horror when she saw the deeds that were done, and Turambar turned his face away and might not look upon her, for his wrath was grown cold and he was sick and weary.

But she hearing the tale said: "Nay, grieve not for me, son of Úrin, but for thyself; for my lord was a hard lord and cruel and unjust, and men might say somewhat in thy defence, yet behold thou hast slain him now at his board being his guest, and Orlin thou hast slain who is of thy mother's kin; and what shall be thy doom?" At those words some were silent and many shouted "death", but Airin said that it was not wholly in accord with the laws of that place, "for," said she, "Brodda was slain wrongfully, yet just was the wrath of the slayer, and Orlin too did he slay in defence, though it were in the hall of a feast. Yet now I fear that this man must get him swiftly from among us nor ever set foot upon these lands again, else shall any man slay him; but those lands and goods that were Úrin's shall Brodda's kin hold, save only

do Mavwin and Nienóri return ever from their wandering, yet
even so may Túrin son of Úrin inherit nor part nor parcel of them
ever." Now this doom seemed just to all save Turambar, and they
marvelled at the equity of Airin whose lord lay slain, and they
guessed not at the horror of her life aforetime with that man; but
Turambar cast his sword upon the floor and bade them slay him,
yet they would not for the words of Airin whom they loved, and
Airin suffered it not for the love of Mavwin, hoping yet to join
those twain mother and son in happiness, and her doom she had
made to satisfy men's anger and save Túrin from death. "Nay,"
said she, "three days do I give thee to get thee out of the land,
wherefore go!" and Turambar lifting his sword wiped it, saying:
"Would I were clean of his blood," and he went forth into the
night. In the folly of his heart now did he deem himself cut off in
truth for ever from Mavwin his mother, thinking that never again
would any he loved be fain to look upon him. Then did he thirst
for news of his mother and sister and of none might he ask, but
wandered back over the hills knowing only that they sought him
still perchance in the forests of the Lands Beyond, and no more
did he know for a long while.

Of his wanderings thereafter has no tale told, save that after
much roaming his sorrow grew dulled and his heart dead, until at
last in places very far away many a journey beyond the river of the
Rodothlim he fell in with some huntsmen of the woods, and these
were Men. Some of that company were thanes of Úrin, or sons of
them, and they had wandered darkly ever since that Battle of
Tears, but now did Turambar join their number, and built his life
anew so well as he might. Now that people had houses in a more
smiling region of the woods in lands that were not utterly far from
Sirion or the grassy hills of that river's middle course, and
they were hardy men and bowed not to Melko, and Turambar got
honour among them.

Now is it to tell that far other had matters fallen out with
Mavwin than the Foalókë had said to Túrin, for her days turning
to better she had peace and honour among the men of those
regions. Nonetheless her grief at the loss of her son by reason of
the cutting off of all messengers deepened only with the years,
albeit Nienóri grew to a most fair and slender maid. At the time of
Túrin's flight from the halls of Tinwelint she was already twelve[17]
years old and tall and beautiful.

Now the tale tells not the number of days that Turambar

sojourned with the Rodothlim but these were very many, and during that time Nienóri grew to the threshold of womanhood, and often was there speech between her and her mother of Túrin that was lost. In the halls of Tinwelint too the memory of Túrin lived still, and there still abode Gumlin, now decrepit in years, who aforetime had been the guardian of Túrin's childhood upon that first journey to the Lands Beyond. Now was Gumlin white-haired and the years were heavy on him, but he longed sorely for a sight once more of the folk of Men and of the Lady Mavwin his mistress. On a time then Gumlin learnt of the with-drawal from the hills of the greater number of those Orc-bands and other fierce beings of Melko's that had for so long made them impassable to Elves and Men. Now for a space were the hills and the paths that led over them far and wide free of his evil, for Melko had at that time a great and terrible project afoot, and that was the destruction of the Rodothlim and of many dwellings of the Gnomes beside, that his spies had revealed,[18] yet all the folk of those regions breathed the freer for a while, though had they known all perchance they had not done so.

Then Gumlin the aged fell to his knees before Tinwelint and begged that he suffer him to depart homeward, that he might see his mistress of old ere death took him to the halls of Mandos — if indeed that lady had not fared thither before him. Then the king[19] said yea, and for his journey he gave him two guides for the succouring of his age; yet those three, Gumlin and the woodland Elves, made a very hard journey, for it was late winter, and yet would Gumlin by no means abide until spring should come.

Now as they drew nigh to that region of Hisilómë where afore-time Mavwin had dwelt and nigh where she dwelt yet a great snow fell, as happened oft in those parts on days that should rather have been ones of early spring. Therein was Gumlin whelmed, and his guides seeking aid came unawares upon Mavwin's house, and calling for aid of her were granted it. Then by the aid of the folk of Mavwin was Gumlin found and carried to the house and warmed back to life, and coming to himself at length he knew Mavwin and was very joyful.

Now when he was in part healed he told his tale to Mavwin, and as he recounted the years and the doughtiest of the feats of Túrin she was glad, but great was her sorrow and dismay at the tidings of his sundering from Linwë[20] and the manner of it, and going from Gumlin she wept bitterly. Indeed for long and since ever she knew that Túrin, an he lived, had grown to manhood she had wondered

that he sought not back to her, and often dread had filled her heart
lest attempting this he had perished in the hills; but now the truth
was bitter to bear and she was desolate for a great while, nor might
Nienóri comfort her.

Now by reason of the unkindness of the weather those guides
that had brought Gumlin out of Tinwelint's realms abode as her
guests until spring came, but with spring's first coming Gumlin
died.

Then arose Mavwin and going to several of the chiefs of those
places she besought their aid, telling them the tale of Túrin's fate
as Gumlin had told it to her. But some laughed, saying she was
deceived by the babblings of a dying man, and the most said that
she was distraught with grief, and that it would be a fool's counsel
to seek beyond the hills a man who had been lost for years agone:
"nor," said they, "will we lend man or horse to such a quest, for all
our love for thee, O Mavwin wife of Úrin."

Then Mavwin departed in tears but railed not at them, for she
had scant hope in her plea and knew that wisdom was in their
words. Nonetheless being unable to rest she came now to those
guides of the Elves, who chafed already to be away beneath the
sun; and she said to them: "Lead me now to your lord," and they
would dissuade her, saying that the road was no road for a woman's
feet to tread; yet she did not heed them. Rather did she beg of her
friend whose name was Airin Faiglindra* (long-tressed) and was
wed to Brodda a lord of that region, and rich and powerful, that
Nienóri might be taken under the guardianship of her husband
and all her goods thereto. This did Airin obtain of Brodda without
great pleading, and when she knew this she would take farewell
of her daughter; but her plan availed little, for Nienóri stood
before her mother and said: "Either thou goest not, O Mavwin my
mother, or go we both," nor would anything turn her from those
words. Therefore in the end did both mother and daughter make
them ready for that sore journey, and the guides murmured much
thereat. Yet it so happened that the season which followed that
bitter winter was very kindly, and despite the forebodings of the
guides the four passed the hills and made their long journey with
no greater evils than hunger and thirst.

Coming therefore at length before Tinwelint Mavwin cast herself down and wept, begging pardon for Túrin and compassion
and aid for herself and Nienóri; but Tinwelint bade her arise and

* In the margin is written *Firilanda*.

seat herself beside Gwedheling his queen, saying: "Long years ago was Túrin thy son forgiven, aye, even as he left these halls, and many a weary search have we made for him. No outlawry of mine was it that took him from this realm, but remorse and bitterness drew him to the wilds, and there, methinks, evil things o'ertook him, or an he lives yet I fear me it is in bondage to the Orcs." Then Mavwin wept again and implored the king to give her aid, for she said: "Yea verily I would fare until the flesh of my feet were worn away, if haply at the journey's end I might see the face of Túrin son of Úrin my well-beloved." But the king said that he knew not whither she might seek her son save in Angamandi, and thither he might not send any of his lieges, not though his heart were full of ruth for the sorrow of Úrin's folk. Indeed Tinwelint spoke but as he believed just, nor meant he to add to Mavwin's sorrow save only to restrain her from so mad and deadly a quest, but Mavwin hearing him spake no word more, and going from him went out into the woods and suffered no one to stay her, and only Nienóri followed her whithersoever she went.

Now the folk of Tinwelint looked with pity on those twain and with kindness, and secretly they watched them, and unbeknown kept much harm from them, so that the wandering ladies of the woods became familiar among them and dear to many, yet were they a sight of ruth, and folk swore hatred to Melko and his works who saw them pass. Thus came it that after many moons Mavwin fell in with a band of wandering Gnomes, and entering into discourse with them the tale was told to her of the Rodothlim, such as those Gnomes knew of it, and of the dwelling of Túrin among them. Of the whelming of that abode of folk by the hosts of Melko and by the dragon Glorund they told too, for those deeds were then new and their fame went far and wide. Now Túrin they named not by name, calling him Mormakil, a wild man who fled from the face of Tinwelint and escaped thereafter from the hands of the Orcs.

Then was the heart of Mavwin filled with hope and she questioned them more, but the Noldoli said that they had not heard that any came alive out of that ransacking save such as were haled to Angamandi, and then again was Mavwin's hope dashed low. Yet did she nonetheless get her back to the king's halls, and telling her tale besought his aid against the Foalókë. Now it was Mavwin's thought that perchance Túrin dwelt yet in the thraldom of the dragon and it might fall to them in some manner to liberate him, or again should the prowess of the king's men suffice then might they slay the worm in vengeance for his evils, and so at his death might he speak words of knowledge concerning the fate of Túrin, were he indeed no longer nigh the caverns of the Rodothlim. Of the mighty hoard that that worm guarded Mavwin recked little, but she spake much of it to Tinwelint, even as the Noldoli had spoken of it to her. Now the folk of Tinwelint were of the woodlands and had scant wealth, yet did they love fair and beauteous things, gold and silver and gems, as do all the Eldar but the Noldoli most of all; nor was the king of other mind in this, and his riches were small, save it be for that glorious Silmaril that many a king had given all his treasury contained if he might possess it.

Therefore did Tinwelint answer: "Now shalt thou have aid, O Mavwin most steadfast, and, openly I say it to thee, it is not for hope of freeing Túrin thereby that I grant it to thee, for such hope I do not see in this tale, but rather the death of hope. Yet it is a truth that I have need and desire of treasury, and it may be that such shall come to me by this venture; yet half of the spoil shalt thou have O Mavwin for the memory of Úrin and Túrin, or else shalt thou ward it for Nienóri thy daughter." Then said Mavwin: "Nay, give me but a woodman's cot and my son," and the king answered: "That I cannot, for I am but a king of the wild Elves, and no Vala of the western isles."

Then Tinwelint gathered a picked band of his warriors and hunters and told them his bidding, and it seemed that the name of the Foalókë was known already among them, and there were many who could guide the band unto the regions of his dwelling, yet was that name a terror to the stoutest and the places of his abode a land of accursed dread. Now the ancient dwellings of the Rodothlim were not utterly distant from the realm of Tinwelint, albeit far enough, but the king said to Mavwin: "Bide now and Nienóri also with me, and my men shall fare against the drake, and all that they do and find in those places will they faithfully report," – and his men said: "Yea, we will do thy bidding, O King," but fear stood in their eyes.

Then Mavwin seeing it said: "Yea, O King, let Nienóri my daughter bide indeed at the feet of Gwedheling the Queen, but I who care not an I die or live will go look upon the dragon and find my son"; and Tinwelint laughed, yet Gwedheling and Nienóri fearing that she spake no jest pled earnestly with her. But she was as adamant, fearing lest this her last hope of rescuing Túrin come to nought through the terror of Tinwelint's men, and none might move her. "Of love, I know," said she, "come all the words ye speak, yet give me rather a horse to ride and if ye will a sharp knife for my own death at need, and let me be gone." Now these words struck amazement into those Elves that heard, for indeed the wives and daughters of Men in those days were hardy and their youth lasted a great span, yet did this seem a madness to all.

Madder yet did it seem when Nienóri, seeing the obstinacy of her mother, said before them all: "Then I too will go; whither my mother Mavwin goeth thither more easily yet shall I, Nienóri daughter of Úrin, fare"; but Gwedheling said to the king that he allow it not, for she was a fay and perchance foresaw dimly what might be.

Then had Mavwin ended the dispute and departed from the king's presence into the woods, had not Nienóri caught at her robe and stayed her, and so did all plead with Mavwin, till at length it was agreed that the king send a strong party against the Foalókë and that Nienóri and Mavwin ride with them until the regions of the beast be found. Then should they seek a high place whence they might see something of the deeds yet in safety and secrecy, while the warriors crept upon the worm to slay it. Now of this high place a woodsman told, and often had he gazed therefrom upon the dwelling of the worm afar. At length was that band of dragon-slayers got ready, and they were mounted upon goodly horses swift and sure-going, albeit few of those beasts were possessed by the folk of the woods. Horses too were found for Nienóri and for Mavwin, and they rode at the head of the warriors, and folk marvelled much to see their bearing, for the men of Úrin and those amongst whom Nienóri was nurtured were much upon horses, and both knave and maid among them rode even in tender years.

After many days' going came now that cavalcade within view of a place that once had been a fair region, and through it a swift river ran over a rocky bed, and of one side was the brink of it high and tree-grown and of the other the land was more level and fertile and broad-swelling, but beyond the high bank of the river the hills drew close. Thither as they looked they saw that the land had become all barren and was blasted for a great distance about the ancient caverns of the Rodothlim, and the trees were crushed to the earth or snapped. Toward the hills a black heath stretched and the lands were scored with the great slots that that loathly worm made in his creeping.

Many are the dragons that Melko has loosed upon the world and some are more mighty than others. Now the least mighty — yet were they very great beside the Men of those days — are cold as is the nature of snakes and serpents, and of them a many having wings go with the uttermost noise and speed; but the mightier are hot and very heavy and slow-going, and some belch flame, and fire flickereth beneath their scales, and the lust and greed and cunning evil of these is the greatest of all creatures: and such was the Foalókë whose burning there set all the places of his habitation in waste and desolation. Already greater far had this worm waxen than in the days of the onslaught upon the Rodothlim, and greater too was his hoarded treasure, for Men and Elves and even Orcs he slew, or enthralled that they served him, bringing him food to slake his lust [?on] precious things, and spoils of their harryings to swell his hoard.

Now was that band aghast as they looked upon that region from afar, yet they prepared them for battle, and drawing lots sent one of their number with Nienóri and Mavwin to that high place[21] upon the confines of the withered land that had been named, and it was covered with trees, and might be reached by hidden paths. Even as those three rode thither and the warriors crept stealthily toward the caves, leaving their horses that were already in a sweat of fear, behold the Foalókë came from his lair, and sliding down the bank lay across the stream, as often was his wont. Straightway great fog and steams leapt up and a stench was mingled therein, so that that band was whelmed in vapours and well-nigh stifled, and they crying to one another in the mist displayed their presence to the worm; and he laughed aloud. At that most awful of all sounds of beasts they fled wildly in the mists, and yet they could not discover their horses, for these in an extremity of terror broke loose and fled.

Then Nienóri hearing far cries and seeing the great mist roll toward them from the river turned back with her mother to the place of sundering, and there alighting waited in great doubt. Suddenly came that blind mist upon them as they stood, and with it came flying madly the dim horses of the huntsmen. Then their own catching their terror trampled to death that Elf who was their escort as he caught at the flying bridles, and wild with fear they sped to the dark woods and never more bore Man or Elf upon their saddles; but Mavwin and Nienóri were left alone and succourless upon the borders of the places of fear. Very perilous indeed was their estate, and long they groped in the mist and knew not where they were nor saw they ever any of the band again, and only pale voices seemed to pass them by afar crying out as in dread, and then all was silent. Now did they cling together and being weary

stumbled on heedless whither their steps might go, till on a
sudden the sun gleamed thin above them, and hope returned to
them; and behold the mists lifted and the airs became clearer and
they stood not far from the river. Even now it smoked as it were
hot, and behold the Foalókë lay there and his eyes were upon
them.

No word did he speak nor did he move, but his baleful eye held
their gaze until the strength seemed to leave their knees and their
minds grew dim. Then did Nienóri drag herself by a might of will
from that influence for a while, and "Behold," she cried, "O
serpent of Melko, what wilt thou with us – be swift to say or do, for
know that we seek not thee nor thy gold but one Túrin who dwelt
here upon a time." Then said the drake, and the earth quaked at
him: "Thou liest – glad had ye been at my death, and glad thy
band of cravens who now flee gibbering in the woods might they
have despoiled me. Fools and liars, liars and cravens, how shall ye
slay or despoil Glorund the Foalókë, who ere his power had waxen
slew the hosts of the Rodothlim and Orodreth their lord, devouring
all his folk."

"Yet perchance," said Nienóri, "one Túrin got him from that
fray and dwells still here beneath thy bonds, an he has not
escaped thee and is now far hence," and this she said at a venture,
hoping against hope, but said the evil one: "Lo! the names of all
who dwelt here before the taking of the caves of my wisdom I
know, and I say to thee that none who named himself Túrin went
hence alive." And even so was Túrin's boast subtly turned against
him, for these beasts love ever to speak thus, doubly playing with
cunning words.[22]

"Then was Túrin slain in this evil place," said Mavwin, but the
dragon answered: "Here did the name of Túrin fade for ever from
the earth – but weep not, woman, for it was the name of a craven
that betrayed his friends." "Foul beast, cease thy evil sayings,"
said Mavwin; "slayer of my son, revile not the dead, lest thine
own bane come upon thee." "Less proud must be thy words, O
Mavwin, an thou wilt escape torment or thy daughter with thee,"
did that drake answer, but Mavwin cried: "O most accursed, lo! I
fear thee not. Take me an thou wilt to thy torments and thy
bondage, for of a truth I desired thy death, but suffer only Nienóri
my daughter to go back to the dwellings of Men: for she came
hither constrained by me, and knowing not the purposes of our
journey."

"Seek not to cajole me, woman," sneered that evil onè. "Liever would I keep thy daughter and slay thee or send thee back to thy hovels, but I have need of neither of you." With those words he opened full his evil eyes, and a light shone in them, and Mavwin and Nienóri quaked beneath them and a swoon came upon their minds, and them seemed that they groped in endless tunnels of darkness, and there they found not one another ever again, and calling only vain echoes answered and there was no glimmer of light.

When however after a time that she remembered not the blackness left the mind of Nienóri, behold the river and the withered places of the Foalókë were no more about her, but the deep woodlands, and it was dusk. Now she seemed to herself to awake from dreams of horror nor could she recall them, but their dread hung dark behind her mind, and her memory of all past things was dimmed. So for a long while she strayed lost in the woods, and haply the spell alone kept life in her, for she hungered bitterly and was athirst, and by fortune it was summer, for her garments became torn and her feet unshod and weary, and often she wept, and she went she knew not whither.

Now on a time in an opening in the wood she descried a campment as it were of Men, and creeping nigh by reason of hunger to espy it she saw that they were creatures of a squat and unlovely stature that dwelt there, and most evil faces had they, and their voices and their laughter was as the clash of stone and metal. Armed they were with curved swords and bows of horn, and she was possessed with fear as she looked upon them, although she knew not that they were Orcs, for never had she seen those evil ones before. Now did she turn and flee, but was espied, and one let fly a shaft at her that quivered suddenly in a tree beside her as she ran, and others seeing that it was a woman young and fair gave chase whooping and calling hideously. Now Nienóri ran as best she might for the density of the wood, but soon was she spent and capture and dread thraldom was very near, when one came crashing through the woods as though in answer to her lamentable cries.

Wild and black was his hair yet streaked with grey, and his face was pale and marked as with deep sorrows of the past, and in his hand he bare a great sword whereof all but the very edge was black. Therewith he leapt against the following Orcs and hewed them, and they soon fled, being taken aback, and though some shot arrows at random amidst the trees they did little scathe, and five of them were slain.

Then sat Nienóri upon a stone and for weariness and the

lessened strain of fear sobs shook her and she could not speak; but
her rescuer stood beside her awhile and marvelled at her fairness
and that she wandered thus lonely in the woods, and at length he
said: "O sweet maiden of the woods, whence comest thou, and
what may be thy name?"

"Nay, these things I know not," said she. "Yet methinks I stray
very far from my home and folk, and many very evil things have
fallen upon me in the way, whereof nought but a cloud hangs upon
my memory – nay, whence I am or whither I go I know not" – and
she wept afresh, but that man spake, saying: "Then behold, I will
call thee Níniel, or little one of tears," and thereat she raised her
face towards his, and it was very sweet though marred with
weeping, and she said with a look of wonderment: "Nay, not
Níniel, not Níniel." Yet more might she not remember, and her
face filled with distress, so that she cried: "Nay, who art thou,
warrior of the woods; why troublest thou me?" "Turambar am I
called," said he, "and no home nor kindred have I nor any past to
think on, but I wander for ever," and again at that name that
maiden's wonder stirred.

"Now," said Turambar, "dry thy tears, O Níniel, for thou hast
come upon such safety as these woods afford. Lo, one am I now of
a small folk of the forest, and a sweet dwelling in a clearing have
we far from hence, but today as thy fortune would we fared
a-hunting, – aye, and Orc-harrying too, for we are hard put to it to
fend those evil ones from our homes."

Then did Níniel (for thus Turambar called her ever, and she
learnt to call it her name) fare away with him to his comrades, and
they asking little got them upon horses, and Turambar set Níniel
before him, and thus they fared as swift as they might from the
danger of the Orcs.

Now at the time of the affray of Turambar with the pursuing
Orcs was half the day already spent, yet were they already leagues
upon their way ere they dismounted once more, and it was then
early night. Already at the sunset had it seemed to Níniel that the
woods were lighter and less gloomy and the air less evil-laden than
behind. Now did they make a camp in a glade and the stars shone
clear above where the tree-roof was thin, but Níniel lay a little apart
and they gave her many fells to keep her from the night chills, and
thus she slept more softly than for many a night and the breezes
kissed her face, but Turambar told his comrades of the meeting in
the wood and they wondered who she might be or how she came
wandering thither as one under a spell of blind forgetfulness.

Next day again they pressed on and so for many journeys more beside until at length weary and fain for rest they came one noon to a woodland stream, and this they followed for some way until, behold, they came to a place where it might be forded by reason of its shallowness and of the rocks that stood up in its course; but on their right it dived in a great fall and fell into a chasm, and Turambar pointing said: "Now are we nigh to home, for this is the fall of the Silver Bowl," but Níniel not knowing why was filled with a dread and could not look upon the loveliness of that foaming water. Now soon came they to places of thinner trees and to a slope whereon but few grew save here and there an ancient oak of great girth, and the grass about their feet was soft, for the clearing had been made many years and was very wide. There stood also a cluster of goodly houses of timber, and a tilth was about them and trees of fruit. To one of these houses that was adorned with strange rude carvings, and flowers bloomed bright about it, did Turambar lead now Níniel. "Behold," said he, "my abode – there an thou listest thou shalt abide for now, but methinks it is a lonely hall, and there be houses of this folk beside where there are maidens and womenfolk, and there wouldst thou liever and better be." So came it afterward that Nienóri dwelt with the wood-rangers,* and after a while entered the house of Bethos, a stout man who had fought though then but a boy in the Battle of Unnumbered Tears. Thence did he escape, but his wife was a Noldo-maiden, as the tale telleth, and very fair, and fair also were his sons and daughters save only his eldest son Tamar Lamefoot.

Now as the days passed Turambar grew to love Níniel very greatly indeed, and all the folk beside loved her for her great loveliness and sweetness, yet was she ever half-sorrowful and often distraught of mind, as one that seeks for something mislaid that soon she must discover, so that folk said: "Would that the Valar would lift the spell that lies upon Níniel." Nonetheless for the most part she was happy indeed among the folk and in the house of Bethos, and each day she grew ever fairer, and Tamar Lamefoot who was held of little account loved her though in vain.

Now came days when life once more seemed to contain joy to Turambar, and the bitterness of the past grew dim and far away, and a fresh love was in his heart. Then did he think to put his fate

---

* In the margin, apparently with reference to the word 'wood-rangers', is written Vettar.

for ever from him and live out his life there in the woodland homes with children about him, and looking upon Níniel he desired to wed her. Then did he often press his suit with her, yet though he was a man of valiance and renown she delayed him, saying nor yea nor no, yet herself she knew not why, for it seemed to her heart that she loved him deeply, fearing for him were he away, and knowing happiness when he was nigh.

Now it was a custom of that folk to obey a chief, and he was chosen by them from their stoutest men, and that office did he hold until of his own will he laid it down again being sick or gone in years, or were he slain. And at that time Bethos was their chief; but he was slain by evil luck in a foray not long after — for despite his years he still rode abroad — and it fell out that a new captain must be chosen. In the end then did they name Turambar, for his lineage, in that it was known among them that he was son of Úrin, was held in esteem among those stout rebels against Melko, whereas[23] he had beside become a very mighty man in all deeds and one of wisdom great beyond his years, by reason of his far wanderings and his dealings with the Elves.

Seeing therefore the love of their new chief for Níniel and thinking they knew that she loved him also in return, those men began to say how they would lief see their lord wed, and that it was folly to delay for no good cause; but this word came to the ears of Níniel, and at length she consented to be the wife of Turambar, and all were fain thereat. A goodly feast was made and there was song and mirth, and Níniel became lady of the woodland-rangers and dwelt thereafter in Turambar's house. There great was their happiness, though there lay at times a chill foreboding upon Níniel's heart, but Turambar was in joy and said in his heart: "'Twas well that I did name myself Turambar, for lo! I have overcome the doom of evil that was woven about my feet." The past he laid aside and to Níniel he spoke not overmuch of bygone things, save of his father and mother and the sister he had not seen, but always was Níniel troubled at such talk and he knew not why.[24] But of his flight from the halls of Tinwelint and the death of Beleg and of his seeking back to Hisilómë he said never a word, and the thought of Failivrin lay locked in his deepest heart well-nigh forgotten.

Naught ever might Níniel tell him of her days before, and did he ask her distress was written on her face as though he troubled the surface of dark dreams, and he grieved at times thereat, but it weighed not much upon him.

Now fare the days by and Níniel and Turambar dwell in peace, but Tamar Lamefoot wanders the woods thinking the world an ill and bitter place, and he loved Níniel very greatly nor might he stifle his love. But behold, in those days the Foalókë waxed fat, and having many bands of Noldoli and of Orcs subject to him he thought to extend his dominion far and wide. Indeed in many places in those days these beasts of Melko's did in like manner, setting up kingdoms of terror of their own that flourished beneath the evil mantle of Melko's lordship. So it was that the bands of Glorund the drake harried the folk of Tinwelint very grievously, and at length there came some nigh even to those woods and glades that were beloved of Turambar and his folk.

Now those woodmen fled not but dealt stoutly with their foes, and the wrath of Glorund the worm was very great when tidings were brought to him of a brave folk of Men that dwelt far beyond the river and that his marauders might not subdue them. It is told indeed that despite the cunning of his evil designs he did not yet know where was the dwelling of Turambar or of Nienóri; and of truth in those days it seemed that fortune smiled on Turambar awhile, for his people waxed and they became prosperous, and many escaped even from uttermost Hisilómë and came unto him, and store of wealth and good things he gathered, for all his battles brought him victory and booty. Like a king and queen did Turambar and Níniel become, and there was song and mirth in those glades of their dwelling, and much happiness in their halls. And Níniel conceived.[25]

Much of this did spies report to the Foalókë, and his wrath was terrible. Moreover his greed was mightily kindled, so that after pondering much he set a guard that he might trust to watch his dwelling and his treasury, and the captain of these was Mîm the dwarf.[26] Then leaving the caves and the places of his sleep he crossed the streams and drew into the woods, and they blazed before his face. Tidings of this came swiftly to Turambar, but he feared not as yet nor indeed heeded the tale much, for it was a very great way from the home of the woodmen to the caverns of the worm. But now sank Níniel's heart, and though she knew not wherefore a weight of dread and sorrow lay upon her, and seldom after the coming of that word did she smile, so that Turambar wondered and was sad.

Now draweth the Foalókë during that time through the deep woods and a path of desolation lies behind, and yet in his creeping a very great while passes, until, behold, suddenly a party of the woodmen come upon him unawares sleeping in the woods among the broken trees. Of these several were overcome by the noxious breath of the beast and after were slain; but two making their utmost speed brought tidings to their lord that the tale aforetime had not been vain, and indeed now was the drake crept even within the confines of his realm; and so saying they fell fainting before his feet.

Now the place where the dragon lay was low-lying and a little hill there was, not far distant, islanded among the trees but itself not much wooded, whence might be espied albeit afar off much of that region now torn by the passage of the drake. A stream there was too that ran through the forest in that part between the drake and the dwellings of the woodmen, but its course ran very nigh to the dragon and it was a narrow stream with banks deep-cloven and o'erhung with trees. Wherefore Turambar purposed now to take his stoutest men to that knoll and watch if they could the dragon's movements in secret, that perchance they might fall upon him at some disadvantage and contrive to slay him, for in this lay their best hope. This band he suffered not to be very great, and the rest at his bidding took arms and scoured about, fearing that hosts of the Orcs were come with the worm their lord. This indeed was not so, and he came alone trusting in his overwhelming power.

Now when Turambar made ready to depart then Níniel begged to ride beside him and he consented, for he loved her and it was his thought that if he fell and the drake lived then might none of that people be saved, and he would liever have Níniel by him, hoping perchance to snatch her at the least from the clutches of the worm, by death at his own or one of his liege's hands.

So rode forth together Turambar and Níniel, as that folk knew them, and behind were a score of good men. Now the distance to that knoll among the woods they compassed in a day's journey, and after them though it were against the bidding and counsel of Turambar there stole a great concourse of his folk, even women and children. The lure of a strange dread held them, and some thought to see a great fight, and others went with the rest thinking little, nor did any think to see what in the end their eyes saw; and they followed not far behind, for Turambar's party went slowly and warily. When first then Turambar suffered her to ride beside him Níniel was blither than for long she had been, and she brightened the foreboding of those men's hearts; but soon they came to a place not far from the foot of the knoll, and there her heart sank, and indeed a gloom fell upon all.

Yet very fair was that place, for here flowed that same stream that further down wound past the dragon's lair in a deep bed cloven deep into the earth; and it came rushing cold from the hills beyond the woodmen's homes, and it fell over a great fall where the water-worn rock jutted smooth and grey from amid the grass. Now this was the head of that force which the woodmen named the Silver Bowl, and aforetime Turambar and Níniel had passed it by, faring home first from the rescuing of Níniel. The height of that fall was very great and the waters had a loud and musical voice, splashing into a silver foam far below where they had worn a great hollow in the rocks; and this hollow was o'ershadowed by trees and bushes, but the sun gleamed through upon the spray; and about the head of the fall there was an open glade and a green sward where grew a wealth of flowers, and men loved that spot.

Here did Níniel of a sudden weep, and casting herself upon Turambar begged him tempt not fate but rather fly with her and all his folk, leading them into distant lands. But looking at her he said: "Nay, Níniel mine, nor thou nor I die this day, nor yet tomorrow, by the evil of the dragon or by the foemen's swords," but he knew not the fulfilment of his words; and hearing them Níniel quelled her weeping and was very still. Having therefore rested a while here those warriors afterward climbed the hill and Níniel fared with them. Afar off they might see from its summit a wide tract where all the trees were broken and the lands were hurt[27] and scorched and the earth black, yet nigh the edge of the trees that were still unharmed, and that was not far from the lip of the deep river-chasm, there arose a thin smoke of great blackness, and men said: "There lieth the worm."

Then were counsels of many a kind spoken upon that hill-top, and men feared to go openly against the dragon by day or by night or whether he waked or slept, and seeing their dread Turambar gave them a rede, and it was taken, and these were his words: "Well have ye said, O huntsmen of the woods, that not by day or by night shall men hope to take a dragon of Melko unawares, and behold this one hath made a waste about him, and the earth is beaten flat so that none may creep near and be hidden. Wherefore whoso hath the heart shall come with me and we will go down the rocks to the foot of the fall, and so gaining the path of the stream perchance we may come as nigh to the drake as may be. Then must we climb if we are able up under the near bank and so wait, for methinks the Foalókë will rest not much longer ere he draweth on towards our dwellings. Thus must he either cross this deep stream or turn far out of his ways, for he is grown too mighty to creep along its bed. Now I think not that he will turn aside, for it is but a ditch, a narrow rut filled with trickling water, to the great Foalókë of the golden caves. If however he belie my counsel and come not on by this path, some few of you must take courage in your hearts, striving to decoy him warily back across the stream, that there we who lie hid may give him his bane stabbing from beneath, for the armour of these vile worms is of little worth upon their bellies."

Now of that band were there but six that stood forward readily to go with Turambar, and he seeing that said that he had thought there were more than six brave men among his folk, yet after that he would not suffer any of the others to go with him, saying that better were the six without the hindrance of the fearful. Then did Turambar take farewell of Níniel and they kissed upon the hilltop, and it was then late afternoon, but Níniel's heart went as to stone with grief; and all that company descended to the head of Silver Bowl, and there she beheld her lord climb to the fall's bottom with his six companions. Now when he was vanished far below she spake bitterly to those who had dared not to go, and they for shame answered not but crept back unto the hill-top and gazed out towards the dragon's lair, and Níniel sat beside the water looking before her, and she wept not but was in anguish.

None stayed beside her save Tamar alone who had fared unbidden with that company, and he had loved her since first she dwelt in Bethos' halls, and once had thought to win her ere Turambar took her. The lameness of Tamar was with him from childhood, yet was he both wise and kindly, though held of little account among those folk, to whom strength was safety and valour the greatest pride of men. Now however did Tamar bear a sword, and many had scoffed at him for that, yet he took joy at the chance of guarding Níniel, albeit she noticed him not.

Now is it to tell that Turambar reached the place of his design after great labour in the rocky bed of the stream, and with his men clambered with difficulty up the steep side of that ravine. Just below the lip of it they were lodged in certain overhanging trees, and not far off they might hear the great breathing of the beast, and some of his companions fell in dread.

Already had darkness come and all the night they clung there, and there was a strange flickering where the dragon lay and dread noises and a quaking if he stirred, and when dawn came Turambar saw that he had but three companions, and he cursed the others for their cravenhood, nor doth any tale tell whither those unfaithful ones fled. On this day did all come to pass as Turambar had thought, for the drake bestirring himself drew slowly to the chasm's edge and turned not aside, but sought to overcreep it and come thus at the homes of the woodmen. Now the terror of his oncoming was very great, for the earth shook, and those three feared lest the trees that upheld them should loosen their roots and fall into the rocky stream below. The leaves too of those trees that grew nigh were shrivelled in the serpent's breath, yet were they not hurt because of the shelter of the bank.

At length did the drake reach the stream-edge and the sight of his evil head and dripping jaws was utterly hideous, and these they saw clearly and were in terror lest he too espy them, for he crossed not over at the spot where Turambar had chosen to lie hid because of the narrowness here of the chasm and its lesser depth. Rather he began to heave himself now across the ravine a little below them, and so slipping from their places Turambar and his men reached as swiftly as might be the stream's bed and came beneath the belly of the worm. Here was the heat so great and so vile the stench that his men were taken with a sore dread and durst not climb the bank again. Then in his wrath Turambar would have turned his sword against them, but they fled, and so was it that alone he scaled the wall until he came close beneath the dragon's body, and he reeled by reason of the heat and of the stench and clung to a stout bush.

Then abiding until a very vital and unfended spot was within stroke, he heaved up Gurtholfin his black sword and stabbed with all his strength above his head, and that magic blade of the Rodothlim went into the vitals of the dragon even to the hilt, and the yell of his death-pain rent the woods and all that heard it were aghast.

Then did that drake writhe horribly and the huge spires of his contortions were terrible to see, and all the trees he brake that stood nigh to the place of his agony. Almost had he crossed the chasm when Gurtholfin pierced him, and now he cast himself upon its farther bank and laid all waste about him, and lashed and coiled and made a yelling and a bellowing such that the stoutest blenched and turned to flee. Now those afar thought that this was the fearsome noise of battle betwixt the seven, Turambar and his comrades,[28] and little they hoped ever to see any of them return, and Níniel's heart died within her at the sounds; but below in the ravine those three cravens who had watched Turambar from afar fled now in terrror back towards the fall, and Turambar clung nigh to the lip of the chasm white and trembling, for he was spent.

At length did those noises of horror cease, and there arose a great smoking, for Glorund was dying. Then in utter hardihood did Turambar creep out alone from his hiding, for in the agony of the Foalókë his sword was dragged from his hand ere he might withdraw it, and he cherished Gurtholfin beyond all his possessions, for all things died, or man or beast, whom once its edges bit. Now Turambar saw where the dragon lay, and he was stretched out stiff upon his side, and Gurtholfin stood yet in his belly; but he breathed still.

Nonetheless Turambar creeping up set his foot upon his body and withdrew Gurtholfin hardly with all his strength, and as he did so he said in the triumph of his heart: "Now do we meet again, O Glorund, thou and I, Turambar, who was once named brave";[29] but even as he spake the evil blood spouted from that wound upon his hand and burnt it, and it was withered, so that for the sudden pain he cried aloud. Then the Foalókë opening his dread eyes looked upon him, and he fell in a swoon beside the drake and his sword was under him.

Thus did the day draw on and there came no tidings to the hill-top, nor could Níniel longer bear her anguish but arose and made as to leave that glade above the waterfall, and Tamar Lamefoot said: "What dost thou seek to do?" but she: "I would seek my lord and lay me in death beside him, for methinks he is dead", and he sought to dissuade her but without avail. And even as evening fell that fair lady crept through the woods and she would not that Tamar should follow her, but seeing that he did so she fled blindly through the trees, tearing her clothes and marring her face in places of thorny undergrowth, and Tamar being lame could not keep up with her. So fell night upon the woods and all was still, and a great dread for Níniel fell upon Tamar, so that he cursed his weakness and his heart was bitter, yet did he cease not to follow so swiftly as he might, and losing sight of her he bent his course towards that part of the forest nigh to the ravine where had been fought the worm's last fight, for indeed that might be perceived by the watchers on the hill. Now rose a bright moon when the night was old, and Tamar, wandering often alone far and wide from the woodmen's homes, knew those places, and came at last to the edge of that desolation that the dragon had made in his agony; but the moonlight was very bright, and staying among the bushes near the edge of that place Tamar heard and saw all that there betid.

Behold now Níniel had reached those places not long before

him, and straightway did she run fearless into the open for love of
her lord, and so found him lying with his withered hand in a swoon
across his sword; but the beast that lay hugely stretched beside she
heeded not at all, and falling beside Turambar she wept, and
kissed his face, and put salve upon his hand, for such she had
brought in a little box when first they sallied forth, fearing that
many hurts would be gotten ere men wended home.

Yet Turambar woke not at her touch, nor stirred, and she cried
aloud, thinking him now surely dead: "O Turambar, my lord,
awake, for the serpent of wrath is dead and I alone am near!" But
lo! at those words the drake stirred his last, and turning his baleful
eyes upon her ere he shut them for ever said: "O thou Nienóri
daughter of Mavwin, I give thee joy that thou hast found thy
brother at the last, for the search hath been weary – and now is he
become a very mighty fellow and a stabber of his foes unseen"; but
Nienóri sat as one stunned, and with that Glorund died, and with
his death the veil of his spells fell from her, and all her memory
grew crystal clear, neither did she forget any of those things that had
befallen her since first she fell beneath the magic of the worm; so
that her form shook with horror and anguish. Then did she start to
her feet, standing wanly in the moon, and looking upon Turambar
with wide eyes thus spake she aloud: "Then is thy doom spent at
last. Well art thou dead, O most unhappy," but distraught with
her woe suddenly she fled from that place and fared wildly away as
one mad whithersoever her feet led her.

But Tamar whose heart was numbed with grief and ruth followed
as he might, recking little of Turambar, for wrath at the fate of
Nienóri filled all his heart. Now the stream and the deep chasm lay
across her path, but it so chanced that she turned aside ere she
came to its banks and followed its winding course through stony
and thorny places until she came once again to the glade at the
head of the great roaring fall, and it was empty as the first grey
light of a new day filtered through the trees.

There did she stay her feet and standing spake as to herself: "O
waters of the forest whither do ye go? Wilt thou take Nienóri,
Nienóri daughter of Úrin, child of woe? O ye white foams, would
that ye might lave me clean – but deep, deep must be the waters
that would wash my memory of this nameless curse. O bear me
hence, far far away, where are the waters of the unremembering
sea. O waters of the forest whither do ye go?" Then ceasing
suddenly she cast herself over the fall's brink, and perished where
it foams about the rocks below; but at that moment the sun arose

above the trees and light fell upon the waters, and the waters roared unheeding above the death of Nienóri.

Now all this did Tamar behold, and to him the light of the new sun seemed dark, but turning from those places he went to the hill-top and there was already gathered a great concourse of folk, and among them were those three that had last deserted Turambar, and they made a story for the ears of the folk. But Tamar coming stood suddenly before them, and his face was terrible to see, so that a whisper ran among them: "He is dead"; but others said: "What then has befallen the little Níniel?" – but Tamar cried aloud: "Hear, O my people, and say if there is a fate like unto the one I tell unto thee, or a woe so heavy. Dead is the drake, but at his side lieth also Turambar dead, even he who was first called Túrin son of Úrin,[30] and that is well; aye very well," and folk murmured, wondering at his speech, and some said that he was mad. But Tamar said: "For know, O people, that Níniel the fair beloved of you all and whom I love dearer than my heart is dead, and the waters roar above her, for she has leapt o'er the falls of Silver Bowl desiring never more to see the light of day. Now endeth all that evil spell, now is the doom of the folk of Úrin terribly fulfilled, for she that ye called Níniel was even Nienóri daughter of Úrin, and this did she know or ever she died, and this did she tell to the wild woods, and their echo came to me."

At those words did the hearts of all who stood there break for sorrow and for dread, yet did none dare to go to the place of the anguish of that fair lady, for a sad spirit abideth there yet and none sets foot upon its sward; but a great remorse pierced the hearts of those three cravens, and creeping from the throng they went to seek their lord's body, and behold they found him stirring and alive, for when the dragon died the swoon had left him, and he slept a deep sleep of weariness, yet now was he awakening and was in pain. Even as those three stood by he spake and said "Níniel", and at that word they hid their faces for ruth and horror, and could not look upon his face, but afterward they roused him, and behold he was very fain of his victory; yet suddenly marking his hand he said: "Lo! one has been that has tended my hurt with skill – who think ye that it was?" – but they answered him not, for they guessed. Now therefore was Turambar borne weary and hurt back among his folk, and one sped before and cried that their lord lived, but men knew not if they were glad; and as he came among them many turned aside their faces to hide their hearts' perplexity and their tears, and none durst speak.

But Turambar said to those that stood nigh: "Where is Níniel, my Níniel – for I had thought to find her here in gladness – yet if she has returned rather to my halls then is it well", but those that heard could no longer restrain their weeping, and Turambar rose crying: "What new ill is this – speak, speak, my people, and torment me not!" But one said: "Níniel alas is dead my lord," but Turambar cried out bitterly against the Valar and his fate of woe, and at last another said: "Aye, she is dead, for she fell even into the depths of Silver Bowl," but Tamar who stood by muttered: "Nay, she cast herself thither." Then Turambar catching those words seized him by the arm and cried: "Speak, thou club-foot, speak, say what meaneth thy foul speech, or thou shalt lose thy tongue," for his misery was terrible to see.

Now was Tamar's heart in a great turmoil of pain for the dread things that he had seen and heard, and the long hopelessness of his love for Níniel, so did rage against Turambar kindle suddenly within him, and shaking off his touch he said: "A maid thou foundest in the wild woods and gave her a jesting name, that thou and all the folk called her Níniel, the little one of tears. Ill was that jest, Turambar, for lo! she has cast herself away blind with horror and with woe, desiring never to see thee again, and the name she named herself in death was Nienóri daughter of Úrin, child of woe, nor may all the waters of the Silver Bowl as they drop into the deep shed the full tale of tears o'er Níniel."

Then Turambar with a roar took his throat and shook him, saying: "Thou liest – thou evil son of Bethos" – but Tamar gasped "Nay, accursed one; so spake Glorund the drake, and Níniel hearing knew that it was true." But Turambar said: "Then go commune in Mandos with thy Glorund," and he slew him before the face of the people, and fared after as one mad, shouting "He lieth, he lieth"; and yet being free now of blindness and of dreams in his deep heart he knew that it was true and that now his weird was spent at last.

So did he leave the folk behind and drive heedless through the woods calling ever the name of Níniel, till the woods rang most dismally with that word, and his going led him by circuitous ways ever to the glade of Silver Bowl, and none had dared to follow him. There shone the sun of afternoon, and lo, were all the trees grown sere although it was high summer still, and noise there was as of dying autumn in the leaves. Withered were all the flowers and the grass, and the voice of the falling water was sadder than tears for the death of the white maiden Nienóri daughter of Úrin that there had been. There stood Turambar spent at last, and there he drew his sword, and said: "Hail, Gurtholfin, wand of death, for thou art all men's bane and all men's lives fain wouldst thou drink, knowing no lord or faith save the hand that wields thee if it be strong. Thee only have I now – slay me therefore and be swift, for life is a curse, and all my days are creeping foul, and all my deeds are vile, and all I love is dead." And Gurtholfin said: "That will I gladly do, for blood is blood, and perchance thine is not less sweet than many a one's that thou hast given me ere now"; and Turambar cast himself then upon the point of Gurtholfin, and the dark blade took his life.

But later some came timidly and bore him away and laid him in a place nigh, and raised a great mound over him, and thereafter some drew a great rock there with a smooth face, and on it were cut strange signs such as Turambar himself had taught them in dead days, bringing that knowledge from the caves of the Rodothlim, and that writing said:

> Turambar slayer of Glorund the Worm
> who also was Túrin Mormakil
> Son of Úrin of the Woods

and beneath that was carven the word "Níniel" (or child of tears); but she was not there, nor where the waters have laid her fair form doth any man know.'

Now thereupon did Eltas cease his speaking, and suddenly all who hearkened wept; but he said thereto: 'Yea, 'tis an unhappy tale, for sorrow hath fared ever abroad among Men and doth so still, but in the wild days were very terrible things done and suffered; and yet hath Melko seldom devised more cruelty, nor do I know a tale that is more pitiful.'

Then after a time some questioned him concerning Mavwin and Úrin and after happenings, and he said: 'Now of Mavwin hath no sure record been preserved like unto the tale of Túrin Turambar her son, and many things are said and some of them differ from one another; but this much can I tell to ye, that after those dread deeds the woodfolk had no heart for their abiding place and departed to other valleys of the wood, and yet did a few linger sadly nigh their old homes; and once came an aged dame wandering through the woods, and she chanced upon that carven rock. To her did one of those woodmen read the meaning of the signs, and he told her all the tale as he remembered it – but she was silent, and nor spoke nor moved. Then said he: "Thy heart is heavy, for it is a tale to move all men to tears." But she said: "Ay, sad indeed is my heart, for I am Mavwin, mother of those twain," and that man perceived that not yet had that long tale of sorrow reached its ending – but Mavwin arose and went out into the woods crying in anguish, and for long time she haunted that spot so that the woodman and his folk fled and came never back, and none may say whether indeed it was Mavwin that came there or her dark shade that sought not back to Mandos by reason of her great unhappiness.[31]

Yet it is said that all these dread happenings Úrin saw by the magic of Melko, and was continually tempted by that Ainu to yield to his will, and he would not; but when the doom of his folk was utterly fulfilled then did Melko think to use Úrin in another and more subtle way, and he released him from that high and bitter place where he had sat through many years in torment of heart. But Melko went to him and spoke evilly of the Elves to him, and especially did he accuse Tinwelint[32] of weakness and cravenhood. "Never can I comprehend," said he, "wherefore it is that there be still great and wise Men who trust to the friendship of the Elves, and becoming fools enough to resist my might do treble their folly in looking for sure help therein from Gnomes or Fairies. Lo, O Úrin, but for the faint heart of Tinwelint of the woodland how could my designs have come to pass, and perchance now had Nienóri lived and Mavwin thy wife had wept not, being glad for the recovery of her son. Go therefore, O foolish one, and return to eat the bitter bread of almsgiving in the halls of thy fair friends."

Then did Úrin bowed with years and sorrow depart unmolested from Melko's realms and came unto the better lands, but ever as he went he pondered Melko's saying and the cunning web of woven truth and falsity clouded his heart's eye, and he was very bitter in spirit. Now therefore he gathered to him a band of wild Elves,[33] and they were waxen a fierce and lawless folk that dwelt not with their kin, who thrust them into the hills to live or die as they might. On a time therefore Úrin led them to the caves of the Rodothlim, and behold the Orcs had fled therefrom at the death of Glorund, and one only dwelt there still, an old misshapen dwarf who sat ever on the pile of gold singing black songs of enchantment to himself. But none had come nigh till then to despoil him, for the terror of the drake lived longer than he, and none had ventured thither again for dread of the very spirit of Glorund the worm.[34] Now therefore when those Elves approached the dwarf stood before the doors of the cave that was once the abode of Galweg, and he cried: "What will ye with me, O outlaws of the hills?" But Úrin answered: "We come to take what is not thine." Then said that dwarf, and his name was Mîm: "O Úrin, little did I think to see thee, a lord of Men, with such a rabble. Hearken now to the words of Mîm the fatherless, and depart, touching not this gold no more than were it venomous fires. For has not Glorund lain long years upon it, and the evil of the drakes of Melko is on it, and no good can it bring to Man or Elf, but I, only I, can ward it, Mîm the dwarf, and by many a dark spell have I bound it to myself." Then Úrin wavered, but his men were wroth at that, so that he bid them seize it all, and Mîm stood by and watched, and he broke forth into terrible and evil curses. Thereat did Úrin smite him, saying: "We came but to take what was not thine – now for thy evil words we will take what is thine as well, even thy life."

But Mîm dying said unto Úrin: "Now Elves and Men shall rue this deed, and because of the death of Mîm the dwarf shall death follow this gold so long as it remain on Earth, and a like fate shall every part and portion share with the whole." And Úrin shuddered, but his folk laughed.

Now Úrin caused his followers to bear this gold to the halls of Tinwelint, and they murmured at that, but he said: "Are ye become as the drakes of Melko, that would lie and wallow in gold and seek no other joy? A sweeter life shall ye have in the court of that king of greed, an ye bear such treasury to him, than all the gold of Valinor can get you in the empty woods."

Now his heart was bitter against Tinwelint, and he desired to have a vengeance on him, as may be seen. So great was that hoard that great though Úrin's company might be scarce could they bear it to the caves of Tinwelint the king, and some 'tis said was left behind and some was lost upon the way, and evil has followed its finders for ever.

Yet in the end that laden host came to the bridge before the doors, and being asked by the guards Úrin said: "Say to the king that Úrin the Steadfast is come bearing gifts," and this was done. Then Úrin let bear all that magnificence before the king, but it was hidden in sacks or shut in boxes of rough wood; and Tinwelint greeted Úrin with joy and with amaze and bid him thrice welcome, and he and all his court arose in honour of that lord of Men; but Úrin's heart was blind by reason of his tormented years and of the lies of Melko, and he said: "Nay, O King, I do not desire to hear such words – but say only, where is Mavwin my wife, and knowest thou what death did Nienóri my daughter die?" And Tinwelint said that he knew not.

Then did Úrin fiercely tell that tale, and the king and all his folk about him hid their faces for great ruth, but Úrin said: "Nay,[35] had you such a heart as have the least of Men, never would they have been lost; but lo, I bring you now a payment in full for the troubles of your puny band that went against Glorund the drake, and deserting gave up my dear ones to his power. Gaze, O Tinwelint, sweetly on my gifts, for methinks the lustre of gold is all your heart contains."

Then did men cast down that treasury at the king's feet, uncovering it so that all that court were dazzled and amazed – but Úrin's men understood now what was forward and were little pleased. "Behold the hoard of Glorund," said Úrin, "bought by the death of Nienóri with the blood of Túrin slayer of the worm. Take it, O craven king, and be glad that some Men be brave to win thee riches."

Then were Úrin's words more than Tinwelint could endure, and he said: "What meanest thou, child of Men, and wherefore upbraidest thou me?[36] Long did I foster thy son and forgave him the evil of his deeds, and afterward thy wife I succoured, giving way against my counsel to her wild desires. Melko it is that hates thee and not I. Yet what is it to me – and wherefore dost thou of the uncouth race of Men endure to upbraid a king of the Eldalië? Lo! in Palisor my life began years uncounted before the first of Men awoke. Get thee gone, O Úrin, for Melko hath bewitched thee, and take thy riches with thee" – but he forebore to slay or to bind Úrin in spells, remembering his ancient valiance in the Eldar's cause.

Then Úrin departed, but would not touch the gold, and stricken in years he reached Hisilómë and died among Men, but his words living after him bred estrangement between Elves and Men. Yet it is said that when he was dead his shade fared into the woods seeking Mavwin, and long those twain haunted the woods about the fall of Silver Bowl bewailing their children. But the Elves of Kôr have told, and they know, that at last Úrin and Mavwin fared to Mandos, and Nienóri was not there nor Túrin their son. Turambar indeed had followed Nienóri along the black pathways to the doors of Fui, but Fui would not open to them, neither would Vefántur. Yet now the prayers of Úrin and Mavwin came even to Manwë, and the Gods had mercy on their unhappy fate, so that those twain Túrin and Nienóri entered into Fôs'Almir, the

bath of flame, even as Urwendi and her maidens had done in ages
past before the first rising of the Sun, and so were all their sorrows
and stains washed away, and they dwelt as shining Valar among
the blessed ones, and now the love of that brother and sister is
very fair; but Turambar indeed shall stand beside Fionwë in the
Great Wrack, and Melko and his drakes shall curse the sword of
Mormakil.'
   And so saying Eltas made an end, and none asked further.

NOTES

1   The passage was rejected before the change of *Tintoglin* to
    Tinwelint; see p. 69.

2   Above the name *Egnor* is written 'Damrod the Gnome'; see Com-
    mentary, pp. 139–40.

3   Here and immediately below the name as first written was
    Tinthellon; this rider must belong to the same time as the note on
    the MS directing that *Tintoglin* be changed to *Ellon* or *Tinthellon*
    (p. 69). See note 32.

4   Associated with this replacement is a note on the manuscript read-
    ing: 'If Beren be a Gnome (as now in the story of Tinúviel) the
    references to Beren must be altered.' In the rejected passage Egnor
    father of Beren 'was akin to Mavwin', i.e. Egnor was a Man. See
    notes 5 and 6, and the Commentary, p. 139.

5   'Túrin son of Úrin': original reading 'Beren Ermabwed'. See notes 4
    and 6.

6   Original reading 'and when also the king heard of the kinship
    between Mavwin and Beren'. See notes 4 and 5.

7   *Linwë (Tinto)* was the king's original 'Elvish' name, and belongs to
    the same 'layer' of names as *Tintoglin* (see I. 115, 131). Its retention
    here (not changed to *Tinwë*) is clearly a simple oversight. See notes
    19 and 20.

8   Original reading 'seeing that he was a Man of great size'.

9   With this passage cf. that in the *Tale of Tinúviel* p. 11, which is
    closely similar. That the passage in *Turambar* is the earlier (to be
    presumed in any case) is shown by the fact that that in *Tinúviel* is
    only relevant if Beren is a Gnome, not a Man (see note 4).

10 'dreams came to them': original reading 'dreams the Valar sent to
    them'.

11 'and his name was Glorund' was added later, as were the subsequent
    occurrences of the name on pp. 86, 94, 98; but from the first on
    p. 103 onwards *Glorund* appears in the manuscript as first written.

12 'with the aid of Flinding whose wounds were not great': original
    reading 'with the aid of a lightly wounded man'. All the subsequent
    references to Flinding in this passage were added.

13   Original reading 'Túrin's heart was bitter, and so it was that he and
      that other alone returned from that battle'. – In the phrase 'reproach-
      ing Túrin that he had ever withstood his wise counsels' 'ever' means
      'always': Túrin had always resisted Orodreth's counsels.

14   Original reading 'although all folk at that time held such a deed
      grievous and cowardly'.

15   Original reading 'and to look upon Nienóri again'. This was emended
      to 'and to look upon Nienóri whom he had never seen'. The words
      'since his first days' were added still later.

16   The following passage was struck out, apparently at the time of
      writing:

      "Indeed," said they, "it is the report of men of travel and rangers
      of the hills that for many and many moons have even the farthest
      marches been free of them and unwonted safe, and so have many
      men fared out of Hisilómë to the Lands Beyond." And this was
      the truth that during the life of Turambar as an exile from the
      court of Tintoglin or hidden amongst the Rothwarin Melko had
      troubled Hisilómë little and the paths thereto.

      (*Rothwarin* was the original form throughout, replaced later by
      Rodothlim.) See p. 92, where the situation described in the rejected
      passage is referred to the earlier time (before the destruction of the
      Rodothlim) when Mavwin and Nienóri left Hisilómë.

17   Original reading 'twice seven'. When Túrin fled from the land of
      Tinwelint it was exactly 12 years since he had left his mother's house
      (p. 75), and Nienóri was born before that, but just how long before
      is not stated.

18   After 'a great and terrible project afoot' the original reading was 'the
      story of which entereth not into this tale'. I do not know whether this
      means that when my father first wrote here of Melko's 'project' he
      did not have the destruction of the Rodothlim in mind.

19   'the king': original reading 'Linwë'. See note 7.

20   *Linwë*: an oversight. See note 7.

21   'that high place': original reading 'a hill'.

22   This sentence, 'And even so was Túrin's boast . . .', was added in
      pencil later. The reference is to Túrin's naming himself *Turambar* –
      'from this hour shall none name me Túrin if I live', p. 86.

23   This sentence, from 'for his lineage . . .' to approximately this point,
      is very lightly struck through. On the opposite page of the MS is
      hastily scribbled: 'Make Turambar never tell new folk of his lineage
      (will bury the past) – this avoids chance (as cert.) of Níniel hearing
      his lineage from any.' See Commentary, p. 131.

24   Against this sentence there is a pencilled question-mark in the
      margin. See note 23 and the Commentary, p. 131.

25   'And Níniel conceived' was added in pencil later. See Commentary,
      p. 135.

26 'and the captain of these was Mîm the dwarf' added afterwards in
    pencil. See Commentary p. 137.

27 The word *tract* may be read as *track*, and the word *hurt* (but with
    less probability) as *burnt*.

28 As it stands this sentence can hardly mean other than that the people
    thought that the men were fighting among themselves; but why
    should they think such a thing? More likely, my father inadvertently
    missed out the end of the sentence: 'betwixt the seven, Turambar
    and his comrades, and the dragon.'

29 Turambar refers to Glorund's words to him before the caves of
    the Rodothlim: 'O Túrin Mormakil, who wast once named brave'
    (p. 86).

30 These words, from 'even he who . . .', were added later in pencil.
    Úrin may also be read as *Húrin*.

31 From this point to the end of Eltas' tale the original text was struck
    through, and is followed in the manuscript book by two brief
    narrative outlines, these being rejected also. The text given here
    (from 'Yet it is said . . .') is found on slips placed in the book. For the
    rejected material see the Commentary, pp. 135–7.

32 Throughout the final portion of the text (that written on slips, see
    note 31) the king's name was first written *Tinthellon*, not *Tintoglin*
    (see note 3).

33 'Elves': original reading 'men'. The same change was made below
    ('Now therefore when those Elves approached'), and a little later
    'men' was removed in two places ('his folk laughed', 'Úrin caused his
    followers to bear the gold', p. 114); but several occurrences of 'men'
    were retained, possibly through oversight, though 'men' is used
    of Elves very frequently in the *Tale of Turambar* (e.g. 'Beleg and
    Flinding both stout men', p. 80).

34 This sentence, from 'But none had come nigh . . .', was added later
    in pencil.

35 This sentence, from 'Then did Úrin fiercely . . .', was added later,
    replacing 'Then said Úrin: "Yet had you such a heart . . ."'

36 This sentence, from "What meanest thou . . .", replaces the original
    reading "Begone, and take thy filth with thee."

Changes made to names in
The Tale of Turambar

Fuithlug < *Fothlug* < *Fothlog*
Nienóri At the first occurrence (p. 71) my father originally wrote
    Nyenòre (Nienor). Afterwards he struck out *Nyenòre*, removed
    the brackets round *Nienor*, and added *-i*, giving *Nienori*. At
    subsequent occurrences the name was written both *Nienor* and

Nienóri, but *Nienor* was changed to *Nienóri* later throughout the earlier part of the tale. Towards the end, and in the text written on slips that concludes it, the form is *Nienor*. I have given *Nienóri* throughout.

Tinwelint < *Tinthellon* (p. 72, twice). See p. 69 and note 3. *Tinwelint* < *Tinthellon* also in the concluding portion of the text, see note 32.

Tinwelint < *Tintoglin* throughout the tale, except as just noted (where *Tinwelint* < *Tinthellon* in passages added later); see p. 69.

Gwedheling < *Gwendeling* at all occurrences (*Gwendeling* unchanged at p. 76, but this is obviously an oversight: I read *Gwedheling* in the text). In the Gnomish dictionary the form *Gwendeling* was changed to *Gwedhiling*; see p. 50.

Flinding bo-Dhuilin < *Flinding go-Dhuilin* This change, made at the occurrence on p. 78, was not made at p. 82, but this was clearly because the form was missed, and I read *bo-Dhuilin* in both cases; the same change from *go-* to *bo-* in the *Tale of Tinúviel*, see p. 51. The form *Dhuilin* is taken by the name when the patronymic is prefixed (cf. *Duilin* p. 79).

Rodothlim < *Rothwarin* at every occurrence.

Gurtholfin < *Gortholfin* at the first occurrences, but from p. 90 *Gurtholfin* was the form first written.

Commentary on
The Tale of Turambar

§1.   The primary narrative

In commenting on this long tale it is convenient to break it into short sections. In the course of this commentary I frequently refer to the long (though incomplete) prose narrative, the *Narn i Hîn Húrin*, given in *Unfinished Tales* pp. 57ff., often in preference to the briefer account in *The Silmarillion*, chapter XXI; and in reference to the former I cite '*Narn*' and the page-number in *Unfinished Tales*.

(i) *The capture of Úrin and Túrin's childhood in Hisilómë* (pp. 70–2).

At the outset of the tale, it would be interesting to know more of the teller, Eltas. He is a puzzling figure: he seems to be a Man (he says that 'our people' called Turambar *Turumart* 'after the fashion of the Gnomes') living in Hisilómë after the days of Turambar but before the fall of Gondolin, and he 'trod Olórë Mallë', the Path of Dreams. Is he then a child, one of 'the children of the fathers of the fathers of Men', who 'found Kôr and remained with the Eldar for ever' (*The Cottage of Lost Play*, I.19–20)?

The opening passage agrees in almost all essentials with the ultimate form of the story. Thus there go back to the beginning of the 'tradition' (or at least to its earliest extant form) the departure of Húrin to the Battle of Unnumbered Tears at the summons of the Noldor, while his wife (Mavwin = Morwen) and young son Túrin remained behind; the great stand of Húrin's men, and Húrin's capture by Morgoth; the reason for Húrin's torture (Morgoth's wish to learn the whereabouts of Turgon) and the mode of it, and Morgoth's curse; the birth of Nienor shortly after the great battle.

That Men were shut in Hisilómë (or Hithlum, the Gnomish form, which here first appears, equated with Dor Lómin, p. 71) after the Battle of Unnumbered Tears is stated in *The Coming of the Elves* (I.118) and in the last of the outlines for *Gilfanon's Tale* (I.241); later on this was transformed into the confinement of the treacherous Easterling Men in Hithlum (*The Silmarillion* p. 195), and their ill-treatment of the survivors of the House of Hador became an essential element in the story of Túrin's childhood. But in the *Tale of Turambar* the idea is already present that 'the strange men who dwelt nigh knew not the dignity of the Lady Mavwin'. It is not in fact clear where Úrin dwelt: it is said here that after the battle 'Mavwin got her in tears into the land of Hithlum or Dor Lómin where all Men must now dwell', which can only mean that she went there, on account of Melko's command, from wherever she had dwelt with Úrin before; on the other hand, a little later in the tale (p. 73), and in apparent contradiction to this, Mavwin would not accept the invitation of Tinwelint to come to Artanor partly because (it is suggested) 'she clung to that dwelling that Úrin had set her in *ere he went to the great war*'.

In the later story Morwen resolved to send Túrin away from fear that he would be enslaved by the Easterlings (*Narn* p. 70), whereas here all that is said is that Mavwin 'knew not in her distress how to foster both him and his sister' (which presumably reflects her poverty). This in turn reflects a further difference, namely that here Nienóri was born before Túrin's departure (but see p. 131); in the later legend he and his companions left Dor-lómin in the autumn of the Year of Lamentation and Nienor was born early in the following year – thus he had never seen her, even as an infant.

An important underlying difference is the absence in the tale of the motive that Húrin had himself visited Gondolin, a fact known to Morgoth and the reason for his being taken alive (*The Silmarillion* pp. 158–9, 196–7); this element in the story arose much later, when the founding of Gondolin was set far back and long before the Battle of Unnumbered Tears.

(ii)   *Túrin in Artanor* (pp. 72–6)

From the original story of Túrin's journey the two old men who accom-

panied him, one of whom returned to Mavwin while the older remained
with Túrin, were never lost; and the cry of Túrin as they set out
reappears in the *Narn* (p. 73): 'Morwen, Morwen, when shall I see you
again?'

Beleg was present from the beginning, as was the meaning of his name:
'he was called Beleg *for* he was of great stature' (see I.254, entry *Haloisi
velikë*, and the Appendix to *The Silmarillion*, entry *beleg*); and he
plays the same rôle in the old story, rescuing the travellers starving in the
forest and taking them to the king.

In the later versions there is no trace of the remarkable message sent by
Tinwelint to Mavwin, and indeed his curiously candid explanation, that
he held aloof from the Battle of Unnumbered Tears because in his
wisdom he foresaw that Artanor could become a refuge if disaster befell,
is hardly in keeping with his character as afterwards conceived. There
were of course quite other reasons for his conduct (*The Silmarillion*
p. 189). On the other hand, Mavwin's motives for not herself leaving
Hithlum remained unchanged (see the passage in the *Narn*, p. 70, where
the word 'almsguest' is an echo of the old tale); but the statement is
puzzling that Mavwin might, when Nienóri was grown, have put aside
her pride and passed over the mountains, had they not become impassable
– clearly suggesting that she never left Hithlum. Perhaps the meaning is,
however, that she might have made the journey *earlier* (while Túrin was
still in Artanor) than she in fact did (when for a time the ways became
easier, but Túrin had gone).

The character of Túrin as a boy reappears in every stroke of the
description in the *Narn* (p. 77):

> It seemed that fortune was unfriendly to him, so that often what he
> designed went awry, and what he desired he did not gain; neither did
> he win friendship easily, for he was not merry, and laughed seldom,
> and a shadow lay on his youth.

(It is a notable point that is added in the tale: 'at no time did he give
much heed to words that were spoken to him'). And the ending of all
word between Túrin and his mother comes about in the same way –
increased guard on the mountains (*Narn* p. 78).

While the story of Túrin and Saeros as told in *The Silmarillion*, and in
far more detail in the *Narn*, goes back in essentials to the *Tale of
Turambar*, there are some notable differences – the chief being that as
the story was first told Túrin's tormentor was slain outright by the
thrown drinking-cup. The later complications of Saeros' treacherous
assault on Túrin the following day and his chase to the death, of the trial
of Túrin in his absence for this deed and of the testimony of Nellas (this
last only in the *Narn*) are entirely absent, necessarily; nor does Mablung
appear – indeed it seems clear that Mablung first emerged at the end of
the *Tale of Tinúviel* (see p. 59). Some details survived (as the comb

which Orgof/Saeros offered tauntingly to Túrin, *Narn* p. 80), while others were changed or neglected (as that it was the anniversary of Túrin's departure from his home — though the figure of twelve years agrees with the later story, and that the king was present in the hall, contrast *Narn* p. 79). But the taunt that roused Túrin to murderous rage remained essentially the same, in that it touched on his mother; and the story was never changed that Túrin came into the hall tousled and roughly clad, and that he was mocked for this by his enemy.

Orgof is not greatly distinct from Saeros, if less developed. He was in the king's favour, proud, and jealous of Túrin; in the later story he was a Nandorin Elf while here he is an Ilkorin with some Gnomish blood (for Gnomes in Artanor see p. 65), but doubtless some peculiarity in his origin was part of the 'tradition'. In the old story he is explicitly a fop and a fool, and he is not given the motives of hatred for Túrin that are ascribed to him in the *Narn* (p. 77).

Though far simpler in narrative, the essential element of Túrin's ignorance of his pardon was present from the outset. The tale provides an explanation, not found later, of why Túrin did not, on leaving Artanor, return to Hithlum; cf. the *Narn* p. 87: 'to Dor-lómin he did not dare, for it was closely beset, and one man alone could not hope at that time, as he thought, to come through the passes of the Mountains of Shadow.'

Túrin's prowess against the Orcs during his sojourn in Artanor is given a more central or indeed unique importance in the tale ('he held the wrath of Melko from them for many years') especially as Beleg, his companion-in-arms in the later versions, is not here mentioned (and in this passage the power of the queen to withstand invasion of the kingdom seems again (see p. 63) less than it afterwards became).

(iii)   *Túrin and Beleg* (pp. 76–81)

That part of the Túrin saga following on his days in Artanor/Doriath underwent a large development later ('Túrin among the Outlaws'), and indeed my father never brought this part of the story to finality. In the oldest version there is a much more rapid development of the plot: Beleg joins Túrin's band, and the destruction of the band and capture of Túrin by the Orcs follows (in terms of the narrative) almost immediately. There is no mention of 'outlaws' but only of 'wild spirits', no long search for Túrin by Beleg, no capture and maltreatment of Beleg by the band, and no betrayal of the camp by a traitor (the part ultimately taken by Mîm the Dwarf). Beleg indeed (as already noticed) is not said to have been Túrin's companion in the earlier time, before the slaying of Orgof, and they only take up together after Túrin's self-imposed exile.

Beleg is called a Noldo (p. 78), and if this single reference is to be given full weight (and there seems no reason not to: it is explicit in the *Tale of Tinúviel* that there were Noldoli in Artanor, and Orgof had Gnomish blood) then it is to be observed that Beleg as originally conceived was an Elf of Kôr. He is not here marked out as a great bowman (neither his name Cúthalion 'Strongbow' nor his great bow Belthronding appear); he is described at his first appearance (p. 73) as 'a wood-ranger, a huntsman of the secret Elves', but not as the chief of the marchwardens of the realm.

But from the capture of Túrin to the death of Beleg the old tale was scarcely changed afterwards in any really important respect, though altered in many details: such as Beleg's shooting of the wolf-sentinels silently in the darkness in the later story, and the flash of lightning that illuminated Beleg's face – but the blue-shining lamps of the Noldor appear again in much later writings: one was borne by the Elves Gelmir and Arminas who guided Tuor through the Gate of the Noldor on his journey to the sea (see *Unfinished Tales* pp. 22, 51 note 2). In my father's painting (probably dating from 1927 or 1928) of the meeting between Beleg and Flinding in Taur-nu-Fuin (reproduced in *Pictures by J. R. R. Tolkien*, no. 37) Flinding's lamp is seen beside him. The plot of the old story is very precisely contrived in such details as the reason for the carrying of Túrin, still sleeping, out of the Orc-camp, and for Beleg's using his sword, rather than a knife, to cut Túrin's bonds; perhaps also in the crushing of Beleg by Túrin so that he was winded and could not speak his name before Túrin gave him his death-blow.

The story of Túrin's madness after the slaying of Beleg, the guidance of Gwindor, and the release of Túrin's tears at Eithel Ivrin, is here in embryo. Of the peculiar nature of Beleg's sword there is no suggestion.

(iv) *Túrin among the Rodothlim; Túrin and Glorund* (pp. 81–8)

In this passage is found (so far as written record goes, for it is to be remembered that a wholly erased text underlies the manuscript) the origin of Nargothrond, as yet unnamed. Among many remarkable features the chief is perhaps that Orodreth was there before Felagund, Lord of Caves, with whom in the later legend Nargothrond was identified, as its founder and deviser. (In *The Silmarillion* Orodreth was one of Finrod Felagund's brothers (the sons of Finarfin), to whom Felagund gave the command of Minas Tirith on Tol Sirion after the making of Nargothrond (p. 120), and Orodreth became King of Nargothrond after Felagund's death.) In the tale this cave-dwelling of exiled Noldoli is a simpler and rougher place, and (as is suggested) short-lived against the overwhelming power of Melko; but, as so often, there were many features that were never altered, even though in a crucial respect the history of Nargothrond was to be greatly modified by contact with the legend of Beren and Tinúviel. Thus the site was from the start 'above a stream' (the later Narog) that 'ran down to feed the river Sirion', and as is seen later (p. 96) the bank of the river on the side of the caves was higher and the hills drew close: cf. *The Silmarillion* p. 114: 'the caves under the

High Faroth in its steep western shore'. The policy of secrecy and refusal of open war pursued by the Elves of Nargothrond was always an essential element (cf. *The Silmarillion* pp. 168, 170),* as was the overturning of that policy by the confidence and masterfulness of Túrin (though in the tale there is no mention of the great bridge that he caused to be built). Here, however, the fall of the redoubt is perhaps more emphatically attributed to Túrin, his coming there seen more simply as a curse, and the disaster as more inevitably proceeding from his unwisdom: at least in the fragments of this part of the *Narn* (pp. 155–7) Túrin's case against Gwindor, who argued for the continuation of secrecy, is seemingly not without substance, despite the outcome. But the essential story is the same: Túrin's policy revealed Nargothrond to Morgoth, who came against it with overwhelming strength and destroyed it.

In relation to the earliest version the roles of Flinding (Gwindor), Failivrin (Finduilas),† and Orodreth were to undergo a remarkable set of transferences. In the old tale Flinding had been of the Rodothlim before his capture and imprisonment in Angband, just as afterwards Gwindor came from Nargothrond (but with a great development in his story, see *The Silmarillion* pp. 188, 191–2), and on his return was so changed as to be scarcely recognisable (I pass over such enduring minor features as the taking of Túrin and Flinding/Gwindor prisoner on their coming to the caves). The beautiful Failivrin is already present, and her unrequited love for Túrin, but the complication of her former relation with Gwindor is quite absent, and she is not the daughter of Orodreth the King but of one Galweg (who was to disappear utterly). Flinding is not shown as opposed to Túrin's policies; and in the final battle he aids Túrin in bearing Orodreth out of the fight. Orodreth dies (after being carried back to the caves) reproaching Túrin for what he has brought to pass – as does Gwindor dying in *The Silmarillion* (p. 213), with the added bitterness of his relation with Finduilas. But Failivrin's father Galweg is slain in the battle, as is Finduilas' father Orodreth in *The Silmarillion*. Thus in the evolution of the legend Orodreth took over the rôle of Galweg, while Gwindor took over in part the rôle of Orodreth.

As I have noticed earlier, there is no mention in the tale of any peculiarity attaching to Beleg's sword, and though the Black Sword is already present it was made for Túrin on the orders of Orodreth, and its blackness and its shining pale edges were of its first making (see *The Silmarillion* pp. 209–10). Its power of speech ('it is said that at times it spake dark words to him') remained afterwards in its dreadful words to Túrin before his death (*Narn* p. 145) – a motive that appears already

---

* From the first of these passages it seems that when Beren came to Nargothrond the 'secret' policy was already pursued under Felagund; but from the second it seems that it came into being from the potent rhetoric of Curufin after Beren went there.

† In *The Silmarillion* she is named Finduilas, and the name Faelivrin 'which is the gleam of the sun on the pools of Ivrin' was given to her by Gwindor (pp. 209–10).

in the tale, p. 112; and Túrin's name derived from the sword (here *Mormagli*, *Mormakil*, later *Mormegil*) was already devised. But of Túrin's disguising of his true name in Nargothrond there is no suggestion: indeed it is explicitly stated that he said who he was.

Of Gelmir and Arminas and the warning they brought to Nargothrond from Ulmo (*Narn* pp. 159–62) the germ can perhaps be seen in the 'whispers in the stream at eve', which undoubtedly implies messages from Ulmo (see p. 77).

The dragon Glorund is named in the 'lengthening spell' in the *Tale of Tinúviel* (pp. 19, 46), but the actual name was only introduced in the course of the writing of the *Tale of Turambar* (see note 11). There is no suggestion that he had played any previous part in the history, or indeed that he was the first of his kind, the Father of Dragons, with a long record of evil already before the Sack of Nargothrond. Of great interest is the passage in which the nature of the dragons of Melko is defined: their evil wisdom, their love of lies and gold (which 'they may not use or enjoy'), and the knowledge of tongues that Men say would come from eating a dragon's heart (with evident reference to the legend in the Norse Edda of Sigurd Fafnisbane, who was enabled to understand, to his own great profit, the speech of birds when he ate the heart of the dragon Fafnir, roasting it on a spit).

The story of the sack of Nargothrond is somewhat differently treated in the old story, although the essentials were to remain of the driving away of Failivrin/Finduilas among the captives and of the powerlessness of Túrin to aid her, being spellbound by the dragon. Minor differences (such as the later arrival of Glorund on the scene: in *The Silmarillion* Túrin only came back to Nargothrond after Glaurung had entered the caves and the sack was 'well nigh achieved') and minor agreements (such as the denial of the plunder to the Orcs) may here be passed over; most interesting is the account of Túrin's words with the dragon. Here the whole issue of Túrin's escaping or not escaping his doom is introduced, and it is significant that he takes the name *Turambar* at this juncture, whereas in the later legend he takes it when he joins the Woodmen in Brethil, and less is made of it. The old version is far less powerfully and concisely expressed, and the dragon's words are less subtle and ingeniously untrue. Here too the moral is very explicitly pointed, that Túrin *should not* have abandoned Failivrin 'in danger that he himself could see' – does this not suggest that, even under the dragon's spell as he was, there was a weakness (a 'blindness', see p. 83) in Túrin which the dragon touched? As the story is told in *The Silmarillion* the moral would seem uncalled for: Túrin was opposed by an adversary too powerful for his mind and will.

There is here a remarkable passage in which suicide is declared a sin, depriving such a one of all hope 'that ever his spirit would be freed from the dark glooms of Mandos or stray into the pleasant paths of Valinor'. This seems to go with the perplexing passage in the tale of *The Coming of the Valar and the Building of Valinor* concerning the fates of Men: see p. 60.

Finally, it is strange that in the old story the gold and treasure was carried out from the caves by the Orcs and remained there (it 'lay by the caves above the stream'), and the dragon most uncharacteristically 'slept before it' in the open. In *The Silmarillion* Glaurung 'gathered all the hoard and riches of Felagund and heaped them, and lay upon them in the innermost hall'.

(v)   *Túrin's return to Hithlum* (pp. 88–91)

In this passage the case is much as in previous parts of the tale: the large structure of the story was not greatly changed afterwards, but there are many important differences nonetheless.

In the *Tale of Turambar* it is clear that the house of Mavwin was not imagined as standing near to the hills or mountains that formed the barrier between Hithlum and the Lands Beyond: Túrin was told that never did Orcs 'come hither deep into the land of Hisilómë', in contrast to the *Narn* (p. 68), where 'Húrin's house stood in the south-east of Dor-lómin, and the mountains were near; Nen Lalaith indeed came down from a spring under the shadow of Amon Darthir, over whose shoulder there was a steep pass'. The removal of Mavwin from one house to another in Hithlum, visited in turn by Túrin as he sought for her, was afterwards rejected, to the improvement of the story. Here Túrin comes back to his old home in the late summer, whereas in *The Silmarillion* the fall of Nargothrond took place in the late autumn ('the leaves fell from the trees in a great wind as they went, for the autumn was passing to a dire winter,' p. 213) and Túrin came to Dor-lómin in the Fell Winter (p. 215).

The names Brodda and Airin (later spelled Aerin) remained; but Brodda is here the lord of the land, and Airin plays a more important part in the scene in the hall, dealing justice with vigour and wisdom, than she does later. It is not said here that she had been married by force, though her life with Brodda is declared to have been very evil; but of course the situation in the later narratives is far more clear-cut — the Men of Hithlum were 'Easterlings', 'Incomers' hostile to the Elves and the remnant of the House of Hador, whereas in the early story no differentiation is made among them, and indeed Brodda was 'a man whom Mavwin trusted'. The motive of Brodda's ill-treatment of Mavwin is already present, but only to the extent that he embezzled her goods after her departure; in the *Narn* it seems from Aerin's words to Túrin (p. 107) that the oppression of Morwen by Brodda and others was the cause of her going at last to Doriath. In the brief account in *The Silmarillion* (p. 215) it is not indeed made explicit that Brodda in particular deserved Túrin's hatred.

Túrin's conduct in the hall is in the tale essentially simpler: the true story has been told to him by a passer-by, he enters to exact vengeance on Brodda for thieving Mavwin's goods, and he does so with dispatch. As told in the *Narn*, where Túrin's eyes are only finally opened to the deception that has been practised upon him by the words of Aerin, who is present in the hall, his rage is more passionate, crazed, and bitter, and indeed more comprehensible: and the moral observation that Túrin's deed was 'violent and unlawful' is not made. The story of Airin's judgement on these doings, made in order to save Túrin, was afterwards removed; and Túrin's solitary departure was expanded, with the addition also of the firing of Brodda's hall by Aerin (*Narn* p. 109).

Some details survived all the changes: in the *Narn* Túrin still seizes Brodda by the hair, and just as in the tale his rage suddenly expired after the deed of violence ('his wrath was grown cold'), so in the *Narn* 'the fire of his rage was as ashes'. It may be noticed here that while in the old story Túrin does not rename himself so often, his tendency to do so is already present.

The story of how Túrin came among the Woodmen and delivered them from Orcs is not found in the *Tale of Turambar*; nor is there any mention of the Mound of Finduilas near the Crossings of Teiglin nor any account of her fate.

(vi)   *The return of Gumlin to Hithlum and the departure of Mavwin and Nienóri to Artanor* (pp. 91–3)

In the later story the elder of Túrin's guardians (Gumlin in the tale, Grithnir in the *Narn*) plays no part after his bringing Túrin to Doriath: it is only said that he stayed there till he died (*Narn* p. 74); and Morwen had no tidings out of Doriath before leaving her home – indeed she only learnt that Túrin had left Thingol's realm when she got there (*The Silmarillion* p. 211; cf. Aerin's words in the *Narn*, p. 107: 'She looked to find her son there awaiting her.') This whole section of the tale does no more than explain with what my father doubtless felt (since he afterwards rejected it almost in its entirety) to be unnecessary complication why Mavwin went to Tinwelint. I think it is clear, however, that the difference between the versions here depends on the different views of Mavwin's (Morwen's) condition in Hithlum. In the old story she is not suffering hardship and oppression; she trusts Brodda to the extent of entrusting not only her goods to him but even her daughter, and is said indeed to have 'peace and honour among the men of those regions'; the chieftains speak of the love they bear her. A motive for her departure is found in the coming of Gumlin and the news he brings of Túrin's flight from the lands of Tinwelint. In the later story, on the other hand, Brodda's character as tyrant and oppressor is extended, and it is Morwen's very plight at his hands that leads her to depart. (The news that came to Túrin in Doriath that 'Morwen's plight was eased' (*Narn* p. 77, cf. *The Silmarillion* p. 199) is probably a survival from the old story; nothing is said in the later narratives to explain how this came about, and ceased.) In either case her motive for leaving is coupled with the fact of the increased safety of the lands; but whereas in the later story the reason for this was the prowess of the Black Sword of Nargothrond, in the tale it was the 'great and terrible project' of Melko that was afoot – the assault on the caves of the Rodothlim (see note 18).

It is curious that in this passage Airin and Brodda are introduced as if for the first time. It is perhaps significant that the part of the tale extending from the dragon's words 'Hearken to me, O son of Úrin . . .' on p. 87 to '. . . fell to his knees before Tinwelint' on p. 92 was written in a separate part of the manuscript book: possibly this replaced an earlier text in which Brodda and Airin did not appear. But many such questions arise from the earliest manuscripts, and few can now be certainly unravelled.

(vii)   *Mavwin and Nienóri in Artanor and their meeting with Glorund* (pp. 93–9)

The next essential step in the development of the plot – the learning by Mavwin/Morwen of Túrin's sojourn in Nargothrond – is more neatly and naturally handled in *The Silmarillion* (p. 217) and the *Narn* (p. 112), where news is brought to Thingol by fugitives from the sack, in contrast to the *Tale of Turambar*, where Mavwin and Nienóri only learn of the destruction of the Elves of the Caves from a band of Noldoli while themselves wandering aimlessly in the forest. It is odd that these Noldoli did not name Túrin by his name but only as the *Mormakil*: it seems that they did not know who he was, but they knew enough of his history to make his identity plain to Mavwin. As noted above, Túrin declared his name and lineage to the Elves of the Caves. In the later narrative, on the other hand, Túrin did conceal it in Nargothrond, calling himself Agarwaen, but all those who brought news of the fall to Doriath 'declared that it was known to many in Nargothrond ere the end that the Mormegil was none other than Túrin son of Húrin of Dor-lómin'.

As often, unneeded complication in the early story was afterwards cleared away: thus the elaborate argumentation needed to get Tinwelint's warriors and Mavwin and Nienóri on the road together is gone from *The Silmarillion* and the *Narn*. In the tale the ladies and the Elvish warriors all set off together with the full intention that the former shall watch developments from a high place (afterwards Amon Ethir, the Hill of Spies); in the later story Morwen simply rides off, and the party of Elves, led by Mablung, follows after her, with Nienor among them in disguise.

Particularly notable is the passage in the tale in which Mavwin holds out the great gold-hoard of the Rodothlim as a bait to Tinwelint, and Tinwelint unashamedly admits that (as a wild Elf of the woods) it is this, not any hope of aiding Túrin, that moves him to send out a party. The majesty, power, and pride of Thingol rose with the development of the conception of the Grey-elves of Beleriand; as I have said earlier (p. 63) 'In the beginning, Tinwelint's dwelling was not a subterranean city full of marvels . . . but a rugged cave', and here he is seen planning a foray to augment his slender wealth in precious things – a far cry from the description of his vast treasury in the *Narn* (p. 76):

> Now Thingol had in Menegroth deep armouries filled with great wealth of weapons: metal wrought like fishes' mail and shining like water in the moon; swords and axes, shields and helms, wrought by Telchar himself or by his master Gamil Zirak the old, or by elven-wrights more skilful still. For some things he had received in gift that came out of Valinor and were wrought by Fëanor in his mastery, than whom no craftsman was greater in all the days of the world.

Great as are the differences from the later legend in the encounter with the dragon, the stinking vapours raised by his lying in the river as the cause of the miscarriage of the plan, the maddened flight of the horses, and the enspelling of Nienor so that all memory of her past was lost, are already present. Most striking perhaps of the many differences is the fact that Mavwin was present at the conversation with Glorund; and of these speeches there is no echo in the *Narn* (pp. 118–19), save that Nienor's naming of Túrin as the object of their quest revealed her identity to the dragon (this is explicit in the *Narn*, and may probably be surmised from the tale). The peculiar tone of Glaurung in the later narrative, sneering and curt, knowing and self-possessed, and unfathomably wicked, can be detected already in the words of Glorund, but as he evolved he gained immeasurably in dread by becoming more laconic.

The chief difference of structure lies in the total absence of the 'Mablung-element' from the tale, nor is there any foreshadowing of it. There is no suggestion of an exploration of the sacked dwellings in the dragon's absence (indeed he does not, as it appears, go any distance from them); the purpose of the expedition from Artanor was expressly warlike ('a strong party against the Foalókë', 'they prepared them for battle'), since Tinwelint had hopes of laying hands on the treasure, whereas afterwards it became purely a scouting foray, for Thingol 'desired greatly to know more of the fate of Nargothrond' (*Narn* p. 113).

A curious point is that though Mavwin and Nienóri were to be stationed on the tree-covered 'high place' that was afterward called the Hill of Spies, and where they were in fact so stationed in *The Silmarillion* and the *Narn*, it seems that in the old story they never got there, but were ensnared by Glorund where he lay in, or not far from, the river. Thus the 'high place' had in the event almost no significance in the tale.

(viii)   *Turambar and Níniel* (pp. 99–102)

In the later legend Nienor was found by Mablung after her enspelling by Glaurung, and with three companions he led her back towards the borders of Doriath. The chase after Nienor by the band of Orcs (*Narn* p. 120) is present in the tale, but it does not have its later narrative function of leading to Nienor's flight and loss by Mablung and the other Elves (who do not appear): rather it leads directly to her rescue by Turambar, now dwelling among the Woodmen. In the *Narn* (p. 122) the Woodmen of Brethil did indeed come past the spot where they found her on their return from a foray against Orcs; but the circumstances of her finding are altogether different, most especially since there is in the tale no mention of the Haudh-en-Elleth, the Mound of Finduilas.

An interesting detail concerns Nienor's response to Turambar's naming her *Níniel*. In *The Silmarillion* and the *Narn* 'she shook her head, but said: Níniel'; in the present text she said: 'Not Níniel, not Níniel.' One has the impression that in the old story what impressed her darkened mind was only the resemblance of *Níniel* to her own forgotten name *Nienóri* (and of *Turambar* to *Túrin*), whereas in the later she both denied and in some way accepted the name *Níniel*.

An original element in the legend is the Woodmen's bringing of Níniel to a place ('Silver Bowl') where there was a great waterfall (afterwards Dimrost, the Rainy Stair, where the stream of Celebros 'fell towards Teiglin'): and these falls were near to the dwellings of the Woodmen — but the place where they found Níniel was much further off in the forest (several days' journey) than were the Crossings of Teiglin from Dimrost. When she came there she was filled with dread, a foreboding of what was to happen there afterwards, and this is the origin of her shuddering fit in the later narratives, from which the place was renamed Nen Girith, the Shuddering Water (see *Narn* p. 149, note 24).

The utter darkness imposed on Níniel's mind by the dragon's spell is less emphasized in the tale, and there is no suggestion that she needed to relearn her very language; but it is interesting to observe the recurrence in a changed context of the simile of 'one that seeks for something mislaid': in the *Narn* (p. 123) Níniel is said to have taken great delight in the relearning of words, 'as one that finds again treasures great and small that were mislaid'.

The lame man, here called Tamar, and his vain love of Níniel already appear; unlike his later counterpart Brandir he was not the chief of the Woodmen, but he was the son of the chief. He was also Half-elven! Most extraordinary is the statement that the wife of Bethos the chieftain and mother of Tamar was an Elf, a woman of the Noldoli: this is mentioned in passing, as if the great significance and rarity of the union of Elf and Mortal had not yet emerged — but in a Name-list associated with the tale of *The Fall of Gondolin* Eärendel is said to be 'the only being that is half of the kindred of the Eldalië and half of Men' (p. 215).*

---

* In a later rewriting of a passage in that tale (p. 164 and note 22) it is said of Tuor and Idril of Gondolin: 'Thus was first wed a child of Men with a daughter of Elfinesse, nor was Tuor the last.'

The initial reluctance of Níniel to receive Turambar's suit is given no explanation in the tale: the implication must be that some instinct, some subconscious appreciation of the truth, held her back. In *The Silmarillion* (p. 220)

> for that time she delayed in spite of her love. For Brandir foreboded he knew not what, and sought to restrain her, rather for her sake than his own or rivalry with Turambar; and he revealed to her that Turambar was Túrin son of Húrin, and though she knew not the name a shadow fell upon her mind.

In the final version as in the oldest, the Woodmen knew who Turambar was. My father's scribbled directions for the alteration of the story cited in note 23 ('Make Turambar never tell new folk of his lineage . . .') are puzzling: for since Níniel had lost all memory of her past she would not know the names Túrin son of Húrin even if it were told to her that Turambar was he. It is however possible that when my father wrote this he imagined Níniel's lost knowledge of herself and her family as being nearer the surface of her mind, and capable of being brought back by hearing the names – in contrast to the later story where she did not consciously recognise the name of Túrin even when Brandir told it to her. Clearly the question-mark against the reference in the text of the tale to Turambar's speaking to Níniel 'of his father and mother and the sister he had not seen' and Níniel's distress at his words (see note 24) depends on the same train of thought. The statement here that Turambar had never seen his sister is at variance with what is said earlier in the tale, that he did not leave Hithlum until after Nienóri's birth (p. 71); but my father was uncertain on this point, as is clearly seen from the succession of readings, changed back and forth between the two ideas, given in note 15.

(ix)   *The slaying of Glorund* (pp. 103–8)

In this section I follow the narrative of the tale as far as Túrin's swoon when the dying dragon opened his eyes and looked at him. Here the later story runs very close to the old, but there are many interesting differences.

In the tale Glorund is said to have had bands of both Orcs and Noldoli subject to him, but only the Orcs remained afterwards; cf. the *Narn* p. 125:

> Now the power and malice of Glaurung grew apace, and he waxed fat [cf. 'the Foalókë waxed fat'], and he gathered Orcs to him, and ruled as a dragon-King, and all the realm of Nargothrond that had been was laid under him.

The mention in the tale that Tinwelint's people were 'grievously harried' by Glorund's bands suggests once again that the magic of the Queen was no very substantial protection; while the statement that 'at length there came some [Orcs] nigh even to those woods and glades that were beloved of Turambar and his folk' seems at variance with Turambar's saying to Níniel earlier that 'we are hard put to it to fend those evil ones from our homes' (p. 100). There is no mention here of Turambar's pledge to Níniel that he would go to battle only if the homes of the Woodmen were assailed (*Narn* pp. 125–6); and there is no figure corresponding to Dorlas of the later versions. Tamar's character, briefly described (p. 106), is in accord so far as it goes with what is later told of Brandir, but the relationship of Brandir to Níniel, who called him her brother (*Narn* p. 124), had not emerged. The happiness and prosperity of the Woodmen under Turambar's chieftainship is much more strongly emphasized in the tale (afterwards he was not indeed the chieftain, at least not in name); and it leads in fact to Glorund's greed as a motive for his assault on them.

The topographical indications in this passage, important to the narrative, are readily enough accommodated to the later accounts, with one major exception: it is clear that in the old story the stream of the waterfall that fell down to the Silver Bowl was the same as that which ran through the gorge where Turambar slew Glorund:

> Here flowed that same stream that further down wound past the dragon's lair [*lair* = the place where he was lying] in a deep bed cloven deep into the earth (p. 105).

Thus Turambar and his companions, as he said,

> will go down the rocks to the foot of the fall, and so gaining the path of the stream perchance we may come as nigh to the drake as may be (*ibid.*).

In the final story, on the other hand, the falling stream (Celebros) was a tributary of Teiglin; cf. the *Narn* p. 127:

> Now the river Teiglin . . . flowed down from Ered Wethrin swift as Narog, but at first between low shores, until after the Crossings, gathering power from other streams, it clove a way through the feet of the highlands upon which stood the Forest of Brethil. Thereafter it ran in deep ravines, whose great sides were like walls of rock, but pent at the bottom the waters flowed with great force and noise. And right in the path of Glaurung there lay now one of these gorges, by no means the deepest, but the narrowest, just north of the inflow of Celebros.

The pleasant place ('a green sward where grew a wealth of flowers') survived; cf. the *Narn* p. 123: 'There was a wide greensward at the head of the falls, and birches grew about it.' So also did the 'Silver Bowl', though the name was lost: 'the stream [Celebros] went over a lip of worn stone, and fell down by many foaming steps into a rocky bowl far below' (*Narn, ibid.*; cf. the tale p. 105: 'it fell over a great fall where the water-worn rock jutted smooth and grey from amid the grass'). The 'little hill' or 'knoll', 'islanded among the trees', from which Turambar and his companions looked out is not so described in the *Narn*, but the picture of a high place and lookout near the head of the falls remained, as may be seen from the statement in the *Narn* (p. 123) that from Nen Girith 'there was a wide view towards the ravines of Teiglin'; later (*Narn* p. 128) it is said that it was Turambar's intention to 'ride to the high fall of Nen Girith . . . whence he could look far across the lands'. It seems certain, then, that the old image never faded, and was only a little changed.

While in both old and late accounts a great concourse of the people follow Turambar to the head of the falls against his bidding, in the late his motive for commanding them not to come is explicit: they are to remain in their homes and prepare for flight. Here on the other hand Níniel rides with Turambar to the head of Silver Bowl and says farewell to him there. But a detail of the old story survived: Turambar's words to Níniel 'Nor thou nor I die this day, nor yet tomorrow, by the evil of the dragon or by the foemen's swords' are closely paralleled by his words to her in the *Narn* (p. 129): 'Neither you nor I shall be slain by this Dragon, nor by any foe of the North'; and in the one account Níniel 'quelled her weeping and was very still', while in the other she 'ceased to weep and fell silent'. The situation is generally simpler in the tale, in that the Woodmen are scarcely characterised; Tamar is not as Brandir the titular head of the people, and this motive for bitterness against Turambar is absent, nor is there a Dorlas to insult him or a Hunthor to rebuke Dorlas. Tamar is however present with Níniel at the same point in the story, having girded himself with a sword: 'and many scoffed at him for that', just as it is afterwards said of Brandir that he had seldom done so before (*Narn* p. 132).

Turambar here set out from the head of the falls with six companions, all of whom proved in the end fainthearted, whereas later he had only two, Dorlas and Hunthor, and Hunthor remained staunch, though killed by a falling stone in the gorge. But the result is the same, in that Turambar must climb the further cliff of the gorge alone. Here the dragon remained where he lay near the brink of the cliff all night, and only moved with the dawn, so that his death and the events that immediately followed it took place by daylight. But in other respects the killing of the dragon remained even in many details much as it was originally written, more especially if comparison is made with the *Narn* (p. 134), where there reappears the need for Turambar and his

companion(s) to move from their first station in order to come up directly
under the belly of the beast (this is passed over in *The Silmarillion*).

Two notable points in this section remain to be mentioned; both are
afterthoughts pencilled into the manuscript. In the one we meet for the
first time Mîm the Dwarf as the captain of Glorund's guard over his
treasure during his absence — a strange choice for the post, one would
think. On this matter see p. 137 below. In the other it is said that Níniel
conceived a child by Turambar, which, remarkably enough, is not said in
the text as originally written; on this see p. 135.

(x)   *The deaths of Túrin and Nienóri* (pp. 108–12)

In the conclusion of the story the structure remained the same from the
old tale to the *Narn*: the moonlight, the tending of Turambar's burnt
hand, the cry of Níniel that stirred the dragon to his final malice, the
accusation by the dragon that Turambar was a stabber of foes unseen,
Turambar's naming Tamar/Brandir 'Club-foot' and sending him to
consort with the dragon in death, the sudden withering of the leaves
at the place of Nienor's leap as if it were already the end of autumn,
the invocation of Nienor to the waters and of Turambar to his sword, the
raising of Túrin's mound and the inscription in 'strange signs' upon it.
Many other features could be added. But there are also many differences;
here I refer only to some of the most important.

Mablung being absent from the old story, it is only Turambar's
intuition ('being free now of blindness' — the blindness that Melko
'wove of old', p. 83)* that informs him that Tamar was telling the
truth. The slaying of Glaurung and all its aftermath is in the late story
compassed in the course of a single night and the morning of the next
day, whereas in the tale it is spread over two nights, the intervening day,
and the morning of the second. Turambar is carried back to the people on
the hill-top by the three deserters who had left him in the ravine, whereas
in the late story he comes himself. (Of the slaying of Dorlas by Brandir
there is no trace in the tale, and the taking of a sword by Tamar has no
issue.)

Particularly interesting is the result of the changing of the place where
Túrin and Nienóri died. In the tale there is only one river, and Níniel
follows the stream up through the woods and casts herself over the falls of
Silver Bowl (in the place afterwards called Nen Girith), and here too, in
the glade above the falls, Turambar slew himself; in the developed story
her death-leap was into the ravine of Teiglin at Cabed-en-Aras, the
Deer's Leap, near the spot where Turambar lay beside Glaurung, and
here Turambar's death took place also. Thus Níniel's sense of dread
when she first came to Silver Bowl with the Woodmen who rescued her

---

* Cf. his words to Mablung in the *Narn*, p. 144: 'For see, I am blind! Did you not know?
Blind, blind, groping since childhood in a dark mist of Morgoth!'

(p. 101) foreboded her own death in that place, but in the changed story there is less reason for a foreknowledge of evil to come upon her there. But while the place was changed, the withering of the leaves remained, and the awe of the scene of their deaths, so that none would go to Cabed-en-Aras after, as they would not set foot on the grass above Silver Bowl.

The most remarkable feature of the earliest version of the story of Turambar and Níniel is surely that as my father first wrote it he did *not* say that she had conceived a child by him (note 25); and thus there is nothing in the old story corresponding to Glaurung's words to her: 'But the worst of all his deeds thou shalt feel in thyself' (*Narn* p. 138). The fact that above all accounts for Nienor's utter horror and despair was added to the tale later.

In concluding this long analysis of the *Tale of Turambar* proper the absence of place-names in the later part of it may be remarked. The dwelling of the Rodothlim is not named, nor the river that flowed past it; no name is given to the forest where the Woodmen dwelt, to their village, or even to the stream of such central importance at the end of the story (contrast Nargothrond, Narog, Tumhalad, Amon Ethir, Brethil, Amon Obel, Ephel Brandir, Teiglin, Celebros of the later narratives).

§2.   *The further narrative of Eltas*
(after the death of Túrin)

My father struck out the greater part of this continuation, allowing it to stand only as far as the words 'by reason of her great unhappiness' on p. 113 (see note 31). From the brief passage that was retained it is seen that the story of Morwen's coming to the stone on Túrin's mound goes back to the beginning, though in the later story she met Húrin there (*The Silmarillion*, p. 229).

The rejected part continues as follows:

Yet it is said also that when the doom of his folk was utterly fulfilled then was Úrin released by Melko, and bowed with age he fared back into the better lands. There did he gather some few to him, and they went and found the caverns of the Rothwarin [*earlier form for* Rodothlim, *see p.* 119] empty, and none guarded them, and a mighty treasury lay there still for none had found it, in that the terror of the drake lived longer than he and none had ventured thither again. But Úrin let bear the gold even before Linwë [i.e. Tinwelint], and casting it before his feet bade him bitterly to take his vile reward, naming him a craven by whose faint heart had much evil fallen to his house that might never have been; and in this began a new estrangement between Elves and Men, for Linwë was wroth at Úrin's words and bid him begone, for said he: "Long did I foster Túrin thy son and forgave him the evil of his deeds, and afterward thy wife I succoured, giving way against my counsel to her wild desires. Yet what is it to me – and wherefore dost thou, O son of the uncouth race of Men, endure to upbraid a king of the Eldalië, whose life began in Palisor ages uncounted before Men were born?" And then Úrin would have gone, but his men were not willing to leave the gold there, and a dissension arose between them and the Elves, and of this grew bitter blows, and Tintoglin [i.e. Tinwelint] might not stay them.

There then was Úrin's band slain in his halls, and they stained with their blood the dragon's hoard; but Úrin escaped and cursed that gold with a dread curse so that none might enjoy it, and he that held any part of it found evil and death to come of it. But Linwë hearing that curse caused the gold to be cast into a deep pool of the river before his doors, and not for very long did any see it again save for the Ring of Doom [*emended to:* the Necklace of the Dwarves], and that tale belongs not here, although therein did the evil of the worm Glorund find its last fulfilment.

(The last phrase is an addition to the text.) The remainder of this rejected narrative, concerning the final fates of Úrin and Mavwin and their children, is essentially the same as in the replacement text given on p. 115 ('Then Úrin departed . . .') and need not be given.

Immediately following the rejected narrative there is a short outline headed 'Story of the Nauglafring or the Necklace of the Dwarves', and this also was struck through. Here there is no mention of Úrin at all, but it is told that the Orcs (emended from *Gongs*, see I. 245 note 10) who guarded the treasury of Glorund went in search of him when he did not come back to the caves, and in their absence Tintoglin (i.e. Tinwelint), learning of Glorund's death, sent Elves to steal the hoard of the Rothwarin (i.e. Rodothlim). The Orcs returning cursed the thieves, and they cursed the gold also.

Linwë (i.e. Tinwelint) guarded the gold, and he had a great necklace made by certain Úvanimor (Nautar or Nauglath). (*Úvanimor* have been defined in an earlier tale as 'monsters, giants, and ogres', see I. 75, 236; *Nauglath* are Dwarves, I. 236). In this Necklace the Silmaril was set; but the curse of the gold was on him, and he defrauded them of part of their reward. The Nauglath plotted, and got aid of Men; Linwë was slain in a raid, and the gold carried away.

There follows another rejected outline, headed 'The Necklace of the Dwarves', and this combines features of the preceding outline with features of the rejected ending of Eltas' narrative (pp. 135–6). Here Úrin gathers a band of Elves and Men who are wild and fierce, and they go to the caves, which are lightly guarded because the 'Orqui' (i.e. Orcs) are abroad seeking Glorund. They carry off the treasure, and the Orcs returning curse it. Úrin casts the treasure before the king and reproaches him (saying that he might have sent a greater company to the caves to secure the treasure, if not to aid Mavwin in her distress); 'Tintoglin would not touch it and bid Úrin hold what he had won, but Úrin would depart with bitter words'. Úrin's men were not willing to leave it, and they sneaked back; there was an affray in the king's halls, and much blood was spilt on the gold. The outline concludes thus:

> The Gongs sack Linwë's halls and Linwë is slain and the gold is carried far away. Beren Ermabwed falls upon them at a crossing of Sirion and the treasure is cast into the water, and with it the Silmaril of Fëanor. The Nauglath that dwell nigh dive after the gold but only one mighty necklace of gold (and that Silmaril is on it) do they find. This becomes a mark of their king.

These two outlines are partly concerned with the story of the Nauglafring and show my father pondering that story before he wrote it; there is no need to consider these elements here. It is evident that he was in great doubt as to the further course of the story after the release of Úrin – what happened to the dragon's hoard? Was it guarded or unguarded, and if guarded by whom? How did it come at last into Tinwelint's hands? Who cursed it, and at what point in the story? If it was Úrin and his band that seized it, were they Men or Elves or both?

In the final text, written on slips placed in the manuscript book and given above pp. 113–16, these questions were resolved thus: Úrin's band was at first Men, then changed to Elves (see note 33); the treasure was guarded by the dwarf Mîm, whom Úrin slew, and it was he who cursed the gold as he died; Úrin's band became a baggage-train to carry the treasure to Tinwelint in sacks and wooden boxes (and they got it to the bridge before the king's door in the heart of the forest without, apparently, any difficulty). In this text there is no hint of what happened to the treasure after Úrin's departure (because the *Tale of the Nauglafring* begins at that point).

Subsequent to the writing of the *Tale of Turambar* proper, my father inserted Mîm into the text at an earlier point in the story (see pp. 103, 118 note 26), making him the captain of the guard appointed by Glorund to watch the treasure in his absence; but whether this was written in before or after the appearance of Mîm at the end (pp. 113–14) – whether it represents a different idea, or is an explanation of how Mîm came to be there – I cannot say.

In *The Silmarillion* (pp. 230–2) the story is wholly changed, in that the treasure remained in Nargothrond, and Húrin after the slaying of Mîm (for a far better reason than that in the early narrative) brought nothing from it to Doriath save the Necklace of the Dwarves.

Of the astonishing feature at the end of Eltas' narrative (pp. 115–16) of the 'deification' of Túrin Turambar and Nienóri (and the refusal of the Gods of Death to open their doors to them) it must be said that nowhere is there any explanation given – though in much later versions of the mythology Túrin Turambar appears in the Last Battle and smites Morgoth with his black sword. The purifying bath into which Túrin and Nienóri entered, called *Fôs'Almir* in the final text, was in the rejected text named *Fauri*; in the *Tale of the Sun and Moon* it has been described (I. 187), but is there given other names: *Tanyasalpë*, *Faskalanúmen*, and *Faskalan*.

There remains one further scrap of text to be considered. The second of the rejected outlines given above (pp. 136–7) was written in ink over a pencilled outline that was *not* erased, and I have been able to disinter a good deal of it from beneath the later writing. The two passages have nothing to do with each other; for some reason my father did not trouble in this case to erase earlier writing. The underlying text, so far as I can make it out, reads:

Tirannë and Vainóni fall in with the evil magician Kurúki who gives them a baneful drink. They forget their names and wander distraught in the woods. Vainóni is lost. She meets Turambar who saves her from Orcs and aids in her search for her mother. They are wed and live in happiness. Turambar becomes lord of rangers of the woods and a harrier of the Orcs. He goes to seek out the Foalókë which ravages his land. The treasure-heap – and flight of his band. He slays the Foalókë and is wounded. Vainóni succours him, but the dragon in dying tells her all, lifting the veil Kurúki has set over them. Anguish of Turambar and Vainóni. She flees into the woods and casts herself over a waterfall. Madness of Turambar who dwells alone . . . . Úrin escapes from Angamandi and seeks Tirannë. Turambar flees from him and falls upon his sword. . . . . Úrin builds a cairn and . . . . doom of Melko. Tirannë dies of grief and Úrin reaches Hisilómë. . . . . Purification of Turambar and Vainóni who fare shining about the world and go with the hosts of Tulkas against Melko.

Detached jottings follow this, doubtless written at the same time:

Úrin escapes. Tiranë learns of Túrin. Both wander distraught . . . in the wood.
Túrin leaves Linwë for in a quarrel he slew one of Linwë's kin (accidentally).
Introduce Failivrin element into the story?
Turambar unable to fight because of Foalókë's eyes. Sees Failivrin depart.

This can only represent some of my father's very earliest meditations on the story of Túrin Turambar. (That it appears in the notebook at the *end* of the fully-written Tale may seem surprising, but he clearly used these books in a rather eccentric way.) Nienóri is here called *Vainóni*, and Mavwin *Tirannë*; the spell of forgetfulness is here laid by a magician named *Kurúki*, although it is the dragon who lifts the veil that the magician set over them. Túrin's two encounters with the dragon seem to have emerged from an original single one.

As I have mentioned before, the *Tale of Turambar*, like others of the *Lost Tales*, is written in ink over a wholly erased pencilled text, and the extant form of the tale is such that it could only be derived from a rougher draft preceding it; but the underlying text is so completely erased that there is no clue as to what stage it had reached in the development of the legend. It may well be – I think it is extremely probable – that in this outline concerning Vainóni, Tirannë, and Kurúki we glimpse by an odd chance a 'layer' in the Túrin-saga older even than the erased text underlying the extant version.

§3. *Miscellaneous Matters*

(i) *Beren*

The rejected passage given on p. 71, together with the marginal note 'If Beren be a Gnome (as now in the story of Tinúviel) the references to Beren must be altered' (note 4), is the basis for my assertion (p. 52) that in the earliest, now lost, form of the *Tale of Tinúviel* Beren was a Man. I have shown, I hope, that the extant form of the *Tale of Turambar* preceded the extant form of the *Tale of Tinúviel* (p. 69). Beren was a Man, *and akin to Mavwin*, when the extant *Turambar* was written; he became a Gnome in the extant *Tinúviel*; and this change was then written into *Turambar*. What the replacement passage on p. 72 does is to change the relation of Egnor and Beren from kinship with Úrin's wife to friendship with Úrin. (A correction to the typescript version of *Tinúviel*, p. 45, is later: making the comradeship of Úrin with Beren rather than with Egnor.) Two further changes to the text of Turambar consequent on the change in Beren from Man to Elf are given in notes 5 and 6. – It is interesting to observe that in the developed genealogy of *The Silmarillion*, when Beren was of course again a Man, he was also again akin to Morwen: for Beren was first cousin to Morwen's father Baragund.

In the rejected passage on p. 71 my father wrote against the name Egnor 'Damrod the Gnome' (note 2), and in the amended passage he wrote that Úrin had known Beren 'and had rendered him a service once in respect of Damrod his son'. There is no clue anywhere as to what this service may have been; but in the second of the 'schemes' for *The Book of Lost Tales* (see I.233–4) the outline for the *Tale of the Nauglafring* refers to the son of Beren and Tinúviel, the father of Elwing, by the name *Daimord*, although in the actual tale as written the son is as he was to remain *Dior*. Presumably *Daimord* is to be equated with *Damrod*.

I cannot explain the insertion of 'Damrod the Gnome' against 'Egnor' in the rejected passage – possibly it was no more than a passing idea, to give the name *Damrod* to Beren's father.

It may be noticed here that both the rejected and the replacement passages make it very clear that the events of the story of Beren and Tinúviel took place *before* the Battle of Unnumbered Tears; see pp. 65–6.

(ii)   *The Battle of Tasarinan*

It is said at the beginning of the present tale (p. 70) that it 'tells of very ancient days of that folk [Men] before the Battle of Tasarinan when first Men entered the dark vales of Hisilómë'.

On the face of it this offers an extreme contradiction, since it is said many times that Men were shut in Hisilómë at the time of the Battle of Unnumbered Tears, and the *Tale of Turambar* takes place – must take place – after that battle. The solution lies, however, in an ambiguity in the sentence just cited. My father did not mean that this was a tale of Men in ancient days of that folk before they entered Hisilómë; he meant 'this is a tale of the ancient days *when* Men first entered Hisilómë – long before the Battle of Tasarinan'.

Tasarinan is the Land of Willows, *Nan-tathren* in *The Silmarillion*; the early word-lists or dictionaries give the 'Elvish' form *tasarin* 'willow' and the Gnomish *tathrin*.* The Battle of Tasarinan took place long after, in the course of the great expedition from Valinor for the release of the enslaved Noldoli in the Great Lands. See pp. 219–20.

(iii)   *The geography of the Tale of Turambar*

The passage describing the route of the Orcs who captured Túrin (p. 77) seems to give further support to the idea that 'the mountains fencing Hisilómë from the Lands Beyond were continuous with those above Angband' (p. 62); for it is said here that the Orcs 'followed ever the line of dark hills toward those regions where they rise high and gloomy and their heads are shrouded in black vapours', and '*there* are they called Angorodin or the Iron Mountains, for beneath the roots of their northernmost fastnesses lies Angband'.

The site of the caves of the Rodothlim, agreeing well with what is said later of Nargothrond, has been discussed already (p. 123), as has the topography of the Silver Bowl and the ravine in which Turambar slew Glorund, in relation to the later Teiglin, Celebros, and Nen Girith (pp. 132–3). There are in addition some indications in the tale of how the caves of the Rodothlim related to Tinwelint's kingdom and to the land

---

* *Tasarinan* survived as the Quenya name without change: 'the willow-meads of Tasarinan' in Treebeard's song in *The Two Towers*, III.4.

where the Woodmen dwelt. It is said (p. 95) that 'the dwellings of the Rodothlim were not utterly distant from the realm of Tinwelint, albeit far enough'; while the Woodmen dwelt 'in lands that were not utterly far from Sirion or the grassy hills of that river's middle course' (p. 91), which may be taken to agree tolerably with the situation of the Forest of Brethil. The region where they lived is said in the same passage to have been 'very far away many a journey beyond the river of the Rodothlim', and Glorund's wrath was great when he heard of 'a brave folk of Men that dwelt far beyond the river' (p. 103); this also can be accommodated quite well to the developed geographical conception – Brethil was indeed a good distance beyond the river (Narog) for one setting out from Nargothrond.

My strong impression is that though the geography of the west of the Great Lands *may* have been still fairly vague, it already had, in many important respects, the same essential structure and relations as those seen on the map accompanying *The Silmarillion*.

(iv)   *The influence of the Valar*

As in the *Tale of Tinúviel* (see p. 68), in the *Tale of Turambar* also there are several references to the power of the Valar in the affairs of Men and Elves in the Great Lands – and to prayers, both of thanksgiving and request, addressed to them: thus Túrin's guardians 'thanked the Valar' that they accomplished the journey to Artanor (p. 72), and more remarkably, Úrin 'called upon the Valar of the West, being taught much concerning them by the Eldar of Kôr – the Gnomes he had encountered – and his words came, who shall say how, to Manwë Súlimo upon the heights of Taniquetil' (p. 77). (Úrin was already an 'Elf-friend', instructed by the Noldoli; cf. the replacement passage on p. 72.) Was his prayer 'answered'? Possibly this is the meaning of the very strange expression 'as the luck of the Valar had it' (p. 79), when Flinding and Beleg found Túrin lying near the point where they entered the Orc-camp.*

Dreams sent by the Valar came to the chieftains of the Rodothlim, though this was changed later and the reference to the Valar removed (p. 83 and note 10); the Woodmen said 'Would that the Valar would lift the spell that lies upon Níniel' (p. 101); and Túrin 'cried out bitterly against the Valar and his fate of woe' (p. 111).

An interesting reference to the Valar (and their power) occurs in Tinwelint's reply (p. 95) to Mavwin's words 'Give me but a woodman's cot and my son'. The king said: 'That I cannot, for I am but a king of the wild Elves, *and no Vala of the western isles.*' In the small part of *Gilfanon's Tale* that was actually written it is told (I. 231) of the Dark Elves who remained in Palisor that they said that 'their brethren had gone

---

* The Gnomish dictionary has the entry: *gwalt* 'good luck – any providential occurrence or thought: "the luck of the Valar", *i·gwalt ne Vanion*' (I.272).

westward to the Shining Isles. There, said they, do the Gods dwell, and they called them the Great Folk of the West, and thought they dwelt on firelit islands in the sea.'

(v)   *Túrin's age*

According to the *Tale of Turambar*, when Túrin left Mavwin he was seven years old, and it was after he had dwelt among the woodland Elves for seven years that all tidings from his home ceased (p. 74); in the *Narn* the corresponding years are eight and nine, and Túrin was seventeen, not fourteen, when 'his grief was renewed' (pp. 68, 76–7). It was exactly twelve years to the day of his departure from Mavwin when he slew Orgof and fled from Artanor (p. 75), when he was nineteen; in the *Narn* (p. 79) it was likewise twelve years since he left Hithlum when he hunted Saeros to his death, but he was twenty.

'The tale tells not the number of days that Turambar sojourned with the Rodothlim but these were very many, and during that time Nienóri grew to the threshold of womanhood' (pp. 91–2). Nienóri was seven years younger than Túrin: she was twelve when he fled from Artanor (*ibid.*). He cannot then have dwelt among the Rodothlim for more than (say) five or six years; and it is said that when he was chosen chieftain of the Woodmen he possessed 'wisdom great beyond his years'.

Bethos, chieftain of the Woodmen before Túrin, 'had fought *though then but a boy* in the Battle of Unnumbered Tears' (p. 101), but he was killed in a foray, since '*despite his years* he still rode abroad'. But it is impossible to relate Bethos' span (from 'a boy' at the Battle of Unnumbered Tears to his death on a foray at an age sufficiently ripe to be remarked on) to Túrin's; for the events after the destruction of the Rodothlim, culminating in Túrin's rescue of Níniel after her first encounter with Glorund, cannot cover any great length of time. What is clear and certain is that in the old story Túrin died when still a very young man. According to the precise dating provided in much later writing, he was 35 years old at his death.

(vi)   *The stature of Elves and Men*

The Elves are conceived to be of slighter build and stature than Men: so Beleg 'was of great stature and girth *as such was among that folk*' (p. 73), and Túrin 'was a Man and of greater stature than they', i.e. Beleg and Flinding (p. 80) – this sentence being an emendation from 'he was a Man of great size' (note 8). See on this matter I. 32, 235.

(vii)   *Winged Dragons*

At the end of *The Silmarillion* (p. 252) Morgoth 'loosed upon his foes the last desperate assault that he had prepared, and out of the pits of Angband there issued the winged dragons, that had not before been seen'. The suggestion is that winged dragons were a refinement of Morgoth's original design (embodied in Glaurung, Father of Dragons who went upon his belly). According to the *Tale of Turambar* (pp. 96–7), on the other hand, among Melko's many dragons some were smaller, cold like snakes, and of these many were flying creatures; while others, the mightier, were hot and heavy, fire-dragons, and these were unwinged. As already noted (p. 125) there is no suggestion in the tale that Glorund was the first of his kind.

III

THE FALL OF GONDOLIN

At the end of Eltas' account of Úrin's visit to Tinwelint and of the strange fates of Úrin and Mavwin, Túrin and Nienóri (p. 116), the manuscript written on loose sheets in fact continues with a brief interlude in which the further course of the tale-telling is discussed in Mar Vanwa Tyaliéva.

And so saying Eltas made an end, and none asked further. But Lindo bid all thank him for his tale, and thereto he said: 'Nay, if you will, there is much yet to tell concerning the gold of Glorund, and how the evil of that worm found its last fulfilment – but behold, that is the story of the Nauglafring or the Necklace of the Dwarves and must wait a while – and other stories of lighter and more happy things I have to tell if you would liefer listen to them.'
Then arose many voices begging Eltas to tell the tale of the Nauglafring on the morrow, but he said: 'Nay! For who here knows the full tale of Tuor and the coming of Eärendel, or who was Beren Ermabwed, and what were his deeds, for such things is it better to know rightly first.' And all said that Beren Ermabwed they knew well, but of the coming of Eärendel little enough had ever been told.
'And great harm is that,' said Lindo, 'for it is the greatest of the stories of the Gnomes, and even in this house is Ilfiniol son of Bronweg, who knows those deeds more truly than any that are now on Earth.'
About that time Ilfiniol the Gong-warden entered indeed, and Lindo said to him: 'Behold, O Littleheart son of Bronweg, it is the desire of all that you tell us the tales of Tuor and of Eärendel as soon as may be.' And Ilfiniol was fain of that, but said he: 'It is a mighty tale, and seven times shall folk fare to the Tale-fire ere it be rightly told; and so twined is it with those stories of the Nauglafring and of the Elf-march[1] that I would fain have aid in that telling of Ailios here and of Meril the Lady of the Isle, for long is it since she sought this house.'
Therefore were messengers sent on the next day to the *korin*[2] of high elms, and they said that Lindo and Vairë would fain see the

face of their lady among them, for they purposed to make a festival and to hold a great telling of Elfin tales, ere Eriol their guest fared awhile to Tavrobel. So was it that for three days that room heard no more tales and the folk of Vanwa Tyaliéva made great preparations, but on the fourth night Meril fared there amid her company of maidens, and full of light and mirth was that place; but after the evening meat a great host sat before Tôn a Gwedrin,³ and the maidens of Meril sang the most beautiful songs that island knew.⁴

And of those one did afterward Heorrenda turn to the language of his folk, and it is thus.⁵

But when those songs had fallen into silence then said Meril, who sate in the chair of Lindo: 'Come now, O Ilfiniol, begin thou the tale of tales, and tell it more fully than thou hast ever done.'

Then said Littleheart son of Bronweg . . . (Tale of Gondolin).
[*sic*]

This then is the *Link* between the *Tale of Turambar* and *The Fall of Gondolin* (an earlier 'preface' to the tale is given below). It seems that my father hesitated as to which tale was to follow *Turambar* (see note 4), but decided that it was time to introduce *The Fall of Gondolin*, which had been in existence for some time.

In this *Link*, Ailios (later Gilfanon) is present ('I would fain have aid . . . of Ailios here') at the end of Eltas' tale of Turambar, but at the beginning of Eltas' tale (p. 70) it is expressly said that he was not present that night. On the proposal that Eriol should 'fare awhile' to Tavrobel (as the guest of Gilfanon) see I.175.

The fact that Eltas speaks of the tale of Beren Ermabwed as if he did not know that it had only recently been told in Mar Vanwa Tyaliéva is no doubt to be explained by that tale not having been told before the Tale-fire (see pp. 4–7).

The teller of the tale of *The Fall of Gondolin*, Littleheart the Gong-warden of Mar Vanwa Tyaliéva, has appeared several times in the *Lost Tales*, and his Elvish name(s) have many different forms (see under *Changes made to names* at the end of the text of the tale). In *The Cottage of Lost Play* he is said (I.15) to be 'ancient beyond count', and to have 'sailed in Wingilot with Eärendel in that last voyage wherein they sought for Kôr'; and in the *Link* to *The Music of the Ainur* (I.46) he 'had a weather-worn face and blue eyes of great merriment, and was very slender and small, nor might one say if he were fifty or ten thousand'. He is a Gnome, the son of Bronweg/Voronwë (Voronwë of *The Silmarillion*) (I.48, 94).

The texts of 'The Fall of Gondolin'

The textual history of *The Fall of Gondolin*, if considered in detail, is extremely complex; but though I will set it out here, as I understand it, there is no need in fact for it to complicate the reading of the tale.

In the first place, there is a very difficult manuscript contained in two school exercise-books, where the title of the tale is *Tuor and the Exiles of Gondolin (which bringeth in the great tale of Eärendel)*. (This is the only title actually found in the early texts, but my father always later referred to it as *The Fall of Gondolin*.) This manuscript is (or rather, was) the original text of the tale, dating from 1916–17 (see I. 203 and *Unfinished Tales* p. 4), and I will call it here for convenience *Tuor A*. My father's treatment of it subsequently was unlike that of *Tinúviel* and *Turambar* (where the original text was erased and a new version written in its place); in this tale he did not set down a complete new text, but allowed a good deal of the old to stand, at least in the earlier part of it: as the revision progressed the rewriting in ink over the top of the pencilled text did become almost continuous, and though the pencil was not erased the ink effectively obliterates it. But even after the second version becomes continuous there are several places where the old narrative was not over-written but merely struck through, and remains legible. Thus, while *Tuor A* is on the same footing as *Tinúviel* and *Turambar* (and others of the *Lost Tales*) in that it is a later revision, a second version, my father's method in *Gondolin* allows it to be seen that here at least the revision was by no means a complete recasting (still less a re-imagining); for if those passages in the later parts of the tale which can still be compared in the two versions shew that he was following the old fairly closely, the same is quite probably true in those places where no comparison can be made.

From Tuor A, as it was *when all changes had been made to it* (i.e. when it was in the form that it has now), my mother made a fair copy (*Tuor B*), which considering the difficulty of the original is extremely exact, with only very occasional errors of transcription. I have said in *Unfinished Tales* (p. 5) that this copy was made 'apparently in 1917', but this now seems to me improbable.* Such conceptions as the Music of the Ainur, which is referred to by later addition in *Tuor A* (p. 163), *may* of course have been in my father's mind a good while before he wrote that tale in Oxford while working on the Dictionary (I. 45), but it seems more likely that the revision of *Tuor A* (and therefore also *Tuor B* copied from it after its revision) belongs to that period also.

Subsequently my father took his pencil to *Tuor B*, emending it fairly heavily, though mostly in the earlier part of the tale, and almost entirely

---

* Humphrey Carpenter in his *Biography* (p. 92) says that the tale 'was written out during Tolkien's convalescence at Great Haywood early in 1917', but he is doubtless referring to the original pencilled text of *Tuor A*.

for stylistic rather than narrative reasons; but these emendations, as will be seen, were not all made at the same time. Some of them are written out on separate slips, and of these several have on their reverse sides parts of an etymological discussion of certain Germanic words for the Butcher-bird or Shrike, material which appears in the Oxford Dictionary in the entry *Wariangle*. Taken with the fact that one of the slips with this material on the reverse clearly contains a direction for the shortening of the tale when delivered orally (see note 21), it is virtually certain that a good deal of the revision of *Tuor B* was made before my father read it to the Essay Club of Exeter College in the spring of 1920 (see *Unfinished Tales* p. 5).

That not all the emendations to *Tuor B* were made at the same time is shown by the existence of a typescript (*Tuor C*), without title, which extends only so far as 'your hill of vigilance against the evil of Melko' (p. 161). This was taken from *Tuor B* when some changes had been made to it, but not those which I deduce to have been made before the occasion when it was read aloud. An odd feature of this text is that blanks were left for many of the names, and only some were filled in afterwards. Towards the end of it there is a good deal of independent variation from *Tuor B*, but it is all of a minor character and none has narrative significance. I conclude that this was a side-branch that petered out.

The textual history can then be represented thus:

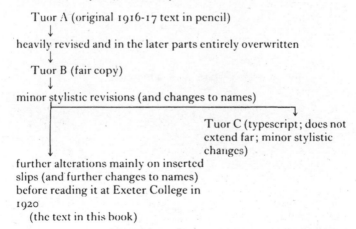

Tuor A (original 1916-17 text in pencil)
↓
heavily revised and in the later parts entirely overwritten
↓
Tuor B (fair copy)
↓
minor stylistic revisions (and changes to names)
↓   → Tuor C (typescript; does not
                                        extend far; minor stylistic
                                        changes)
↓
further alterations mainly on inserted
slips (and further changes to names)
before reading it at Exeter College in
1920
    (the text in this book)

Since the narrative itself underwent very little change of note in the course of this history (granted that substantial parts of the original text *Tuor A* are almost entirely illegible), the text that follows here is that of *Tuor B* in its final form, with some interesting earlier readings given in the Notes. It seems that my father did not check the fair copy *Tuor B* against the original, and did not in every case pick up the errors of transcription it contains; when he did, he emended them anew, according to the sense, and not by reference back to *Tuor A*. In a very few cases I have gone back to *Tuor A* where this is clearly correct (as 'a wall of water rose nigh to the cliff-top', p. 151, where *Tuor B* and the typescript *Tuor C* have 'high to the cliff-top').

Throughout the typescript Tuor is called *Tûr*. In *Tuor B* the name is sometimes emended from *Tuor* to *Tûr* in the earlier part of the tale (it appears as *Tûr* in the latest revisions), but by no means in every case. My father apparently decided to change the name but ultimately decided against it; and I give *Tuor* throughout.

An interesting document accompanies the Tale: this is a substantial though incomplete list of names (with explanations) that occur in it, now in places difficult or impossible to read. The names are given in alphabetical order but go only as far as L. Linguistic information from this list is incorporated in the Appendix on Names, but the head-note to the list may be cited here:

> Here is set forth by Eriol at the teaching of Bronweg's son Elfrith [*emended from* Elfriniel] or Littleheart (and he was so named for the youth and wonder of his heart) those names and words that are used in these tales from either the tongue of the Elves of Kôr as at that time spoken in the Lonely Isle, or from that related one of the Noldoli their kin whom they wrested from Melko.
>
> Here first are they which appear in *The Tale of Tuor and the Exiles of Gondolin*, first among these those ones in the Gnome-speech.

In *Tuor A* appear two versions (one struck out) of a short 'preface' to the tale by Littleheart which does not appear in *Tuor B*. The second version reads:

> Then said Littleheart son of Bronweg: 'Now the story that I tell is of the Noldoli, who were my father's folk, and belike the names will ring strange in your ears and familiar folk be called by names not before heard, for the Noldoli speak a curious tongue sweet still to my ears though not maybe to all the Eldar. Wise folk see it as close kin to Eldarissa, but it soundeth not so, and I know nought of such lore. Wherefore will I utter to you the right Eldar names where there be such, but in many cases there be none.
>
> Know then,' said he, 'that

The earlier version (headed 'Link between *Tuor* and tale before') begins in the same way but then diverges:

> . . . and it is sweet to my ears still, though lest it be not so to all else of Eldar and Men here gathered I will use no more of it than I must, and that is in the names of those folk and things whereof the tale tells but

for which, seeing they passed away ere ever the rest of the Eldar came from Kôr, the Elves have no true names. Know then,' said he, 'that Tuor

This 'preface' thus connects to the opening of the tale. There here appears, in the second version, the name *Eldarissa* for the language of the *Eldar* or *Elves*, as opposed to *Noldorissa* (a term found in the Name-list); on the distinction involved see I.50–1. With Littleheart's words here compare what Rúmil said to Eriol about him (I.48):

'"Tongues and speeches," they will say, "one is enough for me" – and thus said Littleheart the Gong-warden once upon a time: "Gnome-speech," said he, "is enough for me – did not that one Eärendel and Tuor and Bronweg my father (that mincingly ye miscall Voronwë) speak it and no other?" Yet he had to learn the Elfin in the end, or be doomed either to silence or to leave Mar Vanwa Tyaliéva . . .'

After these lengthy preliminaries I give the text of the Tale.

★

Tuor and the Exiles of Gondolin
(which bringeth in the great tale of Eärendel)

Then said Littleheart son of Bronweg: 'Know then that Tuor was a man who dwelt in very ancient days in that land of the North called Dor Lómin or the Land of Shadows, and of the Eldar the Noldoli know it best.

Now the folk whence Tuor came wandered the forests and fells and knew not and sang not of the sea; but Tuor dwelt not with them, and lived alone about that lake called Mithrim, now hunting in its woods, now making music beside its shores on his rugged harp of wood and the sinews of bears. Now many hearing of the power of his rough songs came from near and far to hearken to his harping, but Tuor left his singing and departed to lonely places. Here he learnt many strange things and got knowledge of the wandering Noldoli, who taught him much of their speech and lore; but he was not fated to dwell for ever in those woods.

Thereafter 'tis said that magic and destiny led him on a day to a cavernous opening down which a hidden river flowed from Mithrim. And Tuor entered that cavern seeking to learn its secret, but the waters of Mithrim drove him forward into the heart of the rock and he might not win back into the light. And this, 'tis said, was the will of Ulmo Lord of Waters at whose prompting the Noldoli had made that hidden way.

Then came the Noldoli to Tuor and guided him along dark passages amid the mountains until he came out in the light once more, and saw that the river flowed swiftly in a ravine of great depth with sides unscalable. Now Tuor desired no more to return but went ever forward, and the river led him always toward the west.[6]

The sun rose behind his back and set before his face, and where the water foamed among many boulders or fell over falls there were at times rainbows woven across the ravine, but at evening its smooth sides would glow in the setting sun, and for these reasons Tuor called it Golden Cleft or the Gully of the Rainbow Roof, which is in the speech of the Gnomes Glorfalc or Cris Ilbranteloth.

Now Tuor journeyed here for three days,[7] drinking the waters of the secret river and feeding on its fish; and these were of gold and blue and silver and of many wondrous shapes. At length the ravine widened, and ever as it opened its sides became lower and more rough, and the bed of the river more impeded with boulders against which the waters foamed and spouted. Long times would Tuor sit and gaze at the splashing water and listen to its voice, and then he would rise and leap onward from stone to stone singing as he went; or as the stars came out in the narrow strip of heaven above the gully he would raise echoes to answer the fierce twanging of his harp.

One day after a great journey of weary going Tuor at deep evening heard a cry, and he might not decide of what creature it came. Now he said: "It is a fay-creature", now, "Nay, 'tis but some small beast that waileth among the rocks"; or again it seemed to him that an unknown bird piped with a voice new to his ears and strangely sad – and because he had not heard the voice of any bird in all his wandering down Golden Cleft he was glad of the sound although it was mournful. On the next day at an hour of the morning he heard the same cry above his head, and looking up beheld three great white birds beating back up the gully on strong wing, and uttering cries like to the ones he had heard amid the dusk. Now these were the gulls, the birds of Ossë.[8]

In this part of that riverway there were islets of rock amid the currents, and fallen rocks fringed with white sand at the gully-side, so that it was ill-going, and seeking a while Tuor found a spot where he might with labour scale the cliffs at last. Then came a fresh wind against his face, and he said: "This is very good and like the drinking of wine," but he knew not that he was near the confines of the Great Sea.

As he went along above the waters that ravine again drew together and the walls towered up, so that he fared on a high cliff-top, and there came a narrow neck, and this was full of noise. Then Tuor looking downward saw the greatest of marvels, for it seemed that a flood of angry water would come up the narrows and flow back against the river to its source, but that water which had come down from distant Mithrim would still press on, and a wall of water rose nigh to the cliff-top, and it was crowned with foam and twisted by the winds. Then the waters of Mithrim were overthrown and the incoming flood swept roaring up the channel and whelmed the rocky islets and churned the white sand — so that Tuor fled and was afraid, who did not know the ways of the sea; but the Ainur put it into his heart to climb from the gully when he did, or had he been whelmed in the incoming tide, and that was a fierce one by reason of a wind from the west. Then Tuor found himself in a rugged country bare of trees, and swept by a wind coming from the set of the sun, and all the shrubs and bushes leaned to the dawn because of that prevalence of that wind. And here for a while he wandered till he came to the black cliffs by the sea and saw the ocean and its waves for the first time, and at that hour the sun sank beyond the rim of Earth far out to sea, and he stood on the cliff-top with outspread arms, and his heart was filled with a longing very great indeed. Now some say that he was the first of Men to reach the Sea and look upon it and know the desire it brings; but I know not if they say well.

In those regions he set up his abode, dwelling in a cove sheltered by great sable rocks, whose floor was of white sand, save when the high flood partly overspread it with blue water; nor did foam or froth come there save at times of the direst tempest. There long he sojourned alone and roamed about the shore or fared over the rocks at the ebb, marvelling at the pools and the great weeds, the dripping caverns and the strange sea-fowl that he saw and came to know; but the rise and fall of the water and the voice of the waves was ever to him the greatest wonder and ever did it seem a new and unimaginable thing.

Now on the quiet waters of Mithrim over which the voice of the duck or moorhen would carry far he had fared much in a small boat with a prow fashioned like to the neck of a swan, and this he had lost on the day of his finding the hidden river. On the sea he adventured not as yet, though his heart was ever egging him with a strange longing thereto, and on quiet evenings when the sun went down beyond the edge of the sea it grew to a fierce desire.

Timber he had that came down the hidden river; a goodly wood it was, for the Noldoli hewed it in the forests of Dor Lómin and floated it to him of a purpose. But he built not as yet aught save a dwelling in a sheltered place of his cove, which tales among the Eldar since name Falasquil. This by slow labour he adorned with fair carvings of the beasts and trees and flowers and birds that he knew about the waters of Mithrim, and ever among them was the Swan the chief, for Tuor loved this emblem and it became the sign of himself, his kindred and folk thereafter. There he passed a very great while until the loneliness of the empty sea got into his heart, and even Tuor the solitary longed for the voice of Men. Herewith the Ainur⁹ had something to do: for Ulmo loved Tuor.

One morning while casting his eye along the shore – and it was then the latest days of summer – Tuor saw three swans flying high and strong from the northward. Now these birds he had not before seen in these regions, and he took them for a sign, and said: "Long has my heart been set on a journey far from here; lo! now at length I will follow these swans." Behold, the swans dropped into the water of his cove and there swimming thrice about rose again and winged slowly south along the coast, and Tuor bearing his harp and spear followed them.

'Twas a great day's journey Tuor put behind him that day; and he came ere evening to a region where trees again appeared, and the manner of the land through which he now fared differed greatly from those shores about Falasquil. There had Tuor known mighty cliffs beset with caverns and great spoutholes, and deep-walled coves, but from the cliff-tops a rugged land and flat ran bleakly back to where a blue rim far to the east spake of distant hills. Now however did he see a long and sloping shore and stretches of sand, while the distant hills marched ever nearer to the margin of the sea, and their dark slopes were clad with pine or fir and about their feet sprang birches and ancient oaks. From the feet of the hills fresh torrents rushed down narrow chasms and so found the shores and the salt waves. Now some of these clefts Tuor might not overleap, and often was it ill-going in these places, but still he laboured on, for the swans fared ever before him, now circling suddenly, now speeding forward, but never coming to earth, and the rush of their strong-beating wings encouraged him.

'Tis told that in this manner Tuor fared onward for a great

number of days, and that winter marched from the north some-what speedier than he for all his tirelessness. Nevertheless came he without scathe of beast or weather at a time of first spring to a river mouth. Now here was the land less northerly and more kindly than about the issuing of Golden Cleft, and moreover by a trend of the coast was the sea now rather to the south of him than to the west, as he could mark by the sun and stars; but he had kept his right hand always to the sea.

This river flowed down a goodly channel and on its banks were rich lands: grasses and moist meadow to the one side and tree-grown slopes of the other; its waters met the sea sluggishly and fought not as the waters of Mithrim in the north. Long tongues of land lay islanded in its course covered with reeds and bushy thicket, until further to seaward sandy spits ran out; and these were places beloved by such a multitude of birds as Tuor had nowhere yet encountered. Their piping and wailing and whistling filled the air; and here amid their white wings Tuor lost sight of the three swans, nor saw he them again.

Then did Tuor grow for a season weary of the sea, for the buffeting of his travel had been sore. Nor was this without Ulmo's devising, and that night the Noldoli came to him and he arose from sleep. Guided by their blue lanterns he found a way beside the river border, and strode so mightily inland that when dawn filled the sky to his right hand lo! the sea and its voice were far behind him, and the wind came from before him so that its odour was not even in the air. Thus came he soon to that region that has been called Arlisgion "the place of reeds", and this is in those lands that are to the south of Dor Lómin and separated therefrom by the Iron Mountains whose spurs run even to the sea. From those mountains came this river, and of a great clearness and marvellous chill were its waters even at this place. Now this is a river most famous in the histories of Eldar and Noldoli and in all tongues is it named Sirion. Here Tuor rested awhile until driven by desire he arose once more to journey further and further by many days' marches along the river borders. Full spring had not yet brought summer when he came to a region yet more lovely. Here the song of small birds shrilled about him with a music of loveliness, for there are no birds that sing like the songbirds of the Land of Willows; and to this region of wonder he had now come. Here the river wound in wide curves with low banks through a great plain of the sweetest grass and very long and green; willows of untold age were about its borders, and its wide bosom was strewn with waterlily leaves, whose flowers were not yet in the earliness of the year, but beneath the willows the green swords of the flaglilies were drawn, and sedges stood, and reeds in embattled array. Now there dwelt in these dark places a spirit of whispers, and it whispered to Tuor at dusk and he was loth to depart; and at morn for the glory of the unnumbered buttercups he was yet more loth, and he tarried.

Here saw he the first butterflies and was glad of the sight; and it is said that all butterflies and their kindred were born in the valley of the Land of Willows. Then came the summer and the time of moths and the warm evenings, and Tuor wondered at the multitude of flies, at their buzzing and the droning of the beetles and the hum of bees; and to all these things he gave names of his own, and wove the names into new songs on his old harp; and these songs were softer than his singing of old.

Then Ulmo grew in dread lest Tuor dwell for ever here and the great things of his design come not to fulfilment. Therefore he feared longer to trust Tuor's guidance to the Noldoli alone, who did service to him in secret, and out of fear of Melko wavered much. Nor were they strong against the magic of that place of willows, for very great was its enchantment. Did not even after the days of Tuor Noldorin and his Eldar come there seeking for Dor Lómin and the hidden river and the caverns of the Gnomes' imprisonment; yet thus nigh to their quest's end were like to abandon it? Indeed sleeping and dancing here, and making fair music of river sounds and the murmur of grass, and weaving rich fabrics of gossamer and the feathers of winged insects, they were whelmed by the goblins sped by Melko from the Hills of Iron and Noldorin made bare escape thence. But these things were not as yet.

Behold now Ulmo leapt upon his car before the doorway of his palace below the still waters of the Outer Sea; and his car was drawn by narwhal and sealion and was in fashion like a whale; and amidst the sounding of great conches he sped from Ulmonan. So great was the speed of his going that in days, and not in years without count as might be thought, he reached the mouth of the river. Up this his car might not fare without hurt to its water and its banks; therefore Ulmo, loving all rivers and this one more than most, went thence on foot, robed to the middle in mail like the scales of blue and silver fishes; but his hair was a bluish silver and his beard to his feet was of the same hue, and he bore neither helm nor crown. Beneath his mail fell the skirts of his kirtle of shimmering greens, and of what substance these were woven is not known, but whoso looked into the depths of their subtle colours seemed to behold the faint movements of deep waters shot with the stealthy lights of phosphorescent fish that live in the abyss. Girt was he with a rope of mighty pearls, and he was shod with mighty shoes of stone.

Thither he bore too his great instrument of music; and this was of strange design, for it was made of many long twisted shells pierced with holes. Blowing therein and playing with his long fingers he made deep melodies of a magic greater than any other among musicians hath ever compassed on harp or lute, on lyre or pipe, or instruments of the bow. Then coming along the river he sate among the reeds at twilight and played upon his thing of shells; and it was nigh to those places where Tuor tarried. And Tuor hearkened and was stricken dumb. There he stood knee-deep in the grass and heard no more the hum of insects, nor the murmur of the river borders, and the odour of flowers entered not into his nostrils; but he heard the sound of waves and the wail of sea-birds, and his soul leapt for rocky places and the ledges that reek of fish, for the splash of the diving cormorant and those places where the sea bores into the black cliffs and yells aloud.

Then Ulmo arose and spake to him and for dread he came near to death, for the depth of the voice of Ulmo is of the uttermost depth: even as deep as his eyes which are the deepest of all things. And Ulmo said: "O Tuor of the lonely heart, I will not that thou dwell for ever in fair places of birds and flowers; nor would I lead thee through this pleasant land,[10] but that so it must be. But fare now on thy destined journey and tarry not, for far from hence is thy weird set. Now must thou seek through the lands for the city of the folk called Gondothlim or the dwellers in stone, and the Noldoli shall escort thee thither in secret for fear of the spies of Melko. Words I will set to your mouth there, and there you shall abide awhile. Yet maybe thy life shall turn again to the mighty waters; and of a surety a child shall come of thee than whom no man shall know more of the uttermost deeps, be it of the sea or of the firmament of heaven." Then spake Ulmo also to Tuor some of his design and desire, but thereof Tuor understood little at that time and feared greatly.

Then Ulmo was wrapped in a mist as it were of sea air in those inland places, and Tuor, with that music in his ears, would fain return to the regions of the Great Sea; yet remembering his bidding turned and went inland along the river, and so fared till day. Yet he that has heard the conches of Ulmo hears them call him till death, and so did Tuor find.

When day came he was weary and slept till it was nigh dusk again, and the Noldoli came to him and guided him. So fared he many days by dusk and dark and slept by day, and because of this it came afterwards that he remembered not over well the paths that he traversed in those times. Now Tuor and his guides held on untiring, and the land became one of rolling hills and the river wound about their feet, and there were many dales of exceeding pleasantness; but here the Noldoli became ill at ease. "These," said they, "are the confines of those regions which Melko infesteth with his Goblins, the people of hate. Far to the north – yet alas not far enough, would they were ten thousand leagues – lie the Mountains of Iron where sits the power and terror of Melko, whose thralls we are. Indeed in this guiding of thee we do in secret from him, and did he know all our purposes the torment of the Balrogs would be ours."

Falling then into such fear the Noldoli soon after left him and he fared alone amid the hills, and their going proved ill afterwards, for "Melko has many eyes", 'tis said, and while Tuor fared with the Gnomes they took him twilight ways and by many secret tunnels through the hills. But now he became lost, and climbed often to the tops of knolls and hills scanning the lands about. Yet he might not see signs of any dwelling of folk, and indeed the city of the Gondothlim was not found with ease, seeing that Melko and his spies had not even yet discovered it. 'Tis said nonetheless that at this time those spies got wind thus that the strange foot of Man had been set in those lands, and that for that Melko doubled his craft and watchfulness.

Now when the Gnomes out of fear deserted Tuor, one Voronwë or Bronweg followed afar off despite his fear, when chiding availed not to enhearten the others. Now Tuor had fallen into a great weariness and was sitting beside the rushing stream, and the sea-longing was about his heart, and he was minded once more to follow this river back to the wide waters and the roaring waves. But this Voronwë the faithful came up with him again, and standing by his ear said: "O Tuor, think not but that thou shalt again one day see thy desire; arise now, and behold, I will not leave thee. I am not of the road-learned of the Noldoli, being a craftsman and maker of things made by hand of wood and of metal, and I joined not the band of escort till late. Yet of old have I heard whispers and sayings said in secret amid the weariness of thraldom, concerning a city where Noldoli might be free could they find the hidden way thereto; and we twain may without a doubt [11] find the road to the City of Stone, where is that freedom of the Gondothlim."

Know then that the Gondothlim were that kin of the Noldoli who alone escaped Melko's power when at the Battle of Unnumbered Tears he slew and enslaved their folk [12] and wove spells about them and caused them to dwell in the Hells of Iron, faring thence at his will and bidding only.

Long time did Tuor and Bronweg [13] seek for the city of that folk, until after many days they came upon a deep dale amid the hills. Here went the river over a very stony bed with much rush and noise, and it was curtained with a heavy growth of alders; but the walls of the dale were sheer, for they were nigh to some mountains which Voronwë knew not. There in the green wall that Gnome found an opening like a great door with sloping sides, and this was cloaked with thick bushes and long-tangled undergrowth; yet Voronwë's piercing sight might not be deceived. Nonetheless 'tis said that such a magic had its builders set about it (by aid of Ulmo whose power ran in that river even if the dread of Melko fared upon its banks) that none save of the blood of the Noldoli might light on it thus by chance; nor would Tuor have found it ever but for the steadfastness of that Gnome Voronwë. [14] Now the Gondothlim made their abode thus secret out of dread of Melko; yet even so no few of the braver Noldoli would slip down the river Sirion from those mountains, and if many perished so by Melko's evil, many finding this magic passage came at last to the City of Stone and swelled its people.

Greatly did Tuor and Voronwë rejoice to find this gate, yet entering they found there a way dark, rough-going, and circuitous; and long time they travelled faltering within its tunnels. It was full of fearsome echoes, and there a countless stepping of feet would come behind them, so that Voronwë became adread, and said: "It is Melko's goblins, the Orcs of the hills." Then would they run, falling over stones in the blackness, till they perceived it was but the deceit of the place. Thus did they come, after it seemed a measureless time of fearful groping, to a place where a far light glimmered, and making for this gleam they came to a gate like that by which they had entered, but in no way overgrown. Then they passed into the sunlight and could for a while see nought, but instantly a great gong sounded and there was a clash of armour, and behold, they were surrounded by warriors in steel.

Then they looked up and could see, and lo! they were at the foot of steep hills, and these hills made a great circle wherein lay a wide plain, and set therein, not rightly at the midmost but rather nearer to that place where they stood, was a great hill with a level top, and upon that summit rose a city in the new light of the morning.

Then Voronwë spake to the Guard of the Gondothlim, and his speech they comprehended, for it was the sweet tongue of the Gnomes.[15] Then spake Tuor also and questioned where they might be, and who might be the folk in arms who stood about, for he was somewhat in amaze and wondered much at the goodly fashion of their weapons. Then 'twas said to him by one of that company: "We are the guardians of the issue of the Way of Escape. Rejoice that ye have found it, for behold before you the City of Seven Names where all who war with Melko may find hope."

Then said Tuor: "What be those names?" And the chief of the Guard made answer: "'Tis said and 'tis sung: 'Gondobar am I called and Gondothlimbar, City of Stone and City of the Dwellers in Stone; Gondolin the Stone of Song and Gwarestrin am I named, the Tower of Guard, Gar Thurion or the Secret Place, for I am hidden from the eyes of Melko; but they who love me most greatly call me Loth, for like a flower am I, even Lothengriol the flower that blooms on the plain.' Yet," said he, "in our daily speech we speak and we name it mostly Gondolin." Then said Voronwë: "Bring us thither, for we fain would enter," and Tuor said that his heart desired much to tread the ways of that fair city.

Then said the chief of the Guard that they themselves must abide here, for there were yet many days of their moon of watch to pass, but that Voronwë and Tuor might pass on to Gondolin; and moreover that they would need thereto no guide, for "Lo, it stands fair to see and very clear, and its towers prick the heavens above the Hill of Watch in the midmost plain." Then Tuor and his companion fared over the plain that was of a marvellous level, broken but here and there by boulders round and smooth which lay amid a sward, or by pools in rocky beds. Many fair pathways lay across that plain, and they came after a day's light march to the foot of the Hill of Watch (which is in the tongue of the Noldoli Amon Gwareth). Then did they begin to ascend the winding stairways which climbed up to the city gate; nor might any one reach that city save on foot and espied from the walls. As the westward gate was golden in the last sunlight did they come to the long stair's head, and many eyes gazed[16] upon them from the battlements and towers.

But Tuor looked upon the walls of stone, and the uplifted towers, upon the glistering pinnacles of the town, and he looked upon the stairs of stone and marble, bordered by slender balustrades and cooled by the leap of threadlike waterfalls seeking the plain from the fountains of Amon Gwareth, and he fared as one in some dream of the Gods, for he deemed not such things were seen by men in the visions of their sleep, so great was his amaze at the glory of Gondolin.

Even so came they to the gates, Tuor in wonder and Voronwë in great joy that daring much he had both brought Tuor hither in the will of Ulmo and had himself thrown off the yoke of Melko for ever. Though he hated him no wise less, no longer did he dread that Evil One[17] with a binding terror (and of a sooth that spell which Melko held over the Noldoli was one of bottomless dread, so that he seemed ever nigh them even were they far from the Hells of Iron, and their hearts quaked and they fled not even when they could; and to this Melko trusted often).

Now is there a sally from the gates of Gondolin and a throng comes about these twain in wonder, rejoicing that yet another of the Noldoli has fled hither from Melko, and marvelling at the stature and the gaunt limbs of Tuor, his heavy spear barbed with fish bone and his great harp. Rugged was his aspect, and his locks were unkempt, and he was clad in the skins of bears. 'Tis written that in those days the fathers of the fathers of Men were of less stature than Men now are, and the children of Elfinesse of greater growth, yet was Tuor taller than any that stood there. Indeed the Gondothlim were not bent of back as some of their unhappy kin became, labouring without rest at delving and hammering for Melko, but small were they and slender and very lithe.[18] They were swift of foot and surpassing fair; sweet and sad were their mouths, and their eyes had ever a joy within quivering to tears; for in those times the Gnomes were exiles at heart, haunted with a desire for their ancient home that faded not. But fate and unconquerable eagerness after knowledge had driven them into far places, and now were they hemmed by Melko and must make their abiding as fair as they might by labour and by love.

How it came ever that among Men the Noldoli have been confused with the Orcs who are Melko's goblins, I know not, unless it be that certain of the Noldoli were twisted to the evil of Melko and mingled among these Orcs, for all that race were bred by Melko of the subterranean heats and slime. Their hearts were of granite and their bodies deformed; foul their faces which smiled not, but their laugh that of the clash of metal, and to nothing were they more fain than to aid in the basest of the purposes of Melko. The greatest hatred was between them and the Noldoli, who named them Glamhoth, or folk of dreadful hate.

Behold, the armed' guardians of the gate pressed back the thronging folk that gathered about the wanderers, and one among them spake saying: "This is a city of watch and ward, Gondolin on Amon Gwareth, where all may be free who are of true heart, but none may be free to enter unknown. Tell me then your names." But Voronwë named himself Bronweg of the Gnomes, come hither[19] by the will of Ulmo as guide to this son of Men; and Tuor said: "I am Tuor son of Peleg son of Indor of the house of the Swan of the sons of the Men of the North who live far hence, and I fare hither by the will of Ulmo of the Outer Oceans."

Then all who listened grew silent, and his deep and rolling voice held them in amaze, for their own voices were fair as the plash of fountains. Then a saying arose among them: "Lead him before the king."

Then did the throng return within the gates and the wanderers with them, and Tuor saw they were of iron and of great height and strength. Now the streets of Gondolin were paved with stone and wide, kerbed with marble, and fair houses and courts amid gardens of bright flowers were set about the ways, and many towers of great slenderness and beauty builded of white marble and carved most marvellously rose to the heaven. Squares there were lit with fountains and the home of birds that sang amid the branches of their aged trees, but of all these the greatest was that place where stood the king's palace, and the tower thereof was the loftiest in the city, and the fountains that played before the doors shot twenty fathoms and seven in the air and fell in a singing rain of crystal: therein did the sun glitter splendidly by day, and the moon most magically shimmered by night. The birds that dwelt there were of the whiteness of snow and their voices sweeter than a lullaby of music.

On either side of the doors of the palace were two trees, one that bore blossom of gold and the other of silver, nor did they ever fade, for they were shoots of old from the glorious Trees of Valinor that lit those places before Melko and Gloomweaver withered them: and those trees the Gondothlim named Glingol and Bansil.

Then Turgon king of Gondolin robed in white with a belt of gold, and a coronet of garnets was upon his head, stood before his doors and spake from the head of the white stairs that led thereto. "Welcome, O Man of the Land of Shadows. Lo! thy coming was set in our books of wisdom, and it has been written that there would come to pass many great things in the homes of the Gondothlim whenso thou faredst hither."

Then spake Tuor, and Ulmo set power in his heart and majesty in his voice. "Behold, O father of the City of Stone, I am bidden by him who maketh deep music in the Abyss, and who knoweth the mind of Elves and Men, to say unto thee that the days of Release draw nigh. There have come to the ears of Ulmo whispers of your dwelling and your hill of vigilance against the evil of Melko, and he is glad: but his heart is wroth and the hearts of the Valar are angered who sit in the mountains of Valinor and look upon the world from the peak of Taniquetil, seeing the sorrow of the thraldom of the Noldoli and the wanderings of Men; for Melko ringeth them in the Land of Shadows beyond hills of iron. Therefore have I been brought by a secret way to bid you number your hosts and prepare for battle, for the time is ripe."

Then spake Turgon: "That will I not do, though it be the words of Ulmo and all the Valar. I will not adventure this my people against the terror of the Orcs, nor emperil my city against the fire of Melko."

Then spake Tuor: "Nay, if thou dost not now dare greatly then will the Orcs dwell for ever and possess in the end most of the mountains of the Earth, and cease not to trouble both Elves and Men, even though by other means the Valar contrive hereafter to release the Noldoli; but if thou trust now to the Valar, though terrible the encounter, then shall the Orcs fall, and Melko's power be minished to a little thing."

But Turgon said that he was king of Gondolin and no will should force him against his counsel to emperil the dear labour of long ages gone; but Tuor said, for thus was he bidden by Ulmo who had feared the reluctance of Turgon: "Then am I bidden to say that men of the Gondothlim repair swiftly and secretly down the river Sirion to the sea, and there build them boats and go seek back to Valinor: lo! the paths thereto are forgotten and the highways faded from the world, and the seas and mountains are about it, yet still dwell there the Elves on the hill of Kôr and the Gods sit in Valinor, though their mirth is minished for sorrow and fear of Melko, and they hide their land and weave about it inaccessible magic that no evil come to its shores. Yet still might thy messengers win there and turn their hearts that they rise in wrath and smite Melko, and destroy the Hells of Iron that he has wrought beneath the Mountains of Darkness."

Then said Turgon: "Every year at the lifting of winter have messengers repaired swiftly and by stealth down the river that is called Sirion to the coasts of the Great Sea, and there builded them boats whereto have swans and gulls been harnessed or the strong wings of the wind, and these have sought back beyond the moon and sun to Valinor; but the paths thereto are forgotten and the highways faded from the world, and the seas and mountains are about it, and they that sit within in mirth reck little of the dread of Melko or the sorrow of the world, but hide their land and weave about it inaccessible magic, that no tidings of evil come ever to their ears. Nay, enough of my people have for years untold gone out to the wide waters never to return, but have perished in the deep places or wander now lost in the shadows that have no paths; and at the coming of next year no more shall fare to the sea, but rather will we trust to ourselves and our city for the warding off of Melko; and thereto have the Valar been of scant help aforetime."

Then Tuor's heart was heavy, and Voronwë wept; and Tuor sat by the great fountain of the king and its splashing recalled the music of the waves, and his soul was troubled by the conches of Ulmo and he would return down the waters of Sirion to the sea. But Turgon, who knew that Tuor, mortal as he was, had the favour of the Valar, marking his stout glance and the power of his voice sent to him and bade him dwell in Gondolin and be in his favour, and abide even within the royal halls if he would.

Then Tuor, for he was weary, and that place was fair, said yea; and hence cometh the abiding of Tuor in Gondolin. Of all Tuor's deeds among the Gondothlim the tales tell not, but 'tis said that many a time would he have stolen thence, growing weary of the concourses of folk, and thinking of empty forest and fell or hearing afar the sea-music of Ulmo, had not his heart been filled with love for a woman of the Gondothlim, and she was a daughter of the king.

Now Tuor learnt many things in those realms taught by Voronwë whom he loved, and who loved him exceeding greatly in return; or else was he instructed by the skilled men of the city and the wise men of the king. Wherefore he became a man far mightier than aforetime and wisdom was in his counsel; and many things became clear to him that were unclear before, and many things known that are still unknown to mortal Men. There he heard concerning that city of Gondolin and how unstaying labour through ages of years had not sufficed to its building and adornment whereat folk[20] travailed yet; of the delving of that hidden tunnel he heard, which the folk named the Way of Escape, and how there had been divided counsels in that matter, yet pity for the enthralled Noldoli had prevailed in the end to its making; of the guard without ceasing he was told, that was held there in arms and likewise at certain low places in the encircling mountains, and how watchers dwelt ever vigilant on the highest peaks of that range beside builded beacons ready for the fire; for never did that folk cease to look for an onslaught of the Orcs did their stronghold become known.

Now however was the guard of the hills maintained rather by custom than necessity, for the Gondothlim had long ago with unimagined toil levelled and cleared and delved all that plain about Amon Gwareth, so that scarce Gnome or bird or beast or snake could approach but was espied from many leagues off, for among the Gondothlim were many whose eyes were keener than the very hawks of Manwë Súlimo Lord of Gods and Elves who dwells upon Taniquetil; and for this reason did they call that vale Tumladin or the valley of smoothness. Now this great work was finished to their mind, and folk were the busier about the quarrying of metals and the forging of all manner of swords and axes, spears and bills, and the fashioning of coats of mail, byrnies and hauberks, greaves and vambraces, helms and shields. Now 'twas said to Tuor that already the whole folk of Gondolin shooting with bows without stay day or night might not expend their hoarded arrows in many years, and that yearly their fear of the Orcs grew the less for this.

There learnt Tuor of building with stone, of masonry and the hewing of rock and marble; crafts of weaving and spinning, broidure and painting, did he fathom, and cunning in metals. Musics most delicate he there heard; and in these were they who dwelt in the southern city the most deeply skilled, for there played a profusion of murmuring founts and springs. Many of these subtleties Tuor mastered and learned to entwine with his songs to the wonder and heart's joy of all who heard. Strange stories of the Sun and Moon and Stars, of the manner of the Earth and its elements, and of the depths of heaven, were told to him; and the secret characters of the Elves he learnt, and their speeches and old tongues, and heard tell of Ilúvatar, the Lord for Always, who dwelleth beyond the world, of the great music of the Ainur about Ilúvatar's feet in the uttermost deeps of time, whence came the making of the world and the manner of it, and all therein and their governance.[21]

Now for his skill and his great mastery over all lore and craft whatsoever, and his great courage of heart and body, did Tuor become a comfort and stay to the king who had no son; and he was beloved by the folk of Gondolin. Upon a time the king caused his most cunning artificers to fashion a suit of armour for Tuor as a great gift, and it was made of Gnome-steel overlaid with silver; but his helm was adorned with a device of metals and jewels like to two swan-wings, one on either side, and a swan's wing was wrought on his shield; but he carried an axe rather than a sword, and this in the speech of the Gondothlim he named Dramborleg, for its buffet stunned and its edge clove all armour.

A house was built for him upon the southern walls, for he loved the free airs and liked not the close neighbourhood of other dwellings. There it was his delight often to stand on the battlements at dawn, and folk rejoiced to see the new light catch the wings of his helm — and many murmured and would fain have backed him into battle with the Orcs, seeing that the speeches of those two, Tuor and Turgon, before the palace were known to many; but this matter went not further for reverence of Turgon, and because at this time in Tuor's heart the thought of the words of Ulmo seemed to have grown dim and far off.

Now came days when Tuor had dwelt among the Gondothlim many years. Long had he known and cherished a love for the king's daughter, and now was his heart full of that love. Great love too had Idril for Tuor, and the strands of her fate were woven with his even from that day when first she gazed upon him from a high window as he stood a way-worn suppliant before the palace of the king. Little cause had Turgon to withstand their love, for he saw in Tuor a kinsman of comfort and great hope. Thus was first wed a child of Men with a daughter of Elfinesse, nor was Tuor the last. Less bliss have many had than they, and their sorrow in the end was great. Yet great was the mirth of those days when Idril and Tuor were wed before the folk in Gar Ainion, the Place of the Gods, nigh to the king's halls. A day of merriment was that wedding to the city of Gondolin, and of [22] the greatest happiness to Tuor and Idril. Thereafter dwelt they in joy in that house upon the walls that looked out south over Tumladin, and this was good to the hearts of all in the city save Meglin alone. Now that Gnome was come of an ancient house, though now were its numbers less than others, but he himself was nephew to the king by his mother the king's sister Isfin; and that tale of Isfin and Eöl may not here be told.[23]

Now the sign of Meglin was a sable Mole, and he was great among quarrymen and a chief of the delvers after ore; and many of these belonged to his house. Less fair was he than most of this goodly folk, swart and of none too kindly mood, so that he won small love, and whispers there were that he had Orc's blood in his veins, but I know not how this could be true. Now he had bid often with the king for the hand of Idril, yet Turgon finding her very loth had as often said nay, for him seemed Meglin's suit was caused as much by the desire of standing in high power beside the royal throne as by love of that most fair maid. Fair indeed was she and brave thereto; and the people called her Idril of the Silver Feet* in that she went ever barefoot and bareheaded, king's daughter as she was, save only at pomps of the Ainur; and Meglin gnawed his anger seeing Tuor thrust him out.

In these days came to pass the fulfilment of the time of the desire of the Valar and the hope of [the] Eldalië, for in great love Idril bore to Tuor a son and he was called Eärendel. Now thereto there are many interpretations both among Elves and Men, but belike it was a name wrought of some secret tongue among the Gondothlim[24] and that has perished with them from the dwellings of the Earth.

Now this babe was of greatest beauty; his skin of a shining white and his eyes of a blue surpassing that of the sky in southern lands – bluer than the sapphires of the raiment of Manwë;[25] and the envy of Meglin was deep at his birth, but the joy of Turgon and all the people very great indeed.

Behold now many years have gone since Tuor was lost amid the foothills and deserted by those Noldoli; yet many years too have gone since to Melko's ears came first those strange tidings – faint were they and various in form – of a Man wandering amid the dales of the waters of Sirion. Now Melko was not much afraid of the race of Men in those days of his great power, and for this reason did Ulmo work through one of this kindred for the better deceiving of Melko, seeing that no Valar and scarce any of the Eldar or Noldoli might stir unmarked of his vigilance. Yet nonetheless foreboding smote that ill heart at the tidings, and he got together a mighty army of spies: sons of the Orcs were there with

* Faintly pencilled above in *Tuor B: Idril Talceleb*.

eyes of yellow and green like cats that could pierce all glooms and
see through mist or fog or night; snakes that could go everywhither
and search all crannies or the deepest pits or the highest peaks,
listen to every whisper that ran in the grass or echoed in the hills;
wolves there were and ravening dogs and great weasels full of the
thirst of blood whose nostrils could take scent moons old through
running water, or whose eyes find among shingle footsteps that
had passed a lifetime since; owls came and falcons whose keen
glance might descry by day or night the fluttering of small birds in
all the woods of the world, and the movement of every mouse or
vole or rat that crept or dwelt throughout the Earth. All these he
summoned to his Hall of Iron, and they came in multitudes.
Thence he sent them over the Earth to seek this Man who had
escaped from the Land of Shadows, but yet far more curiously and
intently to search out the dwelling of the Noldoli that had escaped
his thraldom; for these his heart burnt to destroy or to enslave.

Now while Tuor dwelt in happiness and in great increase of
knowledge and might in Gondolin, these creatures through the
years untiring nosed among the stones and rocks, hunted
the forests and the heaths, espied the airs and lofty places,
tracked all paths about the dales and plains, and neither let
nor stayed. From this hunt they brought a wealth of tidings to
Melko — indeed among many hidden things that they dragged
to light they discovered that Way of Escape whereby Tuor
and Voronwë entered aforetime. Nor had they done so save by
constraining some of the less stout of the Noldoli with dire threats
of torment to join in that great ransacking; for because of the
magic about that gate no folk of Melko unaided by the Gnomes
could come to it. Yet now they had pried of late far into its
tunnels and captured within many of the Noldoli creeping there to
flee from thraldom. They had scaled too the Encircling Hills*
at certain places and gazed upon the beauty of the city of
Gondolin and the strength of Amon Gwareth from afar; but into
the plain they could not win for the vigilance of its guardians and
the difficulty of those mountains. Indeed the Gondothlim were
mighty archers, and bows they made of a marvel of power.
Therewith might they shoot an arrow into heaven seven times as
far as could the best bowman among Men shoot at a mark upon the
ground; and they would have suffered no falcon to hover long over
their plain or snake to crawl therein; for they liked not creatures of
blood, broodlings of Melko.

* Pencilled above in *Tuor B: Heborodin*.

Now in those days was Eärendel one year old when these ill tidings came to that city of the spies of Melko and how they encompassed the vale of Tumladin around. Then Turgon's heart was saddened, remembering the words of Tuor in past years before the palace doors; and he caused the watch and ward to be thrice strengthened at all points, and engines of war to be devised by his artificers and set upon the hill. Poisonous fires and hot liquids, arrows and great rocks, was he prepared to shoot down on any who would assail those gleaming walls; and then he abode as well content as might be, but Tuor's heart was heavier than the king's, for now the words of Ulmo came ever to his mind, and their purport and gravity he understood more deeply than of old; nor did he find any great comfort in Idril, for her heart boded more darkly even than his own.

Know then that Idril had a great power of piercing with her thought the darkness of the hearts of Elves and Men, and the glooms of the future thereto – further even than is the common power of the kindreds of the Eldalië; therefore she spake thus on a day to Tuor: "Know, my husband, that my heart misgives me for doubt of Meglin, and I fear that he will bring an ill on this fair realm, though by no means may I see how or when – yet I dread lest all that he knows of our doings and preparations become in some manner known to the Foe, so that he devise a new means of whelming us, against which we have thought of no defence. Lo! I dreamed on a night that Meglin builded a furnace, and coming at us unawares flung therein Eärendel our babe, and would after thrust in thee and me; but that for sorrow at the death of our fair child I would not resist."

And Tuor answered: "There is reason for thy fear, for neither is my heart good towards Meglin; yet is he the nephew of the king and thine own cousin, nor is there charge against him, and I see nought to do but to abide and watch."

But Idril said: "This is my rede thereto: gather thou in deep secret those delvers and quarrymen who by careful trial are found to hold least love for Meglin by reason of the pride and arrogance of his dealings among them. From these thou must choose trusty men to keep watch upon Meglin whenso he fares to the outer hills, yet I counsel thee to set the greater part of those in whose secrecy thou canst confide at a hidden delving, and to devise with their aid – howsoever cautious and slow that labour be – a secret way from thy house here beneath the rocks of this hill unto the vale below. Now this way must not lead toward the Way of Escape, for my heart bids me trust it not, but even to that far distant pass, the Cleft of Eagles in the southern mountains; and the further this delving reach thitherward beneath the plain so much the better would I esteem it – yet let all this labour be kept dark save from a few."

Now there are none such delvers of earth or rock as the Noldoli (and this Melko knows), but in those places is the earth of a great hardness; and Tuor said: "The rocks of the hill of Amon Gwareth are as iron, and only with much travail may they be cloven; yet if this be done in secret then must great time and patience be added; but the stone of the floor of the Vale of Tumladin is as forgéd steel, nor may it be hewn without the knowledge of the Gondothlim save in moons and years."

Idril said then: "Sooth this may be, but such is my rede, and there is yet time to spare." Then Tuor said that he might not see all its purport, "but 'better is any plan than a lack of counsel', and I will do even as thou sayest".

Now it so chanced that not long after Meglin went to the hills for the getting of ore, and straying in the mountains alone was taken by some of the Orcs prowling there, and they would do him evil and terrible hurt, knowing him to be a man of the Gondothlim. This was however unknown of Tuor's watchers. But evil came into the heart of Meglin, and he said to his captors: "Know then that I am Meglin son of Eöl who had to wife Isfin sister of Turgon king of the Gondothlim." But they said: "What is that to us?" And Meglin answered: "Much is it to you; for if you slay me, be it speedy or slow, ye will lose great tidings concerning the city of Gondolin that your master would rejoice to hear." Then the Orcs stayed their hands, and said they would give him life if the matters he opened to them seemed to merit that; and Meglin told them of all the fashion of that plain and city, of its walls and their height and thickness, and the valour of its gates; of the host of men at arms who now obeyed Turgon he spake, and the countless hoard of weapons gathered for their equipment, of the engines of war and the venomous fires.

Then the Orcs were wroth, and having heard these matters were yet for slaying him there and then as one who impudently enlarged the power of his miserable folk to the mockery of the great might and puissance of Melko; but Meglin catching at a straw said: "Think ye not that ye would rather pleasure your master if ye bore to his feet so noble a captive, that he might hear my tidings of himself and judge of their verity?"

Now this seemed good to the Orcs, and they returned from the mountains about Gondolin to the Hills of Iron and the dark halls of Melko; thither they haled Meglin with them, and now was he in a sore dread. But when he knelt before the black throne of Melko in terror of the grimness of the shapes about him, of the wolves that sat beneath that chair and of the adders that twined about its legs, Melko bade him speak. Then told he those tidings, and Melko hearkening spake very fair to him, that the insolence of his heart in great measure returned.

Now the end of this was that Melko aided by the cunning of Meglin devised a plan for the overthrow of Gondolin. For this Meglin's reward was to be a great captaincy among the Orcs – yet Melko purposed not in his heart to fulfil such a promise – but Tuor and Eärendel should Melko burn, and Idril be given to Meglin's arms – and such promises was that evil one fain to redeem. Yet as meed of treachery did Melko threaten Meglin with the torment of the Balrogs. Now these were demons with whips of flame and claws of steel by whom he tormented those of the Noldoli who durst withstand him in anything – and the Eldar have called them Malkarauki. But the rede that Meglin gave to Melko was that not all the host of the Orcs nor the Balrogs in their fierceness might by assault or siege hope ever to overthrow the walls and gates of Gondolin even if they availed to win unto the plain without. Therefore he counselled Melko to devise out of his sorceries a succour for his warriors in their endeavour. From the greatness of his wealth of metals and his powers of fire he bid him make beasts like snakes and dragons of irresistible might that should overcreep the Encircling Hills and lap that plain and its fair city in flame and death.

Then Meglin was bidden fare home lest at his absence men suspect somewhat; but Melko wove about him the spell of bottomless dread, and he had thereafter neither joy nor quiet in his heart. Nonetheless he wore a fair mask of good liking and gaiety, so that men said: "Meglin is softened", and he was held in less disfavour; yet Idril feared him the more. Now Meglin said: "I have laboured much and am minded to rest, and to join in the dance and the song and the merrymakings of the folk", and he went no more quarrying stone or ore in the hills: yet in sooth he sought herein to drown his fear and disquiet. A dread possessed him that Melko was ever at hand, and this came of the spell; and he durst never again wander amid the mines lest he again fall in with the Orcs and be bidden once more to the terrors of the halls of darkness.

Now the years fare by, and egged by Idril Tuor keepeth ever at his secret delving; but seeing that the leaguer of spies hath grown thinner Turgon dwelleth more at ease and in less fear. Yet these years are filled by Melko in the utmost ferment of labour, and all the thrall-folk of the Noldoli must dig unceasingly for metals while Melko sitteth and deviseth fires and calleth flames and smokes to come from the lower heats, nor doth he suffer any of the Noldoli to stray ever a foot from their places of bondage. Then on a time Melko assembled all his most cunning smiths and sorcerers, and of iron and flame they wrought a host of monsters such as have only at that time been seen and shall not again be till the Great End. Some were all of iron so cunningly linked that they might flow like slow rivers of metal or coil themselves around and above all obstacles before them, and these were filled in their innermost depths with the grimmest of the Orcs with scimitars and spears; others of bronze and copper were given hearts and spirits of blazing fire, and they blasted all that stood before them with the terror of their snorting or trampled whatso escaped the ardour of their breath; yet others were creatures of pure flame that writhed like ropes of molten metal, and they brought to ruin whatever fabric they came nigh, and iron and stone melted before them and became as water, and upon them rode the Balrogs in hundreds; and these were the most dire of all those monsters which Melko devised against Gondolin.

Now when the seventh summer had gone since the treason of Meglin, and Eärendel was yet of very tender years though a valorous child, Melko withdrew all his spies, for every path and corner of the mountains was now known to him; yet the Gondothlim thought in their unwariness that Melko would no longer seek against them, perceiving their might and the impregnable strength of their dwelling.

But Idril fell into a dark mood and the light of her face was clouded, and many wondered thereat; yet Turgon reduced the watch and ward to its ancient numbers, and to somewhat less, and as autumn came and the gathering of fruits was over folk turned with glad hearts to the feasts of winter: but Tuor stood upon the battlements and gazed upon the Encircling Hills.

Now behold, Idril stood beside him, and the wind was in her hair, and Tuor thought that she was exceeding beautiful, and stooped to kiss her; but her face was sad, and she said: "Now come the days when thou must make choice," and Tuor knew not what she said. Then drawing him within their halls she said to him how her heart misgave her for fear concerning Eärendel her son, and for boding that some great evil was nigh, and that Melko would be at the bottom of it. Then Tuor would comfort her, but might not, and she questioned him concerning the secret delving, and he said how it now led a league into the plain, and at that was her heart somewhat lightened. But still she counselled that the delving be pressed on, and that henceforth should speed weigh more than secrecy, "because now is the time very near". And another rede she gave him, and this he took also, that certain of the bravest and most true among the lords and warriors of the Gondothlim be chosen with care and told of that secret way and its issue. These she counselled him to make into a stout guard and to give them his emblem to wear that they become his folk, and to do thus under pretext of the right and dignity of a great lord, kinsman to the king. "Moreover," said she, "I will get my father's favour to that." In secret too she whispered to folk that if the city came to its last stand or Turgon be slain that they rally about Tuor and her son, and to this they laughed a yea, saying however that Gondolin would stand as long as Taniquetil or the Mountains of Valinor.

Yet to Turgon she spoke not openly, nor suffered Tuor to do so, as he desired, despite their love and reverence for him – a great and a noble and a glorious king he was – seeing that he trusted in Meglin and held with blind obstinacy his belief in the impregnable might of the city and that Melko sought no more against it, perceiving no hope therein. Now in this he was ever strengthened by the cunning sayings of Meglin. Behold, the guile of that Gnome was very great, for he wrought much in the dark, so that folk said: "He doth well to bear the sign of a sable mole"; and by reason of the folly of certain of the quarrymen, and yet more by reason of the loose words of certain among his kin to whom word was somewhat unwarily spoken by Tuor, he gathered a knowledge of the secret work and laid against that a plan of his own.

So winter deepened, and it was very cold for those regions, so that frost fared about the plain of Tumladin and ice lay on its pools; yet the fountains played ever on Amon Gwareth and the two trees blossomed, and folk made merry till the day of terror that was hidden in the heart of Melko.

In these ways that bitter winter passed, and the snows lay deeper than ever before on the Encircling Hills; yet in its time a spring of wondrous glory melted the skirts of those white mantles and the valley drank the waters and burst into flowers. So came and passed with revelry of children the festival of Nost-na-Lothion or the Birth of Flowers, and the hearts of the Gondothlim were uplifted for the good promise of the year; and now at length is that great feast Tarnin Austa or the Gates of Summer near at hand. For know that on a night it was their custom to begin a solemn ceremony at midnight, continuing it even till the dawn of Tarnin Austa broke, and no voice was uttered in the city from midnight till the break of day, but the dawn they hailed with ancient songs. For years uncounted had the coming of summer thus been greeted with music of choirs, standing upon their gleaming eastern wall; and now comes even the night of vigil and the city is filled with silver lamps, while in the groves upon the new-leaved trees lights of jewelled colours swing, and low musics go along the ways, but no voice sings until the dawn.

The sun has sunk beyond the hills and folk array them for the festival very gladly and eagerly – glancing in expectation to the East. Lo! even when she had gone and all was dark, a new light suddenly began, and a glow there was, but it was beyond the northward heights,[26] and men marvelled, and there was a thronging of the walls and battlements. Then wonder grew to doubt as that light waxed and became yet redder, and doubt to dread as men saw the snow upon the mountains dyed as it were with blood. And thus it was that the fire-serpents of Melko came upon Gondolin.

Then came over the plain riders who bore breathless tidings from those who kept vigil on the peaks; and they told of the fiery hosts and the shapes like dragons, and said: "Melko is upon us." Great was the fear and anguish within that beauteous city, and the streets and byeways were filled with the weeping of women and the wailing of children, and the squares with the mustering of soldiers and the ring of arms. There were the gleaming banners of all the great houses and kindreds of the Gondothlim. Mighty was the array of the house of the king and their colours were white and gold and red, and their emblems the moon and the sun and the scarlet heart.[27] Now in the midmost of these stood Tuor above all heads, and his mail of silver gleamed; and about him was a press of the stoutest of the folk. Lo! all these wore wings as it were of swans or gulls upon their helms, and the emblem of the White Wing was upon their shields. But the folk of Meglin were drawn up in the same place, and sable was their harness, and they bore no sign or emblem, but their round caps of steel were covered with moleskin, and they fought with axes two-headed like mattocks. There Meglin prince of Gondobar gathered many warriors of dark countenance and lowering gaze about him, and a ruddy glow shone upon their faces and gleamed about the polished surfaces of their accoutrement. Behold, all the hills to the north were ablaze, and it was as if rivers of fire ran down the slopes that led to the plain of Tumladin, and folk might already feel the heat thereof.

And many other kindreds were there, the folk of the Swallow and the Heavenly Arch, and from these folk came the greatest number and the best of the bowmen, and they were arrayed upon the broad places of the walls. Now the folk of the Swallow bore a fan of feathers on their helms, and they were arrayed in white and dark blue and in purple and black and showed an arrowhead on their shields. Their lord was Duilin, swiftest of all men to run and leap and surest of archers at a mark. But they of the Heavenly Arch being a folk of uncounted wealth were arrayed in a glory of colours, and their arms were set with jewels that flamed in the light now over the sky. Every shield of that battalion was of the blue of the heavens and its boss a jewel built of seven gems, rubies and amethysts and sapphires, emeralds, chrysoprase, topaz, and amber, but an opal of great size was set in their helms. Egalmoth was their chieftain, and wore a blue mantle upon which the stars were broidered in crystal, and his sword was bent – now none else of the Noldoli bore curved swords – yet he trusted rather to the bow, and shot therewith further than any among that host.

There too were the folk of the Pillar and of the Tower of Snow, and both these kindreds were marshalled by Penlod, tallest of Gnomes. There were those of the Tree, and they were a great house, and their raiment was green. They fought with iron-studded clubs or with slings, and their lord Galdor was held the most valiant of all the Gondothlim save Turgon alone. There stood the house of the Golden Flower who bare a rayed sun upon their shield, and their chief Glorfindel bare a mantle so broidered in threads of gold that it was diapered with celandine as a field in spring; and his arms were damascened with cunning gold.

Then came there from the south of the city the people of the Fountain, and Ecthelion was their lord, and silver and diamonds were their delight; and swords very long and bright and pale did they wield, and they went into battle to the music of flutes. Behind them came the host of the Harp, and this was a battalion of brave warriors; but their leader Salgant was a craven, and he fawned upon Meglin. They were dight with tassels of silver and tassels of gold, and a harp of silver shone in their blazonry upon a field of black; but Salgant bore one of gold, and he alone rode into battle of all the sons of the Gondothlim, and he was heavy and squat.

Now the last of the battalions was furnished by the folk of the Hammer of Wrath, and of these came many of the best smiths and craftsmen, and all that kindred reverenced Aulë the Smith more than all other Ainur. They fought with great maces like hammers, and their shields were heavy, for their arms were very strong. In older days they had been much recruited by Noldoli who escaped from the mines of Melko, and the hatred of this house for the works of that evil one and the Balrogs his demons was exceeding great. Now their leader was Rog, strongest of the Gnomes, scarce second in valour to that Galdor of the Tree. The sign of this people was the Stricken Anvil, and a hammer that smiteth sparks about it was set on their shields, and red gold and black iron was their delight. Very numerous was that battalion, nor had any amongst them a faint heart, and they won the greatest glory of all those fair houses in that struggle against doom; yet were they ill-fated, and none ever fared away from that field, but fell about Rog and vanished from the Earth; and with them much craftsmanship and skill has been lost for ever.[28]

This was the fashion and the array of the eleven houses of the Gondothlim with their signs and emblems, and the bodyguard of Tuor, the folk of the Wing, was accounted the twelfth. Now is the face of that chieftain grim and he looks not to live long – and there in his house upon the walls Idril arrays herself in mail, and seeks Eärendel. And that child was in tears for the strange lights of red that played about the walls of the chamber where he slept; and tales that his nurse Meleth had woven him concerning fiery Melko at times of his waywardness came to him and troubled him. But his mother coming set about him a tiny coat of mail that she had let fashion in secret, and at that time he was glad and exceeding proud, and he shouted for pleasure. Yet Idril wept, for much had she cherished in her heart the fair city and her goodly house, and the love of Tuor and herself that had dwelt therein; but now she saw its destroying nigh at hand, and feared that her contriving would fail against this overwhelming might of the terror of the serpents.

It was now four hours still from middle night, and the sky was red in the north and in the east and west; and those serpents of iron had reached the levels of Tumladin, and those fiery ones were among the lowest slopes of the hills, so that the guards were taken and set in evil torment by the Balrogs that scoured all about, saving only to the furthest south where was Cristhorn the Cleft of Eagles.

Then did King Turgon call a council, and thither fared Tuor and Meglin as royal princes; and Duilin came with Egalmoth and Penlod the tall, and Rog strode thither with Galdor of the Tree and golden Glorfindel and Ecthelion of the voice of music. Thither too fared Salgant atremble at the tidings, and other nobles beside of less blood but better heart.

Then spake Tuor and this was his rede, that a mighty sally be made forthwith, ere the light and heat grew too great in the plain; and many backed him, being but of different minds as to whether the sally should be made by the entire host with the maids and wives and children amidmost, or by diverse bands seeking out in many directions; and to this last Tuor leaned.

But Meglin and Salgant alone held other counsel and were for holding to the city and seeking to guard those treasures that lay within. Out of guile did Meglin speak thus, fearing lest any of the Noldoli escape the doom that he had brought upon them for the saving of his skin, and he dreaded lest his treason become known and somehow vengeance find him in after days. But Salgant spake both echoing Meglin and being grievously afraid of issuing from the city, for he was fain rather to do battle from an impregnable fortress than to risk hard blows upon the field.

Then the lord of the house of the Mole played upon the one weakness of Turgon, saying: "Lo! O King, the city of Gondolin contains a wealth of jewels and metals and stuffs and of things wrought by the hands of the Gnomes to surpassing beauty, and all these thy lords – more brave meseems than wise – would abandon to the Foe. Even should victory be thine upon the plain thy city will be sacked and the Balrogs get hence with a measureless booty"; and Turgon groaned, for Meglin had known his great love for the wealth and loveliness of that burg[29] upon Amon Gwareth. Again said Meglin, putting fire in his voice: "Lo! Hast thou for nought laboured through years uncounted at the building of walls of impregnable thickness and in the making of gates whose valour may not be overthrown; is the power of the hill Amon Gwareth become as lowly as the deep vale, or the hoard of weapons that lie upon it and its unnumbered arrows of so little worth that in the hour of peril thou wouldst cast all aside and go naked into the open against enemies of steel and fire, whose trampling shakes the earth and the Encircling Mountains ring with the clamour of their footsteps?"

And Salgant quaked to think of it and spake noisily, saying: "Meglin speaks well, O King, hear thou him." Then the king took the counsel of those twain though all the lords said otherwise, nay rather the more for that: therefore at his bidding does all that folk abide now the assault upon their walls. But Tuor wept and left the king's hall, and gathering the men of the Wing went through the streets seeking his home; and by that hour was the light great and lurid and there was stifling heat and a black smoke and stench arose about the pathways to the city.

And now came the Monsters across the valley and the white towers of Gondolin reddened before them; but the stoutest were in dread seeing those dragons of fire and those serpents of bronze and iron that fare already about the hill of the city; and they shot unavailing arrows at them. Then is there a cry of hope, for behold, the snakes of fire may not climb the hill for its steepness and for its glassiness, and by reason of the quenching waters that fall upon its sides; yet they lie about its feet and a vast steam arises where the streams of Amon Gwareth and the flames of the serpents drive together. Then grew there such a heat that women became faint and men sweated to weariness beneath their mail, and all the springs of the city, save only the fountain of the king, grew hot and smoked.

But now Gothmog lord of Balrogs, captain of the hosts of Melko, took counsel and gathered all his things of iron that could coil themselves around and above all obstacles before them. These he bade pile themselves before the northern gate; and behold, their great spires reached even to its threshold and thrust at the towers and bastions about it, and by reason of the exceeding heaviness of their bodies those gates fell, and great was the noise thereof: yet the most of the walls around them still stood firm. Then the engines and the catapults of the king poured darts and boulders and molten metals on those ruthless beasts, and their hollow bellies clanged beneath the buffeting, yet it availed not for they might not be broken, and the fires rolled off them. Then were the topmost opened about their middles, and an innumerable host of the Orcs, the goblins of hatred, poured therefrom into the breach; and who shall tell of the gleam of their scimitars or the flash of the broad-bladed spears with which they stabbed?

Then did Rog shout in a mighty voice, and all the people of the Hammer of Wrath and the kindred of the Tree with Galdor the valiant leapt at the foe. There the blows of their great hammers and the dint of their clubs rang to the Encircling Mountains and the Orcs fell like leaves; and those of the Swallow and the Arch poured arrows like the dark rains of autumn upon them, and both

Orcs and Gondothlim fell thereunder for the smoke and the confusion. Great was that battle, yet for all their valour the Gondothlim by reason of the might of ever increasing numbers were borne slowly backwards till the goblins held part of the northernmost city.

At this time is Tuor at the head of the folk of the Wing struggling in the turmoil of the streets, and now he wins through to his house and finds that Meglin is before him. Trusting in the battle now begun about the northern gate and in the uproar in the city, Meglin had looked to this hour for the consummation of his designs. Learning much of the secret delving of Tuor (yet only at the last moment had he got this knowledge and he could not discover all) he said nought to the king or any other, for it was his thought that of a surety that tunnel would go in the end toward the Way of Escape, this being the most nigh to the city, and he had a mind to use this to his good, and to the ill of the Noldoli. Messengers by great stealth he despatched to Melko to set a guard about the outer issue of that Way when the assault was made; but he himself thought now to take Eärendel and cast him into the fire beneath the walls, and seizing Idril he would constrain her to guide him to the secrets of the passage, that he might win out of this terror of fire and slaughter and drag her withal along with him to the lands of Melko. Now Meglin was afeared that even the secret token which Melko had given him would fail in that direful sack, and was minded to help that Ainu to the fulfilment of his promises of safety. No doubt had he however of the death of Tuor in that great burning, for to Salgant he had confided the task of delaying him in the king's halls and egging him straight thence into the deadliest of the fight – but lo! Salgant fell into a terror unto death, and he rode home and lay there now aquake on his bed; but Tuor fared home with the folk of the Wing.

Now Tuor did this, though his valour leapt to the noise of war, that he might take farewell of Idril and Eärendel, and speed them with a bodyguard down the secret way ere he returned himself to the battle throng to die if must be: but he found a press of the Mole-folk about his door, and these were the grimmest and least good-hearted of folk that Meglin might get in that city. Yet were they free Noldoli and under no spell of Melko's like their master, wherefore though for the lordship of Meglin they aided not Idril, no more would they touch of his purpose despite all his curses.

Now then Meglin had Idril by the hair and sought to drag her to the battlements out of cruelty of heart, that she might see the fall of Eärendel to the flames; but he was cumbered by that child, and she fought, alone as she was, like a tigress for all her beauty and slenderness. There he now struggles and delays amid oaths while that folk of the Wing draw nigh – and lo! Tuor gives a shout so great that the Orcs hear it afar and waver at the sound of it. Like a crash of tempest the guard of the Wing were amid the men of the Mole, and these were stricken asunder. When Meglin saw this he would stab Eärendel with a short knife he had; but that child bit his left hand, that his teeth sank in, and he staggered, and stabbed weakly, and the mail of the small coat turned the blade aside; and thereupon Tuor was upon him and his wrath was terrible to see. He seized Meglin by that hand that held the knife and broke the arm with the wrench, and then taking him by the middle leapt with him upon the walls, and flung him far out. Great was the fall of his body, and it smote Amon Gwareth three times ere it pitched in the midmost of the flames; and the name of Meglin has gone out in shame from among Eldar and Noldoli.

Then the warriors of the Mole being more numerous than those few of the Wing, and loyal to their lord, came at Tuor, and there were great blows, but no man might stand before the wrath of Tuor, and they were smitten and driven to fly into what dark holes they might, or flung from the walls. Then Tuor and his men must get them to the battle of the Gate, for the noise of it has grown very great, and Tuor has it still in his heart that the city may stand; yet with Idril he left there Voronwë against his will and some other swordsmen to be a guard for her till he returned or might send tidings from the fray.

Now was the battle at that gate very evil indeed, and Duilin of the Swallow as he shot from the walls was smitten by a fiery bolt of the Balrogs who leapt about the base of Amon Gwareth; and he fell from the battlements and perished. Then the Balrogs continued to shoot darts of fire and flaming arrows like small snakes into the sky, and these fell upon the roofs and gardens of Gondolin till all the trees were scorched, and the flowers and grass burned up, and the whiteness of those walls and colonnades was blackened and seared: yet a worse matter was it that a company of those demons climbed upon the coils of the serpents of iron and thence loosed unceasingly from their bows and slings till a fire began to burn in the city to the back of the main army of the defenders.

Then said Rog in a great voice: "Who now shall fear the Balrogs for all their terror? See before us the accursed ones who for ages have tormented the children of the Noldoli, and who now set a fire at our backs with their shooting. Come ye of the Hammer of Wrath and we will smite them for their evil." Thereupon he lifted his mace, and its handle was long; and he made a way before him by the wrath of his onset even unto the fallen gate: but all the people of the Stricken Anvil ran behind like a wedge, and sparks came from their eyes for the fury of their rage. A great deed was that sally, as the Noldoli sing yet, and many of the Orcs were borne backward into the fires below; but the men of Rog leapt even upon the coils of the serpents and came at those Balrogs and smote them grievously, for all they had whips of flame and claws of steel, and were in stature very great. They battered them into nought, or catching at their whips wielded these against them, that they tore them even as they had aforetime torn the Gnomes; and the number of Balrogs that perished was a marvel and dread to the hosts of Melko, for ere that day never had any of the Balrogs been slain by the hand of Elves or Men.

Then Gothmog Lord of Balrogs gathered all his demons that were about the city and ordered them thus: a number made for the folk of the Hammer and gave before them, but the greater company rushing upon the flank contrived to get to their backs, higher upon the coils of the drakes and nearer to the gates, so that Rog might not win back save with great slaughter among his folk. But Rog seeing this essayed not to win back, as was hoped, but with all his folk fell on those whose part was to give before him; and they fled before him now of dire need rather than of craft. Down into the plain were they harried, and their shrieks rent the airs of Tumladin. Then that house of the Hammer fared about smiting and hewing the astonied bands of Melko till they were hemmed at the last by an overwhelming force of the Orcs and the Balrogs, and a fire-drake was loosed upon them. There did they perish about Rog hewing to the last till iron and flame overcame them, and it is yet sung that each man of the Hammer of Wrath took the lives of seven foemen to pay for his own. Then did dread fall more heavily still upon the Gondothlim at the death of Rog and the loss of his battalion, and they gave back further yet into the city, and Penlod perished there in a lane with his back to the wall, and about him many of the men of the Pillar and many of the Tower of Snow.

Now therefore Melko's goblins held all the gate and a great part of the walls on either side, whence numbers of the Swallow and those of the Rainbow were thrust to doom; but within the city they had won a great space reaching nigh to the centre, even to the Place of the Well that adjoined the Square of the Palace. Yet about those ways and around the gate their dead were piled in uncounted heaps, and they halted therefore and took counsel, seeing that for the valour of the Gondothlim they had lost many more than they had hoped and far more than those defenders. Fearful too they were for that slaughter Rog had done amid the Balrogs, because of those demons they had great courage and confidence of heart.

Now then the plan that they made was to hold what they had won, while those serpents of bronze and with great feet for trampling climbed slowly over those of iron, and reaching the walls there opened a breach wherethrough the Balrogs might ride upon the dragons of flame: yet they knew this must be done with speed, for the heats of those drakes lasted not for ever, and might only be plenished from the wells of fire that Melko had made in the fastness of his own land.

But even as their messengers were sped they heard a sweet music that was played amid the host of the Gondothlim and they feared what it might mean; and lo! there came Ecthelion and the people of the Fountain whom Turgon till now had held in reserve, for he watched the most of that affray from the heights of his tower. Now marched these folk to a great playing of their flutes, and the crystal and silver of their array was most lovely to see amid the red light of the fires and the blackness of the ruins.

Then on a sudden their music ceased and Ecthelion of the fair voice shouted for the drawing of swords, and before the Orcs might foresee his onslaught the flashing of those pale blades was amongst them. 'Tis said that Ecthelion's folk there slew more of the goblins than fell ever in all the battles of the Eldalië with that race, and that his name is a terror among them to this latest day, and a warcry to the Eldar.

Now it is that Tuor and the men of the Wing fare into the fight and range themselves beside Ecthelion and those of the Fountain, and the twain strike mighty blows and ward each many a thrust from the other, and harry the Orcs so that they win back almost to the gate. But there behold a quaking and a trampling, for the dragons labour mightily at beating a path up Amon Gwareth and at casting down the walls of the city; and already there is a gap therein and a confusion of masonry where the ward-towers have fallen in ruin. Bands of the Swallow and of the Arch of Heaven there fight bitterly amid the wreck or contest the walls to east and west with the foe; but even as Tuor comes nigh driving the Orcs, one of those brazen snakes heaves against the western wall and a great mass of it shakes and falls, and behind comes a creature of fire and Balrogs upon it. Flames gust from the jaws of that worm and folk wither before it, and the wings of the helm of Tuor are blackened, but he stands and gathers about him his guard and all of the Arch and Swallow he can find, whereas on his right Ecthelion rallies the men of the Fountain of the South.

Now the Orcs again take heart from the coming of the drakes, and they mingle with the Balrogs that pour about the breach, and they assail the Gondothlim grievously. There Tuor slew Othrod a lord of the Orcs cleaving his helm, and Balcmeg he hewed asunder, and Lug he smote with his axe that his limbs were cut from beneath him at the knee, but Ecthelion shore through two captains of the goblins at a sweep and cleft the head of Orcobal their chiefest champion to his teeth; and by reason of the great doughtiness of those two lords they came even unto the Balrogs. Of those demons of power Ecthelion slew three, for the brightness of his sword cleft the iron of them and did hurt to their fire, and they writhed; yet of the leap of that axe Dramborleg that was swung by the hand of Tuor were they still more afraid, for it sang like the rush of eagle's wings in the air and took death as it fell, and five of them went down before it.

But so it is that few cannot fight always against the many, and Ecthelion's left arm got a sore rent from a whip of the Balrog's and his shield fell to earth even as that dragon of fire drew nigh amid the ruin of the walls. Then Ecthelion must lean on Tuor, and Tuor might not leave him, though the very feet of the trampling beast were upon them, and they were like to be overborne: but Tuor hewed at a foot of the creature so that flame spouted forth, and that serpent screamed, lashing with its tail; and many of both Orcs and Noldoli got their death therefrom. Now Tuor gathered his might and lifted Ecthelion, and amid a remnant of the folk got thereunder and escaped the drake; yet dire was the killing of men that beast had wrought, and the Gondothlim were sorely shaken.

Thus it was that Tuor son of Peleg gave before the foe, fighting as he yielded ground, and bore from that battle Ecthelion of the Fountain, but the drakes and the foemen held half the city and all the north of it. Thence marauding bands fared about the streets and did much ransacking, or slew in the dark men and women and children, and many, if occasion let, they bound and led back and flung in the iron chambers amid the dragons of iron, that they might drag them afterward to be thralls of Melko.

Now Tuor reached the Square of the Folkwell by a way entering from the north, and found there Galdor denying the western entry by the Arch of Inwë to a horde of the goblins, but about him was now but a few of those men of the Tree. There did Galdor become the salvation of Tuor, for he fell behind his men stumbling beneath Ecthelion over a body that lay in the dark, and the Orcs had taken them both but for the sudden rush of that champion and the dint of his club.

There were the scatterlings of the guard of the Wing and of the houses of the Tree and the Fountain, and of the Swallow and the Arch, welded to a good battalion, and by the counsel of Tuor they gave way out of that Place of the Well, seeing that the Square of the King that lay next was the more defensible. Now that place had aforetime contained many beautiful trees, both oak and poplar, around a great well of vast depth and great purity of water; yet at that hour it was full of the riot and ugliness of those hideous people of Melko, and those waters were polluted with their carcases.

Thus comes the last stout gathering of those defenders in the Square of the Palace of Turgon. Among them are many wounded and fainting, and Tuor is weary for the labours of the night and the weight of Ecthelion who is in a deadly swoon. Even as he led that battalion in by the Road of Arches from the north-west (and they had much ado to prevent any foe getting behind their backs) a noise arose at the eastward of the square, and lo! Glorfindel is driven in with the last of the men of the Golden Flower.

Now these had sustained a terrible conflict in the Great Market to the east of the city, where a force of Orcs led by Balrogs came on them at unawares as they marched by a circuitous way to the fight about the gate. This they did to surprise the foe upon his left flank, but were themselves ambuscaded; there fought they bitterly for hours till a fire-drake new-come from the breach overwhelmed them, and Glorfindel cut his way out very hardly and with few men; but that place with its stores and its goodly things of fine workmanship was a waste of flames.

The story tells that Turgon had sent the men of the Harp to their aid because of the urgency of messengers from Glorfindel, but Salgant concealed this bidding from them, saying they were to garrison the square of the Lesser Market to the south where he dwelt, and they fretted thereat. Now however they brake from Salgant and were come before the king's hall; and that was very timely, for a triumphant press of foemen was at Glorfindel's heels. On these the men of the Harp unbidden fell with great eagerness and utterly redeemed the cravenhood of their lord, driving the enemy back into the market, and being leaderless fared even over wrathfully, so that many of them were trapped in the flames or sank before the breath of the serpent that revelled there.

Tuor now drank of the great fountain and was refreshed, and loosening Ecthelion's helm gave him to drink, splashing his face that his swoon left him. Now those lords Tuor and Glorfindel clear the square and withdraw all the men they may from the entrances and bar them with barriers, save as yet on the south. Even from that region comes now Egalmoth. He had had charge of the engines on the wall; but long since deeming matters to call rather for handstrokes about the streets than shooting upon the battlements he gathered some of the Arch and of the Swallow about him, and cast away his bow. Then did they fare about the city dealing good blows whenever they fell in with bands of the enemy. Thereby he rescued many bands of captives and gathered no few wandering and driven men, and so got to the King's Square with hard fighting; and men were fain to greet him for they had feared him dead. Now are all the women and children that had gathered there or been brought in by Egalmoth stowed in the king's halls, and the ranks of the houses made ready for the last. In that host of survivors are some, be it however few, of all the kindreds save of the Hammer of Wrath alone; and the king's house is as yet untouched. Nor is this any shame, for their part was ever to bide fresh to the last and defend the king.

But now the men of Melko have assembled their forces, and seven dragons of fire are come with Orcs about them and Balrogs upon them down all the ways from north, east, and west, seeking the Square of the King. Then there was carnage at the barriers, and Egalmoth and Tuor went from place to place of the defence, but Ecthelion lay by the fountain; and that stand was the most stubborn-valiant that is remembered in all the songs or in any tale. Yet at long last a drake bursts the barrier to the north – and there had once been the issue of the Alley of Roses and a fair place to see or to walk in, but now there is but a lane of blackness and it is filled with noise.

Tuor stood then in the way of that beast, but was sundered from Egalmoth, and they pressed him backward even to the centre of the square nigh the fountain. There he became weary from the strangling heat and was beaten down by a great demon, even Gothmog lord of Balrogs, son of Melko. But lo! Ecthelion, whose face was of the pallor of grey steel and whose shield-arm hung limp at his side, strode above him as he fell; and that Gnome drave at the demon, yet did not give him his death, getting rather a wound to his sword-arm that his weapon left his grasp. Then leapt Ecthelion lord of the Fountain, fairest of the Noldoli, full at Gothmog even as he raised his whip, and his helm that had a spike upon it he drave into that evil breast, and he twined his legs about his foeman's thighs; and the Balrog yelled and fell forward; but those two dropped into the basin of the king's fountain which was very deep. There found that creature his bane; and Ecthelion sank steel-laden into the depths, and so perished the lord of the Fountain after fiery battle in cool waters.[30]

Now Tuor had arisen when the assault of Ecthelion gave him space, and seeing that great deed he wept for his love of that fair Gnome of the Fountain, but being wrapped in battle he scarce cut his way to the folk about the palace. There seeing the wavering of the enemy by reason of the dread of the fall of Gothmog the marshal of the hosts, the royal house laid on and the king came down in splendour among them and hewed with them, that they swept again much of the square, and of the Balrogs slew even two score, which is a very great prowess indeed: but greater still did they do, for they hemmed in one of the Fire-drakes for all his flaming, and forced him into the very waters of the fountain that he perished therein. Now this was the end of that fair water; and its pools turned to steam and its spring was dried up, and it shot no more into the heaven, but rather a vast column of vapour arose to the sky and the cloud therefrom floated over all the land.

Then dread fell on all for the doom of the fountain, and the square was filled with mists of scalding heat and blinding fogs, and the people of the royal house were killed therein by heat and by the foe and by the serpents and by one another: but a body of them saved the king, and there was a rally of men beneath Glingol and Bansil.

Then said the king: "Great is the fall of Gondolin", and men shuddered, for such were the words of Amnon the prophet of old;[31] but Tuor speaking wildly for ruth and love of the king cried: "Gondolin stands yet, and Ulmo will not suffer it to perish!" Now were they at that time standing, Tuor by the Trees and the king upon the Stairs, as they had stood aforetime when Tuor spake the embassy of Ulmo. But Turgon said: "Evil have I brought upon the Flower of the Plain in despite of Ulmo, and now he leaveth it to wither in the fire. Lo! hope is no more in my heart for my city of loveliness, but the children of the Noldoli shall not be worsted for ever."

Then did the Gondothlim clash their weapons, for many stood

nigh, but Turgon said: "Fight not against doom, O my children! Seek ye who may safety in flight, if perhaps there be time yet: but let Tuor have your lealty." But Tuor said: "Thou art king"; and Turgon made answer: "Yet no blow will I strike more", and he cast his crown at the roots of Glingol. Then did Galdor who stood there pick it up, but Turgon accepted it not, and bare of head climbed to the topmost pinnacle of that white tower that stood nigh his palace. There he shouted in a voice like a horn blown among the mountains, and all that were gathered beneath the Trees and the foemen in the mists of the square heard him: "Great is the victory of the Noldoli!" And 'tis said that it was then middle night, and that the Orcs yelled in derision.

Then did men speak of a sally, and were of two minds. Many held that it were impossible to burst through, nor might they even so get over the plain or through the hills, and that it were better therefore to die about the king. But Tuor might not think well of the death of so many fair women and children, were it at the hands of their own folk in the last resort, or by the weapons of the enemy, and he spake of the delving and of the secret way. Therefore did he counsel that they beg Turgon to have other mind, and coming among them lead that remnant southward to the walls and the entry of that passage; but he himself burnt with desire to fare thither and know how Idril and Eärendel might be, or to get tidings hence to them and bid them begone speedily, for Gondolin was taken. Now Tuor's plan seemed to the lords desperate indeed – seeing the narrowness of the tunnel and the greatness of the company that must pass it – yet would they fain take this rede in their straits. But Turgon hearkened not, and bid them fare now ere it was too late, and "Let Tuor," said he, "be your guide and your chieftain. But I Turgon will not leave my city, and will burn with it." Then sped they messengers again to the tower, saying: "Sire, who are the Gondothlim if thou perish? Lead us!" But he said: "Lo! I abide here"; and a third time, and he said: "If I am king, obey my behests, and dare not to parley further with my commands." After that they sent no more and made ready for the forlorn attempt. But the folk of the royal house that yet lived would not budge a foot, but gathered thickly about the base of the king's tower. "Here," said they, "we will stay if Turgon goes not forth"; and they might not be persuaded.

Now was Tuor torn sorely between his reverence for the king and the love for Idril and his child, wherewith his heart was sick; yet already serpents fare about the square trampling upon dead and dying, and the foe gathers in the mists for the last onslaught; and the choice must be made. Then because of the wailing of the women in the halls of the palace and the greatness of his pity for that sad remainder of the peoples of Gondolin, he gathered all that rueful company, maids, children and mothers, and setting them amidmost marshalled as well as he might his men around them. Deepest he set them at flank and at rear, for he purposed falling back southward fighting as best he might with the rearguard as he went; and thus if it might so be to win down the Road of Pomps to the Place of the Gods ere any great force be sent to circumvent him. Thence was it his thought to go by the Way of Running Waters past the Fountains of the South to the walls and to his home; but the passage of the secret tunnel he doubted much. Thereupon espying his movement the foe made forthwith a great onslaught upon his left flank and his rear – from east and north – even as he began to withdraw; but his right was covered by the king's hall and the head of that column drew already into the Road of Pomps.

Then some of the hugest of the drakes came on and glared in the fog, and he must perforce bid the company to go at a run, fighting on the left at haphazard; but Glorfindel held the rear manfully and many more of the Golden Flower fell there. So it was that they passed the Road of Pomps and reached Gar Ainion, the Place of the Gods; and this was very open and at its middle the highest ground of all the city. Here Tuor looks for an evil stand and it is scarce in his hope to get much further; but behold, the foe seems already to slacken and scarce any follow them, and this is a wonder. Now comes Tuor at their head to the Place of Wedding, and lo! there stands Idril before him with her hair unbraided as on that day of their marriage before; and great is his amaze. By her stood Voronwë and none other, but Idril saw not even Tuor, for her gaze was set back upon the Place of the King that now lay somewhat below them. Then all that host halted and looked back whither her eyes gazed and their hearts stood still; for now they saw why the foe pressed them so little and the reason of their salvation. Lo! a drake was coiled even on the very steps of the palace and defiled their whiteness; but swarms of the Orcs ransacked within and dragged forth forgotten women and children or slew men that fought alone. Glingol was withered to the stock and Bansil was blackened utterly, and the king's tower was beset. High up could they descry the form of the king, but about the base a serpent of iron spouting flame lashed and rowed with his tail, and

Balrogs were round him; and there was the king's house in great anguish, and dread cries carried up to the watchers. So was it that the sack of the halls of Turgon and that most valiant stand of the royal house held the mind of the foe, so that Tuor got thence with his company, and stood now in tears upon the Place of the Gods.

Then said Idril: "Woe is me whose father awaiteth doom even upon his topmost pinnacle; but seven times woe whose lord hath gone down before Melko and will stride home no more!" – for she was distraught with the agony of that night.

Then said Tuor: "Lo! Idril, it is I, and I live; yet now will I get thy father hence, be it from the Hells of Melko!" With that he would make down the hill alone, maddened by the grief of his wife; but she coming to her wits in a storm of weeping clasped his knees saying: "My lord! My lord!" and delayed him. Yet even as they spake a great noise and a yelling rose from that place of anguish. Behold, the tower leapt into a flame and in a stab of fire it fell, for the dragons crushed the base of it and all who stood there. Great was the clangour of that terrible fall, and therein passed Turgon King of the Gondothlim, and for that hour the victory was to Melko.

Then said Idril heavily: "Sad is the blindness of the wise"; but Tuor said: "Sad too is the stubbornness of those we love – yet 'twas a valiant fault," then stooping he lifted and kissed her, for she was more to him than all the Gondothlim; but she wept bitterly for her father. Then turned Tuor to the captains, saying: "Lo, we must get hence with all speed, lest we be surrounded"; and forthwith they moved onward as swiftly as they might and got them far from thence ere the Orcs tired of sacking the palace and rejoicing at the fall of the tower of Turgon.

Now are they in the southward city and meet but scattered bands of plunderers who fly before them; yet do they find fire and burning everywhere for the ruthlessness of that enemy. Women do they meet, some with babes and some laden with chattels, but Tuor would not let them bear away aught save a little food. Coming now at length to a greater quiet Tuor asked Voronwë for tidings, in that Idril spake not and was well-nigh in a swoon; and Voronwë told him of how she and he had waited before the doors of the house while the noise of those battles grew and shook their hearts; and Idril wept for lack of tidings from Tuor. At length she had sped the most part of her guard down the secret way with Eärendel, constraining them to depart with imperious words, yet was her grief great at that sundering. She herself would bide, said she, nor seek to live after her lord; and then she fared about gathering womenfolk and wanderers and speeding them down the tunnel, and smiting marauders with her small band; nor might they dissuade her from bearing a sword.

At length they had fallen in with a band somewhat too numerous, and Voronwë had dragged her thence but by the luck of the Gods, for all else with them perished, and their foe burned Tuor's house; yet found not the secret way. "Therewith," said Voronwë, "thy lady became distraught of weariness and grief, and fared into the city wildly to my great fear – nor might I get her to sally from the burning."

About the saying of these words were they come to the southern walls and nigh to Tuor's house, and lo! it was cast down and the wreckage was asmoke; and thereat was Tuor bitterly wroth. But there was a noise that boded the approach of Orcs, and Tuor despatched that company as swiftly as might be down that secret way.

Now is there great sorrow upon that staircase as those exiles bid farewell to Gondolin; yet are they without much hope of further life beyond the hills, for how shall any slip from the hand of Melko?

Glad is Tuor when all have passed the entrance and his fear lightens; indeed by the luck of the Valar only can all those folk have got therein unspied of the Orcs. Some now are left who casting aside their arms labour with picks from within and block up the entry of the passage, faring then after the host as they might; but when that folk had descended the stairway to a level with the valley the heat grew to a torment for the fire of the dragons that were about the city; and they were indeed nigh, for the delving was there at no great depth in the earth. Boulders were loosened by the tremors of the ground and falling crushed many, and fumes were in the air so that their torches and lanterns went out. Here they fell over bodies of some that had gone before and perished, and Tuor was in fear for Eärendel; and they pressed on in great darkness and anguish. Nigh two hours were they in that tunnel of the earth, and towards its end it was scarce finished, but rugged at the sides and low.[32]

Then came they at the last lessened by wellnigh a tithe to the tunnel's opening, and it debouched cunningly in a large basin where once water had lain, but it was now full of thick bushes. Here were gathered no small press of mingled folk whom Idril and Voronwë sped down the hidden way before them, and they were weeping softly in weariness and sorrow, but Eärendel was not there. Thereat were Tuor and Idril in anguish of heart.[33] Lamentation was there too among all those others, for amidmost of the plain about them loomed afar the hill of Amon Gwareth crowned with flames, where had stood the gleaming city of their home. Fire-drakes are about it and monsters of iron fare in and out of its gates, and great is that sack of the Balrogs and Orcs. Somewhat of comfort has this nonetheless for the leaders, for they judge the plain to be nigh empty of Melko's folk save hard by the city, for thither have fared all his evil ones to revel in that destruction.

"Now," therefore said Galdor, "we must get as far hence toward the Encircling Mountains as may be ere dawn come upon us, and that giveth no great space of time, for summer is at hand."[34] Thereat rose a dissension, for a number said that it were folly to make for Cristhorn as Tuor purposed. "The sun," say they, "will be up long ere we win the foothills, and we shall be whelmed in the plain by those drakes and those demons. Let us fare to Bad Uthwen, the Way of Escape, for that is but half the journeying, and our weary and our wounded may hope to win so far if no further."

Yet Idril spake against this, and persuaded the lords that they trust not to the magic of that way that had aforetime shielded it from discovery: "for what magic stands if Gondolin be fallen?" Nonetheless a large body of men and women sundered from Tuor and fared to Bad Uthwen, and there into the jaws of a monster who by the guile of Melko at Meglin's rede sat at the outer issue that none came through. But the others, led by one Legolas Greenleaf of the house of the Tree, who knew all that plain by day or by dark, and was night-sighted, made much speed over the vale for all their weariness, and halted only after a great march. Then was all the Earth spread with the grey light of that sad dawn which looked no more on the beauty of Gondolin; but the plain was full of mists – and that was a marvel, for no mist or fog came there ever before, and this perchance had to do with the doom of the fountain of the king. Again they rose, and covered by the vapours fared long past dawn in safety, till they were already too far away for any to descry them in those misty airs from the hill or from the ruined walls.

Now the Mountains or rather their lowest hills were on that side seven leagues save a mile from Gondolin, and Cristhorn the Cleft of Eagles two leagues of upward going from the beginning of the Mountains, for it was at a great height; wherefore they had yet two leagues and part of a third to traverse amid the spurs and foothills, and they were very weary.[35] By now the sun hung well above a saddle in the eastern hills, and she was very red and great; and the mists nigh them were lifted, but the ruins of Gondolin were utterly hidden as in a cloud. Behold then at the clearing of the airs they saw, but a few furlongs off, a knot of men that fled on foot, and these were pursued by a strange cavalry, for on great wolves rode Orcs, as they thought, brandishing spears. Then said Tuor: "Lo! there is Eärendel my son; behold, his face shineth as a star in the waste,[36] and my men of the Wing are about him, and they are in sore straits." Forthwith he chose fifty of the men that were least weary, and leaving the main company to follow he fared over the plain with that troop as swiftly as they had strength left. Coming now to carry of voice Tuor shouted to the men about Eärendel to stand and flee not, for the wolfriders were scattering them and slaying them piecemeal, and the child was upon the shoulders of one Hendor, a house-carle of Idril's, and he seemed like to be left with his burden. Then they stood back to back and Hendor and Eärendel amidmost; but Tuor soon came up, though all his troop were breathless.

Of the wolfriders there were a score, and of the men that were about Eärendel but six living; therefore had Tuor opened his men into a crescent of but one rank, and hoped so to envelop the riders, lest any escaping bring tidings to the main foe and draw ruin upon the exiles. In this he succeeded, so that only two escaped, and therewithal wounded and without their beasts, wherefore were their tidings brought too late to the city.

Glad was Eärendel to greet Tuor, and Tuor most fain of his child; but said Eärendel: "I am thirsty, father, for I have run far – nor had Hendor need to bear me." Thereto his father said nought, having no water, and thinking of the need of all that company that he guided; but Eärendel said again: "'Twas good to see Meglin die so, for he would set arms about my mother – and I liked him not; but I would travel in no tunnels for all Melko's wolfriders." Then Tuor smiled and set him upon his shoulders. Soon after this the main company came up, and Tuor gave Eärendel to his mother who was in a great joy; but Eärendel would not be borne in her arms, for he said: "Mother Idril, thou art weary, and warriors in mail ride not among the Gondothlim, save it be old Salgant!" and his mother laughed amid her sorrow; but Eärendel said: "Nay, where is Salgant?" – for Salgant had told him quaint tales or played drolleries with him at times, and Eärendel had much laughter of the old Gnome in those days when he came many a day to the house of Tuor, loving the good wine and fair repast he there received. But none could say where Salgant was, nor can they now. Mayhap he was whelmed by fire upon his bed; yet some have it that he was taken captive to the halls of Melko and made his buffoon – and this is an ill fate for a noble of the good race of the Gnomes. Then was Eärendel sad at that, and walked beside his mother in silence.

Now came they to the foothills and it was full morning but still grey, and there nigh to the beginning of the upward road folk stretched them and rested in a little dale fringed with trees and with hazel-bushes, and many slept despite their peril, for they were utterly spent. Yet Tuor set a strict watch, and himself slept not. Here they made one meal of scanty food and broken meats; and Eärendel quenched his thirst and played beside a little brook. Then said he to his mother: "Mother Idril, I would we had good Ecthelion of the Fountain here to play to me on his flute, or make me willow-whistles! Perchance he has gone on ahead?" But Idril said nay, and told what she had heard of his end. Then said Eärendel that he cared not ever to see the streets of Gondolin again, and he wept bitterly; but Tuor said that he would not again see those streets, "for Gondolin is no more".

Thereafter nigh to the hour of sundown behind the hills Tuor bade the company arise, and they pressed on by rugged paths. Soon now the grass faded and gave way to mossy stones, and trees fell away, and even the pines and firs grew sparse. About the set of the sun the way so wound behind a shoulder of the hills that they might not again look toward Gondolin. There all that company turned, and lo! the plain is clear and smiling in the last light as of old; but afar off as they gazed a great flare shot up against the darkened north – and that was the fall of the last tower of Gondolin, even that which had stood hard by the southern gate, and whose shadow fell oft across the walls of Tuor's house. Then sank the sun, and they saw Gondolin no more.

Now the pass of Cristhorn, that is the Eagles' Cleft, is one of dangerous going, and that host had not ventured it by dark, lanternless and without torches, and very weary and cumbered with women and children and sick and stricken men, had it not been for their great fear of Melko's scouts, for it was a great company and might not fare very secretly. Darkness gathered rapidly as they approached that high place, and they must string out into a long and straggling line. Galdor and a band of men spear-armed went ahead, and Legolas was with them, whose eyes

were like cats' for the dark, yet could they see further. Thereafter
followed the least weary of the women supporting the sick and the
wounded that could go on foot. Idril was with these, and Eärendel
who bore up well, but Tuor was in the midmost behind them with
all his men of the Wing, and they bare some who were grievously
hurt, and Egalmoth was with him, but he had got a hurt in that
sally from the square. Behind again came many women with
babes, and girls, and lamed men, yet was the going slow enough
for them. At the rearmost went the largest band of men battle-
whole, and there was Glorfindel of the golden hair.

Thus were they come to Cristhorn, which is an ill place by
reason of its height, for this is so great that spring nor summer
come ever there, and it is very cold. Indeed while the valley dances
in the sun, there all the year snow dwells in those bleak places, and
even as they came there the wind howled, coming from the north
behind them, and it bit sorely. Snow fell and whirled in wind-
eddies and got into their eyes, and this was not good, for there the
path is narrow, and of the right or westerly hand a sheer wall rises
nigh seven chains from the way, ere it bursts atop into jagged
pinnacles where are many eyries. There dwells Thorndor King of
Eagles, Lord of the Thornhoth, whom the Eldar named Sorontur.
But of the other hand is a fall not right sheer yet dreadly steep, and
it has long teeth of rock up-pointing so that one may climb down –
or fall maybe – but by no means up. And from that deep is no
escape at either end any more than by the sides, and Thorn Sir
runs at bottom. He falls therein from the south over a great
precipice but with a slender water, for he is a thin stream in those
heights, and he issues to the north after flowing but a rocky mile
above ground down a narrow passage that goes into the mountain,
and scarce a fish could squeeze through with him.

Galdor and his men were come now to the end nigh to where
Thorn Sir falls into the abyss, and the others straggled, for all
Tuor's efforts, back over most of the mile of the perilous way
between chasm and cliff, so that Glorfindel's folk were scarce
come to its beginning, when there was a yell in the night that
echoed in that grim region. Behold, Galdor's men were beset in
the dark suddenly by shapes leaping from behind rocks where they
had lain hidden even from the glance of Legolas. It was Tuor's
thought that they had fallen in with one of Melko's ranging
companies, and he feared no more than a sharp brush in the dark,
yet he sent the women and sick around him rearward and joined
his men to Galdor's, and there was an affray upon the perilous

path. But now rocks fell from above, and things looked ill, for they did grievous hurt; but matters seemed to Tuor yet worse when the noise of arms came from the rear, and tidings were said to him by a man of the Swallow that Glorfindel was ill bested by men from behind, and that a Balrog was with them.

Then was he sore afraid of a trap, and this was even what had in truth befallen; for watchers had been set by Melko all about the encircling hills. Yet so many did the valour of the Gondothlim draw off to the assault ere the city could be taken that these were but thinly spread, and were at the least here in the south. Nonetheless one of these had espied the company as they started the upward going from the dale of hazels, and as many bands were got together against them as might be, and devised to fall upon the exiles to front and rear even upon the perilous way of Cristhorn. Now Galdor and Glorfindel held their own despite the surprise of assault, and many of the Orcs were struck into the abyss; but the falling of the rocks was like to end all their valour, and the flight from Gondolin to come to ruin. The moon about that hour rose above the pass, and the gloom somewhat lifted, for his pale light filtered into dark places; yet it lit not the path for the height of the walls. Then arose Thorndor, King of Eagles, and he loved not Melko, for Melko had caught many of his kindred and chained them against sharp rocks to squeeze from them the magic words whereby he might learn to fly (for he dreamed of contending even against Manwë in the air); and when they would not tell he cut off their wings and sought to fashion therefrom a mighty pair for his use, but it availed not.

Now when the clamour from the pass rose to his great eyrie he said: "Wherefore are these foul things, these Orcs of the hills, climbed near to my throne; and why do the sons of the Noldoli cry out in the low places for fear of the children of Melko the accursed? Arise O Thornhoth, whose beaks are of steel and whose talons swords!"

Thereupon there was a rushing like a great wind in rocky places, and the Thornhoth, the people of the Eagles, fell on those Orcs who had scaled above the path, and tore their faces and their hands and flung them to the rocks of Thorn Sir far below. Then were the Gondothlim glad, and they made in after days the Eagle a sign of their kindred in token of their joy, and Idril bore it, but Eärendel loved rather the Swan-wing of his father. Now unhampered Galdor's men bore back those that opposed them, for they were not very many and the onset of the Thornhoth affrighted them much; and the company fared forward again, though Glorfindel had fighting enough in the rear. Already the half had passed the perilous way and the falls of Thorn Sir, when that Balrog that was with the rearward foe leapt with great might on certain lofty rocks that stood into the path on the left side upon the lip of the chasm, and thence with a leap of fury he was past Glorfindel's men and among the women and the sick in front, lashing with his whip of flame. Then Glorfindel leapt forward upon him and his golden armour gleamed strangely in the moon, and he hewed at that demon that it leapt again upon a great boulder and Glorfindel after. Now there was a deadly combat upon that high rock above the folk; and these, pressed behind and hindered ahead, were grown so close that well nigh all could see, yet was it over ere Glorfindel's men could leap to his side. The ardour of Glorfindel drave that Balrog from point to point, and his mail fended him from its whip and claw. Now had he beaten a heavy swinge upon its iron helm, now hewn off the creature's whip-arm at the elbow. Then sprang the Balrog in the torment of his pain and fear full at Glorfindel, who stabbed like a dart of a snake; but he found only a shoulder, and was grappled, and they swayed to a fall upon the crag-top. Then Glorfindel's left hand sought a dirk, and this he thrust up that it pierced the Balrog's belly nigh his own face (for that demon was double his stature); and it shrieked, and fell backwards from the rock, and falling clutched Glorfindel's yellow locks beneath his cap, and those twain fell into the abyss.

Now was this a very grievous thing, for Glorfindel was most dearly beloved — and lo! the dint of their fall echoed about the hills, and the abyss of Thorn Sir rang. Then at the death-cry of the Balrog the Orcs before and behind wavered and were slain or fled far away, and Thorndor himself, a mighty bird, descended to the abyss and brought up the body of Glorfindel; but the Balrog lay, and the water of Thorn Sir ran black for many a day far below in Tumladin.

Still do the Eldar say when they see good fighting at great odds of power against a fury of evil: "Alas! 'Tis Glorfindel and the Balrog", and their hearts are still sore for that fair one of the Noldoli. Because of their love, despite the haste and their fear of the advent of new foes, Tuor let raise a great stone-cairn over Glorfindel just there beyond the perilous way by the precipice of Eagle-stream, and Thorndor has let not yet any harm come thereto, but yellow flowers have fared thither and blow ever now

about that mound in those unkindly places; but the folk of the
Golden Flower wept at its building and might not dry their tears.

Now who shall tell of the wanderings of Tuor and the exiles of
Gondolin in the wastes that lie beyond the mountains to the south
of the vale of Tumladin? Miseries were theirs and death, colds and
hungers, and ceaseless watches. That they won ever through those
regions infested by Melko's evil came from the great slaughter and
damage done to his power in that assault, and from the speed and
wariness with which Tuor led them; for of a certain Melko knew of
that escape and was furious thereat. Ulmo had heard tidings in the
far oceans of the deeds that were done, but he could not yet aid
them for they were far from waters and rivers – and indeed they
thirsted sorely, and they knew not the way.

But after a year and more of wandering, in which many a time
they journeyed long tangled in the magic of those wastes only to
come again upon their own tracks, once more the summer came,
and nigh to its height[37] they came at last upon a stream, and
following this came to better lands and were a little comforted.
Here did Voronwë guide them, for he had caught a whisper of
Ulmo's in that stream one late summer's night – and he got ever
much wisdom from the sound of waters. Now he led them even till
they came down to Sirion which that stream fed, and then both
Tuor and Voronwë saw that they were not far from the outer issue
of old of the Way of Escape, and were once more in that deep
dale of alders. Here were all the bushes trampled and the trees
burnt, and the dale-wall scarred with flame, and they wept, for
they thought they knew the fate of those who sundered aforetime
from them at the tunnel-mouth.

Now they journeyed down that river but were again in fear from
Melko, and fought affrays with his Orc-bands and were in peril
from the wolfriders, but his firedrakes sought not at them, both
for the great exhaustion of their fires in the taking of Gondolin,
and the increasing power of Ulmo as the river grew. So came they
after many days – for they went slowly and got their sustenance
very hardly – to those great heaths and morasses above the Land of
Willows, and Voronwë knew not those regions. Now here goes
Sirion a very great way under earth, diving at the great cavern of
the Tumultuous Winds, but running clear again above the Pools
of Twilight, even where Tulkas[38] after fought with Melko's self.
Tuor had fared over these regions by night and dusk after Ulmo
came to him amid the reeds, and he remembered not the ways. In

places that land is full of deceits and very marshy; and here the host had long delay and was vexed by sore flies, for it was autumn still, and agues and fevers fared amongst them, and they cursed Melko.

Yet came they at last to the great pools and the edges of that most tender Land of Willows; and the very breath of the winds thereof brought rest and peace to them, and for the comfort of that place the grief was assuaged of those who mourned the dead in that great fall. There women and maids grew fair again and their sick were healed, and old wounds ceased to pain; yet they alone who of reason feared their folk living still in bitter thraldom in the Hells of Iron sang not, nor did they smile.

Here they abode very long indeed, and Eärendel was a grown boy ere the voice of Ulmo's conches drew the heart of Tuor, that his sea-longing returned with a thirst the deeper for years of stifling; and all that host arose at his bidding, and got them down Sirion to the Sea.

Now the folk that had passed into the Eagles' Cleft and who saw the fall of Glorfindel had been nigh eight hundreds — a large wayfaring, yet was it a sad remnant of so fair and numerous a city. But they who arose from the grasses of the Land of Willows in years after and fared away to sea, when spring set celandine in the meads and they had held sad festival in memorial of Glorfindel, these numbered but three hundreds and a score of men and man-children, and two hundreds and three score of women and maid-children. Now the number of women was few because of their hiding or being stowed by their kinsfolk in secret places in the city. There they were burned or slain or taken and enthralled, and the rescue-parties found them too seldom; and it is the greatest ruth to think of this, for the maids and women of the Gondothlim were as fair as the sun and as lovely as the moon and brighter than the stars. Glory dwelt in that city of Gondolin of the Seven Names, and its ruin was the most dread of all the sacks of cities upon the face of Earth. Nor Bablon, nor Ninwi, nor the towers of Trui, nor all the many takings of Rûm that is greatest among Men, saw such terror as fell that day upon Amon Gwareth in the kindred of the Gnomes; and this is esteemed the worst work that Melko has yet thought of in the world.

Yet now those exiles of Gondolin dwelt at the mouth of Sirion by the waves of the Great Sea. There they take the name of Lothlim, the people of the flower, for Gondothlim is a name too sore to their hearts; and fair among the Lothlim Eärendel grows in the house of his father,[39] and the great tale of Tuor is come to its waning.'

Then said Littleheart son of Bronweg: 'Alas for Gondolin.'

And no one in all the Room of Logs spake or moved for a great while.

NOTES

1   Not of course the great journey to the Sea from the Waters of Awakening, but the expedition of the Elves of Kôr for the rescue of the Gnomes (see I. 26).

2   A *korin* is defined in *The Cottage of Lost Play* (I.16) as 'a great circular hedge, be it of stone or of thorn or even of trees, that encloses a green sward'; Meril-i-Turinqi dwelt 'in a great *korin* of elms'.

3   *Tôn a Gwedrin* is the Tale-fire.

4   There is here a direction: 'See hereafter the Nauglafring', but this is struck out.

5   On Heorrenda see pp. 290ff, 323. A small space is left after the words 'it is thus' to mark the place of the poem in Old English that was to be inserted, but there is no indication of what it was to be.

(In the following notes 'the original reading' refers to the text of Tuor A, *and of* Tuor B *before the emendation in question. It does not imply that the reading of* Tuor A *was, or was not, found in the original pencilled text (in the great majority of cases this cannot be said).)*

6   This passage, beginning with the words 'And Tuor entered that cavern . . .' on p. 149, is a late replacement written on a slip (see p. 147). The original passage was largely similar in meaning, but contained the following:

> Now in delving that riverway beneath the hills the Noldoli worked unknown to Melko who in those deep days held them yet hidden and thralls beneath his will. Rather were they prompted by Ulmo who strove ever against Melko; and through Tuor he hoped to devise for the Gnomes release from the terror of the evil of Melko.

7   'three days': 'three years' all texts, but 'days?' pencilled above 'years' in *Tuor B*.

8   The 'evolution' of sea-birds through Ossë is described in the tale of *The Coming of the Elves*, I.123; but the sentence here derives from the original pencilled text of *Tuor A*.

9   In the typescript *Tuor C* a blank was left here (see p. 147) and subsequently filled in with 'Ulmo', not 'Ainur'.

10 The original reading was: 'Thou Tuor of the lonely heart the Valar will not to dwell for ever in fair places of birds and flowers; nor would they lead thee through this pleasant land . . .'

11 *Tuor C* adds here: 'with Ulmo's aid'.

12 The reference to the Battle of Unnumbered Tears is a later addition to *Tuor B*. The original reading was: 'who alone escaped Melko's power when he caught their folk . . .'

13 In *Tuor A* and *B Voronwë* is used throughout, but this phrase, with the form *Bronweg*, is an addition to *Tuor B* (replacing the original 'Now after many days these twain found a deep dale').

14 The typescript *Tuor C* has here:

> . . . that none, were they not of the blood of the Noldoli, might light on it, neither by chance nor agelong search. Thus was it secure from all ill hap save treachery alone, and never would Tûr have won thereto but for the steadfastness of that Gnome Voronwë.

In the next sentence *Tuor C* has 'yet even so no few of the bolder of the Gnomes enthralled would slip down the river Sirion from the fell mountains'.

15 The original reading was: 'his speech they comprehended, though somewhat different was the tongue of the free Noldoli by those days to that of the sad thralls of Melko.' The typescript *Tuor C* has: 'they comprehended him for they were Noldoli. Then spake Tûr also in the same tongue . . .'

16 The original reading was: 'It was early morn when they drew near the gates and many eyes gazed . . .' But when Tuor and Voronwë first saw Gondolin it was 'in the new light of the morning' (p. 158), and it was 'a day's light march' across the plain; hence the change made later to *Tuor B*.

17 'Evil One': original reading 'Ainu'.

18 This passage, from 'Rugged was his aspect . . .', is a replacement on a separate slip; the original text was:

> Tuor was goodly in countenance but rugged and unkempt of locks and clad in the skins of bears, yet his stature was not overgreat among his own folk, but the Gondothlim, though not bent as were no few of their kin who laboured at ceaseless delving and hammering for Melko, were small and slender and lithe.

In the original passage Men are declared to be of their nature taller than the Elves of Gondolin. See pp. 142, 220.

19 'come hither': 'escaped from Melko' *Tuor C*.

20 'folk': original reading 'men'. This is the only place where 'men' in reference to Elves is changed. The use is constant in *The Fall of Gondolin*, and even occurs once in an odd-sounding reference to

the hosts of Melko: 'But now the men of Melko have assembled their forces' (p. 183).

21   The passage ending here and beginning with the words 'Then Tuor's heart was heavy . . .' on p. 162 was bracketed by my father in *Tuor B*, and on a loose slip referring to this bracketed passage he wrote:

> (If nec[essary]): Then is told how Idril daughter of the king added her words to the king's wisdom so that Turgon bid Tuor rest himself awhile in Gondolin, and being forewise prevailed on him [to] abide there in the end. How he came to love the daughter of the king, Idril of the Silver Feet, and how he was taught deeply in the lore of that great folk and learned of its history and the history of the Elves. How Tuor grew in wisdom and mighty in the counsels of the Gondothlim.

The only narrative difference here from the actual text lies in the introduction of the king's daughter Idril as an influence on Tuor's decision to remain in Gondolin. The passage is otherwise an extremely abbreviated summary of the account of Tuor's instruction in Gondolin, with omission of what is said in the text about the preparations of the Gondothlim against attack; but I do not think that this was a proposal for shortening the written tale. Rather, the words 'If necessary' suggest strongly that my father had in mind only a reduction for oral delivery – and that was when it was read to the Exeter College Essay Club in the spring of 1920; see p. 147. Another proposed shortening is given in note 32.

22   This passage, beginning 'Great love too had Idril for Tuor . . .', was written on a separate slip and replaced the original text as follows:

> The king hearing of this, and finding that his child Idril, whom the Eldar speak of as Irildë, loved Tuor in return, he consented to their being wed, seeing that he had no son, and Tuor was like to make a kinsman of strength and consolation. There were Idril and Tuor wed before the folk in that Place of the Gods, Gar Ainion, nigh the king's palace; and that was a day of mirth to the city of Gondolin, but of (&c.)

The replacement states that the marriage of Tuor and Idril was the first but not the last of the unions of Man and Elf, whereas it is said in the Name-list to *The Fall of Gondolin* that Eärendel was 'the only being that is half of the kindred of the Eldalië and half of Men' (see p. 215).

23   The phrase 'and that tale of Isfin and Eöl may not here be told' was added to *Tuor B*. See p. 220.

24   Original reading: 'a name wrought of the tongue of the Gondothlim'.

25   The sapphires given to Manwë by the Noldoli are referred to in the

tale of *The Coming of the Elves*, I. 128. The original pencilled text of *Tuor A* can be read here: 'bluer than the sapphires of Súlimo'.

26 The passage ending here and beginning with 'In these ways that bitter winter passed . . .' is inserted on a separate sheet in *Tuor B* (but is not part of the latest layer of emendation); it replaces a much shorter passage going back to the primary text of *Tuor A*:

> Now on midwinter's day at early even the sun sank betimes beyond the mountains, and lo! when she had gone a light arose beyond the hills to the north, and men marvelled (&c.)

See notes 34 and 37.

27 The Scarlet Heart: the heart of Finwë Nólemë, Turgon's father, was cut out by Orcs in the Battle of Unnumbered Tears, but it was regained by Turgon and became his emblem; see I. 241 and note 11.

28 This passage describing the array and the emblems of the houses of the Gondothlim was relatively very little affected by the later revision of *Tuor A*; the greater part of it is in the original pencilled text, which was allowed to stand, and all the names appear to be original.

29 The word 'burg' is used in the Old English sense of a walled and fortified town.

30 The death of Ecthelion in the primary text of *Tuor A* is legible; the revision introduced a few changes of wording, but no more.

31 This sentence, from 'and men shuddered', was added to *Tuor B*. On the prophecy see I. 172.

32 *Tuor B* is bracketed from 'Now comes Tuor at their head to the Place of Wedding' on p. 186 to this point, and an inserted slip relating to this bracketing reads:

> How Tuor and his folk came upon Idril wandering distraught in the Place of the Gods. How Tuor and Idril from that high place saw the sack of the King's Hall and the ruin of the King's Tower and the passing of the king, for which reason the foe followed not after. How Tuor heard tidings of Voronwë that Idril had sent Eärendel and her guard down the hidden way, and fared into the city in search of her husband; how in peril from the enemy they had rescued many that fled and sent them down the secret way. How Tuor led his host with the luck of the Gods to the mouth of that passage, and how all descended into the plain, sealing the entrance utterly behind them. How the sorrowful company issued into a dell in the vale of Tumladin.

This is simply a summary of the text as it stands; I suppose it was a cut proposed for the recitation of the tale if that seemed to be taking too long (see note 21).

33 This passage, from 'Here were gathered . . .', replaced in *Tuor B* the original reading: 'Here they are fain to rest, but finding no signs of

Eärendel and his escort Tuor is downcast, and Idril weeps.' This was rewritten partly for narrative reasons, but also to put it into the past tense. In the next sentence the text was emended from 'Lamentation is there . . .' and 'about them looms . . .' But the sentence following ('Fire-drakes are about it . . .') was left untouched; and I think that it was my father's intention, only casually indicated and never carried through, to reduce the amount of 'historical present' in the narrative.

34 'for summer is at hand': the original reading was 'albeit it is winter'. See notes 26 and 37.

35 The original reading was:

> Now the Mountains were on that side seven leagues save a mile from Gondolin, and Cristhorn the Cleft of Eagles another league of upward going from the beginning of the Mountains; wherefore they were now yet two leagues and part of a third from the pass, and very weary thereto.

36 'Behold, his face shineth as a star in the waste' was added to *Tuor B*.

37 This passage, from 'But after a year and more of wandering . . .', replaced the original reading 'But after a half-year's wandering, nigh midsummer'. This emendation depends on the changing of the time of the attack on Gondolin from midwinter to the 'Gates of Summer' (see notes 26 and 34). Thus in the revised version summer is retained as the season when the exiles came to the lands about Sirion, but they spent a whole year and more, rather than a half-year, to reach them.

38 'even where Tulkas': original reading: 'even where Noldorin and Tulkas'. See pp. 278–9.

39 The original pencilled text of *Tuor A* had 'Fair among the Lothlim grows Eärendel in Sornontur the house of Tuor'. The fourth letter of this name could as well be read as a *u*.

Changes made to names in
The Fall of Gondolin

Ilfiniol < *Elfriniol* in the first three occurrences of the name in the initial linking passage, *Ilfiniol* so written at the fourth.

(In *The Cottage of Lost Play* (I.15) the Gong-warden of Mar Vanwa Tyaliéva is named only *Littleheart*; in the *Link* to *The Music of the Ainur* his Elvish name is *Ilverin* < *Elwenildo* (I.46,52); and in the *Link* to the *Tale of Tinúviel* he is *Ilfiniol* < *Elfriniol* as here, while the typescript has *Ilfrin* (p. 7).

In the head-note to the Name-list to *The Fall of Gondolin* he is *Elfrith* < *Elfriniel*, and this is the only place where the meaning of the name 'Littleheart' is explained (p. 148); the Name-list has an entry 'Elf meaneth "heart" (as Elfin Elben): Elfrith is Littleheart' (see I.255, entry Ilverin). In another projected list of names, abandoned after only a couple of entries had been made, we meet again the form Elfrith, and also Elbenil > Elwenil.

This constant changing of name is to be understood in relation to swiftly changing phonological ideas and formulations, but even so is rather extraordinary.)

> In the following notes it is to be understood, for brevity's sake, that names in Tuor B (before emendation) are found in the same form in Tuor A; e.g. 'Mithrim < Asgon in Tuor B' implies that Tuor A has Asgon (unchanged).

Tuor   Although sometimes emended to Tûr in Tuor B, and invariably written Tûr in the typescript Tuor C, I give Tuor throughout; see p. 148.

Dor Lómin   This name was so written from the first in Tuor B. Tuor A has, at the first three occurrences, Aryador > Mathusdor; at the fourth, Aryador > Mathusdor > Dor Lómin.

Mithrim   < Asgon throughout Tuor B; Tuor C has Asgon unchanged.

Glorfalc or Cris Ilbranteloth (p. 150)   Tuor A has Glorfalc or Teld Quing Ilon; Tuor B as written had no Elvish names, Glorfalc or Cris Ilbranteloth being a later addition.

Ainur   As in the first draft of The Music of the Ainur (I.61) the original text of Tuor A had Ainu plural.

Falasquil   At both occurrences (p. 152) in Tuor A this replaces the original name now illegible but beginning with Q; in Tuor B my mother left blanks and added the name later in pencil; in Tuor C blanks are left in the typescript and not filled in.

Arlisgion   This name was added later to Tuor B.

Orcs   Tuor A and B had Orqui throughout; my father emended this in Tuor B to Orcs, but not consistently, and in the later part of the tale not at all. In one place only (p. 193, in Thorndor's speech) both texts have Orcs (also Orc-bands p. 195). As with the name Tuor/Tûr I give throughout the form that was to prevail.

At the only occurrence of the singular the word is written with a k in both Tuor A and B ('Ork's blood', p. 165).

Gar Thurion   < Gar Furion in Tuor B (Gar Furion in Tuor C).

Loth   < Lôs in Tuor B (Lôs in Tuor C).

Lothengriol   < Lósengriol in Tuor B (Lósengriol in Tuor C).

Taniquetil   At the occurrence on p. 161 there was added in the original text of Tuor A: (Danigwiel), but this was struck out.

Kôr   Against this name (p. 161) is pencilled in Tuor B: Tûn. See I.222, II.292.

Gar Ainion   < Gar Ainon in Tuor B (p. 164; at the occurrence on p. 186 not emended, but I read Gar Ainion in both places).

Nost-na-Lothion   < Nost-na-Lossion in Tuor B.

Duilin At the first occurrence (p. 173) < *Duliglin* in the original text of
Tuor A.

Rog In *Tuor A* spelt *Rôg* in the earlier occurrences, *Rog* in the later; in
Tuor B spelt *Rôg* throughout but mostly emended later to *Rog*.

Dramborleg At the occurrence on p. 181 < *Drambor* in the original
text of *Tuor A*.

Bansil At the occurrence on p. 184 only, *Bansil* > *Banthil* in *Tuor B*.

Cristhorn From the first occurrence on p. 189 written *Cristhorn* (not
Cris Thorn) in *Tuor A*; *Cris Thorn Tuor B* throughout.

Bad Uthwen < *Bad Uswen* in *Tuor B*. The original reading in *Tuor A*
was (apparently) *Bad Usbran*.

Sorontur < *Ramandur* in *Tuor B*.

Bablon, Ninwi, Trui, Rûm The original text of *Tuor A* had *Babylon*,
Nineveh, *Troy*, and (probably) *Rome*. These were changed to the
forms given in the text, except *Nineveh* > *Ninwë*, changed to
Ninwi in *Tuor B*.

Commentary on
The Fall of Gondolin

§1. The primary narrative

As with the *Tale of Turambar* I break my commentary on this tale into
sections. I refer frequently to the much later version (which extends only
to the coming of Tuor and Voronwë to sight of Gondolin across the
plain) printed in *Unfinished Tales* pp. 17–51 ('Of Tuor and his Coming
to Gondolin'); this I shall call here 'the later *Tuor*'.

(i) Tuor's journey to the Sea and the visitation
of Ulmo (pp. 149–56)

In places the later *Tuor* (the abandonment of which is one of the saddest
facts in the whole history of incompletion) is so close in wording to *The
Fall of Gondolin*, written more than thirty years before, as to make it
almost certain that my father had it in front of him, or at least had
recently reread it. Striking examples from the late version (pp. 23–4)
are: 'The sun rose behind his back and set before his face, and where the
water foamed among the boulders or rushed over sudden falls, at morning
and evening rainbows were woven across the stream'; 'Now he said: "It is
a fay-voice," now: "Nay, it is a small beast that is wailing in the waste"';
'[Tuor] wandered still for some days in a rugged country bare of trees;
and it was swept by a wind from the sea, and all that grew there, herb or
bush, leaned ever to the dawn because of the prevalence of that wind
from the West' – which are very closely similar to or almost identical with

passages in the tale (pp. 150–1). But the differences in the narrative are profound.

Tuor's origin is left vague in the old story. There is a reference in the *Tale of Turambar* (p. 88) to 'those kindreds about the waters of Asgon whence after arose Tuor son of Peleg', but here it is said that Tuor did not dwell with his people (who 'wandered the forests and fells') but 'lived alone about that lake called Mithrim [< Asgon]', on which he journeyed in a small boat with a prow made like the neck of a swan. There is indeed scarcely any linking reference to other events, and of course no trace of the Grey-elves of Hithlum who in the later story fostered him, or of his outlawry and hunting by the Easterlings; but there are 'wandering Noldoli' in Dor Lómin (Hisilómë, Hithlum) – on whom see p. 65 – from whom Tuor learnt much, including their tongue, and it was they who guided him down the dark river-passage under the mountains. There is in this a premonition of Gelmir and Arminas, the Noldorin Elves who guided Tuor through the Gate of the Noldor (later *Tuor* pp. 21–2), and the story that the Noldoli 'made that hidden way at the prompting of Ulmo' survived in the much richer historical context of the later legend, where 'the Gate of the Noldor . . . was made by the skill of that people, long ago in the days of Turgon' (later *Tuor* p. 18).

The later *Tuor* becomes very close to the old story for a time when Tuor emerges out of the tunnel into the ravine (later called Cirith Ninniach, but still a name of Tuor's own devising); many features recur, such as the stars shining in the 'dark lane of sky above him', the echoes of his harping (in the tale of course without the literary echoes of Morgoth's cry and the voices of Fëanor's host that landed there), his doubt concerning the mournful calling of the gulls, the narrowing of the ravine where the incoming tide (fierce because of the west wind) met the water of the river, and Tuor's escape by climbing to the cliff-top (but in the tale the connection between Tuor's curiosity concerning the gulls and the saving of his life is not made: he climbed the cliff in response to the prompting of the Ainur). Notable is the retention of the idea that Tuor was the first of Men to reach the Sea, standing on the cliff-top with outspread arms, and of his 'sea-longing' (later *Tuor* p. 25). But the story of his dwelling in the cove of Falasquil and his adornment of it with carvings (and of course the floating of timber down the river to him by the Noldoli of Dor Lómin) was abandoned; in the later legend Tuor finds on the coast ruins of the ancient harbour-works of the Noldor from the days of Turgon's lordship in Nevrast, and of Turgon's former dwelling in these regions before he went to Gondolin there is in the old story no trace. Thus the entire Vinyamar episode is absent from it, and despite the frequent reminder that Ulmo was guiding Tuor as the instrument of his designs, the essential element in the later legend of the arms left for him by Turgon on Ulmo's instruction (*The Silmarillion* pp. 126, 238–9) is lacking.

The southward-flying swans (seven, not three, in the later *Tuor*) play essentially the same part in both narratives, drawing Tuor to continue his journey; but the emblem of the Swan was afterwards given a different origin, as 'the token of Annael and his foster-folk', the Grey-elves of Mithrim (later *Tuor* p. 25).

Both in the route taken (for the geography see p. 217) and in the seasons of the year my father afterwards departed largely from the original story of Tuor's journey to Gondolin. In the later *Tuor* it was the Fell Winter after the fall of Nargothrond, the winter of Túrin's return to Hithlum, when he and Voronwë journeyed in snow and bitter cold eastwards beneath the Mountains of Shadow. Here the journey takes far longer: he left Falasquil in 'the latest days of summer' (as still in the later *Tuor*) but he went down all the coast of Beleriand to the mouths of Sirion, and it was the summer of the following year when he lingered in the Land of Willows. (Doubtless the geography was less definite than it afterwards became, but its general resemblance to the later map seems assured by the description (p. 153) of the coast's trending after a time eastwards rather than southwards.)

Only in its place in the narrative structure is there resemblance between Ulmo's visitation of Tuor in the Land of Willows in a summer twilight and his tremendous epiphany out of the rising storm on the coast at Vinyamar. It is however most remarkable that the old vision of the Land of Willows and its drowsy beauty of river-flowers and butterflies was not lost, though afterwards it was Voronwë, not Tuor, who wandered there, devising names, and who stood enchanted 'knee-deep in the grass' (p. 155; later *Tuor* p. 35), until his fate, or Ulmo Lord of Waters, carried him down to the Sea. Possibly there is a faint reminiscence of the old story in Ulmo's words (later *Tuor* p. 28): 'Haste thou must learn, and *the pleasant road that I designed for thee* must be changed.'

In the tale, Ulmo's speech to Tuor (or at least that part of it that is reported) is far more simple and brief, and there is no suggestion there of Ulmo's 'opposing the will of his brethren, the Lords of the West'; but two essential elements of his later message are present, that Tuor will find the words to speak when he stands before Turgon, and the reference to Tuor's unborn son (in the later *Tuor* much less explicit: 'But it is not for thy valour only that I send thee, but to bring into the world a hope beyond thy sight, and a light that shall pierce the darkness').

(ii) *The journey of Tuor and Voronwë to Gondolin* (pp. 156–8)

Of Tuor's journey to Gondolin, apart from his sojourn in the Land of Willows, little is told in the tale, and Voronwë only appears late in its course as the one Noldo who was not too fearful to accompany him further; of Voronwë's history as afterwards related there is no word, and he is not an Elf of Gondolin.

It is notable that the Noldoli who guided Tuor northwards from the Land of Willows call themselves thralls of Melko. On this matter the *Tales* present a consistent picture. It is said in the *Tale of Tinúviel* (p. 9) that

> all the Eldar both those who remained in the dark or who had been lost upon the march from Palisor and those Noldoli too who fared back into the world after [Melko] seeking their stolen treasury fell beneath his power as thralls.

In *The Fall of Gondolin* it is said that the Noldoli did their service to Ulmo in secret, and 'out of fear of Melko wavered much' (p. 154), and Voronwë spoke to Tuor of 'the weariness of thraldom' (pp. 156–7); Melko sent out his army of spies 'to search out the dwelling of the Noldoli that had escaped his thraldom' (p. 166). These 'thrall-Noldoli' are represented as moving as it were freely about the lands, even to the mouths of Sirion, but they 'wandered as in a dream of fear, doing [Melko's] ill bidding, for the spell of bottomless dread was on them and they felt the eyes of Melko burn them from afar' (*Tale of Turambar*, p. 77). This expression is often used: Voronwë rejoiced in Gondolin that he no longer dreaded Melko with 'a binding terror' – 'and of a sooth that spell which Melko held over the Noldoli was one of bottomless dread, so that he seemed ever nigh them even were they far from the Hells of Iron, and their hearts quaked and they fled not even when they could' (p. 159). The spell of bottomless dread was laid too on Meglin (p. 169).

There is little in all this that cannot be brought more or less into harmony with the later narratives, and indeed one may hear an echo in the words of *The Silmarillion* (p. 156):

> But ever the Noldor feared most the treachery of those of their own kin, who had been thralls in Angband; for Morgoth used some of these for his evil purposes, and feigning to give them liberty sent them abroad, but their wills were chained to his, and they strayed only to come back to him again.

Nonetheless one gains the impression that at that time my father pictured the power of Melko when at its height as operating more diffusedly and intangibly, and perhaps also more universally, in the Great Lands. Whereas in *The Silmarillion* the Noldor who are not free are prisoners in Angband (whence a few may escape, and others with enslaved wills may be sent out), here all save the Gondothlim are 'thralls', controlled by Melko from afar, and Melko asserts that the Noldoli are all, by their very existence in the Great Lands, his slaves by right. It is a difference difficult to define, but that there is a difference may be seen in the improbability, for the later story, of Tuor being guided on his way to Gondolin by Noldor who were in any sense slaves of Morgoth.

The entrance to Gondolin has some general similarity to the far fuller and more precisely visualised account in the later *Tuor*: a deep river-gorge, tangled bushes, a cave-mouth – but the river is certainly Sirion (see the passage at the end of the tale, p. 195, where the exiles come back to the entrance), and the entrance to the secret way is in one of the steep river banks, quite unlike the description of the Dry River whose ancient bed was itself the secret way (later *Tuor* pp. 43–4). The long tunnel which Tuor and Voronwë traverse in the tale leads them at length not only to the Guard but also to sunlight, and they are 'at the foot of steep hills' and can see the city: in other words there is a simple conception of a plain, a ring-wall of mountains, and a tunnel through them leading to the outer world. In the later *Tuor* the approach to the city is much stranger: for the tunnel of the Guard leads to the ravine of Orfalch Echor, a great rift from top to bottom of the Encircling Mountains ('sheer as if axe-cloven', p. 46), up which the road climbed through the successive gates until it came to the Seventh Gate, barring the rift at the top. Only when this last gate was opened and Tuor passed through was he able to see Gondolin; and we must suppose (though the narrative does not reach this point) that the travellers had to descend again from the Seventh Gate in order to reach the plain.

It is notable that Tuor and Voronwë are received by the Guard without any of the suspicion and menace that greeted them in the later story (p. 45).

(iii)   *Tuor in Gondolin* (pp. 159–64)

With this section of the narrative compare *The Silmarillion*, p. 126:

> Behind the circle of the mountains the people of Turgon grew and throve, and they put forth their skill in labour unceasing, so that Gondolin upon Amon Gwareth became fair indeed and fit to compare even with Elven Tirion beyond the sea. High and white were its walls, and smooth its stairs, and tall and strong was the Tower of the King. There shining fountains played, and in the courts of Turgon stood images of the Trees of old, which Turgon himself wrought with elven-craft; and the Tree which he made of gold was named Glingal, and the Tree whose flowers he made of silver was named Belthil.

The image of Gondolin was enduring, and it reappears in the glimpses given in notes for the continuation of the later *Tuor* (*Unfinished Tales* p. 56): 'the stairs up to its high platform, and its great gate . . . the Place of the Fountain, the King's tower on a pillared arcade, the King's house . . .' Indeed the only real difference that emerges from the original account concerns the Trees of Gondolin, which in the former were unfading, 'shoots of old from the glorious Trees of Valinor', but in *The Silmarillion* were images made of the precious metals. On the Trees of Gondolin see the entries *Bansil* and *Glingol* from the Name-list, given below pp. 214–16. The gift by the Gods of these 'shoots' (which 'blossomed eternally without abating') to Inwë and Nólemë at the time of the building of Kôr, each being given a shoot of either Tree, is mentioned in *The Coming of the Elves* (I.123), and in *The Hiding of Valinor* there is a reference to the uprooting of those given to Nólemë, which 'were gone no one knew whither, and more had there never been' (I.213).

But a deep underlying shift in the history of Gondolin separates the earlier and later accounts: for whereas in the *Lost Tales* (and later) Gondolin was only discovered *after* the Battle of Unnumbered Tears when the host of Turgon retreated southwards down Sirion, in *The Silmarillion* it had been found by Turgon of Nevrast more than four hundred years before (442 years before Tuor came to Gondolin in the Fell Winter after the fall of Nargothrond in the year 495 of the Sun). In the tale my father imagined a great age passing *between* the Battle of Unnumbered Tears and the destruction of the city ('unstaying labour *through ages of years* had not sufficed to its building and adornment whereat folk travailed yet', p. 163); afterwards, with radical changes in the chronology of the First Age after the rising of the Sun and Moon, this period was reduced to no more than (in the last extant version of 'The Tale of Years' of the First Age) thirty-eight years. But the old conception can still be felt in the passage on p. 240 of *The Silmarillion* describing the withdrawal of the people of Gondolin from all concern with the world outside after the Nirnaeth Arnoediad, with its air of long years passing.*

In *The Silmarillion* it is explicit that Turgon devised the city to be 'a memorial of Tirion upon Túna' (p. 125), and it became 'as beautiful as a memory of Elven Tirion' (p. 240). This is not said in the old story, and indeed in the *Lost Tales* Turgon himself had never known Kôr (he was born in the Great Lands after the return of the Noldoli from Valinor, I.167, 238, 240); one may feel nonetheless that the tower of the King, the fountains and stairs, the white marbles of Gondolin embody a recollection of Kôr as it is described in *The Coming of the Elves and the Making of Kôr* (I.122–3).

I have said above that 'despite the frequent reminder that Ulmo was guiding Tuor as the instrument of his designs, the essential element in the later legend of the arms left for him by Turgon on Ulmo's instruction is lacking'. Now however we seem to see the germ of this conception in Turgon's words to Tuor (p. 161): 'Thy coming was set in our books of wisdom, and it has been written that there would come to pass many great things in the homes of the Gondothlim whenso thou faredst hither.' Yet it is clear from Tuor's reply that as yet the establishment of Gondolin was no part of Ulmo's design, since 'there have come to the ears of Ulmo whispers of your dwelling and your hill of vigilance against the evil of Melko, and he is glad'.

---

* Of the story of Gondolin from Tuor's coming to its destruction my father wrote nothing after the version of 'The Silmarillion' made (very probably) in 1930; and in this the old conception of its history was still present. This was the basis for much of Chapter 23 in the published work.

In the tale, Ulmo foresaw that Turgon would be unwilling to take up arms against Melko, and he fell back, through the mouth of Tuor, on a second counsel: that Turgon send Elves from Gondolin down Sirion to the coasts, there to build ships to carry messages to Valinor. To this Turgon replied, decisively and unanswerably, that he had sent messengers down the great river with this very purpose 'for years untold', and since all had been unavailing he would now do so no more. Now this clearly relates to a passage in *The Silmarillion* (p. 159) where it is said that Turgon, after the Dagor Bragollach and the breaking of the Siege of Angband,

> sent companies of the Gondolindrim in secret to the mouths of Sirion and the Isle of Balar. There they built ships, and set sail into the uttermost West upon Turgon's errand, seeking for Valinor, to ask for pardon and aid of the Valar; and they besought the birds of the sea to guide them. But the seas were wild and wide, and shadow and enchantment lay upon them; and Valinor was hidden. Therefore none of the messengers of Turgon came into the West, and many were lost and few returned.

Turgon did indeed do so once more, after the Battle of Unnumbered Tears (*The Silmarillion* p. 196), and the only survivor of that last expedition into the West was Voronwë of Gondolin. Thus, despite profound changes in chronology and a great development in the narrative of the last centuries of the First Age, the idea of the desperate attempts of Turgon to get a message through to Valinor goes back to the beginning.

Another aboriginal feature is that Turgon had no son; but (curiously) no mention whatsoever is made in the tale of his wife, the mother of Idril. In *The Silmarillion* (p. 90) his wife Elenwë was lost in the crossing of the Helcaraxë, but obviously this story belongs to a later period, when Turgon was born in Valinor.

The tale of Tuor's sojourn in Gondolin survived into the brief words of *The Silmarillion* (p. 241):

> And Tuor remained in Gondolin, for its bliss and its beauty and the wisdom of its people held him enthralled; and he became mighty in stature and in mind, and learned deeply of the lore of the exiled Elves.

In the present tale he 'heard tell of Ilúvatar, the Lord for Always, who dwelleth beyond the world', and of the Music of the Ainur. Knowledge of the very existence of Ilúvatar was, it seems, a prerogative of the Elves; long afterwards in the garden of Mar Vanwa Tyaliéva (I. 49) Eriol asked Rúmil: 'Who was Ilúvatar? Was he of the Gods?' and Rúmil answered: 'Nay, that he was not; for he made them. Ilúvatar is the Lord for Always, who dwells beyond the world.'

(iv)   *The encirclement of Gondolin;*
the treachery of Meglin (pp. 164–71)

The king's daughter was from the first named 'Idril of the Silver Feet' (Irildë in the language of the 'Eldar', note 22); Meglin (later Maeglin) was his nephew, though the name of his mother (Turgon's sister) Isfin was later changed.

In this section of the narrative the story in *The Silmarillion* (pp. 241–2) preserved all the essentials of the original version, with one major exception. The wedding of Tuor and Idril took place with the consent and full favour of the king, and there was great joy in Gondolin among all save Maeglin (whose love of Idril is told earlier in *The Silmarillion*, p. 139, where the barrier of his being close kin to her, not mentioned in the tale, is emphasised). Idril's power of foreseeing and her foreboding of evil to come; the secret way of her devising (but in the tale this led south from the city, and the Eagles' Cleft was in the southern mountains); the loss of Meglin in the hills while seeking for ore; his capture by Orcs, his treacherous purchase of life, and his return to Gondolin to avert suspicion (with the detail of his changed mood thereafter and 'smiling face') – all this remained. Much is of course absent (whether rejected or merely passed over) in the succinct account devised for *The Silmarillion* – where there is no mention, for example, of Idril's dream concerning Meglin, the watch set on him when he went to the hills, the formation on Idril's advice of a guard bearing Tuor's emblem, the refusal of Turgon to doubt the invulnerability of the city and his trust in Meglin, Meglin's discovery of the secret way,* or the remarkable story that it was Meglin himself who conceived the idea of the monsters of fire and iron and communicated it to Melko – a valuable defector indeed!

The great difference between the versions lies of course in the nature of Melko/Morgoth's knowledge of Gondolin. In the tale, he had by means of a vast army of spies† already discovered it before ever Meglin was captured, and creatures of Melko had found the 'Way of Escape' and looked down on Gondolin from the surrounding heights. Meglin's treachery in the old story lay in his giving an exact account of the structure of the city and the preparations made for its defence – and in his advice to Melko concerning the monsters of flame. In *The Silmarillion*, on the other hand, there is the element, devised much later, of the unconscious betrayal by Húrin to Morgoth's spies of the general region in which Gondolin must be sought, in 'the mountainous land between

---

* This is in fact specifically denied in *The Silmarillion*: 'she contrived it that the work was known but to few, and no whisper of it came to Maeglin's ears.'

† It seems that the 'creatures of blood' (said to be disliked by the people of Gondolin, p. 166), snakes, wolves, weasels, owls, falcons, are here regarded as the natural servants and allies of Melko.

Anach and the upper waters of Sirion, whither [Morgoth's] servants had never passed' (p. 241); but 'still no spy or creature out of Angband could come there because of the vigilance of the eagles' – and of this rôle of the eagles of the Encircling Mountains (though hostile to Melko, p. 193) there is in the original story no suggestion.

Thus in *The Silmarillion* Morgoth remained in ignorance until Maeglin's capture of the precise location of Gondolin, and Maeglin's information was of correspondingly greater value to him, as it was also of greater damage to the city. The history of the last years of Gondolin has thus a somewhat different atmosphere in the tale, for the Gondothlim are informed of the fact that Melko has 'encompassed the vale of Tumladin around' (p. 167), and Turgon makes preparations for war and strengthens the watch on the hills. The withdrawal of all Melko's spies shortly before the attack on Gondolin did indeed bring about a renewal of optimism among the Gondothlim, and in Turgon not least, so that when the attack came the people were unprepared; but in the later story the shock of the sudden assault is much greater, for there has never been any reason to suppose that the city is in immediate danger, and Idril's foreboding is peculiar to herself and more mysterious.

(v)   *The array of the Gondothlim* (pp. 171–4)

Though the central image of this part of the story – the people of Gondolin looking out from their walls to hail the rising sun on the feast of the Gates of Summer, but seeing a red light rising in the north and not in the east – survived, of all the heraldry in this passage scarcely anything is found in later writings. Doubtless, if my father had continued the later *Tuor*, much would have re-emerged, however changed, if we judge by the rich 'heraldic' descriptions of the great gates and their guards in the Orfalch Echor (pp. 46–50). But in the concise account in *The Silmarillion* the only vestiges are the titles Ecthelion 'of the Fountain'* and Glorfindel 'chief of the House of the Golden Flower of Gondolin'. Ecthelion and Glorfindel are named also in *The Silmarillion* (p. 194) as Turgon's captains who guarded the flanks of the host of Gondolin in their retreat down Sirion from the Nirnaeth Arnoediad, but of other captains named in the tale there is no mention afterwards† – though it is significant that the eighteenth Ruling Steward of Gondor was named Egalmoth, as the

---

* In the later *Tuor* (p. 50) he is 'Lord of the Fountains', plural (the reading in the manuscript is certain).

† In the version of 'The Silmarillion' made in 1930 (see footnote on p. 208), the last account of the Fall of Gondolin to be written and the basis for that in chapter 23 of the published work, the text actually reads: '. . . much is told in *The Fall of Gondolin*: of the death of Rog without the walls, and of the battle of Ecthelion of the Fountain ', &c. I removed the reference to Rog (*The Silmarillion* p. 242) on the grounds that it was absolutely certain that my father would not have retained this name as that of a lord of Gondolin.

seventeenth and twenty-fifth were named Ecthelion (*The Lord of the Rings*, Appendix A (I,ii)).*

Glorfindel 'of the golden hair' (p. 192) remains 'yellow-haired Glorfindel' in *The Silmarillion*, and this was from the beginning the meaning of his name.

(vi)   *The battle of Gondolin* (pp. 174–88)

Virtually the entire history of the fighting in Gondolin is unique in the tale of *The Fall of Gondolin*; the whole story is summarised in *The Silmarillion* (p. 242) in a few lines:

> Of the deeds of desperate valour there done, by the chieftains of the noble houses and their warriors, and not least by Tuor, much is told in *The Fall of Gondolin*: of the battle of Ecthelion of the Fountain with Gothmog Lord of Balrogs in the very square of the King, where each slew the other, and of the defence of the tower of Turgon by the people of his household, until the tower was overthrown: and mighty was its fall and the fall of Turgon in its ruin.
>
> Tuor sought to rescue Idril from the sack of the city, but Maeglin had laid hands on her, and on Eärendil; and Tuor fought with Maeglin on the walls, and cast him far out, and his body as it fell smote the rocky slopes of Amon Gwareth thrice ere it pitched into the flames below. Then Tuor and Idril led such remnants of the people of Gondolin as they could gather in the confusion of the burning down the secret way which Idril had prepared.

(In this highly compressed account the detail that Maeglin's body struck the slopes of Amon Gwareth three times before it 'pitched' into the flames was retained.) It would seem from *The Silmarillion* account that Maeglin's attempt on Idril and Eärendil took place much later in the fighting, and indeed shortly before the escape of the fugitives down the tunnel; but I think that this is far more likely to be the result of compression than of a change in the narrative of the battle.

In the tale Gondolin is very clearly visualised as a city, with its markets and its great squares, of which there are only vestiges in later writing (see above, p. 207); and there is nothing vague in the description of the fighting. The early conception of the Balrogs makes them less terrible, and certainly more destructible, than they afterwards became: they

---

* In a very late note written on one of the texts that constitute chapter 16 of *The Silmarillion* ('Of Maeglin') my father was thinking of making the 'three lords of his household' whom Turgon appointed to ride with Aredhel from Gondolin (p. 131) Glorfindel, Ecthelion, and Egalmoth. He notes that Ecthelion and Egalmoth 'are derived from the primitive F[all of]G[ondolin]', but that they 'are well-sounding and have been in print' (with reference to the names of the Stewards of Gondor). Subsequently he decided against naming Aredhel's escort.

existed in 'hundreds' (p. 170),* and were slain by Tuor and the Gondothlim in large numbers: thus five fell before Tuor's great axe Dramborleg, three before Ecthelion's sword, and two score were slain by the warriors of the king's house. The Balrogs are 'demons of power' (p. 181); they are capable of pain and fear (p. 194); they are attired in iron armour (pp. 181, 194), and they have whips of flame (a character they never lost) and claws of steel (pp. 169, 179).

In *The Silmarillion* the dragons that came against Gondolin were 'of the brood of Glaurung', which 'were become now many and terrible'; whereas in the tale the language employed (p. 170) suggests that some at least of the 'Monsters' were inanimate 'devices', the construction of smiths in the forges of Angband. But even the 'things of iron' that 'opened about their middles' to disgorge bands of Orcs are called 'ruthless beasts', and Gothmog 'bade' them 'pile themselves' (p. 176); those made of bronze or copper 'were given hearts and spirits of blazing fire'; while the 'fire-drake' that Tuor hewed screamed and lashed with its tail (p. 181).

A small detail of the narrative is curious: what 'messengers' did Meglin send to Melko to warn him to guard the outer entrance of the Way of Escape (where he guessed that the secret tunnel must lead in the end)? Whom could Meglin trust sufficiently? And who would dare to go?

(vii) *The escape of the fugitives*
and the battle in Cristhorn (pp. 188–95)

The story as told in *The Silmarillion* (p. 243) is somewhat fuller in its account of the escape of the fugitives from the city and the ambush in the Eagles' Cleft (there called Cirith Thoronath) than in that of the assault and sack itself, but only in one point are the two narratives actually at variance – as already noticed, the Eagles' Cleft was afterwards moved from the southern parts of the Encircling Mountains to the northern, and Idril's tunnel led north from the city (the comment is made that it was not thought 'that any fugitives would take a path towards the north and the highest parts of the mountains and the nighest to Angband'). The tale provides a richness of detail and an immediacy that is lacking in the short version, where such things as the tripping over dead bodies in the hot and reeking underground passage have disappeared; and there is no mention of the Gondothlim who against the counsel of Idril and Tuor went to the Way of Escape and were there destroyed by the dragon lying in wait,† or of the fight to rescue Eärendel.

---

* The idea that Morgoth disposed of a 'host' of Balrogs endured long, but in a late note my father said that only very few ever existed – 'at most seven'.

† This element in the story was in fact still present in the 1930 'Silmarillion' (see footnote on p. 208), but I excluded it from the published work on account of evidence in a much later text that the old entrance to Gondolin had by this time been blocked up – a fact which was then written into the text in chapter 23 of *The Silmarillion*.

In the tale appears the keen-sighted Elf Legolas Greenleaf, first of the names of the Fellowship of the Ring to appear in my father's writings (see p. 217 on this earlier Legolas), followed by Gimli (an Elf) in the *Tale of Tinúviel*.

In one point the story of the ambush in Cristhorn seems difficult to follow: this is the statement on p. 193 that the moon 'lit not the path for the height of the walls'. The fugitives were moving southwards through the Encircling Mountains, and the sheer rockwall above the path in the Eagles' Cleft was 'of the right or westerly hand', while on the left there was 'a fall . . . dreadly steep'. Surely then the moon rising in the east would illuminate the path?

The name *Cristhorn* appears in my father's drawing of 'Gondolin and the Vale of Tumladin from Cristhorn', September 1928 (*Pictures by J. R. R. Tolkien*, 1979, no. 35).

(viii)   *The wanderings of the Exiles of Gondolin* (pp. 195–7)

In *The Silmarillion* (p. 243) it is said that 'led by Tuor son of Huor the remnant of Gondolin passed over the mountains, and came down into the Vale of Sirion'. One would suppose that they came down into Dimbar, and so 'fleeing southward by weary and dangerous marches they came at length to Nan-tathren, the Land of Willows'. It seems strange in the tale that the exiles were wandering in the wilderness for more than a year, and yet achieved only to the outer entrance of the Way of Escape; but the geography of this region may have been vaguer when *The Fall of Gondolin* was written.

In *The Silmarillion* when Tuor and Idril went down from Nan-tathren to the mouths of Sirion they 'joined their people to the company of Elwing, Dior's daughter, that had fled thither but a little while before'. Of this there is no mention here; but I postpone consideration of this part of the narrative.

§2   *Entries in the Name-list to The Fall of Gondolin*

On this list see p. 148, where the head-note to it is given. Specifically linguistic information from the list, including meanings, is incorporated in the Appendix on Names, but I collect here some statements of other kind (arranged in alphabetical order) that are contained in it.

Bablon 'was a city of Men, and more rightly *Babylon*, but such is the Gnomes' name as they now shape it, and they got it from Men aforetime.'

Bansil 'Now this name had the Gondothlim for that tree before their king's door which bore silver blossom and faded not – and its name had Elfriniel from his father Voronwë; and it meaneth "Fairgleam". Now that tree of which it was a shoot (brought in the deep ages out

of Valinor by the Noldoli) had like properties, but greater, seeing
that for half the twenty-four hours it lit all Valinor with silver light.
This the Eldar still tell of as *Silpion* or "Cherry-moon", for its
blossom was like that of a cherry in spring – but of that tree in
Gondolin they know no name, and the Noldoli tell of it alone.'

Dor Lómin 'or the "Land of Shadows" was that region named of the
Eldar Hisilómë (and this means Shadowy Twilights) where Melko
shut Men, and it is so called by reason of the scanty sun which peeps
little over the Iron Mountains to the east and south of it – there dwell
now the Shadow Folk. Thence came Tuor to Gondolin.'

Eärendel 'was the son of Tuor and Idril and 'tis said the only being that
is half of the kindred of the Eldalië and half of Men. He was the
greatest and first of all mariners among Men, and saw regions that
Men have not yet found nor gazed upon for all the multitude of their
boats. He rideth now with Voronwë upon the winds of the firmament
nor comes ever further back than Kôr, else would he die like other
Men, so much of the mortal is in him.'

(For these last statements about Eärendel see pp. 264–5. The
statement that Eärendel was 'the only being that is half of the
kindred of the Eldalië and half of Men' is very notable. Presumably
this was written when Beren was an Elf, not a Man (see p. 139);
Dior son of Beren and Tinúviel appears in the *Tale of the
Nauglafring*, but there Beren is an Elf, and Dior is not Half-elven.
In the tale of *The Fall of Gondolin* itself it is said, but in a
later replacement passage (p. 164 and note 22), that Tuor was the
first but not the last to wed 'a daughter of Elfinesse'. On the
extraordinary statement in the *Tale of Turambar* that Tamar
Lamefoot was Half-elven see p. 130.)

Ecthelion 'was that lord of the house of the Fountain, who had the fairest
voice and was most skilled in musics of all the Gondothlim. He won
renown for ever by his slaying of Gothmog son of Melko, whereby
Tuor was saved from death but Ecthelion was drowned with his foe
in the king's fountain.'

Egalmoth was 'lord of the house of the Heavenly Arch, and got even out
of the burning of Gondolin, and dwelt after at the mouth of Sirion,
but was slain in a dire battle there when Melko seized Elwing'.
(See p. 258.)

Galdor 'was that valiant Gnome who led the men of the Tree in many a
charge and yet won out of Gondolin and even the onslaught of
Melko upon the dwellers at Sirion's mouth and went back to the
ruins with Eärendel. He dwelleth yet in Tol Eressëa (said Elfriniel),
and still do some of his folk name themselves *Nos Galdon*, for
Galdon is a tree, and thereto Galdor's name akin.' The last phrase
was emended to read: '*Nos nan Alwen*, for *Alwen* is a Tree.'

(For Galdor's return to the ruins of Gondolin with Eärendel see p. 258.)

Glingol 'meaneth "singing-gold" ('tis said), and this name was that which the Gondothlim had for that other of the two unfading trees in the king's square which bore golden bloom. It also was a shoot from the trees of Valinor (see rather where Elfrith has spoken of Bansil), but of Lindeloktë (which is "singing-cluster") or Laurelin [*emended from* Lindelaurë] (which is "singing-gold") which lit all Valinor with golden light for half the 24 hours.'

(For the name *Lindeloktë* see I. 22, 258 (entry *Lindelos*).)

Glorfindel 'led the Golden Flower and was the best beloved of the Gondothlim, save it be Ecthelion, but who shall choose. Yet he was hapless and fell slaying a Balrog in the great fight in Cristhorn. His name meaneth Goldtress for his hair was golden, and the name of his house in Noldorissa *Los'lóriol'* (emended from *Los Glóriol*).

Gondolin 'meaneth stone of song (whereby figuratively the Gnomes meant stone that was carven and wrought to great beauty), and this was the name most usual of the Seven Names they gave to their city of secret refuge from Melko in those days before the release.'

Gothmog 'was a son of Melko and the ogress Fluithuin and his name is Strife-and-hatred, and he was Captain of the Balrogs and lord of Melko's hosts ere fair Ecthelion slew him at the taking of Gondolin. The Eldar named him *Kosmoko* or *Kosomok(o)*, but 'tis a name that fitteth their tongue no way and has an ill sound even in our own rougher speech, said Elfrith [*emended from* Elfriniel].'

(In a list of names of the Valar associated with the tale of *The Coming of the Valar* (I.93) it is said that Melko had a son 'by Ulbandi' called *Kosomot*; the early 'Qenya' dictionary gives *Kosomoko* = Gnomish *Gothmog*, I.258. In the tale Gothmog is called the 'marshal' of the hosts of Melko (p. 184).)

In the later development of the legends Gothmog was the slayer of Fëanor, and in the Battle of Unnumbered Tears it was he who slew Fingon and captured Húrin (*The Silmarillion* pp. 107, 193, 195). He is not of course called later 'son of Melkor'; the 'Children of the Valar' was a feature of the earlier mythology that my father discarded.

In the Third Age *Gothmog* was the name of the lieutenant of Minas Morgul (*The Return of the King* V.6).)

Hendor 'was a house-carle of Idril's and was aged, but bore Eärendel down the secret passage.'

Idril 'was that most fair daughter of the king of Gondolin whom Tuor loved when she was but a little maid, and who bare him Eärendel. Her the Elves name *Irildë*; and we speak of as *Idril Tal-Celeb* or Idril of the Silver Feet, but they *Irildë Taltelepta*.'

See the Appendix on Names, entry *Idril*.

Indor 'was the name of the father of Tuor's father, wherefore did the Gnomes name Eärendel *Gon Indor* and the Elves *Indorildo* or *Indorion.*'

Legolas 'or Green-leaf was a man of the Tree, who led the exiles over Tumladin in the dark, being night-sighted, and he liveth still in Tol Eressëa named by the Eldar there *Laiqalassë*; but the book of Rúmil saith further hereon.'
(See I. 267, entry *Tári-Laisi*.)

§3   *Miscellaneous Matters*

(i)   *The geography of The Fall of Gondolin*

I have noticed above (p. 205) that in Tuor's journey all along the coast of what was afterwards Beleriand to the mouths of Sirion there is an unquestionable resemblance to the later map, in the trend of the coast from north-south to east-west. It is also said that after he left Falasquil 'the distant hills marched ever nearer to the margin of the sea', and that the spurs of the Iron Mountains 'run even to the sea' (pp. 152–3). These statements can likewise be readily enough related to the map, where the long western extension of the Mountains of Shadow (Ered Wethrin), forming the southern border of Nevrast, reached the sea at Vinyamar (for the equation of the Mountains of Iron and the Mountains of Shadow see I. 111–12).

Arlisgion, 'the place of reeds' (p. 153) above the mouths of Sirion, survived in Lisgardh 'the land of reeds at the Mouths of Sirion' in the later *Tuor* (p. 34); and the feature that the great river passed underground for a part of its course goes back to the earliest period, as does that of the Meres of Twilight, Aelin-uial ('the Pools of Twilight', p. 195). There is here however a substantial difference in the tale from *The Silmarillion* (p. 122), where Aelin-uial was the region of great pools and marshes where 'the flood of Sirion was stayed'; *south of the Meres* the river 'fell from the north in a mighty fall . . . and then he plunged suddenly underground into great tunnels that the weight of his falling waters delved'. Here on the other hand the Pools of Twilight are clearly *below* the 'cavern of the Tumultuous Winds' (never mentioned later) where Sirion dives underground. But the Land of Willows, below the region of Sirion's underground passage, is placed as it was to remain.

Thus the view I expressed (p. 141) of the geographical indications in the *Tale of Turambar* can be asserted also of those of *The Fall of Gondolin*.

(ii)   *Ulmo and the other Valar in The Fall of Gondolin*

In the speech of Tuor inspired by Ulmo that he uttered at his first meeting with Turgon (p. 161) he said: 'the hearts of the Valar are

angered . . . seeing the sorrow of the thraldom of the Noldoli and the
wanderings of Men.' This is greatly at variance with what is told in
The Hiding of Valinor, especially the following (I. 208–9):*

> The most of the Valar moreover were fain of their ancient ease and
> desired only peace, wishing neither rumour of Melko and his violence
> nor murmur of the restless Gnomes to come ever again among them to
> disturb their happiness; and for such reasons they also clamoured for
> the concealment of the land. Not the least among these were Vána and
> Nessa, albeit most even of the great Gods were of one mind. In vain
> did Ulmo of his foreknowing plead before them for pity and pardon on
> the Noldoli . . .

Subsequently Tuor said (p. 161): 'the Gods sit in Valinor, though their
mirth is minished for sorrow and fear of Melko, and they hide their land
and weave about it inaccessible magic that no evil come to its shores.'
Turgon in his reply ironically echoed and altered the words: 'they that sit
within [*i.e. in Valinor*] reck little of the dread of Melko or the sorrow of
the world, but hide their land and weave about it inaccessible magic, that
no tidings of evil come ever to their ears.'
How is this to be understood? Was this Ulmo's 'diplomacy'? Certainly
Turgon's understanding of the motives of the Valar chimes better with
what is said of them in *The Hiding of Valinor*.
But the Gnomes of Gondolin reverenced the Valar. There were
'pomps of the Ainur' (p. 165); a great square of the city and its highest
point was Gar Ainion, the Place of the Gods, where weddings were
celebrated (pp. 164, 186); and the people of the Hammer of Wrath
'reverenced Aulë the Smith more than all other Ainur' (p. 174).

Of particular interest is the passage (p. 165) in which a reason is given
for Ulmo's choice of a Man as the agent of his designs: 'Now Melko was
not much afraid of the race of Men in those days of his great power, and
for this reason did Ulmo work through one of this kindred for the better
deceiving of Melko, seeing that no Valar and scarce any of the Eldar or
Noldoli might stir unmarked of his vigilance.' This is the only place
where a reason is expressly offered, save for an isolated early note, where
two reasons are given:
(1) 'the wrath of the Gods' (i.e. against the Gnomes);
(2) 'Melko did not fear Men – had he thought that any messengers
were getting to Valinor he would have redoubled his vigilance and evil
and hidden the Gnomes away utterly.'

---

* It also seems to be at variance with the story that all Men were shut in Hithlum by
Melko's decree after the Battle of Unnumbered Tears; but 'wanderings' is a strange word in
the context, since the next words are 'for Melko ringeth them in the Land of Shadows'.

But this is too oblique to be helpful.

The conception of 'the luck of the Gods' occurs again in this tale (pp. 188, 200 note 32), as it does in the *Tale of Turambar*: see p. 141. The Ainur 'put it into Tuor's heart' to climb the cliff out of the ravine of Golden Cleft for the saving of his life (p. 151).

Very strange is the passage concerning the birth of Eärendel (p. 165): 'In these days came to pass the fulfilment of the time of the desire of the Valar and the hope of the Eldalië, for in great love Idril bore to Tuor a son and he was called Eärendel.' Is it to be understood that the union of Elf and mortal Man, and the birth of their offspring, was 'the desire of the Valar' – that the Valar foresaw it, or hoped for it, as the fulfilment of a design of Ilúvatar from which great good should come? There is no hint or suggestion of such an idea elsewhere.

(iii)   *Orcs*

There is a noteworthy remark in the tale (p. 159) concerning the origin of the Orcs (or *Orqui* as they were called in *Tuor A*, and in *Tuor B* as first written): 'all that race were bred of the subterranean heats and slime.' There is no trace yet of the later view that 'naught that had life of its own, nor the semblance of life, could ever Melkor make since his rebellion in the Ainulindalë before the Beginning', or that the Orcs were derived from enslaved Quendi after the Awakening (*The Silmarillion* p. 50). Conceivably there is a first hint of this idea of their origin in the words of the tale in the same passage: 'unless it be that certain of the Noldoli were twisted to the evil of Melko and mingled among these Orcs', although of course this is as it stands quite distinct from the idea that the Orcs were actually bred from Elves.

Here also occurs the name *Glamhoth* of the Orcs, a name that reappears in the later *Tuor* (pp. 39 and 54 note 18).

On Balrogs and Dragons in *The Fall of Gondolin* see pp. 212–13.

(iv)   *Noldorin in the Land of Willows*

'Did not even after the days of Tuor Noldorin and his Eldar come there seeking for Dor Lómin and the hidden river and the caverns of the Gnomes' imprisonment; yet thus nigh to their quest's end were like to abandon it? Indeed sleeping and dancing here . . . they were whelmed by the goblins sped by Melko from the Hills of Iron and Noldorin made bare escape thence' (p. 154). This was the Battle of Tasarinan, mentioned in the *Tale of Turambar* (pp. 70, 140), at the time of the great expedition of the Elves from Kôr. Cf. Lindo's remark in *The Cottage of Lost Play* (I.16) that his father Valwë 'went with Noldorin to find the Gnomes'.

Noldorin (Salmar, companion of Ulmo) is also said in the tale to have fought beside Tulkas at the Pools of Twilight against Melko himself, though his name was struck out (p. 195 and note 38); this was after the Battle of Tasarinan. On these battles see pp. 278 ff.

(v)   *The stature of Elves and Men*

The passage concerning Tuor's stature on p. 159, before it was rewritten (see note 18), can only mean that while Tuor was not himself unusually tall for a Man he was nonetheless taller than the Elves of Gondolin, and thus agrees with statements made in the *Tale of Turambar* (see p. 142). As emended, however, the meaning is rather that Men and Elves were not greatly distinct in stature.

(vi)   *Isfin and Eöl*

The earliest version of this tale is found in the little *Lost Tales* notebook (see I. 171), as follows:

Isfin and Eöl

Isfin daughter of Fingolma loved from afar by Eöl (Arval) of the Mole-kin of the Gnomes. He is strong and in favour with Fingolma and with the Sons of Fëanor (to whom he is akin) because he is a leader of the Miners and searches after hidden jewels, but he is illfavoured and Isfin loathes him.

(Fingolma as a name for Finwë Nólemë appears in outlines for *Gilfanon's Tale*, I. 238–9.) We have here an illfavoured miner named Eöl 'of the Mole' who loves Isfin but is rejected by her with loathing; and this is obviously closely parallel to the illfavoured miner Meglin with the sign of the sable mole seeking the hand of Idril, who rejects him, in *The Fall of Gondolin*. It is difficult to know how to interpret this. The simplest explanation is that the story adumbrated in the little notebook is actually earlier than that in *The Fall of Gondolin*; that Meglin did not yet exist; and that subsequently the image of the 'ugly miner – unsuccessful suitor' became that of the son, the object of desire becoming Idril (niece of Isfin), while a new story was developed for the father, Eöl the dark Elf of the forest who ensnared Isfin. But it is by no means clear where Eöl the miner was when he 'loved from afar' Isfin daughter of Fingolma. There seems to be no reason to think that he was associated with Gondolin; more probably the idea of the miner bearing the sign of the Mole entered Gondolin with Meglin.

IV

THE NAUGLAFRING

We come now to the last of the original *Lost Tales* to be given consecutive narrative form. This is contained in a separate notebook, and it bears the title *The Nauglafring: The Necklace of the Dwarves*.

The beginning of this tale is somewhat puzzling. Before the telling of *The Fall of Gondolin* Lindo told Littleheart that 'it is the desire of all that you tell us the tales of Tuor and of Eärendel as soon as may be' (p. 144), and Littleheart replied: 'It is a mighty tale, and seven times shall folk fare to the Tale-fire ere it be rightly told; and so twined is it with those stories of the Nauglafring and of the Elf-march that I would fain have aid in that telling of Ailios here . . .' Thus Littleheart's surrender of the chair of the tale-teller to Ailios at the beginning of the present text, so that Ailios should tell of the Nauglafring, fits the general context well; but we should not expect the new tale to be introduced with the words 'But after a while silence fell', since *The Fall of Gondolin* ends 'And no one in all the Room of Logs spake or moved for a great while.' In any case, after the very long *Fall of Gondolin* the next tale would surely have waited till the following evening.

This tale is once again a manuscript in ink over a wholly erased original in pencil, but only so far as the words 'sate his greed' on page 230. From this point to the end there is only a primary manuscript in pencil in the first stage of composition, written in haste – in places hurled on to the page, with a good many words not certainly decipherable; and a part of this was extensively rewritten while the tale was still in progress (see note 13).

The Nauglafring
The Necklace of the Dwarves

But after a while silence fell, and folk murmured 'Eärendel', but others said 'Nay – what of the Nauglafring, the Necklace of the Dwarves.' Therefore said Ilfiniol, leaving the chair of the tale-teller: 'Yea, better would the tale be told if Ailios would relate the matters concerning that necklace,' and Ailios being nowise unwilling thus began, looking upon the company.

'Remember ye all how Úrin the Steadfast cast the gold of Glorund before the feet of Tinwelint, and after would not touch it again, but went in sorrow back to Hisilómë, and there died?' And all said that that tale was still fresh in their hearts.

'Behold then,' said Ailios, 'in great grief gazed the king upon Úrin as he left the hall, and he was weary for the evil of Melko that thus deceived all hearts; yet tells the tale that so potent were the spells that Mîm the fatherless had woven about that hoard that, even as it lay upon the floor of the king's halls shining strangely in the light of the torches that burnt there, already were all who looked upon it touched by its subtle evil.

Now therefore did those of Úrin's band murmur, and one said to the king: "Lo, lord, our captain Úrin, an old man and mad, has departed, but we have no mind to forego our gain."

Then said Tinwelint, for neither was he untouched by the golden spell: "Nay then, know ye not that this gold belongs to the kindred of the Elves in common, for the Rodothlim who won it from the earth long time ago are no more, and no one has especial claim[1] to so much as a handful save only Úrin by reason of his son Túrin, who slew the Worm, the robber of the Elves; yet Túrin is dead and Úrin will have none of it; and Túrin was my man."

At those words the outlaws fell into great wrath, until the king said: "Get ye now gone, and seek not O foolish ones to quarrel with the Elves of the forest, lest death or the dread enchantments of Valinor find you in the woods. Neither revile ye the name of Tinwelint their king, for I will reward you richly enough for your travail and the bringing of the gold. Let each one now approach and take what he may grasp with either hand, and then depart in peace."

Now were the Elves of the wood in turn displeased, who long had stood nigh gazing on the gold; but the wild folk did as they were bid, and yet more, for some went into the hoard twice and thrice, and angry cries were raised in that hall. Then would the woodland Elves hinder them of their thieving, and a great dissension arose, so that though the king would stay them none heeded him. Then did those outlaws being fierce and fearless folk draw swords and deal blows about them, so that soon there was a great fight even upon the steps of the high-seat of the king. Doughty were those outlaws and great wielders of sword and axe from their warfare with Orcs,[2] so that many were slain ere the king, seeing that peace and pardon might no longer be, summoned a host of his warriors, and those outlaws being wildered with the stronger magics of the king[3] and confused in the dark ways of the halls of Tinwelint were all slain fighting bitterly; but the king's hall ran with gore, and the gold that lay before his throne, scattered and spurned by trampling feet, was drenched with blood. Thus did the curse of Mîm the Dwarf begin its course; and yet another sorrow sown by the Noldoli of old in Valinor was come to fruit.[4]

Then were the bodies of the outlaws cast forth, but the woodland Elves that were slain Tinwelint let bury nigh to the knoll of Tinúviel, and 'tis said that the great mound stands there still in Artanor, and for long the fairies called it Cûm an-Idrisaith, the Mound of Avarice.

Now came Gwenniel to Tinwelint and said: "Touch not this gold, for my heart tells me it is trebly cursed. Cursed indeed by the dragon's breath, and cursed by thy lieges' blood that moistens it, and the death of those[5] they slew; but some more bitter and more binding ill methinks hangs over it that I may not see."

Then, remembering the wisdom of Gwenniel his wife, the king was minded to hearken to her, and he bade gather it up and cast it into the stream before the gates. Yet even so he might not shake off its spell, and he said to himself: "First will I gaze my last upon its loveliness ere I fling it from me for ever." Therefore he let wash it clean of its stains of blood in clear waters, and display it before him. Now such mighty heaps of gold have never since been gathered in one place; and some thereof was wrought to cups, to basons, and to dishes, and hilts there were for swords, and scabbards, and sheaths for daggers; but the most part was of red gold unwrought lying in masses and in bars. The value of that hoard no man could count, for amid the gold lay many gems, and these were very beautiful to look upon, for the fathers of the Rodothlim had brought them out of Valinor, a portion of that boundless treasury the Noldoli had there possessed.

Now as he gazed Tinwelint said: "How glorious is this treasure! And I have not a tithe thereof, and of the gems of Valinor none save that Silmaril that Beren won from Angamandi." But Gwenniel who stood by said: "And that were worth all that here lies, were it thrice as great."

Then arose one from among the company, and that was Ufedhin, a Gnome; but more had he wandered about the world than any of the king's folk, and long had he dwelt with the Nauglath and the Indrafangs their kin. The Nauglath are a strange race and none know surely whence they be; and they serve not Melko nor Manwë and reck not for Elf or Man, and some say that they have not heard of Ilúvatar, or hearing disbelieve.

Howbeit in crafts and sciences and in the knowledge of the virtues of all things that are in the earth[6] or under the water none excel them; yet they dwell beneath the ground in caves and tunnelled towns, and aforetime Nogrod was the mightiest of these. Old are they, and never comes a child among them, nor do they laugh. They are squat in stature, and yet are strong, and their beards reach even to their toes, but the beards of the Indrafangs are the longest of all, and are forked, and they bind them about their middles when they walk abroad. All these creatures have Men called 'Dwarves', and say that their crafts and cunning surpass that of the Gnomes in marvellous contrivance, but of a truth there is little beauty in their works of themselves, for in those things of loveliness that they have wrought in ages past such renegade Gnomes as was Ufedhin have ever had a hand. Now long had that Gnome forsaken his folk, becoming leagued with the Dwarves of Nogrod, and was at that time come to the realms of Tinwelint with certain other Noldoli of like mind bearing swords and coats of mail and other smithyings of exquisite skill in which the Nauglath in those days did great traffic with the free Noldoli, and, 'tis said, with the Orcs and soldiers of Melko also.

As he stood in that place the spell of the gold had pierced the heart of Ufedhin more deeply than the heart of any there, and he could not endure that it should all be cast away, and these were his words: "An evil deed is this that Tinwelint the king intends; or who hereafter shall say that the kindreds of the Eldalië love things of beauty if a king of the Eldar cast so great a store of loveliness into the dark woodland waters where none but the fishes may after behold it? Rather than this should be, I beg of thee, O King, to suffer the craftsmen of the Dwarves to try their skill upon this unwrought gold, that the name of the golden treasury of Tinwelint become heard in all lands and places. This will they do, I promise thee, for small guerdon, might they but save the hoard from ruin."

Then looked the king upon the gold and he looked upon Ufedhin, and that Gnome was clad very richly, having a tunic of golden web and a belt of gold set with tiny gems; and his sword was damasked in strange wise,[7] but a collar of gold and silver interlaced most intricate was round his neck, and Tinwelint's raiment could in no wise compare with that of the wayfarer in his halls. Again looked Tinwelint upon the gold, and it shone yet more alluring fair, nor ever had the sparkle of the gems seemed so brilliant, and Ufedhin said again: "Or in what manner, O King, dost thou guard that Silmaril of which all the world hath heard?"

Now Gwenniel warded it in a casket of wood bound with iron, and Ufedhin said it was shame so to set a jewel that should not touch aught less worthy than the purest gold. Then was Tinwelint abashed, and yielded, and this was the agreement that he made with Ufedhin. Half the gold should the king measure and give to the hands of Ufedhin and his company, and they should bear it away to Nogrod and the dwellings of the Dwarves. Now those were a very long journey southward beyond the wide forest on the borders of those great heaths nigh Umboth-muilin the Pools of Twilight, on the marches of Tasarinan. Yet after but seven full moons back would the Nauglath fare bearing the king's loan all wrought to works of greatest cunning, yet in no wise would the weight and purity of the gold be minished. Then would they speak to Tinwelint, and an he liked not the handiwork then would they return and say no more; yet if it seemed good to him then of that which remained would they fashion such marvellous things for his adornment and for Gwenniel the Queen as never had Gnome or Dwarf made yet.

"For," said Ufedhin, "the cunning of the Nauglath have I learnt, and the beauty of design that only can the Noldoli compass do I know – yet shall the wages of our labour be small indeed, and we will name it before thee when all is done."

Then by reason of the glamour of the gold the king repented his agreement with Ufedhin, and he liked not altogether his words, and he would not suffer so great a store of gold to be borne without surety out of his sight for seven moons to the distant dwellings of the Dwarves; yet was he minded nonetheless to profit by their skill. Therefore suddenly he let seize Ufedhin, and his folk, and he said unto them: "Here shall ye remain as hostages in my halls until I see again my treasury." Now Tinwelint thought in his heart that Ufedhin and his Gnomes were of the utmost service to the Dwarves, and no covetice would be strong enough to bring them to forsake him; but that Gnome was very wroth, saying: "The Nauglath are no thieves, O King, nor yet their friends"; but Tinwelint said: "Yet the light of overmuch gold has made many thieves, who were not so before," and Ufedhin perforce consented, yet he forgave not Tinwelint in his heart.

Therefore was the gold now borne to Nogrod by folk of the king guided by one only of Ufedhin's companions, and the agreement of Ufedhin and Tinwelint spoken to Naugladur, the king of those places.

Now during the time of waiting Ufedhin was kindly entreated

in the courts of Tinwelint, yet was he idle perforce, and he fretted inwardly. In his leisure he pondered ever what manner of lovely thing of gold and jewels he would after fashion for Tinwelint, but this was only for the greater ensnaring of the king, for already he began to weave dark plots most deep of avarice and revenge.

On the very day of the fullness of the seventh moon thereafter the watchers on the king's bridge cried: "Lo! there comes a great company through the wood, and all it seems are aged men, and they bear very heavy burdens on their backs." But the king hearing said: "It is the Nauglath, who keep their tryst: now mayst thou go free, Ufedhin, and take my greeting to them, and lead them straightway to my hall"; and Ufedhin sallied forth gladly, but his heart forgot not its resentment. Therefore having speech privily with the Nauglath he prevailed upon them to demand at the end a very great reward, and one thereto that the king might not grant unhumbled; and more of his designs also did he unfold, whereby that gold might fare in the end to Nogrod for ever.

Now come the Dwarves nonetheless over the bridge and before the chair of Tinwelint, and behold, the things of their workmanship they had conveyed thither in silken cloths, and boxes of rare woods carven cunningly. In other wise had Úrin haled the treasure thither, and half thereof lay yet in his rude sacks and clumsy chests; yet when the gold was once more revealed, then did a cry of wonder arise, for the things the Nauglath had made were more wondrous far than the scanty vessels and the ornaments that the Rodothlim wrought of old. Cups and goblets did the king behold, and some had double bowls or curious handles interlaced, and horns there were of strange shape, dishes and trenchers, flagons and cwers, and all appurtenances of a kingly feast. Candlesticks there were and sconces for the torches, and none might count the rings and armlets, the bracelets and collars, and the coronets of gold; and all these were so subtly made and so cunningly adorned that Tinwelint was glad beyond the hope of Ufedhin.

But as yet the designs of Ufedhin came to nought, for in no wise would Tinwelint suffer or him or those of the Nauglath to depart to Nogrod with or without that portion of the unwrought gold that yet remained, and he said: "How shall it be thought that after the weariness of your burdened journeys hither I should let you so soon be gone, to noise the lack of courtesy of Tinwelint abroad in Nogrod? Stay now awhile and rest and feast, and afterward shall ye have the gold that remains to work your pleasure on; nor shall aught of help that I or my folk may afford be wanting in your labour, and a reward rich and more than just awaits you at the end."

But they knew nonetheless that they were prisoners, and trying the exits privily found them strongly warded. Being therefore without counsel they bowed before the king, and the faces of the Dwarf-folk show seldom what they think. Now after a time of rest was that last smithying begun in a deep place of Tinwelint's abode which he caused to be set apart for their uses, and what their hearts lacked therein fear supplied, and in all that work Ufedhin had a mighty part.

A golden crown they made for Tinwelint, who yet had worn nought but a wreath of scarlet leaves, and a helm too most glorious they fashioned; and a sword of dwarven steel brought from afar was hilted with bright gold and damascened in gold and silver with strange figurings wherein was pictured clear the wolf-hunt of Karkaras Knife-fang, father of wolves. That was a more wonderful sword than any Tinwelint had seen before, and outshone the sword in Ufedhin's belt the king had coveted. These things were of Ufedhin's cunning, but the Dwarves made a coat of linked mail of steel and gold for Tinwelint, and a belt of gold. Then was the king's heart gladdened, but they said: "All is not finished," and Ufedhin made a silver crown for Gwenniel, and aided by the Dwarves contrived slippers of silver crusted with diamonds, and the silver thereof was fashioned in delicate scales, so that it yielded as soft leather to the foot, and a girdle he made too of silver blended with pale gold. Yet were those things but a tithe of their works, and no tale tells a full count of them.

Now when all was done and their smithcraft given to the king, then said Ufedhin: "O Tinwelint, richest of kings, dost thou think these things fair?" And he said: "Yea"; but Ufedhin said: "Know then that great store of thy best and purest gold remaineth still, for we have husbanded it, having a boon to ask of thee, and it is this: we would make thee a carcanet and to its making lay all the skill and cunning that we have, and we desire that this should be the most marvellous ornament that the Earth has seen, and the greatest of the works of Elves and Dwarves. Therefore we beg of thee to let us have that Silmaril that thou treasurest, that it may shine wondrously amid the Nauglafring, the Necklace of the Dwarves."

Then again did Tinwelint doubt Ufedhin's purpose, yet did he yield the boon, an they would suffer him to be present at that smithying.

None are that yet live,' quoth Ailios,[8] 'who have seen that most glorious thing, save only[9] Littleheart son of Bronweg, yet are many things told thereof. Not only was it wrought with the greatest skill and subtlety in the world but it had a magic power, and there was no throat so great or so slender whereon it sat not with grace and loveliness. Albeit a weight beyond belief of gold was used in the making, lightly it hung upon its wearer as a strand of flax; and all such as clasped it about their necks seemed, as it hung upon their breasts, to be of goodly countenance, and women seemed most fair. Gems uncounted were there in that carcanet of gold, yet only as a setting that did prepare for its great central glory, and led the eye thereto, for amidmost hung like a little lamp of limpid fire the Silmaril of Fëanor, jewel of the Gods. Yet alas, even had that gold of the Rodothlim held no evil spell still had that carcanet been a thing of little luck, for the Dwarves were full of bitterness, and all its links were twined with baleful thoughts. Now however did they bear it before the king in its new-gleaming splendour; and then was the joy of Tinwelint king of the woodland Elves come to its crowning, and he cast the Nauglafring about his throat, and straightway the curse of Mîm fell upon him. Then said Ufedhin: "Now, O Lord, that thou art pleased beyond thy hope, perchance thou wilt grant the craftsmen thy kingly reward, and suffer them to depart also in joy to their own lands."

But Tinwelint, bewildered by the golden spell and the curse of Mîm, liked not the memory of his tryst; yet dissembling he bid the craftsmen come before him, and he praised their handiwork with royal words. At length said he: "'Twas said to me by one Ufedhin that at the end such reward as ye wished ye would name before me, yet would it be small enough, seeing that the labour was of love and of Ufedhin's desire that the golden hoard be not cast away and lost. What then do ye wish that I may grant?"

Then said Ufedhin scornfully: "For myself, nothing, O Lord; indeed the guestkindliness of thy halls for seven moons and three is more than I desire." But the Dwarves said: "This do we ask. For our labours during seven moons each seven jewels of Valinor, and seven robes of magic that only Gwendelin[10] can weave, and each a sack of gold; but for our great labour during three moons in thy halls unwilling, we ask each three sacks of silver, and each a cup of gold wherein to pledge thy health, O King, and each a fair maiden of the woodland Elves to fare away with us to our homes."

Then was King Tinwelint wroth indeed, for what the Dwarves had asked was of itself a goodly treasury, seeing that their company was very great; and he had no mind thus to devour the dragon's hoard, but never could he deliver maidens of the Elves unto illshapen Dwarves without undying shame.

Now that demand they had made only by the design of Ufedhin, yet seeing the anger of the king's face they said: "Nay, but this is not all, for in payment of Ufedhin's captivity for seven moons seven stout Elves must come with us and abide seven times seven years among us as bondsmen and menials in our labour."

Thereat arose Tinwelint from his seat, and calling summoned his weaponed thanes and warriors, that these surrounded the Nauglath and those Gnomes. Then said he: "For your insolence each three stripes with stinging withes shall ye receive, and Ufedhin seven, and afterwards will we speak of recompense."

When this was done, and a flame of bitter vengeance lit in those deep hearts, he said: "Lo, for your labour of seven months six pieces of gold and one of silver each shall have, and for your labours in my halls each three pieces of gold and some small gem that I can spare. For your journey hither a great feast shall ye eat and depart with good store against your return, and ere ye go ye shall drink to Tinwelint in elfin wine; yet, mark ye, for the sustenance of Ufedhin seven idle months about my halls shall ye each pay a piece of gold, and of silver two, for he has not aught himself and shall not receive since he desires it not, yet methinks he is at the bottom of your arrogance."

Then were the Dwarves paid their reward like common smiths of bronze and iron, and constrained to yield once more therefrom payment for Ufedhin – "else," said the king, "never shall ye get him hence." Then sat they to a great feast and dissembled their mood; yet at the end the time of their going came, and they drank to Tinwelint in elfin wine, but they cursed him in their beards, and Ufedhin swallowed not and spat the wine from his mouth upon the threshold.

Now tells the tale that the Nauglath fared home again, and if their greed had been kindled when first the gold was brought to Nogrod now was it a fierce flame of desire, and moreover they burnt under the insults of the king. Indeed all that folk love gold and silver more dearly than aught else on Earth, while that treasury was haunted by a spell and by no means were they armed against it. Now one there had been, Fangluin* the aged, who had counselled them from the first never to return the king's loan, for

---

* In the margin of the manuscript is written: *Fangluin: Bluebeard.*

said he: "Ufedhin we may later seek by guile to release, if it seem good," but at that time this seemed not policy to Naugladur their lord, who desired not warfare with the Elves. Yet now did Fangluin jeer at them mightily on their return, saying they had flung away their labour for a botcher's wage and a draught of wine and gotten dishonour thereto, and he played upon their lust, and Ufedhin joined his bitter words thereto. Therefore did Naugladur hold a secret council of the Dwarves of Nogrod, and sought how he might both be avenged upon Tinwelint, and sate his greed.[11]

Yet after long pondering he saw not how he might achieve his purpose save by force, and there was little hope therein, both by reason of the great strength of numbers of the Elves of Artanor in those days, and of the woven magic of Gwenniel that guarded all those regions, so that men of hostile heart were lost and came not to those woods; nor indeed could any such come thither unaided by treachery from within.

Now even as those aged ones sat in their dark halls and gnawed their beards, behold a sound of horns, and messengers were come from Bodruith of the Indrafangs, a kindred of the Dwarves that dwelt in other realms. Now these brought tidings of the death of Mîm the fatherless at the hand of Úrin and the rape of Glorund's gold, which tale had but new come to Bodruith's ears. Now hitherto the Dwarves knew not the full tale concerning that hoard, nor more than Ufedhin might tell hearing the speech in Tinwelint's halls, and Úrin had not spoken the full count thereof ere he departed. Hearing therefore these tidings new wrath was added to their lust and a clamour arose among them, and Naugladur vowed to rest not ere Mîm was thrice avenged – "and more," said he, "meseems the gold belongs of right to the people of the Dwarves."

This then was the design; and by his deeds have the Dwarves been severed in feud for ever since those days with the Elves, and drawn more nigh in friendship to the kin of Melko. Secretly he let send to the Indrafangs that they prepare their host against a day that he would name, whenso the time should be ripe; and a hidden forging of bitter steel then was in Belegost the dwelling of the Indrafangs. Moreover he gathered about him a great host of the Orcs, and wandering goblins, promising them a good wage, and the pleasure of their Master moreover, and a rich booty at the end; and all these he armed with his own weapons. Now came unto Naugladur an Elf, and he was one of Tinwelint's folk, and he offered to lead that host through the magics of Gwendelin, for he was bitten by the gold-lust of Glorund's hoard, and so did the curse of Mîm come upon Tinwelint and treachery first arose among the Elves of Artanor. Then did Naugladur [?smile] bitterly, for he knew that the time was ripe and Tinwelint delivered to him. Now each year about the time of the great wolf-hunt of Beren Tinwelint was wont to keep the memory of that day by a hunt in the woods, and it was a very mighty chase and thronged with very many folk, and nights of merriment and feasting were there in the forest. Now Naugladur learnt of that Elf Narthseg, whose name is bitter to the Eldar yet, that the king would fare a-hunting at the next high moon but one, and straightway he sent the trysted sign, a bloodstained knife, to Bodruith at Belegost. Now all that host assembled on the confines of the woods, and no word came yet unto the king.

Now tells the tale that one came unto Tinwelint, and Tinwelint knew him not for the wild growth of his hair – and lo! it was Mablung, and he said: "Lo, even in the depths of the forest have we heard that this year you will celebrate the death of Karkaras with a high-tide greater than even before, O King – and behold I have returned to bear you company." And the king was full of mirth and fain to greet Mablung the brave; and at the words of Mablung that Huan captain of Dogs was come also into Artanor was he glad indeed.

Behold now Tinwelint the king rode forth a-hunting, and more glorious was his array than ever aforetime, and the helm of gold was above his flowing locks, and with gold were the trappings of his steed adorned; and the sunlight amid the trees fell upon his face, and it seemed to those that beheld it like to the glorious face of the sun at morning; for about his throat was clasped the Nauglafring, the Necklace of the Dwarves. Beside him rode Mablung the Heavyhand in the place of honour by reason of his deeds at that great hunt aforetime – but Huan of the Dogs was ahead of the hunters, and men thought that great dog bore him strangely, but mayhap there was something in the wind that day he liked not.

Now is the king far in the woods with all his company, and the horns grow faint in the deep forest, but Gwendelin sits in her bower and foreboding is in her heart and eyes. Then said an Elfmaid, Nielthi: "Wherefore, O Lady, art thou sorrowful at the hightide of the king?" And Gwendelin said: "Evil seeks our land, and my heart misgives me that my days in Artanor are speeding to their end, yet if I should lose Tinwelint then would I wish never to have wandered forth from Valinor." But Nielthi said: "Nay, O Lady Gwendelin, hast thou not woven great magic all about us, so that we fear not?" But the queen made answer: "Yet meseems there is a rat that gnaws the threads and all the web has come unwoven." Even at that word there was a cry about the doors, and suddenly it grew to a fierce noise . . . by the clash of steel. Then went Gwendelin unafraid forth from her bower, and behold, a sudden multitude of Orcs and Indrafangs held the bridge, and there was war within the cavernous gates; but that place ran with blood, and a great heap of slain lay there, for the onset had been secret and all unknown.

Then did Gwendelin know well that her foreboding was true, and that treachery had found her realm at last, yet did she hearten those few guards that remained to her and had fared not to the hunt, and valiantly they warded the palace of the king until the tide of numbers bore them back [and] fire and blood found all the halls and deep ways of that great fortress of the Elves.

Then did those Orcs and Dwarves ransack all the chambers seeking for treasure, and lo! one came and sate him in the high seat of the king laughing loud, and Gwendelin saw that it was Ufedhin, and mocking he bid her be seated in her ancient seat beside the king's. Then Gwendelin gazed upon him so that his glance fell, and she said: "Wherefore, O renegade, dost thou defile my lord's seat? Little had I thought to see any of the Elves sit there, a robber, stained with murder, a league-fellow of the truceless enemies of his kin. Or thinkest thou it is a glorious deed to assail an ill-armed house what time its lord is far away?" But Ufedhin said nought, shunning the bright eyes of Gwendelin, wherefore said she anew: "Get thee now gone with thy foul Orcs, lest Tinwelint coming repay thee bitterly."

Then at last did Ufedhin answer, and he laughed, but ill at ease, and he looked not at the queen, but he said listening to a sound without: "Nay, but already is he come." And behold, Naugladur entered now and a host of the Dwarves were about him, but he bore the head of Tinwelint crowned and helmed in gold; but the necklace of all wonder was clasped about the throat of Naugladur. Then did Gwendelin see in her heart all that had befallen, and how the curse of the gold had fallen on the realm of Artanor, and never has she danced or sung since that dark hour; but Naugladur bid gather all things of gold or silver or of precious stones and bear them to Nogrod — "and whatso remains of goods or folk may the

Orcs keep, or slay, as they desire. Yet the Lady Gwendelin Queen of Artanor shall fare with me."

Then said Gwendelin: "Thief and murderer, child of Melko, yet art thou a fool, for thou canst not see what hangs over thine own head." By reason of the anguish of her heart was her sight grown very clear, and she read by her fay-wisdon the curse of Mîm and much of what would yet betide.

Then did Naugladur in his triumph laugh till his beard shook, and bid seize her: but none might do so, for as they came towards her they groped as if in sudden dark, or stumbled and fell tripping each the other, and Gwendelin went forth from the places of her abode, and her bitter weeping filled the forest. Now did a great darkness fall upon her mind and her counsel and lore forsook her, that she wandered she knew not whither for a great while; and this was by reason of her love for Tinwelint the king, for whom she had chosen never to fare back to Valinor and the beauty of the Gods, dwelling always in the wild forests of the North; and now did there seem to her neither beauty nor joy be it in Valinor or in the Lands Without. Many of the scattered Elves in her wayward journeyings she met, and they took pity on her, but she heeded them not. Tales had they told her, but she hearkened not over much since Tinwelint was dead; nonetheless must ye know how even in the hour that Ufedhin's host brake the palace and despoiled it, and other companies as great and as terrible of the Orcs and Indrafangs fell with death and fire upon all the realm of Tinwelint, behold the brave hunt of the king were resting amid mirth and laughter, but Huan stalked apart. Then suddenly were the woods filled with noise and Huan bayed aloud; but the king and his company were all encircled with armed foes. Long they fought bitterly there among the trees, and the Nauglath – for such were their foes – had great scathe of them or ever they were slain. Yet in the end were they all fordone, and Mablung and the king fell side by side – but Naugladur it was who swept off the head of Tinwelint after he was dead, for living he dared not so near to his bright sword or the axe of Mablung.[12]

Now doth the tale know no more to tell of Huan, save that even while the swords still sang that great dog was speeding through the land, and his way led him as the [?wind] to the land of i·Guilwarthon, the living-dead, where reigned Beren and Tinúviel the daughter of Tinwelint. Not in any settled abode did those twain dwell, nor had their realm boundaries well-marked – and indeed no other messenger save Huan alone to whom all ways were known had ever found Beren and obtained his aid so soon.[13] Indeed the tale tells that even as that host of the Orcs were burning all the land of Tinwelint and the Nauglath and the Indrafangin were wending homeward burdened utterly with spoils of gold and precious things, came Huan to Beren's lodge, and it was dusk. Lo, Beren sat upon a tree root and Tinúviel danced on a green sward in the gloaming as he gazed upon her, when suddenly stood Huan before them, and Beren gave a cry of joy and wonder, for it was long since he and Huan had hunted together. But Tinúviel looking upon Huan saw that he bled, and there was a tale to read in his great eyes. And she said suddenly: "What evil then has fallen upon Artanor?" and Huan said: "Fire and death and the terror of Orcs; but Tinwelint is slain."

Then did both Beren and Tinúviel weep bitter tears; nor did the full tale of Huan dry their eyes. When then it was told to the end leapt Beren to his feet in white wrath, and seizing a horn that hung at his belt he blew a clear blast thereon that rang round all the neighbouring hills, and an elfin folk all clad in green and brown sprang as it were by magic towards him from every glade and coppice, stream and fell.

Now not even Beren knew the tale of those myriad folk that followed his horn in the woods of Hisilómë, and or ever the moon was high above the hills the host assembled in the glade of his abiding was very great, yet were they lightly armed and the most bore only knives and bows. "Yet," said Beren, "speed is that which now we need the most"; and certain Elves at his bidding fared like deer before him, seeking news of the march of the Dwarves and Indrafangs, but at dawn he followed at the head of the green Elves, and Tinúviel abode in the glade and wept unto herself for the death of Tinwelint, and Gwendelin also she mourned as dead.

Now is to tell that the laden host of the Dwarves fared from the place of their ransacking, and Naugladur was at their head, and beside him Ufedhin and Bodruith; and ever as he rode Ufedhin sought to put the dread eyes of Gwendelin from his mind and could not, and all happiness was fled from his heart that shrivelled under the memory of that glance; nor was this the only disquiet that tortured him, for if ever he raised his eyes lo! they lighted on the Necklace of the Dwarves shining about the aged neck of Naugladur, and then all other thoughts save bottomless desire of its beauty were banished.

Thus did those three fare and with them all their host, but so great became the torment of Ufedhin's mind that in the end he might not endure it more, but at night when a halt was called he crept stealthily to the place where Naugladur slept, and coming upon that aged one wrapt in slumbers would slay that Dwarf and lay hands upon the wondrous Nauglafring. Now even as he sought to do so, behold one seized his throat suddenly from behind, and it was Bodruith, who filled with the same lust sought also to make that lovely thing his own; but coming upon Ufedhin would slay him by reason of his kinship to Naugladur. Then did Ufedhin stab suddenly backward at hazard in the dark with a keen knife long and slender that he had with him for the bane of Naugladur, and that knife pierced the vitals of Bodruith Lord of Belegost so that he fell dying upon Naugladur, and the throat of Naugladur and the magic carcanet were drenched anew with blood.

Thereat did Naugladur awake with a great cry, but Ufedhin fled gasping from that place, for the long fingers of the Indrafang had well-nigh choked him. Now when some bore torches swiftly to that place Naugladur thought that Bodruith alone had sought to rob him of the jewel, and marvelled how he had thus been timely slain, and he proclaimed a rich reward to the slayer of Bodruith if that man would come forward telling all that he had seen. Thus was it that none perceived the flight of Ufedhin for a while, and wrath awoke between the Dwarves of Nogrod and the Indrafangs, and many were slain ere the Indrafangs being in less number were scattered and got them as best they might to Belegost, bearing scant treasury with them. Of this came the agelong feud between those kindreds of the Dwarves that has spread to many lands and caused many a tale, whereof the Elves know little tidings and Men have seldom heard. Yet may it be seen how the curse of Mîm came early home to rest among his own kin, and would indeed it had gone no further and had visited the Eldar never more.

Lo, when the flight of Ufedhin came also to light then was Naugladur in wrath, and he let kill all the Gnomes that remained in the host. Then said he: "Now are we rid of Indrafangs and Gnomes and all traitors, and nought more do I fear at all."

But Ufedhin ranged the wild lands in great fear and anguish, for him seemed that he had become a traitor to his kin, blood-guilty to the Elves, and haunted with the [?burning] eyes of Gwendelin the queen, for nought but exile and misery, and no smallest part nor share had he in the gold of Glorund, for all his heart was afire with lust; yet few have pitied him.

Now tells the tale that he fell in with the rangers of Beren's folk, and these gaining from him sure knowledge of all the host and array of Naugladur and the ways he purposed to follow, they sped back like wind among the trees unto their lord; but Ufedhin revealed not to them who he was, feigning to be an Elf of Artanor escaped from bondage in their host. Now therefore they entreated him well, and he was sent back to Beren that their captain might . . . . his words, and albeit Beren marvelled at his [?cowardly] . . . . . .[14] and downward glance it seemed to him that he brought safe word, and he set a trap for Naugladur.

No longer did he march hotly on the trail of the Dwarves, but knowing that they would essay the passage of the river Aros at a certain time he turned aside, faring swiftly with his light-footed Elves by straighter paths that he might reach Sarnathrod the Stony Ford before them. Now the Aros is a fierce stream – and is it not that very water that more near its spring runs swiftly past the aged doors of the Rodothlim's caves and the dark lairs of Glorund[15] – and in those lower regions by no means can be crossed by a great host of laden men save at this ford, nor is it overeasy here. Never would Naugladur have taken that way had he knowledge of Beren – yet blinded by the spell and the dazzling gold he feared nought either within or without his host, and he was in haste to reach Nogrod and its dark caverns, for the Dwarves list not long to abide in the bright light of day.

Now came all that host to the banks of Aros, and their array was thus: first a number of unladen Dwarves most fully armed, and amidmost the great company of those that bore the treasury of Glorund, and many a fair thing beside that they had haled from Tinwelint's halls; and behind these was Naugladur, and he bestrode Tinwelint's horse, and a strange figure did he seem, for the legs of the Dwarves are short and crooked, but two Dwarves led that horse for it went not willingly and it was laden with spoil. But behind these came again a mass of armed men but little laden; and in this array they sought to cross Sarnathrod on their day of doom.

Morn was it when they reached the hither bank and high noon saw them yet passing in long-strung lines and wading slowly the shallow places of the swift-running stream. Here doth it widen out and fare down narrow channels filled with boulders atween long spits of shingle and stones less great. Now did Naugladur slip from his burdened horse and prepare to get him over, for the armed host of the vanguard had climbed already the further bank, and it was great and sheer and thick with trees, and the bearers of the gold were some already stepped thereon and some amidmost of the stream, but the armed men of the rear were resting awhile.

Suddenly is all that place filled with the sound of elfin horns, and one . . . . .[16] with a clearer blast above the rest, and it is the horn of Beren, the huntsman of the woods. Then is the air thick with the slender arrows of the Eldar that err not neither doth the wind bear them aside, and lo, from every tree and boulder do the brown Elves and the green spring suddenly and loose unceasingly from full quivers. Then was there a panic and a noise in the host of Naugladur, and those that waded in the ford cast their golden burdens in the waters and sought affrighted to either bank, but many were stricken with those pitiless darts and fell with their gold into the currents of the Aros, staining its clear waters with their dark blood.

Now were the warriors on the far bank [?wrapped] in battle and rallying sought to come at their foes, but these fled nimbly before them, while [?others] poured still the hail of arrows upon them, and thus got the Eldar few hurts and the Dwarf-folk fell dead unceasingly. Now was that great fight of the Stony Ford . . . . . . nigh to Naugladur, for even though Naugladur and his captains led their bands stoutly never might they grip their foe, and death fell like rain upon their ranks until the most part broke and fled, and a noise of clear laughter echoed from the Elves thereat, and they forebore to shoot more, for the illshapen figures of the Dwarves as they fled, their white beards torn by the wind, filled them [with] mirth. But now stood Naugladur and few were about him, and he remembered the words of Gwendelin, for behold, Beren came towards him and he cast aside his bow, and drew a bright sword; and Beren was of great stature among the Eldar, albeit not of the girth and breadth of Naugladur of the Dwarves.

Then said Beren: "Ward thy life an thou canst, O crook-legged murderer, else will I take it," and Naugladur bid him even the Nauglafring, the necklace of wonder, that he be suffered to go unharmed; but Beren said: "Nay, that may I still take when thou art slain," and thereat he made alone upon Naugladur and his companions, and having slain the foremost of these the others fled away amid elfin laughter, and so Beren came upon Naugladur, slayer of Tinwelint. Then did that aged one defend himself doughtily, and 'twas a bitter fight, and many of the Elves that watched for love and fear of their captain fingered their bow-strings, but Beren called even as he fought that all should stay their hands.

Now little doth the tale tell of wounds and blows of that affray, save that Beren got many hurts therein, and many of his shrewdest blows did little harm to Naugladur by reason of the [?skill] and magic of his dwarfen mail; and it is said that three hours they fought and Beren's arms grew weary, but not those of Naugladur accustomed to wield his mighty hammer at the forge, and it is more than like that otherwise would the issue have been but for the curse of Mîm; for marking how Beren grew faint Naugladur pressed him ever more nearly, and the arrogance that was of that grievous spell came into his heart, and he thought: "I will slay this Elf, and his folk will flee in fear before me," and grasping his sword he dealt a mighty blow and cried: "Take here thy bane, O stripling of the woods," and in that moment his foot found a jagged stone and he stumbled forward, but Beren slipped aside from that blow and catching at his beard his hand found the carcanet of gold, and therewith he swung Naugladur suddenly off his feet upon his face: and Naugladur's sword was shaken from his grasp, but Beren seized it and slew him therewith, for he said: "I will not sully my bright blade with thy dark blood, since there is no need." But the body of Naugladur was cast into the Aros.

Then did he unloose the necklace, and he gazed in wonder at it – and beheld the Silmaril, even the jewel he won from Angband and gained undying glory by his deed; and he said: "Never have mine eyes beheld thee O Lamp of Faëry burn one half so fair as now thou dost, set in gold and gems and the magic of the Dwarves"; and that necklace he caused to be washed of its stains, and he cast it not away, knowing nought of its power, but bore it with him back into the woods of Hithlum.

But the waters of Aros flowed on for ever above the drowned hoard of Glorund, and so do still, for in after days Dwarves came from Nogrod and sought for it, and for the body of Naugladur; but a flood arose from the mountains and therein the seekers perished; and so great now is the gloom and dread of that Stony Ford that none seek the treasure that it guards nor dare ever to cross the magic stream at that enchanted place.

But in the vales of Hithlum was there gladness at the home-coming of the Elves, and great was the joy of Tinúviel to see her lord once more returning amidst his companies, but little did it ease her grief for the death of Tinwelint that Naugladur was slain and many Dwarves beside. Then did Beren seek to comfort her, and taking her in his arms he set the glorious Nauglafring about her neck, and all were blinded by the greatness of her beauty; and Beren said: "Behold the Lamp of Fëanor that thou and I did win from Hell," and Tinúviel smiled, remembering the first days of their love and those days of travail in the wild.

Now is it to be said that Beren sent for Ufedhin and well rewarded him for his words of true guidance whereof the Dwarves had been overcome, and he bid him dwell in . . . . among his folk, and Ufedhin was little loth; yet on a time, no great space thereafter, did that thing betide which he least desired. For came there a sound of very sorrowful singing in the woods, and behold, it was Gwendelin wandering distraught, and her feet bore her to the midmost of a glade where sat Beren and Tinúviel; and at that hour it was new morning, but at the sound all nigh ceased their speaking and were very still. Then did Beren gaze in awe upon Gwendelin, but Tinúviel cried suddenly in sorrow mixed with joy: "O mother Gwendelin, whither do thy feet bear thee, for methought thee dead"; but the greeting of those twain upon the greensward was very sweet. And Ufedhin fled from among the Elves, for he could not endure to look upon the eyes of Gwendelin, and madness took him, and none may say what was his unhappy weird thereafter; and little but a tortured heart got he from the Gold of Glorund.

Now hearing the cries of Ufedhin Gwendelin looked in wonder after him, and stayed her tender words; and memory came back into her eyes so that she cried as in amaze beholding the Necklace of the Dwarves that hung about the white throat of Tinúviel. Then wrathfully she asked of Beren what it might portend, and wherefore he suffered the accursed thing to touch Tinúviel; and told Beren[17] all that tale such as Huan had told him, in deed or guess, and of the pursuit and fighting at the ford he told also, saying at the end: "Nor indeed do I see who, now that Lord Tinwelint is fared to Valinor, should so fittingly wear that jewel of the Gods as Tinúviel." But Gwendelin told of the dragon's ban upon the gold and the [?staining] of blood in the king's halls, "and yet another and more potent curse, whose arising I know not, is woven therewith," said she, "nor methinks was the labour of the Dwarves free from spells of the most enduring malice." But Beren laughed, saying that the glory of the Silmaril and its holiness might overcome all such evils, even as it burnt the [?foul] flesh of Karkaras. "Nor," said he, "have I seen ever my Tinúviel so fair as now she is, clasped in the loveliness of this thing of gold"; but Gwendelin said: "Yet the Silmaril abode in the Crown of Melko, and that is the work of baleful smiths indeed."

Then said Tinúviel that she desired not things of worth or precious stones but the elfin gladness of the forest, and to pleasure Gwendelin she cast it from her neck; but Beren was little pleased and he would not suffer it to be flung away, but warded it in his . . . .[18]

Thereafter did Gwendelin abide a while in the woods among them and was healed; and in the end she fared wistfully back to the land of Lórien and came never again into the tales of the dwellers of Earth; but upon Beren and Tinúviel fell swiftly that doom of mortality that Mandos had spoken when he sped them from his halls – and in this perhaps did the curse of Mîm have [?potency] in that it came more soon upon them; nor this time did those twain fare the road together, but when yet was the child of those twain, Dior[19] the Fair, a little one, did Tinúviel slowly fade, even as the Elves of later days have done throughout the world, and she vanished in the woods, and none have seen her dancing ever there again. But Beren searched all the lands of Hithlum and of Artanor ranging after her; and never has any of the Elves had more loneliness than his, or ever he too faded from life, and Dior his son was left ruler of the brown Elves and the green, and Lord of the Nauglafring.

Mayhap what all Elves say is true, that those twain hunt now in the forest of Oromë in Valinor, and Tinúviel dances on the green swards of Nessa and of Vána daughters of the Gods for ever more; yet great was the grief of the Elves when the Guilwarthon went from among them, and being leaderless and lessened of magic their numbers minished; and many fared away to Gondolin, the rumour of whose growing power and glory ran in secret whispers among all the Elves.

Still did Dior when come to manhood rule a numerous folk, and he loved the woods even as Beren had done; and songs name him mostly Ausir the Wealthy for his possession of that wondrous gem set in the Necklace of the Dwarves. Now the tales of Beren and Tinúviel grew dim in his heart, and he took to wearing it about his neck and to love its loveliness most dearly; and the fame of that jewel spread like fire through all the regions of the North, and the Elves said one to another: "A Silmaril of Fëanor burns in the woods of Hisilómë."

Now fare the long days of Elfinesse unto that time when Tuor dwelt in Gondolin; and children then had Dior the Elf,[20] Auredhir and Elwing, and Auredhir was most like to his forefather Beren, and all loved him, yet none so dearly as did Dior; but Elwing the fairy have all poesies named as beautiful as Tinúviel if that indeed may be, yet hard is it to say seeing the great loveliness

of the elfin folk of yore. Now those were days of happiness in the
vales of Hithlum, for there was peace with Melko and the Dwarves
who had but one thought as they plotted against Gondolin, and
Angband was full of labour; yet is it to tell that bitterness entered
into the hearts of the seven sons of Fëanor, remembering their
oath. Now Maidros, whom Melko maimed, was their leader; and
he called to his brethren Maglor and Dinithel, and to Damrod,
and to Celegorm, to Cranthor and to Curufin the Crafty, and he
said to them how it was now known to him that a Silmaril of those
their father Fëanor had made was now the pride and glory of Dior
of the southern vales, "and Elwing his daughter bears it whitherso
she goes – but do you not forget," said he, "that we swore to have
no peace with Melko nor any of his folk, nor with any other of
Earth-dwellers that held the Silmarils of Fëanor from us. For
what," said Maidros, "do we suffer exile and wandering and rule
over a scant and forgotten folk, if others gather to their hoard the
heirlooms that are ours?"

Thus was it that they sent Curufin the Crafty to Dior, and told
him of their oath, and bid him give that fair jewel back unto those
whose right it was; but Dior gazing on the loveliness of Elwing
would not do so, and he said that he could not endure that the
Nauglafring, fairest of earthly craft, be so despoiled. "Then," said
Curufin, "must the Nauglafring unbroken be given to the sons of
Fëanor," and Dior waxed wroth, bidding him be gone, nor dare to
claim what his sire Beren the Onehanded won with his hand from
the [?jaws] of Melko – "other twain are there in the selfsame
place," said he, "an your hearts be bold enow."

Then went Curufin unto his brethren, and because of their
unbreakable oath and of their [?thirst] for that Silmaril (nor
indeed was the spell of Mîm and of the dragon wanting) they
planned war upon Dior – and the Eldar cry shame upon them for
that deed, the first premeditated war of elfin folk upon elfin folk,
whose name otherwise were glorious among the Eldalië for their
sufferings. Little good came thereby to them; for they fell
unawares upon Dior, and Dior and Auredhir were slain, yet
behold, Evranin the nurse of Elwing, and Gereth a Gnome, took
her unwilling in a flight swift and sudden from those lands, and
they bore with them the Nauglafring, so that the sons of Fëanor
saw it not; but a host of Dior's folk, coming with all speed yet late
unto the fray, fell suddenly on their rear, and there was a great
battle, and Maglor was slain with swords, and Mai . . . .[21] died of
wounds in the wild, and Celegorm was pierced with a hundred

arrows, and Cranthor beside him. Yet in the end were the sons of Fëanor masters of the field of slain, and the brown Elves and the green were scattered over all the lands unhappy, for they would not hearken to Maidros the maimed, nor to Curufin and Damrod who had slain their lord; and it is said that even on the day of that battle of the Elves Melko sought against Gondolin, and the fortunes of the Elves came to their uttermost waning.

Now was naught left of the seed of Beren Ermabwed son of Egnor save Elwing the Lovely, and she wandered in the woods, and of the brown Elves and the green a few gathered to her, and they departed for ever from the glades of Hithlum and got them to the south towards Sirion's deep waters, and the pleasant lands.

And thus did all the fates of the fairies weave then to one strand, and that strand is the great tale of Eärendel; and to that tale's true beginning are we now come.'

Then said Ailios: 'And methinks that is tale enow for this time of telling.'

NOTES

1   This sentence is a rewriting of the text, which had originally:

  "Nay then, know ye not that this gold belongs to the kindred of the Elves, who won it from the earth long time ago, and no one among Men has claim . . ."

  The remainder of this scene, ending with the slaughter of Úrin's band, was rewritten at many points, with the same object as in the passage just cited – to convert Úrin's band from Men to Elves, as was done also at the end of Eltas' tale (see p. 118 note 33). Thus original 'Elves' was changed to 'Elves of the wood, woodland Elves', and original 'Men' to 'folk, outlaws'; and see notes 2, 3, 5.

2   The original sentence here was:

  Doughty were those Men and great wielders of sword and axe, and still in those unfaded days might mortal weapons wound the bodies of the elfin-folk.

  See note 1.

3   The original sentence here was: 'and those Men being wildered with magics'. See note 1.

4   This sentence, from 'and yet another sorrow . . .', was added to the text later.

5   'those': the text has 'the Men', obviously left unchanged through oversight. See note 1.

6 'in the earth' is an emendation of the original reading 'on the earth'.

7 'damasked in strange wise', i.e. 'damascened', ornamentally inlaid with designs in gold and silver. The word 'damascened' is used of the sword of Tinwelint made by the Dwarves, on which were seen images of the wolf-hunt (p. 227), and of Glorfindel's arms (p. 173).

8 The text has 'Eltas', but with 'Ailios' written above in pencil. Since Ailios appears as the teller at the beginning of the tale, and not as the result of emendation, 'Eltas' here was probably no more than a slip.

9 'save only' is a later emendation of the original 'not even'. See p. 256.

10 It is odd that *Gwendelin* appears here, not *Gwenniel* as hitherto in this tale. Since the first part of the tale is in ink over an erased pencil text, the obvious explanation is that the erased text had *Gwendelin* and that my father changed this to *Gwenniel* as he went along, overlooking it in this one instance. But the matter is probably more complex – one of those small puzzles with which the texts of the *Lost Tales* abound – for after the manuscript in ink ceases the form *Gwenniel* occurs, though once only, and *Gwendelin* is then used for all the rest of the tale. See *Changes made to Names*, p. 244.

11 Here the manuscript in ink ends; see p. 221.

12 Against this sentence my father wrote a direction that the story was to be that the Nauglafring caught in the bushes and held the king.

13 A rejected passage in the manuscript here gives an earlier version of the events, according to which it was Gwendelin, not Huan, who brought the news to Beren:

> . . . and her bitter weeping filled the forest. Now there did Gwendeling [*sic*] gather to her many of the scattered woodland Elves and of them did she hear how matters had fared even as she had guessed: how the hunting party had been surrounded and o'erwhelmed by the Nauglath while the Indrafangs and Orcs fell suddenly with death and fire upon all the realm of Tinwelint, and not the least host was that of Ufedhin that slew the guardians of the bridge; and it was said that Naugladur had slain Tinwelint when he was borne down by numbers, and folk thought Narthseg a wild Elf had led the foemen hither, and he had been slain in the fighting.
>
> Then seeing no hope Gwendelin and her companions fared with the utmost speed out of that land of sorrow, even to the kingdom of i·Guilwarthon in Hisilómë, where reigned Beren and Tinúviel her daughter. Now Beren and Tinúviel lived not in any settled abode, nor had their realm boundaries well-marked, and no other messenger save Gwendelin daughter of the Vali had of a surety found those twain the living-dead so soon.

It is clear from the manuscript that the return of Mablung and Huan to Artanor and their presence at the hunt (referred to in general terms at the end of the *Tale of Tinúviel*, p. 41) was added to the tale, and with this new element went the change in Gwendelin's movements immediately after the disaster. But though the textual history is here extremely hard to interpet, what with erasures and additions on loose pages, I think it is almost certain that this reshaping was done while the original composition of the tale was still in progress.

14 The first of these lacunae that I have left in the text contains two words, the first possibly 'believe' and the second probably 'best'. In the second lacuna the word might conceivably be 'pallor'.

15 This sentence, from 'and is it not that very water . . .', is struck through and bracketed, and in the margin my father scribbled: 'No [?that] is Narog.'

16 The illegible word might be 'brays': the word 'clearer' is an emendation from 'hoarser'.

17 'and told Beren': i.e., 'and Beren told'. The text as first written had 'Then told Beren . . .'

18 The illegible word might just possibly be 'treasury', but I do not think that it is.

19 *Dior* replaced the name *Ausir*, which however occurs below as another name for Dior.

20 'Dior the Elf' is an emendation from 'Dior then an aged Elf'.

21 The latter part of this name is quite unclear: it might be read as *Maithog*, or as *Mailweg*. See *Changes made to Names* under *Dinithel*.

Changes made to names in
The Tale of the Nauglafring

Ilfiniol (p. 221) here so written from the first: see p. 201.

Gwenniel is used throughout the revised section of the tale except at the last occurrence (p. 228), where the form is *Gwendelin*; in the pencilled part of the tale at the first occurrence of the queen's name it is again *Gwenniel* (p. 230), but thereafter always *Gwendelin* (see note 10).

The name of the queen in the *Lost Tales* is as variable as that of Littleheart. In *The Chaining of Melko* and *The Coming of the Elves* she is *Tindriel > Wendelin*. In the *Tale of Tinúviel* she is *Wendelin > Gwendeling* (see p. 50); in the type-script text of *Tinúviel Gwenethlin > Melian*; in the *Tale of Turambar Gwendeling > Gwedheling*; in the present tale *Gwendelin/Gwenniel* (the form *Gwendeling* occurs in the rejected passage given in note 13); and in the Gnomish dictionary *Gwendeling > Gwedhiling*.

Belegost At the first occurrence (p. 230) the manuscript has *Ost Belegost*, with *Ost* circled as if for rejection, and *Belegost* is the reading subsequently.

(*i·*)*Guilwarthon*   In the *Tale of Tinúviel*, p. 41, the form is
i·Cuilwarthon. At the occurrence on p. 240 the ending of the
name does not look like *-on*, but as I cannot say what it is I give
Guilwarthon in the text.

Dinithel could also be read as *Durithel* (p. 241). This name was written
in later in ink over an earlier name in pencil now scarcely legible,
though clearly the same as that beginning *Mai* . . . . which appears
for this son of Fëanor subsequently (see note 21).

Commentary on
The Tale of the Nauglafring

In this commentary I shall not compare in detail the *Tale of the
Nauglafring* with the story told·in *The Silmarillion* (Chapter 22, *Of the
Ruin of Doriath*). The stories are profoundly different in essential
features – above all, in the reduction of the treasure brought by Húrin
from Nargothrond to a single object, the Necklace of the Dwarves, which
had long been in existence (though not, of course, containing the
Silmaril); while the whole history of the relation between Thingol and
the Dwarves is changed. My father never again wrote any part of this
story on a remotely comparable scale, and the formation of the published
text was here of the utmost difficulty; I hope later to give an account of it.

While it is often difficult to differentiate what my father omitted in his
more concise versions (in order to keep them concise) from what he
rejected, it seems clear that a large part of the elaborate narrative of the
Tale of the Nauglafring was early abandoned. In subsequent writing
the story of the fighting between Úrin's band and Tinwelint's Elves
disappeared, and there is no trace afterwards of Ufedhin or the other
Gnomes that lived among the Dwarves, of the story that the Dwarves
took half the unwrought gold ('the king's loan') away to Nogrod to
make precious objects from it, of the keeping of Ufedhin hostage, of
Tinwelint's refusal to let the Dwarves depart, of their outrageous
demands, of their scourging and their insulting payment.

We meet here again the strong emphasis on Tinwelint's love of treasure
and lack of it, in contrast to the later conception of his vast wealth (see my
remarks, pp. 128–9). The Silmaril is kept in a wooden casket (p. 225),
Tinwelint has no crown but a wreath of scarlet leaves (p. 227), and he
is far less richly clad and accoutred than 'the wayfarer in his halls'
(Ufedhin). This is very well in itself – the Woodland Elf corrupted by
the lure of golden splendour, but it need not be remarked again how
strangely at variance is this picture with that of Thingol Lord of
Beleriand, who had a vast treasury in his marvellous underground realm
of Menegroth, the Thousand Caves – itself largely contrived by the
Dwarves of Belegost in the distant past (*The Silmarillion* pp. 92–3), and
who most certainly did not need the aid of Dwarves at this time to make

him a crown and a fine sword, or vessels to adorn his banquets. Thingol in the later conception is proud, and stern; he is also wise, and powerful, and greatly increased in stature and in knowledge through his union with a Maia. Could such a king have sunk to the level of miserly swindling that is portrayed in the *Tale of the Nauglafring*?

Great stress is indeed placed on the enormous size of the hoard – 'such mighty heaps of gold have never since been gathered in one place', p. 223 – which is made so vast that it becomes hard to believe that a band of wandering outlaws could have brought it to the halls of the woodland Elves, even granting that 'some was lost upon the way' (p. 114). There is perhaps some difference here from the account of the Rodothlim and their works in the *Tale of Turambar* (p. 81), where there is certainly no suggestion that the Rodothlim possessed treasures coming out of Valinor – though this idea remained through all the vicissitudes of this part of the story: it is said of the Lord of Nargothrond in *The Silmarillion* (p. 114) that 'Finrod had brought more treasures out of Tirion than any other of the princes of the Noldor'.

More important, the elements of 'spell' and 'curse' are dominant in this tale, to such a degree that they might almost be said to be the chief actors in it. The curse of Mîm on the gold is felt at every turn of the narrative. Vengeance for him is one motive in Naugladur's decision to attack the Elves of Artanor (p. 230). His curse is fulfilled in the 'agelong feud' between the kindreds of the Dwarves (p. 235) – of which all trace was afterwards effaced, with the loss of the entire story of Ufedhin's intent to steal the Necklace from Naugladur sleeping, the killing of Bodruith Lord of Belegost, and the fighting between the two clans of Dwarves. Naugladur was 'blinded by the spell' in taking so imprudent a course out of Artanor (p. 236); and the curse of Mîm is made the 'cause' of his stumbling on a stone in his fight with Beren (p. 238). It is even, and most surprisingly, suggested as a reason for the short second lives of Beren and Tinúviel (p. 240); and finally 'the spell of Mîm' is an element in the attack on Dior by the Fëanorians (p. 241). An important element also in the tale is the baleful nature of the Nauglafring, for the Dwarves made it with bitterness; and into the complex of curses and spells is introduced also 'the dragon's ban upon the gold' (p. 239) or 'the spell of the dragon' (p. 241). It is not said in the *Tale of Turambar* that Glorund had cursed the gold or enspelled it; but Mîm said to Úrin (p. 114): 'Has not Glorund lain long years upon it, and the evil of the drakes of Melko is on it, and no good can it bring to Man or Elf.' Most notably, Gwendelin implies, against Beren's assertion that 'its holiness might overcome all such evils', that the Silmaril itself is unhallowed, since it 'abode in the Crown of Melko' (p. 239). In the later of the two 'schemes' for the *Lost Tales* (see I. 107 note 3) it is said that the Nauglafring 'brought sickness to Tinúviel'.*

---

* It is said in the Gnomish dictionary that the curse of Mîm was 'appeased' when the Nauglafring was lost in the sea; see the Appendix on Names, entry *Nauglafring*.

But however much the chief actors in this tale are 'enspelled' or blindly carrying forward the mysterious dictates of a curse, there is no question but that the Dwarves in the original conception were altogether more ignoble than they afterwards became, more prone to evil to gain their ends, and more exclusively impelled by greed; that Doriath should be laid waste by mercenary Orcs under Dwarvish paymasters (p. 230) was to become incredible and impossible later. It is even said that by the deeds of Naugladur 'have the Dwarves been severed in feud for ever since those days with the Elves, and drawn more nigh in friendship to the kin of Melko' (p. 230); and in the outlines for *Gilfanon's Tale* the Nauglath are an evil people, associates of goblins (I. 236–7). In a rejected outline for the *Tale of the Nauglafring* (p. 136) the Necklace was made 'by certain Úvanimor (Nautar or Nauglath)', Úvanimor being defined elsewhere as 'monsters, giants, and ogres'. With all this compare *The Lord of the Rings*, Appendix F (I): 'They [the Dwarves] are not evil by nature, and few ever served the Enemy of free will, whatever the tales of Men may have alleged.'

The account of the Dwarves in this tale is of exceptional interest in other respects. 'The beards of the Indrafangs' have been named in Tinúviel's 'lengthening spell' (pp. 19, 46); but this is the first description of the Dwarves in my father's writings – already with the spelling that he maintained against the unceasing opposition of proof-readers – and they are eminently recognisable in their dour and hidden natures, in their 'unloveliness' (*The Silmarillion* p. 113), and in their 'marvellous skill with metals' (*ibid.* p. 92). The strange statement that 'never comes a child among them' is perhaps to be related to 'the foolish opinion among Men' referred to in *The Lord of the Rings*, Appendix A (III), 'that there are no Dwarf-women, and that the Dwarves "grow out of stone".' In the same place it is said that 'it is because of the fewness of women among them that the kind of the Dwarves increases slowly'.

It is also said in the tale that it is thought by some that the Dwarves 'have not heard of Ilúvatar'; on knowledge of Ilúvatar among Men see p. 209.

According to the Gnomish dictionary *Indrafang* was 'a special name of the Longbeards or Dwarves', but in the tale it is made quite plain that the Longbeards were on the contrary the Dwarves of Belegost; the Dwarves of Nogrod were the Nauglath, with their king Naugladur. It must be admitted however that the use of the terms is sometimes confusing, or confused: thus the description of the Nauglath on pp. 223–4 seems to be a description of all Dwarves, and to include the Indrafangs, though this cannot have been intended. The reference to 'the march of the Dwarves and Indrafangs' (p. 234) must be taken as an ellipse, i.e. 'the Dwarves of Nogrod and the Indrafangs'. Naugladur of Nogrod and Bodruith of Belegost are said to have been akin (p. 235), though this perhaps only means that they were both Dwarves whereas Ufedhin was an Elf.

The Dwarf-city of Nogrod is said in the tale to lie 'a very long journey southward beyond the wide forest on the borders of those great heaths nigh Umboth-muilin the Pools of Twilight, on the marches of Tasarinan' (p. 225). This could be interpreted to mean that Nogrod was itself 'on the borders of those great heaths nigh Umboth-muilin'; but I think that this is out of the question. It would be a most improbable place for Dwarves, who 'dwell beneath the earth in caves and tunnelled towns, and aforetime Nogrod was the mightiest of these' (p. 224). Though mountains are not specifically mentioned here in connection with Dwarves, I think it extremely likely that my father at this time conceived their cities to be in the mountains, as they were afterwards. Further, there seems nothing to contradict the view that the configuration of the lands in the *Lost Tales* was essentially similar to that of the earliest and later 'Silmarillion' maps; and on them, 'a very long journey southward' is totally inappropriate to that between the Thousand Caves and the Pools of Twilight.

The meaning must therefore be, simply, 'a very long journey southward beyond the wide forest', and what follows places the wide forest, not Nogrod; the forest being, in fact, the Forest of Artanor.

The Pools of Twilight are described in *The Fall of Gondolin*, but the Elvish name does not there appear (see pp. 195–6, 217).

Whether Belegost was near to or far from Nogrod is not made plain; it is said in this passage that the gold should be borne away 'to Nogrod and the dwellings of the Dwarves', but later (p. 230) the Indrafangs are 'a kindred of the Dwarves that dwelt in other realms'.

In his association with the Dwarves Ufedhin is reminiscent of Eöl, Maeglin's father, of whom it is said in *The Silmarillion* (p. 133) that 'for the Dwarves he had more liking than any other of the Elvenfolk of old'; cf. *ibid.* p. 92: 'Few of the Eldar went ever to Nogrod or Belegost, save Eöl of Nan Elmoth and Maeglin his son.' In the early forms of the story of Eöl and Isfin (referred to in *The Fall of Gondolin*, p. 165) Eöl has no association with Dwarves. In the present tale there is mention (p. 224) of 'great traffic' carried on by the Dwarves 'with the free Noldoli' (with Melko's servants also) in those days: we may wonder who these free Noldoli were, since the Rodothlim had been destroyed, and Gondolin was hidden. Perhaps the sons of Fëanor are meant, or Egnor Beren's father (see p. 65).

The idea that it was the Dwarves of Nogrod who were primarily involved survived into the later narrative, but they became exclusively so, and those of Belegost specifically denied all aid to them (*The Silmarillion* p. 233).

Turning now to the Elves, Beren is here of course still an Elf (see p. 139), and in his second span of life he is the ruler, in Hithlum– Hisilómë, of an Elvish people so numerous that 'not even Beren knew the tale of those myriad folk' (p. 234); they are called 'the green Elves' and 'the brown Elves and the green', for they were 'clad in green and brown',

and Dior ruled them in Hithlum after the final departure of Beren and
Tinúviel. Who were they? It is far from clear how they are to be set into
the conception of the Elves of the Great Lands as it appears in other
Tales. We may compare the passage in *The Coming of the Elves*
(I. 118–19):

> Long after the joy of Valinor had washed its memory faint [i.e., the
> memory of the journey through Hisilómë] the Elves sang still sadly of
> it, and told tales of many of their folk whom they said and say were lost
> in those old forests and ever wandered there in sorrow. Still were they
> there long after when Men were shut in Hisilómë by Melko, and still
> do they dance there when Men have wandered far over the lighter
> places of the Earth. Hisilómë did Men name Aryador, and the Lost
> Elves did they call the Shadow Folk, and feared them.

But in that tale the conception still was that Tinwelint ruled 'the
scattered Elves of Hisilomë', and in the outlines for *Gilfanon's Tale* the
'Shadow Folk' of Hisilómë had ceased to be Elves (see p. 64). In any case,
the expression 'green Elves', coupled with the fact that it was the Green-
elves of Ossiriand whom Beren led to the ambush of the Dwarves at Sarn
Athrad in the later story (*The Silmarillion* p. 235), shows which Elvish
people they were to become, even though there is as yet no trace of
Ossiriand beyond the river Gelion and the story of the origin of the
Laiquendi (*ibid.* pp. 94, 96).

It was inevitable that 'the land of the dead that live' should cease to be
in Hisilómë (which seems to have been in danger of having too many
inhabitants), and a note on the manuscript of the *Tale of the Nauglafring*
says: 'Beren must be in "Doriath beyond Sirion" on a . . . . . not
in Hithlum.' Doriath beyond Sirion was the region called in *The Silmarillion* (p. 122) Nivrim, the West March, the woods on the west bank
of the river between the confluence of Teiglin and Sirion and Aelin-uial,
the Meres of Twilight. In the *Tale of Tinúviel* Beren and Tinúviel,
called i·Cuilwarthon, 'became mighty fairies in the lands about the north
of Sirion' (p. 41).

Gwendelin/Gwenniel appears a somewhat faint and ineffective figure
by comparison with the Melian of *The Silmarillion*. Conceivably, an
aspect of this is the far slighter protection afforded to the realm of
Artanor by her magic than that of the impenetrable wall and deluding
mazes of the Girdle of Melian (see p. 63). But the nature of the protection
in the old conception is very unclear. In the *Tale of the Nauglafring* the
coming of the Dwarves from Nogrod is only known when they approach
the bridge before Tinwelint's caves (p. 226); on the other hand, it is said
(p. 230) that the 'woven magic' of the queen was a defence against 'men of
hostile heart', who could never make their way through the woods unless
aided by treachery from within. Perhaps this provides an explanation of
a sort of how the Dwarves bringing treasure from Nogrod were able to

penetrate to the halls of Tinwelint without hindrance and apparently undetected (cf. also the coming of Úrin's band in the *Tale of Turambar*, p. 114). In the event, the protective magic was easily – too easily – overthrown by the simple device of a single treacherous Elf of Artanor who 'offered to lead the host through the magics of Gwendelin'. This was evidently unsatisfactory; but I shall not enter further into this question here. Extraordinary difficulties of narrative structure were caused by this element of the inviolability of Doriath, as I hope to describe at a future date.

It might be thought that the story of the drowning of the treasure at the Stony Ford (falling into the waters of the river with the Dwarves who bore it) was evolved from that in the rejected conclusion of the *Tale of Turambar* (p. 136) – Tinwelint 'hearing that curse [set on the treasure by Úrin] caused the gold to be cast into a deep pool of the river before his doors'. In the *Tale of the Nauglafring*, however, Tinwelint, influenced by the queen's foreboding words, still has the intention of doing this, but does not fulfil his intention (p. 223).

The account of the second departure of Beren and Tinúviel (p. 240) raises again the extremely difficult question of the peculiar fate that was decreed for them by the edict of Mandos, which I have discussed on pp. 59–60. There I have suggested that

> the peculiar dispensation of Mandos in the case of Beren and Tinúviel as here conceived is therefore that their whole 'natural' destiny as Elves was changed: having died as Elves might die (from wounds or from grief) they were not reborn as new beings, but returned in their own persons – yet now 'mortal even as Men'.

Here however Tinúviel 'faded', and vanished in the woods; and Beren searched all Hithlum and Artanor for her, until he too 'faded from life'. Since this fading is here quite explicitly the mode in which 'that doom of mortality that Mandos had spoken' came upon them (p. 240), it is very notable that it is likened to, and even it seems identified with, the fading of 'the Elves of later days throughout the world' – as though in the original idea Elvish fading was a form of mortality. This is in fact made explicit in a later version.

The seven Sons of Fëanor, their oath (sworn not in Valinor but after the coming of the Noldoli to the Great Lands), and the maiming of Maidros appear in the outlines for *Gilfanon's Tale*; and in the latest of these outlines the Fëanorians are placed in Dor Lómin (= Hisilómë, Hithlum), see I. 238, 240, 243. Here, in the *Tale of the Nauglafring*, appear for the first time the names of the Sons of Fëanor, five of them (Maidros, Maglor, Celegorm, Cranthor, Curufin) in the forms, or almost the forms, they were to retain, and Curufin already with his sobriquet 'the Crafty'. The names Amrod and Amras in *The Silmarillion* were a late change; for long these two sons of Fëanor were Damrod (as here) and Díriel (here Dinithel or Durithel, see *Changes made to Names*, p. 245).

Here also appear Dior the Fair, also called Ausir the Wealthy, and his daughter Elwing; his son Auredhir early disappeared in the development of the legends. But Dior ruled in 'the southern vales' (p. 241) of Hisilómë, not in Artanor, and there is no suggestion of any renewal of Tinwelint's kingdom after his death, in contrast to what was told later (*The Silmarillion* p. 236); moreover the Fëanorians, as noted above, dwelt also in Hisilómë – and how all this is to be related to what is said elsewhere of the inhabitants of that region I am unable to say: cf. the *Tale of Tinúviel*, p. 10: 'Hisilómë where dwelt Men, and thrall-Noldoli laboured, and few free-Eldar went.'

A very curious statement is made in this concluding part of the tale, that 'those were days of happiness in the vales of Hithlum, for there was peace with Melko and the Dwarves who had but one thought as they plotted against Gondolin' (p. 241). Presumably 'peace with Melko' means no more than that Melko had averted his attention from those lands; but nowhere else is there any reference to the Dwarves' plotting against Gondolin.

In the typescript version of the *Tale of Tinúviel* (p. 43) it is said that if Turgon King of Gondolin was the most glorious of the kings of the Elves who defied Melko, 'for a while the most mighty *and the longest free* was Thingol of the Woods'. The most natural interpretation of this expression is surely that Gondolin fell before Artanor; whereas in *The Silmarillion* (p. 240) 'Tidings were brought by Thorondor Lord of Eagles of the fall of Nargothrond, and after of the slaying of Thingol and of Dior his heir, and of the ruin of Doriath; but Turgon shut his ear to word of the woes without.' In the present tale we see the same chronology, in that many of the Elves who followed Beren went after his departure to Gondolin, 'the rumour of whose growing power and glory ran in secret whispers among all the Elves' (p. 240), though here the destruction of Gondolin is said to have taken place on the very day that Dior was attacked by the Sons of Fëanor (p. 242). To evade the discrepancy therefore we must interpret the passage in the *Tale of Tinúviel* to mean that Thingol remained free for a longer period of years than did Turgon, irrespective of the dates of their downfalls.

Lastly, the statements that Cûm an-Idrisaith, the Mound of Avarice, 'stands there still in Artanor' (p. 223), and that the waters of Aros still flow above the drowned hoard (p. 238), are noteworthy as indications that nothing analogous to the Drowning of Beleriand was present in the original conception.

V

THE TALE OF EÄRENDEL

The 'true beginning' of the *Tale of Eärendel* was to be the dwelling at Sirion's mouth of the Lothlim (the point at which *The Fall of Gondolin* ends: 'and fair among the Lothlim Eärendel grows in the house of his father', pp. 196–7) and the coming there of Elwing (the point at which the *Tale of the Nauglafring* ends: 'they departed for ever from the glades of Hithlum and got them to the south towards Sirion's deep waters, and the pleasant lands. And thus did all the fates of the fairies weave then to one strand, and that strand is the great tale of Eärendel; and to that tale's true beginning are we now come', p. 242). The matter is complicated, however, as will be seen in a moment, by my father's also making the *Nauglafring* the first part of the *Tale of Eärendel*.

But the great tale was never written; and for the story as he then conceived it we are wholly dependent on highly condensed and often contradictory outlines. There are also many isolated notes; and there are the very early Eärendel poems. While the poems can be precisely dated, the notes and outlines can not; and it does not seem possible to arrange them in order so as to provide a clear line of development.

One of the outlines for the *Tale of Eärendel* is the earlier of the two 'schemes' for the *Lost Tales* which are the chief materials for *Gilfanon's Tale*; and I will repeat here what I said of this in the first part (I.233):

> There is no doubt that [the earlier of the two schemes] was composed when the *Lost Tales* had reached their furthest point of development, as represented by the latest texts and arrangements given in this book. Now when this outline comes to the matter of *Gilfanon's Tale* it becomes at once very much fuller, but then contracts again to cursory references for the tales of Tinúviel, Túrin, Tuor, and the Necklace of the Dwarves, and once more becomes fuller for the tale of Eärendel.

This scheme B (as I will continue to call it) provides a coherent if very rough narrative plan, and divides the story into seven parts, of which the first (marked 'Told') is 'The Nauglafring down to the flight of Elwing'. This sevenfold division is referred to by Littleheart at the beginning of *The Fall of Gondolin* (p. 144):

> It is a mighty tale, and seven times shall folk fare to the Tale-fire ere it be rightly told; and so twined is it with those stories of the Nauglafring and of the Elf-march that I would fain have aid in that telling . . .

If the six parts following the *Tale of the Nauglafring* were each to be of comparable length, the whole *Tale of Eärendel* would have been somewhere near half the length of all the tales that were in fact written; but my father never afterwards returned to it on any ample scale.

I give now the concluding part of Scheme B.

Tale of Eärendel begins, with which is interwoven the Nauglafring and the March of the Elves. For further details see Notebook C.*

First part. The tale of the Nauglafring down to the flight of Elwing.

Second part. The dwelling at Sirion. Coming thither of Elwing, and the love of her and Eärendel as girl and boy. Ageing of Tuor – his secret sailing after the conches of Ulmo in Swanwing.

Eärendel sets sail to the North to find Tuor, and if needs be Mandos. Sails in Eärámë. Wrecked. Ulmo appears. Saves him, bidding him sail to Kôr – 'for for this hast thou been brought out of the Wrack of Gondolin'.

Third part. Second attempt of Eärendel to Mandos. Wreck of Falasquil and rescue by the Oarni.[1] He sights the Isle of Seabirds 'whither do all the birds of all waters come at whiles'. Goes back by land to Sirion.

Idril has vanished (she set sail at night). The conches of Ulmo call Eärendel. Last farewell of Elwing. Building of Wingilot.

Fourth part. Eärendel sails for Valinor. His many wanderings, occupying several years.

Fifth part. Coming of the birds of Gondolin to Kôr with tidings. Uproar of the Elves. Councils of the Gods. March of the Inwir (death of Inwë), Teleri, and Solosimpi.

Raid upon Sirion and captivity of Elwing.

Sorrow and wrath of Gods, and a veil dropped between Valmar and Kôr, for the Gods will not destroy it but cannot bear to look upon it.

Coming of the Eldar. Binding of Melko. Faring to Lonely Isle. Curse of the Nauglafring and death of Elwing.

Sixth part. Eärendel reaches Kôr and finds it empty. Fares home in sorrow (and sights Tol Eressëa and the fleet of the Elves, but a great wind and darkness carries him away, and he misses his way and has a voyage eastward).

Arriving at length at Sirion finds it empty. Goes to the ruins of Gondolin. Hears of tidings. Sails to Tol Eressëa. Sails to the Isle of Seabirds.

Seventh part. His voyage to the firmament.

---

* For 'Notebook C' see p. 254.

Written at the end of the text is: 'Rem[ainder] of Scheme in Notebook C'. These references in Scheme B to 'Notebook C' are to the little pocket-book which goes back to 1916–17 but was used for notes and suggestions throughout the period of the *Lost Tales* (see I.171). At the beginning of it there is an outline (here called 'C') headed 'Eärendel's Tale, Tuor's son', which is in fair harmony with Scheme B:

Eärendel dwells with Tuor and Irildë[2] at Sirion's mouth by the sea (on the Isles of Sirion). Elwing of the Gnomes of Artanor[3] flees to them with the Nauglafring. Eärendel and Elwing love one another as boy and girl.

Great love of Eärendel and Tuor. Tuor ages, and Ulmo's conches far out west over the sea call him louder and louder, till one evening he sets sail in his twilit boat with purple sails, Swanwing, Alqarámë.[4] Idril sees him too late. Her song on the beach of Sirion.

When he does not return grief of Eärendel and Idril. Eärendel (urged also by Idril who is immortal) desires to set sail and search even to Mandos. [*Marginal addition*:] Curse of Nauglafring rests on his voyages. Ossë his enemy.

Fiord of the Mermaid. Wreck. Ulmo appears at wreck and saves them, telling them he must go to Kôr and is saved for that.

Elwing's grief when she learns Ulmo's bidding. 'For no man may tread the streets of Kôr or look upon the places of the Gods and dwell in the Outer Lands in peace again.'

Eärendel departs all the same and is wrecked by the treachery of Ossë and saved only by the Oarni (who love him) with Voronwë and dragged to Falasquil.

Eärendel makes his way back by land with Voronwë. Finds that Idril has vanished.[5] His grief. Prays to Ulmo and hears the conches. Ulmo bids him build a new and wonderful ship of the wood of Tuor from Falasquil. Building of Wingilot.

There are four items headed 'Additions' on this page of the notebook:

Building of Eärámë (Eaglepinion).
Noldoli add their pleading to Ulmo's bidding.
Eärendel surveys the first dwelling of Tuor at Falasquil.
The voyage to Mandos and the Icy Seas.

The outline continues:

Voronwë and Eärendel set sail in Wingilot. Driven south. Dark regions. Fire mountains. Tree-men. Pygmies. Sarqindi or cannibal-ogres.

Driven west. Ungweliantë. Magic Isles. Twilit Isle [*sic*]. Little-heart's gong awakes the Sleeper in the Tower of Pearl.[6]

Kôr is found. Empty. Eärendel reads tales and prophecies in the waters. Desolation of Kôr. Eärendel's shoes and self powdered with diamond dust so that they shine brightly.

Homeward adventures. Driven east – the deserts and red palaces where dwells the Sun.[7]

Arrives at Sirion, only to find it sacked and empty. Eärendel distraught wanders with Voronwë and comes to the ruins of Gondolin. Men are encamped there miserably. Also Gnomes searching still for lost gems (or some Gnomes gone back to Gondolin).

Of the binding of Melko.[8] The wars with Men and the departure to Tol Eressëa (the Eldar unable to endure the strife of the world). Eärendel sails to Tol Eressëa and learns of the sinking of Elwing and the Nauglafring. Elwing became a seabird. His grief is very great. His garments and body shine like diamonds and his face is in silver flame for the grief and . . . .

He sets sail with Voronwë and dwells on the Isle of Seabirds in the northern waters (not far from Falasquil) – and there hopes that Elwing will return among the seabirds, but she is seeking him wailing along all the shores and especially among wreckage.

After three times seven years he sails again for halls of Mandos with Voronwë – he gets there because [?only] those who still . . . . and had suffered may do so – Tuor is gone to Valinor and nought is known of Idril or of Elwing.

Reaches bar at margin of the world and sets sail on oceans of the firmament in order to gaze over the Earth. The Moon mariner chases him for his brightness and he dives through the Door of Night. How he cannot now return to the world or he will die.

He will find Elwing at the Faring Forth.

Tuor and Idril some say sail now in Swanwing and may be seen going swift down the wind at dawn and dusk.

The Co-events to Eärendel's Tale

Raid upon Sirion by Melko's Orcs and the captivity of Elwing.

Birds tell Elves of the Fall of Gondolin and the horrors of the fate of the Gnomes. Counsels of the Gods and uproar of the Elves. March of the Inwir and Teleri. The Solosimpi go forth also but fare along all the beaches of the world, for they are loth to fare far from the sound of the sea – and only consent to go with the Teleri under these conditions – for the Noldoli slew some of their kin at Kópas.

This outline then goes on to the events after the coming of the Elves of Valinor into the Great Lands, which will be considered in the next chapter.

Though very much fuller, there seems to be little in C that is certainly contradictory to what is said in B, and there are elements in the latter that are absent from the former. In discussing these outlines I follow the divisions of the tale made in B.

Second part. A little more is told in C of Tuor's departure from Sirion (in B there is no mention of Idril); and there appears the motive of Ossë's hostility to Eärendel and the curse of the Nauglafring as instrumental in his shipwrecks. The place of the first wreck is called the Fiord of the Mermaid. The word 'them' rather than 'him' in 'Ulmo saves them, telling them he must go to Kôr' is certain in the manuscript, which possibly suggests that Idril or Elwing (or both) were with Eärendel.

Third part. In B Eärendel's second voyage, like the first, is explicitly an attempt to reach Mandos (seeking his father), whereas in C it seems that the second is undertaken rather in order to fulfil Ulmo's bidding that he sail to Kôr (to Elwing's grief). In C Voronwë is named as Eärendel's companion on the second voyage which ended at Falasquil; but the Isle of Seabirds is not mentioned at this point. In C Wingilot is built 'of the wood of Tuor from Falasquil'; in *The Fall of Gondolin* Tuor's wood was hewed for him by the Noldoli in the forests of Dor Lómin and floated down the hidden river (p. 152).

Fourth part. Whereas B merely refers to Eärendel's 'many wanderings, occupying several years' in his quest for Valinor, C gives some glimpses of what they were to be, as Wingilot was driven to the south and then into the west. The encounter with Ungweliantë on the western voyage is curious; it is said in *The Tale of the Sun and Moon* that 'Melko held the North and Ungweliant the South' (see I.182, 200).

In C we meet again the Sleeper in the Tower of Pearl (said to be Idril, though this was struck out, note 6) awakened by Littleheart's gong; cf. the account of Littleheart in *The Cottage of Lost Play* (I.15):

> He sailed in Wingilot with Eärendel in that last voyage wherein they sought for Kôr. It was the ringing of this Gong on the Shadowy Seas that awoke the Sleeper in the Tower of Pearl that stands far out to west in the Twilit Isles.

In *The Coming of the Valar* it is said that the Twilit Isles 'float' on the Shadowy Seas 'and the Tower of Pearl rises pale upon their most western cape' (I.68; cf. I.125). But there is no other mention in C of Littleheart, Voronwë's son, as a companion of Eärendel, though he was named earlier in the outline, in a rejected phrase, as present at the Mouths of Sirion (see note 5), and in the *Tale of the Nauglafring* (p. 228) Ailios says that none still living have seen the Nauglafring 'save only Littleheart son of Bronweg' (where 'save only' is an emendation from 'not even').

Fifth and sixth parts. In C we meet the image of Eärendel's shoes shining from the dust of diamonds in Kör, an image that was to survive (*The Silmarillion* p. 248):

> He walked in the deserted ways of Tirion, and the dust upon his raiment and his shoes was a dust of diamonds, and he shone and glistened as he climbed the long white stairs.

But in *The Silmarillion* Tirion was deserted because it was 'a time of festival, and wellnigh all the Elvenfolk were gone to Valimar, or were gathered in the halls of Manwë upon Taniquetil'; here on the other hand it seems at least strongly implied, in both B and C, that Kôr was empty because the Elves of Valinor had departed into the Great Lands, as a result of the tidings brought by the birds of Gondolin. In these very early narrative schemes there is no mention of Eärendel's speaking to the Valar, as the ambassador of Elves and Men (*The Silmarillion* p. 249), and we can only conclude, extraordinary as the conclusion is, that Eärendel's great western voyage, though he attained his goal, was fruitless, that he was not the agent of the aid that did indeed come out of Valinor to the Elves of the Great Lands, and (most curious of all) that Ulmo's designs for Tuor had no issue. In fact, my father actually wrote in the 1930 version of 'The Silmarillion':

> Thus it was that the many emissaries of the Gnomes in after days came never back to Valinor – save one: and he came too late.

The words 'and he came too late' were changed to 'the mightiest mariner of song', and this is the phrase that is found in *The Silmarillion*, p. 102. It is unfortunately never made clear in the earliest writings what was Ulmo's purpose in bidding Eärendel sail to Kôr, for which he had been saved from the ruin of Gondolin. What would he have achieved, had he come to Kôr 'in time', more than in the event did take place after the coming of tidings from Gondolin – the March of the Elves into the Great Lands? In a curious note in C, not associated with the present outline, my father asked: 'How did King Turgon's messengers get to Valinor or gain the Gods' consent?' and answered: 'His messengers never got there. Ulmo [*sic*] but the birds brought tidings to the Elves of the fate of Gondolin (the doves and pigeons of Turgon) and they [?arm and march away].'

The coming of the message was followed by 'the councils (counsels C) of the Gods and the uproar of the Elves', but in C nothing is said of 'the sorrow and wrath of the Gods' or 'the veil dropped between Valmar and Kôr' referred to in B: where the meaning can surely only be that the March of the Elves from Valinor was undertaken in direct opposition to the will of the Valar, that the Valar were bitterly opposed to the intervention of the Elves of Valinor in the affairs of the Great Lands. There may well be a connection here with Vairë's words (I.19): 'When the fairies left

Kôr that lane [i.e. Olórë Mallë that led past the Cottage of Lost Play]
was blocked for ever with great impassable rocks'. Elsewhere there
is only one other reference to the effect of the message from across the
sea, and that is in the words of Lindo to Eriol in *The Cottage of Lost
Play* (I. 16):

> Inwë, whom the Gnomes call Inwithiel . . . . . was King of all the Eldar
> when they dwelt in Kôr. That was in the days before hearing the
> lament of the world [i.e. the Great Lands] Inwë led them forth to the
> lands of Men.

Later, Meril-i-Turinqi told Eriol (I. 129) that Inwë, her grandsire's sire,
'perished in that march into the world', but Ingil his son 'went long ago
back to Valinor and is with Manwë'; and there is a reference to Inwë's
death in B.

In C the Solosimpi only agreed to accompany the expedition on
condition that they remain by the sea, and the reluctance of the Third
Kindred, on account of the Kinslaying at Swanhaven, survived (*The
Silmarillion* p. 251). But there is no suggestion that the Elves of Valinor
were transported by ship, indeed the reverse, for the Solosimpi 'fare
along all the beaches of the world', and the expedition is a 'March';
though there is no indication of how they came to the Great Lands.

Both outlines refer to Eärendel being driven eastwards on his homeward voyage from Kôr, and to his finding the dwellings at Sirion's mouth
ravaged when he finally returned there; but B does not say who carried
out the sack and captured Elwing. In C it was a raid by Orcs of Melko; cf.
the entry in the Name-list to *The Fall of Gondolin* (p. 215): '*Egalmoth*
. . . got even out of the burning of Gondolin, and dwelt after at the mouth
of Sirion, but was slain in a dire battle there when Melko seized Elwing'.

Neither outline refers to Elwing's escape from captivity. Both mention
Eärendel's going back to the ruins of Gondolin - in C he returns there
with Voronwë and finds Men and Gnomes; another entry in the Name-
list to *The Fall of Gondolin* (p. 215) bears on this: '*Galdor* . . . won out
of Gondolin and even the onslaught of Melko upon the dwellers at
Sirion's mouth and went back to the ruins with Eärendel.'

Both outlines mention the departure of the Elves from the Great
Lands, after the binding of Melko, to Tol Eressëa, C adding a reference
to 'wars with Men' and to the Eldar being 'unable to endure the strife
of the world', and both refer to Eärendel's going there subsequently, but
the order of events seems to be different: in B Eärendel on his way back
from Kôr 'sights Tol Eressëa and the fleet of the Elves' (presumably the
fleet returning from the Great Lands), whereas in C the departure of the
Elves is not mentioned until after Eärendel's return to Sirion. But the
nature of these outlines is not conveyed in print: they were written at
great speed, catching fugitive thoughts, and cannot be pressed hard.
However, with the fate of Elwing B and C seem clearly to part company:

in B there is a simple reference to her death, apparently associated with the curse of the Nauglafring, and from the order in which the events are set down it may be surmised that her death took place on the journey to Tol Eressëa; C specifically refers to the 'sinking' of Elwing and the Nauglafring – but says that Elwing became a seabird, an idea that survived (*The Silmarillion* p. 247). This perhaps gives more point to Eärendel's going to the Isle of Seabirds, mentioned in both B and C: in the latter he 'hopes that Elwing will return among the seabirds'.

Seventh part. In B the concluding part of the tale is merely summarised in the words 'His voyage to the firmament', with a reference to the other outline C, and in the latter we get some glimpses of a narrative. It seems to be suggested that the brightness of Eärendel (quite unconnected with the Silmaril) arose from the 'diamond dust' of Kôr, but also in some sense from the exaltation of his grief. An isolated jotting elsewhere in C asks: 'What became of the Silmarils after the capture of Melko?' My father at this time gave no answer to the question; but the question is itself a testimony to the relatively minor importance of the jewels of Fëanor, if also, perhaps, a sign of his awareness that they would not always remain so, that in them lay a central meaning of the mythology, yet to be discovered.

It seems too that Eärendel sailed into the sky in continuing search for Elwing ('he sets sail on the oceans of the firmament in order to gaze over the Earth'); and that his passing through the Door of Night (the entrance made by the Gods in the Wall of Things in the West, see I.215–16) did not come about through any devising, but because he was hunted by the Moon. With this last idea, cf. I.193, where Ilinsor, steersman of the Moon, is said to 'hunt the stars'.

The later of the two schemes for the *Lost Tales*, which gives a quite substantial outline for *Gilfanon's Tale*, where I have called it 'D' (see I.234), here fails us, for the concluding passage is very condensed, in part erased, and ends abruptly early in the *Tale of Eärendel*. I give it here, beginning at a slightly earlier point in the narrative:

Of the death of Tinwelint and the flight of Gwenethlin [see p. 51].
How Beren avenged Tinwelint and how the Necklace became his.
How it brought sickness to Tinúviel [see p. 246], and how Beren and Tinúviel faded from the Earth. How their sons [*sic*] dwelt after them and how the sons of Fëanor came up against them with a host because of the Silmaril. How all were slain but Elwing daughter of Daimord [see p. 139] son of Beren fled with the Necklace.
Of Tuor's vessel with white sails.

How folk of the Lothlim dwelt at Sirion's Mouth. Eärendel grew fairest of all Men that were or are. How the mermaids (Oarni) loved him. How Elwing came to the Lothlim and of the love of Elwing and Eärendel. How Tuor fell into age, and how Ulmo beckoned to him at eve, and he set forth on the waters and was lost. How Idril swam after him.

(In the following passage my father seems at first to have written: 'Eärendel . . . . Oarni builded Wingilot and set forth in search of . . . . leaving Voronwë with Elwing', where the first lacuna perhaps said 'with the aid of', though nothing is now visible; but then he wrote 'Eärendel built Swanwing', and then partly erased the passage: it is impossible to see now what his intention was.)

Elwing's lament. How Ulmo forbade his quest but Eärendel would yet sail to find a passage to Mandos. How Wingilot was wrecked at Falasquil and how Eärendel found the carven house of Tuor there.

Here Scheme D ends. There is also a reference at an earlier point in it to 'the messengers sent from Gondolin. The doves of Gondolin fly to Valinor at the fall of that town.'

This outline seems to show a move to reduce the complexity of the narrative, with Wingilot being the ship in which Eärendel attempted to sail to Mandos and in which he was wrecked at Falasquil; but the outline is too brief and stops too soon to allow any certain conclusions to be drawn.

A fourth outline, which I will call 'E', is found on a detached sheet; in this Tuor is called Tûr (see p. 148).

Fall of Gondolin. The feast of Glorfindel. The dwelling by the waters of Sirion's mouth. The mermaids come to Eärendel.

Tûr groweth sea-hungry – his song to Eärendel. One evening he calls Eärendel and they go to the shore. There is a skiff. Tûr bids farewell to Eärendel and bids him thrust it off – the skiff fares away into the West. Eärendel hears a great song swelling from the sea as Tûr's skiff dips over the world's rim. His passion of tears upon the shore. The lament of Idril.

The building of Earum.[9] The coming of Elwing. Eärendel's reluctance. The whetting of Idril. The voyage and foundering of Earum in the North, and the vanishing of Idril. How the seamaids rescued Eärendel, and brought him to Tûr's bay. His coastwise journey.

The rape of Elwing. Eärendel discovers the ravaging of Sirion's mouth.

The building of Wingelot. He searches for Elwing and is blown far to the South. Wirilómë. He escapes eastward. He goes back westward; he descries the Bay of Faëry. The Tower of Pearl, the magic isles, the great shadows. He finds Kôr empty; he sails back, crusted with dust and his face afire. He learns of Elwing's foundering. He sitteth on the Isle of Seabirds. Elwing as a seamew comes to him. He sets sail over the margent of the world.

Apart from the fuller account of Tuor's departure from the mouths of Sirion, not much can be learned from this – it is too condensed. But even allowing for speed and compression, there seem to be essential differences from B and C. Thus in this outline (E) Elwing, as it appears, comes to Sirion at a later point in the story, after the departure of Tuor; but the raid and capture of Elwing seems to take place at an earlier point, while Eärendel is on his way back to Sirion from his shipwreck in the North (not, as in B and C, while he is on the great voyage in Wingilot that took him to Kôr). Here, it seems, there was to be only one northward journey, ending in the shipwreck of Earámë/Earum near Falasquil. Though it cannot be demonstrated, I incline to think that E was subsequent to B and C: partly because the reduction of two northward voyages ending in shipwreck to one seems more likely than the other way about, and partly because of the form *Tûr*, which, though it did not survive, replaced *Tuor* for a time (p. 148).

One or two other points may be noticed in this outline. The great spider, called *Ungweliantë* in C but here *Wirilómë* ('Gloomweaver', see I.152), is here encountered by Eärendel in the far South, not as in C on his westward voyage: see p. 256. Elwing in this version comes to Eärendel as a seabird (as she does in *The Silmarillion*, p. 247), which is not said in C and even seems to be denied.

Another isolated page (associated with the poem 'The Bidding of the Minstrel', see pp. 269–70 below) gives a very curious account of Eärendel's great voyage:

Eärendel's boat goes through North. Iceland. [*Added in margin*: back of North Wind.] Greenland, and the wild islands: a mighty wind and crest of great wave carry him to hotter climes, to back of West Wind. Land of strange men, land of magic. The home of Night. The Spider. He escapes from the meshes of Night with a few comrades, sees a great mountain island and a golden city [*added in margin*: Kôr] – wind blows him southward. Tree-men, Sun-dwellers, spices, fire-mountains, red sea: Mediterranean (loses his boat (travels afoot through wilds of Europe?)) or Atlantic.* Home. Waxes aged. Has a new boat builded. Bids adieu to his north land. Sails west again to the lip of the world, just as the Sun is diving into the sea. He sets sail upon the sky and returns no more to earth.

The golden city was Kôr and he had caught the music of the Solosimpë, and returns to find it, only to find that the fairies have departed from Eldamar. See little book. Dusted with diamond dust climbing the deserted streets of Kôr.

---

* The words in this passage ('Tree-men, Sun-dwellers . . .') are clear but the punctuation is not, and the arrangement here may not be that intended.

One would certainly suppose this account to be earlier than anything so far considered (both from the fact that Eärendel's history after his return from the great voyage seems to bear no relation to that in B and C, and from his voyage being set in the lands and oceans of the known world), were it not for the reference to the 'little book', which must mean 'Notebook C', from which the outline C above is taken (see p. 254). But I think it very probable (and the appearance of the MS rather supports this) that the last paragraph ('The golden city was Kôr . . .') was added later, and that the rest of the outline belongs with the earliest writing of the poem, in the winter of 1914.

It is notable that only here in the earliest writings is it made clear that the 'diamond dust' that coated Eärendel came from the streets of Kôr (cf. the passage from *The Silmarillion* cited on p. 257).

Another of the early Eärendel poems, 'The Shores of Faëry', has a short prose preface, which if not as old as the first composition of the poem itself (July 1915, see p. 271) is certainly not much later:

> Eärendel the Wanderer who beat about the Oceans of the World in his white ship Wingelot sat long while in his old age upon the Isle of Seabirds in the Northern Waters ere he set forth upon a last voyage.
>
> He passed Taniquetil and even Valinor, and drew his bark over the bar at the margin of the world, and launched it on the Oceans of the Firmament. Of his ventures there no man has told, save that hunted by the orbed Moon he fled back to Valinor, and mounting the towers of Kôr upon the rocks of Eglamar he gazed back upon the Oceans of the World. To Eglamar he comes ever at plenilune when the Moon sails a-harrying beyond Taniquetil and Valinor.*

Both here and in the outline associated with 'The Bidding of the Minstrel' Eärendel was conceived to be an old man when he journeyed into the firmament.

No other 'connected' account of the *Tale of Eärendel* exists from the earliest period. There are however a number of separate notes, mostly in the form of single sentences, some found in the little notebook C, others jotted down on slips. I collect these references here more or less in the sequence of the tale.

(i) 'Dwelling in the Isle of Sirion in a house of snow-white stone.' — In C (p. 254) it is said that Eärendel dwelt with Tuor and Idril at Sirion's mouth by the sea 'on the Isles of Sirion'.

---

* This preface is found in all the texts of the poem save the earliest, and the versions of it differ only in name-forms: *Wingelot/Vingelot* and *Eglamar/Eldamar* (varying in the same ways as in the accompanying versions of the poem, see textual notes p. 272), and *Kôr* > *Tûn* in the third text, *Tûn* in the fourth. For *Egla* = *Elda* see I. 251 and II. 338, and for *Tûn* see p. 292.

(ii) 'The Oarni give to Eärendel a wonderful shining silver coat that wets not. They love Eärendel, in Ossë's despite, and teach him the lore of boat-building and of swimming, as he plays with them about the shores of Sirion.' – In the outlines are found references to the love of the Oarni for Eärendel (D, p. 259), the coming of the mermaids to him (E, p. 260), and to Ossë's enmity (C, p. 254).

(iii) Eärendel was smaller than most men but nimble-footed and a swift swimmer (but Voronwë could not swim).

(iv) 'Idril and Eärendel see Tuor's boat dropping into the twilight and a sound of song.' – In B Tuor's sailing is 'secret' (p. 253), in C 'Idril sees him too late' (p. 254), and in E Eärendel is present at Tuor's departure and thrusts the boat out: 'he hears a great song swelling from the sea' (p. 260).

(v) 'Death of Idril? – follows secretly after Tuor.' – That Idril died is denied in C: 'Tuor and Idril some say sail now in Swanwing . . .' (p. 255); in D Idril swam after him (p. 260).

(vi) 'Tuor has sailed back to Falasquil and so back up Ilbranteloth to Asgon where he sits playing on his lonely harp on the islanded rock.' – This is marked with a query and an 'X' implying rejection of the idea. There are curious references to the 'islanded rock' in Asgon in the outlines for Gilfanon's Tale (see I.238).

(vii) 'The fiord of the Mermaid: enchantment of his sailors. Mermaids are not Oarni (but are earthlings, or fays? – or both).' – In D (p. 259) Mermaids and Oarni are equated.

(viii) The ship Wingilot was built of wood from Falasquil with 'aid of the Oarni'. – This was probably said also in D: see p. 260.

(ix) Wingilot was 'shaped as a swan of pearls'.

(x) 'The doves and pigeons of Turgon's courtyard bring message to Valinor – only to Elves.' – Other references to the birds that flew from Gondolin also say that they came to the Elves, or to Kôr (pp. 253, 255, 257).

(xi) 'During his voyages Eärendel sights the white walls of Kôr gleaming afar off, but is carried away by Ossë's adverse winds and waves.' – The same is said in B (p. 253) of Eärendel's sighting of Tol Eressëa on his homeward voyage from Kôr.

(xii) 'The Sleeper in the Tower of Pearl awakened by Littleheart's gong: a messenger that was despatched years ago by Turgon and enmeshed in magics. Even now he cannot leave the Tower and warns them of the magic.' – In C there is a statement, rejected, that the Sleeper in the Tower of Pearl was Idril herself (see note 6).

(xiii) 'Ulmo's protection removed from Sirion in wrath at Eärendel's second attempt to Mandos, and hence Melko overwhelmed it.' – This note is struck through, with an 'X' written against it; but in D (p. 260) it is said that 'Ulmo forbade his quest but Eärendel would yet sail to find a passage to Mandos'. The meaning of this must be that it was contrary to Ulmo's purpose that Eärendel should seek to Mandos for his father, but must rather attempt to reach Kôr.

(xiv) 'Eärendel weds Elwing before he sets sail. When he hears of her loss he says that his children shall be "all such men hereafter as dare the great seas in ships".' – With this cf. *The Cottage of Lost Play* (I.13): 'even such a son of Eärendel as was this wayfarer', and (I.18): 'a man of great and excellent travel, a son meseems of Eärendel'. In an outline of Eriol's life (I.24) it is said that he was a son of Eärendel, born under his beam, and that if a beam from Eärendel fall on a child newborn he becomes 'a child of Eärendel' and a wanderer. In the early dictionary of Qenya there is an entry: *Eärendilyon* 'son of Eärendel (used of any mariner)' (I.251).

(xv) 'Eärendel goes even to the empty Halls of Iron seeking Elwing.' – Eärendel must have gone to Angamandi (empty after the defeat of Melko) at the same time as he went to the ruins of Gondolin (pp. 253, 255).

(xvi) The loss of the ship carrying Elwing and the Nauglafring took place on the voyage to Tol Eressëa with the exodus of the Elves from the Great Lands. – See my remarks, pp. 258–9. For the 'appeasing' of Mîm's curse by the drowning of the Nauglafring see the Appendix on Names, entry *Nauglafring*. The departure of the Elves to Tol Eressëa is discussed in the next chapter (p. 280).

(xvii) 'Eärendel and the northern tower on the Isle of Seabirds.' – In C (p. 255) Eärendel 'sets sail with Voronwë and dwells on the Isle of Seabirds in the northern waters (not far from Falasquil) – and there hopes that Elwing will return among the seabirds'; in B (p. 253) 'he sights the Isle of Seabirds "whither do all the birds of all waters come at whiles".' There is a memory of this in *The Silmarillion*, p. 250: 'Therefore there was built for [Elwing] a white tower northward upon the borders of the Sundering Seas; and thither at times all the seabirds of the earth repaired.'

(xviii) When Eärendel comes to Mandos he finds that Tuor is '*not* in Valinor, nor Erumáni, and neither Elves nor Ainu know where he is. (He is with Ulmo.)' – In C (p. 255) Eärendel, reaching the Halls of Mandos, learns that Tuor 'is gone to Valinor'. For the possibility that Tuor might be in Erumáni or Valinor see I.91 ff.

(xix) Eärendel 'returns from the firmament ever and anon with Voronwë to Kôr to see if the Magic Sun has been lit and the fairies have come back – but the Moon drives him back'. – On Eärendel's return from the firmament see (xxi) below; on the Rekindling of the Magic Sun see p. 286.

Two statements about Eärendel cited previously may be added here:

(xx) In the tale of *The Theft of Melko* (I.141) it is said that 'on the walls of Kôr were many dark tales written in pictured symbols, and runes of great beauty were drawn there too or carved upon stones, and Eärendel read many a wondrous tale there long ago'.

(xxi) The Name-list to *The Fall of Gondolin* has the following entry (cited on p. 215): '*Eärendel* was the son of Tuor and Idril and 'tis said the only being that is half of the kindred of the Eldalië and half of Men. He was the greatest and first of all mariners among Men, and saw regions that Men have not yet found nor gazed upon for all the multitude of their boats. He rideth now with Voronwë upon the winds of the firmament nor comes ever further back than Kôr, else would he die like other Men, so much of the mortal is in him.' – In the outline associated with the poem 'The Bidding of the Minstrel' Eärendel 'sets sail upon the sky and returns no more to earth' (p. 261); in the prose preface to 'The Shores of Faëry' 'to Eglamar he comes ever at plenilune when the Moon sails a-harrying beyond Taniquetil and Valinor' (p. 262); in outline C 'he cannot now return to the world or he will die' (p. 255); and in citation (xix) above he 'returns from the firmament ever and anon with Voronwë to Kôr'.

In *The Silmarillion* (p. 249) Manwë's judgement was that Eärendel and Elwing 'shall not walk ever again among Elves or Men in the Outer Lands'; but it is also said that Eärendel returned to Valinor from his 'voyages beyond the confines of the world' (*ibid.* p. 250), just as it is said in the Name-list to *The Fall of Gondolin* that he does not come ever further back than Kôr. The further statement in the Name-list, that if he did he would die like other Men, 'so much of the mortal is in him', was in some sense echoed long after in a letter of my father's written in 1967: '*Eärendil*, being in part descended from Men, was not allowed to set foot on Earth again, and became a star shining with the light of the Silmaril' (*The Letters of J. R. R. Tolkien* no. 297).

This brings to an end all the 'prose' materials that bear on the earliest form of the *Tale of Eärendel* (apart from a few other references to him that appear in the next chapter). With these outlines and notes we are at a very early stage of composition, when the conceptions were fluid and had not been given even preliminary narrative form: the myth was present in certain images that were to endure, but these images had not been articulated.

I have already noticed (p. 257) the remarkable fact that there is no hint of the idea that it was Eärendel who by his intercession brought aid out of the West; equally there is no suggestion that the Valar hallowed his ship and set him in the sky, nor that his light was that of the Silmaril. Nonetheless there were already present the coming of Eärendel to Kôr (Tirion) and finding it deserted, the dust of diamonds on his shoes, the changing of Elwing into a seabird, the passing of his ship through the Door of Night, and the sanction against his return to the lands east of the Sea. The raid on the Havens of Sirion appears in the early outlines, though that was an act of Melko's, not of the Fëanorians; and Tuor's departure also, but without Idril, whom he left behind. His ship was *Alqarámë*, Swanwing: afterwards it bore the name *Eärrámë*, with the meaning 'Sea-wing' (*The Silmarillion* p. 245), which retained, in form but not in meaning, the name of Eärendel's first ship *Eärámë* 'Eaglepinion' (pp. 253–4, and see note 9).

It is interesting to read my father's statement, made some half-century later (in the letter of 1967 referred to above), concerning the origins of Eärendil:

This name is in fact (as is obvious) derived from Anglo-Saxon *éarendel*. When first studying Anglo-Saxon professionally (1913–) – I had done so as a boyish hobby when supposed to be learning Greek and Latin – I was struck by the great beauty of this word (or name), entirely coherent with the normal style of Anglo-Saxon, but euphonic to a peculiar degree in that pleasing but not 'delectable' language. Also its form strongly suggests that it is in origin a proper name and not a common noun. This is borne out by the obviously related forms in other Germanic languages; from which amid the confusions and debasements of late traditions it at least seems certain that it belonged to astronomical-myth, and was the name of a star or star-group. To my mind the Anglo-Saxon uses seem plainly to indicate that it was a star presaging the dawn (at any rate in English tradition): that is what we now call *Venus*: the morning star as it may be seen shining brilliantly in the dawn, before the actual rising of the Sun. That is at any rate how I took it. Before 1914 I wrote a 'poem' upon Eärendel who launched his ship like a bright spark from the havens of the Sun. I adopted him into my mythology – in which he became a prime figure as a mariner, and eventually as a herald star, and a sign of hope to men. *Aiya Eärendil Elenion Ancalima* ([The Lord of the Rings] II.329) 'hail Eärendil brightest of Stars' is derived at long remove from *Éalá Éarendel engla beorhtast*.* But the name could not be adopted just like that: it had to be accommodated to the Elvish linguistic situation, at the same time as a place for this person was made in legend. From this, far back in the history of 'Elvish', which was beginning, after many tentative starts in boyhood, to take definite shape at the time of the name's adoption, arose eventually (a) the C[ommon]E[lvish] stem *AYAR 'sea', primarily applied to the Great Sea of the West, lying between Middle-earth and Aman the Blessed Realm of the Valar; and (b) the element, or verbal base (N)DIL, 'to love, be devoted to' – describing the attitude of one to a person, thing, cause, or occupation to which one is devoted for its own sake. Eärendil became a character in the earliest written (1916–17) of the major legends: *The Fall of Gondolin*, the greatest of the *Pereldar* 'Half-elven', son of *Tuor* of the most renowned House of the Edain, and *Idril* daughter of the King of Gondolin.

My father did not indeed here say that his *Eärendel* contained from the beginning elements that in combination give a meaning like 'Sea-lover'; but it is in any case clear that at the time of the earliest extant writings on

---

* From the Old English poem *Crist*: *éalá! éarendel engla beorhtast ofer mid-dangeard monnum sended*.

the subject the name was associated with an Elvish word *ea* 'eagle' – see p. 265 on the name of Eärendel's first ship *Eärámë* 'Eaglepinion'. In the Name-list to *The Fall of Gondolin* this is made explicit: '*Earendl* [*sic*] though belike it hath some kinship to the Elfin *ea* and *earen* "eagle" and "eyrie" (wherefore cometh to mind the passage of Cristhorn and the use of the sign of the Eagle by Idril [see p. 193]) is thought to be woven of that secret tongue of the Gondothlim [see p. 165].'

★

I give lastly four early poems of my father's in which Eärendel appears.

I

Éalá Éarendel Engla Beorhtast

There can be little doubt that, as Humphrey Carpenter supposes (*Biography* p. 71), this was the first poem on the subject of Eärendel that my father composed, and that it was written at Phoenix Farm, Gedling, Nottinghamshire, in September 1914.[10] It was to this poem that he was referring in the letter of 1967 just cited – 'I wrote a "poem" upon Eärendel who launched his ship like a bright spark': cf. line 5 'He launched his bark like a silver spark . . .'

There are some five different versions, each one incorporating emendations made in the predecessor, though only the first verse was substantially rewritten. The title was originally 'The Voyage of Éarendel the Evening Star', together with (as customarily) an Old English version of this: *Scipfæreld Earendeles Æfensteorran*; this was changed in a later copy to *Éalá Éarendel Engla Beorhtast* 'The Last Voyage of Eärendel', and in still later copies the modern English name was removed. I give it here in the last version, the date of which cannot be determined, though the handwriting shows it to be substantially later than the original composition; together with all the divergent readings of the earliest extant version in footnotes.

> Éarendel arose where the shadow flows
>   At Ocean's silent brim;
> Through the mouth of night as a ray of light
>   Where the shores are sheer and dim   4
> He launched his bark like a silver spark
>   From the last and lonely sand;
> Then on sunlit breath of day's fiery death
>   He sailed from Westerland.   8

He threaded his path o'er the aftermath
   Of the splendour of the Sun,
And wandered far past many a star
   In his gleaming galleon.   12
On the gathering tide of darkness ride
   The argosies of the sky,
And spangle the night with their sails of light
   As the streaming star goes by.   16

Unheeding he dips past these twinkling ships,
   By his wayward spirit whirled
On an endless quest through the darkling West
   O'er the margin of the world;   20
And he fares in haste o'er the jewelled waste
   And the dusk from whence he came
With his heart afire with bright desire
   And his face in silver flame.   24

The Ship of the Moon from the East comes soon
   From the Haven of the Sun,
Whose white gates gleam in the coming beam
   Of the mighty silver one.   28
Lo! with bellying clouds as his vessel's shrouds
   He weighs anchor down the dark,
And on shimmering oars leaves the blazing shores
   In his argent-timbered bark.   32

Readings of the earliest version:

1–8   Éarendel sprang up from the Ocean's cup
       In the gloom of the mid-world's rim;
    From the door of Night as a ray of light
       Leapt over the twilight brim,
    And launching his bark like a silver spark
       From the golden-fading sand
    Down the sunlit breath of Day's fiery Death
       He sped from Westerland.

10   splendour] glory
11   wandered] went wandering
16   streaming] Evening
17   Unheeding] But unheeding
18   wayward] wandering
19   endless] magic   darkling] darkening
20   O'er the margin] Toward the margent
22   And the dusk] To the dusk
25   The Ship] For the Ship
31   blazing] skiey
32   timbered] orbéd

Then Éarendel fled from that Shipman dread
   Beyond the dark earth's pale,
Back under the rim of the Ocean dim,
   And behind the world set sail;   36
And he heard the mirth of the folk of earth
   And the falling of their tears,
As the world dropped back in a cloudy wrack
   On its journey down the years.   40

Then he glimmering passed to the starless vast
   As an isléd lamp at sea,
And beyond the ken of mortal men
   Set his lonely errantry,   44
Tracking the Sun in his galleon
   Through the pathless firmament,
Till his light grew old in abysses cold
   And his eager flame was spent.   48

There seems every reason to think that this poem preceded all the outlines and notes given in this chapter, and that verbal similarities to the poem found in these are echoes (e.g. 'his face is in silver flame', outline C, p. 255; 'the margent of the world', outline E, p. 260).

In the fourth verse of the poem the Ship of the Moon comes forth from the Haven of the Sun; in the tale of *The Hiding of Valinor* (I. 215) Aulë and Ulmo built two havens in the east, that of the Sun (which was 'wide and golden') and that of the Moon (which was 'white, having gates of silver and of pearl') – but they were both 'within the same harbourage'. As in the poem, in the *Tale of the Sun and Moon* the Moon is urged on by 'shimmering oars' (I. 195).

II

The Bidding of the Minstrel

This poem, according to a note that my father scribbled on one of the copies, was written at St. John's Street, Oxford (see I. 27) in the winter of 1914; there is no other evidence for its date. In this case the earliest workings are extant, and on the back of one of the sheets is the outline

33   Then] And
38   And the falling of] And hearkened to

46–8   And voyaging the skies
       Till his splendour was shorn by the birth of Morn
       And he died with the Dawn in his eyes.

account of Eärendel's great voyage given on p. 261. The poem was then
much longer than it became, but the workings are exceedingly rough;
they have no title. To the earliest finished text a title was added hastily
later: this apparently reads 'The Minstrel renounces the song'. The title
then became 'The Lay of Eärendel', changed in the latest text to 'The
Bidding of the Minstrel, from the Lay of Eärendel'.

There are four versions following the original rough draft, but the
changes made in them were slight, and I give the poem here in the latest
form, noting only that originally the minstrel seems to have responded to
the 'bidding' much earlier – at line 5, which read 'Then harken – a tale of
immortal sea-yearning'; and that 'Eldar' in line 6 and 'Elven' in line 23 are
emendations, made on the latest text, of 'fairies', 'fairy'.

> 'Sing us yet more of Eärendel the wandering,
> Chant us a lay of his white-oared ship,
> More marvellous-cunning than mortal man's pondering,
> Foamily musical out on the deep.
> Sing us a tale of immortal sea-yearning   5
> The Eldar once made ere the change of the light,
> Weaving a winelike spell, and a burning
> Wonder of spray and the odours of night;
> Of murmurous gloamings out on far oceans;
> Of his tossing at anchor off islets forlorn   10
> To the unsleeping waves' never-ending sea-motions;
> Of bellying sails when a wind was born,
> And the gurgling bubble of tropical water
> Tinkled from under the ringéd stem,
> And thousands of miles was his ship from those wrought her   15
> A petrel, a sea-bird, a white-wingéd gem,
> Gallantly bent on measureless faring
> Ere she came homing in sea-laden flight,
> Circuitous, lingering, restlessly daring,
> Coming to haven unlooked for, at night.'   20
>
> 'But the music is broken, the words half-forgotten,
> The sunlight has faded, the moon is grown old,
> The Elven ships foundered or weed-swathed and rotten,
> The fire and the wonder of hearts is acold.
> Who now can tell, and what harp can accompany   25
> With melodies strange enough, rich enough tunes,
> Pale with the magic of cavernous harmony,
> Loud with shore-music of beaches and dunes,
> How slender his boat; of what glimmering timber;
> How her sails were all silvern and taper her mast,   30
> And silver her throat with foam and her limber
> Flanks as she swanlike floated past!

The song I can sing is but shreds one remembers
Of golden imaginings fashioned in sleep,
A whispered tale told by the withering embers   35
Of old things far off that but few hearts keep.'

III

The Shores of Faëry

This poem is given in its earliest form by Humphrey Carpenter, *Bio-graphy*, pp. 76–7.[11] It exists in four versions each as usual incorporating slight changes; my father wrote the date of its composition on three of the copies, viz. 'July 8–9, 1915'; 'Moseley and Edgbaston, Birmingham July 1915 (walking and on bus). Retouched often since – esp. 1924'; and 'First poem of my mythology, Valinor . . . . 1910'. This last cannot have been intended for the date of composition, and the illegible words preceding it may possibly be read as 'thought of about'. But it does not in any case appear to have been 'the first poem of the mythology': that, I believe, was *Éalá Éarendel Engla Beorhtast* – and my father's mention of this poem in his letter of 1967 (see p. 266) seems to suggest this also.

The Old English title was *Ielfalandes Strand* (The Shores of Elfland). It is preceded by a short prose preface which has been given above, p. 262. I give it here in the latest version (undateable), with all readings from the earliest in footnotes.

East of the Moon, west of the Sun
There stands a lonely hill;
Its feet are in the pale green sea,
Its towers are white and still,
Beyond Taniquetil   5
In Valinor.
Comes never there but one lone star
That fled before the moon;
And there the Two Trees naked are
That bore Night's silver bloom,   10
That bore the globéd fruit of Noon
In Valinor.
There are the shores of Faëry

Readings of the earliest version:

1   East . . . . . west] West . . . . . East
7   No stars come there but one alone
8   fled before] hunted with
9   For there the Two Trees naked grow
10   bore] bear   11   bore] bear

With their moonlit pebbled strand
Whose foam is silver music   15
On the opalescent floor
Beyond the great sea-shadows
On the marches of the sand
That stretches on for ever
To the dragonheaded door,   20
The gateway of the Moon,
Beyond Taniquetil
In Valinor.
West of the Sun, east of the Moon
Lies the haven of the star,   25
The white town of the Wanderer
And the rocks of Eglamar.
There Wingelot is harboured,
While Eärendel looks afar
O'er the darkness of the waters   30
Between here and Eglamar –
Out, out, beyond Taniquetil
In Valinor afar.

There are some interesting connections between this poem and the tale
of *The Coming of the Elves and the Making of Kôr*. The 'lonely hill'
of line 2 is the hill of Kôr (cf. the tale, I. 122: 'at the head of this long creek
there stands a lonely hill which gazes at the loftier mountains'), while 'the
golden feet of Kôr' (a line replaced in the later versions of the poem) and
very probably 'the sand That stretches on for ever' are explained by the
passage that follows in the tale:

Thither [i.e. to Kôr] did Aulë bring all the dust of magic metals that
his great works had made and gathered, and he piled it about the foot
of that hill, and most of this dust was of gold, and a sand of gold
stretched away from the feet of Kôr out into the distance where the
Two Trees blossomed.

18   marches] margent
20–21   To the dragonheaded door, The gateway of the Moon] From the golden feet of Kôr
24   West of the Sun, east of the Moon] O! West of the Moon, East of the Sun
27   rocks] rock
28   Wingelot] *Earliest text* Wingelot > Vingelot; *second text* Vingelot; *third text*
         Vingelot > Wingelot; *last text* Wingelot
30   O'er the darkness of the waters] On the magic and the wonder
31   Between] 'Tween

   In the latest text *Elvenland* is lightly written over *Faëry* in line 13, and *Eldamar* against
Eglamar in line 27 (only); *Eglamar* > *Eldamar* in the second text.

With the 'dragonheaded door' (line 20) cf. the description of the Door of Night in *The Hiding of Valinor* (I. 215–16):

Its pillars are of the mightiest basalt and its lintel likewise, but great dragons of black stone are carved thereon, and shadowy smoke pours slowly from their jaws.

In that description the Door of Night is not however 'the gateway of the Moon', for it is the Sun that passes through it into the outer dark, whereas 'the Moon dares not the utter loneliness of the outer dark by reason of his lesser light and majesty, and he journeys still beneath the world [i.e. through the waters of Vai]'.

IV

The Happy Mariners

I give lastly this poem whose subject is the Tower of Pearl in the Twilit Isles. It was written in July 1915,[12] and there are six texts preceding the version which was published (together with 'Why the Man in the Moon came down too soon') at Leeds in 1923* and which is the first of the two given here.

(1)

I know a window in a western tower
That opens on celestial seas,
And wind that has been blowing round the stars
Comes to nestle in its tossing draperies.
It is a white tower builded in the Twilight Isles,   5
Where Evening sits for ever in the shade;
It glimmers like a spike of lonely pearl
That mirrors beams forlorn and lights that fade;
And sea goes washing round the dark rock where it stands,
And fairy boats go by to gloaming lands   10
All piled and twinkling in the gloom
With hoarded sparks of orient fire

---

* *A Northern Venture*: see I. 204, footnote. Mr Douglas A. Anderson has kindly supplied me with a copy of the poem in this version, which had been very slightly altered from that published in *The Stapeldon Magazine* (Exeter College, Oxford), June 1920 (Carpenter, p. 268). – *Twilight* in line 5 of the Leeds version is almost certainly an error, for *Twilit*, the reading of all the original texts.

That divers won in waters of the unknown Sun —
And, maybe, 'tis a throbbing silver lyre,
Or voices of grey sailors echo up   15
Afloat among the shadows of the world
In oarless shallop and with canvas furled;
For often seems there ring of feet and song
Or twilit twinkle of a trembling gong.

O! happy mariners upon a journey long   20
To those great portals on the Western shores
Where far away constellate fountains leap,
And dashed against Night's dragon-headed doors,
In foam of stars fall sparkling in the deep.
While I alone look out behind the Moon   25
From in my white and windy tower,
Ye bide no moment and await no hour,
But chanting snatches of a mystic tune
Go through the shadows and the dangerous seas
Past sunless lands to fairy leas   30
Where stars upon the jacinth wall of space
Do tangle burst and interlace.
Ye follow Earendel through the West,
The shining mariner, to Islands blest;
While only from beyond that sombre rim   35
A wind returns to stir these crystal panes
And murmur magically of golden rains
That fall for ever in those spaces dim.

In *The Hiding of Valinor* (I. 215) it is told that when the Sun was first
made the Valar purposed to draw it beneath the Earth, but that

 it was too frail and lissom; and much precious radiance was spilled in
 their attempts about the deepest waters, and escaped to linger as secret
 sparks in many an unknown ocean cavern. These have many elfin
 divers, and divers of the fays, long time sought beyond the outmost
 East, even as is sung in the song of the Sleeper in the Tower of Pearl.

That 'The Happy Mariners' was in fact 'the song of the Sleeper in the
Tower of Pearl' seems assured by lines 10–13 of the poem.
   For 'Night's dragon-headed doors' see p. 273. The meaning of *jacinth*
in 'the jacinth wall of space' (line 31) is 'blue'; cf. 'the deep-blue walls' in
The Hiding of Valinor (I. 215).

   Many years later my father rewrote the poem, and I give this version
here. Still later he turned to it again and made a few further alterations
(here recorded in footnotes); at this time he noted that the revised
version dated from '1940?'.

(2)

I know a window in a Western tower
that opens on celestial seas,
and there from wells of dark behind the stars
blows ever cold a keen unearthly breeze.
It is a white tower builded on the Twilit Isles,   5
and springing from their everlasting shade
it glimmers like a house of lonely pearl,
where lights forlorn take harbour ere they fade.

Its feet are washed by waves that never rest.
There silent boats go by into the West   10
all piled and twinkling in the dark
with orient fire in many a hoarded spark
that divers won
in waters of the rumoured Sun.
There sometimes throbs below a silver harp,   15
touching the heart with sudden music sharp;
or far beneath the mountains high and sheer
the voices of grey sailors echo clear,
afloat among the shadows of the world
in oarless ships and with their canvas furled,   20
chanting a farewell and a solemn song:
for wide the sea is, and the journey long.

O happy mariners upon a journey far,
beyond the grey islands and past Gondobar,
to those great portals on the final shores   25
where far away constellate fountains leap,
and dashed against Night's dragon-headed doors
in foam of stars fall sparkling in the deep!
While I, alone, look out behind the moon
from in my white and windy tower,   30
ye bide no moment and await no hour,
but go with solemn song and harpers' tune
through the dark shadows and the shadowy seas
to the last land of the Two Trees,
whose fruit and flower are moon and sun,   35
where light of earth is ended and begun.

Last revisions:
  3   and there *omitted*
  4   blows ever cold] there ever blows
 17   mountains] mountain
 22   the journey] their journey
 29   While I look out alone   30   imprisoned in the white and windy tower
 31   ye] you   33–6 *struck through*

Ye follow Eärendel without rest,
the shining mariner, beyond the West,
who passed the mouth of night and launched his bark
upon the outer seas of everlasting dark.   40
Here only comes at whiles a wind to blow
returning darkly down the way ye go,
with perfume laden of unearthly trees.
Here only long afar through window-pane
I glimpse the flicker of the golden rain   45
that falls for ever on the outer seas.

I cannot explain the reference (in the revised version only, line 24) to the journey of the mariners 'beyond the grey islands and past Gondobar'. *Gondobar* ('City of Stone') was one of the seven names of Gondolin (p. 158).

NOTES

1   Falasquil was the name of Tuor's dwelling on the coast (p. 152); the Oarni, with the Falmariní and the Wingildi, are called 'the spirits of the foam and the surf of ocean' (I. 66).

2   *Irildë*: the 'Elvish' name corresponding to Gnomish *Idril*. See the Appendix on Names, entry *Idril*.

3   'Elwing of the *Gnomes* of Artanor' is perhaps a mere slip.

4   For the Swan-wing as the emblem of Tuor see pp. 152, 164, 172, 193.

5   The words 'Idril has vanished' replace an earlier reading: 'Sirion has been sacked and only Littleheart (Ilfrith) remained who tells the tale.' *Ilfrith* is yet another version of Littleheart's Elvish name (see pp. 201–2).

6   Struck out here: 'The Sleeper is Idril but he does not know.'

7   Cf. *Kortirion among the Trees* (I. 36, lines 129–30): 'I need not know the desert or red palaces Where dwells the sun'; lines retained slightly changed in the second (1937) version (I. 39).

8   This passage, from 'Eärendel distraught . . .', replaced the following: '[*illegible name, possibly* Orlon] is [?biding] there and tells him of the sack of Sirion and the captivity of Elwing. The faring of the Koreldar and the binding of Melko.' Perhaps the words 'The faring of the Koreldar' were struck out by mistake (cf. Outline B).

9   *Earum* is emended (at the first occurrence only) from *Earam*; and following it stood the name *Earnhama*, but this was struck out. *Earnhama* is Old English, 'Eagle-coat', 'Eagle-dress'.

37   Ye] You   40   outer *omitted*
41–3   *struck through*   46   the] those
Line added at end: beyond the country of the shining Trees.

10 The two earliest extant texts date it thus, one of them with the addition 'Ex[eter] Coll[ege] Essay Club Dec. 1914', and on a third is written 'Gedling, Notts., Sept. 1913 [error for 1914] and later'. My father referred to having read 'Eärendel' to the Essay Club in a letter to my mother of 27 November 1914.

11 But *rocks* in line 27 (26) should read *rock*.

12 According to one note it was written at 'Barnt Green [see *Biography* p. 36] July 1915 and Bedford and later', and another note dates it 'July 24 [1915], rewritten Sept. 9'. The original workings are on the back of an unsent letter dated from Moseley (Birmingham) July 11, 1915; my father began military training at Bedford on July 19.

VI

THE HISTORY OF ERIOL OR ÆLFWINE AND THE END OF THE TALES

In this final chapter we come to the most difficult (though not, as I hope to show, altogether insoluble) part of the earliest form of the mythology: its end, with which is intertwined the story of Eriol/Ælfwine – and with that, the history and original significance of Tol Eressëa. For its elucidation we have some short pieces of connected narrative, but are largely dependent on the same materials as those that constitute *Gilfanon's Tale* and the story of Eärendel: scribbled plot-outlines, endlessly varying, written on separate slips of paper or in the pages of the little notebook 'C' (see p. 254). In this chapter there is much material to consider, and for convenience of reference within the chapter I number the various citations consecutively. But it must be said that no device of presentation can much diminish the inherent complexity and obscurity of the matter.

The fullest account (bald as it is) of the March of the Elves of Kôr and the events that followed is contained in notebook C, continuing on from the point where I left that outline on p. 255, after the coming of the birds from Gondolin, the 'counsels of the Gods and uproar of the Elves', and the 'March of the Inwir and Teleri', with the Solosimpi only agreeing to accompany the expedition on condition that they remain by the sea. The outline continues:

(1)   Coming of the Eldar. Encampment in the Land of Willows of first host. Overwhelming of Noldorin and Valwë. Wanderings of Noldorin with his harp.
     Tulkas overthrows Melko in the battle of the Silent Pools. Bound in Lumbi and guarded by Gorgumoth the hound of Mandos.
     Release of the Noldoli. War with Men as soon as Tulkas and Noldorin have fared back to Valinor.
     Noldoli led to Valinor by Egalmoth and Galdor.

There have been previous references in the *Lost Tales* to a battle in Tasarinan, the Land of Willows: in the *Tale of Turambar* (pp. 70, 140), and, most notably, in *The Fall of Gondolin* (p. 154), where when Tuor's sojourn in that land is described there is mention of events that would take place there in the future:

Did not even after the days of Tuor Noldorin and his Eldar come there seeking for Dor Lómin and the hidden river and the caverns of the Gnomes' imprisonment; yet thus nigh to their quest's end were like to abandon it? Indeed sleeping and dancing here . . . they were whelmed by the goblins sped by Melko from the Hills of Iron and Noldorin made bare escape thence.

Valwë has been mentioned once before, by Lindo, on Eriol's first evening in Mar Vanwa Tyaliéva (I. 16): 'My father Valwë who went with Noldorin to find the Gnomes.' Of Noldorin we know also that he was the Vala Salmar, the twin-brother of Ómar-Amillo; that he entered the world with Ulmo, and that in Valinor he played the harp and lyre and loved the Noldoli (I. 66, 75, 93, 126).

An isolated note states:

(2) Noldorin escapes from the defeat of the Land of Willows and takes his harp and goes seeking in the Iron Mountains for Valwë and the Gnomes until he finds their place of imprisonment. Tulkas follows. Melko comes to meet him.

The only one of the great Valar who is mentioned in these notes as taking part in the expedition to the Great Lands is Tulkas; but whatever story underlay his presence, despite the anger and sorrow of the Valar at the March of the Elves (see p. 257), is quite irrecoverable. (A very faint hint concerning it is found in two isolated notes: 'Tulkas gives – or the Elves take *limpë* with them', and '*Limpë* given by the Gods (Oromë? Tulkas?) when Elves left Valinor'; cf. *The Flight of the Noldoli* (I. 166): 'no *limpë* had they [the Noldoli] as yet to bring away, for that was not given to the fairies until long after, when the March of Liberation was undertaken'.) According to (1) above Tulkas fought with and overthrew Melko 'in the battle of the Silent Pools'; and the Silent Pools are the Pools of Twilight, 'where Tulkas after fought with Melko's self' (*The Fall of Gondolin*, p. 195; the original reading here was 'Noldorin and Tulkas').

The name *Lumbi* is found elsewhere (in a list of names associated with the tale of *The Coming of the Valar*, I. 93), where it is said to be Melko's third dwelling; and a jotting in notebook C, sufficiently mysterious, reads: 'Lumfad. Melko's dwelling after release. Castle of Lumbi.' But this story also is lost.

That the Noldoli were led back to Valinor by Egalmoth and Galdor, as stated in (1), is notable. This is contradicted in detail by a statement in the Name-list to *The Fall of Gondolin*, which says (p. 215) that Egalmoth was slain in the raid on the dwelling at the mouth of Sirion when Elwing was taken; and contradicted in general by the next citation to be given, which denies that the Elves were permitted to dwell in Valinor.

The only other statement concerning these events is found in the first of the four outlines that constitute *Gilfanon's Tale*, which I there called 'A' (I. 234). This reads:

(3)   March of the Elves out into the world.
        The capture of Noldorin.
        The camp in the Land of Willows.
        Army of Tulkas at the Pools of Twilight . . . . . . and [?many]
            Gnomes, but Men fall on them out of Hisilómë.
        Defeat of Melko.
        Breaking of Angamandi and release of captives.
        Hostility of Men. The Gnomes collect some of the jewels.
        Elwing and most of the Elves go back to dwell in Tol Eressëa. The
            Gods will not let them dwell in Valinor.

This seems to differ from (1) in the capture of Noldorin and in the attack of Men from Hisilómë before the defeat of Melko; but the most notable statement is that concerning the refusal of the Gods to allow the Elves to dwell in Valinor. There is no reason to think that this ban rested only, or chiefly, on the Noldoli. The text, (3), does not refer specifically to the Gnomes in this connection; and the ban is surely to be related to 'the sorrow and wrath of the Gods' at the time of the March of the Elves (p. 253). Further, it is said in *The Cottage of Lost Play* (I. 16) that Ingil son of Inwë returned to Tol Eressëa with 'most of the fairest and the wisest, most of the merriest and the kindest, of all the Eldar', and that the town that he built there was named 'Koromas or "the Resting of the Exiles of Kôr".' This is quite clearly to be connected with the statement in (3) that 'Most of the Elves go back to dwell in Tol Eressëa', and with that given on p. 255: 'The wars with Men and the departure to Tol Eressëa (the Eldar unable to endure the strife of the world)'. These indications taken together leave no doubt, I think, that my father's original conception was of the Eldar of Valinor undertaking the expedition into the Great Lands against the will of the Valar; together with the rescued Noldoli they returned over the Ocean, but being refused re-entry into Valinor they settled in Tol Eressëa, as 'the Exiles of Kôr'. That some did return in the end to Valinor may be concluded from the words of Meril-i-Turinqi (I. 129) that Ingil, who built Kortirion, 'went long ago back to Valinor and is with Manwë'. But Tol Eressëa remained the land of the fairies in the early conception, the Exiles of Kôr, Eldar and Gnomes, speaking both *Eldarissa* and *Noldorissa*.

    It seems that there is nothing else to be found or said concerning the original story of the coming of aid out of the West and the renewed assault on Melko.

★

The conclusion of the whole story as originally envisaged was to be rejected in its entirety. For it we are very largely dependent on the outline in notebook C, continuing on from citation (1) above; this is extremely rough and disjointed, and is given here in a very slightly edited form.

(4) After the departure of Eärendel and the coming of the Elves to Tol Eressëa (and most of this belongs to the history of Men) great ages elapse; Men spread and thrive, and the Elves of the Great Lands fade. As Men's stature grows theirs diminishes. Men and Elves were formerly of a size, though Men always larger.[1]

Melko again breaks away, by the aid of Tevildo (who in long ages gnaws his bonds); the Gods are in dissension about Men and Elves, some favouring the one and some the other. Melko goes to Tol Eressëa and tries to stir up dissension among the Elves (between Gnomes and Solosimpi), who are in consternation and send to Valinor. No help comes, but Tulkas sends privily Telimektar (Taimonto) his son.[2]

Telimektar of the silver sword and Ingil surprise Melko and wound him, and he flees and climbs up the great Pine of Tavrobel. Before the Inwir left Valinor Belaurin (Palúrien)[3] gave them a seed, and said that it must be guarded, for great tidings would one day come of its growth. But it was forgotten, and cast in the garden of Gilfanon, and a mighty pine arose that reached to Ilwë and the stars.[4]

Telimektar and Ingil pursue him, and they remain now in the sky to ward it, and Melko stalks high above the air seeking ever to do a hurt to the Sun and Moon and stars (eclipses, meteors). He is continually frustrated, but on his first attempt – saying that the Gods stole his fire for its making – he upset the Sun, so that Urwendi fell into the Sea, and the Ship fell near the ground, scorching regions of the Earth. The clarity of the Sun's radiance has not been so great since, and something of magic has gone from it. Hence it is, and long has been, that the fairies dance and sing more sweetly and can the better be seen by the light of the Moon – because of the death of Urwendi.

The 'Rekindling of the Magic Sun' refers in part to the Trees and in part to Urwendi.

Fionwë's rage and grief. In the end he will slay Melko.

'Orion' is only the image of Telimektar in the sky? [sic] Varda gave him stars, and he bears them aloft that the Gods may know he watches; he has diamonds on his sword-sheath, and this will go red when he draws his sword at the Great End.

But now Telimektar, and Gil[5] who follows him like a Blue Bee, ward off evil, and Varda immediately replaces any stars that Melko loosens and casts down.

Although grieved at the Gods' behest, the Pine is cut down; and

Melko is thus now out of the world – but one day he will find a way back, and the last great uproars will begin before the Great End.

The evils that still happen come about in this wise. The Gods can cause things to enter the hearts of Men, but not of Elves (hence their difficult dealings in the old days of the Exile of the Gnomes) – and though Melko sits without, gnawing his fingers and gazing in anger on the world, he can suggest evil to Men so inclined – but the lies he planted of old still grow and spread.

Hence Melko can now work hurt and damage and evil in the world only through Men, and he has more power and subtlety with Men than Manwë or any of the Gods, because of his long sojourn in the world and among Men.

In these early chartings we are in a primitive mythology, with Melko reduced to a grotesque figure chased up a great pine-tree, which is thereupon cut down to keep him out of the world, where he 'stalks high above the air' or 'sits without, gnawing his fingers', and upsets the Sun-ship so that Urwendi falls into the Sea – and, most strangely, meets her death.

That Ingil (Gil) who with Telimektar pursues Melko is to be identified with Ingil son of Inwë who built Kortirion is certain and appears from several notes; see the Appendix on Names to Vol. I, entries *Ingil*, *Telimektar*. This is the fullest statement of the Orion-myth, which is referred to in the *Tale of the Sun and Moon* (see I.182, 200):

of Nielluin [Sirius] too, who is the Bee of Azure, Nielluin whom still may all men see in autumn or winter burning nigh the foot of Telimektar son of Tulkas whose tale is yet to tell.

In the Gnomish dictionary it is said (I.256) that Gil rose into the heavens and 'in the likeness of a great bee bearing honey of flame' followed Telimektar. This presumably represents a distinct conception from that referred to above, where Ingil 'went long ago back to Valinor and is with Manwë' (I.129).

With the reference to Fionwë's slaying of Melko 'in the end' cf. the end of *The Hiding of Valinor* (I.219):

Fionwë Úrion, son of Manwë, of love for Urwendi shall in the end be Melko's bane, and shall destroy the world to destroy his foe, and so shall all things then be rolled away.

Cf. also the *Tale of Turambar*, p. 116, where it is said that Turambar 'shall stand beside Fionwë in the Great Wrack'.

For the prophecies and hopes of the Elves concerning the Rekindling of the Magic Sun see pp. 285–6.

The outline in C continues and concludes thus (again with some very slight and insignificant editing):

(5) Longer ages elapse. Gilfanon is now the oldest and wisest Elf in Tol Eressëa, but is not of the Inwir – hence Meril-i-Turinqi is Lady of the Isle.

Eriol comes to Tol Eressëa. Sojourns at Kortirion. Goes to Tavrobel to see Gilfanon, and sojourns in the house of a hundred chimneys – for this is the last condition of his drinking *limpë*. Gilfanon bids him write down all he has heard before he drinks.

Eriol drinks *limpë*. Gilfanon tells him of things to be; that in his mind (although the fairies hope not) he believes that Tol Eressëa will become a dwelling of Men. Gilfanon also prophesies concerning the Great End, and of the Wrack of Things, and of Fionwë, Tulkas, and Melko and the last fight on the Plains of Valinor.

Eriol ends his life at Tavrobel but in his last days is consumed with longing for the black cliffs of his shores, even as Meril said.

The book lay untouched in the house of Gilfanon during many ages of Men.

The compiler of the Golden Book takes up the Tale: one of the children of the fathers of the fathers of Men. [*Against this is written*:] It may perhaps be much better to let Eriol himself see the last things and finish the book.

Rising of the Lost Elves against the Orcs and Nautar.[6] The time is not ready for the Faring Forth, but the fairies judge it to be necessary. They obtain through Ulmo the help of Uin,[7] and Tol Eressëa is uprooted and dragged near to the Great Lands, nigh to the promontory of Rôs. A magic bridge is cast across the intervening sound. Ossë is wroth at the breaking of the roots of the isle he set so long ago – and many of his rare sea-treasures grow about it – that he tries to wrench it back; and the western half breaks off, and is now the Isle of Íverin.

The Battle of Rôs: the Island-elves and the Lost Elves against Nautar, Gongs,[8] Orcs, and a few evil Men. Defeat of the Elves. The fading Elves retire to Tol Eressëa and hide in the woods.

Men come to Tol Eressëa and also Orcs, Dwarves, Gongs, Trolls, etc. After the Battle of Rôs the Elves faded with sorrow. They cannot live in air breathed by a number of Men equal to their own or greater; and ever as Men wax more powerful and numerous so the fairies fade and grow small and tenuous, filmy and transparent, but Men larger and more dense and gross. At last Men, or almost all, can no longer see the fairies.

The Gods now dwell in Valinor, and come scarcely ever to the world, being content with the restraining of the elements from utterly destroying Men. They grieve much at what they see; *but Ilúvatar is over all.*

On the page opposite the passage about the Battle of Rôs is written:

> A great battle between Men at the Heath of the Sky-roof (now the Withered Heath), about a league from Tavrobel. The Elves and the Children flee over the Gruir and the Afros.
>
> 'Even now do they approach and our great tale comes to its ending.'
>
> The book found in the ruins of the house of a hundred chimneys.

That Gilfanon was the oldest of the Elves of Tol Eressëa, though Meril held the title of Lady of the Isle, is said also in the *Tale of the Sun and Moon* (I.175): but what is most notable is that Gilfanon (not Ailios, teller of the *Tale of the Nauglafring*, whom Gilfanon replaced, see I.197 note 19 and 229ff.) appears in this outline, which must therefore be late in the period of the composition of the *Lost Tales*.

Also noteworthy are the references to Eriol's drinking *limpë* at Gilfanon's 'house of a hundred chimneys'. In *The Cottage of Lost Play* (I.17) Lindo told Eriol that he could not give him *limpë* to drink:

> Turinqi only may give it to those not of the Eldar race, and those that drink must dwell always with the Eldar of the Island until such time as they fare forth to find the lost families of the kindred.

Meril-i-Turinqi herself, when Eriol besought her for a drink of *limpë*, was severe (I.98):

> ıf you drink this drink . . . even at the Faring Forth, should Eldar and Men fall into war at the last, still must you stand by us against the children of your kith and kin, but until then never may you fare away home though longings gnaw you . . .

In the text described in I.229ff. Eriol bemoans to Lindo the refusal to grant him his desire, and Lindo, while warning him against 'thinking to overpass the bounds that Ilúvatar hath set', tells him that Meril has not irrevocably refused him. In a note to this text my father wrote: '. . . Eriol fares to Tavrobel – after Tavrobel he drinks of *limpë*.'

The statement in this passage of outline C that Eriol 'in his last days is consumed with longing for the black cliffs of his shores, even as Meril said' clearly refers to the passage in *The Chaining of Melko* from which I have cited above:

> On a day of autumn will come the winds and a driven gull, maybe, will wail overhead, and lo! you will be filled with desire, remembering the black coasts of your home. (I.96).

Lindo's reference, in the passage from *The Cottage of Lost Play* cited above, to the faring forth of the Eldar of Tol Eressëa 'to find the lost families of the kindred' must likewise relate to the mentions in (5) of the Faring Forth (though the time was not ripe), of the 'rising of the Lost Elves against the Orcs and Nautar', and of 'the Island-elves and the Lost Elves' at the Battle of Rôs. Precisely who are to be understood by the 'Lost Elves' is not clear; but in *Gilfanon's Tale* (I.231) all Elves of the Great Lands 'that never saw the light at Kôr' (Ilkorins), whether or not they left the Waters of Awakening, are called 'the lost fairies of the world', and this seems likely to be the meaning here. It must then be supposed that there dwelt on Tol Eressëa only the Eldar of Kôr (the 'Exiles') and the Noldoli released from thraldom under Melko; the Faring Forth was to be the great expedition from Tol Eressëa for the rescue of those who had never departed from the Great Lands.

In (5) we meet the conception of the dragging of Tol Eressëa back eastwards across the Ocean to the geographical position of England – it becomes England (see I.26); that the part which was torn off by Ossë, the Isle of Íverin, is Ireland is explicitly stated in the Qenya dictionary. The promontory of Rôs is perhaps Brittany.

Here also there is a clear definition of the 'fading' of the Elves, their physical diminution and increasing tenuity and transparency, so that they become invisible (and finally incredible) to gross Mankind. This is a central concept of the early mythology: the 'fairies', as now conceived by Men (in so far as they are rightly conceived), have *become* so. They were not always so. And perhaps most remarkable in this remarkable passage, there is the final and virtually complete withdrawal of the Gods (to whom the Eldar are 'most like in nature', I.57) from the concerns of 'the world', the Great Lands across the Sea. They watch, it seems, since they grieve, and are therefore not wholly indifferent to what passes in the lands of Men; but they are henceforward utterly remote, hidden in the West.

Other features of (5), the Golden Book of Tavrobel, and the Battle of the Heath of the Sky-roof, will be explained shortly. I give next a separate passage found in the notebook C under the heading 'Rekindling of the Magic Sun. Faring Forth.'

(6)   The Elves' prophecy is that one day they will fare forth from Tol Eressëa and on arriving in the world will gather all their fading kindred who still live in the world and march towards Valinor – through the southern lands. This they will only do with the help of Men. If Men aid them, the fairies will take Men to Valinor – those that wish to go – fight a great battle with Melko in Erumáni and open Valinor.[9] Laurelin and Silpion will be rekindled, and the mountain wall being destroyed then soft radiance will spread over all the world, and the Sun and Moon will be recalled. If Men oppose them and aid Melko the Wrack of the Gods and the ending of the fairies will result – and maybe the Great End.

On the opposite page is written:

> Were the Trees relit all the paths to Valinor would become clear to
> follow — and the Shadowy Seas open clear and free — Men as well as
> Elves would taste the blessedness of the Gods, and Mandos be emptied.

This prophecy is clearly behind Vairë's words to Eriol (I. 19–20): '. . .
the Faring Forth, when if all goes well the roads through Arvalin to
Valinor shall be thronged with the sons and daughters of Men.'

Since 'the Sun and Moon will be recalled' when the Two Trees give
light again, it seems that here 'the Rekindling of the Magic Sun' (to which
the toast was drunk in Mar Vanwa Tyaliéva, I. 17, 65) refers to the
relighting of the Trees. But in citation (4) above it is said that 'the
"Rekindling of the Magic Sun" refers in part to the Trees and in part to
Urwendi', while in the *Tale of the Sun and Moon* (I.179) Yavanna
seems to distinguish the two ideas:

> 'Many things shall be done and come to pass, and the Gods grow old,
> and the Elves come nigh to fading, ere ye shall see the rekindling of
> these trees or the Magic Sun relit', and the Gods knew not what she
> meant, speaking of the Magic Sun, nor did for a long while after.

Citation (xix) on p. 264 does not make the reference clear: Eärendel
'returns from the firmament ever and anon with Voronwë to Kôr to see if
the Magic Sun has been lit and the fairies have come back'; but in the
following isolated note the Rekindling of the Magic Sun explicitly means
the re-arising of Urwendi:

(7)   Urwendi imprisoned by Móru (upset out of the boat by Melko and
        only the Moon has been magic since). The Faring Forth and the
        Battle of Erumáni would release her and rekindle the Magic Sun.

This 'upsetting' of the Sun-ship by Melko and the loss of the Sun's
'magic' is referred to also in (4), where it is added that Urwendi fell into
the sea and met her 'death'. In the tale of *The Theft of Melko* it is said
(I. 151) that the cavern in which Melko met Ungweliant was the place
where the Sun and Moon were imprisoned afterwards, for 'the primeval
spirit Móru' was indeed Ungweliant (see I. 261). The Battle of Erumáni
is referred to also in (6), and is possibly to be identified with 'the last fight
on the plains of Valinor' prophesied by Gilfanon in (5). But the last part
of (5) shows that the Faring Forth came to nothing, and the prophecies
were not fulfilled.

There are no other references to the dragging of Tol Eressëa across the
Ocean by Uin the great whale, to the Isle of Íverin, or to the Battle
of Rôs; but a remarkable writing survives concerning the aftermath of

the 'great battle between Men at the Heath of the Sky-roof (now the Withered Heath), about a league from Tavrobel' (end of citation (5)). This is a very hastily pencilled and exceedingly difficult text titled *Epilogue*. It begins with a short prefatory note:

(8)   Eriol flees with the fading Elves from the Battle of the High Heath (Ladwen-na-Dhaideloth) and crosses the Gruir and the Afros.
      The last words of the book of Tales. Written by Eriol at Tavrobel before he sealed the book.

This represents the development mentioned as desirable in (5), that Eriol should 'himself see the last things and finish the book'; but an isolated note in C shows my father still uncertain about this even after the *Epilogue* was in being: 'Prologue by the writer of Tavrobel [*i.e., such a Prologue is needed*] telling how he found Eriol's writings and put them together. His epilogue after the battle of Ladwen Daideloth is written.'
      The rivers Gruir and Afros appear also in the passage about the battle at the end of (5). Since it is said there that the Heath was about a league from Tavrobel, the two rivers are clearly those referred to in the *Tale of the Sun and Moon*: 'the Tower of Tavrobel beside the rivers' (I.174, and see I.196 note 2). In scattered notes the battle is also called 'the Battle of the Heaven Roof' and 'the Battle of Dor-na-Dhaideloth'.[10]
      I give now the text of the *Epilogue*:

And now is the end of the fair times come very nigh, and behold, all the beauty that yet was on earth – fragments of the unimagined loveliness of Valinor whence came the folk of the Elves long long ago – now goeth it all up in smoke. Here be a few tales, memories ill-told, of all that magic and that wonder twixt here and Eldamar of which I have become acquaint more than any mortal man since first my wandering footsteps came to this sad isle.
      Of that last battle of the upland heath whose roof is the wide sky – nor was there any other place beneath the blue folds of Manwë's robe so nigh the heavens or so broadly and so well encanopied – what grievous things I saw I have told.
      Already fade the Elves in sorrow and the Faring Forth has come to ruin, and Ilúvatar knoweth alone if ever now the Trees shall be relit while the world may last. Behold, I stole by evening from the ruined heath, and my way fled winding down the valley of the Brook of Glass, but the setting of the Sun was blackened with the reek of fires, and the waters of the stream were fouled with the war of men and grime of strife. Then was my heart bitter to see the bones of the good earth laid bare with winds where the destroying hands of men had torn the heather and the fern and burnt them to make sacrifice to Melko and to lust of ruin; and the thronging places of the bees that all day hummed among the whins and whortlebushes long ago bearing rich honey down

to Tavrobel – these were now become fosses and [?mounds] of stark red earth, and nought sang there nor danced but unwholesome airs and flies of pestilence.

Now the Sun died and behold, I came to that most magic wood where once the ageless oaks stood firm amid the later growths of beech and slender trees of birch, but all were fallen beneath the ruthless axes of unthinking men. Ah me, here was the path beaten with spells, trodden with musics and enchantment that wound therethrough, and this way were the Elves wont to ride a-hunting. Many a time there have I seen them and Gilfanon has been there, and they rode like kings unto the chase, and the beauty of their faces in the sun was as the new morning, and the wind in their golden hair like to the glory of bright flowers shaken at dawn, and the strong music of their voices like the sea and like trumpets and like the noise of very many viols and of golden harps unnumbered. And yet again have I seen the people of Tavrobel beneath the Moon, and they would ride or dance across the valley of the two rivers where the grey bridge leaps the joining waters; and they would fare swiftly as clad in dreams, spangled with gems like to the grey dews amid the grass, and their white robes caught the long radiance of the Moon . . . . and their spears shivered with silver flames.

And now sorrow and . . . . . has come upon the Elves, empty is Tavrobel and all are fled, [?fearing] the enemy that sitteth on the ruined heath, who is not a league away; whose hands are red with the blood of Elves and stained with the lives of his own kin, who has made himself an ally to Melko and the Lord of Hate, who has fought for the Orcs and Gongs and the unwholesome monsters of the world – blind, and a fool, and destruction alone is his knowledge. The paths of the fairies he has made to dusty roads where thirst [?lags wearily] and no man greeteth another in the way, but passes by in sullenness.

So fade the Elves and it shall come to be that because of the encompassing waters of this isle and yet more because of their unquenchable love for it that few shall flee, but as men wax there and grow fat and yet more blind ever shall they fade more and grow less; and those of the after days shall scoff, saying Who are the fairies – lies told to the children by women or foolish men – who are these fairies? And some few shall answer: Memories faded dim, a wraith of vanishing loveliness in the trees, a rustle of the grass, a glint of dew, some subtle intonation of the wind; and others yet fewer shall say . . . . . 'Very small and delicate are the fairies now, yet we have eyes to see and ears to hear, and Tavrobel and Kortirion are filled yet with [?this] sweet folk. Spring knows them and Summer too and in Winter still are they among us, but in Autumn most of all do they come out, for Autumn is their season, fallen as they are upon the Autumn of their days. What shall the dreamers of the earth be like when their winter come.

Hark O my brothers, they shall say, the little trumpets blow; we hear a sound of instruments unimagined small. Like strands of wind, like mystic half-transparencies, Gilfanon Lord of Tavrobel rides out tonight amid his folk, and hunts the elfin deer beneath the paling sky. A music of forgotten feet, a gleam of leaves, a sudden bending of the grass,[11] and wistful voices murmuring on the bridge, and they are gone.

But behold, Tavrobel shall not know its name, and all the land be changed, and even these written words of mine belike will all be lost; and so I lay down the pen, and so of the fairies cease to tell.

Another text that bears on these matters is the prose preface to *Kortirion among the Trees* (1915), which has been given in Part I 25–6, but which I repeat here:

(9) Now on a time the fairies dwelt in the Lonely Isle after the great wars with Melko and the ruin of Gondolin; and they builded a fair city amidmost of that island, and it was girt with trees. Now this city they called Kortirion, both in memory of their ancient dwelling of Kôr in Valinor, and because this city stood also upon a hill and had a great tower tall and grey that Ingil son of Inwë their lord let raise.

Very beautiful was Kortirion and the fairies loved it, and it became rich in song and poesy and the light of laughter; but on a time the great Faring Forth was made, and the fairies had rekindled once more the Magic Sun of Valinor but for the treason and faint hearts of Men. But so it is that the Magic Sun is dead and the Lonely Isle drawn back unto the confines of the Great Lands, and the fairies are scattered through all the wide unfriendly pathways of the world; and now Men dwell even on this faded isle, and care nought or know nought of its ancient days. Yet still there be some of the Eldar and the Noldoli of old who linger in the island, and their songs are heard about the shores of the land that once was the fairest dwelling of the immortal folk.

And it seems to the fairies and it seems to me who know that town and have often trodden its disfigured ways that autumn and the falling of the leaf is the season of the year when maybe here or there a heart among Men may be open, and an eye perceive how is the world's estate fallen from the laughter and the loveliness of old. Think on Kortirion and be sad – yet is there not hope?

★

At this point we may turn to the history of Eriol himself. My father's early conceptions of the mariner who came to Tol Eressëa are here again no more than allusive outlines in the pages of the little notebook C, and some of this material cannot be usefully reproduced. Perhaps the earliest is a collection of notes headed 'Story of Eriol's Life', which I gave in Vol.

I. 23-4 but with the omission of some features that were not there relevant. I repeat it here, with the addition of the statements previously omitted.

(10)   Eriol's original name was Ottor, but he called himself *Wǽfre* (Old English: 'restless, wandering') and lived a life on the waters. His father was named Eoh (Old English: 'horse'); and Eoh was slain by his brother Beorn, either 'in the siege' or 'in a great battle'. Ottor Wǽfre settled on the island of Heligoland in the North Sea, and wedded a woman named Cwén; they had two sons named Hengest and Horsa 'to avenge Eoh'.

Then sea-longing gripped Ottor Wǽfre (he was 'a son of Eärendel', born under his beam), and after the death of Cwén he left his young children. Hengest and Horsa avenged Eoh and became great chieftains; but Ottor Wǽfre set out to seek, and find, Tol Eressëa (*se uncúpa holm*, 'the unknown island').

In Tol Eressëa he wedded, being made young by *limpë* (here also called by the Old English word *líp*), Naimi (Éadgifu), niece of Vairë, and they had a son named Heorrenda.

It is then said, somewhat inconsequentially (though the matter is in itself of much interest, and recurs nowhere else), that Eriol told the fairies of *Wóden, Þunor, Tíw*, etc. (these being the Old English names of the Germanic gods who in Old Scandinavian form are *Óðinn, Þórr, Týr*), and they identified them with Manweg, Tulkas, and a third whose name is illegible but is not like that of any of the great Valar.

Eriol adopted the name of *Angol*.

Thus it is that through Eriol and his sons the *Engle* (i.e. the English) have the true tradition of the fairies, of whom the *Íras* and the *Wéalas* (the Irish and Welsh) tell garbled things.

Thus a specifically English fairy-lore is born, and one more true than anything to be found in Celtic lands.

The wedding of Eriol in Tol Eressëa is never referred to elsewhere; but his son Heorrenda is mentioned (though not called Eriol's son) in the initial link to *The Fall of Gondolin* (p. 145) as one who 'afterwards' turned a song of Meril's maidens into the language of his people. A little more light will be shed on Heorrenda in the course of this chapter.

Associated with these notes is a title-page and a prologue that breaks off after a few lines:

(11)   The Golden Book of Heorrenda
                         being the book of the
                            Tales of Tavrobel

                         ────────────

                      Heorrenda of Hægwudu

This book have I written using those writings that my father Wǽfre (whom the Gnomes named after the regions of his home Angol) did make in his sojourn in the holy isle in the days of the Elves; and much else have I added of those things which his eyes saw not afterward; yet are such things not yet to tell. For know

Here then the Golden Book was compiled from Eriol's writings by his son Heorrenda – in contrast to (5), where it was compiled by someone unnamed, and in contrast also to the *Epilogue* (8), where Eriol himself concluded and 'sealed the book'.

As I have said earlier (I.24) *Angol* refers to the ancient homeland of the 'English' before their migration across the North Sea (for the etymology of *Angol/Eriol* 'ironcliffs' see I.24, 252).

(12) There is also a genealogical table accompanying the outline (10) and altogether agreeing with it. The table is written out in two forms that are identical save in one point: for Beorn, brother of Eoh, in the one, there stands in the other *Hasen of Isenóra* (Old English: 'iron shore'). But at the end of the table is introduced the cardinal fact of all these earliest materials concerning Eriol and Tol Eressëa: Hengest and Horsa, Eriol's sons by Cwén in Heligoland, and Heorrenda, his son by Naimi in Tol Eressëa, are bracketed together, and beneath their names is written:

conquered Íeg
('seo unwemmede Íeg')
now called Englaland
and there dwell the Angolcynn or Engle.

Íeg is Old English, 'isle'; *seo unwemmede Íeg* 'the unstained isle'. I have mentioned before (I.25, footnote) a poem of my father's written at Étaples in June 1916 and called 'The Lonely Isle', addressed to England: this poem bears the Old English title *seo Unwemmede Íeg*.

(13) There follow in the notebook C some jottings that make precise identifications of places in Tol Eressëa with places in England.

First the name *Kortirion* is explained. The element *Kôr* is derived from an earlier *Qorǎ*, yet earlier *Guorǎ*; but from *Guorǎ* was also derived (i.e. in Gnomish) the form *Gwâr*. (This formulation agrees with that in the Gnomish dictionary, see I.257). Thus *Kôr* = *Gwâr*, and *Kortirion* = **Gwarmindon* (the asterisk implying a hypothetical, unrecorded form). The name that was actually used in Gnomish had the elements reversed, *Mindon-Gwar*. (*Mindon*, like *Tirion*, meant, and continued always to mean, 'tower'. The meaning of *Kôr/Gwâr* is not given here, but both in the tale of *The Coming of the Elves* (I.122) and in the Gnomish dictionary (I.257) the name is explained as referring to the *roundness* of the hill of Kôr.)

The note continues (using Old English forms): 'In Wielisc *Caergwâr*, in Englisc *Warwíc*.' Thus the element *War-* in *Warwick* is derived from the same Elvish source as *Kor-* in *Kortirion* and *Gwar* in *Mindon-Gwar*.[12] Lastly, it is said that 'Hengest's capital was Warwick'.

Next, Horsa (Hengest's brother) is associated with *Oxenaford* (Old English: Oxford), which is given the equivalents Q[enya] *Taruktarna* and Gnomish **Taruithorn* (see the Appendix on Names, p. 347).

The third of Eriol's sons, Heorrenda, is said to have had his 'capital' at Great Haywood (the Staffordshire village where my parents lived in 1916–17, see I. 25); and this is given the Qenya equivalents *Tavaros(së)* and *Taurossë*, and the Gnomish *Tavrobel* and *Tavrost*; also 'Englisc [i.e. Old English] *Hægwudu se gréata, Gréata Hægwudu*'.[13]

These notes conclude with the statement that 'Heorrenda called Kôr or Gwâr "Tûn".' In the context of these conceptions, this is obviously the Old English word *tún*, an enclosed dwelling, from which has developed the modern word *town* and the place-name ending *-ton*. *Tûn* has appeared several times in the *Lost Tales* as a later correction, or alternative to *Kôr*, changes no doubt dating from or anticipating the later situation where the city was *Tûn* and the name *Kôr* was restricted to the hill on which it stood. Later still *Tûn* became *Túna*, and then when the city of the Elves was named *Tirion* the hill became *Túna*, as it is in *The Silmarillion*; by then it had ceased to have any connotation of 'dwelling-place' and had cut free from all connection with its actual origin, as we see it here, in Old English *tún*, Heorrenda's 'town'.

Can all these materials be brought together to form a coherent narrative? I believe that they can (granting that there are certain irreconcilable differences concerning Eriol's life), and would reconstruct it thus:

– The Eldar and the rescued Noldoli departed from the Great Lands and came to Tol Eressëa.

– In Tol Eressëa they built many towns and villages, and in Alalminórë, the central region of the island, Ingil son of Inwë built the town of Koromas, 'the Resting of the Exiles of Kôr' ('Exiles', because they could not return to Valinor); and the great tower of Ingil gave the town its name *Kortirion*. (See I. 16.)

– Ottor Wæfre came from Heligoland to Tol Eressëa and dwelt in the Cottage of Lost Play in Kortirion; the Elves named him *Eriol* or *Angol* after the 'iron cliffs' of his home.

– After a time, and greatly instructed in the ancient history of Gods, Elves, and Men, Eriol went to visit Gilfanon in the village of Tavrobel, and there he wrote down what he had learnt; there also he at last drank *limpë*.

- In Tol Eressëa Eriol was wedded and had a son named Heorrenda (Half-elven!). (According to (5) Eriol died at Tavrobel, consumed with longing for 'the black cliffs of his shores'; but according to (8), certainly later, he lived to see the Battle of the Heath of the Sky-roof.)

- The Lost Elves of the Great Lands rose against the dominion of the servants of Melko; and the untimely Faring Forth took place, at which time Tol Eressëa was drawn east back across the Ocean and anchored off the coasts of the Great Lands. The western half broke off when Ossë tried to drag the island back, and it became the Isle of Íverin (= Ireland).

- Tol Eressëa was now in the geographical position of England.

- The great battle of Rôs ended in the defeat of the Elves, who retreated into hiding in Tol Eressëa.

- Evil men entered Tol Eressëa, accompanied by Orcs and other hostile beings.

- The Battle of the Heath of the Sky-roof took place not far from Tavrobel, and (according to (8)) was witnessed by Eriol, who completed the Golden Book.

- The Elves faded and became invisible to the eyes of almost all Men.

- The sons of Eriol, Hengest, Horsa, and Heorrenda, conquered the island and it became 'England'. They were not hostile to the Elves, and from them the English have 'the true tradition of the fairies'.

- Kortirion, ancient dwelling of the fairies, came to be known in the tongue of the English as Warwick; Hengest dwelt there, while Horsa dwelt at Taruithorn (Oxford) and Heorrenda at Tavrobel (Great Haywood). (According to (11) Heorrenda completed the Golden Book.)

This reconstruction may not be 'correct' in all its parts: indeed, it may be that any such attempt is artificial, treating all the notes and jottings as of equal weight and all the ideas as strictly contemporaneous and relatable to each other. Nonetheless I believe that it shows rightly in essentials how my father was thinking of ordering the narrative in which the *Lost Tales* were to be set; and I believe also that this was the conception that still underlay the *Tales* as they are extant and have been given in these books.

For convenience later I shall refer to this narrative as 'the *Eriol* story'. Its most remarkable features, in contrast to the later story, are the transformation of Tol Eressëa into England, and the early appearance of the mariner (in relation to the whole history) and his importance.

In fact, my father was exploring (before he decided on a radical transformation of the whole conception) ideas whereby his importance would be greatly increased.

(14)   From very rough jottings it can be made out that Eriol was to be so tormented with home longing that he set sail from Tol Eressëa with his son Heorrenda, against the command of Meril-i-Turinqi (see the passage cited on p. 284 from *The Chaining of Melko*); but his purpose in doing so was also 'to hasten the Faring Forth', which he 'preached' in the lands of the East. Tol Eressëa was drawn back to the confines of the Great Lands, but at once hostile peoples named the *Guiðlin* and the *Brithonin* (and in one of these notes also the *Rúmhoth*, Romans) invaded the island. Eriol died, but his sons Hengest and Horsa conquered the Guiðlin. But because of Eriol's disobedience to the command of Meril, in going back before the time for the Faring Forth was ripe, 'all was cursed'; and the Elves faded before the noise and evil of war. An isolated sentence refers to 'a strange prophecy that a man of good will, yet through longing after the things of Men, may bring the Faring Forth to nought'.

Thus the part of Eriol was to become cardinal in the history of the Elves; but there is no sign that these ideas ever got beyond this exploratory stage.

★

I have said that I think that the reconstruction given above ('the *Eriol* story') is in essentials the conception underlying the framework of the *Lost Tales*. This is both for positive and negative reasons: positive, because he is there still named *Eriol* (see p. 300), and also because Gilfanon, who enters (replacing Ailios) late in the development of the *Tales*, appears also in citation (5) above, which is one of the main contributors to this reconstruction; negative, because there is really nothing to contradict what is much the easiest assumption. There is no explicit statement anywhere in the *Lost Tales* that Eriol came from England. At the beginning (I.13) he is only 'a traveller from far countries'; and the fact that the story he told to Vëannë of his earlier life (pp. 4–7) agrees well with other accounts where his home is explicitly in England does no more than show that the story remained while the geography altered — just as the 'black coasts' of his home survived in later writing to become the western coasts of Britain, whereas the earliest reference to them is the etymology of *Angol* 'iron cliffs' (his own name, = *Eriol*, from the land 'between the seas', Angeln in the Danish peninsula, whence he came: see I.252). There is in fact a very early, rejected, sketch of Eriol's life in which essential features of the same story are outlined — the attack on his father's dwelling (in this case the destruction of Eoh's castle by his brother Beorn, see citation (10)), Eriol's captivity and escape — and in this note it is said that Eriol afterwards 'wandered over the wilds of the Central Lands to the Inland Sea, *Wendelsæ* [Old English, the Mediterranean], and hence to the shores of the Western Sea', whence his father had originally come. The mention in the typescript text of the *Link* to the *Tale of Tinúviel* (p. 6) of wild men out of the Mountains of the East, *which the duke could see from his tower*, seems likewise to imply that at this time Eriol's original home was placed in some 'continental' region.

The only suggestion, so far as I can see, that this view might not be correct is found in an early poem with a complex history, texts of which I give here.

The earliest rough drafts of this poem are extant; the original title was 'The Wanderer's Allegiance', and it is not clear that it was at first conceived as a poem in three parts. My father subsequently wrote in subtitles on these drafts, dividing the poem into three: *Prelude*, *The Inland City*, and *The Sorrowful City*, with (apparently) an overall title *The Sorrowful City*; and added a date, March 16–18, 1916. In the only later copy of the whole poem that is extant the overall title is *The Town of Dreams and the City of Present Sorrow*, with the three parts titled: *Prelude* (Old English *Foresang*), *The Town of Dreams* (Old English *Þæt Slæpende Tún*), and *The City of Present Sorrow* (Old English *Seo Wépende Burg*). This text gives the dates 'March 1916, Oxford and Warwick; rewritten Birmingham November 1916'. 'The Town of Dreams' is Warwick, on the River Avon, and 'The City of Present Sorrow' is Oxford, on the Thames, during the First War; there is no evident association of any kind with Eriol or the *Lost Tales*.

Prelude

> In unknown days my fathers' sires
> Came, and from son to son took root
> Among the orchards and the river-meads
> And the long grasses of the fragrant plain:
> Many a summer saw they kindle yellow fires
> Of iris in the bowing reeds,
> And many a sea of blossom turn to golden fruit
> In wallèd gardens of the great champain.

★

> There daffodils among the ordered trees
> Did nod in spring, and men laughed deep and long
> Singing as they laboured happy lays
> And lighting even with a drinking-song.
> There sleep came easy for the drone of bees
> Thronging about cottage gardens heaped with flowers;
> In love of sunlit goodliness of days
> There richly flowed their lives in settled hours –
> But that was long ago,

And now no more they sing, nor reap, nor sow,
And I perforce in many a town about this isle
Unsettled wanderer have dwelt awhile.

The Town of Dreams

Here many days once gently past me crept
In this dear town of old forgetfulness;
Here all entwined in dreams once long I slept
And heard no echo of the world's distress
Come through the rustle of the elms' rich leaves,
While Avon gurgling over shallows wove
Unending melody, and morns and eves
Slipped down her waters till the Autumn came,
(Like the gold leaves that drip and flutter then,
Till the dark river gleams with jets of flame
That slowly float far down beyond our ken.)

For here the castle and the mighty tower,
More lofty than the tiered elms,
More grey than long November rain,
Sleep, and nor sunlit moment nor triumphal hour,
Nor passing of the seasons or the Sun
Wakes their old lords too long in slumber lain.

No watchfulness disturbs their splendid dream,
Though laughing radiance dance down the stream;
And be they clad in snow or lashed by windy rains,
Or may March whirl the dust about the winding lanes,
The Elm robe and disrobe her of a million leaves
Like moments clustered in a crowded year,
Still their old heart unmoved nor weeps nor grieves,
Uncomprehending of this evil tide,
Today's great sadness, or Tomorrow's fear:
Faint echoes fade within their drowsy halls
Like ghosts; the daylight creeps across their walls.

The City of Present Sorrow

There is a city that far distant lies
And a vale outcarven in forgotten days –
There wider was the grass, and lofty elms more rare;
The river-sense was heavy in the lowland air.
There many willows changed the aspect of the earth and skies
Where feeding brooks wound in by sluggish ways,
And down the margin of the sailing Thames
Around his broad old bosom their old stems
Were bowed, and subtle shades lay on his streams
Where their grey leaves adroop o'er silver pools
Did knit a coverlet like shimmering jewels
Of blue and misty green and filtering gleams.

★

O agéd city of an all too brief sojourn,
I see thy clustered windows each one burn
With lamps and candles of departed men.
The misty stars thy crown, the night thy dress,
Most peerless-magical thou dost possess
My heart, and old days come to life again;
Old mornings dawn, or darkened evenings bring
The same old twilight noises from the town.
Thou hast the very core of longing and delight,
To thee my spirit dances oft in sleep
Along thy great grey streets, or down
A little lamplit alley-way at night –
Thinking no more of other cities it has known,
Forgetting for a while the tree-girt keep,
And town of dreams, where men no longer sing.
For thy heart knows, and thou shedst many tears
For all the sorrow of these evil years.
Thy thousand pinnacles and fretted spires
Are lit with echoes and the lambent fires
Of many companies of bells that ring
Rousing pale visions of majestic days
The windy years have strewn down distant ways;
And in thy halls still doth thy spirit sing
Songs of old memory amid thy present tears,
Or hope of days to come half-sad with many fears.
Lo! though along thy paths no laughter runs
While war untimely takes thy many sons,
No tide of evil can thy glory drown
Robed in sad majesty, the stars thy crown.

★

In addition, there are two texts in which a part of *The City of Present Sorrow* is treated as a separate entity. This begins with 'O agéd city of an all too brief sojourn', and is briefer: after the line 'Thinking no more of other cities it has known' it ends:

> Forgetting for a while that all men weep
> It strays there happy and to thee it sings
> 'No tide of evil can thy glory drown,
> Robed in sad majesty, the stars thy crown!'

This was first called *The Sorrowful City*, but the title was then changed to *Wínsele wéste, windge reste réte berofene* (*Beowulf* lines 2456–7, very slightly adapted: 'the hall of feasting empty, the resting places swept by the wind, robbed of laughter').

There are also two manuscripts in which *The Town of Dreams* is treated as a separate poem, with a subtitle *An old town revisited*; in one of these the primary title was later changed to *The Town of Dead Days*.

Lastly, there is a poem in two parts called *The Song of Eriol*. This is found in three manuscripts, the later ones incorporating minor changes made to the predecessor (but the third has only the second part of the poem).

The Song of Eriol

Eriol made a song in the Room of the Tale-fire telling how his feet were set to wandering, so that in the end he found the Lonely Isle and that fairest town Kortirion.

I

> In unknown days my fathers' sires
> Came, and from son to son took root
> Among the orchards and the river-meads
> And the long grasses of the fragrant plain:
>
> Many a summer saw they kindle yellow fires
> Of flaglilies among the bowing reeds,
> And many a sea of blossom turn to golden fruit
> In walléd gardens of the great champain.
>
> There daffodils among the ordered trees
> Did nod in spring, and men laughed deep and long
> Singing as they laboured happy lays
> And lighting even with a drinking-song.

There sleep came easy for the drone of bees
Thronging about cottage gardens heaped with flowers;
In love of sunlit goodliness of days
There richly flowed their lives in settled hours –
    But that was long ago,
   And now no more they sing, nor reap, nor sow;
   And I perforce in many a town about this isle
   Unsettled wanderer have dwelt awhile.

2

Wars of great kings and clash of armouries,
Whose swords no man could tell, whose spears
Were numerous as a wheatfield's ears,
Rolled over all the Great Lands; and the Seas

Were loud with navies; their devouring fires
Behind the armies burned both fields and towns;
And sacked and crumbled or to flaming pyres
Were cities made, where treasuries and crowns,

Kings and their folk, their wives and tender maids
Were all consumed. Now silent are those courts,
Ruined the towers, whose old shape slowly fades,
And no feet pass beneath their broken ports.

★

There fell my father on a field of blood,
And in a hungry siege my mother died,
And I, a captive, heard the great seas' flood
Calling and calling, that my spirit cried

For the dark western shores whence long ago had come
Sires of my mother, and I broke my bonds,
Faring o'er wasted valleys and dead lands
Until my feet were moistened by the western sea,
Until my ears were deafened by the hum,
The splash, and roaring of the western sea –
    But that was long ago
   And now the dark bays and unknown waves I know,
   The twilight capes, the misty archipelago,
   And all the perilous sounds and salt wastes 'tween this isle
   Of magic and the coasts I knew awhile.

★

One of the manuscripts of *The Song of Eriol* bears a later note: 'Easington 1917–18' (Easington on the estuary of the Humber, see Humphrey Carpenter, *Biography*, p. 97). It may be that the second part of *The Song of Eriol* was written at Easington and added to the first part (formerly the *Prelude*) already in existence.

Little can be derived from this poem of a strictly narrative nature, save the lineaments of the same tale: Eriol's father fell 'on a field of blood', when 'wars of great kings . . . rolled over all the Great Lands', and his mother died 'in a hungry siege' (the same phrase is used in the *Link* to the *Tale of Tinúviel*, pp. 5–6); he himself was made a captive, but escaped, and came at last to the shores of the Western Sea (whence his mother's people had come).

The fact that the first part of *The Song of Eriol* is also found as the Prelude to a poem of which the subjects are Warwick and Oxford might make one suspect that the castle with a great tower overhanging a river in the story told by Eriol to Vëannë was once again Warwick. But I do not think that this is so. There remains in any case the objection that it would be difficult to accommodate the attack on it by men out of the Mountains of the East which the duke could see from his tower; but also I think it is plain that the original tripartite poem had been dissevered, and the *Prelude* given a new bearing: my father's 'fathers' sires' became Eriol's 'fathers' sires'. At the same time, certain powerful images were at once dominant and fluid, and the great tower of Eriol's home was indeed to become the tower of Kortirion or Warwick, when (as will be seen shortly) the structure of the story of the mariner was radically changed. And nothing could show more clearly than does the evolution of this poem the complex root from which the story rose.

Humphrey Carpenter, writing in his *Biography* of my father's life after he returned to Oxford in 1925, says (p. 169):

He made numerous revisions and recastings of the principal stories in the cycle, deciding to abandon the original sea-voyager 'Eriol' to whom the stories were told, and instead renaming him 'Ælfwine' or 'elf-friend'.

That *Eriol* was (for a time) displaced by *Ælfwine* is certain. But while it may well be that at the time of the texts now to be considered the name *Eriol* had actually been rejected, in the first version of 'The Silmarillion' proper, written in 1926, *Eriol* reappears, while in the earliest *Annals of Valinor*, written in the 1930s, it is said that they were translated in Tol Eressëa 'by Eriol of Leithien, that is Ælfwine of the Angelcynn'. On the other hand, at this earlier period it seems entirely justifiable on the evidence to treat the two names as indicative of different narrative projections — 'the *Eriol* story' and 'the *Ælfwine* story'.

'Ælfwine', then, is associated with a new conception, *subsequent to* the writing of the *Lost Tales*. The mariner is Ælfwine, not Eriol, in the second 'Scheme' for the *Tales*, which I have called 'an unrealised project for the revision of the whole work' (see I. 234). The essential difference may be made clear now, before citing the difficult evidence: *Tol Eressëa is now in no way identified with England*, and the story of the drawing back of the Lonely Island across the sea has been abandoned. England is indeed still at the heart of this later conception, and is named *Luthany*.[14] The mariner, Ælfwine, is an Englishman sailing westward from the coast of Britain; and his role is diminished. For whereas in the writings studied thus far he comes to Tol Eressëa *before* the dénouement and disaster of the Faring Forth, and either he himself or his descendants witness the devastation of Tol Eressëa by the invasion of Men and their evil allies (in one line of development he was even to be responsible for it, p. 294), in the later narrative outlines he does not arrive until all the grievous history is done. His part is only to learn and to record.[15]

I turn now to a number of short and very oblique passages, written on separate slips, but found together and clearly dating from much the same time.

(15)   Ælfwine of England dwelt in the South-west; he was of the kin of Ing, King of Luthany. His mother and father were slain by the sea-pirates and he was made captive.

He had always loved the fairies: his father had told him many things (of the tradition of Ing). He escapes. He beats about the northern and western waters. He meets the Ancient Mariner – and seeks for Tol Eressëa (*seo unwemmede íeg*), whither most of the unfaded Elves have retired from the noise, war, and clamour of Men.

The Elves greet him, and the more so when they learn of him who he is. They call him *Lúthien* the man of Luthany. He finds his own tongue, the ancient English tongue, is spoken in the isle.

The 'Ancient Mariner' has appeared in the story that Eriol told to Vëannë (pp. 5, 7), and much more will be told of him subsequently.

(16)   Ælfwine of Englaland, [*added later*: driven by the Normans,] arrives in Tol Eressëa, whither most of the fading Elves have withdrawn from the world, and there fade now no more.

Description of the harbour of the southern shore. The fairies greet him well hearing he is from Englaland. He is surprised to hear them speak the speech of Ælfred of Wessex, though to one another they spoke a sweet and unknown tongue.

The Elves name him Lúthien for he is come from Luthany, as they call it ('friend' and 'friendship'). Eldaros or Ælfhâm. He is sped to Rôs their capital. There he finds the Cottage of Lost Play, and Lindo and Vairë.

He tells who he is and whence, and why he has long sought for the isle (by reason of traditions in the kin of Ing), and he begs the Elves to come back to Englaland.

Here begins (as an explanation of why they cannot) the series of stories called the Book of Lost Tales.

In this passage (16) Ælfwine becomes more firmly rooted in English history: he is apparently a man of eleventh-century Wessex — but as in (15) he is of 'the kin of Ing'. The capital of the Elves of Tol Eressëa is not Kortirion but Rôs, a name now used in a quite different application from that in citation (5), where it was a promontory of the Great Lands.

I have been unable to find any trace of the process whereby the name *Lúthien* came to be so differently applied afterwards (*Lúthien Tinúviel*). Another note of this period explains the name quite otherwise: 'Lúthien or Lúsion was son of Telumaith (Telumektar). Ælfwine loved the sign of Orion, and made the sign, hence the fairies called him Lúthien (Wanderer).' There is no other mention of Ælfwine's peculiar association with Orion nor of this interpretation of the name Lúthien; and this seems to be a development that my father did not pursue.

It is convenient to give here the opening passage from the second Scheme for the *Lost Tales*, referred to above; this plainly belongs to the same time as the rest of these 'Ælfwine' notes, when the *Tales* had been written so far as they ever went within their first framework.

(17)   Ælfwine awakens upon a sandy beach. He listens to the sea, which is far out. The tide is low and has left him.

Ælfwine meets the Elves of Rôs; finds they speak the speech of the English, beside their own sweet tongue. Why they do so — the dwelling of Elves in Luthany and their faring thence and back. They clothe him and feed him, and he sets forth to walk along the island's flowery ways.

The scheme goes on to say that on a summer evening Ælfwine came to Kortirion, and thus differs from (16), where he goes to 'Rôs their capital', in which he finds the Cottage of Lost Play. The name Rôs seems to be used here in yet another sense — possibly a name for Tol Eressëa.

(18)   He is sped to Ælfhâm (Elfhome) Eldos where Lindo and Vairë tell him many things: of the making and ancient fashion of the world: of the Gods: of the Elves of Valinor: of Lost Elves and Men: of the Travail of the Gnomes: of Eärendel: of the Faring Forth and the Loss of Valinor: of the disaster of the Faring Forth and the war with evil Men. The retreat to Luthany where Ingwë was king.

Of the home-thirst of the Elves and how the greater number
sought back to Valinor. The loss of Elwing. How a new home was
made by the Solosimpi and others in Tol Eressëa. How the Elves
continually sadly leave the world and fare thither.

For the interpretation of this passage it is essential to realise (the key
indeed to the understanding of this projected history) that 'the Faring
Forth' does *not* here refer to the Faring Forth in the sense in which it has
been used hitherto – that from Tol Eressëa for the Rekindling of the
Magic Sun, which ended in ruin, but to the March of the Elves of Kôr
and the 'Loss of Valinor' that the March incurred (see pp. 253, 257,
280). It is not indeed clear why it is here called a 'disaster': but this is
evidently to be associated with 'the war with evil Men', and war between
Elves and Men at the time of the March from Kôr is referred to in
citations (1) and (3).

In 'the *Eriol* story' it is explicit that after the March from Kôr the Elves
departed from the Great Lands to Tol Eressëa; here on the other hand
'the war with evil Men' is followed by 'the retreat to Luthany where
Ingwë was king'. The (partial) departure to Tol Eressëa is from Luthany;
the loss of Elwing seems to take place on one of these voyages. As will be
seen, the 'Faring Forth' of 'the *Eriol* story' has disappeared as an event of
Elvish history, and is only mentioned as a prophecy and a hope.

Schematically the essential divergence of the two narrative structures
can be shown thus:

(*Eriol* story)	(*Ælfwine* story)
March of the Elves of Kôr to the Great Lands	March of the Elves of Kôr to the Great Lands (called 'the Faring Forth')
War with Men in the Great Lands	War with Men in the Great Lands
Retreat of the Elves to Tol Eressëa (loss of Elwing)	Retreat of the Elves to Luthany (> England) ruled by Ingwë
	Departure of many Elves to Tol Eressëa (loss of Elwing)
Eriol sails from the East (North Sea region) to Tol Eressëa	Ælfwine sails from England to Tol Eressëa
The Faring Forth, drawing of Tol Eressëa to the Great Lands; ultimately Tol Eressëa > England	

This is of course by no means a full statement of the *Ælfwine* story, and is
merely set out to indicate the radical difference of structure. Lacking
from it is the history of Luthany, which emerges from the passages that
now follow.

(19) *Luthany* means 'friendship', *Lúthien* 'friend'. Luthany the only
land where Men and Elves once dwelt an age in peace and love.

How for a while after the coming of the sons of Ing the Elves
throve again and ceased to fare away to Tol Eressëa.

How Old English became the sole mortal language which an Elf
will speak to a mortal that knows no Elfin.

(20) Ælfwine of England (whose father and mother were slain by the
fierce Men of the Sea who knew not the Elves) was a great lover of
the Elves, especially of the shoreland Elves that lingered in the
land. He seeks for Tol Eressëa whither the fairies are said to have
retired.

He reaches it. The fairies call him Lúthien. He learns of the
making of the world, ... of Gods and Elves, of Elves and
Men, down to the departure to Tol Eressëa.

How the Faring Forth came to nought, and the fairies took
refuge in Albion or Luthany (the Isle of Friendship).

Seven invasions.

Of the coming of Men to Luthany, how each race quarrelled,
and the fairies faded, until [?the most] set sail, after the coming of
the Rúmhoth, for the West. Why the Men of the seventh invasion,
the Ingwaiwar, are more friendly.

Ingwë and Eärendel who dwelt in Luthany before it was an isle
and was [*sic*] driven east by Ossë to found the Ingwaiwar.

(21) All the descendants of Ing were well disposed to Elves; hence the
remaining Elves of Luthany spoke to [?them] in the ancient
tongue of the English, and since some have fared . . . . . to Tol
Eressëa that tongue is there understood, and all who wish to speak
to the Elves, if they know not and have no means of learning Elfin
speeches, must converse in the ancient tongue of the English.

In (20) the term 'Faring Forth' must again be used as it is in (18), of the
March from Kôr. There it was called a 'disaster' (see p. 303), and here it
is said that it 'came to nought': it must be admitted that it is hard to see
how that can be said, if it led to the binding of Melko and the release of
the enslaved Noldoli (see (1) and (3)).

Also in (20) is the first appearance of the idea of the Seven Invasions of
Luthany. One of these was that of the Rúmhoth (mentioned also in (14))
or Romans; and the seventh was that of the Ingwaiwar, who were not
hostile to the Elves.

Here something must be said of the name *Ing* (*Ingwë, Ingwaiar*) in
these passages. As with the introduction of Hengest and Horsa, the
association of the mythology with ancient English legend is manifest.
But it would serve no purpose, I believe, to enter here into the obscure
and speculative scholarship of English and Scandinavian origins: the

Roman writers' term *Inguaeones* for the Baltic maritime peoples from whom the English came; the name *Ingwine* (interpretable either as *Ing-wine* 'the friends of Ing' or as containing the same *Ingw-* seen in *Inguaeones*); or the mysterious personage *Ing* who appears in the Old English *Runic Poem*:

> Ing wæs ærest   mid East-Denum
> gesewen secgum   oþ he siþþan east
> ofer wæg gewat;   wæn æfter ran

– which may be translated: 'Ing was first seen by men among the East Danes, until he departed eastwards over the waves; his car sped after him.' It would serve no purpose, because although the connection of my father's *Ing*, *Ingwë* with the shadowy *Ing* (*Ingw-*) of northern historical legend is certain and indeed obvious he seems to have been intending no more than an *association* of his mythology with known traditions (though the words of the *Runic Poem* were clearly influential). The matter is made particularly obscure by the fact that in these notes the names *Ing* and *Ingwë* intertwine with each other, but are never expressly differentiated or identified.

Thus Ælfwine was 'of the kin of Ing, King of Luthany' (15, 16), but the Elves retreated 'to Luthany where Ingwë was king' (18). The Elves of Luthany throve again 'after the coming of the sons of Ing' (19), and the Ingwaiwar, seventh of the invaders of Luthany, were more friendly to the Elves (20), while Ingwë 'founded' the Ingwaiwar (20). This name is certainly to be equated with Inguaeones (see above), and the invasion of the Ingwaiwar (or 'sons of Ing') equally certainly represents the 'Anglo-Saxon' invasion of Britain. Can *Ing*, *Ingwë* be equated? So far as this present material is concerned, I hardly see how they can not be. Whether this ancestor-founder is to be equated with *Inwë* (whose son was *Ingil*) of the *Lost Tales* is another question. It is hard to believe that there is no connection (especially since *Inwë* in *The Cottage of Lost Play* is emended from *Ing*, I.22), yet it is equally difficult to see what that connection could be, since Inwë of the *Lost Tales* is an Elda of Kôr (Ingwë Lord of the Vanyar in *The Silmarillion*) while Ing(wë) of 'the *Ælfwine* story' is a Man, the King of Luthany and Ælfwine's ancestor. (In outlines for *Gilfanon's Tale* it is said that Ing King of Luthany was descended from Ermon, or from Ermon and Elmir (the first Men, I.236–7).)

The following outlines tell some more concerning Ing(wë) and the Ingwaiwar:

(22)   How Ing sailed away at eld [i.e. in old age] into the twilight, and Men say he came to the Gods, but he dwells on Tol Eressëa, and will guide the fairies one day back to Luthany when the Faring Forth takes place.*

---

* The term 'Faring Forth' is used here in a prophetic sense, not as it is in (18) and (20).

How he prophesied that his kin should fare back again and possess Luthany until the days of the coming of the Elves.

How the land of Luthany was seven times invaded by Men, until at the seventh the children of the children of Ing came back to their own.

How at each new war and invasion the Elves faded, and each loved the Elves less, until the Rúmhoth came — and they did not even believe they existed, and the Elves all fled, so that save for a few the isle was empty of the Elves for three hundred years.

(23) How Ingwë drank *limpë* at the hands of the Elves and reigned ages in Luthany.

How Eärendel came to Luthany to find the Elves gone.

How Ingwë aided him, but was not suffered to go with him. Eärendel blessed all his progeny as the mightiest sea-rovers of the world.[16]

How Ossë made war upon Ingwë because of Eärendel, and Ing longing for the Elves set sail, and all were wrecked after being driven far east.

How Ing the immortal came among the Dani OroDáni Urdainoth East Danes.

How he became the half-divine king of the Ingwaiwar, and taught them many things of Elves and Gods, so that some true knowledge of the Gods and Elves lingered in that folk alone.

Part of another outline that does not belong with the foregoing passages but covers the same part of the narrative as (23) may be given here:

(24) Eärendel takes refuge with [Ingwë] from the wrath of Ossë, and gives him a draught of *limpë* (enough to assure immortality). He gives him news of the Elves and the dwelling on Tol Eressëa.

Ingwë and a host of his folk set sail to find Tol Eressëa, but Ossë blows them back east. They are utterly wrecked. Only Ingwë rescued on a raft. He becomes king of the Angali, Euti, Saksani, and Firisandi,* who adopt the title of Ingwaiwar. He teaches them much magic and first sets men's hearts to seafaring westward. . . . . .

After a great [?age of rule] Ingwë sets sail in a little boat and is heard of no more.

It is clear that the intrusion of Luthany, and Ing(wë), into the conception has caused a movement in the story of Eärendel: whereas in the older version he went to Tol Eressëa after the departure of the Eldar and Noldoli from the Great Lands (pp. 253, 255), now he goes to

---

* Angles, Saxons, Jutes, and Frisians.

Luthany; and the idea of Ossë's enmity towards Eärendel (pp. 254, 263) is retained but brought into association with the origin of the Ingwaiwar.

It is clear that the narrative structure is:

- Ing(wë) King of Luthany.
- Eärendel seeks refuge with him (after [many of] the Elves have departed to Tol Eressëa).
- Ing(wë) seeks Tol Eressëa but is driven into the East.
- Seven invasions of Luthany.
- The people of Ing(wë) are the Ingwaiwar, and they 'come back to their own' when they invade Luthany from across the North Sea.

(25)   Luthany was where the tribes first embarked in the Lonely Isle for Valinor, and whence they landed for the Faring Forth,* whence [also] many sailed with Elwing to find Tol Eressëa.

That Luthany was where the Elves, at the end of the great journey from Palisor, embarked on the Lonely Isle for the Ferrying to Valinor, is probably to be connected with the statement in (20) that 'Ingwë and Eärendel dwelt in Luthany before it was an isle'.

(26)   There are other references to the channel separating Luthany from the Great Lands: in rough jottings in notebook C there is mention of an isthmus being cut by the Elves, 'fearing Men now that Ingwë has gone', and 'to the white cliffs where the silver spades of the Teleri worked'; also in the next citation.

(27)   The Elves tell Ælfwine of the ancient manner of Luthany, of Kortirion or Gwarthyryn (Caer Gwâr),[17] of Tavrobel.
            How the fairies dwelt there a hundred ages before Men had the skill to build boats to cross the channel – so that magic lingers yet mightily in its woods and hills.
            How they renamed many a place in Tol Eressëa after their home in Luthany. Of the Second Faring Forth and the fairies' hope to reign in Luthany and replant there the magic trees – and it depends most on the temper of the Men of Luthany (since they first must come there) whether all goes well.

Notable here is the reference to 'the Second Faring Forth', which strongly supports my interpretation of the expression 'Faring Forth' in (18), (20), and (25); but the prophecy or hope of the Elves concerning

* In the sense of the March of the Elves from Kôr, as in (18) and (20).

the Faring Forth has been greatly changed from its nature in citation (6): here, the Trees are to be replanted in Luthany.

(28) How Ælfwine lands in Tol Eressëa and it seems to him like his own land made . . . . clad in the beauty of a happy dream. How the folk comprehended [his speech] and learn whence he is come by the favour of Ulmo. How he is sped to Kortirion.

With these two passages it is interesting to compare (9), the prose preface to *Kortirion among the Trees*, according to which Kortirion was a city built by the Elves in Tol Eressëa; and when Tol Eressëa was brought across the sea, becoming England, Kortirion was renamed in the tongue of the English *Warwick* (13). In the new story, Kortirion is likewise an ancient dwelling of the Elves, but with the change in the fundamental conception it is in Luthany; and the Kortirion to which Ælfwine comes in Tol Eressëa is the second of the name (being called 'after their home in Luthany'). There has thus been a very curious transference, which may be rendered schematically thus:

> (I)   Kortirion, Elvish dwelling in Tol Eressëa.
>   Tol Eressëa ———→ England.
>   Kortirion = Warwick.

> (II) Kortirion, Elvish dwelling in Luthany (> England).
>   Elves ———→ Tol Eressëa.
>   Kortirion (2) in Tol Eressëa named after Kortirion (1) in Luthany.

On the basis of the foregoing passages, (15) to (28), we may attempt to construct a narrative taking account of all the essential features:

- March of the Elves of Kôr (called 'the Faring Forth', or (by implication in 27) 'the First Faring Forth') into the Great Lands, landing in Luthany (25), and the Loss of Valinor (18).

- War with evil Men in the Great Lands (18).

- The Elves retreated to Luthany (not yet an island) where Ing(wë) was king (18, 20).

- Many [but by no means all] of the Elves of Luthany sought back west over the sea and settled in Tol Eressëa; but Elwing was lost (18, 25).

- Places in Tol Eressëa were named after places in Luthany (27).

- Eärendel came to Luthany, taking refuge with Ing(wë) from the hostility of Ossë (20, 23, 24).

- Eärendel gave Ing(wë) *limpë* to drink (24), *or* Ing(wë) received *limpë* from the Elves before Eärendel came (23).

- Eärendel blessed the progeny of Ing(wë) before his departure (23).
- Ossë's hostility to Eärendel pursued Ing(wë) also (23, 24).
- Ing(wë) set sail (with many of his people, 24) to find Tol Eressëa (23, 24).
- Ing(wë)'s voyage, through the enmity of Ossë, ended in shipwreck, but Ing(wë) survived, and far to the East [i.e. after being driven across the North Sea] he became King of the Ingwaiwar the ancestors of the Anglo-Saxon invaders of Britain (23, 24).
- Ing(wë) instructed the Ingwaiwar in true knowledge of the Gods and Elves (23) and turned their hearts to seafaring westwards (24). He prophesied that his kin should one day return again to Luthany (22).
- Ing(wë) at length departed in a boat (22, 24), and was heard of no more (24), or came to Tol Eressëa (22).
- After Ing(wë)'s departure from Luthany a channel was made so that Luthany became an isle (26); but Men crossed the channel in boats (27).
- Seven successive invasions took place, including that of the Rúmhoth or Romans, and at each new war more of the remaining Elves of Luthany fled over the sea (20, 22).
- The seventh invasion, that of the Ingwaiwar, was however not hostile to the Elves (20, 21); and these invaders were 'coming back to their own' (22), since they were the people of Ing(wë).
- The Elves of Luthany (now England) throve again and ceased to leave Luthany for Tol Eressëa (19), and they spoke to the Ingwaiwar in their own language, Old English (21).
- Ælfwine was an Englishman of the Anglo-Saxon period, a descendant of Ing(wë), who had derived a knowledge of and love of the Elves from the tradition of his family (15, 16).
- Ælfwine came to Tol Eressëa, found that Old English was spoken there, and was called by the Elves Lúthien 'friend', the Man of Luthany (the Isle of Friendship) (15, 16, 19).

I claim no more for this than that it seems to me to be the only way in which these *disjecta membra* can be set together into a comprehensive narrative scheme. It must be admitted even so that it requires some forcing of the evidence to secure apparent agreement. For example, there seem to be different views of the relation of the Ingwaiwar to Ing(wë): they are 'the sons of Ing' (19), 'his kin' (22), 'the children of the children of Ing' (22), yet he seems to have become the king and teacher of North Sea peoples who had no connection with Luthany or the Elves (23, 24). (Over whom did he rule when the Elves first retreated to Luthany (18, 23)?) Again, it is very difficult to fit the 'hundred ages' during which the

Elves dwelt in Luthany before the invasions of Men began (27) to the rest of the scheme. Doubtless in these jottings my father was thinking with his pen, exploring independent narrative paths; one gets the impression of a ferment of ideas and possibilities rapidly displacing one another, from which no one stable narrative core can be extracted. A complete 'solution' is therefore in all probability an unreal aim, and this reconstruction no doubt as artificial as that attempted earlier for 'the *Eriol* story' (see p. 293). But here as there I believe that this outline shows as well as can be the direction of my father's thought at that time.

There is very little to indicate the further course of 'the *Ælfwine* story' after his sojourn in Tol Eressëa (as I have remarked, p. 301, the part of the mariner is only to learn and record tales out of the past); and virtually all that can be learned from these notes is found on a slip that reads:

(29) How Ælfwine drank of *limpë* but thirsted for his home, and went back to Luthany; and thirsted then unquenchably for the Elves, and went back to Tavrobel the Old and dwelt in the House of the Hundred Chimneys (where grows still the child of the child of the Pine of Belawryn) and wrote the Golden Book.

Associated with this is a title-page:

(30)   The Book of Lost Tales
            and the History of the Elves of Luthany
                    [?being]
            The Golden Book of Tavrobel
    the same that Ælfwine wrote and laid in the House of a Hundred
Chimneys at Tavrobel, where it lieth still to read for such as may.

These are very curious. Tavrobel the Old must be the original Tavrobel in Luthany (after which Tavrobel in Tol Eressëa was named, just as Kortirion in Tol Eressëa was named after Kortirion = Warwick in Luthany); and the House of the Hundred Chimneys (as also the Pine of Belawryn, on which see p. 281 and note 4) was to be displaced from Tol Eressëa to Luthany. Presumably my father intended to rewrite those passages in the 'framework' of the *Lost Tales* where the House of a Hundred Chimneys in Tavrobel is referred to; unless there was to be another House of a Hundred Chimneys in Tavrobel the New in Tol Eressëa.

Lastly, an interesting entry in the Qenya dictionary may be mentioned here: *Parma Kuluinen* 'the Golden Book – the collected book of legends, especially of Ing and Eärendel'.

★

In the event, of all these projections my father only developed the story of Ælfwine's youth and his voyage to Tol Eressëa to a full and polished form, and to this work I now turn; but first it is convenient to collect the passages previously considered that bear on it.

In the opening *Link* to the *Tale of Tinúviel* Eriol said that 'many years agone', when he was a child, his home was 'in an old town of Men girt with a wall now crumbled and broken, and a river ran thereby over which a castle with a great tower hung'.

My father came of a coastward folk, and the love of the sea that I had never seen was in my bones, and my father whetted my desire, for he told me tales that his father had told him before. Now my mother died in a cruel and hungry siege of that old town, and my father was slain in bitter fight about the walls, and in the end I Eriol escaped to the shoreland of the Western Sea.

Eriol told then of

his wanderings about the western havens, . . . of how he was wrecked upon far western islands until at last upon one lonely one he came upon an ancient sailor who gave him shelter, and over a fire within his lonely cabin told him strange tales of things beyond the Western Seas, of the Magic Isles and that most lonely one that lay beyond. . . .

'Ever after,' said Eriol, 'did I sail more curiously about the western isles seeking more stories of the kind, and thus it is indeed that after many great voyages I came myself by the blessing of the Gods to Tol Eressëa in the end . . .'

In the typescript version of this *Link* it is further told that in the town where Eriol's parents lived and died

there dwelt a mighty duke, and did he gaze from the topmost battlements never might he see the bounds of his wide domain, save where far to east the blue shapes of the great mountains lay – yet was that tower held the most lofty that stood in the lands of Men.

The siege and sack of the town were the work of 'the wild men from the Mountains of the East'.

At the end of the typescript version the boy Ausir assured Eriol that 'that ancient mariner beside the lonely sea was none other than Ulmo's self, who appeareth not seldom thus to those voyagers whom he loves'; but Eriol did not believe him.

I have given above (pp. 294–5) reasons for thinking that in 'the *Eriol* story' this tale of his youth was not set in England.

Turning to the passages concerned with the later, *Ælfwine* story, we learn from (15) that Ælfwine dwelt in the South-west of England and that his mother and father were slain by 'the sea-pirates', and from (20) that they were slain by 'the fierce Men of the Sea'; from (16) that he was 'driven by the Normans'. In (15) there is a mention of his meeting with 'the Ancient Mariner' during his voyages. In (16) he comes to 'the harbour of the southern shore' of Tol Eressëa; and in (17) he 'awakens upon a sandy beach' at low tide.

I come now to the narrative that finally emerged. It will be observed, perhaps with relief, that Ing, Ingwë, and the Ingwaiwar have totally disappeared.

ÆLFWINE OF ENGLAND

There are three versions of this short work. One is a plot-outline of less than 500 words, which for convenience of reference I shall call *Ælfwine A*; but the second is a much more substantial narrative bearing the title *Ælfwine of England*. This was written in 1920 or later: demonstrably not earlier, for my father used for it scraps of paper pinned together, and some of these are letters to him, all dated in February 1920.[18] The third text no doubt began as a fair copy in ink of the second, to which it is indeed very close at first, but became as it proceeded a complete rewriting at several points, with the introduction of much new matter, and it was further emended after it had been completed. It bears no title in the manuscript, but must obviously be called *Ælfwine of England* likewise.

For convenience I shall refer to the first fully-written version as *Ælfwine I* and to its rewriting as *Ælfwine II*. The relation of *Ælfwine A* to these is hard to determine, since it agrees in some respects with the one and in some with the other. It is obvious that my father had *Ælfwine I* in front of him when he wrote *Ælfwine II*, but it seems likely that he drew on *Ælfwine A* at the same time.

I give here the full text of *Ælfwine II* in its final form, with all noteworthy emendations and all important differences from the other texts in the notes (differences in names, and changes to names, are listed separately).

There was a land called England, and it was an island of the West, and before it was broken in the warfare of the Gods it was westernmost of all the Northern lands, and looked upon the Great Sea that Men of old called Garsecg;[19] but that part that was broken was called Ireland and many names besides, and its dwellers come not into these tales.

All that land the Elves named Lúthien[20] and do so yet. In Lúthien alone dwelt still the most part of the Fading Companies, the Holy Fairies that have not yet sailed away from the world, beyond the horizon of Men's knowledge, to the Lonely Island, or even to the Hill of Tûn[21] upon the Bay of Faëry that washes the western shores of the kingdom of the Gods. Therefore is Lúthien even yet a holy land, and a magic that is not otherwise lingers still in many places of that isle.

Now amidmost of that island is there still a town that is aged among Men, but its age among the Elves is greater far; and, for this is a book of the Lost Tales of Elfinesse, it shall be named in their tongue Kortirion, which the Gnomes call Mindon Gwar.[22] Upon the hill of Gwar dwelt in the days of the English a man and his name was Déor, and he came thither from afar, from the south of the island and from the forests and from the enchanted West, where albeit he was of the English folk he had long time wandered. Now the Prince of Gwar was in those days a lover of songs and no enemy of the Elves, and they lingered yet most of all the isle in those regions about Kortirion (which places they called Alalminórë, the Land of Elms), and thither came Déor the singer to seek the Prince of Gwar and to seek the companies of the Fading Elves, for he was an Elf-friend. Though Déor was of English blood, it is told that he wedded to wife a maiden from the West, from Lionesse as some have named it since, or Evadrien 'Coast of Iron' as the Elves still say. Déor found her in the lost land beyond Belerion whence the Elves at times set sail.

Mirth had Déor long time in Mindon Gwar, but the Men of the North, whom the fairies of the island called Forodwaith, but whom Men called other names, came against Gwar in those days when they ravaged wellnigh all the land of Lúthien. Its walls availed not and its towers might not withstand them for ever, though the siege was long and bitter.

There Éadgifu (for so did Déor name the maiden of the West, though it was not her name aforetime)[23] died in those evil hungry days; but Déor fell before the walls even as he sang a song of ancient valour for the raising of men's hearts. That was a desperate sally, and the son of Déor was Ælfwine, and he was then but a boy left fatherless. The sack of that town thereafter was very cruel, and whispers of its ancient days alone remained, and the Elves that had grown to love the English of the isle fled or hid themselves for a long time, and none of Elves or Men were left in his old halls to lament the fall of Óswine Prince of Gwar.

Then Ælfwine, even he whom the unfaded Elves beyond the waters of Garsecg did after name Eldairon of Lúthien (which is

Ælfwine of England), was made a thrall to the fierce lords of the Forodwaith, and his boyhood knew evil days. But behold a wonder, for Ælfwine knew not and had never seen the sea, yet he heard its great voice speaking deeply in his heart, and its murmurous choirs sang ever in his secret ear between wake and sleep, that he was filled with longing. This was of the magic of Éadgifu, maiden of the West, his mother, and this longing unquenchable had been hers all the days that she dwelt in the quiet inland places among the elms of Mindon Gwar – and amidmost of her longing was Ælfwine her child born, and the Foamriders, the Elves of the Sea-marge, whom she had known of old in Lionesse, sent messengers to his birth. But now Éadgifu was gone beyond the Rim of Earth, and her fair form lay unhonoured in Mindon Gwar, and Déor's harp was silent, but Ælfwine laboured in thraldom until the threshold of manhood, dreaming dreams and filled with longing, and at rare times holding converse with the hidden Elves.

At last his longing for the sea bit him so sorely that he contrived to break his bonds, and daring great perils and suffering many grievous toils he escaped to lands where the Lords of the Forodwaith had not come, far from the places of Déor's abiding in Mindon Gwar. Ever he wandered southward and to the west, for that way his feet unbidden led him. Now Ælfwine had in a certain measure the gift of elfin-sight (which was not given to all Men in those days of the fading of the Elves and still less is it granted now), and the folk of Lúthien were less faded too in those days, so that many a host of their fair companies he saw upon his wandering road. Some there were dwelt yet and danced yet about that land as of old, but many more there were that wandered slowly and sadly westward; for behind them all the land was full of burnings and of war, and its dwellings ran with tears and with blood for the little love of Men for Men – nor was that the last of the takings of Lúthien by Men from Men, which have been seven, and others mayhap still shall be. Men of the East and of the West and of the South and of the North have coveted that land and dispossessed those who held it before them, because of its beauty and goodliness and of the glamour of the fading ages of the Elves that lingered still among its trees beyond its high white shores.[24]

Yet at each taking of that isle have many more of the most ancient of all dwellers therein, the folk of Lúthien, turned westward; and they have got them in ships at Belerion in the

West and sailed thence away for ever over the horizon of Men's knowledge, leaving the island the poorer for their going and its leaves less green; yet still it abides the richest among Men in the presence of the Elves. And it is said that, save only when the fierce fathers of Men, foes of the Elves, being new come under the yoke of Evil,[25] entered first that land, never else did so great a concourse of elfin ships and white-winged galleons sail to the setting sun as in those days when the ancient Men of the South set first their mighty feet upon the soil of Lúthien – the Men whose lords sat in the city of power that Elves and Men have called Rûm (but the Elves alone do know as Magbar).[26]

Now is it the dull hearts of later days rather than the red deeds of cruel hands that set the minds of the little folk to fare away; and ever and anon a little ship[27] weighs anchor from Belerion at eve and its sweet sad song is lost for ever on the waves. Yet even in the days of Ælfwine there was many a laden ship under elfin sails that left those shores for ever, and many a comrade he had, seen or half-unseen, upon his westward road. And so he came at last to Belerion, and there he laved his weary feet in the grey waters of the Western Sea, whose great roaring drowned his ears. There the dim shapes of Elvish[28] boats sailed by him in the gloaming, and many aboard called to him farewell. But he might not embark on those frail craft, and they refused his prayer – for they were not willing that even one beloved among Men should pass with them beyond the edge of the West, or learn what lies far out on Garsecg the great and measureless sea. Now the men who dwelt thinly about those places nigh Belerion were fishermen, and Ælfwine abode long time amongst them, and being of nature shaped inly thereto he learned all that a man may of the craft of ships and of the sea. He recked little of his life, and he set his ocean-paths wider than most of those men, good mariners though they were; and there were few in the end who dared to go with him, save Ælfheah the fatherless who was with him in all ventures until his last voyage.[29]

Now on a time journeying far out into the open sea, being first becalmed in a thick mist, and after driven helpless by a mighty wind from the East, he espied some islands lying in the dawn, but he won not ever thereto for the winds changing swept him again far away, and only his strong fate saved him to see the black coasts of his abiding once again. Little content was he with his good fortune, and purposed in his heart to sail some time again yet further into the West, thinking unwitting it was the Magic Isles of the songs of Men that he had seen from afar. Few companions could he get for this adventure. Not all men love to sail a quest for the red sun or to tempt the dangerous seas in thirst for undiscovered things. Seven such found he in the end, the greatest mariners that were then in England, and Ulmo Lord of the Sea afterward took them to himself and their names are now forgotten, save Ælfheah only.[30] A great storm fell upon their ship even as they had sighted the isles of Ælfwine's desire, and a great sea swept over her; but Ælfwine was lost in the waves, and coming to himself saw no sign of ship or comrades, and he lay upon a bed of sand in a deep-walled cove. Dark and very empty was the isle, and he knew then that these were not those Magic Isles of which he had heard often tell.[31]

There wandering long, 'tis said, he came upon many hulls of wrecks rotting on the long gloomy beaches, and some were wrecks of many mighty ships of old, and some were treasure-laden. A lonely cabin looking westward he found at last upon the further shore, and it was made of the upturned hull of a small ship. An ancient man dwelt there, and Ælfwine feared him, for the eyes of the man were as deep as the unfathomable sea, and his long beard was blue and grey; great was his stature, and his shoes were of stone,[32] but he was all clad in tangled rags, sitting beside a small fire of drifted wood.

In that strange hut beside an empty sea did Ælfwine long abide for lack of other shelter or of other counsel, thinking his ship lost and his comrades drowned. But the ancient man grew kindly toward him, and questioned Ælfwine concerning his coming and his goings and whither he had desired to sail before the storm took him. And many things before unheard did Ælfwine hear tell of him beside that smoky fire at eve, and strange tales of wind-harried ships and harbourless tempests in the forbidden waters. Thus heard Ælfwine how the Magic Isles were yet a great voyage before him keeping a dark and secret ward upon the edge of Earth, beyond whom the waters of Garsecg grow less troublous and there lies the twilight of the latter days of Fairyland. Beyond and on the confines of the Shadows lies the Lonely Island looking East to the Magic Archipelago and to the lands of Men beyond it, and West into the Shadows beyond which afar off is glimpsed the Outer Land, the kingdom of the Gods – even the aged Bay of Faëry whose glory has grown dim. Thence slopes the world steeply beyond the Rim of Things to Valinor, that is God-home, and to the

Wall and to the edge of Nothingness whereon are sown the stars. But the Lonely Isle is neither of the Great Lands or of the Outer Land, and no isle lies near it.

In his tales that aged man named himself the Man of the Sea, and he spoke of his last voyage ere he was cast in wreck upon this outer isle, telling how ere the West wind took him he had glimpsed afar off bosomed in the deep the twinkling lanterns of the Lonely Isle. Then did Ælfwine's heart leap within him, but he said to that aged one that he might not hope to get him a brave ship or comrades more. But that Man of the Sea said: 'Lo, this is one of the ring of Harbourless Isles that draw all ships towards their hidden rocks and quaking sands, lest Men fare over far upon Garsecg and see things that are not for them to see. And these isles were set here at the Hiding of Valinor, and little wood for ship or raft does there grow on them, as may be thought;[33] but I may aid thee yet in thy desire to depart from these greedy shores.'

Thereafter on a day Ælfwine fared along the eastward strands gazing at the many unhappy wrecks there lying. He sought, as often he had done before, if he might see perchance any sign or relic of his good ship from Belerion. There had been that night a storm of great violence and dread, and lo! the number of wrecks was increased by one, and Ælfwine saw it had been a large and well-built ship of cunning lines such as the Forodwaith then loved. Cast far up on the treacherous sands it stood, and its great beak carven as a dragon's head still glared unbroken at the land. Then went the Man of the Sea out when the tide began to creep in slow and shallow over the long flats. He bore as a staff a timber great as a young tree, and he fared as if he had no need to fear tide or quicksand until he came far out where his shoulders were scarce above the yellow waters of the incoming flood to that carven prow, that now alone was seen above the water. Then Ælfwine marvelled watching from afar, to see him heave by his single strength the whole great ship up from the clutches of the sucking sand that gripped its sunken stern; and when it floated he thrust it before him, swimming now with mighty strokes in the deepening water. At that sight Ælfwine's fear of the aged one was renewed, and he wondered what manner of being he might be; but now the ship was thrust far up on the firmer sands, and the swimmer strode ashore, and his mighty beard was full of strands of sea-weed, and sea-weed was in his hair.

When that tide again forsook the Hungry Sands the Man of the Sea bade Ælfwine go look at that new-come wreck, and going he saw it was not hurt; but there were within nine dead men who had not long ago been yet alive. They lay abottom gazing at the sky, and behold, one whose garb and mien still proclaimed a chieftain of Men lay there, but though his locks were white with age and his face was pale in death, still a proud man and a fierce he looked. 'Men of the North, Forodwaith, are they,' said the Man of the Sea, 'but hunger and thirst was their death, and their ship was flung by last night's storm where she stuck in the Hungry Sands, slowly to be engulfed, had not fate thought otherwise.'

'Truly do you say of them, O Man of the Sea; and him I know well with those white locks, for he slew my father; and long was I his thrall, and Orm men called him, and little did I love him.'

'And his ship shall it be that bears you from this Harbourless Isle,' said he; 'and a gallant ship it was of a brave man, for few folk have now so great a heart for the adventures of the sea as have these Forodwaith, who press ever into the mists of the West, though few live to take back tale of all they see.'

Thus it was that Ælfwine escaped beyond hope from that island, but the Man of the Sea was his pilot and steersman, and so they came after few days to a land but little known.[34] And the folk that dwell there are a strange folk, and none know how they came thither in the West, yet are they accounted among the kindreds of Men, albeit their land is on the outer borders of the regions of Mankind, lying yet further toward the Setting Sun beyond the Harbourless Isles and further to the North than is that isle whereon Ælfwine was cast away. Marvellously skilled are these people in the building of ships and boats of every kind and in the sailing of them; yet do they fare seldom or never to the lands of other folk, and little do they busy themselves with commerce or with war. Their ships they build for love of that labour and for the joy they have only to ride the waves in them. And a great part of that people are ever aboard their ships, and all the water about the island of their home is ever white with their sails in calm or storm. Their delight is to vie in rivalry with one another with their boats of surpassing swiftness, driven by the winds or by the ranks of their long-shafted oars. Other rivalries have they with ships of great seaworthiness, for with these will they contest who will weather the fiercest storms (and these are fierce indeed about that isle, and it is iron-coasted save for one cool harbour in the North). Thereby is the craft of their shipwrights proven; and these people are called by Men the Ythlings,[35] the Children of the Waves, but the Elves call the island Eneadur, and its folk the Shipmen of the West.[36]

Well did these receive Ælfwine and his pilot at the thronging quays of their harbour in the North, and it seemed to Ælfwine that the Man of the Sea was not unknown to them, and that they held him in the greatest awe and reverence, hearkening to his requests as though they were a king's commands. Yet greater was his amaze when he met amid the throngs of that place two of his comrades that he had thought lost in the sea; and learnt that those seven mariners of England were alive in that land, but the ship had been broken utterly on the black shores to the south, not long after the night when the great sea had taken Ælfwine overboard.

Now at the bidding of the Man of the Sea do those islanders with great speed fashion a new ship for Ælfwine and his fellows, since he would fare no further in Orm's ship; and its timbers were cut, as the ancient sailor had asked, from a grove of magic oaks far inland that grew about a high place of the Gods, sacred to Ulmo Lord of the Sea, and seldom were any of them felled. 'A ship that is wrought of this wood,' said the Man of the Sea, 'may be lost, but those that sail in it shall not in that voyage lose their lives; yet may they perhaps be cast where they little think to come.'

But when that ship was made ready that ancient sailor bid them climb aboard, and this they did, but with them went also Bior of the Ythlings, a man of mighty sea-craft for their aid, and one who above any of that strange folk was minded to sail at times far from the land of Eneadur to West or North or South. There stood many men of the Ythlings upon the shore beside that vessel; for they had builded her in a cove of the steep shore that looked to the West, and a bar of rock with but a narrow opening made here a sheltered pool and mooring place, and few like it were to be found in that island of sheer cliffs. Then the ancient one laid his hand upon her prow and spoke words of magic, giving her power to cleave uncloven waters and enter unentered harbours, and ride untrodden beaches. Twin rudder-paddles, one on either side, had she after the fashion of the Ythlings, and each of these he blessed, giving them skill to steer when the hands that held them failed, and to find lost courses, and to follow stars that were hid. Then he strode away,

and the press of men parted before him, until climbing he came
to a high pinnacle of the cliffs. Then leapt he far out and down
and vanished with a mighty flurry of foam where the great
breakers gathered to assault the towering shores.

Ælfwine saw him no more, and he said in grief and amaze:
'Why was he thus weary of life? My heart grieves that he is
dead,' but the Ythlings smiled, so that he questioned some that
stood nigh, saying: 'Who was that mighty man, for meseems ye
know him well,' and they answered him nothing. Then thrust
they forth that vessel valiant-timbered[37] out into the sea, for no
longer would Ælfwine abide, though the sun was sinking to the
Mountains of Valinor beyond the Western Walls. Soon was her
white sail seen far away filled with a wind from off the land, and
red-stained in the light of the half-sunken sun; and those aboard
her sang old songs of the English folk that faded on the sailless
waves of the Western Seas, and now no longer came any sound
of them to the watchers on the shore. Then night shut down and
none on Eneadur saw that strong ship ever more.[38]

So began those mariners that long and strange and perilous
voyage whose full tale has never yet been told. Nought of their
adventures in the archipelagoes of the West, and the wonders
and the dangers that they found in the Magic Isles and in seas
and sound unknown, are here to tell, but of the ending of their
voyage, how after a time of years sea-weary and sick of heart
they found a grey and cheerless day. Little wind was there, and
the clouds hung low overhead; while a grey rain fell, and nought
could any of them descry before their vessel's beak that moved
now slow and uncertain over the long dead waves. That day had
they trysted to be the last ere they turned their vessel homeward
(if they might), save only if some wonder should betide or any
sign of hope. For their heart was gone. Behind them lay the
Magic Isles where three of their number slept upon dim strands
in deadly sleep, and their heads were pillowed on white sand
and they were clad in foam, wrapped about in the agelong spells
of Eglavain. Fruitless had been all their journeys since, for ever
the winds had cast them back without sight of the shores of the
Island of the Elves.[39] Then said Ælfheah[40] who held the helm:
'Now, O Ælfwine, is the trysted time! Let us do as the Gods and
their winds have long desired — cease from our heart-weary
quest for nothingness, a fable in the void, and get us back if the
Gods will it seeking the hearths of our home.' And Ælfwine

yielded. Then fell the wind and no breath came from East or West, and night came slowly over the sea.

Behold, at length a gentle breeze sprang up, and it came softly from the West; and even as they would fill their sails therewith for home, one of those shipmen on a sudden said: 'Nay, but this is a strange air, and full of scented memories,' and standing still they all breathed deep. The mists gave before that gentle wind, and a thin moon they might see riding in its tattered shreds, until behind it soon a thousand cool stars peered forth in the dark. 'The night-flowers are opening in Faëry,' said Ælfwine; 'and behold,' said Bior,[41] 'the Elves are kindling candles in their silver dusk,' and all looked whither his long hand pointed over their dark stern. Then none spoke for wonder and amaze, seeing deep in the gloaming of the West a blue shadow, and in the blue shadow many glittering lights, and ever more and more of them came twinkling out, until ten thousand points of flickering radiance were splintered far away as if a dust of the jewels self-luminous that Fëanor made were scattered on the lap of the Ocean.

'Then is that the Harbour of the Lights of Many Hues,' said Ælfheah, 'that many a little-heeded tale has told of in our homes.' Then saying no more they shot out their oars and swung about their ship in haste, and pulled towards the never-dying shore. Near had they come to abandoning it when hardly won. Little did they make of that long pull, as they thrust the water strongly by them, and the long night of Faërie held on, and the horned moon of Elfinesse rode over them.

Then came there music very gently over the waters and it was laden with unimagined longing, that Ælfwine and his comrades leant upon their oars and wept softly each for his heart's half-remembered hurts, and memory of fair things long lost, and each for the thirst that is in every child of Men for the flawless loveliness they seek and do not find. And one said: 'It is the harps that are thrumming, and the songs they are singing of fair things; and the windows that look upon the sea are full of light.' And another said: 'Their stringéd violins complain the ancient woes of the immortal folk of Earth, but there is a joy therein.' 'Ah me,' said Ælfwine, 'I hear the horns of the Fairies shimmering in magic woods – such music as I once dimly guessed long years ago beneath the elms of Mindon Gwar.'

And lo! as they spoke thus musing the moon hid himself, and the stars were clouded, and the mists of time veiled the shore, and nothing could they see and nought more hear, save the sound of the surf of the seas in the far-off pebbles of the Lonely Isle; and soon the wind blew even that faint rustle far away. But Ælfwine stood forward with wide-open eyes unspeaking, and suddenly with a great cry he sprang forward into the dark sea, and the waters that filled him were warm, and a kindly death it seemed enveloped him. Then it seemed to the others that they awakened at his voice as from a dream; but the wind now suddenly grown fierce filled all their sails, and they saw him never again, but were driven back with hearts all broken with regret and longing. Pale elfin boats awhile they would see beating home, maybe, to the Haven of Many Hues, and they hailed them; but only faint echoes afar off were borne to their ears, and none led them ever to the land of their desire; who after a great time wound back all the mazy clue of their long tangled ways, until they cast anchor at last in the haven of Belerion, aged and wayworn men. And the things they had seen and heard seemed after to them a mirage, and a phantasy, born of hunger and sea-spells, save only to Bior of Eneadur of the Ship-folk of the West.

Yet among the seed of these men has there been many a restless and wistful spirit thereafter, since they were dead and passed beyond the Rim of Earth without need of boat or sail. But never while life lasted did they leave their sea-faring, and their bodies are all covered by the sea.[42]

The narrative ends here. There is no trace of any further continuation, though it seems likely that *Ælfwine of England* was to be the beginning of a complete rewriting of the *Lost Tales*. It would be interesting to know for certain when *Ælfwine II* was written. The handwriting of the manuscript is certainly changed from that of the rest of the *Lost Tales*; yet I am inclined to think that it followed *Ælfwine I* at no great interval, and the first version is unlikely to be much later than 1920 (see p. 312).

At the end of *Ælfwine II* my father jotted down two suggestions: (1) that Ælfwine should be made 'an early pagan Englishman who fled to the West'; and (2) that 'the Isle of the Old Man' should be cut out and all should be shipwrecked on Eneadur, the Isle of the Ythlings. The latter would (astonishingly) have entailed the abandonment of the foundered ship, with the Man of the Sea thrusting it to shore on the incoming tide, and the dead Vikings 'lying abottom gazing at the sky'.

In this narrative — in which the 'magic' of the early Elves is most intensely conveyed, in the seamen's vision of the Lonely Isle beneath 'the horned moon of Elfinesse' – Ælfwine is still placed in the context of the figures of ancient English legend: his father is Déor the Minstrel. In the great Anglo-Saxon manuscript known as the Exeter Book there is a little poem of 42 lines to which the title of *Déor* is now given. It is an utterance of the minstrel Déor, who, as he tells, has lost his place and been supplanted in his lord's favour by another bard, named Heorrenda; in the body of the poem Déor draws examples from among the great misfortunes recounted in the heroic legends, and is comforted by them, concluding each allusion with the fixed refrain *þæs ofereode; þisses swa mæg*, which has been variously translated; my father held that it meant 'Time has passed since then, this too can pass'.[43]

From this poem came both Déor and Heorrenda. In 'the *Eriol* story' Heorrenda was Eriol's son born in Tol Eressëa of his wife Naimi (p. 290), and was associated with Hengest and Horsa in the conquest of the Lonely Isle (p. 291); his dwelling in England was at Tavrobel (p. 292). I do not think that my father's Déor the Minstrel of Kortirion and Heorrenda of Tavrobel can be linked more closely to the Anglo-Saxon poem than in the names alone – though he did not take the names at random. He was moved by the glimpsed tale (even if, in the words of one of the poem's editors, 'the autobiographical element is purely fictitious, serving only as a pretext for the enumeration of the heroic stories'); and when lecturing on *Beowulf* at Oxford he sometimes gave the unknown poet a name, calling him *Heorrenda*.

Nor, as I believe, can any more be made of the other Old English names in the narrative: Óswine prince of Gwar, Éadgifu, Ælfheah (though the names are doubtless in themselves 'significant': thus *Óswine* contains *ós* 'god' and *wine* 'friend', and *Éadgifu éad* 'blessedness' and *gifu* 'gift'). The Forodwaith are of course Viking invaders from Norway or Denmark; the name Orm of the dead ship's captain is well-known in Norse. But all this is a mise-en-scène that is historical only in its bearings, not in its structure.

The idea of the seven invasions of Lúthien (Luthany) remained (p. 314), and that of the fading and westward flight of the Elves (which indeed was never finally lost),[44] but whereas in the outlines the invasion of the Ingwaiwar (i.e. the Anglo-Saxons) was the seventh (see citations (20) and (22)), here the Viking invasions are portrayed as coming upon the English – 'nor was that the last of the takings of Lúthien by Men from Men' (p. 314), obviously a reference to the Normans.

There is much of interest in the 'geographical' references in the story. At the very beginning there is a curious statement about the breaking off of Ireland 'in the warfare of the Gods'. Seeing that 'the *Ælfwine* story' does not include the idea of the drawing back of Tol Eressëa eastwards across the sea, this must refer to something quite other than the story in (5), p. 283, where the Isle of Íverin was broken off when Ossë tried to wrench back Tol Eressëa. What this was I do not know; but it seems conceivable that this is the first trace or hint of the great cataclysm at the end of the Elder Days, when Beleriand was drowned. (I have found no trace of any connection between the harbour of *Belerion* and the region of *Beleriand*.)

Kortirion (Mindon Gwar) is in this tale of course 'Kortirion the Old', the original Elvish dwelling in Lúthien, after which Kortirion in Tol Eressëa was named (see pp. 308, 310); in the same way we must suppose that the name Alalminórë (p. 313) for the region about it ('Warwickshire') was given anew to the midmost region of Tol Eressëa.

Turning to the question of the islands and archipelagoes in the Great Sea, what is said in *Ælfwine of England* may first be compared with the passages of geographical description in *The Coming of the Valar* (I.68) and *The Coming of the Elves* (I.125), which are closely similar the one to the other. From these passages we learn that there are many lands and islands in the Great Sea before the Magic Isles are reached; beyond the Magic Isles is Tol Eressëa; and beyond Tol Eressëa are the Shadowy Seas, 'whereon there float the Twilit Isles', the first of the Outer Lands. Tol Eressëa itself 'is held neither of the Outer Lands or of the Great Lands' (I.125); it is far out in mid-ocean, and 'no land may be seen for many leagues' sail from its cliffs' (I.121). With this account *Ælfwine of England* agrees closely; but to it is added now the archipelago of the Harbourless Isles.

As I have noted before (I.137), this progression from East to West of Harbourless Isles, Magic Isles, the Lonely Isle, and then the Shadowy Seas in which were the Twilit Isles, was afterwards changed, and it is said in *The Silmarillion* (p. 102) that at the time of the Hiding of Valinor

the Enchanted Isles were set, and all the seas about them were filled with shadows and bewilderment. And these isles were strung as a net in the Shadowy Seas from the north to the south, before Tol Eressëa, the Lonely Isle, is reached by one sailing west. Hardly might any vessel pass between them, for in the dangerous sounds the waves sighed for ever upon dark rocks shrouded in mist. And in the twilight a great weariness came upon mariners and a loathing of the sea; but all that ever set foot upon the islands were there entrapped, and slept until the Change of the World.

As a conception, the Enchanted Isles are derived primarily from the old Magic Isles, set at the time of the Hiding of Valinor and described in that Tale (I.211): 'Ossë set them in a great ring about the western limits of the mighty sea, so that they guarded the Bay of Faëry', and

all such as stepped thereon came never thence again, but being woven in the nets of Oinen's hair the Lady of the Sea, and whelmed in agelong slumber that Lórien set there, lay upon the margin of the waves, as those do who being drowned are cast up once more by the movements of the sea; yet rather did these hapless ones sleep unfathomably and the dark waters laved their limbs . . .

Here three of Ælfwine's companions

slept upon dim strands in deadly sleep, and their heads were pillowed on white sand and they were clad in foam, wrapped about in the agelong spells of Eglavain (p. 320).

(I do not know the meaning of the name *Eglavain*, but since it clearly contains *Egla* (Gnomish, = *Elda*, see I.251) it perhaps meant 'Elfinesse'.) But the Enchanted Isles derive also perhaps from the Twilit Isles, since the Enchanted Isles were likewise in twilight and were set in the Shadowy Seas (cf. I.224); and from the Harbourless Isles as well, which, as Ælfwine was told by the Man of the Sea (p. 317), were set at the time of the Hiding of Valinor – and indeed served the same purpose as did the Magic Isles, though lying far further to the East.

Eneadur, the isle of the Ythlings (Old English *ýð* 'wave'), whose life is so fully described in *Ælfwine of England*, seems never to have been mentioned again. Is there in Eneadur and the Shipmen of the West perhaps some faint foreshadowing of the early Númenóreans in their cliff-girt isle?

The following passage (pp. 316–17) is not easy to interpret:

Thence [i.e. from the Bay of Faëry] slopes the world steeply beyond the Rim of Things to Valinor, that is God-home, and to the Wall and to the edge of Nothingness whereon are sown the stars.

In the *Ambarkanta* or 'Shape of the World' of the 1930s a map of the world shows the surface of the Outer Land sloping steeply westwards from the Mountains of Valinor. Conceivably it is to this slope that my father was referring here, and the Rim of Things is the great mountain-wall; but this seems very improbable. There are also references in *Ælfwine of England* to 'the Rim of Earth', beyond which the dead pass (pp. 314, 322); and in an outline for the *Tale of Eärendel* (p. 260) Tuor's boat 'dips over the world's rim'. More likely, I think, the expression refers to the rim of the horizon ('the horizon of Men's knowledge', p. 313).

The expression 'the sun was sinking to the Mountains of Valinor beyond the Western Walls' (p. 320) I am at a loss to explain according to what has been told in the *Lost Tales*. A possible, though scarcely convincing, interpretation is that the sun was sinking towards Valinor, *whence it would pass* 'beyond the Western Walls' (i.e. through the Door of Night, see I.215–16).

Lastly, the suggestion (p. 313) is notable that the Elves sailing west from Lúthien might go beyond the Lonely Isle and reach even back to Valinor; on this matter see p. 280.

★

Before ending, there remains to discuss briefly a matter of a general nature that has many times been mentioned in the texts, and especially in these last chapters: that of the 'diminutiveness' of the Elves.

It is said several times in the *Lost Tales* that the Elves of the ancient days were of greater bodily stature than they afterwards became. Thus in *The Fall of Gondolin* (p. 159): 'The fathers of the fathers of Men were of less stature than Men now are, and the children of Elfinesse of greater growth'; in an outline for the abandoned tale of Gilfanon (I.235) very similarly: 'Men were almost of a stature at first with Elves, the fairies being far greater and Men smaller than now'; and in citation (4) in the present chapter: 'Men and Elves were formerly of a size, though Men always larger.' Other passages suggest that the ancient Elves were of their nature of at any rate somewhat slighter build (see pp. 142, 220).

The diminishing in the stature of the Elves of later times is very explicitly related to the coming of Men. Thus in (4) above: 'Men spread and thrive, and the Elves of the Great Lands fade. As Men's stature grows theirs diminishes'; and in (5): 'ever as Men wax more powerful and numerous so the fairies fade and grow small and tenuous, filmy and transparent, but Men larger and more dense and gross. At last Men, or almost all, can no longer see the fairies.' The clearest picture that survives of the Elves when they have 'faded' altogether is given in the *Epilogue* (p. 289):

> Like strands of wind, like mystic half-transparencies, Gilfanon Lord of Tavrobel rides out tonight amid his folk, and hunts the elfin deer beneath the paling sky. A music of forgotten feet, a gleam of leaves, a sudden bending of the grass, and wistful voices murmuring on the bridge, and they are gone.

But according to the passages bearing on the later '*Ælfwine*' version, the Elves of Tol Eressëa who had left Luthany were unfaded, or had ceased to fade. Thus in (15): 'Tol Eressëa, whither most of the unfaded Elves have retired from the noise, war, and clamour of Men'; and (16): 'Tol Eressëa, whither most of the fading Elves have withdrawn from the world, and there fade now no more'; also in *Ælfwine of England* (p. 313): 'the unfaded Elves beyond the waters of Garsecg'.

On the other hand, when Eriol came to the Cottage of Lost Play the doorward said to him (I.14):

> Small is the dwelling, but smaller still are they that dwell here – for all who enter must be very small indeed, or of their own good wish become as very little folk even as they stand upon the threshold.

I have commented earlier (I. 32) on the oddity of the idea that the Cottage and its inhabitants were peculiarly small, in an island entirely inhabited by Elves. But my father, if he had ever rewritten *The Cottage of Lost Play*, would doubtless have abandoned this; and it may well be that he was in any case turning away already at the time of *Ælfwine II* from the idea that the 'faded' Elves were diminutive, as is suggested by his rejection of the word 'little' in 'little folk', 'little ships' (see note 27).

Ultimately, of course, the Elves shed all associations and qualities that would be now commonly considered 'fairylike', and those who remained in the Great Lands in Ages of the world at this time unconceived were to grow greatly in stature and in power: there was nothing filmy or transparent about the heroic or majestic Eldar of the Third Age of Middle-earth. Long afterwards my father would write, in a wrathful comment on a 'pretty' or 'ladylike' pictorial rendering of Legolas:

> He was tall as a young tree, lithe, immensely strong, able swiftly to draw a great war-bow and shoot down a Nazgûl, endowed with the tremendous vitality of Elvish bodies, so hard and resistant to hurt that he went only in light shoes over rock or through snow, the most tireless of all the Fellowship.

★

This brings to an end my rendering and analysis of the early writings bearing on the story of the mariner who came to the Lonely Isle and learned there the true history of the Elves. I have shown, convincingly as I hope, the curious and complex way in which my father's vision of the significance of Tol Eressëa changed. When he jotted down the synopsis (10), the idea of the mariner's voyage to the Island of the Elves was of course already present; but he journeyed out of the East and the Lonely Isle of his seeking was – England (though not yet the land of the English and not yet lying in the seas where England lies). When later the entire concept was shifted, England, as 'Luthany' or 'Lúthien', remained pre-eminently the Elvish land; and Tol Eressëa, with its meads and coppices, its rooks' nests in the elm-trees of Alalminórë, seemed to the English mariner to be remade in the likeness of his own land, which the Elves had lost at the coming of Men: for it was indeed a re-embodiment of Elvish Luthany far over the sea.

All this was to fall away afterwards from the developing mythology; but Ælfwine left many marks on its pages before he too finally disappeared.

Much in this chapter is necessarily inconclusive and uncertain; but I believe that these very early notes and projections are rightly disinterred. Although, as 'plots', abandoned and doubtless forgotten, they bear witness to truths of my father's heart and mind that he never abandoned. But these notes were scribbled down in his youth, when for him Elvish magic 'lingered yet mightily in the woods and hills of Luthany'; in his old age all was gone West-over-sea, and an end was indeed come for the Eldar of story and of song.

NOTES

1 On this statement about the stature of Elves and Men see pp. 326–7.
2 For the form *Taimonto* (*Taimondo*) see I. 268, entry *Telimektar*.
3 *Belaurin* is the Gnomish equivalent of *Palúrien* (see I. 264).
4 A side-note here suggests that perhaps the Pine should not be in Tol Eressëa. – For *Ilwë*, the middle air, that is 'blue and clear and flows among the stars', see I. 65, 73.
5 *Gil = Ingil*. At the first occurrence of *Ingil* in this passage the name was written *Ingil* (*Gil*), but (*Gil*) was struck out.
6 The word *Nautar* occurs in a rejected outline for the *Tale of the Nauglafring* (p. 136), where it is equated with *Nauglath* (Dwarves).
7 *Uin*: 'the mightiest and most ancient of whales', chief among those whales and fishes that drew the 'island-car' (afterwards Tol Eressëa) on which Ulmo ferried the Elves to Valinor (I. 118–20).
8 *Gongs*: these are evil beings obscurely related to Orcs: see I. 245 note 10, and the rejected outlines for the *Tale of the Nauglafring* given on pp. 136–7.
9 A large query is written against this passage.
10 The likeness of this name to *Dor Daedeloth* is striking, but that is the name of the realm of Morgoth in *The Silmarillion*, and is interpreted 'Land of the Shadow of Horror'; the old name (whose elements are *dai* 'sky' and *teloth* 'roof') has nothing in common with the later except its form.
11 Cf. *Kortirion among the Trees* (I. 34, 37, 41): *A wave of bowing grass*.
12 The origin of *Warwick* according to conventional etymology is uncertain. The element *wic*, extremely common in English place-names, meant essentially a dwelling or group of dwellings. The earliest recorded form of the name is *Wæring wic*, and *Wæring* has been thought to be an Old English word meaning a dam, a derivative from *wer*, Modern English *weir*: thus 'dwellings by the weir'.
13 Cf. the title-page given in citation (11): *Heorrenda of Hægwudu*. – No forms of the name of this Staffordshire village are actually recorded from before the Norman Conquest, but the Old English form was undoubtedly *hæg-wudu* 'enclosed wood' (cf. the *High Hay*, the great hedge that protected Buckland from the Old Forest in *The Lord of the Rings*).
14 The name Luthany, of a country, occurs five times in Francis

Thompson's poem *The Mistress of Vision*. As noted previously (I. 29) my father acquired the Collected Poems of Francis Thompson in 1913–14; and in that copy he made a marginal note against one of the verses that contains the name *Luthany* – though the note is not concerned with the name. But whence Thompson derived *Luthany* I have no idea. He himself described the poem as 'a fantasy' (Everard Meynell, *The Life of Francis Thompson*, 1913, p. 237).

This provides no more than the origin of the name as a series of sounds, as with *Kôr* from Rider Haggard's *She*,* or *Rohan* and *Moria* mentioned in my father's letter of 1967 on this subject (*The Letters of J. R. R. Tolkien*, pp. 383–4), in which he said:

> This leads to the matter of 'external history': the actual way in which I came to light on or choose certain sequences of sound to use as names, *before* they were given a place inside the story. I think, as I said, this is unimportant: the labour involved in my setting out what I know and remember of the process, or in the guess-work of others, would be far greater than the worth of the results. The spoken forms would simply be mere audible forms, and when transferred to the prepared linguistic situation in my story would receive meaning and significance according to that situation, and to the nature of the story told. It would be entirely delusory to refer to the sources of the sound-combination to discover any meanings overt or hidden.

15 The position is complicated by the existence of some narrative outlines of extreme roughness and near-illegibility in which the mariner is named Ælfwine and yet essential elements of 'the *Eriol* story' are present. These I take to represent an intermediate stage. They are very obscure, and would require a great deal of space to present and discuss; therefore I pass them by.

16 Cf. p. 264 (xiv).

17 *Caer Gwâr*: see p. 292.

18 It may be mentioned here that when my father read *The Fall of Gondolin* to the Exeter College Essay Club in the spring of 1920 the mariner was still *Eriol*, as appears from the notes for his preliminary remarks on that occasion (see *Unfinished Tales* p. 5). He said here, very strangely, that 'Eriol lights by accident on the Lonely Island'.

19 *Garsecg* (pronounced *Garsedge*, and so written in *Ælfwine* A) was one of the many Old English names of the sea.

20 In *Ælfwine I* the land is likewise named *Lúthien*, not *Luthany*. In *Ælfwine A*, on the other hand, the same distinction is made as in the outlines: 'Ælfwine of England (whom the fairies after named

---

* There is no external evidence for this, but it can hardly be doubted. In this case it might be thought that since the African Kôr was a city built on the top of a great mountain standing in isolation the relationship was more than purely 'phonetic'.

Lúthien (friend) of Luthany (friendship)).' – At this first occurrence (only) of *Lúthien* in *Ælfwine II* the form *Leithian* is
pencilled above, but *Lúthien* is not struck out. *The Lay of Leithian*
was afterwards the title of the long poem of Beren and Lúthien
Tinúviel.

21 The *Hill of Tûn*, i.e. the hill on which the city of Tûn was built: see
p. 292.

22 *Mindon Gwar*: see p. 291.

23 *Éadgifu*: in 'the *Eriol* story' this Old English name (see p. 323) was
given as an equivalent to Naimi, Eriol's wife whom he wedded in
Tol Eressëa (p. 290).

24 In *Ælfwine I* the text here reads: 'by reason of her beauty and
goodliness, even as that king of the Franks that was upon a time
most mighty among men hath said . . .' [*sic*]. In *Ælfwine II* the
manuscript in ink stops at 'high white shores', but after these words
my father pencilled in: 'even as that king of the Franks that was
in those days the mightiest of earthly kings hath said . . .' [*sic*]. The
only clue in *Ælfwine of England* to the period of Ælfwine's life is
the invasion of the Forodwaith (Vikings); the mighty king of the
Franks may therefore be Charlemagne, but I have been unable
to trace any such reference.

25 *Evil* is emended from *Melko*. *Ælfwine I* does not have the phrase.

26 *Ælfwine I* has: 'when the ancient Men of the South from
Micelgeard the Heartless Town set their mighty feet upon the soil
of Lúthien.' This text does not have the reference to Rûm and
Magbar. The name *Micelgeard* is struck through, but *Mickleyard*
is written at the head of the page. *Micelgeard* is Old English (and
Mickleyard a modernisation of this in spelling), though it does
not occur in extant Old English writings and is modelled on Old
Norse *Mikligarðr* (Constantinople). – The peculiar hostility of
the Romans to the Elves of Luthany is mentioned by implication in
citation (20), and their disbelief in their existence in (22).

27 The application, frequent in *Ælwine I*, of 'little' to the fairies
(Elves) of Lúthien and their ships was retained in *Ælfwine II* as
first written, but afterwards struck out. Here the word is twice
retained, perhaps unintentionally.

28 *Elvish* is a later emendation of *fairy*.

29 This sentence, from 'save Ælfheah . . .', was added later in
Ælfwine II; it is not in *Ælfwine I*. – The whole text to this point
in *Ælfwine I* and *II* is compressed into the following in *Ælfwine A*:

> Ælfwine of England (whom the fairies after named Lúthien
> (friend) of Luthany (friendship)) born of Déor and Éadgifu.
> Their city burned and Déor slain and Éadgifu dies. Ælfwine a
> thrall of the Winged Helms. He escapes to the Western Sea
> and takes ship from Belerion and makes great voyages. He is

seeking for the islands of the West of which Éadgifu had told him in his childhood.

30   *Ælfwine I* has here: 'But three men could he find as his companions; and Ossë took them unto him.' *Ossë* was emended to *Neorth*; and then the sentence was struck through and rewritten: 'Such found he only three; and those three Neorth after took unto him and their names are not known.' Neorth = Ulmo; see note 39.

31   *Ælfwine A* reads: 'He espies some islands lying in the dawn but is swept thence by great winds. He returns hardly to Belerion. He gathers the seven greatest mariners of England; they sail in spring. They are wrecked upon the isles of Ælfwine's desire and find them desert and lonely and filled with gloomy whispering trees.' This is at variance with *Ælfwine I* and *II* where Ælfwine is cast on to the island alone; but agrees with *II* in giving Ælfwine seven companions, not three.

32   A clue that this was Ulmo: cf. *The Fall of Gondolin* (p. 155): 'he was shod with mighty shoes of stone.'

33   In *Ælfwine A* they were 'filled with gloomy whispering trees' (note 31).

34   From the point where the Man of the Sea said: 'Lo, this is one of the ring of Harbourless Isles . . .' (p. 317) to here (i.e. the whole episode of the foundered Viking ship and its captain Orm, slayer of Ælfwine's father) there is nothing corresponding in *Ælfwine I*, which has only: 'but that Man of the Sea aided him in building a little craft, and together, guided by the solitary mariner, they fared away and came to a land but little known.' For the narrative in *Ælfwine A* see note 39.

35   At one occurrence of the name *Ythlings* (Old English *ýð* 'wave') in Ælfwine I it is written *Ythlingas*, with the Old English plural ending.

36   *The Shipmen of the West*: emendation from *Eneathrim*.

37   Cf. in the passage of alliterative verse in my father's *On Translating Beowulf* (*The Monsters and the Critics and Other Essays*, 1983, p. 63): *then away thrust her to voyage gladly valiant-timbered*.

38   The whole section of the narrative concerning the island of the Ythlings is more briefly told in *Ælfwine I* (though, so far as it goes, in very much the same words) with several features of the later story absent (notably the cutting of timber in the grove sacred to Ulmo, and the blessing of the ship by the Man of the Sea). The only actual difference of structure, however, is that whereas in *Ælfwine II* Ælfwine finds again his seven companions in the land of the Ythlings, and sails west with them, together with Bior of the Ythlings, in *Ælfwine I* they were indeed drowned, and he got seven companions from among the Ythlings (among whom Bior is not named).

39 The plot-outline *Ælfwine A* tells the story from the point where
Ælfwine and his seven companions were cast on the Isle of the Man
of the Sea (thus differing from *Ælfwine I* and *II*, where he came
there alone) thus:

> They wander about the island upon which they have been cast
> and come upon many decaying wrecks – often of mighty ships,
> some treasure-laden. They find a solitary cabin beside a lonely
> sea, built of old ship-wood, where dwells a solitary and strange
> old mariner of dread aspect. He tells them these are the Harbour-
> less Isles whose enchanted rocks draw all ships thither, lest men
> fare over far upon Garsedge [*see note 19*] – and they were
> devised at the Hiding of Valinor. Here, he says, the trees are
> magical. They learn many strange things about the western world
> of him and their desire is whetted for adventure. He aids them to
> cut holy trees in the island groves and to build a wonderful
> vessel, and shows them how to provision it against a long voyage
> (that water that drieth not save when heart fails, &c.). This he
> blesses with a spell of adventure and discovery, and then dives
> from a cliff-top. They suspect it was Neorth Lord of Waters.
>
> They journey many years among strange western islands hear-
> ing often many strange reports – of the belt of Magic Isles which
> few have passed; of the trackless sea beyond where the wind
> bloweth almost always from the West; of the edge of the twilight
> and the far-glimpsed isle there standing, and its glimmering
> haven. They reach the magic island [*read* islands?] and three
> are enchanted and fall asleep on the shore.
>
> The others beat about the waters beyond and are in despair –
> for as often as they make headway west the wind changes and
> bears them back. At last they tryst to return on the morrow if
> nought other happens. The day breaks chill and dull, and they
> lie becalmed looking in vain through the pouring rain.

This narrative differs from both *Ælfwine I* and *II* in that here
there is no mention of the Ythlings; and Ælfwine and his seven
companions depart on their long western voyage from the Harbourless Isle of the ancient mariner. It agrees with *Ælfwine I* in the
name Neorth; but it foreshadows *II* in the cutting of sacred trees
to build a ship.

40 In *Ælfwine I* Ælfheah does not appear, and his two speeches in
this passage are there given to one *Gelimer*. Gelimer (Geilamir) was
the name of a king of the Vandals in the sixth century.

41 In *Ælfwine I* Bior's speech is given to Gelimer (see note 40).

42 *Ælfwine I* ends in almost the same words as *Ælfwine II*, but with a
most extraordinary difference; Ælfwine does not leap overboard,
but returns with his companions to Belerion, and so never comes to

Tol Eressëa! 'Very empty thereafter were the places of Men for Ælfwine and his mariners, and of their seed have been many restless and wistful folk since they were dead . . .' Moreover my father seems clearly to have been going to say the same in *Ælfwine II*, but stopped, struck out what he had written, and introduced the sentence in which Ælfwine leapt into the sea. I cannot see any way to explain this.

Ælfwine A ends in much the same way as *Ælfwine II*:

As night comes on a little breath springs up and the clouds lift. They hoist sail to return – when suddenly low down in the dusk they see the many lights of the Haven of Many Hues twinkle forth. They row thither, and hear sweet music. Then the mist wraps all away and the others rousing themselves say it is a mirage born of hunger, and with heavy hearts prepare to go back, but Ælfwine plunges overboard and swims into the dark until he is overcome in the waters, and him seems death envelops him. The others sail away home and are out of the tale.

43 Literally, as he maintained: 'From that (grief) one moved on; from this in the same way one can move on.'

44 There are long roots beneath the words of *The Fellowship of the Ring* (I.2): 'Elves . . . could now be seen passing westward through the woods in the evening, passing and not returning; but they were leaving Middle-earth and were no longer concerned with its troubles.' '"That isn't anything new, if you believe the old tales,"' said Ted Sandyman, when Sam Gamgee spoke of the matter.

I append here a synopsis of the structural differences between the three versions of *Ælfwine of England*.

A	I	II
Æ. sails from Belerion and sees 'islands in the dawn'.	As in A	As in A, but his companion Ælfheah is named.
Æ. sails again with 7 mariners of England. They are shipwrecked on the isle of the Man of the Sea but all survive.	Æ. has only 3 companions, and he alone survives the shipwreck.	Æ. has 7 companions, and is alone on the isle of the Man of the Sea, believing them drowned.
The Man of the Sea helps them to build a ship but does not go with them.	The Man of the Sea helps Æ. to build a boat and goes with him.	Æ. and the Man of the Sea find a stranded Viking ship and sail away in it together.

A	I	II
The Man of the Sea dives into the sea from a cliff-top of his isle.	They come to the Isle of the Ythlings. The Man of the Sea dives from a cliff-top. Æ. gets 7 companions from the Ythlings.	As in I, but Æ. finds his 7 companions from England, who were not drowned; to them is added Bior of the Ythlings.
On their voyages 3 of Æ.'s companions are enchanted in the Magic Isles.	As in A, but in this case they are Ythlings.	As in A
They are blown away from Tol Eressëa after sighting it; Æ. leaps overboard, and the others return home.	They are blown away from Tol Eressëa, and all, including Æ., return home.	As in A

Changes made to names, and differences in names,
in the texts of *Ælfwine of England*

Lúthien   The name of the land in I and II; in A *Luthany* (see note 20).
Déor   At the first occurrence only in I *Déor* < *Heorrenda*, subsequently *Déor*; A *Déor*.
Evadrien   In I < *Erenol*. *Erenol* = 'Iron Cliff'; see I.252, entry *Eriol*.
Forodwaith   II has *Forodwaith* < *Forwaith* < *Gwasgonin*; I has *Gwasgonin or the Winged Helms*; A has *the Winged Helms*.
Outer Land   < *Outer Lands* at both occurrences in II (pp. 316–17).
Ælfheah   I has *Gelimer* (at the first occurrence only < *Helgor*).
Shipmen of the West   In II < *Eneathrim*.

APPENDIX

NAMES IN THE *LOST TALES* – PART II

This appendix is designed only as an adjunct and extension to that in Part One. Names that have already been studied in Part One are not given entries in the following notes, if there are entries under that name in Part One, e.g. *Melko, Valinor*; but if, as is often the case, the etymological information in Part One is contained in an entry under some other name, this is shown, e.g. '*Gilim* See I.260 (*Melko*)'.

Linguistic information from the Name-list to *The Fall of Gondolin* (see p. 148) incorporated in these notes is referred to 'NFG'. 'GL' and 'QL' refer to the Gnomish and Qenya dictionaries (see I.246ff.). *Qenya* is the term used in both these books and is strictly the name of the language spoken in Tol Eressëa; it does not appear elsewhere in the early writings, where the distinction is between 'Gnomish' on the one hand and 'Elfin', 'Eldar', or 'Eldarissa' on the other.

★

Alqarámë For the first element Qenya *alqa* 'swan' see I.249 (*Alqaluntë*). Under root RAHA QL gives *rá* 'arm', *rakta* 'stretch out, reach', *ráma* 'wing', *rámavoitë* 'having wings'; GL has *ram* 'wing, pinion', and it is noted that Qenya *ráma* is a confusion of this and a word *róma* 'shoulder'.

Amon Gwareth Under root AM(U) 'up(wards)' QL gives *amu* 'up(wards)', *amu-* 'raise', *amuntë* 'sunrise', *amun(d)* 'hill'; GL has *am* 'up(wards)', *amon* 'hill, mount', adverb 'uphill'.

GL gives the name as *Amon 'Wareth* 'Hill of Ward', also *gwareth* 'watch, guard, ward', from the stem *gwar-* 'watch' seen also in the name of *Tinfang Warble* (*Gwarbilin* 'Birdward', I.268). See *Glamhoth, Gwarestrin*.

Angorodin See I.249 (*Angamandi*) and I.256 (*Kalormë*).

Arlisgion GL gives *Garlisgion* (see I.265 (*Sirion*)), as also does NFG, which has entries '*Garlisgion* was our name, saith Elfrith, for the Place of Reeds which is its interpretation', and '*lisg* is a reed (*liskë*)'. GL has *lisg, lisc* 'reed, sedge', and QL *liskë* with the same meaning. For *gar* see I.251 (*Dor Faidwen*).

Artanor GL has *athra* 'across, athwart', *athron* adverb 'further, beyond', *athrod* 'crossing, ford' (changed later to *adr(a), adron, adros*). With *athra, adr(a)* is compared Qenya *arta*. Cf. also the name *Dor Athro* (p. 41). It is clear that both *Artanor* and *Dor Athro* meant 'the Land Beyond'. Cf. *Sarnathrod*.

Asgon   An entry in NFG says: '*Asgon* A lake in the "Land of Shadows" Dor Lómin, by the Elves named *Aksan*.'

Ausir   GL gives *avos* 'fortune, wealth, prosperity,' *avosir, Ausir* 'the same (personified)'; also *ausin* 'rich', *aus(s)aith* or *avosaith* 'avarice'. Under root AWA in QL are *autë* 'prosperity, wealth; rich', *ausië* 'wealth'.

Bablon   See p. 214.

Bad Uthwen   Gnomish *uthwen* 'way out, exit, escape', see I.251 (*Dor Faidwen*). The entry in NFG says: '*Bad Uthwen* [emended from *Uswen*] meaneth but "way of escape" and is in Eldarissa *Uswevandë*.' For *vandë* see I.264 (*Qalvanda*).

Balcmeg   In NFG it is said that Balcmeg 'was a great fighter among the *Orclim* (*Orqui* say the Elves) who fell to the axe of Tuor – 'tis in meaning "heart of evil".' (For *-lim* in *Orclim* see *Gondothlim*.) The entry for *Balrog* in NFG says: '*Bal* meaneth evilness, and *Balc* evil, and *Balrog* meaneth evil demon.' GL has *balc* 'cruel': see I.250 (*Balrog*).

Bansil   For the entry in NFG, where this name is translated 'Fairgleam', see p. 214; and for the elements of the name see I.272 (*Vána*) and I.265 (*Sil*).

Belaurin   See I.264 (*Palúrien*).

Belcha   See I.260 (*Melko*). NFG has an entry: '*Belca* Though here [i.e. in the Tale] of overwhelming custom did Bronweg use the elfin names, this was the name aforetime of that evil Ainu.'

Beleg   See I.254 (*Haloisi Velikë*).

Belegost   For the first element see *Beleg*. GL gives *ost* 'enclosure, yard – town', also *oss* 'outer wall, town wall', *osta-* 'surround with walls, fortify', *ostor* 'enclosure, circuit of walls'. QL under root OSO has *os(t)* 'house, cottage', *osta* 'homestead', *ostar* 'township', *ossa* 'wall and moat'.

bo-   A late entry in GL: '*bo* (*bon*) (cf. Qenya *vô, vondo* "son") as patronymic prefix, *bo- bon-* "son of"'; as an example is given *Tuor bo-Beleg*. There is also a word *bôr* 'descendant'. See *go-, Indorion*.

Bodruith   In association with *bod-* 'back, again' GL has the words *bodruith* 'revenge', *bodruithol* 'vengeful (by nature)', *bodruithog* 'thirsting for vengeance', but these were struck out. There is also *gruith* 'deed of horror, violent act, vengeance'. – It may be that Bodruith Lord of Belegost was supposed to have received his name from the events of the *Tale of the Nauglafring*.

Cópas Alqalunten   See I.257 (*Kópas*) and I.249 (*Alqaluntë*).

Cris Ilbranteloth   GL gives the group *crisc* 'sharp', *criss* 'cleft, gash, gully', *crist* 'knife', *crista-* 'slash, cut, slice'; NFG: '*Cris* meaneth much as doth *falc*, a cleft, ravine, or narrow way of waters with high walls'. QL under root KIRI 'cut, split' has *kiris* 'cleft, crack' and other words.

For *ilbrant* 'rainbow' see I. 256 (*Ilweran*). The final element is *teloth* 'roofing, canopy': see I. 267–8 (*Teleri*).

Cristhorn For *Cris* see *Cris Ilbranteloth*, and for *thorn* see I. 266 (*Sorontur*). In NFG is the entry: '*Cris Thorn* is Eagles' Cleft or *Sornekiris*.'

Cuilwarthon For *cuil* see I. 257 (*Koivië-néni*); the second element is not explained.

Cûm an-Idrisaith For *cûm* 'mound' see I. 250 (*Cûm a Gumlaith*). *Idrisaith* is thus defined in GL: 'cf. *avosaith*, but that means avarice, money-greed, but *idrisaith* = excessive love of gold and gems and beautiful and costly things' (for *avosaith* see *Ausir*). Related words are *idra* 'dear, precious', *idra* 'to value, prize', *idri* (*id*) 'a treasure, a jewel', *idril* 'sweetheart' (see *Idril*).

Curufin presumably contains *curu* 'magic'; see I. 269 (*Tolli Kuruvar*).

Dairon GL includes this name but without etymological explanation: '*Dairon* the fluter (Qenya *Sairon*).' See *Mar Vanwa Tyaliéva* below.

Danigwiel In GL the Gnomish form is *Danigwethil*; see I. 266 (*Taniquetil*). NFG has an entry: '*Danigwethil* do the Gnomes call *Taniquetil*; but seek for tales concerning that mountain rather in the elfin name.'

(bo-)Dhrauthodavros '(Son of) the weary forest'. Gnomish *drauth* 'weary, toilworn', *drauthos* 'toil, weariness', *drautha-* 'to be weary'; for the second element *tavros* see I. 267 (*Tavari*).

Dor Athro See *Artanor, Sarnathrod*.

Dor-na-Dhaideloth For Gnomish *dai* 'sky' see I. 268 (*Telimektar*), and for *teloth* 'roofing, canopy' see *ibid.* (*Teleri*); cf. *Cris Ilbranteloth*.

Dramborleg NFG has the following entry: '*Dramborleg* (or as it may be named *Drambor*) meaneth in its full form Thudder-sharp, and was the axe of Tuor that smote both a heavy dint as of a club and cleft as a sword; and the Eldar say *Tarambor* or *Tarambolaika*.' QL gives *Tarambor, Tarambolaike* 'Tuor's axe' under root TARA, TARAMA 'batter, thud, beat', with *taran, tarambo* 'buffet', and *taru* 'horn' (included here with a query: see *Taruithorn*). No Gnomish equivalents are cited in GL.

The second element is Gnomish *leg, lêg* 'keen, piercing', Qenya *laika*; cf. *Legolast* 'keen-sight', I. 267 (*Tári-Laisi*).

Duilin NFG has the following entry: '*Duilin* whose name meaneth Swallow was the lord of that house of the Gondothlim whose sign was the swallow and was surest of the archers of the Eldalië, but fell in the fall of Gondolin. Now the names of those champions appear but in Noldorissa, seeing that Gnomes they were, but his name would be in Eldarissa *Tuilindo*, and that of his house (which the Gnomes called *Nos Duilin*) *Nossë Tuilinda.*' *Tuilindo* '(spring-singer), swallow' is given in QL, see I.269 (*Tuilérë*); GL has *duilin(g)* 'swallow', with *duil, duilir* 'Spring', but these last were struck through and in another part of the book appear *tuil, tuilir* 'Spring' (see I.269).

For *nossë* 'kin, people' see I.272 (*Valinor*); GL does not give *nos* in this sense, but has *nosta-* 'be born', *nost* 'birth; blood, high birth; birthday', and *noss* (changed to *nôs*) 'birthday'. Cf. *Nostna-Lothion* 'the Birth of Flowers', *Nos Galdon, Nos nan Alwen*.

Eärámë For *ea* 'eagle' see I.251 (*Eärendel*), and for *rámë* see *Alqarámë*. GL has an entry *Iorothram, -um* '= Qenya *Eärámë* or Eaglepinion, a name of one of Eärendel's boats'. For Gnomish *ior, ioroth* 'eagle' see I.251 (*Eärendel*), and cf. the forms *Earam, Earum* as the name of the ship (pp. 260, 276).

Eärendel See pp. 266–7 and I.251.

Eärendilyon See I.251 (*Eärendel*), and *Indorion*.

Ecthelion Both GL and NFG derive this name from *ecthel* 'fountain', to which corresponds Qenya *ektelë*. (This latter survived: cf. the entry *kel-* in the Appendix to *The Silmarillion*: 'from *et-kelē* "issue of water, spring" was derived, with transposition of the consonants, Quenya *ehtelë*, Sindarin *eithel*'. A later entry in GL gives *aithil* (< *ektl*) 'a spring'.) – A form *kektelë* is also found in Qenya from root KELE, KELU: see I.257 (*Kelusindi*).

Egalmoth NFG has the following entry: '*Egalmoth* is a great name, yet none know clearly its meaning – some have said its bearer was so named in that he was worth a thousand Elves (but Rúmil says nay) and others that it signifies the mighty shoulders of that Gnome, and so saith Rúmil, but perchance it was woven of a secret tongue of the Gondothlim' (for the remainder of this entry see p. 215). For Gnomish *moth* '1000' see I.270 (*Uin*).

GL interprets the name as Rúmil did, deriving it from *alm* (< *alðam-*) 'the broad of the back from shoulder to shoulder, back, shoulders', hence *Egalmoth* = 'Broadshoulder'; the name in Qenya is said to be *Aikaldamor*, and an entry in QL of the same date gives *aika* 'broad, vast', comparing Gnomish *eg, egrin*. These in turn GL glosses as 'far away, wide, distant' and 'wide, vast, broad; far' (as in *Egla*; see I.251 (*Eldar*)).

Eglamar See I.251 (*Eldamar*). NFG has the following entry: '*Egla* said the son of Bronweg was the Gnome name of the Eldar (now but seldom used) who dwelt in Kôr, and they were called *Eglothrim* [emended from *Eglothlim*] (that is *Eldalië*), and their tongue *Lam Eglathon* or *Egladrin*. Rúmil said these names *Egla* and *Elda* were akin, but Elfrith cared not overmuch for such lore and they seem not over alike.' With this cf. I.251 (*Eldar*). GL gives *lam* 'tongue', and *lambë* is found in QL: a word that survived into later Quenya. In QL it is given as a derivative of root LAVA 'lick', and defined 'tongue (of body, but also of land, or even = "speech")'.

Eldarissa appears in QL ('the language of the Eldar') but without explanation of the final element. Possibly it was derived from the root ISI: *ista* 'know', *issë* 'knowledge, lore', *iswa, isqa* 'wise', etc.

Elfrith See pp. 201–2, and I.255 (*Ilverin*).

Elmavoitë 'One-handed' (Beren). See *Ermabwed*.

Elwing GL has the following entry: '*Ailwing* older spelling of *Elwing* = "lake foam". As a noun = "white water-lily". The name of the maiden loved by Ioringli' (*Ioringli* = *Eärendel*, see I.251). The first element appears in the words *ail* 'lake, pool', *ailion* 'lake', Qenya *ailo, ailin* – cf. later *Aelin-uial*. The second element is *gwing* 'foam': see I.273 (*Wingilot*).

Erenol See I.252 (*Eriol*).

Ermabwed 'One-handed' (Beren). GL gives *mab* 'hand', *amabwed, mabwed* 'having hands', *mabwedri* 'dexterity', *mabol* 'skilful', *mablios* 'cunning', *mablad, mablod* 'palm of hand', *mabrin(d)* 'wrist'. A related word in Qenya was said in GL to be *mapa* (root MAPA) 'seize', but this statement was struck out. QL has also a root MAHA with many derivatives, notably *mā* (= *maha*) 'hand', *mavoitë* 'having hands' (cf. *Elmavoitë*).

Faiglindra 'Long-tressed' (Airin). Gnomish *faigli* 'hair, long tresses (especially used of women)'; *faiglion* 'having long hair', and *faiglim* of the same meaning, 'especially as a proper name', *Faiglim, Aurfaiglim* 'the Sun at noon'. With this is bracketed the word *faiglin(d)ra*.

Failivrin Together with *fail* 'pale, pallid', *failthi* 'pallor', and *Failin* a name of the Moon, GL gives *Failivrin*: '(1) a maid beloved by Silmo; (2) a name among the Gnomes of many maidens of great beauty, especially Failivrin of the Rothwarin in the Tale of Turumart.' (In the Tale *Rothwarin* was replaced by *Rodothlim*.)

The second element is *brin*, Qenya *vírin*, 'a magic glassy substance of great lucency used in fashioning the Moon. Used of things of great and pure transparency.' For *vírin* see I.192–3.

Falasquil Three entries in NFG refer to this name (for *falas* see also I.253 (*Falman*)):

'*Falas* meaneth (even as *falas* or *falassë* in Eldar) a beach.'

'*Falas-a-Gwilb* the "beach of peace" was *Falasquil* in Elfin where Tuor at first dwelt in a sheltered cove by the Great Sea.' -*a-Gwilb* is struck through and above is written, apparently, '*Wilb or Wilma*.

'*Gwilb* meaneth "full of peace", which is *gwilm*.'

GL gives *gwîl, gwilm, gwilthi* 'peace', and *gwilb* 'quiet, peaceful'.

Fangluin 'Bluebeard'. See *Indrafang*. For *luin* 'blue' sec I.262 (*Nielluin*).

Foalókë Under a root FOHO 'hide, hoard, store up' QL gives *foa* 'hoard, treasure', *foina* 'hidden', *fölë* 'secrecy, a secret', *fôlima* 'secretive', and *foalókë* 'name of a serpent that guarded a treasure'. *lókë* 'snake' is derived from a root LOKO 'twine, twist, curl'.

   GL originally had entries *fû, fûl, fûn* 'hoard', *fûlug* 'a dragon (who guards treasure)', and *ulug* 'wolf'. By later changes this construction was altered to *fuis* 'hoard', *fuithlug, -og* (the form that appears in the text, p. 70), *ulug* 'dragon' (cf. Qenya *lókë*). An entry in NFG reads: '*Lûg* is *lókë* of the Eldar, and meaneth "drake".'

Fôs'Almir (Earlier name of *Faskala-númen*; translated in the text (p. 115) 'the bath of flame'.) For *fôs* 'bath' see I.253 (*Faskala-númen*). GL gives three names: '*Fôs Aura, Fôs'Almir,* and *Fôs na Ngalmir,* i.e. Sun's bath = the Western Sea.' For *Galmir, Aur,* names of the Sun, see I.254 and I.271 (*Úr*).

Fuithlug See *Foalókë*.

Galdor For the entry in NFG concerning Galdor see p. 215; as first written *galdon* was there said to mean 'tree', and Galdor's people to be named *Nos Galdon. Galdon* is not in GL. Subsequently *galdon > alwen*, and *alwen* does appear in GL, as a word of poetic vocabulary: *alwen* '= *orn*'. – Cf. Qenya *alda* 'tree' (see I.249 (*Aldaron*)), and the later relationship Quenya *alda*, Sindarin *galadh*.

Gar Thurion NFG has the earlier form *Gar Furion* (p. 202), and GL has *furn, furion* 'secret, concealed', also *fûr* 'a lie' (Qenya *furu*) and *fur-* 'to conceal; to lie'. QL has *furin* and *hurin* 'hidden, concealed' (root FURU or HURU). With *Thurion* cf. *Thuringwethil* 'Woman of Secret Shadow', and *Thurin* 'the Secret', Finduilas' name for Túrin (*Unfinished Tales* pp. 157, 159).

Gil See I.256 (*Ingil*).

Gilim See I.260 (*Melko*).

Gimli GL has *gimli* '(sense of) hearing', with *gim-* 'hear', *gimriol* 'attentive' (changed to 'audible'), *gimri* 'hearkening, attention'. The hearing of Gimli, the captive Gnome in the dungeons of Tevildo, 'was the keenest that has been in the world' (p. 29).

Glamhoth GL defines this as 'name given by the Goldothrim to the Orcin: People of Dreadful Hate' (cf. 'folk of dreadful hate', p. 160). For *Goldothrim* see I.262 (*Noldoli*). The first element is *glâm* 'hatred, loathing'; other words are *glamri* 'bitter feud', *glamog* 'loathsome'. An entry in NFG says: '*Glam* meaneth "fierce hate" and even as *Gwar* has no kindred words in Eldar.'

   For *hoth* 'folk' see I.264 (*orchoth* in entry *Orc*), and cf. *Goldothrim, Gondothlim, Rúmhoth, Thornhoth*. Under root HOSO QL gives *hos* 'folk', *hossë* 'army, band, troop', *hostar* 'tribe', *horma* 'horde, host'; also *Sankossi* 'the Goblins', equivalent of Gnomish *Glamhoth*, and evidently compounded of *sankë* 'hateful' (root SNKN 'rend, tear') and *hossë*.

Glend Perhaps connected with Gnomish *glenn* 'thin, fine', *glendrin* 'slender', *glendrinios* 'slenderness', *glent, glentweth* 'thinness'; Qenya root LENE 'long', which developed its meaning in different directions: 'slow, tedious, trailing', and 'stretch, thin': *lenka* 'slow', *lenwa* 'long and thin, straight, narrow', *lenu-* 'stretch', etc.

Glingol For the entry in NFG, where the name is translated 'singing-gold', see p. 216; and see I. 258 (*Lindelos*). The second element is *culu* 'gold', for which see I. 255 (*Ilsaluntë*); another entry in NFG reads: '*Culu* or *Culon* is a name we have in poesy for *Glor* (and. Rúmil saith that it is the Elfin *Kulu*, and *-gol* in our *Glingol*).'

Glorfalc For *glor* see I. 258 (*Laurelin*). NFG has an entry: '*Glor* is gold and is that word that cometh in verse of the Kôr-Eldar *laurë* (so saith Rúmil).'

Falc is glossed in GL '(1) cleft, gash; (2) cleft, ravine, cliffs' (also given is *falcon* 'a great two-handed sword, twibill', which was changed to *falchon*, and so close to English *falchion* 'broadsword'). NFG has: '*Falc* is cleft and is much as *Cris*; being Elfin *Falqa*'; and under root FLKL in QL are *falqa* 'cleft, mountain pass, ravine' and *falqan* 'large sword'. GL has a further entry: *Glorfalc* 'a great ravine leading out of Garioth'. *Garioth* is here used of Hisilómë; see I. 252 (*Eruman*). Cf. later *Orfalch Echor*.

Glorfindel For the entry in NFG, where the name is rendered 'Goldtress', see p. 216. For *glor* see I. 258 (*Laurelin*), and *Glorfalc*. GL had an entry *findel* 'lock of hair', together with *fith* (*fidhin*) 'a single hair', *fidhra* 'hairy', but *findel* was struck out; later entries are *finn* 'lock of hair' (see *fin-* in the Appendix to *The Silmarillion*) and *fingl* or *finnil* 'tress'. NFG: '*Findel* is "tress", and is the Elfin *Findil*.' Under root FIRI QL gives *findl* 'lock of hair' and *firin* 'ray of the sun'.

In another place in GL the name *Glorfindel* was given, and translated 'Goldlocks', but it was changed later to *Glorfinn*, with a variant *Glorfingl*.

Glorund For *glor* see I. 258 (*Laurelin*), and *Glorfalc*. GL gives *Glorunn* 'the great drake slain by Turumart'. Neither of the Qenya forms *Laurundo, Undolaurë* (p. 84) appear in QL, which gives an earlier name for 'the great worm', *Fentor*, together with *fent* 'serpent', *fenumë* 'dragon'. As this entry was first written it read 'the great worm slain by Ingilmo'; to this was added 'or Turambar'.

Golosbrindi (Earlier name of Hirilorn, rendered in the text (p. 51) 'Queen of the Forest'.) A word *goloth* 'forest' is given in GL, derived from **gwōloth*, which is itself composed of *aloth* (*alos*), a verse word meaning 'forest' (= *taur*), and the prefix **ngua* > *gwa*, unaccented *go*, 'together, in one', 'often used merely intensively'.

The corresponding word in Qenya is said to be *málos*, which does not appear in QL.

Gondobar   See *Gondolin*, and for *-bar* see I.251 (*Eldamar*). In GL the form *Gondobar* was later changed to *Gonthobar*.

Gondolin   To the entries cited in I.254 may be added that in NFG: '*Gond* meaneth a stone, or stone, as doth Elfin *on* and *ondo*.' For the statement about Gondolin (where the name is rendered 'stone of song') in NFG see p. 216; and for the latest formulation of the etymology of *Gondolin* see the Appendix to *The Silmarillion*, entry *gond*.

Gondothlim   GL has the following entry concerning the word *lim* 'many', Qenya *limbë* (not in QL): 'It is frequently suffixed and so becomes a second plural inflexion. In the singular it = English "many a", as *golda-lim*. It is however most often suffixed to the plural in those nouns making their plural in *-th*. It then changes to *-rim* after *-l*. Hence great confusion with *grim* "host" and *thlim* "race", as in *Goldothrim* ("the people of the Gnomes").' NFG has an entry: '*Gondothlim* meaneth "folk of stone" and (saith Rúmil) is *Gond* "stone", whereto be added *Hoth* "folk" and that *-lim* we Gnomes add after to signify "the many".' Cf. *Lothlim*, *Rodothlim*, and *Orclim* in entry *Balcmeg*; for *hoth* see *Glamhoth*.

Gondothlimbar   See *Gondolin*, *Gondothlim*, and for *-bar* see I.251 (*Eldamar*). In GL the form *Gondothlimbar* was later changed to '*Gonthoflimar or Gonnothlimar*'.

go-   An original entry in GL, later struck out, was: *gon- go-* 'son of', patronymic prefix (cf. suffix *ios/ion/io* and Qenya *yô, yondo*)'. The replacement for this is given above under *bo-*. See *Indorion*.

Gon Indor   See *go-*, *Indorion*.

Gothmog   See pp. 67, 216, and I.258 (*Kosomot*). GL has *mog-* 'detest, hate', *mogri* 'detestation', *mogrin* 'hateful'; Qenya root MOKO 'hate'. In addition to *goth* 'war, strife' (Qenya root KOSO 'strive') may be noted *gothwen* 'battle', *gothweg* 'warrior', *gothwin* 'Amazon', *gothriol* 'warlike', *gothfeng* 'war-arrow', *gothwilm* 'armistice'.

Gurtholfin   GL: *Gurtholfin* 'Urdolwen, a sword of Turambar's, Wand of Death'. Also given is *gurthu* 'death' (Qenya *urdu*; not in QL). The second element of the name is *olfin(g)* (also *olf*) 'branch, wand, stick' (Qenya *olwen(n)*).

It may be noted that in QL Turambar's sword is given as *Sangahyando* 'cleaver of throngs', from roots SANGA 'pack tight, press' (*sanga* 'throng') and HYARA 'plough through' (*hyar* 'plough', *hyanda* 'blade, share'). *Sangahyando* 'Throng-cleaver' survived to become the name of a man in Gondor (see the Appendix to *The Silmarillion*, entry *thang*).

Gwar   See I.257 (*Kôr, korin*).

Gwarestrin   Rendered in the Tale (p. 158) as 'Tower of Guard', and so also in NFG; GL glosses it 'watchtower (especially as a name of Gondolin)'. A late entry in GL gives *estirin, estirion, estrin* 'pinnacle', beside *esc* 'sharp point, sharp edge'. The second element of this word is *tiri(o)n*; see I.258 (*Kortirion*). For *gwar* see *Amon Gwareth*.

Gwedheling See I.273 (*Wendelin*).

Heborodin 'The Encircling Hills.' Gnomish preposition *heb* 'round about, around'; *hebrim* 'boundary', *hebwirol* 'circumspect'. For *orod* see I.256 (*Kalormë*).

Hirilorn GL gives *hiril* 'queen (a poetic use), princess; feminine of *bridhon*'. For *bridhon* see *Tevildo*. The second element is *orn* 'tree'. (It may be mentioned here that the word *neldor* 'beech' is found in QL; see the Appendix to *The Silmarillion*, entry *neldor*).

Idril For Gnomish *idril* 'sweetheart' see *Cûm an-Idrisaith*. There is another entry in GL as follows: *Idhril* 'a girl's name often confused with *Idril*. *Idril* = "beloved" but *Idhril* = "mortal maiden". Both appear to have been the names of the daughter of Turgon – or apparently *Idril* was the older and the Kor-eldar called her *Irildë* (= *Idhril*) because she married Tuor.' Elsewhere in GL appear *idhrin* 'men, earth-dwellers; especially used as a folk-name contrasted with *Eglath* etc.; cf. Qenya *indi*', and *Idhru, Idhrubar* 'the world, all the regions inhabited by Men; cf. Qenya *irmin*'. In QL these words *indi* and *irmin* are given under root IRI 'dwell?', with *irin* 'town', *indo* 'house', *indor* 'master of house' (see *Indor*), etc.; but *Irildë* does not appear. Similar words are found in Gnomish: *ind, indos* 'house, hall', *indor* 'master (of house), lord'.

After the entry in NFG on *Idril* which has been cited (p. 216) a further note was added: 'and her name meaneth "Beloved", but often do Elves say *Idhril* which more rightly compares with *Irildë* and that meaneth "mortal maiden", and perchance signifies her wedding with Tuor son of Men.' An isolated note (written in fact on a page of the *Tale of the Nauglafring*) says: 'Alter name of *Idril* to *Idhril*. The two were confused: *Idril* = "beloved", *Idhril* = "maiden of mortals". The Elves thought this her name and called her *Irildë* (because she married Tuor Pelecthon).'

Ilbranteloth See *Cris Ilbranteloth*.

Ilfiniol, Ilfrith See I.255 (*Ilverin*).

Ilúvatar An entry in NFG may be noticed here: '*En* do the mystic sayings of the Noldoli also name *Ilathon* [emended from *Âd Ilon*], who is Ilúvatar – and this is like the Eldar *Enu*.' QL gives *Enu*, the Almighty Creator who dwells without the world. For *Ilathon* see I.255–6 (*Ilwë*).

Indor (Father of Tuor's father Peleg). This is perhaps the word *indor* 'master (of house), lord' (see *Idril*) used as a proper name.

Indorion See *go-*. QL gives *yô, yond-* as poetic words for 'son', adding: 'but very common as *-ion* in patronymics (and hence practically = "descendant")'; also *yondo* 'male descendant, usually (great) grandson' (cf. Eärendel's name *Gon Indor*). Cf. *Eärendilyon*.

Indrafang GL has *indra* 'long (also used of time)', *indraluin* 'long ago'; also *indravang* 'a special name of the *nauglath* or dwarves', on which see p. 247. These forms were changed later to *in(d)ra, in(d)rafang, in(d)raluin/idhraluin*.

An original entry in GL was *bang* 'beard' = Qenya *vanga*, but this was struck out; and another word with the same meaning as *Indravang* was originally entered as *Bangasur* but changed to *Fangasur*. The second element of this is *sûr* 'long, trailing', Qenya *sóra*, and a later addition here is *Surfang* 'a long-beard, a *naugla* or *inrafang*'. Cf. *Fangluin*, and later *Fangorn* 'Treebeard'.

Irildë See *Idril*.

Isfin NFG has this entry: '*Isfin* was the sister of Turgon Lord of Gondolin, whom Eöl at length wedded; and it meaneth either "snow-locks" or "exceeding-cunning".' Long afterwards my father, noting that *Isfin* was 'derived from the earliest (1916) form of *The Fall of Gondolin*', said that the name was 'meaningless'; but with the second element cf. *finn* 'lock of hair' (see *Glorfindel*) or *fim* 'clever', *finthi* 'idea, notion', etc. (see I. 253 (*Finwë*)).

Ivárë GL gives *Ior* 'the famous "piper of the sea"', Qenya *Ivárë*.'

Íverin A late entry in GL gives *Aivrin or Aivrien* 'an island off the west coast of Tol Eressëa, Qenya *Íwerin* or *Iverindor*.' QL has *Íverind-* 'Ireland'.

Karkaras In GL this is mentioned as the Qenya form; the Gnomish name of 'the great wolf-warden of Belca's door' was *Carcaloth* or *Carcamoth*, changed to *Carchaloth, Carchamoth*. The first element is *carc* 'jag, point, fang'; QL under root KṚKṚ has *karka* 'fang, tooth, tusk', *karkassë, karkaras* 'row of spikes or teeth'.

Kosmoko See *Gothmog*.

Kurûki See I. 269 (*Tolli Kuruvar*).

Ladwen-na-Dhaideloth 'Heath of the Sky-roof'. See *Dor-na-Dhaideloth*. GL gives *ladwen* '(1) levelness, flatness; (2) a plain, heath; (3) a plane; (4) surface.' Other words are *ladin* 'level, smooth; fair, equable' (cf. *Tumladin*), *lad* 'a level' (cf. *mablad* 'palm of hand' mentioned under *Ermabwed*), *lada-* 'to smooth out, stroke, soothe, beguile', and *ladwinios* 'equity'. There are also words *bladwen* 'a plain' (see I. 264 (*Palúrien*)), and *fladwen* 'meadow' (with *flad* 'sward' and *Fladweth Amrod (Amrog)* 'Nomad's Green', 'a place in *Tol Erethrin* where Eriol sojourned a while; nigh to Tavrobel.' *Amrog, amrod* = 'wanderer', 'wandering', from *amra-* 'go up and down, live in the mountains, wander'; see *Amon Gwareth*).

Laiqalassë   See I. 267 (*Tári-laisi*), I. 254 (*Gar Lossion*).

Laurundo   See *Glorund*.

Legolas   See *Laiqalassë*.

Lindeloktë   See I. 258 (*Lindelos*).

Linwë Tinto   See I. 269 (*Tinwë Linto*).

Lókë   See *Foalókë*.

Lôs   See I. 254 (*Gar Lossion*). The later form *loth* does not appear in GL (which has however *lothwing* 'foamflower'). NFG has '*Lôs* is a flower and in Eldarissa *lossë* which is a rose' (all after the word 'flower' struck out).

Lósengriol   As with *lôs*, the later form *lothengriol* does not appear in GL. *Losengriol* is translated 'lily of the valley' in GL, which gives the Gnomish words *eng* 'smooth, level', *enga* 'plain, vale', *engri* 'a level', *engriol* 'vale-like; of the vale'. NFG says '*Eng* is a plain or vale and *Engriol* that which liveth or dwelleth therein', and translates *Lósengriol* 'flower of the vale or lily of the valley'.

Los 'lóriol   (changed from *Los Glóriol*; the Golden Flower of Gondolin). See I. 254 (*Gar Lossion*), and for *glóriol* 'golden' see I. 258 (*Laurelin*).

Loth, Lothengriol   See *Lôs, Lósengriol*.

Lothlim   See *Lôs* and *Gondothlim*. The entry in NFG reads: '*Lothlim* being for *Loslim* meaneth folk of the flower, and is that name taken by the Exiles of Gondolin (which city they had called *Lôs* aforetime).'

Mablung   For *mab* 'hand' see *Ermabwed*. The second element is *lung* 'heavy; grave, serious'; related words are *lungra-* 'weigh, hang heavy', *luntha* 'balance, weigh', *lunthang* 'scales'.

Malkarauki   See I. 250 (*Balrog*).

Mar Vanwa Tyaliéva   See I. 260 and add: a late entry in GL gives the Gnomish name, *Bara Dhair Haithin*, the Cottage of Lost Play; also *daira-* 'play' (with *dairwen* 'mirth', etc.), and *haim or haithin* 'gone, departed, lost' (with *haitha-* 'go, walk', etc.). Cf. *Dairon*.

Mathusdor   (Aryador, Hisilómë). In GL are given *math* 'dusk', *mathrin* 'dusky', *mathusgi* 'twilight', *mathwen* 'evening'. See *Umboth-muilin*.

Mavwin   A noun *mavwin* 'wish' in GL was struck out, but related words allowed to stand: *mav-* 'like', *mavra* 'eager after', *mavri* 'appetite', *mavrin* 'delightful, desirable', *mavros* 'desire', *maus* 'pleasure; pleasant'. Mavwin's name in Qenya, *Mavoinë*, is not in QL, unless it is to be equated with *maivoinë* 'great longing'.

Meleth   A noun *meleth* 'love' is found in GL; see I. 262 (*Nessa*).

Melian, Melinon, Melinir   None of these names occur in the glossaries, but probably all are derivatives of the stem *mel-* 'love'; see I. 262 (*Nessa*). The later etymology of *Melian* derived the name from *mel-* 'love' (*Melyanna* 'dear gift').

Meoita, Miaugion, Miaulë   See *Tevildo*.

Mindon-Gwar   For *mindon* 'tower' see I. 260 (*Minethlos*); and for *Gwar* see p. 291 and I. 257 (*Kôr, korin*).

Morgoth   See p. 67 and *Gothmog*. For the element *mor-* see I. 261 (*Mornië*).

Mormagli, Mormakil   See I. 261 (*Mornië*) and I. 259 (*Makar*).

Nan Dumgorthin   See p. 62. For *nan* see I. 261 (*Nandini*).

Nantathrin   This name does not occur in the *Lost Tales*, where the Land of Willows is called *Tasarinan*, but GL gives it (see I. 265 (*Sirion*)) and NFG has an entry: '*Dor-tathrin* was that Land of Willows of which this and many a tale tells.' GL has *tathrin* 'willow', and QL *tasarin* of the same meaning.

Nauglafring   GL has the following entry: '*Nauglafring* = *Fring na Nauglithon*, the Necklace of the Dwarves. Made for Ellu by the Dwarves from the gold of Glorund that Mîm the fatherless cursed and that brought ruin on Beren Ermabwed and Damrod his son and was not appeased till it sank with Elwing beloved of Eärendel to the bottom of the sea.' For Damrod (Daimord) son of Beren see pp. 139, 259, and for the loss of Elwing and the Nauglafring see pp. 255, 264. This is the only reference to the 'appeasing' of Mîm's curse. — Gnomish *fring* means 'carcanet, necklace' (Qenya *firinga*).

Níniel   Cf. Gnomish *nîn* 'tear', *ninios* 'lamentation', *ninna-* 'weep'; see I. 262 (*Nienna*).

Nínin-Udathriol   ('Unnumbered Tears'). See *Níniel*. GL gives *tathn* 'number', *tathra-* 'number, count', *udathnarol, udathriol* 'innumerable'. *Ú-* is a 'negative prefix with any part of speech'. (QL casts no light on *Nieriltasinwa*, p. 84, apart from the initial element *nie* 'tear', see I. 262 (*Nienna*).)

Noldorissa   See *Eldarissa*.

Nos Galdon, Nos nan Alwen   See *Duilin, Galdor*.

Nost-na-Lothion   See *Duilin*.

Parma Kuluinen   The Golden Book, see p. 310. This entry is given in QL under root PARA: *parma* 'skin, bark; parchment; book, writings'. This word survived in later Quenya (*The Lord of the Rings* III. 401). For *Kuluinen* see *Glingol*.

Peleg   (Father of Tuor). GL has a common noun *peleg* 'axe', verb *pelectha-* 'hew' (QL *pelekko* 'axe', *pelekta-* 'hew'). Cf. Tuor's name *Pelecthon* in the note cited under *Idril*.

Ramandur   See I. 259 (*Makar*).

Rog   GL gives an adjective *rôg, rog* 'doughty, strong'. But with the Orcs' name for Egnor Beren's father, Rog the Fleet, cf. *arog* 'swift, rushing', and *raug* of the same meaning; Qenya *arauka*.

Rôs   GL gives yet another meaning of this name: 'the Sea' (Qenya *Rása*).

Rodothlim   See *Rothwarin* (earlier form replaced by *Rodothlim*).

Rothwarin   GL has this name in the forms *Rothbarin, Rosbarin*: '(literally "cavern-dwellers") name of a folk of secret Gnomes and also of the regions about their cavernous homes on the banks of the river.' Gnomish words derived from the root ROTO 'hollow' are *rod* 'tube, stem', *ross* 'pipe', *roth* 'cave, grot', *rothrin* 'hollow', *rodos* 'cavern'; QL gives *rotsë* 'pipe', *róta* 'tube', *ronta, rotwa* 'hollow', *rotelë* 'cave'.

Rúmhoth   See *Glamhoth*.

Rúsitaurion   GL gives a noun *rûs (rôs)* 'endurance, longsuffering, patience', together with adjective *rô* 'enduring, longsuffering; quiet, gentle', and verb *rô-* 'remain, stay; endure'. For *taurion* see I. 267 (*Tavari*).

Sarnathrod   Gnomish *sarn* 'a stone'; for *athrod* 'ford' see *Artanor*.

Sarqindi   ('Cannibal-ogres'). This must derive from the root SṚKṚ given in QL, with derivatives *sarko* 'flesh', *sarqa* 'fleshy', *sarkuva* 'corporeal, bodily'.

Silpion   An entry in NFG (p. 215) translates the name as 'Cherry-moon'. In QL is a word *pio* 'plum, cherry' (with *piukka* 'black-berry', *piosenna* 'holly', etc.), and also *Valpio* 'the holy cherry of Valinor'. GL gives *Piosil* and *Silpios*, without translation, as names of the Silver Tree, and also a word *piog* 'berry'.

Taimonto   See I. 268 (*Telimektar*).

Talceleb, Taltelepta   (Name of *Idril/Irildë*, 'of the Silver Feet'.) The first element is Gnomish *tâl* 'foot (of people and animals)'; related words are *taltha* 'foot (of things), base, pedestal, pediment', *talrind, taldrin* 'ankle', *taleg, taloth* 'path' – another name for the Way of Escape into Gondolin was *Taleg Uthwen* (see *Bad Uthwen*). QL under root TALA 'support' gives *tala* 'foot', *talwi* (dual) 'the feet', *talas* 'sole', etc. For the second element see I. 268 (*Telimpë*). QL gives the form *telepta* but without translation.

Tarnin Austa   For *tarn* 'gate' see I. 261 (*Moritarnon*). GL gives *aust* 'summer'; cf. *Aur* 'the Sun', I. 271 (*Ûr*).

Taruithorn, Taruktarna   (Oxford). GL gives *târ* 'horn' and *tarog* 'ox' (Qenya *taruku-*), *Taruithron* older *Taruitharn* 'Oxford'. Immediately following these words are *tarn* 'gate' and *taru* '(1) cross (2) crossing'. QL has *taru* 'horn' (see *Dramborleg*), *tarukka* 'horned', *tarukko, tarunko* 'bull', *Taruktarna* 'Oxford', and under root TARA *tara-* 'cross, go athwart', *tarna* 'crossing, passage'.

Tasarinan   See *Nantathrin*.

Taurfuin   See I. 267 (*Tavari*) and I. 253 (*Fui*).

Teld Quing Ilon   NFG has an entry: '*Cris a Teld Quing Ilon* signifieth Gully of the Rainbow Roof, and is in the Eldar speech *Kiris Iluqingatelda*'; a *Teld Quing Ilon* was struck out and replaced by *Ilbranteloth*. Another entry reads: '*Ilon* is the sky'; in GL *Ilon* (= Qenya *Ilu*) is the name of *Ilúvatar* (see I. 255 (*Ilwë*)). *Teld* does not appear in GL, but related words as *telm* 'roof' are given (see I. 267–8 (*Teleri*)); and *cwing* = 'a bow'. QL has *iluqinga* 'rainbow' (see I. 256 (*Ilweran*)) and *telda* 'having a roof' (see I. 268 (*Telimektar*)). For *Cris, Kiris* see *Cris Ilbranteloth*.

Tevildo, Tifil   For the etymology see I. 268, to which can be added that the earlier Gnomish form *Tifil* (later *Tiberth*) is associated in GL with a noun *tíf* 'resentment, ill-feeling, bitterness'.

Vardo Meoita 'Prince of Cats': for *Vardo* see I. 273 (*Varda*). QL gives *meoi* 'cat'.

Bridhon Miaugion 'Prince of Cats': *bridhon* 'king, prince', cf. *Bridhil*, Gnomish name of Varda (I. 273). Nouns *miaug, miog* 'tomcat' and *miauli* 'she-cat' (changed to *miaulin*) are given in GL, where the Prince of Cats is called *Tifil Miothon or Miaugion*. *Miaulë* was the name of Tevildo's cook (p. 28).

Thorndor   See I. 266 (*Sorontur*).

Thornhoth   See *Glamhoth*.

Thorn Sir   See I. 265 (*Sirion*).

Tifanto   This name is clearly to be associated with the Gnomish words (*tif-, tifin*) given in I. 268 (*Tinfang*).

Tifil   See *Tevildo*.

Tirin   See I. 258 (*Kortirion*).

Tôn a Gwedrin   *Tôn* is a Gnomish word meaning 'fire (on a hearth)', related to *tan* and other words given under *Tanyasalpë* (I. 266–7); *Tôn a Gwedrin* 'the Tale-fire' in *Mar Vanwa Tyaliéva*. Cf. *Tôn Sovriel* 'the fire lake of Valinor' (*sovriel* 'purification', *sovri* 'cleansing'; *sôn* 'pure, clean', *soth* 'bath', *sô-* 'wash, clean, bathe').

Gwedrin belongs with *cwed-* (preterite *cwenthi*) 'say, tell', *cweth* 'word', *cwent* 'tale, saying', *cwess* 'saying, proverb', *cwedri* 'telling (of tales)', *ugwedriol* 'unspeakable, ineffable'. In QL under root QETE are *qet-* (*qentë*) 'speak, talk', *quent* 'word', *qentelë* 'sentence', *Eldaqet* = *Eldarissa*, etc. Cf. the Appendix to *The Silmarillion*, entry *quen-* (*quet-*).

Tumladin   For the first element, Gnomish *tûm* 'valley', see I. 269 (*Tombo*), and for the second, *ladin* 'level, smooth' see *Ladwen na Dhaideloth*.

Turambar   For the first element see I. 260 (*Meril-i-Turinqi*). QL gives *amarto, ambar* 'Fate', and also (root MṚTṚ) *mart* 'a piece of luck', *marto* 'fortune, fate, lot', *mart-* 'it happens' (impersonal). GL has *mart* 'fate', *martion* 'fated, doomed, fey'; also *umrod* and *umbart* 'fate'.

Turumart   See *Turambar*.

Ufedhin   Possible connections of this name are Gnomish *uf* 'out of, forth from', or *fedhin* 'bound by agreement, ally, friend'.

Ulbandi   See I. 260 (*Melko*).

Ulmonan   The Gnomish name was *Ingulma(n)* (*Gulma* = *Ulmo*), with the prefix *in-* (*ind-, im-*) 'house of' (*ind* 'house', see *Idril*). Other examples of this formation are *Imbelca, Imbelcon* 'Hell (house of Melko)', *inthorn* 'eyrie', *Intavros* 'forest' (properly 'the forest palace of Tavros').

Umboth-muilin   Gnomish *umboth, umbath* 'nightfall'; *Umbathor* is a name of Garioth (see I. 252 (*Eruman*)). This word is derived from **mbaþ-*, related to **maþ-* seen in *math* 'dusk': see *Mathusdor*. The second element is *muil* 'tarn', Qenya *moilë*.

Undolaurë   See *Glorund*.

Valar   NFG has the following entry: '*Banin* [emended from *Banion*] or *Bandrim* [emended from *Banlim*]. Now these dwell, say the Noldoli, in *Gwalien* [emended from *Banien*] but they are spoken of ever by Elfrith and the others in their Elfin names as the *Valar* (or *Vali*), and that glorious region of their abode is *Valinor*.' See I. 272 (*Valar*).

SHORT GLOSSARY OF OBSOLETE, ARCHAIC, AND RARE WORDS

Words that have been given in the similar glossary to Part I (such as *an* 'if', *fain*, *lief*, *meed*, *rede*, *ruth*) are not as a rule repeated here. Some words of current English used in obsolete senses are included.

acquaint   old past participle, superseded by *acquainted*, 287
ardour   burning heat, 38, 170 (modern sense 194)
bested   beset, 193
bravely   splendidly, showily, 75
broidure   embroidery, 163. Not recorded, but *broid-* varied with *broud-* etc. in Middle English, and *broudure* 'embroidery' is found.
burg   walled and fortified town, 175
byrnie   body-armour, corslet, coat-of-mail, 163
carcanet   ornamental collar or necklace, 227–8, 235, 238
carle   (probably) serving-man, 85; **house-carle** 190
chain   linear measure (a chain's length), sixty-six feet, 192
champain   level, open country, 295, 298
clue   thread, 322
cot   small cottage, 95, 141
damasked   224, **damascened** 173, 227, ornamentally inlaid with designs in gold and silver.
diapered   covered with a small pattern, 173
dight   arrayed, fitted out, 173
drake   dragon, 41, 46, 85–7, etc. (*Drake* is the original English word, Old English *draca*, derived from Latin; *dragon* was from French).
drolleries   comic plays or entertainments, 190
enow   enough, 241–2
enthralled   enslaved, 97, 163, 196, 198
entreat   treat, 26, 77, 87, 236 (modern sense 38)
errant   wandering, 42
estate   situation, 97
ewer   pitcher for water, 226
eyot   small island, 7
fathom   linear measure (six feet), formerly not used only of water, 78
fell in dread   fell into dread, 106
force   waterfall, 105 (Northern English, from Scandinavian).
fordone   overcome, 233
fosses   pits, 288
fretted   adorned with elaborate carving, 297

glamour   enchantment, spell, 314
greaves   armour for the lower leg, 163
guestkindliness   hospitality, 228. Apparently not recorded; used in
    I.175.
haply   perhaps, 13, 94, 99
hie   hasten; **hie thee**, hasten, 75
high-tide   festival, 231
house-carle   190, see **carle**.
inly   inwardly, 315
jacinth   blue, 274
kempt   combed, 75; **unkempt**, uncombed, 159
kirtle   long coat or tunic, 154
knave   male child, boy, 96 (the original sense of the word, long since
    lost).
lair   in **the dragon's lair**, 105, the place where the dragon was lying
    (i.e. happened at that time to be lying).
lambent   (of flame) playing lightly on a surface without burning, 297
league   about three miles, 171, 189, 201
lealty   loyalty, 185
let   desisted, 166; allowed, 181; **had let fashion**, had had fashioned,
    174, **let seize**, had (him) seized, 225, **let kill**, had (them) killed,
    235
like   please, 41; **good liking**, good will, friendly disposition, 169
list   wish, 85, 101; like, 236
or ever   before ever, 5–6, 38, 80, 110, 233–4, 240
or . . . or   either . . . or, 226
pale   boundary, 269
ports   gateways, 299
prate   chatter, speak to no purpose, 75
puissance   power, 168
repair   make one's way, go, 162
runagate   deserter, 15, 44 (the same word in origin as **renegade**, 15,
    44, 224, 232)
scathe   hurt, harm, 99, 233
scatterlings   wanderers, stragglers, 182
sconces   brackets fastened on a wall, to carry candle or torch, 226
scullion   menial kitchen-servant, drudge, 17, 45
shallop   274. See I.275; but here the boat is defined as oarless.
silvern   silver, 270 (the original Old English adjective).
slot   track of an animal, 38, 96 (=**spoor** 38).
stead   farm, 89
stricken   in **the Stricken Anvil**, struck, beaten, 174, 179
swinge   stroke, blow, 194
thews   strength, bodily power, 33
tilth   cultivated (tilled) land, 4, 88, 101
tithe   tenth part, 188, 223, 227

travail   hardship, suffering, 77, 82, 239; toil, 168; **travailed**, toiled,
   163; **travailing**, enduring hardship, 75
trencher   large dish or platter, 226
uncouth   85 perhaps has the old meaning 'strange', but elsewhere (13,
   75, 115) has the modern sense.
vambrace   armour for the fore-arm, 163
weird   fate, 85–6, 111, 155, 239
whin   gorse, 287
whortle   whortleberry, bilberry; **whortlebush** 287
withe   withy, flexible branch of willow, 229
worm   serpent, dragon, 85–8, etc.
wrack   downfall, ruin, 116, 253, 283, 285

INDEX

This index is made on the same basis as that to Part I, but selected references are given in rather more cases, and the individual *Lost Tales* are not included. In view of the large number of names that appear in Part II fairly full cross-references are provided to associated names (earlier and later forms, equivalents in different languages, etc.). As in the index to Part I, the more important names occurring in *The Silmarillion* are not given explanatory definitions; and references sometimes include passages where the person or place is not actually named.

82; in reference to Noldoli 95, 149; distinct from Noldoli 153, 165, 178, 215, 218, 289. References to the language of the Eldar (as opposed to Gnomish) 8, 70, 85, 148–9, 169, 192, 199, 215–16 (see *Eldarissa*, *Elfin*); *Eldar* as adjective referring to the language 148. See *Elves*.

Eldarissa   The language of the Eldar, as distinct from *Noldorissa*. 148–9, 280

Eldaros   =*Ælfhâm*, Elfhome. 301. *Eldos* 302

Elder Days   324

Elenwë   Wife of Turgon. 209

Elf-friend   141 (of Úrin), 313 (of Déor Ælfwine's father).

Elfin   References only to use as name of the language of the 'Eldar' (as distinct from Gnomish). 42, 49, 149, 202, 267; probably used in general sense 304. See *Eldar*, *Eldarissa*.

Elfinesse   21, 38, 43, 47, 59, 130, 240, 313, 321, 323, 325; *children of Elfinesse* 159, 326, *daughter of Elfinesse* 164, 215

Elf-march   The expedition of the Elves of Kôr for the rescue of the Gnomes in the Great Lands. 144, 221, 252; *March of the Elves* 253, 257–8, 278–80, 303–4, 307–8, *March of the Inwir and Teleri* 255, 278, *March of Liberation* 279. See *Faring Forth*.

Elfriniel   Littleheart. 148, 201, 214–16. (Replaced by *Elfrith*.) *Elfriniol* 50, 201. (Replaced by *Ilfiniol*.) See *Ilfiniol*, *Ilfrin*.

Elfrith   Littleheart. 148, 201–2, 216. (Replaced *Elfriniel*.) See *Ilfrith*.

Ellon   A (Gnomish) name of Tinwelint. 69, 116. See *Tinto'ellon*, *Tinthellon*.

Ellu   (1) Name of Tinwelint in Eldarissa. 49–50, 69. (2) Lord of the Solosimpi in Tinwelint's place (later Olwë). 50

Elmavoitë   'One-handed', name of Beren 'in the language of the Lonely Isle.' 34. See *Ermabwed*.

Elmir   One of the two first Men (with Ermon). 305

Eltas   Teller of the *Tale of Turambar*. 69–70, 112, 116, 118–19, 135–7, 144–5, 242–3; see especially 119.

Elu Thingol   50

Elvenfolk   286, 297. *Elvenland* 272

Elves   Selected references (see also *Eldar*, *Fairies*). Used to include Gnomes 22, 26, 35, 38, etc.; distinct from Gnomes 8, 45, 48–9, 216–17. Fate of the Elves 60, 250; stature of Elves and Men 73, 80, 142, 159, 198, 220, 281, 283, 326–7; references to 'fading' 240, 242, 250, 281, 283, 285–9, 293–4, 301, 304, 306, 312–14, 323, 326–7; union with mortals, see *Men*; feud with the Dwarves 230; tongues of 4, 148, 163; written characters 163; and Old English 301–2, 304, 309.

   Wild Elves 77, 95, 113, 128, 243. See *Brown*, *Dark*, *Green*, *Grey-*, *Island-*, *Lost*, *Elves*; for *Hidden*, *Secret*, *Wood(land)* *Elves* see *Woodland Elves*.

Elwë Singollo   Thingol. 50

Trees of Gondolin 160, 171, 184–5, 207–8, 215–16 (see *Bansil*, *Glingol*); the birds that flew from Gondolin to Kôr 253, 255, 257, 260, 263, 278; ruins of Gondolin 215–16, 253, 255, 258, 264; time of the founding of Gondolin 120, 208
Gondolindrim The people of Gondolin. 209
Gondor, Stewards of 211–12
Gondothlim 'Dwellers in Stone', the people of Gondolin. 155–66, 168, 170–4, 176, 179–81, 184–5, 187, 190, 193, 196, 198–200, 206, 208, 211, 213–16, 267; speech of, secret tongue of 158, 164–5, 198–9, 267; stature of 159, 198
Gondothlimbar 'City of the Dwellers in Stone', one of the Seven Names of Gondolin. 158
Gong of Littleheart 6–7, 41, 254, 256, 263; *the Gong-warden* 144–5, 149, 201
Gongs Evil beings, obscurely related to Orcs. 136–7, 283, 288, 328
Gon Indor Name of Eärendel as great-grandson of Indor. 217. See *Indor*, *Indorildo*.
Gorgumoth The hound of Mandos. 278
Gorlim the Unhappy 52
Gothmog (1) 'Strife-and-hatred', lord of Balrogs, son of Melko and captain of his hosts. 67, 176, 179, 183–4, 212–13, 215–16. See *Kosmoko*. (2) Lieutenant of Minas Morgul. 216
Great End 60, 170, 281–3, 285. See *Great Wrack*.
Great Folk of the West Name of the Gods among the Ilkorins. 142
Great Haywood Village in Staffordshire (Tavrobel). 146, 290, 292–3, 328; (Old English) *Hægwudu* 290, 292, 328
Great Journey (of the Elves from the Waters of Awakening) 64, 307
Great Lands The lands east of the Great Sea. 4–6, 60, 64–5, 68, 140–1, 206, 208, 249–50, 255, 257–8, 264, 279–81, 283, 285, 289, 292–4, 299–300, 302–3, 306–8, 317, 326–7. See *Lands Without*, *Outer Land(s)*.
Great Market, The In Gondolin. 182
Great Plains 61
Great Sea (not including many references to *the Sea*, *the Ocean*) 151, 155, 162, 196, 312, 315, 324. See *Garsecg*, *Western Sea(s)*.
Great Wrack 116, 282; *Wrack of Things* 283; *Wrack of the Gods* 285. See *Great End*.
Green Elves 234, 248–9; *the brown Elves and the green* 237, 240, 242, 248; (Elves) 'clad in green and brown' 234, 248. See *Laiquendi*.
Greenland 261
Grey-elves of Doriath 64; of Beleriand 64, 128; of Hithlum 204; of Mithrim 205
Grithnir The elder of Túrin's guardians on the journey to Doriath. 127. See *Gumlin*.
Gruir River in Tol Eressëa, joining the Afros at the bridge of Tavrobel (see 288). 284, 287

West Wind 261

Wielisc See *Wéalas*.

Wing, The Emblem of Tuor, see *Swan*; *White Wing* 172; *men, folk, guard, of the Wing* in Gondolin 174, 176–8, 180, 182, 190, 192

Winged Helms The Forodwaith. 330, 334. See *Gwasgonin*.

Wingildi Spirits of the sea-foam. 276

Wingilot 'Foam-flower', Eärendel's ship. 145, 253–4, 256, 260–1, 263; *Wingelot* 260, 262, 272; *Vingelot* 262, 272

Wirilómë 'Gloomweaver'. 260–1. See *Ungweliant(ë)*.

Withered Dale Where Tevildo encountered Huan. 48, 56

Withered Heath Heath near Tavrobel, after the Battle of the Heath of the Sky-roof. 284, 287

Wóden Old English name of the Germanic god in Old Norse called *Óðinn*; by Eriol identified with Manwë. 290

Wolfriders See *Orcs*.

Wolf-Sauron 55

Woodland Elves Elves of Artanor. Also *Woodelves, Elves of the wood(land), of the forest*, etc. 11, 13, 18, 34–5, 37, 43, 45, 52, 63, 65–6, 69, 73–4, 78, 92, 142, 222–3, 228, 242–3, 245–6; *wood(land) fairies* 23, 35, 63; *hidden Elves* 10; *secret Elves* 11, 73, 123

Woodmen (later *Woodmen of Brethil*) Also *woodfolk, wood(land)-rangers*. 91, 100–8, 112–13, 125, 127, 130–5, 138, 141–2. See *Vettar*.

Yavanna 286. See *Belaurin*, *Palúrien*.

Year of Lamentation 120

Ythlings 'Children of the Waves'. 319–20, 322, 325, 331–2, 334; *Ythlingas* 331; described, 318. See *Eneathrim*, *Shipmen of the West*.

Does Marketing Need Reform?

Dedicated to the memory of the late Peter F. Drucker, pioneering management thinker and the true father of the marketing concept. Ideas that he first articulated over fifty years ago remain as vital and relevant to marketing practice and scholarship today as they were when first written. We hope that this book encourages marketing academics to revisit Drucker's inspirational early writings on marketing and gain a renewed appreciation for essential nobility of the marketing function and its centrality in the lives of consumers and the fortunes of businesses.

Jagdish N. Sheth
Rajendra S. Sisodia

Does Marketing Need Reform?

Fresh Perspectives
on the Future

Jagdish N. Sheth
Rajendra S. Sisodia
Editors

M.E.Sharpe
Armonk, New York
London, England

Copyright © 2006 by M.E. Sharpe, Inc.

All rights reserved. No part of this book may be reproduced in any form
without written permission from the publisher, M.E. Sharpe, Inc.,
80 Business Park Drive, Armonk, New York 10504.

Library of Congress Cataloging-in-Publication Data

Does marketing need reform? : fresh perspectives on the future / edited by
Jagdish N. Sheth and Rajendra S. Sisodia.
   p. cm.
 Includes bibliographical references and indexes.
 ISBN 0-7656-1698-X (cloth : alk. paper) ISBN 0-7656-1699-8 (pbk. : alk. paper)
 1. Marketing. I. Sheth, Jagdish N. II. Sisodia, Rajendra.

HF5415.D623 2006
658.8—dc22
                                                     2005025003

Printed in the United States of America

The paper used in this publication meets the minimum requirements of
American National Standard for Information Sciences
Permanence of Paper for Printed Library Materials,
ANSI Z 39.48-1984.

∞

BM (c) 10   9   8   7   6   5   4   3   2   1
BM (p) 10   9   8   7   6   5   4   3   2   1

CONTENTS

Does Marketing Need Reform?

Breif History of Consumerism
↓ linkedin

The History of Marketing.
- the marketing concept
- the rise of consumerism.
  this is
  - how marketings shame.
- how marketing is now
- marketing that works DONE
- the future, so maybe it isn't
  all 'doom' and gloom
  TRASPARENCY)

CHAPTER 1

INTRODUCTION

Does Marketing Need Reform?

JAGDISH N. SHETH AND RAJENDRA S. SISODIA

More than thirty years ago, Peter Drucker wrote:

> Despite the emphasis on marketing and the marketing approach, marketing is still rhetoric rather than reality in far too many businesses. "Consumerism" proves this. For what consumerism demands of business is that it actually market. It demands that business start out with the needs, the realities, the values of the customer. It demands that business define its goal as the satisfaction of customer needs. It demands that business base its reward on its contribution to the customer. That after twenty years of marketing rhetoric consumerism could become a powerful popular movement proves that not much marketing has been practiced. Consumerism is the "shame of marketing." (1973, p. 64)

Drucker's characterization remains as true today as it ever was. Instead of acting as partners engaged in mutually rewarding co-destiny relationships, too many marketers and consumers continue to be locked into mistrustful, adversarial relationships in which there is a constant tug-of-war to determine which side can benefit disproportionately and unfairly.

It has been evident for many years that "marketing as usual" is simply not working anymore, and that fundamentally new thinking is needed to revive and rejuvenate this most vital and potentially noble of business functions—one that has, unfortunately, become the object of skepticism and distrust among many of its stakeholders.

Our own observations over the past decade or so have led us to conclude that marketing has been losing efficiency as well as effectiveness over time (Sheth and Sisodia 1995, 1996, 2002). In other words, marketing has been and continues to be in the throes of a productivity crisis. Other business functions (most dramatically, operations/manufacturing, but also many management support functions) have made striking advances in both efficiency and effectiveness, and have been able to "do more with less" year after year. Marketing, on the other hand, has managed to "do less with more," demanding and receiving more resources year after year, continually relying on a heavy dose of gimmicks and constant sales promotions, while delivering worse results: flat or declining customer satisfaction levels, shockingly low customer loyalty levels, and increasing numbers of alienated customers.

There was a time when marketing's current modus operandi worked, and worked rather well. It was a time when most customers were young, the rate of household formation was high, national brands were few, national distribution was limited, national media were just emerging, television was in its infancy, latent demand in many product categories was high, and producing products of reasonable quality at low cost was a challenge. None of those conditions prevail anymore. Yet, for marketers and their increasingly irritated customers, it seems every day is *Groundhog Day*—recall the movie in which Bill Murray was condemned to relive the same day every day, without end. Or, as Yogi Berra would say, "It's déjà vu all over again."

Of course, marketing *has* added new things to its bag of tricks, such as pop-up ads (which make Web surfing akin to duck shooting as users attempt to close windows faster than they appear) and a tidal wave of increasingly over-the-top and offensive email messages that fill inboxes to overflowing every morning. The problem is that marketing is too fixated on its bag of tricks. Many of those tricks were novel and may even have been interesting at one time, but they are anything but that today. Moreover, marketing's use of such tricks has increased geometrically as the Internet has greatly lowered the direct cost of doing so; more marketers than ever before are able to use these tricks with ever greater frequency, casting ever wider nets in the hope of catching a few unwary customers.

The side effects of marketing today overwhelm its intended main effects. It seems that the more a customer is marketed to, the more frustrated and irritated he or she becomes, and the more manipulated and helpless he or she feels. This is clearly no way to win customers and influence chief executive officers. Noise pollution, information overload, empty promises, outright exaggerations—marketing's negative effects on society have never been more pronounced.

It does not have to be this way. Sound marketing practices lead to low marketing costs coupled with highly satisfied customers, minimal spillover of marketing communication to groups outside the target market, long-term co-destiny relationships between companies and their customers, and a strong emotional bond between companies and customers. Unfortunately, these have become the rare exception rather than the rule.

The harsh reality facing marketers today is that their bag of tricks has become a useless, even dangerous, relic of a bygone era. The power in the marketplace—economic, informational, and psychological—has shifted to customers. Old-style marketers have themselves become sitting ducks now, and information-savvy customers can—and do—readily exploit them to their own advantage.

MARKETING: THE GOOD, THE BAD, AND THE UGLY

Marketing practice today is rife with three major types of problems, as depicted in Figure 1.1. First, many marketing actions are either exploitative or downright unethical; in those cases, the marketer seeks to benefit by taking unfair advantage of the customer. Second, some marketing actions are so poorly thought out that they leave the company vulnerable to being exploited by increasingly deal-savvy consumers. We refer to these actions as "dumb marketing." And third are those marketing actions that benefit neither customers nor companies, and can only be characterized as utterly wasteful. In some cases (as with advertising so heavily as to induce a backlash against the brand), increased marketing spending not only does no good, it actually harms the company! Anheuser-Busch and Campbell Soup discovered this years ago after conducting numerous advertising experiments (Ackoff and Emshoff 1975; Eastlack and Rao 1989).

Collectively, these three types of actions represent the misalignment of marketing—and, ultimately, all of them are dumb as well as wasteful. As the figure shows, any benefits accruing to marketers or customers at the expense of each other are short-lived at best, and usually lead to subsequent losses that more than offset previous gains.

So why is this happening, nearly half a century after the "marketing concept" became an integral part of the business vocabulary? Marketing is *supposed* to be about aligning company

Figure 1.1 **Marketer and Customer Benefits**

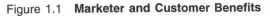

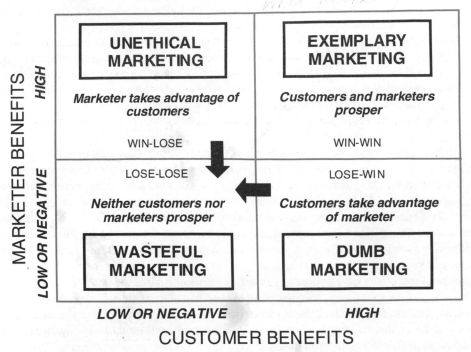

and customer interests. Practiced properly, it should result in happy, loyal customers, motivated and fulfilled employees, and satisfied shareholders. The norm, however, is quite different. Marketing has become synonymous with hype, gimmickry, and the primacy of image over substance; marketers at many companies wittingly or unwittingly end up exploiting their own customers or becoming exploited by them. Marketing swallows up huge resources—the financial resources of companies as well as the time, attention, and efforts of customers—while too often delivering little of value to either side in return. All chickens do eventually come home to roost, and the internal and external consequences of unethical, dumb, and wasteful marketing cannot be escaped forever. Marketing managers must alter their business practices before their companies go out of business or are forced to reform by the heavy hand of regulation. Marketing has become addicted to these unethical, dumb, and wasteful practices. Like any addict, it needs an intervention to break the addiction.

Marketing's current problems are rooted in organizational inertia, misaligned incentive systems, poorly designed value propositions, and outmoded ways of thinking about markets and customers. The culture of marketing, especially in consumer marketing, has become too corrupted and disfigured by short-term thinking and a loss of focus on the fundamental human values that require that companies and customers treat each other as allies and partners in value creation rather than as adversaries and potential victims.

The Bad: Unethical Marketing

To achieve their sales and market share goals, more and more companies are resorting to exploitative and unethical marketing practices. Unethical marketing is that in which the marketer attempts to mislead, misinform, or otherwise take unfair advantage of customers, or knowingly engages in activities that have a harmful effect on society. In these cases, marketers seek to benefit at the *expense of* customers rather than *with* them.

Too many companies try to exploit a customer's emotions, trust, confusion, lack of organization, or lack of knowledge. Companies take advantage of vulnerable customers such as children, the elderly, and the indigent. They convey a false sense of objectivity in their advertising, engage in opportunistic pricing or price gouging, push harmful or unnecessary products, make it difficult for unhappy customers to leave them, create and exploit customer addictions, pressure customers into making hasty decisions, or unduly influence trusted advisors (such as pharmacists and doctors) to give customers poor advice.

Such hit-and-run marketing is so widespread that it sometimes appears to be the norm rather than the exception. Some examples are egregious, others somewhat subtle. Three prominent ones are: brazenly misleading advertisements (e.g., weight loss products), manipulative sales tactics (e.g., automobile retailing), and most forms of multilevel marketing. Telemarketing has earned a deservedly terrible reputation as the last refuge of hit-and-run marketers, and is estimated to result in over $50 billion of consumer fraud annually. Other frequently criticized practices include price gouging (e.g., ink cartridges for printers), advertising to children, and many pharmaceutical marketing techniques.

Unethical marketing may appear to pay off in the short run, but its long-term consequences can be deadly. There are many examples of highly successful companies demonstrating very high standards of marketing ethics. Ethical marketing is financially beneficial in the long run, as it builds customer trust. It is also essential to building employee morale and loyalty, which are prerequisites to delivering superior customer service and customer satisfaction.

The Ugly: Dumb Marketing

Many marketing practices are detrimental to the long-run interests of the marketer, but may offer customers a (usually) temporary benefit. These situations need not involve scams or illegal activities on the part of customers. Rather, they occur when shrewd customers, behaving quite reasonably and rationally, respond to poorly conceived and implemented (i.e., dumb) offers from marketers. For example:

- Some companies indiscriminately try to "buy" customers, as the major long distance companies did in the 1990s, leading many customers to switch providers repeatedly to take advantage of the incentives. The net result was the destruction of brand loyalty in the industry.
- Many customers cherry-pick only deeply discounted "sale" items from retail stores, resulting in a loss for the retailer every time they shop at the store.
- Many marketers use coupons in such a broad, untargeted manner that even those customers who would have readily bought the product at regular price receive a windfall. Traditional coupons are also highly susceptible to fraud by some retailers.
- Retailers that run constant sales (e.g., some chains run three "sales" every week, each with its own expensive advertising circular) or make patently false claims (e.g., advertising "lowest prices of the year" every week) erode their own credibility while rendering the notion of "regular" price meaningless—and spend a great deal of money doing so.
- Blindly copying competitors' marketing tactics without assessing the full long-term impact of doing so.
- Expensive catalogs that go straight into the garbage can.

- Return policies that allow customers to repeatedly purchase and return products for no good reason and without consequences.
- Dumb pricing, as in the airline business, which has totally divorced price from value in setting prices for business versus consumer travel.
- End-of-quarter deals in business-to-business marketing, which cause savvy customers to wait until the end of a quarter to get advantageous terms.

Dumb marketing is not just noisy and annoying; it is very costly to the bottom line and thus detrimental to employees and shareholders, while doing little of ultimate consequence for customers. It is usually motivated by extreme short-term thinking on the part of marketers (e.g., to make their quarterly numbers) or to cover up previous mistakes (e.g., end-of-season clearances on merchandise that customers do not want).

Smart marketers must deal with customers who behave in an unethical way toward them. Some consumers are egregious, habitual, and serial offenders. In most cases, these customers face no repercussions at all; for example, consumers continue abusing some companies' generous return/exchange policies indefinitely. Even if a company eventually detects a pattern and refuses to do business with certain customers (something that rarely happens), such customers can simply start exploiting another company. In doing so, they start with a clean slate, carrying no taint from their previous rejection.

Companies need to be able to identify and tag those consumers who:

- Repeatedly buy and return merchandise, especially apparel, after obviously using it.
- Use multiple names or variations on names in order to qualify for promotional offers multiple times (such as with music and book clubs).
- Habitually make false complaints about customer service in order to get companies to offer them free goods.
- Threaten companies with negative publicity if their (unreasonable) demands are not met.
- Have been verbally or otherwise abusive toward employees.
- Engage in other unacceptable practices such as software piracy, price tag switching, falsely claiming stolen credit cards, and so on.

The Bad and Ugly: Wasteful Marketing

In an age when the mantra of business has been "do more with less," the marketing function has for too long been "doing less with more." In most industries today, the marketing function consumes over 50 percent of corporate resources, up from less than 25 percent around 1950.

At a macro level, marketing represents a tremendous waste of resources that could be better utilized elsewhere. In the United States, companies spend nearly $11,000 per year per family of four on advertising and sales promotion. Does all this marketing spending create incremental value, or does it just influence consumer choice behavior in ways that may not be value decreasers? How much of it fails to do even that? (Out of the fifteen hundred or so advertising messages each person is exposed to daily, how many actually have any impact on attitudes or behavior?) There is strong evidence that as much as 80 percent of that money is wasted or misspent in some way. For example, most sales promotions are so poorly designed and targeted that they achieve redemption rates of 1–2 percent or less, and most of those redeeming are not the ones that the company needs to target. Research clearly shows that many large companies waste billions of dollars on unnecessary and poorly conceived advertising. Most customer loyalty programs don't work; to the contrary, they create customers who are more mercenary than ever.

Some more evidence that marketers are spending resources poorly:

- AdWorks 2, a study conducted by Media Marketing Assessment and Information Resources Incorporated in conjunction with Nielsen Media Research found that television advertising returned only 32 cents for every dollar invested (Merrill 1999, p. 29).
- Roper Starch reports that consumer cynicism and distrust of advertising is growing. Consumers are "tuning out, turning off, and opting out" (quoted in Parker-Pope 1995, p. C1).
- Advertising agency loyalty has declined sharply as client companies look for quick fixes to their advertising woes; the average number of years that clients retain the same agency has declined from eleven years to only two-and-a-half, according to an October 2001 survey by consulting firm Pile & Co. (O'Connell 2001).
- A 1995 study by Information Resources Incorporated found that 70–80 percent of new product introductions fail, with the average failure resulting in a net loss of up to $25 million (Woodward and Clifford 2005).
- Direct marketing response rates have been falling precipitously; for example, according to BAI Global, the response rates for credit-card marketers have steadily declined, from 2.8 percent in 1992 to an all-time low of 0.6 percent in 2000 (Consumer Federation of America 2001).
- Email marketing, one of the newer weapons in the marketer's arsenal, is fast losing its effectiveness; as its use and abuse have soared, response rates over the past five years have fallen from as high as 30 percent to less than 2 percent, and in the most egregious cases of blatant "spamming," a fraction of 1 percent (Jackson 2000).

NOTHING EXCEEDS LIKE EXCESS

Overmarketing is the cause of many of marketing's problems, and the reason for the backlash against many companies and industries, for example, the drug industry. Many companies overadvertise, even more overpromote; for example, Abraham and Lodish (1990) found that 86 percent of sales promotions lose money. Many companies oversell, using pushy tactics, overclaiming benefits, and targeting people who should not be targeted, such as young healthy men with erectile dysfunction drugs.

Overmarketing lowers the quality of life, as it distracts consumers from more relevant pursuits. If companies could eliminate dumb, wasteful, and unethical marketing, how much would be left? What would be the impact? On consumers? On companies? On society? On national competitiveness? We think there would a significant positive impact on each of these.

Marketing, in the aggregate, does benefit the economy; the evidence is pretty strong that societies with high levels of marketing activity are more productive than societies that restrict or do not permit marketing. But more is not necessarily better. Marketing cannot be given a blank check, any more than any other socially useful activity.

Some of the reasons for overspending on marketing are:

- Incremental thinking and marginal analysis
- Short-term thinking—ignoring long-term negative impacts
- Defensive mindsets—irrational fear of competitors
- Continued obsession with conquest sales when the reality is that the business will ultimately prosper only if it can keep existing customers

- Lack of faith in the company's value proposition
- Low hurdles for spending effectiveness
- Dysfunctional budgeting—the "use it or lose it" mindset
- Ignoring overflow effects of excessive marketing on noncustomers—poisoning the well
- Trying harder instead of trying smarter—overspending in one area (e.g., advertising) to compensate for a vulnerability in another (e.g., poor product quality)

Many marketers are locked into a mutually assured distraction (MAD) arms race with their customers. The more customers resist and are able to block marketing efforts, the more these marketers seek to redouble those efforts. To change this MAD pattern, they must change the paradigm—or their mental models, as Jerry Wind suggests in chapter 11 in this volume. At the company level, marketing's job should be to make itself gradually less needed over the life of a product, as awareness and "ever tried" levels rise. In that sense, a good marketer is like a good doctor, who does not make the patient dependent on him or her for continued good health.

CONCLUSION

Must marketing always elicit negative sentiments? Is there something intrinsic to marketing that regardless of how hard we try, consumers are going to resist it? We don't think so. There are many companies that, in fact, are very well liked and even loved by their customers and other stakeholders. These companies show that it is possible to do a lot more with a lot less. We have studied thirty such exemplary marketing companies that, almost without exception, spend much less than their industry peers on marketing, yet have much more satisfied customers. These companies, featured in our book *Firms of Endearment* (Sheth, Sisodia, and Wolfe 2006) have happier employees, suppliers, communities, and investors as well.

Marketing ultimately comes down to a company's attitude toward its customers and how well it serves them. One of the companies we studied is Google. Without spending a dollar on advertising, Google has become the most valuable brand in the world, according to Interbrand. Everything that Google does is demonstrably in the best interests of its customers. It blocks pop-up ads. It will not take a company's money if its ad is not drawing any response. Advertisers can only earn the top position through clickthroughs, not by paying more. Thus, only the most relevant messages move up that chain because the company views advertising as a service to its customers and not as an intrusion or something that exists merely to subsidize the company's free search service. Or consider Jordan's Furniture, a highly successful regional furniture retailer in the Northeast. The average furniture retailer spends approximately 7 percent of gross revenue on marketing and advertising; Jordan's spends only 2 percent. Despite this, it is by far the best-known and most successful company in the business. It turns its inventory over thirteen times a year, compared to one to two times for most furniture retailers. It never has sales; with a philosophy of "underprices" (everyday fair prices), it generates sales of almost $1,000 per square foot, compared to the industry average of $100–200. The company equates retailing with entertainment, has well-paid, highly motivated, and loyal employees, and is a beloved member of its community, receiving dozens of awards for its work (Jordans.com).

So there appears to be no correlation between marketing spending and customer happiness with a company, or necessarily between marketing spending and the creation of valuable marketing assets. When it comes to marketing, it is a matter of doing it right and doing it at the right volume. Or, as Drucker would say, do the right things and do them right. What matters is not the *quantity* of marketing dollars spent, but the *quality* of the marketing thinking that pervades decision making in companies.

All marketers must strive for exemplary marketing, that which is effective, efficient, and ethical. They must figure out how to align the interests of the company with those of its customers, so that they do not have to expend all of their energies getting customers to do things that are ultimately not in their best interests. To achieve this, they will have to shift their priorities and redirect their energies. Marketing has become almost exclusively about representing the company to the customer, and putting a positive spin on everything the company does. It needs to be primarily about representing the customer to the company. Marketers need to achieve deep empathy and emotional understanding of their customers, and then translate that knowledge into company actions that will improve their customers' quality of life. Marketing is a powerful force, backed up by huge resources. It must be entrusted only to those with the wisdom to use it well.

Restoring Marketing Virtues, or Kinder, Gentler Marketing

To conclude, we would quote Martin Luther King, Jr., who said, "We must pursue peaceful ends through peaceful means." This sentiment applies to marketing as well. Forget all the old ideas about marketing warfare, customer conquest and capture, or aggressive marketing tactics of any kind. Indeed, aggressive sentiments and mindsets have no place in marketing. Marketing must be about pursuing desirable ends (delighted customers, undamaged societal interests, fair returns to shareholders) through desirable means. The values of the marketing profession must embrace seemingly forgotten but timeless virtues such as:

- Truth: "Marketing" and "truth" have become words you cannot use in the same sentence; this has to change. If marketing is ever to gain a measure of credibility, the phrase "truthful marketing" cannot be an oxymoron any more.
- Integrity: Companies are becoming painfully aware of the need for uncompromising integrity in their dealings with the financial community, yet many continue to show little concern for maintaining the same standard of integrity in their dealings with customers.
- Authenticity: Many marketing communications are intended to appear as though they are personalized. Of course, the vast majority of customers see right through this façade. Customers can innately sense the human presence (or lack thereof) behind marketing communications. Marketing must strive for authenticity in all customer dealings.
- Trust: This is probably the one virtue that is most lacking in the relationship between companies and their customers. Without mutual trust, it is a joke to speak of "relationship marketing," and an egregious waste to spend hundreds of millions of dollars on "customer relationship management" systems, as many companies have done in recent years to little effect.
- Respect: The legendary advertising executive David Ogilvy wrote, "The customer is not an idiot, she is your wife." Many marketers have indeed been guilty of treating their customers as idiots. Marketers must give respect in order to earn respect. They must respect their customers, of course, but they must also respect their suppliers and even their competitors.
- Reciprocal empathy and vulnerability: To maximize goodwill, marketers and customers must empathize with one another, and both must be (or make themselves) equally vulnerable.
- True dialogue: Most companies are very good (or so they think) at speaking to their customers, but exceedingly few are any good at truly listening to them. Without listening, there is no learning and certainly no relationship.
- Manners: Marketing is rarely polite or deferential; instead, it is usually loud, boorish, in-your-face, insensitive. Marketers constantly interrupt customers' lives with their incessant communications. Marketers routinely bad mouth their competitors, and insult

the intelligence of their customers—hardly the sort of behavior that comprises civilized discourse.

- Forgiveness: Marketers must ask customers for forgiveness, given their past trespasses and indiscretions. Over time, customers will learn to forgive marketers' occasional lapses and see them against the backdrop of overall good behavior. Otherwise, the friction between marketers and customers will remain, as the cartilage between them has worn thin after years of abuse.

- Courage and patience: Changing decades-old practices will take courage, as marketers seek to counter conventional wisdom and the skepticism of colleagues. For example, it takes courage for a company to stop overpromising and underdelivering (as is the norm) and actually start underpromising and overdelivering. It will also take patience; much like a down-on-its-luck professional sports team must go through a painful rebuilding process, the marketing function will have to endure a lengthy adjustment period as it seeks to rebuild its reputation with customers and with other functional areas.

- Gratitude and recognition: Marketers need to show their gratitude and appreciation to their customers, and also put in place mechanisms whereby customers can do the same for their best employees. Some airlines, for example, give their best customers employee appreciation vouchers, which they can hand out to exemplary employees.

- Humility: Marketing must shed its hubris and embrace humility. Consider the definition of the word "hubris": *Exaggerated pride or self-confidence, often resulting in retribution; overbearing presumption; arrogance.* These words fit traditional marketing like a glove.

- Perspective: By adopting a customer-centric perspective, marketing professionals can make marketing a positive force in the quality of life of consumers, instead of the nuisance it is often perceived to be.

REFERENCES

Abraham, Magid M. and Leonard M. Lodish (1990), "Getting the Most Out of Advertising and Promotion," *Harvard Business Review,* 68 (May–June), 50–60.

Ackoff, Russell L. and James R. Emshoff (1975), "Advertising Research at Anheuser-Busch, Inc. (1963–1968)," *Sloan Management Review,* 16 (Winter), 1–15.

Consumer Federation of America (2001), "Industry Profits Surge As Personal Bankruptcies Plummet for the Second Year in a Row," www.consumerfed.org/pdfs/travpr.pdf (accessed September 14, 2005).

Drucker, Peter F. (1973), *Management: Tasks, Responsibilities, Practices.* New York: Harper & Row.

Eastlack, Joseph O., Jr., and Ambar G. Rao (1989), "Advertising Experiments at the Campbell Soup Company," *Marketing Science,* 8 (1), 57–71.

Jackson, Adam (2000), "The Viral Component in Online Creative," *ClickZ Experts*, www.clickz.com/experts/archives/ad/online_ad/article.php/830021 (accessed September 14, 2005).

Jordans.com, www.jordans.com/about/history.asp (accessed September 14, 2005).

Merrill, Cristina (1999), "Machine Dreams," *American Demographics*, 21 (4), 28–31.

O'Connell, Vanessa (2001), "Client Loyalty in Ad Industry Dwindles Along With Sales," *Wall Street Journal (Europe)*, October 15, 28

Parker-Pope, Tara (1995), "Consumers Believe Advertising Misleads, Exaggerates Products—Most Say They Are Skeptical of Industry's Hard Sell, World-Wide Survey Finds," *Wall Street Journal,* July 14.

Sheth, Jagdish N. and Rajendra S. Sisodia (1995), "Feeling the Heat: Making Marketing More Productive," *Marketing Management,* 4 (Fall), 8–23.

——— (1996), "Feeling the Heat: Making Marketing More Productive—Part II," *Marketing Management,* 4 (Winter), 19–33.

——— (2002), "Marketing Productivity: Conceptualization, Measurement and Improvement," *Journal of Business Research,* 55 (May), 349–62.

———, ——— and David. B. Wolfe (2006), *Firms of Endearment.* Philadelphia: Wharton School Publishing.

Woodward, Richard and Richard Clifford (2005), "Eight Out of Ten New Products Fail," www.infores.com/public/uk/newsevents/press/2005/uk_new_072205.htm (accessed September 14, 2005).

PART 1

MIRROR, MIRROR ON THE WALL

Marketing's Image, Excess, and Resistance Problems

Marketing faces three fundamental problems: it suffers from a poor image with consumers as well as with business professionals; it seems to run to excess; and it is now encountering serious resistance from consumers. The chapters in this section address these problems, as well as provide some possible solutions.

Marketing as an institution has been always been under critical surveillance due to its close association with selling, persuasion, and the profit motive. It has, however, invited further criticism recently due to the macro trends of globalization, market-driven government policies (especially after the collapse of communism), and the emergence of the Internet. The Internet is both a richer medium and has greater reach than other mass media. It is a powerful, affordable, and universal medium of information, communication, and transaction that has enabled new and innovative marketing approaches that neither society nor consumers could imagine.

In our first chapter in this section, J. Walker Smith, President of Yankelovich Partners, presents results of a groundbreaking Monitor Omniplus study that examined marketing from a consumer perspective. In other words, what do consumers think of today's marketing practices? Overwhelmingly, 60 percent agreed that their opinion of advertising and marketing had become more negative today than just a few years ago. Sixty-one percent said that the amount of marketing and advertising had gotten out of control. Even worse, 45 percent said that the amount of marketing they are exposed to detracts from their experiences of everyday life. The Yankelovich study also found that the negative perception of marketing held by consumers was not reflected in their survey of marketing directors at well-known companies. Smith believes that this lack of concurrence between consumers and marketers, unless corrected soon, will encourage consumers to be even more resistant to marketing.

A study carried out by Sheth, Sisodia, and Barbulescu also provided similar results about the image of marketing. Using the framework of the "tragedy of the commons," the authors suggest that overutilization of the same marketing tactics and tools by everyone seems to be the underlying reason for the negative image of marketing. This is especially true with respect to telemarketing, junk mail, and pop-up advertising. At the same time, consumers do enjoy free samples and Super Bowl ads. In fact, most of them look forward to them with positive anticipation. It seems that the easier and cheaper it is for a marketing tactic to be executed, the more "junklike" it becomes in the eyes of consumers. This suggests that a way of alleviating this problem would be to raise the cost of marketing approaches such as spam and junk mail.

Finally, the authors also found some significant gaps in the perception of marketing as a business function between marketing professionals and nonmarketing professionals. While both agreed that marketing is a real value-added function, the role of marketing was perceived to be more limited by nonmarketing than marketing professionals.

Johny Johansson's chapter, based on his provocative book *In Your Face: How American Marketing Excess Fuels Anti-Americanism,* suggests that American marketing is morally bankrupt, and that American marketing practices have helped turn the American way of life into its lowest common denominator in terms of quality of life. According to him, we marketers encourage several vices, such as excessive spending, outrageous behavior, and the unmitigated pursuance of individual gratification. We do this because we have the marketing tools to do it, the companies have the financial muscle to do it, and competition gives us a justification to do it. Johansson then supports his argument about the emergence of the lowest common denominator in products (fast foods, SUVs), in promotions (loud and aggressive, instill a "must have" feeling), and in communications media (pop-up ads, cell phone telemarketing, and e-mail spam). He strongly believes that this American approach to marketing is fueling anti-American sentiments worldwide, as American consumer marketing expands globally. His recommendation is to instill moral responsibility among marketing practitioners and academics.

The final chapter in this section by Malhotra, Wu, and Allvine provides thoughtful and empirically based evidence of what Johansson and others have anecdotally asserted. There is clear evidence of excessive buying in America as evidenced by low savings rate, mounting credit card debt, and all-time-high personal bankruptcies. The authors attribute such marketing practices to easy access to credit cards (more recently debit cards) and the lure of advertising and sales promotions. They suggest that we need to redefine the role of marketing in society and that marketing practices should be limited to satisfying consumers' needs that are existent and affordable, rather than creating needs that are unhealthy or unaffordable. In other words, marketing should not convert wants into needs.

CHAPTER 2

COMING TO CONCURRENCE

Improving Marketing Productivity by Reengaging Resistant Consumers

J. WALKER SMITH

The biggest problem confronting marketers today is also their biggest opportunity for tomorrow. Consumer resistance to marketing is a mounting crisis, yet there has never been a better time to win record levels of customer loyalty and commitment.

This mix of problems and opportunities is not as much of a paradox as it sounds. As smart marketers know, problems always create opportunities for companies willing to break the mold and do something different. The best time to secure enduring competitive advantage is when the marketplace is in turmoil. Now is that time.

Simply put, consumers are fed up with marketing saturation and intrusiveness. As a result, consumer resistance to marketing is growing rapidly. So, marketers have the chance, indeed, the necessity, to create competitive advantage for their brands through their marketing practices. Looking ahead, the best marketing won't simply be a better way of promoting a brand and its benefits. The best marketing will actually be a brand benefit itself.

The marketers who prevail will be those who respond to consumer resistance with precision and relevance as well as power and reciprocity—the four elements of P&R^2—instead of more marketing saturation and intrusiveness. This requires true customer-centricity, not the process-centricity that characterizes most marketing organizations.

For the most part, marketers think in terms of the four Ps: product, place, promotion, and price. These are marketing processes. Consumers go unmentioned in the four Ps; they are there only implicitly. Processes come first. This may seem like an insignificant nuance, but it is more than simply splitting hairs. Managers perform the jobs asked of them. When asked to manage processes, that's what managers do. Though consumers are central to marketing, they often take a back seat to processes in the priorities defined for marketing managers. A good illustration of what happens when processes come first is the recent industry response to discoveries about the consumer usage of digital video recorders (DVRs) like TiVo.

Marketers have been alarmed to learn that consumers with DVRs skip 60–80 percent of the ads in the programs they watch (Arlen 2002; *Economist* 2000). In response, many marketers have turned to product placements within TV shows to reach consumers irrespective of whether they skip the ads. By the measure of exposure used to assess TV advertising, this restores the effectiveness of the TV advertising process because the lost viewers are recovered. What it has also done, though, is force consumers to watch these proto-ads whether they want to or not. Putting consumers first by asking what interests or attitudes are expressed when they skip ads and then responding by satisfying those needs and preferences, even if it means abandoning an established process, would lead marketers to respond differently. Making marketing processes work better isn't always the right path for building long-term loyalty and satisfaction.

The elements of P&R^2 (precision, relevance, power, and reciprocity) are what consumers want from marketing. These elements constitute the four cornerstones of concurrence marketing. Concurrence means two things: synchrony, or agreement, and collaboration, or cooperation. The first two elements of P&R^2—precision and relevance—are about getting in sync, or agreement, with consumers in both targeting and messaging. The third and fourth elements—power and reciprocity—are about collaborating, or cooperating, with consumers in product design and marketing execution. Concurrence is a secondary concern with marketing saturation and intrusiveness. Only concurrence can build the kinds of consumer relationships needed to reverse the ongoing decline of marketing productivity.

CONSUMER RESISTANCE TO MARKETING

Marketing resistance is widespread and growing. Yet, few researchers have studied this phenomenon. To fill this knowledge gap, in 2004 Yankelovich Partners conducted a groundbreaking MONITOR OmniPlus study[1] to provide marketers with a baseline understanding of contemporary consumer attitudes toward marketing practices.

In particular, this study examined marketing practice from a marketing perspective. The objective was to look at marketing in the same way that marketers look at any other product or service. Specifically, what are consumers' needs, wants, dissatisfactions, complaints, and aspirations with respect to marketing? What can marketers do to meet these needs and wants and to remedy these dissatisfactions and complaints? How can marketers make marketing practice fit the ways in which consumers aspire to live their lives? And what is the opportunity for greater marketing success from improvements in marketing practice?

The urgency for a new approach to marketing is immediately apparent in the results of the Yankelovich study. The overwhelming majority of respondents expressed a negative opinion about marketing. Sixty percent agreed that their opinion of marketing and advertising has become much more negative than it was just a few years ago. Sixty-one percent said that the amount of marketing and advertising has gotten out of control. Even worse, a sizable 45 percent said that the amount of marketing they are exposed to detracts from their experience of everyday life.

A basis of comparison is available from a major study completed on behalf of the American Association of Advertising Agencies (AAAA) in 1964 regarding attitudes toward advertising.[2] Although a direct comparison of the 1964 AAAA study to the 2004 Yankelovich study is complicated by differences in data collection, question wording, and measurement scaling, a worsening of attitudes is unmistakably clear nevertheless. The percentage with mixed opinions did not change, but the percentage holding a positive attitude declined from 41 percent to 28 percent and the percentage holding a negative attitude increased substantially from 14 percent to 36 percent.

The reason for this worsening of attitudes is no mystery. It is the exponentially greater level of marketing saturation and intrusiveness. In both the 1964 AAAA study and the 2004 Yankelovich study, respondents mentioned the same two principal benefits from marketing and advertising— the social benefit of helping the economy and the personal benefit of getting useful information. (In fact, perceptions of the information value of marketing increased from 1964 to 2004.) On the other hand, the top dislike of 1964 is now mentioned by more people than ever.

In 1964, the biggest complaint that consumers had about advertising was clutter and intrusiveness. Yet, this is the very thing that marketers have done with escalating frequency and intensity over the last forty years. For example, estimates of the number of ads, brand logos, and promotions to which an average person is exposed each day range from three thousand to five thousand, up several-fold from estimates of three hundred to five hundred during the 1970s. Unsurprisingly, then, the percentage of respondents complaining about clutter and intrusiveness has grown sizably, up from 40 percent in 1964 to 65 percent in 2004.

The fervor with which consumers are resisting marketing means a considerable impact on marketing productivity. Fifty-four percent of respondents in the 2004 Yankelovich study reported that they avoid buying products that overwhelm them with too much marketing, 60 percent described themselves as a person who tries to resist or avoid being exposed to marketing and advertising, and 69 percent said that they were interested in products to block, skip, or opt out of exposure to marketing and advertising. To put it another way, the size of the market for marketing resistance products is seven out of ten consumers.

Indeed, consumer resistance to marketing is a defining characteristic of today's marketplace. Contrast the huge percentage of self-confessed resisters in the 2004 Yankelovich survey with the mere 15 percent in the 1964 AAAA study who held the ardent opinion that advertising needed attention and change.[3]

Consumers have always had a love/hate relationship with marketing and advertising. Even as marketing resistance has grown to unprecedented proportions, consumers continue to enjoy entertaining ads and fun events sponsored by marketers. Paradoxically, consumers feel as much affection for marketing as dislike. (Or to put it another way, consumers love advertising but hate marketing.) This only seems like encouraging news. The proper balance between love and hate is a lot of the former and just a little of the latter; as it was forty-plus years ago. But not today.

The Yankelovich data show that while consumers feel the same as ever about the things they love about marketing and advertising, consumers now feel much more annoyed and aggravated by the things they hate about marketing and advertising. Intrusiveness is the culprit. Marketing and advertising have remained informative and entertaining while becoming omnipresent to the point of oversaturating every aspect of consumers' lives. The consumer response to this supersaturation is resistance.

But the proper way to look at the findings from the 2004 Yankelovich MONITOR OmniPlus study on consumer resistance to marketing is to look for opportunities to capture competitive advantage by delivering what consumers want and need. After all, this is how marketing works. Marketers solve problems for consumers. There's no reason why this shouldn't apply to marketing practice as much as to products and services.

THE MODEL IS BROKEN

The root of consumer resistance to marketing is not about bad marketing but about the basic way in which marketing works. The tactics of domination, saturation, and intrusiveness are standard marketing practices. Yet these tactics are the very things that consumers dislike the most. So, consumer resistance is symptomatic of the current marketing model.

Indeed, more often than not, bad marketing is nothing but standard marketing practice carried to an extreme. Arrogant spammers and telemarketers employ the customary practices of interruption and intrusiveness. The only difference is that they are more aggressive in putting these principles into action.

The results from the 2004 Yankelovich study show that marketing resistance has moved beyond the self-selection that is a standard element of the current marketing model. Marketers expect self-selection—if consumers don't care to watch an ad or some other form of marketing,

the current marketing model assumes that they will just ignore it, which is why marketing saturation and intrusiveness are normal practice. Saturation and intrusiveness are designed to penetrate
this veil of indifference and disinterest. Nowadays, however, consumers are unwilling to put up
with and uninterested in taking the time to sort through the barrage of marketing to find the few
messages that are relevant and worthwhile. Instead, with technology at their disposal, more consumers are just opting out of marketing exposure entirely.

The most important change is technology. In the past, whatever dissatisfaction consumers felt
about marketing and advertising, they lacked the means to do anything about it because marketers had all the power. Technology has completely altered that, yet the marketing model that
continues to guide marketing practice is based upon the old balance of power.

To put it more strongly, absent the new technologies, there would be no crisis of marketing
productivity. And these technologies will only get better, if for no other reason than the growing
demand for new and improved tools to resist marketing. Marketers who fight resistance with
more saturation and intrusiveness will lose the battle to the technologies of resistance.

But more than technology has changed. The ways in which consumers live and shop have
changed radically, too. American society is much more heterogeneous and consumer tastes are
much more splintered, which makes active involvement more important to consumers. It is the
only way that consumers can ensure that they get precisely what they want.

Consumers don't depend on marketing as much as before to learn about products and services.
Consumers are smarter than ever—literally, better educated—and have fingertip access to hundreds of sources of information. Consumers have more street smarts, too, having been schooled
by decades of exposure to every marketing trick in the book.

There was a time when advertising was an indispensable source of information. There was a
time when consumers could take time to linger and browse. There was a time when marketing
novelties were eye-catching and arresting. No longer.

Consumers' lifestyle expectations and aspirations have changed, too, and they have grown
accustomed to a more prosperous public life. Pantries, drawers, and driveways are filled with
more stuff than ever before. Consumers are looking for meaning and fulfillment beyond more
things to buy, so emotions, experiences, relationships, service, and aesthetics have become the
central sources of competitive advantage, while reliability, performance, durability, and functionality have come to be taken for granted. Consumers are demanding more from marketers than
great products. Consumers also want a better experience with the marketing for a product. Otherwise, they see marketing as an unnecessary, unwanted, and disagreeable imposition on their scarce
time and resources.

None of this is to suggest that consumers want to quit shopping. They don't. Marketing resistance does not presage an end to consumerism nor even a moderation of demand. Consumers
enjoy the comforts and satisfactions of the products they buy, and they want as much of that as
they can afford. But consumers no longer take it as a given that they must be at the mercy of
marketers in order to enjoy these things.

Consumers also do not want an end to marketing. Consumers understand that the answer to a
flood is not a drought. Consumers just want marketing that is less annoying, less intrusive, less
dominating, less saturating, and more respectful. Consumers want some relief from the dense
marketing smog that covers everything in their lives with a brand logo or a marketing come-on.
Consumers want a different marketing model.

The challenge for marketers is to find a new model that doesn't penalize them for changing
their marketing practices. No marketer should risk self-destruction by pulling back to the point of
hara-kiri. Certainly, results from the 2004 Yankelovich study on consumer resistance don't point

in that direction. Rather, the findings show clearly that marketing based on better principles will be more productive.

MAKING MARKETING PRODUCTIVE

The challenge for marketers is not making marketing work. Marketers are completely conversant in all the tricks of trade. But today, what marketers do to make marketing work doesn't always do so productively. In fact, it often reduces productivity. And marketing productivity is what counts because productivity is more important than efficacy alone when it comes to building value in a business. The issue at hand is getting a bigger bang for the buck.

Marketing productivity is measured as the customer response generated per marketing dollar spent. The consensus of evidence, both anecdotal and quantitative, is clear: marketing productivity is in rapid decline. A dollar spent today buys less response and a smaller audience than the same dollar spent yesterday. There are many factors at work. Specialized niche media have fragmented the audience, so media buying efficiencies have been significantly eroded. More competition has diluted the dominance and customer loyalty once enjoyed by many brands, so more has to be invested in sustaining relationships. Consumers are less dependent upon advertising for information, so advertisers have to invest more to get consumers to watch and read. Consumers are savvier and more knowledgeable about marketing tactics, so constant innovation is required. And marketing clutter has significantly increased, leading marketers to spend a lot more to try to be heard above the noise.

There is another factor as well—the growing consumer resistance to marketing. Consumer resistance is both a cause and an effect of the current productivity challenge. Overwhelmed with a growing deluge of ever more intrusive marketing, consumers have begun to adopt ways of insulating themselves from marketing. As consumer resistance has become more widespread and more sophisticated, marketers have saturated the marketplace with even more marketing. This cycle has created a feedback loop that is spiraling out of control. As more marketing chases more resistant consumers—or to put it another way, as spending rises while response declines—marketing productivity deteriorates at an accelerating rate.

Above all else, marketing resistance is the challenge that marketers need to tackle first. Marketing resistance is not the only cause of today's marketing productivity crisis, but it is now the single biggest barrier to resolving this crisis.

Most of the attention paid to declining marketing productivity focuses on rising costs. This is certainly important, but as long as consumers resist marketing, actions to address the other factors affecting marketing productivity will be piecemeal solutions. For example, reaching a fragmented audience in a more efficient way is essential because it reduces costs, but as long as viewers or readers are resisting the marketing that reaches them, declining marketing productivity will remain a problem. Costs may be reduced, but response will keep dropping.

This is not to suggest that every marketing campaign is unproductive. It is only to point out that the typical performance is below par. Individual marketers hope for breakthroughs notwithstanding the general underperformance of marketing as a whole. And while breakthroughs still happen, these are just exceptions that prove the rule.

Marketing saturation and intrusiveness even affect the trust that consumers have for brands. Too much marketing breeds dissatisfaction, annoyance, and pique, which in turn undermine the trust consumers feel for a brand. This worsens marketing productivity even more. A special Yankelovich MONITOR study on trust found a substantial financial impact from a loss of trust.[4] Ninety-four percent reported that they spend an average of 87 percent less money with companies they don't trust. Or put another way, when consumers lose trust in a company, they pretty much stop doing business with it. Consumers still spend as much in the marketplace as a whole, but not with that company.

Consumer resistance goes even further. In the 2004 Yankelovich study of consumers, 65 percent said that there should be more limits and regulations on marketing and advertising. Of those in favor of more limits, 43 percent preferred limits on times and places, 42 percent preferred limits on total amount, and 14 percent wanted a complete ban on any marketing that they did not agree to see ahead of time.

When asked where they would like to see advertising eliminated entirely, only e-mail (58 percent), public schools (55 percent), and mail (51 percent) were mentioned by a majority of consumers. However, large percentages mentioned other mainstream media and marketing vehicles. Rounding out the top ten were faxes (43 percent), cable TV (40 percent), movie previews (39 percent), Web sites (38 percent), public TV (36 percent), network TV (34 percent), and concerts (30 percent).

Consumers understand that changes in marketing entail trade-offs. Consumers don't want an end to marketing, but if that's the only possible alternative, then many are willing to live with the trade-offs. In exchange for no advertising or commercials, 61 percent of consumers are willing to do more research themselves to find out what's on sale, 41 percent are willing to pay for traditionally free media like network TV or radio, 33 percent are willing to accept a slightly lower standard of living, and 28 percent are willing to pay a significantly greater amount for magazines.

Clearly, large numbers of consumers are ready and willing to do business in a completely different way. These consumers are open to alternatives that enable them to live and shop marketing-free. So, at least for them, devising a new business model seems more far more sensible than continuing to saturate these consumers with more marketing.

For example, the growth of DVRs demonstrates that consumers are willing to pay for the ability to control their television viewing, especially the power to skip over ads. Technology consulting firm Forrester Research forecasts that in five years, over thirty million households will have DVRs, which is more than one-quarter of U.S. households, compared to three million today. And that number could be much higher as cable companies start offering DVRs in their set-top boxes (Olsen 2004).

Consumer resistance is the norm today, not the exception. No matter how well media and marketing are bought, allocated, and measured, marketing productivity will not improve until marketers are able to reengage consumers in more productive and profitable ways.

CONCURRENCE MARKETING

Marketers have a different opinion about the state of marketing than consumers. There is little concurrence. Consumers see a need for change whereas marketers see a need to be persistent and unwavering in their tactics of saturation and intrusiveness. In conjunction with the 2004 Yankelovich research among consumers, Yankelovich interviewed senior marketing directors to assess their take on the current state of marketing.[5] Many of the same questions asked of consumers were asked of these marketing directors.

Marketing directors agreed that there are serious challenges ahead. More clutter (83 percent), higher costs (77 percent), and increasing competition (76 percent) topped their list of concerns. These are the very elements responsible for declining marketing productivity. Yet, far fewer, only 43 percent, agreed that the productivity of marketing spending is declining. And at the very bottom of their list of concerns was consumer hostility to marketing, with a mere 27 percent citing it as a challenge.

Marketers understand the importance of demonstrating a financial return on marketing spending. Eighty-three percent cited it as a top priority. Yet 54 percent also said that the tools available to measure the impact of marketing programs are little better than rudimentary. Hamstrung by the tools available to them, marketers can't always see the impact of clutter, costs, and competition on marketing productivity. Which means that there is no assurance that marketers will address these problems in ways that boost productivity. If productivity is difficult to measure and quantify, more saturation to try to boost sales, which are easier to measure, is a more likely response than better marketing to reengage resistant consumers.

Marketing directors look at the challenges they face in ways that are process-centric not consumer-centric. Clutter, costs, and competition are seen as marketing execution issues related to tactical processes. Most marketers do not believe that they are facing any serious problems with consumers or, even more importantly, any basic challenges to the fundamental model of marketing.

Consumers want things from marketing that marketers don't even recognize as problems. Consumers want more *precision.* Sixty-five percent of consumers agreed that they are bombarded with too much marketing and 52 percent wanted less marketing. Only 8 percent of marketing directors thought that there should be less marketing. In other words, consumers are complaining about the imprecision of marketing saturation while marketers want even more saturation.

The same lack of concurrence is true for *relevance.* Fifty-nine percent of consumers agreed that very little of the marketing to which they are exposed is relevant to them, compared to just one-third of marketing directors who said that most marketing is not genuinely relevant to consumers.

Consumers want more precision and relevance. These are the fundamental elements of sound marketing practice, so it seems almost gratuitous to mention the need for precision and relevance. Yet, consumers are not giving marketers a passing grade on these basic lessons of marketing 101.

Not only do consumers want more of the basics, they want new things as well. To begin with, consumers want *power.* Traditionally, marketers have controlled all of the power. While marketers have been focused on consumers in order to ascertain their needs and wants, marketers have always managed the processes by which consumers have been understood and serviced. Now, consumers want complete control, and they don't feel that they have it. A majority of consumers, 53 percent, said that they are still at the mercy of marketers. In contrast, only 38 percent of marketers thought that consumers should have more control over the content and timing of marketing.

Consumers want *reciprocity,* too. Consumers want to be rewarded for the time and attention they give to marketing. Consumers want more than the value delivered by the product, which is to say that consumers do not want the value they receive to be wholly dependent upon making a purchase. They want value from the marketing experience, too. Yet, 62 percent of consumers said that marketers do not give them enough respect. Which is reflected in the mere 13 percent of marketing directors who thought it would be a good idea to compensate consumers for their time and attention.

Even if marketers don't reciprocate by paying consumers cash for the time they spend with marketing, marketers must do more to compensate them, such as providing truly engaging entertainment, not just jingles. Or truly meaningful information, not more product pitches. Or truly helpful tools, not more selling. Consumers will be more receptive to marketing if they are rewarded in real-time for their time and attention.

With time at more of a premium than ever before, reciprocity must become central to the practice of marketing. This is not about timesaving products. It's about marketing that provides real value in return for time and attention. It's about marketing that makes time better. It's about marketing that is worth it. Marketing practices have to measure up to the value that consumers place on their time.

Marketing abounds with creativity, inspiration, and invention. But the most common ways of putting marketing genius to work today ride roughshod over the fundamentals of precise targeting and relevant positioning, and in doing so, give little, if any, thought to sharing power with consumers or to rewarding them for paying attention. Concurrence marketing based on the principles of P&R^2 is the best way of putting marketing talent to work.

Concurrence means putting consumers in charge, not keeping them on the receiving end as respondents or targets. This is more than just a fancy way of saying the consumer is king. Currently, marketers put consumers first while keeping control through saturation marketing. Concurrence means making consumers at least coequal with marketers, if not more.

Control from the top down is especially problematic when the marketplace is in continual flux. Today, too many things are changing at too fast a rate for a traditional hierarchy of control to be in command of the situation. The marketplace has become so dynamic that it is more than merely evolving; it is protean. It is constantly assuming new shapes and forms. All aspects of the marketplace are caught up in this—the brisk cycling of new products, the fickle nature of consumer preferences, the shifting boundaries of personal and demographic identities, the shooting stars of popular culture, the nonstop deluge of technological upgrades and innovations, and more. The character of the marketplace demands an approach that is more collaborative in which consumers can satisfy their own rapidly changing needs rather than waiting for the marketers, who are always a step behind, to catch up. Pull, not push, will grease the wheels of tomorrow's commerce.

Dominance and control are enforced by practicing and policing marketing as a one-way street. Marketers control the process and make all of the decisions. Consumers take their cues from marketers. Marketers produce. Consumers buy. Marketers listen and observe. Consumers view and react. Everything starts with marketers and then goes in one direction—from marketers *to* consumers.

Getting permission from consumers is a step in the right direction. But permission-based marketing is not enough. Permission raises the bar, yet the typical way in which permission marketing is practiced today does not measure up. Too often, the character of the marketing that follows the grant of permission tends to be exactly what consumers were hoping to escape. Furthermore, once permission is asked for and received, the question is rarely asked again. So, having granted permission, consumers find that, de facto, they are back in the opt-out world they were trying to escape. Permission may seem like a new type of relationship, but when it entails the same marketing as before and puts consumers back in an opt-out position, permission is nothing different.

Most marketing models, new and old, fall short of what consumers now want. The classic hierarchy of effects model, in particular, embraces saturation and intrusiveness. The chain of effects begins with brand awareness, which is built by an overwhelming presence. More awareness is achieved by even greater presence, and that means even more saturation. Competition can diminish presence and awareness, so the model prescribes boosting share of voice, which leads to yet more saturation.

When only a few marketers were competing for time and attention, marketing saturation was not a problem. But now with so many more—and more aggressive—competitors, the classic model no longer works as productively as before. The way to stand out in a supersaturated, highly competitive marketplace is to operate in a distinctive way that invites notice rather than demands center stage. When consumers learn that the only things they will ever hear from a company are things that are directly pertinent and relevant to their interests, they will pay more attention instead of figuring that it's nothing but more clutter.

Marketing is more productive when consumers are seeking out brands than when brands are seeking out consumers. This takes brand charisma. Brands must be lightning rods for emotions and excitement. The easiest way to do that is for a brand to show that it cares more about its consumers than itself. Brands must be advocates for consumers, not rivals for time and attention. Brands must show they care enough to make a sacrifice if that's the best thing for consumers.

Being in sync and being collaborative do that. Through the principles of P&R^2, concurrence marketing makes brands magnetic in their appeal and allure.

In short, consumers are demanding concurrence from marketers. Not as a threat, but as a willingness to do more business with marketers who concur with their attitudes and preferences about what constitutes good marketing. Marketing practices can create enduring competitive advantage for concurrent marketers.

ADDRESSABLE ATTITUDES

If marketers are to succeed in making the shift to concurrence, new tools and organizations will be needed. Current tools and organizations were developed to support and execute marketing saturation In particular, notwithstanding the centrality of consumer to marketing, current tools and organizations put processes ahead of consumers. No surprise, then, that consumer desires for precision, relevance, power, and reciprocity have gone unheeded, and often unheard.

The essential tool for truly putting consumers ahead of processes is that of addressable attitudes. *Addressable attitudes are attitudes that can be linked to individual names and addresses.* When attitudes are addressable, they can be incorporated into all of the databases and systems used for marketing execution, ranging from media buying databases to third-party lists to internal transaction files. When addressable, the attitudes that provide perspective and context for behaviors and demographics can speak with a voice at the individual level.[6]

In the past, demographics and behavioral models sufficed for marketing execution. The inherent imprecision and irrelevance of using demographics to buy media or to select direct mail lists was acceptable because consumers were willing to take on the task of self-selection. The centralized, hierarchical process of control was unable to share power or provide reciprocity not only because it operated in a one-way manner, but also because there were no means of operating any other way. All of this has now changed, so consumer attitudes about needs, preferences, desires, and wants must become central to tactical marketing execution and not just be a broad strategic concern that is a step or two removed from applied marketing practice.

Despite all of the information contained in marketing and media databases, there has been a complete absence of any data about consumer attitudes. This is the biggest gap in marketing, and it forces marketers to live with unproductive imprecision and irrelevance. Historically, direct marketers have focused only on addressability and thus have tried to get by with limited insights into motivations. Brand marketers have always known a lot about motivations but have had no means of pinpointing consumers with particular attitudes.

Addressable attitudes bring together the best of brand marketing and direct marketing by combining the addressability of direct marketing with the attitudinal insights of brand marketing. The productivity of brand marketing is improved through addressability. The productivity of direct marketing is improved through attitudes. Marketing as a whole comes together because addressable attitudes provide a universal platform that works across all forms of marketing. No longer must different types of marketing work with different tools and information.

With addressable attitudes, marketers can reengage resistant consumers. Marketing can be targeted toward consumers who are interested in a particular product instead of consumers with a certain demographic profile, only some of whom are interested. Marketing can be formulated and delivered in a way that is directly relevant to the attitudes, needs, and motivations of specific consumers. Addressable attitudes re-center marketers around insights into what consumers think and want. And what consumers want is power and reciprocity, so integrating these insights into marketing systems would significantly improve the overall tenor of marketplace relationships. In the marketplace of today and tomorrow, the new tool of addressable attitudes is required for marketing organizations to be genuinely insight-centric.

The new organization to complement the new tool is the insight-centric marketing organization (ICO), in which everything follows from insights. Processes and databases have no standing or value apart from insights. In an ICO, processes are not important in and of themselves but only as they fulfill or satisfy what insights reveal about consumers needs, preferences, and attitudes. An ICO puts consumer insights at the center of everything.

Unlike a traditional marketing and sales organization or even a more contemporary customer relationship organization, an ICO is able to practice concurrence marketing. By centering the organization on the insights provided by the study and scoring of addressable attitudes, an ICO will adopt a structure that embodies the essence of concurrence marketing—making the company subordinate to consumers. And when consumers are in charge, they take only what's pertinent and meaningful to them, and marketers are obliged to provide whatever power and reciprocity consumers demand.

If consumer insights are not made central to a marketing organization, then old habits and established processes will continue to predominate. The addressable attitudes tool makes everything in a marketing organization revolve around consumer insights. When attitudes can be infused into all aspects of marketing, from strategy to tactics, consumer insights are assured of coming first, no longer to be ignored or omitted from the everyday operation of marketing processes.

GETTING CONCURRENT

Concurrent marketers are made, not born. Above all else, achieving concurrence takes addressable attitudes and an insight-centric organization. With these tools and organizational structures, the principles of $P\&R^2$ can reengage resistant consumers and reverse the steep, continuing declines in marketing productivity.

The future practice of marketing must be different than that of the past. Marketing has become the white noise of modern life, a background hum left over from the big bang of sixty years of consumerism to which the law of entropy now applies. Without new thinking and fresh energy, it won't be long before it all goes cold.

NOTES

1. This study was a 15-minute recontact telephone interview from February 20 to 29, 2004, among 601 nationally representative empanelled MONITOR 2003 respondents, sixteen-plus years of age. MONITOR, begun in 1971, is the pioneering and longest running tracking of consumer values and lifestyles.

2. This study was a door-to-door survey among a nationally representative sample of 1,846 respondents. It is described more fully in Bauer and Greyser (1968).

3. The authors of the 1964 AAAA study noted that even this 15 percent figure was probably too high an estimate of the size of support for governmental regulatory action (see pp. 383–84). Which means that the size of active resistance today is an even greater multiple of the past.

4. This study was a 22-minute Internet survey from April 6 to April 13, 2004, among a nationally representation sample of 2,606 respondents, ages eighteen-plus, conducted in partnership with the FGI SmartPanel® of MONITOR-coded Internet panelists.

5. This study was a telephone survey from March 19 to April 19, 2004, among senior marketing directors at 153 consumer marketing companies across the full range of company sizes and business categories.

6. Yankelovich introduced the first addressable attitudes product with MindBase and now offers a full range of syndicated and custom addressable attitudes products and solutions.

REFERENCES

Arlen, Gary (2002), "Cache and Cachet, but with a Catch," *Broadband Week*, June 3.

Bauer, Raymond, and Stephen Greyser (1968), *Advertising in America: The Consumer View*. Boston: Harvard Business School Press.

Economist (2000), "A Farewell to Ads?" April 17.

Olsen, Stefanie (2004), "Advertisers Face Up to TiVo Reality," CNET, News.com, April 26.

CHAPTER 3

THE IMAGE OF MARKETING

JAGDISH N. SHETH, RAJENDRA S. SISODIA, AND ADINA BARBULESCU

MARKETING'S IMAGE PROBLEMS

The evidence is increasingly incontrovertible: marketing has a serious and deepening image problem with most of its constituents, external as well as internal. These include customers, the public at large, public watchdog groups, other internal business functions (e.g., R&D, engineering, finance, legal, senior management), chief executive officers, and boards of directors.

Many marketers view today's customers as increasingly capricious: fickle, cynical, disloyal. If they are, can we blame them? Customers have evolved these defense mechanisms as a natural reaction to decades of marketing manipulation, noise, and sheer excess. Through long experience with never-ending sales gimmicks and marketing's history of overpromising and underdelivering, customers have become trained to be highly deal-prone and deeply cynical about marketing claims. Offensive marketing creates defensive, suspicious customers with low and declining brand loyalty, and little tolerance for underperformance. Such customers switch suppliers at the smallest provocation, as evidenced by high churn rates in many industries.

Customers today also have more knowledge, and thus power, than they ever did in the past. In part, this is due to the sheer availability of objective information, which simply did not exist even in the recent past. Lacking any trust in marketers to tell them the truth, customers increasingly feel the need to arm themselves with as much unbiased information as possible. Through the Internet, customers today are also engaged in a never-ending dialogue with each other, answering each other's questions, and guiding each other toward better purchasing decisions, entirely independent of marketers' efforts.

To many traditional marketers, with their antagonistic view of customers, this knowledge is deeply threatening; it allows customers to win every round, to get a better deal with them each time. For more enlightened marketers, however, knowledgeable customers are an advantage, a source of strength and comfort. If a company is confident that it is delivering good quality and value, it can leverage its customers' knowledge and expertise to mutual advantage in numerous ways.

How Marketing Is Viewed

Evidence abounds of growing cynicism among customers, even as companies have invested billions of dollars implementing ambitious CRM (customer relationship management) automation projects hoping to transform themselves into customer-focused enterprises. Customers' trust in the marketing function is lower than ever; especially in the consumer market, few consumers regard themselves as truly being in a relationship with the companies they do business with. For example, a survey by the U.K.-based Marketing Forum/Consumers' Association (cited in Mitchell 2001) found of consumers that:

- 83 percent agreed with the statement that: "As a consumer, companies just see me as someone with money to spend."
- 76 percent agreed that "Many companies see their brands as a way of pushing up prices."
- 78 percent agreed that "Companies like to pretend that their brands are really different, but actually there's rarely any substantial difference between them."
- 70 percent agreed that "I don't trust most advertising of products or services because they're just trying to sell me something."

Hopefully, marketers have at least earned the respect of their colleagues from other functional areas who recognize the difficulty of their challenges, right? Wrong! A survey of how executives from other business functions view the performance of their marketing colleagues found (Mitchell 2001):

- Only 38 percent rated their marketing colleagues as good or excellent.
- Only 18 percent considered marketing executives to be results-oriented (while 71 percent of the marketers perceived themselves in that manner).
- Only 34 percent viewed marketers as strategic thinkers.

DIMENSIONS OF MARKETING'S IMAGE PROBLEM

There is something ironic about the predicament that marketing finds itself in. Marketers are known to be image builders, renowned for their ability to "make a silk purse out of a sow's ear." Over the past few decades, marketing professionals have managed to use the very skills of their livelihood to largely erode their own credibility. How is it that marketing itself is in need of an image makeover (MacDonald 2003)?

Marketing continues to accumulate enormous amounts of negative connotations that, at the current rate, will soon render it a purely derogatory word. This is the direct result of the actions of marketers across the board. Companies have been engaged in harmful practices toward consumers at seemingly unstoppable rates, and consumers have grown weary of ever more egregious attempts to trick them out of their hard-earned money (Santoni 2003). Phony "going out of business" sales, weekly trumpeting of "lowest prices of the year," pyramid schemes, dubious dietary supplements, marketing products known to be harmful—such practices abound because marketing executives are seemingly exempt from responsibility. To justify their lack of liability, marketing executives often claim that corporations are not moral agents and blame increased competitive pressures (Mascarenhas 1995). This attitude suggests that the time may have come to require marketing executives to personally sign off on all aspects of a firm's marketing efforts, just as chief executives now have to personally attest to the validity of their company's financial statements.

One of the biggest contributors to marketing's image problems has been telemarketing. Cheaper computers and long-distance telephony and the ability to locate operations in low-cost locations around the world have decreased the costs of teleselling (for it is not marketing) and escalated the costs to society in wasted time and fraud to the tune of $40 billion a year (FBI.gov). Most telemarketers have little concern for the costs to others as a result of their efforts, and ethical guidelines governing interactions with customers are practically nonexistent (Rosen 2003). Customers have bought devices (with names such as Telezapper and Phone Butler) and paid for services (such as CallWave's Telemarketing Blocking Service) to shield themselves from unwanted calls. Not only is the vast majority of telemarketing annoying and intrusive, a great deal of it is fraudulent. The United States National Fraud Information Center lists fifty different categories of telemarketing fraud, including advance fee loans, telephone company switching, prizes and sweepstakes, work-at-home schemes, pay-per-call services, magazine sales, and fake charities (see www.fraud.org). Telemarketing firms have gone a long way toward imbuing society with the idea that marketing in general is inherently exploitative. Their actions have directly impacted those who attempt to conduct marketing in an ethical way. As is usually the case when an industry fails to adequately police itself, society responds with severe measures. In the United States, the response to the government's "Do Not Call" initiative has been overwhelming, with over fifty-five million phone numbers registered by the end of 2003 (Federal Trade Commission 2004). Under this initiative, companies have 31 days after a phone number is registered to "scrub" their lists, or face penalties that can run to several hundred thousand dollars.

Another major contributor to marketing's poor image has been indiscriminate marketing to children (Linn 2004). Few marketers seem to apply the Golden Rule to their own behavior: would they want their own children exposed to the kind of marketing they are putting out there? Inappropriate marketing to children is a vast area, including fast food, snacks, movies, music, video games, television programs, magazines, and clothing. In each case, the products are physically or psychologically harmful, and they are marketed in aggressive, offensive, and harmful ways. Parents find themselves in continuous battle with marketers, and few are up to the challenge. Parents understandably do not want their young children exposed to sex, violence, and alcohol. Companies covertly introduce violence in products ranging from video games to music. Publications such as *Seventeen, Young Cosmo,* and *Teen People* feature many sexual themes and marketers are quick to advertise in them. Marketers are very aware that children want to appear and act older than they are and consciously target children who are too young for their offerings.

CAUSES OF MARKETING'S IMAGE PROBLEMS

So why do we have these problems in marketing? We strongly believe it is because of a fundamental failure of *marketers* to live up to *marketing*'s ideals. The marketer's job is to align the interest of the customer and the company. However, too often that doesn't happen and neither companies nor customers benefit from marketers' actions. At other times, marketers do things that benefit the company while potentially harming customers or they do things that allow savvy customers to take advantage of the company.

There are several reasons why marketing has come to this pass. First, rising competitive intensity has caused many marketers to cut corners in an increasingly desperate effort to stay afloat amidst a sea of look-alike competitors. Second, most marketers are highly imitative in their actions, and virtually every marketing tactic ever conceived loses its effectiveness with overuse. Third, financial pressures for short-term performance have grown, and marketers have responded with actions (such as excessive sales promotions) that may show immediate (i.e., end-of-quarter) results but have negative long-term consequences. Finally, the performance and image of marketers have actually been harmed rather than helped by the march of technology. Technological developments in telemarketing and e-mail marketing have made these widely abused tools far more efficient than ever before; the problem is that they are also becoming dramatically less effective. Overusing an ineffective resource simply because it is increasingly affordable is an efficient way to alienate large numbers of customers!

Marketing and the Tragedy of the Commons

Marketing's fundamental dilemma is analogous to a "tragedy of the commons." When many people use a common resource, the resource gets overused and ultimately destroyed. For example, consider the case of herdsmen raising cattle on common land. Each of them is a profit-maximizing individual who has the choice of adding animals into that common. The benefit is that they each get the full profit from that animal. The downside, of course, is that there is additional grazing of the common resource. The incentives align in a way to cause every farmer to add more and more animals, resulting in extreme overgrazing and the eventual destruction of the commons.

The analogy with marketing is clear. Our "commons" is the limited attention span of consumers. Collectively, we are vastly "overgrazing" this commons, with the net result that even messages of relevance have a difficult time getting through (Sisodia and Backer 2004).

Economics Nobel laureate Herbert Simon said, "What information consumes is obvious: It consumes the attention of its recipients. So, a wealth of information creates a poverty of attention and the need to allocate that attention efficiently" (Simon 1971). That's what we have, a wealth of marketing information, if you can call it that, and, therefore, consumers will not pay attention to even the right information that they might benefit from, because they simply don't have the time, or there's too much to filter through. There are many reasons why this happens, including the tragedy of the commons. But one of the interesting ones is that the costs are artificially low. The postal service, in fact, subsidizes junk mail by keeping first class postage rates higher. Likewise with e-mail "marketing," which is so cheap that companies can send ten million e-mails for a few hundred dollars. As a result, there is a strong tendency to overuse, and therefore abuse, this medium.

The impact of overmarketing is that people become indifferent. It is similar to overusing an antibiotic; the condition being treated ultimately develops resistance, and the treatment no longer works for anyone.

THE STUDY

To investigate attitudes toward marketing and many of its common practices, we conducted a survey of consumers and business professionals in late 2003. Students working toward their MBAs at Bentley College (Waltham, MA) and Emory University (Atlanta, GA) were asked to use their personal and professional contacts in the online survey. There were three survey instruments: one each for consumers, marketing professionals, and nonmarketing professionals. The surveys consisted of approximately thirty questions, including numerical as well as open-ended qualitative questions. Approximately two thousand surveys were completed, roughly half from business professionals and half from consumers. The business professionals were split in approximately equal numbers between marketing and other functional areas.

Consumers

One of the questions we asked was for respondents to indicate the first five words that came to mind when they thought of "marketing." We then classified these words as negative, neutral or descriptive, and positive. Each respondent's attitude toward marketing was then assessed by developing a score based on these responses. Overall, 65 percent of 973 consumer respondents had a negative attitude toward marketing, about 27 percent were neutral, and only 8 percent were positive. Thus, our findings show an even more negative attitude toward marketing than those of

Table 3.1

Overall Reputations of Professions (1: Terrible; 5: Excellent)

	Mean	Negative (%)	Neutral (%)	Positive (%)
College professors	4.04	5.0	13.6	81.3
Schoolteachers	4.03	5.7	17.4	76.9
Doctors	3.93	5.7	17.6	76.6
Pharmacists	3.82	5.2	25.5	69.4
Accountants	3.22	21.8	36.1	42.1
CEOs (chief executive officers)	2.99	34.7	31.6	33.7
CFOs (chief financial officers)	2.98	35.1	30.9	34.0
Advertising	2.93	31.1	42.2	26.7
Public relations	2.85	34.0	43.8	22.2
Marketers	2.74	38.0	41.9	20.1
Real estate brokers	2.71	39.6	44.4	16.1
Stockbrokers	2.62	44.2	40.8	15.0
Customer service representatives	2.59	48.7	32.9	18.4
Lawyers	2.56	53.3	23.6	23.1
Sales people	2.41	56.4	36.0	7.6
Politicians	1.82	83.4	12.3	4.3
Telemarketing	1.40	91.2	6.9	1.9

Yankelovich in chapter 2 in this volume, which found that approximately 60 percent of consumers had a negative view of marketing.

We expected that respondents with an MBA or other business degree would hold a much more positive view of marketing. After all, unlike the lay public, these individuals have taken at least one marketing course, and would thus be expected to have a greater appreciation for the value and importance of marketing. Such was not the case; only 10 percent had a positive view, while 62 percent were negative. So the overall image of marketing is not very positive, to say the least.

Some of the positive connotations that consumers associate with marketing are creativity, fun, humorous advertising, and attractive people. The negative associations are many, led by telemarketing. Some of the more frequent words include lies, deception, deceitful, annoying, manipulating, gimmicks, exaggeration, invasive, intrusive, and brainwashing.

We asked consumers how they viewed the reputations of different professions, and these results are shown in Table 3.1. We broke out advertising and sales people and some of the other components within marketing as separate professions or occupations. Overall, marketers have a pretty weak reputation, while advertising and public relations come out a little higher. The reputation of sales people is considerably below that of marketers, and is only higher than politicians and telemarketers.

We asked respondents for their views about many common marketing practices, and classified them into negative, neutral, and positive. These results are shown in Table 3.2.

Consumers hold negative attitudes toward many common marketing practices; for example, 94 percent are negative toward telemarketing, and only 2.7 percent are positive. Other marketing practices at the bottom include online pop-up ads (92.2 percent negative) and junk mail (87 percent negative). In general, we may term these three practices "junk marketing." A number of marketing practices are quite positively viewed, which is not a surprise. Consumers enjoy receiving free samples, and most people like Super Bowl ads. Of course, this begs the question of whether a Super Bowl ad is always the right thing to do from the marketer's perspective. Even if viewers are amused by it, is that the right way to spend your limited marketing resources? Perhaps

Table 3.2

Consumer Attitudes Toward Common Marketing Practices

	Negative (%)	Neutral (%)	Positive (%)
Free samples	6.2	14.2	79.6
Advertising during Super Bowl	6.3	15.2	78.5
Airline frequent flyer programs	9.0	28.6	62.4
Frequent user programs in general	12.3	28.9	58.8
Grocery coupons	15.0	27.9	57.1
Department store coupons in newspapers	17.6	24.6	57.8
Packaging innovations, e.g., "fun" size candy bars	13.9	37.9	48.2
"Every day fair pricing" (no sales)	17.7	38.7	43.6
Supermarket "frequent shopper" cards	24.7	23.2	52.0
Noncommissioned sales people	22.1	34.2	43.6
Continuous sales (stores that always have a sale running)	36.4	29.4	34.2
Advertising of prescription pharmaceuticals (TV, magazines)	37.9	33.7	28.4
Sales stating "lowest prices of the year"	48.0	29.1	22.8
Mail-in rebates	52.0	20.6	27.4
Music/video/book "clubs"	46.4	33.0	20.6
Sales people that work on commission	51.0	31.2	17.8
Advertising during children's programs	48.8	38.5	12.7
Fees for service plans (e.g., guarantees and warranties)	52.3	28.8	18.9
Shipping charges	50.9	37.3	11.8
Sales that only last one or two hours	64.8	18.7	16.5
Sweepstakes (e.g., Publishers Clearinghouse)	62.9	25.3	11.7
Third class mail that resembles "real" mail	87.0	10.3	2.7
Internet pop-up ads	92.2	5.3	2.6
Telemarketing calls	94.2	3.1	2.7

not. But because of the amount of creativity that goes into those, people do usually enjoy them, and, in fact, many people (especially women) watch the Super Bowl primarily for that reason. Frequent flyer programs, and frequent user programs in general, are popular with consumers. As marketing tools, there is much evidence that they can be double-edged swords, raising the cost of doing business without necessarily increasing loyalty. Some people carry fifteen or more frequent shopper cards in their wallet, including eight airlines and four supermarkets. So having a frequent user program may not accomplish a marketing objective.

We asked about consumer attitudes toward pricing practices in a number of popular product categories. As Table 3.3 shows, about half of the pricing situations we presented to consumers resulted in an overall positive attitude, half in a negative attitude. With products such as inkjet cartridges and legal services, people don't see a relationship between what they pay and what they get in terms of value received.

We found a number of interesting demographic patterns in the data. Some of these are:

- Older consumers are distinctly more cynical and jaded when it comes to marketing programs, especially sales promotions. As the population ages, and the median age of adults crosses forty-five, these negative attitudes will become the dominant ones, and marketers will have to respond by reducing their reliance on gimmickry.
- Women are more likely than men to watch and listen to most TV ads. They are less likely than men to "surf" (switch channels when ads come on), and more likely to leave the room

Table 3.3

Opinions on Pricing (1: Unrelated to Value Received; 5: Reasonable for Value Received)

	Mean	Negative (%)	Neutral (%)	Positive (%)
Computers	3.65	7.9	32.5	59.6
Consumer electronics (e.g., TVs)	3.54	9.6	37.0	53.4
Grocery items	3.44	14.3	38.1	47.6
Books	3.38	18.3	32.8	49.0
Household appliances	3.33	11.8	49.8	38.4
Office supplies	3.18	19.6	46.5	34.1
Clothes	3.16	24.3	38.7	37.0
Airline tickets	3.08	27.0	38.1	34.9
Over-the-counter drugs	2.99	29.9	40.4	29.6
Home maintenance services	2.77	37.2	42.4	20.3
CDs	2.75	42.3	31.0	26.7
Prescription drugs	2.52	53.0	26.8	20.2
Add-on warranties	2.51	47.2	34.7	18.1
Legal services	2.43	53.7	31.8	14.6
Replacement razor blade cartridges	2.39	52.6	34.1	13.2
Replacement inkjet cartridges	2.28	59.5	27.3	13.1

when ads come on. Nonwhites watch more ads, are less likely to press the "mute" button when ads come on, and are less likely to leave the room when ads come on.

- Whites have a stronger preference than nonwhites (67 percent versus 55 percent) for stores that offer "everyday fair prices" or those that have sales only occasionally over stores that have continuous or very frequent sales.

Business Professionals

We were interested in learning about how marketing and nonmarketing professionals differ in their views of marketing's importance to the corporation, its control over areas commonly perceived to be part of the "marketing mix," and its relationship with other business functions.

We asked both categories of professionals to indicate how senior management views the marketing function. We found a very high degree of concurrence on this question, as Table 3.4 shows. We asked respondents how they personally viewed the importance of marketing, and here we found a significant difference, with marketing professionals rating marketing's importance much higher. Both marketing and nonmarketing professionals regard sales to be the most important business function of all. Marketing professionals view marketing to be the next most vital function (only slightly less important than sales), while nonmarketing professionals ranked it eighth! In terms of productivity (efficiency and effectiveness), marketing professionals had a significantly more positive view of marketing's performance than did nonmarketers.

We also asked business professionals the same question about reputations that we asked of consumers; the only significant difference is in terms of how they view marketers; marketing professionals hold their own profession in significantly higher esteem than do nonmarketing professionals (see Table 3.4). This is consistent with a theme in this book and in the literature that *marketing* is critical, but *marketers* have been doing a poor job living up to its ideals.

Next, we asked respondents to indicate the extent to which marketing has control or influence over activities that relate to the marketing mix, as well the extent to which marketing *should* have

Table 3.4

Differences Between Marketing and Nonmarketing Professionals

	Marketing Professionals	Nonmarketing Professionals	Difference
Senior managementt view of marketing	3.88	3.92	−0.04
Importance of marketing function	4.46	3.98	**0.48**
Importance of sales function	4.54	4.51	0.03
Efficiency of marketing function	3.62	3.21	**0.41**
Effectiveness of marketing function	3.85	3.56	**0.29**
Reputation of marketers	3.40	2.94	**0.46**
Reputation of advertising	3.18	3.17	0.01
Reputation of sales people	2.57	2.46	0.11
Reputation of CEOs	3.53	3.42	0.11
Reputation of CFOs	3.41	3.41	0.00

Note: Bold numbers indicate significant differences.

control. Higher scores indicate a higher degree of control by marketing (see Table 3.5).

The following patterns are noteworthy:

- Marketing professionals believe that marketing needs to have more influence and control over each of the areas listed. The largest areas of concern, where marketing is seen as not having the influence it should, are setting R&D priorities, compensating members, channel selection, setting prices and discounts, and determining the product mix.
- Nonmarketing professionals believe that marketing should have more control over these areas, but by very small margins. For the most part, they appear to hold the view that marketing's influence is about where it needs to be in most of these areas.
- Marketing and nonmarketing professionals show clear and significant differences in terms of how much influence marketing should have in all of these areas. The domains of greatest disagreement are determining the product mix and setting list prices, followed by the related areas of initiating product modifications and determining price discounts.

Clearly, the marketing function has not convinced the rest of the organization about the wisdom of granting it greater control over the elements of the marketing mix. This reflects the widely acknowledged diminished role of marketing within many corporations.

Next, we wanted to probe marketing's relationship with other functional areas (see Table 3.6). We asked respondents to describe the nature of marketing's relationship with each business function, with a score of 1 indicating a "Highly Antagonistic" relationship and 5 a "Highly Cooperative" one.

The following patterns are evident in the data:

- Overall, marketers perceive themselves as having stronger relationships with other functional areas than vice versa.
- Two exceptions to the first perception are sales and public relations. Particularly in the case of sales, nonmarketing professionals perceive a much closer relationship than marking professionals believe to exist.
- Major areas of difference are information technology and customer support. In both cases, marketers see themselves in stronger relationships than do professionals from other functional areas.

Table 3.5

Differences Regarding Marketing Activities

	Marketing respondents			Nonmarketing respondents			Difference between marketing and nonmarketing (should have)
	Marketing has control	Should have control	Difference	Marketing has control	Should have control	Difference	
Advertising	4.31	4.52	0.21	4.25	4.31	0.06	0.21
Promotional tactics	4.23	4.44	0.21	4.17	4.15	-0.02	0.29
Creating product collateral	3.99	4.29	0.30	3.70	3.75	0.05	0.54
Product mix	3.75	4.18	0.43	3.43	3.58	0.15	0.60
Channel selection	3.55	4.11	0.56	3.61	3.69	0.08	0.42
Setting list prices	3.47	3.90	0.43	3.13	3.30	0.17	0.60
Product modifications	3.39	3.90	0.51	3.21	3.40	0.19	0.50
Setting price discounts	3.28	3.80	0.52	3.21	3.31	0.10	0.49
Channel compensation	3.17	3.70	0.53	3.34	3.48	0.14	0.22
Setting R&D priorities	2.91	3.67	0.76	3.13	3.23	0.10	0.44

Table 3.6

Differences Regarding Marketing Relationships with Other Functions

	Marketing professionals' view	Nonmarketing professionals' view	Difference
Public relations	4.28	4.44	–0.16
Business development	4.13	4.05	0.08
Sales	4.04	4.46	**–0.42**
Customer support	3.80	3.50	**0.30**
R&D	3.52	3.32	0.20
IT (information technology)	3.20	2.93	**0.27**
Operations/Manufacturing	3.11	2.94	0.17
Human resources	3.02	2.92	0.10
Legal	2.97	2.74	**0.23**
Finance	2.88	2.63	**0.25**
Mean rating	**3.50**	**3.39**	0.11

Note: Bold numbers indicate significant differences.

- Marketing's relationship with finance is very weak, and this belief is held even more strongly by nonmarketing professionals than marketing professionals. In an era of increasing financial accountability, this should be an area of major concern.

NEEDED: AN EXTREME MAKEOVER

Our research on the image of marketing indicates that the marketing profession needs to urgently address its trust and credibility gaps with customers as well as within the corporation and in society at large. In a later chapter in the volume, we present some ideas on how to reform marketing. The following are some guidelines that deal specifically with the image of marketing:

Rethink marketing's objective function: The objective function of marketing needs to start with a benefit to customers. For example, Internet search engine Google undertakes no new initiative without first assessing its impact on its users and its advertisers. The company's genius lies in coming up with innovations that simultaneously add value to users as well as advertisers and by thinking of advertising as a service to users. Likewise, any new marketing initiative should also be assessed for its impact on customer trust and marketer credibility. Many marketing "gimmicks" may be effective in the short run, but have the effect of eroding trust and credibility in the long run. Such actions must be avoided.

Reform marketing's language: The language of marketers has become thoroughly debased. "Marketer-speak" has become synonymous with shallow, insincere doublespeak. The fine print in advertisements and the "rapid speak" at the end of radio and television ads are the most tangible representations of this. Man cannot live by hype alone, but that seems to be the only currency many marketers know. Ultimately, being enveloped in nonstop hype deadens the soul and takes the joy out of life. Marketers must learn to communicate with customers in a straightforward and sincere way. They have to start saying what they mean and meaning what they say.

Use exemplary marketing as a differentiator: Marketing's poor image today is an opportunity for some companies to stand out by addressing customer perceptions head-on. Essentially, these companies say, "We are customers too, and here is how we like to be treated." For example, Jordan's Furniture, the most successful furniture retailer in the country, refers in its radio advertising to how most mattress marketers mislead customers, and how its "sleep technicians" are different. CarMax, which is transforming automobile retailing, educates customers about the tactics used by traditional dealers. Our hope is that the standards of marketing practice gradually improve to a point that such dishonest approaches would no longer work. Companies would then compete on a higher plane.

Learn to communicate with women: The marketing profession has a particular problem with women. It could truly be said that "marketers are from Mars, customers are from Venus." More and more product categories today are dominated by women customers. Yet very few companies communicate with women in an effective way, and fewer still offer products and solutions that are designed with the unique needs of women in mind. (We are not referring here to product categories that are obviously women's products, but to those that serve both men and women.) Gillette has had a huge success with its Venus line of razors because they were designed for women's unique needs. Car companies such as Volvo and Honda are slowly beginning to tailor their offerings (and the way they are sold) for women, who make up a large majority of their customers. For example, Volvo's design is virtually maintenance free, has extra storage space, has no gas cap and is easy to clean and park.

Focus on "alumni relations": By focusing on creating outstanding and memorable user experiences, marketers can emulate universities and create "alumni" who are lifelong supporters, advocates, and emissaries for the company. Many companies today (such as Harley Davidson and Apple) enjoy the rabid support of user groups. Shouldice, a Canadian hospital specializing in hernia surgery, creates such strong feelings of gratitude and loyalty in its customer that they hold reunions at the hospital (Heskett 1983).

Marketing is a noble business and societal function that serves to align the forces of free markets with the needs and desires of customers. However, its image has been greatly tarnished over time due to errors of omission as well as commission. This is not merely a public relations problem that can be solved through a few well placed and cleverly worded public service announcements. We must rediscover marketing's munificent mission and gradually weed out the practices that detract from it. The essays in this volume provide ample guidance for accomplishing this.

REFERENCES

FBI.gov, "About the Economic Crimes Unit," www.fbi.gov/hq/cid/fc/ec/about/about_tm.htm (accessed September 16, 2005).

Federal Trade Commission (2004), "Do Not Call Registry Complaints," www.ftc.gov/opa/2004/02/dncstats.pdf (accessed September 16, 2005).

Heskett, James L. (1983), "Shouldice Hospital Ltd.," *Harvard Business School Case No. 9-683-068*. Boston: Harvard Business School Publishing.

Linn, Susan (2004), *Consuming Kids: The Hostile Takeover of Childhood.* New York: The New Press.

MacDonald, John D. (2003), "The Feedback Look: The Image of Marketing," MBA student paper, Bentley College, October.

Mascarenhas, Oswald (1995), "Exonerating Unethical Marketing Executive Behaviors: A Diagnostic Framework," *Journal of Marketing*, 59 (April), 43–57.

Mitchell, Alan (2001), "Have Marketers Missed the Point of Marketing?" *Marketing Week*, September 27, 32.

Rosen, Seth (2003), "I'm Not Interested: Telemarketing's Cost to the Image of Marketing," MBA student paper, Bentley College, October.

Santoni, Alejandro (2003), "The Image of Marketing: Overview of Its Current State and Likely Outcome," MBA student paper, Bentley College, October.

Simon, Herbert A. (1971), "Designing Organizations for an Information-rich World", in *Computers, Communications, and the Public Interest*, M. Greenberger, ed. Baltimore: John Hopkins Press, 38–52.

Sisodia, Rajendra and Augustine Backer (2004), "Cybermarketing and the Tragedy of the Commons: An Environmental Policy Perspective," in *Research Reaching New Heights, Proceedings of the AMA Marketing and Public Policy Conference, Salt Lake City, Utah*. Chicago: American Marketing Association.

CHAPTER 4

WHY MARKETING NEEDS REFORM

JOHNY K. JOHANSSON

The data presented by J. Walker Smith of Yankelovich Partners in chapter 2 are certainly disconcerting. Americans seem to dislike marketing more than ever. If 60 percent of consumers have a much more negative view of marketing and advertising now than a few years ago, and 61 percent feel the amount of marketing and advertising is out of control, marketing has problems.

Actually, I was not surprised. I was in fact pleased to find that the figures dovetail with what I am about to present. I will present a qualitative analysis that helps to explain some of the negative marketing sentiments that Smith has documented.

THE ARGUMENT

I am going to make the argument that American marketing is morally bankrupt. American marketing practices have helped turn the American way of life into its lowest common denominator. I don't mean in terms of material welfare, but in terms of quality of life. The watchwords to describe the American way of life are not those of the seven virtues, but rather the seven vices. We marketers encourage unlimited spending, outrageous behavior, and the unmitigated pursuance of individual gratification.[1] And we do this because we have the marketing tools to do it, the companies have the financial muscle to do it, and the competition gives us a justification for doing it. As former President Bill Clinton said in weak defense of his own sexual pursuits: "I did it because I could." American marketers use the same excuse implicitly and sometimes explicitly—and it is equally immoral.

THE EVIDENCE

What is the evidence for this broad assertion? I think there is plenty of evidence, but I will concentrate here on only a few main issues. They include what kinds of products marketers have introduced into the marketplace, how we do promotions, and how the new media are used.

The Products

The most obvious examples of how marketing has driven society to a lowest common denominator come from the products on the market. First, there is the fast food phenomenon, the omnipresent offerings of large portions of unhealthy food that make people obese and even threaten their lives.[2] Then there is the emergence of gas-guzzling vehicles, SUVs and now the oversized Hummer, which not only have helped make Americans the most energy-wasting people on Earth, but also have become mortal threats on our highways.[3] Sure, people should be free to choose in the marketplace, and if they did not like these products they would not be offered. But this assumes that consumer tastes come first, and the products afterward. Not so, clearly, in these cases. The taste for sugar and fat and "a bigger car than yours" are desires carefully cultivated and kindled by marketers. Sure, "needs" are being met—even the Hummer clearly relates to some underlying drive—but the question is whether marketing should appeal to such primal drives.

A slightly different argument can be made against less-controversial products such as computers, cameras, and cell phones. Such technology-based product categories are less driven by customer needs than by the dynamic force of technology. Again, the products come first, the desires afterward. This is not to say that the desires do not relate to needs—we all have a need to communicate with each other, share experiences, and so on, and these products offer more efficient means for filling such a need. But when technology drives the new product innovation, the products will *drive* demand, not meet demand. And our satisfaction is easily dimmed by unnecessary and complicated features that baffle and infuriate us, not to mention the frustration of having to upgrade once you feel comfortable with the system.

Then there is the question of "me-too" products, competing products that are almost indistinguishable except for the brand logos. Because of competitive benchmarking and reverse engineering—not marketing practices, to be sure—product designs are often indistinguishable. Intense competitive rivalry fosters a need to maintain parity with competitors' product features, if for no other reason than to retain brand loyal customers. This happens in product categories from shampoos to autos to popular music. When industry leader Nokia failed to anticipate the unexpected success of flip-phone models, sales dropped sharply.

Of course, marketing and marketers are not solely responsible for what products are introduced into a market. But they do bear a great deal of responsibility for the promotion of the products that are introduced—and for which ones are successful. In our saturated and competitive markets, product differentiation has become almost impossible to sustain against imitation, and the advantages have shifted to the more intangible assets such as brand name and reputation. This means the marketing job has shifted more and more toward increased promotions.

The Promotions

Getting the attention of satisfied customers has never been easy. In our saturated markets, few consumers are in dire need for a product. Promotional messages need to shake people up, create a need or a want, and instill a "must have" feeling. It's done by being loud and aggressive, exciting and tactile, or humorous and generally in-your-face, playing on insecurity or fear, or featuring a celebrity. It requires imagination and creativity to stand out from your competitors, especially since product differentiation can no longer be relied on. It is probably safe to say that advertising in particular has never been challenged to the extent it is today—and for better or for worse, by and large many creative agencies seem to be up to the challenge.

One problem with the massive promotional effort is that when summed across all competitors in a product category and across all markets, the clutter and noise is annoying to most people and an embarrassment to the marketing profession. One would have thought that the arrival of one-to-one marketing and more advanced targeting techniques with database marketing would help eliminate unwanted spillovers to nontarget segments. But either the techniques are not fine-tuned enough, or the effort is decidedly cynical.

Then there is the need to build "brand affinity." The lack of true product differentiation is one reason why brand building has become the new mantra. The emotional attachment is what matters, since functional attributes are similar across brands. And brand logos are the symbolic icons that trigger the soft power of emotional bonds. Building a power brand is perhaps not done through promotions alone, but promotions surely are an important tool. How do you put across a sense of affinity, become the trusted friend of the customer, create a relationship between the customer and your brand, and attract new customers from competitors? Consistently high product quality and after-sales service do help—but many firms do that well today. The key to making one's brand the choice of the customer is through the creation of the appropriate associations, a favorable image, a shared meaning or understanding between the brand and the customer—all tasks of advertising, celebrity endorsements, sponsorships, and other promotional tools. Yes, much of this will seem patronizing and preposterous and an invasion of privacy—but it seems to work in our saturated markets. Again, as more products and markets reach this stage of maturity, the promotional hoopla becomes louder and more invasive than ever.

The Communications Media

A third factor in the emergence of a lower common denominator is the emergence of new communications tools that allow marketers to reach us practically any time and everywhere. We now have e-mail spam, cell-phone telemarketing, and all variety of banner and pop-up ads on the Internet.[4] On a regular May day in 2004, an amazing 70–80 percent of Internet e-mail involved spam (Appriver.com n.d.).

We also, of course, have telemarketing, one-to-one database marketing, direct sales on television, product placement in cinema advertising, infomercials, and event sponsorship.[5] To top it off there is the drive toward integrated marketing communications, the imposed consistency emerging as an unvarying repetition of a simple slogan and logo. Marketing success has managed to make "staying on message" a favorite mantra in many places.

Just as with products and promotion, one can argue that there is nothing inherently negative about the emergence of more channels of communication between seller and buyer. One might even argue that transaction costs have come down, especially with free e-mails and the Internet, and one can also plausibly argue—which has been done—that markets have become more efficient as consumers have better information. The problem, again, is the massive effort across competitors and across products. It is the sheer massiveness that makes it difficult for consumers to process the information, and, by the same token, for companies to make their brand exhortations heard over the clutter. The solution so far has been to increase the volume, use all the channels, and simplify the message so even nonprocessing consumers can hear and remember it. It is, as you will recognize, the same phenomenon that occurred in the 2004 U.S. presidential election campaign. As marketers, we are running such 24/7 campaigns for all products and services on the market. Small wonder if people erupt.

THE EXPLANATIONS

I think it is important to understand what underlies some of these developments. Here I will focus on three major factors: the competition in globalizing markets, the deregulation and privatization of many industries, and the multicultural diversity found in the United States.

Competition

Say what you want about the costs and benefits of globalization, but globalization does increase the supply of products and services in most markets, and it leads to much more competition in local markets. Global competitors meet each other head-to-head in many local markets around the globe, and local firms rise up to defend their niches, or get taken over by global giants. As global competitors introduce new products from their leading countries, technology diffuses rapidly and even local firms have to adopt state-of-the-art product features. The price pressure on margins force more attention to costs, and the best practices from McDonald's, Wal-Mart, and other American high-efficiency operators get implemented in reengineering efforts at the local level. It's the McDonaldization of the business model.[6]

Consumers faced with all the new products and services find the choices confusing, all the more since "me-too" versions make many choices seem cloned from each other. Choices get made on increasingly fickle bases, or by simply buying more of the same thing. This is how competition has created a saturated marketplace where consumers sometimes find they buy something they already have bought but forgot about—shopping is the thing, not the use of the products. This is the arena where the brands and the logos dominate any dispassionate evaluation of functional needs.

All this is not to say that competition is bad. It is not even saying that cutthroat competition is bad—it is likely to bring lower prices to consumers. But, again, the massive promotional effort and variety of choices can easily overwhelm even the most eager shopper—and certainly be a distraction to consumers who are not in the market.

Privatization

This materialistic overkill is now also energized by the emergence of the many new choices consumers have because of deregulation and privatization. Choices now have to be made between competing electric, gas, and water utilities, between different telephone carriers, cable TV packages, and Internet providers, and between assorted health maintenance organizations, hospitals, pharmacies, and retirement packages. As free markets are introduced and the service providers become individual corporations, marketing necessarily becomes more important. Today, even doctors are salesmen.[7] As for consumers, yes, free choice might be great—but it is not always easy to choose when alternatives are many and complicated, for example, the latest Medicare and pharmacy regulations.

With information necessarily based on self-interest on the part of providers, the result is potentially just another source of promotional efforts disguised as information. To sift through the conflicting claims and the costs and benefits of competing suppliers is not easy, even for experts. Not surprising, a new consultancy area has opened up, advising a buyer how to choose the right provider "for you."

Diversity

The U.S. population is singularly diverse. For all its strengths, diversity means that shared meanings and understandings are hard to find, and have to be expressed in very simple language. In itself, this may not be much of a problem. But when there is a need to get heard and understood over the competitive clutter, and when unfamiliar new products and services come on the market, the demands on the language, the media, and the communication skills of the sellers are sorely tested. Even if pinpointed market segmentation is used to focus on specific groups, the integrated marketing communications IMC paradigm and its imposed consistency of branding mantras across all media force a sameness that becomes not only repetitive but also simpleminded, with a high level of stickiness. While a customer orientation would seem to fit nicely with a targeted approach, differentiated by all the diverse segments in the American marketplace, marketers end up staying with simple slogans understood by all—and annoying in equal degree to people everywhere not in the market.

THE EFFECTS

One result of the way American marketing has developed is the antimarketing sentiments we saw demonstrated in Smith's data mentioned earlier here (and in chapter 2). But I think there are other related negatives that need to be acknowledged. Even though marketing is not the only player, here are a few negatives of American society where I think marketing and marketers have played important facilitating roles:

- Shopping has become the most important activity, and the main weekend pastime, for many people. According to market research, twice as many shoppers are out on Saturday and Sunday than at any time during the week (Fetto 2003). Buying products has become an end in itself. Dedicated apparel shoppers catch themselves buying the same item they bought the week before. People are bored when not shopping, and the malls have become entertainment complexes. When shopping, people are "in the market" and all the hoopla complained about here makes more sense.
- Because of bad food habits, American obesity rates are rising. Diabetes is also on the rise, especially among the young.[8] Given the high material welfare, Americans ought to be among the healthiest in the world—we are not. Marketing is behind the fast (and fat) food drive, without doubt.
- Marketing is also behind the stress that exacerbates the consequences of a bad diet. New products introduced into the marketplace create tension among existing consumers, whether or not the marketer intends it. The need to sell the new products in a saturated market makes attention-grabbing, in-your-face approaches necessary—and as consumers we pay the price.
- Americans are not happier than before, although we are probably happier than some others. But most of the evidence I have seen suggests that the materialism created by marketers in America has not noticeably raised happiness levels. Sure, rising aspirations might well have something to do with it—as people come to expect more, they are harder to satisfy. Nevertheless, as the subtitle of the Gregg Easterbrook (2003) book says, there is a progress paradox: "How life gets better while people feel worse."

SOCIETY AND THE MEDIA

Marketing, of course, is only one major culprit in American society's slide toward the lowest common denominator; other factors are at work as well. The entertainment industry seems intent on producing films and television programs that cater to the lowest urges in all of us. The media helps by turning TV news into a contest between celebrities, dominated by sound bites and sensational overreach. Political parties and other institutions that are intended as bulwarks of stability, integrity, and trust seem populated by self-serving public servants and dishonest, if not corrupt, individuals ready to shade the truth for personal advantage and to attract voters. As with marketing excesses, not much of this is new to our society, but the intensity, the extent, and the depth of the deviousness is palpably greater.

Marketing reflects these developments, but I think it also helps create them. The reason is simple: many of the players involved need to market themselves. It is often the marketing impulse that forces people to deny facts, dissemble events, go for the jugular, and play hardball. Today we all have to sell ourselves before selling our ideas or our arguments. In fact, it is often impossible for today's audiences to distinguish between the message and the messenger. We are trained to accept what likeable people say, and ignore those we dislike.[9] Emotion seems to dominate reason, just as the brand's influence supposedly works.

Here I will deal with only one of the most pernicious examples of the corrosive effect of marketing, that is, on the media. The media, especially television news programs, effectively show us what the society is like. The American way of life is what these programs show and tell us it is. But the choice of what to show and what not to show, what to tell and what not to tell, is made by program producers and editors. And these producers and editors have to take into account marketing factors. They may fight against commercial pressure, and surely make efforts to keep their integrity—but when audience numbers dwindle, bottom-line concerns become unavoidable. Newscasts have to attract an audience—and the selection of anchors, stories, length of coverage, and commentators needs to be based ultimately on the salability of the images and the copy.[10] Marketers, in this way, indirectly show and tell us what the American society is like.

I should emphasize that this development is independent of the commercials and the more explicit promotional content in the media. Yes, the media are commercially based—advertising pays for the programs—but that has long been true. Today, however, the limits on the degree to which the commercial impulse have been allowed to interfere with news programming seem more relaxed than ever. News is entertainment. News journalists are celebrities. Networks feature commentators whose main task is to create excitement, simplified sound bites, and the visceral feeling of engaging in a war of words. The "professional" vocabulary now includes words like ridiculous, vapid, ludicrous, stupid—and many more too graphic to mention here. Such speech is now commonplace on television, among politicians, and, not surprisingly, in everyday American life. Civil society has reached a new uncivil low as media attracts audiences by featuring shouting matches between political commentators. Even though I am not talking here about the rest of the world—as my book does—I don't think it is difficult for anyone to appreciate how badly this American style discourse plays out in the foreign policy arena. The belligerence and bullying by the unilateralists might seem justified to the American home market, but it surely antagonizes allies abroad.

Again, the media is only one of the forces corrupted by marketing considerations. Although there is no space to do it here, a similar analysis can be made of the other pillars of American society. One is likely to find a similar weakening of individual integrity and civil discourse as everyone is trying to project themselves to the greatest advantage in the free market society— doctors and lawyers, teachers and professors, musicians and painters. When we all are marketing ourselves for jobs, for marriage, for power, for success, the temptation to cut corners is hard to resist. After all, that's why Botox is so popular. [11]

THE SOLUTIONS

I don't see any easy solutions to the problems facing marketers. They are systemic to the free market, and one can hardly say, "stop the world, I want to get off." At the individual marketer level, I would only ask each one of us to try to stay true to the moral principle of taking responsibility for what we do to others. That is, let us not hide behind some weak "buyer beware" motto. Don't think that "more choice is better anyway," or "they don't have to buy it," or "it never hurts to ask." Recognize that our own research tells us that increased choice can be painful. And the mass of promotion across competitors and product markets surely does not make it any less of a nuisance.

For companies' strategies, it seems logical to shift to a much more educational platform, to help consumers make decisions that work for them, not against them. Don't be a bad influence—don't do it just because you can. The French advertising by McDonald's saying "Kids should not eat at McDonald's more than once a week," is a case in point (*Associated Press* 2002). Yes, this ad was pulled by the company headquarters, but it represented a recognition of the need to update the product line with foods that can be eaten every day (which is what McDonald's has since done). I sometimes wish we in marketing could develop something akin to the total quality management (TQM) movement used for products, which has meant that product quality is better than ever—we really do have great products on the market. It would be nice if we somehow found a way to create a TQM movement that emphasized best practices in the marketing field.

What if we don't act now to reform marketing? The likely outcome is quite clear. Once consumers and legislators reach the tipping point, there will be much more regulation of marketing efforts, or, more precisely, there will be great efforts to lobby for more regulation. One can visualize how the telemarketing "Do-not-call" registry will extend to the Internet. Fat levels in food will be regulated and limits will be set. There will be moves to limit the size of cars on the road. Language and nudity and violence in the media will be policed and rules enforced. The free market will no longer be particularly free and neither will we marketers. The driving force behind these developments will be religious fundamentalists who espouse traditional values and who already abhor marketing and the media. If we don't improve, their agenda will attract many more recruits.

When I first came to this country many years ago to study American marketing I was attracted to marketing as a force for good. Sure, as Vance Packard had pointed out, the "hidden persuaders" were already at work on the American psyche. But the overall marketing effect was one of a relatively innocent rise in material welfare after a devastating world war. Today this is not the case. Marketing has become a major force in creating a belligerent, obese, and indulgent society whose self-gratifying materialism is matched only by its ignorance about other people. In their clearer moments, the American people recognize this, as the Yankelovich data show. We marketers can do better—and we have to help America do better.

NOTES

This chapter is drawn from a book of mine titled *In Your Face: How American Marketing Excess Fuels Anti-Americanism* (Upper Saddle River, NJ: Financial Times/Prentice Hall, 2004). It deals primarily with American marketing effects abroad, and the initial impetus for the book was the recent antiglobalization and anti-American sentiments abroad so widely documented in the media. I wanted to identify the role of marketing in these movements, and as I did the research I discovered a strong antimarketing tendency also here at home. It is this antimarketing sentiment I discuss here.

1. Of course, one might argue that from a macroeconomic point of view this is to society's benefit. For example, the 2004 rebound in stock market share prices was mainly due to continued strong consumer spending, fueled by low interest rates and borrowing against increased housing values.

2. There is plenty of data now that document the obesity problem. See, for example, Schlosser (2001). Still, McDonald's revenues have increased, and earnings rose more than 50 percent in 2004, to $2.3 billion from $1.5 billion the year before (*The Washington Post*, April 25, 2005, Financials, T68).

3. Between July and November 2002 monthly sales of Hummer H1 and H2 doubled. Buyers waited months and paid over sticker price to get earlier delivery (Gross 2004).

4. For those who expected Internet ads to lose their initial glow with the dot-com failures, the news is different. Jupiter Communications estimates that online advertising revenue will reach $16.5 billion by 2005, with about 950 Internet-based marketing messages per user, per day, in five years.

5. Telemarketing does provide jobs, and not only abroad. In fact, retailer L.L.Bean's plan to build a call center in Oakland, California, had to be put on hold because T-Mobile telecommunications already had

advanced plans for a center employing 700 workers in the same location—and there might not be enough workers for two call centers (*Associated Press* 2004).

6. Of course, category killers compete against their own species—by 2004 rumors swirled that Toys "R" Us, one of the original and most successful category killers, might withdraw from the toy business because of competition from Wal-Mart (see *Wall Street Journal* 2004, p. B1).

7. As are professors. Harvard's former president, Derek Bok (2003), made a plea for less commercialization of universities. Perhaps not listening, Harvard picked its current president, Lawrence Summers, from the U.S. Treasury Department.

8. In the last ten years, obesity rates have increased more than 60 percent among U.S. adults. In recent years, diabetes rates among people ages 30 to 39 rose by 70 percent. (www.healthierUS.gov/exercise.html, 2004).

9. The presidential campaign coverage in particular has helped exacerbate this tendency, with voters reportedly tuning in only to those newscasts that predictably echo their own views, not listening to others.

10. The need to attract an audience, of course, affects more than newscasts, and sometimes promotions reach unimaginably lower levels. Clear Channel's Washington DC channel WIHT has staged an "animal sex offender" promotion, a misogynist-homophobic "Running the Bull Dykes" contest, and an "Osama Pinata" contest (Ahrens 2001, p. C01).

11. Botox injections for cosmetic use were approved by the FDA in April 2002. In 2003 there were 2,272,080 Botox injections, up 37 percent since 2002 (American Society for Aesthetic Plastic Surgery *2003 ASAPS Statistics*, www.surgery.org/press/news-print.)

REFERENCES

Ahrens, Frank (2001), "Finding a New Station in Life." *Washington Post,* November 13.

Associated Press (2002), "McDonald's France Says Kids Shouldn't Eat Their Food More Than Once a Week," *Associated Press,* October 31.

———— (2004), "Catalogue Retailer Puts Call-Center on Hold," *Associated Press,* November 24.

Appriver.com (n.d.), Spam and Virus Protections, www.appriver.com/stat_spampct.asp.

Bok, Derek (2003), *Universities in the Marketplace.* Princeton, NJ: Princeton University Press.

Easterbrook, Gregg (2003), *The Progress Paradox.* New York: Random House.

Fetto, John (2003), "Shop Around the Clock." *American Demographics,* September 1.

Gross, Daniel (2004), "Hummer vs. Prius," Slate.MSN.com, February 26.

Packard, Vance (1957), *The Hidden Persuaders.* New York: Random House.

Schlosser, Eric (2001), *Fast Food Nation.* Boston: Houghton-Mifflin.

Wall Street Journal (2004), "Toys 'Were' Us?" August 12, B1.

CHAPTER 5

MARKETING REFORM

The Case of Excessive Buying

NARESH K. MALHOTRA, LAN WU, AND FRED C. ALLVINE

The twentieth century has witnessed the rapid development of marketing as a formal discipline. Marketing is the exchange process by which organizations and individuals obtain what they need and want by identifying value, providing it, communicating it, and delivering it to others (Kotler 2000). Overtime, marketing has become more sophisticated and created numerous benefits to society and individual consumers, directly and indirectly. First, as engine of U.S. economy, marketing helps to sustain the development of a high-income society. Second, by identifying consumer needs and coupling them with multiple channels (e.g., retail stores, telephone, and the Internet), marketing improves the availability and quality of a variety of products. Third, through increasing consumer demand, marketing helps to lower production costs and make products more affordable. Finally, through advertising and other communication alternatives, marketing teaches consumers to become more knowledgeable about products and their rights as consumers.

Despite all the benefits, some negative consequences have developed as a result of the defining role and practice of marketing. One such consequence is excessive buying, which is the focus of this chapter. Excessive buying can be defined as *an individual type of buying behavior whereby consumers repetitively spend more than they should based on financial considerations.* We argue that marketing has encouraged or led to excessive buying in some circumstances, resulting in serious consequences both for society and individual American consumers. First, excessive buying may not be sustainable and a sharp downturn in the economy could have serious economic consequences. Second, those families taking on growing consumer debt can experience economic difficulty, plus negative emotions- such as guilt and anxiety. Marketing needs to address the problem of excessive buying before it causes more serious problems and hurts the image of marketing.

The rest of the chapter is organized as follows: The next section provides evidence of excessive buying. We then discuss how current marketing practices contribute to excessive buying. Thereafter, we propose that both the theoretical and practical aspects of marketing need to be reformed, and provide a new definition of marketing expanding the one recently provided by the American Marketing Association (AMA). We give directions for future research in excessive buying and conclude with some thoughts on the role and realm of marketing.

EVIDENCE OF EXCESSIVE BUYING

Growing Personal Consumption Expenditure

Consumer spending as a percentage of Gross Domestic Product (GDP) has steadily increased since the 1970s (U.S. Bureau of Economic Analysis 2004, pp. 152–53, see Table 5.1). However,

Table 5.1

Growing Personal Consumption Expenditure of the United States, 1970–2003 (in $ billions)

Year	GDP	Personal expenditure	Percent of GDP
1970	1,038.5	648.5	62.4
1975	1,638.3	1,034.4	63.1
1980	2,789.5	1,757.1	63.0
1985	4,220.3	2,720.3	64.5
1990	5,803.1	3,839.9	66.2
1995	7,397.7	4,975.8	67.3
2000	9,817.0	6,739.4	68.7
2001	10,100.8	7,045.4	69.8
2002	10,480.8	7,385.3	70.5
2003	10,983.9	7,752.3	70.6

Note: GDP = gross domestic product.
Source: U.S. Bureau of Economic Analysis 2004.

some policymakers and marketing researchers have recently begun to view the continued increase in consumer spending with apprehension. Concerns have been expressed that a growing portion of American households are engaged in excessive buying, spending more than they can afford.

The Consumer Expenditure Survey 2000 shows that the average incomes before taxes of the lowest and second lowest 20 percent of households were, respectively, $7,683 and $19,071. In contrast, the average annual expenditures for these households were, respectively, $17,940 and $26,550 (U.S. Bureau of Labor Statistics 2002, p. 7). More seriously, the gap between income and expenditures for the lowest 20 percent of households grew even larger in 2001 and 2002. In addition to government statistics, journalists have provided anecdotal accounts of excessive buying. For example, Schor (2000) argues that excessive buying is a result of upward social comparison; Danziger (2002) implies that people use various justifiers (e.g., quality of life, pleasure, home beautification, education, and relaxation) when they buy things they cannot afford. In addition to income-expenditure statistics,[1] excessive buying is evinced by some other facts.

Low Personal Saving Rate

In recent years, the personal saving rate (i.e., savings divided by disposable personal income) in the United States has fallen sharply. It is now at a very low level compared either to U.S. historical experience or to the saving rates of many other industrialized countries. The U.S. saving rate averaged 8.2 percent from 1980 to 1992. It then steadily declined and reached a low of 1.7 percent in 2001 (U.S. Bureau of Economic Analysis 2004, pp. 172–73, see Table 5.2). By contrast, the personal saving rates from 1980 though 2001 averaged 13 percent in Japan, 12 percent in Germany, and 15 percent in France (Marquis 2002).

With a savings rate of 2 percent of after-tax income, most Americans are not planning for retirement and have made no preparation for financial emergencies. Many American consumers are living hand to mouth and do not appreciate the importance of saving.

Table 5.2

Falling Personal Saving Rate (%) of the United States, 1970–2003

Year	Personal saving rate	Year	Personal saving rate
1970	9.4	1997	3.6
1975	10.6	1998	4.3
1980	10.0	1999	2.4
1985	9.0	2000	2.3
1990	7.0	2001	1.7
1995	4.6	2002	2.3
1996	4.0	2003	2.0

Source: U.S. Bureau of Economic Analysis 2004.

Mounting Credit Card Debt

One symptom of excessive buying involves the existence of credit card debt. Consumer credit card debt increased dramatically during the past two decades, with an average annual growth rate of 22.1 percent (Federal Reserve 2004, see Table 5.3). By the end of 2003, the country's credit card debt soared to $734 billion, which is nearly $7,000 per household. Since 40 percent of credit card users pay off their full balances every month, credit card debt of those households who carry balances is close to $12,000 (Mapother 2004).

Of growing concern, credit card debt has increased disproportionately among poor households and college students. According to Bird, Hagstrom, and Wild (1999), from 1983 to 1995, the percentage of poor households with a credit card doubled, and the average balances held on these cards increased as rapidly as that of nonpoor households. In 2001, 83 percent of college students had at least one credit card, with an average credit card balance of $2,327. It is also found that from the time they arrive on campus until after graduation, undergraduate students double their average credit card debt and triple the number of credit cards they carry (Baum and O'Malley 2003).

All-Time High Personal Bankruptcies

Personal bankruptcy set another record during fiscal year 2003: 1.6 million American households filed for personal bankruptcy, compared to 832,374 a decade earlier (the U.S. Courts 2003, see Table 5.4). Unlike the 1960s, when personal bankruptcy was a haven for the young and struggling, much of the increase in personal bankruptcy is now driven by older people, many of who have decades of work experience in white-collar positions. For example, in 2001, per capita filings of individuals ages 45 to 54 increased 58 percent, to 11 per thousand (Hwang 2004). This can be attributed to the fact that many bankrupt baby boomers are not frugal as their Depression-era parents. It is also due to the fact that people are living longer and do not save enough for their longer retirements.

IS MARKETING TO BLAME FOR EXCESSIVE BUYING?

We argue that current marketing practices are partially responsible for the exacerbation of excessive buying for the following reasons.

Table 5.3

Soaring Consumer Credit Card Debt of the United States, 1980–2003 (in $ millions)

Year	Credit card debt	Year	Credit card debt
1980	54,970.1	2000	665,174.1
1985	124,465.8	2001	708,916.9
1990	238,642.6	2002	719,116.3
1995	443,126.9	2003	734,070.5

Source: Federal Reserve 2004.

Table 5.4

1990–2003 Bankruptcy Filings (Twelve-Month Period Ending September)

Year	Personal bankruptcy	Year	Personal bankruptcy
1990	685,429	1997	1,313,112
1991	848,812	1998	1,389,839
1992	905,753	1999	1,315,751
1993	823,374	2000	1,226,037
1994	783,372	2001	1,398,864
1995	832,415	2002	1,508,578
1996	1,058,444	2003	1,625,813

Source: The U.S. Courts 2003.

Supply of Credit Cards

Easy access to credit cards in recent years have pushed many American consumers to purchase what they cannot afford, contributing to soaring household credit card debt. Since the 1990s, the banking industry has dramatically increased its marketing of credit cards to the public. In 2001, major credit card networks (VISA, MasterCard, Discover, and American Express) spent $800 million on advertising. Individual card issuers spent an additional $10 billion marketing credit cards through multiple channels, such as direct mail, telemarketing, and the Internet (www.cardweb.com/cardlearn/faqs/2002/aug/15.xcml).

The number of credit card solicitations in the United States grew from 1.1 billion in 1990 to 4.3 billion in 2003 (see Table 5.5), with 69 percent of American households receiving 4.8 offers per month during 2003 (Synovate Inc. Mail Monitor ®). Recently, an increasing number of credit card marketers have started to offer rewards and cash rebates to attract potential customers. Synovate reported that in 2003 1.27 billion reward and 0.90 billion cash rebate offers were sent out, as compared to 0.81 billion and 0.68 million in 2002.

Credit card marketers also turn to telemarketing and electronic mails to boost their response rates. On average, a telemarketing campaign helps to increase card response rate by two to nine times, as compared to a direct mail campaign (Punch 2002). The Internet, in conjunction with radio and television advertising, has proven to be a good means of acquiring cardholders as well.

Financial deregulation in the 1980s contributed to increased profitability of credit cards. Competition for these profits led to an increasing number of marketers who are willing to take the risk and lend to more marginal borrowers. Lyons (2003) suggests that those experiencing the greatest gains in credit access are black households, female-headed households, and households with low

Table 5.5

U.S. Credit Card Acquisition Mailings, 1990–2003 (in billions)

Year	Number of solicitations	Year	Number of solicitations
1990	1.1	1997	3.0
1991	1.0	1998	3.5
1992	0.9	1999	2.9
1993	1.5	2000	3.5
1994	2.5	2001	5.0
1995	2.7	2002	4.9
1996	2.4	2003	4.3

Source: Synovate Inc. Mail Monitor®.

permanent earnings. To make the situation worse, creditors capitalize on these consumers by charging ridiculously high interest rates. For instance, in a typical *Wall Street Journal* story (Hwang 2004), Jennifer Reid said she found that her annual interest rate suddenly jumped to 24.98 percent, up from 19.98 percent the prior month and far over the initial single-digit rate. Although she did not miss a single payment, she was told that she was seen as a "credit risk" by the creditor since she had accumulated some $5,000 debt on her other two credit cards.

The Lure of Advertising

The U.S. advertising market has expanded in the past two decades. Although rising at a more moderate rate recently (as compared to the second half of the 1990s), U.S. advertising through major media (including newspapers, magazines, television, radio, cinema, outdoor, and Internet) spent $144 billion in 2002 and $147 billion in 2003, accounting for 59.1 and 59.2 percent of the global spending. It is predicted that the expenditure of U.S. advertising through major media will reach $168 billion in 2006 (ZenithOptimedia 2004).

Current U.S. advertising practices expose American consumers to a variety of products and reinforce the materialistic ideal. This creates an upscale lifestyle illusion and intensifies consumers' desire and motivation to buy. A lot of advertising messages portray expensive products as both desirable and common. This leads many consumers who want a certain quality life to gamble their future and make purchases they cannot afford, which results in excessive buying. "Luxury Fever," created by advertising, contributes to families going further into debt.

Housing is an example: "A generation or so ago, a basic 800-square-foot, $8,000 Levittown box with a carport was heaven. By the 1980s, the dream had gone upscale. Home had become a 6,000-square-foot contemporary on three acres or a guttered and rehabbed townhouse in a gentrified ghetto" (Warren and Tyagi 2003, p. 21).

Clothing is another good example of advertising leading consumers to excessive buying. "Many debtors blame their woes squarely on Tommy, Ralph, Gucci, and Prada." This is consistent with what one observes: "Banana Republic is so crowded that we can barely find an empty fitting room. Adidas and Nike clad the feet of every teenager we meet" (Warren and Tyagi 2003, p. 17).

The Lure of Sales Promotions

Sales promotion provides added inducement to purchase by offering price reductions for a limited period of time. Many consumers feel compelled to "buy now" because of the savings they will realize. Marketers usually combine advertising with sales promotion and make huge investments. For instance, the top U.S. spender for advertising and promotion, "Motor Vehicles and Car Bodies" spent $24.73 billion in 2003 (Schonfeld & Associates 2004, p. 197). Many consumers are receptive to such sales promotion efforts and purchase products they cannot afford, resulting in excessive buying.

The impulse-buying literature has long recognized the impact of sales promotion on excessive purchases (Bellenger, Robertson, and Hirschman 1978). A positive, although not always significant, relationship has been found between price promotion and impulsive buying behavior. Consumers are often caught up by a sales situation and buy something they might not normally buy. Being too practical (i.e., being able to buy something at a lower price) leads to the collapse of some consumers' self-control (Thompson, Locander, and Pollio 1990).

Loewenstein (1996) suggests that sales promotion could manipulate the various dimensions of proximity—physical (e.g., the urge to buy is more likely to be triggered in a shopping mall than in one's office), sensory (i.e., buying a cup of latte tempted by its smell), and temporal (i.e., the positive outcomes of making a purchase should be experienced immediately, as opposed to at some distal point in time)—and thus elicit visceral influences on consumers' buying behavior. Many promotions show a product in use, vividly simulating the experience and seducing purchases. For example, smell or taste of free food samples in malls is often accompanied by product orders. Other promotion efforts increase consumers' impatience by reminding them that the product is "yours for the asking" or "only a phone call away." The "no down payment, no interest" promotion campaigns used by many furniture merchants and electronics stores increase product desirability and reduces consumers' willingness to delay gratification, even though they might not be able to afford the purchases.

WHAT REFORMS ARE NEEDED? REDEFINING THE ROLE AND REALM OF MARKETING

We believe that current marketing practices have contributed to the growth of excessive buying and that both the theoretical and practical aspects of marketing need to be reformed.

Theoretical Aspects of Marketing Need to Be Reformed

Marketing was recently defined by the AMA as "an organizational function and set of processes for creating, communicating, and delivering value to customers and for managing customer relationships in ways that benefit the organization and its stakeholders."[2] Compared to the 1985 AMA definition, this definition makes a huge contribution to identifying the impact of marketing on the physical and mental well-being of target consumers. For example, current marketing efforts have led American consumers to excessive buying, resulting in personal financial crisis and mental problems (e.g., feeling anxiety and depression).

We feel that this definition falls short of capturing the social role that marketing plays in the exchange process. Andreasen (1993) suggests that marketing has profound impacts on the physical and mental well-being of the society, in addition to that of its target audiences. In the case of excessive buying, marketing not only creates financial and mental consequences for consumers but it also makes the U.S. economy more vulnerable since excessive spending is not sustainable.

We argue that a "social marketing approach" should be adopted in redefining the role and realm of marketing (Andreasen 2002). We propose that a future definition of marketing recognize the welfare of the society at large and encourage marketers to fulfill the needs of the target consumers in ways that improve society as a whole (Schiffman and Kanuk 2004). There is a need to limit the realm of marketing so that marketing does not lead to the creation of needs, wants, and desires that are unsustainable by the target consumers and society at large, and that ultimately will result in negative and dysfunctional consequences. There is also a need to expand the realm of marketing so that it encompasses those activities that do not in the short run promote an organization's profit objectives, but in the long run contribute to societal welfare. Thus, a new definition of marketing is called for that both limits its role to avoid dysfunctional consequences and expands its role to include societal welfare. We provide such a definition by expanding the new AMA definition as follows: "Marketing is an organizational function and set of processes for creating, communicating, and delivering real, long-term value to customers and for managing customer relationships in ways that benefit the organization and its stakeholders. These organizational functions and processes should not lead to negative and dysfunctional consequences for the target consumers and society at large, but rather should seek to enhance consumer and societal welfare."

Practical Aspects of Marketing Need to Be Reformed

In terms of practice, we suggest that the current role of marketing be limited. Generally speaking, marketers' attention should be focused upon satisfying consumers' existing needs that are affordable rather than creating needs that are unhealthy (e.g., promoting food with high calorie or cholesterol) or unaffordable (e.g., encouraging someone with a $40,000 annual income to buy a $55,000 Mercedes by providing a low-interest loan or accepting a credit card).

More importantly, marketers and the U.S. government should restrict those marketing activities that have undesirable social consequences (e.g., excessive buying) even when market forces imply great potential profits. For instance, the U.S government successfully curtailed tobacco and liquor commercials on TV. To prevent excessive buying from ultimately undermining the U.S. economy and social welfare, marketers should restrain from practices such as setting up expensive stores and overcharging in poor neighborhoods, providing too much credit access to low- or medium-income households, and attracting customers who are at the brink of financial crisis by using seductive sales promotions.

Marketers should resume their social responsibility by involving themselves in marketing activities that improve the welfare of society as a whole. Recently, a few marketers have begun to make efforts in this direction. For example, the "drink responsibly" campaign highlights Anheuser-Busch's effort to promote responsible drinking and fight against alcohol abuse (beeresponsible.com). To improve its image from one as a source of unhealthy choices, the fast food industry has started substituting salads for carb-laden french fries and bottled water for soft drinks. In the case of excessive buying, marketers should encourage sustainable spending by consumers and teach them how to avoid financial embarrassment of excessive buying. In the long run, these campaigns will help to enhance the well-being of stakeholders at all levels (e.g., consumers, local community, and the society).

DIRECTIONS FOR FUTURE RESEARCH

Although prevalent in contemporary American society, the definition and nature of excessive buying remain mysterious to marketing researchers. The biggest challenge lies in defining the construct. Much controversy focuses on whether excessive buying is a perception-based phenomenon or something that can be inferred by "hard" data (e.g., personal debt information). We suggest that, from an academic perspective, excessive buying should be defined as a perception-based construct (consumers repetitively spend more than they should based on financial considerations)[3] for the following two reasons: (1) a perception-based definition helps to rule out the influences of external factors (e.g., geographic locations, income expectations, and socioeconomic status) on consumers' buying behavior, and (2) since many consumers engage in budget planning or at least have a rough idea about how much money they can afford for a product (Heath and Soll 1996), a perception-based definition can be operationalized without invading too much consumer financial privacy.

Research efforts in the following areas will also enhance our understanding of the nature of excessive buying: a psychometric scale to measure excessive buying needs to be developed and the antecedents and consequences of excessive buying need to be examined systematically. Journalists (e.g., Schor 2000 and Danziger 2002) have contributed some anecdotal discussions about the antecedents and consequences. However, we believe that a general theoretical framework is required to integrate the diverse accounts and help us understand the essence of the phenomenon.

CONCLUSIONS

We have seen over the past decades that the U.S. economy has been growing on the backs of consumer buying. Nevertheless, the excessive buying behavior of American consumers cannot continue, since it has wide impacts on their physical and mental welfare and on the well-being of our society. It is suggested that some marketers are at least partially responsible for the prevalence of excessive buying by supplying easy credit card access to lower-income households, creating "Luxury Fever", and seductively promoting sales. In order to avoid societally undesirable phenomena such as excessive buying, we propose that the realm and role of marketing be reformed. We provide such a definition of marketing by modifying the AMA's new definition to both limit its role to avoid dysfunctional consequences and expand its role to include societal welfare.

NOTES

1. Some researchers argue that the discrepancy between income and expenditure can be explained by "missing income" (e.g., income from the stock market) rather than consumer excessive buying. We do not agree with them and provide the evidence later in the chapter.

2. This definition was released by Dr. Robert Lusch, professor of marketing at University of Arizona, during the 2004 AMA Summer Conference, Boston.

3. Researchers might argue that an overoptimistic estimation of their ability to afford may lead consumers to buy excessively. However, most accounts of excessive buying indicate that consumers act against their economic self-interest in full knowledge that they are doing so (e.g., Loewenstein 1996; Danziger 2002), that is, they know that they spend more than they can afford.

REFERENCES

Andreasen, Alan R. (1993), "A Social Marketing Research Agenda for Consumer Behavior Researchers," *Advances in Consumer Research,* 20, 1–5.

——— (2002), "Marketing Social Marketing in the Social Change Marketplace," *Journal of Public Policy & Marketing,* 21 (Spring), 3–13.

Baum, Sandy and Marie O'Malley (2003), "College on Credit: How Borrowers Perceive Their Education Debt," www.nelliemae.com/library/nasls_2002.pdf (accessed August 4, 2004).

Bellenger, Danny N., Dan H. Robertson, and Elizabeth C. Hirschman (1978), "Impulse Buying Varies by Product," *Journal of Advertising Research,* 18 (December), 15–18.

Bird, Edward J., Paul A. Hagstrom, and Robert Wild (1999), "Credit Card Debts of the Poor: High and Rising," *Journal of Policy Analysis and Management,* 18 (January), 125–33.

CardWeb.com, "CARDFAQ's-Frequently Asked Questions," www.cardweb.com/cardlearn/faqs/2002/aug/15.xcml (accessed August 10, 2004).

Danziger, Pemela N. (2002), *Why People Buy Things They Don't Need.* Ithaca, NY: Paramount Market Publishing.

Federal Reserve (2004), "Consumer Credit Outstanding," www.federalreserve.gov/releases/G19/hist/cc_hist_sa.txt (accessed August 9, 2004).

Heath, Chip and Jack B. Soll (1996), "Mental Budgeting and Consumer Decision," *Journal of Consumer Research,* 23 (June), 40–52.

Hwang, Suein (2004), "New Group Swells Bankruptcy Court: The Middle-Aged," The *Wall Street Journal,* July 6, A1.

Kotler, Philip (2000), *Marketing Management,* 5th ed. Upper Saddle River, NJ: Prentice Hall.

Loewenstein, George F. (1996), "Out of Control: Visceral Influences on Behavior," *Organizational Behavior and Human Decision Processes,* 65 (March), 272–92.

Lyons, Angela C. (2003), "How Credit Access Has Changed over Time for U.S. Households," *Journal of Consumer Affairs,* 37 (Winter), 231–55.

Mapother, William R. (2004), "Taming Consumer Debt," *Credit Union Magazine,* 70 (April), 72.

Marquis, Milt (2002), "What's Behind the Low U.S. Personal Saving Rate", *Federal Reserve Bank of San Francisco (FRBSF) Economic Letter*, March 29, 1–3.

Punch, Linda (2002), "A Changed Marketing Game", *Credit Card Management,* 14 (January), 38–41.

Schiffman, Leon G. and Leslie Lazar Kanuk (2004), *Consumer Behavior,* 8th ed. Upper Saddle River, NJ: Pearson Education.

Schonfeld & Associates (2004), *Advertising Ratios and Budgets,* Riverwoods, IL: Schonfeld & Associates.

Schor, Juliet (2000), *Do Americans Shop Too Much?* Boston, MA: Beacon Press.

Synovate Inc. Mail Monitor®, "Credit Card Companies Mail Fewer Offers for Second Consecutive Year," www.synovate.com/en/news/press_detials,php?id=48 (accessed August 9, 2004).

Thompson, Craig J., William B. Locander, and Howard R. Pollio (1990), "The Lived Meaning of Free Choice: An Existential Phenomenological Description of Everyday Consumer Experiences of Contemporary Married Women," *Journal of Consumer Research,* 17 (December), 346–61.

U.S. Bureau of Economic Analysis (2004), "GDP and Other Major NIPA Series, 1929–2003," www.bea.gov/bea/ARTICLES/02February/0204GDP&Other.pdf (accessed August 5, 2004).

U.S. Bureau of Labor Statistics (2002), "Consumer Expenditures in 2000," www.bls.gov/cex/csxann00.pdf (accessed August 9, 2004).

U.S. Courts (2003), "News Release," www.uscourts.gov/Press_Release/fy03bk.pdf (accessed August 4, 2004).

Warren, Elizabeth and Amelia Tyagi (2003), *Two-Income-Trap: Why Middle-Class Mothers and Fathers Are Going Broke.* New York, NY: Basic Books.

ZenithOptimedia (2004), "ZenithOptimedia Charts Global Advertising Recovery," www.fipp.com/1260 (accessed August 24, 2004).

PART 2

ARE MARKETING'S PROBLEMS
SELF-CORRECTING?

This section invites authors to either challenge the negative perception of marketing or suggest ways to reform marketing. The chapters here posit that the problems marketing presently faces are essentially self-correcting and incremental in nature. In other words, they do not call into question any of marketing's fundamental precepts or its raison d'etre.

In his provocative style, marketing historian Stephen Brown suggests that what marketing needs is not reform but restraint. He believes that marketers have taken the customer-driven view too far: "These days, customer satisfaction isn't good enough. The customer must be delighted, engaged, enthralled, enraptured, and, if service quality inflation continues at the current rate, eventually carried away on transports of ecstatic erotic abandon."

Debra Jones Ringold states that "individual consumers are quite capable of navigating markets, exercising choice in a manner consistent with their preferences, and learning from their mistakes . . . . In the aggregate, consumers appear to be 'smarter' than the elite few, outperforming experts in problem solving, forecasting, and decision making." Furthermore, she suggests that profit making is a high calling when seen as a consequence of satisfying customers with products and services of real value. The great virtue of markets is that they create wealth, benefiting all, including the poor. Markets can reduce envy if economic opportunities are available to all. So, while they are not perfect, markets deliver prosperity and freedom, as well as the "opportunity to lead a virtuous life."

Thus, as we contemplate reform according to Ringold, we should work toward creating more-educated and competent consumers, while "recognizing the inherent morality of choice." Reform efforts should be geared toward making markets more responsive to consumer preferences. They should seek to inculcate values such as reciprocity, moral obligation, duty toward community, and trust, working through educational, religious, and familial institutions. Such efforts, Ringold believes, would have a better chance of improving markets and would not be subject to the unintended consequences of many regulatory efforts.

Similarly, Shelby Hunt believes that current marketing practices and theories are perfectly fine, especially if we examine them from a resource-advantage viewpoint. Utilizing the areas of branding and brand equity, Hunt argues that branding not only creates competitive advantage to a firm as a resource, but also protects and enhances consumer welfare. Hunt suggests that marketing as a discipline and a practice has predominantly focused on micronormative (marketing management) issues, but that it needs to also examine macropositive and macronormative issues that will enable it to align with society.

Russ Winer is a firm believer in consumer sovereignty and in the good driving out the bad. He believes that if there is temporary disequilibrium, market forces result in changes toward equilibrium. Also, everything is not "me too" marketing, as many critics have asserted. There is enormous innovation (products such as Apple's iPod and Chrysler 300), and the growing movement toward category management provides more optimal levels of choice. Winer is, however, in agreement that marketing does not have the ears of senior management and corporate boards. This is because we have not marketed marketing very well. That is, the enemy is "us." Instead of financial people pushing for accountability of marketing spending on advertising, customer relationship management hardware and software, promotions, and other marketing tools, it should be marketing people. With regard to reforming academia, Winer suggests greater emphasis be placed on relevant research.

Finally, Dave Stewart believes that although introspection and reflection are useful, it is important that they not become critical to the point of being disparaging. He believes "reform" is a highly value-laden word. According to *Webster's Online Dictionary,* it means "amendment of what is defective, vicious, corrupt or depraved." A more benign definition of reform should focus on the positive and affirmative need for improvement. Stewart's view is that marketing has been remarkably successful as an academic discipline and an area of management practice. Furthermore, the marketing discipline can be justifiably proud that managers in other disciplines speak the language of marketing. The operations manager who speaks of customer-centric service delivery, the finance professor who talks about the value of investing in a customer and the lifetime value of a customer, and the business strategy consultant who emphasizes the roles of differentiation and positioning in business success are merely reflecting the triumph of ideas that originated in marketing. Therefore, marketing does not need reform in the negative sense of the word. It does need to evolve so it can respond to the changes occurring around it, develop the means for encouraging more ethical practice, and reinvent itself to deal with the issues and contingences of the twenty-first century. Stewart believes that what we need to do is to reclaim marketing's role in business and society and reinvent marketing.

CHAPTER 6

DOES REFORM NEED REFORM?

STEPHEN BROWN

BUSINESS AS USUAL

If marketing were human, it would be diagnosed as dangerously manic-depressive, a suitable candidate for electro-convulsive therapy. Its clinical history consists of what can only be described as bipolar outbreaks of incipient megalomania and introspective self-loathing. As every student knows, marketing claims to be king of the world, the solution for a small planet, the be-all-and-end-all of business. Marketing is a universal verity. Marketing is a category of human action. Marketing delivers a standard of living. Marketing is the most important organizational function, so we're told. Marketing subsumes neoclassical economics, though economists may beg to differ. Marketing, according to Regis McKenna's (1991) much-quoted battle cry, is "everything." That's right, *everything*. Or as near as makes no difference.

Set against such bouts of irrational exuberance, marketing is singularly susceptible to severe anxiety attacks and periods of deep despondency. It is often described as in some kind of crisis, quandary, or predicament (Brown 2002). It routinely contends that its proprietary ideas are being (mis)appropriated by adjacent subject areas like strategy, organizational studies, and information technology. It occasionally wonders why neighboring academic disciplines, such as sociology and anthropology, ignore its scintillating scholarly insights. It frequently flagellates itself for losing touch with key constituents or stakeholders, principally practitioners and policymakers. It periodically proclaims that it's time to pull together, get a grip, and turn over a new leaf. It really means it this time.

The reality, of course, is that marketing is neither the bees' knees nor a basket case. It is a massive socioeconomic institution, what cult novelist David Foster Wallace (2004, p. 25) aptly calls, "the great grinding US marketing machine." A moment's reflection reminds us that there are innumerable marketing practitioners, countless marketing students, copious marketing academicians, numberless marketing consultants, illimitable marketing conference, training course, and executive education attendees, most of whom go about their marketing business without suffering existential crises or, for that matter, harboring imperialistic ambitions. They are content, in the main, to make the sale, move the merchandise, meet the target, mind the store, beat the competition, collect the kudos, get the grades, earn the crust, run the department, write the report, secure the tenure, or whatever. They do what they have to do. They get by. They don't have time to reform marketing or, unlike leading learned lights, worry unduly about the need for reform.

SEND NO MONEY

Actually, the really worrying thing about the "Does marketing need reform?" question is that it melds marketing's megalomaniacal and self-abnegating bipolarities. Calls for reform are symptomatic of the latter propensity, since they imply that there is something seriously amiss with marketing. Conversely, the assumption that marketing *can* be reformed is testament to the former trait, insofar as it intimates that our recommended reforms will be embraced by the community of marketers. The simple fact of the matter, however, is that marketing is way too big, way too unwieldy, way too set in its ways to be reformed. And, even if it could be reformed, it is unlikely that the necessary alterations—even if these could be agreed on, which is again unlikely—would be implemented consistently by marketing's many and varied constituents (or even implemented at all). It is delusional to think otherwise.

It is equally delusional to ignore the difficulties, avoid the issues, and imagine that everything in the marketing garden is rosy, when it is decidedly rose-tinted. There's no doubt whatsoever that marketing is facing mounting criticism. It is beset by the attacks of anticapitalist protesters, not least of which are Naomi Klein of *No Logo* fame and Reverend Billy of the "Church of Stop Shopping." It is condemned for targeting tiny tots, tweenagers, and the terminally tubby, to say nothing of tobaccoheads, shopaholics, and the borderline anorexic. It is disparaged by chief executive officers (CEOs) on account of its imprecise and unquantifiable contribution to the bottom line and denounced by academicians of every conceivable disciplinary stripe, marketing included. It is little wonder that a recent Research International survey of attitudes to marketers concluded, "Marketing is disposable and unimportant to strategic development. Its recruits are inferior to those in other disciplines. It is untrustworthy, unreliable, uncooperative, and it lacks leadership" (quoted in Simms 2004, p. 32).

Such critiques, to be sure, aren't new. Consumerism comes in waves, as the history books bear witness, and marketing responds accordingly (Hollander and Rassuli 1993). Societal marketing precepts were forged in the face of an antimarketing uproar (the 1970s oil crises-cum-environmental concerns). The modern marketing concept emerged at a time when commentators considered commerce unconscionable, well-nigh unconstitutional (Galbraith's *Affluent Society,* Packard's *Hidden Persuaders,* and so on). This time last century, marketing was being maligned by muckrakers, pooh-poohed by progressives, and yelled at by yellow journalists (the Trust in Advertising movement duly arose). Marketing has always been a convenient scapegoat for unsuccessful CEOs, self-aggrandizing politicians, and the leading lights of the moral majority. Marketing has been through so many self- and other-inflicted crises that the absence of crisis is cause for concern. Marketers get worried when they're not being worried over, attacked, excoriated, and what have you.

FREE HOME TRIAL

Clearly, critique and crisis are part of marketing's makeup and when the worries and wobbles subside—which they invariably do—the counterreaction is often one of extraordinary ebullience, excitement, and effervescence. We lurch from one extreme to the other. We bounce between delusions of grandeur and the depths of despond. It is arguable, nevertheless, that the malaise is deeper seated this time round, largely because marketing's contemporary maladies stem from its successes rather than its failures. Fifty years ago, when Drucker (1954) first posited the modern marketing concept, the notion of customer orientation was unusual, novel, noteworthy. Its adoption conferred significant competitive advantage on the adopter. Half a century later, however, every organization is customer-oriented, or claims to be. Every mission statement proclaims that customers come first, last, and always. Every marketing department is staffed with MBA-emblazoned or degree-draped executives, all of whom have read Kotler (1967) from cover to cover, can rustle up a marketing plan with the best of them, and spend many a happy weekend on hug-the-customer refresher courses. Parity prevails. Ubiquity rules. Marketing may not be everything, but my goodness, it's everywhere.

Alongside this flattening of the marketing playing field, the game itself is becoming tougher and tougher. Not only are there more products (and services) to choose from than ever before—in every conceivable category, line, and range—but these products (and services) are increasingly indistinguishable. Whether it be detergents, deodorants, dishwashers, or DVDs; chinos, colognes, cornflakes, or cellulite creams; banks, batteries, bottled waters, or barbeque grills; magazines, margarines, motor bikes, or management consultants; SUVs, sneakers, surfboards, or silicon chips; or toothpastes, televisions, theme parks, and tennis rackets, extraordinary abundance and attribute equivalence are the order of the day (Earls 2002). Granted, one of the key functions of marketing is to differentiate the otherwise undifferentiated and insidiously imbue the ostensibly identical with an inimitable aura, image, patina, or personality. But, when marketing itself is omnipresent and the same tools, techniques, and tricks of the trade are available to all, then its ability to do what it's supposed to do is constrained at best and compromised at worst.

Above and beyond the ubiquity of marketing and the perils of plenitude, the customer too is changing. Today's consumers are marketing-literate, marketing-savvy, marketing-weary, and, not least, marketing-wary. They cannot fail to be. After all, our television channels and radio stations are chock-a-block with programs and stories about marketing, consumption, shopper psychology, and all the rest. Standup comics perform lengthy routines on supermarkets, shopping carts, and stereotyped TV ads for shampoo, shaving foam, or sanitary napkins. Glossy magazines routinely apprise their readers of the rationale behind retail store design and the rebranding exercise du jour. Sunday newspaper supplements are replete with reflections on, and deconstructions of, breaking advertising campaigns, as well as industry gossip, impending pitches, and account executive shenanigans. Hollywood movies regularly make use of advertising/marketing/retail store settings—*What Women Want, Crazy People, Clerks, High Fidelity, Scenes From a Mall, You've Got Mail, Working Girl, Soul Man, Pretty Woman, Jerry Maguire, Lost in Translation, Dawn of the Dead, Catwoman*—and, in so doing, reveal the inner workings of the marketing institutions concerned. These inner workings may well be overdramatized caricatures, but they still raise the general public's overall marketing consciousness.

Twenty-first-century consumers, in sum, are wise to marketers' wiles. They are cognizant that the customer is always right. They are aware that customer satisfaction and loyalty are the drivers of corporate competitive strategy. They are fluent in Brandsperanto, Malltalk, Productpatter. They aren't so much Generation X, Y or Z, as Generation®.

WHILE STOCKS LAST

Modern marketing, most would agree, has succeeded beyond its wildest dreams. It has sold itself brilliantly. It is an idea that almost everyone has bought into, consumers included. It is arguable, however, that marketing is beginning to pay the price of success and becoming its own worst enemy. Its scholarly spokespersons are starting to suffer from what some deem groupthink, and others consider arrogance or complacency. For example, when marketing fails in practice—as it often does—the marketing scholars' standard response is that the cause can't possibly be conceptual. It is operational, organizational, or empirical. It is due to managers' inept implementation, incompetent research, incomplete planning, inadequate decision-taking, insufficient attention to quality issues, environmental issues, competitive issues, relationship issues etc., etc., etc. Our customers, in other words, are to blame. The people who buy academicians' ideas are at fault for not following the instructions properly. They're not doing it right! They must try harder next time.

Table 6.1

May Contain Nuts

Experiential	An emergent school of marketing thought that emphasizes ecstasy, emotion, and the delivery of extraordinary consumer experiences. It exploits the "wow" factor, in effect
Environment	An approach that relies on retail store atmospherics, impressive architecture, and the power of space, place, and genius loci. The Niketown phenomenon, in other words
Esthetic	A stance that espouses art, beauty, and design, everything from quirky Alessi kettles and psychedelic Apple iMacs to the Chrysler P.T. Cruiser and the "feel" of a Mont Blanc pen. Art for mart's sake
Ephemeral	A net-driven notion based on buzz-building, fad-forwarding, chat-room churning, brand community boosting, and unleashing the ideavirus. In the beginning was the word of mouth, so to speak
Evangelical	An alternative that taps into the alleged spirituality of consumption. This ranges from the shopping-mall-as-cathedral cliché to the suggestion that CEOs seek solace in the seven deadly sins
Ethical	A perspective predicated on Anita Roddick's precept of trade-not-aid and ecoconscious consumer behavior. Just say no to rapaciousness, exploitation, and waste. Buy a lipstick, save the world
Eccentric	An off-the-wall standpoint that wraps itself in hipness, irreverence, and fun-filled frolics. Instantly recognizable by wacky book titles like *Eat the Big Bananas* or *Hey Wendy's, Squeeze This*
E = MC²	An antidote to eccentricity, which contends that marketing is a science, or would be if it weren't for the bananas brigade. Rigor, rectitude, and reliability are what marketing needs right now. Got that?

Source: Brown 2003, p. 47.

If they were truly committed to marketing they couldn't possibly fail and the fact that they've failed is proof of their lack of commitment. QED.

Obviously, this form of self-justifying self-preservation is completely unacceptable, especially in a field that purports to be customer-oriented. Yet that is exactly what we are seeing now that, to cite a single instance, CRM is starting to turn sour. Fifty years after Drucker's deliberations, the marketing concept has been placed on a pedestal. It is inviolate, untouchable, above criticism. And, while this may have been excusable when marketing was in its infancy—when it really was possible to get things wrong—it no longer holds water when marketing is middle-aged, going on senescent. We can't keep blaming the victims. Perhaps its time to reform the reformers.

In fairness, many scholars are cognizant of marketing's conceptual shortcomings. The shelves of our friendly neighborhood mega bookstores are sagging under the weight of suggested solutions to marketing's ills, some of which are listed in Table 6.1. Summarized under an entirely egregious Eight E's rubric, these range from *Experiential,* a perspective predicated on the emotions of the marketing encounter, to *Esthetic,* which aspires to the condition of art, beauty, and the ineffably sublime.

Welcome and necessary though these exercises in E-type marketing are, the only problem is that they are content to posit more of the same. They are still predicated on the basic premise of customer centricity, the premise that has dominated marketing thought since Drucker's (1954) declaration, Levitt's (1960) popularization, and Kotler's (1967) codification of the marketing concept. Indeed, if the overall message of the marketing E-volutionaries can be briefly paraphrased, it is that marketers need to become *even more* customer-focused than before. These days, customer satisfaction isn't good enough. The customer must be delighted, enchanted, enthralled, enraptured, and, if service quality inflation continues at the current rate, eventually carried away on transports of ecstatic erotic abandon. I gather Tom Peters's latest book might be titled *Getting to Yes, Yes, YES!*

The thinking seems to be that more is always better, that there's no limit to the amount of good lovin' today's customers can take. The brutal fact of the matter, however, is that more isn't always better. Less is sometimes more. Sometimes it's necessary to act cool, play hard to get, and treat 'em mean to keep 'em keen. Sometimes abjuring customers is the best way to attract them. Certainly, many have attributed the success of cult brands like Brioni, Hermès, and Trikkes to their refusal to play the customer-coddling game. Antimarketing marketing, as practiced by Sprite, Diesel, and Madonna among others, is on the up and up. Likewise, the advent of offensive and gross-out marketing—Benetton, FCUK, Opium et al.—dramatically demonstrates that innocuous sales pitches aren't always the most efficacious.

MONEY BACK GUARANTEE

All things considered, the word that best describes marketing's contemporary state is "decadent." This ascription, it must be stressed, is not pejorative, or at least not deliberately so. It refers, rather, to the decadent turn in the arts that emerged at the fin de siècle of the nineteenth century and, some say, reappeared during the fin de siècle of the twentieth (Barzun 2000). Typified by the outlandish esthetic aspirations of Oscar Wilde, Aubrey Beardsley, Arthur Rimbaud, Max Nordau, and so forth, decadence is characterized by an air of exhaustion, enervation, and lassitude. It is artificial, affected, overrefined, self-satisfied, and stylized to the point of pointlessness. It is sickly, it is saccharine, it is strange, it is simultaneously sybaritic and splenetic. It is marked by what Abrams (1993, p. 43) terms, "a special sweet savor of incipient decay."

In this sense, then, marketing is decadent. It fiddles while Rome burns. It appears to be past its prime. It seems to suffer from analysis paralysis, four-Ps fatigue, imagination deficit disorder. It gives the impression of being bereft, bloated, out of ideas, on the slide. It is in a rut, stuck in the mud, spinning its wheels. It is going round in circles, as the recent rapid recent rise of retromarketing attests. The merest glance across the marketing landscape reveals that contemporary commercial culture is replete with retro this, retro that, retro the other—retro autos, retro speedboats, retro telephones, retro fashions, retro housewares, retro communities, retro lawnmowers, retro movies, retro celebrities, retro restaurants, retro casinos, retro television advertisements, and many more besides. According to acerbic comedian George Carlin (1997, p. 110), "Our culture is composed of sequels, reruns, remakes, revivals, reissues, re-releases, re-creations, adaptations, anniversaries, memorabilia, oldies radio and nostalgia record collections."

Needless to say, there has been much debate about the cause of this remarkable retro outbreak. For some, it is due to the midlife yearnings of aging baby boomers, who pine for the products and services of their gilded youth. For others, it is a consequence of twenty-first-century life, the sheer pace of which has prompted an understandable yearning for safer, simpler, less sophisticated times, as well as brands associated with the balmy days of yore. For yet others, it is indicative of marketing's bankruptcy, its lack of creativity, the fact that every conceivable marketing tactic, strategy, stunt, plan, advert, angle, or whatever, has already been tried and there is nothing left to do but recycle the past, plunder the memory banks, and pore over dusty growth-share matrices in the hope that yesterday's dogs will be tomorrow's stars.

Regardless of the reasons, or the question of whether retro is a good thing or bad, the salient point is that retro itself is not new (Brown 2001). Retro goes around in circles, too. There have been several "nostalgia booms" prior to this one, most notably in the 1970s, 1930s, and 1890s. We have been here before and, as noted at the outset of this commentary, the notion that marketing needs reform has also been floated before. Calls for repentance come and go, wax and wane, rise and fall. We have lashed, lacerated, and lambasted ourselves many times over and no doubt will continue to do so in future. Indeed, it is fairly safe to predict that, once we get through the present phase of doom-and-gloom, the manic side of our bipolar personality will reassert itself. Someone will announce a technological breakthrough, a revolutionary insight, a new marketing paradigm, or a counterintuitive mode of thinking that'll transform the discipline, save the world and, naturally, place marketing back on top where it belongs.

WASH, RINSE, REPEAT

While we're waiting, it may be worthwhile—in the spirit of reform and retro—to return to the present debate's point of departure: namely, the fifty-year-old words of Peter Drucker, whose customer-centric, marketing-encompasses-everything ethos is quoted in the "call" (Sisodia and Sheth 2004). Understandably, this inaugural statement means a great deal to marketing scholars, and so it should. However, if we go beyond Drucker's much-cited sound bite and reconsider what the great guru actually says in *The Practice of Management,* two things are crystal clear. The first of these is that marketing should be *proactive* rather than *reactive.* Marketing's purpose, Drucker proclaims, is to make things happen, to lead rather than follow, to deliberately "create a customer." It is not about responding to consumers' expressed needs or taking environmental and competitive conditions into account, important though these are. It is about driving, forcing, leading, commanding, compelling, propelling, arousing, and bulldozing, if need be. Thus, it is arguable that total customer orientation—placing the customer on a pedestal and pandering to their heart's desire, as E-type marketers recommend—is making marketing reactive rather than proactive and, while reactive marketing has its place, it's not what Drucker originally had in mind:

> Markets are not created by God, nature or economic forces, but by business men. The want they satisfy may have been felt by the customer before he was offered the means of satisfying it. It may indeed, like the want of food in a famine, have dominated the customer's life and filled all his waking moments. But it was a theoretical want before; only when the action of business men makes it effective demand is there a customer, a market. It may have been an unfelt want. There may have been no want at all until business action created it—by advertising, by salesmanship, or by inventing something new. In every case it is business action that creates a customer. (Drucker 1954, p. 35)

The other realization that comes from rereading *The Practice of Management* concerns Drucker's contention that his precepts only apply to business organizations, the for-profit sector, the purveyors of economic goods and services. He specifically eschews the application of management principles—marketing included—to the not-for-profit arena and disdains the idea that managerial acumen can be appropriately exercised in the societal sphere.

> The skills, the competence, the experience of management cannot, as such, be transferred and applied to the organization and running of other institutions. In particular, a man's success in management carries by itself no promise—let alone a guarantee—of his being

successful in government. A career in management is, by itself, not a preparation for major political office—or for leadership in the Armed Forces, the Church or a university. (Drucker 1954, p. 8)

Suffice it to say, this proscription runs completely counter to established marketing sentiment, which has long subscribed to the view—since the "broadening" debate of the late 1960s, at least— that the marketing concept can be applied in every conceivable company, context, or circumstance. When something applies to everything, however, it effectively cancels itself out and ultimately applies to nothing. Certainly, marketing's temporary contemporary difficulties cannot be divorced from its "imperial overreach." Indeed, it's got to the ludicrous point where basic marketing principles—acquired at Harvard Business School, no less—are being adapted to husband hunting, of all things. In *The Program,* Greenwald (2004) recommends that wannabe brides market themselves as eligible brands in order to overcome the competition and capture the man of their dreams. One suspects that if Drucker had imagined where his ruminations would lead, he'd have kept his marketing thoughts to himself.

If nothing else, then, rereading *The Practice of Management* reminds us that less is sometimes more. A bit less marketing wouldn't go amiss. "A good thing," as the imperishable Ted Levitt (1991, p. 6) rightly observes, "is not necessarily improved by its multiplication."

Marketing doesn't need reform; it needs restraint.

REFERENCES

Abrams, M.H. (1993), *A Glossary of Literary Terms,* 6th ed. Fort Worth, TX: Harcourt Brace Jovanovich.

Barzun, Jacques (2000), *From Dawn to Decadence: 500 Years of Western Cultural Life.* New York: HarperCollins.

Brown, Stephen (2001), *Marketing—The Retro Revolution.* London: Sage.

—— (2002), "Crisis, What Crisis? Marketing, Midas, and the Croesus of Representation," *Qualitative Market Research, An International Journal,* 6 (3), 194–205.

—— (2003), *Free Gift Inside!!* Oxford: Capstone.

Carlin, George (1997), *Brain Droppings.* New York: Hyperion.

Drucker, Peter (1954), *The Practice of Management.* Oxford: Butterworth-Heinemann.

Earls, Mark (2002) *Welcome to the Creative Age: Bananas, Business and the Death of Marketing.* New York: John Wiley.

Greenwald, Rachel (2004), *The Program: Fifteen Steps to Finding a Husband After Thirty.* New York: Time Warner.

Hollander, Stanley C. and Kathleen M. Rassuli (1993), *Marketing,* Vol. 1. Aldershot, UK: Edward Elgar.

Kotler, Philip (1967), *Marketing Management: Analysis, Planning and Control.* Englewood Cliffs, NJ: Prentice Hall.

Levitt, Theodore (1960), "Marketing Myopia," *Harvard Business Review,* 38 (4), 45–56.

—— (1991), *Thinking About Management.* New York: Free Press.

McKenna, Regis (1991), "Marketing Is Everything," *Harvard Business Review,* 69 (1), 65–79.

Simms, Jane (2004), "You're Not Paranoid, They Do Hate You," *Marketing,* May 19, 32–34.

Sisodia, Raj and Jadish N. Sheth (2004), "Does Marketing Need Reform?" www.bentley.edu/events/markreform/ (accessed August 12, 2004).

Wallace, David Foster (2004), *Oblivion: Stories.* London: Abacus.

CHAPTER 7

THE MORALITY OF MARKETS, MARKETING, AND THE CORPORATE PURPOSE

DEBRA JONES RINGOLD

I subscribe to the view that choice is inherently good and defensibly constrained only when "conduct [is] . . . calculated to produce evil to someone else" (Mill 1947, p. 10). Choice embodies two notions. The first refers to the act of choosing, that is, the freedom to engage in deliberate actions on one's own responsibility. The second refers to the options from which one may choose. Both are prerequisites to moral behavior. In order to do good, there must exist the possibility of choosing between right and wrong and one must have the freedom to do so.

"Every human person . . . has the natural right to be recognized as a free and responsible being. All owe to each other this duty of respect. The *right to the exercise of freedom* . . . is an inalienable requirement of the dignity of the human person" (*Catechism of the Catholic Church* 1995, p. 482, emphasis in original). This duty of respect ought to be extended to consumers.

Bauer (1958, 1964), Calfee and Ringold (1992), and Ringold (1995) have made the argument that individual consumers are quite capable of navigating markets, exercising choice in a manner consistent with their preferences, and learning from their mistakes. Yet, consumer competence is often disparaged, most apparently when consumer behavior reflects economic or social preferences at odds with those of others in the marketplace. Arguably, these assaults on consumer competence derive from the well-documented "third-person effect" exemplified by respondents who assert their own competence while disparaging the ability of others and call for greater regulation to protect the incompetent among us (Rojas, Shah, and Faber 1996; Shah, Faber, and Youn 1999 and citations therein).

Such judgments are at best patronizing. In the aggregate, consumers appear to be smarter than the elite few, outperforming experts in problem solving, forecasting, and decision making (Surowiecki 2004). This result is consistent with Hoch (1988), who finds that experts cannot overcome the "information deficit" that results from their being unlike the typical American consumer, and Posner (2003, p. 206) who argues that "[e]xperts constitute a distinct class in society with values and perspectives that differ systematically from those of 'ordinary' people."

In contrast to economies centrally planned by experts, free economies—communities united by voluntary exchange—create circumstances in which individuals exercise choice, commanding dignity and respect (McGurn 2004). They foster diverse, disaggregated, and competitive economic interests (Novak 1996) and in so doing, decentralize and disperse power (Scherer and Ross 1990). Individuals are free to choose whatever trade or profession they desire, engage in any business enterprise they wish, buy from and sell to anyone they choose (Scherer and Ross 1990) and are largely free to spend their income and other resources in a manner consistent with their values.[1]

Markets are inherently other-regarding (McGurn 2004); producers cater to consumers, differentiating products to appeal to particular tastes. Markets create the wealth that helps the poor escape poverty (Novak 1996). They reduce envy through open economic opportunity and economic growth (Novak 1996). Capitalism fosters trust and cooperation because "trade and exchange are games in which everyone can end up gaining, rather than zero-sum games in which there's always a winner and a loser" (Surowiecki 2004, p. 118). Thus, while markets are not perfect, in the main, they deliver individual prosperity, unprecedented individual freedom, and amidst this prosperity and liberty, the opportunity to lead a virtuous life (D'Souza 2000).

"The purpose of a business firm is to be a community of persons endeavoring to satisfy basic needs at the service of the whole of society . . . [t]he Church acknowledges the legitimate role of profit as an indication that a business is functioning well" (John Paul II, 1992, paragraph 35). This is in part the doctrine offered by Levitt (1986, pp. 5–7), who observed that superior corporate performance is achieved by "figuring out what people really want and value, and then catering to those wants and values. [This] statement of [corporate] purpose . . . provides specific guidance and has moral merit." In denouncing profit as *the* end to which organizational means are put, Levitt (1986, p. xxiii) argues that "profit is a meaningless statement of the corporate purpose. Without customers in sufficient and steady numbers there is no business."

While not the purpose of business, profit is one measure of an organization's ability to effectively satisfy consumers using the most efficient techniques or processes and a minimum amount of inputs. Empirical evidence suggests several mechanisms by which greater customer satisfaction leads to greater shareholder value (see Anderson, Fornell, and Mazvancheryl 2004 and citations therein). For example, higher levels of customer satisfaction lead to greater customer retention and significantly lower transaction, "rework," and customer replacement costs. Higher levels of customer satisfaction lead to higher levels of employee satisfaction and productivity and reduced turnover and labor costs. The longer-term view and greater sensitivity to societal values and priorities characteristic of customer-oriented organizations have been found to foster superior compliance with normative and legal expectations, thus lowering overall operating costs. Best (2004, p. 15) concludes, "[t]he ultimate objective of any given marketing strategy should be to attract, satisfy, and retain target customers. If a business can accomplish this objective with a competitive advantage in attractive markets, the business will produce above-average profits."

Thus, profit making, when conceptualized as a *consequence* of satisfying consumers with products and services of real value, is a high calling. Profit is a useful measure of the corporate contribution to society because it is a metric by which satisfaction is measured in terms of consumer willingness and ability to pay. Given that corporate performance is most universally measured in terms of profits, one can well understand the assertion that "there is one and only one social responsibility of business—to use its resources and engage in activities designed to increase its profits so long as it stays within the rules of the game,[2] which is to say, engages in open and free competition, without deception or fraud" (Friedman 1962, p. 133).

Corporations produce the greatest societal return on investment by focusing on two priorities: (1) developing and deploying the distinctive capabilities necessary to create superior customer value and (2) capturing externalities, reducing transaction costs, and in other ways improving economic efficiency. Thus, "[t]here can be no corporate strategy that is not in some fundamental fashion a marketing strategy, no purpose that does not respond somehow to what people are willing to buy for a price" (Levitt 1986, p. 7).

Kotler (2003, p. 9) defines marketing as "a societal process by which individuals and groups obtain what they need and want through creating, offering, and freely exchanging products and services of values with others." Its importance to the welfare of modern societies is evident. "The wealth of the industrialized nations is based much more on [know-how, technology, and skill] than on natural resources. A person produces something so that others may use it after they have paid a just price, mutually agreed upon through free bargaining. The ability to foresee both the needs of others and the factors best fit to satisfying those needs is another source of wealth in modern society. In this way, the role of disciplined and creative human work and initiative and entrepreneurial ability becomes increasingly decisive" (John Paul II, 1992, paragraph 32). Thus, marketing is the process by which individuals and organizations are compelled to be attuned to satisfying their neighbor's wants and desires.

Organizations seeking to maximize consumer satisfaction depend on consumer definitions of satisfaction, the existence of particular social constructs, and virtue itself to direct these efforts. Fukuyama (1996, p. 11) makes this very case:

> If the institutions of democracy and capitalism are to work properly, they must coexist with certain premodern cultural habits that ensure their proper functioning. Law, contract, and economic rationality provide a necessary but not sufficient basis for both the stability and prosperity of post-industrial societies; they must as well be leavened with reciprocity, moral obligation, duty toward community, and trust, which are based in *habit* rather than rational calculation [emphasis added]. The latter are not anachronisms in a modern society but rather the sine qua non of the latter's success.

Moral lapses within the domain of commerce may be attributable to unrestrained consumer appetites, abdication of personal responsibility, managerial transgressions, or self-centered corporate strategy. More troubling, deterioration of society's stock of habitual virtue may be at the heart of recent corporate scandals. Reformers might well consider how individual consumers can be made more accountable for their choices, how organizations can better keep promises to consumers, and how we can strengthen institutions charged with teaching the ground rules (i.e., reciprocity, moral obligation, duty toward community, and trust) necessary to successful markets and democracy itself.

When addressing these questions, reformers must be careful to buttress society's commitment to the ground rules rather than attempt to alter consumer tastes and preferences at variance with their own. Areeda and Kaplow (1997, p. 9) offer this caution:

> Those who doubt the wisdom or propriety of consumer tastes will have reason to question and perhaps alter the perfectly competitive result. They may seek to have government restrict or tax individual or business choices when existing consumers have "insufficient" regard for future generations or when the "wrong" kinds of commodities are purchased. They may want government to subsidize certain goods and services that they feel individuals and firms undervalue. Finally, they may ask government to affect consumer choice through education and persuasion.

The morality of free markets derives from the opportunity to exercise personal prerogative. The morality of marketing organizations derives from the potential of one group of people to satisfy the wants and needs of another. It is important that we not indict, and attempt to curtail, the processes that foster consumer choice when our quarrel is actually with the choices consumers freely make. Marketing organizations seek to influence, but ultimately respond to, societal preferences. Marketing reflects (i.e., follows, responds to) rather than manipulates (i.e., initiates, leads) societal preferences and values (Holbrook 1987). Efforts to regulate the tastes and preferences of consumers directly contradict traditional notions of consumer sovereignty (Bloom and Smith 1986) and the purpose of organizations as described above. If reformers wish to modify consumer tastes and preferences, let them freely compete for consumer hearts and minds in the marketplace of ideas.

That marketing is the object of public criticism is nothing new. Years ago, Levitt (1986, p. 215) observed that:

> Everywhere marketing is maligned for its pushy, noisy, manipulative intrusions into our lives; its corruptive teachings of greed and hedonism; its relentless pursuit of the consumer's cash, regardless of consequence, save the profit of the seller. Paradoxically, these complaints seem to rise in direct proportion to the . . . implementation of the idea that success is most assured by responding in every fiscally prudent way to what people actually want and value.

Should we be surprised by what he calls "the perverse simultaneity of a triumphant marketing concept that seeks to better satisfy the public and a less satisfied public" (Levitt 1986, p. 225)? Levitt's paradox seems a logical (and desired) consequence of a marketplace committed to consumer satisfaction. With every improvement in the deployment of organizational resources to satisfy specific consumer desires, we "bid up" consumer expectations for better, faster, and cheaper everything. Consumers are never completely satisfied with what is offered them and often disapprove what is offered others. "[W]hile more people are better satisfied by getting a chance to buy what's better tailored to their specific functional or psychosocial wants, [others] get frustrated, annoyed or distracted by marketing programs . . . they don't want, or can't afford but would like to have" (Levitt 1986, p. 225). This is the ever-present challenge that requires the "marketing imagination" of Levitt's title.

Thus, as we contemplate reform, we must embrace, and work to enhance, a marketplace inhabited by competent consumers and organizations in business to serve them, while recognizing the inherent morality of choice. Our efforts are best invested in enhancing the responsiveness of markets, organizations, and marketing to consumer preferences. Reform would therefore be well directed at educational, religious, and familial institutions wherein inculcating the values of reciprocity, moral obligation, duty toward community, and trust can and should influence the manner in which market participants treat one another. After all, market imperfections such as externalities, information asymmetries, moral hazards, transaction costs, and the like result when these basic values or ground rules are abandoned. Moreover, efforts to inculcate these basic values stand a better chance of improving markets than regulatory substitutes and the often-unintended consequences thereof.

NOTES

The comments of Janis K. Pappalardo and G. Frederick Thompson on an earlier draft of this essay are most appreciated.

1. Friedman and Friedman (1980) take issue with this assertion, suggesting that many of our economic freedoms have been eroded by local, state, and federal regulations.

2. Elsewhere, Friedman elaborates "the basic rules of society, both those embodied in law and those embodied in ethical custom" (1970, p. 33).

REFERENCES

Anderson, E.W., C. Fornell, and S.K. Mazvancheryl (2004), "Customer Satisfaction and Shareholder Value," *Journal of Marketing*, 68 (October), 172–85.

Areeda, Phillip and Louis Kaplow (1997), *Antitrust Analysis Problems, Text, Cases*. New York: Aspen Law & Business.

Bauer, Raymond A. (1958), "Limits of Persuasion: The Hidden Persuaders Are Made of Straw," *Harvard Business Review,* 36 (5), 105–10.

——— (1964), "The Obstinate Audience: The Influence Process from the Point of View of Social Communication," *American Psychologist,* 19 (May), 319–28.

Best, Roger J. (2004), *Market-Based Management: Strategies for Growing Customer Value and Profitability,* 3d ed. Upper Saddle River, NJ: Prentice Hall.

Bloom, P.N. and R.B. Smith (1986), *The Future of Consumerism.* Lexington, MA: Lexington Books.

Calfee, J.E. and D.J. Ringold (1992), "The Cigarette Advertising Controversy: Assumptions About Consumers, Regulation, and Scientific Debate," *Advances in Consumer Research,* 19, 557–62.

Catechism of the Catholic Church (1995), 2d ed. Revised in Accordance with the Official Latin Text Promulgated by Pope John Paul II. New York: Doubleday.

D'Souza, Dinesh (2000), *The Virtue of Prosperity: Finding Values in an Age of Techno-Affluence.* New York: The Free Press.

Friedman, Milton (1962), *Capitalism and Freedom.* Chicago: University of Chicago Press.

——— (1970), "The Social Responsibility of Business Is to Increase Its Profits," *New York Times Magazine,* September 13, 32.

——— and Rose D. Friedman (1980), *Free to Choose: A Personal Statement.* New York: Harcourt Brace Jovanovich.

Fukuyama, Francis (1996), *Trust: The Social Virtues and the Creation of Prosperity.* New York: Free Press.

Hoch, Stephen J. (1988), "Who Do We Know: Predicting the Interests and Opinions of the American Consumer," *Journal of Consumer Research,* 15 (December), 315–24.

Holbrook, Morris B. (1987), "Mirror, Mirror, on the Wall, What's Unfair in the Reflections on Advertising," *Journal of Marketing,* 51 (July), 95–103.

John Paul II (1992), *"Centesimus Annus,"* in *A New Worldly Order: John Paul II and Human Freedom,* George Weigel, ed. Washington, DC: Ethics and Policy Center.

Kotler, Philip (2003), *Marketing Management,* 11th ed. Upper Saddle River, NJ: Prentice Hall.

Levitt, Theodore (1986), *The Marketing Imagination.* New York: The Free Press.

McGurn, William (2004), *Is the Market Moral? A Dialogue on Religion, Economics, and Justice,* E.J. Dionne Jr., J.B. Elshtain, and K. Drogosz, eds. Washington, DC: Brookings Institution Press.

Mill, John Stuart (1947), *On Liberty,* A. Castell, ed. New York: Appleton-Century-Crofts.

Novak, Michael (1996), *Business as a Calling: Work and the Examined Life.* New York: The Free Press.

Posner, Richard A. (2003), *Law, Pragmatism, and Democracy.* Cambridge: Harvard University Press.

Ringold, Debra Jones (1995), "Social Criticisms of Target Marketing: Process or Product?" *American Behavioral Scientist,* 38 (February), 578–92.

Rojas, H., D.V. Shah, and R.J. Faber (1996), "For the Good of Others: Censorship and the Third-Person Effect," *International Journal of Public Opinion Research,* 8 (2), 163–85.

Scherer, F.M. and D. Ross (1990), *Industrial Market Structure and Economic Performance,* 3d ed. Boston: Houghton Mifflin.

Shah, D.V., R.J. Faber, and S. Youn (1999), "Susceptibility and Severity: Perceptual Dimensions Underlying the Third-Person Effect," *Communication Research,* 26 (2), 240–67.

Surowiecki, James (2004), *The Wisdom of Crowds.* New York: Doubleday.

CHAPTER 8

ON REFORMING MARKETING

For Marketing Systems and Brand Equity Strategy

SHELBY D. HUNT

Many commentators believe that both marketing practice and marketing academe need reform. As to marketing practice, for example, J. Walker Smith (2004) of Yankelovich Partners points to studies showing that marketing productivity is declining and consumer activism and expectations are growing. For him, the increasing resistance of consumers to conventional mass marketing communications implies that firms must precisely target their messages, avoid using demographic proxies for targeting, ensure that all messages are relevant to consumer needs, and earn the trust of their customers. As a second practice example, Jagdish Sheth (2004) argues that marketing, headed by a "chief customer officer," should shift from being a line and business-unit function to a corporate and staff function. This shift would imply that marketing should (1) report directly to the chief executive officer, (2) have responsibilities for branding, key account management, and business development, and (3) manage outside suppliers (e.g., market research firms and advertising agencies).

As to marketing academe, Robert Lusch (2004), drawing on Vargo and Lusch (2004), argues that marketing has suffered from a goods-centered logic that it inherited from equilibrium economics. For him, marketing should shift toward a dynamic, "service-dominant logic" that (1) focuses on specialized skills and knowledge as operant resources, (2) strives to maximize consumers' involvement in developing customized offerings, (3) aims toward an organizational philosophy that leads in initiating and coordinating a market-driven perspective, (4) stresses service provision in teaching the principles course, and (5) teaches marketing strategy courses based on resource-advantage theory. As a second example, Sheth (2004) believes that marketing academe's problems stem from its esoteric, nonfunded, and ad hoc research. He argues that it should shift toward newsworthy, funded, and programmatic research. On a different theme, William Wilkie (2004), drawing on Wilkie and Moore (2003), points out that, because academic marketing research has become increasingly fragmented, much marketing knowledge is being *lost*. For example, Alderson's (1957, 1965) contributions to understanding marketing systems are unknown to many marketing academics (and underappreciated by most). In terms of the "three dichotomies model" model of marketing (Hunt 1976, 2002), Wilkie argues for more *macropositive* and *macronormative* research. Specifically, he recommends that (1) studies of marketing systems and (2) research on the relationship between marketing systems and society be reinstituted as intrinsic parts of mainstream marketing. These topics, he points out, were central to marketing prior to its shift toward marketing management in the 1950s and 1960s.

Consistent with Wilkie (2004), this chapter argues for the importance in marketing academe of studying marketing systems and society. I do so by using the example of the attacks on marketing's emphasis on brands and brand equity as components of dynamic marketing systems. Consistent with Vargo and Lusch (2004), I use resource-advantage theory as a foundation for exploring whether society benefits or loses from the use of brand marketing. Specifically, this chapter argues *for* the study of dynamic marketing systems and *for* the use of brand equity strategies in such systems.

THE INDICTMENT OF BRANDING

The indictment of brand marketing comes from many quarters. Here, I briefly review the attacks from antiglobalization activists, marketing academics, and equilibrium-oriented economists.

Antiglobalization Activists

Attacks on branding by antiglobalization activists have been greatly influenced by the book, *No Logo,* by Canadian journalist and social activist Naomi Klein (2000). (An Internet search for "No Logo" will yield hundreds of thousands of hits.) Klein's book attacks global brands (especially *American* global brands), and is divided into four sections: No Space, No Choice, No Jobs, and No Logo. The first section documents the pervasiveness of global brands; the second chastises global brands for replacing local alternatives; the third associates global brands with job losses in developed countries; and the fourth sets out an agenda for antiglobalization activists. For Klein, global brands exploit Third World workers (e.g., sweatshops and child labor), increase domestic unemployment, reduce domestic wages, erode workers' rights, censor the media, and debase local cultures by making them more homogeneous. She argues for boycotting global brands, disrupting shareholder meetings, filing lawsuits, and picketing trade conferences. Her hope is that, "as more people discover the brand-name secrets of the global logo, their outrage will fuel the next big political movement, a vast wave of opposition squarely targeting transnational corporations, particularly those with high name recognition" (Klein 2000, p. xviii).

Marketing Academe

In marketing academe, a major attack on brand marketing comes from Johny Johansson (2004a), who inquires: "Is American marketing morally bankrupt?" For him, "the answer is yes." His bankruptcy claim is detailed in his book, *In Your Face* (Johansson 2004b), in which he asks, "What are global marketers doing wrong?" He responds, "The answer seems to lie in their emphasis on global branding" (p. 12). Using Klein's (2000) indictment as a starting point, Johansson links together three movements: (1) antimarketing, (2) antiglobalization, and (3) anti-Americanism. He maintains, "The Americans were the main proponents of war, and they were also the main proponents of globalization. Anti-Americanism and anti-globalization seemed two sides of the same coin, and marketing surely played a common role in both movements" (2004b, p. xviii). Linking anti-Americanism with antiglobalization enables him to explain the fact that 121 of the brands indexed in Klein's *No Logo* were American, and only nineteen were European.

Johansson (2004b) views with favor Klein's charges against American brand marketing. He also faults American marketers and what he calls the American government's "Brand America campaign" for arguing their positions with "arrogant zeal" and an "in-your-face attitude" (p. 17). He accuses American marketers of promoting "materialism and superficiality" (p. 39), and he complains that "the rate of technological innovation is so high that products are obsolete while still perfectly functional" (p. 40). Indeed, " the free market system . . . is out of whack, and our consumer paradise has turned into a quagmire of commercialism, consumption, and materialism (p. 41). For him, "The problem with these brands is that they encourage an *American lifestyle* based on superficiality and fads, all engineered by profit-seeking marketers. It is this new consumerspace with its in-your-face marketing techniques that threatens engrained ways of life and traditional culture" (p. 119). Although Johansson acknowledges that "there is no gainsaying the statistical fact that the standard of living is higher with free markets" (p. 72), he maintains that American proglobalist writers fail to recognize that "in most other societies, particularly those older than America, . . . economic and social progress is much more of a zero-sum game" (p. 158). That is, for him, in most societies, one group's economic gain is another's loss, one group's progress is another's regress.

For Johansson, "In the race to the bottom [in America], marketing has, not unwittingly, played a major role" (p. 159). The "race to the bottom" in America results from its diversity: "Considering the multiracial, multi-ethnic, and multicultural mix of people inhabiting the U.S., the popular choice of the majority naturally involves a 'lowest common denominator'" (p. 159). Why the "lowest common denominator"? Because, he explains, whereas "advanced and sophisticated expressions or products" can be used in racially and ethnically homogeneous societies, in America, "to appeal to a multicultural and multi-ethnic mass market, simple statements about simple things that all can agree on are needed" (p. 159).[1] He concludes his indictment of American brand marketing by, as he puts it, trying to find grounds to "accentuate the positive" (p. 183). Alas, for him, "I would like to say there are some positive signs [in American marketing], but honestly, I don't see any" (p. 183).

Equilibrium Economics

Attacks on branding are also common in neoclassical economics. The hostility of equilibrium economics to branding stems from its reliance on perfect competition theory and the view that brands (i.e., trademarks) are anticompetitive because they promote product differentiation, which, in turn, promotes market power and monopoly. Chamberlin's (1962) seminal analysis provides the standard view in equilibrium economics. He points out that the legal protection of trademarks fosters product differentiation and, therefore, a situation in which prices are higher (p. 88), quantities produced are lower (p. 88), excess capacity is permanent (p. 109), products are inferior (p. 99), and all factors of production are exploited (p. 183). Because, for him (p. 270), "the protection of trademarks from infringement . . . is the protection of monopoly," he inquires whether there are arguments by which the "monopolies protected by the law of unfair competition and of trademarks may be justified" (p. 271).

As to the rights of producers in their own names, Chamberlin (1962, p. 272) first defines a trademark as "any sign, mark, symbol, word or words which indicate the origin or ownership of an article as distinguished from its quality," and he asks: "where does identification leave off and differentiation begin?" His analysis suggests that trademarks in fact stand not just as devices for "mere identification" but also signal levels of quality as well. Therefore, as to whether producers have intellectual property rights in their names:

> There seem to be no grounds upon which he [the producer] may justly claim such protection. Given that the consumer is equally satisfied with the goods of two sellers, the entrance of the second into the field [with the first seller's name] must be regarded as the natural flow of capital under competition to check the profits of the first and to adjust the supply of the commodity to the demand for it at cost. (p. 272)

As to the interests of consumers, Chamberlin (1962) evaluates three arguments that might seem to imply that consumers actually benefit from the legal protection of trademarks: (1) trademarks stimulate variety, (2) trademarks protect consumers from deception and fraud, and (3) trademarks encourage producers to maintain the quality of their goods. As to the first, given the tradeoff between more variety and the efficiency of more competition, he argues against trademark protection because "less monopoly would be created" and "useless differentiation would be discouraged" (p. 273). As to the second and third arguments, he maintains that "equally effective" as trademark *protection* "would be a policy of permitting imitation [of a trademark] only if it were perfect, or of defining standards of quality by law" (p. 273). Whereas he believes the former is "condemned by its impracticality," the latter solution "has large possibilities, especially in the case of staples" (p. 273). Chamberlin (1962) concludes his evaluation by recommending that, if trademarks warrant legal protection at all, it should be limited to five years. Such protection, he argues, would sufficiently prompt innovation and:

> The wastes of advertising . . . would be reduced, for no one could afford to build up goodwill by this means, only to see it vanish through the unimpeded entrance of competitors. There would be more nearly equal returns to all producers and the elimination of sustained monopoly profits. All in all, there would be a closer approach to those beneficent results ordinarily pictured as working themselves out under "free competition." (p. 274)

Chamberlin's (1962) analysis of trademarks graphically illustrates the power of a research tradition to frame both what phenomena are problems and what factors get considered. The fact that consumers use trademarks as heuristics indicating quality is a problem to be solved because of neoclassical theory's exclusive focus on static-equilibrium efficiency. That is, trademarks are a problem because they contribute to product differentiation, which is itself a problem because of its inconsistency with perfect competition and the welfare implications of static equilibrium. In contrast, because property rights are outside the scope of equilibrium analysis, the moral implications of transgressing the rights that producers have in their names is outside the scope of the analysis and not even considered. Similarly, that "trademarks stimulate variety" can be dismissed with a wave of the hand because the variety so stimulated is probably *useless* differentiation. Furthermore, the goal of government is not to protect property rights, but to increase static efficiency by encouraging the imitation of successful innovators through the use of the coercive power of the state to enforce common quality standards. Such coercion, Chamberlin assures us, will be "equally effective" as the use of trademarks in consumers' search for information.

All research traditions have foundational premises. And these premises, as the neoclassical approach to branding reminds us (or should remind us), *count*.

FOR MARKETING SYSTEMS AND BRAND EQUITY STRATEGY

As the preceding shows, the attacks on brand marketing come from numerous and influential sources. Given the great emphasis on brand marketing in both practice and academe, one might expect to find vigorous defenses of branding in texts and journals. Such is not the case. Texts on strategic brand management discuss topics such as how to build brand equity, communicate brand attributes, and manage brand portfolios, but they devote almost no space to the role of brands in the economy or the impact of branding on society. Similarly, the academic literature is largely silent on these issues. For example, the widely cited special issue on branding in the *Journal of*

Marketing Research in May of 1994 contained twelve expositions of branding issues, but not a single article devoted to the role of brands in the economy or society.[2]

As Wilkie points out, prior to the shift toward marketing management in the 1950s and 1960s, texts and articles in marketing, influenced by the commodity, institutional, and functional approaches to marketing, would devote significant space to analyses of marketing systems and the impact of such systems on society. I agree with him that marketing's texts and scholarship have been remiss in not giving more attention to issues such the role of brands in marketing systems. Although this brief chapter cannot address *all* the issues raised by the many critics of brand marketing, what can be offered is a start that focuses on the "anticompetitive" charge leveled at brand marketing in neoclassical economics.

An Inchoation

The fundamental thesis of brand equity strategy is that, to achieve competitive advantage and, thereby, superior financial performance, firms should acquire, develop, nurture, and leverage an effectiveness-enhancing portfolio of brands.[3] Are firms' brand equity strategies pro-competitive or anticompetitive, good for society or bad? Answering this question requires exploring the role of branding in market-based economies. Because market-based economies are premised on self-directed, privately owned firms competing with each other, understanding the role of brands in the economy requires a theory of how firms compete. Here, I use as a foundation the resource-advantage (R-A) theory of competition, first articulated in Hunt and Morgan (1995), later developed in numerous articles, and summarized in Hunt (2000). Resource-advantage theory is particularly appropriate for the task at hand because it is (1) a dynamic theory of competition, (2) recommended by Vargo and Lusch (2004) as a vehicle for teaching strategy, and (3) argued to be toward a general theory of marketing (Hunt 2002). Indeed, one of the grounds for the "general theory of marketing" claim is that R-A theory incorporates key parts of Alderson's "lost" work on marketing systems.

For R-A theory, competition is an evolutionary, dynamic, disequilibrating process that consists of "the constant struggle among firms for comparative advantages in resources that will yield marketplace positions of competitive advantage for some market segment(s), and thereby, superior financial performance" (Hunt 2000, p. 135). The theory stresses the importance of (1) market segments, (2) heterogeneous firm resources, (3) comparative advantages/disadvantages in resources, and (4) marketplace positions of competitive advantage/disadvantage. In brief, market segments are defined as intraindustry groups of consumers whose tastes and preferences with regard to an industry's output are *relatively* homogeneous. Resources are the tangible and intangible entities available to the firm that enable it to produce efficiently and/or effectively market offerings that have value for some marketing segment(s).

Resources can be categorized as financial (e.g., cash resources and access to financial markets), physical (e.g., plants and equipment), legal (e.g., trademarks and licenses), human (e.g., the skills and knowledge of individual employees), organizational (e.g., competences, controls, policies, and culture), informational (e.g., knowledge from consumer and competitive intelligence), and relational (e.g., relationships with suppliers and customers). Each firm in the marketplace has a set of resources that is in some ways unique (e.g., knowledgeable employees or efficient production processes) that could potentially result in a marketplace position of competitive advantage. Just as international trade theory recognizes that nations have heterogeneous, immobile resources, and it focuses on the importance of comparative advantages in resources to explain the benefits of trade, R-A theory recognizes that many of the resources of firms within the same industry are significantly heterogeneous and relatively immobile. There-fore, analogous to nations, some firms will have comparative advantages and others compara-tive disadvantages in efficiently and/or effectively producing particular market offerings that have value for particular market segments.

Specifically, when firms have a comparative advantage (disadvantage) in resources, they will occupy marketplace positions of competitive advantage (disadvantage). Marketplace positions of competitive advantage (disadvantage) then result in superior (inferior) financial performance. Therefore, firms compete for comparative advantages in resources that will yield marketplace positions of competitive advantage for some market segment(s) and, thereby, superior financial performance. Competition is influenced by five environmental factors: the societal resources on which firms draw, the societal institutions that structure economic actions, the specific actions of competitors and suppliers, the behavior of consumers, and public policy.

Firms seek marketplace positions of competitive advantage because they lead to superior fi-nancial performance. In general, firms occupy marketplace positions of competitive advantage when they have an efficiency advantage (i.e., producing market offerings at lower cost than ri-vals), an effectiveness advantage (i.e., producing market offerings that are perceived as being more valuable than those of rivals), or both an efficiency advantage and an effectiveness advan-tage. Therefore, competition is both efficiency- and effectiveness-seeking.

Firms learn through competition because of the feedback from their relative financial perfor-mance signaling relative market position, which, in turn, signals relative resources. When firms competing for a market segment learn from their inferior financial performance that they occupy positions of competitive disadvantage, they attempt to neutralize and/or leapfrog the advantaged firm(s) by acquisition and/or innovation. That is, they attempt to acquire the same resource as the advantaged firm(s), and/or they attempt to innovate by imitating the resource, finding an equiva-lent resource, or finding (creating) a superior resource. Here, "superior" implies that the innovat-ing firm's new resource enables it to surpass the previously advantaged competitor in terms of either relative efficiency or relative value, or both.

Firms can maintain marketplace positions of competitive advantage if they continue to have comparative advantages in resources over their rivals. Some resources are more crucial than oth-ers for developing and maintaining marketplace positions of competitive advantage. Specifically, resources will lead to sustainable competitive advantages when they: (1) cannot be imitated eas-ily, (2) are difficult to substitute for, (3) are not easily traded among firms, and (4) resist efforts by rivals to leapfrog them through major innovation (i.e., through developing superior resources). Resources that meet these criteria include those that (1) are causally ambiguous, (2) are socially and technologically complex, and (3) require time to develop.

Brand Equity Strategy and R-A Theory

Readers should note that brands (trademarks) can be resources under R-A theory, but only if they contribute to the firm's ability to efficiently and/or effectively produce a market offering of value to some market segment(s). That is, the brand must *add value* to the market offering in the eyes of the market segment(s). What, then, for R-A theory, is a "high-equity" brand? A high-equity brand is one that, by triggering highly favorable associations among targeted consumers, adds such value to the market offering that the resulting increase in firm effectiveness moves the market offering to the right in the marketplace position matrix (see figure 9.2 in Hunt 2002). Some brands, of course, actually *reduce* the value of the offering, as when, for example, consumers associate the brand with shoddy merchandise. In such circumstances, a brand would be characterized by R-A theory as a "contra-resource" (Hunt and Morgan 1995). Also, as to R-A theory's resource categories, a brand may be considered to be both a relational and a legal resource. It is a *relational* resource because brand equity is a manifestation of a firm's relationship with consumers. It is a *legal* resource because trademark law prevents competitors from stealing the value of the firm's investment in developing the brand's equity.

Theories are derived from their premises. The perfect competition theory on which equilibrium economics draws to analyze trademarks assumes that consumers have perfect and costless information about the availability, characteristics, benefits, and prices of all products in the marketplace. In contrast, R-A theory posits that consumers within market segments have imperfect information about goods and services that might match their tastes and preferences (see table 9.1 in Hunt 2002). Furthermore, the costs to consumers in terms of the effort, time, and money in identifying satisfactory goods and services (i.e., consumers' search costs) are often considerable. Consequently, one purpose served by the legal protection of trademarks is the reduction of consumer search costs. Specifically, trademarks are societal institutions that reduce search costs by signaling the attributes of market offerings.[4]

Recall that, for equilibrium economics, trademarks are a *problem* because they contribute to product differentiation, which is *itself* a *problem* because of its inconsistency with perfect competition and the welfare implications of static equilibrium. In contrast, the fact that consumers have imperfect information and often use trademarks as heuristics of quality is not a *problem* for R-A theory. First, because heterogeneous, intra-industry demand and supply is viewed as natural by R-A theory, it is only natural that, facing imperfect information, consumers will often use trademarks as indicators of quality. Second, because a trademark is viewed as intellectual property and fully worthy of legal protection, R-A theory views firms' protecting the equity in their trademarks as providing not only (1) a valuable source of information to consumers, but also (2) a powerful incentive for producers to maintain quality market offerings, and (3) a means by which manufacturers of shoddy, defective, or even dangerous products can be held accountable. Third, because R-A theory rejects static-equilibrium efficiency as the appropriate welfare ideal, the heterogeneity of demand and supply does not pose a problem to be solved, but a state of nature—and a desirable one at that. Indeed, R-A theory proposes that the *best* way to view the role of trademarks in market-based economies is that they are quality-control and quality-enhancing institutions. As evidence in favor of R-A theory's view of trademarks, consider the case of trademarks in the Soviet Union.

As Goldman (1960) recounts, the Soviet Union in its first few decades treated advertising and trademarks as capitalist institutions that, consistent with equilibrium economics, promoted inefficiency. As one might expect, with Soviet production goals set in quantitative terms, shoddy products proliferated, despite the huge inspection costs brought about by an army of inspectors. By the 1950s, Goldman (1960) points out, not only was the Soviet Union finding that advertising was an efficient means to inform consumers about products, but Soviet planners, in a desperate attempt to improve quality, made it obligatory that every plant in the Soviet Union place a "production mark" *(proizvodstvennaia marka)* on all output. Goldman (1960) quotes a Soviet planner as justifying making trademarks obligatory for all plants: "This makes it easy to establish the actual producer of the product in case it is necessary to call him to account for the poor quality of his goods. For this reason, it is one of the *most effective weapons* in the battle for the quality of products" (p. 399; emphasis added).

But, Goldman (1960) observed, holding Soviet producers accountable for shoddy quality was not the only benefit of obligatory trademarks. He also noted that a more elaborate and attractive form of mark, *tovarnyi znak,* while sometimes optional, is obligatory for 170 groups of goods and

for all exports. Again, Goldman (1960) quotes a Soviet planner as to the quality-enhancing benefits of the "competition" resulting from mandating the use of trademarks: "Due to its originality,
the trademark makes it possible for the consumer to select the good which he likes . . . this forces
other firms to undertake measures to improve the quality of their own product in harmony with
the demands of the consumer. Thus the trademark promotes the drive for raising the quality of
production" (p. 351).

Therefore, the experience of the Soviet Union supports R-A theory's view that consumers' use
of trademarks as indicators of quality is not a problem to be solved. Instead, trademarks are
institutions that serve as important quality control and quality-enhancing devices in real economies. How important? So important that command economies *mandated* that firms use trademarks, even in those situations where all plants were supposed to produce *homogenous*
commodities. In short, trademarks and product differentiation are not problems for society to
solve; they are institutions that solve societal problems.

CONCLUSION

The preceding analysis supports the reforms suggested by Wilkie (2004) and Vargo and Lusch
(2004). Marketing should supplement its emphasis on the micronormative (i.e., marketing management) aspects of marketing with more research on macropositive and macronormative issues,
with the former focusing on marketing systems as they *are* and the latter focusing on marketing
systems as they *ought to be*, respectively. Using resource-advantage theory as a foundation for
understanding dynamic marketing systems, this chapter has explored the benefits that redound to
marketing systems and society when firms implement brand equity strategies. I have argued that
the best way to view the role of brands in market-based economies is that they are highly important quality control and quality-enhancing, institutions. Therefore, the implementation of brand
equity strategies provides substantial benefits to market-based economies (as well as major benefits to socialist economies, a counterintuitive finding, to be sure).

With respect to the role of brands in society, this essay provides a beginning, not an ending. As
one example of a starting point for other aspects of the controversy over brand marketing, recall
the fact that brands allow consumers and others to identify the firms to be held responsible for the
products they produce. Now recall that Klein (2000) argued that global firms exploit Third World
workers. Without the global brand as a means for *identifying* the global firm, antiglobalization
activists would have great difficulty knowing which products to boycott. As a second example,
recall Johansson's (2004b) belief that antiglobalization is actually anti-Americanism at its roots.
Again, without global brands, the antiglobalization activists would have difficulty knowing which
products are American (and, thus, to be boycotted) and which are European or Japanese (and,
thus, to be favored).[5]

As an assistant professor in the early 1970s at the University of Wisconsin, Madison, I
recall expressing the view to a senior professor that marketing academe has an important role
to play in conducting research on marketing systems and society. His response was that such
research was the province of economics. Business professors, he stated emphatically, should
focus exclusively on the needs of business managers for better decision-making models. I
countered by arguing that business practitioners have needs that extend well beyond the area
of decision-making models. He "replied" by walking away. Marketing has paid a steep price
for "walking away" from such subjects as marketing systems and society. The best interests
of marketing practice, marketing academe, and society are not served by continuing to pay
that price.

NOTES

The author thanks Robert E. McDonald and James B. Wilcox for their helpful suggestions on a draft of this chapter.

1. A reviewer of a draft of this chapter found Johansson's argument here to be offensive, if not insulting. He commented that many readers might be outraged, and he wondered if I perhaps had quoted Johansson inaccurately or out of context. As a check, I showed the quoted material to colleagues familiar with the source. They reread the section in the book in question and affirmed that the quotes are accurate and in context. That is, the quoted material accurately describes Johansson's argument.

2. The excellent article by Low and Fullerton (1994) on the history of brands, brand management, and the brand manager system comes closest. However, the article does not position these topics within the overall marketing system or evaluate the impact of brands on the economy or society.

3. "Effectiveness-enhancing," as used here, has a very specific meaning, which is increasing the value of the market offering, as perceived by consumers in the target market, and, therefore, potentially moving to the right in the marketplace position matrix. See figure 9.2 in Hunt (2002).

4. See Erdem and Swait (1998) for an informative discussion of brand equity as a signaling phenomenon.

5. I am not arguing here that critics' calls for boycotts are justified. Rather, I point out that critics' calls for boycotts are uninformed by reason.

REFERENCES

Alderson, Wroe (1957), *Marketing Behavior and Executive Action.* Homewood, IL: Irwin.

────── (1965), *Dynamic Marketing Behavior.* Homewood, IL: Irwin.

Chamberlin, Edward (1962), *The Theory of Monopolistic Competition.* Cambridge, MA: Harvard University Press.

Erdem, Tulin and Joffre Swait (1998), "Brand Equity as Signaling Phenomenon," *Journal of Consumer Psychology,* 7 (2), 131–57.

Goldman, Marshall I. (1960), "Product Differentiation and Advertising: Some Lessons from Soviet Experience," *Journal of Political Economy,* 68, 346–57.

Hunt, Shelby D. (1976), "The Nature and Scope of Marketing," *Journal of Marketing,* 40 (July), 17–28.

────── (2000), *A General Theory of Competition: Resources, Competences, Productivity, Economic Growth.* Thousand Oaks, CA: Sage.

────── (2002), *Foundations of Marketing Theory: Toward a General Theory of Marketing.* Armonk, NY: M.E. Sharpe.

────── and Robert M. Morgan (1995), "The Comparative Advantage Theory of Competition," *Journal of Marketing,* 59 (April), 1–15.

Johansson, Johny, K. (2004a), "In Your Face: The Backlash Against Marketing Excess," paper presented at the symposium *Does Marketing Need Reform?* Bentley College, Boston.

────── (2004b), *In Your Face: How American Marketing Excess Fuels Anti-Americanism.* Upper Saddle River, NJ: Prentice Hall.

Klein, Naomi (2000), *No Logo: Taking Aim at the Brand Bullies.* New York: Picador.

Low, George S. and Ronald A. Fullerton (1994), "Brands, Brand Management, and the Brand Manager System," *Journal of Marketing Research,* 31 (May), 173–90.

Lusch, Robert F. (2004), "The Service Dominant Logic of Marketing," presentation at the symposium titled *Does Marketing Need Reform?* Bentley College, Boston.

Sheth, Jagdish N. (2004), "How to Reform Marketing," paper presented at the symposium *Does Marketing Need Reform?* Bentley College, Boston.

Smith, J. Walker (2004), "Consumer Resistance to Marketing," paper presented at the symposium *Does Marketing Need Reform?* Bentley College, Boston.

Vargo, Stephen L. and Robert F. Lusch (2004), "Evolving to a New Dominant Logic for Marketing," *Journal of Marketing,* 68 (January), 1–17.

Wilkie, William L. (2004), "Scholarship in Marketing: Lessons from the 'Four Eras' of Thought Development," paper presented at the symposium *Does Marketing Need Reform?* Bentley College, Boston.

────── and Elizabeth S. Moore (2003), "Scholarship in Marketing: Lessons from the 'Four Eras' of Thought Development," *Journal of Public Policy & Marketing,* 22 (2), 116–46.

CHAPTER 9

DOES MARKETING NEED REFORM?

Personal Reflections

RUSSELL S. WINER

A number of prominent marketing practitioners and academics have made appealing arguments that both the practice of marketing and academic marketing research need serious reform. With respect to the former, the complaints include some of the following:

- Marketers produce products that are unhealthy and dangerous and are attempting to foist them on an unsuspecting public;
- Marketers are not innovative anymore;
- The general public is unhappy with marketers;
- There are more choices among products than people need;
- Marketers do not have the ears of company senior management and boards.

With respect to marketing academics, the complaints tend to focus on the old problem of relevance: what we do is relevant and important only to other academics but not to practitioners. Below, I offer some personal reflections on these two topics.

REFORM MARKETING PRACTICE?

Undoubtedly, marketers have a deteriorating image among the general American public (and perhaps in other countries as well). Unhealthy "supersized" products, unwanted telemarketing phone calls, voluminous spam e-mails, SUVs with significant probabilities of rolling over when making sharp turns as well as large appetites for gasoline, and so on combine to give marketing a bad name. Many "me too" products make people wonder if companies are innovative any more. Paralysis in the supermarket when confronted with a hundred varieties of spaghetti sauce leaves shoppers exhausted rather than fulfilled.

Additionally, there are many who bemoan the lack of impact corporate marketers have at the senior management and board levels. These groups are more persuaded by financial wizards who can manipulate earnings, acquire and disgorge companies as "assets," and hedge earnings through sophisticated investments. Often, lawyers who can navigate the arcane world of Sarbanes-Oxley and other modern legislation are chosen to head firms rather than people who have experience in acquiring and retaining customers.

There is, of course, some truth to all of this. However, the picture is generally not as bleak as has been painted. Let me address these issues in turn.

I am a firm believer in consumer sovereignty and that good drives out bad. At some point, a situation in disequilibrium returns to equilibrium, that is, market forces result in change. Let's take the situation of "supersized," unhealthy products. When consumers do not want these any more, companies like McDonald's respond. That is why the company is repositioning itself by offering more salads as part of a healthier menu. Hummer recently introduced a new model, the H3, which is smaller and more fuel-efficient. Many food brands have developed versions of their products with fewer carbohydrates. I am not embarrassed to be in marketing despite the existence of some products that are not particularly useful or healthy. It is not our responsibility to dictate to consumers what they should or should not consume. While I am personally against cigarette smoking, it is a person's right to make that decision and a company's fiduciary responsibility to try to market the product the best they can. If and when insufficient numbers of consumers want cigarettes, the companies will find some other businesses (as most have already).

Unfortunately, with respect to other unpopular marketing practices such as telemarketing and spam e-mails, the reputations of useful direct marketing techniques have been sullied by improper and excessive actions of individuals and companies. Clearly, such direct marketing is effective given the billions of dollars consumers spend in these channels. In these cases, the return to an equilibrium of good practice has been enforced by legislation sparked by consumer complaints as well as technological solutions. However, I believe the net impact of these actions will be positive. Consumers not wishing to receive telemarketing calls can register on the "Do not call list"; increased use of "opt-in" registration and spam filters will help control unwanted e-mail.

Are marketers really not innovative any more? Is everything "me too"? I do not subscribe to that thesis. Apple's iPod is a designer's dream and is selling well. The Chrysler 300 is hot. In fact, innovation in product and design is very popular today. Magazines such as *Cargo* are devoted to new and exciting products. Samsung has opened an interactive showcase in New York's Time Warner Center displaying its new products; the company has clearly successfully positioned itself as a technology and design leader and has grown substantially as a result.

With respect to product assortment and choice, the movement toward category management in drug, grocery, and discount stores should keep such problems to a minimum. Under category management, manufacturers and retailers work together to ensure that the brand and item assortment is optimal for the retailer's profits. If there are too many items displayed in the spaghetti sauce category, some of the variants will have low turnover, low profitability for the retailer, and be replaced by something more profitable.

Finally, I am in agreement with the thesis that marketing does not have the ears of senior management and corporate boards. This is because we have not marketed marketing very well, that is, the enemy is us. Instead of financial people pushing for accountability of marketing spending on advertising, customer relationship management hardware and software, promotions, and other marketing tools, it should be marketing people. Peter Drucker has written for decades about the customer being the most important entity in a business. We are in charge of acquiring and retaining customers. We are the ones producing revenues. The "assets" that are acquired and divested when companies are bought and sold are actually aggregations of customers that have value, both in the long and short run. These messages have not been delivered effectively internally and I agree that it is our fault.

Additionally, marketing managers have only recently showed renewed interest in making marketing accountable, that is, developing financial and other metrics that permit senior management to quantitatively evaluate the efficacy of marketing programs. Again, while we have been performing quantitative analyses of, say, the effects of advertising for decades, we have been asleep at the switch as corporate officers have demanded better financial accountability. Marketing will gain more respect among the top levels of corporations when we are proactive in linking spending to the top and bottom lines and can do this in a convincing, scientifically sound manner.

REFORM ACADEMIA?

Arguments have been made for a long time that most academic research is irrelevant and does not speak to practical business issues. I look at academic research as the R&D of business: a few papers produce hits that have relevant results but most produce failures (in terms of insights to either theory or practice). However, even the failures provide building blocks for future insightful research. Additionally, we have failed as an industry in communicating most of the relevant findings to industry in language that they can understand and apply.

I would also argue that research in marketing can be both relevant and "academic," that is, produce basic, fundamental results. I have made this point earlier (Winer, 1999). One of the solutions to this dual problem (academic and practical implications) is for academics to be concerned about the generalizability of research results beyond the lab into other contexts. This would give practitioners who are interested in applying our work to their problems (and there is much more even today that can be applied) confidence that empirical results relate to other than eighteen- to twenty-two-year-olds at "large Midwestern universities." This also means that academics can produce meaningful, applied research without resorting to writing only case studies or *Harvard Business Review* articles.

I have proposed that experimental papers focusing on internal validity in controlled laboratory environments at least have a mandatory section at the end of each paper indicating what kind of studies are necessary to establish external validity. This would put pressure on consumer behavior researchers to think about external validity as an integral part of their work and not leave it up to someone else, as Bill Wells has said (1993).

Additionally, I have argued that there are readily available sources of information that can be used to extend the generalizability of many consumer behavior studies: scanner panel data. These data (or their predecessor type, diary panel data) have been around for nearly fifty years and are a rich source of information that has been rarely exploited for this purpose. Scanner data represent observations of purchasing behavior of individuals in a real environment. While the environment itself is not the critical factor, scanner data studies that support results found in the lab provide strong evidence of external validity.

As we all know, business schools have been under increasing pressure to be relevant to the business world. This need to be relevant has resulted in a number of changes in business school faculty-hiring practices, for example. It is no longer enough to be only a promising scholar to get a job at a top school. The most sought-after candidates also must have the potential to be excellent teachers so deans can mollify impatient MBA students. This is sometimes referred to as one of the *Business Week* effects, from the magazine's biannual survey of alumni and recruiters resulting in rankings of the top U.S. schools. In addition, business school communications offices are developing newsletters and other materials for distribution to their constituents "translating" faculty research into terms they can understand and, perhaps, even use.

While I deplore many of the *Business Week* effects (for example, new business school deans stating their goal is for theirs to be a "top 10" school), I believe that the pressure on faculty to ultimately develop more relevant research is well placed. Marketing academics should be as well trained in their basic disciplines (usually psychology or economics) as possible and this training should be demonstrated in their research. However, most marketing academics choose marketing doctoral programs and to concomitantly take faculty positions in business schools rather than social science departments. This choice not only implies that we have to teach students who are more interested in the real world than the laboratory world, but that we should be interested in thinking about our research in the same way.

How can we break out of these routines and keep our focus on basic research? I have recommended that more joint ventures be sought between consumer behavior researchers and people with other disciplinary approaches in marketing. Excellent candidates for the latter are marketing scientists. There are a number of marketing scientists who are interested in consumer behavior but who attack problems from the perspective of another tradition. I consider myself one of this group. Rather than running tightly controlled experiments, marketing scientists are more likely to use scanner panel or other secondary data to test consumer behavior hypotheses. Often, the tests involve specifying alternative models of consumer decision making, estimating the models, and then choosing the model with the best fit or out-of-sample predictions as most consistent with the specified behavior. Alternatively, estimated values and statistical significance of the parameters of the models are interpreted as providing evidence of the underlying consumer behavior.

As I noted earlier, secondary data sources such as scanner panel data are particularly appropriate for assessing external validity for a wide variety of consumer behavior. Scanner data present the researcher with actual consumers making purchases in their real environment, the supermarket. However, scanner data are not perfect. We do not know which person in the household is making the purchases (except, of course, for single-person households). This is important: for food items, multiple brand or flavor purchases can represent different household preferences, which are unknown. We also do not have any consumption data. In addition, while the samples are much more representative than they were using the old diary technology and the data are collected effortlessly by panel members, there are always questions about the kind of people who agree to be on these panels, as well as the "mortality" issue of panel dropouts. Finally, and importantly for consumer behavior researchers, there are no process measures (e.g., attitudes) taken because only purchasing behavior is measured. Despite these problems, scanner panel data represent real people making real decisions in a real environment.

Thus, my ideal form of the research process is a lab experiment in conjunction with a natural experiment using scanner panel data. Note that the process does not have to work in the direction experiment->scanner data. It is also possible for results found in scanner data studies to be given internal validity using lab experiments. I do not expect the same person to do both kinds of work; however, partnerships between scholars trained from different perspectives can and have brought complementary insights and skills to bear on a research problem that has resulted in greater generalizability than would have from either alone. In this way, we can have research that moves in the direction of practicality without sacrificing intellectual rigor.

CONCLUSION

Market forces will curb the excesses of harmful and useless products and the extensive, mind-numbing product assortment. We have already seen an explosion in outstanding product design and innovation. However, there is work to be done in better marketing of marketing inside of organizations, making marketing financially accountable, and in making academic research more accessible to practitioners. I am optimistic that these latter changes will occur, and that the futures of both marketing practice and research are bright.

REFERENCES

Wells, William D. (1993), "Discovery-oriented Consumer Research," *Journal of Consumer Research*, 19 (March), 489–504.

Winer, Russell S. (1999), "Experimentation in the Twenty-First Century: The Importance of External Validity," *Journal of the Academy of Marketing Science*, 27 (Summer), 349–58.

CHAPTER 10

REFORM, RECLAMATION, OR IMPROVEMENT

Reinventing Marketing

DAVID W. STEWART

It is useful for a discipline to introspect and reflect on what it has become and how it might change in the future. Such introspection may be especially helpful for a discipline like marketing that is so frequently focused on the external environment of customers, markets, and competition. There is no doubt that other business disciplines now champion such central marketing constructs as customer focus, differentiation, segmentation, and positioning. The fact that other disciplines now embrace key marketing concepts reflects the success of the marketing discipline even as it raises questions about the definition and role of marketing in the future. Reflection on the state of the marketing discipline, its history, and its future can also provide insight, perspective, and direction.

It is also the case that the field of marketing exists within a context that includes unethical and abusive business and marketing practices. Every human enterprise, including government organizations and religious institutions, includes some unsavory characters and practices. There is no doubt that marketing practice, and business in general, includes some unsavory, unethical, and immoral elements. There is no good excuse for this state of affairs even if it reflects, in part, the human condition. Reflection and introspection on the marketing discipline may be helpful in formulating standards, codes of ethics and conduct, educational programs, regulatory practices, and other actions for controlling and reducing the incidence of unethical and immoral practices. Such reflection on the ethical dimensions of marketing may also help inform the discussion of the future of the discipline.

Although introspection and reflection are useful it is important that it not become critical to the point of being disparaging. The word "reform" is highly value laden. The *Merriam-Webster On-line Dictionary* (2004) defines the noun "reform" as:

1. amendment of what is defective, vicious, corrupt, or depraved;
2. a removal or correction of an abuse, a wrong, or errors.

There is no reason to assume that marketing, or business in general, is corrupt and in need of reform in the sense offered in this definition. A more benign definition of reform might focus on the positive and affirmative need for improvement. It is certainly the case that marketing has and will continue to evolve over time and the discipline could and should be improved as a discipline and business practice. Nevertheless, there is much that is positive about marketing and its contributions to the firm, the consumer, and society at large. These positive contributions provide a foundation for constructive change and should not be overlooked in any discussion of the future of the discipline. There is much about the marketing discipline of which its members can be justifiably proud.

THE SUCCESS OF MARKETING

Marketing has been remarkably successful as an academic discipline and area of management practice. As an academic discipline, marketing has developed an impressive body of empirical data, theoretical constructs, and research methods. As an area of management practice marketing has had enormous influence on how businesses define themselves and interact with key constituencies. Although marketing has enjoyed success as a discipline, its very success has resulted in its most important strategic contributions being adopted by and associated with other business functions ranging from operations and finance to strategy. This is a positive outcome. Indeed, Drucker (1993) has defined marketing as the central and unique characteristic of business:

> Marketing is the distinguishing, the unique function of a business. A business is set apart from other human organizations by the fact that it markets a product or a service. (1993, p. 61–62)

> Because its purpose is to create a customer, the business enterprise has two—and only these two—basic functions: marketing and innovation. Marketing and innovation produce results; all the rest are "costs." (1993, p. 61)

> Marketing is so basic that it cannot be considered a separate function (i.e., a separate skill or work) within the business . . . it is, first . . . a central dimension of the entire business. (1993, p. 63)

The marketing discipline can be justifiably proud that managers in other disciplines speak the language of marketing. The operations manager that speaks of customer-centric service delivery, the finance professor that talks about the value of investing in a customer and the lifetime value of a customer, and the business strategy consultant who emphasizes the roles of differentiation and positioning in business success are merely reflecting the triumph of ideas that originated in marketing. The issues of ethics in marketing practice that are the focus of many of the chapters in this volume also reflect a discipline that has been successful in creating a sensitivity and concern for important moral issues within its ranks. Indeed, marketing may be at the forefront of the discussion of such issues as consumer information disclosure, privacy protection, intellectual property safeguarding, and unfair business practices identification and elimination. One of the more vital special interest groups in the American Marketing Association (AMA) focuses on public policy and the AMA publishes one of the more influential journals devoted to public policy issues, the *Journal of Public Policy and Marketing*.

Marketing does not need reform in the negative sense of the word. It does need to evolve, to be responsive to the changes occurring around it, to develop the means for encouraging more ethical practice and to reinvent itself to deal with the issues and contingencies of the twenty-first century. The discipline may also need to reclaim its birthright and more fully embrace its past and future leadership role within the business community and society at large.

MARKETING'S CONTRIBUTION TO BUSINESS AND SOCIETY

Wilkie and Moore (2002, 2003) provide a powerful chronicle of marketing's contributions to the larger economic system and to economic development. Although imperfect, markets work. Markets are generally efficient and effective means for distributing goods and services. The formation and servicing of markets is the engine that produces jobs, creates wealth, and raises the standard of living within a society. A market may fail and may not always produce positive outcomes, but there is ample empirical evidence that there are no good alternatives. Markets may need some regulation, but they remain the best means for distributing goods and services to heterogeneous consumers. The marketing discipline is the repository of knowledge about how real markets work and it possesses unique expertise in at least three areas:

(1) *Empirical Knowledge and Theories of Consumer Behavior and Markets.* There is no area where marketing has been more successful than in the development of a broad and deep body of knowledge and theories about consumer behavior and how markets are defined, are structured, and evolve over time. While it is the case that marketing has borrowed liberally from other disciplines, the reality is that the study of consumer and market behavior represents a well-defined area of social science and a business practice that is uniquely owned by the marketing discipline. When businesses, government organizations, or consumers have questions about markets and consumer behavior, it is marketing that is the repository of this knowledge and it is marketing that is committed to adding to this store of knowledge. Although many of the processes marketing examines are shared with other disciplines that focus on human behavior, marketing focuses on a unique context, the marketplace, and unique dependent variables, purchase and consumption.

(2) *Marketing and Consumer Research Tools.* The marketing discipline has developed unique tools for addressing specific questions about markets and consumer behavior. Although many of these tools have been adapted from other disciplines, their application in a marketing context is unique. When questions about markets and consumers arise, it is marketing that has the toolkit for addressing these questions. The marketing research toolkit is uniquely suited to the context of markets and dependent variables related to purchase and consumption.

(3) *Expertise Regarding the Alignment and Management of Value-Creating Organizational and Interorganizational Relationships.* Although the study of consumer behavior and the use of marketing research have even longer histories, the earliest marketing functions within firms and marketing courses in universities focused on the institutional dimensions of value delivery, especially those concerned with the distribution function. Marketing has a long and rich history of research and practice related to aligning organizations to deliver value to customers. Although other disciplines can claim expertise with respect to intra-organizational behavior, strategic alliances, and the economics of interorganizational relationships, marketing is unique in its focus on alignment for the purpose of value delivery to an end user. In other words, marketing has unique expertise related to the organization of value delivery systems. Especially important elements in these systems are reputation and trust, which are often embodied in a brand.

Although other disciplines have embraced the need for a customer focus and a concern for value delivery, no discipline other than marketing has accumulated the body of knowledge and expertise related to these dimensions of market activity. Rather than ceding expertise to other disciplines and business functions, marketing must proudly reclaim its historical role as the creator and repository of knowledge about markets, consumers, and value delivery systems. Marketing has been far too modest about its own expertise and contributions and should aggressively pursue those activities that would reinforce its reputation for contributing to the welfare of consumers, firms, and society.

RECLAIMING MARKETING'S ROLE

As Webster (2002) has observed, the definition of marketing is no longer as clear as it once was and the discipline has lost the influence it once exerted in business organizations. In contrast to its loss of influence within business organizations, marketing has never been fully recognized or appreciated for its contributions to the welfare of the individual consumer or society. Both the loss of influence in business and the lack of broader appreciation is the fault of the marketing discipline. Many individuals in the discipline, especially those on the academic side, seem almost embarrassed by it and skeptical about the value of markets. There are certainly products and practices that are sources of embarrassment, but these are exceptions in an otherwise positive context. It is ironic that even as other disciplines embrace a customer-centric view of business, marketing raises concerns about its contribution. If marketing is to reclaim its influence and receive recognition of it contributions, the discipline must celebrate and promote those contributions and its expertise.

The success of marketing has produced another outcome that reduces its influence, at least in the short term. In an appropriate pursuit of rigor the discipline has tended in recent years to focus on narrower issues and more tactical problems. In and of itself this is not a bad thing; understanding and explanation require a narrower focus with greater control that eliminates alternative explanations in an otherwise complex environment. Such a focus has added enormously to the body of knowledge and theory that defines the substance and unique contributions of marketing. On the other hand, the focus on narrower problems and tactics has resulted in a relative neglect of larger, strategic questions that link marketing activities to the welfare of the firm, the consumer, and society at large. Titles of marketing papers and books in the past reflected a concern for broader questions. There are few titles today that suggest the kind of linkage to general strategic problems that were suggested by Alderson's 1943 *Journal of Marketing* paper, "The Marketing Viewpoint in National Economic Planning," and his 1957 book, *Marketing Behavior and Executive Action.*

This does not mean that marketers should write more popular business books or forsake the very good work that is being done on marketing tactics or on micro-level consumer behavior. It does mean that the marketing discipline needs to reclaim its legitimate authority with respect to broader strategic and societal issues by returning to questions of strategy and policy. It is certainly the case that greater visibility must be given to the unique expertise and perspective that marketing can provide when addressing these questions.

Marketing has also done a poor job of quantifying its contributions. While there is little debate about the value of a brand, the economic value of a brand and the return on marketing investments required to create that brand have not been defined well by the discipline. The same problem exists with respect to other marketing activities. Even as other business functions have documented economic returns in response to demands for greater accountability, marketing has been very slow to embrace the need for accountability and quantification of return on investment in marketing. This is not because there is a shortage of measures of impact. Rather, marketing has not linked its many measures directly to economic returns nor has it developed a set of generally accepted standards for the measurement of impact. If, as Drucker argues, marketing is the driver of value, it behooves the discipline to demonstrate and quantify that value. Doing so would allow marketing to reclaim its influence and obtain greater recognition for its many positive contributions.

Finally, the very success of marketing has created a splintering of the discipline. There is enormous momentum in the accumulation of knowledge about markets and consumers. This momentum has had the effect of fragmenting the discipline into narrow interest groups that are each aggressively pursuing their research and practice agendas. This is not unexpected when knowledge is increasing at an accelerating rate and it is a sign of a mature discipline. Unfortunately, this fragmentation reduces the identity of marketing as a unified discipline. Marketing's three unique areas of expertise are increasingly isolated from one another. This fragmentation and isolation is part of what has blurred the identity of marketing. Reclaiming marketing's leadership role will require renewing the dialog among the various constituencies that now comprise the marketing discipline and rediscovering the linkages among them. This dialog, in turn, needs to link marketing's expertise to the welfare of consumers, firms, and society at large.

REINVENTING MARKETING

Reclaiming its role as the driver of value delivery will require that marketing continue to build its unique expertise and knowledge base even as it shares that expertise with others. Today's firms are responding to the mantra of customer focus by significantly altering the role of the marketing function. Activities traditionally associated with marketing are increasingly shared with other functions of the firm, including R&D, operations, manufacturing, and finance. Focus on markets and customers has increasingly become a general management function. Various activities associated with the four Ps (Product, Price, Promotion and Place) are increasingly shared with other functions in the firm or have migrated to other functions altogether. R&D and quality assurance, which have always been important participants in the design of products, have taken on many of the product-related activities formerly handled by the marketing function. Product or service specification based on direct customer input to the product design process—with or without the involvement of marketing—has become commonplace. Pricing has increasingly become the domain of financial planners and operations. Operations personnel, often without consultation with the marketing function, handle sophisticated yield management pricing systems and pricing by market conditions in real-time. Promotion remains the domain of marketing, but has become increasingly tactical. Strategic marketing activities, such as building brands, are often the function of strategic planners and general managers. Distribution has become highly specialized and is often a part of what is now called supply-chain management. Supply-chain management is as much the domain of information systems specialists as it is the domain of marketing and logistics specialists. This migration of marketing activities to other functions in the firm varies by firm and industry, but its occurrence is real and unmistakable.

   The migration of marketing activities to other functions within the firm does not mean that marketing is disappearing. Indeed, in many ways, marketing as a discipline and business function is stronger today than ever before. Rather, marketing and other business functions have been evolving in response to changes in the marketplace and the competitive landscape. Although marketing no longer owns the customer, marketing retains its unique expertise and knowledge base. This means that marketing has the opportunity to help firms be truly customer-focused and market-oriented. It also has the opportunity to take on new roles and responsibilities, even as some of its former activities migrate to other functions.

   Marketing, or at least the values and processes long championed by marketing, has become a philosophy of doing business for the rest of the organization. If this philosophy is to work, general management and other functional area must embrace it. The marketing function cannot be the owner of customer contact and information if the organization is to be truly market-oriented and customer-focused. Thus, it was inevitable that traditional marketing activities would migrate from the marketing function to other areas within the firm. Indeed, an organization in which marketing remains the owner of and conduit to customers is by definition not customer-focused or market-oriented; it might be *marketing*-oriented, but this is altogether different and does not provide the benefits associated with customer focus and market orientation. The migration of traditional marketing activities from the marketing function to other functions and general management is a positive development.

Freeing marketing of some of its traditional activities does not diminish the value of marketing. Indeed, the migration of traditional marketing activities to other functions expands the role of marketing and can make it more strategic. Although other functions may be customer-focused and market-oriented, marketing remains the repository of knowledge about customers and customer behavior. This knowledge provides insights into what works and does not work, what obstacles or opportunities exist in markets of various types and in products with particular characteristics. Such knowledge, when made accessible to the larger organization, can provide direction to other functional disciplines and to general management. It can also produce faster and more efficient responses by the firm and its various functional disciplines by eliminating the need to constantly rediscover the obvious. Thus, marketers bring accumulated wisdom about markets and customers to the organization, even as other functional disciplines spend more time with customers in the search for specific solutions to problems.

Any organization that seeks to learn over time and benefit from its experiences must have a repository for its accumulated learning. For knowledge about markets and customers, marketing provides this repository. This means that successful practitioners of marketing will need to have expertise beyond the firm's current markets and products. Rather, marketers will need to have an understanding of general principles of how markets work, how customers respond in given situations, and the underlying psychological, economic, and social processes that drive customer behavior. The fluidity of markets today means that it is important to be able to see the implications of lessons learned in a services business for a product business, the meaning of lessons learned in managing a sales force for the management of distributors, and the implications of lessons learned from advertising and brand building by traditional media for e-commerce. This is because the product business today may be the service business of tomorrow and the direct seller of yesterday may be tomorrow's indirect seller. Learning anew each time the business changes is too painful and inefficient. An important role of marketing in the future will be to reduce the pain and increase the efficiency as the marketplace and the firm evolves.

Marketing also continues to be the repository of expertise about how to best obtain information about and from customers. Thus, marketing continues to play an important role in helping senior managers and other functional specialists acquire the skills needed to obtain useful and timely information from customers. Even as marketing has given away some activities within the firm, it has also taken on new roles that often did not exist before, at least in any formal sense. In markets where relationships are an important part of the firm's offerings, marketing has assumed the role of relationship management. Relationship management is more than tending to the care and feeding of customers; it also involves determining which customers the firm should build relationships with and the nature of the relationship with any particular customer. Relationships are costly, and the deeper the relationship with a customer, the greater the costs of serving that customer in most cases. This means that it is important to choose customers who value the relationship and will pay a premium for it. Thus, market selection has become an even more important function of marketing today. However, unlike in the past, selection in relationship marketing is not a one-time or an infrequent activity. The cost and value of customer relationships must be constantly monitored to assure that both the firm and the customer are benefiting from the relationship. Marketing is about understanding how to manage relationships and how to analyze the economic value of relationship building and maintenance.

Marketing should also play a role in helping the firm understand what it does well and in matching markets and business models to the firm's capabilities. What a firm does well has been variously called its core competencies, competitive advantages, and comparative advantages— among other things. Understanding the things a firm does better than its competition has long been a part of market analysis. In recent years, however, this type of analysis has expanded to include consideration of what the firm should do and what it should have partners do. Thus, a firm must determine whether it should be its own supplier, its own manufacturer, and its own distributor, or focus on only some of these activities.

Marketing is not about just understanding and selecting markets; it is also about developing a deep understanding of how the firm should serve the markets it selects. This understanding requires an identification of all the activities that are necessary for delivering a complete product or service to the customer. It also requires determining which activities the firm is uniquely suited to pursue itself and which activities are best left to partners, suppliers, distributors, and complementors. This analysis of the value chain includes understanding both how to best organize activities to deliver value to the customer (and assure the customer is happy paying for the value received) and what are the economic consequences of various alternative organizations for the firm. This means looking beyond the firm and its immediate competitors to consider such issues as whether a supplier or distributor has the potential to become a competitor, whether a partner might learn enough about the firm's markets, technology, and operations to become a competitor, and whether certain activities are really needed to deliver value to the customer. Such analyses require knowledge of the economics and best practices of alternative value delivery systems. Marketers can help the firm answer the question of how it should participate in the value chain, and where within the larger value chain the firm can maximize its return on investment.

As they contemplate the structure of value delivery systems marketers can also work to assure that relationships with various members of the value delivery system are routinely analyzed and managed appropriately. Such relationships cannot be placed in proper perspective without an understanding of how the relationships—and the associated activities of partners in a relationship—play out in terms of value delivered to specific markets and types of customers. This is a strategic function that has only recently been recognized as critical to the long-term success of the firm. No other function in the firm is as well suited to address such strategic issues as marketing is.

Marketing does not require reform, but it does need to reinvent itself by calling on its unique expertise to address important business and societal issues. It needs to refocus on its core, which is the creation of value for customers and the firm. It needs to integrate its many very successful components into an integrated whole that makes explicit its contributions to the firm, the consumer, and society. In many ways this represents a return to the marketing discipline's roots.

REFERENCES

Alderson, Wroe (1943), "The Marketing Viewpoint in National Economic Planning," *Journal of Marketing,* 7 (April), 326–32.

——— (1957), *Marketing Behavior and Executive Action: A Functionalist Approach to Marketing Theory.* Homewood, IL: R.D. Irwin.

Drucker, Peter F. (1993), *Management: Tasks, Responsibilities, Practices.* New York: HarperBusiness.

Merriam-Webster Online Dictionary (2004), www.m-w.com/cgi-bin/dictionary (accessed August 1, 2004).

Webster, Frederick E. (2002), "The Role of Marketing and the Firm," in *The Handbook of Marketing,* B. Weitz and R. Wensley, eds. London: Sage, 66–82.

Wilkie, William and Elizabeth S. Moore (2002), "Marketing's Relationships to Society," in *The Handbook of Marketing,* B. Weitz and R. Wensley, eds. London: Sage, 9–38.

——— (2003), "Scholarly Research in Marketing: Exploring the 'Four Eras' of Thought Development," *Journal of Public Policy & Marketing,* 22 (Fall), 116–46.

PART 3

RETHINKING MARKETING'S
SACRED COWS

The chapters in this section suggest ways to rethink and reinvent marketing. They differ from those in the previous section in contending that marketing's problems are not incremental but are fundamental and require major rethinking from within the function and possible intervention from the outside.

Like all disciplines and practices, marketing has its own orthodoxies: branding, positioning, differentiation, segmentation, the four Ps (product, place, promotion, and price), the marketing concept, and exchange as the underlying constructs. Jerry Wind strongly and persuasively argues that we must challenge the prevalent mental models of marketing and develop new ones. We need mental models because they guide our research and practice. We need new mental models of marketing because the environment of marketing has changed significantly. He recommends that for marketing to have a seat at the corporate table, it must bridge the walls within and between marketing's functions; expand the focus from consumers to other stakeholders; rethink the value of customer satisfaction measures; combine mass markets with segments of one; empower consumers with information and choice tools, not just choices; identify appropriate metrics and incorporate corporate dashboards; and in general expand marketing from a function to a philosophy.

Wind believes that we must look through the eyes of the developing world and the "bottom of the pyramid" markets; see the potential of technology, empowered consumers, and convergence marketing; and use the dashboard to better integrate marketing perspective into business decision making.

Greg Gundlach focuses on the new American Marketing Association definition of marketing. He believes that its exclusive focus on the marketer's perspective limits the scope and domain of marketing to traditional marketing management. It does not include, for example, consumers doing marketing when they search for products they need at prices they can afford. Also, there are participants other than marketers in the marketing system that are left out of the definition. He suggests that marketing should not adopt a single perspective, so that marketing knowledge can be more objective, similar to what we know in psychology and sociology.

Kumar and Ramani take an inductive, field-oriented, and clinical way to discover new ways of marketing, especially in a changing world. They suggest we learn from firms that are getting it right. This includes viewing customers as individuals and not aggregates; adapting technology as a means to reach and carry out useful dialogs with each potential and current customer; devising active customer empowerment strategies that lead to competitive advantage; and, finally, identifying opportunity areas that legitimately obtain valuable customer information that can help customers enrich their own lives. Kumar and Ramani suggest that companies must transition from a selling orientation to an interaction orientation, and provide a framework for an effective interaction orientation perspective.

Glen Urban suggests that advocacy by companies on behalf of customers is key to a new marketing that will be effective in generating profit, welcomed by consumers, ethically right, and able to get marketing back to its role as a driver of corporate strategy. According to Urban, customer advocacy is analogous to the transition from Theory X to Theory Y in human resource management. He proposes a customer advocacy pyramid and suggests tools for its implementation.

Firat and Dholakia believe that marketing does not need reform, it needs a revolution! They believe that the two core concepts underlying modern marketing (marketing concept and customer satisfaction) are obsolete. Although the concepts of the free market advocated by Adam Smith and David Riccardo were meant to separate the individual from the institutional bondage (the feudal system), it has created more tensions between the individual and the institution, or between the desire to be independent and free and the desire to belong and relate to others. In the postmodern world, they suggest that marketing must shift from a managerial "command and control" approach to a "shared and collaborative" approach with customers and markets; from centralized to diffused marketing; and from ordered to complex marketing. According to them, the new marketing must exhibit fluidity of form; such marketing would resemble a neural network that constantly re(de)constructs itself.

Venkatesh and Peñaloza argue that for a major shift in marketing, we must shift from the study of market*ing* to the study of markets. They credit Johan Arndt, who advocated the study of markets to enrich and extend marketing theory to such nontraditional areas as nonprofit services, and sports and personality markets. They provide an interesting new classification of markets–markets in the mainstream, markets in the emerging global context, and virtual markets–and they describe differences among these types of markets.

CHAPTER 11

CHALLENGING THE MENTAL MODELS OF MARKETING

YORAM (JERRY) WIND

Mental models shape research, teaching, and practice in marketing. By understanding and challenging the current mental models through which we view the discipline, we can gain new insights on improving the theory and practice of marketing and giving it a more powerful role. But to see these opportunities to transform marketing and its role, we first have to understand the central importance of mental models in limiting or expanding our world.

Why should we be concerned about mental models of marketing? What are the current prevailing mental models? Are these current models appropriate given the changes that we see in the business environment? What new mental models of marketing should be considered? These are the topics I explore, leading to a consideration of new models for marketing, and I conclude with a brief section on the implications for research and practice.

WHY MENTAL MODELS OF MARKETING MATTER

Mental models in every area of our lives are much more important than we generally realize. They can limit our world or create opportunities for action. For example, the 9/11 Commission concluded that the greatest failure in the intelligence and other activities preceding the terrorist attacks of September 11, 2001, was a "failure of imagination" (The 9/11 Commission Report, p. 9). It was a failure to "connect the dots." Groupthink may have obscured these connections, contributing to the failure. The passengers and crew on the two planes that hit the World Trade Center towers apparently followed the standard advice for a hijacking. The instructions were to stay quiet, follow the rules, and authorities would eventually negotiate their release. This may be the best chance of survival in a traditional hijacking, but the hijackings of September 11 did not fit this model.

In contrast, the passengers and crew of Flight 93, with information from friends and family by cell phones, recognized that they were facing a different hijacking model. There would be no negotiations. The airplanes in this case were being used as missiles against targets. While no one knows exactly what happened on board that flight, it appears that passengers and crew stormed the cockpit and the plane crashed in western Pennsylvania, far short of its intended target. The new information had led to a fundamentally different view of the situation, and this shift in mental model allowed the passengers and crew to take what seemed to be heroic action. The apparent shift in models aboard Flight 93 created new opportunities for thinking and acting. Mental models have a tremendous impact on how we make sense of and respond to the world.

As one demonstration of the power of mental models, consider a study by Daniel Simons and Christopher Chabris at Harvard University (1999). They asked subjects to count the number of times basketball players with white shirts pitched a ball back and forth in a video. More than half the subjects in this study, and hundreds of other executives to whom I have shown the video, were so engrossed in the task that they failed to notice a black gorilla that walked into the center of the scene and beat its chest. The subjects may have been doing a good job of counting the basketball passes, but a gorilla was right in front of them and they didn't see it. We are so focused on the current task at hand that we do not see what is lurking in the environment right in front of us. How can we break through these models that limit our ability to *see* the gorillas? What are the gorillas running through the field of marketing that we cannot see because we are focused on a specialized task?

The Power of Impossible Thinking

Breaking through our current models can have a powerful impact in many areas of life and work. An example was when Starbucks founder Howard Schultz created the idea for an American café. After all, it was a far-fetched idea. Coffee at the time was a commodity. Brands fought bitter price wars in the supermarkets. Seattle was undergoing a tough economic period. It seemed the worst possible place to launch a new business. But Schultz proved the "power of impossible thinking," creating one of the fastest growing businesses, one of the most recognizable brands, and a phenomenon that changed the way customers think about coffee and even how they live and work (Wind and Crook 2004).

There are many examples of how to shift mental models and the powerful impact of breaking through them. For example, running a four-minute mile was considered impossible until 1954 when runner Roger Bannister ran it in three minutes 59.4 seconds on an Oxford track. Within three years after he broke this barrier, sixteen other runners followed in his footsteps. This progress was not the result of some leap in evolution that made humans run faster, but rather a breakthrough in thinking. After Bannister, runners considered it possible (Bannister 1981; Wind and Crook 2004). Breakthroughs in business such as the creation of overnight delivery by FedEx or the design of the Palm Pilot personal digital assistant required a similar shift in thinking to create different models. The design of the overnight packaging business challenged traditional mail and delivery services with a hub-and-spoke system. The developers of the Palm Pilot realized that they could train the human operators to learn a simplified character set much more easily than designing a machine that could recognize diverse handwriting styles. This was a shift in thinking that built a huge market for devices that were initially slow to take off. What shifts in thinking in marketing might produce similar payoffs?

Challenging Our Models

Before considering how mental models apply to marketing, think about a few ways we can creatively challenge our models in other areas. For example, would you invest in the inner city? Most companies have little interest in the inner city. They see poverty, crime, and drugs. On the other hand, most multinational companies are very interested in emerging markets, which are viewed as a source of future growth as they develop. Companies are racing into China, India, and other parts of the emerging world. Researchers at the Milken Institute, as well as Michael Porter, have pointed out that if we look at inner city markets as "domestic emerging markets" this leads to a fundamental shift in how we see these markets and the opportunities they present (Yago and Pankratz 2000).

To take another example, think about medicine. What are the images that come to mind when you think about alternative, complementary, or integrative medicine? Obviously these are dramatically different images of the way one views medicine and how to be treated. These approaches represent very different views of the nature of disease and health. Or, in the business world, are people an asset or an expense? All chief executive officers (CEOs) talk about how people are our greatest assets, but, what happens during a downturn? The same people are treated as expenses, and the same CEOs fire them. Is inventory an asset or a liability? Standard accounting practice regards inventory as an asset, but then Dell and others challenged this model, seeing it as a liability. This led to the creation of just-in-time systems to limit this liability, fundamentally rethinking their supply chains.

We can consider the same question about marketing: Is it an expense or an investment? It is treated as an expense or overhead in some organizations. But as companies look for new sources of growth, some are turning to marketing for insights. These organizations are seeing marketing as an investment in new ideas and an engine of growth. Is marketing viewed as a set of decisions relating to the four Ps (product, price, place, and promotion), or is it viewed as a pervasive business philosophy at the core of business strategy? These different views of marketing will lead to different strategies and staffing, so the mental models that managers use to view marketing have a tremendous impact.

Rethinking the Thirty-Second Commercial

Most mental models are effective when they are formulated, but they become problematic when the environment changes. Great models often outlive their usefulness. For example, the dominant model of mass marketing in the packaged goods industries was built around the thirty-second commercial. But now, with television fragmented into hundreds of channels, the rise of video games, and the empowerment of the viewer, first with the remote and then with TiVo, the world has changed in fundamental ways. A study of U.S. television viewers found that more than 43 percent were actively ignoring advertising. For people with TiVo and other personal video recorders, more than 71 percent skipped advertising. In some categories, such as credit cards and mortgage financing, more than 90 percent of ads were TiVo'd (Bianco 2004).

Clearly the thirty-second commercial needs to be rethought. Has marketing changed to meet this new reality? Companies are turning to approaches such as events, using word-of-mouth strategies for buzz marketing and product placement. For example, in launching its new Scion brand targeting youth markets, Toyota shunned traditional advertising, spending 70 percent of its promotion on street events (Kroft 2004). Even the remaining ad spending was mostly directed toward the Internet. Video games are using product placement within the context of the game. For example, in the *Tony Hawk Underground* video game, players cannot move up to the third level until they drink a Pepsi. As Robert Kotick, chairman and CEO of video game maker Activision commented during the Milken Institute's Global Forum, "In our medium, people cannot skip the advertising." The dominant model for mass marketing is already being challenged. How does it need to change further? There is clearly a desperate need for innovation in marketing approaches.

These revolutions are not absolute. Paradigm shifts to new models are often a two-way street. Old and new mental models exist side-by-side. Super Bowl advertising spots are unlikely to go away, but television advertising is becoming a smaller and less important part of the overall marketing portfolio for companies. Similarly, the horse-and-buggy model is out of place on the expressway, but even in an age of automobiles and space flight, we see police on horseback in cities and soldiers on horses guiding missiles through the mountains of Afghanistan. Even in an age of e-mail and computer printouts we still use handwritten notes and phone calls. With hundreds of cable television channels, we still listen to the radio and read the newspaper. When new models arrive, the old ones are not necessarily discarded. The Internet didn't completely take over advertising, as some predicted. Instead, it offers another model for getting out messages. As we introduce new models, in marketing or any other area, we mustn't get so carried away with the revolution that we don't recognize the power of the old models. We are better off with a portfolio of models so that we can choose the best one for the task at hand.

WHAT ARE THE CURRENT MENTAL MODELS OF MARKETING?

Current teaching, research, and the practice of marketing are shaped by our mental models. Among the powerful models that have guided the theory and practice of marketing, we might identify ideas and frameworks such as:

- The marketing concept
- Marketing as exchange
- The four Ps (product, price, place, and promotion)
- The three Cs (company, customers, and competitors)
- Customer satisfaction
- Relationship marketing
- Permission marketing
- Collaborative marketing

But the full range of marketing models and approaches is much broader and richer. To take a few examples, the list might be expanded to include:

- Convergence marketing (combining call, click, and visit)
- Guerilla marketing
- One-to-one marketing
- Buzz marketing
- Integrated/holistic marketing
- Cult marketing
- Brand equity
- Brand chronicles

Through the Eyes of Diverse Stakeholders

One way to understand the diverse mental models of marketing is to consider the different views of the field by various stakeholders. Many chief marketing officers (CMOs) and other marketing practitioners are concerned about building their brands, while CEOs may be concerned about issues such as marketing productivity or return on investment in marketing, focusing on increasing accountability for marketing expenditures. Consumers have yet another view of marketing. At one extreme, some view it as disruptive, the telemarketing calls at dinner and relentless, annoying, and tasteless election advertising. On the other hand, some may view it as a value-creating engine that makes them aware of innovative and valuable new products and services. Think about the view of marketing reflected in the *Journal of Marketing Research* and *Marketing Science*. We see a different view presented in textbooks and in general marketing journals such as the *Journal of Marketing* or *Marketing Management*.

There is yet another view in consumer behavior publications such as the *Journal of Consumer Research.*

Like the blind men and the elephant (where one grasped a trunk, another a leg and a third the tail), each of these stakeholders sees one part of the total picture, limited by their mental models. Each has a different view and enormous walls separate their mental models of marketing. Are there unhealthy chasms among these marketing stakeholders? How do we bridge these silos? How do we benefit from these diverse perspectives?

WEAKNESSES OF THE CURRENT MODEL

There are a number of problems that highlight some of the weaknesses of the current model of marketing. Consider a few examples of how this model of marketing falls short.

Gaining a Seat at the Table

Has the narrow focus of academic marketing marginalized the discipline in the organization? Is the academic research of value to business executives or only to other academics? At recent meetings of the CMO Summit, which drew senior marketing executives from major corporations, one of the major concerns was the loss of a seat at the corporate table. Marketing has become marginalized in many organizations precisely at a time when it is more critical than ever as an engine of growth. How did this happen and what can be done about it? Are marketing academics and practitioners becoming too self-centered? The challenge of gaining a seat at the table is basically to have marketing accepted as an integral part of the business-related mental model of the CEO and other top leaders. Marketers need to forge a mental model of marketing that is relevant to the organization and that addresses the areas of concern to the CEO such as growth, innovation, and customer loyalty and retention.

Interdisciplinary Perspectives

As marketing has matured, as any discipline does, it has become more specialized, isolated from the rest of the business, and more deeply engrained in its own mindset. PhD students, for example, do most of their work within marketing with a foundation in a relatively narrow range of disciplines, such as economics and statistics. Left out are other disciplines, such as operations or competitive strategy, that can broaden the base of marketing thinking. The narrow focus of our PhD programs is even more serious, given that most have eliminated the requirement that students have an MBA. Thus, many graduating PhD students have no idea what finance, operations, accounting, and other management functions do and what their concerns and research agendas are, nor do they appreciate the interfaces between marketing and these other business functions. How can doctoral students consider marketing challenges without addressing operations or finance? We need to strengthen the link between marketing and other business functions.

The reality is that there is no business problem that has on it a label that says "marketing problem." All business problems are multidisciplinary, multifunctional problems. Every business problem that we have to address can have marketing, operations, financial, accounting, information technology, and human resources perspectives. We are fooling ourselves if we think we can artificially carve out a marketing problem and ignore the real business one. Marketing is only one component.

Limited Data

Another problem of marketing research and modeling is that it is often driven by available data. It is like the old story of the drunk who is looking for his keys under the streetlamp. He lost them down the block, but looks under the lamp because the light is better there. Marketing research too often focuses where the data are and not on finding the answers to other important questions that may be elsewhere. What about noncustomers? What about share of wallet (the percentage of an individual's total spending in a category)? What about customer behavior in countries that do not have the syndicated data sources available in the United States? What new data do we need to be gathering? What information will lead to true insights about the market rather than about minor variations in the existing customer base?

ARE THE CURRENT MENTAL MODELS OF MARKETING APPROPRIATE FOR THE CHANGING BUSINESS ENVIRONMENT?

As can be seen from this discussion, some of the limitations of the current models of marketing are already beginning to show. Much of the published marketing research and modeling and consumer behavior and economic modeling have questionable relevance to corporate strategy. Chief executive officers are concerned with both increasing the return on investment of marketing *and* harnessing marketing as an engine of growth. Sophisticated CMOs who seek a place at the corporate strategy table recognize the limitations of marketing. As Jim Stengel, global CMO of Procter & Gamble commented, "Today's marketing world is broken. I give us a 'D' because our mentalities have not changed. Our work processes have not changed enough. Our measurement has not evolved" (Neff and Sanders 2004).

It is no wonder that some of the marketing mental models that were developed in the last century are no longer relevant today. There have been dramatic changes in the environment that require us to rethink our approaches to marketing. Among these changes are:

- Post–9/11 global terrorism
- A turbulent global economy
- The pervasive impact of the Internet and the constant advances in information and communication technologies
- Continued advances in science and technology-based inventions
- The empowered hybrid consumer who expects customized products and services, messages, and distribution channels
- The reluctant consumer—with declining response rates, TiVo, and increasingly negative attitudes toward marketing and advertising
- Decreased consumer and employee loyalty
- The vanishing mass market and increased fragmentation of all markets
- A blurring of the line between B2B and B2C
- The rising importance of the developing world
- Opportunities for outsourcing and digital outsourcing/offshoring of marketing services (beyond call centers)
- Increased focus on public/private cooperation (nongovernmental organizations and others)

To what extent do marketing activities have relevance to this world? Is marketing as a discipline ignoring the gorillas in front of it? Do academic marketing publications have any relevance to CEOs, CMOs, and other marketing "customers"?

WHAT NEW MENTAL MODELS FOR MARKETING SHOULD WE CONSIDER?

Given the changing demands of the environment, mental models in marketing need to embrace a variety of new perspectives and address a number of challenges. Among these are:

- *Bridging disciplinary silos:* Bridging the walls among the marketing functions (such as customer service and sales) and marketing and other business functions (such as operations and finance) is critical given the fact that most marketing decisions are interrelated and in turn affect and are affected by the other functions.
- *Expanding the focus from consumers to stakeholders:* Since business decisions are affected not only by consumers but by distributors, suppliers, employees, shareholders, and others who are all heterogeneous, marketing concepts and approaches should not be restricted to consumers but should apply to all stakeholders.
- *Rethinking the value of customer satisfaction measures:* The rising popularity of customer satisfaction measures is leading to increased abuses and to unreliable and invalid data on customer satisfaction. Is it time to reexamine the value of our investments in these measures and consider replacing them with measures of referenceability (to what extent customers are willing to serve as references for our products and services or become our advocates and champions)?
- *Combining mass markets with segments of one:* As the ability to customize and personalize marketing products and messages increases, a rethinking of approaches to customers is needed to develop the right portfolio of custom and mass-marketed products and services.
- *Empowering consumers with information and choice tools:* Capitalize on the opportunities offered by the Internet to provide consumers with search engines and tools that give them the comparative information and decision aids that help them make optimal buying decisions (Urban 2005; Wind and Mahajan 2001).
- *Addressing the failure of most customer relationship management (CRM) implementation efforts:* The high failure rate of CRM initiatives may be a function of overemphasis on technology and a failure to assure that the systems are consistent with underlying business processes. Yet, it may also be the time for a shift in thinking so that instead of the company managing relationships with customers, the customers manage relations with the company, as discussed later.
- *Expanding marketing from a function to a philosophy:* Marketing should not be viewed only as the function responsible for performing the four Ps, but also as a business philosophy centered on understanding and meeting the evolving needs of customers and other stakeholders.
- *Designing products, services, and business models for the developing world:* Simple exporting of existing products, services, and business models to the developing world, ignoring the unique needs and characteristics of these markets, is inviting disaster. Products, services, and strategies need to be tailored to the distinctive conditions of emerging markets.
- *Building brands around consumer solutions:* While the focus of most companies has been on building brand equity and winning brands, this ignores the fact that consumers use multiple brands. An alternative perspective is building *customer brands* centered on the unique combination of products and services that address the specific customer needs. For example, in pharmaceuticals, most people on medication have more than one problem (such as hypertension *and* high cholesterol), yet most prescriptions are branded and marketed by therapeutic category brands. Why not instead create a brand for a consumer who has both hypertension

and high cholesterol, or one for patients with hypertension, high cholesterol, and diabetes?

- *Enhancing the communication mix with branded entertainment, edutainment, electronic games, buzz creation, and so on:* As discussed earlier, the increasing ineffectiveness of traditional marketing through mass media channels is a call for action for more creative communication approaches.

- *Identifying appropriate metrics and incorporating them into corporate dashboards:* Investments in marketing initiatives should be connected to business results. A focus on dashboards (interfaces that highlight key metrics needed to guide the firm in much the way an automobile dashboard serves a driver), forces the establishment of relevant metrics to run the business and on understanding of the drivers of these metrics, as discussed later.

- *Creating integrated customers, prospects, and competitive databases, and augmenting them with management's subjective judgment:* The data tracked by the company needs to include financial, customer, and competitive information, augmented with management's subjective judgment. It is also critical to develop approaches to detect early warning signals of opportunities (such as an increase in consumers' negative word of mouth of a competitor's products and services) and threats (such as an increase in consumers' negative word of mouth of our products and services).

- *Rethinking the role of marketing research and modeling:* The increased complexity of the business environment requires more effective marketing research and modeling approaches, yet critical business decisions such as mergers and acquisitions are being made with no marketing input at all. Equally disturbing is the fact that many decisions are being made on nonprojectable, nongeneralizable focus group interviews. It is critical to develop more effective data mining and other analytics as part of a decision support system (DSS) as well as marketing research and modeling tools that can be easily used by top executives, not only by marketing researchers. Creative applications of the Analytic Hierarchy Process (AHP) and Analytic Network Process (ANP) are good examples of such tools.

- *Combining traditional planning with adaptive experimentation:* Given the uncertainty of the business environment, traditional long-range planning has to be replaced with a more flexible process. This might combine a long-term vision and strategic direction with a set of adaptive experiments. These experiments facilitate continuous learning and assure that over time the strategic initiatives lead the organization toward the desired vision.

- *Transforming the organizational culture, structure, processes, and competencies:* It is not enough to change the mental models of marketing. These models are supported by an organizational architecture that also needs to be addressed. Managers need to recognize the importance of issues such as culture, structure, processes, technology, incentives, resources, and competencies (see, for example, Wind and Main 1998). And make sure that the entire organizational architecture is aligned with the new mental models of marketing.

- *Reexamining the traditional "Make-Buy" decision and the role of outsourcing:* The increased importance of integrated global supply chains and their implications to the creation of the virtual network organizations, as well as the increased importance of outsourcing and offshoring, have significant implications for marketing. It can no longer be assumed that marketing functions are best performed by the firm itself. Organizations have a choice of developing their own marketing capabilities ("making") or purchasing them on the market ("buy"). Who should perform all aspects of marketing has to be examined. These include R&D, new product and service development, customer service, and even sales.

Figure 11.1   **Three Interrelated Models**

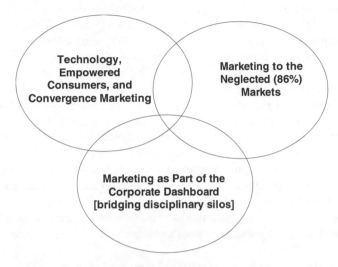

TOWARD NEW MENTAL MODELS OF MARKETING

What are some of the new ways we can look at marketing? While any combination of the preceding sixteen points challenges the current mental models of marketing, let me propose three interrelated models that address some of the needed changes as shown in Figure 11.1.

Looking through the Eyes of the Developing World

Emerging markets are becoming increasingly important, and this creates a need to expand our models, which are primarily designed for the developed world. Traditional views of marketing, designed for developed markets, overlook the 86 percent of the world population in developing markets (Mahajan and Banga 2005). Tata Motors, for example, is working on a $2,000 automobile for consumers in the Indian market who are ready to trade up from a scooter to their first car. (Mahajan and Banga 2005). This is a radically different solution and a very different concept than products targeted toward the first-time car buyer in the developed world. It is not just product design, but advertising, branding, distribution, and many other aspects of marketing that have to be rethought for these markets. Strategies and models that are designed for markets with widespread media penetration, good distribution systems, and sophisticated consumers need to be reconsidered in developing markets.

Do we understand the models that are needed to reach emerging markets? For example, in contrast to the "supersize" culture of the developed world, we need to think small in the developing world. Small sachets of shampoo and other products account for more than $1 billion in sales for Unilever in India alone (Mahajan and Banga 2005). Also, with high rates of immigration, there is a huge ricochet economy that zigzags from the developed world into the developing world as workers abroad send funds and products back home.

With weak infrastructures, companies have to bring their own infrastructure to meet the needs of the market. The progress of the developing world also challenges markets of the developed world. For example, over a million people today are going for medical treatment to the developing world. They are not coming to the Mayo Clinic for better treatment because only a very small segment of the very rich can afford it. People from England and other parts of the world are going to India as medical tourists because it is faster and cheaper, without sacrificing quality (Mahajan and Banga 2005).

C.K. Prahalad, in *The Fortune at the Bottom of the Pyramid* (Prahalad 2004), points out that there are opportunities among the poorest of the poor in these developing markets that are very significant and will become more so as these markets continue to develop. But the bottom of the pyramid requires different solutions than those of the developed world. Consider, for example, artificial limbs. In India alone, there are over five million people who have artificial limbs and there have been fundamental breakthroughs in product design. While the cost of an artificial limb replacement in the United States is over $7,000, designers in India developed a limb for less than $100.

Are these inferior limbs? Actually, they have superior functionality because they are designed to meet the challenges of recipients in the developing world who need to spend eight hours or more per day standing or squatting in the field. They are also installed in one day by less-skilled (and less-expensive) professionals than in the United States. It is a dramatically different product and process to meet the needs of this market. This has required a breakthrough in thinking about artificial limbs. Companies cannot expect to simply take products and strategies from the developed world and export them to the developing world. They need to challenge their mental models.

Seeing the Potential of Technology, Empowered Consumers, and Convergence Marketing

New technology and consumer empowerment have encouraged the development of "hybrid consumers," those who expect to have the best of both worlds in a variety of different areas. This has led to "convergence" along a number dimensions, which requires a rethinking of approaches to these consumers. To reach this hybrid consumer, companies need to address the "five Cs" of convergence marketing (Wind and Mahajan 2001), as illustrated in Figure 11.2.

Converging on "customerization" (make it mine): With opportunities to customize products and one-to-one marketing messages, companies need to manage the convergence of mass-produced, mass-marketed products and services as well as the "customerization" (tailoring of products, services, and messages).

Converging on communities (let me be a part of it): With the advent of online communities, consumers are members of both real and virtual communities. Companies such as online trader eBay have built businesses around virtual communities that lead to real transactions. Sites such as Sulekha.com have connected the Indian community around the globe, while providing networks and entertainment in local cities as well.

Converging on channels (I want to call, click, or visit): Consumers expect to be able to interact with the company seamlessly through multiple channels. Although most Charles Schwab investment customers conduct their business online, the majority of them still want to sit down with a live broker when they set up the account. The customer who books a plane ticket or hotel through online travel service firm Travelocity still may want to pick up the phone to speak with a reservation agent. These channels need to be tightly integrated.

Converging on competitive value (give me more for my money): Companies need to redefine the value equations to reflect the increased expectations of "24/7" service as well as to combine supplier-set pricing with consumer-determined pricing. How can we ignore online sellers Priceline and eBay and their implications for all businesses? There are many more pricing options and ways of delivering value than in the past and we need to integrate these into our marketing strategies.

Converging on choice (give me more tools to make better decisions): In the same way that the introduction of the Sabre reservation system empowered travel agents, online tools and the CMR

Figure 11.2 **The Five C's of Convergence Marketing**

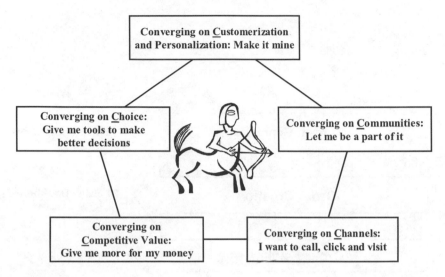

Source: Wind and Mahajan 2001.

approach can empower consumers by putting choice and decision making in their hands. For example, converging on choice means moving to customer managed relationships (CMR) instead of the more company-centric approach of customer relationship management (CRM). In CRM, the company manages its relationship with the customer, whereas in the more consumer-centric CMR, customers are given tools to manage their own relationships with the company, its competitors, and other relevant organizations.

Using Dashboards to Bridge Disciplinary Silos

Another way to take a fresh look at marketing is through dashboards that help to better integrate the marketing perspective into business decision making. On the corporate dashboard, marketing is just one component, yet creating an effective corporate dashboard requires linking marketing to other business drivers and performance outcomes. This means more clearly specifying how the business fits together. Marketing can then be seen as the glue for integrating the rest of the business functions. Managers need a dashboard that is more like a car than a 747, to provide a simple and clear view of progress using a limited number of metrics and controls to run the business (although there can be great complexity beneath the dash). The dashboard, if well designed, allows managers to watch many parts of the business simultaneously. Companies need to achieve the triple goals of creating value for the customers, the employees, and the shareholders. These goals are interrelated, and the dashboard makes this clear.

An example for an integrated corporate dashboard is the one developed by Johnson & Johnson (Figure 11.3). It focuses on three core processes—demand generation, order creation, and order fulfillment—and how they are related to the enabling processes of business strategy and information, people development, finance, and information management.

These are all then linked to performance measures such as sales, income, and capital efficient profitable growth (CEPG). The marketing initiatives in demand generation, for example, can now

Figure 11.3 **Illustrative Strategic Framework for a Corporate Dashboard – Johnson & Johnson 2003**

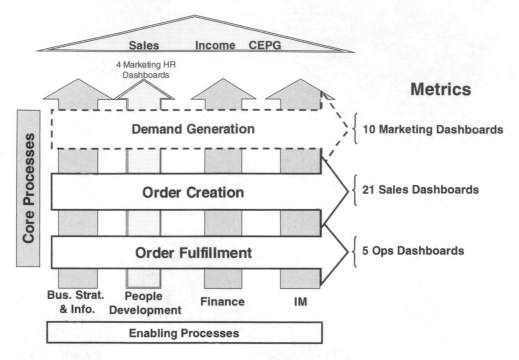

Source: A Wharton School presentation by James DeMaioribus, 2003.

be directly related to performance outcomes. They are not isolated. Dashboards such as these can be a powerful way for organizations to look across business silos and connect marketing perspectives to broader business decisions.

Integrating the Three Models

These three models are just an illustration of some of the new ways of thinking about marketing. As indicated in Figure 11.1, these three models are interrelated and address some of the key changes in our business environment. The Internet and advances in communication technology empower consumers and accelerate the changes in developing markets by offering more direct access to global markets. The rise of emerging markets and convergence marketing are having an impact on the metrics and design of corporate dashboards. And the dashboards themselves can help identify opportunities in all these areas. It is important to note that the dramatically changing environment means marketing is not alone in facing these challenges. Virtually all aspects of business need to address developing markets, convergence, and dashboards. This is both an opportunity as well as a threat. In challenging their mental models, other parts of the business may well subsume many of the old marketing functions. Just look at how the materials management function has totally transformed itself into the all-powerful and dominant "supply chain" role, which has already started to encroach into many other areas of the business, including marketing. This by itself forces marketing to reinvent itself. A transformation of marketing thinking can well redefine itself just like the supply chain.

Figure 11.4 **The New Partnership**

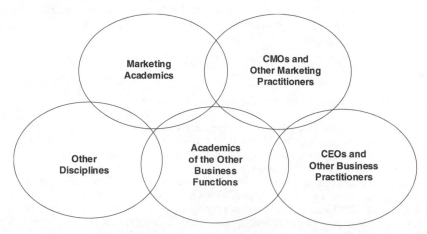

IMPLICATIONS OF THE NEW MENTAL MODELS OF MARKETING FOR THE DISCIPLINE'S RESEARCH AGENDA

New mental models can offer insights on how marketing can become more effective and more integral to the core processes of the organization. Marketing academics and professionals can also learn from other disciplines. Overall, we need to begin thinking more broadly about issues such as joint optimization of marketing and operations. For academic researchers not to be marginalized, kept on the other side of the wall, they need to step out of the narrow confines of the discipline to actively engage with colleagues in other management functions. Marketing researchers need to connect with top executives who are wrestling with real business problems that marketing perspectives can help solve. Marketing practitioners also need to engage in this dialogue with the rest of the organization, to expand their own thinking, and look for opportunities to apply their tools and approaches more broadly. We need to be open and invite the intellectual leaders of other disciplines to join us in finding joint solutions. We have to rigorously measure the effectiveness of marketing-driven strategies so we can see the true results and challenge our views of limits.

In the field of marketing, there already are encouraging model-busting initiatives that we can build on in challenging our mental models. These include the Marketing Science Institute, ART Forum, the CMO Summit, and the INFORMS Society for Marketing Science Practice prize for the outstanding implementation of marketing science concepts and methods (and its publication in *Marketing Science*). These initiatives are starting to bridge and break the walls between research and practice, but we need additional initiatives, especially focused on bridging the silos of marketing and the other business functions, marketing and the other disciplines (including the less commonly relied on disciplines of cultural anthropology, complex adaptive system, architecture, artificial intelligence, etc.), and academic marketing and marketing practitioners. This calls for new partnerships that bridge the traditional silos of marketing, as illustrated in Figure 11.4.

We need to conduct many more such experiments. Experimentation is the way we test the limits of our models and discover useful new ones. We have to understand the power and limits of our current mental models of marketing and look for ways to change them. At the same time, this rethinking of marketing cannot be done in isolation. It requires changing the mental models of business and the integration of marketing insights and philosophy into these broader models. We have undertaken a new project at Wharton's SEI Center for Advanced Studies in Management, "Towards a New Theory of the Firm," to examine shifts in the models of business organizations. Projects such as this could have a significant impact on the practice of marketing. By challenging its current mental models, and changing them when necessary, marketing can identify its own "four-minute mile" barriers and, hopefully, run past them.

REFERENCES

Bannister, Roger (1981), *The Four Minute Mile.* Guilford, CT: Lyons Press.

Bianco, Anthony (2004), "The Vanishing Market," *Business Week,* July 12, 2004, p. 60; reporting on a survey of the fifteen largest U.S. television markets in 2003 by CNW Marketing Research, Inc.

Kotick, Robert (2004), "Media and Entertainment " Milken Institute Global Forum, Los Angeles, April.

Kroft, Steve (2004), "The Echo Boomers", *CBS News,* www.cbsnews.com/stories/2004/10/01/60minutes/printable646890.shtml (accessed October 3).

Mahajan, Vijay and Kamini Banga (2005), *The 86 Percent Solution.* Philadelphia: Wharton School Publishing.

Neff, Jack and Lisa Sanders (2004), "It's Broken," *Advertising Age,* February 16.

Prahalad, C.K. (2004), *The Fortune at the Bottom of the Pyramid.* Philadelphia: Wharton School Publishing.

"The 9/11 Commission Report: Final Report of the National Commission on Terrorist Attacks in the United States, Executive Summary," http://a257.g.akamaitech.net/7/257/2422/22jul20041147/www.gpoaccess.gov/911/pdf/execsummary.pdf.

Simons, Daniel and Christopher Chabris (1999), "Gorillas in Our Midst: Sustained Inattentional Blindness for Dynamic Events," *Perception,* 28, 1059–74.

Urban, Glen (2005), *Don't Just Relate, Advocate: A Blueprint for Profit in the Era of Customer Power.* Philadelphia: Wharton School Publishing.

Wind, Yoram and Colin Crook (2004), *The Power of Impossible Thinking: Transform the Business of Your Life and the Life of Your Business.* Philadelphia: Wharton School Publishing.

——— and Vijay Mahajan (2001), *Convergence Marketing.* Upper Saddle River, NJ: Financial Times/Prentice Hall.

——— and Jeremy Main (1998), *Driving Change: How the Best Companies Are Preparing for the 21st Century.* New York: The Free Press.

Yago, Glen and Aaron Pankratz (2000), *The Minority Business Challenge: Democratizing Capital for Emerging Domestic Markets*, Milken Institute Research Report, September 25.

CHAPTER 12

WHITHER "MARKETING"?

Commentary on the American Marketing Association's New Definition of Marketing

GREGORY T. GUNDLACH

Does marketing need reform? I am pleased to be able to offer commentary on such an important and timely question. In the short space allotted for this chapter, I focus on how "marketing" is defined, viewing such inquiry to be central to the question of whether marketing should be reformed.[1] In particular, I comment on the new definition of marketing recently announced by the American Marketing Association (AMA). I contend that the AMA's definition of marketing advances an exclusively *marketer* perspective of marketing (more so than prior AMA definitions). I briefly discuss the implications of adopting such a perspective for defining marketing, concluding that these implications are of sufficient concern to call for "reform" in how marketing is defined in relation to scholarship.[2] In particular, I argue that scholars should adopt a definition of marketing that does not advance a single perspective, but is independent and of sufficient breadth to be integrative of other perspectives, thereby enabling comprehensive and objective advances in scholarship.

BACKGROUND

With almost forty thousand members, the American Marketing Association is considered by many to be the major association of its kind for many academics and practitioners in the field of marketing. There is no doubt that the AMA has played an important and influential role in the development of scholarship in the field. Few in marketing are not familiar with the AMA's journals, conferences, and other activities. Many academics attend AMA conferences, publish in AMA journals, are members of their special interest groups, and have provided service to the association. Indeed, as an academic association, the AMA positions itself as a "thought leader," seeking to influence marketing's scholarly development and practice.

AMA's Definition of Marketing

Since 1935, as part of its role, the AMA has offered to both academics and practitioners its version of the definition of marketing.[3] In 2004, a new definition was announced. According to the AMA, under this new definition:

> Marketing is an organizational function and a set of processes for creating, communicating and delivering value to customers and for managing customer relationships in ways that benefit the organization and its stakeholders.

The new definition was officially unveiled at the AMA Summer Educators' Conference in Boston in August (*Marketing News* 2004). According to the AMA, it incorporates the contributions of many marketers from around the world, both academics and practitioners.

COMMENTARY

Inspection of the AMA's new definition of marketing reveals that it advances a largely (if not exclusively) *marketer* perspective, viewing marketing as an "organizational function" engaged in by the firm. While in some ways helpful to the marketing manager, from the perspective of scholarship and progress toward a comprehensive understanding of marketing, adoption of an exclusively marketer-based perspective has the unfortunate consequence of omitting other perspectives and their importance for such understanding. As with any subject, adoption of a single perspective for its study has the potential of: (1) constraining the relevant domain of interest, (2) limiting the development and dissemination of knowledge concerning the subject, and (3) biasing knowledge that is developed and disseminated (both through research and teaching).

To be sure, recognition and characterization of the concerns for scholarship that attend an exclusively marketer perspective for marketing are not new to the field and have been advanced by others. More than thirty years ago, Tucker (1974, p. 31), for example, noted the tendency of the field to study consumers from the point of view of the "channel captain," analogizing the use of an exclusively marketer perspective to be equivalent to "the ways that fisherman study fish rather than as marine biologists study them." Echoing continuing concern for the discipline, Anderson (1983, p. 28), described the likely consequences of Tucker's earlier observations, remarking almost ten years later that "Marketing's preoccupation with the concerns of Tucker's 'channel captain' introduces an asymmetry into the study of the phenomenon that can only limit the discipline's perspective and inhibit its attainment of scientific status." More recently, Bazerman (2001) has argued for a consumer-based approach to consumer research, describing the "implicit biases" that attend research in consumer behavior that applies a marketer perspective and focuses on the determinants of consumer purchasing. Beyond marketing, in general, scholarship that adopts a single perspective is a concern for any academic field or scientific discipline (see Kuhn 1962).

Scope and Domain of Marketing

Rather than defining marketing, the AMA's definition describes what most have previously known as the narrower concept of "marketing management."[4] Although consistent with a marketer's view of marketing, marketing management does not fully describe the scope of marketing. Beyond specific functions and processes engaged in by an organization, the concept of marketing encompasses a much broader domain. According to Kotler and Armstrong (2001, p. 13), for example, "[C]onsumers *do* marketing when they search for the goods they need at prices they can afford" (emphasis added). Wilkie and Moore (1999, p. 201) go further, suggesting that "There are participants other than marketers in the aggregate marketing system. Organizational customers and ultimate consumers are key players . . . and governments provide services intended to facilitate system operations."

In terms of scholarship, circumscribing marketing to those activities and processes of the marketer limits and constrains the relevant domain of interest. As Anderson (1983, p. 28) points out, adoption of a single perspective in marketing "limit[s] the discipline's perspective" and may well undermine its ability to attain scientific status. This latter result concerns perceptions regarding the field's ability to obtain scientific legitimacy where it is primarily concerned with the interests of only one segment of society (p. 27).

Knowledge Development and Dissemination about Marketing

Adoption of a single perspective, as found in the AMA's exclusively marketer view, also possesses the potential for limiting the development and dissemination of knowledge regarding marketing. Such potential exists for the study of any subject when approached from a single vantage point. As Wilkie and Moore (1999, p. 199) observed, "[V]iewing a topic from a single perspective highlights certain characteristics, but can hide other aspects that also may be important."

In the above respect, for scholarship, adoption of the AMA's definition may have the unfortunate consequence of focusing knowledge development and dissemination activities narrowly and on subjects that address topics and issues of specific interest to the firm and its managers. While a worthy endeavor in itself and beneficial in many ways, address of important topics and issues of interest to those who view marketing from other vantage points may be overlooked. As observed by Bartels (1983, pp. 34–35) such an emphasis, "means that important aspects of *total* marketing are neglected" (emphasis added). The dissemination of knowledge that is developed from these other vantage points is also likely to be adversely affected as increasing focus is given to knowledge that aids the marketer. Over time, the perception that marketing knowledge is largely limited to only topics and issues of interest to the marketer may ultimately inhibit the flow of its knowledge both within the field and to other fields whose interest in marketing is not similarly circumscribed.[5]

Objectiveness of Marketing Knowledge

Perhaps the greatest concern, however, in the adoption of an exclusively marketer perspective for marketing is the potential that knowledge that is developed and disseminated may represent a biased perspective of "marketing." Such a result, unfortunately, is likely unavoidable given the inherent biases that attend the study of a subject from a particular vantage point. As Tucker (1974, p. 31) counsels, studying marketing from a single point of view, "encourage[s] the sort of myopia common to all specialists" (see also Bazerman 2001). Where a scholar adopts a particular perspective, by definition the scholar approaches the subject from that point of view. Given that the scholar's vantage point is predetermined, they cannot be expected to be objective nor independent in their study of the topic. The consequences of such an outcome for marketing cuts to the core of those principles that undergird our process of scientific inquiry.

CONCLUSION

While providing a definition of marketing that is helpful to marketing practitioners, scholars in marketing should adopt a definition of marketing that does not advance a single perspective. Marketing should be defined independent of any one particular perspective and with sufficient breadth to be integrative of other perspectives. Development of such a definition is necessary for comprehensive and objective advances in marketing scholarship. To this end, Anderson (1983, p. 28) provides a helpful description of the type of definition that should be sought after by scholars in the field:

> On this view, the exchange process itself becomes the focus of attention in much the same way that communication is the focus of communication theorists, and administration is the focus of administrative scientists. The interest must lie in understanding and explaining the phenomenon itself, rather than understanding it from the perspective of only one of the participants.

For scholarship, adoption of a definition of marketing within the discipline that is inclusive of its varying perspectives and focuses on marketing not as a managerial practice, but more broadly as a phenomenon, is likely to pay dividends for the field. These include benefits for the ongoing discovery of knowledge, its dissemination through teaching and other forms of diffusion, the application of such knowledge in practice, and the acceptance and integration of its knowledge by scholars in other academic fields and members of society at large.

NOTES

1. The importance of a definition cannot be overstated. Standing alone, a definition outlines the scope and content of what is defined, fixing its boundaries and describing its subject matter. A formal definition is an authoritative statement of meaning or significance that attaches to and explains the nature and essential qualities of that which is defined. In practice, a definition provides clarity and direction, making clear what might be otherwise indefinite.

2. A related benchmark of critical importance, but not focused upon in this chapter, is the role and responsibility of marketing in society. As Robert Bartels once said, "[A] standard for judging what is or is not marketing must give consideration to the question of the role of marketing in human society" (Bartels 1983, p. 33). Although not emphasizing the implications of defining marketing from an exclusively marketer perspective, several chapters in this book address the question "Does Marketing Need Reform?" through examination of the current state of marketing in society. For insights, readers are encouraged to read the contributions of William L. Wilkie, Rajan Varadarajan, Johny K. Johansson, Jagdish Sheth, Raj Sisodia, and Katherine N. Lemon.

3. The first official definition of marketing was adopted in 1935 by the National Association of Marketing Teachers, a predecessor of the AMA. It was adopted by the AMA in 1948, and again in 1960 when the AMA revisited the definition and decided not to change it. This original definition stood for fifty years, until it was revised in 1985 (see, AMA's website, www.marketingpower.com/content4620.php).

4. In this respect, some have even characterized prior definitions of marketing advanced by the AMA to be definitions of "marketing management" rather than marketing (see Kotler 2001).

5. Indeed, the potential exists that knowledge from this larger domain may not be considered "mainstream" in marketing, leading to the view of such contributions being "outside" the discipline. At the extreme, such endeavors on the part of scholars may not be recognized (e.g., published) or rewarded (e.g., tenure).

REFERENCES

Anderson, Paul F. (1983), "Marketing, Scientific Progress, and Scientific Method," *Journal of Marketing,* 47 (Fall), 18–31.
Bartels, Robert (1983), "Is Marketing Defaulting Its Responsibilities?" *Journal of Marketing,* 47 (Fall), 32–35.
Bazerman, Max H. (2001), "Consumer Research for Consumers," *Journal of Consumer Research,* 27 (4), 499–504.
Kotler, Philip and Gary Armstrong (2001), *Principles of Marketing.* Upper Saddle River, NJ: Prentice Hall.
Kuhn, Thomas (1962), *The Structure of Scientific Revolutions.* Chicago: University of Chicago.
Marketing News (2004), "Marketing Redefined," September 15, 16–18.
Tucker, W.T. (1974), "Future Directions in Marketing Theory," *Journal of Marketing,* 38 (April), 30–35.
Wilkie, William L. and Elizabeth S. Moore (1999), "Marketing's Contributions to Society," *Journal of Marketing,* 62 (Special Issue), 198–218.

CHAPTER 13

INTERACTION ORIENTATION

The New Marketing Competency

V. KUMAR AND GIRISH RAMANI

LEARNING FROM FIRMS THAT ARE GETTING IT RIGHT

Does Wal-Mart feel uneasy that despite its impressive presence and growth, it does not have a successful loyalty program with its customers? Is identifying its valuable customers and rewarding them individually never going to be a part of its marketing strategy? For the moment, Wal-Mart does not care what an individual customer buys at its stores, but by promoting its own website (walmart.com), it does admit that it does not want to be left behind in the online business, where the rule of the game is to enhance the share of your customers' wallet by learning more about each one of them individually. At Sam's Club, the warehouse chain promoted by Wal-Mart, there already exists rich data on each individual customer. We do not know if walmart.com or Sam's Club will at some time overtake the mainline stores' business. But Wal-Mart is willing to be prepared, if and when that day arrives. Thus, the first learning that the changing marketplace offers is:

L1: Think of customers as individuals, and not aggregates.

Amazon.com is at the other end of the marketing spectrum when compared with Wal-Mart. Is it doing the right thing by actively recommending a set of products that its computers decide a customer is likely to be interested in on the basis of purchase history? Whether or not Amazon's recommendations hit home, there seems to be an increasing number of customers who are comfortable with this technoprofiling, and some who even say, "I like the idea that some one cares, even if it is only a machine" (Zaslow 2002). Customers seek more than low prices and product availability; they crave interaction and to be treated as unique, individual customers. Of course, the cost of providing human interaction to every individual customer is prohibitive. However, technology and computing power offer firms an option to stay connected with individual customers. In fact, online relationship building possesses certain advantages that human interactions lack. First, there is consistency in the knowledge and expertise level encountered by the customer over a website, unlike in a face-to-face scenario where these levels could vary depending on the sales person. Second, most customers enjoy a feeling of privacy and freedom in online transactions because they believe that they are not being physically watched by a human being, even though they are aware that computers are likely to be collecting individually identifiable data. So, to more and more customers who are either wary of the human interface or who consider self-help a richer buying experience, the Internet is the ideal way to interact with a firm. In today's economy, the capability of a firm to use technology to respond to individual customers and enrich their interaction experiences is slowly but surely turning out to be a key marketing strength. Thus, we arrive at the second learning that the changing marketplace offers:

L2: Adopt technology as a means to reach and carry out useful dialogues with each potential and current customer.

Tying a customer down through contractual obligations or through technological roadblocks is a sure way to stoke attitudinal disloyalty, while perhaps increasing profits in the short run. Microsoft's current revenues largely depend on machines needing the Windows operating system. The development and release of various versions of Windows is controlled and supervised by Microsoft. IBM, on the other hand, spends billions of dollars promoting Linux, a free operating system, as an alternative to Windows, without earning a penny on it (Maiello and Kitchens 2004). IBM does this in the belief that creating choice is the way to empower customers and fight competition. If users buy in to this as a sincere marketing move, IBM hopes the customer sentiment will upset Microsoft's dominant presence in the operating systems market. While competitors like HP and Dell also gain from this move by selling more Linux-based machines, IBM believes that its initiative to drive Linux will be recognized by its customers in the long run and boost their attachment to the company. Only time will tell whether IBM succeeds or not, but the fact remains that to obtain competitive advantage, firms increasingly need to be seen as empowering their customers.

Internet commerce empowers customers by removing constraints in the buying process, e.g., by allowing customers to compare products and prices, by providing quick and easy access to products that complement and supplement the focal product that a customer sets out to buy (Day and Montgomery 1999; Jaworski, Kohli, and Sahay 2000), and by accepting electronic instructions and payments. Opening up options to customers could upset a firm's carefully laid plans, but this is where a firm needs to radically change its mindset from product centric to customer centric. Outsourcing as a supply-side strategy places few bounds on the capability of firms to offer virtually any product or service to a customer. Why should any firm then be afraid of outsourcing to its customers some responsibility for its destiny? Firms should follow an empowerment strategy that seeks to make their customers feel that they too are investors in the firm. Empowered customers would themselves provide the checks and balances necessary to steady a firm's progress, much like empowered employees of a firm do. A firm that empowered customers by promoting legitimate online music downloads, when most music companies were still unsure of the path to take, is Apple. The wall of Apple iPod customers, although severely critical of the product in online forum communities, creates a protective shield around the brand that any competitor would find hard to penetrate. The proliferation of self-check kiosks at airports is another example of customer empowerment. A breed of customers view these kiosks as a reward for their competence with technology because they can cut long lines, check in their own baggage, select their seats, change their itinerary, and view their frequent flyer miles. Self-check kiosks undoubtedly lead to lower costs for the airlines that promote them. A single ticket agent at a kiosk station can check in three people at once, reducing the number of counter agents by two-thirds (Gage and McCormick 2003). Delta Airlines is therefore happy to see customers increasingly use self-check kiosks at its various airports. Thus, the third learning that the changing marketplace offers is:

L3: Devise active customer empowerment strategies since they lead to competitive advantage.

Proctor & Gamble's (P&G) worldwide success with mass-market products is unparalleled. However, it realizes that to stay on course, it needs to strengthen its ties with its customers who are more information hungry than ever. Two of its initiatives in the online market space indicate its eagerness to interact with its individual customers. The first is Beinggirl.com, which engages early- and late-teen girls by providing informative content in cool teenage-girl vocabulary and style on delicate issues related to puberty and other teen subjects. The website, available in multiple languages in twenty-five countries, connects with potential users of P&G's feminine protection products in a way no mass medium can. Consider this move in light of the fact that in some countries teenage girls may not be able to openly discuss these products with anyone they know, and the power of the website is obvious. The second initiative, reflect.com, allows customization of a complete range of beauty products. To assure customers that it is committed to them, the website offers free recustomization and a money back guarantee without having to return the product. By posing a wide variety of questions, answers to which help the customer create a customized product, the website offers a unique and creative experience, while simultaneously gathering invaluable information for the firm, through voluntary customer participation. These initiatives put P&G in a position to offer successive online and offline interaction experiences that incorporate information from previous interactions with each customer individually and from all interacting customers collectively. Thus, the fourth learning from the changing marketplace is:

L4: Identify opportunity areas that legitimately obtain valuable customer information, in situations where it is demonstrable that this information is what is helping customers enrich their own lives.

The most compelling change in the marketplace today is the questioning of the credibility of the role of marketing. Increasingly, a firm's top management is demanding accountability for every marketing action. In the words of Gary Loveman, chief executive officer of casino hotel company Harrah's, "Broadcasting an ad on television or in a newspaper is admitting you have no idea who your customers are" (Bianco et al. 2004). Accountability, therefore, is linked to knowing each customer and measuring the effect of marketing action in terms of the responses obtained from that customer. The monetary value that a customer is likely to provide a firm over the period of his or her relationship, if assessed, would vastly aid in quantifying the role of marketing in contributing to a firm's profits. Credit card firms, catalog marketers, banks, and more recently, fashion retailers have made efforts to determine "customer lifetime value" in order to prioritize their customers and devise appropriate marketing actions that would result in maximizing profits across the customer base. The ability to define and measure customer lifetime value and use it to take marketing action will increase in importance to firms that would like to see and verify the return on the marketing dollar. Thus, the fifth learning that the changing marketplace offers is:

L5: Firms need to devise methods and implement systems that define and dynamically measure customer value to demonstrate the accountability of marketing actions.

These five learnings help us develop a framework that could be used to describe or analyze the new governing strategic orientation that firms need to be successful in the changing marketplace. This strategic orientation will be determined by the increasingly visible role of individual customers in shaping firms' destinies, omnipresent information and database technology, and the increasing demand for managerial accountability for marketing actions. We call this interaction orientation.

THE PATH FROM SELLING ORIENTATION TO INTERACTION ORIENTATION

Having looked at the learnings from the marketplace, we step back to develop the context in which to view interaction orientation as an important research construct. We trace the path of marketing that began with the *selling concept,* moved to embrace the *marketing concept,* and is now poised to adopt the *customer concept.* The selling concept is characterized by customers *to whom* something is sold (Hoekstra, Leeflang, and Wittink 1999). Selling orientation therefore reflects the belief that consumers will purchase more goods and services if aggressive sales and advertising methods are employed, and suggests an emphasis on short-term sales maximization over long-term relationship building (Noble, Sinha, and Kumar 2002). The marketing concept is characterized by customers *for whom* products and services are developed (Hoekstra et al. 1999). Market orientation of a firm is then a measure of how strongly a firm believes in the marketing concept and how much it supplements this belief with an understanding of the need for processes that enable it to gather information on its customers and competitors, analyze this information, and disseminate the knowledge thus generated with a view to developing a position of competitive advantage. Market orientation is thus viewed as an organizing framework that involves a dual focus on customers and competitors (Hunt and Morgan 1995; Kohli and Jaworski 1990; Narver and Slater 1990). While the marketing concept underscored the importance of customers, and market orientation as a construct has been the subject of numerous studies, these terms when originally conceived did not explicitly recognize the degree to which it would be possible to isolate, address, and interact with each customer on an ongoing basis. Therefore, there is a pressing need to conceive new concepts, constructs, and measures that more truly reflect the role of marketing as it has evolved to today. One such concept that begs to be in the forefront of the research agenda is the customer concept. The customer concept is characterized by the individual customer as the starting point for value-creating marketing activities (Hoekstra et al. 1999). We adapt this thought but define the customer concept more precisely as the conduct of all marketing activities with the individual customer as the central unit of analysis and action. This interpretation of the customer concept emphasizes the analysis and measurement of marketing activities and consequences at an individual customer level. A firm that subscribes to the customer concept is likely to be of the view that interactions with each *individual* customer would determine the course of firm strategy (see Figure 13.1).

We envision the concept of interaction orientation as a combination of a firm's belief in the customer concept and the concomitant processes and practices that the firm adopts to carry out its marketing activities.[1]

By overlaying the received learnings from the changing marketplace onto the knowledge of various strategic orientations provided by the marketing literature, we propose a firm's interaction orientation as a composite construct that reflects the belief in the customer concept, the capacity to offer customer interaction experiences based on a dynamic response system, the willingness to empower customers, and the extent to which customer value management is used to make marketing decisions.

The Components of Interaction Orientation

A firm's business can be thought of as an integration of three critical aspects. The first aspect is the underlying belief with which the firm operates. The second is the set of systems and processes that the firm employs. The third is the collection of managerial practices that a firm

Figure 13.1 **From Selling Orientation to Interaction Orientation**

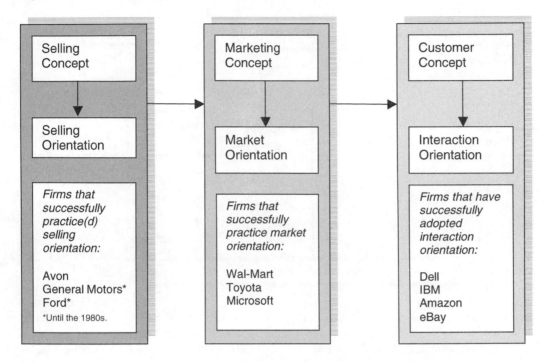

adopts. The four components of interaction orientation emanate from these three aspects (see Figure 13.2).

Belief in the customer concept: This component represents the degree of the embedded belief among managers that the firm should strive to engage each potential and current customer in order to understand the needs of each individual customer. Firms that believe that each customer has unique needs that cannot be satisfied with the same set of products and services focus on consumers more than on products and competitors. Such firms also seek out new customers individually and tend to unify different functional areas looking for ways to satisfy individual customer needs.

Interaction response capacity: This component represents the degree to which the firm is capable of offering successive interaction experiences to each customer by dynamically incorporating feedback from previous behavioral responses of that customer individually, and of other customers collectively. Not so long ago, a key role of marketing was to transform process information into knowledge by developing expert systems and decision models that present analyzed data and decision scenarios on an interactive basis to personnel in the field (Achrol and Kotler 1999). This role has gone beyond field personnel to include end customers. Data have to be analyzed and customer decision scenarios presented to the end customer dynamically. The scenarios in the form of product and service options need to be the result of observing buying patterns of individual customers. Predictions on which product or service a customer is likely to buy next and when need to be incorporated into the scenarios. Another key aspect that determines the degree of interaction response capacity lies in the ability to design, manufacture, and outsource products and services in direct response to customer needs by investing in flexible back-end systems. Dell is a prime example of providing front-end customization as a result of investments in a network of back-end support.

Customer empowerment: It is time to offer customers a greater say in the operations and stra-

Figure 13.2 **The Interaction Orientation Construct**

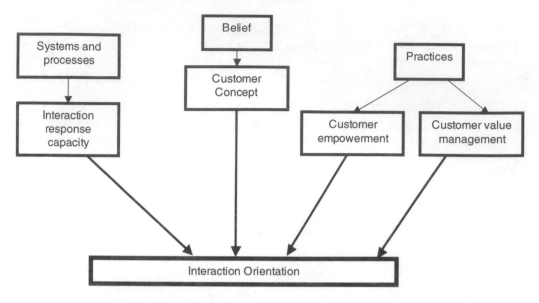

tegic direction of the business. A successful business strategy must be based on empowering individual customers to allow them to develop the experience with the company on their terms (Newell 2003; Prahalad and Ramaswamy 2004). Customer empowerment reflects the extent to which a firm provides its customers avenues to a) connect with the firm and actively shape the nature of transactions, and b) connect and collaborate with each other by sharing information, praise, criticism, suggestions, and ideas about its products, services and policies. Getting customers to interact with each other and facilitating them to highlight issues often results in providing solutions to problems that otherwise require the firm's resources. Hewlett-Packard encourages online peer-to-peer service and the rich information that the members of this online community provide to one another and to Hewlett Packard only helps raise its overall service efficiency.

Customer value management: This component represents the extent to which the firm is able to define and dynamically measure customer value and use it as its guiding metric for marketing resource allocation decisions. Customer value management is defined as providing differentially tailored treatment, based on the expected response from each customer to available marketing initiatives, such that the contribution from each customer to overall profitability is maximized (Kumar, Ramani, and Bohling 2004). Customer value, when measured for the duration of a customer's association with a firm as the sum of cumulated cash flows discounted using the weighted average cost of capital, is called customer lifetime value. A series of studies have shown the success of customer lifetime value as a metric that helps firms decide on retaining or discontinuing a customer, plan suitable marketing and communication channel mixes, and provide time- and product-based cross-sell recommendations for individual customers (Kumar and Venkatesan 2005; Kumar, Venkatesan, and Reinartz 2004; Reinartz and Kumar 2003, 2000, 2002; Venkatesan and Kumar 2004).

THE NEED TO ADOPT AN INTERACTION ORIENTATION

The market orientation construct ended up excluding profitability as its component primarily because of the emphasis that was placed on the view obtained from field managers. Marketing is losing its focus as a business process due to the refusal of managers to accept monetary account-ability of marketing actions (Rust et al. 2004). The increased need to individualize and the in-creased ability of firms to do so offer the marketing management of a firm no protection behind aggregate and backward-looking performance measures like sales volume, sales value, sales growth, market share, and market share growth. By including the concept of customer value in interaction orientation we seek to offer a construct that directly links marketing action to business perfor-mance. The time has come for marketers to hone their measures of customer value. Customer lifetime value should continue to be the subject of active research, and become the guiding metric for practitioners in the real world. However, we may face resistance from marketing managers to endorse the adoption of customer value management concepts, not only due to an aversion to being held accountable, but also due to the organizational and implementation challenges that such a step poses (Kumar, Ramani, and Bohling 2004). On the organizational front, quantifica-tion of the projected return on investment (ROI) needs to be agreed upon across stakeholders and business units, and managers and professionals who have traditionally been responsible for all aspects of the marketing of a single brand now have to be empowered with the ability and respon-sibility across brands, products, and business units. On the implementation front, understanding the data-driven campaign execution output file, choosing the right set of customers in each prod-uct category and in each time frame, and documenting the relationship progression to provide effective feedback to the system requires investments and training. But, if a firm accepts that value-creating customers define a business, measuring the long-term business value of marketing actions at the customer level is the way to guide its progress. The need for firms to develop a high degree of interaction orientation is therefore inexorable.

THE BENEFITS AND RESULTS OF ADOPTING AN INTERACTION ORIENTATION

We focus now on the expected benefits and results of firms adopting interaction orientation. Not all customers are of equal significance or value to a firm. However, in the absence of interactions between a firm and a customer, the relative value of customers is not evident. The tendency then is to overservice low-value customers and underservice high-value customers. An educated cus-tomer is a powerful customer. Actions of knowledgeable and experienced customers can either help or damage a firm's reputations. The ability to take advantage of such customers is made possible by identifying and cultivating them as a resource to the firm. The firm's lack of attention toward a customer results in a lack of interest in the firm by the customer. Without being rewarded in terms of recognition, power, or monetary benefits, customers will not feel that they are stake-holders in the firm. Empowering and rewarding customers according to each ones' expertise and needs, on the other hand, results in discernible mutual benefits. Interaction orientation prescribes that products and services are not predetermined. Thus, a shifting array of products and services mark a firm that adopts this orientation. This makes the firm a moving target for competitors who end up focusing on analyzing its products and miss out on the end customers. Microsoft, in its response to the threat from promoters of Linux such as IBM and Novell, has taken steps to focus on bringing out features similar to Linux in their own products with a view to counter the Linux phenomenon (Murphy 2004). This example suggests the power of interaction orientation as a source of competitive advantage. The confidence in anticipating the course of the business in-creases with the ability to predict the value that each customer is likely to contribute in the future.

In the absence of interactive updating of a firm's customer equity, which is the sum of the lifetime value of all its customers, the firm has to rely on past performance measures and judg-

Table 13.1

The Interaction Orientation Framework: A Summary

The construct	The need	The benefits	The results
1. The extent of belief in the customer concept	1. Include the power and value of a firm's customers as an evaluation criterion	1. Identification and retention of valuable customers	1. Short-term profits
2. The extent of interaction response capacity	2. Integrate marketing action with business performance	2. Development of customers as a skilled resource	2. Sustained competitive advantage
3. The extent of customer involvement and empowerment	3. Provide a constructive measure of marketing accountability	3. Build customer ownership of firm	3. Long-term profits
4. The extent of customer value management practiced	4. A dynamic array of products and services		
	5. Longer planning horizons		

ment to plan into the future. Interaction orientation, which prescribes that the consequences of all marketing actions be measured in terms of its impact on customer value, would improve the accuracy of the prediction of both short-term and long-term performance. Thus the consequential benefits of adopting interaction orientation are: (1) the firm is able to attract and retain the most valuable customers, (2) the firm's customers develop into a skilled resource for the firm, (3) the firm's customers keep competitors away because of their heightened sense of ownership of the firm, (4) the firm develops a dynamically shifting portfolio of products and services, and (5) the firm develops the ability to foresee customer responses and plan marketing activities for longer time horizons.

Since the consequences of interaction orientation are the result of dynamically monitoring business performance at the customer level, it is easy to see that we should be able to observe a greater linkage between where a firm stands in relation to its competitors on the measure of interaction orientation and its relative position on aggregate business performance measures, especially profits and ROI. A recent study documents the effect of adopting a customer-centric approach in increasing ROI (Kumar and Petersen 2004). Thus, interaction orientation directly results in a firm being able to monitor and enhance ROI and short-term and long-term profits.

SUMMARY

Interaction orientation is a set of beliefs, processes, and practices that a firm needs to adopt to compete successfully in the changing marketplace (see Table 13.1). The four components of interaction orientation are believing in the customer concept, offering customer interaction experiences based on a dynamic response system, empowering customers, and using customer value management to make marketing decisions. Interaction orientation is different from market orientation because it seeks to focus on customers as individuals, embraces advancements in technology in order to adopt interactive processes not envisaged earlier, and implicitly builds into all marketing actions the notion of profits. It is a prescription for firms to follow, to successfully negotiate the pressure on marketing to demonstrate accountability. Interaction orientation is therefore the new marketing competency that today's firms need to achieve. While empirical research to test the robustness of this construct is necessary and efforts need to be made to verify the antecedents and consequences of interaction orientation, there is ample evidence from the marketplace that some firms have adopted all or some of the components of interaction orientation into their practices.

Dell Computers, cited by many as the company that has modeled its success by creating successful interaction experiences, knows that computers are not the only product that it is capable of selling. Its deep knowledge of its customers and the expertise in setting up back-end systems has given it the wisdom to introduce products traditionally not its forte. Dell seems to believe that as long as you are engaged in a dialogue with your customers, the range of products and services that you offer them need not be limited. The recent launch of Dell's plasma and high-definition-ready LCD TVs and the customer acceptance of these products is a testimony to the success of its governing strategic orientation—interaction orientation.

NOTE

1. By analogy, the customer concept should lead to a customer orientation and not interaction orientation. However, we prefer the term interaction orientation for two reasons. First, customer orientation as a term is firmly established in the literature as a constituent of the traditional market orientation concept. Second, and more importantly, the term interaction orientation effectively captures the bidirectional and dynamic nature of firm–customer relationships, a phenomenon more prevalent today than in earlier years.

REFERENCES

Achrol, Ravi S. and Philip Kotler (1999), "Marketing in the Network Economy," *Journal of Marketing,* 63 (Special Issue), 146–63.

Bianco, Anthony, Tom Lowry, Robert Berner, Michael Arndt, and Ronald Grover (2004), "The Vanishing Mass Market," *Business Week,* July 12, 60–65.

Day, George S. and David B. Montgomery (1999), "Charting New Directions for Marketing," *Journal of Marketing*, 63 (Special Issue), 3–13.

Gage, Deborah and John McCormick (2003), "Delta's Last Stand," *Baseline*, April 1, www.baselinemag.com/print_article2/0,1217,a=39974,00.asp (accessed September 2005).

Hoekstra, Janny C., Peter S.H. Leeflang, and Dick R. Wittink (1999), "The Customer Concept: The Basis for a New Marketing Paradigm," *Journal of Market-Focused Management,* 4 (June), 43–76.

Hunt, Shelby D. and Robert M. Morgan (1995), "The Comparative Advantage Theory of Competition," *Journal of Marketing,* 59 (April), 1–15.

Jaworski, Bernard, Ajay K. Kohli, and Arvind Sahay (2000), "Market-Driven Versus Driving Markets," *Journal of the Academy of Marketing Science*, 28 (Winter), 45–54.

Kohli, Ajay K. and Bernard J. Jaworski (1990), "Market Orientation: The Construct, Research Propositions, and Managerial Implications," *Journal of Marketing,* 54 (April), 1–18.

Kumar, V. and J. Andrew Petersen (2004), "Maximizing ROI or Profitability," *Marketing Research,* 16 (Fall), 28–34.

———, Girish Ramani, and Timothy Bohling (2004), "Customer Lifetime Value Approaches and Best Practice Applications," *Journal of Interactive Marketing,* 18 (Summer), 60–72.

——— and Rajkumar Venkatesan (2005), "Who Are Multichannel Shoppers and How Do They Perform? Correlates of Multichannel Shopping Behavior," *Journal of Interactive Marketing,* 19 (Spring), 44–62.

———, Rajkumar Venkatesan, and Werner Reinartz (2004), "A Purchase Sequence Analysis Framework for Targeting Products, Customers and Time Period," Working Paper, University of Connecticut.

Maiello, Michael and Susan Kitchens (2004), "Kill Bill," *Forbes,* June 7, pp. 86–90.

Murphy, Victoria (2004), "This Is War," *Forbes,* August 16, 65–68.

Narver, John C. and Stanley F. Slater (1990), "The Effect of a Market Orientation on Business Profitability," *Journal of Marketing,* 54 (October), 20–35.

Newell, Frederick (2003), *Why CRM Doesn't Work: How to Win By Letting Customers Manage the Relationship.* Princeton, NJ: Bloomberg Press.

Noble, Charles H., Rajiv K. Sinha, and Ajith Kumar (2002), "Market Orientation and Alternative Strategic Orientations: A Longitudinal Assessment of Performance Implications," *Journal of Marketing,* 66 (October), 25–39.

Prahalad, C.K. and Venkatram Ramaswamy (2004), *The Future of Competition: Co-Creating Unique Value with Customers.* Boston: Harvard Business School Press.

Reinartz, Werner J. and V. Kumar (2000), "On the Profitability of Long-Life Customers in a Noncontractual Setting: An Empirical Investigation and Implications for Marketing," *Journal of Marketing,* 64 (October), 17–35.

———— (2002), "The Mismanagement of Customer Loyalty," *Harvard Business Review,* 80 (July), 86–94.

———— (2003), "The Impact of Customer Relationship Characteristics on Profitable Lifetime Duration," *Journal of Marketing,* 67 (January), 77–99.

Rust, Ronald T., Tim Ambler, Gregory S. Carpenter, V. Kumar, and Rajendra K. Srivastava (2004), "Measuring Marketing Productivity: Current Knowledge and Future Directions," *Journal of Marketing,* 68 (October), 76–89.

Venkatesan, Rajkumar and V. Kumar (2004), "A Customer Lifetime Value Framework for Customer Selection and Resource Allocation Strategy," *Journal of Marketing,* 68 (October), 106–25.

Zaslow, Jeffrey (2002), "If TiVo Thinks You Are Gay, Here's How to Set It Straight," *Wall Street Journal,* November 26, A1.

CHAPTER 14

CUSTOMER ADVOCACY

A New Paradigm for Marketing?

GLEN L. URBAN

The chapters in this book document that marketing as a field has many serious problems: (1) the effectiveness of marketing tools has declined, (2) marketing today is viewed as intrusive— it is resented by many and increasingly regulated, (3) marketing ethics are being called into question, and (4) marketing has lost its seat at the table with top management. What is needed is a new paradigm for marketing. I cannot claim I have it, but my experience over the past ten years suggests to me that trust and customer advocacy are the keys to a new approach to marketing that will be: (1) effective in generating profit, (2) welcomed by consumers, (3) ethically right, and (4) able to get marketing back to its role as a driver of corporate strategy. In this chapter I describe the forces impelling advocacy, define assumptions for Theory A (A for advocacy), position advocacy versus customer relationship management (CRM), outline some tools for advocacy, and argue that moving to customer advocacy is an easy ethical decision in the long run—but a tough one in the short run.

CUSTOMER POWER: THE DRIVER OF CHANGE

The Internet provides easy access to tremendous amounts of information, and people have been taking advantage of that to become smarter shoppers. They are using digital technologies to gather information, to find competing products, and to talk to other customers. Increasingly, they are using the Internet to avoid pushy marketers and to help them make their own purchasing decisions. The Internet is a great enabler of customer power. What the popular press predicted in the late 1990s would happen with the Internet is actually occurring.

Customers now have access to information about a company and its products from a multitude of sources. In many industries like autos, travel, and health, over two-thirds of consumers go to the Internet for information.[1] Customers can find competing products more easily. Search engines, comparison sites, and online reviews all enable customers to find the best products at the lowest price. Customers can buy from anywhere, regardless of physical location. The Internet simplifies transactions for both consumers and industrial customers. Customers can connect directly with providers to buy goods and services. Prospective customers can find out if a company has mistreated former customers by consulting and collaborating with them through the Internet. Consumers have more control over the flow of marketing messages into their homes and lives. Consumers' distaste for junk mail, telemarketing calls, spam, and pop-up ads means that these pushy messages are more likely to earn ire than profits. Technology empowers consumers by letting them mute or zap TV commercials, screen telephone calls, block pop-up ads, stop telemarketing, or send spam straight to the trashcan.

This is not news to most of us, but we have to realize that this is a fundamental shift in the relationship between companies and consumers. Corporations are not in control anymore—customers are. We always said customers are king and queen, but that traditionally meant that corporations sensed needs, build products to fit them, and then convinced customers to buy them (with one-sided advertising and aggressive promotion). Now customers reject aggressive push/pull tactics and decide themselves based on full information if they want the product and if it fits their needs.

WHAT IS A COMPANY TO DO?

A company could push/pull harder with more entertaining ads, new tricky pop-ups based on more sophisticated data mining, or ads placed intrusively in search outputs or e-mails for microtargeting. In this case more money is spent on advertising and promotion in an effort to overpower the customer even though traditional media effectiveness is decreasing and costs per thousand are going up. But there is another alternative. The firm could recognize that consumers are in control and partner with them based on mutual trust. In this case the firm provides open, honest, and complete information and helps consumers make the right decisions by giving fair advice and comparisons across all products. I call this customer advocacy. The firm advocates for the customer and the customer advocates for the firm.

ADVOCACY THEORY: AN ANALOGY TO MCGREGOR AND THEORY X TO Y TRANSITION

The differences between push/pull and advocacy are profound. Theory P (push/pull) implies one-sided advertising and aggressive promotion while Theory A (advocacy) implies trust building and helping customers. For fifty years we have been in the push/pull era, enabled by TV media and promotion. I believe we are now experiencing a paradigm shift and moving to advocacy.

One of the most significant differences between Theory P and Theory A is the set of assumptions we make about customers. The old paradigm of push/pull marketing assumed that customers do not know what is good for them and we had to convince them to buy our products, while advocacy assumes that customers are responsible and active decision makers—involved and intelligent.

There is an analogy in the transformation of organizational behavior by Theory Y and the transformation of marketing by Theory A. In 1960, McGregor introduced Theory X and Theory Y on the management of employees. Theory X represented an old style of management in which employees were mindless robots that had to be pushed into working through monetary incentives and tight control by management. Theory Y represented a new style of management in which employees were intelligent, responsible individuals that could be trusted to do a good job. More specifically, the traditional view, Theory X, held that employees dislike work, avoid responsibility, and prefer to be told what to do. This led to authority and control as the key factors in organizations. In contrast, McGregor proposed in Theory Y that employees are creative and can exercise self-direction and accept responsibility. This led to participatory management, management by objectives, and team-work as critical success factors in organizations. Quality circles would never have been possible under Theory X, but they flourish under Theory Y. It may be difficult to think of business without management by objectives and teams, but in 1960, good management was based on power and span of control. McGregor was viewed as radical by many traditional managers in 1960.

The contrast between push/pull marketing—Theory P—and advocacy marketing—Theory A—parallels McGregor's Theory X and Theory Y. The key is in changing the assumptions that companies hold about their customers. Just as Theory Y provides a new view of empowered employees, Theory A provides a new view of customers. Theory P views customers as avoiding decision making, having to be coerced to buy, and lacking in imagination. Theory A, on the other hand, provides a view of empowered customers—they accept responsibility, are active decision makers, like to learn, and are creative and imaginative. The implications for Theory A marketing are companies using trust-based marketing and advocating for their consumers. Theory P thinking leads to a view of marketing that says companies must make reluctant, apathetic customers buy products. In contrast, Theory A points to and creates a mutually beneficial relationship with an empowered, responsible, loyal customer following. For example, under Theory A, a company has the opportunity to partner with its customers and use the Internet as an enabler to provide information and offer customized advice. The question is, what do you assume about your customers? You must examine your markets and test your assumptions. In most cases today, Theory A assumptions will be supported.

In the spirit of full information, I must say advocacy is not for all firms. If a firm has a commodity product, maintains a monopoly, or has customers who only care about price, advocacy may not work. But for most firms, where segmentation, differentiation, and innovation are possible, advocacy will have many benefits in the new world of customer power. My view is that there is paradigm shift going on in marketing similar to the Theory Y shift in organizational theory in the 1960s. It may take five to ten years, but the world of marketing will never be the same. Those who practice Theory A now may be viewed as radical, but I believe that Theory A will become the dominant approach to marketing in the future.

THE CUSTOMER ADVOCACY PYRAMID

In the past ten years, firms have been moving toward a new relationship with customers with CRM (customer relationship management). The dream of CRM was to build a long-run relationship with customers that built loyalty by careful communication that the customer wanted and could use to help make decisions. However, most CRM applications are distinctively push marketing. A data warehouse is built, sophisticated data mining tools are applied to find opportunities, and aggressive advertising, direct mail, or telephone marketing is used to get extra sales to pay back the CRM investment. In reality few CRMs are producing a good return on investment and most are not successful.

The positioning of CRM and advocacy can be seen in Figure 14.1. It shows the pyramid of advocacy where Total Quality Management (TQM) and customer satisfaction are at the base. They are necessary conditions for trust and advocacy. If a company wants to honestly recommend its own products, then it must have products that are good enough to recommend. Advocacy is supported in the middle by relationship marketing because CRM provides the tools needed to personalize a company's advocacy relationship with each customer. The pinnacle is advocacy.

As the middle of the pyramid is reached, a company won't use CRM as it did in the past. Instead of targeting promotions and company communications at its customers, it will design CRM to build trusted and partnering relationships with its customers. It will use CRM and related systems to provide balanced, transparent, and relevant information plus unbiased advice on how to make the best decision. CRM, seen in this light, would be better called a Dream CRM strategy since it makes the dream of CRM real. Some people call these customer-managed relations—CMR, not CRM. Likewise, one-to-one and permission marketing shifts in the company's inten-

Figure 14.1 **The Pyramid of Advocacy**

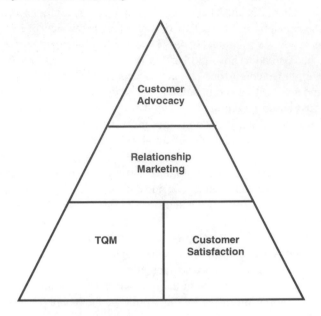

tions toward customers. But instead of creating more microgranularity in spewing out promotions and hyping tangentially relevant company product information, these methods should become a mutual dialogue between individual customers and a firm to maximize customer interest over the available products in the market.

TOOLS FOR ADVOCACY

As a firm climbs the pyramid toward advocacy, a number of tools are available to enable this ascent. Building on quality products and customer service, a firm must establish transparency. This means open, honest, complete, and unbiased information. This does not require any new technology—just get the information and put it in an easy to use format. Now the information needs to be converted into advice. Many virtual trusted advisors are available based on configuration, attribute importance, revealed preferences, and Bayesian updating of requirements.[2] These should be based on comparisons across all products available to the customer—not just the firm's offerings. Many pioneering firms are using such advisors (examples are Amazon, Expedia, Orbitz, Travelocity, and Epinions).

A good example is the General Motors (GM) Auto Choice Adviser (autochoiceadvisor.com or Kbb.com, under "decision aids") that was built based on MIT research in 1997–2000 to build a trust advisor called "Trucktown" (Urban and Hauser 2003). The next step toward advocacy is partnering with customers to design products. Not just measuring needs, but also actively collaborating with lead users to create products. "Listening in" to the dialogue between a trusted advisor and a customer can identify new needs and give customers a design pallet so they can, for example, create their own cars (Urban and Hauser 2003).

With great products and service, the next challenge is to insure trust and advocacy in the channel. All members of the supply chain must be committed and given incentives to represent the customer's welfare. As the firm moves to advocacy, it is not just marketing that is involved. Finance must shift from short-term to long-term payback. Personnel must hire and compensate

Figure 14.2 **My Auto Advocate Internet Site**

employees who believe in advocacy. Engineering must design the best products—that win in open and unbiased comparisons. Production must produce at the highest quality level. And most important, top management must embrace the long-run strategy of advocacy. In many organizations culture must be changed and the chief executive officer must lead the way.

I am working on such a comprehensive shift to customer advocacy at General Motors. We are experimenting in a market research setting with an advocacy system. See Figure 14.2 for a site called "My Auto Advocate" that represents the strategy. It is an opt-in system where, after the customer agrees, they can visit the site and get unbiased advice (Auto Choice Advisor), competitive test drives of more than 150 cars in their Auto Show in Motion Program (over two hundred thousand people attended last year) in a no-sales-pressure environment, into a "drivers forum," brochures and technical specifications for all cars, and links to government sites for safety and environmental characteristics of cars. The navigation is driven by a 360-degree panorama that simulates an auto show and gives access to information sources and comments by the people shown on the screen. A unique feature of the program is paying people with Amazon award certificates (up to $20) for going to the information sources. They get paid for doing their homework—isn't that an interesting idea? Rather than spending billions on advertising, we pay them for looking at the information they should view to make a good decision. Early results indicate over 35 percent of potential car buyers will opt into the advocacy program after one exposure to an ad explaining the benefits and approach. About 50 percent of these will go to the information sources and earn rewards. The net impact for General Motors is increased trust, consideration of GM cars, preference, and market share.

ADVOCACY IS ETHICALLY RIGHT

Personally I have long been offended by many marketing practices and sometimes I am embarrassed that I am working in the field of marketing. So for me customer advocacy is great—it is ethically right! It is honest, open, and transparent, and helps the customer make the best decision.

But why will firms use advocacy? Fortunately advocacy can lead to increased long-run profits because customers become loyal to the firm and will pay for the value of the product (not just look for low price), buy other products from the firm, help design new innovative products, and help convince other customers to buy from the firm (drastically lowering customer acquisition costs). So in the long run it is easy to do the ethical thing—be honest, fair, and unbiased in helping customers and earning profits. This is one of the cases where the right ethical decision is easy. So what is the problem? Well, it may be a "no brainer" in the long run, but in the short run it often involves decreased profits and large investments as the firm reformulates it product line to meet open comparisons. There is also a learning period for customers to develop trust, which may require investments (e.g. better service, Internet trusted advisors, new opt-in communication systems). So the commitment to advocacy takes leadership and courage.

TRANSITION TO CUSTOMER ADVOCACY

Fortunately we see examples of firms pioneering in trust and advocacy. A salient example is eBay, where trust has created an over $40 billion dollar marketplace. I find it particularly interesting that eBay is successful in selling used cars. The use of sellers' ratings, escrow, appeals procedures, and full information have made it attractive to many buyers to purchase a used car over the Internet. Estimates are that eBay sells approximately $12 billion in used cars and most of these are from existing used car dealers who had been the most pushy and abusive marketers. But eBay has taught them how to behave. They must the transparent and honest and back up their claims, or customer ratings will deny them future business and eBay will ban them. Customer power has turned them into upright, trustworthy marketers.

It is not just Internet companies who have shown the way; established firms like General Motors (as discussed earlier), Progressive Insurance, and John Deere have pioneered with advice and product comparisons. For example, John Deere not only provides unbiased advice in selecting a tractor with its "needs analyzer", but also makes honest comparisons to competitors like Kubota. Pioneers are gaining rewards and those who follow will face a disadvantage. The first firm to win customer trust will be difficult to dislodge because customers are reluctant to switch from a trusted supplier. With the market gains from advocacy accruing to the pioneers, other firms may have no choice but to follow and be second best. Advocacy will be a strategic option for most firms, but for followers it may be an imperative to survive in the world of customer power.

A NEW PARADIGM

It is my opinion that advocacy will emerge as the new paradigm. If it does, marketing will have a new set of trust tools that can generate profits. Customers will welcome the new marketing approach and view it as helpful, not intrusive. Customer advocacy will give marketing a prominent position in corporate strategy formulation. It may take ten years, but when it occurs, we will all be proud to be in a new ethical marketing world!

NOTES

1. See Urban (2005), chapter 1, for data and citations on Internet usage and impact.
2. See Urban (2005), chapters 6 and 7, for examples of advisors and methodological tradeoffs.

REFERENCES

McGregor, Douglas (2005), *The Human Side of Enterprise* (1960). Reprint, New York: McGraw Hill.

Urban, Glen (2005), *Don't Just Relate—Advocate: A Road Map to Profit in an Era of Customer Power.* Upper Saddle River, NJ: Prentice Hall.

——— and John Hauser (2003), "Listening in to Find and Explore New Combinations of Customer Needs," *Journal of Marketing,* 68 (April), 72–87.

CHAPTER 15

DOES MARKETING NEED TO TRANSCEND MODERNITY?

A. Fuat Firat and Nikhilesh Dholakia

Does marketing need reform? No, marketing needs a revolution!

The principles and strategies of modern marketing fitted well with the image of the modern individual. Contemporary transformations in modern culture, however, are de(re)constructing markets and consumers in an epochal manner. "Modern marketing" is simply not geared to deal with the ongoing technology-aided and culturally momentous de(re)constructions of markets and consumers.

Two core principles defined modern marketing: the marketing concept and consumer satisfaction. In 1995, Firat, Dholakia, and Venkatesh (1995) argued that these two principles, which led to the practice of providing products for the needs of consumers identified in the markets, were becoming obsolete. Marketers, they argued, had to turn to facilitative processes that allowed consumers to participate in the design, construction, and consumption of products. This idea was later articulated in Firat and Dholakia (1998), and has been echoed by others (cf., Prahalad and Ramaswamy 2000, 2004; Vargo and Lusch 2004), in terms of conceptualizing consumers as co-creators. Contemporary conditions present a radically different market than the one envisioned, constructed, and "managed" in the era that is now identified as modernity (Featherstone 1991; Jameson 1991; Jencks 1987; Lyotard 1984).

To fully appreciate the contemporary transformations in constructions of markets and consumers, and to provide an explanation of why the marketing concept and consumer satisfaction were appropriate principles for modern marketing, first we turn briefly to the history of modern marketization and consumerization.

MODERNITY, MARKETS, AND CONSUMERS

When early economists such as Adam Smith and David Ricardo developed the original ideas that led to the definition of modern markets, they did not provide modern thought with simply an economic category or concept. The usage of the term "free market" by many politicians and leaders shows that the idea of the market has been integral to the whole modern project (Angus 1989) of emancipating the individual human being from all shackles, natural and social. Following the Enlightenment, the idea that humanity could control its own destiny and not be "subject" to powers above steadily gained ascendancy. The modern project became one of improvement of human lives and the building of a grand future, when all human beings could realize their potentials as well as exercise their free wills. In this project is inscribed the clear distinction between the individual and the social, a distinction that was not so fervently made before, and the belief that such a separation is possible and necessary (Dreyfus 1991; Ricoeur 1992).

Prior to the modern era, the individual human being was put on Earth to live (out) her or his preordained lot (fate). With the modern idea(l), the human being is no longer a subject "to" (an)other, but a subject "that" acts on one's own behalf. The capability to act is fundamentally ingrained in science. Through scientific technologies one is able to act upon and even reorient life conditions toward creating the rationally possible, best human existence. The human being becomes the "knowing subject" of modernity, leaving behind the traditional condition of "being subject" to fate and ascribed authority (Rorty 1979).

Enabling this modern "knowing subject" to fulfill her or his potential and exercise free will in realizing the modern project required a thorough reorganization of traditional societies. The market, as conceptualized and constructed in modern society, has been key to this reorganization. As a mechanism that allows those who wish to exchange their resources to find each other when and where needed, the market serves as the fundamental medium of individual freedom (Slater 1997). The idea is that all who meet in the market do so for a momentary exchange. They need not know each other, and other than the momentary exchanging of their resources—most often money of one party for goods or services of another party—they have no obligations to each other prior to or following the exchange. This freedom from obligation lies at the basis of the individual's ability to exercise free will; based only on that individual's own powers of decision, reason, and ability. As such, the individual human being becomes a free agent, acting only on the basis of that individual's needs as he or she sees them.

Modernity did not resolve the tensions between the desire to belong and relate, and the desire to be independent and free. In effect, it heightened the tension. It offered the ambiguous possibility of independence and freedom laced with the oft-contradictory promise of better (social) experiences of "relating and belonging" based on freedom of choice. In modernity, what one belongs to and who one relates with were thought to be matters of free will, not preordained. Thus, belongings and relations that are best suited to one's own choices—regarding life, self, and the humanity's project to be completed—were somehow deemed possible, even as tradition-bound sociality was abandoned.

Given such conceptualization of the modern individual, and the role of the market in its actualization, it is understandable how the modern marketing concept originated and why it fitted well with the modern project. Modern marketing is the activity that helped the modern markets work most efficiently. Along with other phenomena such as commoditization and individualization, consumerization of the modern individual plays a significant role in this efficiency.

Briefly, consumerization is the freeing of the individual from the necessity to produce what one needs or consumes. A feat of marketization, consumerization also contributes to the growth of the market. By becoming a consumer, the individual is able to procure for needs he or she would otherwise not be able to produce for. With ever-greater numbers of individuals becoming consumers of commodities that are not self-produced, products that are mass-produced to meet similar needs of many consumers became the norm. Markets became the efficient mechanisms of exchanging such products. As a consumer, the individual is able to expand beyond capabilities of self-producing, thereby to contemplate a large array of alternatives to satisfy his or her needs, improving choice, and thus improving the exercise of free will. Marketers are able to help "consumerized" individuals who can rationally analyze their needs based on their life conditions. With the growth of consumers who now can contemplate and articulate almost endless numbers of needs, and the rise of corporate entities that can employ scientific production technologies that can produce for these needs, modern marketing's principles are integral to the actualization of the modern project: improvement of human lives in a society of free agents who decide what this improvement means and can reach a consensus based on reason and scientific discovery. Consumers have needs they want to satisfy to progress toward actualization of their life project; and marketing helps in the identification, articulation, and satisfaction of these needs.

AFTER MODERNITY

There is now quite a large consensus among scholars that modernity has run its course or is approaching its end. We are, it is argued, in states variously characterized as late modern, high modern, liquid modern, or postmodern (Bauman 2000; Giddens 1991). Whichever term (and the phenomenon it represents) is preferred, each term—by the inclusion of the word "modern"—indicates extensions of aspects of modernity. That is, we are living in times that, while extending characteristics of the modern, nonetheless transcend and transform it (Massumi 1987).

Natural developments in many of the principles of modernity (that originated to realize the individual free agent) are reflected in human rights, modern democracy, and markets. Technological developments of the last half-century, however, have rendered the principles of modern marketing obsolete. Several significant developments can be mentioned in understanding this phenomenon.

The relationship between organizations and individuals in modern society always had seeds of tension. On the one hand, while consumerization enabled individuals to find satisfaction for many more needs than they could if they had to self-produce for all needs, turning to the market to get satisfaction meant that there was always a gap between individuals' perceptions of needs and what could be acquired in the market to satisfy such needs. They could find numerous alternatives in the market to satisfy a need and select from among them the one that most closely met their need, but necessarily all mass marketed offerings were a step removed from each consumer's need in order to satisfy the need of many. Furthermore, the distance or the boundary that separated a marketing organization from its customers always constituted a challenge to the individual's ability to exercise one's free will. In the end, the decisions regarding the features, ingredients, and so on of the commodities were made by the organization, even if the organization was closely attuned to its customers' needs. Beyond these fundamental tensions between corporate organizations and their consumers, there were of course the practical problems of power and conflicts between these two parties, often highlighted in critiques of marketing. Just based on their sizes, the resources they controlled, and the interests (such as return on investments) they had to serve beyond the satisfaction of consumers' needs, organizations in practice often competed with consumers' interests rather than championed such interests. Complete exercise of free agency required, in effect, consumer control of organizations and the production processes. This is paradoxical in modernity because, as we discussed above, freeing the individual from production processes was originally thought desirable for actualizing free agency.

Furthermore, individuality—a revered consequence of the emancipation of the individual—always conflicted with choice of a mass commodity that, in the end, millions of others also chose. That is, as long as complete customization of alternatives chosen in the market did not exist, complete individuality or exercise of free agency remained in question. Therefore, customization and direct control over organizational production processes were natural and necessary extensions of modern aspirations and the modern organization of society; and as a result, today, these are desired phenomena that are culturally sought. Consequently, the nature of consumption and the constitution of consumers are changing.

Very briefly, these changes entail a complete reorganization of the meanings and roles of production and consumption. Consumption is now the arena where value is created (Baudrillard

1981), and consumers increasingly become postconsumers, involved in the construction of life mode alternatives they coproduce in consumer communities or with marketing organizations. The increasingly individualized forms of life and consumption in modernity are tempered with rising involvement in consumer communities or neotribes (Maffesoli 1996) in order to construct alternative cultures of experiencing life.

CONTEMPORARY MARKETING

Moreover, consumers the world over are becoming increasingly marketing savvy, understanding —tacitly if not via formal business education—the spirit and workings of marketing (Brown 2003). In effect, consumers are maturing, ready and capable of interacting with marketing organizations at a level not possible before; and technologies are enabling this. Like youth who mature, or like politically and socially conscious women who increasingly decipher the working principles of patriarchal society, maturing and savvy postconsumers look for a playful equal relationship, a partnership with organizations. Modern marketing's segmentation-targeting-positioning mode of providing for, satisfying, and taking care of consumers' needs is not an approach that is amenable to this mature desire of postconsumers.

There is also a force for change that comes from the production technologies side of the equation. Increasingly, no product is completely produced in one place or in a singular process. With the growth of a global economy and global markets, much of the production is outsourced, as are many of the managerial operations (Balasubramanian and Padhi 2005). What becomes important for businesses under these circumstances is the expertise of designing the processes that make such worldwide and distributed sets of operations coordinated and seamlessly integrated. Like all other forms of expertise and managerial skills, these design and operational integration skills become distributed and simple to replicate. From corporate centers in New York and London, such skills percolate to workplaces in Hanoi and Hangzhou, and eventually to homes of postconsumers.

These kinds of design and integration skills are also required in life in general. Life skills are becoming marketing skills. After modernity, marketing is the expertise of designing the processes whereby human (postconsumer) communities imagine, construct, and experience meaningful and substantive modes of life. This means transforming and transcending several principles of modern marketing.

CHARACTERISTICS OF NEW MARKETING

A radical reconstruction of marketing means that the core marketing concept, which ultimately determines its practice, is reconstituted. Two issues have dominated the discussions of the modern marketing concept: exchange and consumer centeredness (Bagozzi 1975; Kotler 1972). We shall discuss the various implications of the challenges we see in terms of how these two aspects of the modern marketing concept will likely be affected. These implications are framed in terms of four portending transitions that marketing theory and practice are likely to experience.

Phenomena Essence Transition: Business Activity to Embedded Cultural Practice

Contemporary transformations—as modernity loses steam—reinforce the recognition that marketing was always, and will continue to be a human practice embedded in the culture of community life. This signals a sea change in the meaning of marketing. Conceptualizing marketing as the activity of finding out what consumers need, organizing resources, designing a product that fits the image of the need, communicating its presence, and making it available to the consumers—these processes have likely reached their end. Instead, the concept of embedded marketing has to emerge, where the firm is part of the community to facilitate the efforts of consumer communities to mutually construct their desires and the products they want.

Pushed to the logical extreme, this implies the dissolving of the organization. Corporate entities blur due to the melting away of their boundaries. Rather than a professional business practice controlled by managers to serve its consumers and stakeholders, marketing morphs into an openly accessible cultural practice of the postconsumer communities. The concept of business is also in flux. It is changing from a distinct form of activity of incorporated entities to everyday practices of all corporeal entities. People are engaged in far greater numbers in the business of life than in "business life."

The modern order demarcated markets and corporations. Marketers largely performed a boundary task. Marketing constituted the semipermeable "membrane" between the organ(ization) and the larger (social) body (market). Marketing informed the organization of the needs of the consumers and informed consumers about the products of the organization. The very existence of this specialized membrane confirmed and affirmed the organ(ization)'s separate existence. This membrane is stretching, rupturing, and dissolving and fusing with both sides: the organization and the market. With the dissolving membrane, postconsumer communities are emerging as the new conjoined conglomerate entities of the new era. Somewhat surprisingly and a bit ironically, in its very dissolution, marketing is becoming the most pronounced moment in everyday life as everyone becomes engaged in and with it in all aspects of their lives. The dissolving membrane is permeating both sides—organizations and the postconsumer communities.

The ongoing and ubiquitous pervasiveness of marketing is not just a marketer's indulgence in self-importance. The modern marketing impulse, as discussed by Hirschman (1983), may not be able to respond fully to all dimensions of human existence. Extending Hirschman's ideas reveals some essential paradoxes in the nature of modern marketing. As many nonmarketing scholars recognize (see, for example, Jameson 1991; Jhally 1990; Wang, Servaes, and Goonasekera 2000), in the waning moments of modernity marketing has already taken center stage. It has largely replaced democracy; just as the consumer has replaced the citizen (Moyers 1989). Contemporary representational democracy, guided by "poll-itics," relies heavily on the modern marketing concept. The idea has taken hold that the most efficient form of democracy is when a government fulfills its constituencies' needs in the style of a marketing (business) organization. We also observe the infusion of this idea into education, when students are conceived as "customers." In this displacement of democracy by marketing and citizen by consumer, a key difference between the two may often get lost. Democracy has necessarily been a process of citizen agency; that is, the citizenry acting on its visions and ideals for a meaningful life. Marketing, on the other hand, as a modern business practice consists of organizations catering to consumers and acting on consumers' behalf, but focused on the organization's (economic) success as much as, if not more than, on the satisfaction of the consumers' desires. When democracy is reconceptualized in the modern marketing mode, it reduces the citizen (consumer) from a constructor who produces policy alternatives to someone who selects and pushes buttons—of policy alternatives—offered in his or her name. In such marketing-laced "poll-itics," there is an erosion of the "body politic" and increasing individualization of the desires and acts of the citizen (consumer).

The advent of the postconsumer and of embedded marketing hold the prospect of reempowering the consumer as well as the citizen, going much beyond democracy-diluting "poll-itics." In embedded marketing shaped by contemporary sensibilities, marketing would reemerge as the empowering tool of the postconsumer. Postconsumers and embedded marketing would tend to reestablish democracy in a form that is viable—based on the constitution of postconsumer communities or tribes (Cova 1999; Firat and Dholakia 1998). While the enormous centralizing and centripetal tendencies of "modern poll-itics" would be lost, small-scale (not necessarily "local," given the ability of information technologies to connect people) postconsumer communities would cherish and nurture true democratic processes.

Power-Sharing Transition: Managed to Collaborative Marketing

For marketing, the entrenchment of management came much later than on the factory floor—beginning in the 1950s and 1960s—but it came with cogent sophistication (Kotler 1967; McCarthy 1960). Catering to consumers' needs in efficient, economic terms—while assuring the organization's economic success—was a tightrope act. Hierarchic, rational, ordered, and systematic "management" of market-oriented tasks and people was needed to walk this tightrope. Such a hierarchic orientation, of course, was in tune with modernity's impulse for order and with modernity's overarching project of constructing a grand future for humanity. On the highly visible center stage of media and malls, the marketing "acts" had to be well orchestrated so as to be effective, visible, comprehensible, and popular (Pine and Gilmore 1999). Visible marketing operatives—top executives, sales people, spokespersons, endorsers, and actors in commercials—had to be provided with scripts and direction from the backstage (management) to ensure that the acts were performed well. Haphazard, unscripted, and chaotic acts could waste time and other resources on the stage, and result in the audience (consumers) losing interest and walking away from the performance (product/market).

Under modernity, well-managed marketing processes freed consumers from the burdens of designing, constructing, and disseminating market offerings—tasks that ordinary consumers could not effectively or efficiently perform anyway. Marketing research and management methods were deployed to second-guess consumers—by providing what consumers would likely have constructed for themselves anyway.

Contemporary, "new" marketing needs to shift gears from a managerial mode to a shared, collaborative mode. By collaborating as partners with postconsumer communities in constructing their modes of life, marketing organizations become parts of the cultural ecosystem. Marketing's role becomes that of facilitating and coordinating the efforts of the community's members. This is a coperformer, not a provider role. The shape of such collaborative marketing is just emerging, particularly in technology-aided arenas—in multiperson online games (such as EverQuest), friends-of-friends electronically-aided networks (such as Friendster), some forms of "reality TV," virtual market-oriented communities, "flash" meeting tools such as Meetup.com, certain types of "blogs," and so on.

Power Locus Transition: Centralized to Diffused Marketing

New marketing becomes increasingly a domain of the postconsumers, rather than that of organizations. The postconsumer is a marketer, constantly involved in the imagination, creation, and performance of desires to be experienced as modes of organizing life. The membrane that separated organizations and consumers not only stretches thin but also begins to dissolve. There is growing interchange between the marketers and the postconsumer communities, to the point that the two blend into one. Marketing becomes everyone's activity, emancipated from the somewhat occult practice of professionally anointed managerial cadres, organized and ensconced in firms. It is an omnipresent essence of transactional and exchange-oriented human activity. Such a change, as it unfolds, is no less dramatic than the impact of the Gutenberg press, which moved cloistered knowledge into public spaces. In this emergent era of diffused marketing in postconsumer communities, experimentation with marketing modes flourishes, constantly finding new ways of doing things.

Phenomena Clarity Transition: Ordered to Complex Marketing

A diffused marketing increasingly moves away from a hierarchically ordered form, and eventually away from any form in which an order can be detected. The new marketing is likely to exhibit fluidity of form and a complex system of fluid orders. Such marketing would resemble a neural network that constantly re(de)constructs itself. Marketing precepts and practices would have to exhibit a fluid resilience in adapting to the changing modes found in different (and continually evolving) postconsumer communities.

The role of information, communication, and entertainment technologies in facilitating such transformations is paramount. We have already pointed to the incipient effects of electronic communities of buyers and sellers, content-swapping technologies, and game-playing environments in challenging or dismantling long-held notions of modern marketing. Other technologies such as mobile communications and networked appliances are also transforming various "consumption" arenas—homes, vehicles, shopping centers, parks, streets—into places where postconsumers can, if they so desire, engage in various acts of researching, designing, engineering, producing, and communicating. Peer-to-peer and virtual community technologies would continue to usurp nicely ordered marketplace hierarchies. Marketers who corral and make accessible relevant resources and facilitate conjoint processes involving postconsumers will be the winners in contemporary games.

Together, the above imply that marketing's role will increasingly be to facilitate the means for the playful (co)construction of a theater, a textual and textured culture that is continually made and remade, and allow postconsumers to have a performative engagement with life.

It is important to note briefly that whatever talents and knowledge the new marketing practitioners develop, such knowledge is not likely to follow any unified set of principles or criteria of efficiency or success. The presence of different communities constructing varied life modes and cultures is likely to mean that there would be multiple orders of principle and efficiency. In effect, postconsumers will not encounter an order that dominates and betters all others, but an order of multiple orders.

These are not unfathomable transformations. Nor are they fantasies. Because of their pragmatic orientation, business firms at leading edges of practice are already undergoing such shifts (Pine and Gilmore 1999; Schmitt 1999). The challenge is to start discussing such changes in the academic marketing discipline. These shifts require a clear change of paradigm. Our current world and conditions of existence may already be reaching the precipice where serious thinking about such paradigm change is not an option but a necessity.

REFERENCES

Angus, Ian (1989), "Circumscribing Postmodern Culture," in *Cultural Politics in Contemporary America*, I. Angus and S. Jhally, eds. New York: Routledge, 96–107.

Bagozzi, Richard P. (1975), "Marketing as Exchange," *Journal of Marketing*, 39 (October), 32–39.

Balasubramanian, Ramnath and Asutosh Padhi (2005), "The Next Wave in US Offshoring," *The McKinsey Quarterly*, 1, www.mckinseyquarterly.com/article_page.aspx?ar=1565&L2=1&L3=106 (accessed September 2005).

Baudrillard, Jean (1981), *For a Critique of the Political Economy of the Sign*, C. Levin, trans. St. Louis, MO: Telos.

Bauman, Zygmunt (2000), *Liquid Modernity*. Cambridge, UK: Polity Press.

Brown, Stephen (2003), *Free Gift Inside: Forget the Customer. Develop Marketease*. Chichester, UK: Capstone.

Cova, Bernard (1999), "From Marketing to Societing: When the Link Is More Important than the Thing," in *Rethinking Marketing: Towards Critical Marketing Accountings*, D. Brownlie, M. Saren, R. Wensley, and R. Whittington, eds. London: Sage, 64–83.

Dreyfus, Hubert L. (1991), *Being-in-the-World: A Commentary on Heidegger's "Being and Time,"* Division I. Cambridge, MA: The MIT Press.

Featherstone, Mike (1991), *Consumer Culture and Postmodernism*. London: Sage.

Firat, A. Fuat and Nikhilesh Dholakia (1998), *Consuming People: From Political Economy to Theaters of Consumption*. London: Routledge.

———, and Alladi Venkatesh (1995), "Marketing in a Postmodern World," *European Journal of Marketing*, 29 (1), 40–56.

Giddens, Anthony (1991), *Modernity and Self-Identity: Self and Society in the Late Modern Age*. Stanford, CA: Stanford University Press.

Hirschman, Elizabeth C. (1983), "Aesthetics, Ideologies and the Limits of the Marketing Concept," *Journal of Marketing*, 47 (Summer), 45–55.

Jameson, Fredric (1991), *Postmodernism, or, the Cultural Logic of Late Capitalism*. Durham, NC: Duke University Press.

Jencks, Charles (1987), *What Is Postmodernism?* New York: St. Martin's Press.

Jhally, Sut (1990), *The Codes of Advertising: Fetishism and the Political Economy of Meaning in the Consumer Society*. New York: Routledge.

Kotler, Philip (1967), *Marketing Management: Analysis, Planning, and Control*. Englewood Cliffs, NJ: Prentice-Hall.

——— (1972), "A Generic Concept of Marketing," *Journal of Marketing*, 36 (April), 46–54.

Lyotard, Jean-François (1984), *The Postmodern Condition*. Minneapolis: University of Minnesota Press.

Maffesoli, Michel (1996), *The Time of the Tribes: The Decline of Individualism in Mass Society*. London: Sage.

Massumi, Brian (1987), "Realer than Real: The Simulacrum According to Deleuze and Guattari," *Copyright*, 1 (Fall), 90–96.

McCarthy, E. Jerome (1960), *Basic Marketing: A Managerial Approach*, Homewood, IL: Irwin.

Moyers, Bill (1989), "Image and Reality in America: Consuming Images," *The Public Mind* (television program), Part 1, November 8, Public Broadcasting Service.

Pine, B. Joseph, II and James H. Gilmore (1999), *The Experience Economy: Work Is Theater and Every Business a Stage—Goods and Services Are No Longer Enough*. Boston: Harvard Business School Press.

Prahalad, C.K. and Venkatram Ramaswamy (2000), "Co-opting Consumer Competence," *Harvard Business Review* (January–February), 79–87.

——— (2004), "Co-Creation Experiences: The Next Practice in Value Creation," *Journal of Interactive Marketing*, 18 (3), 5–14.

Ricoeur, Paul (1992), *Oneself as Another*, K. Blamey, trans. Chicago: University of Chicago Press.

Rorty, Richard (1979), *Philosophy and the Mirror of Nature*. Princeton, NJ: Princeton University Press.

Schmitt, Bernd H. (1999), *Experiential Marketing: How to Get Customers to Sense, Feel, Think, Feel, Act, and Relate to Your Company and Brands*. New York: The Free Press.

Slater, Don (1997), *Consumer Culture and Modernity*. Cambridge, UK: Polity Press.

Vargo, Stephen L. and Robert F. Lusch (2004), "Evolving to a New Dominant Logic for Marketing," *Journal of Marketing*, 68 (January), 1–17.

Wang, Georgette, Jan Servaes, and Anuta Goonasekera, eds. (2000), *The New Communications Landscape: Demystifying Media Globalization*. London: Routledge.

CHAPTER 16

FROM MARKETING TO THE *MARKET*

A Call for Paradigm Shift

ALLADI VENKATESH AND LISA PEÑALOZA

The search for new paradigms has been a major source of methodological and theoretical opportunities within the marketing discipline over the years (Arndt 1983; Bagozzi 1975; Day and Montgomery 1999; Deshpande 1983; Howard and Sheth 1969; Kohli and Jaworski 1990; Kotler and Levy 1969; Sheth 2004; Venkatesh 1985). Researchers such as Belk (1991) and McCracken (1988) ushered in the interpretive, humanistic approach to research in marketing. Recently, in an important development that has captured our thinking, Vargo and Lusch (2004) have worked to refashion the field into a new "dominant logic," the basis of which is service orientation (see also Lusch and Vargo 2006). Current trends in global commerce have spurred some serious thinking on how firms can be competitive and stay afloat in this fast-paced environment (Sheth and Sisodia 2002). Years ago, in an ironic anticipation of contemporary global order, Dholakia, Firat, and Bagozzi (1980) proposed a global vision of marketing by referring to their approach as one of "de-Americanization of marketing thought" (p. 75).

In this chapter we argue for a major paradigm shift, from the study of marketing to the study of *market(s)*. Some of our preliminary thoughts on this subject are available in a forthcoming piece (Venkatesh, Peñaloza, and Firat 2006). The basis of our thinking can be traced back to a seminal paper published several years ago by Johan Arndt (1973) where he is concerned with the extension of the marketing concept to nonprofit/nonbusiness sectors. In that paper, he called our attention to the study of *markets* as a disciplinary imperative:

> This extension of marketing [i.e., to the nonprofit sector] has revitalized the discipline and resulted in valuable insights for better management practice in new areas. Nevertheless, so far this conceptual expansion seems to be a broadening of marketing *practice* rather than marketing *theory* . . .
>
> An alternative way of enriching marketing (instead of applying "old" knowledge to "new" problems) is to develop new theories. The aim of this article is to provide foundations for such a development. The article addresses an institution central to marketing thinking, the *market* itself. [emphasis added] (p. 69)

More recently, in a special issue of the *Journal of Marketing* the discussion regarding markets was revived in a series of articles by Buzzell (1999), John, Weiss, and Dutta (1999), and Rosa et al. (1999). In addition, as examples of major developments within the field, attention to the study of markets has continued in other key journals such as the *Journal of Macromarketing, Consumption,*

Table 16.1

Current Disciplinary Typologies in the Marketing Discipline

Typology	Type	Components
1	Major Disciplinary Foci	Consumer marketing Industrial marketing
2	Market Structure Foci	Product marketing Services marketing
3	Consumer Marketing	*Topics* Psychological approaches (Emphasis—Individual) Phenomenological/Experiential approaches (Emphasis—Individual) Sociological/Anthropological approaches (Emphasis—Social/Cultural) Quantitative modeling approaches Game theory approaches Brand management Online shopping behaviors Advertising
4	Industrial Marketing	*Topics* Distribution channels Sales force management Organizational buying/procuring
5	Competitive Strategies	Game theory Economic theories of competition
6	Institutional/Managerial Approaches	Transaction cost analysis Firm-level behaviors/decision making
7	International Marketing	Cross-cultural marketing

Markets and Culture, and *Marketing Theory.* There are also several established journals from across the globe such as the *European Journal of Marketing, Journal of Consumer Policy, International Marketing Review, International Journal of Research in Marketing, Asian Journal of Marketing,* and *Vikalpa* to mention a few, which have touched upon this issue one way or the other.

In light of recent developments in the field that address some fundamental issues concerning the directions for our discipline, we feel that a systematic study of markets is warranted. Our reasons for doing so are multiple and layered. We begin by charting major social and technological developments that call into question, if not render obsolete, existing substantive conceptualizations of the field. The theory of the firm, as a key player in the market, serves to organize our inquiry. More specifically, by viewing the field of marketing through the prism of the firm, we chart out advancements in analytical levels of abstraction, domain, scope, and maneuverability afforded by refocusing the attention of our discipline on the market. Currently, the marketing discipline can be identified in terms of the different disciplinary typologies as shown in Table 16.1. These typologies are not exhaustive but representative of the field. At the risk of simplification, one might say that Typology 3 (Consumer Marketing) represents the dominant paradigmatic focus within our field.

SETTING THE STAGE: STRENGTHS AND VULNERABILITIES OF THE GLOBAL MARKET

In the past decade or so, we have noticed three major developments causing the ground to shift underneath many of the concepts and frameworks that have been espoused within marketing.

First, the center of gravity in the global economic systems is moving rather rapidly to some non-Western regions of this world (Sheth 2004). This in itself may not be a novel development, for Japan has been a major influential force in the world economy for almost thirty years. But, as strong and globally impactful as its economy is acknowledged to be, Japan was never considered a dominant world power in the larger scheme of things presumably because of its relatively small size. What we are now witnessing is the emergence of two major economic powers in the world, China and India, that are also two of the most populous nations; a fact to be noted is that in the global game, indeed size does matter (Sheth 2004). The combined population of the two countries constitutes over one-third of the world's inhabitants and coupled with this, their continued economic growth forces us to speculate about the impending fundamental changes in the global scenario in the years to come. If we introduce Brazil and other South American economies as well as Korea and ASEAN (Association of Southeast Asian Nations) countries into the picture, the story becomes even more dramatic.

A second development has to do with the transformation of the global industrial economy into an information economy (Castells 2001). The emergence of the Internet is now viewed as a major technological revolution that has the potential to alter the future shape of global commerce. The Internet is leveling the playing field within and across the global economic system, and, at the risk of some exaggeration, one might say that the website has become a powerful articulation of one's global market presence.

The third development, somewhat closer to home for our disciplinary interests, relates to the changing nature of macro-organizational structures among firms, consumers, and nation-states. To briefly summarize these changes: Borders are increasingly blurring between firms and consumers, organizational processes are increasingly called into question by major stakeholders to whom firms are beholden, and firms are frequently called upon by critics to perform social activities traditionally performed by governments in the name of social responsibility. In this fast-changing world of global alliances, diasporic movements, and organizational turmoil, marketing as we know it with its oft-repeated mantra of the four Ps (product, place, promotion, and price) and customer satisfaction becomes tiresome, outmoded, and almost beside the point as there is greater need for reconceptualizations and adaptations.

In sum, marketers are on the march globally, and marketing activity has become so prevalent in social life that Slater and Tonkiss (2001) have coined the term "the market society" to describe the contemporary global social order. On one hand, there is growing awareness and appreciation for marketing as an instrument of social change and a facilitator of wealth creation across the globe. Yet, perhaps because of this success and its excesses, marketers are also the target of a plethora of serious charges ranging from antimarketing, to anti-Americanism, to antiglobalization for fueling materialism, commercialism, and the debasement of local cultures (Chua 2003; Johansson 2004).

THE MARKET AND MARKETING

As we shift our attention to the *market* as the primary focus of our discipline, we recognize that *marketing* is something that takes place within a market system and is therefore derivative to the main focus. We differentiate between "market" and "marketing" using the following definitions.

A *market* is a set of institutions and actors located in a physical or virtual space where marketing-related transactions and activities take place. Typically, these institutions and actors include sellers, buyers, customers, retail stores, sales offices, commercial banks, advertising agencies, and the like. Thus the key concepts are a set of institutions or actors, physical or virtual space, discourses, and practices.

Similarly, we define *marketing* as a set of activities undertaken by a firm to stimulate demand for its products or services and to ensure that the products are sold and delivered to the customers. Modern marketing refers to the development of marketing since the early part of the twentieth century. The key concepts are demand creation and demand management. As a result, what we study in marketing is a set of activities relating to the following marketing functions: brand/product management, customer relationship management, advertising/promotion, pricing, sales promotion, personal selling, direct marketing, distribution, marketing research, and new product/market development.

Within the contemporary global context, these definitions highlight the need to shift the disciplinary emphasis, not by disregarding the role of marketing, but by enlarging its scope to the market, and in turn embedding such markets within their social and historical contexts. The discipline of marketing has centered over the past four decades on firm-level actions and managerial perspectives. In such an approach, either the larger context of the market was considered as given or it was assumed to be unchanging or unchangeable. This rather restricted approach has served and outlived its purpose and one consequence of continuing with it will result in ignoring the critical role of the broader institutional context called the market, whether it is local or global. That is, without this understanding of the market no amount of marketing knowledge can sustain our discipline. By the same token, although we shift our focus to the market, we recognize that the key players remain the firm and its customers.

In the following section, we review the literature on the theory of the firm and its relationship to the market. The main argument we present is that while the legacy of marketing is a theory of the firm as contained in the paradigm nurtured in the emblematic work of Kotler, it has simply outlived its purpose and we need to look for new vistas. That is, the current approaches to the firm-level analysis do not take into consideration the emerging global markets, technological forces, and macro-organizational transformations. In addition, because the existing theory is U.S.-centric, it desperately needs to be reoriented in light of emerging global market transformations.

THE THEORY OF THE FIRM: A HISTORICIZED ACCOUNT

In order to keep our discussion focused we limit the theory of the firm as it pertains to developments that relate to our discipline. We begin with neoclassical theory.

Neoclassical Theory of the Firm

The neoclassical or marginal theory of the firm began as an economic theory based upon undifferentiated, purely competitive markets characteristic of the nineteenth century. Essentially, the theory states that the primary objective of an organization is to maximize profits, given a market price and a technologically determined production function. Profit maximization occurs when the firm produces a quantity of output at which its marginal cost equals its marginal revenue (hence the term "marginalism"). A parallel analysis is made in the factor market, in which marginal revenue of a product equals its marginal factor cost. Single-period profit maximization is the goal, so present value and risk considerations are ignored. In the short run, management's tasks are to determine and maintain operations at the equilibrium level of output. In the long run, management can strive to lower its marginal costs, and consequently increase profits until diminishing returns set in.

Over the years, the economic discipline has moved away from a strict neoclassical approach, as described, to other formulations. Thus, for example, the current thinking in the economic discipline recognizes differentiated markets and various degrees of competitive situations from monopolistic to oligopolistic to dispersed; accommodates objective functions other than that of maximization; allows firms to set a market price instead of leaving it to the "invisible hand"; allows for multiperiod profit maximization; and recognizes firm-level decisions and not merely considerations of equilibria.

Markets and Hierarchies

The works of Ronald Coase (1937) and Oliver Williamson (1975) are a slight variation of the neoclassical theory. Both were still concerned with optimization and equilibrium, but the emphasis shifted to the economic theory of organizations. To maximize the value of the firm, the owner chooses an organizational form and thus the shift is made toward profitability and organizational structure. A common starting point in the literature is Coase's (1937) insight that markets and firms are different responses to the problem of transactional governance. Williamson (1975), through his work on transaction cost analysis (TCA), goes on to identify the specific conditions (e.g., uncertainty, asset specificity) that impel the movement of the organizational form from market through hybrid to hierarchy. Transaction cost analysis has been accepted and applied at some level within the marketing discipline (Anderson 1985; Ghosh and John 1999; John 1984; Rindfleisch and Hyde 1997) especially in the context of industrial marketing and marketing channels, but overall, it has not received the attention that it deserves.

Behavioral Theories of the Firm

Cyert and March (1963) built upon the work of Simon (1959) in which the concepts of "bounded rationality" and "satisficing" are introduced. Managers have limits to exploring all the variables that can contribute to goal maximization. Therefore, they satisfice, or set and meet goals which are below maximization levels. Simon argues that the complexity of modern organizations prohibits maximizing behavior. Cyert and March have two major criticisms of the neoclassical theory of the firm. First, it is questioned because it is based upon undifferentiated, purely competitive commodity markets of the nineteenth century. The widespread appearance of differentiated (oligopolistic) markets has shaken the faith of both economists and noneconomists. Second, even if the theory did apply to contemporary market systems, the behavioralists challenge the appropriateness of the questions the neoclassical theory "answers." Observations of managerial behavior demonstrated that labor–management negotiations, collusion, favoritism, and other elements of environmental "noise" are also germane to the study of the firm.

The Marketing Discipline

Aldersonian Perspective

Alderson (1957) presents a theory of the firm based upon the concept of an "organized behavior system." These systems include individual firms, marketing channels, and the aggregate economy. Any prediction or explanation of firm behavior must be analyzed in the context of social systems. As with the human body, firms adapt and change to ensure survival. Various units within the organization perform functions that affect the entire system. Central to his theory are the concepts of power and communication, which explain many of the firm's activities. Power is considered an inherent goal for any organized behavior system. Maintaining or improving the power structure is achieved largely through communication channels (i.e., advertising). This perspective has been described as "functionalism," since the theory attempts to explain a system by examining the functions of the individual parts, yet in some ways the term is a misnomer because it loses sight of a focus on the overall system.

Alderson's view of organizational goals assumes a distinction between implicit and explicit goals. Every behavior system operates under the implicit goals of survival and growth. The two goals are viewed as interrelated in the sense that survival is not generally possible with zero growth. Growth is essential for survival in modern economy. "If the firm does not grow, it cannot compete for the more able candidates among executives and workers. . . . The growing firm also attracts favorable attention from customers and suppliers" (p. 59). Among explicit goals of the firm, Alderson provides many strategic possibilities such as return on investment, cost minimization, and vertical integration. In this process, the firm attempts to create a differentiated product and thereby gain a niche within the larger behavior system, the national economy.

Kotlerian Perspective

Kotler's (2000 [1967, 1971]) adoption of the behavioralist viewpoint (e.g., Simon, Cyert and March) is apparent throughout his texts. Yet his adoption of behavioral theory is distinct from Alderson's. Alderson portrayed a macrotheory of marketing (a systems approach), while Kotler developed a micromanagerial theory that prescribes the practice of the marketing manager. Further, Alderson's work centers on intrafirm and more systemic behaviors, while Kotler's work focuses on firm–consumer and firm–competitor conflicts.

In this latter regard, Kotler drew from the neoclassical theory to provide logic to managerial action. He provides both the theory and practice elements necessary for the marketing manager to utilize marketing tools within the firm. This is a notable accomplishment of blending two approaches of theory and practice, as previous authors provided either theory (Alderson) or practice (McCarthy). Other aspects of Kotlerian paradigm can be summarized in the following.

The marketing mix (the four Ps) consists of controllable variables of managerial effort in the market. With this understanding, Kotler operationalized the marketing effort through manipulation of the marketing mix. By extending this operational principle, Kotler and Levy (1969) broadened the concept of marketing to nonbusiness sectors.

Kotler used existing marketing technologies in the literature (i.e., forecasting models, market share grids, and so on) to provide concrete means of implementing the normative concepts. Thus terms such as synchromarketing and strategic marketing planning become meaningful as they are matched with appropriate techniques to solve marketing problems.

His theory has come closest to operationalizing the marketing concept. Previous textbook authors had presented the marketing concept as central to marketing, yet they failed to systematically describe the process of discovering, meeting, and maintaining satisfaction of customers' needs and wants. By all accounts, Kotler's approach synthesizes and defines the marketing paradigm as practiced today.

The marketing paradigm as enunciated in the work of Kotler and the legacy of marketing have been praised and critiqued over the years (Meamber and Venkatesh 1995). There has been some sharp criticism, especially among scholars based abroad (Brown 2002). Stephen Brown (2002) has posited alternative perspectives to the so-called customer-orientation and to the reductionist as well as universalistic perspectives in U.S.-centric approaches to marketing. We go beyond Brown's exhortations and argue that our focus on marketing should be replaced by a more expanded focus on the market. Ironically, upon some reflection, we feel that Alderson's work, which has been side-lined for a long time, may have much to offer and is probably much more valuable for its insights because he espouses broader institutional and social contexts that are either missing or not prominent enough in more recent work within the discipline.

WHY STUDY THE MARKET (OR MARKETS)?

While we emphasize the need to shift our focus to the study of the market, we also need to remind ourselves that the market does *not* have a universal quality. That is, as we move toward the global economy and confront its pluralistic character, we should really talk about markets and develop theories that apply to all of its systems, properties, and national boundaries. Although the issue of universalization is an important one, we will not address it here. Our focus is simply to recognize the market as a theoretical category and provide different perspectives in studying it.

The different perspectives of the market are presented in Table 16.2. In the second column of the table, we indicate the present emphasis within our marketing discipline. In column 3, we provide some additional comments.

As the table shows, markets can be viewed from three different, if somewhat related, perspectives—markets in the mainstream, markets in the emerging global context, and virtual markets. We will describe each one of them and provide a brief analysis.

Markets in the Mainstream

Markets as Product Markets

Some seminal work of marketing scholars reminds us that product markets can be a very important area of research (Day, Shocker, and Srivastava 1979; Rosa et al. 1999). Product markets are defined by Rosa et al. (1999) as "socially constructed knowledge structures (i.e., product conceptual systems) that are shared among producers and consumers" (p. 64). Product markets sometimes overlap with the notion of industries. Some examples are the automobile market (or industry), the homes market (or housing industry), the toys market, the fish market, entertainment industry, fashion industry, the hospital industry, and so on. In the marketing discipline, there is very little attention paid to the specific industry types or product markets and how they function both empirically and theoretically. The closest approach seems to be to identify the underlying structure (e.g., oligopoly, monopoly) of a firm or a group of firms and discuss the strategies appropriate to the firm(s). This is rather inadequate and misses the point somewhat because what we end up with is an abstraction of the industry type but not the specific empirical characteristics of the industry. One reason for this development is that our discipline has become rather narrow and formalistic and consequently quite rigid, and we are too preoccupied with micro-level managerial practices at the expense of deriving important industry- or market-level insights. Because of our preoccupation with firm-level decisions as the sole point of academic discourse, we have neglected important areas of inquiry concerning industry patterns and trends. We believe that there is a great opportunity to study market-related practices and structural factors in industry sectors.

Market Structures from an Industrial Organization Perspective

There is a growing interest in the industrial organization perspective within the marketing discipline (Ghosh and John 1999). This is particularly true of the work in homogeneous or undifferentiated markets. Basically, the industrial organization perspective relies on the notion that the structure

Table 16.2

Market Descriptions

Perspectives	Current emphasis in the marketing discipline	Comments
A. Markets in the mainstream		
1. Markets as product markets or industry types	Medium	E.g., auto industry, fashion industry, entertainment industry, toy markets
2. Markets from an industrial organization perspective	Low to medium	A limited number of scholars work in this area
3. Markets as hierarchies	Low	There was some initial interest but it is sporadic. Very high interest in other disciplines—industrial economics, and business strategy. Growing interest in economic sociology
4. Markets as a site for competing firms	The highest emphasis	This is really the heart of contemporary marketing paradigm. The rhetoric has shifted to global competitiveness
5. Markets as networks	Low in the U.S., high in the Nordic countries	Has not diffused to non-Nordic countries. A growing area of research in economic sociology
6. Markets as political economies	Low within the marketing discipline	A very important research area in the global context. Growing area in political science
7. Markets as institutional systems	Low	In the pre-Kotlerian era, was a major focus. E.g., Wroe Alderson. George Fisk and so on. Worth reconsidering
8. Markets as brand communities	A growing area of interest in the field	Has become even more important in light of the diffusion of global brands: McDonalds, Sony, Honda, Samsung, Apple, Starbucks, Microsoft, etc.

(continued)

Table 16.2 (*continued*)

Perspectives	Current emphasis in the marketing discipline	Comments
B. Emerging global context		
9. Emerging markets	Growing area of interest especially in light of developments in China, India, Southeast Asia, and South America	Shifting market structures, outsourcing, diffusion of fashion, food, cultural products, as well as technology
10. Market as sign economy	Growing area of interest with the aestheticization of market environments, consumption practices, products, and brands	A fertile area of research because of cross-cultural market forces
11. Markets as informal economies	Low	A great potential for research in the global context
12. Markets as cultural economies	Low	In the field of international marketing there is some attention to this perspective. Anthropologists speak to this most of the time
13. Markets as communities	Low	Usually discussed in the anthropological literature
14. Markets as traditional bazaars	Low to nonexistent	Currently, limited number of studies. Touched on in history
15. Rural and urban markets	Nonexistent	Very relevant to developing economies. Tradition in developmental economics, anthropology
16. Market as ideology	Nonexistent	Popular among critical theorists and postmodernists. A very fruitful area theoretically and empirically
C. New perspectives		
17. Markets as virtual environments	Emerging interest but very micro-oriented approaches	Marketing discipline needs to address this more rigorously. A growing area in communications and management info systems

of an industry influences the conduct of firms in it and ultimately this carries over to the performance of the market (Zellner 1988). A limited number of marketing scholars work in this area.

Markets as Hierarchies

This is really an integral part of the industrial organization approach to the study of markets. Stern and Reve's (1980) political economy approach to marketing channels is one example. John (1984) and Anderson (1985) pioneered this line of thinking in marketing. In addition, social hierarchies such as those based on race/ethnicity, gender, and class are vital topics as the systems of hierarchies are reproduced and or modified within the contexts of markets (Peñaloza 1994, 1996).

Markets as Sites for Competing Firms

This is probably the most dominant approach within the marketing discipline (Choi 1991; Ghemwat 2002; *Marketing Science* 2005). Many marketing scholars are concerned with how firms can compete in the marketplace and how they can use different strategies based on various elements of the marketing mix (price, promotion, etc.). Even here a large part of our scholarly work tends to be normative and very managerially oriented. Recent work in the application of game theory marks a growing attention to this area (Moorthy 1993; Tyagi 2005). Nobody can deny that survival and growth of firms are important indicators of a well-behaved economy. But a rather absorbed preoccupation with matters of success and failure at the expense of various other analytics and historical and institutional details reduces marketing to a purely normative discipline without an opportunity to expand the field into more creative directions. This economic Darwinism is very self-defeating in the long run.

Markets as Networks

There has been a fair amount of work in this area, but it is limited to researchers in the Nordic region (Hultman 1999; Mattson 1997). More specifically, the Uppsala school is known for many leading studies concerning business networks and strategic issues. Although quite popular in the Nordic region and theoretically strong, network approaches to marketing did not diffuse significantly to the other parts of the world. One reason may be that the network approaches typically focus on industrial markets (Anderson and Narus 1984) rather than consumer markets.

Markets as Political Economies

A fertile area of inquiry in the 1980s (Arndt 1983; Stern and Reve 1980), it was the focus of research primarily among European scholars and did not gain much popularity within the very micro-oriented research environment within the United States. Nevertheless, as markets continue to gain social currency and dominate national and local economic policy, this area holds much promise in documenting and analyzing the political dimensions and dynamics of market agents and their activities.

Markets as Institutional Systems

This approach dates back to the contributions of Wroe Alderson (1957) but the field has not pursued this avenue in the past several decades. A good case can be made to revive this approach, as valuable theoretical and methodological gains are to be made in addressing more macro social and organizational dimensions of market activities and structures, such as market governance and formation. Fligstein's (1996) work on market institutions within the discipline of sociology is particularly noteworthy.

Markets as Brand Communities

One of the main activities of a marketing firm has to do with branding. While the literature on branding goes back to the late 1960s, it is only recently that there has been a sustained scholarly interest in brand communities (Muniz and O'Guinn 2001; Schouten and McAlexander 1995). Brand communities are defined by Muniz and O'Guinn as "a specialized, non-geographically bound community, based on a structured set of social relations among admirers of a brand" (p. 412). A very important and growing area of research, it is becoming even more important as markets become more aestheticized (Venkatesh and Meamber 2006).

Markets in Emerging Global Context

Emerging Markets

It is generally acknowledged that one of the major consequences of globalization is the rapid expansion of industrialization into many countries that have been customarily described as Third World and even Fourth World. Scholars writing on emerging global markets are attempting to critically examine the reality of the global changes (Sheth 2004). As new markets emerge and existing markets are transformed, the marketing discipline has to keep pace with these changes and introduce new frameworks and empirical accounts of market practices and behaviors.

Market as a Sign Economy

The legitimacy of the market lies in what value it creates for the producer and the consumer and various intermediaries. Historically, we have seen a progression in terms of how "value" was defined and conceptualized. In primitive societies, products and services were evaluated in terms of their use value. Since the dawn of the industrial revolution, use value has given rise to exchange value. Contemporary marketing paradigm has developed around the creation and management of exchange value (Bagozzi 1975). In recent years, a major shift has occurred in the functioning of markets in relation to consumers. As products become commodified and undifferentiated in terms of their functionalities, what distinguishes one product from another is the image or the symbolism built into it. Assuming that most market offerings (we include services here) become similar to each other or where their functionalities are indistinguishable at the margin, consumers look for a different value element, which we label as *sign* value. In other words, because marketers cannot change their product offerings in the short term or without much financial investment, they try to compete on the sign values they create in their products. This also explains why advertising has become the sine qua non of contemporary marketing. Once we recognize the role of the sign in contemporary marketing, we have to admit the role that culture plays in the shaping of the current economic systems. After all, signs are nothing but products of culture. It is thus logical to define the market system as the sign economy.

Finally, as markets become globalized, and consumer images are transported across cultures, the success of marketing becomes vitally linked to the success of the sign economy (Venkatesh, Peñaloza, and Firat 2006).

Markets as Informal Economies

In many parts of the world, markets do not behave like organized systems—as the term is understood—but operate informally or through invisible networks (Ferman, Henry, and Hoyman 1987; Wilson 1998). Although they are not organized, they are quite robust and possibly historically rooted, and in a few instances operate in parallel to more established market structures. In some places, they are the only institutional arrangements that facilitate market transactions. Even in developed countries like the United States, informal markets operate quite briskly either legally or illegally and function more like an underground economy (Levitt and Dubner 2005). Not much has appeared in the marketing literature on informal markets (for an exception, see Arnould 1995), although this is a very important part of social and cultural order in many parts of the globe.

Markets as Cultural Economies

With the globalization of markets, this is going to be a major area worthy of intense exploration. Currently, some important contributions are emerging within our discipline (Holt 2004; Peñaloza 2000, 2001). Anthropologists and social theorists such as Wilk (1996), Slater and Tonkiss (2001), and Callon (1998) have written rather extensively on the fundamentally cultural nature of economic systems of exchange, shifting disciplinary currents in understanding the increasingly prevalent role of marketing practices in society, and the increasing cultural roles of marketing institutions, respectively. This area offers a great opportunity within international marketing, a field that has been accorded a low status within the mainstream. One reason may be that the work in this area is rather descriptive and highly undertheorized.

Markets as Communities

Much of the work in this area has focused on brand communities (see earlier section); that is, groups of consumers fashioned in terms of the social relations and meanings they generate from corporate and product identities and images (Holt 2004; Muniz and O'Guinn 2001; Peñaloza 2000; Schouten and McAlexander 1995). We envision the next generation of this work to spread beyond consumers' relations to firms and products to include the dual sets of agents, marketers, and consumers acting within the larger configuration of the market.

Markets as Traditional Bazaars

This is a very important area of inquiry and mostly researched by anthropologists. Some exceptions within the marketing discipline are Sherry's (1990) work on the flea market and Peñaloza's (2001) work on a Western stock show. Geertz's (1978) seminal article in the *American Economic Review* lays some anthropological foundations and finds a meeting point for anthropology and economics. The primary issue in these essays is to show how sociocultural factors provide more than the context in which market practices are enacted. That is, market discourses, practices, and beliefs are institutionalized by social and cultural agents as part of their ongoing activities in (re)producing themselves and negotiating extensive social relations.

Markets as Rural and Urban Economic Sectors

Most regions of the world are distinguished by two types of markets, rural and urban. This is certainly true of the less-developed regions of the world, and even the most developed nations retain rural and urban distinctions. If our discipline aspires to have a global appeal, marketing scholars should take note of this two-tier market structure. A good example of research in rural markets is the work by Mitra and Pingali (2000) describing how consumerism is diffusing into the so-called marginalized rural communities and what impact it has on such communities.

Markets as Virtual Environments

With the advent of the Internet, this new market medium has become an explosive area of inquiry (Dholakia, Zhao, and Dholakia 2005; Hoffman and Novak 1996). Although the articles on the Internet have multiplied significantly, only a small number of studies have examined the Internet as a market or a marketplace (Hagel and Armstrong 1997; Varadarajan, Yadav, and Shankar 2005). Most work seems to be focused on consumer behaviors on the Internet (Haugtvedt, Machleit, and Yalch 2005). Yet there is a wide array of opportunities in developing theories of virtual markets that address such issues as the formation of electronic markets, their distribution patterns, channel relationships, power structures, social dynamics, and institutional contexts as applied to the Internet.

Market as Ideology

Finally, and arguably most importantly, markets may be viewed as a constellation of normative beliefs regarding appropriate roles by actors (Colchoy 1998). In the discourse of modern marketing, such roles were circumscribed narrowly for marketers and consumers. However, as marketing discourses and institutions take on larger social significance, such roles are increasingly broadened to include a wide range of national identity, as well as racial/ethnic, gender, age-specific, identity, and behavioral complexes. It is important in this approach to the study of the market to distinguish between normalized marketing beliefs and their manifestations in market discourses and practices.

DISCUSSION AND CONCLUSIONS

This chapter began by charting several trends in ushering in the study of the market as the central topic of study in the field of marketing. We proceeded to trace the trajectory of work on the theory of the firm, and illustrate several extensions to it, by situating it within the context of various approaches to the study of the market.

In forwarding the paradigm of markets, we hope to generate promising new methodological and theoretical work along dimensions of level of abstraction, scope, and maneuverability. First, regarding analytical level of abstraction, the paradigm of markets is more complete in including the smallest holistic unit toward which marketing techniques are oriented.

Second, regarding the scope of study, the market encompasses more than just marketing techniques. While the study of marketing techniques privileges the perspectives of marketing managers, the higher level of markets requires attention to the perspectives of marketers as well as consumers and other operative agents. A better understanding of these various perspectives is a prerequisite to deciphering the various contours and dynamics of markets, historically and at present.

Third, the paradigm of markets enables more conceptual maneuverability in moving around and shifting between the various perspectives included in the fashioning of markets. As noted by C. Wright Mills (1959) in his classic treatise, *The Sociological Imagination,* the move to the paradigm of markets stimulates marketing researchers and practitioners to imagine and develop more creative configurations of markets in better synch with global social and technological trends.

Fourth, it is our hope in shifting the field to the study of markets that marketers may become more responsible, not less. By viewing themselves as inhabiting the markets they produce, and bringing them about in conjunction with other market agents, as opposed to discovering some preexisting consumer segment or merely competing with other businesses, marketers are better suited to developing novel ways of conceptualizing what they do. These insights are critical in moving beyond carrying out existing formulas that have resulted in what Shoenberger (1997) termed the cultural crisis of the firm. While the study of marketing techniques was well-suited to modern markets characterized by large vertically integrated firms, mass markets, standardized distributions of labor, and price mechanisms, the study of markets better comprehends these modern dynamics together with the workings of small firms, organized flexibly in alliances, niche and customized markets, informational processes, and style/identity mechanisms.

Finally, the focus on markets minimizes criticisms against the discipline that it is dominated by a U.S.-centric perspective. As the study of markets becomes global, we take the opportunity to make the discipline more globally relevant and responsive.

To conclude, the shift from marketing techniques to markets moves us from limiting what we study to ways of doing to the larger and more encompassing mode of ways of thinking. Such reconceptualization challenges the field to qualify and circumscribe supposedly universal techniques and concepts, such as the marketing concept and consumer satisfaction, to instead comprehend their different inflections as rooted in sociohistorical particularities. As scholars such as Callon (1998), Slater and Tonkiss (2001), and Bevir and Trentmann (2004) have documented, markets are not universal, self-contained entities, but rather take on distinct discursive forms and material practices across various social contexts and over time. Markets are subject to varying objectives as well, from shareholder wealth, to market growth, to social stability, to quality of life, and to political participation, as political parties deploy and deter them toward different social, economic, and political ends (Fligstein 1996). It is our hope that by enlarging the scope of the field to hone in on the market we will begin to chart a path that opens up exciting new possibilities in better understanding what is arguably the most potent contemporary social force in the world today. It is time to bring to fruition Johan Arndt's prophetic vision (1973).

REFERENCES

Alderson, Wroe (1957), *Marketing Behavior and Executive Action.* Homewood, IL: Richard D. Irwin.

Anderson, Erin (1985), "Transaction Costs Analysis and Marketing," in *Transaction Cost Economics and Beyond,* John Gwoenwegen, ed. Boston: Kluwer Academic, 65–83.

Anderson, James and James A. Narus (1984), "A Model of the Distributor's Perspective of Distributor-Manufacturer Working Relationships," *Journal of Marketing,* 48 (Autumn), 62–74.

Arndt, Johan (1973) "Toward a Concept of Domesticated Markets," *Journal of Marketing,* 37 (Fall), 69–75.

———— (1983), "The Political Economy Paradigm: Foundation for Theory Building," *Journal of Marketing,* 47 (Fall), 44–54.

Arnould, Eric (1995), "West African Marketing Channels: Environmental Duress, Relationship Management and Implications for Western Marketing," in *Contemporary Marketing and Consumer Behavior: An Anthropological Sourcebook,* John Sherry, ed. Thousand Oaks, CA: Sage, 109–68.

Bagozzi, Richard P. (1975), "Marketing as Exchange," *Journal of Marketing,* 39 (October), 32–39.

Belk, Russell, ed. (1991), *Highways and Buyways: Naturalistic Research from the Consumer Behavior Odyssey.* Provo, UT: Association for Consumer Research.

Bevir, Mark and Frank Trentmann (2004), *Markets in Historical Contexts: Ideas and Politics in the Modern World.* Cambridge, UK: Cambridge University Press.

Brown, Stephen (2002), "Vote, Vote, Vote for Philip Kotler," *European Journal of Marketing,* 36 (April), 313–24.

Buzzell, Robert (1999), "Introduction: Market Functions and Market Evolution," *Journal of Marketing,* 99 (October Special Issue), 61–63.

Callon, Michel ed. (1998), *The Laws of the Markets.* Oxford: Blackwell.

Castells, Manuel (2001), *The Internet Galaxy: Reflections on the Internet, Business, and Society.* New York: Oxford University Press.

Choi, S.C. (1991), "Price Competition in a Channel Structure with a Common Retailer," *Marketing Science,* 10 (Fall), 271–96.

Chua, Amy (2003), *World on Fire: How Exporting Free Market Democracy Breeds Ethnic Hatred and Global Instability.* New York: Doubleday.

Coase, Ronald (1937), "The Nature of the Firm," *Economica,* 4 (November), 386–405.

Colchoy, Franck (1998), "Another Discipline for the Market Economy: Marketing as a Performative Knowledge and Know-How for Capitalism," in *The Laws of the Markets,* Michel Callon, ed. Oxford: Blackwell, 194–221.

Cyert, Richard M. and James G. March (1963), *A Behavioral Theory of the Firm.* Englewood Cliffs, NJ: Prentice Hall.

Day, George and David Montgomery (1999), "Charting New Directions for Marketing," *Journal of Marketing,* 63 (Special Issue), 3–13.

———, Allan D. Shocker, and V. Srivastava (1979), "Customer-Oriented Approaches to Identifying Product Markets," *Journal of Marketing,* 43 (July), 8–19.

Deshpande, Rohit (1983), "On Paradigms Lost: On Theory and Method on Research in Marketing," *Journal of Marketing,* 47 (Fall), 101–10.

Dholakia, Nikhilesh, A. Faut Firat, and Richard P. Bagozzi (1980), "The De-Americanization of Marketing Thought: In Search of a Universal Basis," in *Conceptual and Theoretical Developments in Marketing,* Charles W. Lamb and Patrick M. Dunne, eds. Chicago: American Marketing Association, 75–80.

Dholakia, Ruby, Miao Zhao, and Nikhilesh Dholakia (2005), "Multichannel Retailing: A Case Study of Early Experiences," *Journal of Interactive Marketing,* 19 (Spring), 63–74.

Ferman, Louis A., Stuart Henry, and Michele Hoyman, eds. (1987), *The Informal Economy.* Thousand Oaks, CA: Sage.

Fligstein, Neil (1996), "Markets as Politics: A Political-Cultural Approach to Market Institutions," *American Sociological Review,* 61 (August), 656–73.

Geertz, Clifford (1978), "The Bazaar Economy: Information and Search in Peasant Marketing," *American Economic Review,* 68 (2), 28–32.

Ghemwat, Pankaj (2002), "Competition and Business Strategy in Historical Perspective," *Business History Review,* 76 (Spring), 37–74.

Ghosh, Mrinal and George John (1999), "Governance Value Analysis and Marketing Strategy," *Journal of Marketing,* 63 (October), 131–45.

Hagel, John and Arthur G. Armstrong (1997), *Net Gain: Expanding Markets Through Virtual Communities.* Boston: Harvard Business School Press.

Haugtvedt, Curtis P., Karen A. Machleit, and Richard F. Yalch, eds. (2005), *Online Consumer Psychology.* Mahwah, NJ: Lawrence Erlbaum.

Hoffman, Donna L. and Thomas P. Novak (1996), "Marketing in Hypermedia Computer-Mediated Environments: Conceptual Foundations," *Journal of Marketing,* 60 (July), 50–68.

Holt, Douglas (2004), *The Culture of the Brand.* Boston, MA: Harvard University Press.

Howard, John A. and Jagdish Sheth (1969), *A Theory of Buyer Behavior.* John Wiley and Sons.

Hultman, Claes M. (1999), "Nordic Perspectives on Marketing and Research in the Marketing/Entrepreneurship Interface," *Journal of Research in Marketing & Entrepreneurship,* 1 (January), 54–71.

Johannsson, Johnny K. (2004), *In Your Face: How American Marketing Fuels Anti-Americanism.* Fairlawn, NJ: Prentice Hall.

John, George (1984), "An Empirical Examination of Some Antecedents of Opportunism in a Marketing Channel," *Journal of Marketing Research,* 21 (August), 278–89.

———, Allen M. Weiss, and Shantanu Dutta (1999), "Marketing in Technology-Intensive Markets: Toward a Conceptual Framework," *Journal of Marketing* 63 (October Special Issue), 78–91.

Kohli, Ajay K. and Bernard J. Jaworski (1990), "Market Orientation: The Construct, Research Propositions, and Managerial Implications," *Journal of Marketing,* 59 (April), 1–18.

Kotler, Philip (2000), *Marketing Management: Analysis, Planning and Control* (1967, 1971). Reprint, Englewood Cliffs, NJ: Prentice Hall.

——— and Sidney Levy (1969), "Broadening the Concept of Marketing," *Journal of Marketing,* 33 (January), 10–15.

Levitt, Steven D. and Stephen J. Dubner (2005), *Freakonomics: A Rogue Economist Explores the Hidden Side of Everything.* New York: William Morrow.

Lusch, Robert F. and Stephen Vargo, eds. (2006), *The Service-Dominant Logic of Marketing: Dialog, Debate, and Directions.* Armonk, NY: M.E. Sharpe.

McCracken, Grant (1988), *Culture and Consumption: New Approaches to the Symbolic Character of Consumer Goods and Activities.* Bloomington: Indiana University Press.

Marketing Science (2005), Special Issue on Competition and Competitive Responsiveness, 24 (Winter), 1–174.

Mattson, Lars-Gunnar (1997), "Relationship Marketing and the Markets-as-Networks Approach: A Comparison Between Two Evolving Research Traditions." *Journal of Marketing Management,* 13 (December), 447–61.

——— (1998), "Relationship Marketing in a Network Perspective," in *Relationships and Networks in International Markets,* J. Geminden, S. Ritter, and D. Walter, eds. New York: Pergamon Press, 37–47.

Meamber, Laurie A. and Alladi Venkatesh (1995), "Discipline and Practice: A Postmodern Critique of Marketing As Constituted by the Work of Philip Kotler," in *Proceedings of the AMA Summer Educators' Conference,* Vol. 6, B. Stern and G.M. Zinkhan, eds. Chicago: American Marketing Association, 248–53.

Mills, C. Wright (1959), *The Sociological Imagination.* New York: Oxford University Press.

Mitra, Reshmi and Venugopal Pingali (2000), "Consumer Aspirations in Marginalized Communities: A Case Study in Indian Villages," *Consumption, Markets and Culture,* 4 (2), 125–42.

Moorthy, K Sridhar (1993), "Game Theoretical Modeling in Marketing," *Journal of Marketing,* 57 (April), 92–106.

Muniz, Albert M. Jr. and Thomas C. O'Guinn (2001), "Brand Community," *Journal of Consumer Research,* 27 (March), 412–32.

Peñaloza, Lisa (1994), "Altravesando Fronteras/Border Crossings: A Critical Ethnographic Exploration of the Consumer Acculturation of Mexican Immigrants," *Journal of Consumer Research,* 21, (June), 32–54.

——— (1996), "A Critical Perspective on the Accommodation of Gays and Lesbians in the U.S. Marketplace," *Journal of Homosexuality,* 31 (Summer), 9–41.

——— (2000), "The Commodification of the American West: Marketers as Producers of Cultural Meanings at the Trade Show," *Journal of Marketing,* 64 (October), 82–109.

——— (2001), "The Consumption of the American West: Animating Cultural Meaning and Memory at a Stock Show and Rodeo," *Journal of Consumer Research,* 28 (December), 369–98.

Rindfleisch, Aric and Jan B. Heide (1997), "Transaction Cost Analysis: Past, Present, and Future Applications," *Journal of Marketing,* 61 (October), 30–54.

Rosa, Jose Antonio, Joseph F. Porac, Jelena Runser-Spanjol, and Michael S. Saxon (1999), "Sociocognitive Dynamics in a Product Market," *Journal of Marketing* 63 (October Special Issue), 64–77.

Schouten, John W. and James H. McAlexander (1995), "Subcultures of Consumption: An Ethnography of the New Bikers," *Journal of Consumer Research,* 22 (June), 43–61.

Sherry, John (1990), "A Sociocultural Analysis of a Midwestern American Flea Market," *Journal of Consumer Research,* 17 (June), 13–30.

Sheth, Jagdish (2004), "Making India Globally Competitive," *Vikalpa: The Journal of Decision Makers,* 29 (October–December), 1–10.

——— and Rajendra Sisodia (2002), *The Rule of Three: Surviving and Thriving in Competitive Market.* New York: The Free Press.

Shoenberger, Erica (1997), *The Cultural Crisis of the Firm.* Oxford: Blackwell.

Simon, Herbert (1959), "Theories of Decision-Making in Economics and Behavioral Science," *American Economic Review,* 49 (June), 253–83.

Slater, Don and Fran Tonkiss (2001), *Market Society: Markets and Modern Social Theory.* Cambridge, UK: Polity.

Stern, Louis W. and Torger Reve (1980), "Distribution Channels as Political Economies: A Framework for Comparative Analysis," *Journal of Marketing,* 44 (Summer), 52–64.

Tyagi, Rajeev (2005), "Do Strategic Conclusions Depend on How Price Is Defined in Models of Distribution Channels?" *Journal of Marketing Research,* 42 (May), 1–8.

Varadarajan, Rajan, Manjit Yadav, and Venkatesh Shankar (2005), "First-Mover Advantage on the Internet: Real or Virtual?" Marketing Science Institute Working Paper Series, 05-001, Cambridge, MA: Marketing Science Institute, 3–25.

Vargo, Stephen L. and Robert F. Lusch (2004), "Evolving to a New Dominant Logic for Marketing," *Journal of Marketing,* 68 (January), 1–17.

Venkatesh, Alladi (1985), "Is Marketing Ready for Kuhn?" in *Changing the Course of Marketing: Alternative Paradigms for Widening Marketing Theory,* Nikhilesh Dholakia and Johan Arndt, eds. Greenwich, CT: JAI Press, 105–15.

——— and Laurie Meamber (2006), "Arts and Aesthetics: Marketing and Cultural Production," *Marketing Theory,* 6 (January).

———, Lisa Peñaloza, and A. Fuat Firat (2006), "The Market as a Sign System and the Logic of the Market," in *The Service-Dominant Logic of Marketing: Dialog, Debate, and Directions,* Robert F. Lusch and Stephen Vargo, eds. Armonk, NY: M.E. Sharpe.

Wilk, Richard (1996), *Economies and Culture: Foundations for an Economic Anthropology.* Boulder, CO: Westview Press.

Williamson, Oliver E. (1975), *Markets and Hierarchies.* New York: The Free Press.

——— and Scott E. Masten (1999), "Introduction," in *The Economics of Transaction Costs,* Oliver E. Williamson and Scott E. Masten eds. Northhampton, MA: Edward Elgar Publishing, 1–10.

Wilson, Tamar Diana (1998), "Approaches to Understanding the Position of Women Workers in the Informal Sector," *Latin American Perspectives,* 25 (March), 105–19.

Zellner, James A. (1988), "Industrial Organization: Some Applications for Managerial Decisions," *Journal of Agricultural Economics,* 70 (May), 469–74.

PART 4

ADJUSTING TO MARKETING'S
CHANGING CONTEXT

More than any other business discipline, marketing is shaped by its context. Today, that context is changing in three key areas: shifting demographic patterns, the proliferation of information technology that empowers customers, and a heightened sensitivity to ethical issues. The chapters in this section address the impact of these discontinuities on the practice of marketing.

Philip Kotler leads off with an insightful analysis of marketing ethics, posing questions and then providing suggestions for how marketing needs to adjust for its future survival and growth. Marketing has made major contributions over the years in raising material standards of living around the world. It has also created jobs through demand generation. So why is the marketing profession not respected? Kotler believes it has to do with the ethical dilemma marketing faces: Should marketing give the customer what he or she wants or should marketing judge what the customer wants? There are many products that are not necessarily good for the customer. Examples include hard drugs, tobacco, high-calorie fast food, alcohol, and sweets. In addition, there are products that consumers may want, but which may not be good for them or society at large, such as asbestos, lead paint, gas-guzzling automobiles, dangerous guns, pornography, and so on.

Kotler believes that marketing should encourage socially responsible behavior by firms, not just help sell more stuff or produce more profits for a company's shareholders in any legally sanctioned way. This moral compass should enable marketing to become a more noble profession in the eyes of the public.

Monroe and Xia address the issue of unfair prices. People seem to be clearer about what is unfair than what is fair. We know what is unfair when we see it, but it is difficult to articulate what is fair. While perceptions of unfairness are based on discrepancies or inequities, unfairness is also associated with a strong emotional reaction. Monroe and Xia suggest that customers either stop buying or complain or seek revenge, depending on the degree of unfairness and the amount of switching costs.

They suggest that managers must strive toward fair pricing to avoid these negative consequences of perceived unfair pricing. Fair price does not mean one price for everyone. When products are differentiated, when values are delivered, when a good buyer–seller relationship is maintained, and when damage control is implemented, it is likely that customers will trust and believe it is a fair price.

David Wolfe suggests that with aging populations and people living longer today than ever, the new customer majority will demand new marketing paradigms. The primary developmental objective in the spring of life is to gain knowledge and skills to enter adulthood. The primary developmental objective in the summer of life is the social and vocational development of the individual. This season of life is about "becoming somebody." The primary developmental objective of the fall season of life is a search for the meaning of life and legacy. Finally, the primary development objective in the winter of life is to reach a state of wholeness, commonly referred to as self-realization or self-actualization. Wolfe believes that since the new customer majority is transitioning from the fall to the winter of life, marketing needs to embrace inner harmony and spiritual development. He suggests this underscores the success of companies such as New Balance.

Tim Ambler focuses on how marketing processes evolve from founder-driven small entrepreneurial companies to large process-driven corporations, and what can we do to improve them. "Moments of truth" are defined as those marketing activities that make a difference to the firm's bottom line or to its marketing assets. He suggests that the classic planning/implementation/measurement/review cycle be examined from this moments of truth perspective.

Sheth and Sisodia believe that most marketing inefficiency and effectiveness arises from the mismatch between the rising heterogeneity of supply and demand. They offer a radical solution: greater automation of purchase and consumption. It is the ultimate empowering of the customer and probably the best way to create a customer advocacy culture. This automation of consumption requires that there exists a high level of mutual trust and respect between consumers and marketers; marketers and consumers both must invest time and effort to increase their knowledge of each other; both must commit to ethical behavior; blend high tech with high touch for personalization; and engage in variety-seeking behavior to satisfy the epistemic needs of the market. While this may sound like a marketing utopia, the authors provide a realistic future scenario of the automation of consumption that resembles *The Jetsons* cartoon.

Berthon and John provide a forceful argument in favor of using information technology in marketing to increase interaction intensity. They suggest that both the frequency and value of interaction should be measured to improve marketing practice.

CHAPTER 17

ETHICAL LAPSES OF MARKETERS

PHILIP KOTLER

It is interesting to contemplate how much approval and respect different professions get from the public. College professors garner an 81 percent public approval rating and doctors draw a 76 percent rating. Lawyers, not surprisingly, draw only a 23 percent favorable regard. We marketers register 20 percent. Sales people rate very poorly at 6 percent, only to be beaten at the low end by politicians at 4.3 percent and telemarketers at a disturbing 1.9 percent. Clearly, some groups in our profession, particularly sales people and telemarketers, are at the bottom end of the revile scale.

Howard Bowen, in his book *Social Responsibilities of Businessmen,* raised critical ethical questions about marketing that still haunt the profession today. He asks:

- Should he conduct selling in ways that intrude on the privacy of people, for example, by door-to-door selling?
- Should he use methods involving ballyhoo, chances, prizes, hawking, and other tactics which are at least of doubtful good taste?
- Should he employ "high pressure" tactics in persuading people to buy?
- Should he try to hasten the obsolescence of goods by bringing out an endless succession of new models and new styles?
- Should he appeal to and attempt to strengthen the motives of materialism, invidious consumption, and "keeping up with the Joneses? (1953, p. 215)

VIEWS ABOUT THE MARKETER'S GOALS

How do marketers view their role in society? Sergio Zyman (1999), former head of marketing at Coca-Cola, states baldly that the marketer's job is "to sell more stuff." I can't think of a less inspiring statement of the goal of our profession than being able "to sell more stuff." To many, more stuff means more waste, more congestion, more environmental degradation.

A second view of the marketer's goal is to produce more profits for company shareholders in any legally sanctioned way. The problem is that many marketers pursue this goal without considering the ethical and social consequences of their actions. Company cynics go so far as to say: A high-minded socially-conscious person would not be effective in marketing. A company shouldn't hire such a person.

ETHICAL SYSTEM PERSPECTIVES

How can we define ethical marketing? The problem is that there are many clashing views on what constitutes ethical behavior. They include the following five perspectives:

- Ethical egoism: Your only obligation is to take care of yourself (Protagoras and Ayn Rand).
- Government requirements: The law represents the minimal moral standards of a society (Hobbes and Locke).
- Personal virtues: Be honest and good and caring (Plato and Aristotle).
- Utilitarianism: Aim for the greatest good for the greatest number (Bentham and Mill). (Thus a nuclear power plant is defensible even if it may cause cancer to a few but benefits society as a whole.)
- Universal rules: "Act only on that maxim through which you can at the same time will that it should become a universal law" (Kant's categorical imperative).

THE MARKETING DILEMMA

Marketers face a dilemma. The dilemma stems from the two central axioms of marketing: (1) give the customer what he or she wants, and (2) don't judge what the customer wants. But this produces two complicating issues.

- What if the customer wants something that is not good for him or her?
- What if the product or service, while good for the customer, is not good for society or other groups?

There are many products that are not necessarily good for the customer. Examples would be hard drugs, tobacco, high-calorie fast foods, alcohol, and sweets. In addition, there are products that the customer may want but which may not be good for him or her or society as a whole. This would include asbestos, lead paint, gas guzzling automobiles, dangerous guns, pornography, and so on.

Industrialized economies generate many products that challenge global sustainability. In the United Kingdom there is a group that is trying to define "sustainable marketing," marketing that contributes to, rather than subtracts from, environmental sustainability. Consider the following three culprits:

- *Disposable products.* Profits can be made by companies that produce disposable products such as cheap pens and throwaway cameras. A movie with Alec Guinness called *The Man in the White Suit* (1951) showed how the shirt industry tried to destroy a company that made a shirt than lasted forever.
- *Product obsolescence.* Companies can make profits by introducing more advanced models that obsolete earlier models before their usefulness has expired.
- *"More is better" doctrine.* The public is encouraged to "Keep up with or get ahead of the Joneses" in terms of material acquisitions.

THE FOUR QUESTIONS

So here we pose four questions.

- Why do companies make questionable products?
- What can these companies do to make these products safer?
- What can be done to discourage consumption of questionable products?
- Do socially responsible companies achieve higher long-run profit as a result of their caring attitude?

Why Do Companies Make Questionable Products?

Let's ask this question about tobacco companies, which long fought regulation and long denied the harmful effects of tobacco usage. These companies cared more about profits than human life. Suppose a new smoker starts at the age of thirteen, smokes for fifty years, and dies at sixty-three from lung cancer. If he spends $500 a year on cigarettes, he will spend $25,000 over his lifetime. If the company's profit rate is 20 percent, that new customer is worth $5,000 to the company (undiscounted). What company doesn't want to attract a customer who contributes $5,000 to its profits?

By this scenario, tobacco companies win the most by creating young smokers. They also win by trying to increase the volume of cigarettes annually smoked by each smoker. The heavy user segment is every company's target. A high-level Coca-Cola manager in Sweden told me that her aim is to get people to start their day drinking Coca-Cola instead of orange juice. Companies constantly strive to get more and more people to use more and more of what they sell.

Consider McDonald's. The company works hard to interest us in buying a larger hamburger and a larger order of french fries and a larger Coke, all of which contribute to the nation's growing obesity problem and the medical ailments this consumption leads to.

Marketers are hired by companies specifically to use marketing tools to sell more of the company's products and services. Marketers are skilled in identifying which consumer groups are more susceptible and vulnerable. We assemble the best thirty-second TV commercials and print ads and sales incentives to persuade them.

What Can Companies Do to Reduce Adverse Effects of Their Products?

Suppose a company making a questionable product wants to reduce its adverse affects. Beer companies now tell people not to overdrink or drive after drinking. They cooperate in enforcement programs to prevent underage people from buying beer. They adopt this position out of enlightened self-interest and should be applauded.

Consider the efforts by McDonald's. Some years ago they started offering salads and the choice of a leaner hamburger to minimize public criticism. Neither offering was successful. The leaner hamburger didn't taste good and the salad was a pretty poor version of a salad. Recently they added tastier salads to their menu and this has been well-received. They have recognized the profit potential of this move. The mother who brings her child to McDonald's may not want to eat a hamburger, so now she has more reason to patronize the restaurant. Companies with questionable products should try to figure out how to moderate the use of their products along healthier lines.

What Can Public Interest Groups Do to Reduce the Consumption of Questionable Products?

Public interest groups can do things that reduce the consumption of questionable products. Here are six major public initiatives:

- *Encourage companies to make their products safer.* Laws have been passed that impose strict product liability penalties on companies that have been careless about making unsafe toys, cars, or prescription drugs.
- *Ban or restrict the sale or use of the product or service.* Gun dealers are under strict regulations about to whom they can sell guns. The sale of hard drugs is strictly banned.

- *Ban or limit advertising or promotion of the questionable product or service.* Many countries ban or limit the advertising of cigarettes or alcoholic products.
- *Increase "sin" taxes to discourage consumption.* Governments usually impose high taxes on alcoholic drinks and tobacco to discourage their consumption.
- *Run public education campaigns.* Public school systems introduce lessons to students aimed at encouraging sensible consumption behavior on their part.
- *Run social marketing campaigns.* Social marketing campaigns are run to raise consciousness about unhealthy behavior and to encourage healthy behavior.

Are Socially Responsible Companies Likely to Achieve Higher Profits in the Long Run?

It would be a powerful argument for encouraging more socially responsible marketing if the evidence showed that socially responsible companies became more profitable. To answer this, we must first identify the more socially responsible companies and then see if they are more profitable and, if so, if this is partly attributable to their more caring behavior.

Each year *Business Ethics* publishes a list of the one hundred best American companies out of one thousand that are evaluated (*Business Ethics* 2003, p. 6).[1] They evaluate the degree to which the companies serve well seven stakeholder groups: shareholders, community, minorities and women, employees, environment, non-U.S. stakeholders, and customers. Information is also gathered on company lawsuits, regulatory problems, pollution emissions, charitable contributions, staff diversity counts, union relations, employee benefits, and employee awards. Companies are removed from the list if there are significant scandals or improprieties.

The top twenty U.S. companies cited for high corporate citizenship in 2003 were General Mills, Cummins Engine, Intel, Procter & Gamble, IBM, Hewlett-Packard, Avon Products, Green Mountain Coffee, John Nuveen, St. Paul, AT&T, Fannie Mae, Bank of America, Motorola, Herman Miller, Expedia, Autodesk, Cisco Systems, Wild Oats Markets, and Deluxe. Now, are these same firms more profitable? Previous studies differ in their findings on this question (Waddock and Graves 1997). They either find no correlation or fail to distinguish cause and effect in a positive correlation. It may be that highly profitable firms have more surplus resources to give back to society, rather than that their good citizen orientation was a factor leading to higher profits. Cause and effect is very hard to disentangle. The conclusions are:

- The correlations between financial performance (FP) and social performance (SP) are sometimes positive, sometimes negative, and sometimes neutral, depending on the study.
- Even when FP and SP are positively related, which causes which?
- The most probable finding is that financially profitable firms invest slack resources in social caring and then discover that social caring leads to better financial performance, in a virtuous circle.

WHAT ARE THE EARMARKS OF A SOCIALLY RESPONSIBLE FIRM?

Here are my views of the earmarks of a socially responsible firm. Such firms:

- Live out a deep set of company values that drives company purpose, goals, strategies, and tactics.
- Treat customers with fairness, openness, and quick response to inquiries and complaints.
- Treat employees, suppliers, and distributors fairly.

- Care about the environmental impact of its activities and supply chain.
- Behave in a consistently ethical fashion.

Such companies typically put a set of four P (product, place, promotion, and price) questions to their contemplated actions. For every company action (Paine 2003) they ask:

- Is the purpose worthwhile?
- Is it consistent with company principles?
- Does it impact favorably on people (stakeholders)?
- Does the company have the power to do it well?

MARKETING'S BOTTOM LINE

Nothing said here should detract from the major contributions that marketing has made over the years to raising the material standards of living around the world. One doesn't want to go back to the kitchen where the housewife cooked five hours a day, scrubbed dishes by hand, and washed and dried clothes in the open air. We value the invention and progressive improvement of refrigerators, washing machines, dryers, radio, TV, and computers—all these good things.

There is a second positive contribution of marketing. Marketing is the discipline that is responsible for job creation. Our success in demand creation results in job creation. If we slow down demand creation, we slow down job creation and, therefore, incomes. That is all right if we want to move to a "less is more philosophy" as a society, where we emphasize living a good life with less material support. But today we are pretty glued to a materialistic lifestyle and we depend on marketing for job creation.

At the same time, we need to clean up some of our activities. I would hope that more marketing professors could act as social critics of certain marketing practices and provide the sobering considerations that should guide good company marketing practice.

NOTE

1. The research was done by Kinder, Lydenberg, Domini (KLD), an independent rating service.

REFERENCES

Bowen, Howard R. (1953), *Social Responsibilities of the Businessman.* New York: Harper & Row.
Business Ethics (2003), "One Hundred Best Corporate Citizens 2003," *Business Ethics* (Spring).
Paine, Lynn Sharp (2003), *Value Shift: Why Companies Must Merge Social and Financial Imperatives to Achieve Superior Performance.* New York: McGraw-Hill.
Waddock, Sandra A and Samuel B. Graves (1997), "The Corporate Social Performance–Financial Performance Link," *Strategic Management Journal,* 18 (4), 303–19.
Zyman, Sergio (1999), *The End of Marketing As We Know It.* New York: Harper Business.

CHAPTER 18

THE PRICE IS UNFAIR!

Reforming Pricing Management

KENT B. MONROE AND LAN XIA

The question of price fairness has become an important issue as criticisms of gasoline and prescription drug prices rise and the use of fees, "smart" vending machines, and the practice of dynamic pricing to enhance profitability become public knowledge (Ayres and Nalebuff 2003; Matanovich 2004; Thornton 2003). When Coca-Cola was considering installing smart vending machines, which would vary the price of a soft drink according to demand or the outside temperature, the resulting uproar was a public relations nightmare for the firm (Hays 1999). And Amazon.com did some back peddling when a customer discovered that the price of same-title DVDs differed across purchase occasions (Adamy 2000). More recently, the uproar of assessing fees (some hidden) as a mechanism of increasing revenues has led to cries of "unfair." These examples indicate that both the price offered and the rationale for a given price may induce perceptions of price unfairness, further damaging the public's perception of marketing.

THEORIES OF PERCEIVED FAIRNESS

As firms embrace and use smart pricing tools, more transactions will result in different customers paying different net prices. Combining price segmentation tactics with different types of price promotions suggests that at any point in time, no item will sell at exactly the same price to all customers (Marn and Rosiello 1992). Thus, more customers may perceive discrepancies between (1) the prices they pay and their reference prices, (2) the prices they pay and the prices comparable other buyers pay, or (3) the prices charged by different sellers for the same product or service. An important question then is when are such discrepancies perceived to be unfair?

Our notions of unfairness are typically clearer, sharper, and more concrete than those of fairness. We know what is unfair when we see it but it is difficult to articulate what is fair. While perceptions of unfairness are based on discrepancies or inequalities, unfairness is also associated with a strong emotional reaction. An unfairness perception and the potential negative emotions usually are directed to the party that is perceived to cause the unfair situation. For price unfairness, the primary target of the perception and the emotions is the seller. Hence the actions that buyers take when they perceive that prices are unfair are usually directed toward the seller.

Distributive and Procedural Fairness

The principle of *distributive fairness* maintains that individuals judge the fairness of a relationship or exchange based upon the allocation of rewards resulting from their contributions to the relationship. Thus, equal ratios of profits to investments between all parties involved in an exchange relationship, both those directly involved (i.e., buyer and seller) and indirectly involved (i.e., two buyers purchasing from the same seller), result in perceived fairness, whereas unequal ratios create perceptions of unfairness. *Procedural fairness* concerns judgments whether processes are based on prevailing norms and behaviors. Subjective procedural fairness pertains to how a process affects the fairness perceptions of those involved.

An important point established by price behavioral research is that buyers' price judgments are comparative in nature (Monroe 2003). That is, to be able to judge whether a price is fair or acceptable, buyers must compare that price to a reference price. Perceptions of price unfairness may arise when buyers perceive that their inputs (i.e., price paid) are unequal relative to a comparable other party (seller or other customer) given the same output (i.e., product or service purchased).

Information on how the sellers determine prices, including the use of different pricing strategies and segmentations of customers, may help buyers refine their unfairness perceptions. For example, a given price inequality may be perceived as unfair when a seller seeks to maximize its profits by segmenting according to customers' willingness to pay, but as fair when the seller offers different prices to customers with different characteristics (e.g., offering discounts to senior citizens).

Price fairness judgments often are based on both the outcome and other information related to the specific outcome (i.e., procedure). Information on outcomes and procedures may interact and the order in which the information is received (i.e., outcome or procedure information is received first) may influence perceptions of price fairness. If buyers receive information first about the way prices have been determined, their subsequent judgments of the fairness of the actual prices will depend more on how they judged the process used to determine the prices. If the process is judged to be fair, then it is less likely that prices that deviate from expectations will be judged to be unfair. On the other hand, if buyers first perceive that the prices they pay are equivalent (or not equivalent) to the comparative other (whether the seller or other buyers), then they are more likely to judge the price to be fair (or unfair).

Equity Theory

Equity theory expands the perspective of distributive fairness by positing that individuals compare themselves to similar or referent others: another person, an organization, a class of people, or the individuals themselves relative to their earlier experiences. People are more likely to compare themselves to similar others, although dissimilar references may be used as bases for comparisons. In the context of price fairness, a buyer's perception may vary depending on the choice of a reference. The tension resulting from an inequitable relationship prompts both parties to seek means to restore equity within the relationship through a variety of ways including altering the quantities and importance of the inputs and outputs for one or both parties, leaving the relationship, or changing the reference other. However, in a buyer–seller relationship, buyers may place more importance on their personal outcomes than their inputs when forming fairness judgments, but expect the seller's inputs to be high in order for the exchange to be considered fair (Oliver and Swan 1989). Hence, advantaged inequity and disadvantaged inequity are associated with different emotions. Buyers may feel uncomfortable or guilty when they are advantaged, but feel anger or outrage when they are disadvantaged.

Principle of Dual Entitlement

The main premise of dual entitlement is that one party should not benefit by causing a loss to another party. If either party does not receive what they believe is their entitlement, the relationship will be perceived as unfair. For example, in telephone surveys to identify standards of fairness that apply to price setting by firms, 82 percent of the respondents judged a price increase for snow shovels the morning after a snowstorm to be unfair, while 21 percent of respondents viewed an increase in grocery prices following an increase in wholesale prices as being unfair (Kahneman, Knetsch, and Thaler 1986).

Dual entitlement principles propose that a firm perceived to be unfair in its transactions will encounter punishment in the form of customers switching to competing products and services or customers avoiding the firm, even though they may incur costs to themselves by doing so. The dual entitlement principle operates in the context of cost and benefit distribution between the buyer and seller so it has natural applications to price fairness. However, dual entitlement does not indicate what references consumers may choose and the different consequences of these choices (Bolton, Warlop, and Alba 2003).

Attribution Theory

Attribution theory provides a basis for how people rationalize an ambiguous situation. In the context of price fairness judgments, a buyer may experience difficulty judging whether a price is fair. A source of this difficulty is the ambiguity concerning *why* the outcomes occurred and *who* is responsible for them. The basic premise of attribution theory is people attempt to make causal inferences about observed actions or events (Weiner 2000). These inferences in turn influence their perceptions and behaviors. It is suggested that buyers respond more unfavorably if the cause of a perceived negative outcome is due to a firm's volitional intentions or actions. On the other hand, buyers may be more likely to accept price inequalities over which the sellers have no control or that are due to factors external to the seller.

Attributions help buyers sort the information regarding how and why the seller set a particular price. The inferences developed based on the available information may help buyers refine their price fairness judgments. If a negative motive is perceived by buyers, they will evaluate the firm and its behavior unfavorably. Firms that develop goodwill through marketing practices and quality products earn customer loyalty leading to repeat purchases. A change in pricing policy or in prices that is perceived to be unfair may damage this goodwill.

It has been demonstrated that not all cost-based price increases will be perceived as fair. Price increases resulting from internally based cost increases are perceived as less fair than externally caused cost increases (Vaidyanathan and Aggarwal 2003). In addition, some internally caused cost increases are perceived as less fair than other costs, for example, promotion costs (Bolton, Warlop and Alba 2003). However, cost-induced price increases due to external reasons such as general inflation cost increases would be considered relatively fair.

CONSEQUENCES OF PERCEIVED PRICE UNFAIRNESS

Available research results indicate that perceived unfairness has a negative influence on purchase intentions (Campbell 1999; Martins 1995). In addition, unfairness perceptions may lead to complaints (Xia, Monroe, and Cox 2004). We now outline a set of actions that buyers may take when they perceive prices to be fair or unfair. These actions are influenced by the severity of the unfairness that the buyers perceive. Consequently, buyers' actions will vary depending on their intentions and the damage to sellers will vary accordingly.

Perceptions of fairness or unfairness are accompanied by cognitions of equality or inequality. When severe unfairness perceptions occur, the cognition of inequality is also accompanied by a strong negative emotion. Buyers may respond to perceived unfairness either by seeking compensation for their monetary sacrifice or by trying to gain revenge and damage the seller.

It is not costless when buyers act to cope with an inequitable situation. If they decide to leave the relationship they may incur switching costs. There is the cost of time and effort if they decide to complain or disseminate negative word-of-mouth information to other people. And there are monetary costs if they decide to take legal action. Hence, the cost of action moderates the potential actions that buyers may take when perceiving an unfair situation. In addition, when considering what actions to take, buyers may also estimate their relative power and the likelihood that they will succeed in executing the potential actions.

No Action

No action refers to the situation when perceived unfairness has no significant influence on buyers' planned transactions with the seller. An advantaged inequality or a slightly disadvantaged inequality may not induce a strong negative emotion although they perceive a price inequality. Therefore, an outcome that is less fair may not necessarily induce consumers to take any actions. For example, Urbany, Madden, and Dickson (1989) found that 89 percent of respondents perceived a bank's failure to pass on a cost decline to patrons a year after an ATM fee implementation was unfair. However, the majority of the respondents would not choose to change banks because of the costs of switching.

Self-Protection

When buyers perceive that an inequality within an exchange is unacceptable, they may choose to leave the relationship. Or, if they decide to stay in the relationship because the switching costs are high or they still value their relationship with the seller, they may attempt to resolve the situation by actions such as a complaining to the seller.

How do buyers decide which method will most effectively reduce inequity within a buyer-to-seller relationship? Huppertz, Arenson, and Evans (1978), measuring perceived fairness of hypothetical retail exchange scenarios, discovered that subjects were more likely to complain when price inequity was high and service inequity low than when both price and service inequity were high. When both price and service levels were inadequate, the majority of the respondents chose to leave the store. Similarly, it has been found that buyers are more likely to complain when their involvement with the seller is high, but are more likely to leave when their involvement is low (Urbany, Madden, and Dickson 1989). Therefore, in the context of price inequality, buyers may complain, ask for a refund, or just leave the relationship, depending on their assessment of which action is most likely to restore the equality with the least cost.

Revenge

When a strong negative emotion rises with the perception of price unfairness, leaving the relationship or complaining may not be sufficient to address the inequality situation. Hence, to cope with the emotional aspect of unfairness, buyers may seek revenge. In this situation, the intention of action is to damage the seller and get even. Such actions can even be at the buyer's expense instead of compensating the buyer's perceived loss. It has been shown that consumers would gain revenge for a company's wrongdoing by switching to the company's direct competitor even when that is a suboptimal choice for them (Bechwati and Morrin 2003).

Finally, in addition to the damage to the specific exchange between the buyer and the seller, perceived unfairness may also have a long-term effect. Firms that invest in developing goodwill through marketing practices and quality products or services earn customer loyalty, which, in turn, results in repeat purchases. A price differential that is perceived to be unfair may damage this goodwill and encourage buyers to avoid the relationship.

IMPLICATIONS FOR PRICING MANAGERS

"Managers who view fair process as a nuisance or as a limit on their freedom to manage must understand that it is the violation of fair process that will wreak the most serious damage on corporate performance" (Kim and Mauborgne 1997, p. 71). Price fairness perceptions may be formed prior to a transaction or after. If fairness perceptions occur before a transaction, a perception of unfairness may reduce purchase intentions. When these perceptions occur after a transaction, a perception of unfairness may influence future transactions.

A Fair Price Does Not Mean One Price for Everyone

Although perceptions of price unfairness are based on perceived price differences, a goal of fair pricing does not mean a one-price policy for everyone and it does not mean customers do not accept price changes or price differences. For example, when Microsoft implemented its product upgrade pricing policy, they offered new customers switching from competing products the same as loyal customers upgrading their current Microsoft software. The practice led to displeased loyal customers because they expected to pay a *different* (lower) price than new customers. That is, these customers would have welcomed differential pricing based on loyalty.

Offering customers different prices for essentially the same product or service is not new. A key question is what makes these situations more acceptable or perceived to be fairer than Amazon.com's pricing experiments or Coca-Cola's smart vending machines? We now offer some guidelines for achieving and maintaining perceived fair prices within the context of differential pricing.

Differentiate Products and Services

When two transactions are completely comparable, the effect of observed price differences on perceptions of price unfairness will be larger than in other situations. Therefore, perceptions of price unfairness can be mitigated by decreasing the comparability of the transactions. For example, airplane tickets may differ in terms of cancellation policies or time of purchase corresponding to different prices. Resorts offer in-season and out-of season rates and models within a product line differ by features and benefits delivered. These variations in benefits delivered or time of use of a service decrease the comparability of similar transactions and the importance that customers may place on price differences when judging the fairness of a price. Contrarily to this principle, Amazon.com charged the same customer a higher price for the same product based on his purchasing history. There was no differentiation between the products or service in the two transactions and Amazon.com received negative customer and media response when the practice was discovered (Adamy 2000). Differentiating products to serve different segments of customers is not a new practice. Such customization, by differentiating the products or services offered, decreases the comparability between transactions, and reduces the potential for perceptions of unfairness.

Signal Cost and Communicate Benefits and Values Delivered

While cost-based pricing rules are perceived by buyers to be fairer than market-based pricing rules (Maxwell 1999), nevertheless, consumers have very little knowledge of a seller's actual costs and profit margins (Bolton, Warlop, and Alba 2003). If sellers are not willing to openly communicate their cost structures and margins with customers, they can signal both their pricing procedures as well as the value of their products or services.

Signaling enables sellers to reduce the uncertainty that exists within the exchange relationship with respect to product's quality and the seller's costs (Kirmani and Rao 2000; Monroe 2003). Sellers may communicate costs or their inputs to the exchange relationship in several ways. For example, advertising and public relations campaigns that demonstrate the firm's commitment to acquiring top-of-the-line raw materials for its products suggest to consumers that the sellers' costs are relatively high. Also, announcing the increased price of raw materials or consumer price index adjustments to workers informs buyers of the firm's costs.

Managers may resist more open communications about their pricing; however, to avoid misinterpretations of a firm's intents and actions by either rival sellers or buyers, clear and unambiguous signals need to be provided. Recognizing that information technology makes it easier for price information to be known across buyers and sellers, it no longer makes sense for sellers to hide the reasoning behind their pricing decisions.

In addition to signaling costs, sellers may switch buyers' attention away from cost to focus on the values that the product or service delivers. By focusing on the benefits and value provided, the firm can relate its price to customer usage and value received. Instead of selling price or price differences firms need to emphasize the differences in value offered (quality and benefits received relative to price paid). For example, a higher airfare may be associated with flexible travel dates, ability to seek a refund, and friendly cancellation policies. On the other hand, using differential pricing may not be effective if customers do not value the product or service differences. When providing differentiated products and services to different customer segments, managers should communicate the benefits and values and help customers perceive the different values that are equitable with different offers.

Maintain a Good Buyer–Seller Relationship

The emphasis buyers place on a firm's intentions and trust encourages firms to develop and maintain good relationships with their customers. Sellers should avoid exploiting their customers, especially their loyal customers, thereby strengthening the exchange relationship. For example, when demand exceeded the supply of Cabbage Patch dolls during the 1986 holiday season, retailers maintained prices to avoid losing customer goodwill (Martins 1993).

Allowing or creating a shortage situation during periods of heightened demand or increased costs enables a firm to maintain goodwill and continue long-term relationships with loyal customers. For example, restaurants located in tourist areas may maintain their price structure to avoid punishing local customers, even though they could profit by increasing prices to meet the short-term increase in demand. In addition, as demand increases for products such as bottled water and building materials after the occurrence of a natural disaster, local retailers may maintain prices for necessity items. Local retailers interested in maintaining goodwill to sustain customer relationships will use queues in lieu of price increases.

Building trust with buyers enhances buyers' fairness perceptions. However, customers request that the seller value this relationship by offering fair prices. Therefore, maintaining such a good reputation and the sellers' trust is more important. When the price is fair, good reputation and trust enhance perceptions of fairness. However, when customers perceive the pricing procedure or a price to be unfair, good reputation and trust will not save the seller. In contrast, customers may perceive the action of the sellers as a betrayal of their trust and exacerbate perceptions of unfairness. Sellers must find ways to determine fair, value-oriented prices that are grounded in real market and buyer knowledge.

Damage Control When Perceptions of Unfairness Arise

While it is important to prevent unfair price perceptions, it is equally important to control the damage when perceptions of unfairness occur. When the major concern of buyers is financial, sellers may control the potential damage by offering buyers a refund, an additional monetary reward, or other financial compensation. However, when the unfairness perception is accompanied with a strong negative emotion, financial compensation may not be sufficient. Sellers need to offer a venue that allows the buyers to vent their anger. The key of such a venue lies in the interaction between the buyers and the sellers' representatives. When treated appropriately (i.e., polite and with respect) during the interaction, the buyers may reinstate their normal emotional state (Bowman and Narayandas 2001). Although buyers may still choose to leave the exchange relationship, they may not be as motivated to seek revenge, which is an action that potentially brings the most damage to the sellers. Hence, sellers may need to proactively reach their customers when severe unfair price perceptions arise and try to reduce the damages by redressing the situation with an appropriate method.

CONCLUSION

"In the short term, customers may well buy according to economic rationales: if the price is below my perceived value I buy it, if not I don't. But in the long term, customers are motivated to find their way out of what they perceive to be unfair situations. . . . In the long term being perceived as 'fair' is important, to prevent detrimental buyer behavior and buyer-seller relationship[s]" (Dolan and Simon 1996, pp. 138, 273). Pricing managers need to reform their myopic vision about maximizing short-term margins and carefully consider the long-term effects of perceived unfair pricing procedures and price differences. Understanding how customers perceive prices and form value judgments is necessary to fulfill this important prescription.

REFERENCES

Adamy, J. (2000), "E-tailer Price Tailoring May be Wave of Future," *Chicago Tribune,* September 25, 4.

Ayres, I. and Barry J. Nalebuff (2003), "In Praise of Honest Pricing," *MIT Sloan Management Review,* 45 (Fall), 24–28.

Bechwati, Nada Nasr and Maureen Morrin (2003), "Outraged Consumers: Getting Even at the Expense of Getting a Good Deal," *Journal of Consumer Psychology,* 13 (4), 440–53.

Bolton, Lisa E., Luk Warlop, and Joseph W. Alba (2003), "Consumer Perceptions of Price (Un)Fairness," *Journal of Consumer Research,* 29 (March), 474–91.

Bowman, Douglas, and Das Narayandas (2001), "Managing Customer-Initiated Contacts with Manufacturers: The Impact on Share of Category Requirements and Word-of-Mouth Behavior," *Journal of Marketing Research,* 38 (August), 281–97.

Campbell, Margaret C. (1999), "Perceptions of Price Unfairness: Antecedents and Consequences," *Journal of Marketing Research,* 36 (May), 187–99.

Dolan, Robert J. and Hermann Simon (1996), *Power Pricing.* New York: The Free Press.

Hays, Constance L. (1999), "Price Strategy in Coke Test: What's It Worth to You?" *International Herald Tribune,* October 29, 20.

Huppertz, John W., Sidney J. Arenson, and Richard H. Evans (1978), "An Application of Equity Theory to Buyer-Seller Exchange Situations," *Journal of Marketing Research,* 15 (2), 250–60.

Kahneman, Daniel, Jack L. Knetsch, and Richard Thaler (1986), "Fairness and the Assumptions of Economics," *Journal of Business,* 59 (4), 285–300.

Kim, W. Chan and Renee Mauborgne (1997), "Fair Process: Managing in the Knowledge Economy," *Harvard Business Review,* 75 (July–August), 65–75.

Kirmani, Amna and Akshay R. Rao (2000), "No Pain, No Gain: A Critical Review of the Literature on Signaling Unobservable Product Quality," *Journal of Marketing,* 64 (April), 66–79.

Marn, Michael V. and Robert L. Rosiello (1992), "Managing Price, Gaining Profit," *Harvard Business Review,* 70 (September–October), 84–94.

Martins, Marielza (1993), "Promoting Product Value Through Price Fairness," *Pricing Strategy & Practice,* 1 (April), 16–21.

——— (1995), "An Experimental Investigation of the Effects of Perceived Price Fairness on Perceptions of Sacrifice and Value," unpublished doctoral dissertation, Department of Business Administration, University of Illinois.

Matanovich, Tim (2004), "Fees! Fees! Fees!" *Marketing Management,* 13 (January/February), 14–15.

Maxwell, Sarah (1999), "The Social Norms of Discrete Consumer Exchange: Classification and Quantification," *American Journal of Economics and Sociology,* 58 (4), 999–1018.

Monroe, Kent B. (2003), *Pricing: Making Profitable Decisions.* Burr Ridge, IL: McGraw-Hill/Irwin.

Oliver, Richard L. and John E. Swan (1989), "Consumer Perceptions of Interpersonal Equity and Satisfaction in Transaction: A Field Survey Approach," *Journal of Marketing,* 53 (April), 21–35.

Thornton, Emily (2003), "Fees! Fees! Fees!" *Business Week,* September 29, 99–104.

Urbany, Joel E., Thomas J. Madden, and Peter R. Dickson (1989), "All's Not Fair in Pricing: An Initial Look at the Dual Entitlement Principle," *Marketing Letters,* 1 (January), 17–25.

Vaidyanathan, Rajiv and Praveen Aggarwal (2003), "Who Is the Fairest of Them All? An Attributional Approach to Price Fairness Perceptions," *Journal of Business Research,* 56 (6), 453–63.

Weiner, Bernard (2000), "Attributional Thoughts About Consumer Behavior," *Journal of Consumer Research,* 27 (December), 382–87.

Xia, Lan, Kent B. Monroe, and Jennifer L. Cox (2004), "The Price Is Unfair! A Conceptual Framework of Price Unfairness Perceptions," *Journal of Marketing,* 68 (October), 1–15.

CHAPTER 19

MARKETING TO THE NEW CUSTOMER MAJORITY

DAVID B. WOLFE

In 1989, an event of epochal proportions happened in the United States, but never made a single headline. Even today, more than a decade and a half later, this historic event draws little attention. The event? For the first time in history, most adults were age forty and older.

My main objective in this chapter is to share with you some of the implications this event holds for marketing and a few thoughts about how we as marketers might best deal with those implications. To the extent any of us believe that marketing needs reform, we'll never figure out how to accomplish that without understanding how the New Customer Majority has changed the rules of marketing.

In his book *Management Challenges for the 21st Century* (1999), Peter Drucker said the number one issue facing business is coping with the worldwide decline in birth rates. This has dramatically changed age ratios, making young people a smaller percentage of the population and older people a larger percentage.

We hear all the time that people are living much longer today than ever before. That's true, but it's also untrue. It's true if we're talking about the life expectancy of children from the day of their birth—which is how life expectancy figures are generally figured. But it's not true if we're talking about the life expectancy of adults. The life expectancy of a person who turned sixty-five this morning is only about thirty months greater than a person who turned sixty-five in 1940. Perhaps more astonishing, the life expectancy of a person who turned eighty-five this morning is less than a year greater than it was for a person who turned eighty-five in 1900.

More than three-quarters of longevity gains since 1900 have accrued to people under the age of eighteen. Only about seven years has been added to the life expectancy of adults at age eighteen. And despite common perceptions, we've added nothing to the human lifespan over the past century—or, in fact, over the past ten thousand years. Lifespan refers to how long you *can* live; longevity refers to how long you *do* live. So far, science has not broken through the time barrier nature imposed on humankind many millennia ago.

With that introduction, which might have unsettled a few of your beliefs about aging and longevity, I want to turn your attention to some of the effects that changes in demography will have on marketing—indeed, on the whole of society.

THE BIRTH DEARTH MEANS A SALES DEARTH FOR MANY PRODUCTS

The number of twenty-five- to forty-four-year-olds is shrinking. This age group, which historically contributes more to the consumer economy than any other twenty-year age cohort, will shrink by more than four million consumers in this decade. By 2010, spending by this age group will fall by $104 billion. This should force many companies to examine the question, "Where will our sales growth come from?"

People in this age group, particularly twenty-five- to thirty-four-year-olds, spend the most per capita on vehicles, while thirty-five- to forty-four-year-olds olds spend the most per capita on housing and housing-related products. However, population shrinkage in these age groups means sales of vehicles, homes, and home products will fall in this decade—as well as in scores of other product categories.

How can companies best cope with these conditions? For many, the best response will be to tie sales goals to the life forces of the burgeoning older population that makes up the New Customer Majority. The numbers are pretty eye-popping. In 2003, while the eighteen- to thirty-nine-year-old age cohort numbered 85 million, the forty-plus set was far larger at 128 million. In 2010, there will have been less than 1 percent growth during this decade in the eighteen- to thirty-nine-year-old group compared with 63 percent growth among adults forty and older whose numbers are projected to rise to 138 million by 2010.

So why is more than 90 percent of marketing dollars targeting the incredible shrinking adolescent and young adult markets?

Look at the numbers—the dollars and cents numbers: By 2010, spending in households headed by people under forty-five is projected to be $1.62 trillion—a lot of money, for sure. But consider the fact that people forty-five and over are projected to spend an estimated $2.63 trillion in 2010. As the late U.S. Senator Everett Dirkson would say, "A billion here, a billion there—pretty soon it adds up to real money" (Quotations page).

Let me ask you, where do you think most marketing dollars should be spent today?

OLDER MARKETS CHALLENGE MARKETERS WITH DIFFERENT BEHAVIORS

As I've already noted, the aging consumer universe is changing the calculus of supply and demand in dozens of product and service lines. At forty-five or fifty-five or sixty-five or older, a person's bundle of needs is quite different from his or her needs as a young adult.

Older people also behave differently. Changes in goals, values, and in what they want from life changes behavior as well as needs. Life satisfaction is more often sought in experiences than in things. The narcissistic and materialistic influences that drive much of the behavior of younger people tend to ebb among older people.

Trackers of consumer trends have recently been using the word "surprising" to describe shifts in leading consumer attitudes and behavior. However, I see nothing surprising in consumer behavior today because the outlines of what we're seeing in leading consumer attitudes and behavior were predictable years ago. I know this because I predicted many of the leading behavioral attributes reflected in marketplace behavior today over fifteen years ago in my book, *Serving the Ageless Market* (Wolfe 1990).

Moreover, what I predicted then was predictable as long as nearly three decades ago—starting around the mid-1960s when the birth control pill first became broadly available. The pill led to a drastic decline in fertility in 1965—falling off by 130 basis points—then falling below population replacement levels in 1974—the year after *Roe vs. Wade*. This collapse in fertility rates generated changes in age ratios that ultimately led to the adult median age reaching midlife levels nearly three decades in the future.

The emergence of the New Customer Majority has transformed the leading attitudes and behaviors from reflections of the social and cultural patterns of youth to those of people in midlife and older.

For instance, Yankelovich President J. Walker Smith writes in this volume that resistance to marketing influences has become stronger. This is not a happenstance event; it's not because people are more highly educated today; it's not because people have more choice and more money to make choices—all reasons that have been cited as the source of greater consumer resistance to marketing. Increased resistance to marketing is rooted in the patterns of human development that manifest in midlife. People in the second half of life have always been more resistant to the efforts of others to persuade them to some course of action. Maslow wrote extensively about this more than fifty years ago. So, it is quite natural that with most adults now in middle age or older, consumer behavior overall would reflect greater resistance to marketers.

Older people generally look less to the external world for behavioral cues. They become more introspective, thus less dependent on others for information. They become more individuated, thus less like their peers, and more autonomous in acting out their lives—all of which makes members of the New Customer Majority more challenging to figure out, as well as more resistant to marketing. As everyone in the marketing game should know, the young are both more predictable and more receptive to marketing.

CONDITIONS CALL FOR A MAJOR PARADIGM SHIFT IN MARKETING

Marketing desperately needs to undergo a major paradigm shift because more and more, old ways of doing things are proving ineffective. A paradigm shift is not simply a new way of doing what you've always been doing. It's a new way of looking at something. It's a new mindset. It's a change in assumptions, concepts, values, and practices in response to nontraditional challenges that resist solutions by traditional means.

The twentieth-century marketing paradigm was product-centric. Marketing was mostly about huckstering—moving as much product as possible in as short a time as possible at the least cost possible cost. The twenty-first century marketing paradigm is customer-centric. It transforms marketers from hucksters to healers. It's about helping people process their lives to reach higher states of well-being.

It may sound a bit weird to be talking about marketers as healers, but I think you'll be more comfortable about this new idea—about this paradigm shift in marketing in just a few minutes.

Marketers as healers view consumers in new ways. They understand how a person's season of life influences his or her consumer needs and behavior. They understand the characteristics that define behavior in a given season of life. This enables the marketer to be more effective in sensing customers' needs.

Let's spend a few moments examining life through the lens of personality development through four seasons.

Each season of life has a primary developmental objective. We don't just develop until we're voting age. We develop all our life along a path that has been laid down in our genetic makeup. Just as a child first turns over, crawls, talks, and walks as a matter of natural course, all our lives we are on a natural course that takes us to one developmental milestone after another.

The primary developmental objective in the spring of life—from birth to age twenty or so is gaining knowledge and skills to enter adulthood with reasonable prospects for social and vocational success.

There is also a primary life activity focus in each season of life that concentrates energy in service of the primary developmental objective of the season. The primary activity focus in spring is play. Play is nature's way of drawing the young into experiences that promote the acquisition of skills that will be needed in adulthood.

Another dimension of each season is the narrative theme of a person's life story that shapes the outlines of his or her worldview and thereby exerts considerable influence on values, attitude, needs, and behavior. The narrative theme of spring, *fantasy,* is strongly present in children's games and in their daily play. Fantasy also plays a major role in the life stories of adolescents, coloring their dreams, ideas, relationships, personal appearances, social activities, and imaginings about various adult roles they fancy themselves fulfilling in the future.

Moving on, the primary developmental objective in summer is the social and vocational development of the individual—social actualization, as it were. This season is about *becoming* somebody, the overarching task a person needs to turn to after full-time entry into a career.

The primary life activity focus in summer is work. Work provides the measure of one's production. The manner in which it is pursued and the output that results determines the value of who the young person is in the eyes of peers, colleagues, and society at-large.

The narrative theme of one's life story in summer is a blend of romance and heroics: "Nothing will stop me. I can do all I set my mind to. The world is my oyster, and I intend to harvest many pearls." While the child expects good things to flow from without, the young adult adopts a take-charge attitude in the belief that good things happening depend on their own efforts.

People who are in the fall of life—which begins with the onset of midlife—have become the dominant consumer group, both in population size and spending power. Their needs are predisposed by the primary developmental objective of fall, which is development of the inner self—the spiritual self, as it were. Currently, aging boomers represent more than 90 percent of people in the midlife years.

The primary life activity focus in fall is balancing work and play in ways that leave enough psychic energy to explore the meaning of one's life. The pivotal questions in fall are, "What is the meaning of life—of my life? And what will be my legacy?"

The narrative theme in fall is reality. It is a theme driven by the need to bring the real self that has been concealed behind a social mask to the surface to divine the ultimate meaning of life. This process often generates deeply held episodes of disappointment: "I haven't accomplished what I thought I would when I was twenty-five," is one common sentiment. Another common feeling is, "I've accomplished more than I ever thought I would, but I feel an emptiness. Something is missing."

The midlife shift in worldview is a predictable dimension of human life that has been recognized for millennia. It's discussed in Vedic literature extending back nearly four thousand years. The Roman philosopher Seneca wrote of it. Shakespeare addressed it in his plays and sonnets. More recently, Carl Jung spent considerable time investigating this milestone in human development. So did Abraham Maslow and Erik Erikson. Given this, one of the great mysteries in marketing is why the marketing community ignores what these great minds have known for millennia about changes in midlife that have altered the lives and behavior of the adult age group that now dominates the marketplace?

Developmental psychology has virtually no standing in marketing at all. Yet it has more to inform us as marketers than any other branch of behavioral science.

Moving on, the primary developmental objective in the winter of life is to reach a state of wholeness that Jung referred to as *self-realization* and Maslow as *self-actualization.* The primary life focus is reconciliation, coming to terms with the sweet and the bitter of life and making peace with the self within, all others in our life, and with the world at large. The theme of our life story is irony: acceptance.

NEW BALANCE: A MARKETER THAT GETS IT.

As we've just discussed, in the second half of life, behavior is oriented to the needs of the inner self. Madison Avenue seems to have little awareness that an inner self even exists. And yet, it is a huge driving force in consumer behavior today. A company that has picked up on this better than any company I'm aware of is the sneaker maker New Balance. In 1990, it was the United States's number twelve sneaker maker; in 1996 it was number eight; in 2003, number three. It accomplished this in a field that, due to the birth dearth, was not growing, by touching the midlife soul and doing so in a way that resonated with all age groups. This is what I refer to as ageless marketing.

New Balance's ageless marketing strategies have not only given it a commanding position in forty-plus markets, its market share among youth has been growing by leaps and bounds, outpacing even mighty Nike.

Here in this New Balance ad, like a typical Harley-Davidson ad, you can't make out the individual features of the women jogging along a country road. That makes it easier for more people to dial themselves into the picture. Look at the body copy:

One more woman renewing her life is the dream.
One more woman discovering strength is beauty.
One more woman believing in herself.
One less woman walking in someone else's footsteps.
Those words are reflective of the sentiments of a typical midlife soul.

The new marketing paradigm recognizes that the possibility for real differentiation in the marketplace comes less from the product than in the past, and more in how you collaborate with consumers' need to heal, to be whole, to be complete.

People commonly get disoriented in midlife as they shift from a social-actualization track to a self-actualization track. It can be very confusing to a person undergoing this personal paradigm shift, which switches them from socially focused to inner-self-focused. New Balance marketing addresses this seasonal stress by in effect saying, "We hear the bubbling anxiety that has come across you as you try to reorient your life to a more mature state."

If you look at the differences between New Balance and Nike in values, I think this begins to come clear: Winning versus self-improvement, roar of the crowd versus inner harmony, extreme effort versus balanced effort, smell of sweat versus the smell of nature, physical development versus spiritual development. Nike appeals to the youthful, narcissistic, masculine self. New Balance appeals to the mature, other-centered experiential self—to the feminine self.

Each season of life takes us to higher and more complex psychological states of being. This is consistent with biologists' definition of "growth": the movement of an organism from a lower and simpler state to a higher and more complex state. Thus thirty-year-olds operate at a higher and more complex state than they did at twenty, at a higher and more complex state at forty than at thirty, the same at age fifty in comparison to age forty, and so on.

This presents a real problem to marketers because so many people involved in creating and placing marketing messages are in their twenties and thirties, creating messages targeting people in their fifties and sixties and older, people twice or more their age. The young copy writer, operating at a lower and simpler state, looks at life through the lens of his or her own value structure, trying to talk to people who look at life through a different lens. So, if we are serious about taking on the task of reforming marketing, we must deal with this issue.

THE NEW "S" WORD IN MARKETING

Maslow reflected the movement of people toward higher and more complex states in his hierarchy of basic human needs: Physiological, safety and security, love and belonging, self-esteem, esteem of others, and of course, self-actualization. Melinda Davis, writing in her book *The New Culture of Desire* (2002) says—I think quite appropriately—"Human behavior is now being ruled by a new pleasure imperative, a new primal desire, that is at least as powerful as the one that brought us into the world" (p. 2). Wow! Something more powerful than sex? That's what she's saying. And I agree.

In Jungian definitions, the libido is a persistent urge we have to recreate ourselves in all we do whether we're an artist, a pianist, a physician, or a marketer. And in the second half of life, we begin shifting away from the biological urge to reproduce ourselves to a metaphysical urge to reproduce ourselves. This is really what self-actualization is about.

I propose that the new "S" word in marketing and sales—due to the overwhelming dominance of middle-age consumers—is "self-actualization." Until we grasp what that means in practical terms, we're not going to be able to reform marketing. To make this a bit more vivid, self-actualization is an advanced state of psychological maturity in which behavior is more realistic, more practical, more dependent on context, and more resistant to persuasion.

People on a self-actualizing track focus more on peak experiences than on "things." They become more introspective and more authentic as they begin dissolving their persona (Latin for *mask*) that served them well when young and seeking the best advantage in their social and business ambitions. In midlife, many people develop a sense that they want to be more "real." And as they demand more authenticity of themselves, they demand more authenticity in those they do business with.

This was dramatically illustrated in *More* magazine (2002) in which actress Jamie Lee Curtis agreed to appear only if they presented her as she was with no special lighting, no makeup, and no air brushing, in sweat halter and shorts that revealed her sprouting love handles. Read her words: "I don't have great thighs. I have great big breasts, and a soft fatty little tummy; glam Jamie, the perfect Jamie is such a fraud. The more I like me, the less I want to pretend to be other people" (p. 92).

Jamie Lee Curtis at age forty-three is on the same track that people in every generation of self-actualization follow. So, forget what you hear about how baby boomers are different. That has been so overstated that we have a corrupt vision of boomers' behavior in this fall season of their lives. They're more like their parents than commonly acknowledged. It's in their genes.

REFERENCES

Davis, Melinda (2002), *The New Culture of Desire.* New York: The Free Press.
de Laszlo, Violet, (1990) *The Basic Writings of C.G. Jung.* Princeton, NJ: Princeton University Press.
Drucker, Peter (1999), *Management Challenges for the 21st Century.* New York: Harper Business.
Erikson, Erik (1980) *Identity and the Life Cycle.* New York: W.W. Norton.
Maslow, Abraham H. (1968) *Toward a Psychology of Being.* New York: Van Nostrand Reinhold Company.
The Quotations Page, www.quotationspage.com/quote/170.html (for Senator Dirksen quote, accessed September 2005).
Wallace, Amy (2002), "True Thighs," *More,* September, 92.
Wolfe, David (1990), *Serving the Ageless Market.* New York: McGraw-Hill.

CHAPTER 20

QUESTIONS MARKETERS NEED TO ANSWER

TIM AMBLER

Much as marketers like to believe that they are contributing to the happiness of customers and the wealth of society, the brutal truth is that they are employed to make money for, or otherwise achieve the goals of, their employers. How they do that, and how their performance can be measured, have only recently become top issues both in practice and academia. That in itself is remarkable. Normative approaches, originally derived in the main from microeconomics, have long instructed marketers on what they should do, and innumerable case studies have documented practice. Other marketing academics have been explaining how parts of the mix, such as advertising, work and how consumers behave. These issues are important but this chapter delves into marketer behavior and accountability in order to uncover the key questions marketers need to address.

Based largely on personal experience, this chapter cites no references even though I owe a huge debt to my academic colleagues. My sources are the twenty-five years spent marketing alcoholic drink brands, and other products, followed by fifteen years in academia trying to understand and explain that experience. Perhaps this perspective is moderated, for better or worse by age, but, rather in the manner we check later waves of responses to surveys against earlier ones, comparing these opinions with papers written thirty years ago did not reveal much change in the fundamentals. Technological developments such as data capture and processing, quantitative analysis, diversity of choice, and concepts such as the marketing asset, call it "brand equity" or what you will, have indeed changed, but how marketers spend their time has changed much less. Marketers no longer stagger into meetings with "guard books" of advertising and PowerPoint is a mixed blessing, but we are concerned with deeper human and corporate matters and those evolve more slowly than technology.

The chapter is therefore concerned with what marketers do, their marketing process, their capabilities, and how they are evolving. If we understand all that a little better, asking the right questions may improve practice and guide theoreticians toward relevance.

The structure is as follows. "Moments of truth" are defined as those marketing activities that make a difference to the firm's bottom line or to its marketing assets. Financial performance is defined for the purpose of this chapter as the short-term increase in profitability, or net cash flow, plus the change in the marketing asset, which I call brand equity. So the marketer's year is made up of moments of truth and a mass of other activities that may be necessary but that do not directly contribute to performance.

Marketer activity in a small start-up enterprise differs from that in a vast multinational. Size matters: broadly speaking, small businesses are time rich and money poor, whereas large companies have access to all the money they need, but may lack the time to acquire it or use it well. Innovation may be stronger, pro rata, in start-ups, and large companies grow also by acquisition. To establish the range, both ends are explored. This leads to the provisional list of questions to be

Figure 20.1 **The Marketing Year**

answered. The chapter then considers the extent to which the sector, for example, financial services versus packaged goods, moderates the questions. Developed economies have shifted from manufacturing to services and information technologies. Marketing in a financial services context may add value in different ways compared to packaged goods.

The chapter concludes with a short discussion of the four questions that emerged.

THE MARKETING YEAR

The classic planning—implementation—measurement—review cycle holds good in practice, driven by the firm's financial calendar. Even in small firms, where some stages will be informal, expenditure has to be tracked and cash availability will influence the extent of activity. Figure 20.1 charts the key steps.

The process begins with new marketing ideas, whether gleaned from customer insight, marketer intuition, business contacts, or experience. Strategy most often emerges implicitly and few companies today have separate strategy departments. In one way or another, some degree of change consensus emerges along with the budget required to implement it. This may be annually or quarterly or ad hoc. The formal plan typically revolves around advertising and other promotional activity because those budgets are conspicuous. Changes to product (defined here as goods and other services and packaging) or pricing may follow other cycles if they have a pattern at all. More likely they are responses to external pressures.

Figure 20.1 shows the firm's marketing year, not necessarily the marketer's year. British Airways only recently made pricing a responsibility of their chief marketing officer (CMO) and services firms do not usually allow marketers to control the product offering itself. This confusion between marketing (what the whole firm does to delight customers, and acquire new ones profitably) and what the firm's marketers do, lies at the heart of the difficulty of measuring marketing performance. Marketers may talk four Ps (product, place, promotion, and price) but they practice, and are accountable for, just those they have been allocated by the firm.

Even in a brand-oriented organization like Diageo, the Smirnoff brand manager may be officially responsible for all four Ps in his country, but in practice, global considerations will constrain flexibility. He cannot change the product or the packaging and pricing must conform to global strategy. The performance of the Disney CMO in France will be greatly affected by changes to the Disney brand equity worldwide.

In large firms and small, some specialist marketing activities, such as advertising or promotions or direct marketing, will be outsourced to agencies. The marketer is still accountable, but the reality of her role is to brief the agency and then accept or reject their proposals.

The functions of sales and marketing may be combined, but in any case both plans and implementation emerge from interaction between the two. Retail aside, the marketer classically is concerned with the end user, or consumer, whereas the sales person is concerned with the immediate buyer. This is equally true, albeit not often recognized, in business-to-business: the shop floor operative who uses the product is not usually the same person as the buyer for the firm. So the marketer battles for a larger share of the budget for "pull" marketing whereas the sales person demands more for "push."

The marketing year can be described in any number of ways but the cycle shown as Figure 20.1 is intended to highlight marketing activities, the moments of truth, which truly impact performance. That may all seem somewhat prosaic but two points should be noted. First, the seasonal process described may not at all match the timing of when great new ideas emerge. An inventive promotion with a large financial payback may strike six months after the annual plan is concluded. A brilliant idea for briefing the ad agency may arise from working with the agency on the original brief. It should not, but it does. And even the smallest company has no financial problems with marketing activity that has immediate payback. It is not unusual for crisis to cause creativity.

Second, the very routine of the formal annual process described in Figure 20.1 can drive out creativity. Days spent in predictable planning meetings numb the gray matter. The techniques for wresting the biggest budget from the bureaucracy are very different from the inspired marketing that will excite customers.

This leads to the first question of whether marketers have analyzed how they spend their resources relative to the moments of truth. Would a better allocation of time and energies, for example, less time planning and more on briefing agencies or measuring performance, improve performance? What have been the moments of truth over the past, say, three years and how did they arise?

Marketer time and energy are in short supply. Unless their use is actively challenged, to an outsider marketers may look as if they are running around the same wheel without it necessarily going anywhere. This is equally true for small and large companies but, as the chapter now describes, the wheels are very different.

SMALL COMPANIES

In most small (less than ten employees) companies, the marketing role is undertaken by the chief executive officer (CEO) or the key sales person. Few small firms have written plans beyond what is required by the bank manager or the key investor. In other words, any plan is written for someone else, not necessarily as a way to determine the best course of action. Formal performance measurement rarely goes beyond the annual accounts and reporting on the cash situation. In start-ups, emotion swings from panicking about the absence of orders to panicking about the capacity to deliver. Experienced small companies have settled into a more stable state but many want to stay small. Some want to grow and some want to sell out to larger companies, but other CEOs do not want the paraphernalia, meaning paperwork and routines, of large businesses. We see increasing numbers of public companies reverting to private status to escape all the reporting the law now requires and the internal procedures of large firms, including marketing processes.

In short, small companies rarely follow textbook marketing process. We writers of textbooks would like to think that hinders their performance but the evidence for that is weak at most.

Are the most successful small companies customer centric? They obviously recognize that they depend on customers and inward cash flow, but I have come to doubt the conventional wisdom that firms, or even their marketers, should be customer driven. Let us explore the idea that start-ups are ego driven, not ego with arrogance but ego with empathy. A few examples:

- Bill Gates started Microsoft in his own home to satisfy his own needs as a computer user. To a large extent, Microsoft still innovates in the same way: not asking customers what they want, but deducing what would be attractive from Gates's and his R&D people's own intuitions.
- A number of coffee enterprises began simply because the entrepreneur believed he could provide better coffee. The customer has not been short of coffee suppliers for a century or two and yet within the last ten years new CEOs continue to leap, Tarzan-like, into the coffee marketing jungle. For example, David McKernan created Java Republic in Dublin in 2001 based on the quality of the green beans, a "21-minute slow roast," freshness, and ethical standards. That gave the business the quality and distinctiveness they needed (they claim to be the most expensive coffee in the world) but the other reality is that David McKernan is an extrovert who would have found one limelight or another.
- Similarly, Richard Branson created Virgin Atlantic in his own image. Some people find British Airways pompous and nannyish . Virgin Atlantic differentiates itself by being fun and having fun at the expense of the senior competitor. Even today, flying Virgin declares a youthful independence. Did the customers have any idea they wanted such an airline before it was created? Of course not.
- Finally, Michelle Mone was born into a poor Glasgow slum district but with a big personality. At fourteen she was telling market stallholders how to do business. At fifteen she became the family's only breadwinner. She had the looks to become a fashion model but a mouth that cut her catwalk career short, or so she told the annual conference of the Irish Marketing Institute in February 2005. She joined the marketing department of Labatts brewery but knew that she wanted her own business. The spark appeared the evening she found her own bra uncomfortable and could not find anything better in the shops. Ten years later, her "Ultimo" brand of bras and swimwear is a top global brand and she has bought out previous market leaders.

These four minicases have one thing in common: marketing is not driven by consumer research or insights but by the ego-driven founder passionately seeking fame as well as fortune and exploiting empathy with the end user. The product has to solve the problem that the entrepreneur has identified but that the consumer had no inkling of.

The question is whether this adding-value formula is true for small businesses in general.

LARGE COMPANIES: INTERACTING WITH THE EXTERNAL MARKET

However dominant the CEO, large company marketing cannot be driven personally. Different parts of the organization must be free to innovate and at the same time coordinate what they do. They have to cultivate the former without allowing the need for coordination to either to stifle initiative or to allow transient marketers to bring bedlam. Marketers stay with small businesses for long periods, often because they have shares in them or other ties with the founding families.

The tension between autonomy and coordination only complicates the marketer's life in a large company. Indeed, the internal marketplace can become so dominant that it crowds out time for the external, namely, getting close to customers and understanding them and competitors. One U.K. company, "X," employs about a thousand marketers on one brand in virtually one country and yet almost all marketing activities are outsourced to agencies and consultancies. Those who think that marketing one brand in one market should need only one person may consider X to be an extreme case. Perhaps it is, but the lessons apply to all large companies to some extent. This is an observation, not a criticism. Marketing by X, like that of many other large companies, is top class despite the excessive bureaucracy and introversion. Whether "despite" or "because of" is the question, but my answer is clear. We are talking complexity, not chaos.

The complicating factors include:

- Learning competes with knowledge. Innovation involves replacing the known with experimentation that may or may not prove correct. Owners of knowledge resent attempts to prove them wrong. The short tenure of marketers in large companies biases them toward innovation, or mere novelty, relative to their peers in other functions. If their competition is too one-sided, be it toward learning or knowledge, performance suffers. In theory, the planning process provides the battleground for testing new ideas against existing knowledge but in practice plans are part of gaining financial support. Extensions and new brand launches, for example, tend to appear in plans only after the launch decision has been made.
- Paradoxically, knowledge (exploitation) can also create the demand for new learning (exploration). The idea of "levels" of learning has long been around. Level 1 knowledge allows the firm to exploit existing assets, capabilities, and resources in a pressured environment that may not be available for level 2 developments, namely, exploiting the knowledge that change is needed to improve the firm's position in a dynamic environment. At this second level, knowledge does not compete with but encourages learning and exploration; however, that needs slack resources from the operational first level.
- Very large marketing departments mean that the job has been divided into numerous specialties. A strategy team will devise the broad goals and pass them to other teams to take forward. The receiving team may not wholly accept what they are given. Instead of clear end-to-end accountability, the process becomes a game of pass the parcel with the parcel being transformed as it is transmitted. No one is finally responsible.
- Another large group of meetings involves the vertical dimension of the hierarchy. The rate of managerial turnover adds to the desire by senior management to pass wisdom down to their new hires and by juniors to impress their seniors. Planning is only one of the activities involving hierarchical meetings. Campaign approvals and reporting are others. Those unused to the ways of large companies are often astonished to find that no one is too clear who exactly has responsibility for any decision or outcome, nor can those involved explain after the event exactly who made the decision and how. In reality, decisions arise through talk-out, in other words, consensus is assumed when opponents have given up the argument.
- Internal communications are not confined to meetings. In large companies, e-mail has become more of a curse than a blessing, with some managers receiving hundreds every day. If they go away for a few days, the problem of sifting out the ones they really need to read and react to becomes formidable. Maybe in the future expert systems will provide electronic personal assistants and take care of the problem but, in the meantime, internal communications compound the inward focus of many marketers.

A company with one thousand marketers is spending two million hours a year without necessarily doing any marketing if it is all outsourced to agencies and consultants. They may be effective, depending on the quality of the marketing output, but they are certainly not efficient. And the bigger concern is that the process is internally, not market, oriented. When it comes to customer centricity, rhetoric rarely matches reality.

This caricature is drawn from life and highlights a central problem for large companies: complexity that causes marketers to look inward, not to the market. This context includes suppliers, whether consultants, agencies, or market researchers as insiders, not least because of their inevitable tendency to massage the client. I'm not suggesting that agencies distort the truth, the best ones are candid, but the fact remains that their clients provide their cash flow. The external agents are drawn into the internal party.

So the big question for large company marketers is how much time they give the realities of the marketplace. Do they go out with sales people? Take calls in call centers?

Observe what happens at the points of delivery? Deal personally with complaints? Compare service delivery with that offered by competitors?

The second question is how much time can they extract from the daily round of level 1 process for level 2, namely, exploring, experimenting, and improving level 1 processes.

LARGE COMPANIES: INTERACTING WITH THE INTERNAL MARKET

After challenging excessive internal focus, it may seem contrary to call for more internal marketing. Marketers interacting with each other is quite different from promoting the marketing concept around the rest of the firm. The need for this arises from the earlier distinction between marketing as a whole firm activity and the narrower role given by large companies to specialist marketers. The firm's marketing addresses two constituencies: existing and prospective customers. Motivating existing customers to stay, to buy more, and to buy better depends on their whole brand experience, not just experience of promotions and advertising. See Figure 20.2 for examples of so-called customer touch-points. In this diagram, marketing is shown as driving all aspects of the customer's experience of the brand and thereby growing brand equity.

In a thoroughly market-oriented organization, the marketers will be canvassing colleagues who are already converted. Little additional effort should be needed although coordinating the different aspects of brand experience from the customer's point of view is almost always demanding. Other companies, whether they claim to be customer centric or not, present a greater challenge. Can marketers afford to take resources from their day jobs, as others will see it, to promote what these same others may regard as a partisan view of the business?

As ever, the CEO's attitude is crucial. More unusually, the attitude of the human resources function is critical too. Some regard internal marketing (communications) as part of their role and resent interference. Others welcome the professional skills that marketers can provide and the overarching need for the company to improve brand experience.

No simple answer is likely, so we are left, once again, with a question: how much resources, namely, time, creativity, and energy, should marketers divert from the external to the internal marketplace? •

ARE THE ANSWERS TO THESE QUESTIONS LIKELY TO BE MODERATED BY SECTOR?

This section first brings together the four key questions thus far before considering potential sector effects:

- Is it generally true, at least for small businesses, that marketing success is not driven by consumer research or insights but by the ego-driven founder passionately seeking fame as well as fortune and exploiting empathy with the end user?

Figure 20.2   **Brand Experience**

- How much time should large company marketers devote to immersion in the external marketplace as distinct from following internally driven processes?
- How much time can they extract from the daily round of level 1 process for level 2, namely, exploring, experimenting, and improving level 1 processes?
- How much resources, namely, time, creativity, and energy, should marketers divert from the external to the internal marketplace (other employees)?

The first question looks at the personal influence of a dominant CEO, which seems to be more likely to be key than business size or sector. One of the examples was Microsoft, hardly a small company, and IBM could be cited as another, albeit in the same sector. Other examples can be found across all sectors and, while examples are not proof, there seems little reason to believe that this question is sector sensitive.

The second question is about market orientation that has been repeatedly shown to correlate with profit performance irrespective of sector, albeit weakly. Exploration necessarily means some degree of market immersion but not necessarily a rapid payback. One would expect the returns on exploration to vary considerably by sector. In rapidly changing technology, exploration is both more necessary and better and more quickly rewarded when it is right. Slow-moving sectors, however, are likely to have poor returns on exploration. That makes market immersion possibly less financially attractive but no less necessary.

The third question is mostly invisible to marketers, which itself is a good enough reason for raising it here. Marketing capabilities, even dynamic capabilities, have received much academic attention but perhaps with little change in practice. Company processes die hard, not least because practitioners accept them as the company culture, the way the company does business. Marketers aim to work within their company's culture and rarely see it as their job to change it. After complaining about the more absurd aspects for some months after joining, the culture becomes part of the wallpaper. In any case, the typical marketer's job tenure is not long enough to worry about such matters.

My evidence for this is based more on personal observation than formal research, although my work on metrics shows how little changes. I recently presented senior marketing executives with the results from formal work into valuing market research benefits. They were accepted without question and only later did I reveal the work was over thirty years old. Marketing plans are written much as they were in the 1960s. More use of PCs and PowerPoint, of course, but those are technology, not marketing processes.

The question here is whether these observations have changed for some sectors relative to others. My personal sample is not large enough to be sure, but the impression is that company size matters more than sector. Some sectors, such as professional services, are newer to formal marketing than others, such as packaged goods. One would expect to find some correlations in the size of a marketing department with the length of time formal marketing has been part of the culture and with sector. And one would certainly expect the lack of change in capabilities to be related to firm size. But that would make the sector effect only indirect at most.

Finally, the fourth question considers the formalization of internal marketing. This has long seemed a fine idea in theory and various agencies, such as People in Business, have been around since 1990 to provide specialized expertise. Few now survive. Some built business for a while, sold out to large communications groups such as WPP or Omnicom, and then disappeared. Others simply folded. We can be sure that, in their fight for survival, they tackled all sectors. Their general demise (though a handful still exist) indicates that there was little or no sector bias.

CONCLUSION

Technology has certainly changed the appearance of marketing capabilities, namely, the way marketing is conducted, and to some extent it has changed the reality, for example, database mining and quantitative analysis. But the highly technical aspects are conducted by only a few experts. Most marketers operate with the basic tools provided by Microsoft Office.

Technology aside, the major development has been our understanding of marketing assets. Short-term profit performance has always been, and always will be, measured as best as firms can, but the recognition of the need to adjust that by the change in brand equity is new. So our fifth and last question is:

- Does your firm have a compact (e.g., dashboard) and comprehensive presentation of all key brand equity metrics, reconciled with the firm's business model?

The difficulty for most firms with this question is relating changes in intermediate variables, such as awareness or intention to purchase, with behavioral metrics such as sales or market share.

The five key questions assembled here are important matters for CMOs to consider. They are moderated by the size of the business, or marketing team, but do not seem to be moderated by sector.

CHAPTER 21

MARKETING'S FINAL FRONTIER

The Automation of Consumption

JAGDISH N. SHETH AND RAJENDRA S. SISODIA

The marketing function has gone through a number of transitions over the years in a search for more efficient as well as more effective operating models. One of the key drivers of change has been the need to create a more efficient match between supply and demand, since many potential sales are lost due to the lack of the right inventory at the right time and place. To this end, many business-to-business companies in the past decade have moved toward the practice of "automatic replenishment" or "vendor-managed inventory," in which manufacturers take on the responsibility for managing inventory at the retail level. Monitoring starting inventory levels and sell-through volumes, manufacturers automatically ship additional merchandize when stock is depleted. The advantages of this approach are several: out-of-stock situations are greatly reduced, and many administrative costs associated with ordering, invoicing, and billing are reduced or eliminated. Implemented effectively, this approach results in higher levels of product availability at the point of purchase, with much lower average levels of inventory. The track record has been very strong; 80 percent of retailers now use some form of automatic replenishment, and companies have reported an up to 400 percent increase in inventory turns and 75 percent reduction in out-of-stock situations.

LOOKING FOR A BETTER WAY IN CONSUMER MARKETS

Beset with inefficient and ineffective marketing approaches, the consumer market is now ripe for the widespread deployment of this approach. We strongly believe that marketing efficiency as well as effectiveness in consumer markets can be greatly increased through the routinization and automation of purchase and consumption. With creativity, imagination, and sound marketing, these arrangements could go considerably beyond "automatic replenishment" and become commonplace in the near future.

The opportunities and pressures that make this an appealing concept have been building for quite some time. Rising incomes, escalating time pressures, and a critical mass of affordable and powerful enabling technologies are driving the trend toward the automation of consumption. The affluent class now represents more than 35 million households out of 110 in the United States. Purchases of so-called luxury goods and services are growing at about four times the rate of overall spending (Silverstein and Fiske 2003). Over 60 percent of women over the age of sixteen

Adapted with permission from *The CRM Project: Defying the Limits*, Montgomery Research, 2000.

and 70 percent of mothers with children under age eighteen worked full-time in 2004, making households more wealthy but time-poor (U.S. Department of Labor 2005).

The automation of consumption can take place directly between consumers and manufacturers for larger purchases, and through intermediaries for smaller purchases. Suppliers of large items or major services will have a great opportunity to become the "one-stop-shop" supplier of choice for an ever-widening array of goods and services.

The automation of consumption, first and foremost, is aimed at simplifying life for buyers as well as sellers. For example, buyers should be freed of the burden of monitoring inventory levels of frequently purchased goods. It is about understanding customers so deeply and thoroughly that marketers can anticipate their needs and wants, often even before the customers themselves are consciously aware of those needs and wants. It reflects a "customer business development" mindset (becoming common in business marketing situations) applied to the consumer market, wherein marketers and consumers continually look for opportunities to elevate the mutual gains from their relationship. It is, in brief, autopilot marketing, in which most human intervention may only be required at take-off (relationship creation) and landing (relationship termination, in the event that it ceases to make economic sense).

Marketing efforts in the past have been inordinately geared to *acquiring* customers, with insufficient attention given to how best to retain and maintain those customers. As a result, most customer–provider relationships are intermittent, stop-and-go affairs. Rather than building on previous interactions, every encounter is treated like a new beginning. It is a well-known principle in physics that it is much harder to get a stationary object to start moving than it is to keep a moving object moving. In other words, "static friction" greatly exceeds "kinetic friction." In most marketing, however, the customer relationship starts from a standstill position every time, and is thus subject to a high level of static friction. Experience curve effects, that is, the benefits of mutual learning, are lacking, since every transaction is similar to the first transaction. The marketer fails to become more efficient and effective in meeting the customer's needs over time; likewise, customers continue to perform like novices in the relationship.

The current buying mode for many customers is "just in case" purchasing; large amounts of opportunistically acquired inventory accumulate in the basement. The automation of consumption will lower systemwide costs and improve value delivery to customers. This should result in higher overall profits; a well-honed approach will lead to large amounts of new value creation generally. Consider the benefits from Baxter's ValueLink system, which delivers hospital supplies directly to nurse stations and operating rooms rather than to a central warehouse. This allows hospitals to convert warehouses into clinical space. Likewise, consumers will be able convert inert storage space into usable living space.

CONFRONTING CUSTOMER CYNICISM

Many marketers view today's customers as increasingly capricious: fickle, cynical, disloyal. Customers have evolved these defense mechanisms as a natural reaction to decades of marketing manipulation, noise, and sheer excess. Through long experience with never-ending promotions and marketing's long history of overpromising and underdelivering, customers have been trained to be highly deal-prone and cynical about marketing claims. They have low and declining brand loyalty, and little tolerance for underperformance. They switch suppliers at the smallest provocation, as evidenced by extremely high churn rates in many industries; in the telecommunications industry, for example, churn rates range from 30 to 50 percent per year in sectors such as cellular telephony and small business long distance service.

Customers today also have more knowledge, and thus power, than ever before. In part, this is due to the sheer availability of more objective information (much of it from new third party providers) than before. It is also due to customer cynicism; lacking trust in marketers, they feel the need to "arm" themselves with as much unbiased information as possible.

To many traditional marketers, with their antagonist view of customers, this knowledge is a threat; it allows customers to win every round, to "get a better deal" with them each time around. For more enlightened marketers, however, knowledgeable customers are an advantage. If a company is confident that it is delivering good quality and value, it can leverage its customers' knowledge and expertise to mutual advantage. Such customers may be more demanding in terms of quality and value, but typically have fewer requirements for customer service and support.

CONSUMER STRESS AND DISTRESS

Our consumption-driven society is taking a heavy toll on many consumers, not because there is too much consumption, but because of the additional burden it places on consumers seeking to make reasonably informed purchase decisions. One of the ironies of how markets have evolved in the past few decades is that even as consumers have been presented with many more choices in the marketplace, the actual differences between the offerings have shrunk. With the widespread adoption of standardized production approaches such as TQM (total quality management) and ISO 9000 (a set of standards for global quality assurance and quality control systems), average product quality has improved, but so has the level of standardization and conformity across products. Even generic products offer good quality and a high level of standardized capabilities. Consumers are thus faced with the prospect of engaging in a great deal of shopping behavior (given the abundance of pseudochoices and seemingly random price differentials across stores and over time) with little incremental value to gain. There is little actual product differentiation (most differentiation today is image-based rather than innovation-based), and almost no customization or personalization in what customers do buy. To make matters worse (for consumers as well as marketers), advertising intensity correlates negatively with real product differentiation, so that the products most often advertised have little meaningful to say.

The result: the true ROI (return on investment) on shopping effort is very low, given the amount of time and physical and mental effort expended and the high level of commoditization in many product categories. The greatest tangible benefit of shopping effort to consumers is usually a defensive one: to ensure that they did not fall victim to opportunistic marketing tactics, and, hopefully, to try and take advantage of some ill-conceived tactics. Many customers also face high opportunity costs for their shopping effort (alternative uses of time to pursue personal as well as professional goals). If such customers forego extensive shopping effort, they risk being victimized by unscrupulous marketers.

No wonder, then, that consumers find many buying situations stressful—cars, groceries, clothing, financial products—and very few enjoyable. Many are paralyzed by simply too much choice—too many cereals, too many clock radios, too many TV channels. As a result, there is also a large body of evidence (e.g., the University of Michigan's Customer Satisfaction Surveys) that overall customer satisfaction is low and declining in many industries. Not surprisingly, customer loyalty levels are also very low, and most customers feel little long-run loyalty to even preferred suppliers.

Any alternative model, such as the automation of consumption, must be highly efficient in its use of *all* resources, not just time. It must also be built on a high level of mutual trust and respect, and the nearly complete absence of opportunistic action by both sides.

SUCCESS FACTORS

Mutual Trust and Respect

The automation of consumption requires that there exists a high level of mutual trust and respect between customers and marketers. Without trust, both sides will withhold information and access that is essential to value-creation. Especially early in a customer relationship, it is extremely important that the marketer strive for "zero defects." This requires investment in capable and reliable information systems, with enough built-in redundancy to ensure that customers get exactly (or more than) what they were promised and what they expect. Once a high level of trust is established, customers will develop a degree of tolerance for occasional, unavoidable lapses in service quality. However, marketers must put in place a "recovery strategy" to deal with these lapses, so that they do not lose the customer, but in fact establish an even higher level of trust. Respect is another important dimension that is almost completely lacking in most marketer–customer relationships. As legendary advertising pioneer David Ogilvy said, "The consumer is not a moron; she is your wife" (1985, p. 170). Unfortunately, few companies show evidence that they respect their customers, and even fewer customers respect the companies they do business with (let alone admire or feel affection for them). Yet, without mutual respect, a beneficial long-term relationship is unlikely to result.

Mutual Learning and Authenticity

Marketers and consumers both have to invest the time and effort needed to increase their knowledge about each other. Training classes for consumers may become commonplace, as they are for business customers today. Ultimately, if customer relationships are to be long, strong, and productive, marketing will need to become humanistically competent as well as technically competent. Consumers want relationships with providers that are authentic and empathetic, a need that grows more important with age. If the promise is the attention of a personal relationship, but the delivery is impersonal, customers will have a hard time feeling a human presence in the relationship and the marketers will be back in the era of transaction marketing and nonexistent "average" consumers.

Ethical Behavior

With the automation of consumption, there may be many possibilities for unethical opportunistic action on both sides that would violate and ultimately destroy the trust between customers and companies. The customer surrenders the right to make ongoing choices, to verify the accuracy of shipments, to ensure pricing fairness. Companies invest upfront for benefits that they expect to receive later. It is an easy but myopic step for either side to take advantage of this for short-term gain.

High Tech—High Touch Customization and Personalization

Today's customers are increasingly heterogeneous; they do not fit into traditional stereotyped categories, and they certainly do not respond to mass market approaches. Marketers must provide customized as well as personalized services to customers. The must also monitor changes in customers' lives to ensure that their services remain relevant and optimized. Along with the use of self-learning expert systems and sophisticated fulfillment systems, marketers must also ensure that there is a human face to their services. The more technology consumers adopt, the more they look to balance this with countervailing human elements. The dehumanizing potential of technology is such that marketers must be very careful. Used correctly, technology can add to rather than detract from human value. Consumers in an automated consumption relationship will not harvest all of their freed-up time for extra work; much of it will be used for meaningful social interaction (rather than anonymous interaction as happens in a supermarket).

Epistemic Value

Like any relationship, one based on the automation of consumption is subject to maturing and the onset of boredom. If the relationship becomes excessively routinized, it will be taken for granted. Marketers must take the lead in revitalizing and dematuring relationships, by understanding consumer variety-seeking behavior. For example, as illustrated in the scenario at the end of the chapter, they can inject elements of surprise into the service.

OVERCOMING INNOVATION RESISTANCE

Consumers everywhere tend to resist change. It is important to understand the psychology of resistance and use this knowledge in the development and promotion of innovations such as the automation of consumption. A failure to understand the psychology of innovation resistance has led to the failure of numerous innovations. The two most useful psychological constructs in understanding the psychology of innovation resistance are: (a) habit toward an existing practice or behavior, and (b) the perceived risks associated with innovation adoption.

The strength of habit associated with an existing practice or behavior is the single most powerful source of resistance to change. Given entrenched habits, individuals are not likely to voluntarily pay attention to innovation communications or try them out. In fact, the perceptual and cognitive mechanisms of such individuals are geared toward preserving the habit. This is because the typical human tendency is to strive for consistency and maintain the status quo rather than to continuously search for and embrace new behaviors (the exception is among true innovators, who are more likely to be social deviants and abnormal in their epistemic drive). In other words, the formation and sustenance of habits is much more prevalent than innovativeness among people.

The habit toward an existing practice includes all the behavioral steps involved in the process of selecting, acquiring, and using an existing alternative. In consumer behavior, it includes all the behavioral acts associated with shopping (time and place choices), procuring (money and effort choices), and consuming (storage, packaging, and serving choices) the product. In other words, habit includes the total behavioral stream as a system rather than just the terminal act.

A second major determinant of innovation resistance is the perception of different risks associated with the adoption of an innovation. There are three major types of risks: (1) aversive physical, social, or economic consequences; (2) performance uncertainty; and (3) perceived side effects associated with the innovation.

In order to implement the major behavioral change that would be required for the automation of consumption, marketers need to devise sophisticated strategies to break existing consumer habits and supplant them with new ones. They also need to alleviate the actual as well as the perceived risks associated with moving to this mode of consumption.

CONCLUSION

The benefits of the automation of consumption are summed up in Mobil's phrase in its advertisements for its Speed Pass service: It's "like buying time without paying for it." The automation of consumption can work with all kinds of products, including commodities. The key is that the *experience* must not be commoditized, even though the core products may well be.

Several objections can be raised about what is described here. First, there is concern that a high level of automation will lead to widespread deskilling and dependence on others rather than self-reliance. Clearly, we have already lost skills that our forefathers used to have, but gained new ones. This is an interesting philosophical issue, but it goes to the heart of this phenomenon: Ricardo's Theory of Comparative Advantage, which is arguably the basis for much of how our economic life is organized. This theory clarifies the benefits of specialization and resource allocation. Ricardo demonstrated not simply that a country should export what it has in abundance and import what it has in scarcity, he showed that it should concentrate its resources on what it does efficiently and trade its surplus for what its neighbor does efficiently. If the neighbor makes a cheaper car, a country's response should not be to impose tariffs on it to protect its own inefficient car industry. Its response should be to buy cars from the neighbor, get out of the car business, and put its own resources to better use (Ricardo 1996).

Second, it is argued that many consumers derive a certain amount of enjoyment and sense of accomplishment by performing tasks such as cooking, yard work and even cleaning. Clearly, for some consumers, these dimensions are important and will outweigh other factors. However, we suggest that many of these automated activities will come back (or already exist) in the form of hobbies, which people will engage in for pleasure rather than out of necessity.

Finally, there is concern expressed about the likely loss of jobs and a decline in competitive intensity. The creation of new jobs and the substitution of some jobs for others are both central characteristics of a competitive economy. "Creative destruction" is far preferable in the long run to a job preservation mind-set, as that can severely impede progress. It can be argued that the likely lowering of competitive intensity is a good thing; there is simply too much frenzied competition in many sectors, with huge amounts of resources deployed simply to counter competitive actions, with little benefit to consumers. The automation of consumption could restore some much-needed stability to business relationships.

Clearly, the automation of consumption is a double-edged sword that could hurt as many marketers as it helps. Only those marketers that are able to make a rational, substantive case to the customer will benefit in a big way. In other words, the adoption of this marketing approach will disproportionately benefit companies with superior offerings, and create a near winner-take-all situation. Building on mutual learning and beneficial lock-in, those companies will enjoy the benefits of customer loyalty and longevity. With little random switching and churn, they will enjoy more predictable revenue streams. The automation of consumption is akin to what Seth Godin has called "subscription marketing," wherein customer revenues become a form of annuity (Godin 1999, p. 102). These companies will also be more profitable since they will lower their marketing costs across the board, and will enjoy the benefits of sharper experience curves with individual customers. Over time, companies will learn how to serve these customers more efficiently and effectively, and individual customers will increase their purchases while placing fewer demands on customer service.

Incremental value must be shared with customers; savvy consumers will demand it. Customers with a high lifetime value to the company will demand and receive special consideration. Currently, investment in customers usually stops after they have become customers, and loyal customers typically subsidize those that are less loyal, as well as the acquisition of new ones. Without being forced, smart companies will proactively invest resources in those relationships with the greatest long-term value.

FUTURE PERFECT: ASSISTED LIVING FOR ALL?

The scenario following ends with a listing of some of the concepts, issues, and technologies that are involved in making the scenario work.

On the morning of October 23, 2015, John A. Consumer woke to the sound and smell of his automatic coffeemaker. After he stumbled into the kitchen, John poured himself a cup of coffee, thinking to himself that some of the oldest conveniences were still the best. Of course, this was no 1990s Mr. Coffee machine; this machine had a large canister of gourmet coffee beans on top, a built-in grinder and was connected to the filtered water supply. It automatically discarded its coffee grounds into the sink disposal. It was, in short, the perfect appliance—effortless, unobtrusive, and completely reliable.

As he opened the fridge, John marveled anew at how it was always well stocked and had just about everything he could want. The thrice-weekly delivery from the Fresh Direct service had replenished his fridge and pantry with fresh bread, milk, produce, and other items the previous day. They had picked up his laundry and delivered his shirts from the previous trip. They had also left some new firewood by the fireplace, and returned his repaired (and polished) shoes.

It had been two years since John had been inside a supermarket; at first, he thought he would miss it (squeezing the tomatoes and all that). But now he never gave it a second thought. Besides, he had never been very good at picking the sweetest honeydew melons or cantaloupes. Now, they were just right every time. And he was actually paying less for his groceries now than he had before. Guess those huge, well-lit, air-conditioned supermarkets cost a lot to run.

In the beginning, John spent about twenty minutes a week placing his online order. As he got more comfortable, though, and as his buying patterns became more discernable to the computer at Fresh Direct, he found that the shopping list offered to him when he first logged on was actually more appealing than what he would have created himself. Gradually, John had found himself making fewer and fewer changes to the list. About a year after he started using the service, John decided to let it go solo. Now he looked forward to the deliveries, knowing that each one always contained two or three surprises that were guaranteed to delight him (if not, he would get his money back, of course). John found that, as a result, he had tried new foods that he never would have thought to try earlier, and liked most of them a lot. Sometimes, it was an exotic fruit, or an unusual kind of cheese, even some new imported beer. Once a month, they even replenished his coffee machine with some great new beans, leaving a little pamphlet about it next to the machine. They did this with all of their "Just for You" selections.

Best of all were the fully prepared meals. John had invited a few friends to come to dinner that night, and he had asked for a meal for six. As he looked at the neatly packed containers and the two bottles of Italian wine, he saw the printed menu that had been sent with the meal. "Rustic Tuscany," it said across the top. John was tempted to open a couple of boxes and take a peek (and perhaps a taste), but he resisted. The price was great—just a little more than it would have cost him just to buy the ingredients. He could have tried to make the meal himself, but the cost of his time (very high) and the value of his cooking expertise (very low) made that an unappetizing proposition.

John took his croissant and coffee into his study, and turned on his computer. As was his habit, he started by checking his e-mail. There was an e-mail from Paul Frederick & Co., informing him that they had selected four new shirts they thought he would like. John looked at the high-resolution images on his screen and liked what he saw. If he did nothing, the shirts would show up in his SmartBox in a couple of days, monogrammed and in his size, of course. The next e-mail was from Jaguar. John's current Jag was coming off lease in a couple of months. The e-mail offered him a great lease rate on the hot new S-class that he knew had a long waiting list. But that was only for first-time buyers. If he wanted the car, they would bring it to his house and take away the old one on the day the lease ended. John was tempted to say "Yes!" on the spot, but reluctantly decided he should think it over a bit. Not that he expected to change his mind . . .

The third e-mail was from Scott Burka over at Delbe Home Services. This was John's favorite service of all. John had never been much of a handyman or a gardener, though he liked living in a big house and enjoyed looking at a well-tended garden as much as anyone else. For a ridiculously low $125 a year, Delbe took over everything to do with the house and the yard. When he had signed up, Scott from Delbe had done a complete inspection of the house, noting down all the makes, models, and condition of his appliances, heating and air conditioning systems, the condition of his carpets, hardwood floors, roof, outside and inside paint, and a dozen other things John did not even know you were supposed to worry about. Delbe then set up a Web page with all of this information, and updated it every time any work was done on the house. John rarely felt the need to go to this other "home" page; still, he had it in his bookmarks, and it was sure nice to know that it was there. Once every couple of months, using his own key, Scott came through and did a quick inspection. He sent service people to the house to take care of problems before John even knew he had them. Best of all, he didn't have to wait around for them to show up. John got a monthly e-mail from Scott updating him on what had been done and what was coming up and the money was paid automatically. The rates were as good as or better than those John would have paid had he dealt directly with the service contractors. In return for steady business, Scott had negotiated lower rates with them. If there was ever a problem, Scott handled it with the service technicians. Scott had also arranged for a cleaning service, and was now looking into offering a bundled cleaning/home maintenance/insurance package that would be like an HMO for the home. John thought that was a great idea and fully expected to sign up when the service was offered. John had raved so often about Delbe's comprehensive services that literally a dozen of his friends were now customers of Delbe's, or were on a waiting list.

The next message was from John's personal financial manager, with a full report on the previous month's activities in his account. John was starting to feel like one of those mega-rich athletes whose financial affairs are completely handled by a management company, and who simply receive a monthly allowance for incidental expenses—except there was no chance that John's money could get sunk into some fly-by-night scam. John was not mega-rich, by any means, though each monthly e-mail provided a gratifying report on his steady progress toward that goal. For a guy who had never quite mastered the art of balancing his checkbook, it was certainly comforting for him to know that all his bills were checked and paid on time. The only time John needed to think about them was when there was something unusual, in which case the item was automatically flagged for his attention. All of his spending was automatically categorized and entered into his Quicken register, and his monthly reports would on occasion point out that he had exceeded his budget in some category or another. Even his tax return was prepared and filed automatically. John's savings were automatically routed into appropriate investments by the "Financial Engines Investment Advisor," a very popular computerized service developed by a Stanford professor who was an economics Nobel laureate. As with every one of John's automated services, he had been assigned a personal advisor who could answer all his questions. As he grew familiar with the services, John found himself calling less frequently, though his all advisors always sent him personalized greetings on his birthday and other occasions.

The last e-mail was from his car. When he bought the car, John knew that it was equipped with a GPS device as well as the ability to send data and e-mail wirelessly, but he hadn't thought much of it. Not anymore. The car had saved him from some sticky situations more than once. John still found it hard to get used to these e-mails, though. The e-mails came infrequently, only when the car had something on its mind. Today, it had several things to convey. First, it reminded him (somewhat plaintively, he thought) that his lease was about to expire, and what it would cost him to buy the car if he wanted to. Second, it reminded him that it was due for an oil change, and that it had already scheduled several possible times with the dealership. John clicked next to the one that worked for him. Finally, the car pointed out that it needed new tires within the next thousand miles, and offered a direct link to Costco with the recommended tire size information already incorporated. With a few clicks, John purchased the tires and set up an installation time to coincide with the oil change.

The holiday season was approaching and John was starting to feel a little tense about all the gifts he still had to buy. But he was trying out a new system that he thought would make life a little easier. A nifty new website (MsManners.com) reminded him of upcoming occasions for giving gifts, and also suggested some ideas for each one. John had gone through a somewhat lengthy interview process when he signed up, and his "agent" knew what he expected to spend on each individual and on a given occasion. It also knew which of the recipients were friends, relatives, or professional contacts. So far, it had worked well; John had been able to send gifts with a single click, selecting from the offered choices and quickly personalizing a message for each. The company used John's personal font to create "handwritten" messages.

With Christmas looming, John thought he would also try out wishlist.com, a universal gift registry that he had been subtly promoting to his nieces, nephews, siblings, and others for several months. Wishlist.com was a universal registry; it allowed *all* people, not just those getting married, to create their own equivalent of a bridal registry. Sure enough, John found that about a dozen of his friends and relatives had in fact signed up. John quickly scanned each person's wish list; he smiled to himself at some of the entries ("Yeah, sure, George, someone's going to buy you a 96" HDTV," he thought to himself), but was able to quickly select items that were in his budget range. On two occasions, he decided to split the cost of an especially large gift with several of his relatives.

John glanced up at the clock. It was only 8:30 A.M.; he still had an hour before he had to make that video conference call to Bucharest. Glancing out the window, John saw a delivery truck pulling away from his driveway—an increasingly familiar sight nowadays. This particular truck was marked FedEx, but John knew that all the major delivery companies now used each other's trucks to deliver packages, so that the FedEx truck contained many packages that had originated with UPS, the U.S. Postal Service, AirBorne, or a variety of other smaller players. It was like completing a long distance phone call; the receiver did not have to be a subscriber of the same company that the sender used.

Putting on his slippers, John went into the garage. A small door in one of the side walls opened directly into his SmartBox, which sat unobtrusively next to his garage; it was even painted a matching color. Punching in his code, he opened the door and entered the small shed. The light went on, and he could see that he had received several packages the previous day, left there by delivery people using a code to enter the SmartBox from the outside. One was from Amazon.com. John had joined their "Must Read" club, though he now downloaded most of his books electronically into his eBook reader. The difference between this and the old "Book of the Month" club was that the book was specifically chosen for him, rather than the same book that was going out to everyone. In the one year he had been a member, John had yet to get a book that he hadn't liked a great deal. He didn't know how they did it, but it sure worked. John also saw a package from drugstore.com, containing some toiletries (they always knew when his blades and shaving cream were running low), a couple of prescription refills (he never had to remember to fill those anymore), and a sixty-day supply of a customized multivitamin his doctor had e-mailed in.

As John shaved and showered, he mused about how his life had become so much less crazed and stressful in the last few years. Gone were the weekly grocery shopping trips, the long lines, handling products a dozen times before he used them, the midnight milk runs. No more marathon bill-paying sessions on the last day of the month; John hadn't written a check in years. No more worrying about balancing the checkbook. No more need to keep track of when the car needed an oil change or new tires (the car "called in" its own service needs, and an e-mail showed up on his computer about when he could bring it in, or have it picked up from the office). Most of all, no more nagging worries about the house; "Do I need to change the air conditioning filter? It is time to service the furnace? Do the gutters need cleaning? Does the lawn need fertilizing? Is that insect damage in the shrubs?" Good old Scott was there to take care of all that.

Thinking back, John found it hard to imagine what life had been like in 2005; it seemed eons ago, a primitive, harried time. Now he had plenty of time to work out, socialize with his friends, even do volunteer work. And yet, he was working as much or more than before, making a lot more money, and enjoying it more as well . . .

Just then, the alarm went off, and John was jolted back into his *real* reality. He was back in 2005, and as he lay in bed thinking about his day, John groaned to himself. The house was a mess, he needed to do a huge grocery shopping trip, the lawn was too long, it was the last day of the month, he had no clean shirts, and several friends were supposed to come to dinner that evening. How was he going to finish that project at work? Shuddering, John pulled the sheet back over his face and shut his eyes tight, hoping to get back to that beautiful dream.

EPILOGUE

In addition to the issues discussed in this chapter, the scenario also illustrates the following:

- Scope-based, one-stop-shop service provision: We will see the emergence of new kinds of intermediaries, who may be described as customer-focused service integrators. These companies will produce very few products or services themselves; their function will be to own and manage the customer relationship, and serve as the value-adding hub around which customers and service providers can interact.
- Responsiveness to special demands as well as routine replenishment: Companies cannot simply optimize for routine replenishment; their systems must be able to effectively respond to special demands.
- Producer economies of scale and the industrialization of service: The automation of consumption can only work if there is net value added. This would happen through the realization of efficiencies by providers that can leverage scale and specialized technologies to deliver higher quality service at lower cost than the alternatives available to the customer.
- Outsourcing of memory functions: Customers need to be relieved of the mental costs of monitoring and scheduling.
- Optimal matching of products and customers: Customers often make suboptimal decisions in selecting products because they lack the time or information to select the right alternative. Automated systems should be able to outperform customers in this regard.
- Mass personalization: Mass customization without personalization is sterile and emotionally uninvolving. Marketers need to be able to offer true personalization.

Everything that is described here is technologically feasible today, and the infrastructure to create and deliver the services exists today or is being developed. Many of the companies mentioned already exist (Fresh Direct, Paul Frederick, Financial Engines, Delbe, Wishlist.com, SmartBox).

The real challenge is customer behavior: how to get consumers to adopt this way of doing business. Besides the obvious benefits to marketers and consumers, there are also benefits to society in the form of greatly reduced marketing noise and wasted efforts. As Don Peppers has said, today's marketing has simply evolved into targeted harassment.

Clearly, the scenario described here applies to certain segments and not to the market as a whole. However, we do believe it will be quite broad-based, and will encompass middle-income consumers as well as high-income consumers. The cost savings that are inherent in this mode of operating (lower marketing costs, greatly reduced inventory levels and the related real estate expenses, better matching of supply and demand) mean that many of these conveniences can be provided at little or no premium compared to traditional ways; in many cases, they will cost less.

Marketing needs to concern itself with larger quality-of-life issues rather than the usual trivialities of cents-off coupons and advertising taglines. The automation of consumption represents one important way for marketing to make a greater positive impact on peoples' lives.

REFERENCES

Godin, Seth (1999), *Permission Marketing: Turning Strangers Into Friends And Friends Into Customers.* New York: Simon & Schuster.

Ogilvy, David (1985), *Ogilvy On Advertising.* New York: Vintage Publishing.

Ricardo, David (1996), *Principles of Political Economy and Taxation.* New York: Prometheus Books (Original work published in 1817).

Silverstein, Michael and Neil Fiske (2003), *Trading Up: The New American Luxury.* New York: Portfolio Publishing.

U.S. Department of Labor (2005), "Women in the Labor Force: A Databook," www.bls.gov/cps/wlf-databook2005.htm (accessed October 2005).

CHAPTER 22

THE MARKETING-IT PARADOX

Interactions from the Customer's Perspective

PIERRE BERTHON AND JOBY JOHN

Information technology (IT) promises to deliver both increased firm efficiencies and customer satisfaction (Day 1992). Yet the paradox is that in recent years, despite accelerated investment in service industries such as banking, both productivity and customer satisfaction have deteriorated (Olazabal 2002). In this chapter we propose a solution to this paradox. We argue that it is *interaction value* that produces customer satisfaction and ultimately competitive advantage, and contend that interaction should be central to any marketing reform.

Interaction is defined as "reciprocal action, or influence of persons or things on each other" (OED 2005). Extending this, we define business interactions as purposeful, contextual exchanges involving two or more parties. Context may include specificity in terms of time, place, or persons, while purpose may include specificity in terms of direction, evaluation, and memory.

If interactions are purposeful, contextual exchanges involving two or more parties, *interaction intensity* represents the *value* of interactions in a marketing exchange. The relationship between interactions and information is pivotal; essentially it is through interactions that information is on the one hand consumed (i.e., existing information utilized) and on the other produced (i.e., new information created). Thus *interactive information intensity* can be defined as the value of interactions that consume and produce information.

The increasing importance of interactions in information-intensive contexts is most evident in marketing, the business function that is central to the interface with the customer. As the opportunities to interact with the customer have increased, so potentially has the interaction intensity or the value of interactions to the customer and the firm. Because information technology can facilitate increasingly synchronized, memorized, and individualized marketing interactions, which if properly managed can result in real-time, intimate conversations between parties (cf. Deighton 1996). Figure 22.1 is a graphic representation of how information technology has changed the type of marketing from broadcast marketing to real-time marketing in the information age.

Information technology increasingly allows the firm to store, access, and process huge amounts of information on customers faster and cheaper than previously possible. Similarly, customers increasingly have access to a greater amount of information on firms. This information is produced and consumed during IT-enabled customer–firm interactions. Thus, firms find themselves looking for decision-making heuristics to guide huge investments in information technology. Often these information technology decisions are made without a clear understanding of how to

Figure 22.1 **Interaction Intensity, Synchronicity, and Marketing**

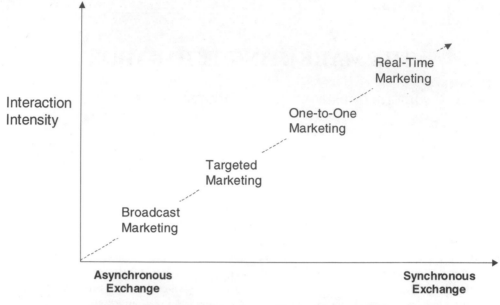

deploy them for maximum returns. For example, traditional "brick and mortar" firms forced to embrace the internet as a new medium find themselves struggling to come to grips with how to incorporate the new technology into their existing way of doing business (*Economist* 2001). The experience of these firms has been less than satisfactory. We suggest that customer-centric firms will be successful in the design and implementation of information technology if they focus on how *interactions* with the customer use and produce information *to add value.*

Information to the firm has two value components: value-in-use and exchange-value (Repo 1986). One or both types of value may be realized through interactions with other parties (i.e., customers, suppliers, and so on). Moreover, interactions can generate *new* information, and thus potential future value or simply "potential-value." The return on investment of information technology is thus inextricably bound to interactions, for it is through interactions that information is applied (value-in-use), exchanged (exchange-value), and generated (potential-value). Overall, the return on investment in IT is the sum of the values that can be generated across a stream of IT-enabled interactions.

Interactions themselves also have two value perspectives: informational-value and customer-value. The former corresponds to the value of the information used and produced in the interaction; the latter, the value that the interaction provides to the customer and thus his or her corresponding value-accrual (current and future monetary streams) to the firm. Thus, in adopting an interaction-intensive perspective, firms need to focus on both customer and informational value. We argue that interaction value assessment needs to be an important input into decisions regarding investments in IT. To do this managers need an in-depth understanding of types of interaction and their value dimensions.

The purpose of this chapter is to add an interaction-intensive complement to the information-intensive narrative, and in doing so enrich our understanding of the challenges and opportunities provided by information technology. We introduce a generic set of concepts about interactions, and focus the insights primarily to the customer-firm dyad. The chapter is set out as follows. First, we explore the relationship between information and interaction intensity. Second, we examine the value dimensions of interactions, and apply this to the interaction of firms and customers. Finally, we present the manager with suggestions on how to increase the value from interactions with customers.

INTERACTIONS AND INFORMATION

As defined earlier, interaction intensity is the value added by interactions along a value chain. It complements Glazer's (1991) definition of information intensity as the value added by information as part of exchange processes. As intimated above, the two concepts are closely related, for it is *through* interactions that information is both used and created.

However, the relationship runs both ways. For, as interactions migrate from the physical to the informational (i.e., from matter-intensive interactions to information-intensive interactions), the potential *cost* of each interaction falls and the potential for *automation* increases to 100 percent. When informational interactions are fully automated, cost tends to zero. Here, we have essentially frictionless interactions, where cost is uncoupled from frequency of interaction. Thus, we have potentially infinite scalability of interaction frequency.

However, as automation is typically adopted asymmetrically between parties, costs also tend to accrue asymmetrically. For example, the cost of sending of junk e-mails is essentially zero to the firm, but far from costless to the consumer. In other instances, benefits of automated interactions to the consumer can outweigh the costs. Thus, in the instance of automated updates on stock prices to a trader, the cost of checking the prices is outweighed by the benefit. This dynamic is explored in more detail later. The point is that interaction intensity in information-intensive environments is a double-edged sword. To be used effectively it needs to be understood.

INTERACTION VALUE DIMENSIONS

We defined "interactions" as purposeful, contextual exchanges involving two or more parties, where context may encompass specificity in terms of time, place, or person(s), and purpose specificity in terms of direction, evaluation, and memory. Thus, value in an interaction is a function of seven components or dimensions, four for context, and three for purpose. They are outlined in detail in Table 22.1. *Context* comprises (1) the currency (time) of the interaction, or how temporally relevant it is; (2) the configuration (place) of the interaction, or how relevant it is to a particular place or setting; (3) the customization (person) of the interaction, or how tailored to a specific individual it is; (4) the communitization (persons) of the interaction, or how personalized it is to a group or collective. *Purpose* comprises (5) the continuation (memory) of the interaction, or the degree to which it utilizes memories of previous interactions; (6) the control (direction) of the interaction, or the extent to which the customer in real time directs the interaction; and (7) the contact or content quality (evaluation) of the interaction. These value dimensions can be applied to both the *form* and the *content* of an interaction, where form can encompass elements of both structure and process.

Each dimension captures a distinctive aspect of interactions and is about a specific type of value that can be derived from an interaction. These dimensions are both independent and combinatory and reflect both the efficiency as well as the effectiveness of the interaction. Thus, it is possible to have anything from a one-way to a seven-way combination of the dimensions.

We may now return to the paradox identified at the start of the chapter—that of decreasing

Table 22.1

Interaction Value Dimensions

Dimension	Definition	Example
Currency	Up-to-period (time [virtual and real] sensitive interaction)	From a computer a consumer request the latest stock price for Apple Computers
Configuration	Up-to-place (space [virtual and real] sensitive interaction)	A consumer requests via mobile phone advice on finding a vegetarian restaurant within walking distance. Using GPS, your position is determined and a list of vegetarian restaurants, their ratings, distances, and the directions transferred to your phone screen
Customization	Up-to-person (individual tailored interaction, over and above time and place)	A tailor adjusts a business suit to the precise measurements of a customer
Communitization	Up-to-party (group sensitive interactions, over and above individual)	When selecting a new hire for a university marketing department, the often disparate wants, needs, and whims of the faculty need to be integrated
Continuation	Up-to-past (long-term/integrative learning interaction—the long-term learning, which integrates past and future in an interaction)	When booking a room at Hilton Heathrow, staff is alerted to the fact that as regular customer, who is asthmatic, you always request a nonsmoking room, with special pillows and bedclothes
Control	Up-to-me (the extent to which the customer—in real time—directs the interaction [this is a function of the flexibility of the interaction design])	You decide to go away for the weekend, and contact your telephone provider to specify that you want all your phone calls diverted to your mobile for two days
Content	Up-to-expectation (the experiential quality of the interaction)	At a top cordon bleu French restaurant that you frequent with your partner, you experience the waiting staff as courteous and unobtrusive

customer satisfaction, coupled with lower labor productivity within banks despite increased investment in IT. Using the interaction value dimensions identified, we can explore whether information technology has been used to add value to bank–consumer interactions:

- *Currency*—technology is supposed to speed up transactions, yet it takes three days for a transfer of funds to take effect; two to three days for a cash deposit made at an ATM to show up in your account; a day or more for a payment made via the Web to show up as paid.
- *Configuration*—technology supposedly makes location insignificant, yet ATMs, branches, and bank websites actually have very different capabilities in terms of service delivery.
- *Customization*—technology makes available customer-specific information, yet frontline staff typically do not recognize the customer or are unable to customize interactions with customers based on a customer's credit risk or value to the bank.
- *Continuity*—technology enables tracking of customer activity, yet if a customer makes regular business trips overseas, banks generally do not adjust their services to offer travelers checks or financial services tailored to the needs of the international business traveler.

- *Control*—technology should add value by putting the consumer in control, yet as many bank customers will testify, technology has often reduced their ability to direct interactions. For example, try closing a bank account online or from an ATM.
- *Contact*—technology is supposed to reduce the heterogeneity of the interaction quality of human-delivered services. Yet dirty, out-of-money, out-of-order ATMs with illegible screens, dodgy keypads, and another customer breathing down your neck all render the interaction experience less than salutary.

The managerial imperative is to design, and deliver, ideally differentiated interactions that are mutually beneficial to both the customer and the firm. To do this, firms will need to explore a number of issues. First, understand the customer's priorities in terms of the value dimensions. Second, identify possible trade-offs between dimensions. Third, identify the benefits of interactions from the firm's perspective. Finally, design and deliver differentiated interactions for which customers will be prepared to pay a premium.

For example, how much value does the customer place on the context of a particular interaction? Is the customer prepared to trade off context for currency? What value does the firm accrue if the interaction is provided? Thus, if the firm can provide an economically viable interaction in a context that adds value to the customer, the firm should consider finding ways to provide that offering. Below, we describe a number of examples of the value of customer–firm interactions in terms of the dimensions delineated in Table 22.1.

FleetBoston instituted the "customer experience crusade" (Hechinger 2001). The firm hired new staff to be stationed in the lobbies of its large-volume banks to serve as "meeter-greeters" assisting customers with their banking problems. Staff in these new positions are trained to anticipate and accost customers who look like they might need help, thereby preempting a potential service failure. Imagine the opportunities to serve clients at these interactions with the help of information technology such as hand-held wireless terminals that could access and conduct cashless transactions on these customers' accounts. The value of the interaction is manifested in its currency, context, and customization.

Alaska Airlines customer service agents enabled by miniature computers and printers approach travelers in front a flight information display and offer to look up their flight status, check them in, and hand them their boarding passes (Carey 1999). Once again the value of the interactions is evident in its currency, context, and customization.

The BBC in its coverage of the 2002 Winter Olympics extended its interactive TV service (Bennion 2002). Consumers could select from multiple simultaneous feeds from Salt Lake City to display up to three live feeds on the screen at once, in addition to up-to-the-minute results, medal tables, and event schedules (currency and customization). Future developments include the storing of preferences and viewing habits so that the service learns and customizes delivery (continuation).

Finally, interactions that are not mutually beneficial should be terminated. For example, the Securities and Exchange Commission forced online brokerages to intervene and disallow investors from day trading if their balances fell below a certain level. The brokerage firm benefits by preventing potential bad debts arising from impending margin calls in a down-market, and customers benefit by not risking their already depleting cash reserves and depreciating equity value.

INTERACTION VALUE

For a manager, the decision whether to place resources into an interaction with the customer will generally depend on the perception of its ultimate (long-term) economic value. The customer evaluates an interaction and determines whether or not to enter into it based on its perceived value to him or her. As discussed, the value perceived in an interaction is manifested in the seven value dimensions of the interaction. The costs incurred by the customer in time, effort, and money are weighed against the benefits derived along the seven value dimensions of the interaction.

The total value of a set of interactions can be seen as a function of the number of interactions between parties over a period. Thus, the value of a set of interactions is the sum of the benefit of all interactions (to the firm or customer) minus the sum of the cost of all interactions (to the firm or customer). The value of a set of interactions can also be seen as the product of the number of interactions and the net average benefit of interaction and average cost of interaction.

For this analysis, it can be observed that the value of a set of interactions can be increased in one of three ways: First, by increasing the value of each interaction (holding frequency constant). Second, by increasing the frequency of interaction (holding the value of each interaction constant). Third, by increasing both the value and the frequency of each interaction. Of course, the challenge is that value and frequency can be inversely related. In some cases, the value increases with frequency while in others value might decrease with frequency. There are also examples where the value is independent of frequency.

CONCLUSIONS AND IMPLICATIONS

With information technology, we are able to interact with each other in a multitude of different new ways. Technology in this information age has actually changed services and created new ones. Essentially, in a service economy the core difference compared to the manufacturing economy is the extent and variety of interaction between provider and customer. Indeed, we argue that the paradox of information technology actually decreasing customer satisfaction can be explained by a lack of focus and understanding of customer interactions. Managers need to take the customer-centric view in analyzing the value of the interactions that are made possible with information technology.

Information technology has increased not just the variety of modes of interactions, but also the frequency of interactions. Increasing the frequency of the interactions does not necessarily increase value or satisfaction. Therefore, we argue that an analysis of the relationship between the frequency and the value of the interaction completes the exercise. Is the value of the interaction directly and not inversely proportionate to the frequency of the interaction?

With this customer-centric view that focuses on the value of customer interactions, managers will find themselves using a structured approach in making information technology decisions. The approach we have outlined and discussed clearly applies to all business interactions, both internal and external, as well as upstream and downstream. We have chosen to focus on a specific type of interaction, the customer–firm interaction. We have also used more information technology-enabled interactions to allow the reader to apply the thinking to the information age context. We need to reiterate that ultimately the focus is the interaction and the information that is generated and used in that interaction, whether enabled by information technology or not.

REFERENCES

Bennion, Jackie (2002), "BBC Put Viewers in the Lung Seat," *Wired,* February 22, 129.

Carey, Susan (1999), "New Gizmos May Zip Travelers Through Airport Lines," *Wall Street Journal,* January 4, A13.

Day, George S. (1992), "Continuous Learning About Markets," *Strategy and Leadership,* 20 (September/August), 47.

Deighton, John (1996), "The Future of Interactive Marketing," *Harvard Business Review,* 74 (November–December), 151–62.

Economist (2001), "Older, Wiser, Webbier," June 28, 45–46.

Glazer, Rashi (1991), "Marketing in an Information Intensive Environment: Strategic Implications of Knowledge as an Asset," *Journal of Marketing,* 55 (October), 1–19.

Hechinger, John (2001), "FleetBoston Financial Shifts Focus From Deals to Clients," *Wall Street Journal,* May 18, B4.

OED (2005), *Oxford English Dictionary.* Oxford: Oxford University Press.

Olazabal, Nedda G. (2002), "Banking the IT Paradox," *McKinsey Quarterly,* 1, 47–51.

Repo, A. (1986), "The Dual Approach to the Value of Information: An Appraisal of Use and Exchange Values," *Information Processing and Management,* 22 (5), 373–83.

PART 5

MARKETING AND ITS STAKEHOLDERS

While the previous section focused on how to improve marketing by focusing on customers, this section includes marketing scholars' views on both the need and the desirability of taking a multiple stakeholder perspective on marketing. Stakeholders include employees, investors, suppliers, and society at large, especially the underprivileged segments of society (lately referred to as the "bottom of the pyramid," a phrase coined by C.K. Prahalad).

Lemon and Seiders argue that current marketing practice is skewed toward a short-term orientation and a relatively narrow concept of the customer. They suggest taking a longer time horizon and a broader view of the customer to encompass other stakeholders in marketing practice. For example, broadening from the core customer orientation to augmented customer orientation, it is possible to include the impact of marketing on nontargeted customer, unqualified customer, and future potential customer segments. Similarly, taking a long-term viewpoint, marketing practice can be assessed and measured in terms of its unintended consequences. The rewards for anticipating and avoiding the negative unintended consequences of market impacts are a function of controlling the risk. To be viewed as a good citizen is argued to have inherent, though somewhat intangible, rewards, the most apparent of which is the strengthening of brand equity. Lemon and Seiders lament the tyranny of current marketing metrics that encourage a short-term and narrow orientation. They suggest how value equity, brand equity, and relationship equity can be measured in ways that take into account a longer-term and augmented definition of customer orientation.

Russ Belk suggests that we need to focus on the vast number of consumers, especially in Africa and Asia, who have not benefited from globalization. While consumer desire has been democratized, especially after the collapse of communism and the spread of free market democracy, the growing inequality makes the global standard package of consumer goods no more than an impossible dream for the majority of the world's population. He suggests that we need to focus on affordability and accessibility of products and services to "bottom of the pyramid" markets. Furthermore, we must stimulate the entrepreneurial skills of the poor through microlending to eradicate poverty on a global basis. Pressure must be brought to bear to reorganize world trade and financial institutions to better represent the have-nots of the world. Global junk foods should be restrained from out-promoting more nutritious local foods. Dumping of unsafe products like high-nicotine cigarettes should be as difficult in the less affluent world as it is in the more affluent world.

Douglas and Craig also focus on international marketing. They strongly recommend that we must make marketing less U.S. centric. This can be done by conducting more research in other countries; testing the validity of U.S.-based theories and models in other countries; conducting what they call "emic" studies (focusing research on the unique characteristics of each country); developing multicountry research teams; understanding the role of marketing in transitional economies; and examining the relevance and role of marketing in emerging markets.

Chipp, Hoenig, and Nel also provide similar views. They focus on South Africa and suggest how marketers there and in other developing countries can avoid some of the mistakes made in developed countries.

Finally, Stringfellow and Jap suggest how marketing can regain its strategic importance in business by doing more internal marketing. It should break down the walls surrounding the marketing fortress and venture into other functional areas.

CHAPTER 23

MAKING MARKETING ACCOUNTABLE

A Broader View

? 6 ?

KATHERINE N. LEMON AND KATHLEEN SEIDERS

Marketing practice has long been skewed toward a short-term orientation and a relatively narrow concept of *customer*, with a focus on the immediate: immediate results and the immediately reachable customer. As marketers, we have adopted innovative technologies and acquired new capabilities that enable us to be even more productive in the short-term and more attuned to increasingly narrow customer markets. For example, we can deliver more effective promotions that produce faster and more formidable spikes in sales; we can collect finer information that allows us to segment, target, and execute at the most micro level.

Although we are more progressive and sophisticated marketers, our generally short-term, narrow customer orientation has interfered with our ability to consider and evaluate important marketing impacts that are widely felt over time. The marketing practices of a variety of industries —from pharmaceuticals to food—are justly criticized for their negative effects on the natural environment, population-wide health, and global culture. Despite the fact that such impacts may manifest as unforeseen and unintended consequences of otherwise compelling business decisions, accountability still falls to us.

The implications of a short-term perspective and narrow stakeholder view, as business behaviors, have been recognized in the literature for some time. Driven by emphasis on quarterly financial results, a short-term focus has characterized the behavior of public corporate firms for decades (Piety 2004). Corporate reward and compensation systems flow from financial metrics that evaluate markets in terms of periodic market share, revenue, earnings, share price, and rate of growth. Excessive emphasis on short-term performance has been linked to injudicious cuts in capital investment, research and development, pension funds, and such events as the Enron debacle (Deakin and Konzelmann 2003; Harrison and Fiet 1999). Collingwood (2001) argues that the *earnings game*—managing quarterly earnings for the investment community—skews corporate decision making and offers no true or enduring advantage to financial markets.

The flaws inherent in a narrow stakeholder perspective also have been compellingly articulated. Stakeholder theory, which argues that firms are responsible to multiple constituencies, has become institutionalized in the strategic management literature (see Freeman 1984). It is stakeholders, both as traditionally defined (i.e., customers, stockholders, suppliers, and employees) and more broadly defined (i.e., local communities, nonprofit organizations, and governments) that determine corporate reputation, of which corporate responsibility is one measure (Murphy and Laczniak 2006; Waddock 2006). Stakeholder theory links to the issue of short-term orientation, as decisions that are made to satisfy analysts' financial performance demands may please

Figure 23.1   **The Augmented Customer Orientation Matrix**

Customer Orientation

	Core	*Augmented*
Long	Some Relationship-Based and B2B Firms	Few Firms
Short	All Corporate Firms and Most Organizations	Nonprofit Organizations

Time Horizon for Marketing Impacts

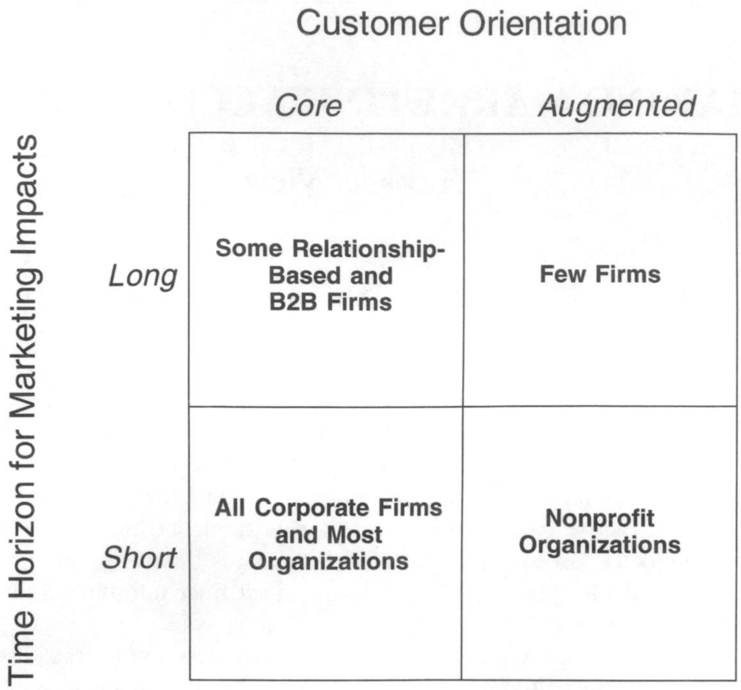

the market but have strongly negative consequences for various stakeholder groups (Post, Preston, and Sachs 2002). While responsibility management has become more systematic within organizations, "the borders of responsibility are difficult to define" (Waddock 2004, p. 26).

Just as stakeholder theory argues the need to balance the requirements and demands of various constituent groups, marketing practice would benefit from a more broadly defined concept of customer. Figure 23.1, the Augmented Customer Orientation Matrix, illustrates how the two dimensions of time horizon and breadth of customer focus interact to influence marketing decisions and reflect a firm's core marketing values.

The vertical axis is easily interpretable, as marketing impacts can be viewed with a *short time horizon*—the immediate influence of marketing actions—or a *long time horizon*—influence that becomes visible only in some mid- or longer-term future. The horizontal axis is somewhat more complex: the term *core customer orientation* identifies normal practice where the overwhelming emphasis is on the primary, qualified target customer. *Augmented customer orientation* identifies a perspective in which an organization considers the effects of its marketing practice on a broader set of constituencies, including nontargeted customers, unqualified customers, and future potential customer segments. In this chapter, we explore approaches by which organizations can begin to consider the short-term and long-term effects of their marketing actions on both core customers and the currently unintended, or "augmented customers."

Most companies' marketing practices and values are positioned in the lower left area of the matrix, with a short time horizon for marketing impacts and a core (narrow) customer orientation. Objectives are driven by targets based on short-term metrics and the need for immediate results; if firms don't succeed in this condition, they likely will not survive. Some organizations extend beyond this baseline area and also operate in other conditions. In industries where customer lifetime value is a dominant driver, that is, some business-to-business and relationship-based services, firms are compelled to also operate in the upper left condition, with a core customer orientation but with attention to the longer-term impacts of their marketing on existing customers.

The lower right area, where the time horizon is short and customer focus is augmented, is not well occupied within the corporate sector. Nonprofit organizations, however, have short-term financial constraints but must operate with an augmented customer orientation in their need to reach groups beyond their core target of contributors. In the upper right area, where the time horizon for marketing impacts is long and the customer orientation is augmented, the population of firms and other organizations is very sparse. Operating in this condition involves learning to evaluate and value products and services for their long-term marketing impacts, and recalibrating customer orientation to include strategies designed for more remote and lesser-known customer groups. Although departing from the traditional marketing mindset, firms that make this investment could better anticipate and control the unintended negative consequences of their marketing actions.

THE QUESTION OF UNINTENDED CONSEQUENCES

Although managers are criticized for marketing's unintended consequences, we suggest that these impacts are often triggered by inadequate assessment of potential future scenarios. The probability of unintended consequences is unrecognized by firms and their marketing managers for a variety of reasons, and it is useful to consider the costs and rewards of adopting a longer-term, augmented customer view of marketing impacts. On the cost side, there is the potential expense of resolving legal disputes, the threat of negative publicity, and the uncertainty and risk of being dependent on a public relations solution. (However, putting controversial scenarios to rest can be managed, and the cost of public, political, and policy reactions lessens considerably if all companies in the industry follow similar practices.) A different set of costs would be represented by firm resources that would be needed to expand time horizon and customer orientation priorities.

The rewards for anticipating and avoiding the negative unintended consequences of marketing impacts are a function of controlling the risk. To be viewed as a *good citizen* is argued to have inherent though somewhat intangible rewards, the most apparent of which is the strengthening of brand equity. Of course, many firms seek more straightforward ways of building brand equity through good citizen behavior. Cause marketing, alliances with nonprofits, direct corporate philanthropy, corporate-named activist foundations, and programs that encourage employees to donate time to charitable organizations all are more easily realized alternatives. While we acknowledge that these are important activities that influence brand equity and corporate reputation, they do not address a firm's core business activities and the consequences of its marketing actions.

Beyond the costs and rewards, we recognize the extreme difficulty managers face in attempting to assess their organization's marketing impacts. As Freeman (1984) notes, the costs and benefits of some actions—such as those that prevent disasters—may be invisible and ignored by organizational reward systems. Moreover, Drumwright and Murphy (2004) report that the least proximate types of problems—those that occur at the aggregate level of society and relate to unintended consequences—are the most characterized by moral myopia. This suggests that marketers will need an organizational infrastructure as well as systematic processes to bring such problems into better focus.

Perhaps most challenging is the fact that the most far-reaching negative impacts occur at the industry level, for example, the computer industry's rapidly obsolete products have exacerbated ecological waste problems and fast food chains have long promoted high-fat, high-caloric diets that have contributed to widespread obesity. While some firms send the message that they are more virtuous than their competitors, and the largest companies are targets for greater criticism, these essentially are industry-wide issues: unintended consequences produced by ingrained and even core industry practices, perpetuated by intense competition and the low likelihood that the cooperation needed to address a socially important issue will emerge.

CURRENT MODELS AND METRICS ENCOURAGE A NARROW VIEW

Current marketing approaches and market forces almost push firms into a short-term, core customer view. In particular, the metrics by which firm success is measured are almost all short-term focused. In addition, reward structures within firms (and at the market level) encourage short-term thinking and narrow customer focus. Finally, it is difficult for firms to assess the effects of their marketing actions on the augmented customer.

In terms of metrics, consider the tools crucial in today's measurement-hungry business culture. Current sales, current profit, and market share are tracked not only quarterly, but monthly, weekly, and even daily in most firms. This extreme focus on short-term metrics almost *requires* firms to take a short-term view of their marketing efforts. Reward systems at the firm level encourage this short-term focus. Within most firms, individuals responsible for marketing strategies and implementations often change positions every 18 to 24 months. For example, the average tenure for chief marketing officers at the top one hundred branded companies is 22.9 months, compared to 53.8 months on average for chief executive officers (Booker 2004). Informal discussions with marketing executives in many *Fortune* 500 firms suggest that this tenure is typical throughout marketing organizations. Marketing managers often begin a new job, develop an extensive marketing strategy (e.g., for a new product, service, or campaign), and then move on to another position before the strategy is implemented or evaluated.[1] Given the short tenure in each position, with the goal of promotion in mind, individuals are not rewarded for taking a long-term perspective in terms of marketing strategy.

Market-level reward systems also encourage short-term focus. Public firms must consider the effects of their actions on stock price. Currently, short-term metrics and results significantly influence investors and the value of the firm. In addition, a focus on the core customer (rather than a broader view) may also encourage short-term growth. Taken together, the firm's perceived need for short-term positive results and demonstrated, continued growth—in order to satisfy the investment community—leads to firms focusing their efforts in the lower left quadrant of the Augmented Customer Orientation Matrix.

Firms are also hampered in their ability to take a broader customer view by difficulties in evaluating the effects of marketing activities on unintended audiences. How does one assess the positive or negative impact of an advertisement or new product offering on the augmented customer? Current metrics and approaches do not provide an adequate approach for measuring these effects.

CONSIDERING THE LONG-TERM AND AUGMENTED CUSTOMER VIEW: NEW APPROACHES

Our goal in this chapter is to suggest some ways in which marketing executives can begin to move toward consideration of a longer-term view of marketing's effects and consider the broader effects of marketing on unintended consumers. In particular, we believe that firms can move in these directions by adopting changes in terms of metrics, strategy, and marketing models.

New marketing metrics that take a longer-term view have begun to have a significant impact on marketing. In particular, many firms are beginning to consider customer lifetime value as a crucial metric when evaluating marketing actions (Gupta and Lehmann 2005; Rust, Lemon, and Zeithaml 2004). Given that a firm's customers represent critical assets, measuring customer lifetime value and customer equity (both long-term, forward-looking measures) is becoming as important as measuring current sales and market share. In addition, firms should also lengthen the time horizon for evaluating the effects of marketing efforts. For example, firms should consider lagged effects of marketing actions (price changes, advertising, new product launch) on performance, as well as current effects. Finally, it is not sufficient to incorporate new measurements. Reward systems must also be updated to include these metrics. Two firms that have incorporated customer lifetime value metrics into their reward systems are Vanguard and Harrah's (Lal and Carrolo 2001; Quelch and Knoop 2003). Their marketing evaluation systems enable them to assess and reward performance based upon changes in customer retention and customer lifetime value.

Strategically, firms can broaden their perspective in at least two ways. First, in strategy development, new models enable the firm to consider the effects of marketing actions on these longer-term metrics (Rust et al. 2004; Venkatesan and Kumar 2004). Second, in customer selection and strategy development, firms should consider the augmented customer view, not just a core customer view. Firms should try to envision the effects of their strategic decisions (short-term and long-term) on nontargeted customers, unqualified customers, and future potential customer segments. This broader view may enable the firm to uncover opportunities or threats from the marketplace much earlier than if they focus more narrowly.

New models may guide firms as they move toward a long-term, augmented customer view. In particular, the customer equity framework (Rust, Zeithaml, and Lemon 2000) may prove a starting point, as it offers a customer-focused framework with a long-term perspective. The customer equity approach suggests that customer equity, defined as "the total of the discounted lifetime values summed over all of the firm's current and future customers" (Rust et al. 2004, p. 110), should be the key metric to evaluate marketing actions. In addition, the approach suggests that there are three key drivers of customer equity, and that, broadly, all marketing actions will fall under one of the three drivers: value equity (objective evaluation aspects such as quality, price, convenience), brand equity (subjective evaluation aspects such as brand awareness, brand attitude, and brand ethics) and relationship equity (aspects that increase customer switching costs, such as loyalty programs, customization and customer knowledge, and salesperson relationships). Rust et al.'s (2000) customer equity approach can be seen in Figure 23.2.

In applying the broader view advocated in this chapter, we can consider which drivers and subdrivers may be associated with more positive long-term consequences and a better consideration of multiple constituencies. For example, under value equity, consider each of the subdrivers: quality, price, and convenience. Aspects of quality that have broader implications include the impact of the firm and its products and services on the environment (e.g., recycled materials, fuel efficiency, pollution, product disposal costs), on individuals (e.g., organic food options, pharmaceutical side effects), and ultimately on societies (e.g., exporting culture through entertainment, influencing developing economies through the introduction of sustainable or unsustainable new technologies). In terms of convenience and price, location and attributes of distribution may influence the effect of a marketing strategy on both intended and unintended audiences. For example, recent turmoil in the United States over whether or not to allow individuals (or states) to reimport pharmaceuticals from Canada has implications for distribution and pricing (Anonymous 2005). The fallout from this issue could have substantial effects on pharmaceutical firms' pricing practices globally, and will have significant consequences on the ability of individuals in the affected countries to acquire these medications.

Figure 23.2 **The Customer Equity Framework**

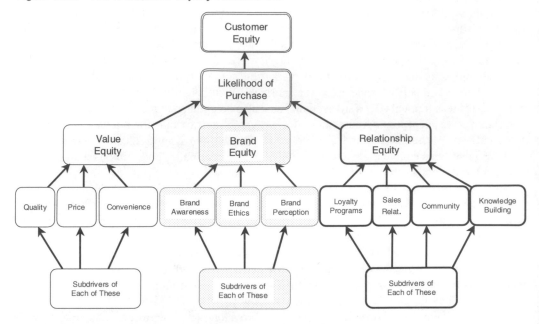

Sources: Based on Rust et al. 2004 and Rust et al. 2000.

Brand equity offers substantial opportunity for the firm to broaden its view. Specifically, recent research has suggested that customers' perceptions of firms' corporate citizenship can influence customer equity (Rust et al. 2004). This suggests that, by engaging in actions that have a positive effect on the community, firms can improve long-term performance. Second, firms should consider the long-term effects of their actions on brand perceptions. Poor short-term decisions (for example, potentially offensive advertising, ethical breaches, or rushing products to market) may have lasting effects on customers' perceptions of the brand. Finally, firms may find opportunities to build brand awareness among constituencies that are outside their core customer segments. This brand awareness may create opportunities for future brand, product, or market extensions.

Relationship equity focuses on the firm's direct relationship with its customers. Firms should consider the long-term effects of any changes that may affect customer perceptions of this relationship. For example, reorganizations that move sales or service personnel from one account to another may have negative, long-term effects on customer relationships. Additionally, firms should consider the long-term consequences of outsourcing aspects of customer–firm interaction, such as customer service, unless they can ensure the quality of the outsourced resource. On the positive side, firms can build communities of customers (consider Harley-Davidson's Harley Owners Groups, for example). These communities should provide a long-term positive return for the firm, and may also lead to new opportunities in untapped customer segments.

In the limited space available, we have tried to provide a short overview of how a broad return on a marketing model, such as the customer equity framework, can provide a starting point for firms to move toward a long-term, augmented customer view. Other emerging models may also be helpful for firms moving in this direction. For example, Bhattacharya and Sen's (2004) model, which investigates how consumers respond to firms' corporate social initiatives, provides insight into these issues as well.

NEXT STEPS

Moving forward, we see a need for the development of marketing models that evolve past the consideration of the core customer view—that begin to consider the augmented customer view. In particular, such models could investigate the effects of marketing actions on the firm's (and the broader community's) social (Coleman 1990; Lin 2001) or intellectual capital. In terms of social capital, defined as "resources embedded in a social structure than are accessed and/or mobilized in purposive action" (Lin 2001, p. 29), firms should consider how their marketing actions enhance or diminish the level of social capital in the communities they influence. For example, Saxton and Benson (2005) show a strong relationship between the number of nonprofits in a country and social capital. This suggests that increasing social capital may have far-reaching effects on a much broader set of consumers. In terms of intellectual capital, typically defined as the sum of all knowledge firms utilize for competitive advantage (Nahapiet and Ghoshal 1998; Subramaniam and Youndt 2005), firms could also measure the effects of their marketing actions on the intellectual capital of the broader community. Cardy (2001) suggests initial steps toward this approach. He builds upon the customer equity framework discussed above, and suggests that firms should evaluate the effects of human resources actions on "employee equity" with the underlying metric of employee lifetime value (i.e., employee retention and loyalty).

These suggestions require substantial research by the academic community and significant investments on the part of firms before they can truly be implemented. What, then, can firms do now to broaden their perspective, moving toward a long-term, augmented customer view? First, firms can evaluate their metrics. Shifting toward long-term metrics, or at least including such metrics in overall measurement and evaluation approaches is a significant first step. Second, firms should examine specific drivers or subdrivers of customer equity—drivers that firms can influence, drivers that will have effects on the augmented customer, and drivers that are likely to have effects in the long-term. Third, firms can include a section in their strategic plan that examines the effects of marketing strategies on nontargeted customer segments. It would be relatively straightforward for most firms to implement these three actions. This would result in greatly expanded horizons for the firm, and a significant shift up and to the right in the Augmented Customer Orientation Matrix. Why should firms take these actions? We propose that firms that are early movers in considering the long-term and taking an augmented view of the customer will see emerging trends first, will envision new opportunities earlier than rivals, and will gain and maintain substantial competitive advantage.

NOTE

1. These ideas based upon the authors' informal conversations with individuals at several firms in many industries, including consumer packaged goods, business-to-business manufacturing, high technology, and pharmaceuticals.

References

Anonymous (2005), "Cross-border Headache," *Economist*, January 15, 36.

Bhattacharya, C.B. and Sankar Sen (2004), "Doing Better at Doing Good: When, Why and How Consumers Respond to Corporate Social Initiatives," *California Management Review*, 47 (Fall), 9–24.

Booker, Ellis (2004), "'Accountability': the CMO's Watchword," *B to B*, 89 (November), 8–10.

Cardy, Robert L. (2001), "Employees as Customers?" *Marketing Management*, 10 (September/October), 12–13.

Coleman, J.S. (1990) *Foundations of Social Theory*. Cambridge, MA: Belknap Press.

Collingwood (2001), "The Earnings Game," *Harvard Business Review*, 79 (June), 65–73.

Deakin, Simon and Suzanne J. Konzelmann (2003), "After Enron: An Age of Enlightenment," *Organization*, 10 (August), 583–88.

Drumwright, Minette E. and Patrick E. Murphy (2004), "How Advertising Practitioners View Ethics," *Journal of Advertising*, 3 (Summer), 7–24.

Freeman, R. Edward (1984), *Strategic Management: A Stakeholder Approach*. London: Pitman Books Limited.

Gupta, Sunil and Donald Lehmann (2005), *Managing Customers as Investments: The Strategic Value of Customers in the Long Run*. Philadelphia: Wharton School Publishing.

Harrison, Jeffrey S. and James O. Fiet (1999), "New CEOs Pursue their Own Self-Interests by Sacrificing Stakeholder Value," *Journal of Business Ethics*, 19 (April), 301–309.

Lal, Rajiv and Patricia Martone Carrolo (2001), "Harrah's Entertainment, Inc.," Harvard Business School Publishing Case Number 9-502-011. Boston: Harvard Business School Publishing.

Lin, N. (2001), *Social Capital*. Cambridge, UK: Cambridge University Press.

Murphy, Patrick E. and Gene R. Laczniak (2006), *Marketing Ethics*. Upper Saddle River, NJ: Pearson Prentice Hall.

Nahapiet, J. and S. Ghoshal (1998), "Social Capital, Intellectual Capital, and the Organizational Advantage," *Academy of Management Review*, 23 (April), 242–66.

Piety, M.G. (2004), "The Long-Term: Capitalism and Culture in the New Millennium," *Journal of Business Ethics*, 51 (May), 103–119.

Post, James E., Lee E. Preston, and Sybille Sachs (2002), "Managing the Extended Enterprise: The New Stakeholder View," *California Management Review*, 45 (Fall), 6–29.

Quelch, John and Carin-Isabell Knoop (2003), "Marketing at the Vanguard Group," Harvard Business School Publishing Case Number 9-504-001. Boston: Harvard Business School Publishing.

Rust, Roland T., Katherine N. Lemon, and Valarie A. Zeithaml (2004), "Return on Marketing: Using Customer Equity to Focus Marketing Strategy," *Journal of Marketing*, 68 (January), 109–27.

———, Valarie A. Zeithaml and Katherine N. Lemon (2000), *Driving Customer Equity: How Customer Lifetime Value Is Reshaping Corporate Strategy*. New York: The Free Press.

Saxton, Gregory D. and Michelle A. Benson (2005), "Social Capital and the Growth of the Nonprofit Sector," *Social Science Quarterly*, 86 (March), 16–35.

Subramaniam, Mohan and Mark A. Youndt (2005), "The Influence of Intellectual Capital on the Types of Innovative Capabilities," *Academy of Management Journal* 48 (June), 450–63.

Venkatesan, Rajkumar and V. Kumar (2004), "A Customer Lifetime Value Framework for Customer Selection and Resource Allocation Strategy," *Journal of Marketing*, 68 (Fall), 106–25.

Waddock, Sandra (2004), "Parallel Universes: Companies, Academics, and the Progress of Corporate Citizenship," *Business and Society Review*, 109 (Spring), 5–42.

——— (2006), *Leading Corporate Citizens: Vision, Values, Value Added*. Irwin, NY: McGraw-Hill.

CHAPTER 24

OUT OF SIGHT AND OUT OF OUR MINDS

What of Those Left Behind by Globalism?

RUSSELL BELK

As was once true of the British Empire, the sun never sets on McDonald's, Microsoft, or Mickey Mouse. And as so many adventure movies set in the colonial era put it, the natives are getting restless. The agitated natives in the current era of global marketing are not only those who have had too much of the neocolonialist exploits of our multinational corporations, but also those who have had too little of the benefits of globalism, both as producers and as consumers. This chapter is about these latter-day left-outs who live in parts of the world or parts of our own cities that are largely undiscovered lands for the current captains of postindustrial industry and other sailors of the seas of globalism.

It is true that the globe is shrinking. Faster travel and faster communications make the once distant and mysterious native more and more accessible. Yet there is an asymmetry to this accessibility. For those of us in the more affluent world, it is relatively easy to tap into global flows of finance, ideologies, technology, people, and media (Appadurai 1996) as well as global flows of consumption (Ger and Belk 1996). We can buy Nikes made in Vietnam, hire Mexican *maquila* workers, listen to music from Mozambique, invest in Colombian coffee futures, and vacation in Bermuda. We can use a computer with chips from China and software with source code from India to access the Internet so we can follow our favorite Russian tennis star. As the last examples suggest, some of those in the less-affluent world participate in global flows as well, but most often as sellers of commodities (including their labor and skills), rather than as full-fledged consumers, much less as multinational marketers. They have neither the access nor the means to afford most of the glittering consumer goods of the world's economy, even when they help make them. Thus the village women, or *dagongmei,* drawn to work and live in the factories of Chinese Special Economic Zone cities, cannot afford to buy the clothes they make for the export market (Ngal 2003). Consumption for them is like it is for someone serving a life sentence in prison. The global images of consumers that they see on television and in magazines may as well depict life-forms in a different galaxy. Nevertheless, as Stiglitz (2003) pointed out, even though a low-paying job in a Nike factory seems like exploitation to many in the West, it may still be far better than staying on the farm and growing rice. It offers something that at least hints at participation in the global consumer village that they now know is out there. Their consumption may involve only a tube of lipstick, a pair of jeans, or a fashion magazine, but it gives them the illusion that they are on the path to becoming a part of the global society of consumption (Belk 1999; Canclini 2001; Ong 1987).

Much of Asia has benefited from globalism, and the new wealth and opportunities it has generated are slowly trickling down and making many Asian poor less poor. Even though many Asians are becoming better able to participate in global consumer culture, this is not the case in sub-Saharan Africa, much of South America, and many other impoverished nations where globalism has made things worse rather than better. Compared to the late 1970s, twenty countries in sub-Saharan Africa now have lower real per capita incomes (Giddens 2003). And despite world yearly economic growth of 2.5 percent throughout the 1990s, the number of people living on less than US$2 a day grew by nearly one hundred million (World Bank 2000). As this paradox of economic statistics implies, the gap between the rich and the poor of the world is growing ever larger. Coupled with the widened window on the world opened by global media networks and expanded telecommunication technologies, one predictable result is the growing envy, resentment, and hatred of the haves by the have-nots of the globe. Amy Chua's (2003) provocative contention is that since the demise of communism, the export of free market democracy together with growing gaps between the rich and the poor, which often divide along ethnic and religious lines, have propelled us into a state of growing violence, warfare, and terrorism. This is true not only between nations but within nations as well. Consumer desire has been democratized while growing inequality makes the global standard package of consumer goods no more than an impossible dream for the majority of the world's population. And the natives are indeed growing restless.

WHAT'S WRONG WITH GLOBALISM?

Globalism and globalization are on the lips of many people these days and have become a topic of considerable interest in a variety of disciplines. There are many takes on globalism, some of which are positive, but most of which are negative or mixed. Initial fears that globalization would destroy cultures and homogenize the world have largely been dismissed as glocalization, hybridization, or creolization are accepted as more accurate depictions of the results of increased global marketing (Featherstone 1990; Ritzer 2004; Robertson 1992). This does not mean that globalization is not contentious or troublesome. Samuel Huntington (1993) sees it leading to a clash of civilizations that he characterizes as the West versus the rest. Benjamin Barber (1995) viewed globalism as promoting a new tribalism that he labeled "Jihad versus McWorld." Stiglitz (2003) sees the global economic policies enacted by the World Bank and the International Monetary Fund (IMF) as bankrupting the less-affluent world for the benefit of the more-affluent world. Thomas Friedman (2000, 2005) offers one of the few positive interpretations, celebrating globalization as liberating, empowering, and peace-promoting. No two nations with a McDonald's or that are part of the same global supply chain have ever gone to war or ever will, he suggests. Others have focused on such phenomena as global tourism (Urry 1990), cosmopolitanism (Breckenridge et al. 2002), global popular culture (Rollin 1989), and the collapse of time and space in global postmodernity (Featherstone and Lash 1999; Harvey 2000). The present treatment is narrower than any of these. It focuses on the global marketing organization and the global brand.

Protests at Seattle, Davos, Cancun, and elsewhere at meetings of the World Bank, the International Monetary Fund, the World Trade Organization (WTO), and the G7/G8 are one indication that all is not well in the global marketplace. It is significant that visible targets of the protestors have included prominent retail brands like Starbucks, McDonald's, the Gap, and Nike. While the protestors have multiple agendas, most are not against globalization per se. They instead advocate a more equitable, humane, and environmentally sustainable globalization that benefits the people and places that have been left out and left behind or whose condition has been substantially worsened by globalization (e.g., Danaher and Burbach 2000; Held and McGrew 2002;

Klein 1999, 2002; Thomas 2000; Wallach and Sforza 1999). The most salient criticisms from a marketing perspective are Naomi Klein's (1999) critique of global brands. These brands, she argues, roll roughshod over the sweatshop and temporary McJob labor hired to make or sell them and they use their corporate power to overwhelm the consumer. They co-opt cool, advertise in school, sponsor stars with irresistible allure, brand-bomb neighborhoods with their retail outlets, appropriate sacred icons like Gandhi, and in general colonize every area of our lives. And they do all this while bullying their way into every profitable corner of the globe, whether to take advantage of low wages and lax labor and environmental laws or still innocent consumers who can be made to lust after the Western modernity that they cast themselves as bestowing. While we in marketing know that much of this view exaggerates the power of promotion and inaccurately relegates the consumer to a passive role as pawn in the marketer's game, we nevertheless need to pay close attention to this message and consider the grains of truth on which it is based. This is especially true for dominant brands and in highly visible product categories like movies, the news, software, soft drinks, coffee shops, athletic shoes, clothing, fast foods, cigarettes, toys, discount stores, and gasoline. The larger and more successful the brand and the more omnipresent the product category, the more likely a target it becomes for urban legends, consumer boycotts, and sometimes violent protest (Fine 1992). These are the tactics by which the weak attempt to fight back and voice their frustration (de Certeau 1984).

Multinational marketing organizations have a much greater potential role in either exacerbating or changing this situation than might at first be imagined. In terms of financial resources, many multinationals have greater clout than most nations of the world (Barnett and Cavanagh 1995; Frank 2000; Sklair 1991). They also have greater name recognition than many nations, enjoy greater geographic dominion, and engender greater feelings of loyalty among their constituents. On the production side, the power and competitive nature of large multinational corporations means that they exercise absolute authority over their foreign factories and subcontractors. They are like feudal lords living large while those who depend on them for employment eke out meager wages, at least until lower-cost labor becomes available elsewhere (Bauman 1998). This is not to suggest that all multinational corporations lack a sense of corporate responsibility to workers or are unresponsive to consumers. Nor is the continued antiglobal protest against corporations like Starbucks and Nike entirely justified by the revised business practices of these firms (Starbucks now sells some Fair Trade coffee and Nike has made some of its Asian factories showplaces for good labor and environmental practices). But the point is that multinational consumer companies can and must do more to address global inequality and to combat charges of cultural insensitivity, homogenization, and environmental devastation. Together with governments, nongovernmental organizations (NGOs), and international regulatory agencies, multinational corporations can do far more to help those who have thus far been ignored or crushed by globalism.

WHAT CAN BE DONE?

Consider the case of providing low-cost drugs for low-income Africans afflicted with HIV/AIDS. A combination of antiretroviral drugs is available that makes HIV/AIDS a treatable disease for those who can afford the US$500 to $1,000 per month cost. Although Africa has 70 percent of the adults and 80 percent of the children with HIV infections in the world, the vast majority of the 25.3 million AIDS-infected Africans cannot even come close to affording this cost (Kuadey 2004). A number of African countries have declared national states of emergency and sought to produce or purchase low-cost generic versions of these drugs—something that is allowed by the World Trade Organization TRIPS (Trade-Related Aspects of Intellectual Property Rights) agreement of

1995. However, they have been stopped from doing so by WTO red tape, threats of trade sanctions by the United States, and lobbying by the large Western drug companies that hold the patents on the AIDS drugs. The drug companies argue that they have invested billions of dollars in developing these drugs and that to have any hope of recouping these costs they cannot allow low-cost generic versions. At the Thirteenth World AIDS conference in Durban, the South African government, even offered to pay royalties of 2 percent to 5 percent to the drug companies for using their patents. During late 2003 world pressure forced an agreement to allow generic versions of the drugs where they are needed most in Africa, the United Nations has moved to obtain money to help impoverished African nations with drug costs, and the United States has committed money to making low-cost brand name (nongeneric) drugs available in Africa. Oxfam has called these actions "largely cosmetic" (Oxfam 2003). It remains to be seen what the effects of these political actions will be, but as of November 2003, only 7 percent of those in need of AIDS/HIV drugs in the world were receiving them (AVERT 2003).

While multinational pharmaceutical companies have a legal right to pursue profits from the drugs they have developed, to value profits above the lives of more than 25 million Africans is unconscionable. Barring unimaginable levels of world aid, there is no way that these people will ever be able to buy the drug brands on which the pharmaceutical giants hold patents. South Africa's offer of royalties would mean profits where there would otherwise be none. But even without profit, a larger ethical view of this dilemma would split it from the exchange economy and place it within the gift economy (Vaughan 1997). Those who would couch this as paternalism confuse it with compassion and also misread the gender of giving. The years that the drug companies have spent trying to avoid giving in to world opinion have already cost millions of lives in the less-affluent world, while simultaneously stimulating hatred of the pharmaceutical industry. Africa has not only suffered economically from globalism, it has paid an unthinkable price in human lives. If ever there was an area where marketing needs reform, this is it.

But let us consider a very different case where human lives are not at stake: counterfeit luxury branded goods in the less-affluent world. Again multinational brands such as Rolex, Louis Vuitton, and Hugo Boss argue that their intellectual property rights are being violated and demand action by their own governments, the WTO, and the governments of nations where counterfeits are being produced. The goods here are not AIDS cocktails, but extravagant luxury items. The counterfeit versions sell on the streets of the less-affluent world for such low prices that it is clear that they are not the real version of the brand. Since almost none of those who buy these cheap versions would otherwise be buying the much higher-priced authentic versions, it could be argued that the luxury brands are not really being harmed by the counterfeits, while ingenious imitators in less-affluent countries are benefiting from the desire of consumers in their countries to gain some measure of dignity by buying an imitation status good. Those who would counterargue that the image of the brand is diluted by having cheap imitations around may fail to appreciate the ability of high-end consumers to distinguish the real from the fake (Wong and Ahuvia 1998). I am currently engaged in a seven-country study of consumer ethics with Timothy Devinney and Giana Eckhardt in which we find that consumers in both more-affluent countries like Sweden and the United States and less-affluent countries like China and India frequently feel morally justified in buying fake luxury goods because they regard the high prices charged for the originals to be immoral, especially when the workers who produce these goods in the less-affluent world are paid nowhere near world class wages (Belk, Eckhardt, and Devinney 2005). While the case may not be as clear for unauthorized versions of music and films, and consumers would feel very differently if they were unknowingly driving a car or flying in an airplane with counterfeit parts, it also seems clear that multinational luxury goods manufacturers have been overzealous in attempting to protect their trademarks and copyrights. Attempting to do so can also sometimes result in a great deal of negative publicity for the firm, as with the seemingly endless "McLibel" case (as it was called by the popular press) in the United Kingdom in which McDonald's lost the battle for public opinion by prosecuting two environmentalists for distributing allegedly libelous pamphlets (Schlosser 2001). With luxury goods, it could additionally be argued that imitation is the most sincere form of flattery. That is, the desirability of having the authentic version may sometimes be enhanced rather than diminished by the presence of knock-off versions. So even though compared to HIV/AIDS drugs, luxury goods may seem frivolous, there are also multiple reasons for the multinational firms that make the authentic versions to be more forgiving of those who copy them.

The mention of McDonald's in the preceding paragraph also provides an entry point for considering another criticism that is often leveled against multinational marketers: that they are homogenizing (or sometimes Westernizing or Americanizing) the world by the ubiquity of their offerings. I have already suggested that this charge of cultural imperialism is now largely dismissed by anthropologists and others who suggest that glocalization, hybridization, or creolization is the more likely result of globalized marketing. While it might seem that Disney movies, American television shows, CNN news, and Western music have proliferated everywhere, this observation fails to recognize both local and regional adaptations and local re-interpretations of the meanings of global products. As Liebes and Katz (1990) found in studying how people in different parts of the world watched the U.S. television series *Dallas*, local meanings may be quite different from those formed by the U.S. audience. Other studies of the reception of Western films and television in Trinidad (Miller 1990), Belize (Wilk 1993), the Dominican Republic (Klein 1991), Tonga (Gailey 1990), and Aboriginal Australia (Michaels 1988) have found these portrayals of Western life to be a catalyst for criticizing more than emulating the West.

McDonald's in Asia provides a good example of both how its foods and characteristic operating model have changed to adapt to local preferences (Watson 1997). Thus, in Beijing for example, rather than being an informal eat-and-run place, McDonald's is a place to hang out, do homework, and (for women especially) linger. In adapting to the local, the multinational company also creates a warmer image and may even come to be thought of as local. Thus one group of Japanese Boy Scouts visiting Chicago was surprised to find that the United States has McDonald's too. But Chua (2003) suggested that the firm must do more than localize their offerings in order to deflect local resentment, including engaging in local charitable donations and other income-redistributing activities. Using local managers rather than expatriates is another obvious way that the multinational firm can come to be perceived as sincerely local rather as a patronizing foreign outsider.

As Johansson (2004) pointed out, unlike most domestic marketing that acknowledges the marketing concept and makes a real effort to deliver what the consumer wants when introducing a new product or service, most global marketing assumes that what is wanted at home will be wanted abroad. In order to go farther in helping those left out of globalism, a firm might not only tailor its offerings to local preferences, but actually design products geared to the less-affluent consumer. In a book called *What Can Multinationals Do for Peasants?* (Serrie and Burkhalter 1994), a number of useful illustrations of locally appropriate technologies and products are offered in areas such as agriculture, cooking, transportation, and power. Not all products need to be localized, but many are, even if it is something as simple as selling in smaller, more affordable containers and being certain not to violate local values and religious precepts in ingredients and advertising. As Prahalad (2004) argues, because there are so many poor people in the world it is possible to target appropriate low-cost products and services to them that can result in high sales and high profits—to do well by doing good. A striking example is the success of Kama Sutra condoms in India, despite the availability of free condoms from the government and other sources (Mazarella 2003). Prahalad (2004) also emphasizes utilizing and stimulating the creative and entrepreneurial skills of the world's poor. While smaller in scale than the projects he advocates, a good example of doing so is found in the microfinance operations of the Grameen Bank, initially established in Bangladesh. The Grameen Bank has funded numerous small and very small business enterprises in the world's most impoverished areas. A project might involve lending money to a woman who uses it to buy a cellular phone and phone service and then rents the phone out to local customers who need to make calls. Or she might start a walk-in Internet service or a small shop selling groceries. Such projects help the poor to help themselves in earning a living. They may stop short of founding what will become multinational firms, for that is not their intent. But as the communication examples illustrate, these projects can bring people more in touch with the world by connecting them to others, while at the same time empowering them locally. And the Grameen Bank itself has become a multinational success story by catering to the poor and offering an alternative to loan sharks.

CONCLUSION

Much more is needed than I have outlined here. Pressure must be brought bear to reorganize world trade and financial institutions to better represent the have-nots of the world. Even more international debt forgiveness for the world's most impoverished nations is essential. Global junk foods should be restrained from out-promoting more nutritious local foods (Belk 1988). Dumping of unsafe products like high-nicotine cigarettes should be as difficult in the less-affluent world as it is in the more-affluent world. International tourism must be managed in a way that helps revenues stay in the less-affluent world rather than be extracted from it by multinational airlines, travel agencies, auto rental firms, hotel chains, and food suppliers (Belk and Costa 1995). The United States and Europe must curtail subsidizing their agriculture so their prices can undercut Third World farmers. The United States must stop imposing trade tariffs even as it forces less-powerful countries to drop their own tariffs (Black 2001). The IMF and the World Bank must reverse disastrous requirements for sudden structural readjustment in the less economically developed world. Even seemingly innocent efforts like donating used clothing for the less-affluent world can have disastrous negative effects like destroying indigenous textile industries (Bloemen 2002). These and similar suggestions need to be applied not just to poor nations, but to less-affluent parts of rich nations as well. And in order to consider any of these reforms and shifts in perspective, marketing must be reformed in such a way that the bottom line reaches beyond dollars and euros to the bottom of our hearts. The sun must never be allowed to set on our souls.

REFERENCES

Appadurai, Arjun (1996), *Modernity at Large: Cultural Dimensions of Globalization.* Minneapolis: University of Minnesota Press.

AVERT (2003), "The WHO 3 by 5 Strategy," www.avert.org/3by5.htm (accessed June 2005).

Barber, Benjamin R. (1995), *Jihad vs. McWorld: How Globalism and Tribalism Are Reshaping the World.* New York: Times Books.

Barnett, Richard and John Cavanagh (1995), *Global Dreams: Imperial Corporations and the New World Order.* New York: Touchstone.

Bauman, Zygmunt (1998), *Globalization: The Human Consequences.* New York: Columbia University Press.

Belk, Russell (1988), "Third World Consumer Culture," in *Marketing and Development: Toward Broader Dimensions,* Erdogan Kumcu and A. Fuat Firat, eds. Greenwich, CT: JAI Press, 103–27.

——— (1999), "Leaping Luxuries and Transitional Consumers," in *Marketing Issues in Transitional Economies,* Rajiv Batra, ed. Norwell, MA: Kluwer, 38–54.

——— and Janeen Arnold Costa (1995), "International Tourism: An Assessment and Overview," *Journal of Macromarketing,* 15 (Fall), 33–49.

———, Giana Eckhardt, Timothy Devinney (2005), "Consumer Ethics Across Cultures," *Consumption Markets & Culture,* 8 (September), 275–90, with accompanying DVD.

Black, Stephanie (2001), *Life and Debt,* 86-minute video. Kingston, Jamaica: Tuff Gong Pictures.

Bloemen, Samantha (2002), *T-Shirt Travels,* 57-minute video. Nesconset, NY: Grassroots Pictures.

Breckenridge, Carol A., Sheldon Pollock, Homi K. Bhabha, and Dipesh Chakrabarty, eds. (2002), *Cosmopolitanism.* Durham, NC: Duke University Press.

Canclini, Néstor García (2001), *Consumers: Globalization and Multicultural Conflicts.* Minneapolis: University of Minnesota Press.

Chua, Amy (2003), *World on Fire: How Exporting Free Market Democracy Breeds Ethnic Hatred and Global Instability.* New York: Doubleday.

Danaher, Kevin and Roger Burbach, eds. (2000), *Globalize This! The Battle Against the World Trade Organization and Corporate Rule.* Monroe, ME: Common Courage Press.

de Certeau, Michel (1984), *The Practice of Everyday Life.* Berkeley: University of California Press.

Featherstone, Mike, ed. (1990), *Global Culture: Nationalism, Globalization and Modernity.* London: Sage.

——— and Scott Lash, eds. (1999), *Spaces of Culture: City, Nation, World.* London: Sage.

Fine, Gary Alan (1992), *Manufacturing Tales: Sex and Money in Contemporary Legends.* Knoxville: University of Tennessee Press.

Frank, Thomas (2000), *One Market Under God: Extreme Capitalism, Market Populism, and the End of Economic Democracy.* New York: Doubleday.

Friedman, Thomas L. (2000), *The Lexus and the Olive Tree: Understanding Globalization.* New York: Anchor Books.

——— (2005), *The World Is Flat: A Brief History of the Twenty-First Century.* New York: Farrar, Straus, and Giroux.

Gailey, C. (1990), "Rambo in Tonga: Video Film and Cultural Resistance in Tonga," *Culture,* 9, 20–33.

Ger, Güliz and Russell Belk (1996), "I'd Like to Buy the World a Coke: Consumptionscapes of the 'Less Affluent World,'" *Journal of Consumer Policy,* 19 (September), 271–304.

Giddens, Anthony (2003), *Runaway World: How Globalization Is Reshaping Our Lives.* New York: Routledge.

Harvey, David (2000), *Spaces of Hope.* Berkeley: University of California Press.

Held, David and Anthony McGrew (2002), *Globalization/Anti-Globalization.* Cambridge, UK: Polity.

Huntington, Samuel P. (1993), "The Clash of Civilizations?" *Foreign Affairs,* 72 (April), 22–49.

Johansson, Johny K. (2004), *In Your Face: How American Marketing Excess Fuels Anti-Americanism.* Upper Saddle River, NJ: Prentice Hall.

Klein, Alan M. (1991), *Sugarball: The American Game, the Dominican Dream.* New Haven, CT: Yale University Press.

Klein, Naomi (1999), *No Logo: Taking Aim at the Brand Bullies.* New York: Picador.

——— (2002), *Fences and Windows: Dispatches from the Front Lines of the Globalization Debate.* New York: Picador.

Kuadey, Kwame (2004), "The Politics of AIDS Drugs in Africa," www.aidsandafrica.com (accessed September 2005).

Liebes, Tamar and Elihu Katz (1990), *The Export of Meaning: Cross-Cultural Readings of Dallas.* New York: Oxford University Press.

Mazarella, William (2003), *Shoveling Smoke: Advertising and Globalization in Contemporary India.* Durham, NC: Duke University Press.

Michaels, Eric (1988), "Hollywood Iconography: A Warlpiri Reading," in *Television and Its Audience: International Research Perspectives,* Philip Drummond and Richard Patterson, eds. London: BFI, 109–24.

Miller, Daniel (1990), "'The Young and the Restless' in Trinidad: A Case of the Local and the Global in Mass Consumption," in *Consuming Technologies: Media and Information in Domestic Spaces,* Roger Silverstone and Eric Hirsch, eds. London: Routledge, 163–82.

Ngal, Pan (2003), "Subsumption or Consumption? The Phantom of Consumer Revolution in 'Globalizing' China," *Cultural Anthropology,* 18 (November), 469–92.

Ong, Aihwa (1987), *Spirits of Resistance and Capitalist Discipline: Factory Women in Malaysia.* Albany: State University of New York Press.

Oxfam (2003), "WTO Patent Rules Will Still Deny Medicines to the Poor," August 27, www.oxfam.org/eng/pr030827_wto_patents.htm (accessed September 2005).

Prahalad, C.K. (2004), Th*e Fortune at the Bottom of the Pyramid: Eradicating Poverty Through Profits.* Upper Saddle River, NJ: Wharton School Publishing.

Ritzer, George (2004), *The Globalization of Nothing.* Thousand Oaks, CA: Pine Forge Press.

Robertson, Roland (1992), *Globalization: Social Theory and Global Culture.* London: Sage.

Rollin, Roger, ed. (1989), The *Americanization of the Global Village: Essays in Comparative Popular Culture.* Bowling Green, OH: Bowling Green State University Popular Press.

Schlosser, Eric (2001), *Fast Food Nation.* New York: Houghton Mifflin.

Serrie, Hendrick and S. Brian Burkhalter, eds. (1994), *What Can Multinationals Do for Peasants? Studies in Third World Societies.* Williamsburg, VA: College of William and Mary.

Sklair, Leslie (1991), *Sociology of the Global System.* Baltimore: Johns Hopkins University Press.

Stiglitz, Joseph E. (2003), *Globalization and Its Discontents.* New York: W.W. Norton.

Thomas, Janet (2000), *The Battle in Seattle: The Story Behind the WTO Demonstrations.* Golden, CO: Fulcrum.

Urry, John (1990), *The Tourist Gaze: Leisure and Travel in Contemporary Societies.* London: Sage.

Vaughan, Genevieve (1997), *For-Giving: A Feminist Criticism of Exchange.* Austin, TX: Plain View Press.

Wallach, Lori and Michelle Sforza (1999), *The WTO: Five Years of Reasons to Resist Corporate Globalization.* New York: Seven Stories Press.

Watson, James, ed. (1997), *Golden Arches East: McDonald's in East Asia.* Stanford, CA: Stanford University Press.

Wilk, Richard (1993), "'It's Destroying a Whole Generation': Television and Moral Discourse in Belize," *Visual Anthropology,* 5 (Fall/Winter), 229–44.

Wong, Nancy Y. and Aaron C. Ahuvia (1998), "Personal Taste and Family Face: Luxury Consumption in Confucian and Western Societies," *Psychology & Marketing,* 15 (August), 430–41.

World Bank (2000), *Global Economic Prospects and Developing Countries 2000.* Washington, DC: World Bank.

CHAPTER 25

EXPANDING THE PERSPECTIVE

Making U.S. Marketing Relevant for the New World Order

SUSAN P. DOUGLAS AND C. SAMUEL CRAIG

As the globalization of business becomes increasingly prevalent, marketing must respond to the rapid changes that are occurring throughout the world. Dramatic expansion of the communications and distribution infrastructures is resulting in more interchanges and linkages between cultures and marketing communities in different parts of the world. Many U.S. firms have moved into international markets, and some such as Coca-Cola, IBM, Ford, and Colgate derive a major proportion of their profits from markets outside the United States. Increasingly, start-up firms are born global as technological advances facilitate rapid communication across geographically distant and disparate locations.

Yet, while U.S. businesses are rapidly becoming global in their orientation, marketing academia remains firmly U.S. centric. Attention is focused on problems and issues relevant to the United States such as use of couponing, scanner data, choice models, Web browsing behavior, sophisticated statistical models, and so on. Reliance is placed on U.S. data to develop and test theories and models that are grounded in practices and realities observed in the United States. Even where issues relating to markets outside the United States are examined, these same models and theories are typically applied without regard to their relevance elsewhere or the implications of differences in the nature of market behavior and its environmental context.

As U.S. hegemony comes increasingly into question, the time is ripe to move beyond this U.S.-centric perspective and to pay greater attention to issues, ideas, and approaches in countries outside the United States. Rather than assuming that trends in other countries will parallel those in the United States, more importance should be attached to examining differences in environmental conditions in other countries, as, for example, the fragmentation of the market infrastructure in developing countries and how this impacts the evolution of marketing activities. In addition, more focus is needed on issues unique to other countries such as the importance of the consumerist movement in places like Sweden and Denmark, the role of government influences on marketing activities in other countries, or the challenges associated with the shift from a command to a market-driven economy in transitional economies. Further, investigation is needed of the marketing implications of the increasing interlinking and integration of markets around the world, and whether the relevant unit to study may be a geographic region or area of the world rather than a country. Only if such issues are addressed will the United States continue to contribute to the advancement of marketing thought and keep pace with the emerging trends of the new millennium.

THE INTERNATIONALIZATION OF MARKETS

With current advances in communications and technology and the increased movement of people, goods, ideas, and images across the world, markets are becoming increasingly interlinked with marketing activities extending beyond national borders. This requires more attention to world markets as a whole rather than treating markets on a country-by-country basis (Craig and Douglas 2004). Media networks such as CNN and BBC World span national boundaries in response to increasing international travel and interest in events in other countries, while publications such as *Time, Business Week,* and the *Wall Street Journal* have editions tailored to different regions of the world. The MTV channel spans the world with different programming adapted to each region, such as Brazil, India, and so on. Increasingly, U.S. firms are expanding operations in other countries, establishing programs and strategies at a regional or global level. Icons of U.S. culture such as McDonald's, Nike, and Starbucks are to be found throughout the world. Equally, U.S. films constitute a major export and dominate box offices in most countries worldwide.

As U.S. firms expand into other countries they develop internal mechanisms for the exchange of information, ideas, and products from one part of the world to another. Activities are coordinated at the regional or global levels to exchange information and ideas through meetings or information systems. A new product that has been successful in one location or a promotion that has worked in one context may be tried in another. Experience relating to a similar market environment, for example, dealing with the problems of distribution to small, undercapitalized retailers may be exchanged from one area to another.

While business has become increasingly global in its scope, academia in the United States has largely failed to come to terms with the new reality in establishing research priorities. One way of assessing the amount of academic research and consequently interest in international topics is the number of articles categorized as dealing with international or comparative marketing in the *Journal of Marketing.* Articles appearing in one of the field's premier journals should to some extent reflect the general level of attention being paid to international topics. In the period from 1990 to 2003, 1,002 articles appeared in the *Journal of Marketing.* Of these, only 3 percent (32) dealt with international or comparative marketing and in some years there was only one or none.

The dearth of articles dealing with international and comparative topics further reinforces the notion that U.S. academics are focusing narrowly on marketing topics germane to the United States. If, however, marketing theories and research are to progress and to reflect the growing internationalization of the strategies, organization, and activities, greater attention is needed to internationalizing the scope of U.S. research and writing. Research and theoretical contributions from researchers in other countries need to be better incorporated into the existing base of U.S. literature and opportunities created for the exchange of ideas, information, and methodological approaches among marketers from different countries.

MAKING MARKETING LESS U.S. CENTRIC

In order for such goals to be achieved, a number of steps need to be taken by U.S. researchers to broaden perspectives beyond the current U.S.-centric focus. These are described in the following sections.

Greater Emphasis on Conducting Research in Other Countries

Greater attention is needed to conducting research in countries outside the United States. This should go beyond examining issues typically studied in the United States, such as consumer information processing or branding strategy or the impact of new technology, to look at some of the issues arising from the fundamentally different social and political structures in other regions of the world such as Latin America or Eastern Europe. While much research conducted in the United States assumes the existence of a free enterprise economy, the role of public policy or government influences is considerably more pervasive in other countries. This may result in greater regulation of marketing activities such as, for example, the composition and labeling of products and their sale to different consumer segments such as children, the poor, or the elderly; the regulation of retail prices and wholesale and retail margins; the prohibition of advertising of certain products on TV, or the regulation of advertising copy; the regulation of use of couponing and other types of promotional activities, store opening hours and location, and so on.

In some countries such as Japan or Italy the predominance of small family businesses may have important implications for how marketing activities are organized. as compared with countries such as Germany and the United Kingdom, where large-scale businesses with professional management are more common. Retail distribution is more fragmented in the former countries, with resultant longer channels of distribution and the shift of functions such as inventory management and the breaking bulk or building assortments further back in the channel.

At the same time, this research should go beyond studying issues relating to other large industrialized countries similar to the United States to studying other types of countries such as smaller industrialized countries, which may have different characteristics and research issues. These differences may be particularly marked in relation to issues such as ethnocentrism, attitudes toward foreign products and brands, and so forth.

Testing the Validity of U.S.-Based Theories and Models in Other Countries

Radical differences in the very fabric of society and the way in which it functions call into question the relevance of marketing theories and models developed in response to conditions in the United States. Rather than blindly assuming that these provide an appropriate framework for research in all contexts, it is important to explicitly test their salience and validity in other contexts (Craig and Douglas 2005). This requires carefully examining the underlying assumptions of the theory or model developed in the United States to see whether these also hold in other countries studied. These might, for example, relate to the structure of society, the role of vertical versus horizontal relationships or the underlying value system of a society.

The strength of vertical relationships in Japanese society has, for example, important repercussions on the structure of channel relationships and the ties between different intermediaries in the channel. Similarly, in examining the dimensions of national culture identified by Hofstede (2001) based on research conducted in the West, a new dimension of long versus short-term orientation was identified in China based on values suggested by Chinese scholars. These appeared related to the teachings of Confucius and reflected persistence and thrift as opposed to personal stability and respect for traditions.

Where the assumptions of the theory do not hold, the relevance of the theory or model outside the United States needs to be reexamined. For example, Cerha (1985) found that the horizontal two-step flow of personal influence developed by Katz and Lazarsfeld in the United States (1955) did not hold in Sweden due to the flatter societal structure. If, on the other hand, the assumptions do hold, then the relevance of the theory can be tested by examining its predictive ability in another country or context. For example, the relevance of consumer ethnocentrism in countries outside the United States can be tested to see whether or not ethnocentric consumers have negative intentions to purchase foreign goods and show preference for domestic products.

Conducting "Emic" Studies

A further imperative is to conduct research in other countries adopting an "emic" perspective. Adopting this perspective focuses research on studying the unique characteristics of each country and on identifying and probing these in-depth (Berry 1989). This is in marked contrast to an "etic" approach, which is primarily concerned with identifying and assessing universal attitudinal and behavioral concepts and developing pan-cultural or "culture-free" measures of these (Berry 1989). More broadly, indigenous psychological theories may be applied rather than imposing those developed based on Western values and beliefs. Adopting this approach entails identifying culture-specific concepts and developing culture-specific measures of these. Each facet is understood in its own terms and interpreted in relation to its context rather than making a comparison relative to other countries or cultures.

Developing Multicultural Research Teams

For progress to be made both in improving understanding of issues specific to other countries and in identifying relevant theories and models to guide research, the research team should incorporate members from each of the different countries in which research is conducted. While each researcher will tend to have a different perspective embedded in his or her own cultural background and research training, he or she will also be able to provide input with regard to issues characteristic of his or her own country and how to adapt existing models to accommodate such issues.

Multicultural research teams also provide a means for "decentring" the research design together with the theories and concepts that both guide research and are generated from it (Craig and Douglas 2005). Participation of researchers from different cultural backgrounds in the initial phases of the research design will help ensure that emic theories and constructs provide input to the research design. Such multiple perspectives are also critical in interpreting results and their implications across different cultural contexts.

Examining the Relevance and the Role of Marketing in Emerging Market Countries

Over half the world's population lives in twenty-four emerging countries, including China, India, Indonesia, and Brazil. Yet the role of marketing in such countries is sadly neglected. Marketing is nonetheless a vital engine of economic and social development. It establishes a conduit for the flow of goods and services and creates value for both producers and consumers integrating the wants, needs, and resources of consumers with the capacities and resources of producers through a sequence of exchanges.

At the same time, by establishing such networks marketing creates purposeful, risk-taking managers and entrepreneurs in such emerging countries. It becomes a creator of small businesses and a catalyst for economic development and growth. Marketing thus plays a vital role in the formation of a vibrant and thriving middle class who are consumers of products and services and at the same time are essential to those products and services being brought to the marketplace. Yet little attempt has been made to examine or explore the broader social and economic role marketing has played as a stimulus for change in such nations.

Equally few attempts have been made to examine what specific issues are relevant in these nations and whether concepts developed and studied in industrialized countries also apply in these contexts. Yet lower levels of income, lack of consumer information, and poorly developed marketing infrastructure suggest that relevant issues may be strikingly different. Further attention to identifying and examining such questions is clearly needed.

Understanding the Role of Marketing in Transitional Economies

With the breakup of the Soviet Union in the late 1990s, a substantial number of countries changed from command economies where the government controlled and regulated industry and commerce to market economies where private enterprise prevails. This has resulted in sweeping changes throughout society. Instead of a limited supply of goods dictated by the functioning of a planned economy, marketing has now begun to play an important role in the creation and satisfaction of demand. Consumers who once were confronted by a limited range of choices (if any at all) are now facing an increasingly wide range of alternatives and, in addition, are bombarded by Western-style advertising.

The way in which this transition is occurring and its causes and effects in different countries need to be further examined. The lessons to be learned for marketing remain obscure. Experience in these countries may, for example, provide a natural experiment in understanding how attitudes toward advertising and other promotional activities are formed and change over time. Similarly, some valuable insights might be gained in understanding the issues and difficulties faced by producers in adjusting to this new regime. The growth of branding and competitive pricing tactics has important implications for the efficiency and productivity of the marketing system. Study of these issues in the transitional economy context may provide important insights into the mechanisms underlying the effective functioning of a marketing system.

CONCLUSIONS

Academic marketing has been at the cutting edge of developments in the United States. However, the world has changed and academic marketing must respond to the changes by embracing this new reality. United States academics must begin to examine marketing as it exists beyond the confines of their country and investigate the challenges faced by marketers in other parts of the world. Failure to do so will be unfortunate, not only because of the loss to our understanding of what is happening in the larger world, but also to our insights about the generality of marketing laws and theories. As Reavis Cox (1965, p. 161) presciently remarked forty years ago, "Paradoxical though it may seem, what we stand to gain most from studying other marketing systems, is not so much what they tell us about others but what they force us to learn about ourselves in order to understand what we see abroad."

REFERENCES

Berry, J.W. (1989), "Imposed Etics-Emics-Derived Etics: The Operationalization of a Compelling Idea," *International Journal of Psychology,* 24 (6), 721–35.

Cerha, J. (1985), "The Limits of Influence," *European Research,* 2 (July), 141–51.

Cox, Reavis (1965), "The Search for Universals in Comparative Studies of Domestic Marketing Systems," in *Marketing and Economic Development,* Proceedings of the 1965 Fall Conference, Peter D. Bennett, ed. Chicago: American Marketing Association, 143–62.

Craig, C. Samuel and Susan P. Douglas (2004), "Beyond National Culture: Consequences of the Changing Dynamic of Culture," Working paper, Stern School of Business, New York University.

——— (2005), *International Marketing Research,* 3rd ed. Chichester, UK: John Wiley & Sons.

Hofstede, Geert (2001), *Culture's Consequences: Comparing Values, Behaviors, Institutions and Organizations Across Nations,* 2nd ed. Thousand Oaks, CA: Sage.

Katz, Elihu and Paul F. Lazarsfeld (1955), *Personal Influence.* New York: The Free Press.

CHAPTER 26

WHAT CAN INDUSTRIALIZING COUNTRIES DO TO AVOID THE NEED FOR MARKETING REFORM?

KERRY CHIPP, SCOTT HOENIG, AND DEON NEL

Many chapters in this volume have identified pressures for reform in marketing in the industrial countries (which can be approximated by the Organization for Economic Cooperation and Development) so that the profession can fully take on its role as a productive element in companies and society at large. These pressures may also apply to the academic sectors of marketing (mostly universities and other forms of training programs) that are closely linked to the profession.

In this chapter we consider similar concerns in the context of an industrializing economy to better understand where elements of this critique may prevail in this setting. We do this because we feel that marketers in developing areas, faced with growing skepticism toward the profession in both the developed and developing sectors of the world's economy, have a special need to understand the areas where the discipline has succeeded and failed so as to restimulate developed sectors in their own economies and not make the same mistakes with new segments. And, marketers in industrialized economies can gain some insight from successes and failures marketers have encountered in other parts of the world.

We focus on the geographic area of South Africa. This setting is similar in many ways to other industrializing areas of the world, such as those found in various countries in South America and Southeast Asia. South Africa has an advanced, competitive, and growing industrial and services sector, which must serve quickly changing segments of consumer and industrial markets; a significant portion of the economy characterized by small entrepreneurial operators, certain of which are transforming into larger concerns; a high level of unemployment, some of which is transforming into underemployment and full employment; and substantial academic presence monitoring these changes.

We identify a number of major sources of reform pressures, and examples of initiatives that have developed and could be developed that may avoid future need for reform. We discuss these issues using observations from interviews with business and academic leaders around the Johannesburg area, combined with our collective experiences with managers and other participants in each sector.

THE GENERAL SITUATION

Marketing in South Africa has much the same purpose for firms as that in other companies across the world: to enhance revenues by connecting to customers with various services and products, using well-targeted communication, distribution, and pricing, subject to prevailing economic, market, social, political, and legal constraints. When the industry is competitive, this also involves creating some form of sustainable differentiation to maximize long-term profitability. One way this differentiation can be maintained is through continual innovation in product, process, and the organization of marketing itself.

Small, medium, and large enterprises in South Africa are no exception to the industrialized world in that they face many external and continually changing marketing challenges from each of these areas: the competitive and legislative environments, the markets and customers they serve, and organizing and staffing their marketing function to effectively address these external challenges. The economy and subsequent markets are forecast to continue their current longest span of continuous growth since 1945 (currently at 4 percent annually) through at least 2007 or 2008 (*Sunday Times* 2004). As a whole the markets served by the companies are not large ones, with a population of 44 million, 27 percent of whom are unemployed (with 57 percent below the poverty line), but becoming more employed as the economy grows (*Sunday Times* 2004). In many industries competition is moderate to strong with a few large firms (often either large South African companies or even larger multinationals) dominating the markets. The high unemployment, combined with South Africa's active and ongoing transformation from its apartheid past, has caused the South African government to underline the need for firms to include a social element in their business ethos, both in what they do and in their work practices. As a result, there is a strong motivation to employ social appeals in corporate marketing policy.

To add to these pressures, South Africa has, in many respects, a dual economy. As such it can be viewed as a global microcosm with two distinct sectors, that is, a highly developed segment that has similar levels of development and goes through similar trends as those in the developed world, and an underdeveloped and developing sector whose patterns closely follow that of underdeveloped and emerging markets. Correspondingly, the country has a sophisticated marketing apparatus in place, which coexists with many market segments that are not fully dealt with, understood, or tapped. These segments are generally low-income and high-risk, but with good growth potential. South African corporations are now forced to deal with all segments as future growth, global developments, and government initiatives all point in this direction.

The challenge, therefore, for marketers in South Africa is to continually find new ways to meet the demands of customers and marketplace conditions characteristic of a rapidly changing developing economy, outmaneuvering whatever competition may be present. Those who have succeeded have demonstrated that marketing tools can be used effectively, moreover, that marketing, when employed effectively, has little need of reform.

In this setting, therefore, marketing has an enhanced need to constantly refocus, in both form and product. In order to achieve this, marketers must sharpen their vision and continually renew their energy to keep their actions in alignment with the basics of their profession. In areas of business that this is not applied, seeds for reform are sown.

The conditions described demonstrate that marketing in an industrializing economy differs in some areas from typical marketing in an industrialized economy in both form and content; namely a greater variety is evident. Marketers must seek to connect with and satisfy at the one end a sophisticated, global, Westernized segment along a continuum to a rural, remote, underdeveloped segment at the other end. These conditions, enjoined with legislated and other environmental pressures to include social upliftment as part of corporate strategy, create the special challenges that must be addressed in this setting for marketing to be effective.

SUCCESS FACTORS IN THIS INDUSTRIALIZING COUNTRY SETTING

It is in this context that we turn to the key success factors found in our interviews with South African managers: *understanding and connecting with customers; innovation* through products and services, markets and marketing strategies; and effective *internal organizing, staffing, and training* to support the marketing function. Again, these factors appear to be no different from what managers in other parts of the world find, except that their effective execution seems to require an enhanced level of supervision and continual refocusing to address the rapidly changing local conditions. Furthermore, the execution of marketing processes is often at a different level to those found elsewhere. Each of these key success factors (which also helps prevent the need for reform) will be discussed in turn.

Understanding and Connecting with Customers

This appears to involve two main elements: companies need to continually monitor changes in segments to keep abreast of developments in the lifestyles and attitudes of each market; and they must resegment quickly using this information. Several ongoing studies have effectively measured lifestyles and cultural backgrounds across the entire population of South Africa, and have categorized the multiple lifestyles using highly advanced methodologies. One ongoing study in particular, the All Media and Product Survey (AMPS), sponsored by the South African Advertising Research Foundation (SAARF), regularly samples adults representatively from all of the wide range of economic groupings in South Africa to develop profiles ranging from those living in subsistence conditions to the wealthy business professional. This study gathers information that contains a remarkable variance in factors such as languages understood and spoken, household and personal income, household composition, consumption of various types of food and beverages, media usage, entertainment events attended, family and religious celebrations and types, and technology (such as cell phone and satellite dish) usage. This study is annual and conducted on a nationally representative sample of 12,400. It is done on a not-for-profit basis and the data is available through many secondary companies that design access and management programs around the study. Thus, the survey itself provides a national reference for all marketing managers and media owners, ensuring that all marketers in the country are abreast of developments within the market. Many of its terms, such as SAARF Universal Living Standards Measure (SULSM), which supersedes ethnic and other groupings, have entered into the national marketing lexicon.

This kind of information allows marketers to understand better how, with technological improvements available and increases in income level, niches vary, not only across profiles, but also in the ongoing make-up of the profiles themselves. As an example, AMPS includes a yearly lifestyle segmentation study, which tracks movements in the way in which people spend their discretionary time. Once lifestyle groups are ascertained, they are assumed to be in vacillation rather than to be fixed for extended periods—a different approach to many of the international lifestyle segmentation studies. It is through the responsive use of information of this type that marketers can see consumers and better understand how to more effectively connect with them.

A common element needed to connect with customers across these segments in South Africa (and possibly other industrializing countries) appears to be the desire for a trusting and longer-term relationship with merchants and companies that culminates in the need for a social element in corporate and marketing policy. This creates conditions quite unlike those found elsewhere, with the morality and ethics of marketing coming into sharper focus. Part of the reason for this lies in a global backlash against Westernized "hard sell" approaches and an increased consumer resistance to marketing in all its forms. And, a major portion of South Africa's reconciliation process during its ongoing transformation from a primarily white-dominated state to a democracy that actively promotes multiculturalism involves emphasizing the need for trust between the different ethnic backgrounds.

Fostering this trust therefore can be a tool for companies to achieve maximum consumer buy-in to their marketing strategies, which generally are not aggressive or focused on the hard sell. Rather, communication with customers and potential customers tends to have a long-term relationship focus in mind. As part of this, respecting privacy also is becoming more important as a means to foster trust, and reducing the memories of control from the formerly intrusive intelligence service of the South African police of the apartheid era.

Many companies have used social concerns as part of their appeal to gain consumers' trust, which not only adds to the firm's image, but also creates an atmosphere of authenticity in company communications. This type of appeal appears to have some success, as one marketing manager we interviewed stated, "people aren't getting meaning out of money anymore." In this setting, many have found that a creditworthy social donation is more effective than a price reduction.

Such social appeals are, however, not vague and distant. Successful firms have built marketing models that connect with causes or concerns that are close to consumers' hearts. More than this, though, is that these concerns come with little or no costs, whether these are monetary or non-monetary. Woolworth's, a successful retailer, focuses on the niches present in the upper end of the market. Woolworth's concern is consumer health, which is packaged together with environmental health. Both are socially responsible causes, but, nonetheless, those that affect the consumer in a visible manner. MySchool is a profit-making social marketing firm, which makes money by rewarding everyday parental purchases at regular retailers, with a contribution to the consumer's favorite charity: their child's school.

Innovation

Continuous *innovation* lies at the heart of developing-country marketing models to serve multiple goals involving the creation of new markets or penetrating existing markets involving quickly changing niches. South African companies are often compelled, either through necessity or government directive, to deal with lower-end markets that many organizations elsewhere would find too high in risk. Banks, for example, have been forced to supply services to the lowest-income sector, individuals who are traditionally "unbanked." This directive has seen banks design an entire range of products directed at this high-risk, low-return market. Not only are the markets high-risk, but, as already discussed, to enter many of them, companies must gain trust and promote socially active causes in the face of a nontrusting past. This forces companies to rethink their marketing strategies and develop uniquely adapted product, service, communication, pricing, and distribution tactics. Many successful organizations have done so through accurately targeting a niche market or group of niche markets, for both the fast-moving consumer goods markets and the financial and other services markets, which include insurance, banking, telecommunications, and tourism.

Product and service development has seen the most success when a long-term, innovative, relationship-driven approach has catered to changing niches. In the industrialized world, more specialized retailers, such as Anita Roddick's Body Shop, also use innovative ways of approaching product offerings, most of which speak to key consumer concerns, such as the environment, health, and community development. But the South African experience has demonstrated that this is also possible for services, which do not appear to be ready candidates for the social and health conscious environment, to act on this trend. Discovery Health, a short-term medical insurance company, changed the common, but disliked, model of selling short-term insurance into one more welcomed by customers: through offering insurance as a health product. This company actively promotes healthy lifestyles among its members by linking their loyalty club to various healthy behaviors. Members are awarded points for attending a gym, having regular check-ups, stopping smoking, and other positive health orientated actions. In addition, this insurance company has negotiated reduced rates for health and fitness clubs for its members, so that they pay a nominal fee to belong to their local gym. This example underscores many of the key issues: the company is seen as active in caring for its members, it builds relationships and trust; its focus is long term and it has followed the niche trend toward health and fitness. It is authentic because members can clearly see the benefits for a health insurer in keeping them healthy. This concept has been successfully introduced into other developed countries.

Such practice follows closely on other innovations that have centered on the necessity, given the social and historical conditions in the country, of companies developing social forms of marketing. But South African environmental conditions are such that various government directives have encouraged, if not mandated, a social focus in the policies of the formal business sector. Social programs have been developed and communicated in innovative ways, such as the above examples of Discovery Health, Woolworth's, and MySchool. Regardless of these innovative approaches, however, these initiatives are seen to be authentic; they tie in closely with the core business function of the company concerned. Authenticity lends weight to reputation and avoids the embarrassments suffered by other organizations when their business practices are scrutinized and fall short. Such authenticity is a further step away from the hard-sell and it lends an additional aspect to the corporation so that it is no longer seen as merely short-term profit driven, or purely out for itself, thus this helps curtail the skepticism that greets many marketing communiqués.

Distribution is another area where the variety of approaches, both in form and content, is clearly evident. Large retail brands, such as Coca-Cola, are sold in far more direct means than found in the developed world. To distribute products, successful marketers have developed unusual and innovative channels that provide goods or services at access points most convenient to the customer, as well as meeting social objectives. Some banks now have both high-contact access points for low-income consumers, as well as Internet for high-income, low-contact customers. Large corporations have reduced the underemployed and gained large community participation in their brands through changing the distribution of their products from larger retailers to small sellers. Coca-Cola, for instance, provides one-person street and suburb vendors with refrigeration and stock, while the wireless telecomm providers (Cell C, MTN, Vodacom) distribute the sale of cellular airtime in a similar manner. And in many of the townships (such as Soweto), many "spazas" (home shops) are seen selling various products or services that are popular with their neighbors, as a means to both improve distribution and enhance individual income. This novel approach to distribution involves a great deal of work with consumers and also goes some way to reducing underemployment. Indeed, the informal sector takes care of a much product delivery through street stalls, sellers at street corners and traffic lights, and the sale of everything from furniture to plants along main roads. At a single traffic light, vendors offering products and distributing pamphlets often surround consumers in cars, selling everything from newspapers to sunglasses, and, when it is raining, umbrellas.

While there is undoubtedly a strong entrepreneurial spirit in the country, both with young organizations such as MySchool, there appears to be a major threat to many of the entrepreneurs from an overemphasis on short-term focus. Some local financiers have the need to see fast returns on their money, or are hesitant to invest without large guarantees, or, alternatively, large shares in budding enterprises. Certain entrepreneurs see the purchase of their successful new enterprises by large corporations as a goal—a fast way of earning money and then exiting the environment. Such practices can stifle competition and innovation in the long term. Moreover, if not managed properly, the ways in which smaller enterprises have connected with consumers may be easily destroyed when customers see that they are dealing with a large corporation with an ethos that is perceived to be different than that of the enterprise's founders.

Internal Organization, Staffing, and Training

The third success factor concerns internal organization, staffing, and training that allows the marketing function to be effective in the changing setting. This involves two main components: the actual operation and staffing of the companies and the preparation of future employees by the academic institutions. It is in these areas that we heard the greatest concern voiced for improvement from the managers we talked with, centering on attitudes of management and corresponding corporate culture, which often can prevent marketing from taking its full role in the company. A short-term focus in management, along with an emphasis on choosing top management personnel from the financial disciplines (such as accounting), was often seen as leading to a cost saving, and immediate results-driven focus. Marketing often was considered as little more than a functional department rather than a corporate philosophy and, as a consequence, its value limited to the four Ps (product, place, promotion, and price) and customer relationship management (CRM). In firms that have deemphasized the subtleties of internal marketing, the roles of all employees in creating customer relationships, in developing innovative ways to collect valid and reliable data on consumers, of building reputation in branding, and, most importantly, of innovating in the marketing process, can all be in jeopardy.

To staff marketing positions, career paths and employee packages must attract top talent. Unfortunately, in the firms we interviewed, marketing frequently was not viewed as a breeding ground for the highest-quality personnel. Corporate career advancement often was not found to be orientated toward long-term benefits, and it did not appear to tolerate failure or encourage risk-taking behavior, two key components needed when targeting new markets or trying new approaches. In addition, training through rotation, which enables the marketer to more effectively interface with all areas of the corporation, was generally not provided. Each of these areas needs to be addressed so that marketers can better ensure that their programs are more sustainable and future orientated.

Educational institutions also have a role to play. Our review found that little has been done to encourage the culture of innovation in marketing thought, both in undergraduate and graduate programs. Much focus has been on content rather than process and the four Ps have become prescriptive, doing little to review critiques of marketing. Marketing education overall lacked focus on the process of innovation and risk management, the very concepts that were viewed as necessities in marketing reform, and it did not conceptualize the role of the marketer within the broader organization.

Some organizations we interviewed felt that the future prevention of the need for marketing reform lay in developing a scholarship-oriented business education for marketing graduates, ensuring that the general fundamentals of business science, in both quantitative and qualitative areas, as well as the value of disciplined thought in problem solving, are communicated. But such an approach begs the question of the business generalist as a preferred educational product over the marketing specialist. Thus some attention needs to be directed toward a clearer delineation of the contribution of the marketing specialist. Such a demarcation may also help reestablish the role of marketing as a philosophy in the broader organization and its importance for the entire organization rather than just the marketing function. And, if a critique of marketing practice is embedded in marketing education, future marketers may be more inclined to view marketing as a dynamic and responsive process so that they avoid rehashing weary marketing models to an oversold and jaded market.

CONCLUSION

The success factors we have listed in this discussion are by no means mutually exclusive—in fact, it appears that the more of these factors companies use, whether large or small, the more success they may have in their marketing efforts. Large corporations that effectively organize to seek innovative ways to deal with high-risk markets in their approaches thereby foster consumer belief in their products and marketing messages. And small entrepreneurs who use their skills to quickly adapt and connect with clientele by tapping into causes that are close to their hearts can also be successful. By doing this, both large and small companies are helping solve a social problem at the same time as marketing their products.

Is there anything revolutionary that can be learned from the South African setting about ways to prevent the need for marketing reform in developing, or even more developed, country settings? Not really, except that when a simple but vigilant and energetic focus is placed on the fundamentals of the marketing process, little reform is needed. Conversely, when this is ignored, calls for reform may be triggered.

Nevertheless, the strong drivers toward entering high-risk markets, with one eye on social concerns, may force marketers in this area to draw on more innovative approaches in daily marketing practice than they otherwise would have. Correspondingly, the wide variety of market conditions forces a greater range of approaches. Most significantly, the success of the hard-sell is absent; marketing must appear to be authentic and address the key social issues of its market in order to succeed. Thus, the tools used may not be entirely new; so perhaps it is the marketers who need reforming rather than the discipline. A lot of the youth and zeal of new markets, such as South Africa's, can help marketers recapture their lost vision.

REFERENCE

Sunday Times (Johannesburg) (2004), "Good Times Roll for SA," November 21.

CHAPTER 27

LEVERAGING MARKETING'S INFLUENCE IN TEAM AND GROUP SETTINGS

ANNE STRINGFELLOW AND SANDY D. JAP

Marketing should play a powerful and influential role in the firm. However, marketing has become marginalized in many firms. We believe that marketing can increase its influence in business organizations, not simply to gain power for its own sake, but in order to maximize firmwide outcomes. This chapter examines potential sources of leveraging marketing influence at various levels in firms, providing several suggestions for improving marketing's influence throughout. After a brief discussion of the marginalization of marketing, we consider the sources of influence. Thereafter, we examine firms' need for marketing influence. This is followed by a discussion of suggested methods for improving marketing's influence, particularly in team and group settings. The chapter concludes with an overview of the implications for reforming marketing.

MARKETING'S MARGINALIZATION

Evidence in the United States and European markets suggests that the marketing function is marginalized across firms and industries. For example, in the United States, the average compensation of a U.S. marketing executive is only 69 percent of that of a finance executive, and only 91 percent of that of a manufacturing executive (Pfeffer 1994), indicating that firms value marketing executives less than finance or manufacturing executives. Research on British companies indicates that other functions perceive marketing as being concerned only with tactical matters such as advertising and promotions instead of strategic issues (Shipley 1994). Indeed, marketing is so poorly perceived in industrial and business-to-business companies that its importance as a function ranks only above human resources (Meldrum and Palmer 1998).

Additionally, when one considers the path to the chief executive officer (CEO) door, a background in finance is a more powerful predictor of becoming a CEO than is a background in marketing. Among the hundred largest firms listed on the London stock exchange (the FTSE 100), twice as many CEOs come from finance backgrounds as from marketing backgrounds (Lewis 2002a). Moreover, marketers are also scarce on top management teams. In the United States, only one of the top twenty Fortune 500 companies has a chief marketing officer (Melkman 2004), and in Great Britain only five of the FTSE 100 companies have a board-level marketing position (Simms 2003).

Members of technical functions, such as finance and engineering, regard marketing as intuitive and nontechnical (Benjamin 1993). Apparently, the quantitative aspects of marketing are not prominent and the technical aspects are underappreciated. It may also be the case that the marketing function suffers from a common fallacy—that because one has experienced something, he or she can then be an expert at it. In other words, since one has been a customer, one must therefore know something about how to sell. Of course, we recognize that this line of reasoning is not any more appropriate than concluding that if one had been born in a garage, one must therefore be a car.

Collectively, the evidence overwhelmingly indicates that marketing suffers from a lack of recognition in many firms. However, there are CEOs who recognize that marketing has access to customer needs and is therefore in the best position to determine how a firm's resources could be utilized to meet these needs while maximizing profits. These CEOs recognize the central role that marketing could play in the organization and "want marketers to become full partners, understand the whole business, and come up with ideas linked to driving profits" (Lewis 2002b, p. 3). This is marketing's rightful place in the firm and marketing must move toward it.

MARKETING'S VALUE

We believe that the marginalization of the marketing function in a firm is a grave and serious mistake. Marketing, along with R&D, are vital "rainmaking" functions that develop new product ideas and new markets that can translate into sustainable competitive advantages, such as added value for customers and increased growth for the firm. In fact, research has shown that marketing influence at the top management level is associated with a firm's innovation and growth (Barker and Mueller 2002). It has also been demonstrated that, on average, firms that are marketing-oriented experience improved firm performance. For example, one study conducted on British firms showed a 5.3 percent greater total shareholder return in firms in which the CEO had marketing experience (Ambler 2003). Another study using data from Japan showed that business performance (relative profitability, relative size, relative growth rate, and relative share of market) was correlated positively with customer evaluations of firms' customer orientation (Deshpandé, Farley, and Webster 1993). Finally, research conducted in the United States found a significant positive relationship between customer orientation and subjective measures of firm performance (Jaworski and Kohli 1993; Slater and Narver 2000). Taken together, these findings suggest that the marginalization of marketing is not in the firm's best interest, and that marketing influence should reverberate throughout the entire firm, for the overall health of the company.

Marketing is particularly important when (1) competition levels are high, (2) environments are dynamic, and (3) customers are concentrated. In highly competitive environments, technical superiority in products may be insufficient to assure profitability. Marketing expertise is necessary to insure that the product continues to create value in the eye of the customer. Consistent with this, Workman (1993) found that high-tech firms were unable to sustain their competitive advantage over time without improvements in their marketing capabilities.

Marketing is also essential in highly dynamic environments where customer requirements are changing rapidly. Advantages accrue to organizations that match their internal complexity to the level of complexity of the external environment (Lawrence and Lorsch 1967). The notion of requisite variety (Weick 1979) suggests that combining diverse knowledge produces better innovation outcomes, particularly in fast-changing environments. Since different functions scan different parts of the environment and obtain different types of knowledge (Arrow 1974), in highly dynamic environments marketing's detailed knowledge of the customer must influence the firm's strategy. Otherwise, the firm will pursue goals and objectives that cause it to be left behind as customer needs move on.

Marketing's influence is particularly vital when the firm's target segments consist of a few large customers. Here, close relationships with customers are vital so that marketers may discover latent opportunities to creatively anticipate and meet customer needs. This is the path to improved profitability and sustainable competitive advantages. However, recognition of value-adding opportunities is necessary, but not sufficient, for profitability. What is needed, in order to take advantage of the opportunities, is that marketing enhance its influence over other key functional areas of the firm.

A common theme throughout this section is the idea that in circumstances where customers—including every individual and organization that can influence the sale of the product—are vital to the firm, then marketing must also be vital. Clearly, this is because managing the firm's relationship with customers and external publics, both upstream, downstream, and horizontally, is the essence of the marketing function. Hence, the only firm where marketing's marginalization is warranted is the firm that has no need for customers. Such a firm does not exist.

GROWING MARKETING'S INFLUENCE

We have shown that marketing is an important contributor to growth, and that in highly competitive, dynamic industries or firms with a concentrated customer base, marketing influence is particularly vital to firmwide success. How then can the marketing function improve its influence within the firm? We ask this question not for the promotion of marketing for its own sake, or even at the expense of other functional areas, but with an eye toward group outcomes.

There is no gain for marketing to be promoted at the expense of the group. In fact, there are numerous studies that suggest that unequal power among group members can negate the benefits of bringing diverse opinions to decision making. Instead, in any team setting, whether it be a top management team or a procurement team, marketing plays a vital role in preventing dysfunctional group dynamics such as *groupthink*—which occurs when the group converges too quickly on a solution and neglects consideration of other key factors (Janis 1972). In addition, marketing's minority external view may improve the quality of group decisions since majority opinions are enhanced by the existence of consistent counterarguments from a minority (Nemeth 1986). To this end, marketers must prevent an overemphasis on other functional areas without a consideration of potential marketing contributions to the group effort. For example, in a new product development team, marketing's influence may be necessary to highlight the possibility of revenue enhancement and prevent an overemphasis by the group on manufacturing processes and cost-cutting efforts.

Thus, we see that throughout the firm, marketing plays a critical role in its interactions with finance, accounting, manufacturing, R&D, and other critical functional areas in team settings such as new product development, procurement, and top management. In order for marketing's influence to grow within the firm, marketers must promote their influence within these settings in order to improve the group's overall outcomes. To this end, we outline several ways in which marketing might accomplish this goal. Throughout the discussion, there is the assumption that marketing's power should not grow at the expense of group outcomes or at the expense of any particular function. Instead, the emphasis is on enhancing marketing's influence while *simultaneously* improving group outcomes.

Truth Supported Wins

Individuals across functions tend to be "selective preceptors" (Dearborn and Simon 1958) with a tendency to rely on their functional background as the dominant approach for solving problems. This tendency introduces a host of specific values and beliefs that color the worldviews of its members, analogous to the effect of national cultures. These values and beliefs are often tacit, rather than explicit, and may lead to unintended misunderstandings. Marketing is faced with the task of how to best combat this. Research has shown that in many team settings, the "lone voice in the wilderness" is generally an unsuccessful approach to winning influence on the team. Instead, marketing should look to at least one other function and convince that individual of the value of a marketing approach. In this way, truth that finds support in at least two members is more likely to influence the group's outcomes (McGrath 1984).

Understand Their Culture

Another strategy to convince other functions of marketing's utility is to identity marketing's specialist knowledge of customer needs in a language that other functions can understand. In this way they can recognize marketing's expertise. In order to persuade functions that are more quantitatively based, marketers should also use quantitative metrics to argue their position. In doing so, they can more effectively communicate marketing principles, highlight key tradeoffs, and improve the predictive power of the group outcomes.

As an example, consider marketing's influence on new product development teams. This influence is generally lower in technologically oriented organizational cultures (Atuahene-Gima and Evangelista 2000; Workman 1993). However, this does not necessarily mean that marketing cannot be influential. In fact, Workman (1993) observed that marketing was able to gain some measure of influence in a major technology company. These marketers gained credibility, not by their knowledge of marketing, but by showing their understanding of products and technology, and demonstrating to the engineers how they could add value. In this case their expert power was supplemented by their persuasiveness power, which stemmed from knowledge of how to "sell" their ideas to an engineering audience.

Expand the Pie

Another avenue for expanding marketing's influence in procurement teams, new product development teams, and top management teams is to move the focus of the group from "pie-division," or negotiations over how to share the rewards of their joint efforts among the various functions, to "pie-expansion," which involves growing the overall level of rewards for all parties (Jap 1999, 2001). Thus, instead of negotiating about the group's location on an efficiency frontier (pie-division), the focus of the group's activities is on moving the efficiency frontier away from the origin (pie-expansion). This can be accomplished in several ways. One approach would be for marketing to highlight and target new markets and segments for the firm to pursue. Also, the marketing function could propose a plan to develop strong relationships with key customers to identify latent and emerging needs that could be creatively and uniquely satisfied by the firm. In this way, revenue is grown and profits improved. Another approach would be to develop strategic sourcing agreements with the supply base to cut costs and provide sourcing stability in the long run.

Group Metrics

From the onset of any team formation, key marketing metrics should be a part of the group's performance metrics. In light of marketing's rainmaking functions, factors such as customer relationship equity, revenue enhancements, and other customer-focused activities designed to detect, monitor, and respond to customer needs over time should be key elements of the group's overall outcomes. These metrics serve to keep track of the outcomes of marketing actions and provide justification for investments in marketing activities with long-term payoffs.

Breadth and the Path to the Corner Office

Previously we mentioned that one reason for the ongoing scarcity of CEOs with a marketing background is these candidates' lack of breadth. Research has shown that factors in determining the expert power of members of top management teams are the number of functional areas in which experience was gained, and the number of different positions held in a firm (Finkelstein 1992). Managers with a breadth of functional experience are promoted more quickly and to higher levels (Bunderson 2003). This is because successful CEO candidates possess "metafunctional expertise," which refers to "a broad understanding of the roles played by and the relationships among the different functions on a multifunctional team combined with some depth of expertise in those functions of greatest strategic import" (Bunderson 2003, p. 459). Hence, marketing executives must ensure that they gain significant exposure to line management and other functional areas to ensure their eligibility for promotion to CEO level. Assignments with direct profit and loss responsibility should be chosen in preference to a string of pure marketing assignments. Another approach for encouraging breadth is at the educational stage, where marketing educators can expose their students to the importance of generalist skills and experience outside of the marketing function. By exposing oneself to the functional perspectives and jargons, top managers can improve their ability to state their case in a way that appeals to managers with different backgrounds.

Another path to the CEO office comes with the creation of "C-level" marketing positions. Given the critical role that marketing plays with respect to managing the customer relationship and the firm's increasing dependence on this relationship, it follows that more firms should appoint chief marketing officers (CMOs). Indeed, recent evidence indicates that this is a growing trend in firms that recognize the value of their customers. For example, in July 2003, General Electric (GE) appointed Beth Comstock to a newly created chief marketing officer position. When announcing the appointment, GE Chairman and CEO Jeff Immelt said: "We are making GE a more externally focused, market-driven company to better serve our customers and their future needs" (General Electric 2003). The food and beverage industry has also recently seen the appointment of a number of chief customer officers (CCOs) tasked with building earnings per customer. Examples include Campbell's soup, Coca-Cola, and Kellogg's (Johnson and Schultz 2004). This recognition of the importance of customers and the marketing function to the financial health of the firm is well overdue.

CONCLUSION

We have reviewed marketing's influence in organizations and formulated several suggestions for leveraging the influence of marketing in firms. The goal of these suggestions is not to increase the power of the marketing function at the expense of other functional areas. Rather, it is an attempt to ensure that marketing fulfills its proper role in organizational group settings by effectively representing the perspective of the customer.

What emerges from the discussion is that, in many situations, marketers could be more influential because of their marketing expertise and proven track record (their expert power). At the top management level, the focus is often on gaining influence with the chief financial officer. Here, the current movement toward demonstrating returns on investment (ROI) in marketing represents a step in the right direction. At the product development team level, the focus is usually on representing customer interests to technically trained peers. In either case, and particularly in situations where marketing is not the dominant organizational culture, marketers' ability to frame arguments in terms understood by members of the other function (their persuasiveness power) and to build common ground with representatives of other functional areas (their referent power) determines the extent of their influence.

What does this mean for reforming marketing? To us it strongly suggests a need for marketers to break down the walls surrounding the marketing fortress and to venture out into other functional areas. We may return to the fortress with renewed understanding of areas where marketing can add value to the organization. Alternatively, we may never return to the fortress, choosing rather to serve as missionaries to spread the marketing message throughout the organization, and possibly ending up as CEOs along the way. In either case, the influence of marketing will increase, bringing with it increased returns for the organization.

REFERENCES

Ambler, Tim (2003), "Are You a Wimp or a Warrior?" *Marketing,* October 23, 22–23.

Arrow, Kenneth (1974), *The Limits of Organization.* New York: Norton.

Atuahene-Gima, Kwaku and Felicitas Evangelista (2000), "Cross-Functional Influence in New Product Development: An Exploratory Study of Marketing and R&D Perspectives," *Management Science,* 46 (October), 1269–84.

Barker, Vincent L. III and George C. Mueller (2002), "CEO Characteristics and Firm R&D Spending," *Management Science,* 48 (June), 782–801.

Benjamin, Beth A. (1993), "Understanding the Political Dynamics of Developing New Products," Working paper, Stanford Graduate School of Business.

Bunderson, J. Stuart (2003), "Team Member Functional Background and Involvement in Management Teams: Direct Effects and the Moderating Role of Power Centralization," *Academy of Management Journal,* 46 (August), 458–74.

Dearborn, DeWitt C. and Herbert A. Simon (1958), "Selective Perception: A Note on the Departmental Identifications of Executives," *Sociometry,* 21 (June), 140–45.

Deshpandé, Rohit, John U. Farley, and Frederick E. Webster Jr. (1993), "Corporate Culture Customer Orientation, and Innovativeness in Japanese Firms: A Quadrad Analysis," *Journal of Marketing,* 57 (January), 23–37.

Finkelstein, Sydney (1992), "Power in Top Management Teams: Dimensions, Measurement, and Validation," *Academy of Management Journal,* 35 (August), 505–38.

General Electric (2003), "GE Taps Beth Comstock as Chief Marketing Officer to Lead Corporate Commercial Programs," Press release, July 15.

Janis, Irving L. (1972), *Victims of Groupthink: A Psychological Study of Foreign-Policy Decisions and Fiascoes.* Boston: Houghton-Mifflin.

Jap, Sandy D. (1999), "'Pie-Expansion' Efforts: Collaboration Processes in Buyer-Supplier Relationships," *Journal of Marketing Research* 36 (November), 461–75.

——— (2001), "Pie-Sharing in Complex Collaboration Contexts," *Journal of Marketing Research* 38 (February), 86–99.

Jaworski, Bernard J. and Ajay K. Kohli (1993), "Market Orientation: Antecedents and Consequences," *Journal of Marketing,* 57 (July), 53–60.

Johnson, Craig R. and Don E. Schultz (2004), "A Focus on Customers," *Marketing Management,* 13 (September/October), 20–26.

Lawrence, Paul R. and Jay W. Lorsch (1967), *Organization and Environment.* Homewood, IL: Irwin.

Lewis, Ellen (2002a), "Marketers Must Show Shareholder Value," *Brand Strategy,* 164 (October), 3.

——— (2002b), "The Faltering Faith in Marketers' Business," *Brand Strategy,* 166 (December), 3.

McGrath, Joseph E. (1984), *Groups: Interaction and Performance.* Englewood Cliffs, NJ: Prentice Hall.

Meldrum, M.J. and R. Palmer (1998), "The Future of Marketing in Industrial and Technological Organizations," Working paper, Cranfield University.

Melkman, Alan (2004), "Increasing Marketing's Influence in the Boardroom," *MCE Knowledge,* http://64.233.179.104/search?q=cache:_LrjxMHFgFwJ:www.mce.be/knowledge/394/7+melkman+boardroom&hl=en (accessed August 2004).

Nemeth, Charlan Jeanne (1986), "Differential Contributions of Majority and Minority Influence," *Psychological Review,* 93 (January), 23–32.

Pfeffer, Jeffrey (1994), *Competitive Advantage Through People.* Boston: Harvard Business School Press.

Shipley, David (1994), "Achieving Cross-Functional Co-Ordination for Marketing Implementation," *Management Decision,* 32 (October), 17–20.

Simms, Jane (2003), "How to Drive Business Success . . . and Your Own Career," *Marketing,* September 18, 22–23.

Slater, Stanley F. and John C. Narver (2000), "The Positive Effect of a Market Orientation on Business Profitability: A Balanced Replication," *Journal of Business Research,* 48 (April), 69–73.

Weick, Karl E. (1979), *The Social Psychology of Organizing.* Reading, MA: Addison-Wesley.

Workman, John P., Jr. (1993), "Marketing's Limited Role in New Product Development in One Computer Systems Firm," *Journal of Marketing Research,* 30 (November), 405–21.

PART 6

ACADEMIA, HEAL THYSELF

Reforming Marketing Scholarship and Education

This section is a collection of thoughts about the academic side of marketing, focusing on how marketing academics need to change their scholarship as well as their instruction to make them more valuable to marketing professionals, consumers, and society at large.

In a very thoughtful article, William Wilkie suggests that we need to go back to the study of aggregate marketing systems (AGMS), which consist of three actors: producers, consumers, and government entities. For the last half century, marketing has focused too much at the managerial and consumer levels, resulting in a fragmentation of the discipline. In the process, marketing has lost its impact and influence on all three stakeholders. As research specialization has increased, this risk has increased. Knowledge outside a person's specialty may first be viewed as noninstrumental, then as nonessential, then as nonimportant and finally as nonexistent in terms of meriting attention.

Gary Lilien considers the state of marketing to be a tale of two cities: it is at the best of times and it is also at the worst of times. He believes that part of the reason is that marketing as practiced by most marketers and as taught and researched by most academics is a narrow, silo-based operation addressed either in a predominantly quantitative or predominantly conceptual manner. Really good marketing requires, according to Lilien, a deep integration of science and creativity. It is, indeed, perhaps the most schizophrenic of business activities. It requires skill in problem identification, problem framing, and creativity as well as discipline to collect appropriate data, create metrics and benchmarks, and develop demonstration of economic value.

Rajiv Grover believes that it is market*ers* who need reform and not market*ing*. There are two reasons concerned academicians are insisting on marketing reform. The first relates to their perception that most academic marketing research is irrelevant to marketing issues in organizations and, to their exasperation, such research is held in higher regard in the discipline. The second source of their discontent stems from their perceptions of marginalization of the authority of practicing marketers by nonmarketers, as evidenced by the involvement of the latter in making marketing decisions. According to Grover, though not obvious, the two sources of discontent are related, with the first being the cause of the second.

Grover suggests five potential approaches to make future research more managerially relevant and, therefore, more impactful: selecting the right problems for research, modifying the intellectual rigor perception, coordinating varied research efforts in a particular area or knowledge domain, developing a distinctive identity for marketing, and creating support from the business sector. Similarly, he recommends that our teaching, especially in MBA programs, should be modified to include and integrate both strategy and operations. In his view, we teach too much strategy and not enough operations.

Jagmohan Raju finds that marketing in practice is becoming more marginalized, as evidenced by the declining tenure of the chief marketing officer (CMO). But marketing as a discipline in academia is growing, as evidenced by student enrollments and increasing size of departments of marketing, as well as by the number of manuscripts submitted to major marketing journals. He believes that since marketing is an applied discipline, marketing academia can enhance the prestige and position of marketing practitioners by choosing the audience (academics vs. practitioners), doing the right things versus doing things right (relevance vs. rigor), encouraging Ph.D. students to go for industry careers in addition to academic careers, valuing consulting activity in annual performance evaluations, and teaching what we discover in our research.

In a very insightful and provocative chapter, Morris Holbrook suggests that too much emphasis on customer orientation and confusion about who is our customer has created enormous problems in classroom teaching. In the old-fashioned elementary school he attended, the customer was the teacher and the producer was the student. The student produced homework, wrote exams, and the teacher as a customer rewarded the student as a producer with appropriate grades, promotion, and graduation.

This changed to a system where the school became the producer and corporations became customers. Schools produced job candidates and the corporation rewarded the school with employment opportunities. This revised model "freely acknowledges that careerism has come to dominate the academic process and that the inherently selfish interests of big business play a major role in shaping educational policy without any real regard for the moral or intellectual development of individual character." This perspective elicits great outrage from students, who do not want to be regarded as products. Students would rather be viewed as customers, similar to patients in a hospital, parishioners of a church, voters in an election, or inmates at a prison.

This has led to the third emerging view that sees the school as a producer that offers MBA degree diplomas, networking opportunities, and career counseling in exchange for tuition dollars, generous donations, and favorable evaluations from its students, regarded as customers.

Holbrook suggests a fourth and preferred model. He suggests school as producer, student as a channel, and society as the customer. The school produces knowledge and transmits it through the students to society. In return, society offers respect and good will to the student and the student offers appreciation to the school. In this supply chain model, the major purpose of the university lies in the creation and dissemination of knowledge.

Rajan Varadarajan, drawing on his experience as editor of two major academic journals in marketing (*JM* and *JAMS*), suggests that reviewers and editors of scholarly journals must insist that authors provide managerial, public policy, and scholarly implications of their research. He also suggests a tighter integration of marketing strategy and consumer behavior research. Finally, he suggests examining the current marketing curriculum, especially for doctoral students, to see if it includes rapidly changing environmental forces and their implications on marketing theory and practice.

CHAPTER 28

THE WORLD OF MARKETING THOUGHT

Where Are We Heading?

WILLIAM L. WILKIE

Does marketing need reform? is a welcome question. I have become increasingly convinced that there are critical issues in our field that require attention and discourse within the college of marketing and I raise several of these that I see as most pressing. In this chapter I address three essential points, one as background, and two as key issues for us to consider, discuss, and hopefully rectify:

- As a background perspective, in my view the academy of marketing needs its own identity in certain of these discussions—we need to be more specific in our referents when analyzing our field. It is interesting to recognize that in recent years, when discussing "marketing," we often implicitly equate marketing practice and marketing academics, as if the problems, opportunities, and issues are equivalent in these spheres. While the two do have a symbiotic relationship, clearly there are also occasions for which issues, perspectives, and behaviors will be sharply distinct. My personal interests are in the realm of marketing thought, which links closely to marketing academia. Thus my discussion here will involve issues and possible reforms for marketing academia.
- One central issue for academics to address is, Is there any need for aggregate perspectives in our conception of the field of marketing? If we consider this only briefly, it becomes clear that our modern conceptions of marketing are really not aggregate in nature—they are very much centered on individual managers, firms, or consumers. As a result, we likely do not possess the best mental frameworks with which to be addressing some of the problems confronting our field, such as those raised elsewhere in this volume. So in this chapter I'd like to explicitly direct our attention to the concept of an aggregate marketing system as an organizing framework from which we might better consider our field as a whole. Further, in this regard the new definition of marketing from the American Marketing Association appears especially problematic: comments on its potential deficiencies are also offered in this discussion.
- The second key issue involves the question, Is knowledge being lost from our field? Again, only brief reflection allows us to recognize that our scholarship attends easily and eagerly to knowledge accreting in our field (i.e., the exciting new discoveries at the frontier). However, I've become increasingly concerned that this directed attention to incremental advances in specific sectors is also leading to a situation in which we are in the process of losing knowledge in other sectors of the field. It appears, moreover, that this is happening both at indi-

vidual levels and as a community of scholars. In this regard, we also appear to be allowing (encouraging?) a suppressive publication infrastructure to develop—one that is discouraging future contributors and their potential contributions to knowledge across a broad swath of our field.

ISSUE ONE: WHAT HAS HAPPENED TO AN AGGREGATE PERSPECTIVE IN MARKETING?

The Aggregate Marketing System

Before delving into specifics, some brief background may be helpful. The commentary in this chapter springs from a long-term project in which I and my colleague Elizabeth Moore have been exploring the question, What *is* marketing, anyway? One of the two primary reports of our project findings to date appeared in the *Journal of Marketing's Special Millennium Issue,* under the title, "Marketing's Contributions to Society" (Wilkie and Moore 1999).[1] There, in order to capture the concept of "society," we built on perspectives from an earlier era and proposed the concept of an aggregate marketing system (AGMS)—a huge, powerful, yet intricate complex operating to serve the needs of its host society. The AGMS is recognized to be different in each society, as it is an adaptive human and technological institution reflecting the idiosyncrasies of the people and their culture, geography, economic opportunities and constraints, and sociopolitical decisions. The three primary sets of actors within the system are seen to be: (1) marketers, (2) consumers, and (3) government entities, whose public policy decisions are meant to facilitate the maximal operations of the AGMS for the benefit of the host society.[2]

Our initial goal was to explore the AGMS of the United States. Early in the process we recognized that much of the marketing system operates behind the scenes, known only to those persons involved in pieces of the operation itself. It is challenging, therefore, for outside observers to fully appreciate the scope and nuances of marketing, a useful reminder to us academics as well.[3] Three early insights that we gained were that marketing's contributions (1) accumulate over time, (2) diffuse through a society, and (3) occur within the context of everyday life. This makes it difficult to distinguish them at any given point in time, so we took a one-hundred-year glimpse at what the U.S. AGMS is delivering to daily life today versus one hundred years ago, when the academic field of marketing was beginning to form. Here's a little of what we found:

> At the turn of the century in 1900, few homes had running water, so the average housewife had to carry nine thousand gallons per year from the well source outside. Only 3 percent of homes had electricity: for the rest this meant reading with no electric lighting and keeping house with no labor-saving household appliances, and, of course, no radio or television. Food purchasing and preparation took forty-two hours per week, versus less than ten hours today. Home heating was often limited to only the kitchen, versus central heating today, and there was no home air conditioning. Virtually no one had a gas-powered vehicle: there are some two hundred million motor vehicles registered in the United States today, all having been delivered through the AGMS. Infant mortality was common at the time, about one in every ten births, and life expectancy in 1900 was only forty-seven years. Today's health and well-being has improved dramatically, with infant mortality much less than 1 percent and life expectancy at almost eighty years. Similar comparisons exist on many other fronts as well: it is clear that the AGMS has delivered a substantially better standard of living to its society across time. (Wilkie and Moore 1999)

But why give so much credit to marketing for these advances? Clearly it isn't responsible for discoveries, inventions, or production operations. Our point was that today we are simply not conceiving of marketing as a system in the world, and that if we were to do so we would easily see that it is, *in tandem with other systems such as research and development, finance and banking, production, and so forth,* clearly engaged in both delivering a standard of living to society and constantly supporting innovations to raise these standards.

In order to examine marketing as a system, we began by learning directly in detail from marketers who were doing it, then illustrated this with a vignette we called "Breakfast at Tiffany's." We join Tiffany Jones in New York, have breakfast with her family, and inquire how this breakfast has managed to come about. Imagine Tiffany sitting in her apartment, picking up her cup of coffee, blowing across the top of the cup. How did this cup of coffee get here? We trace the process, discussing the planting of coffee, where it is planted, why it is planted, how it is sold by contract, how it is harvested, how it is graded, processed, bagged, warehoused, and transported to the United States by sea, mixed, roasted, packaged, then shipped through the channels of distribution to retail, where Tiffany has purchased it. We then move to her breakfast pastry and repeat the system analysis, though this one is much more complex because there is new product development involved, plus fifteen ingredient sourcing systems similar to that for coffee. We then point to each of the foods being consumed by each family member, as well as to the kitchen support system (appliances, cutlery, utilities, etc.), which also had been provided by the AGMS at prior points, and which are still delivering benefits through use.

During this illustration we note the set of structured, practiced activities that are already developed in an infrastructure sense. This is a marketing system at work, in the sense that there is buying and selling occurring at all stages, with temporal dimensions, planning, employment, capital investment, movement, production, risk taking, financing, and so on, all taking place with the expectation of transactional exchanges occurring to fuel the system's continuing operation. We further point out that the AGMS is routinely providing these kinds of breakfasts for a hundred million households every day, and that this is just a miniscule portion of its total activity. It is very clear that the AGMS is huge, practiced, and powerful. In our discussion of aggregating these separate systems into a whole we attempted statistical estimates of sizes, and arrived at some thirty million Americans— about one in five workers—directly employed in the marketing operations of the AGMS. This raises some very interesting challenges for us in conceptualizing the field, unless we've already conceived that there are thirty million marketers in the United States alone!

Of considerable import for this book is what came next in our analysis, namely an assessment of the various activities embedded in our illustration of the systems for these two products. It turned out that *we found seventy-five marketing-related activities embodied in those two little examples.* For each one, we asked whether a marketer in the firm is (1) primarily responsible, or (2) has an influence, or (3) doesn't even have an influence. The results were instructive: of the seventy-five marketing system activities, we saw that marketing managers control only about thirty, or less than half. They do have influence on most of the others (consumer usage and some aspects of governmental operations were viewed as uncontrollable), but they are not in control, and this is not what we're calling marketing today. *My personal lesson from this was that this property of the system demands a perspective on marketing that reaches far beyond a controllable decision of someone called a marketing manager.* At a minimum, it requires an inclusive appreciation of business organizations and processes, as clearly has been recognized elsewhere in this book, and also requires an appreciation of roles that the government plays in facilitating development of the system's infrastructure and operations. In brief, it calls for a larger conception of marketing.

A Historical Perspective on Marketing Thought

Have we ever had such larger conceptions in the field? Yes, clearly this used to be the case. My basic perspectives are captured in a Fall 2003 *Journal of Public Policy & Marketing* article titled "Scholarly Research in Marketing: Exploring the 'Four Eras' of Thought Development" (Wilkie and Moore 2003).[4] In this effort we examined the evolution of marketing thought across the last one hundred years, including the growth of the knowledge infrastructure (journals, associations, conferences, etc.) and trends and paradigms characterizing thought progression in the field. We found that writings on marketing and society were common in the first half of the century. For example, consider these quotes from two leading marketing thinkers of the time, who apparently viewed their scholarly and professional roles more broadly than we do today:

> It is the responsibility of the marketing profession, therefore, to provide a marketing view of competition in order to guide efforts at regulation and to revitalize certain aspects of the science of economics. . . . For surely no one is better qualified to play a leading part in the consideration of measures designed for the regulation of competition. (Alderson 1937, pp. 189, 190)

And, from Ralph Breyer:

> [M]arketing is not primarily a means for garnering profits for individuals. It is, in the larger, more vital sense, an economic instrument used to accomplish indispensable social ends. . . . A marketing system designed solely for its social effectiveness would move goods with a minimum of time and effort to deficit points. In doing so, it would also provide a fair compensation, and no more, for the efforts of those engaged in the activity. At the same time it would provide the incentive needed to stimulate constant improvements in its methods. These are the prime requisites of social effectiveness. (1934, p. 192)

Then, about 1950, the world of marketing thought began to undergo a major academic paradigm shift in modes of thinking. Era III had begun, now featuring (a) an overt *marketing-as-management* orientation, and (b) an overt *reliance on the behavioral and quantitative sciences as means of knowing.*[5] These approaches to marketing thought have now been dominant for a half century in the field: as noted at the start, our modern conceptions of marketing are no longer aggregate in nature—they are very much centered on individual managers, firms, brands, and consumer behaviors. In this regard, the new definition offered by the American Marketing Association is worthy of serious consideration.

AMA's New Definition of Marketing (2004)

Recently the American Marketing Association convened a process (under Professor Robert Lusch) to update the definition of marketing. The first formal AMA definition had been developed in 1935, and was retained for fifty years until being modified in 1985, and then modified again in 2004.[6] Here are the three definitions:

> (Marketing is) the performance of business activities that direct the flow of goods and services from producers to consumers. (1935)

(Marketing is) the process of planning and executing the conception, pricing, promotion, and distribution of ideas, goods and services to create exchanges that satisfy individual and organizational objectives. (1985)

(Marketing is) an organizational function and a set of processes for creating, communicating and delivering value to customers and for managing customer relationships in ways that benefit the organization and its stakeholders. (2004)

Examining the direction of these definitions reveals a narrowing of focus over the time, quite in accord with the historical trends just noted (and discussed at length in Wilkie and Moore 2003). Notice that until 1985 the field's definition was pluralistic, thereby easily translatable to more aggregated issues such as competition, system performance, and contributions to consumer welfare. The 1985 change then firmly turned focus toward the manager's tasks as embodied in the four Ps (product, place, promotion, and price); interestingly, by focusing on the concept of mutually satisfactory exchanges it also implicitly defined marketing to be in the best interests of consumers. Overall, these changes made it more difficult to adopt more aggregated perspectives on the field.

The new 2004 definition is much in the same spirit, with a singular focus on the individual organization acting alone. This is not simply my reading, but is also clear from the leaders of the initiative. For example, according to the head of the AMA's Academic Division:

What we (now) have is more strategic. Now it says marketing is really something that makes the organization run. (in Keefe 2004, p. 17)

Some Concerns about Equating Marketing with Management

To be clear about my personal position, let me say that I quite agree that the conception of marketing as a strategic and tactical activity undertaken within individual organizations is a most reasonable view for marketing managers to take, and for academics to use when appropriate. My concern, however, is with this as such a dominant conception of our field that it forecloses other directions for thought development. In essence, I see a sole focus on the firm to be *incomplete,* in that some broader questions go unanswered precisely because the managerial perspective within a firm does not need to consider these questions in order to act in that firm's interest. For example, let us consider the following items.

The Competitive Nature of the AGMS. A sole focus on the firm does not provide constructs with which to assess marketing more broadly. For example, when eight or twelve firms compete in a market, how do we assess the marketing that is occurring? It would appear inefficiencies would be natural in such settings, yet these are not assessed with this focus. Extended to public policy, moreover, what does this conception of marketing have to offer to antitrust theory and enforcement?

Marketing's Inputs into Consumers' Resource Allocation Decisions. One of the major tasks confronting every consumer is to decide on how to allocate his or her budget for purchases, as well as the time and effort to be expended on each. But what if we ask, How well do marketers help consumers with their budget and effort allocation decisions? Our short answer: Very poorly. *In the aggregate (i.e., all marketers taken together) our marketing system simply proposes far too much consumption for any individual to come close to undertaking.* The system acts as if consumer resources and wants are infinite and insatiable: every product and service category is advocated as worthy of consumption for virtually every consumer. *It thus becomes mandatory for every consumer to ignore most marketing programs, resist many others, and respond positively to only a relative few* (see Wilkie 1994, chap. 2, for a discussion of this perspective). My point here is that the extreme heterogeneity of marketing activity cannot possibly serve an individual consumer well in terms of personal allocation choices (excepting in a partially informative sense), and that *this characteristic surely makes it difficult to equate each marketer's best interest with each consumer's best interest.*

Marketing within Specific Categories and Inputs to Consumer Decisions. This same issue arises if we narrow our focus to firms within specific product or service categories. Within each category, marketers as a set are offering each consumer *highly conflicting advice* as to which sources (both brand and retailer) to select. The system's marketers are also often employing intrusive persuasive attempts, demanding attention and consideration from consumers who would not be best served by the option being advocated. (Let me stress that I do not offer this as a criticism, but as a descriptive characteristic of our marketing system that is simply not evident enough from the managerial perspective on marketing.)

Further, it seems to me that the greatest risk of equating the field of marketing with the managerial decisions being made inside all organizations is that *the goals of those organizations are also being adopted by marketing thinkers, but without any external or neutral appraisal.* This leads to something akin to a lack of direction, or blanket approval, regarding the reality of what the marketing world in total is undertaking.

Let us consider some issues that come to mind as we ponder this issue, and ask whether this is a satisfactory solution for marketing scholarship. For example, when we implicitly adopt the goals of an organization engaged in marketing, exactly whose perceived interests are being served, and does this matter to us? The many egregious examples found in political campaigning, lobbying, fraudulent schemes, bid rigging, energy gouging, channel stuffing, and so on are sufficient to alert us to the fact many organizations are highly imperfect entities with a highly mixed set of motivations. Also, in most organizations persons other than marketers are setting priorities, and not necessarily with marketing's sensitivities to consumers. For example, I recently heard of an analysis showing that—across providers—most users of cell phones end the month with a large number of unused calling minutes and that most customers were not enrolled in the plan best for them in terms of their actual phone usage. Is this successful marketing, then?

In general, I'm suggesting that the impacts that marketing is having on the world are a legitimate concern for scholarship in our field, and much of this will relate to the twin issues of marketplace competition and pressure for profitability and stock market price gains in organizations. Further, any such assessments of marketing performance are likely to benefit if more aggregated perspectives are called upon.

Finally, I should mention that this line of thinking has helped me to realize how interesting it is that "the marketing concept" was introduced just at the beginning of the shift to the managerial view of the field, and has been a bulwark in characterizing marketing ever since. Because we have overtly characterized our field's mission as meeting the needs of customers, we have not had to consider what's actually being undertaken by the huge numbers of marketers who are working in parallel day after day after day, in terms of the actual meeting of consumers' wants and needs. Again, this would seem to be a much more reasonable task were we also to be thinking of marketing in a larger, systemic sense.

In closing this section, I think it is important to note that defining marketing in a larger sense was in fact considered in the development process for the AMA's new definition for the field.

When interviewed about the definition, Professor Lusch spoke directly to this point:

> Some view [marketing] as a managerial activity, but others view it as a broad societal activity . . . Europeans and Australians, for example, were most likely to argue that marketing is a societal process . . . I don't disagree, but . . . because it's used to introduce students to the discipline, we needed something comprehensible. (in Keefe 2004, p. 18)

I have long admired Professor Lusch's views and work, and realize that he had to make conscious choices with this definition. However, it is telling that the AMA seems to be pointing toward introductory students with the definition. This does not seem to be an appropriate guide for directing scholarly pursuits in marketing, so perhaps my concerns about the definition are actually not very serious. For what it's worth, however, I'd like to officially weigh in on the side of those who were suggesting that marketing is best understood when its societal impacts are being formally considered, as in the context of an aggregate marketing system.

ISSUE TWO: IS KNOWLEDGE BEING LOST FROM OUR FIELD?

In the space remaining, I will briefly point to some other key points involving knowledge development in the field. First, the importance of a solely managerial perspective on the AMA's restrictive definition has little to do with their focus itself, which I like. Instead, the danger lies in subsequent impacts on effort, attention, and transmission of marketing knowledge. Within the context of an increasingly specialized and fragmented academic field of marketing, two brief quotes capture my concern:

> It is troubling to realize that knowledge does not necessarily accumulate in a field—that knowledge can disappear over time if it is not actually transmitted. (Wilkie 1981)

> As research specialization has increased, this risk has increased—knowledge outside a person's specialty may first be viewed as non-instrumental, then as non-essential, then as non-important, and finally as non-existent in terms of meriting attention. (Wilkie 2002).

In our exploration of the four eras of thought development it became clear that many research insights and findings did not get passed on, but were "left behind" as researchers turned their attention to new areas of interest. This finding prompts us to look more closely at whence the academic marketing thought leaders of the future will come, and how their scholarly training and predispositions will be shaped. How are they being educated to think about the field of marketing? Specifically, for me, are they being educated in the societal domain of marketing issues?

To examine this question, we undertook a survey of AMA-Sheth Doctoral Consortium participants (Wilkie and Moore 1997). The results were most interesting. Somewhat surprising to me, personal interest in the topic was high: two-thirds of these doctoral candidates felt that this area should be covered in PhD education, and wanted to learn about it. However, fewer than one in ten had ever taken a course in the subject. Further, they reported their self-ratings of expertise to be low, regular readership of the journals most pertinent to marketing and society as very low, and their participation in the conferences for this area as very low. Finally, many of these respondents answered that they do not see this area as professionally relevant for them, at least at the current stage of their careers.

Doctoral programs sorely need to reconsider this issue, but this will not happen unless marketing scholars are willing to admit that knowledge is being lost from this field. My true concern in this regard is not for the aware scholar who opts to make an informed choice to avoid societal issues, but instead is for later generations of scholars (today's and the future's doctoral students) who may not gain enough background to even realize that a choice is available to them.

CONCLUSION: IT IS TIME FOR A MARKETING ACADEMIC SUMMIT TO ENHANCE SCHOLARSHIP IN OUR FIELD

The interest in this book and the turnout for the Bentley Symposium that precipitated it is further evidence of unrest within marketing academia, and a need to explore means to create a better context for scholarship in the future. Worthy topics that I personally would suggest for consideration include: (1) the character of business schools' vocational objectives for university faculty members, (2) the "publish or perish" system's incentives and time constraints, (3) the character of the modern journal publication system, (4) the nature and objectives of research-oriented doctoral programs, especially the extent to which failure to provide sufficient background in intrinsic domains of marketing thought may be leading to problems for the future of the field, and (5) the implications, problems, and opportunities presented by the twin forces of globalization and the Internet. Such a summit is feasible. Similar efforts have been undertaken before in our field in the form of task forces on thought development, with interesting and impressive results (e.g., AMA Task Force 1988; Myers, Massy, and Greyser 1980). It seems clear that a new effort is needed today.

NOTES

1. Interested readers may download a copy directly from web2.business.nd.edu/Faculty/wilkie.html.

2. As pointed out in the classic volume by Vaile, Grether, and Cox many years ago (1952), marketing systems perform two distinct macro-tasks for their societies: (1) delivering the standard of living for the citizenry, and (2) creating a marketplace dynamism that fosters and supports continual innovation and improvement such that the standard of daily life is enhanced over time.

3. Studies have shown that the less familiar a person is with the marketing field, the more likely he or she is to equate marketing with advertising or selling, the most visible portions of marketing to laypersons. As a person learns more, the view deepens and he or she begins to appreciate the richness of the field (Kasper 1993).

4. A copy of this article is also available at http://web2.business.nd.edu/Faculty/wilkie.html.

5. This was followed by Era IV (1980 to the present), which has maintained these core modes for thought development, but now with a fragmentation of the mainstream of marketing thought (Wilkie and Moore 2003).

6. A very informative article (Keefe 2004) in the *Marketing News* can be consulted for more information on this topic.

References

Alderson, Wroe (1937), "A Marketing View of Competition," *Journal of Marketing,* 1 (January), 189–90.

American Marketing Association Task Force (1988), "Developing, Disseminating, and Utilizing Marketing Knowledge," *Journal of Marketing,* 52, 1–25.

Breyer, Ralph F. (1934), *The Marketing Institution.* New York: McGraw-Hill.

Kasper, Hans (1993), "The Images of Marketing: Facts, Speculations, and Implications," working paper 93-015, Maastricht, Netherlands: University of Limburg.

Keefe, Lisa M. (2004), "What Is the Meaning of 'Marketing'?" *Marketing News,* September 15, 17–18.

Myers, John G., William F. Massy, and Stephen A. Greyser (1980), *Marketing Research and Knowledge Development.* Englewood Cliffs, NJ: Prentice-Hall.

Vaile, Roland S., E.T. Grether, and Reavis Cox (1952), *Marketing in the American Economy.* New York: Ronald Press Co.

Wilkie, William L. (1981), "Presidential Address," in *Advances in Consumer Research,* Vol. 8, K. Monroe, ed. Ann Arbor, MI: Association for Consumer Research, 1–5.

———— (1994), *Consumer Behavior,* 3rd ed. New York: Wiley.

———— (2002), "On Books and Scholarship: Reflections of a Marketing Academic," *Journal of Marketing,* 66 (July), 141–52.

———— and Elizabeth S. Moore (1997), "Consortium Survey on Marketing and Society Issues: Summary and Results," *Journal of Macromarketing,* 17 (2), 89–95.

———— and ———— (1999), "Marketing's Contributions to Society," *Journal of Marketing,* 63 (Special Millennium Issue), 198–218.

———— and ———— (2003), "Scholarly Research in Marketing: Exploring the 'Four Eras' of Thought Development," *Journal of Public Policy and Marketing,* 22 (Fall), 116–46.

CHAPTER 29

MARKETING

A Tale of Two Cities

GARY L. LILIEN

Charles Dickens began his *Tale of Two Cities* with the line "It was the best of times, it was the worst of times." So it seems to be for the marketing profession today, both on the academic and on the practice side. The chapters in this volume address the question, does marketing need reform? I don't have a clear answer for that question, but marketing at least needs a better press agent.

Throughout my career, my colleagues and I in marketing have felt like the Rodney Dangerfields of business. We get no respect. Many years ago, Peter Drucker noted "business has only two functions: innovation and marketing." No wonder he added that "marketing is too important to be left to marketers." Why has it come to this? Why does marketing (but neither finance nor operations nor human resources) need reform?

Part of the reason is that marketing as practiced by most marketers and as taught and researched by most academics is a narrow, silo-based operation addressed either in a predominantly quantitative (bring in the data miners!) or predominantly conceptual (bring in the agency creatives!) manner.

Really good marketing is not like that at all. Indeed, really good marketing requires a deep integration of science and creativity. It is, indeed, perhaps the most schizophrenic of business activities. It requires skill in problem identification, problem framing, and creativity as well as the discipline to collect appropriate data, create metrics and benchmarks, and develop demonstrations of economic value.

As the information age has lowered the cost of documenting value in most organizational functions, and as management-by-dashboard has become more pervasive, firms are less tolerant of business as usual and are demanding business as possible. Marketing has generally been slow to react, but react it must.

This quantitative/creative schizophrenia brings to mind what C.P. Snow (1993) originally raised in a 1953 essay where he discussed the dichotomy between science and literature, and his belief in the need for closer contact between them. Both of Snow's "Two Cultures" must thrive within the marketing profession for it to be healthy. And the challenge is how to stimulate healthy schizophrenia within the profession. To paraphrase Snow, we have to humanize the scientist and simonize the humanist in the marketing profession for it to prosper. Indeed, as Hoch (2001) pointed out, a combination of formal models and intuition outperforms either pure approach to marketing decisions.

Marketing problems need both approaches. A classic story from the early days of operations research (OR) recalls the OR group (the techie or quant group) that was brought in to improve the elevator service in a recently opened office building. Building management was receiving numerous complaints about unacceptably slow service and the OR group carefully analyzed and reprogrammed the elevators, but was only able to achieve a marginal improvement in (objective) service. Finally one member of the group had a bright idea—the complaints indicated that folks in the building "felt they were waiting too long." That is a perception and not a technically defined metric. So they cleverly addressed the perception by installing mirrors in each floor landing in the building, providing some distraction for those awaiting service. The complaints about the slow service ceased because the marketing "quals" had reframed the problem in a way that was much easier to address.

Ideas like this have been adopted in the Disney Company's work on "guestology," where engineers work alongside psychologists, designing systems that are both efficient from an engineering perspective and from the customer's perspective as well. Queues generally move (people are happier when they perceive progress); customers are told how long they will wait (there are signs that say, "When you reach this point, you have 10 minutes to wait") and Disney generally beats the posted waiting time (you will wait about 8 minutes when they say you will wait 10—a gain relative to expectations) yielding happy customers.

Most real marketing problems have a quantitative and a qualitative component. Design engineers are given budgets and goals. The products engineers develop will be used by people. How should the design requirements incorporate the humanistic or customer-use element? We need humanists in marketing to answer that question properly.

And for the creative, or (purely) intuitive marketer—business is moving much too quickly, generating much too much important data to make decisions based on intuition. Each day, global airlines reoptimize their fares and seat allocations on all their routes and route-segments for a year in advance. That task, involving tens of millions of decision-variables, cannot possibly be addressed by intuition alone.

Marketing must be reformed in such a way that it addresses the world through the eyes of the scientist at some times and through the humanist at others, when appropriate. The benefits are potentially enormous, but if such a perspective were easy, many more people would use their scientist/humanist bifocals so that they could look through the correct lens at the right time

While I don't have a prescription for marketing reform here, whatever prescription emerges should address the following ideas.

Embrace Schizophrenia

Lorange (2005) closed his "memo to marketing" with the following:

> Marketing . . . must become a model for innovation rather than follow a strategy of incrementalism based on the mere administration of brands . . . *it must learn to embrace ambiguity by recognizing the importance of data and intuition*. The goal is to be at the forefront of seeing new business opportunities based on facts and insights . . . the task of marketing has become increasingly difficult—and more important than ever before. (p. 20, emphasis added)

Note that Lorange cites marketing as a key engine for organizational innovation and he challenges the function to embrace the necessary schizophrenia or ambiguity needed to achieve that position. This echoes the point that Clancy and Krieg (2000) made when they stated that "counterintuitive marketing grounded in rigorous analysis of unimpeachable data is the key to success" (p. xii).

Escape from the Silo

When Drucker said that marketing was too important to be left to marketers, he was calling for marketing to get out of its silo. Wind (2005) presents a case for marketing as the "engine of business growth." But a necessary condition for that engine to generate power is that it becomes cross-functional. Increasingly, marketing will not be able to create value or insights on its own but will be able to do so only in concert with other disciplines and functions of the firm—finance, R&D, operations, distribution. The opportunity here is for marketing to catalyze changes in organizational architectures and entire business models, creating truly significant rather than marginal value. The challenge is for the marketing profession—both the practitioner and the academic—to learn how to survive and thrive outside the comfort of its traditional silo.

Demonstrate and Document (D&D) Value

Anderson and Narus (2003) stress the importance for the marketing function to continually demonstrate and document (D&D) value. These are two separate steps—-the developments needed to demonstrate value and the associated documentation. Most of what masquerades as such demonstrations today are "success stories"—the firm ran program X and sales were 14 percent higher than a year earlier. But how do we know that without program X sales would not have been 20 percent higher? This success story or folk wisdom approach—a post-only research design—is bad science and unacceptable as credible evidence for effectiveness. Marketing must continually run experiments as part of its way of doing business, with appropriate selection of pre- and post-measurements and test versus control situations. New marketing campaigns often provide attractive venues for such situations, and are especially effective test beds when using direct channels or the Internet. In any case, the D&D approach requires specification of metrics (the documentation or dashboard items) as well as the selection of the test and control venues as part of doing business.

Enterprise Value Resides in Customer Knowledge

Peppers and Rogers (2001, for example) have helped popularize the notion that a firm can no longer maintain a competitive advantage in most industries through technological leadership. Technology and business models are too easily and rapidly copied. Rather, they argue that deep customer knowledge is an asset that cannot readily be copied—a relationship, by definition, takes time to build. Marketing, the owner of the customer interface, has the ability to help the firm execute that real option, that is, help turn that customer knowledge into a sequence of correctly designed and targeted offerings (created by the firm or within the firm's value net) to generate long-term, noncopy-able value.

I have suggested that marketing does need reform—that we are in a new age of marketing myopia (acknowledgments to Ted Levitt). The symptoms of myopia are clear; the prescription requires courage and imagination. If we have the courage and imagination, marketing can lead business advances in academia and practice in the years to come; if we don't, marketing will forever be wondering who moved our cheese.

REFERENCES

Anderson, James C. and James A. Narus (2003), *Business Market Management: Understanding, Creating and Delivering Value,* 2d ed. Upper Saddle River, NJ: Prentice Hall.

Clancy, Kevin J. and Peter C. Krieg (2000), *Counterintuitive Marketing*. New York: The Free Press.

Hoch, Stephen J. (2001), "Combining Models with Intuition to Improve Decisions," in *Wharton on Making Decisions,* Stephen J. Hoch, Howard C. Kunreuther, and R.E. Gunther, eds., New York: John Wiley and Sons, 81–102.

Lorange, Peter (2005), "Memo to Marketing," *MIT Sloan Management Review,* (Winter), 16–20.

Peppers, Don and Martha Rogers (2001), *One to One, BtoB.* New York: Doubelday.

Snow, C.P. (1993), *The Two Cultures.* Cambridge: Cambridge University Press.

Wind, Yoram (2005), "Marketing as an Engine of Business Growth: A Cross-Functional Perspective," *Journal of Business Research,* 58, 863–73.

CHAPTER 30

MARKETING OR MARKETERS

What or Who Needs Reforming?

RAJIV GROVER

Of late, part of the academic marketing community has shown growing interest in reforming the discipline of marketing. It might even be justifiably argued that some progress toward this end has already been made. The interest in reform in the concerned academicians seems to have arisen from two main sources of discontentment. The first source relates to their perception that an appreciable level of research conducted in academic marketing is irrelevant to marketing issues in organizations and, to their exasperation, such research is held in higher regard in the discipline. The second source of their discontentment stems from their perception of marginalization of the authority of practicing marketers by non-marketers, as evidenced by the involvement of the latter in making marketing decisions.

Though not fairly obvious, the two sources of discontentment are related, with the first being the cause of the second. A lack of research with useful managerial implications (that are clear and *definitive* at some level of abstraction) produces a corresponding lack of availability of cutting-edge, practically applicable teaching materials. The dearth of teaching materials, in turn, results either in repetition of concepts in marketing courses or in delivery of educational content that is half-baked and, hence, inapplicable. In either case, the student takeaways from marketing courses tend to be rather simplistic. This simplistic view of marketing translates into a confidence in nonmarketing professionals about their capability to make marketing decisions.

With the practical relevance of its efforts forming the key basis of the need for reform in the marketing discipline, the essential work that needs to be done may be seen as two-fold. First, the discipline needs to adopt specific approaches for ensuring that marketing knowledge that is "useful"—of practical value—is continuously and efficiently generated and appropriately disseminated on a real-time basis. Second, the discipline needs to ensure that there are structural and functional mechanisms in place that serve to facilitate progress toward those approaches.

The call for generating new outputs of relevant knowledge cannot be answered without changes in inputs (outputs result from inputs). Those inputs are represented by the outlook, behaviors, and research and teaching activities of the academicians in the discipline. Thus, for appropriate reform to occur in the marketing discipline, there needs to occur a reform in the academicians. In other words, academic marketers themselves need to change and transform some of their research and teaching activities in order to bring about a change in the marketing discipline.

This chapter discusses how marketing academicians might reform the discipline by reforming their own research and teaching. It recounts what the past has been and what the future might be with the academicians undertaking certain steps to shape it proactively. It specifically addresses the issues of practical relevance of the discipline's efforts, providing a brief historical perspective of how academic marketing grew to stray away from practice, and then listing potential approaches that academic marketers might consider for generating and disseminating marketing knowledge that would be perceived as more useful in terms of practical relevance.

THE ISSUE OF PRACTICAL OR MANAGERIAL RELEVANCE IN ACADEMIC MARKETING

There have been extended debates in the marketing discipline on whether the discipline's research and teaching efforts should be concerned with practical or managerial implications at all. The pure-theorists claim that like physicists, biologists, or mathematicians, academic marketers are also scientists, and thus practical relevance should not be interjected into their research discussions. The proponents of practical relevance, on the other hand, maintain that if practical relevance is not of much import, then such marketing academicians should practice their profession in other academic departments—departments that directly support or are directly relevant to their research, whether they are statistics, psychology, sociology, or any other. The advocates of practical relevance argue that as long as marketing academicians want to be in marketing, and marketing is a distinct function in business organizations, the results of the efforts of marketing academicians must be material to business organizations. In their estimation, although a publication might not have direct managerial utility, it should at least be able to articulate how the direction of research could eventually impact or improve marketing practice in the broader world.

Evidence now indicates that a preponderance of marketing academicians have begun to give some attention to the issue of practical relevance in their papers and dissertations. Even though the incorporation of this issue in research may still many times be superficial, slow, or force-fitted, the debate over it seems to be slowly becoming muted and less contentious.

In order for marketing academicians to be able to consider some approaches and mechanisms for reform, an appreciation of how academic marketing got to where it is would be appropriate.

The Past: How the Research and Teaching Pendulum Swung

The academic discipline of marketing grew as an "applied" field, historically developing by borrowing theories from other disciplines. Many would agree that economics was the "mother" discipline for marketing, and that some other disciplines, such as psychology, social psychology, sociology, anthropology, and statistics, were significant contributors to the field. During the initial stages of the growth of marketing, most of the academic research in the discipline consisted of direct application of theories or methodologies from these disciplines to the problems in marketing. Given that marketing was a new and virgin territory and that there were thus many potential ideas that researchers could bring in, most of the issues that were chosen for research (generally from the parent disciplines) produced knowledge that had not been previously available and was, hence, perceived as useful by marketers both in practice and academics.

With business schools struggling to attain respect among other schools by demonstrating that their research was based upon accepted research protocols (i.e., accepted in other fields) and was not "atheoretical," the trend of borrowing and applying methodologies from other disciplines continued and picked up pace. Similar to some other business disciplines, academic marketing too carried on its pursuit of avoiding being cast as a vocational field, focusing on inserting (whether discriminately or indiscriminately) theoretical rigor in its teaching and research. It thus kept moving away from practice, with the issues that were researched made artificially simple to allow them to be resolved in a manner that embraced conventional methodological rigor.

The nature of the problems or issues selected for research in the early stages stemmed from the background and training of the initial scholars in marketing, which were acquired from areas outside of marketing. Furthermore, the discipline did not strive to ensure that the candidates recruited into the doctoral programs were aware of or sensitive to the needs of the marketing world. The irrelevance of the problems researched persisted and did not diminish any with time since the newer problems investigated and studied were almost always based upon previous research that had solved innocuous problems in the first place. The cycle so continued (and does so to this day to a certain extent). In that vein, the research and teaching pendulum continued to swing, and, in the eyes of some, had swung to quite the extreme when researchers in marketing loathed the thought of having to provide any real *marketing*—let alone *managerial*—implications of their research! Thus, though there were improvements over time in the types of problems selected for analysis, progress in the field was not as significant as might have been with the right channels in place, such as direct interactions with managers.

As time went on, research in marketing started falling into three broad areas—quantitative/analytical, behavioral, and managerial/strategic. Besides the general distancing of academia from practice, some academicians, especially those in the managerial/strategic areas, thought that research in the quantitative and behavioral areas was particularly lacking in practical marketing implications. For these managerial researchers, insult was added to injury when the areas of quantitative and behavioral research started commanding greater respect in the discipline than managerial research. Furthermore, because of the associated prestige and the types of intellect required by these two research areas, an increasing number of budding academicians started gravitating toward them.

In the perception of some academicians, however, it was not only the two areas of quantitative and behavioral research that went adrift in terms of their bearing on real-life business issues—the managerial/strategic research area also drifted in that direction. These academicians cited, for example, the effort of managerial/strategic-area researchers to build a *unifying theory* of marketing to be a wild goose chase. That marketing could have any theory, let alone a unifying one, or any laws did not seem feasible to them. They felt that even if erroneously expounded, such a theory would be amenable to being easily proven false by practitioners.

All in all, many saw the divide between academics and practice widening, with academics being unable to keep pace with the requirements of practice.

Shaping Future Research: Swinging the Research Pendulum in the Other Direction

There has been a growing and increasingly prevailing sentiment among many in the marketing discipline that the research and teaching pendulum should be brought back and made to swing in the direction of practical relevance and of generation/dissemination of more applicable knowledge. In that light, five potential approaches are discussed below for academic marketers to consider incorporating into the future focus of their research. These are:

- Selecting the right problems for research
- Modifying the intellectual rigor perception
- Coordinating the varied research efforts in a particular area or knowledge domain
- Developing a distinctive identity for marketing
- Getting support from the business sector

Selecting the Right Problems to Research

Selecting the right marketing problems for research would be the first key step for academic marketers to consider taking toward generating meaningful applications and solutions for business. Problems selected for research should represent those for which businesses or industries of one type or another seek solutions. In that context, it is not important which of the areas of research—managerial, behavioral, or quantitative—is more useful. Rather, any type of research can prove valuable as long as there are demonstrable benefits from it for some businesses or industries.

For identifying meaningful problems, it would be necessary for researchers to stay in touch with and interact with the practicing world. This does not necessarily imply that all researchers need to be in commune with practicing managers all the time. What the academicians would need to ensure is that the discipline has constant exposure to the business community and that there are a sufficient number of avenues set up for a regular flow of information and issues from the business world. They would thus need to establish adequate channels for the orchestration of such interactions (examples of which are currently represented by the Marketing Science Institute and the Product Development and Management Association).

An argument presented against this approach of finding solutions for the real problems of the business industry is that it falls in the domain of management consultants. That argument can be countered by distinguishing that management consultants attempt to resolve specific problems for individual clients and, unlike academicians, do not have the distinct focus or goal of advancing knowledge frontiers that can be generalized or are oriented for the greater good. In that regard, their motivations for solving problems, and hence their solutions, are quite different from those determined by academicians.

Modifying the Intellectual Rigor Perception

The educational curriculum that prospective marketing academicians go through imparts to them a regimen of certain research methodologies, instituting in them a preference for those methodologies when conducting research work. Thus, while organizations such as the Marketing Science Institute represent commendable efforts that are underway to bridge the academic and business worlds, the bias for orienting their work toward acceptable types of methodological rigor many times prevents marketing academicians from appropriately or completely attacking the marketing problems brought to fore by such organizations. Certain types of methodological rigor have come to be coveted by many researchers and have also come to be equated by the discipline with intellectual rigor. Unfortunately, such methodological rigor alone may not be conducive to resolving many real-world business problems. To make matters worse for the potential of real-world problem resolution, the brightest and the best students tend to be attracted to the rigorous-methodology/constrained-problem domain because of its equation with intellectual rigor. Real-world problems thus miss the opportunity of being worked on by these high-caliber researchers.

It is proposed here that marketing academicians attempt to modify their disposition on traditional methodological rigor and not construe such rigor to be the sole indicator of intellectual rigor. The scientific and intellectual rigor that a particular research is based on should be determined on a case by case basis, depending upon the problem being resolved. Eventually, researchers should strive to ensure that the marketing discipline *encourages, expects,* and *respects* the employment of appropriate creative techniques that are scientifically thorough for resolving a given real, complex problem.

Apart from rigor at the paper level, individual researchers should strive for another type of rigor—at the level of individual program of research. Such rigor would entail a controlled approach by the researcher in gradually chipping away at the shortcomings and assumptions of the individual's past research. With researchers conscious of and working toward resolving complex issues, the coordination of research at the discipline level becomes easier. This issue is addressed next.

Coordinating the Numerous Research Efforts of a Particular Area or Knowledge Domain

Knowledge can be efficiently produced if individual research efforts on an issue serve as the building blocks of possible solutions for that problem. In that light, researchers do evaluate each and every effort of theirs in terms of the potential for making a contribution to a particular problem or domain. An extension of that consideration points to a need for an instillation of a certain degree of orderliness that could possibly be brought about by timely, periodic snapshots of the state of affairs and further needs in a given domain. Without attempts at some form of coordination of individual research initiatives, there is a danger of chaos, of the possible attempts at resolving an issue going adrift, or of the domain or issue losing its very significance.

Perhaps the domain of relationship marketing (RM) would serve as a good case in point in the preceding context. When relationship marketing came to the fore, there was a flurry of papers claiming the wonders of the new paradigm and its ability to be a panacea for all that ailed marketing. Three or four years into the introduction of the concept to marketing, twenty-nine definitions of RM had been proposed, out of which ten had used the word "relationship" itself! Definitions were constructed using any of the following phrases: refers to, achieved by, purpose of, objective of, associated with, attempts to, assumes, reflects, emphasizes, and involves. Some papers claimed that RM was between two parties; others proposed it as between more than two parties. Some thought that RM was relevant only in the long term; others thought that it was appropriate even in the short term. But more importantly, when scholars tried developing it as a science, constructs proposed were all over the place in terms of whether they were antecedent, consequence, or mediating variables. For example, Opportunistic Behavior and Relationship Benefits were each modeled as both antecedent and consequence variables and Commitment and Trust were each modeled as both consequence and mediating variables. The unfortunate outcome of the situation was that there was no final resolution. Perhaps there can be no possibility of a resolution being achieved through this linear track of thinking. The truth may be that there is a positive feedback cycle between the two variables, of commitment breeding trust and of trust breeding commitment. Perhaps the choice of linear hypothesis, as compared to the positive feedback loop hypothesis, was dictated by the methodological correctness with which it could be tested, the data requirements and measurement challenges being arduous for the constant feedback model. A simple but erroneous conceptual model was thus advanced because it could be tested in the traditional methodologically rigorous manner.

The result of RM being all over the map and positioned as having no significant limitations in scope was that it faced pushback from many and absolute rejection by others. It would have been beneficial if, instead, at some point early in RM's popularity, a leading journal had published an article on the caveats of RM, including issues such as: When is RM not applicable? Do all consumers want a relationship with a frequently bought consumer nondurable brand? How is extracting value from a relationship over time different from pricing strategies that incorporate low up-front costs and fees for membership, subscription, or licensing? What role do intangibles play in relationships, and how is this role any different from the notion of intangibles in the concentric-circles model of augmented product?

Based upon the lessons learned from issues such as RM, it would seem that a deliberation of a given issue as a whole and a coordination of the full range of research efforts related to its various parts would go a long way toward overcoming the deficiencies and assumptions of the individual efforts.

Developing a Distinctive Identity for Marketing

The kind of research proposed in the preceding sections would be risky and more time-consuming for any academician and would be associated with lower chances of making it successfully through the journal review process—*unless the research and publication parameters are changed in the discipline.* The latter is precisely what is being presented here as a key to developing a distinctive identity for the marketing discipline.

Changes in the research and publication parameters to reward innovative ways of addressing marketing issues that face businesses would not only bridge the gap between the academic and business worlds, but also move toward giving marketing its own identity. Senior researchers would have to lead by example for the change, by publishing articles with the kind of themes being advocated here as well as by encouraging modifications in the acceptance criteria of marketing journals. Journal editors and reviewers would also have to become more accepting of such research. Baby steps in this direction, individually and collectively by all in the discipline, can be envisioned to produce an upward spiral that would eventually culminate in marketing acquiring its own identity. This, in turn, can be anticipated to bring about a better recognition of the contributions of the marketing discipline and thereby, a greater level of self-confidence in the academicians regarding those contributions (rather than a search for approval from economists or psychologists).

Getting Support from the Business Sector

With the discipline meticulously tackling appropriate problems and exuding confidence about the value of its research, marketers will have a stronger base for approaching businesses regarding funding of their research. It is heartening to note that despite the recognized limitations of the research and teaching conducted by business schools, business schools are still heavily supported by business entities. One can only anticipate with enthusiasm what that level of support would be if the work that marketers put out in the field is more relevant to the business sector. Needless to say, researchers could base such work, in addition to any innovative methods, upon judiciously chosen and appropriately modified theories and methods from other disciplines as necessary. (The important point is that the dog—the problem—should wag the tail—the methodology—rather than the other way around.)

SHAPING FUTURE TEACHING: SWINGING THE TEACHING PENDULUM IN THE OTHER DIRECTION

Having addressed to some degree how academic marketers can ensure *generation* of useful knowledge, it would be in order to discuss some points regarding how they can ensure the appropriate *dissemination* of such knowledge. From that perspective, marketing may be considered as made up of two streams or components—the strategy stream and the operations stream.

The Two Components of Marketing: Strategy and Operations

The strategy component of marketing comprises the philosophy that professes that the basic approach of conducting business should be based upon satisfying the needs of customers—whether current or future and whether expressed or latent. It claims that such philosophy assures the long-term financial viability of a business. The component incorporates macro issues such as target segments, positioning, value propositions, brand equity, and so on. It entails knowledge that, to a large degree, is tacit.

The operations component of marketing is the part that involves the all-important details of every one of the marketing functions and marketing know-how, for example, how to listen to the voice of the market, how to research advertising effectiveness, how to measure brand equity, how to develop pricing strategies, how to develop and test optimal promotional strategies, how and when to establish relationships, and so forth. The details may be carved up in any of a variety of ways—as customer linking, bonding and sensing, as four Ps (product, place, promotion, and price), as attracting and satisfying customers, as creating and fulfilling demand, or as a new paradigm of relationships. All these relate to and provide answers for an organization's day-to-day operations. Marketing models (quantitative, behavioral, or others) and research techniques constitute a significant part of this component. Knowledge in this component is mostly explicit.

Teaching the Two Components

In disseminating marketing knowledge, marketers err on two dimensions. First, in their pedagogical approach, they do not differentiate enough between the strategy and operations components of marketing. Rather, they incorporate the two components into one unit and then treat that unit either as a science or as an art, neither of which is a perfectly accurate approach. Second, in teaching the operations component, marketers do not cover the necessary materials in sufficient detail to guard against their potential misapplication. Topics belonging in the realm of this second component are not taught with all the caveats spelled out. Nor are they comprehensively covered from all angles to provide solutions for all product-market nuances. Because of such treatment, many solutions that are proposed in marketing are either discarded altogether or applied erroneously.

It is proposed that marketers consider it essential to delineate the strategy and operations components of marketing in teaching courses and in other methods of dissemination of marketing knowledge. As already mentioned, the knowledge base represented by the two components is quite different—implicit in strategy and explicit in operations. Delincation of the two components would ensure that they can be focused upon individually toward the goal of boosting the impact and perception of marketing in every sphere, whether as a research and teaching subject in business schools or as a function in business organizations. As it stands today, the strategy component is so ingrained in the DNA of routine business that its learning and practice is warranted for all top managers and chief executive officers (CEOs), as well as for nonmarketing departments, such as finance, manufacturing, and R&D. The operational component, on the other hand, is expected to be executed exclusively by marketing professionals.

The strategy component of marketing, given its tacit nature, should to be taught as much like an art as a science. A close analogy to this might be found in cooking, where a master chef needs to gain expertise about the science of food and also master the art of cooking. An interesting mix of art and science, the knowledge of the strategy component appeals to, and is pertinent and useful to, both marketers and nonmarketers. If marketers want to advocate the philosophy that for any firm, the route to long-term financial viability is through satisfying customer needs, then the strategy component becomes basic in business. As such, it should be taught to all business students as a fundamental course in marketing rather than as a capstone course to marketing majors. If taught to all, practiced by all, and considered useful by all, the concept of marketing strategy will, in most likelihood, be adopted and absorbed by other disciplines. And the more other disciplines borrow from marketing, the more marketing will be able to establish its own identity—representing a potential cause for celebration. That situation would be similar to economists enjoying a borrowing of their concepts by other fields. Marketers must, however, watch out for the associated temptation of resting on their laurels, and just like economists keep their wares current, they must too.

As far as the operations component of marketing is concerned, both the breadth and depth of what is imparted by academic marketers in its education can be improved, with the potential caveats and pros and cons in its practical application pointed out more effectively and thoroughly. As mentioned earlier, this component has heavyweight contents—quantitative and other models, research, simulation, and decision support systems, to name a few, to aid in marketing decisions. For any meaningful learning to occur in this regard, students ought to be *actually* engaged in real operational steps and processes, examples of which include: allocating and buying media for the dollar amount budgeted by a particular advertising strategy, writing storyboards, conducting research to test the effectiveness of a message, learning and applying different advertising response models and reviewing their pros and cons, testing the effectiveness of various promotional strategies and campaigns, designing measurements systems for customer satisfaction and its drivers, and segmenting a particular product market with real data in a real competitive landscape. The point is that it is not sufficient for students to know, for example, only the hierarchy of effects and the other psychological components of advertising. There is more to advertising in the business world than its scientific basis. The same is true for other areas of marketing.

If teaching courses for the operations component are not constructed with more in-depth consideration to potential real-world applications, there is a danger that either materials from the strategy component will be repeated in these courses or that the relevance of the information disseminated will miss its mark. Additionally, without attaining a good grasp of this component, marketers in business are apt to misapply and misuse models that form a key part of the component.

The structure of marketing electives generally presents ample scope and time for allowing incorporation of the aforementioned details. Marketing courses for MBAs and undergraduates are generally less demanding and exacting than courses in subjects such as finance. There seems to be a hierarchy or pecking order in subject majors, with students who have quantitative abilities tending to opt more for a major in finance or accounting. By increasing the level of its expectations from students and by delivering more intensive content, marketing can expect to impact that trend and attract more students who are seeking a challenging stream of work. It needs to be pointed out though that the recommendations for more intensive content, rather than based upon an intent to make the discipline difficult, are based upon a recognition of the value such knowledge content can bring to business. In the current environment, because such information is not routinely available in business and does not make up a routine part of marketing, not only are *marketers* marginalized but also *marketing* tends to be looked at in a skeptical or unsure manner by senior managers. As one CEO said, "when executives from other disciplines ask for dollars, I know what I am getting in return; with marketing, I never know if the money will be well spent."

Thus, academic marketers may consider redesigning marketing education such that marketing strategy details are taught as a part of a fundamental marketing course to all business students, and marketing operations is taught in all its depth and breadth to marketing majors.

INSTITUTING FACILITATING MECHANISMS FOR THE PROPOSED APPROACHES

With some potential approaches for the reform of their research and teaching having been identified for academic marketers, the following suggestions are presented regarding some mechanisms they might institute for facilitating progress in that direction.

Reframing and Redefining the Role of Journal Editors

Editors of marketing journals can contribute in a significant way to moving the discipline forward. The discipline would benefit from structuring editorial positions such that in addition to having responsibilities for receiving articles for review, forwarding them to reviewers, collating reviewer comments, making final decisions, and executing other gate-keeping functions for research publications, these positions are expected to play an expanded leadership role. Editorial function may thus be defined to encompass a requirement for setting some vision for the knowledge domains researched in the discipline and for leading and coordinating research in a purposeful direction, in a well thought out and concerted manner. In the context of this chapter then, it would follow that editors should encourage attempts at investigation of the kinds of problems discussed herein and bring about required changes in acceptance criteria and acceptable methodologies for research publications.

A New Body to Steer Research and Teaching

An avenue through which marketing academicians might move their cause forward is with one or more formal bodies of relevant experts—boards, panels, committees, or commissions (similar to the Financial Accounting Standards Board, but with a rather different scope)—responsible for laying down research and teaching guidelines, standards, criteria, and so on. By having a permanent structure for setting and resetting direction in this manner on an ongoing basis, marketing academicians would ensure that there exists a forum for discussion of critical marketing issues and that marketing knowledge domains make more meaningful contributions. The efforts of such a steering force would allow the agenda of the academicians to be reviewed and revised as necessary, and might also earn better recognition for the discipline.

For greater effectiveness, it would be appropriate for the suggested body or bodies to have diverse representation from all hierarchical levels of marketing researchers, teaching instructors, and editors, as well as marketing professionals from the business sector. A rotating membership (of a two- or three-year term) would probably be most effective in ensuring a broader input base and continual generation of fresh perspectives.

Publication of a Textbook on the State of the Art of Marketing

Marketing academicians might find that their concerns regarding reform are partially addressable through publication of a textbook that takes stock of existing marketing knowledge (including marketing models, theories, and methods) and that outlines where marketing knowledge is deficient and what kinds of information are still missing at this juncture. A snapshot of the existing knowledge base and the current marketing environment would be helpful to both students as well as academicians. For students, it would point out what and how to practice and where to be careful. For academicians, the book would serve as an excellent source of potential ideas for research.

CHAPTER 31

REVITALIZING THE ROLE OF MARKETING IN BUSINESS ORGANIZATIONS

What Can Poor Academics Do to Help?

JAGMOHAN S. RAJU

Many chapters in this volume have convincingly argued that marketing as a practice profession faces many challenges and dangers. A number of leading organizations have abolished, or have seriously considered abolishing, marketing departments partly because academics and other thought leaders have convinced companies that "marketing is far too important to be left only to the marketing departments."[1] In a recent conference organized at Wharton, it was suggested that the life span of a chief marketing officer (CMO) is relatively short, and many CMOs believe that one of the more serious challenges they face is justifying their existence. Marketing budgets are being cut at many corporations because these businesses find it hard to justify the return on such expenditures. All in all, these are not good signs.

On the other hand, it appears that marketing as a discipline in the world of academics is not doing badly at all. In fact, a fairly strong case can be made that it has never been better. Casual observation, discussions with colleagues from other universities, and anecdotal evidence has led this author to come to the following conclusions.

1. By and large, over the past twenty years, the average size of the marketing departments has increased at major business schools.
2. More marketing courses are being taught, and furthermore, marketing courses are in great demand.
3. Marketing academics are holding important leadership positions at many business schools. In fact, the list of marketing academics holding leadership positions (deans, deputy deans, vice deans, associate deans and similar important administrative titles) has never been higher.
4. The number of manuscripts submitted to major marketing journals is at an all-time high. The last few years have seen some of the most dramatic increases. Numbers reported at *Marketing Science,* the *Journal of Marketing Research,* and *Management Science* suggest increases of up to 100 percent over the last five years.
5. The number of PhDs granted in marketing worldwide is at healthy levels. Further-

Originally published in the *Journal of Marketing,* Vol. 69, No. 3, 2005. Published with permission from the American Marketing Association.

more, the demand for these graduates, while varying from one year to the next, remains quite strong.

It appears that the life on one side of the street is quite different from the life on the other side.
It makes one wonder why the two are so different, but it may also explain why some academics
are surprised (if not shocked) when they are made aware of what is happening on the business
side. Should one care about what is going on the other side? This chapter will attempt to argue
that one should and provides some ideas as to what can be done.

WHY MARKETING PRACTITIONERS ARE IN TROUBLE

A strong argument can be made that one reason why marketing in the world of practice is
floundering is because practitioners did not fully utilize what was developed by academics and
other marketing thought leaders. Therefore, they deserve the state they are currently in. However, one also cannot rule out the possibility that maybe what academics and marketing thought
leaders gave to the practitioners was not good enough—or potent enough—compared to what
thought leaders in other disciplines gave to their practitioners. To determine which of the two
explanations is the cause requires considerable work. A more pragmatic approach would be to
reconcile that there is some truth to each of these reasons. If one buys into the idea that there is
some truth to the latter argument, those of us who are in academics may need to change. Furthermore, no matter what the reason for the plight of the practitioner, to the extent that marketing is an applied discipline, and one of our key end-customers is the practitioner, we need to do
what we can to make sure our customers are healthy. It is with this objective that this author
humbly makes the following suggestions.

Choosing Our Audiences

Most marketing academics live and thrive in a university setting. Our colleagues are individuals from basic disciplines. Many of us come from basic disciplines, and this lineage has done
wonders for our field. However, instead of focusing on pleasing economists or mathematicians,[2] we need to keep in mind that one of our key constituencies is the practitioner. We clearly
cherish when our work gets published in the *Journal of Applied Mathematics,* but we need to be
equally proud of studying problems that matter to practitioners and provide solutions that they
can implement. The second issue worth thinking about is: who is the right audience within a
company? By and large, historically our audience in companies has been individuals engaged
in marketing research. I think we need to go higher. The following section addresses this in
more detail.

Doing It Right vs. Doing the Right Thing

Our discipline pays great attention to the precision of arguments and the methodology used in our
work. But often times, this can lead to incrementalism. We should be more open to studying
problems that matter—even if we need to make some limited compromises in terms of the precision with which we study these. Approximate answers to important problems or issues are just as
useful (if not more useful) than precise answers to unimportant narrow problems (Lodish 1974).
This balance will also allow us to appeal to senior levels in the organization—our current audience is at a more junior level.

Directing the Output of Our PhD Programs

Our PhD programs are designed to train future academics. This is a very desirable motive because there is an acute shortage of marketing academics. However, we should encourage (or at least not discourage) our PhD students from entering the business world. Many leading corporations are led by individuals who have PhDs in chemistry, life sciences, and engineering. Why not PhDs in marketing? Corporations can gain if they are led by individuals who have an in-depth knowledge, and an appreciation, of how one goes about understanding customer needs and developing products, services, and programs that allow a company to profitably satisfy such needs. Furthermore, it does not hurt if audience members understand our language because they have been taught to do so.

Valuing Consulting Activity

Virtually all academics in medical schools spend some time taking care of patients. In fact, in most cases, it is a part of their responsibility. This not the case in business schools. Do our "patients" not need any help, or are we incapable of helping them? Or do we not care one way or the other? These are questions that we need to address head-on.

Teach What We Study and Discover in Our Research

All of us want, and try very hard, to teach what we study and discover in our research. However, the structure and design of our courses often limit our intentions. A large majority of students who we teach take just one course in marketing—a course that goes by different names in different schools, but that is often referred to as "Introduction to Marketing." In most schools, this course deals with developing a marketing plan using some well-known and very useful frameworks that have stood the test of time. However, as one compares our approach with the first courses taught in other disciplines, there appear to be some differences. The first course in finance does not deal with developing a financial plan for a company. The first course in operations management does not attempt to write an operations plan. This author believes that we try to cover too much, and therefore focus more on breadth than depth, limiting our ability to link teaching with research. What if our first course was titled "Customer Analysis?" Such a course should put equal weight on behavioral and quantitative methods, and could be co-taught if necessary.

Measure the Value of Marketing Activities

Many other contributors have spoken about the issue of measuring the value of marketing activities and this is critical. Our focus here should not be to measure the value of a particular marketing input (say advertising) or a particular marketing asset (say the brand), but also to measure the value of better methods and models we develop. For example, what is the value of better allocation of resources, such as of the sales force across territories and of advertising across products?

Finally, it may not hurt if we were more comfortable with our own identity. Our field has made a number of important contributions to the business world, to society, and to science. We need to be more comfortable with who we are. We could even be more proud of who we are. If we have a good article that fits equally well in two outlets, we may want to consider publishing it in a marketing journal rather than in an economics journal. If we have two equally good PhD students we are considering hiring, one from psychology and the other from marketing, we may want to go with the one from marketing. If we are more comfortable with, and possibly more proud of, our own identity, it will surely help us, and it may also rub off onto the practitioners.

NOTES

1. While many have used similar phrases in different contexts, this particular phrase is assigned to Jack Trout.

2. The words "economist" or "mathematician" can be substituted with the words "psychologist" or "statistician" if the reader prefers.

Reference

Lodish, Leonard M. (1974), "Vaguely Right Approach to Sales Force Allocations," *Harvard Business Review,* 52 (January–February), 119–25.

CHAPTER 32

DOES MARKETING NEED REFORM SCHOOL?

On the Misapplication of Marketing to the Education of Marketers

MORRIS B. HOLBROOK

When Ted Levitt famously penned his updating of conventional wisdom borrowed from Peter Drucker under the title "Marketing Myopia" back in 1960, this canonical *Harvard Business Review* article raised some important issues concerning the weaknesses of Levitt's professed fealty to an extreme form of customer orientation. The problem with excessive obeisance to the customer—various critics correctly noted—is that what customers want may be too expensive to produce profitably (the highest possible quality at the lowest possible price); may be illegal, environmentally dangerous, unethical, or otherwise damaging to society (styrofoam, cigarettes, SUVs); or may not be anticipated as desirable until actually offered on the market (compact discs, laptop computers, iPods, Listerine). Pretty soon, most thoughtful commentators had begun to agree that success requires a balance of the customer orientation (external focus) and the product orientation (internal focus) weighed against other imposing environmental forces (the systems view) toward the end of enhancing profits in order to survive (the ecological imperative). Many ways developed to say essentially the same thing—namely, that effective marketing strategy for a brand, product, or firm seeks an ecological niche in the marketplace so as to achieve a differential advantage based on a distinctive competence that supports prosperity or what I like to call survival with dignity.

This episode in the history of marketing thought would have been instructive and salubrious if it had been settled and put to rest then and there. But the specter of overzealous customer orientation—like the ghouls in a low-budget grade-B horror movie—refuses to die, rising zombie-like from the grave of dead metaphors to walk again among us as a potential threat to our clear vision of what we are doing and why. Indeed, more recently, the misplaced doctrine of customer orientation has infected a number of areas where the people in charge ought to know better—medicine, religion, politics, the penal system, and . . . most lamentably . . . education. To a frightening extent, university administrators have come to regard the student as a customer whose satisfaction should guide the purposes and operations of the educational institution. In league with the hedonic bent of our inherently greedy society—seeking always the good life via a lucrative participation in the free enterprise system—this student customer tends to place a woefully misguided premium on two major criteria: entertainment and career advancement. As the college years advance toward their potential culmination in a professional degree such as an MBA, the balance tends to shift from the former (entertainment) to the latter (careerism) so that the MBA mind obsesses about nothing so much as what every scrap of information (as distinct from knowledge) will contribute to the student customer's fund of bankable skills (as distinct from growth of intellectual capabilities). In this climate, the student customer views the school as a vendor of career-relevant diplomas. Business-related publications (*Forbes, US News & World Report, Business Week*) evaluate schools according to how much their academic degrees are worth on the job market (the net present value of future earnings less tuition and the opportunity costs of foregone income). In short, all pretense of academic values surrenders to an ethos that emphasizes an anti-intellectual preoccupation with the bottom line or, in other words, with the highest monetary payoff for one's educational dollar.

Nowhere does this anti-intellectual ethos of career-oriented customer orientation take root more strongly than in a business school. And—ironically in the extreme—nowhere do we find a devotion to customer orientation in the academic community voiced more vociferously or with more sanctimonious subservience to the student as customer than among those very marketing professors whose allegiance to student satisfaction runs in a direction diametrically opposed to the more soundly conceived principles of effective marketing strategy that they teach in the classroom. As one appalling example, consider the widespread adoption of required core courses in marketing offered to students grouped into clusters that take all their classes together. Such a system maximizes the student satisfaction that stems from incessantly networking with one's classmates. But, by necessitating the standardization of course offerings across sections, it runs directly counter to every known principle of market segmentation. Professors unlucky enough to teach such a course find themselves producing a standardized mass-marketed commodity that paradoxically embodies the often-lamented majority fallacy—that is, the demonstrably false premise that a single offering can please everybody or, in other words, the single greatest marketing error that it is possible to commit.

In this brief chapter, I shall use these regrettable aspects of business education in general and marketing instruction in particular as a cautionary tale to illustrate the pitfalls of what can happen if we push marketing too far (into areas where it does not belong) or, more accurately, if we misconstrue the meaning of the marketing concept (by confusing it with a misbegotten version of customer orientation).

The particular manifestation in which customer orientation rears its ugly head in the field of education in general and of marketing education in particular entails a view of the academic institution as a business that provides services to its students regarded as customers. This misconception of the academic project has evolved over the course of time from earlier perspectives that emphasized rather different aspects of the key exchange relationships involved.

Once upon a time, back in the distant days when I was a boy in elementary school, we used to regard the student as a producer who offered homework assignments, exam papers, and term projects to the teacher as customer in return for good grades, promotion to the next-higher class, and eventual graduation. This admittedly old-fashioned model looked something like this:

Old-Fashioned Model

PRODUCER	CUSTOMER
Student	Teacher
Homework, Exams, Projects ➔	⬅ Grades, Promotion, Graduation

From a societal viewpoint, this outmoded conception of student-as-producer and teacher-as-customer left a lot to be desired. One might argue that, under the old-fashioned model, students felt the need to work for grades and other academic honors rather than for self-improvement or intellectual fulfillment. One might lament the absence of a thrust toward learning-for-its-own-sake. One might suggest that teachers gained an unfair power advantage over those under their tutelage. But, that said, the old model did retain some sense of the faculty's responsibility for determining what themes and topics best suited the needs of its students—much as a doctor is responsible for prescribing a treatment appropriate to the disease at hand or, at least, was thus accountable before the days when increasingly customer-oriented pharmaceutical companies such as (say) Merck began to spend more on television commercials for (say) Vioxx than Pepsi or Budweiser spend advertising their cola and beer products in hopes that patients will go to their physicians with special requests for pills promoted by the media. (And let's not get started on the subject of Viagra, Levitra, and Cialis.)

Whatever the merits of the old model, it began to lose sway as baby boomers chased dwindling employment opportunities in an increasingly competitive job market. Soon an MBA became a near-requisite ticket for success on the career ladder. The leading business schools came to be viewed by corporate recruiters as refined screening devices for identifying the most promising job candidates. The value added by an elite B-school depended less on what it taught its students than on its savvy in recruiting, selecting, and matriculating the best and the brightest. Under this revised interpretation of a school's mission, the model of the relevant exchange process took a new form in which the academic institution produced job candidates by turning its raw materials (students) into finished products (graduates) in return for employment offers from corporations as its major customers. This revised model now appeared as follows:

Revised Model

PRODUCER	CUSTOMER
School	Corporation
Job Candidates ➜	← Employment Offers

The only thing that I like about this revised model is that it possesses the advantage of openly calling a spade a spade and thereby explicitly naming the particular type of manure that the educational system happens to be shoveling. That is, the revised model freely acknowledges that careerism has come to dominate the academic process and that the inherently selfish interests of big business play a major role in shaping educational policy without any real regard for the moral or intellectual development of individual character. Interestingly, today's students find this revised model offensive even though the vast majority of them support it with their own overt behavior. To greet a student who has missed several classes due to a busy interviewing schedule with the news that he or she has behaved like the true product of a diploma mill would be tantamount to suicide in the end-of-term student evaluations. When a colleague once mentioned the revised model in class as an alternative view of the academic system at a major business school, students expressed such unrestrained rage that a dean forced this teacher to apologize to his class. The dean did not explain why merely stating a simple fact of life should require an apology. The reason, of course, is that—put in its briefest and bleakest terms—students do not want to be regarded as products. Rather—like patients in a hospital, parishioners of a church, voters in an election, or inmates at a prison—they wish to be regarded as customers.

Thus, the emerging view sees the school as a producer that offers MBA-degree diplomas, networking opportunities, and career counseling in exchange for tuition dollars, generous donations, and favorable evaluations from its students regarded as customers. This customer-oriented model takes the following form:

Customer-Oriented Model

PRODUCER		CUSTOMER
School		Student
Diplomas, Networking, Careers ➜	⬅ Tuition, Donations, Evaluations	

The pernicious nature of this customer-oriented model appears almost too obvious to require discussion. Suffice it to say that it represents an ugly logic in which the rewards of education take the most banausic possible form—premised on the purely utilitarian benefits of money, status, and power—while the reciprocal contributions of the student customers are as perfunctory, instrumental, and lacking in moral foundation as it is possible to imagine. Yet when the dean of a major business school recently referred to the activities of what one used to call Student Affairs under the new heading Customer Services, not a single voice rose in protest. Rather, the logic that students receive the soulless transfer of wealth-engendering career opportunities in return for their tuition dollars has taken root so strongly that no one even notices the enormity of the ethical and intellectual transgressions routinely transpiring when, to paraphrase the old adage, the inmates are running the asylum.

By now the potentially exasperated reader will have begun to wonder whether I have something better to offer. Am I just complaining and bemoaning the inequities of the new regime in academia? Or have I got something up my sleeve that I claim as an improved model? The answer is that I do not believe that the blame for this calamitous decline down the path toward customer orientation in business academia lies with marketing as a discipline—neither with marketing professionals nor with marketing educators. Rather, I believe that the fault lies with a mistaken view of marketing strategy or with a misapplication of the marketing concept. To repeat a point made earlier, the problem results from a misunderstanding of the proper role played by customer orientation as a force to balance product orientation in conjunction with other environmental factors toward the attainment of an ecological niche that permits survival.

In this connection, it makes sense to view the student as a customer but as a customer of a type altogether different from that normally assumed. Specifically, I believe, the student should be viewed as a customer whose role is analogous to that played by the channels of distribution in conventional marketing thought. That is, the student acts as an intermediary by whom the school's production of knowledge is transmitted and transferred to members of society in a position to benefit from it. This supply-chain model takes the following shape:

Supply-Chain Model

PRODUCER	CHANNEL	CUSTOMER
School	Student	Society
Knowledge ➜	Knowledge ➜	
	⬅ Appreciation	⬅ Goodwill, Respect

In this supply-chain model, the major purpose of the university lies in the creation and dissemination of knowledge. Put differently, the school and its faculty work toward the creation of new ideas, concepts, and insights that may or may not prove useful to the members of society facing real-world problems in general and to the members of the business community seeking profitable applications in particular. The student's role, as a leading member of the channels of distribution, is to assimilate the relevant knowledge and to transmit its contents to those members of society in a position to achieve useful applications. In return, society will reward the academic institution and its faculty with goodwill and respect transmitted through the school's former students in the form of appreciation for their privilege of participating in the educational experience. Very often, of course, the transmission and application of knowledge through students in the manner envisioned here will involve ideas, concepts, and insights of relevance to the practical solutions of business problems by business corporations. At other times, the knowledge transmitted may be of the type that sheds light on issues of social concern or that enriches the intellectual environment of the community at large. In either case, the role of the student is only partially that of a customer—a customer only in the sense of an intermediary whose purpose, like that of Wal-Mart or Home Depot or even PETCO, is to serve the members of a larger community of end users. In this sense, the marketing enterprise of relevance to an academic institution involves a push-through rather than a pull-through strategy. Students can take comfort in the implication that they resemble a pet owner (acting as part of the channel of distribution) more than they resemble a Cocker Spaniel (the end user).

So, in the end, the marketing concept stands unscathed. Marketing, it turns out, does not need reform school so much as schools need to reform their view of the process wherein they create and transmit knowledge to society at large, whether in the context of learning in general or in that of business education in particular. In this sense, all academic activities involve the instruction of those who will ultimately perform a role as channels of distribution in the marketing of ideas, concepts, and insights of potential relevance to other members of society. Thus the challenge to our discipline within the context of a university lies in reforming the misapplication of marketing to the education of marketers.

REFERENCE

Levitt, Theodore (1960), "Marketing Myopia," *Harvard Business Review,* 38 (July/August), 45–56.

CHAPTER 33

MUSINGS ON THE NEED FOR REFORM IN MARKETING

RAJAN VARADARAJAN

But what is most special about the American research university is that it is a place where authority of ideas, rather than the idea of authority, reigns supreme. At Harvard, we consider it an extremely important accomplishment when a 25-year-old graduate student who has been here a mere 18 months makes a discovery that disproves the pet theory of a 55-year-old professor who has been here 30 years. Indeed, the professor whose theory has been disproved might be the first to congratulate that graduate student. (Summers 2003, p. 144)

I grant that scientists often fall in love with their own constructions. I know; I have. They may spend a lifetime vainly to shore them up. A few squander their prestige and academic capital in the effort. In that case—as economist Paul Samuelson once quipped—funeral by funeral, theory advances. (Wilson 1998, p. 52)

It's reasonable to presume that the impetus for either a marketing scholar or a community of marketing scholars to pose the question, does marketing need reform? could conceivably be discontent with the current state of, for example:

- marketing practice
- applied research in marketing
- laws and regulations governing the practice of marketing
- scholarly research in marketing
- marketing education at institutions for higher education

In this chapter, I address the question of the need for reform in marketing in the following contexts. Concerns voiced by marketing academicians regarding the:

- Diminishing influence of the marketing discipline (and marketing scholars) in the academic discourse on strategy
- Diminishing influence of the marketing function (and marketing managers) in organizations
- Specter of deficiencies in scholarly research in marketing or marketing education leading to the marginalization of the marketing function (and marketing managers) in organizations

ALLEGED LOSS OF INFLUENCE OF MARKETING IN ACADEMIC DISCOURSE ON STRATEGY: ACRIMONY IN THE IVORY TOWER REVISITED

Reminiscing about marketing's loss of influence in the academic discourse on strategy, Day (1992, p. 324) noted: "Within academic circles, the contribution of marketing, as an applied management discipline, to the development, testing, and dissemination of strategy theories has been marginalized during the past decade." Among the reasons for the loss of influence, according to Day, are the following:

- Preemption of marketing frameworks, concepts and methods by other fields of inquiry.
- Tendency to employ theories and frameworks of other academic disciplines, and the attendant lop-sided balance of trade in influential ideas.
- Ceding of territory by shifting the balance of research activity further toward micro issues.
- Tardiness in addressing important issues and tendency to stay too long with outmoded characterizations of strategy processes and issues.[1]

Also published in the issue containing Day's (1992) article is an article by Sheth (1992) titled, "Acrimony in the Ivory Tower: A Retrospective on Consumer Research," and two invited commentaries by Bagozzi (1992) and Chakravarti (1992). Considering in tandem the issues addressed in these writings, I have often wondered whether the editorial policies of some of the scholarly journals in our field also shoulder some of the blame for marketing's loss of influence in the academic discourse about strategy. Specifically, the editorial policies of scholarly journals in the field of consumer research that seem to be predisposed to exclude managerial implications of research from the scope of articles published. The predicament of marketing educators caught between the following editorial policy positions is unenviable:

- In order for a manuscript to be considered for review and publication in the journal, the author must clearly articulate the managerial implications of the research reported.
- Even if the author has valuable insights to share about the managerial implications of the research reported, the journal is neither interested nor inclined to provide journal space for such insights to be disseminated in the article.

What are the likely consequences of mandating authors to elaborate on the managerial implications of their research regardless of whether they are interested in or equipped to do so? An editorial by Cunningham and Enis (1983, p. 6) is instructive on this issue. They noted: "In sharp contrast to the analytical rigor characterizing the research design of many papers, the discussion of managerial implications is often nothing more than speculation. Too few researchers discuss their work with practitioners and even fewer involve them in the project, for example, as 'feasibility advisors.'"

What about the likely consequences of explicitly excluding managerial implications from the scope of published articles? The message to the researcher seems to be, "keep the knowledge of the managerial implications related to your scholarly research on consumer behavior to yourself, or explore other avenues for dissemination of any such insights." From the standpoint of the advancement of the field, some likely long-term consequences are:

- Inefficiencies in knowledge dissemination and utilization.
- Researchers, neither being trained nor encouraged to give careful thought to the managerial implications of their research.
- Advancement of "demand side perspective of marketing strategy" being adversely impacted.

The "implications" section of a manuscript is a researcher's *informed* point of view on issues such as the following.[2] Given the conceptual underpinnings and empirical research findings of a research study in marketing, what changes should be considered by:

- *Firms* in how they behave (compete, conduct their business, etc.) in the marketplace?
- *Public policy agencies* in regard to how firms should be allowed to behave (can compete, can conduct their business, etc.) in the marketplace?
- *Researchers in marketing* in regard to how they conduct scholarly research or in the focus of their scholarly research?
- *Marketing educators* in regard to what they teach in the classroom or how they teach?
- *Consumers* in regard to their behaviors pertaining to product acquisition, consumption, possession, and disposition.

Interestingly, of the above, it is only the implications of the conceptual underpinnings and research findings for *firm* behavior that seem to be a source of controversy in the field of consumer research. Although *implications for firm behavior* and *managerial implications (implications for managerial behavior)* refer to one and the same issue, for some reason, the latter phrase does not seem to resonate too well among some academic constituencies in our field. Perhaps, doing away with the term "managerial implications" and using the term "implications for firm behavior" instead, might be conducive to allaying the concerns of some researchers.[3] Regardless of the phrase used, the reference here is to implications for the behavior of the firm at various levels such as the brand, product category, product-market, business unit, and so on. That is, changes that a manager, acting on behalf of the firm, should consider instituting in light of the conceptual underpinnings of the study and empirical research findings.

Current State of Marketing Strategy Informed by Consumer Behavior Theory and Research

Strategy exists at multiple levels in an organization, chief among them the corporate, business unit, and functional levels. *Corporate strategy* refers to a firm's decisions pertaining to the business arenas in which to compete. A firm's corporate strategy decision manifests as its business portfolio and relative emphasis (resource allocation) among businesses in the firm's portfolio. *Competitive strategy* refers to strategy at the business unit level and is concerned with where and how individual businesses in the firm's portfolio should compete in the marketplace in order to achieve and maintain defensible competitive positional advantage(s)—cost leadership and differentiation. *Functional level strategies* are integral components of a business's overall competitive strategy concerned with facilitating the achievement of competitive positional advantage(s) by the business. The issue of marketing's influence in the academic discourse on strategy arises in the following contexts:

- the distinctive and overlapping domains of corporate, business, and marketing strategy (e.g., Varadarajan and Clark 1994), and

- the role of marketing in strategy (formulation process, content, and implementation) at the corporate and business unit levels (e.g., Webster 1992)

More so than these, an even more fundamental issue that we should be concerned about is the current state of marketing strategy, informed by consumer behavior theory and research. Marketing strategy, as a field of study, can be viewed as primarily concerned with describing, understanding, explaining, and predicting the competitive *marketplace behavior* of a business to facilitate the achievement of a competitive advantage. Illustrative of questions fundamental to the field of marketing strategy are the following:

- What *explains* the marketplace behavior of competing businesses?
- How *should* a business compete in the marketplace given the characteristics of the industry in which it competes and the characteristics of customers that constitute its target market?

As implied by the second question, a business's marketing strategy decisions are impacted by both supply side and demand side considerations. The *supply side perspective of marketing strategy* refers to how a business should behave in the context of the structural characteristics of the industry in which it competes (e.g., number of competitors, size of competitors, entry and exit barriers, and industry growth rate), its competitors' history of past behavior, and so on. The *demand side perspective of marketing strategy* refers to how a business should behave in the context of the characteristics of its target customers (e.g., attitudes, beliefs and preferences; number and size; purchase frequency; and sensitivity and responsiveness to various marketing instruments), their history of past behavior, and so on. The term "should behave" here refers to "competitive behavior conducive to achieving superior marketplace and financial performance."

Over the past quarter century, the impact of insights from industrial organization economics and strategic management literature on the supply side perspective of marketing strategy has been considerable. However, the state of the demand side perspective of marketing strategy appears to be somewhat stagnant or neglected.[4] The content of marketing strategy courses (at all levels— bachelors, master's, and doctoral) is also indicative of a similar imbalance, characterized by extensive coverage of marketing strategy informed by supply side perspectives and sparse coverage of marketing strategy informed by demand side perspectives.

Against this backdrop, a question that merits addressing is, what would it take to change this lopsided situation? In my view, it would require consumer researchers in our field taking the lead in exploring the implications of research on consumer and customer behavior issues for firm behavior. As alluded to earlier, firm behavior encompasses behavior at various levels such as brand, market segment, product category, product market, and business unit. A stronger link between consumer behavior theory and research and marketing strategy problems could pave the way for a marketing strategy knowledge base that is infused with valuable insights on the implications of research-based knowledge on consumer and customer behavior for firm behavior.

At the most fundamental level, the interface of consumer behavior and *marketing* strategy encompasses issues such as:

Consumer behavior and positioning strategy
Consumer behavior and advertising strategy
Consumer behavior and sales promotion strategy
Consumer behavior and pricing strategy
Consumer behavior and product strategy

Consumer behavior and branding strategy
Consumer behavior and brand extension strategy
Consumer behavior and co-branding strategy
Consumer behavior and Internet strategy
Customer satisfaction and marketing strategy
Customer loyalty and marketing strategy
Brand loyalty and marketing strategy
Customers' quality perceptions and marketing strategy

Undisputedly, many of these issues have been explored in considerable depth, and textbooks on consumer behavior provide valuable insights into marketing strategy informed by demand side considerations. However, in some quarters, the resistance to *accelerating diffusion of such knowledge* through scholarly journals seems to persist. Is the chasm really wide and unbridgeable?

The history and origins of some journals devoted to consumer research issues sheds insights into the reasons why their editorial policies exclude managerial implications from the scope of manuscripts published in them. Scholarly journals do periodically revisit their editorial policies and institute changes as warranted. All one can hope for is that the concerns voiced in this section would receive some consideration when journals revisit their editorial policies. The rationale for singling out implications of research for *firm behavior* (changes that firms should consider instituting in regard to how they behave/compete/conduct their business in the marketplace) from the scope of articles published is not self-evident.

ALLEGED DIMINISHING INFLUENCE OF THE MARKETING FUNCTION IN ORGANIZATIONS: SHOULD MARKETING ACADEMICIANS BE CONCERNED?

Concerns over the diminishing influence of the marketing function in organizations have been repeatedly voiced by marketing academics over the years. Illustrative of such concerns are the following excerpts:

> For the past two or three decades, marketing has effectively ceded its strategic responsibilities to other organizational specialists who have not, until recently, been guided by the voice of the customer. (Webster 1997, p. 49)

> CMOs are far from complacent about marketing's role in the firm, this study finds. To secure corporate-level influence, marketing must develop tools to quantify its contribution to firm growth and profitability, reinforce its traditional strength in branding, and broaden its view to encompass not just new products, but new business opportunities. (Webster, Malter, and Ganesan 2003, p. 29)

> Consequently, marketing's share of voice at the corporate level has declined. Research now demonstrates that, at large companies only 10 percent of executive meeting time is devoted to marketing. As the attention and imagination of CEOs have shifted to other functions, marketing academics have bemoaned marketing's declining influence within the firm. (Kumar 2004, p. 3)[5]

Merlo, Whitwell, and Lukas (2003) use the phrase "Marketing's Tribulations in the Marketing Literature" (table 1, pp. 340–42) to characterize the large body of literature focusing on issues pertaining to the standing of marketing in organizations and in academe. In their synthesis and critique, they delineate four recurring concerns advanced in literature on marketing's perceived lack of influence: (1) lack of strategic focus, (2) poor awareness, detached from reality, (3) poor reputation and marginalization, and (4) lack of effective measures of the performance impact of marketing. Besides distinguishing between two broad literature streams that assess the impact of marketing on organizational performance and analyze the role of marketing within the firm as a functional unit, respectively, they characterize a third stream as literature that *bemoans* marketing's lack of influence as an organizational philosophy or as function.

Marketing's Declining Influence within the Firm: Opportunity for Scholarly Research or Cause for Concern?

Even if assertions concerning the diminishing influence of the marketing function in organizations made in some studies were to be true, whether marketing academicians should *bemoan* marketing's declining influence within the firm would depend on the underlying causes. If the decline were a consequence of the commissions and omissions of marketing academicians in the areas of scholarly research or the content of marketing education imparted to students in classrooms at institutions for higher learning, there is certainly a need to be concerned. (More on this in a later section.) On the other hand, if factors *other than* deficiencies in scholarly research in marketing or the content of marketing education are the primary root cause, there is no reason for marketing academicians to *bemoan*. Instead, it should be viewed as an opportunity for scholarly research. Our primary obligation as academics is to engage in disinterested pursuit of truth— *describing, understanding, explaining,* and *predicting* marketing phenomena of interest. The following quote from a recent article titled, "Why We Built the Ivory Tower?" succinctly conveys this point of view:

> After nearly five decades in academia, and five and a half years as a dean at a public university, I exit with a three-part piece of wisdom for those who work in higher education: do your job; don't try to do someone else's job, as you are unlikely to be qualified; and don't let anyone else do your job. In other words, don't confuse your academic obligations with the obligation to save the world; that's not your job as an academic; ... Marx famously said that our job is not to interpret the world, but to change it. In the academy, however, it is exactly the reverse: Our job is not to change the world, but to interpret it. (Fish 2004, Section A, p. 23)[6]

In other words, if evidence were to suggest that the influence of the marketing function in organizations is on the decline, the principal focus of marketing academicians should be on understanding, explaining, and predicting this phenomenon by researching questions such as:

- What explains the relative influence of different organizational functions in firms?
- What explains changes in their relative influence (i.e., decreasing versus increasing influence)?
- What explains the emergence of dominant coalitions in firms (certain organizational functions emerging as more dominant and wielding greater power than other functions)?
- What explains the marketing function being more influential in certain types of firms, industries, cultures, and so on, than in others?
- How are various macroenvironmental trends likely to impact on the relative influence of the marketing function in organizations in the future? Will it diminish or increase, and why?

Extant literature in management on dominant coalitions and the relative power of organizational functions can serve as a foundation for exploration of questions such as these.

Concerns over the lack of influence at the corporate level are not unique to marketing. Gartner Inc., a U.S.-based consulting firm, surveyed 450 non-information technology business managers on their perceptions of the relative influence of various organizational functions in the boardroom. The study found that of the eight organizational functions considered, information technology was ranked seventh and human resources eighth in terms of impact on setting strategic direction for the company. The study also provides suggestions on steps that chief information officers could undertake to enhance their influence in the boardroom (*Financial Times* 2004).

Whether questions in the genre of what managers in various functional areas can do or should do in order to elevate their stature in the eyes of the CEO and the boardroom belong under the rubric of scholarly research pursuits in business disciplines is debatable. On the other hand, questions in the genre of what explains various functional area managers engaging in behaviors to enhance their stature in the eyes of the CEO and the boardroom? clearly belong under the rubric of scholarly research pursuits in business disciplines.

Marketing's Declining Influence within the Firm: Fact or Myth?

The *empirical evidence* presented in support of a decline in the influence of the marketing function in organizations (e.g., Ambler 2003; Webster et al., 2003) must be viewed as preliminary at best, and with caution. For the most part, the studies tend to be exploratory and descriptive, based on samples that cannot be construed as representative of the larger population, and limited to firms in North America or Western Europe. On the other hand, *at the conceptual level,* the number of macroenvironmental trends that can be invoked to argue that the importance of marketing in organizations is likely to be on an ascendant rather than a descendant trajectory is quite substantial. Consider, for instance, the following:

- Globalization of markets—the challenges faced by firms in serving customers worldwide
- Globalization of industries and emergence of global competitors
- Growing importance of managing a firm's market-based assets—brand equity, channel equity, and customer equity—from the standpoint of organizational growth, survival, and long-term financial performance
- Growth of the Internet and the attendant increase in the number of e-informed and e-empowered customers
- Growth of the Internet and the growing power of electronic word of mouth
- Rising customer expectations and rising customer satisfaction threshold

The marketing thrust of a number of recent additions to the business lexicon, such as listed here, also portend an increasingly important role for the marketing function in organizations:

- CRM—customer relationship management
- MKTGM—marketing knowledge management
- MKTM—market knowledge management (market is used here as more encompassing—customer knowledge, competitor knowledge, marketing knowledge, etc.)

CRM, MKTGM, and MKTM entail market and marketing knowledge acquisition, dissemination, and organizational responsiveness in a 24/7/365 competitive business environment.

In summary, increasingly firms tend to view "planet earth" as the target market for their product offerings and often use the same brand names to market their product offerings worldwide. In a growing number of industries, in the face of installed capacity (supply) exceeding demand, stimulating demand or striving for a larger share of current demand are competitive imperatives. The growing market for digitized information products presents a whole new set of challenges and opportunities to firms. Unlike physical products whose supply is constrained by installed capacity, once created, the available supply of digitized information products is virtually unlimited. Unlike other organizational functions such as manufacturing, procurement, and R&D, which engage in activities that result in a firm incurring costs, the marketing function in organizations is entrusted with primary responsibility for revenue generation. Such considerations suggest that observations concerning the diminishing influence of the marketing function in organizations must be viewed with caution.

IS THE MARKETING FUNCTION IN ORGANIZATIONS ON A TRAJECTORY FOR DEVOLVING INTO A DEPARTMENT OF AD COPY AND CENTS-OFF COUPONS?

In an editorial essay, as an introduction to a special section of a recent issue of the *Journal of Marketing* on "Linking Marketing to Financial Performance and Firm Value," Lehmann (2004, p. 74) noted:

> Put simply, if marketing wants "a seat at the table" in important business decisions, it must link to financial performance. Otherwise, by focusing on the measures it is most comfortable with (e.g., awareness, attitude, sales), it will continue to lose ground to other areas, in fields such as product development (e.g., research and development, design) and to devolve into a department of "ad-copy and cents-off coupons." The task is not easy, but the reward is great.

As noted earlier, if allocation of an increasingly larger percent of marketing resources to programs such as cents-off coupons by businesses is based on considerations *other than* deficiencies in scholarly research in marketing and marketing education, then the phenomenon should be viewed as an opportunity for scholarly research in marketing. Research focusing on issues such as the following can inform marketing practice as well as shed insights into potential biases in managerial decision-making processes that result in marketing managers making suboptimal decisions.

- What explains the behavior (change in behavior) of firms in respect to their pattern of deployment of marketing resources?
- What organizational characteristics and environmental characteristics explain differences in the pattern of allocation of total promotional resources to short-term marketing programs such as consumer and trade sales promotion versus long-term brand-building programs such as advertising?

However, Lehmann (2004), in his recent editorial essay, as well in his earlier works (e.g., Lehmann 1997), cautioned that deficiencies in scholarly research in marketing and marketing education could eventually lead to the marginalization of the marketing function in organizations. Is Lehmann's cautionary note concerning marketing function devolving into a department of ad copy and cents-off coupons within the realm of possibilities? Over the long term, deficien-cies in the state of scholarly research in marketing and marketing education imparted to students at institutions for higher learning is likely to have an adverse impact on the standing of the mar-keting function in organizations under the following scenarios:

* The curriculum content of various business disciplines (what is typically taught in business schools in various courses and subject areas such as marketing, finance, and accounting) having an impact on their relative influence in organizations.
* Scholarly research in various business disciplines such as marketing, finance, and account-ing having an impact on their relative influence in organizations, both directly as a conse-quence of research utilization and indirectly as a consequence of the impact of scholarly research on what is taught in the classroom.
* The perceived relative contribution of various organizational functions to the bottom line of firms having a direct bearing on their relative standing in organizations.

Does the current state of scholarly research in marketing and marketing education suffer from severe deficiencies? An answer to this question must await a task force of marketing scholars undertaking a comprehensive and objective assessment of deficiencies in the substantive, theo-retical, and methodological research traditions at the marketing discipline level and various sub-disciplines such as advertising, consumer behavior, marketing channels, marketing ethics, and marketing strategy. As regards deficiencies in the realm of marketing education, questions such as the following must be addressed:

* In order to perform effectively in the rapidly changing marketplace, what competencies and skills must marketing practitioners of tomorrow possess?
* To what extent are marketing academicians informed and responsive in their roles as re-searchers and educators to changes in the environment and organizations that impact on the competencies and skills that marketing practitioners of tomorrow must possess?
* How well are the competencies and skills that marketing practitioners of tomorrow must pos-sess are currently being imparted in marketing coursework at institutions for higher learning?
* To what extent are students currently enrolled in doctoral programs in marketing receiving the kind of training they need in order to impart cutting-edge and relevant marketing knowl-edge critical to tomorrow's marketing practitioner?

In regard to both calls for reforms in the realms of scholarly research in marketing and market-ing education, certain caveats need to be borne in mind. For instance, in the context of calls for research linking marketing to financial performance and firm value, there is the need to guard against going overboard. Indeed, metrics matter, but financial metrics is not the be-all and end-all. Marketing science is at peril when researchers focusing on measures that are appropriate in the context of the research questions being addressed and the underlying theory (e.g., attitudes and beliefs) are criticized as focusing on the measures they are most comfortable with and disre-garding financial metrics. Marketing science is also at peril when researchers force-fit constructs (i.e., financial performance constructs) that do not belong in the nomological network.

Although I do not have a verbatim quote that I can cite here, since my years as a doctoral student I have been privy to occasional remarks by marketing academicians, the gist of which can be summarized as follows: "Marketing academicians are not the hired hands of for-profit busi-ness organizations. Hence, there is no need to belabor about either the managerial relevance or managerial implications of our scholarly research pursuits." Representative of points of view in direct contrast to the above include Webster and colleague's (2003) article titled, "Can Marketing Regain Its Seat at the Table?" and Lehmann's (2004, p. 72) cautionary note: "Put simply, if marketing wants 'a seat at the table' in important business decisions, it must link to financial performance." Clearly, with any reform initiatives there is a need to guard against being swayed too much by either the "we are not the hired hands of for-profit business organizations" or the "if marketing wants a seat at the table" stance.

With regard to marketing education, calls for changes in business curriculum content have been frequent and have been addressed in numerous published works, mostly in the context of the MBA degree program. For instance, in an article titled, "The Upwardly Global MBA," based on a survey of 100-plus executives in more than 20 countries, Andrews and Tyson (2004) identify the repertoire of knowledge, skills, and attributes that MBA degree programs should be designed to equip the students with.[7] However, the initiative for reform in specific reference to the field of marketing must necessarily come from and be led by the community of marketing educators. Interestingly, Andrews and Tyson use the term "customer-driven education" in reference to higher education, a credence product (or a product that's salient on credence attributes). This brings to fore an important issue: what is or should be the role for customers (stakeholders such as students and employers) in the design and development of credence products such as higher education?

CONCLUSION

My musings on the alleged loss of influence of marketing in academic discourse on strategy, the diminishing influence of the marketing function in organizations, and the specter of the marginalization of the marketing function in organizations presented in this chapter are intended to stimulate further debate and discussion on the topic. Even if warranted, the pace of *major reforms at the macro level* in the realms of scholarly research in marketing and marketing education might be somewhat slow in light of the need for collective deliberation and contemplation. However, *incremental reform at the micro level* is an everyday occurrence, with some marketing scholar somewhere in the world instituting some changes in his/her scholarly research pursuits and instructional material. The following quote by Dr. Leslie Aiello succinctly conveys this point: "I always tell my students that I've taught for 30 years and I've never given the same lecture twice. Hardly a year goes by when something new isn't found" (Wade 2004, p. D2).

NOTES

1. See Varadarajan (1992) for my commentary on Day (1992).

2. A more detailed discussion of this and other related issues (a broader construal of relevance and implications of scholarly research in marketing) can be found in Varadarajan (2003).

3. From the standpoint of the advancement of the discipline, neither of the following extreme positions that some marketing academicians seem to hold (advocate) is likely to serve us well: (a) The litmus test for assessing the relevance of a scholarly research in marketing is its managerial implications; or (b) The managerial implications of scholarly research in marketing is not an issue that we should be concerned about, since marketing academicians are not the hired hands of business organizations.

4. It is conceivable that the body of research-based knowledge of marketers, advertising agencies, market research firms, and consultants on consumer and customer behavior and its implications for marketing strategy practice is quite extensive. However, such knowledge is proprietary and does not reside in the public domain.

5. Here, Kumar (2004) cites Ambler (2003) in support of only 10 percent of executive meeting time being devoted to marketing.

6. I recognize that in marketing as well as in other disciplines, academicians are involved to varying degrees in research that has the potential to change the world in ways big and small. However, applied (policy) research, whether in marketing or in other fields, should be informed by basic (pure) research. Miller (1991, p. 4), points to the following distinctions between the two:

- **Basic (Pure) Research**
  Nature of problem: Seek new knowledge about phenomena to establish general principles that explain them.
  Goal of research: Produce new knowledge including discovery of relationships and the capacity to predict outcomes under various conditions.

- **Applied (Policy) Research**
  Nature of problem: Seek to understand social problems and to provide policy-makers with well-grounded guides to remedial action.
  Goal of research: Produce knowledge that can be useful to policymakers who seek to eliminate or alleviate social problems.

7. I often wonder whether during the past quarter century, at every major university, the MBA program structure and curriculum might have been revised more often than any other master's program offering of that university.

References

Ambler, Tim (2003), *Marketing and the Bottom Line.* London: FT Prentice Hall.

Andrews, Nigel and Laura D. Tyson (2004), "The Upwardly Global MBA," *Strategy + Business,* (Fall), 1-10.

Bagozzi, Richard P. (1992), "Acrimony in the Ivory Tower: Stagnation or Evolution?" *Journal of the Academy of Marketing Science,* 20 (Fall), 355–59.

Chakravarti, Dipankar (1992), "Appraising Consumer Research: There's More to Vision than Meets the Eye," *Journal of the Academy of Marketing Science,* 20 (Fall), 361–66.

Cunningham, William H. and Ben M. Enis (1983), "From the Editor," *Journal of Marketing,* 47 (Summer), 5–6.

Day, George S. (1992), "Marketing's Contribution to the Strategy Dialogue," *Journal of the Academy of Marketing Science,* 20 (Fall), 323–29.

Financial Times (2004), "Chief Information Officers Stay Out in the Cold," August 4, 6.

Fish, Stanley (2004), "Why We Built the Ivory Tower?" *New York Times,* May 21, Section A, 23.

Kumar, Nirmalya (2004), *Marketing as Strategy.* Boston: Harvard Business School Press.

Lehmann, Donald R. (1996), "Some Thoughts on the Futures of Marketing," in *Reflections on the Futures of Marketing,* Donald R. Lehmann and Katherine E. Jocz, eds. Cambridge, MA: Marketing Science Institute, 121–35.

——— (2004), "Metrics for Marketing Matter," *Journal of Marketing,* 68 (October), 73–75.

Merlo, Omar, Gregory Whitwell, and Bryan A. Lukas (2003), "Toward a Conceptual Understanding of the Alleged Decline of Marketing's Influence Within Organizations," *Proceedings of the American Marketing Association's Marketing Educators' Winter Conference,* G. Henderson et al., ed., 337–46.

Miller, Delbert C. (1991), *Handbook of Research Design and Social Measurement.* Newbury Park, CA: Sage.

Sheth, Jagdish N. (1992), "Acrimony in the Ivory Tower: A Retrospective on Consumer Research," *Journal of the Academy of Marketing Science,* 20 (Fall), 345–53.

Summers, Lawrence H. (2003), "The Authority of Ideas," *Harvard Business Review,* 81 (August), 144.

Varadarajan, Rajan (1992), "Marketing's Contribution to the Strategy Dialogue: The View from a Different Looking Glass," *Journal of the Academy of Marketing Science,* 20 (Fall), 335–43.

——— and Terry Clark (1994), "Delineating the Scope of Corporate, Business and Marketing Strategy," *Journal of Business Research,* 31 (October–November), 93–105.

——— (2003), "Musings on Relevance and Rigor of Scholarly Research in Marketing," *Journal of the Academy of Marketing Science,* 31 (Fall), 368–76.

Wade, Nicholas (2004),"Miniature People Add Extra Pieces to Evolutionary Puzzle," *New York Times*, November 9, D2.

Webster, Frederick E., Jr. (1992), "The Changing Role of Marketing in the Corporation," *Journal of Marketing,* 56 (October), 1–17.

——— (1997), "The Future Role of Marketing in the Organization," in *Reflections on the Futures of Marketing,* Donald R. Lehmann and Katherine E. Jocz, eds. Cambridge, MA: Marketing Science Institute, 39–66.

———, Alan J. Malter, and Shankar Ganesan (2003), "Can Marketing Regain Its Seat at the Table?" *MSI Reports: 2003 Working Paper Series. 03-003,* 29–47.

Wilson, Edward O. (1998), *Consilience: The Unity of Knowledge,* New York: Knopf.

PART 7

A NEW MISSION FOR MARKETING

Marketing remains a fundamentally noble calling, as it seeks to align the interests, needs, and desires of individuals with those of profit-seeking corporations and other societal institutions. The chapters in this concluding section help to end this book on a positive note by reminding us how essential marketing is and how it can reclaim the high ground within companies, with customers, and in society.

According to Fred Webster, many marketing scholars put forth arguments that marketing competence in the form of a customer orientation, market knowledge, and a focus on customer value would be the key to business performance and profitability in today's dynamic market environments. Unfortunately, there is now widespread concern and mounting evidence that marketing has lost, not gained, the expected influence in the firm. Instead, the sales function has become much more powerful and has been allocated resources once controlled by marketing, as firms have increasingly focused on short-term tactics and sales revenue more than long-term market development strategy and profitability. Marketing's role appears to have been diminished in terms of both effectiveness and trust.

Webster suggests that to regain its influence within management circles, marketing managers and educators need reorientation. On the business side, marketing managers must learn what their company's financial statements mean and how they are created. They must identify the real marketing drivers of financial results and shareholder value. Similarly, marketing educators need to reassess the relationship between their research and their teaching. He highlights three sets of issues: the dangerously false idea that rigor and relevance are in conflict; the need to train PhD students with an understanding of the total field of marketing as an academic discipline with historical roots; and the need to train MBA and undergraduate students for the future, not just the present.

Berry and Mirabito suggest that marketing has had a positive, defining impact on society. Marketers have influenced the creation of myriad goods and services that have lessened the drudgery of housework, enhanced consumer's self-confidence and sense of style, and enabled consumers to use their time—a finite resource—in more productive and satisfying ways. However, despite these contributions, the net impact of marketing on the quality of life has shifted, subtracting rather than adding value. The enormous power for social good that marketing once wielded has diminished and has even been misused. Misuse of social power leads to decline of social power. And this is happening with marketing.

According to Berry and Mirabito, marketing can operate on a customer need-centered or customer desire-centered basis, or it can strive to balance needs and desires. Need-centered marketing stresses helping customers improve their lives over a long time horizon. Desire-centered marketing stresses satisfying customers' immediate wants. Need-centered marketing shapes and reshapes markets. Desire-centered marketing caters to customers' present demands. Customers dictate and marketers oblige.

Berry and Mirabito believe that marketing as a profession and as a discipline has lost its way—and much of its credibility and influence—by emphasizing the satisfaction of customers' desires at the expense of customer needs. Desire-centered marketing can never be as effective as need-centered marketing. The most powerful brands have been built on satisfying customers' needs. The authors suggest that marketing must take the high road because its true mission is to improve peoples' quality of life, where quality is measured as the percent of time a person spends in a state of well-being. Furthermore, this is not a "feel-good" mission but rather a mission that strengthens financial performance and credibility among shareholders. The right marketing is the soul of an organization, guiding, cajoling, teaching, and inspiring other decision makers to act and invest on behalf of creating customer well-being. The right marketing is the voice of the customer inside the organization, the customer's advocate, the customer's friend. The right marketing strengthens with deeds marketing's credibility, influence, and future vitality in an organization and in society.

Keller and Kotler suggest embracing a "holistic marketing concept" in which the customer is not the only stakeholder. Holistic marketing recognizes that everything matters with marketing—customers, employees, other companies, competition, as well as society as a whole. It therefore includes internal marketing, relationship marketing with multiple stakeholders, integrated marketing, and performance marketing.

Grove, John, and Fisk recommend a renewed focus on *people* in marketing. The role of people in marketing is vital, especially in services industries. The people factor creates greater intimacy between the producers and the consumers, which is how it used to be in the pre-industrial age. The authors recommend that it would be beneficial to augment the scientific method that is so prevalent in the field with insights from the arts. By integrating aspects of art into marketing, the field may be able to escape the passionless, nearly dehumanized marketing approaches that are currently in vogue in the field.

Haeckel believes that industrial age marketing is obsolete and we need to think from the postindustrial age perspective. He suggests that the best way to implement the marketing concept is to embrace a sense and respond perspective. Its premise is that rapid, unpredictable, and often discontinuous change is baked into the logic of an information economy. As a result, businesses must learn to respond effectively to what individual customers need/want/prefer now, rather than execute efficiently plans that are based on predictions about what markets will want in the future. He uses the analog of a bus driver versus the taxi driver. The bus driver has a predictable, fixed route and fixed stops and knows what the destination is. It does not matter whether there are passengers waiting to take the bus. On the other hand, the taxi driver cannot start without a customer because without a customer he doesn't know where to go. The essence of the postindustrial economy is an exchange of information *about* value from customers *for* the production of value from producers. Haeckel believes value creation should not start with capabilities but instead with development of a design system with subsystems. Second, these subsystems should be designed for interaction between them. In sense and respond designs, coherent, system-level behavior arises from quasi-autonomous, self-organizing behavior. This is a network approach to value creation.

Finally, Sheth and Sisodia focus on three stakeholders of marketing: practitioners, academics, and policymakers. They suggest that marketing should be reorganized as a corporate staff function similar in structure and impact to finance, human resource, and information technology. As a corporate staff function it should report directly to the CEO. Also, it should have corporate-wide responsibility for branding; managing external suppliers of marketing such as ad agencies, market research companies, and outsourced call centers; managing business development; and acting as a coordinator and facilitator of marketing across different business units. As a staff function, marketing should have both capital and operating expenditure budgets, similar to the information technology function. Sheth and Sisodia also recommend focusing on newsworthy research and encouraging programmatic contractual research that is peer reviewed. Lastly, they suggest the establishment of a National Academy of Marketing as well as certification and recertification of marketing professionals to enhance the public perception of marketing.

CHAPTER 34

MARKETING

A Perpetual Work in Progress

FREDERICK E. WEBSTER, JR.

In broad terms, marketing management can be defined as the process by which the firm responds to a changing marketplace. The past two decades have certainly been a period of rapid marketplace change, seen in the following environmental forces:

- global competition
- organizational cost-cutting and down-sizing
- heightened emphasis on short-term financial measures of business performance including return on investment and quarterly earnings per share
- increased use of outsourcing, often to offshore vendors
- order-of-magnitude improvements in information processing speed and telecommunications
- the Internet revolution including the boom, bust, and rebirth of electronic commerce
- rapid growth of discount mass merchants such as Wal-Mart, Home Depot, and Target

As organizations have changed in response to their environment, it would be logical to expect that marketing would also change. Given the presence of tougher competition, more demanding customers, and increasingly powerful channel members, marketing should have been leading organizational change. In fact, several marketing authors in the 1990s (for example, Day 1992; Haeckel 1999; McKenna 1991; Srivastava, Shervani, and Fahey 1999; and Webster 1992) put forth arguments that marketing competence in the form of customer orientation, market knowledge, and a focus on customer value would be the key to business performance and profitability in these dynamic market environments. Unfortunately, there is now widespread concern and mounting evidence that marketing has lost, not gained, the expected influence in the firm. Instead, the sales function has become much more powerful and has been allocated resources once controlled by marketing as firms have increasingly focused on short-term tactics and sales revenue more than on long-term market-development strategy and profitability (Webster, Malter, and Ganesan 2003). Marketing's role appears to have been diminished in terms of both effectiveness and trust. This brief chapter will examine some of the causes and consequences.

CAUSES OF THE DECLINE OF MARKETING

The causes of marketing decline are both internal and external to the firm and, within the firm, both within and outside of the traditional marketing function.

Forces External to the Firm

We began by noting the macrotrends in the environment that have influenced the changing role of marketing within the firm. Here we expand briefly on their influence on the marketing function.

The increasingly competitive environment has forced firms to find areas where costs can be reduced without doing damage to top-line revenues or bottom-line profits. Financial results are measured and reported on a quarterly basis according to commonly accepted accounting standards and disclosure rules of the securities exchanges. The long-standing focus on quarterly-earnings-per-share has been sharpened by the increased portion of equity investments held by pension funds, mutual funds, and fund managers who are likewise focused on short-term performance by their measurement and reporting requirements. Everybody wants to be above average in performance when compared with various indices and this leads to heightened trading activity and rapid movements in and out of stocks caused by only small changes in revenue and earnings projections and results.

As top management and financial management officers seek ways to enhance these measures of performance, marketing expenditures are an obvious place to look. Many marketing budget items, such as investments in new product development, geographic market expansion, brand-image-building advertising, or new retail display materials, can be reduced or eliminated without an immediate effect on the financial numbers. While astute marketing managers would like to be able to argue that their spending is an investment in the long-term growth and profitability of the business, they usually lack compelling conceptual models or economic and financial data to defend themselves. Nonmarketing managers see marketing budgets as "expenses," not investments, and "expenses" get "cut." By and large, marketing managers have not had the tools to argue convincingly that their investments in market research and market development will produce superior returns.

Outsourcing of manufacturing, often to partners in the less-developed countries, as a cost-cutting strategy is well known, but it sometimes comes with a loss of control over product and service quality. Branded products manufacturers have been under intense pressure from their mega-retailer partners such as Wal-Mart to do more manufacturing offshore. Increasingly, customer service activities involving telecommunications and data processing have also been sent to India, Russia, and other places where there is a pool of low-cost labor that is highly competent and familiar with the English language. Credit card companies, catalogue marketers, and computer hardware and software firms have all made good use of such partnerships. In the drive to reduce costs, long-term strategic marketing goals of building customer satisfaction, loyalty, and profitability may receive secondary consideration as these elements of the marketing mix are managed from an operations, not a marketplace, perspective.

Nonmarketing Forces within the Firm

As these outside competitive, cost-cutting pressures impact upon the firm, the organization changes in important ways. Strategic planning departments, once thought to be critical to long-term success in business development and optimal resource allocation, disappeared very rapidly in the early 1980s when it was realized that their efforts were expensive and time-consuming and often resulted in disastrous delays in strategic response to a changing marketplace. In many of the more sophisticated corporations that had led the strategic planning revolution, marketing had been co-mingled with strategic planning to enhance long-term business development, to bring more customer focus into the strategic planning process, and to tie strategic business unit marketing strategies to overall corporate strategy. Unfortunately, few of these firms gave much thought to preserving the organizational marketing capability part when formal strategic planning was put to the ax.

It was common for planning and marketing responsibilities to be removed from the corporate level and decentralized into strategic business units in pursuit of the twin objectives of reduced costs and enhanced market responsiveness. It was not often the case, however, that marketing responsibilities were assigned to a marketing professional, a manager with previous training and experience in the marketing discipline. Especially in industrial firms, the recipient of new marketing duties was likely to be a person in field sales or someone with a technical background such as an applications engineer or a product/market manager. The result was usually a decline in the total level of marketing competence and skills within the organization.

It is worth noting the implicit assumption here that marketing is something easy to learn, something "anybody can do," an assumption that would not be made about most other critical management functions. There is a serious lack of appreciation of the nature and value of marketing knowledge and skills as organizational assets. Rather, marketing is often seen as a personality characteristic and skill set, not as a body of knowledge and management competence. It is a fair criticism that marketing managers are often not finance-literate. It is also true, but less commonly said, that very few managers from other functions are marketing-literate.

Responding to the dominating influence of mega-retailers, marketing strategy and brand management responsibilities have migrated to the field sales organization. However, in most companies, sales and marketing are organizationally distinct functions. One is much more likely to see a vice president of sales and a vice president marketing than a single executive vice president of marketing and sales.

Forces within Marketing as a Function and a Discipline

Marketing as a management function and an academic discipline must share responsibility for its diminished power and effectiveness. Marketing educators and marketing practitioners have not done a very good job of conveying the relevance of marketing knowledge as a distinct discipline. Marketing scholars have preferred to talk to one another rather than to managers; marketing managers themselves have a hard time distinguishing between marketing and sales and often revert to the sales mentality under the pressures to make the revenue and profit numbers. Short term drives out attention to long term every time.

From the perspective of top management and other functional managers within the firm, marketing often seems incapable of justifying its budget requests with analytically based marketing programs and demonstrated results from earlier expenditures. Marketing managers have often countered with the argument that they do not have the market research funds to measure postprogram results. The measurement of marketing productivity is now recognized as the single greatest challenge, and opportunity, facing marketing managers.

On the academic side, we can cite several factors that have led to a perception, not unfair or unrealistic, that published research in marketing has had decreasing relevance for all but a small portion of managers who must deal with the myriad of marketing problems and decisions. These factors can be briefly summarized as follows:

- Top-level marketing journals have editorial policies discouraging the publication of conceptual papers and results based on qualitative, observational, clinical research methods. Important areas in the development of marketing thought have been ceded to the strategic management discipline and to general management journals.

- Consumer behaviorists have been reluctant to publish in marketing journals and have favored tightly controlled laboratory experiments with student subjects over less-structured research with actual consumers in field settings. These results are often not generalizable to actual marketplace behavior. Some scholars have even argued explicitly that research with managerial relevance is *by definition* tainted and not to be trusted.
- The availability of large-scale databases has encouraged research on marketing tactics intended to produce immediate and relatively easily tracked sales results within stores, on Internet sites, or in telephoned responses. Sales promotion has received a disproportionate share of attention relative to other marketing variables. Armed with proven statistical models and empirical results, marketing managers find it easier to justify price cuts and other tactical expenditures than strategic investments in the future of the business.
- Marketing scholars have tended to ignore field sales management as a research venue even as selling budgets grow in importance relative to marketing expenditures. Many business schools have dropped sales management courses from their curricula as the definition of the intellectual domain of marketing evolves, intentionally or otherwise, toward exclusion of field sales.
- There is a longstanding bias toward consumer products and services to the exclusion of business products and services. Most research studies involve consumer goods, with a heavy emphasis on frequently purchased packaged goods. Managers in industrial marketing firms have few opportunities to use academic marketing research and the marketing literature to guide their work and to gain support for their efforts within the firm.

CONSEQUENCES OF MARKETING'S DECLINING INFLUENCE

The decline of marketing can be seen in several specific outcomes within organizations. Most basically, marketing as a distinct function has often all but disappeared within many organizations. One manager in a firm we studied noted that in his company, the marketing function had essentially "run the corporate bureaucracy" in the past and represented the majority of the middle management layer in the organization.

Another manager stated, "It once seemed obvious that Marketing Management was destined to assume ultimate influence—and control—over the American corporation. With few exceptions, that has not happened."

As marketing responsibilities were dispersed throughout the organization, some people argued that this was actually consistent with the original marketing concept and its assertion that marketing was really not a separate function at all but "the whole business seen from the customer's point of view." It was presumed that the entire organization would become more customer-focused and market-driven, a highly desirable outcome. One of our respondents commented "Every part of the company now says '*We* are the customer interface.'" However, the pressures of running a business often take the "designated marketer's" eye off the ball and there is actually less advocacy for the long-term interest of the customer and a decline in overall marketing competence. Paradoxically, quoting another manager, "As the marketing point-of-view pervades the corporation, Marketing as a function seems destined to dwindle."

Such marketing competence as has remained at the corporate level has tended to focus on global, not day-to-day or product-level, brand management, which is now the responsibility of people in the field who work closely with the trade, and on advertising and other forms of marketing communication that are best purchased and controlled from a centralized perspective. These remaining marketing staffs tend to be quite small, often only one senior-level manager with a small support group.

The major dimensions of the multiple issues that now face marketing managers can be summarized as follows:

- Managing the trade-off between long-term and short-term goals
- Deciding which marketing activities should be budgeted as capital investments vs. expenses
- Arguing forcefully that price cuts that impact the revenue line should not be treated as "below the line" marketing expenses
- Making clear, within the organizational structure of their firm, which marketing functions require centralized, specialized marketing competence and which marketing activities are cross-functional processes that require decentralized marketing direction
- Advocating for customer-orientation vs. product- and technology-orientation and making customer value the strategic objective of all activities
- Defining the real customer of the company, whether it is the end-user or the reseller, and managing the brand and customer relationships within this strategic framework
- Defining clearly the roles and responsibilities of sales and marketing and the relationship between the two

HOW MARKETING CAN REGAIN A SEAT AT THE TABLE

If marketing management is to regain its influence within management circles and to justify its status as a distinct academic discipline within the management profession, there is a clear need for reorientation. That reorientation requires some major shifts in direction both from management and from thought leaders within the marketing field.

On the business side, marketing managers (encouraged by their CEOs and financial colleagues) must learn what their company's financial statements mean and how they are created. They must identify the real marketing drivers of financial results and shareholder value. This may require substantial investments of time and money in gathering market data, tracking the results of multiple variables within marketing programs, and analytical modeling of both a conceptual and statistical nature. Considerable attention should be devoted to understanding the links between customer value and shareholder value through strategic pricing. Likewise, it is critically important to measure brand equity and to relate this to the value of the firm.

The marketing measurement issues are at the core of the development of the field at the moment. Three presentations to the American Marketing Association's 2004 Summer Educators Conference by marketing consultants, whose work keeps them at the interface of marketing thought and marketing practice, were recently summarized by the editor of *Marketing Management* (Neal 2004):

- Return on investment measures are necessary but not sufficient; marketers need to evaluate investments in brands, communications, and customers against other strategic objectives for the firm and to assure that they are managed in an integrated framework of marketing and business strategy.
- Measures of sales volume, profit, cash flow, etc., do not relate directly to marketing performance; specific marketing measures are needed for such key variables as brand equity, the most valuable business asset for many firms.
- Marketing as investment vs. expense is only part of the problem facing marketing managers; equally important is the fact of the declining productivity of marketing expenditures, reflecting not only the economics of diminishing returns caused by media fragmentation and proliferation but a fundamental loss of trust of marketing by both consumers and company

managers. Marketing must become both more precise and more relevant, for consumers as well as for companies.

Marketing educators need to reassess the relationship between their research and their teaching. We can highlight three sets of issues: the dangerously false idea that rigor and relevance are in conflict; the need to train PhD students with an understanding of the total field of marketing as an academic discipline with historical roots; and the need to train MBA and undergraduate students for the future, not just the present.

The false dichotomy between rigor and relevance in academic research has a number of negative consequences. We have noted the lack of impact on management practice from research that is too narrowly focused on relatively unimportant problems and emphasizes methodology over results. Marketing is fundamentally a business practice, not a subbranch of economics, and as such is an applied discipline by definition. At the same time, management practice has suffered from a lack of analytical rigor. It has often been said that there is nothing as useful as a good theory. At this critical juncture in the development of marketing as a discipline, new emphasis must be placed on conceptual and theoretical developments that will move the field forward.

The great universities have always been based on the traditions of rigorous research. This is not the place to debate the proper balance of research with teaching, except to recognize that great researchers are not always great teachers and great universities need both. The most respected scholars will always be those who can do both exceptionally well. There is something troubling about a growing practice at some leading business schools to specify professorships for teaching, labeling their holders as second-class citizens who couldn't cut the research mustard. The most exciting teachers are those who are excited by their own research and can convey that excitement about their knowledge of their field because they are contributing to it. Likewise, great researchers, whose ideas have the longest-lasting impact, have been motivated by a basic desire to solve important problems. They envision "clients" who will benefit from their work and those clients are seldom other researchers who are working on the same problems. Authors might think about this when a paper rejected by one journal is submitted to another, only to be submitted for review again to one or more of the same reviewers. Journal editors should think twice when they see that only a few members of their editorial board are likely to be interested in and knowledgeable about the underpinnings of a particular paper. Incest produces ugly outcomes.

On the teaching side, it is important to look at the state of PhD education as a starting point because these programs are producing the teachers of tomorrow. What are *they* being taught? Marketing department chairs report that they have great difficulty in identifying programs that are preparing PhD students to do research and teaching in the area of marketing strategy. The field is currently overwhelmed by modelers and behavioral decision theorists. Important work for sure but not the whole story! As Wilkie and Moore (2003) have forcefully argued, stewardship for marketing as an academic field of study has not characterized scholarship for the past two or three decades. Fortunately, some leading programs are now incorporating seminars on the development of conceptual knowledge in the field and a review of its historical development. These young PhDs should be highly marketable because of their enhanced ability to convey a body of received knowledge to tuition-paying marketing students as well as to contribute to it.

In teaching marketing to our undergraduate and MBA students, we must recognize a common problem and resolve to address it: the sad fact is that many students elect marketing majors because they have little tolerance for quantitative material as found in courses in accounting, finance, economics, statistics, and mathematics. Marketing teachers need to reinforce the importance of the underlying logic and rigor of analytical methods and to teach their application and relevance to solving marketing problems. Students, like researchers, must be taught to abandon the false dichotomies of theory and practice, rigor and relevance. Of course, this is easier said than done, but it *must* be done. Marketing teachers must incorporate sound accounting and financial concepts into their teaching, which will likely require that they themselves get some additional training and make some additional intellectual commitments to broadening their understanding of marketing.

Marketing educators need a current, complete, and correct understanding of the nature of marketing practice if they are to avoid the failure of teaching students concepts, techniques, and skills that are relevant for jobs that are rapidly disappearing or no longer exist. We must accept our share of responsibility for the fact that marketing has lost influence with both managers and consumers. To quote Rajiv Grover at the Bentley College symposium which was the genesis for this book: "The main reason that marketing is getting marginalized is because much of our research and teaching has become orthogonal to practice" (2004).

MAKING PROGRESS IN DEVELOPING THE DISCIPLINE

Marketing will always be a work in progress unless it dies as a distinct discipline. If academic research is to contribute to the development of the discipline in significant ways, there needs to be a broadening of its objectives and its horizons. The intended audience of research results must be enlarged to incorporate real-world users of the research, a focus on real-world problems both long term and short term, and larger numbers of business managers across multiple disciplines as well as within marketing. Marketing authors should take on responsibility for familiarizing future general managers with fundamental marketing concepts and techniques, updating these concepts and techniques for the realities of the present and future market environment. Researchers must be sure that their work is idea- and theory-driven, not just data-driven. The marketing field in general must make a new commitment to integrating consumer behavior theory and research with marketing problems and practice. Researchers, especially those with a primary interest in strategy and organization, should continue to develop the paradigm of marketing as organizational processes, not separate business functions. It is important to work on the definition of the borders of the field of marketing, to specify which organizational processes are within the intellectual domain of marketing and which are not. More interdisciplinary research with colleagues from organizational behavior and strategic management is certain to produce interesting and important results with practical significance.

Senior marketing managers have expressed concern about how marketing will develop in the future (Webster et al. 2003). Change in most firms seems to be driven more by dissatisfaction with the status quo, not a clear vision of what marketing should be or where it is going. Even if marketing will always be changing in response to an ever-changing market environment, it will be stronger if it has a clear sense of purpose and direction.

REFERENCES

Day, George S. (1992), "Marketing's Contribution to the Strategy Dialogue," *Journal of the Academy of Marketing Science,* 20 (Fall), 323–29.

Grover, Rajiv (2004), "Marketing or Marketers: What or Who Needs Reforming?" Presentation at the Bentley College Symposium *Does Marketing Need Reform?* Boston, MA, August 9.

Haeckel, Stephan H. (1999), *Adaptive Enterprise: Creating and Leading Sense-and-Respond Organizations.* Boston: Harvard Business School Press.

McKenna, Regis S. (1991), "Marketing Is Everything," *Harvard Business Review,* 61 (January/February), 65–79.

Neal, Carolyn P. (2004), "From the Editor," *Marketing Management,* 13 (September/October), 2.

Srivastava, Rajendra K., Tassaduq A. Shervani, and Liam Fahey (1999), "Marketing, Business Processes, and Shareholder Value: An Organizationally-Embedded View of Marketing Activities, and the Discipline of Marketing," *Journal of Marketing,* 63 (Special Issue), 168–79.

Webster, Frederick E., Jr. (1992), "The Changing Role of Marketing in the Corporation," *Journal of Marketing,* 56 (October), 1–17.

———, Alan S. Malter, and Shankar Ganesan (2003), "Can Marketing Regain Its Seat at the Table?" Marketing Science Institute Working Paper No. 03–113, *MSI Reports* (Issue No. 3).

Wilkie, William L., and Elizabeth S. Moore (2003), "Scholarly Research in Marketing: Exploring the 'Four Eras' of Thought Development," *Journal of Public Policy in Marketing,* 22 (Fall), 116–46.

CHAPTER 35

RECAPTURING MARKETING'S MISSION

LEONARD L. BERRY AND ANN M. MIRABITO

Over the years, marketers have had a positive, defining impact on society. Marketers have influenced the creation of myriad goods and services that have lessened the drudgery of housework, enhanced consumers' self-confidence and sense of style, and enabled consumers to use their time—a finite resource—in more productive and satisfying ways. Supply chain managers have wrung excess costs out of distribution systems, reducing unnecessary expenses to customers. Advertisers have entertained television audiences with novel and informative campaigns.

Despite these contributions, however, the net impact of marketing on the quality of life has shifted, subtracting rather than adding value. Clever products and promotions encourage consumers to overeat, take on debt, and fritter away their money on lottery tickets. The enormous power for social good that marketing once wielded has diminished and has even been misused. Misuse of social power leads to the decline of social power. And this is happening with marketing.

Most marketers—indeed, most firms—want to create value for consumers. They know that customers reward firms whose products solve their problems. To be sure, most important new products are designed to satisfy customer needs and desires. But markets are dynamic and firms must be prepared to anticipate and respond to changing needs and desires. Many firms that initially focus on creating differential value for the customer shift their focus to maximizing short-term value for the firm after they have launched a successful product. Firms that focus on near-term results inevitably become more internally focused and more reactive. Reinvention loses out. Costs rise as marketers resort to heavy advertising spending and expensive promotions to sell products less well suited to the changing market.

Marketers are not alone in shifting focus from creating customer value to protecting firm resources as products mature. Financial stewards may shift emphasis from reporting financial results to framing financial results. Operations managers may shift emphasis from improving quality to cutting costs, outsourcing, and downsizing.

THE ROAD MOST TRAVELED

Marketing can operate on a customer need-centered or a customer desire-centered basis, or it can strive to balance needs and desires. Need-centered marketing stresses helping customers improve their lives over a long time horizon. Desire-centered marketing stresses satisfying customers' immediate wants. The two approaches often lead customers to different mindsets, to different habits. Need-centered marketing shapes and reshapes markets. Desire-centered marketing caters to customers' present demands; customers dictate and marketers oblige. Desire-centered marketing follows short-term trends.

We believe that marketing as a profession and as a discipline has lost its way—and much of its credibility and influence—by emphasizing the satisfaction of customers' desires at the expense of customer needs. Desire-centered marketing can never be as effective as need-centered marketing. The most powerful brands have been built on satisfying customers' needs. Many of those brands risk becoming dinosaurs because marketers have failed to shift the brand's focus as customers' needs shifted. Instead, too many companies have responded with tactics designed to flog value out of the existing offering, rather than with strategic reinvention to maintain congruency with customers' needs. The history of several product categories illustrates this thesis.

Cigarette manufacturers originally supplied a product to help customers relax. During World War II, the U.S. government gave billions of cigarettes to soldiers because cigarettes were considered calming. As scientists began to understand the carcinogenic properties of cigarettes, the tobacco companies missed the opportunity to create healthful products that might promote relaxation.

Similarly, in an era of uncertain water quality and limited refrigeration, Coca-Cola's concoction of caffeine, sugary syrup, and water met consumers' needs for a nonalcoholic, portable refreshment. Today's consumers have easy access to safe beverages, but they are threatened with the risk of obesity. Coca-Cola's product line may satisfy consumers' desires for a crisp, refreshing drink but does little to help consumers with their need to eat healthy, nutritious foods.

McDonald's is another case in point. Consider how McDonald's fortune slipped as its mission shifted from satisfying needs to satisfying desires. At the time McDonald's was born, restaurants were known for uneven quality and cleanliness, and they often reeked of alcohol and stale cigarettes. McDonald's filled consumers' need for a family-friendly restaurant offering consistently prepared wholesome food—beef, potatoes, cheese—at attractive prices in a clean facility. The jingle and golden arches appealed to consumers' desire for fun. Thus, McDonald's success came from fulfilling essential needs and desires.

The company lost much of its luster among virtually all of its stakeholders in recent years, however, not because of weak advertising campaigns but because of the company's failure to respond to changing nutritional standards. Instead of crafting healthier menus, the company focused on developing promotional deals, toy giveaways, and marginally innovative sandwiches.

Today, McDonald's is trying to recapture its former icon status with fresh salads, more chicken products, and children's Happy Meals featuring sliced apples and milk as alternatives to fries and soft drinks. The company has quickly become one of the largest buyers of fresh apples, grape tomatoes, and spring mix greens in the country. It may succeed in making sliced apples a popular snack. However, the fast food giant remains burdened with overcoming the stigma of being the leader of an industry that seemingly specializes in bad-for-you food.

MARKETING'S MISSION

Marketing's true mission is to improve people's quality of life, where quality of life is measured as the percent of time a person spends in a state of well-being. This is not a feel-good mission, but rather a mission that strengthens financial performance and credibility among stakeholders. Most people respond favorably to marketing that improves the quality of their lives and vice versa. Firms that add to rather than subtract from the quality of life are more likely to enjoy customer loyalty, stakeholder trust, regulatory freedom, and high employee morale and productivity. Firms that subtract from the quality of life should expect the opposite effects.

Improving the quality of life is the only mission that enhances marketing rather than diminishes it. By not adhering to that mission, marketing has taken on an ugly public face. Approximately 60 percent of all households in the United States registered their telephone numbers on the

Federal Trade Commission's National Do Not Call Registry during its first year of operation to avoid telemarketers phone calls. Telemarketing, once a powerful selling tool, has lost much of its punch and much of its freedom. Clearly, the majority of consumers do not regard telemarketing as useful and many consider it annoying or manipulative. When given the opportunity to stop the calls, an astonishing percentage of consumers seized it. The Do Not Call Registry seems a rather impressive wake-up call that marketing needs to reconsider its reason for being.

The future of marketing need not be bleak. Properly conceived and channeled, marketing can do so much good. Who in the organization is better equipped to lead the firm to customer value-creating offerings than the marketer?

Marketers and the organizations they represent can use marketing to harness the power of social profit in pursuit of financial profit. Companies create social profit when their actions produce net benefits to society. Social profit accumulates when customers, employees, and communities are better off because of a company's actions. Whereas many companies would not be missed if they suddenly disappeared, companies creating social profit would be missed because their actions contribute to the greater good. Social profit creates benefits beyond financial profit, and the benefits are not confined to the organization.

Social profit and financial profit are mutually reinforcing in the long run. Customers are willing to pay for products and services that genuinely benefit them. Too often, however, obsession with short-term financial profits drives consideration of social profit—and marketing's long-term influence and viability—right into the ground. It doesn't have to be this way.

TAKING THE HIGH ROAD

Many marketers have chosen to take the high road. A few examples will illustrate how some companies have prospered by adhering to marketing's primary mission.

Auto insurance is a necessary service but not a wanted one. No one looks forward to buying auto insurance or making a claim after an accident. Progressive, the third-largest auto insurer in the United States and among the most profitable large companies in the country, would clearly be missed were it to disappear. Few companies have been more imaginative or bolder in satisfying customers' needs and desires for a service as nonhedonic as auto insurance. Perhaps no other auto insurer has done more to build customers' trust for a service prone to mistrust.

Progressive readily provides prospective customers the insurance policy rates of competitors alongside its rates. In 2002, Progressive began scrolling its rates and competitors' rates on the company website, facilitating easy price comparisons. Competitors' rates appear even when they are lower than Progressive's. For more than ten years, Progressive has used immediate response vehicles (IRVs) to transport claims representatives to an accident site quickly to assess damage and, in some cases, to pay the claim on the spot. Progressive is expanding its network of service centers where customers can bring their damaged vehicles and obtain a rental car. Progressive arranges for the repairs and gives customers a text-message pager that transmits car repair updates. In the truest spirit of marketing, Progressive has improved the customer auto insurance experience enough to at least partially decommoditize a commodity service. "We have a high tolerance for innovation and experimentation," explains Glenn Renwick, the company's chief executive officer (Coolidge 2005).

Progressive satisfies desires in an industry that typically focuses only on satisfying needs. Chuck E. Cheese's restaurants, on the other hand, satisfy needs in an industry that typically emphasizes satisfying desires.

Parents with young children face a big challenge when it comes to finding a fun venue for an evening out. Most family restaurants rely on chicken fingers and crayons to engage younger guests. Placemat word games and coloring may entertain elementary school children but often do not provide sufficient stimulation to engage preschoolers. For about the same price as dinner in other family restaurants, Chuck E. Cheese's restaurants offer families with young children pizza and a salad bar, a live stage show, a chance to hug lovable mouse Chuck E. Cheese, and hours of fun in the restaurant's playroom. The playroom captures the excitement and hullabaloo of a carnival but on a scale appropriate for small children. Visit a Chuck E. Cheese's and you will see toddlers enchanted by the miniature merry-go-round and various car and truck rides. Preschoolers become pinball wizards, play skeetball, and toss basketballs. Children fly a pedal-propelled airplane a breathtaking three feet in the air. Virtual reality rides include wave runners, motorcycle races, and roller coasters.

Chuck E. Cheese's offers fun, value, and safety. Families are invited to enjoy the playroom facilities even if they don't buy the food. Some of the attractions are free, such as the sky tube overhead climbing structure and a toddler play zone. Other games and rides cost only one token (about a quarter), and most games offer tickets that children can cash in for souvenir prizes. Rides are small enough to allow children to safely climb on and off. The children revel in the autonomy of choosing rides and Mom and Dad enjoy dinner and conversation while supervising their children from a short distance away. The Kid Check program gives parents an extra cushion of security that a preschooler will not wander off. A staff member greets guests at the door and stamps the wrists of all members of each group with an identifying code. When it's time to go, the staff checks the wrists of each group member under a black light to make sure that "everyone who comes together, leaves together."

More than two hundred thousand children each year celebrate their birthdays at Chuck E. Cheese's. Indeed, Chuck E. Cheese's novel concept has proven to be a winning business model. The restaurant reports record revenues and earnings and its stock outperforms the restaurant industry (CEC Entertainment, Inc. 2003).

RECAPTURING THE MAGIC

Marketing academicians must play a key role in guiding the redemption of the profession. Marketing academics introduce college students who will become managers to the discipline. Educators have the underappreciated opportunity to create (or correct) students' impressions about marketing's role in society and in organizations as well as to explore its promise to effect positive change.

To teach the "right" marketing, academics must first understand it themselves. Far too often, educators teach the wrong marketing. The wrong marketing is persuading people to buy; the right marketing is helping people to live well. The wrong marketing is catering exclusively to customers' desires; the right marketing is finding creative ways to fulfill customers' desires without neglecting their needs. The wrong marketing focuses on creating value for the firm; the right marketing focuses on creating value for the customer and the broader community in which the customer lives and the firm operates, earning a financial return, stakeholder trust, and loyalty as a result. The wrong marketing is led; the right marketing leads. The wrong marketing emphasizes the now; the right marketing emphasizes a stronger future. The wrong marketing is selfish; the right marketing is generous.

The right marketer is the soul of an organization, guiding, cajoling, teaching, and inspiring other decision makers to act and invest on behalf of creating customer well-being. The right marketer is the voice of the customer inside the organization, the customers' advocate, the customers' friend. The right marketer strengthens with deeds marketing's credibility, influence, and future vitality in the organization and in society.

Marketing can be great again; its luster can be regained, but only if those who teach and practice it embrace its core purpose, which is to improve the quality of life.

REFERENCES

CEC Entertainment, Inc. (2003), Annual Report. CEC Enterprises, Inc., www.chuckecheese.com (accessed February 2005).

Coolidge, Carrie (2005), "The Innovator," *Forbes* 135 (January), 150.

Chapter 36

HOLISTIC MARKETING

A Broad, Integrated Perspective to Marketing Management

Kevin Lane Keller and Philip Kotler

Too often marketing is conducted in a fragmented, piecemeal fashion that results in suboptimal brand performance. Marketers overlook or fail to adequately incorporate important concerns that impact or are impacted by their decisions. Holistic marketing is the design and implementation of marketing activities, processes, and programs that reflect the breadth and interdependencies of their effects. Holistic marketing recognizes that "everything matters" with marketing—customers, employees, other companies, competition, as well as society as a whole—and that a broad, integrated perspective is necessary. Marketers must attend to a host of different issues and be sure that decisions in any one area are consistent with decisions in other areas. Four components of holistic marketing are internal marketing, integrated marketing, relationship marketing, and performance marketing. This chapter introduces the concept of holistic marketing and briefly addresses these four components.[1]

THE HOLISTIC MARKETING CONCEPT

Marketing has become markedly more complex. The straightforward, well-honed mass marketing techniques of previous decades are no longer as effective as they once were. Marketers now must make a host of difficult, interrelated decisions, dealing with numerous issues internal and external to the company.

As a consequence, marketing is done very differently now from how it was done in years past. Marketing is no longer done by just the marketing department. Companies are reviewing internal structures and processes and how they conduct their marketing. Because mass market advertising is not as effective as before, marketers are exploring new forms of communication, such as experiential, entertainment, permission, and viral marketing. Firms now sell goods and services through a wide variety of direct and indirect channels. Customers are increasingly telling companies what types of products or services they want and when, where, and how they want to buy them. To satisfy these customer needs, marketers are developing strong ties to various partners and channel members. Goals and objectives have become much more multidimensional as marketers attempt to maximize their financial return on investments while also being socially responsible, community involved, legally appropriate, and so on.

Without question, a whole set of forces have appeared in recent years that call for new marketing and business practices. Marketers now must do many things, and do them right. Companies need fresh thinking about how to operate and compete given a new marketing environment and the realities of the modern economy. Marketers in the twenty-first century are recognizing the need to have a more complete, cohesive approach that goes beyond traditional applications of the marketing concept.

Holistic marketing is the design and implementation of marketing activities, processes, and programs that reflect the breadth and interdependencies of their effects. Holistic marketing recognizes that "everything matters" with marketing—customers, employees, other companies, competition, as well as society as a whole—and that a broad, integrated perspective is necessary. Marketers must attend to a diverse range of different issues and be sure that decisions in any one area are consistent with decisions in other areas.

Holistic marketing is thus an approach to marketing that attempts to recognize and reconcile the scope and complexities of marketing activities. Figure 36.1 provides a schematic overview of four broad themes characterizing holistic marketing.

- *Internal marketing,* ensuring everyone in the organization embraces appropriate marketing principles.
- *Relationship marketing,* ensuring rich, multifaceted relationships are created with customers, employees, investors, channel members, and other marketing partners.
- *Integrated marketing,* ensuring that multiple means of creating, delivering, and communicating value are employed and combined in the optimal manner.
- *Performance marketing,* ensuring that the financial, brand equity, social, legal, ethical, community, and environmental effects of marketing decisions are all adequately accounted for.

We next briefly highlight some key issues in each of these four areas.[2]

INTERNAL MARKETING

Marketing is no longer the responsibility of a single department—it is a company-wide undertaking. Marketing drives the company's vision, mission, and strategic planning. Marketing succeeds only when all departments work together to achieve goals: when engineering designs the right products, finance furnishes the right amount of funding, purchasing buys the right materials, production makes the right products in the right time horizon, and accounting measures profitability in the right ways. Such interdepartmental harmony can only happen, however, when there is a clear understanding of customers and the company's marketing orientation and philosophy toward serving them.

Holistic marketing incorporates *internal marketing,* ensuring that everyone in the organization fully understands, accepts, and implements appropriate marketing principles. Internal marketing involves hiring, training, and motivating employees who want to serve customers well and market effectively. Marketing activities within the company are as important—if not even more so—than marketing activities directed outside the company. In fact, skillful internal marketing helps to ensure that external marketing can be done properly so that marketing programs fulfill and even surpass customer expectations.

Internal marketing must take place at different levels. At a very core level, the various marketing functions—personal selling, advertising, customer service, brand management, marketing research—must work together. There cannot be internal conflict within the marketing team such that the sales force thinks brand managers are pushing the wrong products at the wrong price or that brand managers think that the advertising director is pushing the wrong ad campaigns, and so

Figure 36.1 **Holistic Marketing Dimensions**

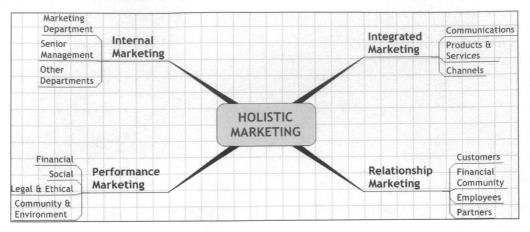

on. All these marketing functions must be coordinated from the customer's point of view. At a broader level, marketing must also be embraced by other departments in the organization. Marketing is not a department so much as a company orientation, and marketing thinking must be pervasive throughout the company.

Internal marketing also involves bottom-up and top-down marketing. Bottom-up marketing involves marketing managers directing marketing activities to maximize sales and brand equity for individual products for particular markets. Although such close, detailed marketing supervision can be advantageous, creating strong brands for every different possible product and market in this way is an expensive and difficult process and, most importantly, ignores possible synergies that may be obtainable.

Top-down marketing, on the other hand, involves marketing activities that capture the big picture and recognize the possible synergies across products and markets to brand products accordingly. Such a top-down approach seeks to find common products and markets that could share marketing programs and activities and only develops separate brands and marketing programs and activities as dictated by the customer or competitive environment.

Unfortunately, if left unmanaged, firms tend to follow the bottom-up approach, resulting in many brands marketed inconsistently and incompatibly. Marketing in a top-down fashion requires centralized and coordinated actions from high-level marketing supervisors to establish brand architecture, assemble brand portfolios, and provide marketing leadership. Given this guidance, bottom-up marketing can then concentrate on achieving deep consumer understanding, building strong customer bonds, and promoting product innovation.

RELATIONSHIP MARKETING

Increasingly, a key goal of marketing is to develop deep, enduring relationships with all people or organizations that could directly or indirectly affect the success of the firm's marketing activities.

Relationship marketing has the aim of building mutually satisfying long-term relationships with key parties in order to earn their trust or retain their business. Although customer relationship management is at its heart, relationship marketing is more than that. Relationship marketing requires cultivating the right kinds of relationships with the right constituent groups. Four key constituents for marketing are customers, employees, marketing partners (channels, suppliers, distributors, dealers, agencies) and members of the financial community (shareholders, investors, analysts). Relationship marketing builds strong economic, logistical, and social ties among relevant parties.

Successful relationship marketing offers the potential for smoother operations and superior customer solutions. The ultimate outcome of relationship marketing is the building of a marketing network—the company and all its supporting constituents and stakeholders with whom it has built mutually beneficial relationships. Marketing networks are invaluable company assets. Increasingly, competition is not between companies but between marketing networks.

Developing strong relationships requires understanding the capabilities and resources of different groups, as well as their needs, goals, and desires. Each party must be treated differently. Rich, multifaceted relationships with key constituents create the foundation for a mutually beneficial arrangement for both parties.

INTEGRATED MARKETING

The marketer's task is to devise marketing activities and assemble fully integrated marketing programs to create, communicate, and deliver value for customers. Complicating the development of integrated marketing programs is that marketing activities come in all forms.

Integrated marketing is based on two premises: (1) Many different marketing activities should be employed to create, communicate, and deliver value and (2) all marketing activities should be coordinated to maximize their joint effects such that the whole is great than the sum of its parts. In other words, the design and implementation of any one marketing activity is done with all other activities in mind.

Products and services are at the heart of value-creating marketing activities. To communicate and deliver value, two key components of an integrated marketing program are integrated communications and integrated channels. An integrated communication strategy involves choosing communication options that singularly build equity and drive sales, but that also reinforce or complement each other. A marketer might selectively employ television, radio, and print advertising, public relations and events, and public relations and website communications so that each makes its own contribution, as well as improves the effectiveness of other communications in the program. Marketers must mix and match communication options to build brand equity, that is, choose a variety of different communication options that share common meaning and content but which also offer different, complementary advantages.

Integrated channel strategy involves ensuring that direct and indirect channels work together to maximize sales and brand equity. Direct channels involve selling through personal contacts from the company to prospective customers by mail, phone, electronic means, in-person visits, and so on. Indirect channels involve selling through third party intermediaries such as agents or broker representatives, wholesalers or distributors, and retailers or dealers.

Direct and indirect channels offer varying advantages and disadvantages that must be thoughtfully combined to both sell products in the short run as well as maintain and enhance brand equity in the long run. As with communications, the key is also to mix and match channel options so that they collectively realize those two goals. Thus, it is important to assess each possible channel option in terms of its direct effect on product sales and brand equity as well as its indirect effect through interactions with other channel options.

In many cases, winning channel strategies are those that develop "integrated shopping experiences" and cleverly combine direct and indirect channels. For example, consider the variety of channels by which Nike sells their athletic shoes, apparel, and equipment products:

- *Branded Niketown stores.* Niketown stores offer a complete range of Nike products and serve as showcases for the latest fashions.
- *Niketown.com.* Consumers can place Internet orders for a range of products on Nike's e-commerce site.
- *Retail.* Nike products are sold in retail locations such as shoe, sporting goods, department, and clothing stores.
- *Catalog retailers.* Nike's products appear in numerous shoe, sporting goods, and clothing catalogs.
- *Outlet stores.* Outlet stores feature discounted Nike merchandise.
- *Specialty stores.* Nike equipment from product lines such as Nike Golf and Nike Hockey are sold through specialty stores like golf pro shops or hockey equipment suppliers.

Integrated channels of this kind must be managed in a way to maximize coverage and effectiveness, while minimizing cost and conflict. Marketers must address the tradeoff of having too many channels (leading to conflict among channel members or a lack of support) or too few channels (resulting in market opportunities being overlooked).

PERFORMANCE MARKETING

Finally, holistic marketing incorporates *performance marketing* and understanding all the different effects arising from marketing. Performance marketing involves assessing brand equity, customer equity, and financial returns from marketing activities and programs as well as addressing broader concerns and their legal, ethical, social, and environmental context.

Marketers increasingly are being asked to justify their investments to senior management. Marketing, however, works in a variety of direct and indirect ways, affecting brand awareness, image, attitudes, intentions, behaviors, and so on. As a consequence, marketers need to employ a wide variety of measures to assess their marketing efforts. Marketing metrics can help firms quantify and compare their marketing performance along a broad set of dimensions. Marketing research and analysis can then assess the financial efficiency and effectiveness of different marketing activities. Finally, firms can employ organizational processes and systems to make sure that the value from the analysis of these different metrics is maximized by the firm.

Accountability to key stakeholders forces marketers to be able to justify the short- or long-run financial effects of marketing activities. Yet, effects of marketing clearly extend beyond the company and the customer to society as a whole. Marketers must carefully consider the role that they are playing and could play in terms of social welfare in its broadest sense. Marketing performance requires that companies determine the needs, wants, and interests of target markets to satisfy them more effectively and efficiently than competitors, but in a way that preserves or enhances customers' and society's well-being. At times, they must balance and juggle the often-conflicting criteria of company profits, customer satisfaction, and public interest. Marketers can engage in cause marketing and other socially responsible marketing programs that provide mutually beneficial outcomes in that regard.

CONCLUSIONS

As marketing becomes more complex, marketers run the danger of overlooking or ignoring too many important factors in their decisions, arriving at suboptimal, piecemeal solutions as a result. The problem is exacerbated by industry marketing gurus and the popular press who promote overly simplistic solutions through aggressively promoted books and other means.

Holistic marketing eschews such approaches by recognizing and addressing the multidimensional nature of marketing. Holistic marketing requires that marketers adopt a broad perspective and address the scope and complexities of marketing activities to improve marketing management. In particular, superior holistic marketing is evident when companies effectively employ internal marketing, relationship marketing, integrated marketing, and performance marketing.

Holistic marketing requires broad, cohesive thinking. Holistic marketing also necessitates that marketers transcend conventional, but dated, marketing thinking. For example, a traditional depiction of marketing activities is in terms of the four Ps of the marketing mix: product, price, place, and promotion. From a holistic marketing perspective, such terminology is a narrow way to highlight what matters most with marketing. To capture the four components of holistic marketing more completely, a more appropriate set of four Ps might be: people, processes, programs (which would include the old four Ps), and performance.

NOTES

1. This chapter is based, in part, on material that appears in Kotler and Keller (2006).

2. An early conception of holistic marketing by Kotler, Jain, and Maesincee (2002) viewed it as "integrating the value exploration, value creation, and value delivery activities with the purpose of building long-term, mutually satisfying relationships and co-prosperity among key stakeholders" (p. 31). According to this view, holistic marketing maximizes value exploration by understanding the interrelationships between the customer's cognitive space, the company's competence space, and the collaborator's resource space; it maximizes value creation by identifying new customer benefits from the customer's cognitive space, utilizing core competencies from its business domain, and selecting and managing business partners from its collaborative networks; and it maximizes value delivery by becoming proficient at customer relationship management, internal resource management, and business partnership management.

References

Kotler, Philip and Kevin Lane Keller (2006), *Marketing Management*, 12th ed. Upper Saddle River, NJ: Prentice Hall.

Kotler, Philip, Dipak C. Jain, and Suvit Maesincee (2002), *Marketing Moves*. Boston: Harvard Business School Press.

CHAPTER 37

BACK TO THE FUTURE

Putting the People Back in Marketing

STEPHEN J. GROVE, JOBY JOHN, AND RAYMOND P. FISK

The question has been posed: "Does Marketing Need Reform?" It's a question that is likely to generate as many responses as there are folks who take the time to mull over the query. Inherent in the question is the supposition that something is wrong or amiss with the current state of marketing. After all, the dictionary defines *reform* as "improve by some alteration" and "change from worse to better" (www.m-w.com). Given that definition, we argue that, yes indeed, marketing does need reform, but it's more a matter of refocus than cataclysmic change. The reform that we believe is needed is a rediscovery of the importance and impact of the people component of the marketing enterprise. Whether it's the individuals who enact an organization's marketing effort or the customers themselves, the significance of the human element as a critical component of marketing has somehow eroded in the academic field of marketing. It's time to restore people to their proper place in marketing.

HOW WE GOT HERE

The changes that have occurred over the years to marketing as an academic field and as an organizational activity are obvious and profound. Marketing has become much more systematic and precise by embracing scientific methods of inquiry. Simply flipping through the pages of the *Journal of Marketing,* the *Journal of Marketing Research* or the *Journal of Consumer Research* will attest to this point. For a variety of reasons, it seems that marketing has grown to be more focused on measurable outcomes as well. Tangible and finite results are paramount and deemed to be the strongest indicator of market success. Wall Street's imperative of quarterly earnings and sales growth is no small influence on the responsibility of marketers. Finally, there is a greater and more pronounced emphasis on the implementation of technology in marketing. Whether it's the ability to collect, access, and distribute data quickly and efficiently or the ease and reliability that it offers organizations and their customers, technology commands a special status within the marketing enterprise. Indeed, it is perhaps the force of information technology that has created the increased emphasis on metrics and the quantification of all things human.

Collectively, there is little doubt that these changes have helped to establish marketing's credibility as both a discipline and a practice. However, we are convinced that this transformation has occurred with a significant tradeoff or expense. The people that comprise the marketing exchange—the employee and the customer—have been recast in a narrower and less realistic form as the various changes in marketing have occurred. Ultimately, perhaps by default, the human side of marketing has been devalued or dismissed. It may simply be a matter of a changing emphasis as marketing evolves rather than a conscious decision, but the accent on the people element of marketing has nevertheless eroded. It is our contention that there is a need to reconstruct marketing by returning the full importance of people to the character of marketing.

THE ROLE OF PEOPLE IN MARKETING

The people of marketing that we are particularly concerned about as the discipline's transformation has occurred are the customers and the employees that represent the organization to the customers. Both have seemingly been bleached of their spirit and soul as organizations focus on such phenomena as return on quality, lifetime value, harnessing information technology, and e-commerce. The former are, of course, essentially the raison d'etre for the marketing organization. After all, without customers, marketing doesn't exist. The latter are the organizational boundary spanners that directly interact with the customer. As such, they serve as conduits of information to and from the customer, and from the customer perspective they *are* the organization.

Nevertheless, whether the folks in question are household consumers or industrial buyers, service personnel, sales representatives, or retail employees, they are people that have often been reduced to a number or a function. Left by the wayside are their inherent human qualities and broader importance. The transformation occurs through stages. In the case of the "people" in an organization, the depersonalization follows a path that leads from the person in toto, to the person by name, to his/her job position, to one's status as employee, to his/her role as a workforce asset, to one's utility as an organizational asset, to—finally—his/her ability to generate revenue or wealth for the organization (see Figure 37.1). At each successive stage in this progression, more and more of the "whole" person is lost until at the final stage the human features are virtually nonexistent. The dehumanizing progression is equally as pronounced in the transformation of the person in the customer realm as marketing recasts the person through the intermediary stages of market, segment, target, buyer, and customer asset. The human element and whole person nature of the individual is diminished at each point along the slippery slope of depersonalization.

To underscore our point, one needs only to examine the newly fashioned definition of marketing offered by the American Marketing Association:

> Marketing is an organizational function and a set of processes for creating, communicating and delivering value to customers and for managing customer relationships in ways that benefit the organization and its stakeholders. (Keefe 2004, p. 17)

In this definition, the person as customer is narrowly cast as "customer value" to the organization and its stakeholders while the role of people in the organization's effort to develop and manage customer relationships is unclear at best. Or worse, the definition is presumptuous in asserting the notion that customers want to be "managed." When did marketing become so oblique?

THE CUSTOMER IS *KING?*

Marketing's objectification of people is visible and pronounced in how it approaches its most important concern—the customer. Consider the case of widely acclaimed and broadly supported marketing practice, customer relationship management (CRM). Over the past fifteen years, customer relationship management has taken center stage among marketing's critical activities, yet it is often void of any true regard for the customer as a person. Arguably, CRM should be the

Figure 37.1   **Slippery Slope of Depersonalization**

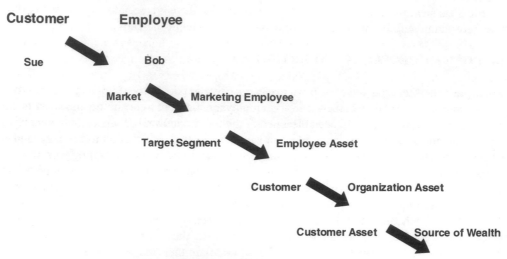

embodiment of the marketing concept to the fullest. Organizations that adopt the tenets and philosophical underpinnings of CRM profess to be committed to the customer. The rhetoric runs rampant. Terms such as customer equity, lifetime value of the customer, customer assets, and the like pepper the CRM discourse. Indeed, customer relationship management is built on old school thinking: the customer is *king;* the customer is *sovereign.* Yet for all of its spotlight on the customer, CRM typically ignores the people aspect of the customer. Much as Bambi the deer is simply venison to the hunter, Bob the person is often merely a buyer to the marketer—even the marketer that embraces CRM. Customers are myopically and narrowly viewed in terms of revenue generation. (See Figure 37.1.) This shortcoming may in fact be behind the recent realization by many firms that CRM has failed to deliver on its promise. Built largely on information technology that focuses at the transactional level and the particulars of purchase and sale, CRM programs typically provide little or no meaningful knowledge of the customer as a person upon which true relationships are built (see Dorsch et al. 2001). The essence of the customer—the people part—cannot be found in a database that tracks purchase patterns and preferences over time or calculate the cost of a lost customer in dollars and cents. It is becoming increasingly clear that unless companies fundamentally change the way they view their customers, CRM technologies will continue to fail. This is indeed unfortunate since today's information technology provides companies and customers with tremendous opportunities and capabilities to establish and maintain true relationships by augmenting face to face interaction and providing the means to create distance relationships that are potentially more personal than are currently pursued.

THE *PEOPLE* FACTOR?

As a further illustration of the dilemma we posit, consider the following with respect to employees. Some years ago, services scholar Len Berry (Berry 1988) addressed the importance of employees in service delivery as the "people factor," recognizing that the service workers who interact with the customer are a significant source of differentiation. Ostensibly, that observation can be extended beyond services to all of marketing. In the context of our arguments here, Berry was at least infusing the employee component of exchange with the need for the human element—a pronouncement that is underscored by his and his colleagues' research on service quality (see Parasuraman et al. 1988). After all, three of the five dimensions of service quality that they uncovered in their comprehensive study are directly related to human characteristics (i.e., empathy, assurance, and responsiveness) and the other two, in part, reflect human aspects as well (i.e., tangibles and reliability). Yet, even the "people factor" concept as it relates to service quality places primary importance on what the person as employee represents in terms of a finite and specific set of characteristics to facilitate an exchange that benefits the organization. While it is easy to see how such characteristics are important for service success, to reduce the person to his/ her potential in those few areas fails to appreciate the whole person and the numerous other sources of individuality that may be relevant. Personal attributes such as desire, concern, gregariousness, flexibility, genuineness, approachability, initiative, innovativeness, and so many more are overlooked or dismissed.

The role that is played in the marketing exchange by the *whole* person is lost when the organization's focus is on only a few characteristics. How many times have positive attributes of people as employees been overlooked and the benefits of an optimal interaction with the customer sacrificed because marketing decision makers have neglected the *true* spirit of the people factor? Whether employees perform in a service, sales, or retail capacity, their value and the human capital they represent simply cannot be reduced to a personality inventory, a fixed collection of desired skill and characteristics or monetary terms. Workers connect with their customers for a variety of reasons, many of which may not be captured by such means. Personnel decisions regarding hiring, rewarding, or terminating employees based on a rigid set of criteria may sacrifice potential relationships that employees who don't possess the approved profile are able to form and nurture with particular customers—customers who may find the "Stepford Wife"-like employee unappealing. Much may be lost in terms of customer equity. Moreover, the subjugation of unique personal character has potentially far reaching societal implications (see Ritzer 1993).

Simply put, customers don't have relationships with organizations—they have relationships with people. Clients are loyal to people who work for an organization—not to the organization itself. Real customer knowledge and the ability to establish relationships reside with people. Tacit knowledge held by employees is likely to be more meaningful and valuable than the explicit knowledge about customers captured by information technology and stored in computer databases. Prior to the industrial revolution, business organizations were much closer to their customers as employees brought to bear all their (tacit) knowledge in all interactions with the buyer. Mass production and the mass consumption that it spawned resulted in the transformation of business such that marketers became removed from the end customer. Direct exchange between manufacturers and the customer became a thing of the past as intermediaries in the distribution and logistics chain developed. Lost in transition was meaningful personal interaction. Clearly, information technology has revolutionized organizations' knowledge management capabilities, yet it has also reduced the complexity of people to sheer numbers and shallow statements. Customers and employees are more than just numbers and words that appear on an organization's balance sheet or computer files.

WHAT CAN BE DONE?

Marketing is (or *should* be) about people. Organizations and their markets are comprised of people—not things, not creators of wealth, not financial assets, not some numbers representing lifetime value or the like. Yet, the bureaucratization of society and its institutions has replaced the human element of interaction with people as a means to an end (see Ritzer 1993), and the institution of marketing has not escaped that fate.

What can be done to recenter the marketing field on people? Perhaps, as a start, it would be beneficial to augment the scientific method that is so prevalent in the field with insights from the arts. By integrating aspects of art into marketing, the field may be able to escape the passionless, nearly dehumanized marketing approaches that are currently in vogue in the field

Centuries before the development of the scientific method, human beings created and reveled in art of various types. In their highest forms, the arts are often considered to enhance and enrich human life. The arts reflect and express the human condition, and they connect with people because of that. In many ways, art is a communication medium that speaks to people personally. Isn't this what marketing should do? Consider, for instance, the performing arts—those arts characterized by live human performance such as theater. For years we have championed the metaphor of theater as a means to comprehend, to think about, and to implement marketing activities such as service delivery and personal selling (Grove, Fisk, and John 2000). These and many other marketing endeavors are essentially human performances that embody theatrical expression by employees and customers alike. Principles found in theater can provide fertile ground to grow and nourish the ability to relate to customers as people and to bond with them emotionally. By recognizing and embracing the potential contribution that theater can pose for nurturing the people aspect of marketing, it may be possible to assuage the erosion of the human element in the field. Lessons learned from other art forms such as music may have similar effects. Infusing marketing with a softer, more ethereal character to complement the harder, more exacting manner that currently exists is desirable.

The philosopher Aristotle once mused, "the aim of art is to represent not the outward appearance of things, but their inward significance" (BrainyQuotes.com)—an aspect of buyer–seller interaction that is often lost in marketing as a science. However, it bears noting that our criticism is not with the tenets of marketing as a science per se, rather, it is with its exclusionary prominence. By elevating positivism, marketing has reduced other ways of knowing, thinking about, and practicing the enterprise to a lesser or nonrelevant status. Fields such as psychology and sociology entertain multiple paradigms and arguments are offered for alternate views of understanding phenomena in those fields. We argue that to embrace the human element more fully, marketing should follow their example. Marketing is, after all, multidisciplinary in nature and should continue to draw from its rich and diverse heritage. By doing so, and specifically looking to the arts, the people or human aspects of marketing might be rediscovered.

Some are likely to say that the perspective on marketing that we have posed here is based on a romanticized view of the past—that the marketing we have described never truly existed. Others may offer that it is an impossible dream to think that marketing can return to a time or world that can no longer be found. Regardless, our position is that marketing needs reform that stresses the human element of the enterprise. It is foolhardy to believe that the type of change we believe is necessary, can, or will, happen overnight. It is more likely that significant reform rests on an incremental, yet continuous, emphasis of the value and importance of workers and customers as people that will eventually blossom into the marketing we envision.

REFERENCES

Berry, Leonard L. (1988), "How to Improve the Quality of Service," (audiotape presentation), Chicago: Teach 'Em, Inc.

BrainyQuotes.com (n.d.), www.brainyquote.com/quotes/a/aristotle104151.html (accessed September 2005)

Dorsch, Michael J., Les Carlson, Mary Anne Raymond, and Robert Ranson (2001), "Customer Equity Management and Strategic Choices for Sales Managers," *Journal of Personal Selling and Sales Management,* 21 (Spring), 157–66.

Grove, Stephen J., Raymond P. Fisk, and Joby John (2000), "Service Theater: Impression Management Guidelines," in *Handbook for Services Marketing and Management*, Terri Swartz and Dawn Iaccobucci, eds. Thousand Oaks, CA: Sage, 13–21.

Keefe, Lisa M. (2004), "What Is the Meaning of 'Marketing'?" *Marketing News,* September 15, 16–18.

Parasuraman, A., Valarie A. Zeithaml, and Leonard L. Berry (1988), "SERVQUAL: A Multiple Item Scale for Measuring Consumer Perceptions of Service Quality," *Journal of Retailing,* 64 (Spring), 12–37.

Ritzer, George (1993), *The McDonaldization of Society.* Newbury Park, CA: Pine Forge Press.

Merriam Webster Online Dictionary (2004), www.m-w.com.

CHAPTER 38

MARKETING REFORM

A Meta-Analytic, Best Practice Framework for Using Marketing Metrics Effectively

JOHN U. FARLEY AND PRAVEEN K. KOPALLE

In a discussion session with marketing managers from a broad array of industries at an Marketing Science Institute conference on marketing metrics in London, the consensus was the following: (1) while an ever-growing amount of marketing-related data is flowing into marketing departments, it is often not used because the capability is not available to produce useful and timely summaries, and (2) despite the demands of senior management for hard evidence about marketing's contribution to performance, the means necessary to demonstrate linkages between various measures of marketing activities and firm performance are not available.

MARKETING METRICS AND MARKETING REFORM

Important parts of the marketing world were under heavy pressure to reform even as this symposium met. One of the most important pressures for such reform has been generated within the firm but outside of marketing. There is widespread demand from the top managements and from other parts of organizations for the development and implementation of marketing performance metrics that allow marketing managers to quantify their contribution to firm performance. (Another major pressure for marketing reform is technologically driven; it is the somewhat delayed but nonetheless rapid growth of interactive marketing [Barwise and Farley 2004b]. While this is beyond the scope of the present discussion, it will have the important side effect of generating orders of magnitudes of additional and potentially useful data about buyers and potential buyers.)

We discuss structuring ongoing analysis of marketing data (metrics) in a form resembling a series of designed meta-analyses based on a form of best practices analysis.

WHY THE GROWTH IN USE OF MARKETING METRICS?

Marketing metrics are hardly new. A study of marketing expenditure by leading marketing firms in five industrial countries (Barwise and Farley 2004a) found that most firms regularly report one (or more) of six marketing metrics to the board of directors. Examples range from the obvious—use of market share by 79 percent and perceived product/service quality by 77 percent of the sample firms—to the less obvious—estimated customer or segment lifetime value, used by only 40 percent of the sample. There are significant country differences, with German firms claiming to be the heaviest users and Japanese firms the lightest. There is a consistent pattern of intended increased use in the future for all metrics in all countries, and the metrics are complementary.

Ambler (2003) lists five theoretical perspectives that are relevant to the current growing interest in marketing metrics:

1. *Control theory*, which suggests the need for ex-post information on marketing programs as an essential part of the cycle of analysis, planning, implementation, and control.
2. *Agency theory*, which focuses on the contract between a principal and an agent and specifically on the need for the terms of the contract to be structured to provide incentives to the agent to meet the principal's objectives.
3. *Brand equity*, developed as a concept in the late 1980s, plays a major role in growing recognition that intangible assets account for a large and increasing proportion of shareholder value. Marketing metrics are part of a wider quest for a "balanced scorecard" of performance (Kaplan and Norton 1996).
4. *Market orientation,* where research suggests that market-oriented firms tend to enjoy superior performance.
5. *Institutional theory*, which suggests that as marketing metrics become more widespread among firms, the use of metrics is likely to become an institutional norm, which will encourage further uptake among late-adopting businesses (Meyer and Rowan 1977).

Metrics are generally believed to be linked to short- and long-term financial performance (Ambler 2003), but the prologue to this chapter indicates limited efforts in practice to measure relationships of metrics to performance, much less to track them for stability over time. In terms of published literature, most metrics have yet to be shown to be systematically associated with current and future financial performance (Lehmann 2002).

DESIGNED META-ANALYSIS AND GENERALIZING ABOUT MARKETING METRICS

In this chapter, we propose a "designed meta-analytic" approach to generalizing the performance impact of various marketing metrics. It is meta-analytic to the extent that the focus of the designed system can be used to develop generalizations about marketing performance across various dimensions—markets, countries, segments, time, and so on. Looking forward, the designed meta-analysis can also be used, through statistical decomposition of various effects, to estimate likely results in yet unstudied research environments—a fact that gives it particular potential for analysis of international situations in which some countries or markets have been studied but others have not.

Conventional meta-analysis studies related to the marketing mix have focused on much-researched topics like advertising effectiveness. Most published marketing meta-analyses are ex-post, based on available parameter values from relating various metrics to performance (e.g., advertising to sales and thence to profits). A considerable improvement may be realized when questions of assessing parameter differences are built into the analysis in the first place—in both collecting and simultaneously estimating response parameters from the raw data. We propose such a built-in approach to developing marketing metrics.

The idea of such "designed meta-analysis," presented in Deshpandé and Farley (1998), involves incorporating differentials in intercepts and slopes that connect explanatory variables or characteristics of measurements to one or more dependent variables. Examples from such analyses include response parameters of firm performance to various operationalizations of measured market orientation, as well as country-specific differentials in parameters relating perfor-mance to market orientation, innovativeness, or corporate culture (Deshpandé, Farley, and Webster 2000).

The designed approach can also be used to test the appropriateness of combining data on the same variables from different sources or using slightly different questions to measure the same phenomenon. (Such source and measurement differences seem to be the rule rather than the exception in comparative marketing studies. These differences often seem to stymie efforts to make generalizations using straightforward statistical comparisons.) In a market-focused study of performance of large Vietnamese firms (Deshpandé and Farley 1999), for example, one sample drawn randomly from a population of firms and another drawn from managers in a senior man-agement executive program did not differ in terms of average responses or estimated sensitivities of firm performance to those responses. Therefore the samples could be combined.

USE OF BEST-PRACTICES IN MODEL SPECIFICATION

"Best practices" thinking in this chapter refers to the elements and the nature of the specified model (for example, a marketing mix model) that can be used to structure the designed meta-analysis. Best-practice analysis approaches generalization directly through identifying how "best" decisions are made, in contrast to the meta-analytic goal of providing best estimates of parameters on which to base decisions. This approach is in the spirit of benchmarking (searching for best practices, innovative ideas, and effective operating procedures), which has a history almost as long as modern manufacturing.

A best practice approach can be especially helpful for generating exploratory models. For example, the market mix models discussed later in this chapter are based on discussions with consultants familiar with the products and markets, combined with in-depth survey of the trade literature dealing with the various product/market combinations.

AN EXAMPLE: DESIGNED META-ANALYSIS OF INSTITUTIONAL FINANCIAL SERVICES

As an example, we use the relatively unstudied business-to-business markets for two financial services (bonds and foreign exchange) in two countries that are leaders in these businesses (the United Kingdom and the United States). The data, provided by Greenwich Associates, cover three years of their annual interviews with representative samples of major customers in these markets. Table 38.1 shows results of estimated change of probability of choice of a given supplier resulting from a 10 percent increase of each of the marketing inputs. (The model is a logit specification that captures the two-stage process of the choice and use of a dealer. The model itself and the estima-tion procedures are discussed in depth in Farley, Hayes, and Kopalle [2004]).

The table summarizes succinctly the results of estimated market response in over twenty-two thousand choice situations (certainly a large amount of data) that recur over time in the two countries and two markets. The metrics, elements of a marketing mix specification, include price, promotion (principally sales effort), and product differences. The response values are larger in the more heterogeneous bond markets. For the manager, price is critical in all four markets. Promotion is also important, but product differentiation generally has less impact. The responses were significantly different between markets and countries, but they did not change over the three years studied. (With very large samples such as these, relatively small differences will be signifi-cant; for example, a Pearson correlation of .02 is significant at .05.)

Table 38.1

Percent Change in Probability of Choice (Usage) for a 10 Percent Change in Each Marketing Mix Variable in the Four Country and Market Combinations

	Price	Promotion	Product
U.K. bond	0.231	0.079	−0.004
U.S. bond	0.311	0.131	0.068
U.K. foreign exchange	0.072	0.050	0.029
U.S. foreign exchange	0.102	0.092	0.092

ON PARAMETER STABILITY OVER TIME

Parameters of the sort shown in Table 38.1 are more easily generalized if they are stable over time. If they are, there is no need to start from scratch in each time period.

It is thus worth noting that parameters of the metrics such as in Table 38.1 do tend to be stable over periods of time as they were in this case, although the meta-analysis should continue to check for stationarity as its use is repeated over time. For example, in a more comprehensive meta-analysis of determinants of firm profitability over time, published response parameters relating firm performance to advertising and R&D were stable over a period of half a century (Capon, Farley, and Hoenig 1996).

CONCLUSIONS

It is pretty clear that the considerable published research linking marketing metrics to performance has relatively little currency with managers of the type represented in our prologue. Our guess is that this is rather typical. Academic researchers might learn from Delaine Hampton (2004) of P&G, who expressed the view at the 2004 Marketing Science Conference that academic journal publication represents about 20 percent of the distance of an idea to implementation, while managers expect researchers to bring ideas (approximately) 80 percent of the way. There is no clear, quick way of closing this gap, but a systematic framework for repeatedly modeling different time periods, different products, and different markets measured in different ways for different managers (such as the one we suggest here) may be helpful, at least in making the common approach familiar to users of results.

A related point is that marketing managers as well as their managers will probably underestimate the calendar time and resources (man years of time, for example) required to develop systems that continuously relate metrics to measures of firm performance and firm values. This makes it especially important to develop consistent frameworks that can be used and that will become familiar across units of the firm for this purpose. An interesting, somewhat analogous case related to this point is in the area of modeling and designing sales territories. Zoltners and Sinha (2004) report a more or less steady increase in sophistication of sales districting procedures over a period of years, but always based on additional improvement of the basic approach developed at the outset of the work.

For the future, there may be scope for efficient frontier benchmarking (Horsky and Nelson 1996) based on simulations using models like the example discussed earlier. This may lead to more attention to optimization involving metrics. Also for the future, relatively straightforward expansion of product/market combinations for applying a designed meta-analysis type of modeling should broaden the array of environments in which such an approach might be considered acceptable within a given firm.

REFERENCES

Ambler, Tim (2003), *Marketing and the Bottom Line,* 2d ed. London: Prentice Hall.

Barwise, P. and J.U. Farley (2004a), "Marketing Metrics: Status of Six Metrics in Five Countries," *European Management Journal,* 22 (June), 257–62.

——— (2004b), "The State of Interactive Marketing in Seven Countries: Interactive Marketing Comes of Age," *Journal of Interactive Marketing,* 19 (Summer), 55–67.

Capon, N., J.U. Farley, and S. Hoenig (1996), *Toward an Integrative Explanation of Corporate Financial Performance.* Norwell, MA: Kluwer Academic.

Deshpandé, R. and J.U. Farley (1998), "Measuring Market Orientation: Generalization and Synthesis," *Journal of Market-Focused Management,* 2 (September), 237–51.

——— (1999), "Culture, Customers and Contemporary Communism: Vietnamese Management Under Doi Moi," *Asian Journal of Marketing,* 7 (1), 4–19.

——— and F.W. Webster (2000), "Triad Lessons: Generalizing Results on High Performance Firms in Five Business-to-Business Markets," *International Journal of Research in Marketing,* 17 (December), 353–62.

Farley, J.U., A.F. Hayes, and P.K. Kopalle (2004), "Choosing and Upgrading Financial Service Dealers in the U.S. and U.K.," *International Journal of Research in Marketing,* 21 (December), 359–75.

Hampton, D. (2004), "Adoption of Marketing Science: What Success Looks Like for One Marketing Organization." Paper presented at the 2004 Marketing Science Conference, Erasmus University, Rotterdam, Netherlands.

Horsky, D. and P. Nelson (1996), "Evaluation of Sales Force Size and Productivity Through Efficient Frontier Benchmarking," *Marketing Science,* 15 (4), 301–20.

Lehmann, D.R. (2002), "Linking Marketing Decisions to Financial Performance and Firm Value," *Executive Overview* (March). Cambridge, MA: Marketing Science Institute.

Kaplan, R.S. and D.P. Norton (1996). *The Balanced Scorecard: Measures that Drive Performance.* Boston: Harvard Business School Press.

Meyer, J.W. and B. Rowan (1977), "Institutionalized Organizations: Formal Structure as Myth and Ceremony," *American Journal of Sociology,* 83 (September), 340–63.

Zoltners, A. and P. Sinha (2004), "Sales Territory Design: 30 Years of Modeling and Implementation." Working paper, Kellogg School of Management, Northwestern University.

CHAPTER 39

DESIGNING A BUSINESS FROM THE CUSTOMER BACK

A Post-Industrial Management Competence

Stephan H. Haeckel

I am honored by the opportunity to add my two cents to this ritual of existential angst that marketing celebrates periodically—over a span of at least thirty years and counting, in my experience.

It strikes me as bizarre that, just as companies are beginning seriously to confront the issues of discovering and coproducing value with customers, the marketing function is increasingly focused on justifying its existence. The marketing concept, now a half-century old, is becoming the business concept. But marketing departments, the natural home of customer-centric knowledge and initiatives, seem to have largely devolved into a sales support function—and an expensive one at that. One chief executive officer recently discovered that his marketing department, having outsourced most of the real work of advertising and communications, was still spending two-thirds of its budget *internally!* Unable to imagine what possible value was being created by an internal staff that didn't actually *do* anything, he immediately simplified marketing's problem of justifying itself by reducing the marketing budget by 50 percent.

How did this happen? How did it come to pass that the highest priority for academic research in the minds of MSI Trustees has become "marketing measurements"—a.k.a. self-justification arguments and techniques? And this precisely in a time that straddles the historical transition from an industrial to a postindustrial economy. If ever business needed academic help in reconceptualizing the theory and practice of managing its relationship with customers, it is now.

Let me suggest that the way for marketing to earn its keep in the twenty-first century is to return to its mid–twentieth-century roots: to the marketing concept. One might frame the challenge as one of reinterpreting for the Information Age the axiom that businesses exist to create and keep customers. I will use this chapter as a call to action for the Academy, because I don't think the current generation of business leaders is likely to do this on its own—too much Industrial Age baggage and too many three-month performance horizons. So implementing a managerial transformation will probably fall to the next generation of executives—the one that business schools are now educating. But for that to happen, academics must be prepared to provide the next generation of leaders with a postindustrial MBA curriculum (PIMBA). This PIMBA will be a new managerial framework, based on new axioms, concepts, and profoundly different prescriptions. I will briefly indicate some of the major discontinuities and differences between it and the current legacy framework.

We're about halfway across the great divide between an industrial and a postindustrial society and economy. The transition was formally, forcefully, and convincingly announced by an aca-

Figure 39.1   **Managerial Implications of Unpredictability**

	Demise of Efficiency Managerial Framework	**Emergence of Adaptive Managerial Framework**
STRATEGY	**Strategic plan OF action**	**Strategic design FOR action**
STRUCTURE	**Functional hierarchy**	**Network of modular capabilities**
GOVERNANCE	**Command and Control**	**Context and Coordination**

demic, Daniel Bell, thirty-two years ago. Since then, the academic and business practitioner communities have identified new forms of behavior, new technologies, new techniques, and new leadership qualities to address the imperatives of the postindustrial economy. But we are trying to bolt these new adaptive ideas, technologies, and behaviors into an Industrial Age managerial framework that systematically discourages them.

Peter Drucker (1991), who codified the Industrial Age managerial framework of the mid–twentieth century, wrote that "No new theories on which a big business can be built have emerged . . . but the old ones are no longer dependable."

There is now at least one successor candidate—the name I have given it is *sense and respond.* Its premise is that rapid, unpredictable, and often discontinuous change is baked into the logic of an information economy. As a result, businesses must learn how to respond effectively to what individual customers want/need/prefer *now,* rather than execute efficiently plans that are based on predictions about what markets will want in the future.

If you buy that as a premise, then the concepts of strategy, structure, and governance must change radically (Figure 39.1). Strategy, instead of being a plan of action, becomes a design *for* action. Structure no longer follows strategy, it *becomes* strategy—a strategy for transforming a network of capabilities into a system for coproducing customer value.

And finally, organizational governance changes from command and control, where the knowers are at the top and the doers are at the bottom of an organizational hierarchy of authority, to context and coordination, where leadership declares a global context within which people can improvise and self-synchronize to produce coherent behavior at the enterprise level. The purpose of this context declaration is to make unambiguously clear the answers to three questions: what are we here to accomplish; how do we relate to each other; and what are the boundaries that govern, but do not dictate, the actions we take in pursuing organizational purpose.

Figure 39.2 depicts Rashi Glazer's way of representing that change (1999). Rashi, as many know, talks about "smart markets." Smart markets are the postindustrial, information intensive

Figure 39.2 **Smart Versus Dumb Markets**

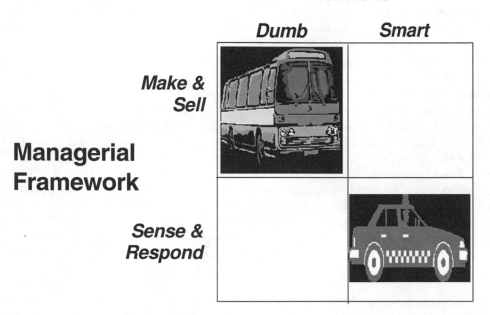

Markets

markets in which products, customers, and firms become highly interactive and adaptive and information-intense. Dumb markets are not "stupid," but dumb in the sense of not being able to talk, not being interactive. Of course, there still are dumb markets, but we've got one hundred years of theory and practice to instruct us on how to organize a business to address those markets. I call that collective construct "make and sell." Plan, develop, make, and sell the products that you (and by the way, your competitors) can reliably predict the customer will need.

That frames strategy as a game against competition, and from Michael Porter (1980) we have learned that this is the right way to think about strategy in a world that is sufficiently predictable.

Rashi and I use the icon of a bus to represent a company that uses advanced market research techniques to find out where most customers plan to be and where they plan to go; hires rocket scientists to figure out the most efficient way to get most customers from where they say they're going to be to where they say they're going to go; then invests in buses and hires drivers who they train to do what? To execute the schedule. The schedule is an early binding of capabilities that then is executed with maximum, ideally six-sigma efficiency. A few years ago, the *Times* of London reported on a productivity initiative by the London Bus Authority. It seems the authority had raised the bar so high that only one bus driver was able to meet all the requirements: He got the bus out of the barn on time, stopped everywhere he was supposed to at the time he was supposed to, got the bus back to the barn on time, used no more gas than the plan called for, and ran over no more pedestrians than the plan called for. The only thing he was unable to do—because there was no time—was to open the doors to let customers on and off. But he made his numbers, and his measurements had nothing to do with getting customers to where they wanted to go. In fact, customers were, truth be told, a nuisance. They would sometimes get sick, or want to change a $20 bill, or want to get off between stops—all of which were unpredictable and all of which were terribly inefficient. But this bus driver was an A performer precisely because he closed the door to customers. (How many businesses do you know today that use 800 numbers and websites to shut the doors on customers because it's considered too expensive to have real people address their problems? And because of this, how much more do you like doing business with a Lands End or the insurance company USAA—where you talk with a human being who has access to what these companies already know about you, and who seems genuinely interested in helping you do business with them?)

Back to our bus driver, who can start work every morning without a customer. He doesn't need a customer because he has a schedule. A taxi driver, on the other hand, operates in sense and respond mode, and cannot start work without a customer. Why is that? Because without a customer she doesn't know where to go. Who does know? Only the customer. And that to me is the fundamental transaction of the postindustrial economy; an exchange of information *about* value from customers for the production *of* value from producers. The tricky part of this is that in smart markets with smart products that change dynamically, customers often can't tell you what they need. They need diagnostic help. I have no idea what the best digital camera would be for me. I have no idea what the right telephone plan is for me. And I have no idea what kind of anti-spam software to use; nor do I trust any of those providers to give me an honest answer about it. I darkly suspect they want to sell me what they happen already to have made. How likely are you to agree to codevelop value with someone you think is more interested in extracting value from you?

That leads to the question of what we mean by value. Specifically, what do we mean by customer value? Much of the literature today takes it to mean value of the customer to the firm, measured as lifetime value (LTV), or by loyalty. But increasing the lifetime value of a customer cannot be the design point of a firm—LTV is a firm's *reward* for producing value *to* a customer.

If a firm is to operate as a system, you can't design it to produce a reward for operational excellence; and you can't design a system to optimize the function of one of its parts. It must be designed to produce a state change in an external system. Value to the customer is value produced for an external system, a value that can, and in this view of the world should, become the design point for a business. In a recent executive education session Glazer and I proposed what we modestly called the "fundamental equation of business."

$$V = V_p + V_c$$
V = Total Value Produced
V_p = Value to the Producer = LTV = Price – Cost
V_c = Value to the Customer = $\text{Benefits}_{\text{Relative}}$ – $\text{Price}_{\text{Relative}}$

Value is the sum of value delivered to the customer, and value received by the producer. Value to the customer is benefits minus price, where *benefits* means the dollar value assigned to tangible and intangible effects, and *price* incorporates, similarly, such things as monetary price, inconvenience, and other intangible negatives. Value to the producer is price minus cost, which also incorporates such intangibles as loyalty effects and opportunity costs.

Total value can be thought of as a waterfall, and the purpose of the collaboration between customer and producer is to maximize the height of that waterfall by increasing the dollar value of the benefits received by the customer, and by reducing the cost to the producer of delivering them. The game with customers is to maximize total value through the exchange of information about value (from the customer), and the structuring (by the producer) of a value-producing system that incorporates customer and producer capabilities. Having maximized the height of the waterfall, the price is set, instance by instance, which determines for each instance how much of the value created will flow to the customer, and how much to the producer.

The concept of an organization designed to collaboratively produce customer value implies that a distinction is made between the design point of the organization, and the reward for a good design, which is what shareholders get. If you don't make that distinction, and you think enhanced shareholder value is the design point, you end up doing things like buying back your own stock, investing in the discovery and exploitation of loopholes in the tax law, and doing creative accounting—all of which are logical things to do if your design point is increasing the share price to the stockholders. Such logic is reflected in the strategy of several insurance companies, who now see underwriting risk not as its value proposition, but as a means of raising cash to invest in the money market. Making money has become, literally, their real business.

Networks are the generic structure of postindustrial organizations. They provide the basis for a modular design, and they provide connectivity. But they don't provide interoperability and coherence. The way to add these attributes is to transform a network of capabilities into a value-producing system, using the principles of systems design. These principles, which are related to but different than "systems thinking," specify the *interactions* between accountable roles necessary to produce a desired affect on a customer.

Applying the principles of systems design to create collaborative organizational structures for action will be a core competence of postindustrial managers. Two of these design principles are regularly violated in current business practice. The first: that you always design a system by decomposing its function into subsystems, and the subsystems into lower-level subsystems. You never, ever start with the capabilities you have, and try to bolt them together into a system. And yet that's what frequently happens in post merger integration projects. That's also what happens in most reorganizations. We look at the capabilities we've got, and we try to figure out how we can integrate those into a value-producing system. That is a flagrant violation of a first principle of systems design.

A second frequently violated principle: do not design the actions of the components, design the *inter*actions between them. The interactions between them are—at least in the sense and respond prescription—the exchange of deliverables between organizational roles. Optimizing processes focuses on designing and presequencing the *actions* of components, as opposed to specifying the interactions between them. Process optimization makes great sense in stable environments where efficient replication produces economies of scale. But in environments of unpredictable change, six-sigma execution of a process to accomplish what has become the wrong thing is a recipe for disaster.

The systems design of roles and accountabilities that transforms a network of capabilities into a value-producing system is the strategy document of sense and respond organizations. It is a design for action, not a plan of action. It uses some but not all of the capabilities in a given network, because some of them won't make the cut after decomposition of the value proposition into its constituent capabilities. The strategic design shows the interactions between, not the activities of, people who are accountable for the production of specified outcomes, and who are evaluated by the role receiving those outcomes. It is these interactions that produce the system-level effect, a state change in the form of an effect that constitutes additional value to the customer.

Strategy as a system design for action *dissolves*, rather than solves, perennial issues that have plagued managers for decades. The issue of organizational alignment disappears, because alignment of the component parts is precisely what is specified in a systems design. Synergy is unavoidably produced, because the interaction of component roles produces an effect that cannot be produced by any subset of roles.

Clarity about roles, accountability, and authority, lack of suboptimization and fragmentation:

These follow naturally from a systems design. But some make and sell "best" practices are flat out bad practices, because they are antisystematic: for example, line of sight measurements, which call for the same outcome from multiple subsystems, creating redundancy and making accountability for the outcome ambiguous. And one would never ask a question such as, what is the return on marketing investment? any more than one would ask the question of an automobile designer or owner, what is the return on investment of a gasket or a carburetor? Because they are parts of a system, the loss of any of them makes the system incapable of delivering its function.

In sense and respond designs, coherent, system-level behavior arises from quasi-autonomous, self-organizing behavior. ("Quasi" because these behaviors are governed, though not dictated, by the declared organizational context.) The manager/designer does not specify any level of sub-system design beyond that he/she feels comfortable with. Double-click on any one of those roles, and you will see their subsystem design, a design that can be a make and sell, highly optimized process that deals efficiently with a stable set of inputs and outputs, or can be another, highly adaptive subsystem within which improvisation is the norm. Because all roles are dispatched using a universal and general commitment management process, *how* the role produces its outcomes is not a strategic issue.

The effective incorporation of customer and supplier capabilities occurs because they become a part of the same design, as the decomposition of the design point customer value determines which capabilities are needed from the customer and which from the supplier. Once you've invested in instantiating the design, each customer request can reconfigure the organization. Supply and value capabilities become "chains" only at the last possible moment—when dispatched by a customer-facing role. This achieves late-binding of capabilities. Products are the earliest form of binding of capabilities, designed and manufactured far in advance of a request by customers. Process design is a way of achieving later binding, where the sequence in which capabilities are linked is specified in advance. But dispatching capabilities in response to (or better yet, in anticipation of) a current request, like a taxi company does, provides maximum adaptability.

Ideally, dispatching is not only reactive to an articulated current request—but follows from the kind of sensing and responding that a doctor does when diagnosing your stomach ache as appendicitis. The doctor is not predicting that you need an appendectomy. The doctor is telling you what you need before you know it. He or she can interpret the data that you're sending out with your EKGs and blood tests and from his/her palpations and probes.

The metrics that have emerged from early adopters of this managerial framework include:

- Response cycle time reduction
- Response quality (as evaluated by the effect created on customers)
- Scope and number of requests successfully addressed
- Organic growth in revenue and profits
- Win rates, auditability
- Employee morale

The first metric is the length of response cycle time relative to the opportunity change cycle. That's a vital sign, because keeping up with change is a survival trait. The second metric establishes that response quality is not measured by traditional customer satisfaction metrics; It is measured by the state change in value *to* the customer. The effect on the customer may or may not occur if you delivered the product or service you promised. But that effect is the design point, and the key question is did the customer realize improved responsiveness, quality, operational results, and so on?

The scope and number of requests successfully addressed is the focus of the third metric. It is important to keep track of the number of times you have to say no bid (because, for example, the risk is too great, or the capabilities aren't there). If the same request keeps recurring, this suggests how you might expand the value scope. And because your capabilities are modular, you have combinatorial mathematics working for you. If you incorporate a new capability into a new systems design to create greater value, you get a substantial increase in the number of possible requests that you can profitably respond to. That's a significant potential improvement in a firm's ability to grow organically.

The last two metrics are internal indicators of organizational health that should improve as a by-product of success in co-creating value with customers.

I have given a very high-level synopsis of the sense and respond managerial framework in order to make the point that a basis already exists for educating postindustrial managers on a new managerial theory whose premise is increasing amounts of unpredictable change. My exhortation to those in the marketing academy is to seize the initiative in introducing this to the next generation of managers. After all, designing adaptive customer-backed businesses is becoming a strategic competence and marketing ought to be the function that co-opts it. First, that's supposed to be our job: minimizing the gap between what the customer needs and what the firm can respond to. Second, according to Harvard's Kash Rangan, the competence of organizational design has not been picked up by any of the other disciplines in the business school. And third—perhaps most important—I'm convinced we really know how to do this. We now have a few case studies, and the start of a learning curve. But while we know the principles, we don't have a sufficient body of experience from which to develop best practices regarding the new set of choices managers must make in this new framework. There is an enormous number of researchable propositions awaiting empirical testing by the readers of this volume.

REFERENCES

Drucker, Peter F. (1991), "How to Be Competitive Though Big," *Wall Street Journal*, February 7, A14.
Glazer, Rashi (1999), "Winning in Smart Markets," *Sloan Management Review*, 40 (4), 59–61.
Haeckel, Stephen H. (1999), *Adaptive Enterprise: Creating and Heading Sense-and-Respond Organizations*. Cambridge: Harvard Business School Press.
Porter, Michael E. (1980), *Competitive Strategy*, New York: The Free Press.

CHAPTER 40

HOW TO REFORM MARKETING

JAGDISH N. SHETH AND RAJENDRA S. SISODIA

Marketing is a vital and highly visible institution in free market societies around the world. However, it is suffering from major problems with each of its major constituents: a lack of respect within the corporation and a lack of trust by consumers. Taken together, these two major deficiencies have placed marketing in society's doghouse as, more often than not, a shallow, wasteful, and polluting influence.

Why is this happening? We believe that this is because marketing has become excessively driven by a short-term managerial agenda, and has lost sight of its fundamental mission: to represent the customer's interest to the company. Just as the role of government is to represent the public's interest and to align other societal interests with that goal, the role of marketing is to represent the interests of customers, and to align the interests of other stakeholders with that goal.

THE POWER TO HEAL—OR HARM

Marketers should think of themselves as healers; after all, their job is to meet the functional and psychological needs of their customers, and leave them satisfied and even delighted. They should adopt this perspective at the individual as well as at the societal level. The best doctor is not the one who makes the patient dependent on him or her, but who makes the patient well. The most successful doctor is one whose patients need to see her least—because she knows how to cure them, and how to keep them well.[1] Marketing's job should be analogous to that of an outstanding physician.

Marketing tactics are like potent drugs with potentially serious side effects. It is important to understand that there are in fact no "main effects" and "side effects"—these are just convenient labels we apply to connote which effects we choose to observe and measure and which ones we would rather ignore. Unfortunately, the side effects of marketing today—noise pollution, customer irritation, excessive consumption, unhealthy lifestyles—tend to overwhelm its intended main effects. If that is the case, we need to reconsider the diagnosis and treatment.

Indications: As with any drug, we must understand the proper indications that call for its use. What is the appropriate marketing response to each condition? Some responses may alleviate the symptoms in the short term, but may deepen the problem in the long term. For example, General Motors now finds it virtually impossible to sell most of its cars without deep discounts and constant promotions; its latest offer was to extend its employee discounts to all customers.

Dosage: Every medicine is also a poison, and determining the right dosage is critical. In many cases, the initial dosage varies from a maintenance dosage. The volume of advertising, for example, must be monitored very carefully. Too much advertising has been shown to cause a backlash among consumers (like an allergic reaction). For example, in a series of controlled experiments,

Anheuser Busch found that increasing advertising spending beyond certain levels led to declining sales (Ackoff and Emshoff 1975).

Resistance: Related to the above, the overuse of a drug builds up resistance in the user, and this resistance often extends to society at large. More and more customers are becoming not only resistant to many strains of marketing, but are becoming actively allergic as well; not only do they not respond to many marketing efforts, they actively resist them (see the chapter by J. Walker Smith in this volume). E-mail marketing, for example, started with 30 percent response rates. Its overuse and abuse led to response rates dropping precipitously and ultimately to a thriving spam-blocker business to protect users from the continuing onslaught of unwelcome messages.

Interactions: Certain drugs work well in combination, some cancel each other out, and others can interact in deadly ways. Likewise, well-integrated marketing efforts work to reinforce each other, while disjointed efforts waste resources and can lead to enormous losses.

Vaccines vs. Cures vs. Treatments: The best medicines are vaccines, which prevent a disease from occurring in the first place. The next best are cures; the key here is early detection in order for the cure to be effective. The least desirable option is an ongoing treatment: a medicine that needs to be taken as long as the condition persists. Such medicines simply alleviate the symptoms but do not attack the underlying cause. They generate huge amounts of revenue for the companies that sell them. Many such medicines cause dependency; users who stop using them may find themselves worse off than they were before they started using them. Marketing should try to create programs that are more like vaccines and cures, and only rely on ongoing treatments when there is no alternative. For example, if marketers create a superior value proposition for customers, positive word-of-mouth carries the product forward, without the need for constant advertising and sales promotions, both of which are costly and have negative side effects.

Lifestyle Changes: Drugs may be an attractive and easy short-term solution, but a better way to address many chronic and seemingly incurable problems is through lifestyle changes. Sometimes conditions such as high cholesterol, high blood pressure, diabetes, and many others can be greatly helped through lifestyle changes, including diet and exercise. The side effects of these treatments are all positive, unlike the drugs. Likewise, companies should strive to make changes that will reduce their need for constant advertising, frequent sales promotions, and other expensive marketing habits. If General Motors had more "must have" products and a better reputation for quality, it wouldn't suffer the heartburn of anemic sales. Many companies are hooked on excessive price promotions (perpetual "sales"). By moving to an "everyday fair price" approach, they can create a much saner marketing environment.

Marketing managers should look to heal their customers by developing a holistic understanding of their needs. However, many have become too prescription happy, and are always ready to reach into their bag of tricks to find a tool that will "fix" a problem. They must refocus on overall wellness and wean themselves and their customers from dependency on harmful short-term fixes.

MARKETING SIMPLICITY

> *Along the way, of course, I was going to be adding to the world's knowledge of man, no doubt. But there was already a lot of that, to put it mildly. Possibly, there was enough.*
> —Norman Rush (*Mating*)

How much more do we need to know about the micromanipulation of consumer behavior? To paraphrase Rush, possibly we know enough. We are hyperanalytical and heroically rigorous about trivialities. Meanwhile, the big, important questions go begging, and marketing's increasingly ugly public persona, like the graying image of Dorian Gray in the mirror or the proverbial elephant in the living room, is for the most part studiously avoided.

We need to rediscover our own essence, to become a truly self-justifying profession. A firefighter may never have the slightest doubt that he or she is doing something socially valuable. But marketers are routinely filled with angst about what they do, how they do it, how much it costs, who it benefits, who it hurts. Getting a cheap laugh by showing lizards talking or having a horse release gas into a candle (just two of last year's Super Bowl ads) does not represent the epitome of what marketing can contribute to society.

But marketing *can* be a self-justifying profession! And we can and must celebrate such marketing when we see it. Produce great (not just good) products, sell them *only* to people who would benefit from them, treat your employees, suppliers, retailers, and other business partners with respect and decency, be a good citizen wherever you are—and make good, but not obscene, profits doing all that.

Quite simple really.

ALIGNING MARKETING AND SOCIETY

Marketing's raison d'etre is an eminently noble one: it alone is charged with the responsibility to align the interests of corporations and their customers (and by extension, society as a whole). It can be the civilizing influence on the brute force of capitalism. But the reality of how marketing has been practiced, in toto, is that it has abrogated its responsibility toward customers and has become the handmaiden of short-term corporate interests. No wonder that it has lost trust with consumers. Marketing has become too focused on competitors, and as a result has given short shrift to customers. The growing influence of the strategy literature on marketing thought and practice has caused many marketers to lose sight of a fundamental truth: without delighted customers, no amount of strategizing ultimately matters.

We should not underestimate the power of market forces and that of marketing to shape virtually every aspect of a society's mores, attitudes, and culture. Used wisely and with restraint, marketing can harness and channel the vast energies of the free market system for the good of consumers, corporations, and society as a whole. Used recklessly, it can cause significant harm to all of those entities as well.

Mainstream marketing ignores societal concerns at its own great peril. Marketing and society have been moving on increasingly divergent paths, and this will result in escalating conflict and criticism of marketing as a profession and a discipline. To remedy this, we must look at the role of marketing from three stakeholder perspectives—those of policymakers, academics, and practitioners. Taking such a holistic view is important, since a piecemeal solution will not suffice. All three stakeholders of marketing must take the initiative to revitalize and reenergize marketing by making it a positive force for society at large.

Policymakers

Neither legislation nor regulation seems to be working well to curb abusive marketing practices. Most laws that pertain to marketing practices are seldom enforced; others are enforced only when lawsuits are filed. Marketing policymaking is currently reactive and driven by political agendas.

The primary problems that marketing faces in the public policy arena are that nonmarketing experts are generally chosen to lead important regulatory agencies, and (partly as a result), marketing is subject to ad hoc, reactive, issue-driven legislation and regulations rather than well-conceived initiatives designed to foster long-term improvements and direction-setting.

The heads of most federal agencies dealing with marketing issues are political appointees, unlike the heads of agencies such as the Centers for Disease Control (CDC) and the National Institutes of Health (NIH), which are scientific appointments. The marketing profession has the clout both as an industry and as an academic discipline to seek the appointment of regulatory policymakers with a scientific orientation rather than a political agenda.

We advocate establishing a National Academy of Marketing similar in reputation to National Academy of Science, the National Endowment for the Arts, and the NIH. These preeminent agencies all have a scientific orientation to policymaking. The timing could not be better. After the collapse of communism, fostering a market orientation has become an important issue world-wide. Many prime ministers and presidents of countries are very much marketing-minded now, even to the extent of "branding" and "positioning" their own countries. We should seek to make marketing more relevant to society by encouraging nonprofit marketing, nation branding, and citizen relationship marketing. We should seek to establish public–private partnerships to make marketing a socially relevant science, so that capable people are attracted to marketing. We should also invest in developing primary and secondary education curriculum that socializes good marketing approach and practices.

We need to reestablish marketing's identity as a noble profession, rather than a parasitic one that feeds on people's insecurities and adds little to society. Most importantly, we must establish rules and regulations for licensing marketing professionals, comparable to financial service providers. It is interesting to note that today the selling of financial products is highly regulated, and customers are afforded a number of protections. But the ways in which products such as automobiles are sold is hardly regulated; anyone can be a marketer, and can seemingly say anything they want to customers.

Marketing must become a full-fledged profession on par with, for example, the accounting and medical professions. It is time to require the mandatory certification and recertification of marketing practitioners. Consider the fact that the Institute for Supply Management (formerly known as the National Association of Purchasing Managers) has a well-established certification program, and requires that managers renew it every five years through continuing education. In business-to-business marketing, marketers have to deal with highly professional, certified purchasing managers. It is important that marketers are at least as professional in how they market as purchasing managers are in how they buy.

Instead of resisting all government regulations and scrutiny, as is the instinctive reaction of most companies, the marketing profession should support well thought out regulations that eliminate shoddy practices and are thus to the advantage of companies that practice "good" marketing. Marketing academics and practitioners should work hand in hand with the government to ensure that marketing policymaking is purposeful and forward looking and has a scientific rather than a political orientation.

Academics

The three main issues with current academic research in marketing are (1) it is too heavily focused on consumer-oriented concepts and theories; (2) it has become too driven by an explicitly managerially driven agenda; and (3) it is too highly specialized and esoteric.

The first point is fairly straightforward; academics need to better understand and appreciate business-to-business marketing, which in general works much better than consumer marketing. Let us consider the second point.

Should Marketing Academics Serve Managers or Customers and Society?

As marketing academics, whose interests do we serve? and whose interests should we serve? These are not merely academic questions—they go to the very heart of what makes marketing relevant to a corporation and worthwhile to society.

It is a fair criticism of the academic marketing discipline to say that we have not had the impact on business practice that our colleagues in accounting, finance, and operations have had. We believe the reason for this is that we have abandoned our unique role in the world—as the voice of the customer—and have become just another business function serving the narrowly defined short-term interests of companies.

It is clear that, for the most part, marketing academics have been trained to serve the interests of marketing managers. Wilkie and Moore (2003) describe how the present era of marketing scholarship has been characterized by the strong dominance of the managerial perspective, which holds that "the major purpose for academic work is to enhance the effectiveness of managers' marketing decisions" (p. 132). Most of our efforts are aimed at helping marketing managers make better decisions. The extent to which we have succeeded in doing so is open to debate, but the proposition that this is what we have been driven by is not.

In many ways, this is as it should be—after all, it is ultimately marketing managers who pay our salaries by hiring our students. However, a crucial question arises as to the definition of the term "effectiveness" in this context. Is it synonymous with "maximizes sales and profitability," or does it imply decisions that are simultaneously in the customers' as well as the company's best long-term interests? We submit that only the latter perspective represents a worthy and sustainable delineation of what should concern us as marketing academics.

In our introduction to this volume, we used the chart repeated here to suggest that too much of marketing practice is dumb, unethical, or wasteful (Figure 40.1). The job of marketing managers is to align the interests of customers and society with those of the company. The job of marketing academics is likewise to facilitate that alignment. If academics seek to overtly advance the short-term bottom-line interests of managers and companies, they do them a great disservice. They become complicit in the myriad ways in which modern marketing practice often runs counter to marketing's own first principles: that the definition of success begins with doing right by the customer and ends with the achievement of a healthy bottom line.

This needs to change. Marketing should be less about representing the company to the customer and more about representing the customer to the company. Unfortunately, the latter perspective has been getting short shrift by corporate boards as well as journal editorial boards. We believe that the *primary* goal of marketing academics should be to serve the interests of customers first and managers second.

By donning the customer-perspective hat more or less permanently, marketing academics can go a long way toward making marketing a positive force that enhances the quality of life of consumers. Our research efforts should be aimed at measuring the degree of the customers' resentment at exploitative pricing and promotional tactics, and the spillover it has on the company's other businesses. We should be pointing the way toward *enlightened marketing practices* (analogous to sustainable economic development, which seeks to safeguard the physical environment while permitting vigorous economic activity). The "environment" we should be seeking to safeguard is the rapidly depleting pool of goodwill that consumers possess toward most companies. Our equivalent of global warming is rising customer cynicism. The ozone layer of mutual trust between customers and marketers has steadily been burned away—as a result of the marketing profession's many small and large abuses over the decades. Marketing managers are too close to

Figure 40.1 **Marketer and Customer Benefits**

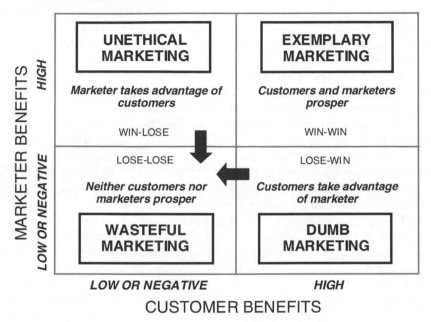

the battle lines to be able to see this problem in its full dimensions. They are too consumed with daily hand-to-hand combat with their competitors—even, it often seems, with their customers.

Some years ago, Bill Wilkie conducted a survey of PhD students in marketing, and found a high level of interest in the societal aspects of marketing. However, the same survey showed that the vast majority of students had received little or no exposure to societal issues in their doctoral education (Wilkie and Moore 2005). This is a very important omission, since the doctoral students of today are the educators of future managers. We must take the critically important step of requiring all doctoral students in marketing to take a course on Marketing and Society, and should encourage more of them to make this an important component of their research agenda.

Academics are urged by the editors of some marketing journals to include a section in their articles under the heading Managerial Implications. Perhaps editors should also ask for a section titled Customer and Societal Implications. Of course, it could be argued that this should be implicit under Managerial Implications; after all, good marketing managers are supposed to align customer and company interests.

Focus on Programmatic, Newsworthy Research

In addition to explicitly adopting more of a customer perspective, as discussed above, marketing academics should undertake funded, programmatic, and newsworthy research rather than highly specialized, esoteric, and ad hoc research. Editorial boards and editors of journals must insist on a high level of relevance, not just rigor. Even important research in marketing is not seen as newsworthy. As a result, practitioners as well as policymakers largely ignore the outcomes of most academic marketing research. Other professional disciplines do a far superior job generating newsworthy research. The day an important article is published in the *New England Journal of*

Medicine or the *Journal of the American Medical Association,* it gets national and global attention. It should be the responsibility of the editors of marketing journals, not just authors, to ensure this kind of publicity.

Research in marketing is usually nonfunded ad hoc research, not programmatic research. Tremendous talent gets wasted, as highly capable people end up doing mostly mundane work. An example of programmatic research in marketing was Columbia University's Buyer Behavior project, for which half a million dollars was raised from companies. A series of articles, books, and dissertations resulted. The Marketing Science Institute performs an extremely valuable role in aligning faculty research topics with the expressed needs of companies. However, most research projects in marketing are funded out of university or business school research budgets, with no long-term strategic direction.

We should establish a peer review process for research proposals for external funding. The biggest potential funders in this country are corporations. At Pillsbury and General Mills, the most exciting work on consumer behavior is not being done by marketing but by R&D scientists in what they call the kitchens. Procter & Gamble has many times more PhDs than most university science departments. Nokia and Motorola excel at understanding what their customers are looking for. Researchers at these companies are focused on understanding consumers as users, unlike academic marketing, which tends to focus largely on consumers as buyers.

We should have more postdoctoral programs to initiate programmatic research, as is common in medicine and engineering. Our PhD graduates have no experience managing programmatic research. To encourage such a long-term perspective, we should lengthen the tenure clock to at least ten years. Finally, editorial boards and editors of leading journals must insist on a high degree of societal relevance in addition to scientific rigor. This will make our research more newsworthy and relevant to the needs of consumers, companies, and society.

Practitioners

For practicing managers, there are three key issues. First, they need to rediscover the customer-centric essence of marketing. Second, marketing is measured by its impact on the profit and loss (P&L) statement; instead, a balance sheet perspective is needed. Third, marketing is organized in most companies as a tactical sales support function, but needs to be elevated to a strategic staff function. Taken together, the latter two factors cause marketing to be driven primarily by short-term agendas.

Rediscover the Joy of Marketing

Marketing is the one business function that is explicitly charged with maintaining an outward focus on markets and customers rather than on internal factors. However, other business functions have steadily become more externally oriented and customer-driven over time, while ironically, marketing seems ever more driven by concerns divergent from customer interests.

Too many marketers have lost sight of the fundamental guiding principles of their calling. For marketing *should* be viewed as a calling, not just another profession, since it alone defines itself on the basis of enabling the greater well-being of customers. The only people who should become marketers are those that care *passionately* about customers. Instead, unfortunately, the profession seems to attract more than its share of individuals with a passionate focus on their own short-term gains.

Marketers must focus on enhancing customers' quality of life, rather than maximizing the sales of their company's products. They need to understand how quality of life is defined by each customer, and tailor what they do accordingly. Marketers should go beyond the narrow and the mundane that preoccupy them, and learn how to leverage their considerable powers to make their customers truly happy.

In practical terms, this means that instead of figuring how to create products that maximize profits for them, managers should focus on the process of creating products and marketing programs that deliver high levels of real value to customers. Instead of studying which advertising tactic is most likely to, in essence, trick a customer into trying a product, they should focus on what kinds of communications are useful and valuable to a customer, and which ones are simply irritating or misleading.

Taking such a perspective does not mean that marketing managers would be doing their companies a disservice, or helping customers to take undue advantage of their company. If we believe that the path to enduring business success must without exception go through the intermediate stage of true customer contentment, then this in fact is the best way to achieve a higher level of business success.

There are a number of companies that represent the best of what marketing can do. These companies inspire tremendous devotion and loyalty—even love—from their customers. Instead of obsessing about share of market or share of wallet, these companies strive for a high "share of heart"—of *all* of their stakeholders, not just customers. Without fail, such companies are led by visionary individuals with a strong emphasis on human values, and are deeply involved in their communities. Their employees are highly competent, enthusiastic, and joyful. Their shareholders are amply rewarded as well; most are also customers, and many are employees. Almost without exception, these companies accomplish all this while spending less on marketing than their peers. We feature thirty such companies and describe the secrets of their success in our forthcoming book *Firms of Endearment* (Sheth, Sisodia, and Wolfe 2006).

Elevate Marketing to a Corporate Staff Function

Marketing needs to move from the P&L statement to more of a balance sheet approach. Unfortunately, most marketing executives don't understand balance sheets. It is abundantly clear that marketing can and does create assets of considerable tangible value. Many retailers today are creating new brands based on their strong market presence. If they want to, they can sell those brands to a manufacturer or anyone else. For example, Sears's brands such as Craftsman, Kenmore, and Diehard probably have more value than the market cap of the entire company.

Today, advertising, product design, market research, sales promotions, public relations, and even selling and distribution are usually handled by specialist providers. In fact, the bulk of marketing dollars are spent on outside suppliers; much of marketing has become strictly a coordination function within the corporation. However, few marketing managers have much expertise on how best to manage suppliers or properly coordinate their activities. They also lack an adequate understanding of the proper demarcation of activities that *should* be performed in-house and those that are best outsourced.

We believe that the best way to get marketing to adopt a long-term perspective is to change it from a line function primarily concentrated at the business unit level to a corporate staff function. One company that has already done this is Alcoa. As a corporate staff function, marketing should be considered as strategic as finance.

In most companies today, the most powerful person after the chief executive office (CEO) is the chief financial officer (CFO), not the COO (chief operating officer) or president. The CFO is a staff position, but is very powerful. Similarly, the head of information technology (IT), the chief information officer, doesn't report to the CFO anymore, but rather directly to the CEO. Similarly, the general counsel reports to the CEO and the board. The fourth major staff function is human resource management. These functions are organized in such a way that, in addition to having corporate staff, they are also distributed into the functional, regional, and product organizations. They become part of the operating "atmosphere" of the company, providing guidance, inculcating values, nurturing, ensuring adherence to standards, and so on. Corporate staff functions are managed from a compliance as well as a strategic perspective, and marketing should be no exception.

There should be a board-level standing committee that oversees marketing, similar to the Audit, Compensation, and Governance committees. The head of corporate marketing should be called the chief customer officer (CCO) instead of chief marketing officer to minimize internal perception and image problems about marketing, and should report directly to the CEO. The CCO should be responsible for branding, key account management, and business development. Importantly, marketing must be given both capital expenditure and operating expenditure budgeting responsibilities and authority, similar to the IT function.

CONCLUSION

The world has changed a great deal in the past two decades, but marketers have adapted to it in only superficial ways. Not only must marketers accept the reality that customers today are far more empowered than ever before, they must embrace it to fashion a "new deal" with customers, one predicated on respect, integrity, and a long-term vision.

Current demographic megatrends add to the urgency of the need to do so. Every market in the world is evolving rapidly. Emerging markets such as China and India are growing fast, but consumers there already have access to cutting-edge information tools that enable them to blunt the edge of traditional marketing weapons. Developed markets (e.g., North America, Europe, Japan) are characterized by much slower growth and a simultaneous maturing of the population, blurring of gender distinctions, and the rise of feminine values in society and hence the marketplace. Increasingly, consumers are in the more highly evolved later stages of life, which is reflected in every aspect of how they lead their lives. Marketing must learn how to relate to such consumers.

The problem, of course, is that as people have matured and markets have evolved, marketing has not; it remains stuck in a juvenile time warp of gimmickry and shallow imagery. While people have become more preservation and conservation minded, marketers have remained wasteful spendthrifts. While people have become more spiritual in outlook, marketing remains crassly materialistic. While people focus more on achieving their own potential, marketing remains obsessed with "keeping up with the Joneses." While people are digging deeper to discover the substance of people and things, marketing remains fixated on outward appearances. While people are more concerned with authenticity in every aspect of their life, marketing is riddled with inaccuracy and insincerity.

Clearly, marketers have to change a great deal to adjust to this new world order.

NOTE

1. Today's pharmaceutical industry appears to be completely driven by creating lifelong treatments for chronic conditions rather than searching for cures or preventive measures. Many products today are being designed with recurring revenues in mind—a variant of the old razor and blade approach, complete with monopoly margins on the supplies (e.g., filters for refrigerators, ink cartridges for printers, etc.).

References

Ackoff, Russell L. and James R. Emshoff (1975), "Advertising Research at Anheuser-Busch, Inc. (1963–1968)," *Sloan Management Review*, Winter, 1–15.

Sheth, Jagdish N., Rajendra S. Sisodia, and David B. Wolfe (2006), *Firms of Endearment*. Philadelphia: Wharton School Publishing.

Wilkie, William L. and Elizabeth S. Moore (2003), "Scholarly Research in Marketing: Exploring the "4 Eras" of Thought Development," *Journal of Public Policy and Marketing*, 22 (2), 116–147.

—— and —— (2005), "The American Marketing Association's New Definition of Marketing: Perspectives on its Implications for Scholarship and the Role and Responsibility of Marketing in Society," Presentation at the Marketing and Public Policy Conference, Washington, DC, May.

ABOUT THE EDITORS AND CONTRIBUTORS

EDITORS

Jagdish N. Sheth is the Charles H. Kellstadt Professor of Marketing in the Goizueta Business School at Emory University. He is internationally known for his scholarly contributions in consumer behavior, relationship marketing, competitive strategy, and geopolitical analysis. In 2004, Dr. Sheth was awarded both the Richard D. Irwin Distinguished Marketing Educator and the Charles Coolidge Parlin Awards, the two highest awards given by the American Marketing Association. Dr. Sheth is a prolific author, with several hundred articles and books published.

Rajendra S. Sisodia is Professor of Marketing at Bentley College. He has a PhD in Marketing from Columbia University. In 2003, he was cited as one of "50 Leading Marketing Thinkers" by the Chartered Institute of Marketing. His book *The Rule of Three* (with Jag Sheth) was a finalist for the 2004 Best Marketing Book Award from the American Marketing Association. Forthcoming books include *Firms of Endearment* (with Jag Sheth and David Wolfe), *Tectonic Shift: The Geopolitical Realignment of Nations* and *The 4 As of Marketing* (both with Jag Sheth).

CONTRIBUTORS

Fred C. Allvine is Professor Emeritus, College of Management, Georgia Institute of Technology. His research and teaching interests include economics, competition, and investment in addition to marketing. He coauthored a book, *The New State of the Economy,* which is also the subject of a course he teaches. In addition, he has published several books and articles concerned with competition in the petroleum industry.

Tim Ambler is Senior Fellow at London Business School. His research covers international marketing and the measurement of brand equity, marketing, and advertising performance. His books include *Marketing and the Bottom Line, Doing Business in China, The SILK Road to International Marketing,* and *Marketing from Advertising to Zen.* He has published in the *Journal of Marketing, Journal of Marketing Research, International Journal of Research in Marketing, Journal of Advertising Research* and *International Journal of Advertising.*

Adina Barbulescu is a doctoral student in Marketing at Goizueta Business School, Emory University. She is originally form Romania and holds an MBA from Bentley College in Massachusetts.

Russell Belk is N. Eldon Tanner Professor of Business at the University of Utah. He is past president of several professional associations and a fellow in the Association for Consumer Research. He has received the Paul D. Converse Award, two Fulbright Fellowships, and honorary professorships on four continents. His more than 350 publications involve the meanings of possessions, collecting, gift-giving, and materialism, and are often cultural, visual, qualitative, and interpretive.

Leonard L. Berry is a Distinguished Professor of Marketing at Texas A&M University. He is a former national president of the American Marketing Association, and has twice been recognized with Texas A&M's highest honors: Distinguished Achievement Awards in teaching as well as in research. His books include, *Discovering the Soul of Service: The Nine Drivers of Sustainable Business Success, On Great Service: A Framework for Action, Marketing Services: Competing Through Quality,* and *Delivering Quality Service: Balancing Customer Perceptions and Expectations.*

Pierre Berthon is the Clifford F. Youse Professor of Marketing at Bentley College. His teaching and research focus on electronic commerce, marketing information processing, organization and strategy, and management decision-making. He has published in *Sloan Management Review, Journal of Business Research, Journal of the Academy of Marketing Science, Journal of International Marketing, Long Range Planning, Business Horizons, Industrial Marketing Management, California Management Review, Journal of Interactive Marketing, European Journal of Marketing, Journal of Advertising Research,* and others.

Stephen Brown is Professor of Marketing Research at the University of Ulster, Northern Ireland. Best known for *Postmodern Marketing,* he has written several books including *Free Gift Inside* and *Wizard: Harry Potter's Brand Magic.* His articles have been published in the *Harvard Business Review, Journal of Marketing, Journal of Consumer Research,* and many more.

Kerry Chipp teaches marketing in the School of Economics and Business Sciences at the University of the Witwatersrand. She has taught in market research, e-commerce, marketing theory, philosophical thought in marketing, and consumer behavior. She is the joint author of the book, *E-commerce: A Southern African Perspective.* She has contributed to numerous journal articles and conference papers and has been very involved in social marketing in South Africa.

C. Samuel Craig is the Catherine and Peter Kellner Professor of Marketing and International Business at New York University's Stern School of Business. His research focuses on the entertainment industry, global marketing strategy, and methodological issues in international marketing research. He coauthored *Consumer Behavior, Global Marketing Strategy,* and *International Marketing Research.* His research has appeared in the *Journal of Marketing Research, Journal of Marketing, Journal of Consumer Research, Journal of International Business Studies,* and other publications.

Nikhilesh Dholakia is Professor of Marketing, E-Commerce, and International Business at the University of Rhode Island. His research deals with technology, innovation, market processes, and consumer culture. He has written *Consumption and Marketing: Macro Dimensions* and *Consuming People: From Political Economy to Theaters of Consumption.* With A. Fuat Firat, he won the Charles Slater award from the *Journal of Macromarketing.* He has also chaired doctoral dissertations that have won the MSI/Clayton and ACR/Sheth Foundation awards.

Susan P. Douglas is the Paganelli-Bull Professor of Marketing and International Business at New York University's Stern School of Business. She coauthored *Global Marketing Strategy and International Marketing Research,* and has published in the *Journal of Marketing, Journal of Consumer Research, Journal of Marketing Research, Journal of International Business Studies, Columbia Journal of World Business, International Journal of Research in Marketing, Journal of International Marketing,* and other publications.

John U. Farley is C.V. Starr Senior Research Fellow at the Tuck School of Business at Dartmouth, Dartmouth College. He served on the faculties of Carnegie-Mellon, Columbia, and the China Europe International Business School, and he is professor emeritus of the Wharton School. He has coauthored six books and has published widely in marketing and in the behavioral and management sciences. He has a BA from Dartmouth College in Russian, an MBA from the Amos Tuck School, and a PhD from the University of Chicago.

Raymond P. Fisk is Professor and Chair of the Department of Marketing at the University of New Orleans. He has taught in Arizona, Florida, Oklahoma, and internationally in Austria, Chile, Finland, Ireland, Jamaica, and Portugal. He has written numerous books and articles, primarily on the topic of services marketing. He is Past President of the American Marketing Association Academic Council and Past President of the New Orleans and Central Florida AMA Professional Chapters. He also started the AMA Academic Services Marketing Special Interest Group.

A. Fuat Firat is Visiting Professor of Marketing at the University of Southern Denmark–Odense. His research interests cover areas such as macro consumer behavior and macromarketing; postmodern culture; transmodern marketing strategies; gender and consumption; marketing and development; and interorganizational relations. He has written books including *Consuming People,* coauthored with Nik Dholakia, and is Co-Editor-in-Chief of *Consumption, Markets & Culture.* He has won Best Paper awards from *Journal of Consumer Research* and *Journal of Macromarketing.*

Stephen J. Grove is Professor of Marketing at Clemson University. His research interests include interactive aspects of service encounters, environmental issues, and promotion of services. He has published in *Journal of Retailing, Journal of the Academy of Marketing Science, Journal of Public Policy and Marketing, Journal of Macromarketing, Journal of Business Research, Journal of Services Research, Journal of Advertising, European Journal of Marketing, Journal of Services Marketing,* and others. He is coauthor of *Interactive Services Marketing.*

Rajiv Grover is the Head of the Department and holder of the Terry Chair of Marketing at the Terry College of Business, The University of Georgia in Athens, Georgia. His research and teaching philosophy focuses on resolution of managerial problems. His interests lie in the areas of market-focused management and strategy; new product development; customer satisfaction; market research; and organizational networks and relationships. He is the author of *Theory and Simulation of Market-Focused Management.*

Gregory T. Gundlach is the Visiting Eminent Scholar in Wholesaling, Professor of Marketing, and Director of the Center for Research and Education in Wholesaling at the University of North Florida. He is also a Senior Research Fellow at the American Antitrust Institute. Before coming to the University of North Florida, Professor Gundlach was the John Berry, Sr. Professor of Business at the University of Notre Dame.

Stephan H. Haeckel is President of Adaptive Business Designs. He is the author of *Adaptive Enterprise.* He has published in the *Harvard Business Review, Sloan Management Review, Planning Review, Long Range Planning, Marketing Management, IBM Systems Journal,* and the *Journal of Interactive Marketing.*

Scott Hoenig is Visiting Professor at the Fisher Graduate School of International Business at Monterey Institute of International Studies in California. His primary research interest lies in documenting the determinants of sustainable corporate financial performance, in both domestic and international settings. This chapter was written while he was considering these issues in an industrializing country setting as Visiting Fellow at the School of Economic and Business Sciences, University of Witwatersrand in Johannesburg, South Africa.

Morris B. Holbrook is the W.T. Dillard Professor of Marketing in the Graduate School of Business at Columbia University. He has taught courses in areas such as marketing strategy, consumer behavior, and commercial communication in the culture of consumption. His research focuses on issues related to communication in general and to aesthetics, semiotics, hermeneutics, art, entertainment, music, motion pictures, nostalgia, and stereography in particular. Recent books include *The Semiotics of Consumption, Consumer Research,* and *Consumer Value.*

Shelby D. Hunt is the Jerry S. Rawls and P.W. Horn Professor of Marketing at Texas Tech University, Lubbock, Texas. He is the author of numerous books, including *Foundations of Marketing Theory, Controversy in Marketing Theory,* and *A General Theory of Competition.* He has written numerous articles on competitive theory, macromarketing, ethics, channels of distribution, philosophy of science, and marketing theory. Three of his *Journal of Marketing* articles won the Harold H. Maynard Award.

Sandy D. Jap is the Caldwell Research Fellow Associate Professor of Marketing at the Goizueta Business School, Emory University. Her research focuses on the development and management of interorganizational relationships. She has published in *Management Science, Journal of Marketing Research, Journal of Marketing, Sloan Management Review, California Management Review,* and *Harvard Business Review.* She has won numerous research awards and is a member of the editorial boards of the *Journal of Marketing Research* and the *Journal of Marketing.*

Johny K. Johansson is McCrane/Shaker Professor of International Business and Marketing, McDonough School of Business, Georgetown University. A native of Sweden, he is a graduate of the Stockholm School of Economics and University of California at Berkeley. He specializes in international marketing strategy and consumer decision making, and is the author of *In Your Face: How American Marketing Excess Fuels Anti-Americanism, Global Marketing,* and coauthor of *Relentless: The Japanese Way of Marketing.*

Joby John is Professor and Chair of the Marketing department at Bentley College. His research interests include service orientation and marketing of services, customer-focused management, cross-cultural research, and offshoring. He has published in the *European Journal of Marketing, Journal of Healthcare Marketing, International Marketing Review, Journal of Marketing Education, Healthcare Management Review, Journal of Professional Services Marketing, Journal of Services Marketing,* and others. He coauthored a textbook, *Interactive Services Marketing,* and wrote *Fundamentals of Customer-focused Management: Competing Through Service.*

Kevin Lane Keller is the E.B. Osborn Professor of Marketing at the Tuck School of Business at Dartmouth College. He wrote *Strategic Brand Management* and coauthored *Marketing Management* with Philip Kotler.

Praveen K. Kopalle is Associate Professor of Business Administration at the Tuck School of Business at Dartmouth, Dartmouth College. Research includes new products/innovation, pricing and promotions, customer expectations, and e-commerce. Published or forthcoming in the *Journal of Consumer Research, Journal of Marketing Research, Marketing Science, Strategic Management Journal, Organizational Behavior and Human Decision Processes, Journal of Retailing, Journal of Product Innovation Management, Managerial and Decision Economics, Marketing Letters, Applied Economics,* and the *International Journal of Electronic Commerce.*

Philip Kotler is the S.C. Johnson & Son Distinguished Professor of International Marketing at the Kellogg School of Management, Northwestern University. Author of *Marketing Management: Analysis, Planning, Implementation and Control; Principles of Marketing; Marketing Models; Strategic Marketing for Non-Profit Organizations; The New Competition; High Visibility; Social Marketing; Marketing Places; Marketing for Congregations; Marketing for Hospitality and Tourism; The Marketing of Nations;* and *Kotler on Marketing.* He has published over one hundred articles in leading journals.

V. Kumar is the ING Chair Professor of Marketing at the University of Connecticut. His research focuses on multichannel shopping behavior, international diffusion models, customer relationship management, customer lifetime value analysis, sales and market share forecasting, international marketing research and strategy, coupon promotions, and market orientation. He has published more than seventy-five articles in the *Harvard Business Review, Journal of Marketing, Journal of Marketing Research, Marketing Science,* and *Operations Research.* He is the author of *International Marketing Research.*

Katherine N. Lemon is Associate Professor of Marketing at Boston College's Carroll School of Management. Her research areas include customer equity, customer asset management, and marketing strategy, and her research appears in leading marketing journals including the *Journal of Marketing, Journal of Marketing Research, Marketing Science, Journal of Service Research,* and the *Journal of Product Innovation Management.* Her book, *Driving Customer Equity* (with Rust and Zeithaml) received the first annual (2003) AMA Foundation AMA-Berry Book Prize.

Gary L. Lilien is Distinguished Research Professor of Management Science in The Smeal College of Business Administration at Pennsylvania State University. His research interests are in business marketing, marketing engineering, market segmentation, new product modeling, marketing-mix issues for business products, bargaining and negotiations in business markets, modeling the industrial buying process, and innovation diffusion modeling. He has authored or coauthored twelve books and more than ninety professional articles, and was Editor-in-Chief of *Interfaces* for six years.

Naresh K. Malhotra is Regents' Professor, Georgia Institute of Technology. He has published more than ninety papers in the *Journal of Marketing Research, Journal of Health Care Marketing, Journal of the Academy of Marketing Science, International Marketing Review, Journal of Consumer Research, Marketing Science, Journal of Marketing, Journal of Retailing,* and others, as well as two very successful marketing research textbooks. He has received numerous awards and honors for research, teaching, and service to the profession.

Ann M. Mirabito is a doctoral candidate in marketing at Texas A&M University. She has extensive executive-level marketing management experience with responsibilities for brand management, customer relationship marketing, product development, and public policy in consumer and business-to-business firms including Time-Life Books and Frito-Lay. She holds an MBA from Stanford University and a BA in Economics from Duke University.

Kent B. Monroe is Distinguished Visiting Scholar, Department of Marketing, Robins School of Business, University of Richmond, Richmond, and the J. M. Jones Distinguished Professor Emeritus, Department of Business Administration, University of Illinois at Urbana-Champaign. He is the author of *Pricing: Making Profitable Decisions*, 3rd ed. and has offered executive training programs on pricing throughout the world. His current research focuses on price perceptions, price fairness and buyers' processing of price information.

Deon Nel is the Anglo Vaal Industries Professor of Marketing at the School of Economic & Business Sciences at the University of the Witwatersrand. Previously, he has been with the Henley Management College in the United Kingdom, Graduate School of Business of the University of Cape Town; the University of Stellenbosch Business School and Aston Business School in the United Kingdom, where he taught MBA and executive courses in marketing strategy, services marketing and international marketing.

Lisa Peñaloza is Associate Professor of Marketing at the University of Colorado, Boulder. Her research is concerned with how consumers and marketers interact, constituting and navigating culture in the marketplace. Her recent work includes a documentary film exploring consumer behavior and market practice in a Mexican American community. Her research has appeared in the *Journal of Consumer Research, Journal of Marketing, Public Policy and Marketing, International Journal of Research in Marketing,* and *Consumption, Markets and Culture.*

Jagmohan S. Raju is the Joseph J. Aresty Professor at the Wharton School. His research areas include competitive marketing strategy, pricing, retailing, sales force compensation, corporate image advertising, and strategic alliances. Professor Raju is the President of the INFORMS Society for Marketing Science and the Marketing Editor of *Management Science.* He has received several teaching awards, and his research papers have won the John DC Little Best Paper award (twice), the Frank Bass Dissertation Paper Award (twice) and several other recognitions.

Girish Ramani is currently a PhD student at the University of Connecticut. His research interests include Customer Lifetime Value, Strategic Orientations of Firms, Interactive Marketing, and Customer Relationship Management. His teaching interests are in the areas of Marketing Research, Customer Relationship Management, New Product Management, and Marketing Strategy. He has published articles in the *Journal of Interactive Marketing* and the *Journal of Integrated Communications.*

Debra Jones Ringold is Professor of Marketing and Associate Dean at the Atkinson Graduate School of Management, Willamette University. Her research has appeared in the *Journal of Marketing, Journal of Public Policy and Marketing, Organizational Dynamics, Journal of Marketing, Sloan Management Review, Academy of Management Executive, Journal of Retailing, Journal of Public Policy and Marketing,* and *Annals of Internal Medicine.* Research interests include retailing strategy, services marketing, and food marketing. She is currently chair-elect of the AMA Board.

Kathleen Seiders is Associate Professor of Marketing at Boston College. Her research interests include retailing strategy, services marketing, and food marketing. Her work has been published in *Organizational Dynamics, Journal of Marketing, Sloan Management Review, Academy of Management Executive, Journal of Retailing, Journal of Public Policy and Marketing, Annals of Internal Medicine,* and other journals. Her coauthored paper "Understanding Service Convenience" (*Journal of Marketing*) received the 2003 AMA Services Marketing SIG Best Paper Award.

J. Walker Smith is president of Yankelovich Partners, Inc. He is coauthor of *Coming to Concurrence, Rocking the Ages: The Yankelovich Report on Generational Marketing, Life Is Not Work, Work Is Not Life: Simple Reminders for Finding Balance in a 24/7 World.* Described by Fortune magazine as "one of America's leading analysts on consumer trends," Walker holds three degrees from the University of North Carolina at Chapel Hill including a doctorate in Mass Communication Research.

David W. Stewart is the Robert E. Brooker Professor of Marketing in the Marshall School of Business at the University of Southern California. He has served as Chairman of the Department of Marketing and Deputy Dean of the Marshall School. He is a past editor of the *Journal of Marketing.* He is a past president of the Academic Council of the American Marketing Association, and has also served on the board of the AMA Foundation.

Anne Stringfellow is an assistant professor in the Global Business Department at Thunderbird, The Garvin School for International Management in Glendale, Arizona. She holds a PhD in marketing from the University of Florida and her work has been published in *Management Science, Journal of Retailing,* and *Journal of Operations Management.* Her research interests include cross-functional and multicultural teams, new product development, and the impact of offshoring on customer relationships.

Glen L. Urban has been a member of the MIT Sloan School of Management faculty since 1966, was Deputy Dean at the school from 1987 to 1991, and Dean from 1993 to 1998. His research focuses on management science models that improve the productivity of new product development. He has won several prestigious awards, including two O'Dells and the Paul D. Converse Award for outstanding contributions to the development of the science of marketing.

Rajan Varadarajan is Distinguished Professor of Marketing and the Ford Chair in Marketing and E-Commerce, Texas A&M University. He has served as the editor of the *Journal of Marketing* and the *Journal of the Academy of Marketing Science.* He is author of more than sixty articles in the *Journal of Marketing, Journal of the Academy of Marketing Science, Strategic Management Journal, Sloan Management Review, California Management Review, Business Horizons, Journal of Business Research,* and other journals.

Alladi Venkatesh is Professor of Management and Associate Director of CRITO at the University of California. His research focused on the impact of new media and information technologies on consumers/households. Current work involves electronic commerce and the consumer sector, and the future of the networked home. He has published in the *Journal of Consumer Research, Management Science, Communications of the ACM, Journal of Product Innovation and Management, International Journal of Research in Marketing,* and *Telecommunications Policy.*

Frederick E. Webster, Jr. is Charles Henry Jones 3rd Century Professor of Management, Emeritus, at the Tuck School, as well as a Visiting Scholar at the Eller School of Business and Public

Administration at the University of Arizona. His work has focused on the role of marketing in the organization, value-based views of marketing strategy, and the links between organization culture, customer orientation, and business performance. He has published articles in the *Journal of Marketing, Business Horizons,* and the *Harvard Business Review.*

William L. Wilkie is the Aloysius and Eleanor Nathe Professor of Marketing at the University of Notre Dame. His research centers on marketing and society, consumer behavior, and advertising. Professor Wilkie has received the American Marketing Association's highest honor, the Distinguished Marketing Educator Award, and has been honored with Notre Dame's President's Award and BP/Amoco Outstanding Teacher Award. One of his articles has been named a "Citation Classic in the Social Sciences" by the Institute for Scientific Information.

Yoram (Jerry) Wind is Lauder Professor and Professor of Marketing at the Wharton School and the Chancellor of the International Academy of Management. He has published more than twenty books and over 250 articles. He has received all the major marketing rewards including: The Charles Coolidge Parlin Award (1985), AMA/Irwin Distinguished Educator Award (1993), the Paul D. Converse Award (1996), and the Elsevier Science Distinguished Scholar Award of the Society of Marketing Advances (2003).

Russell S. Winer is the Deputy Dean and William Joyce professor of Marketing at the Stern School of business, New York University. He has written three books: *Marketing Management, Analysis for Marketing Planning,* and *Product Management* and has authored more than sixty articles for prestigious journals.

David B. Wolfe is an internationally recognized consumer behavior expert who originated the field of developmental relationship marketing (DRM). Author of *Serving the Ageless Market* and *Ageless Marketing*, he has lectured in Asia, Africa, Europe and North America, and has published numerous articles in magazines and journals such as *Advertising Age, American Demographics, Journal of Consumer Marketing, Journal of Business Strategy,* and *Journal of Health Care Marketing.*

Lan Wu is a Doctoral Candidate in the College of Management, Georgia Institute of Technology. Her research has been published in the *International Marketing Review* and other publications. She is the winner of Outstanding Teaching Award and the recipient of other honors.

Lan Xia is an Assistant Professor of Marketing at Bentley College. Her primary research interest is in consumer behavior including consumer perceptions of pricing and promotion tactics, consumer information processing, and memory issues. She has published articles in the *Journal of Marketing, Journal of Consumer Psychology, Journal of Interactive Marketing*, and the *Journal of Product & Brand Management.*

INDEX

343